By Tad Williams

OTHERLAND

VOLUME FOUR

Sea of Silver Light

TAD WILLIAMS

www.orbitbooks.co.uk

An *Orbit* Book

First published in Great Britain by Orbit 2001
This edition published by Orbit 2002

Copyright © 2001 by Tad Williams

The moral right of the author has been asserted.

Jacket art by Michael Whelan.
For colour prints of Michael Whelan's paintings, please contact:
Glass Onion Graphics
P.O. Box 88
Brookfield, CT 06804
www.michaelwhelan.com

A CIP catalogue record for this book
is available from the British Library.

ISBN 1 84149 064 4

Typeset by Palimpsest Book Production Limited,
Polmont, Stirlingshire

Printed and bound in Great Britain
by Mackays of Chatham plc, Chatham, Kent

Orbit
An imprint of
Time Warner Books UK
Brettenham House
Lancaster Place
London WC2E 7EN

My father still hasn't actually cracked any of the books – so, no, he still hasn't noticed. I think I'm just going to have to tell him. Maybe I should break it to him gently.

'Everyone here who hasn't had a book dedicated to them, take three steps forward. Whoops, Dad, hang on a second . . .'

Find Tad Williams' next groundbreaking fantasy epic,
Shadowmarch, at:
www.shadowmarch.com

Shadowmarch will only be available online.

For more information on Otherland, Tad's other books,
and touring schedules, visit the Tad Williams website at:
www.tadwilliams.com

These people saved my life. Without their help, I would never have finished these books. You may apply the appropriate punishments.

The List So Far:

Barbara Cannon, Aaron Castro, Nick Des Barres, Debra Euler, Arthur Ross Evans, Amy Fodera, Sean Fodera, Jo-Ann Goodwin, Deborah Grabien, Nic Grabien, Jed Hartmann, Tim Holman, Nick Itsou, John Jarrold, Katharine Kerr, Ulrike Killer, M. J. Kramer, Jo and Phil Knowles, Mark Kreighbaum, LES.., Bruce Lieberman, Mark McCrum, Joshua Milligan, Hans-Ulrich Möhring, Eric Neuman, Peter Stampfel, Mitch Wagner, Michael Whelan.

To which must be added another group of the brave and the good:

Melissa Brammer, Dena Chavez, Rick Cuevas, Marcia de Lima, Jim Foster.

As always, shout-outs to all my homies on the Tad Williams List-serve and the message boards of the TW Fan Page and Guthwulf.com's MS&T Interactive Thesis.

And of course, no acknowledgments would be truly acknowledgmentacious without mentioning my wonderful wife Deborah Beale, my lovely and talented agent Matt Bialer, and my brilliant and patient editors Betsy Wollheim and Sheila Gilbert. My kids Connor and Devon didn't really help much, but they sure make life more interesting (and the need to finish and sell books more acute), and Connor did type a bunch of consonants into my manuscript at random for me to use later, so I guess they belong in here as well.

OTHERLAND: City of Golden Shadow

Synopsis

Wet, terrified, with only the companionship of trench-mates *Finch* and *Mullet* to keep him sane, *Paul Jonas* seems no different than any of thousands of other foot soldiers in World War I. But when he abruptly finds himself alone on an empty battlefield except for a tree that grows up into the clouds, he begins to doubt that sanity. When he climbs the tree and discovers a castle in the clouds, a woman with wings like a bird, and her terrifying giant guardian, his insanity seems confirmed. But when he awakens back in the trenches, he finds he is clutching one of the bird-woman's feathers.

In South Africa, in the middle of the twenty-first century, *Irene 'Renie' Sulaweyo* has problems of her own. Renie is an instructor of virtual engineering whose newest student, *!Xabbu*, is one of the desert Bushmen, a people to whom modern technology is very alien. At home she is a surrogate mother to her young brother, *Stephen*, who is obsessed with exploring the virtual parts of the world communication network – the 'net' – and Renie spends what little spare time she has holding her family together. Her widowed father *Long Joseph* only seems interested in finding his next drink.

Like most children, Stephen is entranced by the forbidden, and although Renie has already saved him once from

a disturbing virtual nightclub named Mister J's, Stephen
returns to the net. By the time Renie discovers what he
has done, Stephen has fallen into a coma. The doctors
cannot explain it, but Renie is certain something has
happened to him online.

American *Orlando Gardiner* is only a little older than
Renie's brother, but he is a master of several online
domains, and because of a serious medical condition,
spends most of his time in the online identity of *Thargor*,
a barbarian warrior. But when in the midst of one of his
adventures Orlando is given a glimpse of a golden city
unlike anything else he has ever seen on the net, he is
so distracted that his Thargor character is killed. Despite
this terrible loss, Orlando cannot shake his fascination
with the golden city, and with the support of his software agent *Beezle Bug* and the reluctant help of his online
friend *Fredericks*, he is determined to locate the golden
city.

Meanwhile, on a military base in the United States, a
little girl named *Christabel Sorensen* pays secret visits to
her friend, *Mr Sellars*, a strange, scarred old man. Her
parents have forbidden her to see him, but she likes the
old man and the stories he tells, and he seems much more
pathetic than frightening. She does not know that he has
very unusual plans for her.

As Renie gets to know !Xabbu the Bushman better, and
to appreciate his calm good nature and his outsider's viewpoint on modern life, she comes to rely on him more and
more in her quest to discover what has happened to her
brother. She and !Xabbu sneak into the online nightclub,
Mr J's. The place is as bad as she feared, with guests
indulging themselves in all manner of virtual unpleas-
antness, but nothing seems like it could have actually
physically harmed her brother until they are drawn into

a terrifying encounter with a virtual version of the Hindu death-goddess Kali. !Xabbu is overcome, and Renie, too, is almost overwhelmed by Kali's subliminal hypnotics, but with the help of a mysterious figure whose simulated body (his 'sim') is a blank, with no features at all, she manages to get herself and !Xabbu out of Mister J's. Before she goes offline, the figure gives her some data in the form of a golden gem.

Back (apparently) in World War I, Paul Jonas escapes from his squadron and makes a run for freedom through the dangerous no-man's-land between the lines. As rain falls and shells explode, Paul struggles through mud and corpses, only to find he has crossed over into some nether-region, stranger even than his castle dream – a flat, misty emptiness. A shimmering golden light appears, and Paul is drawn to it, but before he can step into its glow, his two friends from the trenches appear and demand that he return with them. Weary and confused, he is about to surrender, but as they come closer he sees that Finch and Mullet no longer appear even remotely human, and he flees into the golden light.

In the twenty-first century, the oldest and perhaps richest man in the world is named *Felix Jongleur*. His physical body is all but dead, and he spends his days in a virtual Egypt he has built for himself, where he reigns over all as *Osiris*, the god of Life and Death. His chief servant, both in the virtual and real world, is a half-Aboriginal serial murderer who has named himself *Dread*, who combines a taste for hunting humans with a strange extrasensory ability to manipulate electronic circuitry that allows him to blank security cameras and otherwise avoid detection. Jongleur discovered Dread years before, helped to nurture the young man's power, and has made him his chief assassin.

Jongleur/Osiris is also the leader of a group of some of the world's most powerful and wealthy people, the *Grail Brotherhood*, who have built for themselves a virtual universe unlike any other – the Grail Project, also called Otherland. (This latter name comes from an entity known as the 'Other' which has some important involvement with the Grail Project network – an artificial intelligence or something even stranger. This powerful force is largely in the control of Jongleur, but it is the only thing in the world that the old man fears.)

The Grail Brotherhood are arguing among themselves, upset that the mysterious Grail Project is so slow to come to fruition. They have all invested billions in it, and waited a decade or more of their lives. Led by the American technology baron *Robert Wells*, they grow restive about Jongleur's leadership and his secrets, like the nature of the Other.

Jongleur fights off a mutiny, and orders his minion Dread to prepare a neutralization mission against one of the Grail members who has already left the Brotherhood.

Back in South Africa, Renie and her student !Xabbu are shaken by their narrow escape from the virtual nightclub known as Mister J's, and more certain than ever that there is some involvement between the club and her brother's coma. But when she examines the data-object the mysterious figure gave her, it opens into an amazingly realistic image of a golden city. Renie and !Xabbu seek the help of Renie's former professor, *Dr Susan Van Bleeck*, but she is unable to solve the mystery of the city, or even tell for certain if it is an actual place. The doctor decides to contact someone else she knows for help, a researcher named *Martine Desroubins*. But even as Renie and the mysterious Martine make contact for the first time, Dr Van Bleeck is attacked in her home and savagely beaten, and all her equipment destroyed. Renie rushes to the hospital, but after pointing Renie in the direction of a friend, Susan dies, leaving Renie both angry and terrified.

Meanwhile Orlando Gardiner, the ill teenager in America, is hot in pursuit of the golden city that he saw while online, so much so that his friend Fredericks begins to worry about him. Orlando has always been odd – he has a fascination with death-experience simulations that Fredericks can't understand – but his current behavior seems excessive. When Orlando announces they are going to the famous hacker-node known as TreeHouse, Fredericks' worst fears are confirmed.

TreeHouse is the last preserve of everything anarchic about the net, a place where no rules dictate what people can do or how they must appear. But although Orlando finds TreeHouse fascinating, and discovers some unlikely allies in the form of a group of hacker children named the *Wicked Tribe* (whose virtual guise is a troop of tiny winged yellow monkeys), his attempts to discover the origins of the golden-city vision arouse suspicion, and he and Fredericks are forced to flee.

Meanwhile Renie and !Xabbu, with the help of Martine Desroubins, have also come to TreeHouse, in pursuit of an old, retired hacker named *Singh*, Susan Van Bleeck's friend. When they find him, he tells them that he is the last of a group of specialist programmers who built the security system for a mysterious network nicknamed 'Otherland,' and that his companions have been dying in mysterious circumstances. He is the last one alive.

Renie, !Xabbu, Singh, and Martine decide they must break into the Otherland system to discover what secret is worth the lives of Singh's comrades and children like Renie's brother.

Paul Jonas has escaped from his World War I trench only to find himself seemingly unstuck in time and space. Largely amnesiac, he wanders into a world where a White Queen and a Red Queen are in conflict, and finds himself pursued again by the Finch and Mullet figures. With the help of a boy named *Gally* and a long-winded, egg-shaped bishop, Paul escapes them, but his pursuers murder Gally's children friends. A huge creature called a Jabberwock provides a diversion, and Paul and Gally dive into a river.

When they surface, the river is in a different world, a strange, almost comical version of Mars, full of monsters and English gentleman-soldiers. Paul again meets the bird-woman from his castle dream, now named *Vaala*, but this time she is the prisoner of a Martian overlord. With the help of mad adventurer *Hurley Brummond*, Paul saves the woman. She recognizes Paul, too, but does not know why. When the Finch and Mullet figures appear again, she flees. Attempting to catch up to her, Paul crashes a stolen flying ship, sending himself and Gally to what seems certain doom. After a strange dream in which he is back in the cloud-castle, menaced by Finch and Mullet in their strangest forms yet, he wakes without Gally in the midst of the Ice Age, surrounded by Neandertal hunters.

Meanwhile in South Africa, Renie and her companions are being hunted by mysterious strangers, and are forced to flee their home. With the help of Martine (whom they still know only as a voice) Renie, along with !Xabbu, her father, and Dr Van Bleeck's assistant *Jeremiah*, find an old, mothballed robot-plane base in the Drakensberg Mountains. They renovate a pair of V-tanks (virtuality immersion vats) so Renie and !Xabbu can go online for an indefinite period, and prepare for their assault on Otherland.

Back on the army base in America, little Christabel is

convinced to help the burned and crippled Mr Sellars with a complex plan that is only revealed as an escape attempt when he disappears from his house, setting the whole base (including Christabel's security chief father) on alert. Christabel has cut what seems an escape hole in the base's perimeter fence (with the help of a homeless boy from outside), but only she knows that Mr Sellars is actually hiding in a network of tunnels beneath the base, free now to continue his mysterious 'task.'

In the abandoned facility under the Drakensberg Mountains, Renie and her companions enter the tanks, go online, and break into Otherland. They survive a terrifying interaction with the Other which seems to be the network's security system, in which Singh dies of a heart attack, and find that the network is so incredibly realistic that at first they cannot believe it is a virtual environment. The experience is strange in many other ways. Martine has a body for the first time, !Xabbu has been given the form of a baboon, and most importantly, they can find no way to take themselves offline again. Renie and the others discover that they are in an artificial South American country. When they reach the golden city at the heart of it, the city they have been seeking so long, they are captured, and discover that they are the prisoners of *Bolivar Atasco*, a man involved with the Grail Brotherhood and with the building of the Otherland network from the start.

Back in America, Orlando's friendship with Fredericks has survived the twin revelations that Orlando is dying of a rare premature-aging disease, and that Fredericks is in fact a girl. They are unexpectedly linked to Renie's hacker friend Singh by the Wicked Tribe just as Singh is opening his connection to the Grail network, and drawn through into Otherland. After their own horrifying encounter with the Other, Orlando and Fredericks also become Atasco's prisoners. But when they are brought to the great man, along with Renie's company and others, they find that it is not Atasco who has gathered them, but Mr Sellars – revealed now as the strange blank sim who helped Renie and !Xabbu escape from Mister J's.

Sellars explains that he has lured them all here with the image of the golden city – the most discreet method he could devise, because their enemies, the Grail Brotherhood, are so vastly powerful and remorseless. Sellars explains that Atasco and his wife were once members of the Brotherhood, but quit when their questions about the network were not answered. Sellars then tells how he discovered that the secret Otherland network has a mysterious but undeniable connection to the illness of thousands of children like Renie's brother Stephen. Before he can explain more, the sims of Atasco and his wife go rigid and Sellars' own sim disappears.

In the real world, Jongleur's murderous minion Dread has begun his attack on the Atascos' fortified Colombian island home, and after breaking through the defenses, has killed both Atascos. He then uses his strange abilities – his 'twist' – to tap into their data lines, discovers Sellars' meeting, and orders his assistant *Dulcinea Anwin* to take over the incoming line of one of the Atascos' guests – the online group that includes Renie and her friends – so he can take on the identity of that usurped guest, leaving Dread hidden as a spy in the midst of Renie and friends.

Sellars reappears in the Atascos' virtual world and begs Renie and the others to flee into the network while he tries to hide their presence. They are to look for a man named Jonas, he tells them, a mysterious virtual prisoner Sellars has helped escape from the Brotherhood. Renie and company make their way onto the river and out of the Atascos' simulation, then through an electrical blue glow into the next simworld. Panicked and overwhelmed by too much input, Martine finally reveals her secret to Renie: she is blind.

Their boat has become a giant leaf. Overhead, a dragonfly the size of a fighter jet skims into view.

Back in the mountain fortress, in the real world, Jeremiah and Renie's father Long Joseph can only watch the silent V-tanks, wonder, and wait.

OTHERLAND: River of Blue Fire

Synopsis

Paul Jonas still seems to be adrift in time and space. He has recovered most of his memory, but the last few years of his life remain a blank. He has no idea why he is being tossed from world to world, pursued by the two creatures he first knew as *Finch* and *Mullet*, and he still does not know the identity of the mysterious woman he keeps encountering, and who has appeared to him even in dreams.

He has survived a near-drowning only to find himself in the Ice Age, where he has fallen in with a tribe of Neandertals. The mystery woman appears to him in another dream, and tells him that to reach her he must find 'a black mountain that reaches to the sky.'

Not all of the cave dwellers welcome the unusual stranger; one picks a quarrel that results in Paul being abandoned in the frozen wilderness. He survives an attack by giant cave hyenas, but falls into the icy river once more.

Others are having just as difficult and painful a time as Paul, although they are better informed. *Renie Sulaweyo* originally had set out to solve the mystery of her brother *Stephen's* coma with her friend and former student *!Xabbu*, a Bushman from the Okavango Delta. With the help of a blind researcher named *Martine Desroubins*, they have found their way into Otherland, the world's biggest and strangest virtual reality network, constructed by a cabal of powerful men and women who call themselves the *Grail Brotherhood*. Summoned by the mysterious *Mr Sellars*, Renie meets several others who have been affected by the Grail Brotherhood's machinations – *Orlando Gardiner*, a dying teenager, and his friend *Sam Fredericks* (who Orlando has only recently discovered is a girl), a woman named *Florimel*, a flamboyant character who calls himself *Sweet William*, a Chinese grandmother named *Quan Li*, and a sullen young man in futuristic armor who uses the handle *T4b*. But something has trapped them within the network, and the nine companions have been forced to flee from one virtual world to the next on a river of blue fire – a virtual path that leads through all the Otherland simulation worlds.

The newest simworld is much like the real world, except that Renie and her companions are less than a hundredth of their normal size. They are menaced by the local insects, as well as larger creatures like fish and birds, and the members of the group become separated. Renie and !Xabbu are rescued by scientists who are using the simulation to study insect life from an unusual perspective. The scientists soon discover that, like Renie and !Xabbu, they are trapped online. Renie and !Xabbu meet a strange man named *Kunohara*, who owns the bug world simulation, but claims he is not part of the Grail Brotherhood. Kunohara poses a pair of cryptic riddles to them, then vanishes. When a horde of (relatively gigantic) army ants attacks the research station, most of the scientists are killed and Renie and !Xabbu barely escape from a monstrous praying mantis.

As they flee back to the river in one of the researchers'

aircraft, they see Orlando and Fredericks being swept down the river on a leaf. As they attempt to rescue them, Renie and !Xabbu are pulled through the river gateway with them, but the two groups wind up in different simulations.

Meanwhile, in the real world outside the network, other people are being drawn into the widening Otherland mystery. *Olga Pirofsky*, the host of a children's net show, begins to suffer from terrible headaches. She suspects that her online activities might have something to do with it, and in the course of investigating her problem, begins to learn of the apparently net-related illness that has struck so many children (including Renie's brother). Olga's research also draws the attention of a lawyer named *Catur Ramsey*, who is investigating the illness on behalf of the parents both of Orlando and Fredericks, since in the real world both teenagers have been in a coma ever since their entrance into the Otherland network.

John Wulgaru, who calls himself *Dread*, and whose hobbies include serial murder, has been an effective if not one hundred percent loyal employee of the incredibly wealthy *Felix Jongleur*, the man who heads the Grail Brotherhood (and who spends most of his time in his Egyptian simulation, wearing the guise of the god Osiris). But in the course of killing an ex-member of the Brotherhood at Jongleur's orders, Dread has discovered the existence of the Otherland network, and has even taken over one of the sims in Renie's marooned company. As his master Jongleur is caught up in the final arrangements for the Otherland network – whose true purpose is still known only to the Brotherhood – Dread busies himself with this new and fascinating puzzle. As a spy among Sellars' recruits, Dread is now traveling through the network and trying to discover its secrets. But unlike those in Sellars' ragtag group, Dread's life is not at risk: he can go offline whenever he wishes. He recruits a software specialist named *Dulcie Anwin* to help him run the puppet sim. Dulcie is fascinated by her boss, but unsettled by him, too, and begins to wonder if she is in deeper than she wants to be.

Meanwhile, a bit of Dread's past has surfaced. In Australia, a detective named *Calliope Skouros* is trying to solve a seemingly unexceptional murder. Some of the terrible things done to the victim's body are reminiscent of an Aboriginal myth-creature, the Woolagaroo. Detective Skouros becomes convinced that there is some strange relationship between Aboriginal myths and the young woman's death she is investigating.

Back in the Otherland network, Renie and !Xabbu find themselves in a weird, upside-down version of the Oz story, set in the dreary Kansas of the original tale's opening. The Otherland simulations seem to be breaking down, or at least growing increasingly chaotic. As Renie and !Xabbu try to escape the evil of Lion and Tinman – who seem to be two more versions of Paul Jonas' Finch and Mullet – they find a pair of unlikely allies, the young and naive *Emily 22813* and a laconic Gypsy named *Azador*. Emily later reveals that she is pregnant, and says Azador is the father. Separated from Azador during one of the increasingly frequent 'system spasms,' they escape Kansas, but to their surprise, Emily (who they had thought was software) travels with them to the next simulation.

Orlando and Fredericks have landed in a very strange world, a kitchen out of an ancient cartoon, populated by creatures sprung from package labels and silverware drawers. They help a cartoon Indian brave search for his stolen child, and after battling cartoon pirates and meeting both a prophetic sleeping woman and an inexplicable force –

entities that are really Paul Jonas' mystery woman and the network's apparently sentient operating system, known as the *Other* – they escape the Kitchen and land in a simulation that seems to be ancient Egypt.

Meanwhile, their former companions, the blind woman Martine and the rest of the Sellars' recruits, have hiked out of the bug world to discover themselves in a simulation where the river is made not of water but air, and where the primitive inhabitants fly on wind currents and live in caves along vertical cliffs. Martine and the others name the place Aerodromia, and although they are nervous about trying it at first, they soon discover that they can fly, too. A group of natives invite them to stay in the tribal camp.

Paul Jonas has passed from the Ice Age into something much different. At first, seeing familiar London sights, he believes he has finally found his way home, but soon comes to realize that he is instead traveling through an England almost completely destroyed by Martian attack – it is, in fact, the setting of H. G. Wells' *War of the Worlds*. Paul now realizes that he is traveling not just to worlds separate in time and space, but to some that are actually fictitious. He meets a strange husband and wife called the *Pankies*, who seem to be another guise of his pursuers Finch and Mullet, but offer him no harm. (Paul is also being pursued by a special software program called the *Nemesis* device, but he is not yet aware of it.) Then, when Paul and the Pankies stop at Hampton Court, Paul is led into the maze by a strange man and then shoved through a gateway of glowing light at the maze's center.

On the other side Paul finds himself in the setting of Coleridge's famous poem, *Xanadu*, and the man who brought him there introduces himself as *Nandi Paradivash*.

Nandi is a member of a group named the *Circle*, who are working against the Grail Brotherhood. Paul finally learns that he is not insane, nor caught in some kind of dimensional warp, but is rather a prisoner in an incredibly realistic simulation network. But Nandi has no idea why the Brotherhood should be interested enough in Paul – who worked in a museum and remembers his other life as being very ordinary – to pursue him throughout Otherland. Nandi also reveals that all the simulations through which Paul has been traveling belong to one man – Felix Jongleur, the Grail Brotherhood's chairman. Before Nandi can tell him more, they are forced to separate, Nandi pursued by Kublai Khan's troops, Paul passing through another gateway into yet another simworld.

Things are no less complex and confusing in the real world. Renie's and !Xabbu's physical bodies are in special virtual reality tanks in an abandoned South African military base, watched over by *Jeremiah Dako* and Renie's father, *Long Joseph Sulaweyo*. Long Joseph, bored and depressed, sneaks out of the base to go see Renie's brother Stephen, who remains comatose in a Durban hospital, leaving Jeremiah alone inside the base. But when Joseph arrives at the hospital, he is kidnapped at gunpoint and forced into a car.

The mysterious Mr Sellars lives on a military base, too, but his is in America. *Christabel Sorensen* is a little girl whose fatehr is in charge of base security, and who, despite her youth, has helped her friend Sellars escape the house arrest her father and others have kept him in for years. Sellars is hiding in old tunnels under the base, his only companion the street urchin *Cho-Cho*. Christabel does not like the boy at all. She worries for the feeble Mr Sellars' safety, and is torn by guilt for doing something she knows would make her mother and father angry. But when her mother discovers her talking with Sellars through specially modified sunglasses, Christabel is finally in real trouble.

Martine, Florimel, Quan Li, Sweet William, and T4b have been enjoying the flying world, Aerodromia, but things get uncomfortable when a young girl from the tribe is kidnapped. Martine and the rest don't know it, but the girl has been stolen, terrorized, and murdered by Dread, still pretending to be one of Martine's four companions. The people of Aerodromia blame the newcomers for the disappearance, and dump them all into a labyrinth of caverns they call the Place of the Lost, where they find themselves surrounded by mysterious, ghostly presences which Martine, with her heightened nonvisual senses, finds particularly upsetting. The phantoms speak in unison, telling of the 'One who is Other,' and how he has deserted them instead of taking them across the 'White Ocean,' as promised. The voices also identify the real names of all Martine's company. The group is fascinated and frightened, and only belatedly realizes that Sweet William has disappeared – evidently to protect the guilty secret of his true identity. Something large and strange – the Other – abruptly enters the darkened Place of the Lost, and Martine and the others flee the horrifying presence. Martine searches desperately for one of the gateways that will allow them to leave the simulation before either the Other or the renegade Sweet William catches them.

At the same time, Orlando and Fredericks discover that the Egyptian simulation is not a straightforward historical recreation, but a mythical version. They meet a wolf-headed god named *Upaut*, who tells them how he and the whole simworld have been mistreated by the chief god, Osiris. Unfortunately, Upaut is not a very bright or stable god, and he interprets Orlando mumbling in his sleep – the result of a dream-conversation Orlando is having with his software agent, *Beezle Bug*, who can only reach him from the real world when he dreams – as a divine directive for him to try to overthrow Osiris. Upaut steals their sword and boat, leaving Orlando and Fredericks stranded in the desert. After many days of hiking along the Nile, they come upon a strange temple filled with some terrible, compelling presence. They cannot escape it. In a dream, Orlando is visited by the mystery woman also seen by Paul Jonas, and she tells them she will give them assistance, but as the temple draws them closer and closer, they find only the *Wicked Tribe*, a group of very young children they had met outside the network, who wear the sim-forms of tiny yellow flying monkeys. Orlando is stunned that this is the help the mystery woman has brought them. The frightening temple continues to draw them nearer.

Paul Jonas has passed from Xanadu to late-sixteenth-century Venice, and soon stumbles into *Gally*, a boy he had met in one of the earlier simulations, and who had traveled with him, but Gally does not remember Paul. Seeking help, the boy brings him to a woman named *Eleanora*; although she cannot explain Gally's missing memories, she reveals that she herself is the former real-world mistress of an organized crime figure who built her this virtual Venice as a gift. Her lover was a member of the Grail Brotherhood, but died too soon to benefit from the immortality machinery they are building, and survives now only as a set of flawed life-recordings. Before Paul can learn more, he discovers that the dreadful Finch and Mullet – *the Twins*, as Nandi named them – have tracked him to Venice: he must flee again, this time with Gally. But before they can reach the gateway that will allow them to escape, they are caught by the Twins. The Pankies also make an appearance, and for a moment the two mirror-pairs face each other, but the Pankies quickly depart, leaving Paul alone to fight the Twins. Gally is killed, and Paul barely escapes with his life. Still trying to fulfill the mystery woman's summons from his Ice Age dream, he travels to a simulation of ancient Ithaca to meet someone called 'the weaver.' Still shocked and saddened by Gally's death, he learns that in this new simulation he is the famous Greek hero Odysseus, and that the weaver is the hero's wife, Penelope – the mystery woman, again. But at least it seems he will finally get some answers.

Renie and !Xabbu and Emily find that they have escaped Kansas for something much more confusing – a world that does not seem entirely finished, a place with no sun, moon, or weather. They have also inadvertently taken an object from Azador that looks like an ordinary cigarette lighter, but is in fact an access device, a sort of key to the Otherland network, stolen from one of the Grail Brotherhood (*General Daniel Yacoubian*, one of Jongleur's rivals for leadership). While studying the device in the hopes of making it work, !Xabbu manages to open a transmission channel and discovers Martine on the other end, trapped in the Place of the Lost and desperately trying to open a gateway. Together they manage to create a passage for Martine and her party, but when they arrive, believing they are being pursued by a murderous Sweet William, they find that it is William himself who has been fatally injured, and grandmotherly Quan Li who is really the murderer Dread in virtual disguise. His secret revealed, Dread escapes with the access device, leaving Renie and the others stranded, perhaps forever, in this disturbing place.

OTHERLAND: Mountain of Black Grass

Synopsis

Renie Sulaweyo, her Bushman friend *!Xabbu*, and several more of the volunteers recruited by the strange *Mr Sellars* have been reunited in the weirdest part of the Grail network they have yet discovered – a world that seems somehow unfinished. They are stranded there because the murderer named *Dread*, who was masquerading as one of their company, has taken the access device – a virtual object that appears to be a cigarette lighter – that they have been using to travel between simulated worlds.

While they try to discover a way out, two of the more mysterious members of their company, *Florimel* and *T4b*, finally explain their backgrounds. Florimel is an escapee from a German religious cult, and has come to the network because her daughter is one of the children (like Renie's brother *Stephen*) who has fallen into one of the mysterious Tandagore's Syndrome comas. T4b, whose real name is Javier Rodgers, is a former street kid and gang member, now living with his grandparents. A young friend of his has also fallen prey to a coma.

Renie and the others find the unfinished world in which they are marooned increasingly uncomfortable – at one point, they see something that looks just like !Xabbu's baboon sim, but isn't. When a huge hole suddenly opens right in the middle of the ground, almost swallowing the blind woman *Martine* and somehow obliterating one of T4b's virtual hands, they decide they must escape immediately. Martine, !Xabbu, and Renie, working together, manage to open a gateway even without the lighter.

After they step through the gateway, following in Dread's virtual tracks, the search-and-destroy program named *Nemesis*, which was put into the network to locate another fugitive, *Paul Jonas*, tries to decide whether to follow them or not. It is confused – there are things happening on the network that interfere with the original clarity of its programmed drives, anomalies that are making it do strange, unprecedented things.

The amnesiac fugitive Paul Jonas is living out a version of the *Odyssey* in which he is Odysseus, returned to his home island of Ithaca after the Trojan War. But Penelope, the wife of Odysseus (who also appears to be yet another incarnation of the mysterious woman Paul thinks of as '*the Angel*') does not seem to be playing by the same set of rules. In an effort to shake her up and get some answers – another incarnation of the Angel has told him that the Penelope-version will tell him how to find the 'black mountain' he must reach – he performs an invocation of what he thinks is Hades, the death god of ancient Greece. Instead, he summons the Angel herself, confronting Penelope with a near-twin. Next, a new force answers his invocation – not Hades, but the *Other*, the dark intelligence behind the Grail network. Terrified, Paul flees onto the ocean, but his boat is destroyed.

Meanwhile, *Orlando Gardiner* and his friend *Sam Fredericks* are in a simulation of ancient Egypt – a simworld that is the one place on the network that *Felix Jongleur*, the world's oldest man and master of the Grail Brotherhood, considers his home. They have been hidden from Jongleur's subordinates by a woman named *Bonnie Mae Simpkins*, who is a member of a group called the Circle. She tells them how her husband and many other Circle members have been killed trying to penetrate the mysteries of the Grail network. Now the last few members in Egypt are besieged in a temple. Bonnie Mae recruits the god *Bes* to lead her and Orlando and Fredericks there, hoping that her Circle friends can help the two teenagers escape Egypt through an activated gateway.

People offline are just as involved in these events as those trapped on the network. *Catur Ramsey*, a lawyer who works for Sam Fredericks' parents, finds himself drawn deeper and deeper into the Otherland mystery. With the help of Orlando's software agent, a cartoon bug named *Beezle*, Ramsey follows the online trail of the two comatose teenagers. A Canadian woman named *Olga Pirofsky* that he contacts, who works for one of Jongleur's many companies, has also become involved. What started for her as troubling headaches have now become dream-visitations by mysterious children. Olga fears she might be going mad.

In North Carolina, the little girl *Christabel Sorensen*, who helped Sellars escape and hide under the military base where they both live, has been caught by her security chief father, *Major Sorensen*. Sellars uses the little homeless boy *Cho-Cho* to ask Christabel to arrange a conversation with her parents. Sellars tells – and shows – Christabel's parents enough to convince them to help him escape the base entirely. With Sellars hidden in the back of their van, and Cho-Cho pretending to be Christabel's cousin, they all set out for a rendezvous with Catur Ramsey, who has also been contacted by Sellars.

Back in the Otherland network, Renie, !Xabbu, and the others have come through their jury-rigged gateway, following Dread's trail into a mysterious simworld known only as the House. They quickly dicover it's called that because the world is nothing *but* a house – an endless collection of halls and rooms, with separate civilizations living only floors apart from each other. They are assisted in their queries by a brotherhood of monks who maintain the House's monstrous library, but Martine is kidnapped by Dread, and with the aid of one of the monks they set out in search of her – and the murderer.

Someone else searching for the murderer Dread – although in the real world, not the virtual – is *Calliope Skouros*, an Australian homicide detective. In the course of investigating one of Dread's earliest killings, she begins to find out just what a strange and unpredictable killer he is. Although Dread – also known by his birth-name, John Wulgaru – is listed as dead in police records, Calliope begins to suspect that he is alive.

Dread is not only alive, but has returned to Sydney, setting up operations only miles from Detective Skouros. He has brought the American programmer *Dulcie Anwin* to Australia to help him make sense of the Otherland network, whose existence he discovered while eliminating one of Felix Jongleur's Grail Brotherhood rivals. Dulcie finds herself strangely attracted to Dread – she knows he is a criminal, but has no idea of his true proclivities – and Dread is more than willing to use that attraction for his own benefit. He has big plans for the network, and plans to use his experience there as a basis for overthrowing his employer, Jongleur. He sets Dulcie up in a loft and puts her to work.

In South Africa, Renie's father *Long Joseph Sulaweyo* and friend *Jeremiah Dako* have been guarding her and !Xabbu while they lie helpless in the V-tanks they have used for long-term access to the network. But Long

Joseph, cut off from drink, miserable, and distracted, left the abandoned army base to head for Durban and was kidnapped outside the hospital where his son Stephen lies comatose. The kidnapper turns out to be Renie's ex-boyfriend *Del Ray*, whose own life has been ruined by the help he gave Renie. He is desperate to find Renie so he can get a group of thugs (whom Dread hired on behalf of Jongleur) off his back. But when Joseph and Del Ray leave the hospital after going back to see Joseph's son, they are trailed by a mysterious black van. Then, when they return to the army base dug deep into one of the Drakensberg mountains, they find the thugs are there ahead of them. Joseph and Del Ray sneak into the base through the air duct Joseph used in his escape. Inside the base, Jeremiah has been contacted by Mr Sellars, who wants to help them, but things do not look good. All but weaponless themselves, they are now besieged by heavily-armed killers.

Shipwrecked Paul Jonas is bound for Troy, which means he is living out the *Odyssey* more or less backward. After getting help building a raft – and other sorts of solace – from a hospitable goddess, he puts to sea again. He survives the attack of the monster Scylla and the whirlpool Charybdis, then finds another survivor floating uncon-scious in the waves. The stranger turns out to be *Azador*, a mysterious Gypsy who had traveled earlier with Renie and !Xabbu and the strange girl *Emily* from the Oz simu-lation, and from whom Renie accidentally took the access device/lighter. Together, Paul and Azador defeat a danger-ous cyclops and land on the island of Lotos, where they fall under the spell of the narcotic flowers. The Angel wakens Paul and helps them escape, but only after a hallu-cinating Azador has told Paul that he too is being pursued by the Grail Brotherhood, that he has escaped from their immortality machines, but many of his Gypsy kin have not. Free of Lotos, they sail on to Troy.

In the House-world, Renie and her companions have had little luck finding the kidnapped Martine (who is being psychologically tortured by Dread) and have themselves been captured by one of the tribes who make the House's attic their home. To their surprise, they find *Hideki Kunohara* sharing the robbers' revelries. Kunohara, one of the landlords of the Grail network, whose own giant world of insects they had crossed earlier, seems bemused to see them, but intercedes for them with the robbers. Paul Jonas' Angel appears to them all in a supernatural fashion, frightening away the robbers and alarming even Kunohara, who refuses to help Renie and the others any more than he already has, saying that he cannot risk the displeasure of the powerful Grail Brotherhood.

Renie and her companions at last find Martine, but only after !Xabbu has disappeared while searching for her (his baboon sim a more useful form for exploring the rooftops of the House). But Martine is not alone: Dread has prepared a trap for them. When they open the door, he shoots T4b and Florimel, then battles with Renie across a steep rooftop. Just when it seems he has won, !Xabbu returns, and then Florimel finds one of Dread's discarded guns. As Dread prepares to kill Renie, Florimel shoots him. He dies – but only online, leaving the stolen virtual body behind. For the moment Dread has been pushed out of the Grail network, and Renie and her companions are battered but safe.

Ancient arch-mogul Felix Jongleur has been very busy preparing for the Ceremony – the moment at which the members of the Grail Brotherhood will become immortal within the virtual worlds they have built for themselves. He has not been spending much time in his favorite mythical-Egypt simulation, and does not realize how far out of hand things have become there. His servants Tefy and Mewat – the Egyptian versions of his subordinates *Finney* and *Mudd*, who have been chasing Paul Jonas all through the network – are now forced to besiege a temple full of people resisting their cruel reign.

Inside the besieged temple, Orlando Gardiner and Sam Fredericks meet other members of the Circle, including *Nandi Paradivash*, a specialist who is trying to make sense of the network's dying gateway system. There is something very wrong with the Grail network. Its mysterious operating system, the Other, is acting in a peculiar fashion, and many of the simworlds seem to be falling apart.

Tefy and Mewat attack the temple, first bringing in a trio of rogue Egyptian gods to fight with the temple's two sphinx-guardians, then sending in a horde of tortoise men and flying snakes to finish the job. Orlando fights bravely, but cannot keep Sam from being captured by Tefy and Mewat. The unpleasant pair have recognized the teenagers as real people from outside the network, and are about to take them away to be tortured when Jongleur himself returns in the form of Osiris, chief god of Egypt. In the chaos, Orlando and Fredericks escape through one of the gateways Nandi has opened, out of Egypt and into Troy, where they have been urged to go by another incarnation of Paul Jonas' Angel.

Paul has already made his way to Troy, where – as Odysseus – he fits right in with the Greeks besieging the city. But when he is sent to the tent where the hero Achilles and his friend Patroclus wait, unwilling to fight against the Trojans, he decides something about the two doesn't seem to fit the simulation. After much sparring, he reveals his true name to them. Achilles and Patroclus are in fact Orlando and Sam, who recognize the name 'Jonas' from something Sellars had told them. The meeting becomes a happy one, although Paul's spirits sag a little when he learns the two teenagers are in just as much trouble, and are just as lost, as he is.

Renie and the others use the lighter recaptured from Dread to leave the House and go to Troy. Unlike Orlando and Paul, when they enter the simulation they are assigned to the Trojan side in the besieged city, aware that their friends may be outside the gates, but with no way to recognize them. They are quickly sent on a deadly raid against the Greeks.

Paul Jonas has a dream in which the Angel appears to him again and tells him to go outside the camp. He meets Renie and the others. They talk for a long time, comparing stories, trying to make sense of what they have learned. Paul decides to bring them back to the Greek settlement in the guise of prisoners so they can be reunited with Orlando and Sam, but even as they reach the camp the Trojans launch a frightening attack.

Caught in the middle of a fierce battle, cut off from Orlando and Sam, they can only struggle to stay alive. In the meantime, Sam, in a misguided effort to keep up the morale of Achilles' despairing troop and buy the sick Orlando some time to get better, dresses herself in the famous armor of Achilles and, masquerading as their chieftain, leads Achilles' soldiers out to fight the Trojans. The masquerade is so successful that the Trojans are driven back toward the walls of Troy. Orlando wakes to find himself alone. When he realizes what has happened, he scavenges armor and weapons and sets out across the plain toward the city, despite his own fast-failing health, desperate to save his friend Sam. He discovers her about to be killed by the Trojan hero Hector, and only barely manages to overcome him, then collapses in front of the walls.

Martine, who has been given a role as one of the Trojan royal family, is desperate to keep her friends alive. Hearing of the fighting in front of the walls, she nearly tricks some Trojan guards into opening the gates, but when they balk, she is forced to order T4b to kill the guard captain. The gates are opened, and to Martine's shame the Greeks come roaring into Troy, burning, raping, and killing. Although she and the others are all reunited, and even though the Trojans being killed are merely programs, she feels she has done a terrible thing.

Meanwhile, the Grail Brotherhood have begun their Ceremony, although Jongleur is irritated by the absence of his employee, Dread. Jongleur and technocrat *Robert Wells* explain to the concerned Grail members that they will not truly transfer their minds directly to the network. Instead, duplicate versions of themselves, virtual minds which have been made to copy every detail in the original minds, will come to life online – but in order to assure that only one version of each Brotherhood member exists, they must kill off their physical bodies. Because they are not aware that Jongleur, Wells, the financier *Jiun Bhao*, and American military man *Daniel Yacoubian* are not actually going through with the Ceremony this time – because they want to see how well the process works, these four will only pretend to awaken their virtual bodies and murder their real physical selves – the other members of the Brotherhood are at last convinced.

But Dread has other plans for the Grail network. He has decided to force his way back into the network, and with the help of Dulcie Anwin and a copy he has made of the access device/lighter, he tries to enter the system. He is resisted with terrible force by the security systems of the Other, but in the course of their battle – Dread employing his own telekinetic talent, which he calls his 'twist' – Dread discovers that the network has mechanisms to inflict something like pain on the Other, mechanisms which the Grail Brotherhood has used to force the intelligent operating system to do their will. Dread uses this pain to bludgeon the Other into retreat. Victorious, Dread can now influence and even direct the entire Grail network.

Renie, Paul, !Xabbu, and the others fight their way across the dying city. When Paul meets Emily, a longtime companion of Renie and the others, he is stunned to recognize her as another version of the Angel. A name suddenly comes back to him – 'Avialle' – and he is over-whelmed by returning memories.

Suddenly he can remember being hired by Felix Jongleur to work as a tutor in Jongleur's huge office-tower home in Louisiana. And he also recalls his first meeting with his pupil – Jongleur's daughter, Avialle Jongleur. But he can remember no more.

Despite apparently being followed by someone, they enter an abandoned temple and make their way to an altar at the center of a maze, where the Angel appears to them again and tells them they are too late – that she no longer has the strength to take them to where the Other wishes them to go. Paul offers her anything she needs, but does not expect what happens next. The Angel takes the life-force from Emily, who was only some kind of copy of herself, and then opens a gateway. When they go through, Paul and Renie and the others find themselves on a trail on the side of a bizarre and not-quite-real black mountain. They trek to the top, where they find a bound giant lying in a wide valley. The giant is in terrible pain, but is singing a song about an angel. Martine recognizes the song. It was sung to her by the mysterious child in the Pestalozzi Institute, thirty years before, on the day she lost her sight.

The suffering giant does not harm them, but opens a window through which Paul and Renie and the others can see the virtual Egyptian temple where Jongleur and the rest of the Brotherhood are beginning the Ceremony. Some Brotherhood members are still reluctant, but one of their number, a man named Ricardo Klement, undergoes the process and seems to be born satisfactorily into his new, young, virtual body. The others gleefully perform the Ceremony to kill off their physical bodies and resurrect themselves online, but although their physical selves do die, the virtual bodies remain uninhabited. Jongleur and the rest are spared because they have not undergone the Ceremony, but they are stunned and terrified. Something has gone very wrong.

Orlando, whose own physical body is also dying, can watch no more. He steps through the window and into the temple, where he confronts Jongleur and the other three Grail survivors. Sam and Renie follow to try to save him, and Renie tries to bluff Jongleur with the lighter that Yacoubian recognizes as his own stolen access device, which he has since replaced. Yacoubian, in Egyptian god-form, attacks Orlando.

The Grail system, already under a strain, now seems to begin to fall apart. The temple in Egypt and the top of the black mountain begin to merge. Simultaneously, the giant begins to writhe and bellow in pain – it is being attacked by something. A moment later, in the middle of all this chaos, it becomes clear that the attacker is Dread, who is trying to take control of the system from the Other.

Paul's Angel appears, weeping, as reality breaks down altogether. With the help of T4b, Orlando appears to kill the monstrous Yacoubian, but Orlando himself has used up his strength, and is smashed beneath Yacoubian's giant form when he falls.

The hand of the giant rises and then falls down on top of Renie, !Xabbu, Sam, Orlando, and others. They disappear. Then the reality of the top of the black mountain turns inside out again. Martine, sensitive to the network in ways the others can't quite understand, screams that the children are in pain, dying. Paul is overcome and blacks out.

Afterward, Renie wakes up to discover that she no longer wears the sim she had chosen, but seems to be in her own body again. !Xabbu has also shed his baboon form for his own real shape, as has young, female Sam Fredericks, who no longer appears to be a man. But they are not back in the real world. They are still stuck on the now-empty black mountaintop. The suffering giant has vanished. All their other companions are gone. Only Orlando Gardiner's dead body, still wearing the Achilles sim, remains.

But others are on the mountain, even if their friends are not. Felix Jongleur appears, wearing the body of a middle-aged man, accompanied by Ricardo Klement, who, although he has survived the Ceremony, appears to be brain damaged. After Dread's conquest of the operating system, Jongleur too is trapped in the network. He acknowledges that Renie and her friends have every reason to want to attack him, but suggests that they are better off making common cause. He leads them to the edge of the black mountain and points down.

They are miles high, in the middle of nothing. They cannot see the bottom of the mountain, or any ground at all, because everything below them is hidden in a strange, silver cloud. This is no part of the network he created, Jongleur assures them.

OTHERLAND

VOLUME FOUR

Sea of Silver Light

Contents

Third

THE DYING HOUR

Fourth

SORROW'S CHILDREN

Fifth

INHERITORS

Foreword

HE was tossed, fragmented, part of the outward-collapsing whirl of shattered light. His own identity was gone – he was spun into pieces like a universe being born.

'You're killing him!' his angel had cried as she herself flew apart into a million separate ghosts, each one shimmering with its own individual light – a shrieking flock of tiny rainbows . . .

But as the world collapsed, a piece of his past returned to him. It came first as a single visionary flash – a house surrounded by gardens, the gardens themselves bounded by a wild forest. The sky was patchy with dark clouds, brilliant streaks of sunshine falling between them, the grass and leaves beaded with the recent rain. Light dazzled in the drops of water and fragmented into gleams of many colors so that the trees seemed part of a fairy-garden, a magical wood from a childhood tale. During that fraction of an instant before the memory grew wider and deeper he could imagine no more peaceful a haven.

But it was all, of course, far stranger than that.

THE elevator was so swift and smooth that at times Paul

Jonas could almost forget that he lived inside a great spike, that his journey to the top each morning lifted him close to a thousand feet above the Mississippi Delta. He had never much cared for tall buildings – one of the many ways he felt himself slightly out of step with his own century. Part of the appeal of the Canonbury house had been the old-fashioned scale of it – three stories, a few flights of stairs. It was a place he could actually escape from if there was a fire (or so he flattered himself). When he opened the windows of his flat and looked down into the street he could hear people talking and even see what they had in their shopping baskets. Now, except for the winds of the Gulf's hurricane season whose screaming voices could be heard even through thick fibramic, winds strong enough to make the huge tower rock gently, he might as well be living in some kind of intergalactic spaceship. At least until he reached the part of the building where he did his tutoring each day.

The elevator door glided open, revealing another portal. Paul keyed in his code and pressed his hand against the palm-reader, then waited for long seconds while the reader and other less obvious safeguards did their job. When the security door slid out of the way with a little suck of air, Paul stepped through and pushed open the secondary door, this one on metal hinges and of decidedly old-fashioned design. The smell of Ava's house washed over him, a combination of scents so evocative of another era as to be almost claustrophobic – lavender, silver polish, sheets kept in cedar chests. As he stepped into the foyer he moved in a few strides from the smooth, edgeless efficiency of the present into something that, were it not for the vibrant young woman at the heart of it, could be a museum or even a tomb.

She was not waiting for him in the parlor. Her absence

startled him, an unexpected thing that made the whole strange ritual suddenly seem as mad as he had thought it to be in his first weeks on the job. He checked the glass and ormolu clock on the mantelpiece. A minute after nine, but no Ava. He wondered if she might be ill, and was surprised by the stab of worry that came with the thought.

One of the downstairs maids, capped and aproned in white, silent as a ghost, slid past the hall doorway with her arms full of folded tablecloth.

'Excuse me,' he called. 'Is Miss Jongleur still in bed? She's late for her lessons.'

The maid looked at him, startled, as though merely by speaking he had broken some ancient tradition. She shook her head before disappearing.

After half a year, Paul still had no idea whether the household help were trained actors or simply very strange.

He knocked at her bedroom door, then knocked again, louder. When no one answered, he cautiously pushed open the unlatched door. The room, half-boudoir, half-nursery, was empty. A row of porcelain-faced dolls stared at him dumbly from the mantelpiece, glassy eyes wide beneath the long lashes.

On his way back across the parlor he caught a glimpse of himself in the framed mirror above the mantel: an unexceptional man dressed in clothes far more than a century out of date, in the middle of an over-ornamented parlor room that might have come straight out of a Tenniel illustration. Something only a hair more subtle than a shudder passed through him. For just a moment, but in a most unsettling way, he felt that he was trapped in someone else's dream.

It was bizarre, of course, even a little frightening, but he still could never quite get over how much cleverness had

gone into it. From the house's front door his view across
the formal garden and its maze of paths, past the hedges
and over the woods beyond, was exactly what he would
have expected to see surrounding the country house of a
reasonably well-to-do French family of the late nineteenth
century. The fact that the sky overhead was not real, that
rains and morning mists came from a sophisticated sprin-
kler system, that the shifting of daylight into evening or
the Bo Peep wandering of clouds were created by lighting and holographic illusion, almost added to the charm.
But the idea that this entire house and grounds had been
built on the top floor of a skyscraper largely for one
person, a sealed time capsule in which the past was simulated if not actually returned, was more disturbing.

It's like something from a story, he thought – and not
for the first time, by any means. *The way they keep her
up here. Like the giant's wife in that beanstalk story, or
. . . who was the princess with the hair? Rapunzel?*

He spent a short while exploring the garden, whose
formal, old-fashioned French design was softened by what
he could only think of as that woody, overgrown English
influence that was almost indistinguishable from neglect.
There were several places where the high hedges hid
benches, and Ava had told him that sometimes she liked
to bring her sewing out and work on it while she listened
to the birds sing.

At least the birds are real, he thought as he watched
a few of them flitting from branch to branch above his
head.

The winding paths were all empty. Paul was beginning
to feel a quiet rising of panic, despite all good sense. If
there was ever anyone less likely to stumble into danger
than Avialle Jongleur, it was hard to imagine: she was
watched by the most sophisticated surveillance equipment

available and surrounded by her father's private army. But she had never simply missed a morning's session, never even been late. Her time with Paul seemed to be the highlight of her day, although he didn't flatter himself that it was due to any overwhelming qualities of his own. The poor child had precious few chances to see other human beings.

He turned off the gravel-strewn paths onto the narrow track that led into the overgrown orchard Ava called 'the wood.' Here the ground became as uneven as real terrain, and the plums and crab apples that ringed the garden gave way to stands of silver birch and an increasing tangle of oaks and alders, which were thick enough to hide the house when he looked back and provide at least the illusion of privacy, although Paul knew from one of Finney's very pointed lectures that the surveillance extended everywhere. Still, he could not help feeling he had crossed over some invisible line: this far from the house the trees shouldered together closely and the false sky could only be seen through chinks in the foliage far above. Even the birds kept to the highest branches. The spot seemed strangely isolated. Paul found it hard to keep his earlier folktale impressions out of his head.

He found her sitting on the grass beside the stream. She looked up at his approach, smiling her secretive smile, but said nothing.

'Ava? Are you all right?'

She nodded. 'Come here. I want to show you something.'

'It's time for your lessons. I worried when you weren't waiting for me at the house.'

'That was very kind of you, Mr Jonas. Please, come here.' She patted the grass beside her. He saw that she was at the center of a wide ring of mushrooms – a fairy

ring, as his Grammer Jonas had called them – and the
sense of being in some sort of unfolding tale crept over
him again. Ava's eyes were wide and full of . . . something. Excitement? Anticipation?

'You'll get your dress wet, sitting on the grass,' he said
as he reluctantly moved forward.

'The trees kept the rain off. It's quite dry here.' She
pulled her hem aside and tucked it beneath her leg, making
a space for him to sit, and accidentally – or was it? –
revealing a bit of the petticoat beneath, as well as a pale
gleam of ankle above her shoe. He found himself struggling not to react. He had discovered the first day of
lessons that Ava was a flirt, although it was hard to tell
how much was genuine and how much was simply her
anachronistic manners, which dictated perfect decorum
on the surface, but by doing so made every exchange
even more loaded. A female friend of his back in London
had once spent a drunken evening telling him why
Regency novels were so much sexier than anything written in the less-inhibited centuries since: 'It's all about the
tight focus,' she had insisted.

Paul was beginning to agree with her.

Seeing his discomfiture, Ava grinned broadly, an
expression of unmeasured enjoyment which reminded Paul
again that she was little more than a child, and which
paradoxically made him even more uncomfortable. 'We
really should be getting back,' he began. 'If I had known
you wanted your lessons outside today, I would have
prepared . . .'

'All is well.' She patted his knee. 'It is a surprise.'

Paul shook his head. She clearly had something
planned, but he was angry with himself for losing control
of the situation. It would have been difficult enough, being
private tutor to an attractive, lonely, and very young

woman, but in the bizarre circumstances of the Jongleur fortress the whole thing became even more of a strain. 'This isn't appropriate, Ava. Someone will see us . . .'

'No one will see. No one.'

'That's not true.' Paul wasn't sure how much she knew about the surveillance. 'In any case, we have work to do today . . .'

'No one will see us,' she said again, this time with surprising firmness. She lifted a finger to her lips, smiled, then touched her ear. 'And no one will hear us, either. You see, Mr Jonas, I have a . . . friend.'

'Ava, I hope we are friends, but that's not . . .'

She giggled. The waves of black hair, confined today by pins and a straw hat, framed her amused expression. 'Dear, dear Mr Jonas – I'm not talking about you.'

Puzzled, more worried than ever, Paul stood. He extended a hand for Ava. 'Come with me. We can talk about this later, but we must get back to the house.' When she did not accept his help, he shook his head and turned to leave.

'No!' she cried. 'Don't step out of the circle!'

'What are you talking about?'

'The circle – the ring. Don't step out. My friend won't be able to protect us.'

'What are you talking about, Ava? Are you talking about fairies? Protect us how?'

She pouted, but it was reflexive. Paul thought he saw a real concern there as well – something almost like fear. 'Sit down, Mr Jonas. I will tell you everything, but please don't step outside the ring. As long as you stay here with me, we are both safe from prying eyes and listening ears.'

Overwhelmed, and with the distinct impression that things were going in a very bad direction, Paul never-theless sat back down. Ava's relief was obvious.

'Good. Thank you.'

'Just tell me what's going on.'

She picked at a dandelion. 'I know my father watches me. That he can see me even when I do not know he's there.' She looked up at him. 'It's been true all my life. And the world I read about in books – I know I will never see it, not if he has his way.'

Paul squirmed. He had only recently begun to realize that he himself was more of a jailer than a teacher.

'Even in the harems of the Middle East, the women have each other for company,' she went on. 'But who do I have? A tutor – although I am very fond of you, Mr Jonas, and my other tutors and nannies were also kind – and a doctor, a most dry and unpleasant old fellow. Not to mention maids who are almost too frightened even to speak to me. And those abhorrent men who work for my father.'

Paul's discomfort was rising again. What would Finney or the brutal Mudd think of him sitting here listening to Jongleur's daughter talking this way? 'The fact is,' he said as calmly as he could, 'people do watch you, Ava. Listen to you. And they're doing it right now . . .'

'No, they are not.' Her tight smile was defiant. 'Not now. Because at last I have a friend – a friend who can do things.'

'What are you talking about?'

'You will think me mad,' she said, 'but it's true. It's all true!'

'What is?'

'My friend.' She suddenly fell silent and could not meet his eye. When she did, something strange smoldered there. 'He is a ghost.'

'A what? Ava, that's impossible.'

Tears bloomed. 'I thought you of all people would hear me out.' She turned away.

'I'm sorry, Ava.' He reached out and touched her shoulder, only inches from her smooth, soft neck and the straggling dark curls where her hair had pulled free of the pins. The gurgling of the stream seemed quite loud. He jerked his hand back. 'Look, please tell me what's going on. I can't promise I'll believe in ghosts, but just tell me, will you?'

Still with her face turned from him, her voice very low, she said, 'I didn't believe it myself. Not at first. I thought it was one of Nickelplate's little tricks.'

'Nickelplate?'

'Finney. It's my name for him. Those glasses, the way they gleam – and haven't you heard him when he walks? His pockets are full of something metal. He jingles.' She scowled. 'I call the fat one Butter-ball. They are monstrous, both of them. I hate them.'

Paul closed his eyes. If she was wrong about being overheard, as he felt sure she must be if she thought her protection came from a ghost, then it wouldn't be long before he would be hearing this conversation replayed, probably as part of his exit interview.

I wonder if I'll get severance . . .

'The voice whispered in my ear,' Ava was saying. 'At night, while I lay in bed. As I said, I thought it was one of their tricks and I did not reply. Not at first.'

'You heard a voice in your sleep . . . ?'

'It was not a dream, Mr Jonas. Dear Paul.' She smiled shyly. 'I am not so foolish. It spoke to me very softly, but I was quite awake. I pinched myself to make sure!' She held up her pale forearm to show him where she had done it. 'But I thought it a trick. My father's employees are always saying vile things to me. If he knew, he would surely have them discharged, wouldn't he?' She almost seemed to be pleading. 'But I never tell him, because I am afraid he would not believe me – would think it merely girlish spite. Then they would make it even more difficult for me, perhaps discharge you and bring in some horrible old woman or cruel old man to be my tutor, who knows?' She scowled. 'That fat one, Mudd, he told me once that he would love to get me into the Yellow Room one day.' She shivered. 'I do not even know what that is, but it sounds dreadful. Do you know?'

Paul shrugged uncomfortably. 'Can't say that I do. But what are you telling me? A voice spoke to you? And said that we're safe to speak here?'

'He is a lonely ghost, if that's what he is – a little boy, I think, perhaps a foreigner. He speaks that way, very seriously, very strangely. He told me he had been watching me and he was sorry I was so lonely. He said he wanted to be my friend.' She shook her head in slow wonder. 'It was so odd! It was more than just a voice – it was as though he stood right by me! But although it was dark, there was enough light to see the room was empty.'

Paul was more than ever convinced that something was gravely wrong, but had not the slightest idea of what to do about it. 'I know you don't think it was a dream, Ava, but . . . but it must have been. I just can't believe in ghosts.'

'He hid me. He told me to go out for a walk in the evening, and that he would show me how he could keep me safe from being found. And he did! I went for a walk here in the wood and soon there were maids all over the garden and tramping through the trees. Even Finney came and joined in the search – he was very angry when they finally discovered me sitting on a stone doing my sewing. "I frequently go for walks in the late afternoon, Mr Finney," I told him. "Why are you so upset?" He could not admit that whatever methods they used for spying on me had failed, of course – he merely made an excuse, something urgent that he needed to speak to me about, but it was transparently a ruse.'

'But is that enough . . . ?' Paul began.

'And last night my friend showed me the rooms where you live,' she said hurriedly. 'I know, it is a most terrible incursion on your privacy. I apologize. They are much less grand than I had suspected, I must say. And your furniture is all very smooth and plain – nothing like what I have in my house at all.'

'What do you mean, showed you?'

'The mirror through which my father speaks to me, when he bothers to do so – it has never been of any other use, but last night my friend used it to show me *you*, dear Mr Jonas.' She gave him a girlishly wicked little flash of her teeth. 'I am grateful, for my modesty and yours, that you were fully dressed the entire time.'

'You saw *me*?' Paul was dumbfounded. She had stumbled on some way to use the one-way wallscreen in her study to connect to the general house surveillance.

'You were watching something on the wall – a moving picture of your own. It had animals in it. You were wearing a gray robe. Drinking a glass of something – wine, perhaps?'

Paul had a dim recollection of having half-watched some kind of nature documentary. The other details were correct, too. His earlier worry was growing into something far larger and more frightening. Had someone hacked into the house system? Could it be some elaborate precursor to a kidnapping attempt? 'This . . . this friend of yours . . . Did he tell you his name? Did he tell you what . . . what he wanted?'

'He has told me no name. I am not sure he remembers his name, if he had one.' Her face grew solemn. 'He is so lonely, Paul. So lonely!'

He was dimly aware that she was using his first name now, that some crucial barrier had been breached between them, but at this moment it seemed the smallest of his worries. 'I don't like it, Ava.' Another thought occurred to him. 'You talk to your father? In the mirror?'

She nodded slowly, her eyes now focused on the slow-swaying branches high above. 'He is such a busy man. He always says he wishes he could come to see me, it is only that there are so many demands on his time.' She tried to smile. 'But he speaks to me often. I'm sure that if he knew how his employees treat me, he really would be quite angry.'

Paul sat back, trying to make sense of it all. He himself had only once had a face-to-face interview with Jongleur – or face-to-screen, to be more accurate – and had felt fairly sure that the dapper, sixtyish man who had quizzed him sharply about his daughter's habits and behavior was not a true image: no anti-aging technology in the world could make more than a century and a half look like that. Still, it was one thing for the man to keep up a facade for employees – but his own daughter?

'Has he ever come to see you? Ever? In person?'

She shook her head, still staring at the light bleeding through the leaves.

This is too bizarre. Ghosts. A father who only appears in a mirror. What in the bloody hell am I doing in a madhouse like this?

'We have to get back,' he said aloud. 'I don't care if anyone can see us or not – it's too long for us to be missing, out of the house.'

'Whatever they use to spy on us,' she said blithely, 'they will only see us having a lesson here outside, you reading and me making notes.' She grinned. 'My friend promised me.'

'Even so.' He stood up. 'This is all a bit too strange for me, Ava.'

'But I want to talk to you,' she said, her wide-eyed face suddenly anxious again. 'Truly talk. Don't leave, Paul! I . . . I am lonely, too.'

Her hand, he suddenly realized, was gripping his. Helplessly, he allowed himself to be tugged back into a sitting position once more. 'Talk about what, Ava? I know you're lonely – I know this is a terrible life for you, in some ways. But there's nothing I can do. I'm just an employee myself, and your father is a very powerful man.' But was it true, he wondered? Were there not laws of some kind? Even a rich man's child had rights – was there not some parental responsibility to allow one's offspring to live in the century into which she had been born? It was hard to think: the noise of the stream was so insistent, the light beneath the trees so oddly diffuse, as though he labored under some kind of supernatural glamour.

What should I do? Quit and file a lawsuit? Take it to UN Human Rights? Wasn't Finney pretty much warning me about that when he hired me? A sudden thought, like a splash of icy water – *What really happened to the last tutor? They were displeased with her, they said. Very displeased.*

The grip of Avialle Jongleur's pale fingers had not diminished. When his eyes met hers, he saw for the first time the true desperation, almost madness, under the girlish flightiness.

'I need you, Paul. I have no one – no one real.'

'Ava, I . . .'

'I love you, Paul. I have loved you since you first came to my house. Now we are truly alone and I can tell you. Can't you love me, too?'

'Jesus.' He pulled away, shocked and almost ill with

sadness. She was crying, but her face held both misery and something harder and sharper, something as fierce as anger. 'Ava, don't be silly. I can't . . . we can't. You're my pupil. You're still a child!'

He turned to go. Even in his confusion he found himself stepping carefully over the ring of white, fleshy mushrooms.

'A child!' she said. 'A child could not hurt for you the way I do – ache for you.'

Paul hesitated, compassion battling with quiet terror. 'You don't know what you're saying, Ava. You've met almost no one. You've had nothing to read but old books. It's understandable . . . but it just can't be.'

'Don't go.' Her voice rose to a raw pitch. 'You must stay here!'

Feeling like nothing less than a traitor, he turned and walked away.

'I am not a child!' she shouted from inside the magic circle. 'How can I be a child, when I have already had a child of my own . . . ?'

THE long skein of memory abruptly tore and was gone. Ravaged, feeling a regret so fierce it was almost physical pain, Paul fell from the recovered past into the darkly fractured now.

THE first thing he realized as he sat up, heart pounding, was that he could still hear rushing water, even though the echo of Ava's last bizarre pronouncement was completely gone. The second realization, which followed a split-instant later, was that he was sitting on the ground at the foot of an immense, impossibly huge tree.

'Oh, God!' he groaned, and for a moment hid his face in his hands, fighting the urge to weep. When he pulled his hands away the tree was still there. 'Oh, God, not again!'

The rough cylinder that rose beside him was as wide as an office tower, the gray bark stretching up what must have been hundreds of meters in the air before the first branches spread out from the central column. But there was something odd about the spectacle that only the massive disorientation of waking from the memory-dream had prevented him realizing immediately.

There was not one gigantic tree as in his first battle-field hallucination, a single magical pillar stretching up to the clouds: there were hundreds, all around him.

Blinking, he stood up, slipping a little on the loose ground.

It's real, he thought. *It's all real – or at least it's no dream this time.* He turned slowly, taking in the details he had not been able to absorb upon opening his eyes. It was not just the trees that were titanic. From where he stood, perched on a raised mountain of leaf fragments and loose soil, he could see that everything around him was immense – even the blades of grass were ten meters high, bellying in the breeze like narrow green sails. Farther away, through a stand of swaying flowers each as large as the rose window of a cathedral, lay an expanse of green water, the source of the pervasive rushing noise – water wide as an ocean, but rippling around huge sticks and house-size stones in a way that told him it was actually a river.

I've shrunk. What in the bloody hell is going on? He struggled for a moment, trying to regain some of the perspective lost by the surge of returning memory. *Before what happened that day in the fairy ring came back to me, where was I?*

On the mountaintop. With Renie and Orlando and all

*the rest. And with God, or the Other, or whatever that
was. Then the angel came – the other Ava came – and
. . . and what?* He shook his head. *Who's doing these
things to me? What did I do to deserve this?*

He looked around for his companions, wondering if
any of them had wound up in this place with him, but
other than the mighty river, nothing stirred unless the
wind moved it. He was alone among the oversized stones
and trees.

*This must be the bugworld place Renie and the others
told me about.* His attention was suddenly drawn to a
round rock only a few paces away, a near-spherical pebble
about his own size, half-buried in the mulchy slope. He
had glanced at it briefly in his first inspection . . . but
now it was uncurling.

Startled, Paul scrambled a few steps up the slippery
hill, back toward the trunk of the gigantic tree, but when
he recognized the unfolding shape, a gray-brown shell in
close-fitting segments, he felt a little better.

It's just a wood louse. A pillbug, as some called them
– harmless, inoffensive. Though relieved, he was still
uncomfortable seeing something usually found huddled in
a pea-size ball under a plant pot now swollen to his own
dimensions. A moment later, as the unfolded wood louse
rolled over onto its belly and its dozens of legs stretched
out to steady it on the uneven ground, he saw that the
limbs were all different lengths, and that many of them
ended in awkward hands with stumpy, disturbingly manlike
fingers.

A chill ran through him as the creature reared up.
Worse than the fingered hands was the front of the
thing's head, a dim parody of a human face, as though
parts not meant to serve such purposes had been crushed
together into a mask – a brow-ridge above a dark, eyeless

flatness on either side of the hint of a nose, a raggedly gaping mouth framed by tiny, atrophied mandibles.

Paul stumbled back as the thing lurched toward him, its strange arms reaching out like a crippled beggar's. So strongly did its pathetic, misformed face and halting gait speak of supplication that when it moaned '*Fooood!*' at him in a voice clearly not designed for human speech, he began to raise his hands in the same show of helplessness he had guiltily displayed to the itinerants of Upper Street back in London. Then a half dozen more of the creatures came rustling and squirming up out of the mulch, pushing their way to the surface to join the first in its pursuit, all crying, '*Food! Foooood!*' and Paul Jonas realized that the first mutation had not been begging, but ringing the family dinner bell.

First:

A VOYAGE IN
THE HEART

'Wynken, Blynken, and Nod one night
Sailed off in a wooden shoe —
Sailed on a river of crystal light
Into a sea of dew.'
— Eugene Field, 1850–1895

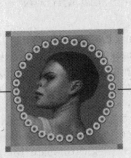

CHAPTER 1

Strange Bedfellows

NETFEED/NEWS: Little League Hostages Freed – Angry Father Killed (visual: body of Wilkes beside camper van)
VO: Gerald Ray Wilkes, like many Little League parents, thought his son's team was victimized by a bad call. Unlike most of them, though, Wilkes decided to take drastic action. After beating the unpaid umpire unconscious, he forced the opposing team of eleven- and twelve-year-olds into his van at gunpoint, then led authorities on a two-state chase. He was eventually stopped by a roadblock outside Tompkinsville, Kentucky, where he was shot when he refused to surrender . . .

RENIE dodged Sam's first blow and ducked the second almost as easily, but the third bounced hard off the side of her head. Renie cursed and leaned away. Sam was crying and swinging blindly, but Renie didn't want to take any chances – if the sim body was a fair representation of her real self, Sam Fredericks was a strong, athletic girl. Renie grabbed her around the waist and threw her to the strangely soapy ground, then struggled to secure the girl's arms in a clinch. She failed, and was slapped on the side of the head again. Renie was having trouble keeping her own anger in check.

'Damn it, Sam, stop! That's enough!'

She finally managed to grab one of the girl's arms and used the leverage to shove Sam's head down against the ground, then climbed atop her and pulled her other arm up behind her back. For a moment the girl bucked, trying to throw her off, then her limbs went slack and her weeping took on a deeper, more heartbroken sound.

Renie kept her weight on Sam for almost a minute, until she felt the girl's convulsive sobbing begin to gentle. Hoping the worst was over, she took the risk of letting go one of the girl's arms so she could rub the spot where Sam had hit her. Her jaw clicked as she worked it. 'Jesus Mercy, girl, I think you broke my face.'

Sam twisted her head back to look at Renie, eyes wide. 'Oh my God, I'm so sorry!' She burst into tears again.

Renie stood up. The skimpy strips of cloth she wore had nearly been pulled off her body in the struggle, as had Sam's, and both of them were streaked with pseudo-dirt. *Some people would pay a lot to see this kind of thing*, Renie thought sourly. *Back at Mister J's, they'd put a lot of good coding into this effect – half-naked women wrestling in the dirt.* 'Get up, girl,' she said aloud. 'We're supposed to be looking for rocks, remember?'

Sam rolled over and stared up at the odd gray sky, face wet, eyes desolate. 'I won't do it, Renie! I *can't* do it – even if you break both my arms. He's a murderer. He killed Orlando!'

Renie silently counted to ten before speaking. 'Look, Sam, I let you scream at me – I even let you hit me and I didn't smack you back, no matter how much I wanted to. Do you think this feels good?' She touched her tender jaw. 'It's been difficult for all of us. But we're going with that nasty old man because we have to – and I'm not going to leave you here. End of discussion. Now, are you going to make me tie you up and carry you all the way down this damned mountain, tired as I am?' Suddenly realizing that she was indeed exhausted, she slumped down next to the girl. 'Are you really going to do that to me?'

Sam looked at her solemnly, struggling for self-control. Her breath hitched; she waited until she could speak. 'I'm sorry, Renie. But how can we go anywhere with . . . with . . . ?'

'I know. I hate the bastard – I'd like to throw him off the mountain myself. But we're going to have to live with Felix Jongleur until we get some answers to what's going on. What's that old saying about keeping your friends close and your enemies closer?' Renie squeezed the girl's arm. 'This is a war, Sam. Not just a single battle. Putting up with that terrible man . . . well, it's like being a spy behind foreign lines or something. We have to do it because we have a bigger purpose.'

Sam looked down, unable to hold Renie's gaze. 'Chizz,' she said after long moments, but she sounded like death. 'I'll try. But I'm not going to talk to him.'

'Fine.' Renie clambered to her feet. 'Come on. I didn't just bring you out here to talk to you alone. We still have to . . .' She broke off as a shape moved slowly around one of the broken spikes of stone which were the primary features of the barren landscape. The handsome young man who stood there said nothing, but only stared back, empty-eyed as a goldfish in a bowl.

'What the hell do you want?' Renie asked him.

The dark-haired man did not answer for a moment. 'I . . . am Ricardo Klement,' he said at last.

'We know.' Just because he was brain-damaged didn't mean he had earned any of Renie's sympathy. Before the Ceremony went awry, he had been another one of the

Grail murderers, just like Jongleur. 'Go away. Leave us alone.'

Klement blinked slowly. 'It is good . . . to be alive.' After another pause he turned and disappeared among the rocks.

'This is so utterly horrible,' Sam said weakly. 'I . . . I don't want to be here anymore, Renie.'

'Neither do I.' Renie patted her shoulder. 'That's why we have to keep going, find our way home. No matter how much we want to give up.' She grabbed Sam's arm and squeezed again, trying to make her hear, force her to understand. 'No matter how much. Now come on, girl, get on your feet – let's go find some more rocks.'

!Xabbu was using the stones they had already gathered to construct a wall around Orlando's naked sim, something that looked more like a lidless coffin than a cairn. The pseudo-stones, like the rest of the environment on the black mountain, were slowly changing: with every hour that passed they looked less like the thing they were supposed to be, more like a sort of cursory 3D sketch. Orlando's Achilles sim, though, had retained its almost supernatural realism: lying in the improvised tomb, he did indeed look like a fallen demigod.

Confronted with her friend's empty shell, Sam was crying again. 'He *is* dead, isn't he? I keep wanting it not to be true, but that's probably how everyone feels, right?'

Renie recalled the achingly bleak months after her mother's death. 'Yes, it is. You'll be seeing him, hearing him, only he won't be there. But it gets better after a while.'

'It'll never get better. Never.' Sam leaned down to touch Orlando's stony cheek. 'But he is dead, isn't he? Really, really dead.'

Renie was finding it almost as difficult as Sam to contemplate leaving behind a body that still looked so full of life. There had been other strange signs too. Unlike all the other sims she had seen whose living owners had died, Orlando's garments had remained soft and supple despite the marble-like solidity of the body beneath. This strange state of affairs had even made Renie wonder for a while if he might not still be living, just lost somehow in his own deep coma back in real life, but numerous surreptitious experiments – performed when Sam was otherwise distracted so as not to raise her hopes – had made Renie as certain as she could ever be in this strange place that there was no animation left in that petrified form.

Orlando's last gift to them had allowed Renie and Sam to salvage enough cloth to make crude garments, which helped Renie feel a little less vulnerable in the presence of the cold-eyed Jongleur and the vacantly childish Klement. In turning over Orlando's stiffened sim to untangle the remains of his tattered chiton, they had even found his broken sword, the hilt still bearing a few inches of blade, which had made it much easier to turn the dirty white fabric into loincloths and crude bandeau tops.

The damaged sword was the only weapon among the mountaintop survivors, perhaps the only weapon in this entire simworld, and obviously far too valuable a tool to leave behind. Renie would have preferred to carry it herself, trusting her own wariness to keep it from falling into Jongleur's hands, but Sam had been so pathetically grateful to have some keepsake from Orlando that Renie had not had the heart to argue very much; Sam now wore it thrust through the waist of her loincloth. With only a bit more than a hand's breadth of blade left, it would not make much of a weapon, although it had given Renie a

nasty scratch on her leg while she and Sam had been
wrestling. Still, she had to admit that in such spare circumstances the shattered blade had the look of a legendary
object.

Renie shook her head, irritated at herself for getting
mystical. Undecaying body or not, their friend was still
dead. Orlando's sword might once have been the scourge
of an imaginary gaming world, but now it would be
used for digging or for sawing wood . . . if they ever
found any. As for the miraculous cloth, it had been
turned into a pair of primitive bikinis from a bad cave-
man flick. (!Xabbu had refused to take any of the tiny
amount of fabric to clothe his own nakedness, and when
Renie had offered some to Jongleur, more to protect her
and Sam's own sensibilities than as a kindness, he had
only laughed.)

So we'll head down the mountain this way, she thought.
*Three naked men and two women looking like something
out of a Neandertal lingerie advertisement. And for all we
know, we're the only people left alive in this whole virtual
universe . . . except for Dread. Oh, yes, we're in great
shape . . .*

!Xabbu took the new stones they had collected, but he
seemed distracted. Before asking him why, Renie made
sure Jongleur was out of earshot. The master of the Grail
Brotherhood stood some distance away, staring out into
the weirdly depthless sky from the rim of the cliff. Renie
couldn't help wondering again what it would feel like to
shove him over the edge.

'You look worried,' she told !Xabbu as he shored up
the walls around Orlando's body. 'How are we supposed
to cover the top of this, by the way?'

'I am worried because I do not think we have time to
do that. I think we must leave Orlando's grave this way

and begin our journey soon. I am sorry – I wanted to do better.'

'What are you talking about?'

'We have all seen what has happened to this place just since we have been here – how things are losing their edges, their color. While I was out looking for more stones, I discovered something that worried me. The trail is losing truth, too.'

She shook her head, confused. 'What do you mean?'

'Maybe I have used the wrong word. I am talking of the trail which we climbed to come here, with Martine and Paul Jonas and the others, before everything became so strange – the trail along the mountainside. It is changing as everything else here is changing, Renie, but there was not much . . . what is the word? There was not much truth, much . . . reality to it in the first place. Already it looks old and blurry.'

Despite the permanent room-temperature ambience, Renie felt a chill. Without that path they would be trapped on top of a miles-high mountain that was rapidly losing its coherence. And what if gravity was the last thing to go?

'You're right. We leave soon.' She turned to Sam, who was brooding over Orlando's empty sim. 'Did you hear that? We're running out of time here.'

The girl was dry-eyed now, but the composure did not go very deep. It was still strange for Renie to see Sam's true face. It had been even stranger to discover that Sam had a black father, and a distinct African look to her features despite her tawny hair. Her teenage dialect had been so compellingly middle-American that even Renie herself had unconsciously typed the girl (even when everyone had still thought her a boy) as white. 'He still looks so . . . perfect,' Sam said quietly. 'What's going to happen to him if this place goes away?'

Renie shook her head. 'I don't know. But remember, that's not him, Sam. That's not even his body. Wherever Orlando is, he must be in a better place than this.'

'We need a little rest before we go anywhere,' !Xabbu said. 'We have none of us slept since the night before Troy was destroyed, and that seems a long time ago. It will be no help to hurry down the mountain if we are not making good choices – if we stumble and fall because we are so tired.'

Renie started to object, but of course he was right: they were all exhausted – in fact, it was !Xabbu himself who usually got the least sleep and insisted on taking the most strenuous duties. It might only be a sim and not his true body, but he was still sagging with weariness. Even Sam's emotional volatility, unsurprising after what they had all been through, might be improved with rest.

'Okay,' she said. 'We'll take a few hours to sleep. But only if you go first.'

'I am used to being without sleep, Renie . . .'

'I don't care if you're used to it. It's your turn. I'll stand first watch, then I'll wake Sam up for the second. So just lie down, will you?'

!Xabbu shrugged and smiled. 'If you say so, Beloved Porcupine.'

'Stop that.' She looked around. 'It would be nice if it ever got dark here.' She remembered the terror of sudden nightfall in the other unfinished land. 'Well, maybe not. Anyway, just close your eyes.'

'You could sleep too, Renie.'

'And not have anyone keeping an eye on Jongleur? *Chance not*, as the young people say.'

!Xabbu curled up on the ground. Trained by his nomadic people to snatch the opportunity when it was available, within moments his breathing slowed and his muscles relaxed.

Renie reached out once and touched his hair, still awed to have the old !Xabbu back again. Or a virtual version of him. She glanced at Felix Jongleur, still staring out into the sky like a ship's captain watching the weather, then at Sam, crouched silently beside Orlando's cairn. Although her knee was touching Renie's leg, the girl seemed farther away than Jongleur.

'You get some sleep too,' Renie told her. 'Sam? Do you hear me?'

The girl looked up, a flash of anger on her face. 'You're not my mother, seen?'

Renie sighed. 'No, I'm not. But I am a grown woman and I'm trying to help. And if you ever want to see that mother of yours again, you must stay alert and healthy.'

Sam's look softened. 'Sorry. Sorry I'm being so stupid. I just . . . I want this all to be over. I want to go home.'

'We're doing our best. Lie down for a while, even if you don't sleep.'

'Chizz.' She stretched out beside Orlando's body and closed her eyes, one hand touching the low stone wall. It gave Renie a superstitious shiver to see it.

I can't even remember, she thought, *what it felt like when life was normal.*

Both !Xabbu and Sam were still sleeping soundly after something like an hour had passed, as deeply as her brother Stephen had used to sleep after a long day of childish hyperactivity. Sam was snoring quietly, and Renie was reluctant to wake her up. She felt a brief desire for a cigarette, and realized with surprise that it had been a long time since she had thought about smoking.

Just too damned busy trying not to get killed, she decided. *Effective, but there must be easier ways to quit.*

Jongleur had his back against a rock some ten meters away and appeared to be sleeping himself, or at least his head was sunk on his chest and his eyes were closed. Renie could not help thinking he looked like a vulture waiting with the patience of millions of years of blind evolution for something to die. The fifth member of the involuntary fellowship, Ricardo Klement, had not reappeared, and even though it disturbed Renie to think about him trudging around the mountaintop, God only knew what kind of thoughts flickering through his damaged brain, it was better than having to look at him.

It was the mountaintop itself that now caught Renie's attention. For all that had happened here, for all that she and !Xabbu had worried about its ongoing dissolution, she had not really looked it over very carefully. Sleepless in the eternal, directionless light, she let her gaze wander across the spiky terrain.

The mountain was not only losing detail, it was losing color as well – or, since it had originally been all the same shiny black material, it might have been more precise to say it was gaining colors. The scumble of dark, unreflective soil beneath her had not changed too much, but the uneven peaks and pillars of stone were less solidly black, as though someone had thrown water on an ink drawing before it was entirely dry. Some of the spikes of rock had merely lightened to dark gray, but others now showed threads of other hues, purples and nightsky blues, and even the suggestion here and there of a dark brown like dried blood.

But that doesn't really make any sense, Renie told herself. *That's not how virtual landscapes decay. If they don't just go nonfunctional, then some of the components might work longer than others and you get an odd effect like a schematic or a wire-frame after all the other detail is gone, but you don't just have color wash out. Things don't go blurry. It's crazy.*

But here they were, and what *hadn't* been crazy since they'd first crossed with the old hacker Singh into this virtual madhouse of a universe? Nothing here behaved as normal code should behave.

Renie squinted. The mountaintop seemed quite real – in some ways more so than when they had first come – but there was no question that the place was losing coherence. Some of the jutting spikes were little more than blobs now, and in other places the canyons that cut into the rim of the valley had begun to sag along the edges like pudding.

It's not a real landscape – in fact, it never was. The more she looked at its sparse verticality and blurry gray sky, dead as a bad piece of theater scenery, the more it seemed like something purely of the imagination. An Expressionist painting, perhaps. A cartoon. A dream.

Yes, that's what it truly looks like, she thought. *And that's what the other unfinished place looked like too. Not like real places, but like one of those landscapes that the brain throws out as a backdrop for a dream.*

A thought suddenly came to her, something as strange and prickly as static electricity, and she found herself sitting up straight. After a few minutes, with other ideas grabbing onto the first as though magnetized, she badly wanted to share. She gave !Xabbu a gentle shake. He came awake immediately.

'Renie? Is it my turn? Is everything . . . ?'

'I'm fine, I just . . . I had an idea. Because of what you always say. A dream is dreaming us, you know?'

'What do you mean?' He drew himself up until he could look closely at her face.

'You always say that a dream is dreaming us, right? And I always thought of that as being, I don't know, *philosophical.*'

He laughed quietly. 'Is that a bad word, Renie?'

'Don't make fun of me, please. I'm admitting my own faults. I'm an engineer, for God's sake – or at least that's my training. I tend to think of things like philosophy as being what you do after the real work is finished.'

The look he gave her was amused, crinkling around the eyes. 'And so?'

'I was just thinking about this place and how much like a dream it is. How nothing is quite normal, but in a dream that doesn't matter because you're waiting for something important to happen. And then I suddenly just thought, what if this place *is* a dream?'

!Xabbu cocked his head. 'What do you mean?'

'Not a dream, really, but strange and unreal for the same reason that a dream is. Why is it that things happen all funny in dreams, things look funny? That nothing is ever quite . . . complete? Because your subconscious isn't actually very good at recreating the stuff the conscious mind usually sees, or else it just doesn't care.'

Sam stirred in her sleep, disturbed by the urgency in Renie's tone, so she dropped her voice to a whisper. 'I think the Other built this place. I think it meant us to come here, and it built this place out of its own mind, like a dream. What did Jonas call it? A metaphor.' Spoken aloud, it did not seem as obviously true. It was hard to conceive of their own existence having any importance to that vast, suffering figure.

'Made this from its mind? But if this Other runs the system, then it has access to anything – all of those worlds, each one perfect.' !Xabbu frowned, thinking. 'It seems strange it should build anything so unreal.'

'But that's just it,' Renie said excitedly. 'It didn't build those other worlds. Those were made by people – programmers, engineers, real people who know what a real world is supposed to look like, and how to make even an imaginary world look real. But what does the Other know? It's just an artificial intelligence of some kind, right? It sees patterns, but it's not a human. It doesn't know what would seem real to us and what wouldn't, just the general shape of things. It would be like giving a book to a very intelligent child who can't read, then telling him, 'Now you make one of these books for yourself.' The kid might have all the right letters to use from the one you gave him, but he couldn't make them into a story. So it would be a weird thing that just *looked* like a book. Get it?'

!Xabbu thought about it for a long moment. 'But why? Why would the Other create a new world?'

'I don't know. Maybe just for us. Martine said she'd met it before, remember? That she'd been part of an experiment with it when she was a girl? Suppose the thing recognized her. Or maybe for some reason it just wanted to see what we were. This is an alien intelligence we're talking about, so who knows? It might be artificial, but it seems to be a lot more complex than any ordinary neural net.'

Renie sensed something at her shoulder and turned. Felix Jongleur stood over them, his face hardened in a frown. 'We have waited long enough. It's time to begin our descent. Wake the girl.'

'We were just . . .'

'Wake her. We are leaving now.'

Ordinarily, faced with a naked middle-aged man, Renie would have been only too happy to keep her eyes on his face, but it was surprisingly difficult to meet Jongleur's cold gaze. Now that the first heat of her rage at the man had begun to dissipate she was discovering an uncomfortable fact: he frightened her badly. He had a deep, hard strength, the kind of unbending core that served nothing but its own will. His dark eyes showed not an iota of human concern, but there was nothing animalistic in them – rather, he seemed a creature that had moved past simple humanity. She had heard politicians and financial titans described as implacable, as forces of nature, and she had always seen it as just a flattering metaphor. Now, faced with the master of the Grail in person, she was beginning to understand that a black charisma like his owed nothing to artistic descriptions.

She darted a look at !Xabbu, but her friend's thoughts were hidden: when he chose to be, he was just as inscrutable in his own skin as he had been behind the mask of the baboon sim.

Jongleur turned his back on them and moved a few paces away, the picture of impatience controlled. Renie leaned over and nudged Sam Fredericks awake.

'We have to go, Sam.'

The girl roused herself slowly. She crouched for a moment, then her eyes swung to Orlando's body lying in its close-fitting coffin of stones.

'!Xabbu,' Renie whispered. 'Go bother Jongleur for a minute so Sam can say goodbye to her friend. Ask the old bastard some questions – not that he'll give you any answers, but it will keep him busy.'

!Xabbu nodded. He walked to Jongleur and said something, then swept his arm out toward the pearly, horizonless sky, exactly like someone discussing the weather or the view. Renie turned back to Sam.

'We have to leave him behind now.'

The girl nodded. 'I know,' she said quietly, staring down at Orlando. 'He was so good. Not just nice – sometimes

he was kind of hardcase, majorly sarcastic. But he really
wanted . . . w-wanted to be g-g-good . . .'

Renie put an arm around her. There was nothing to be
done, really.

'Goodbye, Orlando,' Renie said at last, quietly.
'Wherever you are.' She led Sam away from the cairn,
fussing at the girl's hair and ragged garments to distract
her. 'You'd better get your brain-damaged friend,' she told
Jongleur, 'because he's wandering around out there somewhere. We're leaving now.'

Something even darker and colder than usual moved
across the man's face. 'You think I should go fetch Klement
as though he were some schoolyard chum of mine? You
are a fool. I need the three of you, so we will all go together,
but I see no such use for him. If he wants to join us, then
I will not stop him – unless he does something that endan-
gers my safety – but if he stays here instead while this place
reverts to raw code, it matters little to me.'

He turned and strode away toward the trail down the
mountain, making himself the leader by default.

'Such pleasant company,' Renie muttered. 'Okay, it's
time. Let's go.'

The great bowl-shaped valley where the giant form of the
Other had lain was empty now, one side collapsed in a
long, ragged edge, as though something had taken a bite
out of it. Jongleur walked ahead of them all, ramrod
straight, his posture and stride those of a man even
younger than the middle age his looks suggested. Renie
wondered if the hard-planed face was really Jongleur's
own, as it had looked sometime a century or more ago.
If so, it just added to one of the strangest mysteries of
all – why had they wakened here with sims so much like
their real bodies?

It doesn't make sense. When we first entered the network, I had the sim I'd chosen, and so did T4b and Sweet William, but Martine was just in a generic body from Atasco's simulation and !Xabbu was a baboon. What the hell was that about? And Orlando and Fredericks had their own choice of sims, avatars from their adventure game – but didn't Fredericks tell me that Orlando's sim was not quite the same as usual? Older or younger or something?

But just as their original sims showed no obvious pattern, the fact that they now wore bodies much like their own true forms seemed just as strange. *Could we actually be in our real bodies?* she thought wildly. But she could remember quite clearly that moment of awakening in the tank in her true physical form, and although the difference was subtle, it was a difference. The shape she now wore might look like her real body, down to small details, scars, and even the knobbiness of a knuckle she had broken in childhood, but it wasn't real at all.

So what's going on? If it's the Other's dream, why do we look like this? It's like magic. Renie blew out air, frustrated. No matter how strange and unrelated the facts seemed, there had to be patterns, but she couldn't see any of them yet.

As the small company reached the outermost pinnacles of the mountaintop, Renie noticed that Ricardo Klement had at some point joined the party, following a hundred meters or so behind them like an unquiet ghost.

The trail still curved down from the summit and along the shiny black slope, apparently all the way down into the mysteriously glinting clouds that ringed the mountain, but Renie could see that !Xabbu had not exaggerated. The striations that had made the path safe had lost much of their definition, and although the trail itself still seemed substantial, the crispness of its outer edge was gone, as though the stone were some kind of licorice ice cream that had been out of the freezer a little too long.

'I still wonder why the Other would want to bring us to a place like this,' she said quietly to !Xabbu as they started down the trail after Jongleur. 'And maybe to that first unfinished world, too.' She couldn't help remembering how part of the ground in that other world had suddenly vanished, trapping Martine and shearing off T4b's hand. What if the same instability happened here? She decided not to waste time brooding about something she couldn't prevent.

T4b's hand, though – that was an interesting anomaly. It had been replaced by another hand, a glowing thing that had done terrible damage to one of the Grail people, who had seemed otherwise invincible. Could T4b's hand somehow have been replaced by a bit of the Other itself, or at least of its ability to shape the network? A wild-card piece of the operating system at the end of his virtual arm?

She shared the thought with !Xabbu. 'But even if the Other made both of these places – carved them out of the raw material of the network, so to speak – it doesn't really tell us anything. If it's been captured or taken over or something by Dread, that might be why this particular construct is starting to lose resolution, but it doesn't explain why that other unfinished world started falling apart underneath us.'

!Xabbu cut her off. 'Look here. I do not remember the path being like that before.' The trail in front of them was suddenly only wide enough for them to pass single file. 'We should save our talking and thinking until we have found a wide place on the trail and stopped for the night.'

'We're not going to sleep on this mountain, are we?' Sam protested. 'It only took us a couple of hours to climb up!'

'Yes,' !Xabbu told her, 'but I think that was from a spot very high up the mountainside. Going down to the bottom may be a much longer trip.'

'If we make it down safely,' Renie said, edging past the narrow space and its much too expansive view of the sheer black mountainside below her feet, 'then I won't mind if it takes a week.'

Even after hours of plodding descent, they seemed no closer to the bank of white cloud. They were all tired – Renie, who had not slept, was perhaps the weariest of all. It was not surprising that an accident should happen.

They had reached one of the narrower stretches of trail, not the worst they had seen – in places they had been forced to edge sideways along the path with their backs against the hard stone of the mountainside – but slender enough that two of them could not safely stand side by side. Sam was just behind Renie; !Xabbu and Felix Jongleur were the first and second in line. Klement, who at times had trailed a long way to the rear, was now so close he could reach out and touch the last in line, which for some reason was exactly what he did.

Sam, startled and frightened by Klement's fingers trailing through her hair, lurched forward, trying to push her way past on Renie's inside shoulder. For a moment the two of them tangled; then, trying to give the girl room, Renie put her foot down too far to the outside and the edge of the trail crumbled beneath her like stale bread. For a moment Renie could only flail her arms, a reflex absolutely useless for anything except to increase the odds of dragging Sam over the side as well. Renie shrieked and then tumbled outward, aware even as her heart seemed to stop that the sight of !Xabbu's shoulder and his head turning – far too late to help – was the last of him she would ever see. Then something closed on her wrist like a manacle and she slammed down against the path with her legs dangling over nothingness, her breath smashed out in one great gasp.

In the scrambling and shouting of her companions as they struggled to drag her back over the edge, Renie did not understand until she was safe again that it was Felix Jongleur's hand that had seized her, his wiry body that had kept her from slipping away until !Xabbu and Sam could pull her back to safety.

Stretched on her stomach, blood sizzling through her head like electricity, Renie struggled to refill her lungs. Jongleur looked down on her like a scientist examining a dying lab rat. 'I'm not certain I would have bothered to do it for one of your other companions,' he said, then turned and continued down the path.

Despite her shock and nausea, Renie spent a long moment trying to decide how she should feel about that.

There was no darkness on the mountain, and the strange Van Gogh stars that had hung above them during their ascent did not reappear. That first journey seemed weeks behind them, but Renie thought it must have been less than forty-eight hours since she and !Xabbu and Martine and the rest had emerged from the Troy simulation onto this very trail. Now all those others were gone – vanished or dead. Out of the entire company that had been gathered by Sellars, only three were left: !Xabbu, Sam, and herself.

The climb up the mountain had been brief, but this reverse journey held the promise of being much longer.

Depressed by the way the silvery distant clouds seemed
to grow no closer, increasingly exhausted, they continued down the trail long past the point of safety, searching for a place to stop. An hour longer than Renie would
have believed she was able to walk, they finally reached
a fold in the mountainside, a deep elbow joint in the
trail a few meters wide and a few meters deep where
they could rest away from the cliff face. It was a bleak
campsite, without food or water or even fire, since
!Xabbu had found nothing anywhere that could be used
as fuel, but just the chance to lie down and rest in
safety seemed as good to Renie as any meal she had
ever eaten. Since her near-fall she had been so frightened she would not move out of arm's reach of the
mountain face, and had spent most of the last part of
the descent trailing her fingers along the black stone,
rubbing her skin raw to make certain that she was on
the inside of the path.

Renie made Fredericks curl up at the back of the crevice
so that she could put herself between Jongleur and the
broken sword Fredericks carried, then laid her own head
on !Xabbu's shoulder. Jongleur made a space for himself
farther up the cut where he quickly fell asleep sitting
against the stone with his chin on his chest. Klement
crouched at the opening of the crevice, looking out on
the gray sky, his expression quite unreadable.

Renie was asleep within seconds.

She was teetering on the edge. Stephen was only a few
meters away, a dim shape floating on air currents she
could not feel, as though he wore wings; for all his fluttering movements he never came within reach. She thrust
her arm out as far as she could and for a moment thought
she touched him, but then her footing gave way and she

was falling, plunging, with nothing beneath her but shriekingly empty darkness . . .

'. . . *You there? Can you . . . me? Renie?*'

She fell gasping out of the dream and into a greater madness. Martine's voice was buzzing from her own breast, as though her friend were somehow trapped inside Renie's body. For a long, disoriented moment she could only stare at the black stone walls and the sliver of gray sky before she remembered where she was.

The voice hummed against her skin once more. !Xabbu sat up. Sam stared, groggy and dumbfounded. '*Can . . . us? We're . . . bad shape . . . !*'

'The lighter!' Renie said. 'Jesus Mercy!' She fumbled the device out of the strip of cloth she wore across her chest. 'It's Martine – she's alive!' But even as she lifted it up, trying to angle it into the thin light so she could see it and remember the operating sequences they had discovered, a shadow crashed against her and knocked the lighter from her hand, sent it clattering toward the back of the crevice. Felix Jongleur stood over her, fists clenched.

'What the hell are you doing?' she screamed, already scrambling on her hands and knees after the device.

'. . . *Answer us, Renie,*' Martine pleaded. Renie's hand closed on the lighter again. '*We're . . . without . . .*'

'If you try to activate that,' said Jongleur, 'I will kill you.'

Sam came up from her crouch brandishing Orlando's broken blade. 'Leave her alone!'

Jongleur did not even look at her. 'I am warning you,' he told Renie. 'Do not touch it.'

Renie was frozen, irresolute. Something in Jongleur's tone told her he would do what he threatened, even with the sword buried in his back. Even so, she leaned slowly toward the lighter, fingers spread. 'What's wrong with you?' she growled. 'Those are our friends!'

'*Martine! Is . . . you, sweetness?*' said a new voice – a terrifyingly familiar one, the signal stronger than Martine's, but also slipping in and out. '*I've missed . . . you have any of my other . . . with you?*'

Renie snatched her hand back as though the lighter had begun to glow white-hot.

'*I'm a bit busy . . . old darling, but I'll . . . some friends to find you. Don't move! They'll . . . in minutes. Actually, go . . . move if you want . . . it . . . good.*'

Dread's buzzing laugh filled the small space. 'He's after them!' Renie almost shouted. 'We have to help!'

Jongleur curled his fingers into a fist. 'No.'

After ten seconds had passed in strained silence, Renie reached for the device and picked it up. It seemed cold and inert now, a dead thing. 'Those people are our friends,' she said furiously, but Jongleur had stepped away, back toward the entrance to the crevice. !Xabbu and Sam stared at him as though he had suddenly sprouted horns and a tail. Only Klement had not moved from the place where he sat silently against the wall.

'Those people have just revealed themselves on an open communication band,' Jongleur said. 'They have just announced their helplessness – not to mention their position – across the entire Grail channel. But they are not the only ones with access to that channel, as you also heard. If you had tried to give away my position to him, I would have killed you without a moment's hesitation.'

Renie stared, hating him, but fearful of his cruel certainty. 'And why should we care about that? It's you he wants.'

'All the more reason you shall not give me away.'

'Really?' She was enraged now by her own cowardice.

'Well, you talk big, but there are three of us and only one of you, unless you're expecting help from your idiot friend. As for Dread, he's no worse a threat to us than you are – less, because he's just an ordinary psychopath.'

'Ordinary psychopath?' Jongleur lifted an eyebrow. 'You know nothing. John Dread with no greater weapon than his bare hands would be one of the most dangerous people in the world, but now he has the power of my entire system at his disposal.'

'All right. So he's dangerous. So now he's the little tin god of the Grail network. So what?' Renie pointed a trembling finger. 'You and your selfish old friends, destroying children so you could live forever, so you could build yourself the most expensive toy in the history of the world. I hope your friend Dread *does* bring the whole thing down in flames, even if we go with it. It will be worth it, just to see the last of you.'

Jongleur eyed her, then !Xabbu and Sam. The girl cursed under her breath and turned away, but !Xabbu held Jongleur's gaze with little expression until the older man turned back to Renie.

'Be silent and I will tell you something,' he said. 'I built myself a place. It does not matter what kind of place, but it was something I created for myself, separate from the Grail system. It was my respite when the stress and worry of this project became too much. A system completely removed from the Grail matrix – in fact, a dedicated system, if you know what that is.'

'I know what that is,' Renie said scornfully. 'What's your point?'

'The point is that no one but me could access this virtual environment. Then one day, not long ago, I discovered that someone *had* accessed it, corrupted it, ruined what I had built there. I only realized after much consideration that the

Other itself had penetrated that dedicated system – something it should not have been able to do.'

He paused. Renie could make no sense out of what he was saying. 'So?'

Jongleur shook his head in mock-sorrow. There was a glint in his eye; Renie realized that the monster was actually enjoying this in some strange way. 'I have overestimated you again, I see. Very well, I will explain. The only way the Other could have reached into that environment is through my own system – by stealing or co-opting my own security procedures out of my house system. My *personal* system, not the Grail system. And now the Other is under the control of John Dread.'

Renie's chill had returned. 'So . . . so what you're saying is that the Other . . . isn't isolated on the Grail system anymore.'

Jongleur's smile stretched his lips but went no farther. 'That is correct. So while you consider where your loyalties lie, take this into your counsels. That far-from-ordinary-psychopath Dread not only has control of the most powerful and complex operating system ever developed, that system itself has already managed to reach out of its Grail Project bottle and into my house network. Which means that the Other – and Dread, as its controlling force – can reach anywhere on the global net.'

He stepped out of the crevice and onto the path, turned toward the downhill slope, then paused.

'The damage Dread can do here is nothing compared to what he'll do when he discovers his new reach.' Jongleur spread his hands wide. 'Just imagine. The whole world will be at his fingertips – air traffic control, critical industries, stockpiles of biological weapons, nuclear launch facilities. And as you have already discovered, Johnny Dread is a very, very angry young man.'

CHAPTER 2

Execution Sweet

NETFEED/NEWS: Sect Refuses Marker Gene for Messiah
(visual: Starry Wisdom headquarters, Quito, Ecuador)
VO: The religious sect Starry Wisdom has gone to court to gain an
exemption from UN rules on marker genes in human clones. The religious group intends to clone a duplicate of their late leader, Leonardo
Rivas Maldonado, but claims that the marker genes the UN mandates
to separate clones from originals would compromise their religious
rights.
(visual: Maria Rocafuerte, Starry Wisdom spokesperson)
Rocafuerte: 'How can we create our loving master again in a body
that is sullied by an incorrect gene? We are trying to remake the
Vessel of the Living Wisdom to lead us in these final days, but the
government wants us to change that vessel for the sake of obtrusive,
antireligious regulations.'

THIS is so bad, this is so bad, was all Christabel could
think.

The van bumped up over the sidewalk and slowed down
at the opening, so the soldier who was driving could do
something with a big metal box standing there. A woman
wearing a bathing suit and a robe, pushing a baby in a

stroller along the walkway beside the building, was trying
to look in through the van's windows, but it didn't seem
like she could see Christabel at all through the glass. After
a few seconds the woman turned away. The van rolled
down the ramp into darkness.

Christabel knew she must have made a noise, because
her daddy leaned over and said 'It's just a garage, honey.
Don't be afraid. Just a garage for a hotel.'

They had been driving for what seemed like a long
time, driving out of the town and into a place where there
were more hills than houses, so that she had seen the
hotel coming for a long time – a big, wide, white building that stretched high up into the air, with flags flying
in front. It looked like a nice place, but Christabel did not
feel good about it.

The younger soldier sitting across from them looked at
her, and for a moment she thought he was going to say
something, maybe something kind, but then his mouth
got tight and he looked away. Captain Ron, who was also
sitting across from them, just looked unhappy, like his
stomach hurt.

Where's Mommy? she wondered. *Why did she drive
away in our van? Why didn't she wait for us?*

To keep Mister Sellars a secret, Christabel suddenly
knew. Just because her Daddy and Mommy – and this
new person, Mr Ramsey – all knew about him now didn't
mean that everyone did.

Something she hadn't really thought about came to her
as the van stopped. *That means Captain Ron doesn't know
about Mister Sellars either – about how he came with us
in our car, with that terrible boy, too. None of the army
men know about it. That's why Daddy kept saying not to
talk to anyone.*

She had to hold her breath, because the being-scared

suddenly felt so big. She hadn't understood. She had thought Daddy was angry at Captain Ron, angry because Ron didn't want him to take time off from work. Now she knew that he wasn't angry, he was keeping a secret. A secret she might have told one of the army men if they had asked her.

'Are you all right, honey?' her father asked. The van doors hissed open, and one of the soldiers stepped out. 'Just take the man's hand when you get down.'

Mr Ramsey leaned close to her ear. 'I'll be right behind you, Christabel. Your daddy and I will make sure everything's going to be okay.'

But Christabel was beginning to learn a scary thing about grown-ups. Sometimes they said things would be all right, but they didn't *know* they'd be all right. They just said it. Bad things could happen, even to little kids.

Especially to little kids.

'Very slick,' Captain Ron said as the door slid open in the garage wall, but he didn't sound happy. 'Our own private elevator to the exec suite.'

What kind of sweet? Christabel started to cry. *Exec.* She'd heard the word before. She didn't remember just what it meant, but she was pretty sure it must mean something about executions. She knew about them – she saw more things on the net than her parents knew about. *Execution sweet*, that was what Captain Ron was really saying. She wondered if it was a poison candy bar or something that they kept just for bad kids – maybe a poisoned apple, like in 'Snow White.'

Her father put his hand in her hair, touching the back of her head. 'Honey, don't cry. Everything will be all right. Ron, does she have to come along? Can't we put this off until I can get hold of her mother or someone else to take her?'

Christabel grabbed her daddy's hand, hard. Captain Ron just shrugged, a big, heavy movement of his shoulders. 'I got orders, Mike.'

It was crowded and hot with all of them in the elevator – herself, her father, Mr Ramsey, Captain Ron, and the two other soldiers – but Christabel didn't want the ride to end, didn't want to see what an execution sweet looked like. When the doors pinged and opened, she started crying again.

The room inside wasn't what she expected, which had been something like one of the terrible gray-painted prisons she'd seen on net-shows, like the one Zelmo and Nedra had been in on *Hate My Life*. Captain Ron had kept calling it a hotel, and that's what it looked like, a big, big hotel room with a floor as big as their lawn at home, covered in pale blue carpet, with three couches and tables and a wallscreen that took up one huge wall, and a kitchen at the far end, and doors in the other walls. There was even a vase of flowers on one of the tables. The only thing that seemed as bad as she had expected was the really big man in dark glasses who stood in the doorway waiting for them. Another man who looked a lot like him was sitting on one of the couches, although now he stood up. They both were dressed in funny black suits, tight and a little shiny, and both had things strapped on their chests and hips that looked like guns or something even worse and more complicated and scarier.

'ID,' said the man waiting at the door in a low slow voice.

'And just who the hell are you?' Captain Ron asked. For the first time his unhappiness seemed like something else – like he was angry, or maybe even scared.

'ID,' the big man in the wraparound glasses said again, just the same, like he was one of the store window advertisements in Seawall Center. The soldiers with Captain Ron moved a little. Christabel saw one of them drop his hand to his side, near where his gun was. Christabel's heart began to go really, really fast.

'Hang on,' her daddy said, 'let's all just . . .'

One of the doors on the far side of the big room swung open. A man with a mustache and short gray hair walked out. Christabel could see a whole other big room behind him, with a bed and a desk and a big window with the curtains drawn. The man wore a bathrobe and striped pajamas. He was smoking a cigar. For a moment, Christabel thought she had seen him on the net because even in such funny clothes he looked so familiar.

'It's all right, Doyle,' the man with the mustache said. 'I know Captain Parkins. And Major Sorensen, too – oh, yes.'

The big man in black walked back across the room to the nearest couch. He and the other shiny-suit man sat down together, not saying anything, but there was something about them that made Christabel think of a dog pretending to sleep at the end of a leash, just waiting until a kid got close enough to jump at.

'And I even remember *you*, darlin'.' The man in the mustache smiled and leaned forward to pat Christabel on the head. She remembered him then, the tan-faced man in her daddy's office. 'What are you doing here, little girl?' Her father's hand tightened on hers, so she didn't pull away from him, but she didn't say anything either.

The man straightened up, still smiling, but when he spoke again his voice was cold, like someone had just opened the freezer door and let the air puff out in Christabel's face. 'What's this child doing here, Parkins?'

'I'm . . . I'm sorry, General.' Captain Ron had sweat stains under his arms that had got bigger since they had left the elevator. 'It was a difficult situation – the girl's mother was out shopping and couldn't be located, so since you said this was going to be informal . . .'

The general laughed, a snort. 'Oh, yes, informal. But I didn't say it was going to be a goddamn picnic, did I? What, are we going to have father-daughter sack races? Hmm? Captain Parkins, were you thinking we should have a picnic?'

'No, sir.'

Mr Ramsey cleared his throat. 'General . . . Yacoubian?'

The man's eyes swiveled across to him. 'And you know what?' the general said softly. 'I *definitely* do not recognize you, citizen. So maybe you should just get back on the elevator and get the hell out of my suite.'

'I'm a lawyer, General. Major Sorensen is my client.'

'Really? This is the first time I've ever heard of a military officer bringing legal representation to a casual meeting with his commanding officer.'

Now it was Ramsey who smiled, just a small one. 'Clearly you have a broad definition of the word "casual," General.'

'I'm a brigadier general, sonny. I think you'll find that things have a way of being what I say they are.' He turned to Parkins. 'All right, Captain, you've done your job. Take your men and get the hell back to whatever you're supposed to be doing. I'll take it from here.'

'Sir?' Captain Parkins seemed confused. 'But my men, sir . . . you said to bring a couple of MPs . . .'

'You don't think Doyle and Pilger can handle anything that might come up?' The general shook his head. 'Those boys are carrying more armament than a combat helicopter.'

'Are they also US Army, General?' asked Ramsey loudly. 'For the record?'

'Ask me no questions, lawyer, and I'll tell you no lies,' chuckled the general.

Christabel's daddy's hand was trembling on her shoulder, which was making her almost more frightened than anything else that had happened today. Now he finally spoke. 'General, there's really no need for either my daughter or Mr Ramsey to be involved in this . . .'

'Mike,' Ramsey said, 'don't give away your rights . . .'

'. . . So I wish you'd just let them go,' her father said, ignoring him. 'Send them with Captain Parkins, if you like.'

The general shook his head. Although his face was very tan and his mustache was very small and neat, he had a crinkly look around his eyes that looked like pictures Christabel had seen of Santa Claus. But she thought that he was more like some kind of backward Santa, someone who instead of bringing presents would come down the chimney and take little boys and girls away in a sack. 'Oh, no, I don't think so,' he said. 'I'm very interested to hear what everyone has to say – even the little girl. So you and your men just paddle off, Captain Parkins. The rest of us have some talking to do.' He leaned past them and pushed the gold elevator button in its little frame in the wallpaper.

'If it's just the same with you, sir,' Captain Ron said suddenly. 'I'll stay. Then if you need Major Sorensen or his daughter taken somewhere, I'll be available. Mike's a friend of mine, sir.' He turned quickly to the two soldiers, who were looking very wide-eyed, but still not saying anything. 'You and Gentry go down and wait in the van. If I'm not going to need you, I'll call and let you know you can head back to base.'

The door hissed open. For a moment everyone just looked at each other, the soldiers, the men in black on the couch, Captain Ron and Ramsey and her daddy and the general. Then the general smiled again. 'Fine. You heard the captain, boys.' He gestured the soldiers into the elevator. They were still staring out when the door slid closed. For some reason, seeing the young soldiers in their shiny helmets disappear, she felt like she had the first day her mommy had left her alone at kindergarten. She reached up and took her father's hand again and squeezed it tight.

'Make yourselves at home,' the general said cheerfully. 'I have a rather important conference to finish, but I'll be done in half an hour or so, and then we'll all have a long chat.' He turned toward the two men in black. 'Make sure our guests are comfortable. But make sure they remain our guests until I'm offline. Gently, though. Gently.'

He turned and began to head back toward the bedroom.

'General Yacoubian, sir,' Christabel's daddy said. 'I want to ask you again if my daughter and Mr Ramsey could be released. It would just be a lot easier for everyone . . .'

The general turned around, and Christabel thought his eyes were as bright and strange as a bird's. 'Easier? It's not *me* who has to make things easier, Sorensen. It's not me who has to answer the questions.' He started toward the room, then stopped and turned again. 'See, someone named Duncan from your office copied me on a request for labwork – something I should have been copied on automatically, but for some reason you held it back from me. Made for interesting reading, I have to say. A bit of scientific analysis you had done on some sunglasses. Very interesting sunglasses, they were, too. Ring a bell?'

Captain Ron looked completely confused, but Christabel's daddy turned as pale as if something had leaked out of him.

'So just sit tight and keep your mouth shut until I'm

ready for you.' The general smiled again. 'You might say some prayers, too, if you know some.' He turned and walked back into the bedroom, then shut the door.

There was a long silence. Then one of the men in black, the man called Pilger, said, 'If the kid's hungry, there's some peanuts and chocolate in the minibar,' before turning back to watch the wallscreen again.

*T*HE *thing is*, Dulcie told herself, *I don't really know him all that well.*

She was surveying the routine maintenance levels of Dread's system, which he kept in a state rather similar to his household decor – sparse and colorless. Where her own system had the equivalent of notes and unfinished projects lying around everywhere, not to mention all kinds of strange coding bric-a-brac – everything from long out-of-date utilities and code-busters which she'd hung onto just in case she ever bumped into such a system again to algorithmic representations so interesting she saved them almost as objects of beauty – Dread had nothing out of place, nothing that was not absolutely necessary, nothing that gave any hint of his personality at all.

He's so guarded. One of those anal-retentive types. Probably rolls all his socks the same way. But after spending her childhood in her mother's aggressively bohemian care – most mornings young Dulcinea Anwin had not only needed to clear plates of spoiling food from the previous night's dinner party off the kitchen counter before making her own breakfast, but also had to make a circuit of the house putting out candles that had been left burning and evicting guests who had fallen asleep in strange places – she thought that a certain rigidity about order was not the worst trait a man could have.

She had finished running diagnostics on their project's

house system, which, despite the rather uncommon strains Dread was putting on it at the moment, was holding up nicely, and she was busy making records of some of the events from their incursion into the Grail system for future study when she bumped across something odd.

It was a partition of sorts in Dread's own system, a boxing-off of data, but that wasn't the unusual thing about it. All systems were divided for organizational purposes, and most people who spent a lot of time working directly online were as idiosyncratic about how they arranged their system environments as they were with their RL homes. What she had seen of Dread's space was in fact so nonidiosyncratic she was almost disturbed by it: he had never bothered to change any of the settings, names, or infrastructure of the original system package, for one thing. It was a little like realizing the pictures on your manager's desk were the fake ones of smiling catalog models that had come with the frames. No, there was nothing unusual about partitioning your storage. What was interesting about this partition was that it was invisible, or supposed to be. She checked the directories, but there was no listing to correspond with the fairly extensive secured area' onto which she had stumbled.

A little secret door, she thought. *Why, Mr Dread, you do have some things you want to keep private after all.*

It was sort of cute, really – a boy thing, like a hidden treehouse. No girls allowed. But of course, Dread was a beginner with this stuff, and Dulcie was a very, very hard girl to hide things from.

She hesitated for a few moments – not very long at all, really – reminding herself that it was wrong, that not only did her boss have a right to his privacy, he was also a man who did a lot of dangerous things for dangerous people, people who took their security very seriously. But

Dulcie (who almost always lost these arguments with herself) found the idea more a challenge than a discouragement. After all, didn't she run with a dangerous crowd herself? Hadn't she shot someone only a few weeks ago? The fact that she was having regular nightmares about it, and now wished she had invented an excuse not to do it – faulty gun, jammed door lock, epileptic seizure – didn't mean she was suddenly unfit to run with the big boys.

Besides, she thought, *it will be interesting to have a peek into his mind. See what he really thinks about. Of course, it might just be his account books. Anybody this much of a neat freak might be pretty serious about hiding their double-entry stuff.*

But the small bit of poking and prying she allowed herself failed even to turn up a keyhole, let alone a key. If there was something interesting on the other side of the door, she was not going to find it out so easily. With the faintly shamed feeling that had visited her as a young girl rooting through her mother's bureau drawers, she erased all records of her investigations and dropped back out of the system.

Her employer's secret compartment was still nagging at her half an hour later as she stood over his sleeping form, which lay nestled like a piece of dark jewelry in the white padding of the coma bed.

It's true – I really don't know anything about him, she thought, looking down at his heavy-lidded eyes, at the minute movement of his irises between the mesh of black lashes. *Well, I know he's not the most stable person in the world*. It was hard not to remember each and every one of his flashes of anger. *But there's something else in him, too – something calm, something knowing. Like a big cat, or a wolf*. It was hard to avoid animal analogies

– Dread's compact grace somehow did not seem quite civilized.

She was watching the way his cocoa-colored skin took and softened the clinical glare of the overhead lights when Dread's eyes popped open.

'Hello, sweetness,' he said, grinning. 'Bit jumpy today, aren't you?'

'My God . . . !' She fought to regain her breath. 'You could have warned me. You've been out of communication for almost twenty-four hours.'

'Been busy,' he said. 'Things are hopping.' His grin widened. 'But now I'm going to show you a little something. Come join me.'

It took her a moment to understand it was not an invitation to climb into the coma bed – an unpleasant thought even had her feelings about the man himself been less ambivalent: the low murmur of its engines and the constant slow movement of the bed surface made her think of some kind of sea creature, an oyster without a shell. 'You mean . . . on the network?'

'Yes, on the network. You're a bit slow today, Anwin.'

'Just a few thousand things to do, that's all, and about two hours of sleep.' She tried to keep her voice light, but this teenage jocularity was making her tense. 'What do I do . . . ?'

'Access the way I did, and make sure you're in full wraparound – you're going to need it. When you hit the first security barrier, your password is "Nuba." N-U-B-A. That's all.'

'What does it mean?'

He was smiling again. 'One of our abo words, sweetness. Comes from up north, Melville Island.'

'What, is it insulting or something?'

'Oh, no. No.' He closed his eyes as though drifting back

into sleep. 'Just the term they use for an unmarried woman. Which you are, right?' He chuckled, savoring something. 'See you when you get there.' He visibly relaxed, dropping back into the system like a swimmer sliding under the water.

It took her a long moment to realize that she was still shaking a little, startled by his sudden appearance. *Like he was watching me,* she thought. *Just standing behind me, watching me, waiting to give me a little scare. The bastard.*

She poured herself a glass of wine and drank it off in a couple of swallows before lying down on the couch with the fiberlink.

Dulcie had barely uttered the code word when the nothingness of the first system level abruptly took on color and depth. The initial dazzle was so bright that for a second she wondered if she was staring into the sun, then the huge bronze door in front of her swung open and she stepped through into darkness.

The darkness was not complete: the far end of the corridor had an unsteady glow that drew her forward. A dull murmur washed out to her, deep and slow as an ocean pawing at a stony beach. As the light grew and she began to glimpse the large chamber beyond, a shadowed space filled with tight-packed, round shapes like a field of sunken megaliths, she could not help feeling that she had stumbled into a dream. A look at her own legs and bare feet, muscular and bunioned from years of dance class, told her otherwise. Who ever saw their own feet in a dream? Her hands, too, were recognizably her own, the freckles on her long fingers visible even in the dim light.

It's a sim of . . . me, she realized, even as she stepped out into the great chamber.

The rush of muttering voices rose around her. A thousand people, maybe more, were kneeling on the floor of the massive room, their rhythmic, whispering chant rising to the distant ceiling. Oil lamps burned in niches all along the walls, making everything flicker like some visual recording from the earliest days of technology. A clear space between the huddled bodies led across the pale marble; none of the bent figures even looked up as Dulcie walked past them.

At the far end of the chamber a silent, motionless figure sat enthroned on a dais like a statue in a pagan temple, a long silver rod clutched in its hand. The creature was larger than a man, and although its body was human-shaped, the skin was absolutely black and as glossy as Chinese lacquer. The snouted, prong-eared head was that of some doglike beast.

As she neared the dais the whispering voices dropped into silence. The dog-creature's head was lowered, eyes hooded as if in sleep, muzzle against the massive chest, and she had begun to think it really was a statue when the great yellow eyes fluttered open.

All the kneeling shapes suddenly bellowed in perfect unison: '*Cheers, Dulcie!*' The room thundered with echoes, covering the sound of her startled shriek. '*You're looking damn nice today,*' they added, loud as artillery fire, toneless as a punch press.

Silence fell again as she took a staggering step to maintain her balance. The thing on the dais stood up, rising to almost ten feet, and the muzzle gashed open in a long-toothed leer. 'Like it? Just my way of saying "Welcome!"'

I wonder if you can wet yourself in VR. Aloud, she said, 'That's just charming. Took a few years off my life.'

'What do you want from the Lord of Life and Death – flowers? Singing and dancing? Well, that can be arranged, too.' He lifted the silver rod and a fluttering snow of rose petals began to descend from the roof. With a great scraping and murmuring, the thousands of shaven-headed priests rose from their kneeling positions and began clumsily to dance. 'Any particular music you'd like?'

'I don't want anything.' Dulcie looked up through the flurrying petals, trying to ignore the disturbing spectacle of a thousand blank-eyed, sandaled priests doing a spastic soft-shoe. 'What the hell is this place?'

'It's the Old Man's home away from home.' He waved, and the priests lowered themselves to the floor once more. The last few rose petals were still drifting down. 'His favorite simulation – Abydos, I think it's called. Ancient Egypt.'

It was more than a little disturbing to be carrying on a conversation with a jackal-headed man almost twice her own height, like something from a game or interactive theater. 'The old man – you mean your . . . employer, right? And who are you supposed to be? Sparky the Wonder Dog?'

He showed her his teeth again. 'This is the sim I always wore here. Of course, I was taking orders then, and now I'm the one giving them.' He lifted his voice. 'Roll over! Play dead!' The priests dropped to their bellies, rotated once, then lay motionless with their knees and elbows in the air. 'It's amusing, in a sort of way, especially when I think how much it would piss the old wanker off.' He gestured to one of the nearest priests, who leaped to his feet and scuttled to the dais. Dulcie stared at the sim curiously. He certainly looked like a real person, right down to the gleam of sweat on his shaved head. 'This is Dulcie,' Dread told the priest. 'You love her. She is your goddess.'

'I love her,' the priest intoned, although he did not look

at the object of his newfound affection. 'She is my goddess.'

'Would you do anything for her?'

'I would, Lord.'

'Then show her how much you love her. Go on.'

The priest struggled to his feet – he was one of the fat, middle-aged variety, and a bit short of breath – and waddled to one of the wall niches. As Dulcie watched with growing horror, the priest snatched out the oil lamp and upended its contents over his head; in a moment he was running with flames. His white robe caught and blazed up. His round head seemed to float in a halo of fire. 'I love you, my goddess,' he croaked even as his features began to blacken.

'Oh my God, stop, put him out, stop!' she screamed.

Dread swung his long-muzzled face toward her in surprise, then lifted his rod. The blazing figure disappeared. All the other priests still lay on their backs like dead locusts in a field. 'Christ, girl, they're only code.'

'I don't care,' she said. 'That doesn't mean I want to see something like that.'

The jackal shape vanished, leaving the real Dread, ordinary size and dressed all in loose-fitting black, standing on the top step of the throne. 'Didn't mean to upset you, sweetness.' He sounded more annoyed than contrite.

'I just . . .' She shook her head. 'What's going on here, anyway? You said this was the . . . Old Man's place. Where is he? What have you been doing since you got into the system?'

'Oh, this and that.' His human grin was only slightly less feral. 'I'll explain more later, but first I want to take you on a little tour. Just for fun.'

'I don't want to watch any more burning priests, thank you.'

'There's lots of things more interesting to see than that.' He raised his hand in the air and the silver rod abruptly shrank to a small silver cylinder. 'Let's go.'

'That's the lighter!' she said. 'What . . . ?'

But the high hall of Abydos-That-Was and its thousand patient priests had already vanished.

It was indeed a tour. From their first stop in the streets of Imperial Rome, complete with the shouts of street vendors and the wind off the Tiber rank with the scents of human sweat and urine, Dread moved Dulcie in short order to sweltering afternoon on an African plain inhabited by strange creatures as large as elephants, but which Dulcie had never seen before, and then in quick succession through the plum-treed gardens of some clearly mythical China, to a cliffside position overlooking a waterfall a mile or more high, and at last to the white weirdness of the ultimate north, where the convulsing Aurora Borealis hung over their heads like a fireworks show stuck on extra slow speed.

'My God,' she said, watching her breath hang as vapor in the air, 'it's staggering! I mean, I knew there were a lot of simworlds – we saw quite a few through the Quan Li sim, but . . .' She shivered, mostly out of reflex. Due to some wrinkle in the simworld, or to Dread's control of it, the temperature here felt no cooler than an early spring evening. 'And you can just go anywhere . . .?'

'Go anywhere, do anything.' His grin was now only half a smile, the expression of the proverbial canary-catching cat. He rolled the lighter in his fingers. 'I won't need this much longer. And you can do whatever you want too, if you behave yourself and keep me happy.'

She felt a tingle of warning. 'What does that mean, exactly . . . ?'

'Do your job. Stay out of trouble.' He paused to stare at her in a way that made her squirmingly uncomfortable. It was almost as though the attempted incursions into his hidden storage had appeared on her forehead like stigmata. 'You have no idea what I've got going here.'

She looked out at the endless ice fields, the northern lights shimmering. 'But what about your employer? Where did he go? How is it that you have access to everything . . . ?' Nearby, a piece of ice the size of a football field groaned and shifted, lifting a jagged edge above the permafrost and tipping the entire plate on which Dulcie and Dread stood. She grunted in fear, staggered, and put her hand on Dread's arm for support.

He opened his eyes wide. 'You don't have to worry,' he said, although he seemed to be enjoying her discomfiture. 'Even if you get killed here, you'll just drop offline. We're the only people left with on-and-off access.'

'What about the owners? What are they called, the Grail people?'

He shrugged. 'Things have changed a bit.'

'And you can control the system? You can make things happen?'

He nodded. He seemed as pleased as a child, and Dulcie realized that just like a child, he was anxious to show off. 'Anything you'd like to see?'

'Have you let those other people off the network, then?'

'Other people . . . ?'

'The ones we were traveling with – Martine, T4b, Sweet William. If you can control the access to the network, you should be able to set them free . . .' She realized suddenly that she missed them. After living with them day in and day out for weeks, she knew them better than she knew most of the people in her real life. They had been so miserable, so frightened and trapped . . .

Dread's blank look had become something even deeper and more distant. She pulled at his sleeve. 'You are going to set them loose, aren't you?' When he did not answer, she tugged again. He snatched his arm away with a quick violence that almost yanked her off her feet.

'Shut up,' he snapped. 'Someone's using the main broadcast channel.'

As she watched, in a white world silent but for the deep shifting of ice, his lips moved minutely as he subvocalized to the invisible someone. A slow smile stretched his face. He seemed to say something else, then his fingers flicked momentarily across the lighter. He turned to her slowly, eyes bright.

'Sorry about that. Something I'll have to see to later.' He nodded. 'What were you saying?'

'About the others – the ones the Grail had trapped online.'

'Ah, yes. As a matter of fact, I've just been too busy to see to Martine and the rest. But I'll be getting to them directly. You're right – I need to deal with them.' He closed his eyes for a moment. When he opened them again, his curious elation had been banked like the coals in a fire. 'Come along – we've got one more thing to see.'

Before she had time even to open her mouth the polar icecaps had dissolved and the two of them were hovering in midair above a vast and unbroken expanse of ocean. The sun was sinking toward the horizon, scalloping the wavetops in brassy light, but otherwise there was nothing to see for miles, not even seabirds.

'What's this . . . ?' she began, but he flicked up his hand, demanding quiet.

They hung above the endless green for long moments, then Dulcie saw that the pattern of the waves was beginning to change just before them, the regular crisscross of breakers churning into something more chaotic. As she watched, openmouthed, the churn became a great boiling, the waves lifting into plumes dozens, perhaps even hundreds of meters tall, flinging gobbets of froth into the air. Then, like the nose cone of a missile launched from some inconceivably huge submarine, the first tower top pierced the surface of the angry seas.

It lasted over an hour. For most of that time Dulcie was aware of nothing but the unfolding spectacle before her. The city heaved up from the waters with a surging roar, as though the earth itself were painfully giving birth – the spires of its tallest buildings first, tangled in great ropes of kelp, the walls of the citadel following closely behind, their armor of barnacles glittering wetly as they emerged into the sun. When the citadel had breasted, water sluicing down its roofs and walls before thundering into the ocean, turning the waters into white foam as far as she could see, the mountain and the rest of its clinging city arose, the drowned streets gleaming as they came back into the light.

When it was over, and the monstrous empty husk of island Atlantis had returned from the depths, Dread slipped his arm companionably around her shivering shoulders and leaned close to her ear.

'Play your cards right, sweetness,' he whispered, 'and someday all of this will be yours.' He reached down and patted her on the buttocks. 'I'll even dry it off for you. Now, if you'll excuse me, I've got a few loose ends to deal with. Just keep out of trouble, and make sure that my loft doesn't catch on fire or anything, right? Cheers.'

An instant later she was lying on the couch in the converted Redfern warehouse, muscles cramped and head pounding. Across the room, Dread's unmoving form lay like a corpse set out for viewing.

It was only when she had finished her shower and was sipping her second glass of wine of the afternoon that she realized she had just been taken on what must have been the strangest first date in history.

'HERE, honey,' Catur Ramsey told the little girl. 'Come here and look at the giraffes.'

She stared at him doubtfully, then at her father, who was standing on the far side of the suite. Sorensen nodded, so she came over and curled up on the couch beside Ramsey. He lifted the hotel guide and touched the picture of the Tanzanian resort; instantly the image sprang to life. Ramsey muted the soundtrack. 'See how tall they are?' he asked her. 'They eat the leaves on the very tops of the trees.'

Christabel frowned, her big, serious brown eyes curtained by her lashes. He could see she was nervous, but doing her best to control it. Catur Ramsey found himself impressed yet again by the composure of such a young child. 'Does it hurt their necks to stretch like that?' she asked.

'Oh, no. Doesn't hurt them any more than it hurts you to reach up and take something off a shelf. That's what they're born to do.'

She bit her lip as the brochure cycled through to a picture of a young, happy, wealthy-looking family dining on the veranda overlooking the waterhole while impala and zebra moved gracefully in and out of the spotlights bathing the veldt.

Ramsey was not feeling any happier himself. He eyed his pad, wishing he could try to call out again, but the shorter of the two men in black, the one called Pilger – shorter, but still over six feet and muscled like a professional wrestler – was watching him, broad face set in an expression of misleading indifference. Ramsey was furious with himself that he hadn't brought his t-jack.

Christabel's father, Major Sorensen, had wandered over to the suite's kitchen unit and was fiddling with the touch controls on the range. The big man named Doyle, the general's other bodyguard, or whatever they were, looked over from the European football game he was watching on the wallscreen. 'What are you doing?' he asked.

'I'm just making my daughter a cup of cocoa,' Sorensen said scornfully, but Ramsey saw something anomalous in his body language. He had no idea what the major might be doing but he hoped the men in black weren't paying close attention. On the other hand, he hoped that Sorensen wasn't planning anything heroic – Doyle and Pilger were armed to the teeth, and even Sorensen's friend Captain Parkins, sitting stiffly in a chair in his uniform, scowling at the floor, was armed. It was Parkins who had arrested them in the first place, after all, and now they were cooling their heels waiting for General Yacoubian. That made it three large men with guns against himself and Sorensen, both unarmed, and a little girl who probably didn't even have the training wheels off her bike.

'Daddy,' Christabel said suddenly, unable to pretend interest in the lioness that was chasing down a wildebeest for the fifth time through the loop, 'when can we go home? I want to see Mommy.'

'Soon, honey.'

Sorensen still had his back to them, waiting for the water to boil, and Ramsey felt a shiver of unease. Doyle and Pilger might look like they were doing anything but performing their professional duty, but Ramsey had met their sort before, both on the military bases of his youth and in the cop bars in which he sometimes found himself in his adult profession. Not to mention that physiques like theirs probably owed something to metabolic enhancement. The one named Doyle certainly had more than a bit of yellow in the whites of his eyes, which could mean any number of unsavory things. If he had gone through one of the military biomod programs, it meant that even if Sorensen threw a pot of boiling water over him, the bodyguard would still be capable of snapping several necks, pain and third-degree burns not-withstanding.

Oh, man, Ramsey found himself silently begging. *Major, please don't do anything stupid.*

He was beginning to wonder just what exactly he had let himself into. Yacoubian clearly knew something that scared Sorensen to death – the man's blood had all but drained into his feet when the general started talking about sunglasses – and they were none of them going anywhere without the general's permission. Ramsey was furious that he had not had more time to talk to Sorensen, and had not even met the strange Sellars before this whole thing had blown up; it was like walking unprepared into a capital murder trial, then finding out that you were the one on trial.

His nervous thoughts were interrupted by Christabel scrambling past him toward her father. Sorensen turned and waved her away. 'It's hot, Christabel,' he said sharply. 'I'll bring it to you when it's ready.'

Her face screwed up, and her eyes filled. Ramsey looked helplessly to Captain Parkins, who was still glaring down at the blue carpet as though it had done something to offend him, then went and took her hand and led her back to the couch. 'It's okay, honey. Come sit with me. Tell me about your school. Who's your teacher?'

Something thumped in the far room. For a moment, Ramsey thought he heard the general's voice raised in anger. The two bodyguards flicked each other a look, then turned back to the game. Ramsey wondered who the general's conference was with, and why it was more important than the interrogation of Sorensen. The general had clearly expended a great deal of energy to track the girl's father: it seemed strange he would keep the matter waiting for half an hour or more. Ramsey looked up at the wallscreen. Closer to an hour. What was this all about?

Something banged the connecting door hard, like someone had taken a sledge to it. Ramsey had only a moment to wonder why such an expensive suite would have doors thin enough to shudder just from someone banging their fist against it in the middle of a phone-conference argument, then Doyle jumped to his feet. He moved across the suite in perhaps two strides, just as frighteningly quick as Ramsey had feared he would be, and stood before the door to the general's room, listening. He knocked twice, loud.

'General? Are you all right?' He flicked a glance back to Pilger, who had risen now too, then knocked again. 'General Yacoubian? Do you need some assistance, sir?' He leaned to the door, straining to hear a reply. After a moment, he pounded again, wide hand flat on the door. 'General! Open up, sir!'

'What are they doing?' Christabel asked, beginning to cry again. 'Why are they shouting . . . ?'

Doyle took a step back, grabbed Pilger's shoulder to brace himself, then lifted his booted foot and slammed it against the door. 'Bolted,' he grunted. This time they both kicked the door at the same time, which crunched and fell inward. Pilger splintered it off its broken hinges while Doyle snatched the huge machine-pistol from his shoulder holster and stepped through, the weapon already locked in firing position as he disappeared from Ramsey's view.

His voice came from a few meters inside the room. '*Shit!*'

Pilger stepped through after him, his weapon also drawn. Ramsey waited a moment. When no sounds of firing were heard, he stood and moved cautiously toward the door, trying to get an angle to see what was happening. Captain Parkins was leaning forward in his chair, mouth open.

'Christabel!' Sorensen shouted from somewhere behind him. 'Don't get up! You stay on that damned couch!'

Doyle was squatting over the body of General Yacoubian, which lay sprawled on the floor between the door and the suite's large bed, his bathrobe rucked around his legs and open over his white-furred chest. The general's tan skin had turned a strange shade of gray. His tongue dangled from his mouth like a piece of rag. Doyle had begun CPR; for a surreal moment, Ramsey wondered how the body-guard had pushed hard enough in just a few seconds to make that broad purple welt on the general's breast.

'Ambulance to the garage,' Doyle said between his teeth. 'This is massive. And get the kit.'

Pilger was already hurrying back into the main room, his finger pushing against the jack on his neck. He spat a sequence of code into midair, then suddenly turned and waved his gun across the room. 'All of you, lie on the floor. Right now!' Without waiting to see whether his order was obeyed, he kneeled and pulled a black valise out from under the couch, then headed back toward the bedroom. He popped its catches and slid it toward Doyle, who was still working on the general; with each blow, Yacoubian bounced on the carpet. Pilger drew a syringe out of one of the valise's inner pockets. As he checked its label, he saw Ramsey standing in the doorway. The gun came up in his other hand.

'Goddamn it, I said I wanted you all down on the *floor!*'

'Daddy?' Christabel was crying back in the main part of the suite. 'Daddy!'

Even as Catur Ramsey backed away, helplessly watching the frighteningly large hole at the end of Pilger's gun barrel, something flared in the corner of his eye. He flinched, but there was no sound of a shot. He looked to the right and saw something that made no sense at all: Major Michael Sorensen was standing on a chair in the suite's kitchen holding a burning napkin clutched in a pair of ice tongs. He was lifting it up to the ceiling, like some bizarre parody of the Statue of Liberty with her torch.

'I told you all to lie *down!*' shouted Pilger, who could not see this inexplicable sight. Even as Doyle plunged the hypodermic into the middle of the dark bruise on Yacoubian's chest, Pilger's gun tracked from one side of the doorway to the other, then tilted down at Ramsey's knees. Something clattered, then hissed.

Suddenly it was snowing purple.

The tiles of the ceiling had folded back like venetian blinds. Dozens of nozzles racked down, spewing clouds of pale lavender fire-retardant dust. The lights of the room began to flick on and off and a painfully loud buzzing filled the air. Sorensen leaped past Ramsey and snatched his daughter up off the floor, then sprinted toward the elevator door where he began to press the button, over and over.

Doyle was pasting the second of two defibrillation patches to the general's still unmoving chest, but Pilger came out of the bedroom with gun drawn, waving his arm so he could see through the fog of choking purple. He shoved his gun against the back of Major Sorensen's head, inches from Christabel's terrified face. 'You don't want it to go down this way, do you?' he snarled. 'Your brains splashed all over your little girl? Just step away from the door and lie down.'

'No. None of it's going to go down this way.' Captain Ron Parkins had drawn his own service automatic and was pointing it at Pilger's head. Parkins' face was red with frightened anger. 'We're not going to be disappeared by you bastards, whoever you are. These people are under my authority, not yours. You go tend to the general. We're leaving.'

In the moment that followed, silent except for the low moan of the alarm, the elevator door swished open. Ramsey, who had both Pilger and Captain Parkins between himself and safety, struggled to slow his rattling heart-beat. It was already hard to breathe, and although most of the purple dust had settled to the floor, there was enough left in the air that he could feel the mother of all sneezes coming on. *That would just be the capper*, he thought. *Sneeze and set off a gun battle.*

'Let us go,' Sorensen said quietly, Pilger's gun still against the base of his skull. 'The general's dead. You may have more of your people coming to help clean up the mess, but now the fire alarm's gone off, so there are a lot of people on the way that you *don't* own. Just turn around. He's dead. This isn't worth it anymore.'

Pilger stared at him, then flicked his eyes sideways to the silvery snout of Captain Parkins' gun. His lip curled. He lowered his pistol, then turned and walked back into the bedroom without another look at them. The general's body was twisting on the floor as Doyle turned the defibrillator dial. Ramsey fought the urge to faint dead away.

'Get out here,' growled Captain Parkins. They were five miles from the hotel, the van stopped in front of the light

rail station. 'You can get a cab from here, a train, whatever the hell you want. Just get going.'

'Ron – thank you, man, thank you.' Sorensen helped
his daughter down from the van. The two young soldiers,
who had fought to keep astonishment off their faces when
three men and a girl stepped out of the elevator powdered
in purple from head to foot, sat a little straighter.

'I don't want to know,' Parkins said angrily. 'But even
if I lose my bars for this, I just . . . I couldn't . . .'

'I don't think you're ever going to hear about it again,
Ron. At least not through official channels.' Christabel's
father brushed some of the powder from her hair; she
looked up quickly as though to make certain it was his
hand, not a stranger's. 'Trust me – you don't want to
know anything more about this than you have to, anyway.'

'No, I don't.'

Ramsey stepped down beside them, still amazed that
he was alive and free and under the open sky again.
'Thank you, Captain. You saved our lives.'

Parkins threw up his hands in confusion. 'Jee-zuss!' He
turned to Sorensen. 'Just . . . Mike, just take care of that
wife and little girl of yours. On second thought, maybe I
will ask you to explain this to me one day. What do you
think?'

Major Sorensen nodded. 'As soon as I figure it out,
you'll be the first to hear.'

Christabel was shivering despite the warm sun in front
of the railway station. As the military van drove away
Ramsey took off his wind-breaker, shook a cloud of dust
from it, and draped it over her shoulders. It was only as
he followed the child and her father toward the taxi line
that he realized he was shivering as badly as she was.

CHAPTER 3

Restless Natives

NETFEED/INTERACTIVES: IEN, Hr. 4 (Eu, NAm) – 'BACKSTAB'
(visual: Yohira receiving implant)
VO: Shi Na (Wendy Yohira) is a prisoner in the New Guinea cult
headquarters of the evil Doctor Methuselah (Moishe Reiner). Can
Stabbak (Carolus Kennedy) save her before she joins the cult in their
mass suicide ritual? Casting 28 cult members, 5 tribespeople, 2 Doctor
Methuselah 'special toadies.' Flak to: IEN.BKSTB.CAST

IT was strange how it had come back to him, the new swathe of memory suddenly revealed, as though the roof of an ancient tomb had collapsed and let sunlight stream onto its contents for the first time in centuries. At the same time, the memories seemed new and painfully raw, like growing skin exposed beneath a scab.

Of course, he wasn't going to get much chance to think about it . . .

Paul leaped away up the slithering leafmold hill even as the first of the wood lice just missed clutching his leg in a ripple of malformed paws. He could barely keep his feet:

the skeletal remains of leaves were bigger than he was, slippery to climb as the bones in an elephant's graveyard. A dozen more wood lice emerged along the slope, the whole pack moving in that deceptive, staggering way. Their deformed legs might be different lengths, but that was small handicap on such terrain, and their dozens of tiny grasping hands were a perfect adaptation for chasing a stumbling, two-footed prey.

Paul dragged himself up onto a great curl of root that emerged from the leafmire like the back of a whale breaching the waves. He could see that even if he reached the base of the trunk, still about a hundred paces away, there was no escape on the far side except along another descending slope of the same half-decayed mulch, a slope littered with the bodies of other sleeping wood lice, curled like ribbed Easter eggs. He staggered on anyway.

'*Come back,*' one of the creatures groaned behind him, and some of its companions took up the cry. '*Huuuungry! Eat you!*'

Despite the recognizable English words, the voices were so completely inhuman that he felt utter despair wash over him like a cold rain. Even if he escaped, something else would get him eventually. He was alone in a hostile world – a hostile *universe*. Whether he lived another ten minutes or ten days, he would probably never see another human being, would have only rasping, homicidal monstrosities like these for company until the inevitable end.

The whine of his pursuers became a fierce hiss, a change of tone so sudden and complete that Paul stopped in surprise. The wood lice were all rearing up on their hindmost segments, their distorted little hands waving frantically at him. Or at something behind him.

Paul turned. A man stood at the base of the tree, his

dull robe almost invisible against the vast expanse of gray bark, so that for the first instant he seemed an apparition, a trick of the light making a face out of a whorl in the tree's rough hide. He was no bigger than Paul, but he seemed oddly careless of the approaching wood lice as he walked down the humped spine of the tree root.

'*Huuunngryyy!*' they chanted, like terrible children.

As the man drew closer, Paul had a better view of the stranger's compact frame and distinctly Asian features and guessed that this must be the one Renie and the others had described – Kunohara, the insect world's creator.

The black-haired man glanced briefly at Paul, showing neither interest nor irritation, then stopped just where the root curved sharply down into the leafmold, so that he faced the swarm of creatures like Moses preaching from the mount. But if these were Kunohara's people, they did not seem much disposed to obey him.

'*Eat you!*' they cried, hunching up the slope.

Kunohara shook his head in disgust, then lifted his hand. A great gust of wind abruptly curled down from the sky, then swept along the ground and past the base of the tree – a wind so howlingly fierce that most of the fallen leaves and other detritus were ripped away in an instant. With piping shrieks of frustration or terror, the wood lice, too, were lifted and flung off into nothingness; some managed to cling to larger objects for a few moments, but within a few heartbeats even those were sucked away. Then the gale died.

Paul stood, astonished. Although the closest of the creatures had been only a few paces away from him, and had been hurled sideways like a bullet fired from a gun, he had felt no wind at all.

Of the dozens, one wood louse remained, squirming

helplessly on the ground at Kunohara's feet. 'They even speak . . .' the man said quietly, but he almost sounded shocked. Kunohara snaked his fingers into the plates behind the creature's head, pushing deep. Something crunched and the thing lay still.

'You saved me,' Paul said. 'Those things would have killed me . . .'

The man peered at him, then lifted the curled corpse of the mansized wood louse. He turned his back on Paul and lowered his head. Paul had the distinct impression that his savior was about to vanish.

'Wait! You can't just leave!'

The smaller man paused. 'I did not bring you here.' His English was very precise. 'In fact, you are trespassing. I did not need to rescue you, but these . . . monsters offend me. You are free to leave the way you came in.'

'But I don't even know how I got here.'

'That is nothing to me.' He shrugged and hefted the dead bug. 'It is bad enough, finding my blameless isopods corrupted like this. I will not also be made a park ranger in my own home.'

'What do you mean, corrupted?' Paul was desperate to keep the man from leaving. He sensed that his rescuer was not toying with him – he genuinely intended to leave him alone in the wilderness. The wood lice were gone, but the thought of what other horrors might be lurking was almost enough to make Paul throw himself on the other man to keep him from going, to cling to his legs like a frightened toddler. 'You're Kunohara, aren't you? This is your simulation world.'

The other did not reply, but the look of heightened caution that flitted across his face was enough to tell Paul he was right.

'Look, can you at least tell me if you know anything

about where my friends are? You've met them before –
here and in the House world.'

Kunohara snorted. It was hard to tell whether it was
a noise of amusement or disgust. 'So you are one of
Atasco's orphans,' he said. 'I am almost sorry now I saved
you. You and your friends have brought ruin on me.' He
turned his back again, waving his hand dismissively. 'Go
and find your own road to hell.'

'What are you talking about? At least tell me if you've
seen them! Are they here somewhere?'

Kunohara turned around, his look of anger shifting to
something more subtle, if not more friendly. 'I have not
seen you before with those other fools – and you have
not been in my world before either, I think. So who are
you?'

Paul felt himself at another crossroad. This man
Kunohara was clearly no friend to Renie and the others,
and Paul was reluctant with good reason to tell people
his own name. But he could feel Kunohara slipping away
from him. In a moment the man would be gone, leaving
Paul alone in a place where he was no bigger than an
ant.

'No, I haven't been here before,' he said. 'My name is
Paul Jonas.'

Both of Kunohara's eyebrows now rose. 'So you are
the man for whom Jongleur tore the system apart. Why
does he want you? You do not look like much.' He threw
his hands apart, a gesture of frustration or resignation.
'Come.'

'Come . . . where?'

'To my house on the river.' For the first time, Kunohara
smiled, but it was scarcely more than a brief grimace. 'I
might as well ask you a few questions before I give you
back to the local crustacea.' He nodded his head once and

the environment blurred around them so swiftly and unexpectedly that for a moment Paul thought the ground had
literally been yanked from beneath his feet. A moment
later everything jumped back into place again and Paul
gasped at a world gone suddenly pear-shaped.

The sky curved over him like a weirdly gleaming bowl,
and the towering trees which had stretched upward like
pillars holding the heavens now bent above him like
bystanders examining an accident victim. Paul felt a solid
floor beneath his feet, and turned slowly to discover an
entire room behind him, multileveled, furnished sparsely
but attractively with screens and low furniture. Beyond
the furnishings, the stairs, and the different levels of floor-
ing, the world seemed to distort again, but instead of trees
and sky, the other half of the wide space seemed to cower
beneath a curved wall of foaming water.

The effect was so bizarre that it took long seconds
before Paul realized that the curvature of sky and trees
and water was because the room was . . .

'. . . A big . . . bubble?'

Kunohara shook his head, but only because he was
amused. 'It is not so big, really – it is you and I who are
small. The bubble floats in an eddy between two cataracts
of the river.' He gestured to the wall of water which seemed
to hang above the back of his bubble-house. 'There, see
the river pour down? It is most pleasant to watch its
motion – turbulence is paradoxically soothing, whereas
too much regularity can be maddening.'

'I don't get it.' Paul swiveled to look out what he thought
of as the 'front' of the house, with its leaning trees and
broad if distorted view of the river spreading out below
the cataract, then turned back to the curtain of foaming
water behind them. He could feel the boil of water pushing steadily at the bubble, although the movement it

imparted to the house was surprisingly gentle, like the rolling of a sailboat at anchor. 'If this place is just a bubble, and there's water pouring down behind us, why don't we go over the waterfall?'

'Because this is my world.' Kunohara was beginning to sound irritated again. 'It is easy enough to keep the bubble floating in one place, balanced in the eddy, circling gently to the side of the main current.'

Paul thought it would be even easier just to make the house out of something more substantial and stick it down, or use some programmer's magic code to ensure that the bubble would stay rigidly in one place no matter what, but clearly Kunohara found something to like in the sound and feel of the moving water, the delicate way the bubble swayed and spun. Paul was just glad he was not prone to seasickness. He turned from the view and examined the rest of the multileveled room, the floor covered in rugs and soft mats, the tables low to the ground in the ancient Japanese style.

'Are you interested in the natural sciences?' Kunohara asked suddenly.

'Certainly.' Paul was anxious to keep his host happy. Polite chit-chat beat the hell out of being thrown back to the ravenous pseudo-bugs any day. 'I mean, I'm no expert . . .'

'Go to those stairs. Wave your hand on the topmost step, so, then go down.'

Paul paused at the top of the staircase, looking down into a lower level of Kunohara's house, this one seemingly not much different than the other, except that the floor was made from some dark, glassy substance. Paul waved his hand and the lights in the lower room went out, and he suddenly realized that he was looking not at a dark floor, but at the bottom of the bubble, gazing directly down through its transparency into the river.

Without the reflections obscuring his view he could see the rocky bottom of the river-pond beneath him, which to his eyes seemed as craggy and distant as a mountain range seen from a passenger seat on a jet. From time to time vast shapes slid between stones on the riverbottom, creatures which made Paul flinch in atavistic fear, although he knew that they must be very small fish by any normal standards. There were also a few semitransparent animals a little like attenuated, spider-legged lobsters or even more unusual shapes. Paul moved down to the bottommost step and stood there, reluctant to step onto the glassy material even though he could see a low couch and other furnishings below him, indicating that the floor could hold weight. One of the lobster-things floated up and bumped its head against the bubble, black bead eyes swiveling on stalks, whip-thin legs scrabbling across the curving surface, perhaps wondering why it could not reach something it could see.

'*Penaeus vannemei*, postlarval stage,' Kunohara said from behind him. 'Baby shrimp. I changed the refraction of the bubble here on the bottom, so what you are seeing is a bit magnified. Really they would be much smaller even than we are in our present size.'

'You've got . . . it's very impressive.' Paul did not say so, but although the bubble-house was striking, it was also strangely modest for one of the gods of a virtual universe. 'A beautiful house.'

Paul waved his hand at the topmost step; when the lights came back on, he saw his own reflection stretched along the curve of the wall like a sideshow mirror. Despite the unfamiliar jumpsuit, the man looking back was definitely him, the Paul Jonas he remembered, although with enough of a beard to give him the look of a shipwreck survivor.

But why do I always look like me, he wondered? *When everyone else keeps changing? Someone said !Xabbu was even a monkey for a while.*

Shaking his head, he mounted the stairs and discovered the dead wood louse Kunohara had brought back floating in the center of the room, suspended in an hexahedron of white light as though fossilized in amber. Paul's host walked around it, staring; when he gestured, the bug revolved in place. A pale scrimshaw of *kanji* text ran across the surface of the transparent container.

'Is it . . . something you haven't seen before?'

'Worse. It is something that should not be.' Kunohara grunted. 'Can you drink?'

'Can I?'

'Do you have the receptors? What would you like? You are a guest. Courtesy demands I offer you something, even if you and your friends have ruined my life.'

Kunohara had twice accused Paul and his companions of causing him harm, but he wasn't ready yet to pursue the subject. 'I can drink. I don't know if I can get drunk, so I suppose it doesn't matter.' He had a sudden thought. 'You wouldn't happen to have any tea, would you?'

Kunohara's smile this time was only a few degrees short of friendly. 'Forty or fifty varieties. Green teas, which are my favorite, but also black – orange pekoe, congou, souchong. I have oolong, too. What do you want?'

'I'd kill for English tea.'

Kunohara frowned. 'Strictly speaking, there are no "English" teas, unless they have begun growing it in the high tropical hills of the Cotswolds while I was not looking. But I have Darjeeling and even Earl Grey.'

'Darjeeling would be lovely.'

Paul had no doubt that Kunohara could have magicked the tea into existence just as he had magicked them into the bubble, but his host was clearly a man of carefully preserved idiosyncrasies – both Kunohara and his environment were a strange combination of the naturalistic and absurd. An old-fashioned fire burned in a brazier in a depression in the floor filled with sand, but although there was no visible way for the smoke to vent from the bubble, the air in the room was smoke-free. As Kunohara hung a pot of water above the low flames and Paul sat down on a mat beside the fire pit to wait, he found himself overwhelmed by yet another absurdist juxtaposition – one moment about to be murdered by mutants, five minutes later waiting for water to boil for tea.

'What are those . . . things?' he asked, gesturing at the hovering wood louse.

'They are perversions,' Kunohara said harshly. 'A new and terrible interference with my world. Another reason for me to despise your companions.'

'Renie and the others had something to do with those monsters?'

'I have found strange anomalies in my world for some time – mutations that made no sense, and which could not have come from the normal functioning of the simulation – but this is something else. Look at it! An ugly parody of humanity. These have been created deliberately. Someone with power – someone in the Grail Brotherhood, I do not doubt – has decided to punish me.'

'Punish you? Mutations?' Paul sat back, shaking his head. He was beginning to realize that even if the tea behaved as it did in the real world, it was not going to be enough to clear his head. He was exhausted. 'I don't understand any of this.'

Kunohara stared at the wood louse in scowling silence.

Steam chuffed from the kettle, spread in a cheerful cloud, then vanished, as though overwhelmed by the chill

coming from Paul's host. Paul accepted the cup which
Kunohara conjured out of midair, then watched as he
poured boiling water over an infuser. The fumes rising
from the steeping tea were the first thing Paul had experienced in longer than he could remember that made him
feel like there might be some point to the world. 'I'm
sorry,' he said. 'Maybe I'm being dense, but I'm very, very
tired. It's been the long day to end all long days.' He
laughed, and heard a tiny edge of hysteria in his voice.
He leaned his head over the cup to breathe in the vapor.
'Can you just tell me what terrible thing my friends did
to you?'

'Exactly what I expected them to do,' Kunohara
snapped. 'In fact, it is myself I am angry with as much
as them. They pitted themselves against a far superior
force and lost, and now it is the rest of us who will pay
the price.'

'Lost?' Paul took his first sip. 'Oh, my God, this is
wonderful.' He blew on the tea and sipped again, trying
to make sense of what Kunohara was saying. 'But . . .
but nobody's lost anything yet, as far as I can tell. Except
the Brotherhood. I think most of them are dead now.' He
stopped, suddenly fearing that in his weariness he had
said too much. Was Kunohara one of the Brotherhood, or
just someone who rented space from them?

His host was shaking his head. 'What nonsense is this?'

Paul stared at him. There was, of course, no way to
know what someone was really thinking behind his face
back in the real world, let alone here. But, he reminded
himself, it might have been as little as an hour since he
and Renie and the others had experienced . . . whatever
it was they had experienced. It was too late in the day,
and he himself was too helpless, to offend potential allies.

'You're saying you don't know what happened to us?

That we saw the Grail Brotherhood have their ceremony
– that we met the Other? This is all news to you?'

Paul had the not-inconsiderable pleasure of watching
Kunohara's hard face melt into an expression of astonishment. 'You met . . . the operating system? And you
are alive?'

'Apparently.' It was not, Paul reflected, as sarcastic a
remark as it sounded.

Kunohara lifted the teapot. Admirably, his hand did
not tremble. 'It seems clear you know things I do not.'

'From what my friends told me, it was usually the other
way around. Perhaps this time you'll be a little more
generous with your own information.'

Kunohara looked shaken. 'I will answer your questions,
I promise. Tell me what happened to you.'

Hideki Kunohara listened carefully to Paul's story, stopping him often for clarification. Even in a drastically
streamlined version it was still a long tale: by the time
he was describing the climb up the black mountain, the
world outside the bubble had passed from twilight into
evening and stars hung in the black heavens above the
river. Except for the flicker of the fire, Kunohara had
allowed his house to grow dark too; there were moments
when Paul forgot he was inside the shining, curved walls
and could almost believe himself back on one of the Greek
islands with Azador, huddled by a campfire beneath naked
sky.

Exhausted now and wanting to finish, Paul did his best
to keep to what was important, but with so many mysteries it was hard to know what to leave out. Kunohara
seemed particularly interested in the silver lighter, and
disappointed to hear it had apparently been lost on the
mountaintop. At the mention of Dread and the murderer's

boastful announcement of his control over the operating system, his expression became dark and remote.

'But this is all most, most strange,' he said when Paul had paused to finish his fourth cup of Darjeeling. 'All of it. I had some inkling of what the Brotherhood intended. They approached me about it long ago, and they seemed surprised that although I could have afforded to join their inner circle, I chose not to.' He met Paul's look with a grim smile. 'I said I would answer your questions, but that does not mean I must explain everything of myself. My reasons for not wanting to pursue the Brotherhood's immortality are my own.'

'You don't have to apologize for that,' Paul said hastily. 'I'd like to think that if it was offered to me, and I knew how many children would have to suffer and even die, that I'd say no, too.'

'Yes, the children,' Kunohara nodded. 'There is the matter of the children, too.' For a moment he sat in distracted silence. 'But the Other, that is truly astonishing. I had long suspected that some kind of unique artificial intelligence underlay the system, and even that in some ways it had begun to change the environments. As I said, there have been unlikely mutations in my own biosphere almost since the beginning. At first I attributed them to processing errors because of the mounting complexity of the network, but I began to doubt that. Now these latest . . .' He paused and closed his eyes for a moment. In the silence, Paul felt his own weariness tugging him down like a heavy burden. 'You saw them,' Kunohara finally said. 'Those mutant *isopoda* were no chance corruption of the programming. They even speak!' He shook his head. 'I suspect that this creature who calls himself Dread has truly bent the system to his own will and is beginning to play with his new toy.'

The idea of the monstrous personality that Renie had described having such power over the network sent a chill through Paul.

'And your own story is just as strange,' Kunohara said abruptly. 'You were actually employed by Felix Jongleur?'

'That's what I remember, but beyond that point there's still some kind of block. The rest is all blank, except for the angel – except for Ava.'

'Jongleur's daughter.' Kunohara frowned. 'But how could that be? The man is nearing the end of his second century of life. From what I know, his body has been almost entirely useless for many decades, floating in a tank, kept alive by machiens – far longer than the age of the girl you apparently tutored. Why should he want a child?'

Paul sighed. 'I hadn't even thought of that. I don't understand any of it. Not yet.'

Kunohara slapped his hands on his legs and stood. 'There will be much to consider and discuss tomorrow, but I see that you are falling asleep. Find yourself a place to stretch out. If you need anything you have only to ask the house, but I think you will find the beds are comfortable. I will darken the wall of the place you choose so the morning sun will not wake you too soon.'

'Thank you.' Paul got laboriously to his feet. 'I said it before, but I'll say it again. You saved my life.'

Kunohara shrugged. 'As you may yet save mine. Information is the most valuable capital in this network. I have always maintained sources of my own, of course, out of necessity. Sharing this network with Jongleur and his associates is like living in the Florence of the Medicis. But I must confess that we have come to a time when my knowledge is failing me.'

Paul staggered across the room toward an alcove where a bed that was little more than a padded mat lay unrolled on the floor. 'One more question,' he said as he slumped onto it. 'Why were you so certain we'd lost? That the Brotherhood had won?'

Kunohara paused at the entrance to the alcove. His face was again a stoic mask. 'Because things have changed.'

'Those new mutants?'

He shook his head. 'I did not know of them until I saw your distress. But shortly before that happened, I discovered that I have been affected by the same thing you others have experienced, despite being one of the founders of this virtual universe.' His smile seemed almost mocking. 'I can no longer leave the network. So I too can die here, it seems.' He gave a brief bow. 'Sleep well.'

Paul woke in the middle of the night, disoriented from yet another dream of being chased across clouds by a giant whose every step made tremors. He sat upright, heart speeding, and discovered he was still bouncing, although it was less than in the terrifying dream-pursuit, but as he saw the quiet, restful shapes of Kunohara's house around him, he relaxed. It was raining outside, the drops huge from his perspective. They thudded down on the bubble walls and stirred up the waters of the eddy, but Kunohara had apparently buffered the force so that Paul felt it as no more than a mild jouncing.

He had just lain down again, trying to make his mind a companionable blank in the hope of finding a more soothing dream this time, when a loud and weirdly familiar voice filled the room.

'Are you there? Can you hear me? Renie?'

He scrambled to his feet. The room was empty – the voice had come from thin air. He took a few steps and banged his shin on a low table.

'*Renie, can you hear us? We're in bad shape . . . !*'

It was the blind woman, Martine, and she sounded frightened. Paul pawed at his head, confused and frustrated by the voice from nowhere. 'Kunohara!' he shouted. 'What's going on?'

Light began to glow all around him, a dim, sourceless radiance. His host appeared, dressed in a dark robe. He too seemed disoriented. 'Someone . . . someone is using the open communication band,' he said. 'The fools! What do they think they are doing?'

'*What* communication band?' Paul demanded, but the other man was making a series of gestures. 'Those are my friends! What's going on?'

A group of view-windows sprang open in midair, filled with darting sparks of light that might have been numbers or letters or something even more obscure, but they seemed to make sense to Kunohara, who scowled. 'Seven hells! They are here – in my world!'

'What's going on?' Paul watched as Kunohara opened a new and larger window. This one was full of dark forms; it was a moment until Paul realized he was looking at a section of the macrojungle by moonlight. Rain was splashing down with a force like artillery shells. Paul could make out several dim shapes huddled beneath an overhanging leaf. 'Is that them? How are they talking to us?'

'*Please answer us, Renie,*' Martine's voice moaned. '*We're stuck somewhere without . . .*'

The sound abruptly died. Before Paul could open his mouth to ask more questions, another disembodied voice cracked through the room, deeper and stronger than the first. He had heard this one before too, Paul realized with mounting horror, but only once – from the sky above the black glass mountain . . .

'*Martine! Is that you, sweetness?*' The big bad wolf

discovering that bricks were no longer being issued to pigs could not have sounded more pleased. '*I've missed you! Do you have any of my other old mates with you?*'

Martine had lapsed into what was doubtless terrified silence, but the gloating voice did not seem to mind.

'*I'm a bit busy at the moment, my old darling, but I'll send some friends to find you. Don't move! They'll be with you in a few minutes. Actually, go ahead and move if you want – it won't do you a bit of good.*' Dread laughed, a clear, wholehearted sound of enjoyment. The figures Paul could see in the open view-window shrank back even farther into the shadows beneath the leaf.

He turned and grabbed Kunohara's arm. 'We have to help them!'

In the dim light, Kunohara's profile seemed carved from unmoving stone. 'There is nothing we can do. They have brought this on themselves.'

'You saved *me!*'

'You did not reveal yourself to those who would destroy me. In any case, I think it is too late for them anyway, no matter what this Dread chooses to do. They have been found by a nearer enemy.'

'What are you talking about?'

Kunohara pointed at the window. The leaf where Martine and the others huddled still bounded beneath the heavy raindrops, but a huge shadow had crossed into Paul's field of view, a towering mass of jointed legs and armor that seemed, eclipse-like, to swallow the projected image.

'It is a whip scorpion,' said Kunohara. 'At least they will not suffer long.'

CHAPTER 4

In Silver Dreaming

NETFEED/NEWS: Free Speech for Talking Toys?
(visual: Maxie Mouth Insult Doll, manufacturer's demo)
VO: Parents of a nine-year-old boy in Switzerland are suing the local school authorities, saying that their child is being punished for insubordinate speech when the real culprit is a talking toy named Maxie Mouth, manufactured by the FunSmart company.
(visual: Funsmart VPPR Dilip Rangel)
RANGEL: 'Maxie Mouth is a full-range interactive toy. It talks – that's what it does. Sometimes it says bad things. No matter how unpleasant the remarks may have been, they are not the fault of the owner, who is a minor child. It's one thing to confiscate the toy – we've seen a lot of that – another thing to hold a child responsible for what the toy calls a teacher. Who is apparently a fairly oppressive old bitch, by the way . . .'

THERE could be no mountain so tall. It was inconceivable.

'If this were the real world,' Renie gasped to !Xabbu in the agonizing middle of what seemed to be their fourth or maybe fifth full day descending the mountain, 'then the top would have been above the atmosphere, in outer

space. There wouldn't have been any air. The cold would
have flash-frozen our bones in our bodies.'

'Then I suppose we should be grateful.' He did not
sound convinced.

'Chance not,' Sam muttered. ''Cause if we were poking
up into outer space, we'd be dead and we wouldn't have
to do this hiking *fenfen* any more.'

This was a rare exchange. The exhaustion and misery
of the journey were too great, the danger too constant,
to encourage talking. The path still led them in a monotonous clockwise spiral down the massive black cone, but
as it receded back into the mountain, or simply melted
slowly into nothingness, the trail became too narrow for
anything except single file, too treacherous for them to
attempt any speed greater than a trudging walk with eyes
flicking between the edge of the trail and the back of the
person just ahead.

Sam had slipped twice, saved both times because they
were now marching so closely together that everyone was
within arm's reach of someone else. Jongleur had almost
fallen once too, but !Xabbu had shot out a hand and
grabbed the man's arm, allowing him to topple backward
instead of forward. !Xabbu had acted without thought,
automatically, and Jongleur did not thank him. Renie
could not help wondering what she would do if the Grail
master stumbled again and she were the only one who
could save him.

After Jongleur's near-miss, they made it a practice to
rotate positions during the dwindlingly frequent wide
spots along the path, so that the four of them took turns
at the front, ensuring that whoever was leading would be
relatively alert. Only Ricardo Klement was left out of the
rotation – consigned to the rear, where his somnambu-
listic stops and starts would threaten no one but himself.

It was an indescribably dreary trip. Other than the occasional odd shapes of the black stone itself, its bulges and candledrip flutings, there was nothing to look at, no plant life, not even the distraction of weather. The sky that so closely and fearfully surrounded them was less interesting than a concrete wall. Even the distant beauty of the silvery-white cloudbank below them, with its unstable shimmering and gleams of rainbow light, quickly lost the power to engage, and in any case it was far too dangerous to look over the edge for more than a few seconds. Weary feet frequently stumbled: the trail, though monotonous, was not uniform.

By the time they had gone through their third miserable night's sleep in one of the mountainside's narrow crevices – 'night' signifying only the period during which they stopped walking, because the black peak remained in perpetual twilight – even the violent angers of the first camp had disappeared. Felix Jongleur barely mustered the energy for the few necessary communications, apparently avoiding even contempt as a waste of resources. Renie's fear and dislike of him did not disappear, but in the dull slog of routine and the occasional shock of accident it receded into something at the back of her mind, a small, cold thing that slept. Even Sam, despite her loathing of Jongleur, began to lower her guard a little. She still would not speak to him, but if she stumbled and he was the one in front of her, she would reach out and steady herself on his naked back. The first time she had shivered in disgust, but now, like almost everything else, it had become only another part of their bleak routine.

'I just realized something,' Renie said quietly to !Xabbu. Since they had not found a place wide enough to sit, they were taking their rest standing up, backs against the mountain's side. With no sun to warm it or night to chill it, the temperature of the stone was indistinguishable from that of her own skin. 'We were supposed to climb this.'

'What do you mean?' He lifted one of his feet carefully and massaged the sole.

She sneaked a look at Jongleur, who stood a few meters away down the slope, spine and head pressed back against the smooth rock face. 'Paul's angel,' she whispered. 'Ava. She said something about how we were supposed to get to the mountaintop ourselves, but there wasn't time. And then she made that gateway and dropped us right onto the path. Do you see? They wanted us to climb this whole thing. Imagine that! Having to go *uphill* even farther than we've already gone down.' She shook her head. 'The bastards. It probably would have killed half of us.'

!Xabbu too was shaking his head, but in puzzlement. 'But who wanted that? Who are *they?*'

'The angel. And the Other, I guess. Who knows?'

He pursed his lips, then wiped a hand across his eyes. Renie thought he looked wrung out – more weary than she had ever seen him. 'It is like the journeys our people must make, where we must sometimes travel for months in the bush – but that is for survival.'

'So is this, I guess. But it still makes me angry, someone setting up an obstacle course like this. 'Oh, and let's have them climb a hundred-kilometer mountain, too. That'll keep them busy for a while.' Bastards.'

'It's a quest.' Sam's voice was flat.

Renie looked at her in surprise. By the girl's slumped position, Renie had judged her too exhausted for conversation. 'What do you mean, Sam?'

'A quest, seen? Like in the Middle Country. If you want to get something, you have to go on some utterly long journey and earn bonus points and kill monsters.' She sighed. 'If I ever get out of here, I'm never going in that *fen*-hole Middle Country again.'

'But why would we be sent on a quest? I mean, we already *are* on one, in a sense.' Renie scowled, willing herself to think when her weary brain wanted only to lie torpid in its skullbath of nutrients. 'Sellars brought us in to find out what was going on. But those gameworld quests always have a purpose, an explanation. 'Get this and win the game.' We had no idea what we were looking for – and we still don't.'

Her gaze flicked to Jongleur, as still as a lizard on a rock. Something tugged at her memory. 'It was Ava who kept sending Paul places, wasn't it? And she did it for you and Orlando, too, right?'

'That was her in the Freezer, yeah.' Sam shifted position. 'And in Egypt. So I guess so.'

'Oh my God,' Renie said. 'I've just realized something.' Her voice sank to a whisper. 'If Paul Jonas was right, then Ava is *Jongleur's daughter.*'

!Xabbu cocked an eyebrow. 'But we knew that already.'

'I know, but it hadn't really sunk in. That means the answers to most of our questions might be sitting there in that horrible man's head.'

'Let's open it up with a sharp rock and find out,' Sam suggested.

Jongleur's eyelids slid up and he turned to regard them. Renie wondered if her own sim face would register a guilty flush. 'If you have the energy to whisper like schoolchildren,' he said, 'then you no doubt have the strength to begin walking again.' He pushed himself upright and began to limp down the path.

'You seem very disturbed, Renie,' !Xabbu said quietly as they stepped out after Jongleur.

'Well, what if it's true? What if the answers to

everything – the children, and why we're stuck here, and what's going to happen – what if he already knows everything we've been killing ourselves to find out?'

'I do not think he will help us, Renie. He might trade for information from us, but only if it was useful to him, and we have no idea what he needs.'

Renie could not shake a certain sick feeling. 'I can't help thinking about what Sam just said. Not trying to crack open his skull, but about using force. If he's stuck in a virtual body like we are, then he's vulnerable – and we outnumber him. Don't we owe it to all those children, to our friends, to find out what he knows? Even if we have to . . . to torture it out of him?'

!Xabbu looked truly disturbed. 'I do not like that thought, Renie.'

'Neither do I, but what if the fate of the world really is at stake?' Sam had fallen back a couple of paces, and now Renie lowered her voice until her mouth was almost against !Xabbu's ear, which made walking single file even more dangerous. 'It sounds so melodramatic, but it could be true! What if that's the only way? Don't we have to consider it?'

!Xabbu did not reply. He looked, if it were possible, more exhausted now than before they had stopped to rest.

Renie certainly understood !Xabbu's reluctance even to talk about the possibility of torturing Jongleur for information – not just in abhorrence of what they would themselves become in taking such a step, but also because of real fear about what might come of it. Jongleur was a hard, ruthless man. Watching his measured pace a few steps ahead, the ropy, hard muscles of his naked body moving beneath the skin, she had the feeling that bending him to their will might not be a process without casualties on their own side – a price Renie was unwilling to pay. And although Ricardo Klement had shown no interest in anything so far, that was no guarantee he would stand passively by and let them attack Jongleur. But even if they managed to subdue the Grail master and threaten him with pain or even death, what then? She did not know for certain that Jongleur really was as vulnerable to virtual execution as she and her companions; perhaps he was only pretending for some reason of his own, and dying in this place would merely fling him into some other sim, or back into his ancient physical body. Then they would have lost any chance at the information, not to mention having become the failed assassins of the most powerful man in the world – not a position with much long-term security.

She would not, could not rule out the possibility of using mortal force on him – not as long as the lives of Stephen and countless others were at stake – but all in all, it didn't seem like a gamble that should be undertaken before everything else had failed.

What else, then? If Jongleur were a normal man, they could bargain, trade something he wanted for information. But the only thing she could see that he needed was escape from this place and revenge on his unruly servant, Dread. Neither of those were in Renie's power to grant.

So what do you give the man who has everything? she thought in sour amusement. Was there something that Jongleur also needed to know? Something that Renie and her companions had to give? What might possibly interest him?

His daughter, she thought suddenly. *How does she fit into this?* Suddenly Renie knew why the whole thing had bothered her. *Whatever she's doing, it doesn't seem meant to help her father. The opposite, if anything. Didn't Paul*

say Jongleur's goons have been chasing him? But it seems
like she's been trying to keep Paul away from the Twins
when surely she could just hand him over if she wanted.
In fact, he said she was afraid of them, too. So what was
her relationship with Jongleur? It certainly didn't appear
to be an old-fashioned, Daddy's-Little-Girl scenario.

There was definitely something there. Renie felt a surge
of grateful energy. Something to chew on, some useful
work for her brain.

We don't really know anything about this Ava. Why
was she also Emily, for God's sake – a minor sim in an
Oz simulation? Why did she help Orlando and Fredericks
in the Kitchen and Egypt, but never did anything for me
and !Xabbu? And why has she elected herself Paul's
guardian angel when it's her own father who's tearing up
the network trying to find him?

She continued her downward march like a zombie, one
slow foot in front of the other, but inside she felt alive
for the first time in days.

They found a hollow in the mountainside relatively soon
after the last stop, but since there was no guarantee
another suitable spot would present itself anytime soon,
they decided to make camp, which meant nothing more
than dragging themselves off the trail to sleep.

Renie was the first to wake. She rolled over and looked
at Sam twitching in uneasy slumber. The girl was bearing up as well as could be expected, but Renie was worried:
she suspected the teenager's restraint was due mostly to
the flattening of exhaustion. Acting on impulse, she gently
withdrew the ruined sword from Sam's waistband, then
sat back and waited for Jongleur to wake.

!Xabbu and the hard-faced man began to stir at the
same time. Felix Jongleur seemed to be having a bad

dream – his hands clenched and unclenched, and his lips were moving as though he were trying to speak. It made Renie feel more than a little happy to think that something might be preying on the monster's conscience.

Jongleur started upright, muttering, 'No, the glass . . .' then looked around blearily. His gaze touched on Ricardo Klement, lying a meter away, eyes open but otherwise almost lifeless. Jongleur shuddered and rubbed his face.

'So,' Renie said suddenly and loudly. 'What's with you and Paul Jonas, anyway?'

Jongleur froze like a startled animal, then his face became as carefully expressionless as the mask he had worn as lord of ancient Egypt. 'What did you say?'

'I asked what your problem is with Paul Jonas.' She kept her own voice aggressively casual, but her heart was beating fast.

Jongleur was on his feet in an instant, moving aggressively toward her. 'What do you know of him?'

Renie was ready. The broken sword blade flashed up, inches from his face. Jongleur froze again, staring, lip curled and showing teeth.

'I don't think you should come any closer,' she said. 'What are you, anyway – French? There's still a little accent to your English. Maybe you're used to those North African black women, the ones whose husbands tell them what to do. Well, I'm not that kind of African, old man. Back up and sit down.'

He moved no closer, but did not retreat either. 'Accent? A poor jibe from you, with your school grammar draped over the township *patois*.' His hands were knotted, knuckles like little white eggs. Renie could tell that the autocrat was only one bad decision on her part from trying to use them on her, sword or no sword. 'What do you know of Jonas?' he demanded again.

'That's not the way we're going to play this game.' She saw that !Xabbu was sitting up now, watching her carefully, silently. 'You said before that we weren't going to get any information from you for free. Okay, I suppose that's fair. We know a lot about Paul Jonas. You know a lot about the network. Let's trade.'

He had mastered his rage now, although the cords in his neck and arms were still pulled tight. 'You think much of yourself, woman.'

'No. I know my limitations – that's why I don't feel very comfortable about our arrangement. You need our help to get down this god-forsaken mountain, but what do we get back for it? If we do make it down and you disappear on us, we have nothing but another enemy on the loose.'

Jongleur narrowed his eyes. 'I saved your life.'

Renie snorted. 'That would carry more weight if I didn't know you'd just as happily push me as catch me. And we've saved yours since then, anyway. None of this has anything to do with what I'm talking about. Let's share, shall we?'

Sam also sat up now, a child to whom waking into bizarre situations was sadly becoming second nature. Nevertheless, this time she was watching the proceedings with a curiously feverish intensity. !Xabbu moved close to the girl, perhaps to keep her from intervening in this edgy bit of diplomacy. Renie felt strengthened by his trust.

'What do you want to know?' Jongleur said. 'And what do you have to trade?'

'You already know what we have to trade. Paul Jonas. We know him – we know him well. In fact, we've traveled with him.' She watched carefully and was rewarded by a flicker deep in Jongleur's eyes. 'Why don't you tell us about the Other?'

'Ah. You have learned some things, then.'

'Not enough. What is it? How does it work?'

His laugh was as harsh and sudden as a shark bite. 'You must be more of a fool than I thought. I spent enough money to dwarf the national product of your miserable country developing this system, put years of my life into it, and had dozens of people killed to protect my investment. Do you believe I would give that away for nothing?'

'Nothing? Is Paul Jonas really nothing?' She frowned – his face had gone cold again. 'He was with us, you know. You were within a dozen meters of him back on the mountaintop, when everything started falling apart.' She saw his expression of disbelief and laughed harshly. 'He *was!* Right there, and you didn't even know it.'

Jongleur was clearly wrestling with the idea. For the first time she saw a real crack in his facade of power, a shadow of unhappiness. 'It does not matter,' he said at last. 'He is not here now. I want Jonas himself, not old news. Can you deliver him to me?'

Renie hesitated for a moment, trying to figure out which way to take it. 'Maybe.'

Jongleur's smile was slow and humorless. 'You lie. This conversation is over.'

Stung, Renie tightened her grip on the sword hilt. 'Oh, yes? Before we even get a chance to talk about your daughter Ava?'

To her astonishment, Jongleur actually staggered a step backward. His face went bloodless, so that his dark eyes seemed to bulge out of the sockets. 'You speak her name to me again and I will kill you, blade or no blade,' he said in a grating whisper. He was struggling for control and barely succeeding, and that was the most frightening thing Renie had seen so far. 'You know nothing of

anything . . . in far over your head. Not . . . not another
word! You understand?' He turned and moved out onto
the path. Just before he stepped out of sight, he turned
and thrust a quivering finger toward her. '*Not another
word!*'

When he was gone, silence fell in the small enclosure.
Sam was looking at Renie with wide eyes.

'Okay,' Renie suddenly felt very shaky. 'Okay, if that's
the way he wants it. He's a murdering bastard anyway,
so it's not like we're going to be friends.' She hesitated
for a moment, then handed the broken sword back to
Sam. 'In case he's angry enough to push me off the edge
or something. Keep it safe.'

'Chizz,' said Sam in a muted voice.

Jongleur stayed well ahead of them for hours, although
he was almost always within sight, shoulders stiff, face
resolutely forward. A part of Renie wanted to speak mock-
ingly of his behavior – the most powerful man in the
world, who had climbed over the bodies of countless
people to get to the top, had stalked off like an angry
child when the game did not go his way. But that snide
inner voice, she recognized, came from the part of her
that feared the man and which wanted desperately to
bolster her own courage. A more sensible portion of her
realized she had touched something deep and cata-
strophically dangerous in Jongleur. She had seen his quick
and frightening angers, but this had been something
different, an ice-cold fury that she feared would not dissipate.

She had goaded a bad man, it seemed, and made him
into a personal enemy.

Things might have been worse with Jongleur had the
mountain not still demanded all their attention. The path

was growing worse, a slow but obvious devolution, and they were all disheartened. Almost half the time now was spent edging along the narrow trail with their backs against the stone, forced to stare at the ugly drop down into the weird silvery mist. Even Jongleur appeared to decide on practicality after a while, dropping back until he was only an arm's length in front of !Xabbu, but they found no place wide enough for a safe transfer of leadership for many hours.

After they did, !Xabbu led for a long time, holding down his speed so Renie and the others could keep up, although even the Bushman was visibly flagging. They had several near-accidents because of fatigue, but what was even more depressing was how clear it was that they had reached the very end of the trail's usefulness. At this pace, Renie felt sure, the equivalent of another day in this hourless place would find them with their faces pressed against the mountainside, edging along on tiptoes.

She was wrong. It took nowhere near that long.

They found one more spot wide enough for a short, standing rest and a change of order in the line. Renie stepped to the front while !Xabbu waited until all but Ricardo Klement had passed before moving back into the file, so that the small man followed Jongleur, who crept along behind Sam. Renie almost thought she could feel the Grail master's dark stare burning into the back of her head, but she couldn't afford to waste energy on such fancies: the dwindling path was scarcely wide enough for her to set both feet on it side by side, and she had to lean constantly to the inside to keep her balance.

More hours went by. Renie was staggeringly tired, her back cramping from the awkward, leaning angle, eyes and feet so sore that the idea of a misstep into emptiness was almost alluring. Maddeningly, the sea of glinting fog seemed no closer, but Renie could not bear to think about that – the short-term reality was even more worrisome. She had already stumbled and lurched forward sickeningly several times, once so badly that only Sam catching at the cloth of her makeshift outfit allowed her to regain her balance and avoid sliding down the path toward certain disaster. But even if they found a place to change leaders, Sam could not be any less tired than Renie herself. !Xabbu would unhesitatingly take the lead again if asked – she knew that with the same certainty she knew her finger would meet her thumb when she brought them together – but she did not want him risking himself either. The fact was, no one should be leading anymore. They desperately needed a place to stop and lie down. Another standing line change would let them rest, but they were beyond mere rest now – they had to have sleep. And trying to sleep leaning against the lukewarm stone would be an invitation to disaster.

There was no point in discussing any of this, she realized. She slowed and bent with deliberate care to try to knead a cramp out of her calf. It felt like someone had stuck a dagger into the muscle. She wanted to scream, but knew that her grip on sanity and control was far too tenuous to start anything like that. Everything was now balanced on the finest of points.

'We have to stop,' she said out loud. 'I've got a cramp. Just give me a moment.'

'If we stop, we will all cramp,' Jongleur snapped from behind Sam. 'Then we will all go over the edge. We must keep going forward or die. If you fall, you fall.'

She bit back angry words. He was right. If she paused any longer she would never get herself going again. Wincing, she put the weight back on her tensed, throbbing calf and took a careful step. It held up, although it still felt like it was pulled so tight the very fibers of her muscle might tear loose.

'Renie, be careful,' !Xabbu called.

She lifted her outside hand in the air, trying for a jaunty, don't-worry wave, but could not summon the strength to do much more than flap it limply.

Step. Hobble. Step. Renie had to blink to keep the tears from blinding her. *Hobble. Step.* They were going to die here – one by one, with herself probably the first to go. Whoever had designed this place was a sadistic monster who should have all his nerve endings set on fire. *Step. Hobble. Step.*

Within a very short time the path began to narrow even farther, declining to a strip not much wider than the length of Renie's foot. The only stroke of luck in the entire miserable universe was that the mountainside tilted away from her at a bit of an angle here, so that as she forced herself to turn sideways, putting an even more agonizing burden on her burning calf muscle, she could learn forward slightly, away from the rim of the tiny ledge and the drop into nothingness.

No one spoke. There was nothing to say, and no strength left with which to say it.

After what might have been an agonizing quarter hour of crablike shuffling. Renie glanced sideways and cursed bitterly. Again, tears filled her eyes, and this time she just clung to the face of the mountain and waited for them to wash away, ignoring the screaming pain in her leg. The mountainside bulged out just ahead, so that the tiny strip of path clung to a smooth stone wall that no longer angled away from the drop, but actually leaned outward a bit past the vertical. She tried to summon the strength to move forward for a better look, but her legs were shaking so badly it was all she could do simply to hold on.

'Renie?' !Xabbu said, worry even piercing the weight of exhaustion in his voice. 'Renie?'

'It's no use,' she wept. 'It sticks out – it sticks out here, the side of the mountain sticks out. We're trapped.'

'Is there still a path?' he demanded. 'Talk to us, Renie.'

'Maybe we can go back up . . . ?' Sam said, but her tone was hopeless.

Renie could only shake her head, her fingers cramping, too, as she kept them locked on a vertical protrusion of the mountainside. 'No use . . .' she whispered sadly.

'Don't move,' !Xabbu said. 'I am coming forward.'

Renie, who had thought there was nothing left in all the universe that could be worse than this, felt a crackle of terror. 'What are you talking about . . . ?'

'Don't move,' !Xabbu said. 'Please, do not anyone move. I will try to step between your feet.'

Renie was barely holding on now, staring helplessly at the flat, featureless black stone in front of her. *Jesus Mercy*, she thought, *he's all the way at the back. He was the last leader before me.* 'Don't do it, !Xabbu!' she called, but she could already hear grunting and stirring to her right, where the rest of the company clung as she did to the almost naked cliff. Renie closed her eyes. She heard him coming closer but could not bear to think too hard about what he must be doing, making his way outside of Jongleur and Sam, leaning over them to touch the wall, only his almost superhuman balance keeping him on the tiny path.

'Carefully, Renie, my dear, brave Renie,' he was saying now. 'I am right beside you. I am going to put my foot between your feet. Do not move. Hold on.'

Terrified, she opened her eyes and looked down, saw !Xabbu's brown leg come down between hers, only his toes gripping the edge. Below them – the nothing, the silver nothing. His fingers arched and touched, and spread like a spider's legs beside her own clenched hand, and his other foot came down beside the first, leaving him perched between her heels on the sliver of stone path. For a moment, as his other hand touched and spread so that he leaned against her, just barely brushing against the skin of her back, his balance as fragile as a spiderweb, she had the thought that if she leaned backward they could both just fall away, swoop down into the pale mist like angels, and all the pain would be over.

'Hold your breath, my Beloved Porcupine,' he whispered, his mouth warm against her ear. 'Just for a little moment. Please, please.'

She closed her eyes again and clung, praying to anything and everything, tears running down her cheeks and neck. He moved his foot . . . his hand . . . his other hand . . . then his other foot, and he was not touching her anymore.

But if we're going to die, she thought, quietly, mournfully mad, *I wish it could have been like that, together, together* . . .

She could hear him slowly edging along the shelf beyond her. 'You must move,' he called back quietly. 'Everyone keep moving. It will do no good if I manage to get around but you are all still here. Follow.'

Renie shook her head – didn't he know? Her limbs were locked, trembling. She was like a dead insect, her outside a rigid shell, her insides melted away.

'You must, Renie,' he said. 'The others cannot move until you do.'

She wept a little more, then tried to make her hand unclench. It was a claw, hard and stiff. She slid it a few centimeters to one side, then struggled to make it grasp again. After a moment, biting her lip until it bled to keep her mind off the pain in her extremities, she slid her foot a tiny way along the ledge. Her leg burned like fire and her knee began to buckle.

'Keep moving,' !Xabbu said from somewhere ahead of her. She stared at the black rock. *Stephen*, she told herself. *He has nobody else. Help him.*

She slid the other foot. The pain, although shatteringly bad, did not grow worse. She breathed through her nose and inched the other hand along, then started the whole horrible process again.

Renie risked a look to the side and wished she hadn't. !Xabbu had reached the place where the mountain bulged out, and was performing a terrifyingly intricate series of maneuvers – crouching to get his head beneath the worst of the outcrop, then moving sideways at a snail's pace, bent at the waist, with only his toes on the path and fingers resting lightly on the stone so he could keep most of his weight forward. As he moved, centimeter by agonizing centimeter, he made minute adjustments of balance, tilting head and shoulders a tiny degree here, an equally tiny degree there, moving slowly around the protrusion. Renie felt tears come again and wiped her burning eyes on her upraised arm.

!Xabbu vanished around the edge. She slid a few more steps, then reached the spot where the outward tilt began. She clung, knowing it was all pointless, waiting in dull horror for the cry that would mean he had fallen.

Instead, he spoke. 'There is a place here.'

It took a moment before she could calm the sob waiting to burst out. 'What?'

'A place. A flat place. If you can only make it around the edge. It is a place to lie down, Renie! Hold on! Tell the others!'

'Liar.' She gritted her teeth. She knew it had to be false

– she would do the same herself, say anything to help the others find the strength to try to get around this horrible obstacle. 'There's nothing but more of the same.'

'I am telling you the truth, Renie.' His voice was hoarse. 'By the heart of Grandfather Mantis, I am telling you the truth.'

'I can't make it!' she wailed.

'You can. Come as far toward me as you can. Lean to the side instead of back, to keep your balance. Try to reach your hand around to me. When you touch me, don't be frightened. I will hold your hand tightly and help keep you up.'

'He says there's a place to stop on the other side,' Renie told the others, trying to sound like she believed it. There was no reply, but she could see Sam Fredericks from the corner of her eye, feel the girl's exhaustion and panic. 'A safe place. Just a tiny bit farther.' She relayed !Xabbu's directions so the others would know what to do when they got there, not believing for a moment any of it would work, then slid a little closer to the outcrop. She leaned as !Xabbu had instructed, pushed her throbbing feet a little closer to the bump. For a moment she thought she had leaned too far, and only the stiffness of her limbs kept her from making a fatal grasp for a better handhold. She hugged the black stone tight, edged her left arm as far around it as she could, out of sight . . .

. . . And something touched it. Despite !Xabbu's warning, the surprise was so great she almost lost her grip again, but the fingers around her wrist were tight and sure. She sidestepped again, having to lean back a little now as the stone bulged out above her, and suddenly she felt her balance shift back, back toward nothingness. She had only a moment to draw breath for the pointless reflexive scream, then her arm was jerked hard and she scraped

along the stone. Her right foot slipped off the path, but
the rest of her caromed out, swinging on the pivot of her
other foot, and !Xabbu was there, still holding on with
blessed, blessed strength as he flung himself backward
into a wide cleft in the mountainside so that she tumbled
in on top of him. He quickly dragged himself out from
under her; a moment later Renie heard him shuffling back
to the edge of the fold in the mountainside, calling to
Sam, but Renie herself could only lie facedown on the
floor and cling as hard as she had gripped the mountainside, rubbing her face against the precious horizontal
stone.

She was dimly conscious of !Xabbu bringing the others
in safely. Sam fell gasping beside her, whimpering at the
cramping of her fingers and toes. A more stolid Jongleur
followed and tumbled silently to the ground. Even as the
adrenaline diminished and her heart began to slow, Renie
suddenly realized that !Xabbu had gone back to the rim
of the crevice, risking his life to help the brain-damaged
Ricardo Klement to safety. She struggled to her knees,
every muscle shrieking in protest, and crawled to the edge.
!Xabbu was leaning out at an angle that made her heart
begin triphammering again, talking slowly and softly to
someone she could not see, his slender arm stretched out
of sight around the outcropping.

'I'm behind you, !Xabbu.' Her voice was a dry croak.
'Do you want me to grab your hand?'

'No, Renie.' His voice was muffled against the rock. 'I
need it where it is for balance. But if you held my leg, I
would be grateful. Let go quickly if I ask.'

As her fingers closed around his ankle he leaned out
farther. Renie could only watch for a moment before
having to shut her eyes. The sky's strange lack of depth
did not prevent vertigo.

It's just as well T4b isn't here, she thought, the distracted thought keeping a greater terror at bay.

For a moment, as !Xabbu's muscles tensed beneath her touch and he leaned out even farther on his fingernail grip, she thought her pulse would explode in her chest. Then the naked body of Klement came wobbling around the edge of the stone and !Xabbu crouched and pulled backward, toppling onto Renie as he pulled Klement in on them both.

They all lay gasping for a while, until Renie found the strength to help !Xabbu away from the edge of the cleft, deeper into the dimple in the mountain's side. It was scarcely three meters to the place where Sam lay almost wedged into the back, but after that ribbon of trail the space seemed palatial.

Renie slept then, a brief dive beneath the surface of consciousness. When she woke, she dragged herself toward !Xabbu where he sat propped against the black stone and put her head against his chest, nudging until she found a spot in the hollow under his chin. The beat of his heart was soothing, and she realized she never wanted to let go of him.

'We're in trouble,' she whispered.

He said nothing, but she could feel his attention.

'We can't go out on that trail again. There's nothing left of it.'

She thought he drew breath to argue, but then she felt his head slowly nodding, the curve of his throat and jaw enfolding the line of her own skull like a cupping hand. 'I think you are right.'

'So what's left? We stay here until the thing dissolves out from under us?' She looked at Sam, as rigid as a cata-tonic, staring at her own hands. Jongleur too seemed lost in some inner world, all of them now wandering as distantly as Ricardo Klement. 'What else can we do?'

'Wait. Hope.' !Xabbu brought his arm up and drew her closer. His fingers rested lightly above her heart, on the upper slope of her breast. 'We will be together, no matter what comes.'

She burrowed even deeper against him, and realized that she wanted not just to be held, but to kiss him, weep against his face, make love to him. But not here. Not inches from slow-breathing Jongleur, not under Ricardo Klement's aquarium gaze.

And if not here, where? she thought with a brushstroke of sad humor. *If not now, when?* For it seemed fairly certain there was nothing left. Still, bone-deep weariness and the presence of hateful strangers had turned the thought grotesque. She would content herself with child-like pleasures, with being held, with falling asleep in what for the moment was as much safety as she could imagine.

'Tell a story,' she murmured instead. 'We need one, !Xabbu.'

She felt his head turn slowly from side to side. 'I cannot think of any stories, Renie. I am so tired. My stories are gone.'

It seemed the saddest thing she had ever heard. Unseeing, she touched his face as sleep came and took her again.

Even after all the unreason she had experienced, all the visions and hallucinations, she came up out of the blackest, most unknowing depths into the active force of the dream and realized immediately that this was perhaps the strangest one yet.

Usually when she dreamed, she was the active one, even if those actions were frustrated; in some of the worst she was a helpless observer, a bodiless phantom condemned to watch over a life it could no longer enjoy. But this was different. This dream came *at* her, washing over her with the force of moving water, a river of experience that had swallowed her down and was rushing her along, battering her until she felt she might drown in it.

If there had been coherent images she might have found it easier to resist the terrible flow, to feel some tiny chance of control, but the whirling chaos roared over her and through her, unstoppably. Streaks of color, snatches of incomprehensible sounds, flashes of nerve-scraping heat and cold, it went on until she felt so overwhelmed that she could only pray for some sleep deeper than this terrible active dream, anything that would blank out the sensation, stop the terrible screaming input.

Death. The word registered only for a moment, like a headline on a gust-snagged newspaper. *Death. Calm. Quiet. Dark. Sleep.* In the uncontrolled anarchy of sensation, trapped on this brakeless thrill ride, it had a dreadful allure. But the life inside her was really very strong: when the darkness did come, it terrified her.

It was a cold, oozing dark, a clammy black static grip that, after the initial relief, was only slightly better than the surging horror it had replaced, for not only the swirl of images vanished, but most of her thoughts as well. Reality fragmented and disconnected, became a series of pointless movements that she realized were only the earlier discord stifled and slowed.

She floated in the midst of a living shadow. There was nothing but herself, surrounded by an unimaginable blackness. She could not think, not properly. She could only wait, while time or perhaps some incompetent impostor did its work.

The emptiness was aeons long. Even imagination died. Aeons long.

Then at last she felt something – a fluttering in the void, Oh, God, it was real, it was! Something distant, but actually separate from herself. No, *many* somethings, small and alive, tiny blessed warm things where before there had been nothing but cold.

She reached out eagerly, but the fluttering things darted away, frightened of her. She reached again and the presences retreated even farther. Her sorrow grew so large and painful that she was certain all that kept her coherent would burst and she would spill inside out into the darkness, disperse, collapse. She lay in cold misery.

The things returned.

This time she was careful, as careful as she could be, reaching out to them slowly, gently, feeling them in their terrible fragility. After a while they came to her without coaxing. She handled them with almost infinite caution, enfolded each one as gently as she could, a century between thoughts, a millennium between excruciatingly restrained movements. Even so, some proved too vulnerable, and with tiny cries they were no more, bursting in her grasp like bubbles as they gave up their essences. It tore at her heart.

The others flitted away, alarmed, and she was terrified, certain they would leave her forever. She called to them. Some came back. Oh, but they were delicate. Oh, but they were beautiful.

She wept, and the universe slowly convulsed.

The dream had been so deep and powerful and strange that for a long time she did not realize she had returned to consciousness. Her mind still seemed lost in lonely darkness: for almost a minute after she remembered her

name, Renie did not open her eyes. At last some returning sensation in her skin and muscles pricked her and she
unlidded, stared, then cried out.

Gray, swirling silver-gray. Flickers of light, the smearing of broken spectra, a fine dust of luminance . . . but
nothing else. The shimmery cloudstuff that had girdled
the mountain seemed to be all around her now, an ocean
of silver emptiness, although she could sense something
hard and horizontal beneath her. She was not bodiless –
it was not a dream this time. Her hands crawled over her
own flesh and to the ground on either side, a ground she
could not even see. She was lost in a heavy, shining fog,
everything and everyone else gone.

'!Xabbu? Sam?' She crawled a little way over the hard
but curiously smooth invisibility beneath her, then remembered the edge of the crevice and stopped, fighting against
complete panic. '*!Xabbu! Where are you?*'

An echo had been one of the few lifelike features that
the degenerating black mountainside had retained, but
there was no echo now.

Renie moved forward again, exploring with nervously
twitching fingers, but even after she had crawled what
must have been a dozen meters she had encountered
neither the stone of the cliff face nor the open space at
the crevice's rim. It was as though the mountain had just
melted away around her, leaving her on some inexplicable table-top in the glimmering fog.

She crawled another dozen meters. The ground she
could not see was as smooth as something glazed in a
kiln, but real enough to hurt her knees. She called her
companions' names over and over into absolute silence.
At last, desperate, she climbed to her feet.

'*!Xabbu!*' she shrieked until her throat was sore.
'!Xabbu! Can you hear me?'

Nothing.

She walked a half-dozen careful paces, testing each footstep before setting it down. The ground was absolutely flat. There was nothing else – no precipice, no vertical stone slab of mountain, no sound, no light except the ubiquitous pearly gleam of the mist. Even the fog had no substance: it shimmered wetly but was not wet. There was nothing. There was Renie and nothing. Everything gone.

She sat down and clutched at her head. *I'm dead*, she thought, but outside the dream, the idea of death was not a soothing one. *And this is all there is. Everyone lied.* She laughed, but it sounded like something wasn't working properly inside her. *Even the atheists lied.* 'Oh, damn,' she said out loud.

A flicker of shadow caught her eye – something moving in the fog.

'Xabbu?' Even as she spoke, she felt she shouldn't have. Hunted – they were all hunted now. Still, she could not smother the reflex entirely. 'Sam?' she whispered.

The shape eased forward, resolving out of nothing like a magical apparition. She was prepared for something as bizarre as the setting; it took her a moment to recognize what it was that shared the silver void with her.

'I am . . . Ricardo,' said the blank-eyed man. 'Klement,' he added a moment later.

CHAPTER 5

The Last Fish to Swallow

NETFEED/NEWS: *Church Refuses Exorcism for 'Bogeyman'*
(visual: child on bed in La Paloma Hospital)
VO:*The Archdiocese of Los Angeles has refused the request of a group of close to three dozen Mexican-American parents to perform an exorcism on their children, who claim to have had identical nightmares about a dark spirit they call 'El Cucuy' – the bogeyman. Three of the affected children have committed suicide, and several of the others are being treated for clinical depression. Social help agents say the villain is not a demon, but the medical result of too much time spent on the net.*
(visual: Cassie Montgomery, LA County Human Services)
MONTGOMERY: *'We can't trace the source yet, but I don't think it's a coincidence that most of these young people are latchkey kids and heavy net users. It seems pretty clear that something they've seen or experienced online is provoking these bad dreams. The rest I chalk up to garden-variety hysteria.'*

'**W**HAT'S even more important,' the guide said, smiling her professional smile from behind thick goggle-style sunglasses, 'is that we now have healthy breeding populations of many threatened birds – the gallinule, or marsh hen, the roseate spoonbill, the Lousiana heron, and the beautiful snowy egret, just to name a few. Now Charleroi will take us into the deep swamp. Maybe we'll see some deer, or even a bobcat!' She was good at her job: it was clear she could manifest the same energy for that line every trip, day in and day out.

Not counting the guide and the young man nominally steering the boat, whose suntanned arms bore the serpentine traces of unignited subdermals and whose facial expression also suggested that some necessary light beneath the flesh had not been switched on, there were only six passengers on this slow weekday afternoon, a red-faced British couple and their small noisy son who was cutting at the duckweed with a souvenir lightstick, a pair of young married professionals from somewhere in the middle of the country, and Olga Pirofsky.

'Please keep your hands out of the water.' The guide retained her smile even as her voice hardened to something less cheerful. 'This isn't an amusement park, remember – our alligators are not mechanical.'

Everyone except Olga laughed dutifully, but the boy still did not stop swiping at the water until his father said, 'Lay off, Gareth,' and smacked him on the back of the head.

Strange, so strange, Olga thought. *So strange, all the years and miles of my life, to wind up here.* A bank of cypress loomed ahead in the fast-dissolving morning mist, a gathering of phantoms. *Here at the end.*

Three days now since she had reached the end of the journey, or perhaps since the journey itself had deserted her. Everything was stasis, pointless as the quiet little guideboat moving along its preprogrammed route across the resurrected swamp. Sleepless through the silent nights, only able to slip into unconsciousness when dawn touched the window blinds of her motel room, Olga could scarcely find the energy to eat and drink, let alone do anything more strenuous. She didn't even know what impulse had led her to buy a ticket for the tour, and nothing so far had made it worth missing the few hours of sleep she might have had in its place. She could see the object of her quest from almost anywhere in the area, after all – the black tower dominated the vicinity as thoroughly as a medieval cathedral its village and fields.

Three days without the voices, without the children. She had not felt so bereft since those distant and terrible days when Aleksandr and the baby had died.

And I can't even remember now what that felt like, she realized. *A big emptiness, that's all that's left. Like a hole, and my life since then has just been little things I throw into that hole, trying to fill it up. But I can't feel it.*

She never had felt it, she realized – not fully, not truly. Even now it was a blackness that was out of reach, on the other side of some kind of membrane of deliberate ignorance, a thin wall separating her from a horror as complete as the vacuum of space.

If I had ever let it through, she thought, *I would be dead. I thought I was strong, but no one is that strong. I kept it away.*

'Since the completion of the intracoastal Barrier,' the guide was saying, 'thousands and thousands of acres of waterway which were being lost to erosion and increasing salinity have been returned to their pristine state, preserved for future generations to enjoy.' She nodded, as though she herself had climbed out of bed every morning, smeared on her sunblock, donned her waders, and assembled the barrier.

But it is beautiful, Olga thought, *even if it's all an illusion.* The boat was murmuring through a patch of vibrantly lavender water hyacinths. Small paddling birds moved unhurriedly out of their way, clearly familiar with what by now must be a generations-old routine. The cypresses were looming closer. The sun had lifted a full span in the east above the Mississippi Sound and the gulf beyond, but the light could not penetrate too deeply among the trees and their knee-high blanket of mist. The darkness between them looked restful, like sleep.

'Yes,' said the male half of the professional couple suddenly, 'but didn't making the Intracoastal whatever . . . Barrier . . . didn't that utterly ruin like almost all the wetlands that were already there?' He turned to his wife or girlfriend, who tried to look interested. 'See, the corporation that owns all this dredged out Lake Borgne over there completely. It was only a few meters deep, then they opened it up to the sea, sank the pilings for that island with the corporate headquarters, all that.' He looked up to the guide, a little defiance on his thin face. Olga decided he was an engineer, someone to whom management was usually the enemy. 'So, yeah, it was part of the deal that they had to patch the rest of this up, make it a nice little nature park. But it pretty much killed the fishing all around.'

'You an environmentalist or something?' the British man asked flatly.

'No.' He was a little defensive now. 'Just . . . I just follow the news.'

'The J Corporation didn't have to do anything,' the guide said primly. 'They had permission to build in Lake Borgne. It was all legal. They just . . .' she was reaching, veering an uncomfortable distance off her usual *recititativo* . . . 'they just wanted to give something back. To the community.' She turned and looked at the young pilot, who rolled his eyes but then added a little speed. They began to pass the first cypress stumps, pointy islands breasting the dark water like miniature versions of the mountain that haunted Olga's dreams.

There's nowhere left to go, she thought. *I've reached the tower, but it's all private property. Someone even said that the corporation that owns it has a whole standing army. No tours, no visitors, no way.* She sighed as the cypresses slid toward them through the mist, enfolding the little boat in mist and angled light.

It was indeed, as the promotional material had claimed, like a watery cathedral, a hall of vertical pillars and hangings, the cypress trees draped with moss like a freeze-frame of liquid flow, the water itself still as a drumhead but for the threading wake of the boat. She could almost imagine that they had passed not just out of the direct sun, but out of the direct surveillance of time itself, had slipped back through millennia to a time when humans had not even touched the vast continents of the Americas.

'Look,' said the tour guide, her precisely animated diction puncturing the mood like a needle, 'an abandoned boat. That's a *pirogue*, one of the flat boats the swamp trappers and fishermen used to use.'

Olga turned resignedly to see the skeletonized hull of the little craft, its ribs colonized with hyacinths like the capitals of an illuminated breviary. It was beautifully picturesque. Too picturesque.

'A prop,' the young professional man whispered to his companion. 'This wasn't even swamp until ten years ago – they literally built it after they finished the Lake Borgne project.'

'It was a hard life for the people who made their living in the swamp,' the guide continued, ignoring the man. 'Although there were periodic economic booms in the area,

based around fur or cypress wood, the downturns were
generally longer. Before J Corporation created the
Louisiana Swamp Preserve, it was a dying way of life.'

'Don't look like there's a lot of people making a living
here now,' the British man offered, and laughed.

'Gareth, leave the turtle alone,' his wife said.

'Ah, but there *are* people still making a living in the
old-fashioned way,' the guide responded cheerfully,
pleased that she had been given an easy one. 'You'll see
on the last stop on our tour, when we reach the Swamp
Market. The old crafts and skills haven't been forgotten,
but preserved.'

'Like a dead pig in a jar of alcohol,' the engineer said
quietly, displaying what Olga thought was an unexpected
gift for simile.

'If it comes to that,' the guide said, finally allowing her
own defensiveness to show through, 'Charleroi's people
come from this same area, didn't they?' She turned to the
young pilot, who gazed back at her with infinite weariness. 'Isn't your family from right around here?'

'Yah.' He nodded, then spat over the side. 'And look at
me today.'

'Piloting a boat through the swamp,' the tour guide
said, her point proved.

As the guide went on to list in great detail the red-
shouldered hawk, ibis, annhinga, and other creatures
winged and otherwise who frequented the reclaimed
swamp, Olga let her mind wander away, lazy as the track
through the floating duckweed of yesterday's final tour,
which their own boat was following with only the smallest of deviations. A bird the guide identified as a bittern
made a sound like a hammer striking a board. The
cypresses began to thin, the mist to burn away.

They slipped from the grove to find the stern black

finger of God held up before them, dominating the horizon beyond the swamp's vegetative carpet.

'Lord,' said the Englishwoman. 'Gareth, look at that, darling.'

'It's just that building,' the child said, rooting in the daypack for something else to eat. 'We saw it before.'

'Yes, that's the J Corporation tower,' the guide said, as proud of the distant structure as she had been of the Intracoastal Barrier. 'You can't see from here, but the island in Lake Borgne contains an entire city, with its own airport and police force.'

'They basically make their own law,' the professional man told his partner, who was dabbing her forehead with a handkerchief. He didn't bother to whisper this time. 'The guy who owns it, Jongleur, is one of the richest guys in the world, no dupping. They say he pretty much owns the government down here.'

'That's not very fair, sir . . .' the guide began, flushing.

'Are you kidding?' The man snorted, then turned to the British family. 'They say that the only reason Jongleur doesn't admit he owns the government outright is because then he'd have to pay taxes on it.'

'Isn't he the one who's two hundred years old?' the British woman asked as her husband chortled at the idea of owning your own government. 'I saw about him on the tabnets – he's a machine or something.' She turned to her husband. 'I saw it. Made me go cold all over, thinking about it.'

The guide waved her hands. 'There is a great deal of exaggeration about Mr Jongleur, most of it cruel. He's an old man and he's very ill, it's true.' She put on what Olga thought of as the Sad Newsreader Face, the one that net people donned when presenting schoolbus

crashes or senseless homicides. 'And of course he's influential – the J Corporation is the biggest employer in the
New Orleans area, and has interests worldwide. They're
a major stockholder in many companies, household
names – Commerce Bank, Clinsor Pharmaceutical,
Dartheon. Obolos Entertainment, for that matter, the children's interactive company. What's your name,' she asked
the little boy, 'Gareth, isn't it? Surely you know Uncle
Jingle, don't you, Gareth?'

'Yeah. "Snot fair!"' He laughed and slapped his mother's
shin with his lightstick.

'See? J Corporation is involved in lots of things, vested
in wholesome and consumer-friendly companies all over
the world. We are, as we like to say, a "people corporation" . . .'

The rest of the spiel was lost to Olga – in fact, she had
stopped hearing what the woman said after the mention
of Obolos. In all her years working for the company she
did not remember being told anything about J Corporation.
But, of course, who paid attention? In a world where every
corporate fish was both eater and eaten, who could even
tell which fish had swallowed last?

I should have researched the tower, I should have . . .

But it had been a religious experience, a revelation,
not a school assignment. The children's voices had
demanded she come, and so she had put away her worldly
goods and come.

Uncle Jingle – Uncle Jingle comes from the black tower.

Olga Pirofsky spent almost two more hours in the tiny
boat, surrounded by faces whose mouths moved but whose
voices she could no longer bear to listen to, an interstellar traveler landed among babbling aliens.

*Uncle Jingle is murdering the children. And I helped
him do it.*

'I don't understand here,' said Long Joseph. 'Where is this Sellars? You said he was on the phone – you said he was calling and calling on the phone. But now he don't call at all, anytime.'

'He said he'd call back.' Jeremiah spread his hands helplessly. 'He said there were things going on . . . we're not the only ones with problems.'

'Yeah, but I bet we are the only ones locked up in a mountain while a bunch of Boer murderers trying to burn their way in and kill us.'

'Just settle down, would you? You're making my head hurt.' Del Ray Chiume had returned from his brief inspection tour. 'Don't pay any attention to him,' he told Jeremiah. 'Just read us the notes you made – it's not like we have a lot of time to waste arguing.'

Long Joseph Sulaweyo didn't like anything much about the way this was going. It was bad enough being trapped in a deep underground base in the middle of nowhere, with only three bottles of anything decent to drink to last God only knew how long, and people outside who wanted to kill him, but now it appeared that Del Ray – Del Ray who *Joseph himself* had brought here – was making common cause with Jeremiah Dako, ganging up against him.

Joseph could make no sense of it, unless Del Ray, too, was secretly a girly-man as well, and the deep fraternal bond was stronger than other loyalties. *Maybe that is the real reason he broke up with my Renie.*

'So I am supposed to trust my life to this *kak?*' he demanded.

'Don't start with me, Joseph Sulaweyo,' Jeremiah said. 'Not after you just disappeared for days without an explanation, leaving me to handle everything.'

'I had to go see my son.' But he could not escape a

small flitting shadow of guilt. He would not want to be
cooped up in this place alone. Perhaps it had not been
easy for Jeremiah either. 'All right, then, who is this Sellars
man? What business does he have with us, that he calls
up from nowhere and tells us what to do?'

'The business is trying to save our lives,' Jeremiah
growled. 'And if you hadn't shown up when you did, he
would have been the only thing to keep me from being
murdered by those men out there.'

'That and several feet of battleship steel plate.' Del Ray
was trying to sound cheerful but hadn't quite succeeded.
'There are worse places to be under siege than in a hardened military bunker.'

'Not if we don't get things in order,' Jeremiah said
primly. 'Now, are you going to listen?'

Joseph had not entirely buried his suspicions. 'But if
this man is away in America like you say, how did he
find this place? It is supposed to be a big secret.'

'I'm not exactly sure. He knows a lot about Renie and
!Xabbu and the French woman – he even knew something about that old man Singh. Sellars says he's dead.'

'Why he say a thing like that?' Joseph felt a thrill of
superstitious fear. It had been so strange holding the empty
line, waiting for the voice out of nowhere – the voice that
never came. 'This man Sellars really tell you he is dead?'

Jeremiah stared, then gave a snort of exasperation. 'He
said *Singh* was dead. Singh. The old man that helped
Renie and the others. Now will you shut up and listen to
what I've written here? There are men trying to break
into this place. A folding bed crammed in the elevator
door is not truly a long-term solution.'

Joseph waved his hand. That was one thing about these
homosexual men – like women, they always got so stressed
up about things. 'Talk, then. I will listen.'

Jeremiah snorted again, then looked at the notes he had scribbled in old-fashioned pencil on the concrete pillar. 'Sellars says that we can't just block the elevator – that they could come down the shaft. We have to seal off this entire section of the base. He says that the plans show how to do that. But we also have to prepare for a long siege, so we have to bring everything we need down to this place. Joseph, that means you have to haul as much food and water as you can down from the kitchen. We don't know how long we have until they manage to get through the outer doors, so we have to be ready to seal the thing up as quickly as possible. If we get it ready, then have more time, we'll bring down more food and water.'

'What, you want me just to haul those plastic water things like a day laborer? Who is going to look for the guns – Del Ray? You should see him with a pistol in his hand. He is more dangerous to us than to those bad men.'

Joseph closed his eyes for a moment. Del Ray said something nasty under his breath. 'It's hard to believe there were moments I actually almost missed your company,' Jeremiah said. 'First, there are no guns, just like there aren't any office supplies. Almost anything small enough to be carried away was taken when they closed this place down. They only left food and water because they thought they might use it someday as a bomb shelter or something. Second, even if we had guns, we couldn't stop these people. You said yourself they were armored like a Special Operations team. Sellars says the best thing for us to do is to seal this off and wait them out.'

Long Joseph wasn't sure whether he was sorry or not that he wouldn't be shooting it out with the Boer hitmen. 'So what is *he* going to be doing?' he asked, cocking a thumb at Del Ray.

'Depends. Mr Chiume, do you know anything about
computer systems, electronics?'

Del Ray shook his head. 'My degree was political
science. I know how to use a pad, but that's about it.'

Jeremiah sighed. 'I was afraid of that. Sellars said there
are lots of patches to be made so that he can help us
more. I guess I'll just have to muddle through them myself,
if I can figure out his instructions. God, I hope he calls
back soon.'

'Patches?'

'This is a very old-fashioned system here, twenty, thirty
years old or more. I don't know what exactly he plans to
do, but he said it was important.' He tried to smile. He
looked very gray and drawn. 'Well, then, Mr Chiume, I
suppose you will have generator duty.'

'Call me Del Ray, please. What am I supposed to do?'

'If we're going to be locked down here in the lab, we
need the generator, because those men up there will
certainly be trying to turn off the main power. We have
to have power just to get air in and out of here, not to
mention keeping the tanks running.' He gestured toward
the huge shapes on the floor a level beneath them, tangled
in their cables like stones overgrown with clinging vines.
'Sellars said we're lucky they have a hydrogen-storage
generator down here, not a reactor, because the military
would have taken the hot material out of a reactor and
we'd have nothing except the main power source.'

'I still do not understand,' grumbled Long Joseph, his
mind full of the unattractive picture of himself carrying
dozens of heavy plastic water jugs and food canisters
down from the upper level. 'What does he know of my
Renie? How would she know someone from America, him
get all involved with this, with us?'

Del Ray shrugged and answered for Jeremiah. 'What

are any of us doing here in this strange place? Why did
a bunch of thugs come to my door and threaten to kill
me because my ex-girlfriend was talking to a French
researcher? It's a strange world and it's getting stranger.'

'That is the first thing you say all day that makes sense,'
declared Joseph.

Joseph felt sweaty and irritable, but what was more
disturbing was how the empty, echoing halls of the Wasp's
Nest base made the sweat turn cold on his skin. Joseph
did not like to think of himself as the type to be shivering with fear – although it had happened to him more
than once in his life – but neither could he pretend that
everything was going to be okay either.

Not going to talk your way out of this one, man, he
told himself as he trundled the handtruck into the elevator. Before pushing the down button he cocked an ear,
wondering if they would be able to hear when the thugs
outside finally broke the code on the massive front door,
or whether it would simply swing open silently, allowing
the killers to walk in like cats coming through a window
by night. All was quiet now; he could not even hear the
sounds of Jeremiah and Del Ray two floors below. Only
his own labored breathing gave the place life, made it
something other than a hole surrounded by stone, as uninhabited as an empty seashell.

The elevator door clunked open. Groaning quietly,
Joseph levered the cart into position and began to drag
the water supplies along the landing. He could see
Jeremiah's feet sticking out from beneath the console,
surrounded by various components and cables, and he
was reminded briefly of Elephant's storage-bin version of
a mad scientist's lab. *'It's not a secret anymore,'* the fat
man had said about the military base, and he had been

right. Not that Joseph was ever planning to look him up and congratulate him on his accuracy.

'This is all the water,' he shouted to Jeremiah's feet. 'I am going to bring down the food next. Don't know why – it is nothing but packaged rubbish. Want to kill ourselves after a few more weeks just from eating that.'

Jeremiah slid out from under the console wearing a frown on which Joseph could have opened a beer bottle, if he had been lucky enough to have one. 'Yes, it's a great shame. Which is why I'm certain that while you were out trotting around southern Africa, and I was cooped up here watching over your helpless daughter, you bought a few treats for me, yes? Some expensive candy bars, perhaps? A dozen *koeksisters* from the bakery? Something to compensate for leaving me hanging, stuck with nothing but the food you so accurately describe as rubbish?'

Joseph, from long experience with his daughter and others, recognized an argument he was not going to win; he hurried on with the cart to the spot where he had begun his pyramid of water jugs. On the way back, with Jeremiah safely under the console once more and Del Ray nowhere in sight, he paused to look down onto the laboratory floor. The silent shapes of the v-tanks, dusty, dead objects on a museum shelf, abruptly brought tears to the corner of his eyes. Surprised, he rubbed them away.

But one thing, he silently told the nearest pod. *One thing is, they are never going to get you unless they go through me first. Somehow I get you back out into the sun again.* He was surprised to hear himself making a speech in his own head, but even more surprised to realize what he was saying was true. 'You hear me, girl?' he whispered. 'Not unless they go through me.'

He was afraid Del Ray or Jeremiah would see him, and

in any case, the place was stony and miserable as a tomb. He hurried back to the elevator.

CALLIOPE Skouros made a face and put the coffee back down. It wasn't so much that it tasted bad, although it did, the steaming product of one of those little flash-brew drink packets, but that she'd downed so much coffee the night before that even after five hours of ineffective sleep she could still feel yesterday's caffeine hustling around in her system like one of those horrible cheery people who live to organize neighborhood events.

Calliope was in a pretty good mood, though. While there wasn't exactly sweeping victory on the waitress front, there was definite progress. Elisabetta (bearer of tattoos and all that coffee) had revealed her name, and now dropped by Calliope's table to chat even when an occasional miscalculation of the seat-yourself policy put the detective in another server's section. To her surprise and pleasure, Calliope had discovered that there was more to the young woman than simply her rough, attractive look. She was an art student – of course – but seemed to have a lot on her mind, and was even willing to listen for short stretches when she could be distracted from the eternal waitress complaints of lousy bosses, sore feet, and problems with rent and transportation.

Interestingly, over several nights' worth of fleeting conversation, the other major component of waitress-misery had not come up: so far there had been no mention of lazy, ignorant, or violent boyfriends. In fact, there had been no mention of boyfriends (or girlfriends) of any kind.

This had better turn into something, Calliope thought, considering the prospect of months lurking amid the garish, beach-party ambience of Bondi Baby. *Otherwise, the caffeine alone's going to kill me.*

'I'd offer a penny for your thoughts, partner mine . . .' Stan Chan slipped into the narrow, wallscreened place the cops all referred to as 'the green room' and threw his coat over the back of a chair; as usual, the tiny room was practically a sauna. 'But I'm sure that I'd be undervaluing. You look utterly deep today. What are they worth? Swiss credits? Real estate?' He gazed at the screen, which showed a dark, thin, scar-covered man. The room where the prisoner sat was empty but for an old table and several chairs, the walls a hideously cheerful orange fibramic tile designed to repel graffiti and, it was reputed, blood. 'Speaking of valuable things, is this our friend 3Big?'

Stan was occasionally a bit much in the morning, even when Calliope's head wasn't churning with the perfectly legal equivalent of a couple pops of hotwire. 'Can you talk a little more quietly? Yeah, that's him. He's been boxed all night, and now we're going to chat with him.'

'Lovely.' Her partner really was in a frighteningly good mood. She wondered if he'd had another date or something. 'Can I be nasty? Is it my turn?'

'Your turn.'

'You're a mate.' He paused, frowning, and poked her in the ribs. 'You're not wearing your flakkie, Skouros.'

'In the station?' She hated wearing the gel-filled vest, an item commonly referred to around the office as 'bulletproof underwear.'

'Regulations. After all, while he was in the holding cell our friend in there might have manufactured a pistol out of soap and floor lint.'

'Yeah, right. No wonder you like to wear yours – it makes you look like you actually have muscles. It just makes me look fat.'

'I think of you as the husky angel of Justice.' His face

turned briefly serious. 'You really need to wear that thing, Skouros.'

'Okay, I will. Now let's do some work, Mr Nasty.'

Stan snapped his fingers to douse the green room lights so that only darkness would show in the doorway behind them as they stepped through into the glare of the orange tiles. The prisoner looked up at them, his face emptied of anything except for a lip-droop of casual disgust. Calliope liked that – she enjoyed it more when they pretended to be hard.

'Good morning, Edward,' she said brightly as she and Stan slid into the chairs across from the prisoner. 'I'm Detective Skouros, this is Detective Chan.'

The dark man did not reply, but brought a finger up to stroke the long scars on his cheek.

Calliope decided to be puzzled. 'You are Edward Pike, aren't you? I'm sure this is the right interview room.' She turned to Stan. 'Guess this one will have to go back to the box while we figure out the mistake.'

'Nobody call me Edward but my mother, and she dead two years,' he said sullenly. '3Big, that's how I go. 3Big.'

'Yeah, this is him, fear not,' Stan said. 'Ugly little street beast, just picked up carrying six dozen carts of D-jak wipers in a customized flak belt. Retail weight of Indonesian charge – you're going to do ten years for that, 3-boy, and it won't be in one of the nice places either.'

'It was for personal use, seen?' The denial was pro forma – everybody knew they were fencing until the public defender showed up. 'I need rehabilitation. Got a bad 'diction, me.'

Stan made a spitting noise. 'That's going to play, yeah. Judge take one look at you, notice that you were within half a kilometer of a school, she's going to recommend we put you in one of the refuse barges and sink you in the ocean.'

Calliope sat quietly for a few minutes and watched her partner moving through the formally aggressive steps of the dance. Edward '3Big' Pike was a habitual, so he knew the motions as well as Stan. He wasn't the worst sort they had to deal with – lots of priors for receiving and handling, and one decent stretch in Silverwater for dealing, but as far as she knew he hadn't ever killed anyone who hadn't tried to kill him first, which in Darlinghurst Road terms practically made him Robin Hood. He was known for being a bit smarter than the average King's Cross street beast, and the fact that he'd only gone down once for dealing testified to that. Calliope wondered if there might be a little pride wrapped up in that, another place they could insert the thin end of the wedge.

Stan had the man snarling and defensive, which meant it was about time for her to start her pitch. 'Detective Chan?' She made her voice a little harsh. 'I don't think this is the right way to deal with the situation. Why don't you go get a drink of water?'

'Nah, I don't think so.' Stan gave the prisoner a stare of radiant contempt. 'But if you think you can deal with this curb creature, be my guest.'

'Look, Mr Pike,' Calliope began, 'technically you belong to Street Crime, so we don't have any formal jurisdiction over you. But if you help us out with a little information – and if it's *good* information – we might be able to get them back down to simple possession. With your priors you'll still do some time, but it won't be anything too bad.'

He was interested but trying not to show it, his heavy-lidded eyes burning brightly behind the surprisingly long lashes. 'What you want? Not going to roll over on no one, me. Coming out the box early won't mean nothing if I get sixed first time I touch the Darling.'

'We just want some information. About an old acquaintance of yours, someone you spent some time with back in Minda Juvenile. Johnny Wulgaru . . . ?'

His face was blank. 'Don't know him.'

'Also known as Jonny Dark – Johnny Dread?'

Now something did move beneath the stony features, something swift as mercury rolling in a pan. 'You talking about John More Dread? Talking about Dread?' A complicated series of emotions ran across him, ending in a nervous scowl. 'What you want with him? He's carked it, right? Dead?'

'Supposed to be. Have you heard otherwise?' She looked, but he had fallen back behind the street mask once more. 'We're just trying to clear up an old homicide. A girl named Polly Merapanui.'

He was on safer ground now. 'Don't know her. Never heard nothing about her.' He blinked and reconsidered. 'She the one that got her eyes cut out?'

Calliope leaned forward, keeping her voice casual. 'You know something about it?'

He shrugged. 'Saw it on the net.'

'We just want to know if you heard anything about Johnny Dread connected with that crime. Anything at all.'

'Not going to roll on nobody, me.'

Stan Chan leaned in. 'How can you be rolling on anyone if he's dead, you little shit? Talk some sense.'

3Big gave Calliope a look of wounded dignity. 'This your dog? Because if he don't stop biting my knackers, you might as well put me back in the box.'

Calliope waved Stan back into his chiar. 'Just tell me what you remember about John Dread.'

The prisoner smirked. 'Nothing. I forgot everything.

And if I ever hear anything about him after today, I forget that too. He was one *sayee lo* bastard. Wouldn't talk slice to him for hard money.'

Calliope kept asking questions, augmented by suggestions about 3Big's heritage and social life from Stan that were occasionally rather surreal. If it was a fencing match, the prisoner was not playing to win, but simply not to be scored upon, an unsatisfying experience that went on so long that the last of the caffeine rush finally wore off, leaving Calliope tired and irritable.

'So he's dead, and you haven't seen him for years anyway. That's what you're telling me, right?'

He nodded. 'For true.'

'Then why do I get the feeling you're holding out? You're facing a long stretch, Mr Pike. Eddie. Three Bug, or whatever bullshit you want to call yourself. If I were where you are, I'd be climbing across this table right now, trying hard to kiss my big Greek backside, because there aren't going to be many people offering you anything in the next little while. Unless it's someone in the shower when you go back to Silverwater, handing you a chocolate bar to bend over.' He was clearly a little surprised by how abruptly she had abandoned the pretense of helpfulness, but he maintained his smirk. 'So why won't you talk?'

'I'm talking.'

'Talk about something real, I mean. We could scrape three to five years off your sentence if you told us something useful about John Dread.'

He looked at her for a strangely long time. Stan Chan started to say something, but Calliope touched his knee under the table, asking for patience. 3Big fidgeted with his scars again, sighed, then dropped his hands to the tabletop.

'Look, woman,' he said slowly. 'I tell you something for free. I don't know nothing about Dread. But even if I did know something, I wouldn't tell you shit. Not for good behavior time, not for reduction, not for nothing.'

'But if he's dead . . . !'

He shook his head, his gaze hidden now, curtained behind those long lashes like a panther in a canebrake. 'Don't matter. You don't know Dread, you never met him. You cross him, he come back out of the ground and kill you three ways. If there was ever someone be a *mopaditi*, come back and six you in the dark, Dread do it.'

'Mopaditi. What does that mean?'

He had retreated far back now, surveying them as though from the depths of a cave. 'Ghost. When you dead, but you don't go away. I'll go back to the box now.'

'Well, that was useless.' Stan Chan waited expectantly.

'Hang on.' Calliope took out her hearplug and popped it into its padded slot in her pad. She wondered again if it was time to invest in a can. It was tedious lugging the pad around, even the new, waferthin Krittapong she had bought herself as a birthday present. 'Doctor Jigalong is out of town. I've left her messages at work and home.'

'About "mopaditi"?'

'Yeah. I haven't heard that in street slang before, have you?'

'No.' He put his feet up on the desk. 'That's what, eight, nine of these people we've rousted? Not getting much.'

'We got something there.'

Stan gave her the eyebrow. 'You mean because he used an aboriginal word? In case you didn't notice, Skouros, the man was indeed of aboriginal heritage himself. Don't you say "hopa!" or "retsina" or even "acropolis" every now and then? I've been known to use the occasional ethnic expression myself – I think I called you "round-eye" just the other day . . .'

'He reacted when I asked him about Johnny Dread. He was surprised.' Something else was bothering her too, some detail, maddeningly out of reach.

'Well, the man *is* officially dead. Might be reason for surprise, being questioned about someone you thought was dead.'

'Might be. But there was something weird about his reaction. Maybe he's heard something on the street.'

'Maybe won't get us over the hump, Skouros. What next? Charming as it may be, we're running out of street culture to investigate.'

Calliope shook her head, perplexed and distressed and, with the caffeine finally drained out of her system and nothing gone in to replace it, feeling generally pretty godawful.

Sleeplessly out of skew, she sat on the couch and accessed the interview from the department system to run it on her wallscreen. She had decided for her own good to stay away from Bondi Baby. It wasn't even so much the near-obsessive interest in the waitress Elisabetta, but the fact that she had realized she was actually beginning to look forward to the gooey desserts the place served.

Not going to lose any weight that way, Skouros, she told herself. *Better to stay home.* She hadn't shopped in days, so there was little except crispbread to imperil her determination. She watched the questioning all the way through, then jumped back to the spot where she had first mentioned their quarry's name.

'*You talking about John More Dread?*' 3Big said, then said it yet again as Calliope backed up and played it over. '*. . . Talking about Dread?*'

That's it, she thought. *John More Dread. Haven't heard that one before.* But why should one more alias – for a suspect who already had many – catch in her thoughts this way, like a splinter working its way under the skin? *More Dread. More Dread. Where have I heard that before?*

The thought of the photo taken at Feverbrook Hospital drifted back to her, the blur of dark presence, the formless, smoky face.

3Big Pike said a ghost. If there's anyone who'd come back as a ghost . . .

She closed her eyes and opened them, trying to use the familiarity of her apartment to push back the feeling of being watched. Of being haunted.

SHE was back on the balcony again. The tower drew her as though she were a moth and its black immensity some kind of inverse light. Even now, with the voices gone, when she was somehow farther from it than she'd been even back in Juniper Bay, she could not ignore it.

A sparkle of red signal lights ringed the top like a crown of embers, and on the uppermost floors a few windows glowed, illuminated singly or in small clusters. Otherwise, it was only visible against the night sky because of the searchlights that swept across the empty parking lot, glancing off the shiny, irregular exterior as they tracked across the rows of painted stalls.

The voices were gone. The children were gone. Were they one and the same? Olga Pirofsky had been immersed in the dreamy unreality of her southward journey for so long that she could not quite remember. She was exhausted, too. The nights when the children had pulled her and hurried her, whispering their lives into her dreaming ear, had somehow been far more restful than the dead black hours she had experienced after they had fallen silent. Now she woke each day slow-thinking and hollow, feeling like a helium balloon that had finally leaked the last of its buoyancy and could only roll along the carpet, sagging, useless.

So what now? she asked herself. She could not pull her eyes from the tower, the center of its own dark kingdom. *Go home? Kill yourself?*

But she had no home anymore. Misha was gone, and Juniper Bay seemed like another planet – like the circus, like the dear, sweet murdered days when she had still been with Aleksandr. And she had pushed away those who might have helped her, Roland McDaniel and her other few friends from work, that nice lawyer Mr Ramsey. There was nothing left for her but silence.

The voices had brought her practically to the foot of this dreadful black mountain before deserting her. Somehow it was all tangled together – the children, the tower, and the grinning, corpse-white features of Uncle Jingle, the mask she herself had worn so long she wondered if it had not somehow shaped the face beneath.

She opened her pad and sat down at the tiny pressboard motel desk. She found her gaze repeatedly swinging to the window, and at last clapped her hands to close the drapes, unable to think with the distraction of that dark warning finger.

Tired, but happy to have made a decision, Olga began to write her open-ended suicide note.

CHAPTER 6

Talking to Machines

IT was like a horror flick, but worse, because it was really happening.

Tiny human shapes quailed before a vast and monstrous thing – a whip scorpion, Kunohara had called it. Paul could see Martine and her miniaturized companions huddled deep in the underside folds of a great leaf that shuddered over their heads as rain thumped down like bombs. He reached out, but it was only a view-window – he could do nothing to help them. The whip scorpion took a step closer, slouching in the cradle of its towering, jointed legs. A slender feeler like a stiffened riding crop reached out toward them – slowly, almost tenderly.

'You destroyed those mutants,' Paul shouted. 'Why can't you save my friends?'

'The mutants did not belong here. There is nothing wrong with the scorpion.' Hideki Kunohara almost sounded offended. 'It is only following its nature.'

'If you won't help them, then send me. At least let me go to them.'

Kunohara regarded him with oblique disapproval. 'You will be killed.'

'I have to try.'

'You scarcely know those people – you told me so yourself.'

Tears started in Paul's eyes. Anger expanded like steam, threatening to blow off the top of his head. Dimly, he could hear the threadlike shrieks of Martine and the others as the monstrous scorpion levered itself nearer. 'You don't understand anything. I've been lost – months, maybe years. Alone! I thought I was out of my mind. *They're all I have!*'

Kunohara shrugged, then raised his hand. An instant later the bubble, the view-window, and Kunohara's stolid face all vanished, replaced by a scene of terrifying strangeness.

He was somewhere on the forest floor, trunks of mountainous trees stretching up all around him into the night, so large as to be almost invisible. Rain hissed and thudded all around, drops big as rubbish bins, some even the size of small cars; when they smashed against the mulch of the forest floor, everything jumped.

Paul had a sudden and horrifying recollection of the trenches of Amiens, cowering under the impersonal destruction of the German heavy guns; lightning flashed as if to further the illusion, dazzlingly bright as a phosphorus flare. Something moved on his right with a loud leathery creak he could hear even above the thumping of rain-drops; the ground shifted beneath him. Paul turned and felt his heart try to climb out of his chest.

The whip scorpion shuffled another step closer to the base of the leaf and froze, motionless except for its questing feelers. By Paul's scale it was as big as a fire engine but much higher, a low, wide body slung between a gantry of jointed legs. It had no tail that he could see, but the pincers that folded like bumpers below its head were jagged with thorny spikes that would hold prey as inescapably as a crocodile's jaws. Two bright red spots low on its head, visible as the lightning flared again, gave an impression of malevolent eyes, of something summoned from its sleep in the pits of hell and angry at having been wakened.

A stream of water rolled off one of the high leaves onto the scorpion. It hugged the ground as the torrent splashed down, waiting with cold patience for the inundation to stop. For a moment Paul could see past it, to the hollow beneath a drooping leaf the size of a ski chalet, to pale human faces reflecting like pearls in the faint moonlight. He took a few steps toward them even as the scorpion ratcheted up to its full height again.

'Martine!' His voice was swallowed in the bombardment of rain. He reached and snatched up a fibrous piece of wood as long as his arm, a tree-needle or a thorn, and flung it at the scorpion. It fell harmlessly against one of the monster's legs but the movement attracted attention. The scorpion stopped and waved one of its whips in Paul's direction. Suddenly aware of what he had done, he went rigid. The feeler, like a horn drawn out twenty meters long yet not much wider than Paul's leg, swept by only an arm's length from where he stood motionless, heart knocking in triple time.

What have I done? His thoughts were as distracted and swift as his heart. *I've killed myself. I can't do anything for them, and now I've killed myself, too.*

The scorpion took a rasping step toward him. The whip brushed his chest and almost knocked him over. The shadow swung above him, turning, the legs angled out on either side like a forest of leaning trees. He saw the massive pincers flex outward slowly, then snap back.

Before he could close his eyes to cloak the horror of his coming end, the scorpion suddenly wheeled to the side. A tiny human figure had burst from beneath the leaf and was stumbling away across the uneven ground. The whip scorpion moved after it with appalling speed.

The little shrieking figure staggered as the many-legged darkness covered it. The scorpion's front end dipped and the pincers snatched up its kicking prize, piercing it and smashing it into an impossible configuration before levering it up to the furious machinery of the jaws.

Paul could only stare in stupefied horror. The pursuit and kill had taken only seconds. One of his friends was dead and now the vast monster was turning, leg by leg, back toward him.

Something swept down out of the trees, a column of misty whiteness that shoved the huge creature flat against the ground. Ice began to form all across the monster's carapace and crystallize in powdery chunks on the joints of its legs.

'*Seven hells, nothing works anymore!*' Kunohara's voice rasped in Paul's ear, then the man himself was standing beside him. Ignoring the mammoth, rigid scorpion, Kunohara grabbed Paul's shoulder, then beckoned to the people still cowering under the leaf. 'Step out,' he shouted. 'Come and join hands – I do not know how far my personal field extends.'

Still light-headed with shock, Paul watched three dim shapes tumble out onto open ground. Someone clutched his hand, then another avalanche of rain swept down, sending bits of leaves whirling into the air even as everything abruptly vanished.

He was sprawled on the virtual tatami mats of the bubble-house in dark night, with bodies all around him. A moment later the lights warmed and Paul crawled toward the nearest of the groaning figures.

'What was *that* barking *fen?*' a large shape said, squelching wetly as it sat up. 'And where's this?'

Considering that the last time they had been together the teenager had tried to strangle him, Paul would never have dreamed he would be so happy to see T4b, but as soon as he saw the hand with its pale glow sticking out of the baggy one-piece outfit, he felt a kind of joy. He tugged at the skinny, black-haired sim, a form quite different than the Trojan warrior Paul had met before. 'Javier? That is you, isn't it? Who else is there? Where's Martine?'

'Paul Jonas?' The voice was Florimel's. 'Yes, where *is* Martine?'

'Over here.' T4b crouched beside the third figure. 'Don't look good, her.'

Martine Desroubins tried to speak, coughed, then succeeded. 'I will survive. The transition . . . it overwhelmed me. Paul Jonas, is that truly you? Where are we? I can't make sense of it.'

'Yes, it's me.' He had been counting heads, but no matter

how he tried, he could not make it more than three. He
was terrified to ask the next question, but had to know.
'Where are the others? Did that horrible thing . . . did the
scorpion get them all?'

Florimel sat upright, wearing a fairly generic middle-
aged woman's sim, but recognizable by her wounded eye
and missing ear. 'We have not seen Renie, !Xabbu,
Orlando, or Fredericks since . . . since whatever happened
on the black mountain.'

Paul tried frantically to think of which of the companions he might have forgotten. 'But who . . . ? I saw that
monster catch someone . . . !'

'It was one of the Grail Brotherhood,' Florimel said,
'— a man named Jiun. I suppose he thought he could
escape while the creature was distracted by you. He
misjudged.' She looked around again. 'Where is this place?
How did we come here?'

'Jiun Bhao?' Kunohara said from behind them. All but
Paul turned in surprise. 'Jiun Bhao, the scourge of Asia,
eaten in my garden by a whip scorpion?' He threw back
his head and laughed.

'Pretty locked-up sense of humor, you,' T4b commented,
but he sounded grudgingly impressed by Kunohara's hilarity, which now had their host bent double, hugging his
own middle.

'So is it you we owe our gratitude, then?' Martine asked
their host.

'You certainly took your time before deciding to help,
Kunohara,' Paul said angrily.

The man wiped his eyes. 'Oh, I am sorry, but it is too
sweet. Do you know how many small enterprises Jiun
has gobbled himself? How many lives he has crushed in
his own claws? Jiun Bhao, eaten by a scorpion, in the
rain.' He shook his head. 'But you are unfair to me, Jonas.

I would not have left you to die. I thought I could bring you all back from here, but there are grave problems with the higher levels of my system – doubtless more effects of the larger catastrophe – and I could not move you or your companions remotely. I would even have destroyed the scorpion from a distance if I could, although the creature itself is blameless, but few of my system commands are functioning. That is why I had to come in person, so you could be touching me when I transported back.'

'So now we are your guests,' Florimel said slowly. 'Or are we prisoners?'

'No more than I am.' Kunohara sketched a bow. 'However, that may prove rather less freedom than any of us would wish.'

'There's something I don't understand,' said Paul. 'Martine, I heard your voice. How were you . . . broadcasting like that?'

The blind woman held up a shiny silver object in her fatigue-trembling hand.

'The lighter!' he said. 'But I thought Renie took it from you . . .'

'It is not the same lighter,' Martine said wearily. 'I will explain later, if you don't mind.'

Kunohara scowled at the device. 'You have already done damage by making your presence known with that.' He squinted at the stylized monogram. 'Yacoubian – the idiot. With his cigars and his short attention span. I should have guessed.'

'It would do him no good now, even if he had it,' Florimel said with some satisfaction. 'Not unless they smoke cigars in hell.'

Kunohara frowned. 'I will not ask you to give it to me – over such things a delicate alliance might founder. But if you dare to use it again and risk leading your enemy down on top of me, I will eject you from this house and send you back to the scorpion. He is doubtless thawed by now.'

'We don't want to use it.' Martine's words were slurred by exhaustion. 'None of its other functions work now anyway, as far as I can tell. Just the communication.' She yawned. 'We only want to sleep.'

'Very well, then.' Kunohara waved his hand. 'Sleep. You too, Jonas, since you were wakened by your friends' call. I am not happy with the foolish thing you people have done, but the step is taken now. I will discover what I can and wake you again soon enough.'

He vanished, leaving them alone in the wide, curving room with the sounds and distorted motion of the river. T4b looked critically at the modest furnishings and the corpse of the mutated wood louse, which still hung in midair in its little box of light at one end of the room.

'Beats hiding under a leaf, maybe,' he said, and stretched out on the floor mat.

'*CODE Delphi*. Start here.

'I am hurrying to record these thoughts. God alone knows when I will have a chance again – everything seems tenuous now, tinged with catastrophe, as though this entire virtual world has tipped from its normal orbit. But I must make the effort to do things well, no matter how I feel time slipping away. Perhaps this is what it feels like to be Renie, always driven to move forward . . .

'I believe I had recorded most of the events in Troy and atop the black mountain when we were interrupted by the scorpion. Now I will try to make some kind of sense out of how we left the mountain and what has happened since. There is little chance that I will ever recover these subvocalizations tossed out into the ether of the network, but I have always ordered my life this way, although usually with a more conventional journal; and it is a crutch I prefer not to do without.

'That is a thought, is it not? All my life, I have found my solace and my sanity in talking to machines, and through them to myself. Psychologically transparent, I suppose, and rather grim.

'Enough.

'In the final moments on the peak of the black mountain, as what we could perceive of reality fractured around us, I found myself consumed by images and feelings – powerful sensations as overwhelming as a demonic possession. I suspect now, after talking to Florimel and the others, that somehow my altered senses were perceiving the attack on the Other by Dread – to me it was a phantasm of bird shapes and shadows and the voices of screaming children, and surges of pain and horror for which there are no words. Whether or not the Other is the lonely thing I met in the controlled darkness of the Pestalozzi Institute when I was a child, and no matter what it has done to the old hacker Singh or anyone else, I feel pity for it – yes, pity, even if it is only some kind of highly evolved machine. I can think of almost nothing more pathetic than hearing it sing that old nursery rhyme, that bit of an old fairy tale. But whether it is good or bad or something less straightforward, its agonies nearly killed me.

'As the Other fought to protect itself against Dread's attack, things were happening all around me which I have had to reconstruct from the accounts of others. T4b's successful attack on one of the Grail Brotherhood – apparently an American general named Yacoubian, the true owner of our access device – will bear much considering,

since somehow the strange thing that happened to our
young companion's hand when we were in the patchwork
simworld before the House allowed him to . . . I do not
know. Disrupt Yacoubian's control over the virtual environment? Break down the protective algorithms that all the
Brotherhood until recently enjoyed?

'In any case, soon after that, the Other's giant hand
came down, apparently obliterating Renie, !Xabbu,
Orlando, and Sam, and perhaps also Jongleur, the Grail
master who wore the Osiris sim. But I am not certain I
believe that, and neither is Florimel. It seems strange
to think that a manifestation of the operating system
would do something as crude as swat our companions
like flies.

'In any case, with Florimel practically dragging me, we
hurried to help T4b, who had been knocked aside by the
monster and lay stunned just a few meters from the edge
of the titan hand. That hand abruptly vanished – I felt
the Other's presence vanish at the same time, a sudden
vacuum in my head that I cannot begin to describe –
leaving behind no trace of our companions, only the body
of the falcon-headed Yacoubian. Florimel, who was far
more composed than I was, saw something lying in
Yacoubian's oversized fingers. It was another lighter, identical to the one Renie had taken with her into death or
wherever she has gone – apparently Yacoubian had
replaced his lost original. Even as Florimel bent and
snatched it up, the world fell apart again.

'The Other was gone. I felt Paul's angel, Ava, shattered
into fragments around us, each one suffering, a terrible
chorus of pain almost as devastating as the Other's. The
reality of the network was collapsing in some way I still
cannot define, literally coming to pieces. I reached out
for anything that might save me, as a drowning woman

might snatch in desperation at a chunk of wood far too small to help her float.

'But what I found was indeed enough to save us from perishing in the overflow of chaos. How can I explain it? If I had a hope someone other than myself might actually hear these thoughts someday, I would perhaps try harder, but I cannot summon that belief.

'It was a . . . something. The words do not matter, since words cannot describe it – it was a ray of light, a silvery thread, a string of coherent energies. A connection of some kind between where we were and . . . somewhere else, that was all I knew for certain. The closest thing to it I have experienced was the terrifying moment in the Place of the Lost when I reached out through the nothingness to find !Xabbu on the other end. But this time there seemed to be no one on the far side of the shining filament. As all around me degenerated into meaningless information, only that bright thread remained constant, although it, too, was beginning to lose its cohesion. I snatched at it – again, there are no proper words – as I had done before with !Xabbu's extension of his personality, and I clung. I tried to fix my mind on all my companions – Renie, Florimel, Paul, all of them – tried to see their patterns in the information storm so I could pull them along with me on that slender lifeline. But the abilities I have here are not science, they are more like art, and once more the words fail me. If I knew how consistently to do the things I can sometimes do, I myself would be one of the gods of this place. In any case, I saved only a few.

'And so we came through and found ourselves dropped without warning into the stormy night of Kunohara's world, wearing our old sims from when we first entered the system, but dressed in identical coveralls with a patch reading "The Hive" on the breast – apparently some kind of default garb here in Kunohara's world. It is too bad we were only granted the clothes and not the research installation itself. It would have been nice to have a roof and walls. Instead, we huddled under leaves for shelter from the crushing rain, prey to any monsters who might brave such weather to go hunting. And indeed, we nearly found ourselves eaten by one such creature, until Paul Jonas and Kunohara intervened. I am glad I could not see the thing. Sensing its size and power was bad enough.

'And now we are here in Kunohara's house, where after a short sleep we talked for many, many hours. I am tired again, but I must continue with this a little longer while the others are resting, because who knows when I will next have the chance to sort through my experiences? This network refutes any notion of natural inertia – if something *can* happen here, it almost undoubtedly will.

'When we awakened in the relative safety of this strange bubble, we explained to Paul what had happened since he was separated from us on the mountaintop. I suppose somehow I was able to drag him with us along that gleaming track. Kunohara would not talk to me about what it might have been that led us here, but I have my . . . no, I will keep things in their proper order.

'In any case, our host is a strange man. He spent the afternoon drinking, some virtual liquor that he offered to us with a shrug. Only T4b accepted, but did not finish his glass. Kunohara seems fey and fatalistic – the knowledge that he is trapped here, subject to the same fears and mortal dangers the rest of us have lived with for weeks, seems to have affected him badly.

'As we explained to Paul, when Florimel, T4b, and I first found ourselves returned to Kunohara's microworld, we also discovered we had not come alone. Two of the

Grail Brotherhood had been pulled through with us, no longer dressed as Egyptian gods, but given some kind of default sims – Florimel tells me both were quite generic, more like composites than actual people. She was the one who guessed they must be of the Grail, and with the help of T4b and his strange hand – after all, they had seen what it had done to their comrade Yocoubian – she convinced them to cooperate. The network's former masters had discovered that they no longer had any control over their own system, and I think they were rather shocked and disoriented.

'The less confused of the two was Robert Wells. It was incredibly strange to be huddling in the dirt beneath a monstrous leaf with one of the world's most powerful men, and just as surprising to discover his companion was a no less impressive figure, the Chinese financier Jiun Bhao. Jiun could not completely grasp what had happened, and seemed to think that Florimel, T4b, and I were there to help him get back offline, or failing that, into one of his own simulation worlds. We quickly disabused him of that idea. He spent most of the hours we were together in sullen, almost childish silence.

'Wells was a sharper character, and quickly made it clear he had information to trade if we would help him. He did not specify what information, and I regret now that we did not take the time to barter, but we had already received frighteningly close scrutiny from a hunting centipede, and Florimel and I were more concerned with making our position defensible than trying to find out what Wells might know.

'Ahhh. Too many words, Martine. I am telling this more slowly than when we explained it to Paul and Kunohara. Soon the scorpion found us. In desperation, I tried to use the lighter, and heard the voice of that monster Dread

telling us that he would be . . . how did he put it? *Sending
some friends to find us.* Thank God we are no longer stuck
in the place where I used the communicator. I do not ever
want to see that . . . that . . .

'It is hard to talk when I think of him, remember being
his prisoner, his voice speaking cheerfully of so many
ghastly things. Stop, Martine. Make sense of what you
have, what you know and remember.

'Whether he was more frightened of Dread or the scorpion, I cannot say, but Robert Wells decided to run, and
vanished behind us into the thick vegetation. Jiun waited
a few moments longer to desert us, but he chose the wrong
direction. I cannot say I will lose much sleep over the
death of a cruel, self-serving old man like Jiun, but I wish
I knew where Wells might be. It is doubtless cold-blooded
to say so, but I would be happier if I felt sure he would
meet the same fate as Jiun Bhao. I could tell even in our
brief hours together that Wells is frighteningly clever.

'Kunohara was highly amused by what happened to
Jiun, but did not seem overly concerned about Wells being
loose in his simworld. Actually, it is hard to tell what
Kunohara thinks at all. Paul says he believes our host is
ready to share information, but I have seen little of it,
and as the day goes on, he grows more silent and strange.
Despite his promise, he has still told us little we do not
already know. What kind of ally is this? Only slightly
better than the enemies we already have. With so many
of our friends lost or dead, it is hard not to resent him
and his self-pity.

'At times this Kunohara reminds me of a boy I knew
in university, highly popular and very daring – he would
do anything for applause. But always I heard in his voice
a note of darkness. He died trying to climb the wall of a
ten-story residence building and everyone said it was a

terrible, sad accident, but I thought when I heard it that he was searching for that accident, and finally found it.

'Kunohara, especially with this quiet drunkenness upon him, seems to me like that boy . . .

'The others are stirring again, and there is much to discuss. I will have to continue these thoughts later.

'*Code Delphi.* End here.'

PAUL was surprised by how much better he felt simply having Martine and the others sitting beside him. *Kunohara's right – I barely know these people*, he thought. *But it doesn't feel like that.*

'So, Mr Kunohara.' There was an edge in Martine's voice. 'Now perhaps it is your turn to share a little information. After all, your life is now as much in danger as ours.'

Kunohara smiled, acknowledging her point. 'I have never harmed you. As I told your friends, it was a risk simply to speak to you. You have the sort of enemies someone like me tries to avoid.'

'You can't avoid them anymore,' Florimel said bluntly. 'So talk to us. What do you know about all this?'

Kunohara sighed and folded his legs beneath him. Outside the bubble the first morning light was warming the sky from black to violet. The river was almost completely obscured by mists – they might have been floating through the clouds in a balloon. 'I will tell you what I can, but it is not much. If you do not already know who I am and how I came to be here, I see no sense in explaining. I have built this place because I could, and have lived in uneasy truce with the Grail Brotherhood for a long time. I will not pretend I did not know what they were doing, or what crimes they committed, but I have done nothing wrong myself. It is not my duty to save the world.'

Florimel made a low noise that might have been an angry growl, but Kunohara ignored her.

'All I wanted – all that I still want – is to be left alone. I am not particularly fond of people. It is strange now to see my quiet, private house turned into a barracks, but there is nothing to be done about it. It is hard to ignore someone who keeps appearing in one's garden, however much one might wish it.'

'You said you knew what the Grail Brotherhood were doing,' Martine said. 'Tell us. We have had to rely on guesswork.'

'I think by now you must know all that I do. They have made an immortality machine for themselves and killed to keep it secret, although it has done them little good so far. Despite all their planning they did not account for this maniac employee of Felix Jongleur's who, from what you tell me, seems to have somehow hijacked the operating system.'

'But what *is* the system?' Florimel said. 'It has a name of sorts. They call it the Other. What is it?'

'By now you probably know more about it than I do.' Kunohara showed a thin smile. 'Jongleur has kept it secret even from the rest of the Brotherhood. How it was constructed, what its principle of operation is, only Jongleur knows. It is as though it sprang from nowhere.'

'It didn't spring from nowhere,' Martine said suddenly. 'I met it myself twenty-eight years ago.'

Having heard her say something about this on the mountaintop, Paul was the only one who did not look at her in surprise. Martine quickly told her story. Despite her calm, dry voice, it was not hard to hear the terror of that long-ago child reverberating in her words.

Kunohara shook his head wonderingly. 'So however it is constructed, Jongleur has been programming it in some way for perhaps three decades. As though teaching it to be human.' He frowned, considering; his strange mood seemed to have abated, at least for the moment. 'He must have gained something by both mimicking and using human consciousness as the root of his system.'

'That's right!' Paul said urgently. 'God, I had nearly forgotten. This man Azador – Renie and !Xabbu met him, too – he told me that the system used the brains of children, Gypsy children, and also . . . what did he call them? The unborn?' The memories were dim, distorted by his dreamlike experiences on the island of Lotos. 'Why do you seem so surprised?' he asked Kunohara, who was looking at him very oddly. 'We knew they were using children somehow – that's what brought most of these people here in the first place.'

Kunohara realized he was staring and made a show of poking the fire. 'So this is what they have constructed, then? A sort of net of linked human brains?'

'But what does "unborn" mean?' Florimel seemed to be struggling to hold down anger. 'Stillborn children? Aborted fetuses?'

'We have only hearsay from . . . from the person Jonas mentioned,' Kunohara said. 'But it would not surprise me if the most basic array of neural nodes were unimprinted brains of that sort, yes.' He shrugged liquidly. 'The South American, Klement, he made his fortune in the black market for human organs.'

'Chizz that those old scanners sixed out, then,' said T4b with sudden loathing. 'Wish those Grail-knockers had even more exit-pain, like.'

'It is a horrible idea,' scowled Florimel. 'Horrible. But why would they need living children, too? Why would they need to take someone like Renie's brother, or . . . or my Eirene?'

'Matti, too,' T4b said. 'Just a poor little micro – didn't scuff no one.'

'Hard to know,' said Kunohara. 'Perhaps they derive some different value from a more developed brain.'

'How do they do it anyway?' Florimel demanded. 'You can't just suck someone's mind out like a vampire stealing blood. This place is madness on top of madness, but it still has rules. It still exists within the real universe of physics . . .'

'I want to ask Mr Kunohara another question.' Martine's quiet but firm voice shut Florimel off like a faucet. 'You have said that we know all we need to know about you, but I'm not certain I believe that. If nothing else, there are still the riddles you set for us. Why? And what did they mean?'

Kunohara looked at her coolly. It was interesting and a little depressing, Paul thought, to see how quickly the owner of this particular world had sized up Martine as his most formidable challenge, relegating Paul and the others to bystander status. 'In my own way, I tried to help. I am a meddler, I suppose, and thus not the perfect type to be a hermit, after all. You came crashing through my world as innocent as sheep and I thought it might help you to think a little about what was happening. But as I said before, I could not afford to assist you too obviously. I have remained safe both here and in the real world largely because of the indifference of Jongleur and his cabal.'

'So you taunted us with riddles.' Martine sat back, her face bland. 'Dollo's Law and . . . what was the other? Something Japanese. Kishimo . . . something.'

'Kishimo-jin.' He nodded his head.

'Oh! I remembered what Dollo's Law is,' Florimel said suddenly. 'It took a long time to come back to me, but I remember it from university biology now. It is something about evolution not going backward – but I still can make no sense of why you should say it to us.'

'Life does not retreat.' Kunohara closed his eyes and took a sip of his drink. 'Evolution does not go backward. Once a certain complexity has been reached, it is not undone. The parallel is that it will tend to become more complex – that life, or whatever self-replicating pattern you choose, will only grow more complicated.'

'School?' T4b groaned. 'School, is this? Six me now, save me pain.'

Martine ignored him. 'So what are you saying?'

'That the system is growing more complex than even the Brotherhood had wished. I had suspected that in some way the operating system was evolving, might perhaps be developing a consciousness.' He took another sip. 'It appears I was a few decades late in noticing.'

'And the other little . . . riddle?' Martine's voice seemed unusually harsh to Paul. Kunohara might not be the most charming of men, but he had rescued them and given them shelter, after all.

'Kishimo-jin. A monster, an ogre – a creature out of a Buddhist fairy tale. She was a demon who devoured children, until the Buddha converted her. Then she became their special protector.'

'Even with an explanation,' Martine said drily, 'we are still puzzled. By a monster that devours children, you are alluding to the Other? What does this tell us?'

Kunohara smiled slightly, apparently enjoying the give and take. Paul thought that although the man might not like people, he did seem to like sparring. 'Let us consider what you have told me. Yes, this system eats children, you could say. But have you failed to notice how obsessed it is with children and childhood in all forms? Have you

not met, as I have in my travels through other simulations, the childlike figures who do not seem to belong in
the worlds in which they are found?'

'The orphans!' Paul almost shouted. When he discovered everyone was looking at him, he cleared his throat.
'Sorry. That's my name for the ones like the boy Gally I
met in two different simulations. They're not ordinary
people like us – they don't know who they are outside of
the simulation. When I was with Orlando and Fredericks,
we wondered if they might be something to do with the
children in comas.'

'The Lost,' Martine said quietly. 'Like homeless souls,
they were. Javier heard someone he knew.'

'T4b,' he corrected her, but his heart wasn't in it. 'Heard
Matti. Too far crash, that was.'

'In any case, the operating system – the Other – does
seem obsessed with such things, does it not?' Kunohara
looked to Martine. 'Children, and things of childhood . . .'

'Like children's stories.' Blind Martine could not return
his gaze, but she clearly acknowledged his serve. 'You
spoke to the others about that. That there was some kind
of . . . story-force at work. Some shaping force.'

'You said a "meme,"' Florimel said. 'I have heard the
word but do not know it.'

'Perhaps we are looking at that meme even now,' their
host said. 'Perhaps I have invited it into my house.'

It hurt Paul to see Martine suddenly look so pale. 'Don't
play games with us, man,' he said. 'What do you mean
by that?'

'A meme,' Martine said faintly. 'It is a word that means
a kind of . . . idea-gene. It is a theory from the last century,
brought up and argued many times over. Communism was
such a meme, some would say. An idea that reproduced
itself over and over in human consciousness, like a

biological trait. Eternal life would be another – a meme that has kept itself alive admirably, over hundreds of generations . . . as witness the Grail Brotherhood and their obsession with it.'

'Speed me,' T4b said grumpily. 'This bug-knocker saying that someone here is a Communist? I thought those were all like sixville, dinosaur-type.'

'Mister Kunohara is suggesting that I, along with the others in that long-ago experiment at the Pestalozzi Institute, may have infected the Brotherhood's operating system with the idea of stories – that we have given this fast-evolving machine a notion of casuality based on things like the Brothers Grimm and the fairy tales of Perrault.' Martine put her fingers to her temples, pressing. 'It is possible – yes, I can admit that it is possible. But what does it mean for us?'

The drink was agreeing with Kunohara for the moment – he looked sleek and satisfied. 'It is hard to say, but I think the evidence is everywhere. Look at the things that come up again and again in your experience – look at the way you have been helped and prompted by this apparition which you tell me is Jongleur's daughter. Whatever she is, she is clearly tied closely to the Other, and she appears to you again and again, like a . . . what would be the word from your French tales, Ms Desroubins? Like a fairy godmother. Or an angel, as Jonas puts it.'

'But even if it's true,' said Florimel, 'even if the operating system is trying to make everything into a little story, *the operating system isn't in charge anymore*. As far as we know, whatever small independence it had under the Grail people is gone – it has been completely subverted by that murdering swine, Dread.' She lifted her hand to her face. 'Look at this! I have lost an ear and an eye –

even if I survive to return to the real world, I might be half-blind, half-deaf. Even worse, this killer may have insured that there is no cure for my daughter. So it is meaningless to sit here talking about story this and story that. Where is Dread? How do we get to him? Where *were* we, in that place where the Other manifested itself? You are a landlord in this virtual universe, Kunohara. You must be able to find things out, travel, communicate.' She took a deep, ragged breath; when she spoke again, her voice was quieter but no less harsh. 'We asked you once before if you meant to help us, and you said you were too afraid of the Brotherhood – you would not risk your life. Well, your life is truly in danger now. So will you help us?'

What seemed to Paul like a very long time passed. A dull glow had kindled behind the mists outside: the sun was rising over Kunohara's imaginary world, although it was still hidden in fog.

'You overestimate me,' Kunohara said at last. 'My control of my own system is very small now – any abilities I had to manipulate the larger Grail system infrastructure disappeared a day ago, probably at the time the Other was subjugated by our mutual enemy. I still do not know what powers I have left in my own world, but I have certainly lost most of my oversight capabilities. I also cannot simply insert or remove things from the system as I normally could.' He turned to Paul. 'That is why I could not wipe the mutants out of the system, or even move the whip scorpion to somewhere else. I was forced to use my ability to manipulate weather, an awkward tool at best.'

'So what are we to do, then?' Florimel asked, but her voice had lost its edge. 'Simply give up? Sit here drinking tea and wait to die?'

'We must understand the system. Without understanding, we are indeed doomed. The Other has created, or at least influenced, the structure of the entire network, and even if this man Dread has somehow taken control over the system, the patterns must remain.'

'And what patterns are those?' Martine asked. She had not spoken in a while. She seemed distracted, and tilted her head as though she listened to something the rest of them could not hear.

Kunohara drained his drink and stood up. 'Stories. A quest of sorts. And other things, too. Children and childhood. Death. Resurrection.'

'And labyrinths,' Paul said, remembering. 'I thought of that back on Ithaca. Many of the control points, the gateways, things like that – they center around mazes or places having to do with death. But I thought that was just the Brotherhood's sense of humor.'

'It could be, in part,' Kunohara said. 'Or even a more practical reason. Because of the risk of getting lost, they are often places that people will avoid, which gives the Grail users greater privacy. But I have seen enough of the various worlds to think that too many repetitions of themes might also mean that the operating system has weighted things in that direction – that these are signs of an emergent order, if you will.' He seemed quite involved and excited now, almost feverish. 'In the House world, for instance, where I met most of you again. I knew its builders, and much of the artistry of the place was theirs, but the Lady of the Windows? Who also seems a manifestation of your own guardian angel, Jonas? I cannot believe that was built into the original world. No, rather I think it emerged – was brought into being by patterns in the larger system. And look at where you found another gateway in Troy, and an important one – the Temple of

Demeter. In the house belonging to the mother of the death-god's bride, at the center of a maze. Both of the tropes Jonas described, in one.'

Paul thought he heard now what had caught Martine's attention, a low throbbing hum, barely distinguishable above the murmur of the river. But something else now seemed foremost in Martine's mind. She sat up straighter. 'That's right,' she said. 'You knew we had been summoned there, didn't you? When they met you in the House, Florimel said there was no maze in Troy, but you knew otherwise.'

Kunohara nodded, but looked wary. 'As I said, it was one of the first simulations the Brotherhood constructed.' He frowned. 'But how do you know what we said? You were still a prisoner. You were not there.'

'Exactly.' Martine's face was hard. 'It is always strange when people know things who were not present to see them. And you know much about our time in Troy. Paul, did you tell Mr Kunohara that we were in the Temple of Demeter?'

Martine's open enmity toward their host had been making him uncomfortable, and he was about to say something to set the conversation back on the right track when he realized she had a point. 'Not . . . not specifically. I skipped over a lot . . . because I was in a hurry to tell him what happened to the Grail Brotherhood.' He felt as though he had suddenly been set adrift once more, his destiny in the hands of others. He turned to Kunohara. 'How *did* you know?'

It was hard to tell exactly what the man's exasperation signified: he was hard to read at the best of times. 'Where else could it have been? I practically sent you there myself!'

T4b sat up straight, balling his fists. 'Workin' for those Grail people, him? After all, he dupping us?'

'He could be telling the truth,' Martine said, raising her hand to calm T4b. 'But I wonder. I think perhaps you are not telling us *all* the truth, Mr Kunohara.' She blinked, distracted for a moment, but did her best to finish her thought. 'You did know where we were going, as you said. I suspect that you also had an informant there in Troy and beyond – perhaps even one of our number, although that is an unpleasant thought – and that it was the communication link between you and that informant which I was able to follow back here when everything came apart on the mountaintop.'

The moment of tension between the two of them, which made the whole room feel hot and close, did not last. Just when it seemed Kunohara must either admit his guilt or launch an angry rebuttal, Martine jerked her head back, staring sightlessly toward the arc of the ceiling and the blanket of gray mist that obscured everything. The humming was now too loud to ignore.

'There are many shapes above us,' she said, her voice twisted by surprise. 'Many . . .'

Something thumped heavily on the uppermost curve of the bubble, a dark blotch that made the mists outside swirl. Jointed legs flailed, scrabbling as though they sought to dig through the transparent surface. There were more noises of impact, a few at first, then dozens in rapid succession. Paul tried to scramble to his feet, but the urge to flight was already arrested: slow squirming shapes were all over the bubble and more were landing every moment. Kunohara clapped his hands once and the lights inside the bubble grew bright, so that for the first time they could see the things pressed against the curving roof.

By the shape of the bodies, the long armored abdomens and the blur of beating wings just above their shiny thoraxes, they might have been wasps – but if so, something had gone very wrong. Like the mutated wood lice, there seemed no limit to how many legs they had or how those limbs were arranged. As they crowded in ever-increasing numbers across the bubble, they pressed semihuman faces against the surface, distorted features stretching and squeezing even more alarmingly as they tried to force their way through the barrier.

T4b sprang up, looking for somewhere to retreat, but the wasps covered almost every centimeter of the glassy walls, the foggy sky now replaced with a firmament of plated limbs and drooling, mandibled mouths.

'It's Dread,' Martine said, her voice a hopeless murmur. 'Dread sent them. He knows we're here.'

The weight of the wasp-things was so great now that it seemed to Paul the bubble must collapse at any moment: so many had collected already that they crawled across each other in tangled piles. Some of those caught on the bottom and being crushed to death ran barbed stingers out of their abdomens, driving them over and over into the substance of the bubble, which actually tented inward – giving, but not yet breaking.

Paul grabbed at Kunohara. 'Get them off! For God's sakes, freeze them, whatever. They're going to burst through any moment.'

Their host was wild-eyed but clearly struggling for calm. 'If I blast them with wind or ice, I will destabilize the house as well and destroy it or send it spinning down the river. We would all be killed.'

'You and your bloody realism!' Florimel shouted. 'You rich idiots and your toys!'

Kunohara ignored her. As Paul watched he began to move through a series of meaningless gestures, like nothing so much as someone practicing *tai chi* in a quiet park. For a moment he could not help thinking that the man had gone completely mad; then he realized that Kunohara, his mastery compromised, was running through an inventory of commands, trying to make something work.

'Nothing,' Kunohara snarled, and turned in cold fury on Martine. 'You, with your accusations. I thought you had doomed yourself by using that device, but you have led them here to my house and doomed me as well.' He gestured; a view-window opened in midair. For a moment Paul could not make sense of the boiling, lumpy mass depicted in the window, then he saw that it was a bird's-eye view of the bubble-house, so covered now with the wasp-things that it had lost almost all suggestion of its true shape.

'Look,' Kunohara said bitterly. 'They are building a bridge between us and the land.'

He was right. The massed wasps were extending a tangle of their own squirming bodies out across the moving surface of the river, a squad of suicide engineers giving their own lives to connect the free-floating bubble to the riverside. The wasps on the bottom of the growing pseudopod must be drowning by the hundreds, Paul thought, but more kept dropping out of the air to join them and keep the bridge growing.

But growing toward what? Paul struggled to see through the mist to the dark riverbank, alive with blowing grasses. Kunohara must have had the same thought, for he gestured again and the focus of the window changed, bringing the sandy bank into closer view. There was no grass; it was a solid line of beetle shapes, creatures as horribly distorted as the wasps, an army of thousands upon thousands of malformed crawlers waiting for the wasp-bridge to reach them. Even now, hundreds at the front of the clicking, bumping throng were forming a corresponding chain, climbing atop one another and clutching even as they drowned, struggling out to meet the wasps.

But even this horror was not the worst. On a lump of mossy stone at the river's edge stood a pair of contrasting shapes, like generals surveying the progress of a campaign. Kunohara's focus drove closer. Despite the more important threat of the wasps, who now formed a solid wall of carapace and claw all over the bubble-house, Paul could not tear his eyes from the two figures.

One was a massively bloated caterpillar, its pillowy segments the color of corpse flesh, with a face even more disturbingly humanoid than those of the mutant army, tiny porcine eyes and a mouth full of jagged teeth. Beside it teetered a cricket white as paper, rubbing its legs together in some unheard music. Its long face was as queerly personalized as the caterpillar's, except for the blank spot where eyes should have been.

'The Twins,' Paul said. 'Oh, God. He's sent the Twins after us.'

'There is another,' said Florimel. 'See, riding on that beetle.'

Paul stared at the pale human shape, bumping on the back of a shiny shell. 'Who is it?'

Kunohara was scowling. 'Robert Wells, I suspect. A pity the scorpion did not get him, too.'

The tiny figure waved his arm, sending another squadron of beetles marching down to the water's edge to give their lives to the growing chain.

'The bastard is having fun,' observed Kunohara.

CHAPTER 7

The Man from Mars

NETFEED/DRAMA-LIVE: 'Warrior of Sprootie School'
(visual: Wengweng Cho's practice room)
CHO: Chen Shuo, the time has come for action! My daughter Zia has been stolen by the evil Wolf's Jaw school, and they mean to practice their spiritually incorrect and deadly martial arts style on her.
(audio over: gasps)
SHUO: By the sacred Sprootie, we must not let such a thing happen!
CHO: You are a brave man and a true warrior. Quickly, now, take my treasured throwing stars and go with haste to save my daughter.
SHUO: I will come back to you with the severed head of the Wolf's Jaw master, and with your daughter Zia safe.
(audio over: applause, cheers)
SHUO (to himself): But I must pray that my devotion to the sacred Sprootie will give me strength to achieve this task, because the minions of the Wolf's Jaw school are many and devious. Still – where Sprootie is, bravery is!
(audio over: even louder applause)

MRS Sorensen – Kaylene, she had told him her name was – had just come back from checking on the two children in the connecting room, which gave everyone a chance to catch their breath. Catur Ramsey, in particular, was grateful for the pause. He had never had such a strange day in his entire life, which included a college flirtation with psychedelics.

'Christabel seems okay,' she reported. 'She's sleeping. The little boy's curled up on the floor. I got him bathed again, but I couldn't even get him to use the other bed.'

'She's been through a lot,' said Michael Sorensen. 'If I had imagined . . . God almighty, what have we gotten ourselves into?'

The strange, wizened figure in the rented wheelchair looked up. 'I am truly sorry to have involved your family, Mrs Sorensen. Desperation forces us to do shameful things.'

The woman wrestled for a moment against her obvious urge to say something polite, and won. She had clearly not recovered from the horror of hearing Major Sorensen's cleaned-up version of what had happened in Yacoubian's suite. While Ramsey had tried to entertain a shell-shocked Christabel and the rather sullen little Hispanic boy, she had taken her husband to the adjoining room and, as Sorensen put it afterward, 'let me know she wasn't very happy about how things were going.'

In his own exhausted state, Ramsey was having trouble coping with the tension and unhappiness in the room, not to mention the bizarre story that Sellars had just told, full of the kind of conspiracy theories that even the loopier chat nodes would scorn. He needed a few moments to clear his head.

'I'm going out to grab a soft drink,' he said. 'Anybody want anything?'

Kaylene Sorensen shook her head wearily, but Ramsey couldn't help noticing the flicker of suspicion across her husband's face. It stung. 'Oh, for God's sake, Sorensen, if I were going to bail out on you or betray you or something, don't you think it would be easier for me to wait and do it when I go back to my own motel?'

To his credit, Sorensen looked shamefaced. 'I didn't mean to look that way. I'm just . . . it's been difficult, today.'

Ramsey forced a smile. 'It sure has. Back in a second.'

He caught himself as he started to swipe his card through the drink machine's reader.

Sorensen's paranoia is better sense than you've got, he told himself. *That was a real brigadier general that had us kidnapped out of a public restaurant. Whatever this is, it isn't entirely someone's overheated imagination.* He found he had a few coins, and even briefly considered trying to wipe his prints off them before dropping them into the slot.

Sellars' story, whether Sorensen and his family believed it or not, was patently impossible. Ramsey had been dubious but had tried to remain open-minded about the idea that Tandagore's Syndrome might be a purposeful human creation. He had even begun to suspect that there really was some connection between Orlando Gardiner's condition and the reports of the boy's software agent about some kind of network where Orlando was conscious but trapped. He had been willing, in short, to believe in a strange set of circumstances, even collusion between powerful people. But this? This was something out of a fever dream – a conspiracy among many of Earth's richest men and women to become gods. It was beyond belief that such a thing could exist, let alone that it could be kept silent for years, especially when the mechanism seemed to depend on destroying innocent children. The whole insane notion was like something out of a potboiler – a gruesomely overblown net drama. It simply could not be.

If he had been hearing it all for the first time, Catur Ramsey would have courteously thanked everyone for their time after ten minutes and gone home, keeping his thoughts about the sanity of these people to himself. But he had been living with the strange online world of Orlando Gardiner for weeks, and had begun to think of a software agent in the shape of a cartoon bug as a reliable informant. Before she closed up her house and disappeared, he had heard a woman who by her own admission had spent time in a mental health facility tell him that one of the world's most successful children's entertainment companies was part of a hideous experiment on those selfsame children, and he had begun to wonder if she might be correct. It wasn't as though he was close-minded – hadn't he first met Sellars in the back alleys of a VR gameworld? Where he, Catur Ramsey, respectable attorney, had been running around dressed as a barbarian swordsman? He had to admit that Sellars had told him things about Orlando Gardiner and Salome Fredericks that even Ramsey himself, with total access to both families, hadn't yet discovered.

He sipped his drink and watched the traffic slide past.

Sellars was asking him to believe in something that made the worst pamphleteering nonsense about Freemasons and Rosicrucians seem unambitious. And just to cap it all off, what had Major Sorensen said about Sellars? That he wasn't even human?

For a moment he truly considered walking to his car and driving home. Telling Jaleel and Enrica Fredericks that he'd found nothing to explain their daughter's coma, deleting Olga Pirofsky's name from his call list. Putting the whole thing into the 'who knows what the hell that was about?' category and getting back to his other clients, his more-or-less life.

But he could not forget the face of Orlando Gardiner's mother, bright-eyed with tears, or her voice as she told him that they had always thought they'd have a chance to say good-bye to their son. He had just heard that same voice two hours ago, cracked and hoarse now, whispery as dry grass, leaving a message on his system with a date for Orlando's memorial service. He had promised them he'd find out what he could. He had promised.

He hesitated for only a few more seconds, then crumpled the squeeze-pak and dropped it into the trash slot beside the machine.

Sellars was inhaling something from a damp rag. He looked up when Ramsey came in and smiled, a horizontal distortion of his strange, rippled face. 'The Sorensens will be back in a moment,' he said. 'The little girl had a bad dream.'

'She's been through a lot,' Ramsey said. 'Too much for a kid her age.'

Sellars dipped his head sadly. 'I had hoped her part in this was finished.' He inhaled from the rag again. 'Please forgive me. My lungs . . . they do not function as well as they should. It will be better when I can get filters for my humidifier. I need to keep my breathing tubes moist.' Something in Ramsey's expression brought back the smile, larger now, as Sellars let his withered hands fall to his lap. 'Ah, I see something is troubling you. My lungs? Or just me? Let me guess – Major Sorensen told you something about me?'

'Not much. And that's sure not the worst of what's bothering me. But just because you brought it up, yeah. He said . . .' Suddenly, ludicrously, it seemed a simple piece of discourtesy. Ramsey swallowed and forged ahead. 'He said that you weren't really human.'

Sellars nodded, looking like some ancient mountain hermit. 'Did he tell you my nickname on the base? "The Man from Mars." In fact, they were calling me that before Major Sorensen was born.' The smile surfaced and then was gone. 'It's not true, of course – I've never been near Mars.'

Ramsey suddenly felt weak in the knees. He reached out for support and found the arm of a chair, then lowered himself onto the seat. 'Are you telling me . . . that you're some kind of alien? From space?' Now, as though a lens had changed, he could picture the disturbing texture of Sellars' skin as something far stranger than scar tissue – the mottled pinkish hide of some unknown animal. The scrawny old man with the misshapen head and strange yellow eyes would have made a wonderfully grotesque illustration in a children's book, but at the moment it was hard to tell which sort of supernatural creature he would have been, kindly or cruel. When the door to the adjoining room suddenly popped open, Ramsey flinched badly.

'Kaylene just fixed some sandwiches,' said Michael Sorensen. 'Ramsey, you should eat something – you look sick.'

His wife came through behind him carrying a picnic tray, the too-perfect picture of traditional womanhood from an earlier century. Ramsey could not relax; suddenly everything seemed sinister.

'I was just about to tell Mr Ramsey my story,' Sellars said. 'No, thank you, Mrs Sorensen, I eat very little. Has your husband told you about me yet, Mrs Sorensen? Surely you have wondered.'

'Mike's . . . Mike's told me a bit.' He clearly still made her uncomfortable. 'Are you sure I can't get you anything . . . ?'

'Come on!' Ramsey's resources had been stretched to

the fraying point. 'I'm just sitting here, waiting to hear this man tell me he's an outer space alien. Meanwhile, everybody's talking about sandwiches! Sandwiches, for God's sake!'

Kaylene Sorensen frowned and lifted a finger to her lips. 'Mr Ramsey, please – there are two little children sleeping next door.'

Ramsey shook his head, subsiding into his chair. 'Sorry. Sorry.'

Sellars laughed. 'Did I say I was an alien, Mr Ramsey? No, I said that my nickname was the Man from Mars.' He held the rag close to his mouth, inhaled, then reached out and dipped it in a cup before bringing it to his mouth again. 'It is an interesting story, and might conceivably help you understand a little more of the strange tale I've already given you today.'

'Even if you claim you're the Grand Duke of Alpha Centauri,' Ramsey said feelingly, 'I don't think things could get any weirder than they are.'

Sellars smiled gently at him, then smiled also at Kaylene Sorensen, who had settled in next to her husband on the couch. 'You've all been through a great deal. I hope you can understand how important it is . . .'

Ramsey cleared his throat

'Yes, sorry. I've had little company lately except Cho-Cho – not much practice for adult conversation.' He stretched his knotted fingers before him. 'First, I will reassure Mr Ramsey that, whatever may have happened to me since, I started out as human as anyone. Alien has many definitions, but I am decidedly not the outer space sort.

'In fact, for the first thirty or so years of my life, the only interesting thing you could say about me at all was that I was a pilot – a fighter pilot. I flew for the US Navy in the Middle East, and later in the Taiwan action, then in peacetime I trained new pilots. I was not married, was not even particularly close friends with my comrades, although during combat I trusted them with my life every day, and they did the same with me. I was a naval aviator. That was my life, and I was more or less content with it.

'This is before any of you were born, so you may not remember the dying days of what used to be called the manned space program – how the private consortia who funded most of it decided there was a lot more money to be made in satellites and remote mining than actually putting a live human being into a ship and sending him or her somewhere. Also, the world's populations weren't very interested in the whole matter – I think the human race had begun to turn inward, in a way. But the idea of exploration and colonization didn't die completely, and one rather quiet project went forward after the rest of the better-known operations had folded. It had to get private funding, of course, but it was still nominally under United States government control, back in the days when the UN didn't even have a space program.

'Word went around that military fliers with no close family ties, willing to undertake dangerous duty, were being evaluated for something called PEREGRINE. I was bored with training and, looking back on it, a bit bored with my life, so even though I suspected I was past the optimum age – everything I heard suggested it was a very physically-based selection process, which usually meant reflexes – I thought it couldn't hurt to volunteer.' Sellars smiled again, self-mockingly this time. 'When I found out I was one of the first dozen selectees, I was pretty impressed with myself.

'It's tempting to tell the whole story in proper detail,

because it's interesting in itself, and no one but me really knows the truth now. No books, no net documentaries, no records at all to speak of. But everyone here is tired, so I'll try to keep it brief. PEREGRINE turned out to be a novel approach to human space exploration, a program that would permit human crews not only to travel long distances – with cold sleep along the way, but with connections still to the ship – but also to be able to explore likely planets in a more robust way than the old-fashioned astronauts. There were several planets they were interested in – one in 70 Virginis is the only one I remember now. Many of the signals have since proved misleading, and humankind seems to have lost its interest in exploration – a great shame, I think – but at the time it was very exciting. In any case, even back then we had instruments that could survey planets far more elaborately than anything a live human could do, but the people in charge of the program thought that you could never get the same level of funding and public support for exploration unless you were sending a real, live, breathing human whose life was being risked on behalf of the whole human race. You can almost hear the speeches, can't you?

'So, PEREGRINE. We reported to Sand Creek, a secret base in South Dakota . . .'

'I've heard of that,' Ramsey said slowly. 'Sand Creek . . .'

'No doubt you have. It's been talked about a lot over the years. But whatever you've heard is almost certainly not true.' Sellars closed his eyes. 'Where was I? Ah, yes. We began undergoing a very complicated process to make us capable of all kinds of rigors – and, most importantly, to hard-interface our brains with the ship's computer systems. You almost never hear that word "computer" anymore, do you? They're part of everything now. They used to be boxes with keyboards, you know.' He shook his head, so that it looked like a dry sunflower wobbling on its stalk. 'Technology wasn't very sophisticated – this was half a century ago, after all. Much of what they did was surgical – actually opened me up and applied micro-circuitry directly to my skeleton, implanted various devices, you name it. People take it for granted now that they can connect to the net with a neurocannula, but then the idea that a human being could channel computer information directly into the brain was mostly considered science fiction. Except at Sand Creek, where they were actually doing it.

'So they . . . built me, as it were. Rebuilt me, certainly, strengthened my bones and shielded my skin and vari-ous organs to better resist gravitational hardships and radiation, implanted tiny chemical pumps that would add synthesized calcium and other important supplements to my body if I had to go a long time in zero gravity . . . all kinds of things. But even more profound was the way they wired me – head to toe, like a Christmas tree! They used the latest alloys and polymers – although with all the changes in molecular engineering since then, the orig-inal stuff they put in me would seem positively antique now. But at the time, we PEREGRINE volunteers were works of art. That's when I first learned to love Yeats – the line about the emperor's mechanical birds in "Sailing to Byzantium" caught at me:

> ". . . Once out of nature I shall never take
> My bodily form from any natural thing,
> But such a form as Grecian goldsmiths make
> Of hammered gold and gold enameling . . ."

He paused for a moment, lost in thought. 'I cannot tell you what it was like the first time I simply closed my eyes and found myself online. The net was tiny and primitive then, the early days of virtual interfaces, but still . . . ! Still . . . ! Already, without leaving Earth, we were explorers, flying where others had only crawled. We PEREGRINE volunteers began to talk about the net among ourselves as though it were a place, a universe that others could only visit, like tourists staring through a fence, but which truly belonged to us. When you can swim through information as though it were a physical medium, when access is instantaneous, you begin to see things, learn things . . .' His voice was getting dry and thin; he stopped and inhaled from the rag. 'I promised myself I would not be diverted, didn't I? I apologize. In any case, our ships were built at the same time we ourselves were built – in parallel, as it were – custom-tailored to our particular physiological needs. They were small, sophisticated, using primarily antimatter drives for the long, black distances, but able to use other sources of power as well, including solar wind. There was to be one for each of us, each named for an explorer – the *Francis Drake*, the *Matthew Peary*, I cannot remember them all now and it's too sad to try. Mine was the *Sally Ride*. A lovely name for a ship, and a lovely ship she would have been – my bride, you might say, on a permanent honeymoon. But it did not happen that way. We only had a few orbital flights, practice runs, before . . . Oh, dear, am I boring you?'

Michael Sorensen had fallen asleep sitting up on the couch, his head lolling on his wife's shoulder. 'He's just exhausted,' she said apologetically, as though he had nodded off at some suburban card party. 'He must know all this already, doesn't he?'

'All but the fine details,' Sellars told her gently. 'He's looked through my file a few times since I made contact, I'm sure.'

'I think it's fascinating,' she assured him, although she looked quite tired herself. 'I . . . I had no idea.'

'Please go on,' Ramsey said.

'Well, you both must know something about what happens when you work for the government, and this was in the early days of the private/public partnership, so-called. The administration in Washington changed. The UN grew snippy about a major project with so little international participation. And the corporate angels began to grumble about how much money was being spent with no returns in the foreseeable future. PEREGRINE was nearly canceled several times.

'There were nights later on, years worth of nights, when I used to wish with all my heart it had been.

'The solution was not really surprising, especially with large defense corporations involved. It was decided to streamline the operation, to get "more bang for the buck," I think the phrase of the day was. It would have been very difficult to make the project smaller at that fairly advanced stage, so instead they folded it together with something called HR/CS – Human Robotic Combat Systems. I think that project also had a code name – "Bright Warrior" or "Bright Spear" or something, but the engineers started calling it HARDCASE and the name stuck. This was straight military, what was probably one of the first attempts to create biomodified soldiers – basically humans who could be plugged into extremely sophisticated combat armor, who could use these systems as extensions of their own bodies, go places even an ordinary armored soldier couldn't go. You get the idea – it was like something out of an old comic book. The military was much more intent on their timeline, so the shared resources – mostly engineers, medical personnel, and supercomputer time – began to flow in their direction. The pace of PEREGRINE slowed dramatically.

'All of which wouldn't have meant all that much, except that HARDCASE had a much different approach, especially to recruiting. Their process was much closer to what I had imagined would be used on PEREGRINE, focusing on reflexes and even more esoteric things, synaptic variations, certain types of chemical and immune system receptivities, and so on. And even psychologically they were looking for a different kind of subject. We were pilots, had been chosen primarily as such – some of the PEREGRINE subjects had never flown a combat mission, but they were all fliers, much like the original astronaut corps. HARDCASE needed soldiers. You might even say that, ultimately, they needed killers. They tried to be more discriminating than that, but that infinitesimal slant shadowed it from the beginning, I think.

'Even so, if Barrett Keener's problems had been physical – a tumor, say, or a serotonin imbalance, it would have been caught immediately. Both PEREGRINE and HARDCASE subjects were routinely tested for such things, and we spent most of our time hooked up to analytical devices as a matter of course. But in those days pure schizophrenia was still largely a mystery, and Keener was the sort of paranoid who made hiding his growing illness part of the focus of his madness. Although very few people who worked with the man could honestly say they liked him, not a single one of the psychologists or doctors at Sand Creek or any of his HARDCASE co-subjects guessed that he was slowly going insane. Not until it was too late.

'I see the look on your face, Mr Ramsey. No, you haven't ever heard of Keener. You'll find out why in a moment.

'I can be brief about this, and I would prefer to be. I lost many friends on the day of Keener's rampage. There were plenty of safeguards built into the system, but although the military and its contractors had considered the possibility of sabotage, and had even considered the frightening possibility that one of the HARDCASE subjects might have a breakdown, no one had considered that both might happen. Keener, caught in the grip of a strengthening psychotic delusion, had been preparing for weeks. The HARDCASE complex at Sand Creek was an arsenal – the cybernetic battle-suits themselves each carried the firepower of a Powell tank, and there was a stockpile of other ordnance for combat-testing purposes. But as deadly as the battle-suits were, for someone like Barrett Keener with a background in munitions there was even more damage that could be done. He spent weeks preparing in secret, determined to avenge some incomprehensible insult, or strike some unimaginable blow for delusional freedom, descending deeper and deeper into a black spiral of hatred.

'I have pieced together much of what happened from secret reports. It was night when it began, and most of the personnel on the base were asleep. I happened to be up – I've never needed a lot of sleep – working with the night-shift technicians in the construction bay. We heard the explosions first. We barely had time to wonder what was going on when Keener himself, his battle-suit already in full thermo-dispersal flare, blew through the walls of the construction hangar. He wasn't singling us out – we were simply on his destructive path from one end of the base to the other. Despite the surprise and the firestorm from the bombs he had already triggered, there had been at least a little resistance before he got to us. Keener had already survived a direct hit from a grenade launcher with only scorch marks and a slow freon leak at one of the suit joints to show for it. With the glow of his heat dispersal units and the cloud of leaking vapor, he looked like an angry god. We didn't have a chance. As he stepped through the wall he opened up with a mini-railgun and the place literally fell apart around us.

'It was horrible. I cannot bear to think about it much. In the early days I tried to imagine things I could have done differently, ways I could have saved my comrades – tortured myself with a thousand different scenarios. Now I know that it was only blind luck that I even survived. I was close enough to one of the ships under construction that I was able to scramble inside the shell when the first of Keener's incendiary ordnance went off. I had time only to see Keener marching out across the rubble of the construction bay, armor blazing like the sun as it struggled to process the additional heat, then the rest of the thermal grenades he was spraying began exploding and everything went away.'

Sellars brought a knuckle slowly up to the corner of his dry eye. Ramsey wondered if it were only an old gesture helplessly repeated, or if the man felt tears he could not shed. He wondered which would be worse.

'Two technicians inside the ship and I were the only ones in the bay that survived the attack, and neither of them lasted out the month – they were too badly burned. We all were burned, roasted like meat in an oven, but I had shielded organs and modified skin – the engineers didn't. I was lucky enough, or unlucky enough, to survive. Just barely.

'After leaving a path of destruction all the way across the base, Keener actually escaped Sand Creek. Through a lucky accident his built-in flight jets were incapacitated by machine gun fire from one of the sentry posts, so he set out on foot. He was headed toward the closest town, a place called Buffalo, I think, and God knows what he would have done when he got there, but they scrambled jets from the nearest air base and caught him within a mile or so of Sand Creek, in open prairie. They lost a plane, but Barrett Keener was finally killed by air-to-ground missiles. To be more precise, even though there were no direct hits on him, the explosions finally pushed his suit past its dispersal limit and it went up like a small-bore thermonuclear device. It took years, I hear, before anything grew on the spot. The soil was virtually turned to glass.

'So . . . a madman committed a very, very expensive suicide, and the rest of us were left behind to deal with it. I was the only surviving test subject of PEREGRINE. Keener had been even more thorough with his HARDCASE comrades, placing shaped charges in the barracks, and every one of them died in their beds when the building went up. The entire Sand Creek base was in ruins – one hundred and eighty-six killed, three times that many wounded. The ships were ruined, billions of dollars worth of work and research gone, so the military-corporate fellows cut their losses and ended the program. HARDCASE was buried too – or at least that was the official story. Of course, Keener had managed to do a very impressive amount of damage with only a single suit, and the less ambitious combat suits that soldiers wear today look very similar to the HARDCASE regalia, so perhaps they simply changed the name of the program and started again some-where else.'

'How . . . how *horrible,*' breathed Kaylene Sorensen.

'I've never seen anything about this,' Ramsey said, trying to keep from sounding too doubtful, if nothing else out of respect for the obvious pain on Sellars' ruined face. 'Not a whisper.'

'It was buried very, very deep. People knew about the base at Sand Creek of course, but not what was being done there or what ultimately went wrong. The official story was that it was closed because of a bad fire, with some residual radiation contamination forcing them to seal the site. Some of the dead, like the PEREGRINE volunteers, whose postings had been secret in the first place, were siphoned off to other operations and their deaths reported there. It was a failure of colossal proportions, not to mention that it would have brought down countless billions in lawsuits if the truth came out. They buried it. They couldn't just make it disappear completely, of course, which is why there are rumors about what happened there to this very day.'

'And they buried you, too?'

'As best they could. I had no relatives. In fact, they thought I was dead the first twelve hours or so, because . . . because the scene in the construction bay was so bad. When I survived, it became easier just to lose me.'

'They made you a prisoner!' Ramsey couldn't help feeling angry.

'Not at first. No, with all that time and effort put into me, quite literally, they wanted to find some other use for me. But my project was gone, I myself was burned, crippled, my circuitry badly damaged. I was functionally useless – and, unlike the other survivors, I was also incontrovertible living testimony to what had happened there. If an ordinary soldier violated his confidentiality agreement, you might be able to discredit him as a crackpot, but what about a man with millions of dollars of state-of-the-art cybernetic implants in his body? Yes, eventually they imprisoned me, but I am actually grateful, Mr Ramsey. In another country or another time they might simply have cut their losses and silenced me in a more definitive manner.'

Ramsey did not know what to say. In the silence, Major Sorensen huffed and sat up, glancing around. Not knowing he had been asleep for almost ten minutes, he did his best to look as though he had just closed his eyes to concentrate better. Sellars looked at him for a moment with what almost seemed like fondness before continuing.

'It's been a long time. What happened then isn't so important, except to me. But what does matter is what happened afterward. After the first few years' rounds of hospitals and research facilities, they decided there was nothing useful left to do with me, so they moved me to the base – the one where you babysat me, Major Sorensen, although I arrived there a long time before you even joined the service. In fact, one of the small ironies of the whole terrible mess was that even though I was Navy, my imprisonment somehow came out of the accounting for HARDCASE, so I wound up on an army base.

'The only thing the top brass really wanted from me was silence, so I lived for years in an environment that might have been something from an earlier century – no telephone, no television, no electronic connection to the outside world. But after I had been ten years on the base, my cultivated show of patience had lulled them. I was allowed a wallscreen, since a one-way, extremely low speed media connection could hardly cause much trouble when the recipient was allowed no input devices.

'I had been waiting years for this, of course. I was so bored, and in those days so angry at what had been done to me, that I had freedom on my mind the way a slave chained to a galley oar does. My only exercise was mental – you can see my legs, my withered arms, what Keener's incendiaries did to me – but I was a pilot, damn it! In a few minutes I had lost everything – my ship, my health, my freedom – but I had in me still that drive, that need. If I was denied the skies, I could fly through information space, the way my PEREGRINE fellows and

I had discovered. It might not be the same as walking the streets like other citizens, but it would still be escape of a very real sort.

'It was true that I had no devices to access the net. No visible ones, in any case. But even then my caretakers understood very little about my capabilities . . . and, more importantly, my obsession for escape. It was easy enough to steal a length of fiberlink from the men who installed the wallscreen. When they were gone, it was almost as easy for me to perform a brief if messy operation with a magnifying glass, a butter knife I had ground down to razor-sharpness, and various other implements, including old-fashioned solder. It would have looked horrible to anyone but me, the wires going directly into a long and bloody incision in my arm, but I connected up to the old input control point from the PEREGRINE days and began using some of my implanted systems to force a machine-language connection, reversing through the wallscreen downlink.

'I won't bore you with all the details. My keepers on the base eventually noticed what I was doing – I was so enraptured with my newfound freedom that I was not as cautious as I should have been. They brought four MPs to subdue me – me, all one hundred and ten shriveled, pre-metric pounds! – and ripped out the wallscreen. Doctors sewed me back up. See, here is the scar. They put a big flashing marker on my file ordering that nothing which might allow me that kind of connection was ever to be given me again, and I was subjected to periodic random searches for decades.

'But what they didn't know was that it was already too late. In the early hours of my newfound freedom, I located and downloaded a raft of specialized gear to my internal systems, including a very clever little black market number that permitted me to make remote connection to nearby networks, using my own metallicized bones as an antenna. Long before the telematic jack became a chic accessory for the busy new-rich, I had one of my own, invisibly hidden inside me.

'Since then, I have continually upgraded myself, all without the knowledge of my captors. Not everything could be done by software alone, but to a man who can go anywhere and converse with anyone, not much is out of reach. In a fit of reflexive honesty, the military had kept my pension for any survivors that might turn up. I made it disappear with a smail numbers trick, then moved it into some other areas and began growing it – legitimately, always legitimately. I don't know why that matters, but it does. I have never stolen from anyone. Well, except information. I'm not the world's richest man by any stretch, but I have a tidy sum now, and for a long time I bent it all toward self-improvement. Upgrades?' Sellars suddenly laughed, a genuine bark of amusement. 'I am the Upgraded Man! Do you remember my chess-by-mail game, Major Sorensen?'

The man narrowed his eyes. 'We examined the hell out of that. No codes. No trick writing. Nothing.'

'Oh, it was a perfectly legitimate game – we made sure of that. But you can put quite a bit of expensive black-market nanomachinery in the period after the word "check," which is how one of my contacts was able to send me the last things I needed to be able to upgrade my system and survive without constant hydration. I tore out and ate a tiny little piece of paper and the little machines went to work. I would not have lasted a day in that tunnel under the base without that improvement.'

'You bastard,' Sorensen said admiringly. 'We were wondering what you were going to do after you broke out. We had every medical supply place in three states on the watch.'

'But why?' Ramsey asked. 'Why did you wait so long to escape? I mean, you've been there thirty years or so, haven't you?'

Sellars nodded. 'Because after I'd gained full-time access to the net, and had read every file, explored every record, my anger began to fade. A terrible thing had happened to me, an injustice – but what did that really mean? Now that I had a sort of freedom, what more did I want? Look at me, Mr Ramsey. It was clear that I was never going to be able to live a normal life. I still harbored deep resentments, but I also began to put my endless free time into other things. Exploration of the fast-growing worldwide data sphere – the net. Amusements of various sorts. Experiments.

'It was in the course of one such experiment that I found the first track of the Grail Brotherhood . . .'

'Hang on a bit,' said Ramsey. 'What sort of experiments?'

For a moment Sellars hesitated, then his waxy face seemed to harden. 'I do not wish to talk about that. Do you want me to go on, or have you heard enough for one day?'

'No, please continue. I didn't mean to offend you.' But Catur Ramsey's radar was still flashing. It almost seemed like the old man wanted to be asked again, but Ramsey had no experience reading the odd features. *But there's something there*, he thought. *Something important, at least to Sellars. Is it important to us, too?* It was impossible to guess. He filed it away for later. 'Please, go on.'

'I have already explained much of what I discovered then. What the Brotherhood seemed to be doing, the weapons at its disposal, all were bad enough. But now, just in the last forty-eight hours, everything has gone completely off the rails. I am having a terrible time trying to make sense of anything and my whole Garden is in an uproar.'

'Garden?' said Kaylene Sorensen before anyone else could. 'What garden?'

'I apologize. It is the way I order my information – a metaphor, in a sense, but a very real thing to me as well. If you like, I will show it to you someday. It was . . . really quite beautiful once.' He shook his head slowly. 'Now it is blighted. Order is gone. Something drastic has happened to the Grail network, and also to the Brotherhood itself. The newsnets tell me that several people I believe to be part of their leadership have all died within the last few days, their empires suddenly in chaos. Is this part of some move toward immortality – of conveying themselves into the virtual universe forever, as I suspected that they planned? If so, it seems odd they would leave such disruption behind, since they must surely still need some kind of economic power to maintain that huge, expensive network.'

'You're only guessing about that,' said Michael Sorensen. 'About a lot of things.'

'I am only guessing about almost *everything*,' said Sellars, amused and disgusted, and at that moment finally won much of Catur Ramsey's trust. 'But the probability factors are too high to ignore, and have been since I first encountered this ghastly plot. I'm terrified, trying to grope at something behind a big thick black curtain and guess what it is. But I *am* certain that whatever it might be, it's bad and getting worse – unfortunately, that's the guess I'm most confident about. Do you think I would have involved a child like your daughter if I could believe for an instant I might be wrong? Me, who had his own life ruined by trusting those who should have known better and planned better? Major Sorensen, Mrs Sorensen, I can never earn forgiveness for endangering your daughter, so I haven't asked. But I can promise you that I only did it because I felt that the stakes were so frighteningly high . . .' He stopped and shook his hairless head. 'No, that would not make it better. She is your child, after all.'

'And we won't let anything happen to her,' Christabel's mother said fiercely. 'That's the one risk I won't allow.' She stared at her husband; it was not a gentle look. 'Not anymore.'

'I think we understand the basic situation.' A part of Ramsey was amazed that he was still sitting here, even more amazed to find he was about to take a central part in something that by any rational standard should be considered a mass delusion. 'So the question is . . . what can we do?'

'Let me bring you up to date on the poor and probably hopeless measures I began,' Sellars said. 'My little group of explorers. I still have hopes for them, and until I know otherwise, I'll assume that they are all still alive, still active.'

'Oh my God,' said Ramsey suddenly. 'Sam Fredericks. Orlando Gardiner. They're yours . . . I mean, I'd almost forgotten, when we first spoke you said you knew something about them. Is that what you meant – you sent them into this network?'

Sellars shook his head. 'In a way. But yes, they are part of the small group of people I brought together. I hope they still are.'

'Then you didn't know.' Ramsey hesitated. 'Orlando Gardiner died two days ago.'

Sellars did not reply immediately. 'No, I . . . I did not

know,' he said at last, his voice soft as a dove's call. 'I
have been . . .' He paused again for a surprisingly long
time. 'I had feared . . . that it might all be too much for
him. Such a brave young man . . .' The old man shut his
eyes tight. 'If you don't mind, I will take a moment to
use the bathroom.'

The wheelchair turned and rolled silently across the
carpet. The bathroom door closed behind it, leaving
Ramsey to stare at the Sorensens, who stared back.

CHRISTABEL was having a bad dream, running from men
in black clothes who were chasing her down a long staircase. They were carrying a long fire hose which trailed
behind them like a snake, and she knew that they wanted
to catch her and point its metal nose at her and choke
her with its purple smoke. She tried to scream for her
mother and father, but she couldn't get the breath to do
it, and when she looked back the pale-faced men were
always closer, always closer . . .

She woke up thrashing in pillows and a sheet and
almost screamed again. She twisted herself free, frightened by the strange room, the unfamiliar pictures on the
wall, the heavy curtains which only let a tiny bit of light
into the room, yellow light with dust bouncing in it. She
opened her mouth to call her mother and the face came
up over the edge of the bed.

It was worse than her bad dream, and she fell back
with a feeling like a cold hand had grabbed inside her,
and just like in the dream she couldn't even make a noise.

'Hay-soos, weenit,' the face said, 'wha's your problem?
Trying to sleep down here.'

Her breaths were little and small – she could imagine
her sides moving fast like a rabbit's – but she recognized
the face, the broken tooth, the black hair sticking up.

Some of the worst of the being-scared went away.

'I don't have a problem,' she said, angry, but it didn't sound very good.

The boy smiled an angry smile. 'Know if I had a big ol' nice bed like that one, *claro*, wouldn't see *me* havin' no *pesadilla*, start crying and everything.'

He was talking about food, it sounded like. She didn't understand. She didn't want to understand. She got up and hurried to the door that led to the next room and opened it. Her mommy and daddy and the new grown-up, Mister Ramsey, were all talking to Mister Sellars. They all looked tired and something else, too, like the time that her parents and Ophelia Weiner's parents had thought there was going to be a war about Aunt Artica, which Christabel had thought was a dumb name for a place but not worth having a war about, and all the grown-ups had that same look on their face during dinner.

Mister Sellars was saying, '. . . A South African military program that actually employed a few of the original PEREGRINE designers – they were working with remote aviation, pilots using virtual control modules – but the project was defunded years ago. I found out about it while tracking the PEREGRINE records, and it came in handy. I was able to nudge them into using it, in part because the base was secret and they would be safe there, but somehow the Grail seems to have tracked them down and now they are under siege.' He finally noticed her standing in the doorway and gave her a gentle smile. 'Ah, Christabel, it's good to see you. Did you have a nice nap?'

'Honey, are you okay?' her mommy said, standing up. 'We're just out here talking. Why don't you see if there's anything on the net?'

The fullness and bigness of her parents and Mister Sellars talking about grown-up things, of all of them being somewhere away from home in a strange place, in a motel, suddenly rose up inside her and made her want to cry. She didn't want to cry, so instead she said, 'I'm hungry.'

'You still have your sandwich from earlier – you only took a bite. Here, I'll pour you some juice . . .' and her mommy came back with her to the room where she'd woken up and for a little while things were better again. After Christabel had a paper plate with the sandwich and some raisins, Mommy took a bag of cookies out of her purse and gave two to Christabel and two to the boy, who grabbed them fast, like her mommy might decide to take them back again.

'We grown-ups have to talk a while longer,' she said. 'I want you kids to stay here and watch the net, okay?'

The boy just looked at her like a cat, but Christabel followed her to the door. 'I want to go home, Mommy.'

'We'll go home soon, sweetie.' When she opened the door, Christabel's daddy's voice came through.

'But that doesn't make sense,' he was saying. 'If the network's harming children, causing this Tandagore thing, then why should the boy be able to get on and offline without being . . . hurt, whatever?'

'In part because I have been grappling with the security systems in my own particular way to allow that to happen,' said Mister Sellars. 'But there is something more at work. The system seems almost to have a . . . an affinity, that is the word. An affinity for children.'

Christabel's mommy, who had been listening, suddenly looked down and saw that Christabel was still standing beside her in the doorway. A frightened look went across Mommy's face, the oh-my-god look Christabel hadn't seen for a while, the last time when Christabel had carefully picked up the sharp broken pieces of a wine glass that fell on the kitchen floor and brought them in both hands to show her parents.

'Go on, honey,' her mother said, and almost shoved her back into the room with the terrible boy. 'I'll come in and check on you in a little while. Eat your sandwich. Watch the net.' She closed the door behind her. Christabel felt like crying again. Her mother usually didn't like it when she watched the net, unless it was something Mommy and Daddy had picked out that was educational.

'I'll eat it if you don't want it, weenit,' the boy said behind her.

She turned and saw that he was holding her sandwich in his hand. After all the baths her mommy had been making him take even his fingernails were clean, but she could just tell that no matter how many times he went in the tub, he was still covered with invisible germs. The thought of eating her sandwich now was impossible.

'You have it,' she said, and walked slowly to sit on the edge of the bed. The wallscreen wasn't very big, and the only thing on KidLink was a stupid Chinese game with people running around and all talking out of time with the way their mouths were moving. She stared at it, feeling empty and lonely and sad.

The little boy finished her sandwich, and without asking ate her raisins and cookies, too. Christabel didn't even feel angry – it was strange to see someone eat like that, like they hadn't ever eaten before and didn't know if they'd ever get to do it again. She wondered how he got so hungry. She knew Mister Sellars had lots of meals in packages down in the tunnels, and he was a nice man. He wouldn't have told the boy not to eat. It didn't make sense.

'What you staring at, *mu'chita?*' he said with a mouth full of cookie.

'Nothing.' She turned back to the wallscreen. The Chinese people were making themselves into a big pile to reach something hanging high in the air. The pile fell down and some of the people had to be carried away with the audience cheering. Christabel wished her parents would come in and tell her it was time to go home. She didn't like what was going on any more. She sneaked a look at the boy. He was licking the plate where the sandwiches had been. That was really gross, but it bothered her in a different way, too.

'When we go home,' she said suddenly, 'maybe . . . maybe my mom will give you some food. You know, to take with you.'

He looked at her and shook his head like she had said something stupid.

'Ain't nobody going home, *chica*. We on the run. No more mama-papa house for you, not ever, *m'entiendes?*'

She knew he was lying, knew that he was saying it to make her feel bad, but she could not stop herself from crying anyway. What was worse was that when her mommy came in and asked Christabel what was wrong, and she told her, Mommy didn't say it was a lie, didn't say they were going home right away so don't worry, didn't even yell at the terrible boy. She didn't say anything at all, just held Christabel on the bed. It should have made her feel better, but it didn't, it didn't, it didn't.

CHAPTER 8

Listening to the Nothing

ALMOST dying on the mountain had been bad enough.
Now Sam Fredericks' exhausted sleep was invaded
by the most bizarrely powerful nightmare she had ever
experienced.

The bad dream seemed to go on forever, a flood of
terror and solitude and confusion so real and so lengthy
that at last, in some paradoxical way, even horror became

as boring as a hundred-year trip in the back seat of her parents' car. The only respite from the hammering monotony of fear and loneliness were the small phantoms, swift and cautious as birds, that finally appeared to her out of the long darkness, as though she had passed some terrible pointless test and was now being rewarded. She could not see them but she could feel them all around her, each gentle and insubstantial as a shallow breath. They might almost have been fairies, wispy bits of beauty like something from one of her childhood screen stories. Spirits, perhaps. Whatever they were, she finally felt relieved and at peace. She wanted to hold them close, but they were all as fragile as a butterfly wing, as the trembling puff of a dandelion: to clutch at them was to destroy them.

When she came up at last from the endless dream, Sam Fredericks' first realization – as it had been with every awakening since it had happened – was that Orlando was dead. He was not merely dying (a familiar shadow she had learned to squint into invisibility) but dead. Gone. Not coming back, not ever – no new stories, no new memories. No more Orlando.

But this time, the terrible sadness only lasted until she opened her eyes and saw the endless silver-shot nothing that surrounded her. Surprise was turned to something worse by the look on !Xabbu's careful, devastated face as he told her that Renie was gone.

'But what happened? This so utterly, utterly, *utterly* scans.' At least an hour seemed to have passed and nothing had changed. Sam had not been one of the visitors to the weatherless stasis Renie had named Patchwork Land; to her, the most astonishing thing about this enveloping silver-gray void was the simple fact of its persistence, limitless and unchanging. 'Is Renie still back on the mountain? In fact, where's the mountain?'

'I have no answers, Fredericks,' !Xabbu said.

'Sam. Call me Sam – oh, please.' She had run out of strength to plan, to do. Orlando had died. In all the time she had been trapped in the network, Sam Fredericks had never allowed herself seriously to consider that there might come a time when that would happen – when she would have to go on without him. How could such a thing even be possible? But here it was, the world around her just as strange and incomprehensible as it had been when Orlando was still alive, but now there was no Orlando to push her along, to growl at her, to tell her stupid jokes because he knew that being pissed off by stupid jokes was as good a method of keeping going as being entertained by good ones, and a lot easier on the one telling the jokes.

Sam felt a congestion inside her, a painful swelling of the heart. She would never again get to tell him those obvious things in that way that drove him crazy – an obviousness of such perfection that he could never tell if she was kidding or not. The tightness inside her felt like something that needed to be born, but did not want to come out. It was astonishing to discover how much you could miss someone whose real face you'd never seen.

What would he say now? she wondered. Everything vanished, Renie gone, Sam trapped in the middle of literally nowhere?

'*Neck-deep in* fenfen *and waiting for the tide to rise,*' – that was what he'd told her once in the Middle Country, when they'd turned from stuffing their pockets full of treasure to discover a twenty-meter-long snake forcing its way in through the underground chamber's only exit.

That's where I am now, Gardino, she thought. *For real this time. Waiting for the tide to rise . . .*

!Xabbu saw the tears running down her cheek and crouched beside her, then wrapped her in his slender strong arms. Just as the weeping threatened to overwhelm her, a tall shape appeared out of the mist.

'I knew she was the most reliable of you,' Jongleur said disdainfully, 'but I would not have thought you two would collapse so quickly in her absence. Have you no backbone at all? We must go on.'

The bony-faced man was such a horror Sam could not even look at him, but !Xabbu grew tense beside her. 'It is foolish to go when we have no idea where we are going,' the small man said. 'Did you have any better luck searching than I did?'

Jongleur hissed out breath, as though he had sprung a small leak. 'No. There is nothing. If I had not taken my steps carefully and followed backward along the same track, you might never have seen me again.'

'Wouldn't that be sad.'

Jongleur ignored her. 'That is doubtless what happened to your companion. Wandered off after we made the transition to whatever this place is, and cannot find her way back.'

'Renie would not do such a thing,' !Xabbu said firmly. 'She is too smart for that.'

Jongleur flicked his hand dismissively. 'Still, she is lost, however you choose to explain it. As is Klement.' His smile was wintry. 'I suppose we can be fairly certain they have not eloped.'

!Xabbu rose to his feet. He was a full head shorter than Jongleur, but something in his posture made the taller man step backward. 'Unless you have something useful to say, you will stop talking about her. Now.'

Jongleur peered down at him, annoyed but momentarily surprised. 'Get hold of yourself, fellow. It was merely a remark . . .'

'No more remarks.' !Xabbu stared at Jongleur for a long moment while Sam watched them both, suddenly and uncomfortably aware that without !Xabbu she would be alone with this ancient monster. Jongleur stared back. At last, !Xabbu put his hand down and touched her arm. 'He is right only in one thing, Sam. We can wait a little longer for Renie, but even if she is nearby, we might not find her. Sound does not carry well in this place. She could pass a hundred meters from us and we would not know it. At some point we must move on and hope that we find her along the way.'

'We can't . . . just go without her!'

For a moment !Xabbu's composure slipped, giving Sam a glimpse of the pain he was hiding. 'If . . . something has happened to her . . .' He stopped and darted a look at Jongleur, clearly unwilling to show such things in the man's presence. 'If we cannot find her, we owe it to her to go on. Don't forget, it was her love for her brother that brought her into this place. She would want us to try to help him even without her.'

He spoke with his normal calm, but such desolation lay just behind the words that Sam felt as though her own river of sorrow had met another at least as great – that if they were not both very careful, the combined waters might overflow the banks and flood the world.

The poor visibility meant that she had to stay fairly close to Jongleur while !Xabbu did his work, and it was all she could do to keep her loathing of the man in check. His proud face seemed made of stone, a chiseled monument – like Sam's own father at his stiffest and angriest, but

without the redeeming sense of humor she could always
tease out of him. She could not help wondering how someone with Jongleur's wealth and power could turn himself
into a *thing*, could bend so many lives with his cruelty
. . . for what? Just to keep himself alive? To enjoy centuries
more of cold, unhappy power? Sam had trouble at the
best of times understanding why old people would want
to continue on, long past the point they could do anything
that she could imagine as worth doing; someone like
Jongleur, who had already lasted into a third human life
span, was beyond her grasp.

Orlando had been afraid of dying, too – terrified of it,
she realized now, and all those death-simulations had been
meant to desensitize him to what was coming so unfairly
soon. But even if he had been given the chance to escape
that death, would he have done what this man had done,
taken the lives of innocent others to preserve his own?
She couldn't believe it. She didn't believe it. Not her
Orlando, who believed in the Ring-Bearer's Quest the way
those people in the Circle believed in God. Not Orlando
Gardiner, who had told her that being a true hero was
still the most important thing, even if no one ever found
out about it. He had really believed it didn't matter what
else happened, or what anyone thought about you – it
only mattered what you knew about yourself.

Even her father had told her once, when she was
battling her mother over her name, '*If you want to be
Sam, be Sam – just be the best damn Sam you can.*' His
serious scowl had suddenly become a laugh. '*Someone
ought to put that in a children's book.*'

Missing her father and her wide-eyed, nervously affectionate mother suddenly became a hurt at least as great
as the pain of losing Orlando, and for a moment a shadow
threatened to overtake her completely. Sam stared at

Jongleur sitting a few meters away and could not tell if the dimness was the mist or her own teary eyes, but she knew that whatever happened, she didn't ever want to be like him, angry and frozen and alone . . .

A movement startled her out of her thoughts. !Xabbu's small form appeared from the gray. He sat down beside her gingerly, as though he ached.

'Well?' snapped Jongleur.

!Xabbu ignored him. He took Sam's hand – she hadn't quite become used to his frequent, careful touching, but she still found it reassuring – and asked her how she was feeling.

'Better, I think.' She smiled a little, realizing it was true. 'Did it work?'

He wearily returned the smile. 'As I often say to Renie, the skills I have are not the sort that turn on and turn off. But I think I am making sense of things, yes, perhaps a bit.'

Jongleur made a quiet hissing noise. 'Any other man of my generation would find it comical to see me staking my life on two Africans and, unless I miss my guess about this girl, a Creole – and we have already lost one of the Africans.' He rolled his eyes. 'But I have never been a bigot. If some instinct of yours will show the way out of this place, then damn you, tell us.'

!Xabbu shot him a look of real dislike – one of the strongest things Sam had seen from him. 'It is not "instinct," not in the sense you mean. Everything I know about finding my way has been learned, taught to me by my father's family. They taught me other things you do not seem to know either, like kindness and good sense.' He turned his back on Jongleur, who seemed stuck between outrage and sour amusement. 'I am sorry to have left you with this man, Sam, but I had to move far enough away

that I could not see you, could not even hear the two of
you breathing. All in this network is stranger than in the
real world, and it has been hard at the best of times to
make sense of things. But this place is even more difficult – until a little while ago, I would have said there
was nothing at all to sense beside ourselves. It might still
be true – like a starving man hoping to scent game, I
might have convinced myself of what is not true.'

'You think you . . . smelled something?'

'Not exactly, Sam. For a long time I just sat, trying,
as I said, to forget the sounds and smells of you and . . .
and this man. For some of the time, I hoped I might hear
Renie calling far away.' He shook his head sadly. 'But after
a time I gave up and just . . . opened myself. It is not
mystical,' he said hurriedly, peering over his shoulder at
Jongleur. 'Rather it is being able truly to hear, to smell,
to see – the things people in the city world seldom do,
because everything they need comes to them, hurries
toward them as though it were shot out of a gun.' His
face grew solemn as he searched for words. 'After a while,
I began to feel something. Perhaps it is a little like Martine,
how she senses things – it takes a while to understand
the patterns here – but I think it is simply that I finally
had the stillness and . . . what is the word? Alone-ness?
I finally had a chance to hear.' He squeezed Sam's hand
again and stood up. 'That way,' he said, pointing outward
into a portion of the pearly void no different than any
other. 'It could be that my mind is making things up, but
I feel there is something there, in that direction.'

'Something?' Jongleur's voice was measured, but Sam
could hear his anger just under the surface. In a flare of
insight, she saw how it must eat away at a man like him
to have to rely on anyone at all, let alone someone he
must think of as little better than a savage.

How old is he really, anyway? Sam wondered, and almost shivered. *Maybe two hundred years? Did they still have, like, slaves when he was growing up?*

'What I sense is . . . something,' !Xabbu said. 'There is no other word. I am not speaking that way to disturb you. It is a thickening, perhaps, or greater movement, or distant changes in what is more orderly here, or . . . something. Like the ghost of a track in sand, all the rest blown away by the wind. It might be only a shadow. But that is where I am going, and I think Sam will go with me.'

'Utterly right.' Besides, what was the alternative? Waiting here forever in this fog, hoping something helpful would happen? That wasn't what Orlando or Renie would have done.

Jongleur looked carefully at !Xabbu. Sam did not need any particular insight this time to read the man's mind. He was trying to decide whether !Xabbu was lying to him, or was crazy, or maybe just wrong. Sam could never feel pity for a nasty creature like Jongleur, but she could almost guess what it would be like to suspect everyone and everything. It was an ugly, miserable thing to imagine.

'Lead, then.' Jongleur, even naked, conveyed the impression of a king granting a favor to a peasant. 'Anything is better than this.'

THE third time, Renie almost didn't find her way back. It was strange to be using the shambling, brain-damaged Ricardo Klement as her lodestone, even stranger to experience a flush of pleasure and relief when she saw his seated form appear out of the nothingness.

But what if he'd moved? she asked herself. *Even if I found him again, I wouldn't be coming back to the same spot. It might be a spot !Xabbu and Sam had already checked, and they might be looking for me in the old spot . . .*

This was all presuming that her two friends were still alive – that they hadn't simply been swallowed or drezzed somehow by the network, whatever damned part of it this was. But she couldn't afford to think about that alternative much.

She couldn't really risk wandering anymore, either. Not that it made any difference – the seamless, monotonous gray went on and on, the invisible earth or floor continued, flat as a tabletop; silence and emptiness reigned. So she would either stay put, or move and keep moving.

It would have been an exaggeration to say Klement seemed glad to see her – her lifted his head slightly at her return – but there was no question he knew she was there: his eyes followed her, and he changed his position subtly after she sat down a few meters away, as if to designate a space between them – space that in a world with anything in it at all might have held a campfire.

Renie would have given one of her arms for a campfire. She would have added another limb and perhaps even a few organs to have !Xabbu and Sam seated around that fire with her.

I shouldn't have been thinking about how few of us there were left – tempting fate. Now look what's left. Me. And . . . that.

Ricardo Klement gazed back at her, so still and silent that it was like looking at a picture in a museum. The last thing you would ever imagine was that it would speak.

'What . . . are you?' Klement asked.

Renie flinched in surprise; it took her a moment to respond. 'What am I?' It was hard to talk: her voice was hoarse from shouting for her lost companions. 'What do you mean? I'm a woman. I'm an African woman. I'm someone you and your group of rich friends . . . hurt.' There were no words to express the feelings in her about

Stephen, and the helplessness of the last hours had only made it worse than usual.

Klement stared. There was something moving behind the eyes, but it was deep, deep down. 'That is . . . a long name,' he said at last. 'It seems . . . long.'

'Name?' *Jesus Mercy*, she thought, *that Ceremony scorched his brains properly, didn't it?* 'That's not my name, it's what I . . .' She stopped and took a breath. 'My name . . . ?' She wasn't sure she wanted to tell him, although she had given up on anonymity long ago. There was something galling in the way this thing, whatever had gone wrong with its mind, presumed to a kind of childlike innocence. Did this increase in conviviality mean that the old Ricardo Klement was beginning to surface, or simply that the new, damaged version was becoming more comfortable with its faculties?

'My name is Renie,' she said at last.

Klement did not respond, but did not take his eyes off her either, as though forming an elaborate visual picture to go with the newly-filed name.

Renie sighed. This damaged man was the least of her problems. After what seemed like half a day in the void, nothing had changed. She had shouted until her voice was a husk, she had walked dozens of small circuits, all to no result. There wasn't anything you could call land, let alone landmarks, no directed light, no sound other than that which she made herself. *But if I stay here, I'll die here. Or else Stephen's heart will finally fail and he'll die in that hospital bed, which will make what happens to me pointless.* With the endless gauzy mist before her, it was hard not to see her dear Stephen's face, but it was the bad face that came to her – the sightless eyes and ashy skin, the slack jaw propped by the respirator. *Drying up, curling. Like a fish pulled out of the water and thrown*

*in the dirt. Dear God, please don't let that be the last
Stephen that I see.*

But if she couldn't accomplish anything, what good
was she? It was hard to understand how a Renie lost in
nothingness, with nothing to act upon, even existed. Still,
what choice did she have? She had no tools, nothing but
the lighter, and although she had tried several times to
open a gateway, it remained as frustratingly inert as
before.

'Where . . . is this . . . place?' Klement asked.

Renie cursed silently, then decided she deserved at least
this small pleasure and cursed again out loud. She would
have to be prepared for his occasional startling remarks,
it seemed.

'I don't know. I don't know anything. Jongleur already
said we weren't in the network, and this is . . . even *more*
not in the network, I guess.' She peered at him. 'You don't
understand any of this, do you?'

'That is also a long name. Names of places . . . speaking them . . . usually they are not so long.'

She sighed and shook her head. She was beginning to
think she liked him better when all he could say was 'I
am Ricardo Klement.'

Renie turned her mind back to the pressing problem
of being nowhere at all, and spent a silent quarter of an
hour or so going back over everything that had happened
since she had last been with !Xabbu and the others, but
she could find nothing on which to form a theory of how
they had become separated. The slippery grayness around
her looked very much like the silver cloudbank they had
seen girdling the mountain, but that did not explain how
the mountain itself had vanished, or where her companions had gone. She had simply slept, then woke up in
this different circumstance. Could the strange dream have

something to do with it? She tried to remember the details, the rushing chaos, the long darkness, the heartening appearance at last of those ephemeral presences, but it already seemed vague and distant. In any case, it explained nothing.

So it was a conundrum. A sort of locked-room problem in reverse, if this had been a mystery story – not how to get into a locked room, but how to get out of total nothingness into something . . . into anything at all.

The only things she possessed were the scraps of clothing she had made from Orlando's garments and the lighter. But the lighter would not summon gateways, which would be the most obviously useful thing to do. Could it help her in some other way?

If I had a cigarette, I could light it, she thought grumpily.

A sudden thought came to her. The pale emptiness around her, unnatural and apparently endless – could this be the White Ocean that Paul Jonas and others had spoken about? The network's children had talked of it as a mythical place, something to cross to get to a kind of promised land. Did that mean there was something on the other side of this emptiness? That was a heartening thought. But even if it were true, that still didn't give her any idea how to get there.

She pulled the lighter from between her breasts and held it up. All the studying of it that she, !Xabbu, and Martine had done while preparing to leave the House had actually taught them very little of its true capabilities – as though a group of aliens had discovered a car and, after much trial and error, learned how to turn on the headlights. Further experimentation might teach her more, might even present her with some way out of her current dilemma, but did she dare risk it? She had scoffed at

Jongleur's concerns, but that had mostly been out of loathing for the man. Hearing Dread's voice purring from the lighter – whispering out of something that had been pressed against her skin moments earlier – had made her feel like insects were crawling on her. Could she actually risk announcing her presence to him by trying the communication gear built into the device? The only person she knew besides Dread who was somehow accessing the communications band was Martine, and she had not sounded as though she were in a position to help anyone else.

And what if I reached her? What would I tell her? 'Martine, come find me, I'm in the middle of a bunch of gray stuff.'

She lifted the lighter and turned it, reflexively trying to catch light that would never angle down in this place. She looked at the ornate 'Y', the letter tangled in raised vines and leaves as though it were a statue in a forgotten garden. What had Jongleur said the bastard's name was? Yacoubian. The one who pretty much killed Orlando. She fought a roil in her guts. *I hope whatever T4b did to his head hurts him like sin. I hope it never gives him a moment's peace.*

She wondered briefly if Yacoubian, too, might be listening silently to the communication band of the device, just waiting for her to reveal herself. The thought was unpleasant, but the idea of Dread sitting somewhere, waiting like a cat for one of the mice to show its whiskers, was far worse.

Just listening to the dead air, grinning . . .

The idea came an instant later. Renie leaped up and started to put a little distance between herself and Klement, then stopped and – out of some not quite explicable sense of loyalty – told him, 'I'm just going a short distance away. I need quiet. Don't say anything, anything at all. I'll be back in just a moment.'

He watched her go, incurious as a cow chewing grass.

When she was far enough away that she could still see his dim silhouette, but had created a sense of privacy for herself, she held the lighter up again. Back in the House they had discovered how to bring up the communication band, but she wasn't sure she recalled the sequence. She stared at it with a sense of dull fear, but triggered the combination of touches she remembered. When she had finished, nothing bad happened, but nothing much good happened either. The lighter remained inert and silent. The environment around her seemed unchanged.

Cautiously, holding her breath, she held it up to her ear, then held it out before her and moved it in a slow arc. She could hear nothing but more silence. She let her breath out, then listened again. When she had confirmed her result, she turned herself a few degrees to her right and began the process again.

Dowsing, she thought, amused and disgusted. *If I ever have to explain this to someone, I'd better come up with something that sounds closer to engineering.*

But there was more to her search than superstition or despair, and nearly halfway through her slow rotation she heard something. It was so faint that she could think of it only as a slightly noisier silence on the communication band, but she definitely thought she could hear a tiny hiss, a noise that, however minuscule, had not been there before.

She swung the lighter a little farther through the arc until the tiny sound was gone again, then continued the rest of the way around, just to be sure. When she came back to the direction she had been facing before, the sound also came back.

If she was going to risk her life on something, she wanted to be as certain as she could be. She looked back to make sure Klement was still where she had left him, a lump of almost invisible shadow perhaps fifteen meters away, then she took off her upper garment and tossed it a meter or so in front of her, in the direction which seemed to produce the noise. She closed her eyes, spun around several times to disorient herself, then began rotating slowly through a circle again, using the lighter as her compass needle. When she felt sure she could hear the soft murmur again, she opened her eyes.

The piece of pale cloth lay right in front of her.

'Right!' She was pleased with herself, but even more pleased to think she had something on which to focus once more. She tied her top on and was about to head off when she turned to look back at Klement. He had not moved. He was so still, it seemed like he might never move again.

I should just leave the murdering bastard here, she thought. *I'll probably curse myself later if I don't.* But the idea of deserting the almost childlike Klement in the middle of this deathly nowhere suddenly seemed wrong, although she could not tell herself why.

Renie shouted, 'I'm going off in this direction. I'm not coming back. If you want to follow me, you'd better do it now.'

Positive that she had just done something gravely stupid, but still feeling lighter in her heart than she had for hours, she marched out in pursuit of a whisper.

WALKING through the endless silver-gray, Sam decided, was in some ways worse than just sitting in it. The plodding along was bad enough – she liked sports, which had a point, but had never much cared for running and hiking, just moving her legs to be moving them – but the lack of landmarks and weather, the failure of the sourceless light to change, made it seem like some torment specifically designed to make Sam Fredericks crazy. For the first time since entering the network she really began to miss eating, not for its own sake, but to mark time passing.

No water, no food, no stopping. After what must have been the first couple of hours, it became a perpetual chant in her head, like the advertising slogan for some particularly awful vacation package. It was also a slight exaggeration, since they did take breaks to rest, in part to allow !Xabbu to pause and listen for whatever vague thing it was that was leading him onward, but the pauses were not much of an improvement on the walking. For part of each stop she was left alone with a silent Jongleur, which was a bit like being left in a room with an unfriendly dog: even when no direct threat was offered, the suggestion of it was always present. Thrown back on her own resources, Sam found it hard to pull her mind away from Orlando and her parents, both now so far out of reach that it was hard to believe her mother and father, unlike Orlando, were still alive and she might see them again someday.

Felix Jongleur marched with the stiff determination of a religious pilgrim. Sam was young and strong, and she guessed he was working hard to keep up with her, but he refused to show it; instead, he made a point of acting impatient when they stopped to let !Xabbu metaphorically sniff the breeze. In a less unpleasant man the stoicism might have been admirable, but to Sam it just made him seem even more coldly removed from normal humanity. She found herself choking back her own weary complaints so as not to show weakness in front of him.

Felix Jongleur might have been struggling to keep up

with Sam, but it was clear that !Xabbu was holding himself
back to avoid leaving them both behind.

After all the time she had known him in the baboon
sim, she was only now starting to grow used to the change.
In some ways, !Xabbu in his real body seemed even more
exotic than in the form of a monkey. For all his small
stature – he was both shorter and more slender than Sam,
who was herself slim and only normal height – he seemed
quite tireless, moving with such graceful economy that it
sometimes seemed he could walk in his sleep if he needed
to.

'Where do Bushmen come from?' she asked suddenly.
When !Xabbu did not immediately answer she felt a pang
of worry. 'Oh, is that an utterly rude question?'

His slanted eyes were so narrow the brown irises were
almost invisible until something made them open wide in
surprise or amusement. She could not tell which of those
her second question had produced. 'No, no. It is not rude,
Sam. I am just trying to think of the answer.' He touched
his chest. 'In my case, a small country called Botswana,
but people with my blood are scattered throughout the
southern part of Africa. Or do you mean originally?'

'I guess so, yeah.' She moved closer, matching her stride
to his; she did not want to include Jongleur in the conversation.

'No one knows for certain. In my school days I was
told we migrated down from the northern part of the
continent long, long ago – a hundred thousand years ago,
perhaps. But there are other theories.'

'Is that why you can walk, like, forever? Because you're
a Bushman?'

He smiled. 'I suppose so. I was raised in two traditions,
and both made for hard lives, but my father's people –
the old, old tradition, the nomadic hunters – sometimes

walked and ran for days on the track of game. I am not as strong as they were, I think, but I had to harden myself when I lived with them.'

'Were? You mean they're not around anymore?'

Something moved across his brown face, a shadow in this place with no shadows. 'I could not find them when I looked for them again a few years ago. There were few left, in any case, and the Kalahari is harsh. It could be that there are no more people who live the old life.'

'Impacted! Then you're like . . . the last of the Bushmen.' Even as she said it, she realized what a terrible thing that would be.

To his credit, !Xabbu did his best to smile again. 'I do not think of myself that way, Sam. I was only a visitor to the original way of life, for one thing. I lived with them just a few years. But it could be that no one else will learn the old ways as I did, that is true enough.' He seemed lost for a moment. In the silence, Sam could hear Jongleur's harsh, even breathing behind them. 'It is not surprising. It is a life I value, but I do not think many others would agree. If you were one of that tribe, Sam, you would find it very hard.'

There was something in the way he said it that poked at Sam's heart – he seemed needy, something she had never seen in him before. Perhaps it was Renie's disappearance. 'Tell me about it,' she said. 'Would I have to hunt lions with a spear or something?'

He laughed. 'No. In the delta, where my mother's people live, they sometimes fish with spears, but in the desert the killing of large animals is done with a bow and arrow. I do not know anyone who has ever killed a lion, few who have ever seen one – they are dying out, too. No, we shoot poison arrows, then track the animal until the poison has killed it.'

She thought that was a bit unfair, but didn't want to say so. 'Do girls do it?'

!Xabbu shook his head. 'No, at least not among my father's people. And even men only go hunting big animals from time to time. Mostly they snare smaller game. The women have other duties. If you were one of my tribe, an unmarried girl like you, you would help with the children – watch them, play games with them . . .'

'That doesn't sound so bad. What would I wear?' She looked down at her improvised bikini, a last sad reminder of Orlando. 'Something like this?'

'No, no, Sam. The sun would burn you up in a day. You would wear a *kaross* – a kind of dress made from the hide of an antelope with the tail still on it. And besides watching the children, you would help the other women dig for melons and roots and grubs – things I think you would not much like to eat. But nothing goes to waste in the Kalahari. We use our bows to make music as well as shoot arrows. And our thumb pianos –' he mimed the playing of a small, two-handed instrument, '– we also use as workbenches for braiding rope. Everything is used as many ways as possible. Nothing goes to waste.'

She considered this for a moment. 'I think that part is good. But I don't know if I'd want to eat grubs.'

'And eggs from ants,' he said solemnly. 'We eat those too.'

'Yick! You're making that up!'

'I swear I am not,' he said, but he was smiling again. 'Sam, I fear for that life, and I would miss ant eggs were I never to eat them again, but I know most people would not want to live in that way.'

'It sounds so hard.'

'It is.' He nodded suddenly a little distant, a little sad. 'It is.'

*   *   *

The endless march at last found a temporary ending. Jongleur was limping, although he refused to admit he was suffering. Sam, who was footsore and exhausted herself, had to surrender her pride and suggest that it was time to stop.

She was getting frighteningly good at falling asleep without pillow or blanket – the many back-country trips Pithlit had made with Thargor had already prepared her a bit – and the invisible ground was no harder than some other places she'd slept, but even exhaustion couldn't bring her peace. The dreams of darkness and solitude returned, not quite as vivid as before, but still enough for her to wake several times, discovering on the last that !Xabbu was kneeling beside her in the pearly false dawn, a concerned look on his face.

'You cried out,' he said. 'You said that the birds would not come to you . . . ?'

Sam couldn't remember anything about birds – the details of the dream were already beginning to recede – but she did remember the loneliness, and how desperate she had been for companionship, some contact that might warm the long, cold dark. When she told him, !Xabbu looked at her strangely.

'That is much like the dreams I have had,' he said. He turned to look at Felix Jongleur, who was coming up from his own sleep with a host of small twitches and whimpers. !Xabbu went to him and shook him awake.

'What do you want?' Jongleur snarled, but Sam thought there was something weak and frightened beneath his words.

'My friend and I have had the same dream,' !Xabbu told him. 'Tell us how you dreamed.'

Jongleur pulled away as though burned. 'I will tell you nothing. Don't touch me.'

!Xabbu stared at him intently. 'This could be important to us. We are all trapped in this place together.'

'What is inside my head is mine alone,' Jongleur said
loudly. 'Not yours – not anyone's!' He struggled to his
feet and stood, fists clenched and face pale. Sam was
suddenly reminded how strange it was that they should
all wear such lifelike forms, that everything should be so
much like the real world while still being completely
unreal.

'Keep them, then,' !Xabbu said in disgust. 'Keep your
secrets.'

'A man without secrets is no man at all,' Jongleur spat
back.

'*Tchi seen*,' said Sam. 'He's scannulated. Forget him,
!Xabbu. Let's get going.' But she was puzzled by the change
from Jongleur's normally icy expression. For a moment
he had looked like a man pursued by demons.

The idea of sharing a dream was still bothering her as
they walked. 'How could that be?' she asked him. 'I mean,
it's one thing for us to see the same things, because they're
all pumped into our heads by the system. But you can't
pump in thoughts and dreams and *fenfen* like that.' She
frowned. 'Can you?'

!Xabbu shrugged. 'Since we have been in this network,
there have been nothing but questions.' He turned to
Jongleur. 'Tell us, since you will not talk of dreams, how
it is that we are kept on this network against our will?
You call yourself a master, a god even, but now you, too,
are trapped here. How can such a thing be? With all that
expensive equipment of yours, you may be little more
than a mind in the wires, perhaps – but me? I am not
even wearing a neurocannula, if that is the word. The
system has no direct contact to my brain.'

'There is always direct contact between the outside and

the brain,' Jongleur responded sourly. 'Constantly. You of all people, with your talk of ancient tribal ways and living close to nature, should know that it has been going on since the beginning of time. We do not see unless light transmits messages to the brain, or hear without sound imposing patterns on it.' He smirked. 'It is happening all the time, all through life. What you mean is that there is no direct electronic contact between your brain and this network – no wires. And that is meaningless in this situation.'

'I do not understand,' !Xabbu said patiently. Sam had thought he was taunting the older man out of anger, but she thought now he was working toward something else. 'What do you mean – are you saying there are other ways of putting thoughts in my mind?'

Jongleur rolled his eyes. 'If you think I am going to reveal the secrets of my expensive operating system as part of this childish catechism, you are mistaken. But any schoolchild, even one from the backwaters of Africa, should be able to guess what it is that keeps us online. Have you gone offline?'

'I have,' Sam said grimly. The memory was horrible.

'And what happened?' He looked at her fiercely, intently, like some grandfather from hell. 'Come, tell me. What happened?'

'It . . . hurt. I mean just majorly scorching.'

Jongleur rolled his eyes. 'I have been forced to endure ten generations of teenage slang. That alone would be enough to discourage a lesser man from wanting to live as long as I have. Yes, it hurt. But you didn't manage to get offline by yourself, did you?'

'No,' Sam said grudgingly. 'Someone unplugged me. Back in RL.'

'Yes, in "real life." How appropriate.' Jongleur showed

his teeth – a sort of chilly grin. 'Because you couldn't find the way to do it yourself, just as I can't now. And do you think that is because, as those religious fools in the Circle believe will happen one day, we have been translated into Paradise, into incorruptible bodies, innocent of such things as neurocannulae? Do you think so?'

'No.' Sam scowled at him. 'Chance not.'

'Then why else can't you find something you know perfectly well is there? Think, child!' He turned to !Xabbu. 'Have I lost you? Can you not guess?'

The Bushman looked back at Jongleur coldly. 'If we could guess, we would have already done so without your lecture, which explains nothing.'

Jongleur threw his hands up in a gesture of mock-frustration. 'Then I will bore you no longer. Solve the riddles yourself.' He slowed until he was several paces behind them once more.

'I *hate* him,' Sam said in whispered fury.

'Do not waste your strength, and especially do not let anger blind you to him. He is clever – I was a fool to think I could draw him out so simply. He has plans of his own, I am sure, and will not easily give anything for anyone else's benefit.'

Sam fingered the length of broken sword thrust through the waist of her garment. 'All the same, I hope he gives me an excuse to use this on him.'

!Xabbu squeezed her arm hard. 'Do nothing reckless, Sam. I tell you as a friend. Renie would tell you the same if she were here. He is a dangerous man.'

'I'm dangerous too,' said Sam, but in a voice so quiet even !Xabbu didn't hear.

They had stopped three times for sleep when !Xabbu finally made his discovery.

Sam and !Xabbu had experienced similar dreams each time, though never exact duplicates. Jongleur continued to make uneasy noises in his sleep, but remained silent about it when awake.

The tramping through the endless, featureless overcast had itself turned into a kind of dreary dream – faced with such unending nothing, Sam had several times slid over into hallucination. Once she saw the front doors of her school in West Virginia, as clearly as if she stood at the bottom of the steps. She even raised her hands to pull them open, braced for the noise of the echoing hallways, then found that she was reaching out toward nothingness and that !Xabbu was looking at her with concern. She also saw Orlando and her parents several times, distant but unmistakable shapes. Once she saw her grandfather trimming a hedge.

Even !Xabbu seemed oppressed by the monotony, the terrible dull pale cloudiness of everything, the continuous pointless now; even he grew increasingly silent and withdrawn. Thus, when he paused suddenly and awkwardly in the middle of one of his investigations, interrupting what had by now become a sort of boringly familiar dance of turning and listening, turning and listening, Sam thought maybe he too had been caught by a hallucination – a vision of Renie, perhaps, or some feature of his people's desert home.

'I do not believe it!' Surprisingly, he had an eager tone in his voice that had been missing for some time. 'Unless I am losing my mind.' He laughed. 'Come, this way.'

Jongleur, who had been showing little more animation than a sleep-walker, dutifully followed, setting one foot after the other as though reading it from an instruction manual. Sam hurried to catch up with !Xabbu.

'What is it?' she said. 'Did you hear something?'

'I need quiet, Sam.'

'Sorry.' She fell back a little way. *Please let him be right*, she thought, watching the poised, flexible tension of his naked back. *Please let him find something. I hate this gray. I hate it so much . . .*

!Xabbu abruptly stopped and crouched. The silvery void was all around him, unchanged and seemingly unchange-able. The small man grew wide-eyed, waving his fingers at nothing visible, paddling them in small circular motions at ground level, until Sam suddenly became terrified that he had lost his mind.

'What are you doing?' She almost shouted it.

'Feel, Sam, feel!' He dragged her down beside him and shoved her hand into the perfectly empty patch of noth-ing identical with every other cubic meter of nothing that stretched away in all directions. 'There. Do you see?'

She shook her head, fearful. Jongleur had stumped up and now paused, looking down on them as though they were beggars he had discovered living in his rose garden. 'I don't see anything,' she moaned.

'I am sorry. I spoke badly – there is nothing to see. But maybe you can feel or hear it . . .' He held her hands in his own and gently moved them back and forth just above the ground. 'Anything?' When she shook her head, he pulled his own hands away from hers. 'Try again. Concentrate.'

It took long moments, but at last she felt it – the faintest, most negligible force, a weak current of skin-temperature air, perhaps, or a vibration so meager she could barely distinguish it from the tremble of her own pulse in her fingers. 'What . . . what is it?'

'A river,' !Xabbu said triumphantly. 'I am certain it is. Or at least it will be.'

CHAPTER 9

Hannibal's Return

NETFEED/INTERACTIVES: HN, Hr. 6.5 (Eu, NAm) – 'Teen Mob!'
(visual: Mako and Crank Monkey searching alley for Klorine)
VO: Suicidal Klorine (Bibi Tanzy) has just discovered she is not her
parents' biological daughter. She takes an overdose of pills, but none
of the Teen Mob know where she is. Her friends Crank Monkey and
Mako only have two hours to find her before it's too late. Producers
claim: 'Surprise Ending of the Year!' Casting 12 Madness Mall employees, pharmacist.
Flak to: HN.TNMB.CAST

'**W**E should have guessed,' said Florimel bitterly, staring into the view-window at the distant, beetle-riding shape. 'Someone like Robert Wells will always find a way to get himself onto the winning side.'

They all stood frozen, helpless. Even Kunohara had stopped trying to make his ruined system function. The crush of mutated wasps swarming over the bubble-house filled Paul with claustrophobic terror – any moment the barbed stingers dimpling the transparent walls would break through and the whole thing would dissolve into tatters, dropping the squirming mass directly on top of them. But what could they do? They were surrounded, but even if they got out, the Twins were waiting. Once he was out of the bubble and onto open ground, they would hunt him down without mercy . . .

'You still have not answered my question, Kunohara.' Martine's voice was raw – Paul could hear her fighting to keep her words steady. 'We must rely on each other or we have nothing. Did you have an informant among us?'

He turned on her angrily. 'You have no right to question me! You and your carelessness have brought this down on us all.' He glared, then turned back to the window. 'I will go out. Wells at least I can talk to, although I doubt I can trust him.'

'Gonna sell us out, him,' T4b growled, but bluster could not hide his fright. 'Don't let him do it!'

Paul astonished himself by saying, 'Then I'll go with him.'

Even Kuhohara looked surprised, but there was cold rage in his eyes as well. 'Why? Do you think if this child was correct with his accusations of treachery, you could stop me?'

'That's not why. Those creatures – the Twins. They've been hunting me all along. If it's me they're looking for, well . . . maybe without me the others would be safe.' It sounded even more foolish spoken out loud, but he could not simply wait here for everything to collapse.

'I'm not sure I understand you,' Kunohara said. 'But if you are with me, you are in no greater danger out there than here.'

'Maybe you could just . . . take us all away.' Paul was already regretting having volunteered. 'Wouldn't that be better? Move us all somewhere else, like you brought us back from where the scorpion was?'

'And give up my house to them?' Kunohara looked at

him with scorn. 'This is what I have left to keep me alive. This is my local interface – the seat of my power, at least what little of it remains. If I flee and they destroy this place, we would not last half an hour out in that world.' He shook his head, face a grim mask. 'Do you still wish to come out to parley with me?'

Paul took a breath. 'I think so, yes.'

The house vanished, replaced by a cold, windy river-bank. The outcropping of stone on which they now stood was surrounded by deformed beetles and wasps, the buzzing so loud he feared it would make him sick to his stomach. The bubble which they had just left was invisible beneath a crawling mass of insects.

'*Wells!*' Kunohara shouted at a human figure watching the action from the edge of the stone. '*Robert Wells!*'

The man sitting astride a beetle as proportionately large as an elephant turned at the call. He kicked with his heels at the creature's shell until it slowly turned toward them, moving with an almost mechanical dignity. The human rider leaned forward, squinting.

'Ah,' he said brightly. 'Doctor Kunohara, I presume?'

Paul understood what Martine had meant – Wells' sim did indeed look slightly less than realistic. The pale hair and the general shape of the face echoed what he had seen in newsnet footage of the technocrat, but there was something unfinished, almost doll-like about the features.

Kunohara was tight-lipped. 'Yes, it is me. But I do not recall inviting you here, Wells. You are even wearing one of my scientists' jumpsuits, I see. What of the agreement I had with the Brotherhood?'

Wells looked briefly and incuriously at Paul before turning back to Kunohara. 'Oh, the Brotherhood. Well, *that* ship ran into a bit of an iceberg, if you haven't heard.' He laughed breathily. Paul did not know the man, but thought he seemed strange, almost a little mad. 'Oh, yes, the Old Man screwed that up pretty damn thoroughly. Then got bumped off by one of his own employees, no less. A corporate power play, I suppose you'd call it, although the timing was unfortunate.' His not-quite-human smile didn't fade. 'Everything's gone to hell now, really. But it's not all bad. We just have to stay in the saddle until everything calms down again.'

Kunohara's expression had not changed. 'You make jokes, Wells, but as you do so, you are trying to destroy my home, the things I have built here.'

Wells swayed a little as the beetle changed positions beneath him. 'Not me! I'm just along for the ride. It's my new friends you want to talk to.' He put his fingers to his mouth and whistled. Paul's heart raced as two mismatched figures appeared over the edge of the stone. It was all he could do not to run, to trust Kunohara's failing abilities instead. 'It's not even you they're after, Kunohara, it's your guests,' Wells said. Now he looked at Paul again, the smile lazy and a bit disconnected. 'Apparently they've gotten on the wrong side of the new management. If you'd just hand them over to the boys,' he cocked his head at the approaching pair, 'I'm sure you'd be welcome to join us.' He leaned forward and winked. 'Time to choose up sides, you know. At the moment, it's not a hard choice at all.'

Paul hardly registered Wells' words. He was fixed in sickly fascination on the two creatures moving toward them, the sagging, fleshy caterpillar and the albino cricket – Mullet and Finch – no, that had only been their names in the trenches. Mudd and Finney.

A spark of memory. Mudd and Finney . . . a dark room, two mismatched shapes . . .

It was gone. Paul shuddered. They were as horrible to

look at as they always were, no matter the incarnation, and every sensible instinct shrieked at him to run as fast and far away from them as he could – but still, something was subtly different this time. Only as they reached Wells and stopped on either side of the beetle did Paul begin to understand what it was.

'What do you want?' the Finney-cricket asked in a scraping, petulant voice. 'The new master says hurry. He is impatient for us to secure these creatures.'

'If we help him,' the Mudd-caterpillar rumbled, 'he will give us the little queen.'

'Yes, the little queen.' The eyeless cricket rubbed its forelegs together in pleased anticipation. 'We have hunted for her so long . . . !' It turned its smooth head toward Kunohara and Paul. 'And what are these things? Prisoners?'

'Do we eat them?' the caterpillar inquired, rearing up so that the front half of its huge heavy body towered over them both.

Paul took a step back in alarm, but there was a surge of elation, too. *I'm right*, he thought. *I don't feel that terrible, sickening fear I've felt in the past – and look at them! They don't even recognize me.*

Wells appeared to consider the caterpillar's request for a moment. 'No, I think not. Kunohara, at least, will be a useful source of conversation in this godforsaken place.' He smiled and nodded. 'But you really better let them have the others, Doctor K. This pair are pretty damn single-minded . . .'

'We will bring the new master the ones who spoke through the air,' the blind cricket rasped, 'and then he will let us have our little queen. Our lively, lovely larva.'

'I miss her,' the caterpillar said, something like a fond smile twisting its tusky mouth. 'So pale, so fat . . . ! When we find her, I will nibble on all of her dozens of little toes!'

Paul now knew for certain that these versions of the Twins were not the remorseless creatures who had stalked him through so many worlds, but something more like the Pankies, oblivious to him, consumed with a quest of their own. A memory of Undine Pankie came to him then, her doughy face transfixed by some grotesque instinct just like the caterpillar's, babbling about '*my dear Viola . . .*'

Viola. Something tickled his thoughts. Viola. Vaala. Avialle.

Ava.

'. . . I must insist you turn them away, Wells,' Kunohara was sputtering. 'This is my house, my domain, and whatever has changed, I still insist on my rights. No guests of mine will be taken from under my roof.'

Wells nodded, the soul of reason. 'Oh, sure, I understand. But what's that old saying about cutting off your nose to spite your face? You don't really want to go up against the new boss, Kunohara. As for me, I have no pull with him at all – not yet, anyway. Nothing personal, but I just can't help you.'

The cricket and the caterpillar, slow and self-absorbed as their thoughts were, nevertheless had begun to pay attention. 'This is the one?' the cricket whined, pale blind face turning to Kunohara. 'This is the one who keeps us from the others?'

With a squelching noise like a giant water mattress, the caterpillar moved closer. A ripple passed through its legs as those nearest Paul stretched toward him, the tips curling and clenching. 'They keep us from the little queen . . . ?'

'Enough,' Kunohara said, and gestured. A moment later

the stone outcrop was gone and Paul, caught by surprise, stumbled and sat down in the middle of Kunohara's bubble-house.

'What happened?' asked Florimel. 'We couldn't hear . . .'

Paul turned on Kunohara. 'Why didn't you blast them – snow or wind or something, one of your god-tricks? We were far enough away from the house . . .'

'Something blocked me in their presence.' Kunohara was clearly troubled. 'Their new master, this Dread it must be, has protected them. He is playing tricks with my world.' The worried look changed to a scowl. 'But I will not be destroyed so easily. Not in my own home.'

The wasps had become more agitated on top of the bubble, the slowly moving tapestry of chitin now sped until it was almost a liquid blur, their buzzing so intense it made the air in the transparent house vibrate.

'Op that!' T4b shouted. He took a hurried step back and knocked Paul staggering. Just above their heads the weight of the swarming creatures had begun to push the arch of the dome downward. 'Don't get out of here, be six-meat, us!'

One of the stingers finally ripped through the fabric of the dome and the pressing weight began to widen the tear. Even Kunohara stared in shock as one of the deformed creatures slid into the hole in the fast-collapsing membrane. It hung above them for a moment, kicking its huge black legs like a horse dangling from a chandelier.

'Downstairs,' Kunohara shouted. He snatched at Paul's arm and shoved him toward the steps leading to the lower chamber. The others tumbled after them as the first wasp finally fell through and landed on the floor of the upper room. It stood, eyes staring blankly from its caricature human face, then several of its fellows rattled down on

top of it, knocking Kunohara's furnishings into splinters
as they struggled mindlessly to disentangle themselves.

When all the humans had reached the room below,
Kunohara flicked his fingers at the door atop the stairwell to close it behind them; when it did not respond, he
snatched at it and began pulling it down. T4b and Florimel
leaped up to help him, but a flailing leg pushed through
before they could close it. With a shout he barely recognized as coming from his own mouth, Paul snatched the
first thing he could find, a small table, and hammered on
the leg until it snapped. Gray liquid spurted through the
trapdoor, but Kunohara and the others were able to ram
it shut and latch it.

Overwhelmed, Paul stared at the severed leg lying on
the transparent floor, still twitching slightly. Beneath his
feet, perhaps stirred by what was happening on the
surface, the spidery postlarval shrimp swarmed toward
the transparent bottom of the bubble, stalk-eyes swiveling, legs stroking. The rumbling hum from the upper
room grew louder. The trapdoor began to bulge inward
beneath the weight of the creatures swarming in through
the torn roof.

'Sixed, us,' T4b panted. 'Take some of them crawlies
with us, though.'

'No.' Kunohara pointed to a place on the floor. 'Stand
there.'

Martine was holding her hands to her ears, overwhelmed by the buzzing. 'What are you going to do?'

'The only thing left to do,' Kunohara said, raising his
voice as the din overhead grew even louder. 'Their field
of defense now surrounds this place, too – I cannot even
transport myself! But with you gone, perhaps I can still
salvage something.' He took Martine's arm and directed
her roughly toward the spot he had indicated.

'What, he give us to the bugs?' T4b shouted. 'Chance not . . . !'

Kunohara hissed with fury and desperation. 'Have you not already brought enough ruin on me? Must you insult me, too? Get on that damned spot!'

Paul seized T4b and shoved him to the place where Martine and Florimel already stood. The floor abruptly bulged downward into a round concavity. T4b slipped and dragged Martine and Florimel to the bottom as well. 'Gonna drown us, him!' T4b shrieked.

Paul looked back at Kunohara, whose returned glance explained nothing, then abandoned himself to trust and slid down into the growing blister. As the bubble-material bulged outward, the water of the river abruptly surrounded them, the congregation of translucent shrimp now only inches away.

Paul shouted back at Kunohara, 'What about you?'

'There is another thing I must do, otherwise they will simply catch you floating here. Brace yourselves.' He turned his back on Paul and began another series of elaborate gestures. As if in response, thunder boomed outside, momentarily outstripping the angry murmuring of the wasps. Lightning flared, a murky flash seen through the water that now almost totally surrounded them. The bulge had become a small bubble, connected only by a shrinking hole to the rest of the house. Paul was crushed between Florimel and T4b, scarcely able to move. Kunohara dropped his hands like a conductor at the finish of a symphony and the hole through which Paul was watching him abruptly narrowed, then disappeared. With a sudden bounce that made Paul's stomach drop toward his feet the bubble popped free of the house that had birthed it and rose swiftly toward the river's surface.

The pressure was so strong that the sphere actually

shot entirely out of the water before falling back, throwing Paul and his companions into each other, elbows and
heads and knees all making painful contact. The momentary sense of freedom was short-lived. They had surfaced
only a small distance from the house and its swarming
blanket of insects. Rain was pounding down on all sides
now, huge drops that smashed the surface of the river
into a froth and bounced their tiny, spherical life raft like
a child's ball.

Paul untangled himself from his companions and
pressed his face against the bubble wall. Even the hammering rain had not slowed the Twins' assault: the bridge to
the land was now complete, a hundred thousand wasps
and beetles twined together across the agitated water. In
a lightning-illuminated moment he saw the cricket and
the caterpillar making their way unhurriedly down the
stone outcrop and onto the landward end of the insectile
chain, like conquerors mounting a castle's drawbridge.
Paul couldn't be sure, but he thought he saw Wells spurring
his beetle behind them.

'They have seen us!' Florimel shouted, and for a
moment Paul had no idea what she meant – the Twins
and Wells were surely too far away to attach any significance to their bubble, surrounded as it was by others
kicked up naturally in the rain-pummeled water. Then he
saw that some of the mutated wasps were swimming
toward them, floundering across the water with purpose
in their movements if not on their blank faces. Several
had already been swept away by the roiling waters, but
dozens more were still paddling on with the awkward
determination of dogs.

Their spherical ark was splashed by another massive
raindrop and slipped sideways, bobbing and spinning. Paul
had to brace himself against its curvature to keep his

balance. When he could see out again, another glare of lightning showed him the Twins, now poised atop the shattered parabola of Kunohara's bubble. The mantle of wasps squirmed wildly, perhaps struggling to make an entrance for their commanders. A river-tossed stick almost half the size of the house bumped past, caught in the current, and scraped away a few of the hundreds of wasps clinging to the house. Leaves and bits of wood and grass were scattered across the surface of the river. Paul looked up to the cataract behind the house and saw that a great clot of debris had formed, an accidental dam of twigs and leafmold, trembling with the force of the water rushing over it and through its interstices.

The rains, he thought distractedly, *so much rain. There must be a lot of water and other things trapped behind that rubbish.*

What had Kunohara said? *'There is another thing I must do . . .'*

'Oh my God!' Paul shouted. 'Hold on – brace yourselves!'

'We are already fighting just to keep upright . . .' Florimel began, but Paul put his foot against her hip and pushed her back against the curve of the bubble. 'Just brace yourself. It's going to be . . .'

As the lightning flashed again, he saw the great wedge of debris lurch and change shape across the top of the cataract. For a moment the waterfall was almost completely choked off – a change so great that even the misshapen pair on top of Kunohara's house turned to look behind them. As the effect of this throttling of the flow reached Paul and the others the current grew momentarily mild and their bubble settled deeper in the water. Then the clot broke apart and the river surged over the fall like a fist made of green water and white foam, smashing down on Kunohara's house and the insects, driving the whole mass beneath the surface in an explosion of spray.

The wall of water rushed across the surface of the pool toward Paul and his companions, caught them up, then hurled them screaming out over the lower cataract, so that for a moment they were freefalling through the air above the dark, rain-whipped river like a star that had plummeted from the heavens.

THE destruction of Rome was in full swing now, and the smoke of the burning could be seen as far away as the vineyards of Campania – a defeat of staggeringly unprecedented proportions. But the Romans, citizens and slaves, could have been forgiven for being caught unprepared, since the massive assault had arrived out of nowhere, and almost three hundred years late.

Before this day had dawned, Tigellinus had reigned two years as emperor. The onetime horse trader was still popular, not so much because of his own acts, although he had been a careful steward, but because of the hatred in which the people of Rome had come to hold his predecessor Nero, the last of the Julio-Claudian emperors, in the days before his assasination. It was not just Tigellinus, many Romans suggested – even one of his horses would have been an improvement over Nero.

In fact, as of the day before, all had seemed more than well in the Mother of all Cities. A March tramontane wind had swept the skies clean, and spring had seemed to sprout almost immediately in its wake, luring buds out of the branches of the chestnut trees, turning the hills green. Strangely, even the College of Augurs had offered no warning of anything amiss – the most recent sacrifices had gone smoothly, and all the signs had suggested a happy year for the emperor and his people. The empire itself was quite secure. There were still skirmishes at the outer fringes of the Roman world, but generally the idea of war had become little more than the setting for stories told by old soldiers in the wineshops who had fought in Britain or the forests of Gaul. No one had expected any sort of attack, let alone one by a long-dead enemy – especially when that enemy's city had been dust almost as long as he had.

On that late March morning, Hannibal's army had simply appeared as if sprung from a god's hand. Hundreds of years earlier, the Carthaginian's crossing of the Alps had caught the Romans by surprise. This time, Hannibal Barca and his armies had found some even more startling way of traveling. The first anyone knew of his presence was black smoke trailing in the sky just north of the city and the first terrified refugees fleeing down the main roads into Rome itself. Within a few hours fires were burning in many places inside the city walls and the corpses of citizens were being defiled on the Field of Mars.

The city was largely undefended. The Senate had fled south down the Via Appia at the first reports of invasion, some of the senators making themselves notable by crushing other refugees beneath the wheels of their carts in their hurry to escape. The most respected men of the day were far from Rome, in large part because Tigellinus had preferred it that way, all Rome's defenders and generals scattered. And, of course, Hannibal's old enemies Scipio and Marcellus were centuries dead.

The Praetorian Guard fought nobly, but against ten thousand shrieking Carthaginians they could do little; Hannibal's armies cut their way down the Via Triumphalis like a knife through hot fat. Emperor Tigellinus was dragged from the Golden House with his arms bound behind him. Hannibal himself climbed down from his

black horse and beat the emperor to death with a stick –
a mark of respect, of sorts.

The most bizarre thing in what would become a week
of horrors too great to comprehend, was not just that the
monster Hannibal of Carthage should rise from his ancient
grave, but that he should storm Rome with an army of
men who looked so much like himself – in fact, some
survivors swore that every soldier was absolutely identical. It was at least certain that instead of the diverse band
of mercenaries he had used the first time he had come
down into Italy in the days of the Republic, Ligurians and
Gauls, Spaniards and Greeks, this time there was a strange
uniformity to his troops – each and every one small but
well-knit, with black skin, long dark hair, and a strange
Asian cast to his eyes. Wherever they were from, they
burned and pillaged and murdered with a cruelty so savage
and arbitrary that even in the early hours of the assault
some Romans swore that the very pits of the Earth had
opened and belched forth this army of demons. By the
end of the first day, scarcely anyone would have argued.

The few who saw him and survived said that Hannibal
himself had the same dark skin and oddly hooded eyes
as his troops. Other than his gold-shod horse and his
banner, went the horrified whispers, Hannibal was only
distinguishable from his minions by the silver staff he
carried at all times, and by the fact that he alone, of all
his implacable army, seemed to find the ghastly events
amusing. He laughed as the young men of equestrian
families were brought before him to be butchered, laughed
just as hard when their sisters and mothers begged for
mercy, as though the whole terrible rampage were a kind
of performance conducted for his benefit alone.

He is no human, but an evil god, survivors murmured
to each other as they huddled in sewers and basements.

He may call himself Hannibal, but even the scourge of Cannae was never so cruel.

As the sun set on the first day of his conquest, the evil one came to the heart of the city, the Forum Romanum, and built himself a palace there. Flies in their millions hovered over the place, darkening the red skies like storm clouds. The demon built his house from corpses and near-corpses, piling them high, skewering them face-up on tall wooden stakes to make his walls, so that each dying man's last sight was of another body being rammed down on top of his own.

At the center the arch-monster Hannibal ordered a throne built from skulls of all sizes, skulls which only hours before had held the diverse thoughts of living folk; when it was finished he sat upon it, surrounded by the high walls of his new palace – walls that screamed and bled and begged – and had the prisoners of Rome brought before him, one by one, then in bunches as the evening wore on, and to each he ordered some terrible thing done.

The old Stoic Seneca, who had advised three emperors, and who himself was the first to admit that many considered him the conscience of Rome, stood brave but weeping before the enemy's throne and quoted Euripides in Hannibal's grinning dark face, saying, *'My mother was accursed the night she bore me, and I am faint with envy of all the dead.'*

The demon laughed loud at this, and had the old man's arms and legs carefully taken off so he should not kill himself, then kept him at the foot of his throne like a dog and made him witness to all that happened afterward.

And indeed, in the end, there was not one of the living who did not at last come to envy those who had already been killed . . .

* * *

It was hard work being God, Dread had begun to realize.

He stood in pale sunlight before his throne room in the Forum and sniffed the dawn air, his keen nostrils sifting the scents of smoke and blood and putrefaction for something more subtle, without knowing quite what it was he sought. His soldiers, a thousand mirrors of himself, kneeled in the Via Sacra, waiting silently for orders. He sniffed again, trying to understand what he was missing, what he was pursuing on the breeze on this lovely spring morning, made only a little less so by the odor of a thousand unburied corpses. Perhaps the faint trace of purpose, of a real challenge.

Destruction for its own sake was beginning to pall, he decided as he surveyed the charred rooftops of Rome. Already he had obliterated half a dozen of the Old Man's favorite simulations, not to mention a select few belonging to some of the network's other masters, and he was beginning to find such exercises boring. It had been exciting at first – he had spent several days engineering the rape of Toyland, testing his cruel imagination to such a degree that near the end, as he lay sated in the midst of the wreckage like a lion beside its kill, he had an almost unheard-of moment of self-doubt, wondering if the elaborate tortures he had visited on Mary Quite Contrary and Little Bo Peep and Tom the Piper's Son, his thundering devastation of their fairy-tale land, might be evidence of some latent pedophilia. The idea had disturbed him – Dread found child molesters a particularly pathetic lot – and when he had moved on to his next target, savaging a charming little comic simulation of 1920s London, he had been careful to limit his more personal and arcane pursuits to those clearly of adult age. But now, several simworlds on, after pursuing the flower of Roman womanhood through fields and burning villas in

this latest world, until both bravery and weeping surrender no longer intrigued him, and after a program of
terror that was starting to become mechanical, Dread was
definitely growing bored.

He picked one of the Dread-soldiers at random and
gave it a non-functional copy of his silver staff.

'You're Hannibal now, mate,' he told his simulacrum.
'Here's your first job. Release the gladiators and give them
all knives and swords and spears.' He frowned. It was hard
to care anymore, impossible to forget he was just talking
to a poor copy of himself. 'Oh, and destroy all the food
stores. When that's finished, you and the rest of the
soldiers withdraw, form a perimeter around the city, and
we'll see what the survivors get up to.'

He did not wait for an answer – what did it matter?
– but flicked himself back into the heart of the system.

The problem was, it was so easy to destroy things here,
but hard to keep it interesting. Initially, of course, just the
idea of wreaking this kind of havoc within the Old Man's
staggeringly expensive simulations had been pleasure
enough, almost like giving the ancient bastard a good
beating, and the endless power to cause horror on such a
scale had its own intriguing allure. Now he was beginning to feel the limitations of the exercise: soon his
complete license to roam the worlds of the network and
do to them what he wanted would lose all savor. In any
case, it was not true destruction: unless he froze them in
eternal and somewhat boring devastation, or destroyed the
code behind them (a very different and far less viscerally
satisfying kind of revenge), the simulations eventually
would simply cycle through and start over and all the
destruction he had committed would be wiped away as
though it had never happened.

Dread floated in midair in the immense but mostly featureless complex he had built for himself, an open-plan structure crafted entirely of smooth white virtual stone. Outside the windows stretched unclouded blue sky and the endless Outback scrubland he had seen on netshows in his childhood but had never visited, the emptiness that filled the center of his native country.

It was not enough simply to hold gross power over the network, he was beginning to think. With the whip of pain – or its analog, since there could be nothing like true pain for an artificial intelligence, however lifelike – he had demanded it give him unlimited control, repeatedly scorching the operating system until it abandoned all protections against him. But even though control had been given to him, there were still too many limitations, and it galled him to realize that although he had equaled Jongleur's power over the system, he still could not surpass it. He could not locate an individual user, for one thing – the system was too complex for that, too distributed. If the blind woman Martine had not announced her presence over an open communication channel, he would not have known she was alive, let alone been able to guess where she was. He regretted now that he had been busy with Dulcie at the time: a quick check of the Kunohara simworld revealed that his former companions' whereabouts were again unknown. He should never have left it to anyone else, even Jongleur's own agents. *Especially* Jongleur's own agents. Dread was developing a greater understanding of the Old Man's frustration with incompetent subordinates.

Confident, cocky, lazy, dead, he reminded himself. The Old Man had thought himself unquestioned master of the network and he had lived to regret it. Dread decided he needed to pay better attention to avoid making similar mistakes. But who could threaten him?

It was not all bad, he reflected – if nothing else, locating Martine and the rest of his former companions would be the first challenge he had found in days. And Jongleur himself seemed to have disappeared from the system entirely, even disconnected from his own system's port into the network. Was he dead, or simply offline and lying low? Dread knew his victory would not be complete until his onetime employer groveled before him. It would be a fine day when it came. Even the devastation of Toyworld and Atlanta and Rome would seem like a picnic compared to what Dread was planning for Felix Jongleur.

Oh, and the Sulaweyo bitch. Not only was the virtual Renie out there somewhere in the Grail network, but Klekker and his boys should be getting hold of her real body very soon now. He made a mental note to check on the progress of the Drakensberg operation. *Won't that be interesting? I'll have her offline and online, both – her body and her mind. It could be . . . very special.*

Dread let the halls of his ice-white palace fill with music, a children's chorale from out of the random choice of his system. The singers, innocent as bees making honey, brought back to him the final hours of Toyland, a thought that at this moment he found aesthetically unpleasant. He dropped the voices in pitch and felt relaxation flow through him.

God, or at least the Grail network's bloody-handed equivalent, rested a while from his heavy labors.

The thing is, he thought after a while, *I can't do without little Dulcie Anwin just yet. I don't know how to make new things, I don't really know how to modify things in any big way. The operating system is like a door – if I lean on it, it opens or closes, but the options are pretty limited.*

He had tried giving it natural language commands, but

either the system was not set up that way or it was
pretending not to understand. All the pain he could inflict
on it had not made it communicate, which had left him
only able to reshape things that already existed – mutation
gradients, sim replacement algorithms. Such limitations
were frustrating, and the need to work with the vagaries
of a network that should have been his like a cheap whore
offended him.

One thing was clear: if he wanted to find Renie
Sulaweyo and Martine Desroubins and the others, he
needed to be able to use the system in a more sophisticated way. Jongleur's own agents were hopelessly flawed,
based on what was happening in the bugworld. Dread
was also beginning to think nothing else in this virtual
world could be nearly as interesting as getting his own
hands on the real people who had defied him. And he
would take such magnificent revenge when he did!
Something fabulous and inventive and achingly slow.
Surely the mind that had imagined flaying the leading
citizens of Rome, then turning their skins into hot air
balloons set aloft with their families clinging to the
bottomless baskets – surely a mind of such artistry could
deal with his few remaining enemies in a way that would
be truly awesome, even . . . beautiful?

Dread slipped into a half-sleep, floating in his white
palace, chasing ideals of pain and power that others could
not even imagine.

*THE elevator seemed to take a long time to go down ten
floors. Anger made him tight all over, hot and full of
pressure. When the door at last whispered open, Paul
thought he might explode out into the reception area like
boiling blood out of a hemorrhaging artery.*

There was no one at the reception desk, which was

just as well – he didn't much like the pale, angular young woman who usually sat there, and didn't want her to see him screaming like a maniac. He walked around the curved room, just composed enough not to trip over any of the stylish and expensive Rostov Modern furniture, and laid his hand on the door panel.

His first reflexive thought at seeing them huddled close together at the desk, the small neat head almost touching the shiny bald one, surprised even him.

They know all the secrets. All the bad secrets.

He stood in the doorway, suddenly aware of his own breach of propriety, his own relative powerlessness, and the self-righteous fury cooled. But there was another side to his upset, the silly, embarrassing part of him that believed all those childhood ideals, the ones he had dragged with him through school like a ragged coat despite manifest evidence that it was going to lose him more friends than it gained. No sneaking, no grassing – he still believed it. Duty and fair play. All that high-minded public school nonsense, which the children who had been born to it had discarded while they were still in short pants, but which to a scholarship boy like himself was exotic and precious.

He looked at the two of them, silent and oblivious to the intruder, undoubtedly communing through some cordless connection – Paul himself didn't even have a neurocannula, further proof of his old-fashioned hopelessness – and could not help feeling exactly like a schoolboy again. He had come to scold the older boys for not playing fair, but now that he was alone with them, he knew that what he was going to get was a terrible beating.

Don't be stupid, *he told himself.* Besides, they don't even know I'm here. I can just turn around and come back later . . .

The eyes of the small one came up, flashing behind the

spectacles, giving the lie to his self-reassurance.

'Jonas.' Finney stared at him as though he had arrived naked. 'You are in my office. The door was closed.'

His companion Mudd was still oblivious, staring at nothing, a grin of disturbing pleasure stretching his lips.

'It's just . . .' Paul realized he was short of breath, his heart beating now not from anger but from something closer to fear. 'It's . . . I know I should have phoned first . . .'

Finney's face was so pinched with disapproval that Paul actually felt his anger smoldering up again. This wasn't school. Nobody was going to thrash anyone. And he had a bone to pick with this little shrew-faced man.

Mudd abruptly surfaced, touching his hand to his neck and then turning his piggy eyes toward Paul. 'Jonas? What the hell are you doing down here?'

'I've just talked to a friend of mine.' Paul stopped to take a breath, then realized he was better off forging ahead while his courage held. 'And I have to say, I'm very upset. Yes, very upset. You had no right.'

Finney tilted his head as though Paul were not only naked but frothing. As the angle changed, the nearly invisible overhead lights turned his spectacles into two blank bars of white. 'What on earth are you babbling about?'

'My friend Niles Peneddyn. He was the one who recommended the job to me.' Paul took another breath. 'He said you contacted him.'

One of Finney's eyebrows rose, thin as a fly's leg. 'He recommended the job to you? That's droll, Jonas. He recommended you to us – and a good thing, because Mr Peneddyn, unlike yourself, is of a well-known family and has excellent connections.'

It was a line of insult he knew well. He did not let it distract him. 'Yes. Yes, that's him. He said you contacted him.'

'So?'

Mudd leaned his huge hip against the desk like an elephant scratching its hide on a tree trunk. 'What exactly is your problem, Jonas?'

'I just talked to him. He was very concerned. He said you told him there was a problem in my relationship with my pupil.'

'He recommended you to us. We wanted to make sure there was no mistake – that he had not simply done a favor for someone he didn't really know.'

'What problem?' Paul had to struggle not to shout. 'How dare you do that? How dare you call my friend and suggest that there's something . . . irregular in my conduct?'

If the moment had not been of such high seriousness, Paul would have almost thought Finney was hiding a laugh. 'Oh, and that upset you?'

'You're damn right it upset me!'

A few moments went by. In the silence, Paul's memory of his own voice grew louder and louder, until he began to suspect he had actually shouted at his multizillionaire employer's right-hand man.

'Listen, Jonas,' Finney said at last, all trace of humor certainly gone now. 'We pay close attention to all our responsibilities – Mr Jongleur is a very, very bad man to displease. And we happen to believe that there are . . . tendencies in your relationship with your pupil we don't like.'

'What tendencies are you talking about? And what are you basing this on?'

Finney ignored Paul's second question. 'There seems to be too great an emotional attachment developing. Between you and Miss Jongleur. We don't approve, and rest assured, her father would most definitely not approve either.'

'I . . . I have no idea what you're talking about.' he shook his head, but his courage was flagging. They must know something about the secret meetings, he felt sure – he should never have let himself get into such a position. Damn his own tendency to let things happen to him! But if they guessed even a little bit of what was going on, wouldn't their response be far more draconian than simply a call to Niles . . . ?

Paul struggled to find his indignation again. Because he actually hadn't done anything wrong, had he? After all? 'I . . . damn it, this is my job. And she's just a child!'

Finney pulled a sour smile. 'She is fifteen years old, Jonas. Not a child in most senses of the word.'

'In the legal sense. In the professional sense. My God, as far as I'm concerned, too. In my own sense.'

'Don't tell us about children, Jonas,' said Mudd with heavy amusement. 'We know all about children.'

'What are you basing this on?' Paul asked. 'Did Ava say something? She's a young girl kept locked up like a storybook princess – she's . . . well, she's a little eccentric, perhaps, imaginative. But I would never . . .'

'No, you would never,' Finney said, cutting him off. 'You definitely would never. Because we would know. And you would spend the rest of your life regretting it.' He leaned forward, and even laid his pale fingers on Paul's arm, as though about to tell him a useful secret. 'The rest of your very short life.'

'A short life, but a merry one!' said Mudd, and laughed out loud.

Bizarrely, as the office door closed behind Paul, he heard Finney join in the laughter. It was a strange, terrible sound.

When the door opened on the top floor, the swelling scent of gardenias washed into the elevator. A moment *later, before he had taken more than a few steps into the hall. Ava had thrown herself at him, wrapping her arms around him so tightly it took him long seconds to pull free.*

'Oh, darling,' she said, her eyes so bright they might have been harboring tears, 'do they know about us?'

'Jesus, Ava.' Paul quickly led her outside into the garden. 'Are you mad?' he whispered. 'Don't do that.'

The look of melodramatic sorrow on her face turned into something infinitely more subtle, infinitely more painful to see. She rushed past him and disappeared into the trees that took up most of the vast towertop. A fireworks display of white and yellow birds leaped into the air, disturbed by her headlong flight . . .

He woke to find his head on Florimel's lap, although at first it was hard to separate the throbbing ache from the lap. All his bones hurt too, and he made a little noise of pain as he tried to sit up. Florimel calmly pushed him back down again. With a strip of cloth tied over her wounded eye and ear, she looked piratical. The up-and-down motion of the bubble, which was doing Paul's head no good, added to the buccaneering illusion.

'She was so . . . unstable,' he said. 'I'd forgotten, but it's no wonder all the things she's told me have been so hard to understand.'

'He's delirious,' Florimel told Martine.

'No, no. I'm talking about Ava – about Jongleur's daughter. Another memory just came back, I guess while I was unconscious. Like a dream, but it wasn't a dream.' He was bursting to tell them all that he'd remembered, but suddenly realized there was a here and now quite separate from the returned memories, no matter how sharp and new they felt. 'Where are we? On the river?'

Martine nodded. 'Bobbing along. No sign of Wells or the Twins or their monster insects.'

'Yes,' Florimel said, 'and Martine and T4b and I all survived, too, although we're sore and badly bruised. Thank you for asking.'

'Sorry.' Paul shrugged and winced. 'Kunohara?'

Florimel shook her head. 'I cannot believe he lived through the collapse of his house. We never saw it come back to the surface after the river took it.'

'Fishfood,' said T4b, not without satisfaction. 'Pure.'

'So where are we heading? Is there any way to control this thing?' The ride was actually fairly comfortable, the bubble so much a part of the river that there was little jostling. He had heard once that riding in a dirigible felt the same way, because the ship moved with the air currents, not through them.

Florimel grunted in disgust. 'Control it? Look around – do you see a rudder? A steering wheel?'

'What do we do then?' He sat up, resting his back against the curve of the wall, and moved carefully to disentangle himself from Florimel. They all faced each other, feet touching at the bottom of the bubble, the river water flowing along beneath them as though they hung in open space. 'Just wait until we snag on a sandbar or something?'

'Or until we reach the end of the river and pass through a gateway,' Martine said. 'Orlando told us that many of the gates are no longer functioning. We will have to hope that if the next simworld is closed off we will be able to find another. One that is safe.'

'Is that all we're going to do? Just wait and see?'

'We could worry about how much air we have in here,' Florimel observed. 'But that wouldn't do us any good either.'

'I would rather talk about Kunohara,' Martine said. 'If

he had denied he had an informant with us in Troy, and if it had felt to me even slightly likely that he told the truth, that would have been the end of it. But you heard him – he had no answer.'

'We were being attacked by giant wasps,' Paul pointed out, compelled for some reason to defend the man. 'He saved our lives.'

'That is not the issue.' Martine was firm. Paul found himself a little alarmed – what had happened to the quiet voice, the almost ghostly presence? 'If he was playing a double game, it might make a difference to us – and if one of *us* has kept a secret . . .' She did not finish, but did not need to. Paul knew without being told what it had meant to these people to discover that a murderer had traveled with them in Quan Li's body, a murderer they had treated as a trustworthy friend.

'Perhaps,' said Florimel. 'But suspicion can be devastating, too. And we are only half of those who were in Troy.'

'Just tell me,' Martine said. 'Tell me that you had no secret relationship with Kunohara. I will believe you.'

Florimel did not look pleased. 'Martine, you are not like us. Don't pretend you will not look at us with your little lie-detector rays.'

'I have no lie-detector rays.' Her smile was bitter, her voice hard. 'Tell me, Florimel.'

'I have had no dealings with Kunohara that the rest of you have not been part of.' Her voice was angry, and Paul thought there was a great deal of pain, too. This network, with its masks and labyrinths, was hard on friendship.

'Paul?' Martine asked.

'The same. This is the first time I've met him – I didn't know him when I was in Troy.'

Martine turned to T4b, who had been unusually silent. 'Javier?' She waited a moment, then prompted him again.

He looked like a spring coiled too tight. 'Just tell the truth, Javier.'

'Off my face, you,' he snarled. Even Paul felt there was something defensive in his voice. 'Got nothing to do with Kuno-whatever. Just like Flor-mel said, the rest of you seen it all.' He seemed to feel Martine's continuing gaze as an assault. He swiveled his head angrily. 'Stop *staring!* No dupping, I told you! Off my face.'

Martine looked troubled, but before she spoke, someone else did.

'Martine? I heard you before – can you hear me now?'

It sounded so much like the familiar voice was right beside him that for a moment Paul found himself wondering how anyone could be in the bubble without being seen. Then as Martine pulled out the lighter, he understood.

'Renie? Is that you?' Florimel made an angry shushing gesture at her, but the blind woman shook her head. 'Dread knows where we are,' Martine said quietly. 'And he will until we get out of this world, so it doesn't matter.' She raised her voice. 'Renie? We hear you. Talk to us.'

When it came again, the voice was quieter, not distorted but diminished, with clean holes in the flow of speech. *'We never left . . . mountain,'* she said. *'We're in . . . must be . . . ocean. But I've lost !Xabbu and . . .'*

'We can't understand you very well. Where are you exactly?'

'. . . Think I'm . . . like the heart of the system.' For the first time, Paul could hear the terror subdued beneath collapsing control. *'But I'm . . . trouble – bad trouble . . . !'*

There was nothing after that, no matter how many times Martine begged her to speak again. At last Martine put the lighter away and they sat in silence, carried as froth on the river surface, hurrying toward the end of one world among many.

CHAPTER 10

The Land of Glass and Air

NETFEED/BUSINESS: Death of Figueira Leaves Shipbuilding Firm High and Dry
(visual: Figueira breaking bottle across bow of tanker)
VO: The sudden death of Maximiliao Figueira, chairman and CEO of Figueira Maritima SA, Portugal's largest shipbuilding firm, has left the company reeling.
(visual: Heitor do Castelo, FM company spokesman)
DO CASTELO: 'We are all shocked. For his age, he was in excellent health, but what is even more confusing is how little preparation he seems to have made for the event of his death. He was not a man to delegate, so we had hoped he had prepared for this eventuality a little more thoroughly. We will persevere and retain our leading position in the industry, but I must honestly admit we are scrambling to untangle some very confusing arrangements . . .'

A T first it seemed like a kind of trick !Xabbu was playing, leading them carefully along the banks of a river that only he could see, but after a while even Sam could perceive clearly what her companion had sensed so much earlier.

It started as lines in the never-ending gray, faint as

pencil markings but less substantial: when Sam approached one, or even changed her angle of view, the mark was gone. It was only as the lines became longer and more numerous that she saw they were rims of shadow delineating big basic shapes – rolling curves like distant hills and a line marking the river-shape !Xabbu had been following. Although there was nothing like a sun, and in fact still very little differentiation between ground and sky, the light for the first time was beginning to have an implied direction.

With the alteration of the light also came a change in the color of things. The gray became livelier and more slippery. A faint sheen moved through it, gleaming here and there like the skin of an eel. Although all around her still was strange and mostly formless, Sam felt a loosening in her heart. The endless nothing finally seemed to be coming alive.

'It's like swimming in a silver ocean,' she said wonderingly. For a long time the void above their heads had been indistinguishable from the void beneath their feet; now, showing the first gleaming striations that might eventually become clouds, it was beginning to take on a suggestion of expansiveness. Sam recognized the paradox: as long as there had been nothing to look at, emptiness did not seem to stretch very far. Now it was as though someone were pulling back a blanket, opening up their view of things. 'It's like being underwater. *Ho dzang!* I feel like I can breathe again.'

!Xabbu smiled at the odd combination of images. 'I think the river has a sound now, too.' He held up his hand. Sam stopped; even Jongleur paused. 'Do you hear it?'

She did, a faint whisper of moving water. 'What does all this mean?'

'I think it means that we are going to reach something

more friendly to us than all that emptiness.' !Xabbu dabbled his hand experimentally where the confluence of emerging shadow suggested the river must be, but drew it back dry. He shrugged. 'But we have a distance still to walk, it seems, before that happens.'

'No, I mean . . . what's happening with this place? It's so scanny, just this nothing, then . . . *something*. Like it was growing here.'

He shook his head. 'I cannot say, Sam. But I think it is not so much growing as that we are moving closer to the place it is most concentrated, if that makes sense.' He looked at Jongleur, half-mocking. 'Maybe you can explain to us?'

The sharp-faced man seemed for a moment about to say something dismissive, but when he spoke, he was surprisingly quiet. 'I do not know. This is all a mystery. The Brotherhood built nothing like this in the network, nor did anyone else.'

'Then we should continue,' said !Xabbu. 'If we are not clever enough to understand the mystery, perhaps it will be enough if we are simply strong enough to walk until we reach its heart.'

Jongleur looked at him for a moment, then nodded his head slowly. He waited until !Xabbu had set out along the translucent riverbank again before moving into a steady, trudging gait behind him.

It was strange, Sam thought, how unobtrusively an entire world could swell into being. It was like music, the kind her parents listened to, with violins and other old instruments starting almost silently then growing before you noticed it into a huge noise.

The silvery phantom landscape was now shot through with colors, although they appeared only for short

moments, rippling and disappearing as she moved, sometimes to be replaced by other equally unexpected hues.
The glassy, ghostly hills traced on the far horizon gleamed
deep purple, taking on weight and substance until she felt
she could see every detail; then, as she walked another
twenty paces, the purple seemed to retreat inward, leaving behind only a sketch of the hillcrest, colorless as a
shed snakeskin. A moment later, just when the shapes had
almost vanished against the equally pale and undefined
sky, there would be a faceted glimmer of deep tan, almost
orange, and for that brief instant there would be hills
again and the world had something like a normal shape.

To the extent Sam could make sense of it, she and the
others seemed to be moving toward those hills along the
gentle slopes of a long and meandering valley, following
the river's course upstream. When the river itself took
color, she could see that it had cut a deep track in the
land, twisting between stones that in their phantom stage
looked almost like huge and irregular chunks of ice. Some
of the larger ones lay across the river's path like bricks
of glass, and here the water foamed as it spilled over and
around them until it found the low ground once more. A
few ghost-trees clustered along the banks and on the
higher knolls, but most of the land seemed to suggest
grassy meadows. Only her own breathing, and occasionally a muttered curse from Jongleur as he stumbled over
some feature of the increasingly solid landscape, rivaled
the sound of the river. No insects hummed, no birds sang.

'It's like someone's inventing it,' she said when they
had stopped again to rest. She was sitting on one of the
flat rocks with the river roiling and whispering just an
arm's length away. !Xabbu had no further need to sniff
the air and listen; he sat beside her companionably,
dangling his feet. Sam had reached down and found that

the water still did not quite feel like water: the sensation was cool but dry, as though chilled silk were being dragged continuously across her skin. 'It's like a coloring book for kids,' she continued, 'and someone's just starting to test a few colors, just getting started.'

'I think rather it is the other way around.' His face turned serious. 'I think perhaps that this place was once all full of color and shape. Do you remember the black mountain? Solid and very real at first, then later it began to fade away? I think that has happened here, too.'

Sam felt her first pang of real fear in hours. If !Xabbu was right, they were walking into reality faster than it was dissolving, but could that last forever? Or would they eventually find themselves, as they had on the mountain, with all of creation vanishing around them again? Would they have to go on and on that way, through abortive worlds that coalesced and then deteriorated around them, without a stable place where they could ever just stop and live like people?

Jongleur had been standing a few paces ahead up the riverbank. He turned now and walked slowly back toward them, his expression distant.

'It reminds me of North Africa,' he said. 'When I was young, I spent a year there, in Agadir. Not the landscape that is growing around us – that looks almost European, or it would if it were filled in. But the light, it reminds me of the desert towns in the early morning – the silver dunes, the white light angling off the houses, everything washed out and pale as linen.' He turned back from surveying the hills to see that Sam and !Xabbu were both staring at him. His mouth curved sourly downward. 'What, did you think I was never young? That I have never seen anything but the inside of a biomedical support pod?'

Sam sat up. 'No. We didn't think you cared about

anything you didn't own. That you didn't have somebody build for you.'

For a second he appeared about to smile, but he still commanded his virtual face as stringently as he had his Egyptian mask. 'A touch, I confess it. But a mistaken attack if you seek to wound me. Am I cold, hard, monstrous? Of course. Have I done my terrible deeds deliberately to oppress the downtrodden, or merely to increase my own pile of luxuries, like a dragon sitting on its hoard? No. I have done what I have done because I love life.'

'What?' Sam was happy to let him hear the disgust in her voice. 'That's uttermost *fenfen* . . .'

'No, child, it is not.' He turned away, looking to the distant limpid hills. 'I did not say that I loved *all* life. I am not a hypocrite. Most of the Earth's crawling billions mean as little to me as the insects and smaller creatures that you crush beneath your feet in the grass mean to you. It is *my* life that I love, and that includes the beauty I have seen and felt. It is my memories, my experiences, that I wish to preserve against death. The happiness of other human beings means little to me, it's true – but it would mean even less to me if I were dead.' He turned slowly. His eyes on her were uncomfortably sharp. Sam's hatred of the man had distracted her from what he truly was, but at that moment she could feel the strength in him, knew that this was a force that had knocked down governments as though they were bowling pins. 'What about you, child? Do you think you will live forever? Would you not like to?'

'Not if I had to hurt other people to do it.' She was suddenly close to tears. 'Not if I had to hurt *children* . . . !'

'Ah, perhaps not. But unless you are presented with that option you will never know for certain, will you? And especially not until you are presented with that option while knowing that Death is standing just behind you . . .'

!Xabbu, who had been listening to the conversation, was suddenly not listening any more. He stood up, staring forward past Jongleur and up the riverbank.

'What is it?' she asked. '!Xabbu, what is it?'

Instead of answering he hurried up the bank, running gracefully, bounding over near-invisible stones like a deer. In a few moments he had reached a cluster of small colorless trees that plumed above the bank like the smoke of several fires. He reached up and snatched at one of the branches, stared at what he held in his hand, then hurried back down the riverside.

'Look!' he cried, skipping past Jongleur to Sam. 'Look at this!'

She leaned in. Nestled in his palm was a tiny bit of white cloth lopped in a knot. It took her a moment to make sense of it. 'Chizz! Is that . . . ?'

!Xabbu held it against the strip of cloth tied around her hips. 'It is the same.' He laughed, a wild sound unlike anything she had heard from him. 'It is from Renie! She was here!' He did a little half-dance, pressing the scrap of fabric against his chest. 'She left it as a sign. She knew we would follow the river.' He turned to Jongleur, his mood so good it sounded as though he were bantering with a friend. 'I told you she was clever. I told you!' He turned back to Sam. 'We must walk now as long as we can, in case she has stopped somewhere ahead of us.'

Sam of course agreed, but could not smother a sigh of weariness as she got down from the stone. !Xabbu was already walking briskly upriver once more. Sam fell in behind him. Jongleur shook his head, but followed.

For the first moments the little man's happiness had

been infectious, and Sam had felt her own spirits lifting higher than they had been since before Orlando's death, but now a finger of worry was poking at her – something she could not bear to mention to !Xabbu, but which troubled her more and more.

In the Girl Scouts they always tell you that if you get lost, you stay in one place, she told herself. Sam hadn't been a great Girl Scout, but she had learned what she had to, especially the things that seemed sensible and useful. *Do they have Girl Scouts in Africa, wherever Renie's from?* She wasn't sure, but !Xabbu was right – Renie was smart. Somehow Sam thought Renie would know about the stay-in-one-place rule. Which meant maybe there was a reason she hadn't stayed there, in that spot she'd marked by the river.

Maybe she had to leave because something was after her.

As the light altered from depthless gray to something as slippery and bright as mercury, as she walked doggedly out of nothing into *something*, Renie knew she should have felt more – should have been full of excitement, exhilaration, relief. This was the reason she had been stopping every few hundred yards to wave the lighter like a dowser's rod. Finding this growing reality should have been a triumph, but she found herself moving more and more slowly instead, as if bowed beneath a heavy burden.

The thing was, this place still made no sense.

And I don't do well with things like that. She looked back to see Ricardo Klement picking his way across the uneven ground, if you could call it that, putting one foot before the other like an overwound automaton that would carry on until it walked over the edge of something and disappeared, legs still grinding.

Like my father. He made no sense either, with his self-destructive slide into alcohol and defeat. Yes, his wife had died. Yes, it was horrible. But his wife was also Renie's mother, yet Renie had managed to get up every day after it happened and take care of what needed to be done. That made sense. Surrender, slow decay, that didn't. Death would get you no matter what, and who knew what would happen then? Better to fight on.

But it seemed some people couldn't.

My father would like it here, she thought. *Wouldn't have to try at all, not even pretend. Just lie on the ground and wait for the world to change around him.* She hated it as soon as she thought it, hated her own bitterness.

As she stood taking her first rest in over an hour, Klement reached her and stopped, so much like the machine she had imagined him to be that at first she did not even look at him, any more than she would look at an oven that had finished its cycle and shut off.

'Tell me,' Klement said in his painfully uninflected way. 'Why . . . is it important, up and down?'

'What?'

He made a stiff gesture that might have indicated his own body, or the span of nascent ground to silvery sky. 'Is it because . . . this? Up and down?'

She found she could not bear to look at whatever was struggling behind his eyes, trapped, lost. 'I don't know what you're talking about.' She turned from him and started to walk again. Klement seemed rooted in place. After a moment, just as Renie was about to stop again, he lurched into motion, following where she had walked as though trying to touch the same footfalls. She shook her head. Perhaps he was so damaged that no part of his earlier self remained, but even if it were so, that still did not make him pleasant company.

So what was this place? Jongleur had said it was not part of the network, but how could that be? It wasn't magic. There had to be an explanation.

Something was murmuring wetly a short distance away. Renie hiked up a translucent rise, noting with interest how much it changed things simply to be able to move out of the strictly horizontal, and saw a shimmering line that looked less substantial than what lay on either side of it.

A river, she thought, then: *Could it be* the *river?*

She waited until she felt sure Klement had seen her, then descended to the river's bank. She had a direction now – upstream, whatever that might mean – and was determined to follow it. She knew !Xabbu would do the same if he was ahead of her, which meant their chances of finding each other would now be improved substantially. The thought lightened her heart.

When nothing makes sense, she thought, *at least there are people you love, people you need.*

But if this senseless world was something the Other had invented, then what did that really mean? A construction within the network, somehow, but not *of* the network? And why should it mimic reality – why should there be hills and a sky, as in the Patchwork Land, and here even a river? Had the operating system been working with some dim notion that humans needed a human place to be? But why did the operating system need humans at all?

The river valley, in its tenuous way, had begun to resemble a real valley in a real world, with grass and stones and even a few stands of trees. Even the sky, which for days had been as blank as an undeveloped level in a VR system, had begun to take on depth, although it was still murky and the light diffuse, as though this entire ghost world were built inside a giant pearl.

What if !Xabbu's not ahead of me? she suddenly thought. *What if he's lost in the gray – he and Sam didn't have the lighter, after all. I should stop, wait for a while. But what if they're ahead?* She considered building a sign out of sticks or some of the glass-clear reeds growing at the river's edge, but knew that if they were to follow along behind her walking even a little way up the slope, they might miss a sign constructed from this environment entirely – it would be like trying to see melting ice in a glass of water. She should wait until the things around her had more substance. Then she could build a sign out of sticks, write anything she wanted – *Help! I'm Being Held Prisoner By My Own Frustration!* Or maybe even, *Wanted, More Reality.*

She sat down on what had once been – or someday would be – a log, giving Klement a chance to catch up again. A copse of phantom trees swayed around her in an unfelt wind, but made no noise, not even the merest whisper of leaves brushing leaves.

After what seemed like a quarter of an hour, Klement had not appeared.

Reluctantly, Renie struggled up the bank to the top, looking back across the rolling land she had just crossed, but there was no sign of him and little chance he could be hidden in the monochrome expanse. She cursed bitterly – not because she feared for him or missed his company, but because she had taken a sort of responsibility for him, then had allowed carelessness to undercut her yet again. After waiting almost as long atop the bank as she had waited below, she trudged back down to the stand of trees.

I have to mark the spot, she decided. *Even if I don't go look for him, I have to at least let !Xabbu and the others know I've come this way.* But there remained the problem of how to do it. As she thought, she distractedly

pulled at the flimsy garments she had made for herself –
the more real the landscape, the more vulnerably under-
dressed she felt – and suddenly realized what she would
use to advertise her presence.

She was tying the strip of pale cloth on a thin branch
that protruded far beyond its shadowy neighbors, thinking that if she had to do this many more times she would
be naked again in short order, when something moved in
the branches just beside her head. She leaped back in
surprise.

It was a bird . . . or at least something birdlike, smaller
than her clenched fist. It seemed only slightly more real
than the landscape, with a tenuous shape and colors as
evanescent as a scatter of broken glass. She watched it
move down the branch toward her, then cock its head –
a hint of an eye, the blurry suggestion of a beak. For a
moment its familiar movements almost made her feel as
though things might make sense again, then the bird
dipped its head and said, '*Didn't think.*'

Renie gasped and took a few backward steps. This was
a crazy place, she told herself: anything was possible,
therefore nothing should be surprising. 'Did you say something?' she asked.

The bird changed its position again and piped, '*Didn't
think I would.*' An instant later it sprang into the air in
a tiny explosion of rainbow light, then flew off across
the river.

Renie had only a moment to decide. She looked at the
wisp of white cloth bobbing on the branch, then back
down the valley, a world of glass frozen in eternal twilight.
She ran in pursuit of the bird, a speck now against the
inconstant sky.

She found a shallow place and splashed across the river.

As she reached the farther bank she noticed that the light had shifted in a subtle way. The environment had suddenly grown quite solid, as though she had passed through some kind of barrier that held the pressure of reality firmly in place, but that was the least of the distractions. The new world around her was so strange that she could scarcely keep the flitting bird in view.

Rolling hills and meadows had given way to a landscape of folds and peaks, as though some great upheaval had shoved the substance of the earth together into gigantic wrinkles. The terrain was rough and rocky, the vegetation reduced to tangles of wind-twisted pines and rugged shrubbery cloaked in mist. The burgeoning sunshine was lost now behind thick overcast, so that even though the world had grown more substantial, it was not a great deal more colorful.

She paused at the top of a rise, panting, watching the bird's flight. Her quarry had grown more solid, too, although at this distance she could make out little of its color. It alighted on a twisted pine branch hundreds of meters below her down the hillside. Its voice floated up, saying *. . . I would . . . I would . . .* softly and regretfully as a tired child.

The track down between two ragged outcroppings was steep, but Renie had run too hard and too long to turn back. This was the first voice other than her friends' that she had heard since the mountain had disappeared, the first new living thing that she had encountered.

As she made her way down the hill the bird sat placidly on the branch as though waiting for her. The mists eddied in a slow but surprisingly chill breeze – she was discovering that not all aspects of returning reality were equally welcome – and she thought she could detect hidden forms built into the curves of land, odd, almost humanoid shapes like vast bodies underneath the soil. It was hard to tell in thin light and mist, but it reminded her uncomfortably of the monstrous figure of the Other that had greeted them on the mountaintop. She shivered and brought her attention firmly back to the rocky soil beneath her feet.

The bird tipped its head to watch her awkward approach. It had color and shape now, a bundle of reddish-brown feathers with a bright black eye, but there was still something unusual about it, something not quite complete.

'*Didn't think I would ever get there,*' the bird said suddenly.

'Get where?' Renie asked. 'Who are you? What is this place?'

'*We walked for a long time,*' the bird chirped sadly. '*Didn't think I would ever . . .*' It suddenly stood and fluttered its wings as if about to fly. Renie's heart sank, but the bird merely settled back on the branch. '*Didn't think I would ever get there,*' it observed again. '*Mama said it would take a while. We walked for a long time.*'

'Walked where? Can you talk to me? Hello?' Renie took a slow step closer and lowered her voice. 'I don't mean you any harm. Please talk to me.'

The bird looked at her again, then suddenly leaped from the branch and flashed away down the hillside. '*Didn't think I would . . . !*' it called shrilly before it disappeared into the mist.

'Jesus Mercy!' Renie sank down onto the stony ground, close to tears. She had traded a place beside the ghost-river for nothing except an exhausting run and a cold, foggy hillside; she would need a long rest before she could manage the climb back up. 'Jesus Mercy.'

It was only when her chin bumped against her chest and she jerked her head upright that she realized she had fallen asleep – whether for seconds or minutes, she could not tell, but the misty landscape seemed distinctly darker now, the shadows deeper in the folds of the hillside, sky shaded from pearl to a stormy gray. Renie staggered to her feet, keenly aware of the chilly winds ranging the slope and of her own skimpy clothing. She shivered, cursing quietly but miserably at the thought of spending a night in the open. She and her companions had been spoiled by the room-temperature ambience of the unfinished land.

She clambered a short way back up the hill, then stood to have a look around before the light began to fail. The fog that clung to the ground had mounted higher. Her friends could have passed only a stone's throw away while she slept without noticing her.

When she turned her head, she thought she could hear the river not too far away, invisible in some fold of the hill. She began to move sideways along the hillside toward the sound, leaning into the angle of the slope as her feet searched for solid earth. She could at least be grateful, since she had no shoes, that the hill was more soft dirt than sharp stones.

The river remained elusive. In fact, she couldn't see anything that looked like the low, rolling country she had just left.

Lost. And it's getting dark fast.

She had paused to catch her breath on a shelf of rock when she heard the strange sound. The wind had died, but a thin howl still skirled along the hilltop above her, a kind of drawn-out bubbling whistle. The skin at the back of Renie's neck tightened. When a second wailing noise arose from a spot ahead of her and distinctly farther down the slope, her unease curdled into fear. The first voice seemed to hear it and reply, keening and gobbling like some sort of underwater hyena, and Renie's heart stuttered in her chest.

There was no time to analyze – she knew only that she did not want to be caught between whatever these two things were. She turned and scrambled back across the hillside, missing footholds in the diminishing light so that twice she came very close to a long and perhaps mortal fall.

Just move, keep moving . . . She had a strange and inexplicable certainty that whatever entities moaned along the slopes above and behind her were not just making noise for its own sake, but were hunting for . . . something. For Renie herself, if she was extremely unlucky. Or perhaps for anything warm that moved, which wasn't a lot better.

The chill wind numbed her skin, enabling her to ignore the countless scratches and bumps of her awkward clamber, but she could feel the cold sucking the strength out of her as well and knew she could not keep up such a pace for long. The cry of the thing on the hilltop seemed farther away now, but the answering moan was at least as loud as before if not louder; Renie chanced a look back and then wished she hadn't. Something pale was moving along the hillside as though following her tracks.

Barely visible through the murk, it flapped and billowed like a man in a bedsheet, but seemed larger than that and much more terrifyingly alien. Unstable shadows moved across its ghostly surface – a horrible suggestion of a face, swimming in and out of focus. As she stared, transfixed, a dark uneven hole opened in the middle of the features to emit the mournful, bubbling cry. As the thing on top of the hill responded, farther away but not by any means far enough for her to head upslope, Renie bolted forward along the hillside, sacrificing caution for speed. The sound of the pursuers filled her with icy dread. Anything, even tumbling to her death down the hill, would be better than being caught by such pale, formless things.

She nearly got her wish when she plunged her foot through a mat of fallen branches that she thought was solid ground. She lost her balance, swung her arms for a moment, then fell and began to roll. Only sheer luck saved her – a tree, bent almost double by years of wind and gnarled as an old man's hand, stood right in her path. As she freed herself from the tangling branches, scratched bloody in a dozen places, another throbbing cry floated up, but it sounded more distant now.

A moment's fierce joy at the idea that she had rolled so far down was suddenly dashed when she realized that this noise came from below her – a third hunter. In confirmation, two more calls echoed from the slope above her head, rising in pitch as though they sensed the end of their run, their quarry's failing strength.

Renie crouched, gasping shallowly, full of useless, terrified thoughts. They had surrounded her – perhaps from pure brute instinct, perhaps because they had planned to do so from the start. She was caught between them now: already she thought she could see the nearest, a wan, deathly shape only a little thicker than the mist, bobbing leglessly along the slope like a jellyfish in an ocean current, moving slowly but inexorably toward her. Her heart was thumping like a high-speed rhythm track.

She realized she was clutching at the lighter and pulled it out of her thin garment. It was useless, but even so she was desperate to hear a voice, any voice. She suddenly couldn't imagine what danger she had thought so great that she had avoided using it before.

'Hello, M-martine, a-a-anyone?' Fear was taking her breath; she could barely speak. 'Is someone listening? Please, answer me?' Silence – even the spectral searchers had fallen still. As she tried the command sequence again, all Renie could see was swirling mist, gray tree-shadows.

'Martine? I heard you before – can you hear me now?'

The voice that came back was diminished but surprisingly clear, so much so that Renie felt a moment of pointless hope, as though her friends might only be a few meters distant, might suddenly come rushing out of the fog to rescue her. '*Renie? Is that you? Renie? We hear you. Talk to us.*'

'Jesus Mercy,' Renie said quietly. 'It's you, Martine.' She struggled for composure – it was almost certain her friends could do nothing for her now. She must tell them what she could, tell them what she had seen and experienced. 'We never left the mountain,' she began. 'We woke up and you were gone. We're in what must be the White Ocean the others talked about. But I've lost !Xabbu and Sam and now I'm lost, too.'

'. . . *Can't understand you very well,*' Martine replied. '*Where are you exactly?*'

She was nowhere. She was in the realms of terror. She had to force herself to remember what she had thought about so long. 'I think . . . oh, God, I think we're in the heart of the system.' The tears started again. 'But I'm in trouble – bad trouble . . . !'

Something crackled in the branches behind her. Renie leaped in startled terror and dropped the lighter.

Second:

GHOST SONGS

'Boys and girls come out to play,
The moon is shining as bright as day.
Leave your supper and leave your sleep,
And join your playfellows in the street.'
                                    — Traditional

CHAPTER 11

Yours Very Sincerely

NETFEED/NEWS: Club Patrons Get Mother Goosed
(visual: advertisement for Limousine)
VO: Visitors to the virtual adults-only club Limousine got a surprise when service was interrupted for almost an hour by what some users suggest was a disguised or artificial voice reciting nursery rhymes.
(visual: anonymated Limousine customer)
CUSTOMER: 'Yeah, it sounds funny, but really it was pretty grue-some. I mean, it didn't sound . . . normal.'
VO: Happy Juggler, the corporation that owns Limousine and several other online clubs, call it 'just the most recent in a series of irritat-ing pranks.'
(visual: Jean-Pierre Michaux, HJN Corporation spokesperson)
MICHAUX: 'It prevented us delivering service in our most productive time slots, and also, let's face it, half our users are fathers and even some mothers who've finally put the kids to bed and are hoping for a little diversion and relaxation. Nobody in that situation wants to have to sit and listen to more damn nursery rhymes.'

JEREMIAH stacked the last vacuum bag and stood survey-ing his handiwork. It wasn't quite a kitchen – who was he fooling, it was nothing like a kitchen – but it would have to do. Piles of cans, boxes, and bags of rations, several plastic jugs of water, the single working portable halogen ring he'd salvaged from one of the upstairs common rooms, a kettle, and about three weeks' supply – if they were stingy with it – of perhaps the most precious commodity of all, instant coffee. Trapped in the underground base without any of the real stuff, he had long since taught himself to drink the self-heating swill without gagging, and had even begun to look forward to his morning cup. Now he was even more anxious to preserve a few last rituals of normality.

He squinted at his makeshift larder, which filled most of an upright metal cabinet. All in all, it would serve. And if they were to be trapped down in this lowest level so long the coffee ran out, well, then perhaps the thugs upstairs wouldn't seem such a bad alternative.

He couldn't even make himself smile. He checked the batteries in his flashlight, firmed up the corners of one of his stacks, and stood.

Good Lord, I am a walking stereotype. Under siege, fighting for our lives, and who promptly takes over the kitchen as mother-elect?

He made his way around the circular walkway to the control consoles where Del Ray sat frowning at the screen like a literary critic forced to review cheap genre fiction. Long Joseph lurked sullenly behind him, two squeeze bottles of wine sitting on the table. Jeremiah felt a moment of actual pity for the man. If Jeremiah himself was feeling miserable about having to ration several weeks' worth of coffee, imagine how Joseph must feel about having to make a day's worth or less of his usual poison last for God alone knew how long?

'How is it going?' he asked.

Del Ray shrugged. 'I can't get the security monitors to work. They should, but they don't. I warned you, this is not really my area of expertise. How's your end?'

'As good as it's going to get.' Jeremiah pulled out one of the swivel chairs and sat down. 'I wish we'd had that old fellow Singh get those cameras all running when we had the chance. But who knew we'd need them?'

'Maybe your friend Sellars will call back,' said Del Ray, but he didn't sound like he believed it. He pushed one of the buttons on the console, then gave it a frustrated whack. 'Maybe he can do something about this disaster.'

'My Renie was here, she would have that wired up before you can jump and turn around,' Long Joseph said suddenly. 'She know all that stuff. Has a degree from the university and all.'

Del Ray glowered, but it quirked unexpectedly into a tiny smile. 'Yes, she would. And she'd get a lot of pleasure cleaning up the mess I've made with it and telling me about it.'

'She would. She is one smart girl. Ought to be, with all that money for her education.'

Del Ray's smile widened a bit as he met Jeremiah's gaze. *Education she paid for herself, if I remember correctly,* Jeremiah thought. He remembered Renie talking about her years of bondage to the university dining hall.

'Hang on a moment,' he said, turning to Joseph. 'Did I hear correctly? Were you bragging about Renie?'

'What do you mean, bragging?' Joseph asked suspiciously.

'I mean, acting like you're actually proud of her?'

The older man scowled. 'Proud of her "Course I am proud of her. She is a smart girl, like her mama was.'

Jeremiah almost shook his head in wonderment. He wondered if the man had ever said anything like that when Renie was around to hear it, instead of waiting until she was encased in plasmodal gel in the depths of a fibramic casket. Somehow he doubted it.

'Damn.' Del Ray pushed his chair back from the console. 'I give up. I can't fix it. This waiting is making me crazy. I thought that at least if we could see what they're doing up there, instead of just sitting here . . .'

'You don't want all those cameras,' Joseph growled. 'That will do no good against bad men like those. I told you, we should be finding guns to shoot those piglockers with.'

Jeremiah grunted in exasperation. 'There *aren't* any guns. You know that already. Nobody's going to decommission a military base and leave the guns lying around.'

Joseph hooked a thumb toward Del Ray, who was slumped in his chair, staring up at the ceiling of the vast underground chamber as though trying to do the work of the inactive monitors by himself. '*He* have a gun. I told you, you should give that gun to me. You didn't see him, waving it around, all in a fright, hand so sweaty I thought he might shoot my head off just by accident.'

'Not this again,' Jeremiah moaned.

'I'm just telling you! I don't think this mother's boy ever fired a gun at all! I was in the Defense Force, you know.'

'Oh, yes,' said Del Ray, eyes still closed, 'I'm sure you shot a lot of other people's chickens after you and your mates had downed a few.' He rubbed at his face. 'Even if it wasn't hand-coded for me, you'd be the *last* person I'd . . .'

The sudden silence was strange. Jeremiah was just about to ask Del Ray if he was all right when the young man abruptly sat upright in his chair, eyes wide.

'Oh my God,' he said. 'Oh my God!'

'What is it?' Jeremiah asked.

'The gun!' Del Ray grabbed at his hair as though he would pull it from his scalp. 'The gun! It's in my jacket pocket!'

'So?'

'I left it upstairs! When I was stacking water bottles yesterday. I was hot. I took the damn thing off, then when I got downstairs you asked me about the cameras, and . . . shit!' He stood up, his hand still on his head as though he was afraid it might otherwise tumble from his shoulders.

'See . . . ?' Joseph began, unable to disguise his pleased tone, but Jeremiah rounded on him.

'Don't say anything.' He turned back to Del Ray. 'Where is it? The kitchen?'

Del Ray nodded miserably.

'Do we really need it?' Jeremiah looked around. 'I mean, once they are down here, is it any real use to us?'

'Is it any real use?' Del Ray stared at him. 'What if they get in here? Are we going to throw bags of flour at them? We need every advantage we have. I have to go get it.'

'You can't. We closed off the elevator – shut those armored security doors like Sellars told us to do. There's no other way up. And we are not going to take the chance of opening them again.'

Del Ray stood looking at the floor for a moment, then straightened, some of the panic suddenly gone from his face. 'Hold on. I don't think I left it in the kitchen after all. I think I just left it outside the elevator on the top floor of our part of the base. I stored most of the water bottles and the extra generator up there, and I think that's where I took my jacket off.'

'I will get it,' said Long Joseph brightly, but both men turned on him.

'Shut up.'

'Yes, shut up, Joseph.'

Del Ray started off toward the stairs. 'It's too bad we

had to seal off the elevator at both ends – it would be nice if we could keep it to use just down here for dragging stuff up and down.'

'Too noisy,' Jeremiah called after him. 'If we are lucky, they won't even know there are more rooms down here.' He suddenly realized how loud his voice was.

Too noisy, you say, and listen to you! What if they're up there with stetho-scopes or something, listening to the floor, looking for us . . .

The idea of the faceless mercenaries – Jeremiah alone of the three had not seen them – crawling along the floor, tapping on the concrete like woodpeckers, was deeply disturbing.

We don't even know they're inside, he told himself. Maybe they can't get through that big front door, like a bank's vault. It took Renie and her hacker friends at least this long to get it open.

Still, the vision would not go away. He looked at Joseph, who was sucking a measured amount of Mountain Rose with a face full of wounded dignity, and decided he had better find something with which to keep himself occupied.

Del Ray had levered open the console and its array of security monitors, revealing a mare's nest of cables that looked like something from an ancient telephone switchboard. Jeremiah sat in the chair the younger man had vacated and meditatively flicked switches. The console had power – all the monitor screens had little red lights glowing beneath them – but the screens themselves were blackly empty.

Joseph was right. If Renie was here she'd have this running in a few minutes.

He tugged at the bundle of cables. All but a few were connected. He took one of those that wasn't and tried it in a few of the open slots, but nothing changed. A second provided nothing different, but as he pulled up the third another came tangled with it, and as it brushed something in the board, the screens momentarily hiccuped with light, then went black again.

Excited, Jeremiah pulled the end of the trailing cable free and began to touch it to the open connections in succession. Suddenly the monitors jumped into life again. Jeremiah attached the cable, warm with pride. Now they could see outside their bunker. They were no longer forced to wait blindly.

Before he could tell Long Joseph of his triumph, something caught Jeremiah's attention. One of the monitors displayed a rectangle of trees and scrub brush, framed by blackness. Puzzled, he stared at it for long moments before he realized what he was seeing.

It was the base's massive front gate, seen from a camera just inside. The gate was open.

Three loud cracks came from somewhere above Jeremiah's head. Long Joseph leaped up, swearing, so startled that he dropped his squeeze bottle of wine to the floor. Jeremiah's skin turned cold.

'Del Ray!' he shouted. 'Del Ray, is that you?'

For once Joseph kept his mouth shut as they both listened. Nothing came to them but the echo of Jeremiah's own voice.

'Is he shooting that gun?' asked Joseph in a hoarse, nervous whisper. 'Or someone shooting at him?'

Jeremiah felt as though his own cry had emptied all the air from his chest: he could only shake his head. For a moment he stood, frightened and confused, trying to decide whether they should shut off the lights and hide. He turned to the console and tried to make sense of the almost monochrome images, seeing what he thought were flickers of movement here or there, but never able to make out anything definitive.

Which one shows upstairs, where Del Ray went?

He recognized the elevator bay at last – not by the elevator itself, which was only a dark shadow along the wall, but because of the old sign posted beside it, a stern warning about the weight the elevator could handle that he had seen so many times he sometimes found himself muttering it under his breath.

He only had time to think, for the very first time in all the weeks he had been immured in the underground base, *Seems funny that there is no freight elevator for a place with this much equipment*, then he saw the dim outline of a pair of legs stretched on the floor, disappearing off-screen. It was too dark to be absolutely sure, but Jeremiah knew with an indisputable horror whose legs and feet those were, lying so still beside the darkness of the elevator door.

DEAR *Mr Ramsey,*

The first time you walked into my house, I thought you were a very nice man. I know it may not have seemed that way, that I may have seemed suspicious. Just listening to me without letting your thoughts show on your face was a kind thing to do, because I am sure you must have thought I was a crazy old woman.

When you read what I have to tell you now, you will be very certain that you were right. I don't mind. When I started to get old, I used to feel bad because men didn't look at me the same way any more, that I wasn't a young girl. I was never pretty, but I was young once, and men do look. When it stopped I felt a little bad, but I thought at least they will take me seriously now. Then when all the things happened to me, the headaches and the problems and my ideas about this Tandagore disease, people stopped even looking at me like I had a brain in my head. But you treated me like a real person. You are a nice man, I was right about you.

I am doing something that is hard to explain and if I am wrong I will wind up in a jail somewhere. If I am right, I will probably be killed. It is a long distance to go to prove a point, I bet you are saying.

But this letter is to tell you that if I am crazy, it doesn't feel like it to me, and that I am doing this with the knowledge that it doesn't seem to make sense. But if you heard the voices I hear in my head, or that I used to hear, you would do what I am doing too. I know you would, because I can tell what kind of man you are.

Before I tell you the other things, that reminds me of something I wanted to say to you. I feel very light now, as if I have taken off a heavy coat and am walking through the snow. Later I may freeze, but for now I am just happy to have that heavy weight off my back. The weight is pretending, you see, and instead I am telling the truth. So I will tell you something that I would never have said to you otherwise. You should get married. You are a good man who works too hard, always in your office, never at your home. I know you will say, what is this crazy old Polish-Russian lady talking about, but you need to find someone to share your life with. I don't even know if you like men or women, and you know what? It doesn't matter to me. But find someone to live with you, that you want to go home for. If you can, have children. Somehow children make sense out of life.

Now I will tell you the rest, about the voices and about Obolos Corporation and Felix Jongleur. Then even if you still think I am crazy, you will understand why I am doing what I am doing. I am telling you just so that someone knows it.

Do you know, if my baby had lived, he would have been just about your age? I think about things like that too much.

And when I have finished explaining there will only be one more thing for you to do. I think there is something called a power of attorney? And since you are an attorney, you would know about this. If I disappear, then please will you sell my things? Mostly only small things and not worth the trouble, but there is Obolos stock and my house. I have no living relatives and that stock now feels to me like something unclean – 'treyf,' as my mother would have said. Will you sell them both, please, and give the money to the children's hospital in Toronto?

I am sitting here at this desk, looking at this screen, and it is very hard to find a place to begin to explain. The voices had not come to me when you and I first met. If they are just something in my own head, something to do with the headache, then I will have made a fool of myself. But you know what? I don't care. There are children hurting, both those with the terrible coma disease and I think maybe others too – the voices who speak to me. It is for the children I must risk it. If I am wrong it is only one more old woman locked away. If I am right, no one will believe me, not even you, but at least I will have tried to do something.

The voices, and now the black tower. It is like a castle from one of my mother's stories. It frightens me very much. But I will go there and I will get inside and I will try to find the truth . . .

'. . . And it ends, 'Yours very sincerely, Olga Pirofsky,' Ramsey finished.

Kaylene Sorensen broke the silence. 'That poor woman!'

'That poor woman, indeed.' Sellars leaned forward, eyes half shut. He had rolled his wheelchair back into the most shadowed corner of the room, but even the small amount of sunlight arrowing in beneath the drapes seemed to make him uncomfortable. 'She's brave, though. She is walking into the lion's den.'

'You don't think they'll really kill her, do you?' Ramsey's hands were still shaking; Olga's letter had disturbed him deeply. 'That wouldn't be very smart of them. Surely if they catch her trespassing on J Corporation property they'll just toss her out, maybe have her arrested?'

Sellars shook his head sadly. 'If Jongleur and his associates had nothing to hide, that would certainly be the case. But do you think your client will go quietly if they do catch her? Or will she make loud claims that will attract more attention than a trespasser usually gets?' He sighed. 'Here is another question. What can she tell them about you?'

'What?' Ramsey was caught unprepared. 'I don't get you.'

'If this mess is everything he claims it is,' Major Sorensen interjected, 'then Sellars is right – they'll question her. And if they're that ugly, they *will* get information. You don't want to think about that part too much, but trust me – you saw the kind of boys General Yacoubian was running around with. What does she know about you, Ramsey – about . . . all this?'

Catur Ramsey suddenly noticed that his heart was

racing. He took a step backward and sank into one of the shiny metal chairs. The cheap servo-motors tried to adjust the seat to fit him, but gave up about halfway through the process. 'Christ.'

'What I don't get, though,' Sorensen continued, 'is all this crap about "voices." Is it like you talking to my daughter and to me, Sellars? Is someone tricking her? Or is she just . . . well, you know . . . nuts?'

'I don't know,' the old man said. He looked as troubled as Ramsey felt. 'But I suspect it is something stranger and more complicated than either.'

'Good Lord, we have to stop her!' Ramsey shoved himself to the edge of the chair, prompting a whine of indignation from the internal mechanism. 'We can't just let her walk into that, whether she's a risk to me or not. I didn't have a chance to tell her half the things I'd found out. I don't know about these voices either, but somehow she's stumbled into this thing – completely separate from you, Sellars, all on her own – and she still thinks she might be imagining it.' He thought about it and slumped back. 'God, the poor woman.'

'Did you respond to what she sent you?' Major Sorensen asked.

'Of course I did! I sent her back a message to call me immediately – not to go one step without talking to me first.' He saw the look on the military man's face and felt his stomach go sour. It took a couple of seconds for him to understand why. 'Shit. I gave her the number for this motel.'

To his credit, Sorensen did no more than shake his head once in irritation before standing up. 'Right. First thing, we move. Kaylene, why don't you round up the kids and I'll start throwing stuff in the car. Sellars, we're going to have to return the chair, and we may not be able to rent another. I'm afraid you're going back in the wheel-well when we travel, too. The military may not be actively searching for us right now, especially if we really were a private matter of Yacoubian's, but you're still way too easily noticed and remembered.'

'Where are we going, Mike?' Kaylene Sorensen, a veteran military spouse, was already tossing things into bags. 'Can't we just go home? We can find Mr Sellars someplace to hide, can't we? Maybe he could stay with Mr Ramsey for a while. Christabel has to get back to school.'

Even Catur Ramsey could see past her husband's carefully maintained expression to the misery in his eyes. 'I don't think we're going back there for a while, honey. And at the moment, I don't have any idea where we're heading – just out of here.'

'I need to call Olga again before we leave,' Ramsey said. 'If there's any chance of keeping her from trying to get into that place, I owe it to her.'

'On the contrary,' Sellars said abruptly. He had been sitting very still, eyes almost closed, like a lizard sunning on a rock. Now he lifted his head to show his strange yellow gaze. 'On the contrary, we must not stop her. And I also know where we must go – some of us, anyway.'

'What are you talking about?' Sorensen demanded.

'I told you that there have been many odd things going on with the Grail Brotherhood in the last few days. I have been watching carefully, trying to make some sense of the events that are sealed away from me within the network, and have seen evidence of uncertainty within the Brotherhood's various holdings and private domains. Jongleur's little kingdom is no different. There are definite suggestions of a tremor in the routines, of confusion at the top.'

'So?' Ramsey was impatient.

'So instead of trying to keep your Ms Pirofsky away from the J Corporation, I think we should instead help her to get *in*, Mr Ramsey. I have been forced to use innocents to help me often enough in this grim task – the Sorensens can testify to that. Olga Pirofsky is at least already determined to take the risk. We will see what we can do to help, and to protect her while she is in there.'

'That's . . . that's crazy.' Ramsey got up so quickly he almost knocked over the coffee tray. 'She doesn't deserve that – she doesn't know what she's getting into!'

For a moment there was a kind of flash in the straw-colored eyes, a sudden glimpse of the aerial predator Sellars had once been. 'Nobody deserves this, Mr Ramsey. But others have dealt the cards – we have no choice but to play the hand.' He turned to the Sorensens, who had both stopped to watch, the major with a certain reluctant professional interest, his wife with growing discomfort. 'I cannot compel you two, but I know where I am going, and I rather suspect that when he thinks it through, where Mr Ramsey is going as well.'

'And that is . . . ?'

'Mike, don't even talk to him,' Kaylene Sorensen said. 'I don't want to hear this. It's crazy . . . !'

'To New Orleans, of course,' said Sellars. 'To the very lair of the Beast. Our plight is so desperate that in retrospect it now seems an obvious endgame move. I wish I had thought of it earlier.'

THEY were moving again. Christabel wasn't sure why, but that never mattered much when things like this were happening. She wondered if when she was older people would tell her things, explain things, or if being grown-up she would just *know*.

What almost seemed like the saddest thing of all, sadder even than leaving the new motel just when she had figured out where the candy bar machine was, was that Mister Sellars was going to have to go back into the place in the back of the van where Daddy normally kept the spare tire. It seemed such an awful place, so tiny.

The old man was sitting in the doorway of the van, waiting for her father to finish some other things and help him in, when Christabel found him.

'It's all right, little Christabel,' he said when she told him her worries. 'I don't mind, really. I don't use my body for much these days, anyway. As long as my mind is free – what is it Hamlet says? "Were I bounded in a nutshell, still could I count myself a king of infinite space . . ." – something like that.' For a moment he looked very sad. If he was supposed to be making her feel better, Christabel thought, he wasn't doing a very good job.

'Mommy said you have wires inside you,' she said at last. 'Is that true?'

Sellars laughed quietly. 'I suppose I do, my young friend.'

'Do they hurt?'

'No. I have pain, but it's more to do with my burns, with . . . with other old injuries. And most of the wires aren't really wires anymore. I've had lots of help changing things inside me. There are plenty of gearmakers hungry for a challenge, more than a few out-of-work nano-engineers in need of a few extra credits.'

Christabel wasn't at all sure what he was talking about. 'Nano-engineers' made her think of Ophelia Weiner's Nanoo dress. The thought of a lot of train-drivers in party dresses that changed color and shape didn't explain anything, so she let it slide away, another thing a kid just worked around. 'You mean you had wires, but you don't anymore?'

'Wires are sort of old-fashioned, especially when there are so many other ways to transmit information. I'm confusing you, aren't I? Well, do you remember when I had you bring me soap to eat?'

She nodded, pleased to be back on familiar ground.

'I sometimes have to eat funny things like that, because my body is making something new for me, or repairing something that's not working very well. I eat little bits of polymer sometimes, too – plastic, you'd call it. Or I have to get more metal. Sometimes there are pills that will help, but usually they don't have enough of what I need. I used to have to eat a couple of copper pennies a week, but that's past now.' He nodded at her and smiled. 'It doesn't matter, Christabel. I have funny insides, but I'm still me. I don't mind what's in *your* insides – can you still be my friend, too?'

She nodded her head rapidly. She hadn't meant anything bad at all, certainly not that she wouldn't be his friend. Her mother's passing remark had been worrying her all day – the thought of sharp wires sticking in Mister Sellars' insides had almost made her cry.

'Oh, just a moment, Christabel,' Sellars told her, then waved for Mister Ramsey to come over.

Christabel could tell that the dark-skinned man was not happy because he didn't smile at her, and even though she had only known him a while, she could tell he was the kind of man who almost always smiled at kids. 'I feel terrible,' he told Mister Sellars. 'I've been a real idiot. It's just still so hard to take all this stuff seriously! Having to worry about being traced – it's like some bad netflick.'

'No one blames you,' Sellars told him gently. 'But I wanted to ask you something before I descend into my traveling *sanctum sanctorum*. Have you heard anything back from Olga Pirofsky since we spoke this morning?'

'No. Nothing.'

'May I make a suggestion? If you were her, doing something as dangerous and questionable as she is doing, and your attorney sent you a message that said, "Don't do anything until you talk to me," what would you assume?'

She could see Ramsey trying hard to think, like Christabel herself when she hadn't been listening to the teacher but got asked a question anyway. 'I don't know. I guess that my attorney was going to try to talk me out of this crazy thing.'

'Exactly. And if you were her, would you bother to reply?'

Now, even though Mister Sellars was talking in his usual quiet, hooty voice, Mister Ramsey looked like Christabel when the teacher yelled at her. 'No. No, I guess wouldn't. Not if I'd already made up my mind.'

'I think that's probably the case. If I may make a suggestion, you might send her another message saying something along the lines of, 'I know what you're doing and believe it or not I think you're right and I want to help you get inside as safely as possible. Please get in touch with me.'

'Right. Right.' Ramsey turned and walked away fast, back toward his motel room.

'Well, little Christabel,' said Mister Sellars, 'I see your father coming to help strap me into my pilot's seat. The best captains always lead from behind, you know. Or even beneath.' He laughed, but Christabel thought he was less happy than she had almost ever seen him. 'I'll be out before you know it. Have a good trip and I'll see you soon.'

The boy was already in the car. Christabel was too confused and worried by everything to pay very much attention.

'What your problem, _mu'chita?_' he asked.

She just ignored him, trying to understand why Mister Sellars had seemed so different than usual – so dark underneath the smile, so quiet and tired.

'Hey, I'm talking to you, weenit!'

'I know,' she said. 'I'm thinking. Talk to yourself.'

He called her names but she ignored him. She knew that if her mother had not been in and out of the car, shoving in bags and cases, he would probably have poked her or pinched her. She wouldn't have cared if he did. Mister Sellars was very sad. Something bad was happening – something even worse than the worst things she had worried about before her parents found out.

'Okay, okay, just tell me what you thinking about, okay?'

She looked up, surprised by the sound of the boy's voice. He didn't look angry, or at least that wasn't all she could see.

'Mister Sellars. I'm thinking about Mister Sellars,' she said.

'He one strange _viejo._'

'He's scared.'

'Yeah. Me, too.'

For a moment she didn't realize what she had heard. She had to look up to make sure it was the same mean-faced boy with the missing tooth. '_You're_ scared?'

He stared for a moment as though waiting for her to make fun of him. 'Not stupid, me. I heard some of what they been talking about. Army men trying to kill them, all that. That's all locked up, seen? The _azules_, the police and stuff, most times they don't go after people like your mama and papa, they go after kids like me, or maybe big crooks, whatever. And if your dad actually snuck _el viejo_ out of an army base, and brought his family along, even a little *gatita* like you – well, you *know* that's trouble major.' He looked out the car window. 'Think I'm going to get out of here soon.' He turned back to her suddenly. 'You tell anyone, I'll kill you. No dupping.'

A few days before, thinking about the little boy running away would have made Christabel happy enough to dance. Now it just made her even more lonely and frightened than she had been.

Something was very, very wrong, but Christabel had no idea what it was.

Long Joseph carried a huge, red-painted fire ax, and was creeping along the corridor with what he probably believed was the warlike stealth of his Zulu ancestors. Jeremiah Dako still hadn't found any weapon better than the table leg with which he had almost brained Joseph and Del Ray during their unexpected entrance, but he couldn't imagine many situations in which they were going to get a chance to hit anyone anyway.

Jeremiah had not much wanted to bring Joseph with him, but it would have been impossible to convince the man to stay with the equipment and their slumbering charges, Renie and !Xabbu, and since it would be hard to carry Del Ray back by himself, Jeremiah had made only a token argument. To Joseph Sulaweyo's credit, he was at least keeping his mouth shut for once.

Now the man stopped at an intersection of aisles and made a theatrically broad gesture, fingers to his lips, other hand pointing at the right-hand corridor. The silliness of it all – Jeremiah knew perfectly well where they were, and where Del Ray was lying so unmovingly – suddenly brought home to him their terrible danger.

There are men out there who want to kill us. Men with

guns and God knows what else. Maybe even the same men who beat Doctor Susan so that she died.

If he stopped to think about it any longer he knew his legs would collapse beneath him, but there was a flame of anger burning now, too. Jeremiah put a hand against Joseph's chest and, returning the older man's wide-eyed stare of outrage with the most purposeful look he could muster, slid past him to the turning of the corridor. He got down on his hands and knees and crawled forward until he could see Del Ray's feet, one of them only wearing a sock, the shoe lying half a meter away. It made Jeremiah feel quietly sick.

Go on, man. Nothing else to be done. Go on.

Certain that any moment someone was going to step out of the shadows – which would somehow be worse, he could not help thinking, than someone simply shooting him – Jeremiah crept toward Del Ray . . . or at least toward his legs . . .

Oh, my God, what if he has been shot in half by one of those machine guns?

He slid another few meters forward over industrial carpet so old and threadbare he could feel exposed patches of cold concrete pass beneath his belly, until at last he was close enough to reach out and touch Del Ray's unshod foot. It *felt* warm and alive, but that meant little – everything had happened only a few minutes earlier. Eyes closed, even more frightened now, he let his hand travel up the outside of Del Ray's leg until, to his great relief, he felt the bunched fabric of the man's shirt, then his arm, shoulder, and even the base of his chin. He was in one piece, anyway.

Jeremiah had just lifted up his hand to beckon Joseph forward when someone hissed in his ear. 'Where they shoot him? In the belly? Between the eyes?'

When Jeremiah's heart had slid back down from his mouth into its normal spot, he turned and glared. 'Just shut up! We have to get him out of here.'

'Tell you one problem,' Joseph whispered. 'There is a big pipe on his arm, over here.'

Jeremiah, feeling a little braver now that a minute had gone by out in the open and no one had put a bullet in his spine, rose until he could kneel beside Del Ray. He touched the young man's chest, which seemed to be moving, then found a living pulse at the base of his jaw. His relief suddenly turned sour when he brought back his hand and found it covered with something dark and sticky.

'Oh, Christ! He's bleeding from the head.'

'Then he is dead,' said Joseph, not unkindly. 'Nobody gets a shot in the head, then they go back to work on Monday.'

'Shut up and help me move him. We have to get him back where I can have a better look at him.'

Joseph had been right – there was indeed a long piece of heavy pipe, about the thickness of a wine bottle, lying across Del Ray's arm. They pushed it off, not without effort, and although Jeremiah flinched when it clanked to the floor, he also began to feel a little relief. Perhaps Del Ray hadn't been shot. Perhaps this thing had fallen on him, clubbing him down in the dark.

Jeremiah looked up and his heart threatened to stop again. A jackstraw clutter of the heavy iron pipes hung down from the ceiling above their heads, all at strange angles, most only connected now at one end, as though some huge hand had reached up and pulled them away from their moorings. The clutter of metal looked as though it might come down at any moment. He gestured urgently to Joseph and they began to drag Del Ray back toward the corridor.

At the last moment Jeremiah remembered the gun. He hesitated, fearful of spending another second out in the open, of letting Del Ray's wounds go untended any longer. What good would a single pistol and a few bullets do them? Joseph made impatient noises. Jeremiah hesitated, then turned and crept back, moving as quietly as he could beneath the Damoclean assortment of broken pipes. Del Ray's jacket was lying almost hidden in shadow. Jeremiah tugged it toward him, patted the pockets until he felt the telltale chunk of smooth, heavy metal, then sprinted away from the treacherous spot.

While Joseph checked the vital signs on the V-tanks, Jeremiah stretched Del Ray full length on a blanket laid out on a conference table in one of the side rooms. He could feel a distinct swelling on the left side of the young man's head, a bump underneath a long but seemingly shallow laceration. His fingers came away slick with blood. Jeremiah would have liked to believe that was the only injury, but much of Del Ray's shirt around the collar and behind his shoulders was dark and damp as well. He hoped it was only that the young man had been lying in the blood of his own head wound, but he could not be sure.

Might have been shot first, then grabbed at a loose pipe on his way down.

Satisfied that Del Ray was at least breathing, Jeremiah began to cut the shirt away with his pocketknife. Long Joseph came in from the main room and watched, his expression hard to read, but he stepped forward when Jeremiah asked, helping to turn Del Ray's wiry body over so that Jeremiah could investigate his back.

Jeremiah splashed water from a squeeze bottle on a ragged strip of shirt and began wiping away the blood, grateful that they still had the overhead fluorescents –

the idea of doing this by flashlight and perhaps missing a vital wound chilled him. He was relieved to find no evidence of another injury. He took a small bottle from the first-aid kit and splashed it on a comparatively clean piece of Del Ray's shirt, then began cleaning the head wound.

'What is that stuff you putting on there?' Joseph asked.

'Alcohol. Not the kind you can drink.'

'I know that,' said Joseph, disgusted.

Probably from experience, Jeremiah thought, but kept it to himself. The edge of the cut was ragged, but gentle probing with his fingers revealed no deep hole, nothing that might be an entrance wound. Feeling better than he had in the last hour, he made a pad of wet shirt and used one of the severed sleeves to tie it in place, then with Joseph's help turned Del Ray back over.

The younger man's groan was so pitiful that for a moment Jeremiah froze in horror, positive he had done something terribly wrong. Then Del Ray's eyes fluttered open. The pupils wandered for a moment, unfixed, confused by the bright bank of fluorescents.

'Is . . . is that you?' Del Ray said at last. He could have meant anyone, but Jeremiah was not going to split hairs.

'Yes, it's us. We brought you back safe. You seem to have been hit on the head. What happened?'

He groaned again, but this time it was more a sound of frustration than pain. 'I'm . . . I'm not sure. I was just coming back from the elevator when something up on the ceiling went *boom!*' He squinted and tried to turn away from the lights, but the pad kept his head from rolling. Jeremiah leaned forward to shade his eyes. 'I think . . . I think maybe they're using some kind of explosives up there. Trying to blast through to our part of the base.' He winced and slowly brought a hand up to his head, his

eyes widening slightly as he felt the bandages. 'What . . .
how bad is it?'

'Not bad,' Jeremiah said. 'A pipe fell down, I think. If
they set something off upstairs, that would make sense. I
heard loud noises, three of them, I think – *bang, bang, bang!*'

'What, so they are trying to bomb us out now?' Joseph
said. 'Foolish. They not going to get me out so easy. They
blow a hole, I come out of it and knock in some heads.'

Jeremiah rolled his eyes. 'He's right about one thing,
though,' he told Del Ray. 'I don't think they'll get through
that concrete or that heavy door on the elevator – not
right away, anyway.'

Del Ray murmured something, then tried to sit up.
Jeremiah leaned forward to restrain him but the younger
man would not be stopped. His skin had paled and he
was shaking, but he seemed otherwise almost normal.

'The question is,' Del Ray said at last, 'how long do we
have to hold them off? A week? We might be able to do
it. Forever? That's not going to work.'

'Not if you are going to get knocked out, walking into
pipes,' declared Joseph. 'I told you, you should let me go
and do that.'

Tired and irritated, Jeremiah could not resist. 'You
know, Del Ray, it's been a real pleasure to see you with
your shirt off. Joseph was right – you're a very handsome young man.'

'What?' Long Joseph Sulaweyo leaped up, almost spitting with indignation. 'What are you talking about? I
didn't say nothing like that! What are you talking about?'

Jeremiah was laughing too hard to push it any farther.
Even Del Ray managed a wincing smile as the older man
stomped off to the other room, presumably to drown the
insult to his manliness in a few swallows of his precious
wine.

'I shouldn't do it,' Jeremiah said when he was gone, but could not restrain a last quiet chuckle. 'He's not all bad, and we need to stick together. Help each other.'

'You helped me,' said Del Ray. 'Thanks.'

Jeremiah waved it off. 'It's nothing. But I was scared. I thought they'd broken in, shooting. They're still out there, though, and we're still safe in here – for the moment. Ah!' Reminded, he bent and picked up Del Ray's jacket off the floor. 'And we even have a gun.'

Del Ray took the heavy pistol out of his pocket and turned it over, looking at it as though it were some completely new object. 'Yes,' he said. 'One gun, but only two bullets.' He wiped a tiny trickle of blood off his ear and gave Jeremiah a mournful look. 'When they *do* manage to get in, that's not even enough to shoot ourselves.'

CHAPTER 12

The Boy in the Well

'LIKE school, this is,' said T4b miserably.

It had been a long time since Paul had been in school, but he knew what their Goggleboy companion meant.

They had been trapped in the bubble for what felt to
Paul like hours, perhaps half a day. In a different situation the bobbing journey atop the swell of the river would
have been fascinating: the current had pushed them past
a great deal of Kunohara's jungle, past huge man-grove
trees with roots sunk deep into the water, monstrously
tangled edifices of bark proportionately large as entire
cities. Strange fish had nosed them, leviathans up from
the river mud to investigate, but fortunately none had
decided the strange bubble was worth trying to swallow.
Birds with wingspans like jumbo jets and colored like an
explosion in God's own fireworks factory, a rat the size
of a warehouse, water beetles big as motorboats – they
had floated past all kinds of wonders. But the four of
them were trapped in a sphere scarcely large enough to
allow them all to sit with their legs stretched out, and
they were bored, stiff, and miserable.

Worse, Renie's unfinished message seemed to hang in
the sealed air of the bubble like a curl of poisonous gas.
She was in trouble somewhere and her friends could do
nothing.

With nothing to do but rest and talk, they had puzzled
and argued for hours, but Paul thought they were no
closer to solving any of the riddles that haunted them.
He had related all that he had remembered so far of his
life in Jongleur's tower, but although the others had been
fascinated, they could offer nothing to help him make
sense of what the fragments meant.

'So what happens?' T4b said, breaking the long silence.
'Just go on, us, all rub-a-dub-dub like this, forever?'

Paul smiled sadly. Personally, he had been thinking of
Wynken, Blynken, and Nod adrift in their wooden shoe,
but the idea was much the same.

'We will go through to the next simulation,' Florimel

said wearily. 'When we get to the gateway, Martine will try to manipulate it to send us back to Troy, so that we might perhaps cross through to the place where Renie and the others are. We have said all this before.'

Paul looked to Martine, who at the moment didn't appear capable of manipulating anything more complicated than a bath towel or a spoon. The blind woman sagged, her earlier confidence gone, or at least worn down for the moment. Her lips were moving, as though she were talking to herself. Or praying.

I hope she doesn't give up, he thought in sudden fear. *Without Renie to push us along, she's all we have. Florimel's smart and brave, but she doesn't think ahead like the two of them, she gets angry and discouraged. T4b – well, he's a teenager, and not a very patient one at that.*

But what about me? Even the thought of taking responsibility for the lives of these people made him feel a little queasy. *Yes, but that's shit, man, and you know it. You've been through things in the last weeks that nobody – nobody! – in the real world has experienced, let alone survived. Chased by monsters, fought in the bloody Trojan War. Why shouldn't you take the lead if it were necessary?*

Because it feels like it's hard enough just being Paul Jonas, he answered himself. *Because it's hard enough getting by when it feels like a big piece of my life is missing. Because I'm damned tired, that's why.*

Somehow, they didn't sound like very good excuses.

Martine stirred and sat up. 'I am troubled,' she said. 'Troubled by many things.'

'And who is not?' Florimel snorted.

'This thing about Kunohara having an informant among us?' Paul asked her.

'No. There is nothing we can do about that if it is true, and I am willing to believe you all when you say you know nothing about it.' But her sightless gaze seemed to pause for a moment on T4b, who shifted uncomfortably. 'I am troubled by the song that the . . . the operating system, as I suppose I must call it, was singing. A song that I think I taught it to sing.'

'You can call it the Other,' said Florimel. 'Many others seem to, and it is easier to say.'

Martine waved her hand in impatience. 'It does not matter. The fact is, I am troubled because it might hold answers to some of our questions, but I can remember very little about that time, those events.'

Paul shrugged. 'We don't know anything except what you've told us.'

'And that is as much as I wish to tell. I was . . . experimented upon. I communicated remotely with what I thought was another child – a strange, even frightening child, but also somehow pitiful. I played games with it, as I assume other children in the institute did. I taught it stories, songs. I think that I taught it the song it was singing . . .' She broke off, staring at nothing.

'And now you think this playmate of yours was an AI?' Paul finished for her. 'They were . . . training the operating system to be like a human, for some reason.'

T4b shook his head. 'Locktacious. Those old Grail-knockers scan freely, huh?'

'Stories,' Martine said quietly. 'Yes, there was a story that went with the song. What was it? God, it was so long ago!'

'I do not remember the song,' Florimel said. 'Much that happened on that mountaintop – it was all very confusing. Frightening.'

Martine raised her hands as though trying to keep her

balance. The others fell silent. When she spoke Paul expected some revelation, but instead the blind woman said, 'We are almost there.'

'What? Where?'

'The end of this simulation. I can feel the . . . the falling-off. The ending.' She swiveled her head. 'I must have quiet. I wish we could land and go through slowly, but we have no way to control our movement, so I must take this as it comes. If I can get us to Troy, I will. If not, there is no telling where we may find ourselves.'

They were all still for a moment, the bubble rising and falling with the movement of the river.

'Will we have a boat on the other side?' Florimel asked hoarsely.

Martine shook her head in irritation, hardly listening, intent on something none of the others could perceive.

'What do you mean?' Paul asked.

'This was not a standard craft,' Florimel said. 'We walked out of this simulation the first time we were here. Renie and !Xabbu used one of the entomological institute's planes, which was translated into something else on the far side of the gateway. But what is this?' She spread her arms. 'It is a bubble, something that did not exist until Kunohara made it. Will it be something on the far side? Or will it just . . . disappear?'

'Jesus.' Paul reached out and clutched Martine's hand. 'Everybody grab on. At least that way we'll go into the water together.' The blind woman did not seem to notice. Florimel took her other hand, then they both linked with T4b, who had gone pale and as silent as Martine. The water seemed to be moving faster now, the bubble jouncing through streaks of white foam. 'I think we're heading toward another waterfall.' Paul tried hard to keep his voice steady.

'Going all blue, like,' T4b growled, trying as hard as Paul. 'Sparkly.'

'Hold tightly.' Florimel closed her eyes. 'If we do go in the water, take a big breath. Do not struggle, do not swim until you know what is up or down.'

'If we can tell,' Paul said, but it was nearly a whisper. Beside him Martine had gone rigid, locked onto some incomprehensible signal.

The current was definitely moving faster now. The bubble bounced from one swift-moving eddy to another, barely dimpling the surface of the water. A lurch turned them all sideways, and for a moment Florimel and T4b rose up above Paul's head before tumbling down on top of him in a bruising pile of elbows and knees. Somehow they managed to keep their hands locked; a moment later the bubble had righted itself, leaving them sprawled on their backs once more, panting and silent.

Blue fire began to rise around them in glittering cascades. The bubble rose, fell, skimmed, and spun.

Where next? Paul thought wildly as they were flung head over heels again. *Good God, where next?*

A fog of blue sparks surrounded them completely. Martine grunted in pain and fell sideways into Paul's lap just as the bubble evaporated around them and black water splashed in on all sides.

'We're still alive,' Paul said. He spoke the words aloud in part because he was still not entirely certain it was true. Their bubble was gone and already he missed it dearly. It had been replaced by a small boat, a crude craft that seemed like something to be poled rather than rowed, although there were no implements on board to do either. The storm that had greeted them at the gateway had swept past, but it had left them drenched and the air was frosty. Paul could already feel his wet clothes crackling with ice.

The river around them was black. The land, such of it as they could see through the mists, was all white. They were surrounded by snow.

'How is Martine?' asked Florimel.

Paul pulled her upright against him. 'Shivering, but I think she's okay. Martine, can you hear me?'

T4b squinted out across the apparently polar landscape. 'Don't look like that Troy place to me.'

Martine groaned quietly and shook her head. 'It is not. I could not find the Trojan simulation in the information at the gateway.' She wrapped her arms tight around her body, still shivering. 'I had to work so fast! Many of the gateways are closed – the information system for the gateway was like a building with most of its lights out.'

'So where *are* we?' Florimel asked. 'And if we can't get to Troy, what are we going to do?'

'Freeze, if we don't make a fire,' Paul said through clenched teeth; he was shivering now. 'Time later to worry about other things if we manage to survive. We'll have to go ashore.' He wished that he felt as confident, as certain as he was trying to sound. This simworld along the riverbanks reminded him of nothing so much as the Ice Age, although he hoped it wasn't so; it was impossible to forget the giant hyenas that had chased him into an icy river much like this one. He did not want to encounter any more primitive megafauna.

'There is nowhere here to make a fire, and nothing to make one with.' Florimel pointed at the hummocks of snow which seemed to extend from the riverbanks all the way to the dim, fogbound mountains. 'Do you see any trees? Any wood?'

'Those hills up ahead,' Paul said. 'Where the river turns

– who knows what's behind them, or even under them?
Maybe this is some kind of futuristic simworld, and there
are underground houses with atomic furnaces or something. We can't just give up. We'll freeze.'

'Not necessarily,' Florimel said sharply. 'None of us is
like Renie and !Xabbu, with their real bodies suspended
in liquid. Our bodies are all resting at room temperature
somewhere. How can we freeze? Our nerves can be fooled
into feeling cold, but that is not the same as actually
being cold.' Despite her words, she too was now wracked
with trembling. 'Psychosomatically we can be convinced
perhaps to radiate more heat, as though we had fever, but
surely we cannot be forced to freeze ourselves?'

'By that logic,' Martine pointed out through chattering
teeth, 'we could not be bitten in half by a giant scorpion,
either – it would only be a tactile illusion. But none of
us were very eager to test that assumption, were we?'

Florimel opened her mouth, then shut it.

'We need to find something to use as paddles, anyway,'
Paul said. 'It will take us days to drift through at this
rate.'

'Only thing for sure is turning all ice,' T4b grumbled.
'Rest of you can jawjack about it. Want to get warm, me.'

'We should huddle close,' Martine said. 'Whatever the
somatic truth, I can perceive heat leaving your virtual
bodies very quickly.'

They crowded into the center of the boat. For once
even T4b, not the most companionable of their number,
had no complaints. The boat moved, but the current was
sluggish, the black river flat as glass.

'Somebody talk,' Paul said after a while. 'Keep our minds
off this. Martine, you said you remembered a story that
went with that song the . . . the Other was singing.'

'That is just the p-problem.' She was shivering so badly

now she could hardly speak. 'I don't re-re-remember it. It's been so long. It was just an old fairy tale. About a b-boy, a little boy who fell down a hole.'

'Sing the song.' Worried for her, Paul began rubbing her arms and back, trying to make some heat by friction. 'Maybe that will tell us something.'

Martine shook her head, but began in a low, trembling voice to sing. *'An . . . an angel touched me, an angel touched me . . .'* She frowned, thinking. *'A river . . .* no, *the river washed me and now I am clean.'*

Paul remembered it clearly now, the eerie sound echoing across the black mountaintop. 'And you think that it's significant somehow . . . ?'

'I know that story,' Florimel said abruptly. 'It was one of Eirene's favorites. From the Gurnemanz collection.'

'You know it from a German book?' Martine said, surprised. 'But it is an old French fairy tale.'

'What's that?' T4b asked.

'A f-fairy tale . . . ?' Martine was stunned despite her suffering. 'You d-d-do not know what a fairy tale is? My God, what have they done to our ch-children?'

'No,' said T4b disgustedly. 'What's *that?*'

He was pointing at a mound of snow perhaps a thousand meters ahead of them, one of the outriders to the cluster of snowy hills Paul had seen earlier.

'It's a pile of snow.' Paul said it a trifle rudely, but he wanted to hear what Florimel had to say about the story. A moment later he was startled and embarrassed to see the glint of something that was not snow or ice. 'Good Lord, you're right, it's a tower. A tower!'

'What, think I'm blind, me?' T4b growled. A moment later he frowned and turned to Martine. 'Didn't mean no slapdown.'

'Understood.' She frowned into the distance. 'I

p-perceive no signs of life at all. I ca-ca-can barely sense that there is anything there at all beside ice and snow. What do you see?'

'It's the top of a tower.' Paul squinted. 'It's . . . very narrow. Like a minaret. Decorated. But I can't see anything of what's underneath. Damn, this current is slow!'

'A minaret, yes,' said Florimel.

'Maybe this is the Mars I visited before,' Paul said excitedly. 'That strange sort of late-Victorian adventure world. It had a lot of Moorish-looking architecture.' His gaze slipped to the countless miles of deadening white spread over both sides of the river. 'But what *happened?*'

'Dread,' said Martine quietly. 'The man called Dread has happened to this place, I would bet.'

They were all straining to see something now, all except for Martine who had let her trembling chin sink to her chest. As they drew closer to the great mound of snow and its single protruding spire, Paul saw something on the bank beside them, a much smaller shape half-covered by white drifts. 'What the hell is that?'

T4b, who was leaning so far out of the boat the little craft was tipping to one side, said, 'It's one of those *Tut-Tut and the Sphinx* things, like – you know, that netshow for micros? That animal they ride with bumps?'

Paul, whose grasp of popular culture had been diminishing rapidly since he left boarding school, could only shake his head. 'It's a sphinx?'

'He means a camel,' Florimel said. If she had not been pressing her teeth together to keep them from chattering, she might have laughed. 'It is a frozen camel. Did they have camels on your Mars?'

'No.' Now that they were closer, he saw the boy was right again. The dead camel was on its knees at the river's edge, teeth exposed in a hideous grin, the skin stretched so tight on its neck and head that it seemed mummified, but it was definitely a camel. 'We must be in Orlando's Egypt. Or something like it.'

Martine stirred. 'That man c-called Nandi. If we are in Egypt, p-p-perhaps we could find him. Orlando and Fredericks said he was the Circle's special expert on the gateways. He might be able to help us reach Renie and the others.'

'If he's here, gotta be a popsicle,' T4b suggested.

'Ancient Egypt with minarets?' asked Florimel sourly. 'In any case, I have changed my mind about trying to outlast this cold. So let us head toward that tower or none of this speculation will matter, because we, too, will be . . . popsicles.'

'We'll have to paddle with our hands,' Paul said. 'We'll have to get there fast or we'll all get frostbite.'

'We will take our hands out in turn to warm up,' Martine said. 'Two paddling, two warming. Now.'

For a moment, as he plunged his fingers into the dark river, Paul felt nothing but clean chill, like an alcohol-swabbing before an injection. Then his skin began to burn like fire.

It was only snow and not ice they had to kick through to reach the open arched door of the building beneath the looming, white-shrouded tower, a piece of luck for which Paul was terribly grateful. Within a few moments they were standing in a decorated antechamber, painted head to ceiling in a beautiful, elaborate scarlet, black, and gold fretwork of repeating shapes. They did not stop to look, but continued forward, bending over the freezing hands they all held pressed against their bellies.

Three more doors and three more decorated chambers led them to a smaller room whose walls were lined with shelves full of leather-bound books, and the glorious discovery of a tiled fire pit and a stack of wood.

'It's damp,' Paul said as he stacked logs in the fireplace with clumsy, stinging fingers. 'We need something to use as kindling. Not to mention a match.'

'Kindling?' Florimel pulled a book down from the shelf and began tearing out pages. It seemed somehow sacrilegious to Paul, but after a moment's consideration he decided he could live with the feeling. He looked at a page and saw that it was in English, but English rendered in a spidery print that had the feeling of Arabic script. As he crumpled pages and arranged them around the wood, he saw a pretty lacquer box tucked into an alcove in the tile on the outside of the fireplace. He opened it, then held it up. 'It's flint and steel, I think, and thank God for that. I wish !Xabbu were here. Anyone else know how to use this?'

'We did not even have electricity at Harmony Camp until I was ten years old,' said Florimel. 'Give it to me.'

Perhaps a quarter of an hour passed, the sound of clicking teeth gradually subsiding, before Paul was willing to take his hands away from the wonderful heat of the fire. After a bit of exploration he turned up a storeroom full of soft rugs which he and the others wrapped around themselves like cloaks. Warmer now and feeling almost human, he picked up one of the discarded books and opened it.

'It's definitely supposed to be Arabic – this book is dedicated to His Majesty the Caliph, Haroun al-Rashid. Hmmm. It seems to be a story about Sinbad the Sailor.' Paul looked up at the shelves. 'I think this is a library of the Thousand and One Arabian Nights.'

'Ain't spending no thousand nights here in this popsicle pit,' T4b said. 'Lock that. Lock that *tight*.'

'That's just the name of a book,' Paul told him. 'A famous old collection of stories.' He turned to Florimel and Martine. 'Which reminds me . . .'

'I said I could not remember the story,' Martine began.

'But I said I could.' Florimel pushed herself back a little way from the fire. Bundled in the stiff carpet, and with the makeshift bandage covering her eye and a large portion of the side of her head, she looked more than ever like some medieval hedge-witch.

Which is funny, Paul thought, *since the witch of the group is Martine.* It was an odd realization, but no less true for being odd.

'I will tell it as I remember it.' The German woman scowled, exaggerating her already daunting appearance. 'It is only memorized because my daughter asked to hear it – and several of that Gurnemanz collection's other stories – many, many times, so don't interrupt me or I will lose the rhythm and forget parts of it. Martine, I am sure it will be different than the version you knew, but tell me about it afterward, will you?'

Paul saw the ghost of a smile flicker on the blind woman's face. 'That is fair, Florimel.'

'Good.' She arranged her damp but drying robes beneath her, opened her mouth, then shut it again and glared at T4b. 'And I will explain the parts you don't understand after I'm done. Do you hear me, Javier? Don't interrupt or I will throw you out into the snow.'

Paul expected anger, or at least teenage indignation, but the boy seemed amused. 'Chizz. Bang those squeezers. Listening, me.'

'Right. Very well then, here it is as I remember it.'

'Once upon a time there was a boy who was the apple of his parents' eye. They loved him so fiercely that they were frightened something would happen to him, so they got him a dog to be his companion. The dog was named Sleeps-Not, and was fierce and loyal.

'Even with the love of two parents and the mercy of God, not all accidents can be avoided. One day, while his father was out working in the fields and his mother was busy preparing the afternoon meal, the boy wandered far from the house. Sleeps-Not tried to stop him, but the boy cuffed the dog and sent him away. The dog ran back to summon the boy's mother, but before she could reach him, the boy fell down into an abandoned well.

'The boy fell and rolled and tumbled a long, long time, and when he finally struck the bottom of the well he was in a cavern very deep in the earth, by the side of an underground stream. When his mother discovered what had happened she ran to get her husband, but no rope they had in the house would reach down to the bottom. They brought all the other villagers as well, but even with their ropes all tied together they could not reach the bottom where the boy was trapped.

'The boy's parents called to him that he must be brave, that somehow they would find a way to get him out of the deep, deep hole. He heard them and was a little heartened, and when they had dropped some food down wrapped in leaves to cushion the fall, he decided to make the best of it.

'Late at night, when his parents and the other villagers had finally gone in to sleep and the boy thought he was alone again at the bottom of the well, he began to weep and to pray to God.

'No one heard him but Sleeps-Not, and when that loyal dog heard his little master crying, he rushed off to roam the wide world in search of someone who could help the boy in the well.

'The boy's parents dropped food to him every day, and he had water to drink from the underground stream, but he was still sad and lonely, and every night, when he thought that no one was listening, he wept. With his dog Sleeps-Not out searching for help, there was no one to hear him at first, except the Devil, who after all lives deep in the ground. The Devil cannot cross rushing water, so he could not reach the little boy and take him down to Hell, but he stood in the darkness on the far side of the river and tormented the boy with lies, telling him that his parents had forgotten him, that everyone above the ground had given up hope of getting him out long ago. The boy's weeping became greater and greater until an angel heard him and appeared to him in the darkness in the form of a pale and fair woman.

'"God will protect you," the angel told the boy, and kissed him on the cheek. "Put yourself into the river and all will be well."

'The boy did as he was told, and then climbed out again wet and shivering, and sang this song: "An angel touched me, an angel touched me, the river washed me and now I am clean."

'The second night the Devil sent a serpent up from the dark depths to attack the boy, but Sleeps-Not had found a hunter, a brave man with a gun, and brought him to the top of the well. Although the hunter could not bring the boy up from the hole, with his keen eyes he saw the serpent coming and killed it with a shot from his gun, and the boy was safe. Again the boy said his prayers and stepped into the river, and again stepped out again, singing: "An angel touched me, an angel touched me, the river washed me and now I am clean."

'The next night the Devil sent a ghost to attack the boy, but Sleeps-Not had brought a priest to the top of the well, and although he could not bring the boy up from his hole, the priest saw the ghost coming and threw down his rosary, dispatching the spirit back to hell. The boy said prayers of thanks and stepped into the river, then came out singing: "An angel touched me, an angel touched me, the river washed me and now I am clean."

'The next night the Devil sent all the hosts of hell after the boy, but Sleeps-Not had brought a peasant girl to the top of the well. It seemed there was little she could do to save the boy from all the hosts of hell, but in truth she was not a peasant girl but the angel who had first helped him, and she flew down into the well holding a fiery sword and the hosts of hell drew back, afraid.

'"God will protect you," the angel told the boy, and kissed him on the cheek. "Put yourself into the river and all will be well."

'The boy stepped into the water, but when he would have come out again, the angel raised her hand and shook her head. "God will protect you," she said. "All will be well."

'At this the boy realized what he was expected to do, and instead of stepping out of the water he let go and allowed the river to carry him. It took him a long way through darkness, but always he could feel the angel's kiss on him, keeping him warm and safe, and when at last he came out into the light again, it was no less a light than that of Paradise itself, which shines from God's face. And soon enough his dog Sleeps-Not and his two loving parents joined him in that place, and unless I am wrong, they are all there still.'

'I am certain I got some details wrong,' Florimel said after they had all spent a few silent moments listening to the pop and hiss of the fire. 'But that is close to what I read

so many times to . . . to my Eirene.' She scowled and
rubbed at the corner of her good eye. Caught between
sympathy and courtesy, Paul looked away.

'Know how you said you'd explain parts that didn't
make sense?' T4b asked.

'Which parts didn't you understand?'

'Total.'

Florimel grunted a laugh. 'I think you are saying that
to be funny. You are not foolish, Javier, and that is a
story meant for children.'

He shrugged, but didn't take offense. Paul could not
help wondering if the sullen teenager might be slowly
turning human. Perhaps the simple fact of being out of
armor was having an effect.

'Is it as you remember it, Martine?' Florimel asked. 'The
same story? Martine?'

The blind woman shook her head as though awakening from a day-dream. 'Oh. Sorry, yes, it is much the
same, I think – it has been a long time. Perhaps a few
differences. The dog in my childhood version was named
"Never-Sleeps," and I think the hunter was a knight . . .'
She trailed off, still absorbed in some inner conversation.
'I am sorry,' she said after a moment, 'but . . . but as I
hear it now, hear the song and the story that go with it,
I am reminded of what was for me a very bad time.' She
waved her hands, forestalling sympathy. 'No, but that is
not all. Also it has made me think.'

'About the song?' Paul asked.

'About everything. About what Kunohara said – that
the reason for the operating . . . for the Other's strange
patterns might be that I taught it a story. But I think that
is too simple. I think that many of the children at the
institute must have told it stories – I am fairly certain I
told it other fairy tales myself. Telling stories was one of

the things the doctors often asked us to do, perhaps as a measure of our memory and general mental health. If the operating system and its growing intelligence has been corrupted by this one particular folktale, I do not think it is because it was the only tale, the only song, that it ever heard.'

Paul blinked. A great wave of weariness was rolling over him. After the perils of Kunohara's bugworld and their escape along the river, he was only now feeling how exhausted he truly was. 'I'm sorry. I don't understand.'

'I think it has taken this story to heart, if you will excuse an inappropriate metaphor, because more than any other, this story had resonance.' Martine looked weary, too. 'For the Other, this was the one that spoke most clearly of its own situation.'

'Are you saying it thinks it's a little boy?' Florimel said, an edge of angry amusement in her voice. 'A little boy with a dog? In a hole?'

'Perhaps, but that is rather simplifying it.' Martine bowed her head for a moment. 'Please, give me the chance to think out loud, Florimel. I do not have the strength to take much argument.'

The other woman flushed a little, but nodded her head. 'Go on.'

'It may not think it is a boy, a human child, but if this truly is an artificial intelligence, something that has become almost human, imagine how it *does* feel. What did Dread say, in that moment on the mountain when he appeared like a giant? "Your system is still fighting me, but I have learned how to hurt it." A metaphor . . . or not? Perhaps when the system, with its growing individuality, did things the Brotherhood did not want it to do, they had to check its efforts with something it perceived as pain.'

Paul had a sudden, nightmarish memory of the Other straining against its bonds, an agonized, Promethean figure. 'It thinks of itself as a prisoner.'

'A prisoner in the dark. Yes, perhaps.' Martine took a breath. 'A thing being punished for no reason – tormented as the Devil torments people, for the pure enjoyment of another's suffering. And so it has sat in its darkness for years – at least three decades, maybe more – hoping that one day it would be saved from its pain and set free, and singing a song that a little boy sang at the bottom of a deep, black well.' Her face suddenly contorted in anger and unhappiness. 'It is terrible to think about, no?'

'You think it has done these things . . . against its will?' Florimel asked. 'That what it did to my Eirene and the other children, to your friend Singh – all these things it was forced to do, like a slave? Like a conscripted soldier?' She looked shocked. 'It is hard to think that way.'

'Oh, Jesus, the angel.' Paul could hardly breathe. 'In the story. Is that why . . . why Ava appears the way she does? Because the Other thinks she's an angel?'

'Perhaps.' Martine shrugged. 'Or because that is the only way it can imagine a human female who is not part of the legions of pain-bringers. And there is the image of the river as well – certainly we must all find *that* familiar by now.'

'But even if you are right, what good does this do us?' Florimel said, breaking a long moment's silence. 'The Other is defeated, at least the part of it that thinks. Dread has taken over the system. Look at this place – the Baghdad of Haroun al-Rashid, all vanished under a glacier. *Dread* is not an unwilling monster. He has turned this whole imaginary universe upside down just to amuse himself.'

'Yes, and with the Brotherhood dead or dispersed, he is our true enemy.' Martine leaned back against the wall.

'I'm afraid you are right, Florimel – my idea means little. If nothing we did before could affect the Other, I cannot imagine how we can do anything to discomfort Dread.'

Paul sat up. 'Aren't you forgetting something? Like the fact that we have friends who are still out there? Maybe we can't do anything to bring down the system, maybe we can't touch this murderer-turned-virtual-god I've heard so much about, but we can bloody well try to find Renie and the others.'

For a moment it looked like Martine would lose her temper – Paul saw color bloom on the cheeks of her sim-face. 'I have not forgotten, Paul,' she said stiffly. 'It is my curse that I forget almost nothing.'

'I didn't mean it that way. But if we can't do anything to stop Dread, we can at least try to get out of this network. The Grail Brotherhood is dead as a doornail, so what are we fighting against anyway? You lot may have volunteered, sort of, but I sure as Christ didn't.' Paul felt his anger swirling uselessly and tried to calm himself. 'Right, then. So what's our next step? If the Troy simu-lation is offline, how can we get to Renie and the others?'

'We do not know that same trick would work twice anyway,' Florimel pointed out. 'It was my impression that the Other somehow wanted us to come to it – that it made some kind of special gateway for us. If the artificial intel-ligence is enslaved now, or at least defeated, then I doubt . . .'

She paused because Martine had held up her hand, fingers spread, like a sentinel who hears a stealthy foot-step outside the camp.

'I think you are right,' Martine said slowly. 'I think, along with Paul's angel, the Other tried to bring us to itself, somehow. It wanted something from us.'

'But we have no idea what that might be,' said Paul.

'Just wait for a moment!' The blind woman's angry flush returned. 'My God, let a person think. It . . . the Other . . . wanted us for some reason. To help it free itself? As in the story?'

Paul frowned, trying to understand where her thoughts were going. 'It . . . it takes the story literally? It wants us to get it out of its hole?'

'Out of its imprisonment, yes, it could be.'

'Which one of us is the dog?' Florimel said with heavy sarcasm. 'I hope we are not expected to volunteer.'

'The dog. Of course!' Martine nodded her head violently. 'Oh, could it really be? Perhaps I am right. Let me say this, however foolish it sounds.' She raised her hands to her head, eyes tightly shut. 'Renie told me once that all the sims I have worn within this network look very . . . unexceptional. Is that true? Almost like generic sims.'

'Yes, I suppose,' said Florimel. 'So?'

'She told me that only in Troy did I look like a specific person. But that was because in Troy I was given a specific character made for the simulation – Cassandra, the king's daughter. All the rest of the time I have been in some version of this original peasant sim from Temilún, and it is not as detailed as yours is, Florimel, or as the false Quan Li's was.'

'Granted. What does that mean?'

'We are all of us interfacing with this system as almost pure information, yes? Whatever our real bodies might look like, we exist on this system only as minds – as sense-memory and conscious thought, correct? And the system sends information back to us along the same neural pathways.'

Paul looked over at T4b, expecting the teenager to be annoyed by the long, complex discussion, but the boy had his head turned away, watching the fire. For a moment, Paul envied his detachment. 'But that's basically the definition of this sort of VR environment, isn't it?' he asked. 'Gives people input at the sensory level, bypassing information coming from what would normally be the real world.'

'Ah.' Martine sat up straighter. 'But there is no such thing as "this sort of environment." We have seen that already – it is unique! Unique in that we cannot find a way to go offline, unique in that we cannot find our own neurocannulae, or even the cruder input-output devices Renie and !Xabbu are using, *even though we know they are there*. And when Fredericks tried to go offline, he . . . no, she, I almost forgot! . . . suffered terrible pain.'

Florimel grunted. 'You are still not explaining. . . .'

'Perhaps the network – or more specifically, the operating system, the Other – can interface with not just our conscious thoughts, but our subconscious thoughts as well.'

'What? You mean, read our minds?'

'I do not know how it might work, or what the limits might be, but think! If it could reach into our subconscious, it could implant suggestions that we cannot go offline. Like hypnosis. It could convince us, below the conscious level, that removing ourselves from the network would cause us great pain.'

'Jesus.' Paul suddenly began to see it taking shape. 'But that would mean . . . that it wanted you all to stay on the network. What about your friend Singh? It killed him.'

'I do not know. Perhaps the security system part of the Other, the part that guarded entry to the network, was under more direct control by the Grail Brotherhood. Perhaps it was only when we had made our way inside that the Other could truly see us, contact us.' She was growing excited. 'If it was trying to act out a story somehow, the story of the boy in the well, it might well have decided we were the allies it was looking for!'

'It makes a kind of sense,' Florimel said slowly. 'Although there is much to think about before I am ready to agree. But you haven't explained about the dog, yet. I said something about the dog in the story, and that set you onto talking about sims, about how your own sims worked . . . ?'

'Yes. Do you know what your face looks like?'

Florimel flinched. 'Are you speaking of my injuries?'

'No, in everyday life. Do you know what your face looks like? Of course you do. You have mirrors, you have photos of yourself. Any normal person knows what he or she looks like. Paul, have you seen your sims? Do they resemble you?'

'Most of them. Except when I was someone specific, as you said, like Odysseus.' He looked at her, puzzled, then a moment later it came clear. 'You don't know what you look like, do you?'

Martine shook her head. 'Of course not. I have been blind since I was a child. I know I don't look like that anymore, but what the years since have done to me, I have no idea, except by touch.'

Florimel was staring at her. 'You are saying that the Other . . . read your mind?'

'In a way, perhaps. It may have tried to take some sense from each of us of who we were, what we looked like – or wanted to look like. Didn't Orlando say that he looked like an earlier version of his own character? Where did that come from, if it wasn't from the mind of Orlando himself?'

Paul's weariness was still powerful, but the unfolding vistas of this new line of thought could not be ignored. 'I wondered, when he told me. I wondered about a lot of this, but there hasn't been any shortage of unanswered questions.'

'Of course,' Martine said. 'We have been fighting for our lives each and every day, in circumstances no one else in history has had to endure. It has taken a long time for, as you English say, the penny to drop.'

Paul smiled wanly. 'So what do we do with this knowledge, if it's all true?'

'I am not done yet.' She turned to Florimel. 'You asked about the dog. Orlando was not the only one of our group to find his Otherland sim a surprise. Do you remember what !Xabbu told us?'

'That . . . that he had been thinking about baboons . . .' Florimel began, then stopped, her expression now honestly dumbstruck. 'He had been thinking about baboons, because of some tribal story or some such . . . but he had not planned to be one.'

'Exactly. But someone . . . something . . . chose that appearance for him. Do you know what the old name for baboon was?'

Paul nodded, impressed. 'The European sailors used to call them "dog-faced apes," didn't they?'

'They did. So imagine the Other, trapped in darkness, praying and singing in the small corner of its own intellect where it could hide from its cruel masters. It remembers a story, one of the most vivid things it knows, something that has been with it since a time that was perhaps as close to a childhood as it ever had. A story about a boy in darkness, tortured and frightened. As it sifts through the thoughts of the latest group of intruders, while its security programming deals with the gross physical facts of the intrusion, it perceives that one of them has an image firmly in his mind – perhaps even a sort of self-image – of a four-legged creature with a head like a dog's head. And, if by probing at the subconscious it can sense anything of its subjects' true nature, it may even have perceived !Xabbu's kindness and loyalty.

'Perhaps it had a plan before that moment, perhaps !Xabbu or something else about us triggered the thought. But from that moment on the Other was not trying to destroy us – or at least the "child" part of it, the thinking, feeling part, was not. It was trying to find us. It was trying to bring us to it. It was praying to be rescued.'

'Jesus.' Paul was dimly aware he'd already said this a few times, but could not help saying it several more. 'Jesus. So the mountain . . . ?'

'A neutral ground, perhaps?' Florimel offered.

'Perhaps. Perhaps a spot near – if we can use such physical terms about this network – to the Other's own secret place, to the center of its "self." If we had been able to remain there, if Dread had not interfered, it might have spoken to us.'

Paul stiffened. 'And so Renie was right. She and the others really are in the heart of the system?'

Martine slumped back. 'I do not know. But if we want to get there, we will have to find some other way, since Troy seems to be barred to us now.'

'We will think of something,' Florimel said. 'Great God, I had not expected to feel this way about the thing that crippled and stole my Eirene, but if what you guess is true, Martine . . . oh! It is a terrible thought.'

Martine sighed. 'But before anything more, we need sleep. I have quite overwhelmed myself, and I did not have much strength in reserve.'

'Hang on.' Paul reached out and touched her arm. He could feel it trembling with fatigue. 'Sorry, but one last thing. You said something about Nandi.'

'The one Orlando met.'

'I know. I met him, too – I'm sure I told you. I think you were right. If anyone can help us puzzle out the gates, it's him.'

'But we don't know where he is,' said Florimel. 'Orlando and Fredericks last saw him in Egypt.'

'Then that's where we need to go. At the very least, it gives us something to aim for!' He squeezed Martine's forearm gently. 'Did you notice whether it was one of the . . . available destinations? When you were looking for Troy?'

She shook her head sadly. 'Too little time. That is why I accepted this place when I couldn't find Troy – it was the default setting.' She reached out and patted his hand, then turned away, searching with her fingers for a clear spot to lie down and sleep. 'But we will look for it at the next gateway.' She yawned. 'And you are right, Paul – at least it is something.'

As she curled herself tighter in her blanket, and Florimel did the same, Paul turned to T4b.

'Javier? You haven't said much.'

The boy still didn't have a great deal to say. He had clearly been asleep for quite a while.

CHAPTER 13

King Johnny

NETFEED/NEWS: *Jiun Would Not Want State Funeral, Heirs Claim*
(visual: *Jiun at Asian Prosperity Zone ceremony*)
VO: *The heirs of Jiun Bhao, Asia's most influential mogul, say that
the state funeral planned for the businessman is inappropriate.*
(visual: *nephew Jiun Tung at press conference*)
JIUN TUNG: *'He was a very modest man, the embodiment of Confucian
values. He would want what was due to a man of his position, nothing more.'*
(visual: *Jiun meeting group of farmers*)
VO: *Some observers suggest that the family is being more modest
than their late patriarch actually was, and that what they really object
to is the state's expectation that the Jiun family pay for part of the
massive ceremony. . . .'*

CALLIOPE drummed her fingers on the countertop. She
was definitely, definitely going to give up caffeine,
go for the no-octane varieties. Tomorrow. Or right after
that.

Every noise from the other room seemed louder than
it was. It was so strange to hear someone else in her
apartment. Calliope's mother hated leaving her little house,
fearful of crowds and unfamiliar places. Stan hadn't visited

in months, mostly because they saw so bloody much of
each other at work: even friendly partners didn't want to
spend any more time in each other's company than they
had to.

Calliope had just decided to pour herself a drink of
something counter-effective to coffee – although, as wired
as she felt at the moment, it would probably take some
kind of morphine derivative to slow her down – when
the bedroom door popped open. Elisabetta, the waitress-
muse, leaned in the doorway, only a yellow towel covering the completeness of her tattooed glory. She held
another towel in her hand and waved it at Calliope. 'I
took one for my hair, too. All right?'

Detective Sergeant Calliope Skouros could only nod.
The towel-clad apparition vanished back into the steamy
bedroom. God, the girl was beautiful. Maybe not in the
runway-model sense, but strong and just vibrating with
youth and life.

*Did I look like that once? Did I have that glow, just
because of how old I was? Or rather, how old I wasn't?*

*Stop it, Calliope. You're not that bloody old, you just
work too hard. And you eat too much crap. Find a life,
like Stan always says. Go to the gym. You've got good
bones.*

As she mulled over the dubious value of good bones,
something her mother had always assured her she had
when a younger Calliope was feeling particularly unpretty,
Elisabetta appeared again from the bedroom, a towel
around her head, the rest of her now dressed in a black
knit top and a pair of black 'chutes slashed with insets
of glowing white.

'These are so. . . .' She waved at the silky trousers. 'I
mean, I know they're utterly cutting, but they're so much
more comfortable than that latex shit.'

'Cutting . . . ?' asked Calliope, knowing even as she did so that she was just confirming her own official middle-agedness.

Elisabetta grinned. 'Cutting edge. Meaning old-fashioned. It's just something this friend of mine says.' She gave her hair a last rub, then ceremoniously draped the towel over the door handle. Which, Calliope reflected, for someone in her early twenties probably represented 'not leaving a mess.'

'It was really nice of you to let me use your shower. It's so far back to my place, and the traffic. . . .' She bent for her bag, then straightened up. 'Oh, and thanks for the drink, too.'

'No problem. I enjoyed it.' Calliope considered some further affirmation but could not come up with anything that didn't sound utterly stupid in mental rehearsal. *I love your company and I have weird fantasies about you all the time? I'd like to be genetically reengineered to have your babies? I drink three gallons of coffee a day just to watch you walk around dropping salads on peoples' tables, so it was quite nice to have you naked at my place, even in the next room?*

'I really want to go to this party. My friend's housesitting, and the people told her it was okay to have it – they've got this amazing place, with walls, like a castle. And you can have fireworks every night. They're not real, they're just holograms or something, but my friend says it's wonderful.' She pushed damp hair out of her eyes and looked at Calliope. 'Hey, maybe you'd like to go. You want to?'

Something squeezed at her heart a little bit. 'I'd love to.' Something else squeezed – her conscience? 'But I can't. Not tonight. I have to meet someone.' *Am I closing a door?* she wondered nervously. 'My partner. My work partner. About work.'

Elisabetta regarded her solemnly for a moment, then returned to the task of rummaging around in her bag. But when she looked up, she wore a smile that was both amused and ever, ever so slightly shy. 'Hey, do you like me?'

Calliope carefully leaned back on her chair, just to stop herself drumming her fingers nervously on the tabletop. 'Yes, Elisabetta. I do. Of course I do.'

'No, I mean do you *like* me?' The smile was still shy, but challenging, too. Calliope was not entirely sure she wasn't being teased or mocked in some way. 'Are you . . . are you interested in me?'

Further obfuscation was not going to work, although it was tempting. Calliope realized that after almost a decade and a half of police work, after sitting in interrogation rooms facing rapists and robbers and murderous psychopaths, she couldn't think of a thing to say. After what seemed like half an hour, but was probably three seconds, she cleared her throat.

'Yes.' That was as much as she could manage.

'Hmmm.' Elisabetta nodded, then slung her bag over her shoulder. She still seemed to be enjoying some secret joke. 'I'll have to think about that.' As she reached the door, she turned, her smile wide now. 'Got to fly – see you later!'

Calliope sat in her chair for a long minute after the door whooshed closed, unmoving, as stunned as if she had been hit by a car. Her heart was hammering, although nothing had really changed.

What the hell am I supposed to do now?

'Technically,' Stan Chan said after a short silence, 'this should be the portion of the conversation where you ask me, "and how was the big meeting, Stan?" I mean, now that we've spent twenty minutes or so talking about some waitress I don't remember.'

'Oh, Jesus, Stan, I'm sorry.' She stared at the bowl of cocktail crispies, then defiantly took another handful. 'I really am. I haven't forgotten about it. It's just . . . I've been out of circulation a long time, what with one thing and another. I forgot how much like shooting some weird drug it is. Does she like me, should I care, what does *that* little thing mean . . . ? Damn, see, I'm doing it again. Tell me about what happened, please. I'm getting sick of listening to myself, anyway.'

'That's why you and I make such good partners. We agree on so many things.'

'Die, China-boy.'

'You'll never take me down, you goat-chasing lemon.'

'I'm glad we've got that straightened out.'

Stan nodded happily, then sobered. 'I'm afraid that's going to be the highlight of the evening.'

'So they didn't go for it.' One of the reasons she had been wasting time with waitress-trivia had been a bad feeling about Stan's meeting with the department brass.

'Not only didn't they go for it, they pretty much made it clear that they thought a couple of garden-variety homicide dicks should keep their noses out of things they couldn't understand.'

'Meaning the Real Killer case.'

'Yep.'

'Did you ask them about the Sang-Real thing I was thinking about? The whole King Arthur and the Grail idea?'

'Yes, and they informed me that they'd thought of it themselves a long time ago, and had beaten it into the dust. Looked up Arthurian scholars, checked the seating lists for *Parzival* in case the guy's a closet Wagner nut, every angle they could think of. I have to admit, it sounds like they were pretty thorough.'

'So basically, then, the answer was "piss off."'

'That sums it up pretty well, Skouros. They already decided once that Merapanui wasn't anything to do with their serial killer. And the captain was there, too – did I mention that? She thinks it's a lot more likely that minor villain Buncie got his dates wrong than he saw Johnny Dread alive after his check-out certificate, and she's also beginning to wonder why we're putting so much time into this case, since it's five years old and – in your own words when they gave it to us, Skouros – "as dead as good manners."' He shrugged.

'The captain . . .' Calliope leaned forward, thoughts of Elisabetta's shoulders shining with water drops vanishing quickly as she realized what Stan was trying to tell her. 'Oh, God. Does that mean . . . ?'

Stan nodded. ''Fraid so. She basically said we should wrap it up and put it away. She asked me if we'd found any actual evidence that our Johnny was still among the living, and I had to admit we hadn't.'

'But . . . damn.' Calliope slumped. There wasn't any, of course, not hard evidence, not the kind you could even take to a prosecutor. She felt like she had been hit in the stomach with a club. The whole thing was a structure built on guesswork – the kind of paranoid fantasy that kept thousands of net nodes busy. But she knew it wasn't pure fantasy – that the hunches were built on *something*. And Stan knew it, too. 'Didn't you argue?'

'Of course I did.' For a moment he showed a flash of genuine hurt. 'What do you take me for, Skouros? But she pointed out that while we were devoting so much time to this five-year-old case, people were getting murdered in new and original ways all the time, and the department is understaffed as it is. It was hard to argue with her.'

'Yeah. I'm sorry, Stan. You were the one who had to listen to it.' She scowled and picked a piece of ice out of her drink, rubbing it along the table so it left a trail of moisture. 'It's probably just as well I wasn't there. I probably would have screamed at her.'

'Well, did you put the afternoon to some other good use? Besides inviting people over to use your shower?'

She winced. That hurt – despite all the unpaid overtime she had put in lately, she had fretted over leaving half an hour early just to catch the end of Elisabetta's shift at Bondi Baby. 'I didn't just spend the entire day trying to get laid, Chan, honestly. But if they're going to pull us off Merapanui, there's not much point talking about what I found, because it isn't much.'

'Not pull – pulled.'

'You mean . . . we're off it?'

'We're reassigned as of 1800 hours today.' Stan did not often show real emotion, but his quicksilver features turned leaden. 'It's over, Calliope. Sorry, but the captain made it very clear. Merapanui goes back in the "do not resuscitate" file and Monday morning we go back to work on the latest street-beast bashings and alley slashings.' He grinned bleakly. 'We would have solved it, partner. We just ran out of time.'

'Shit.' Calliope was not going to cry, even in front of Stan, but the wave of frustration and anger that washed through her definitely made her eyes smart. She slammed the piece of ice down on the table-top; it squirted from her fingers and caromed off a napkin holder onto the floor. 'Shit.'

There wasn't much else to say.

* * *

IT was always strange, this sensation of intrusion. She thought of it as being somehow very male, which probably explained why most hackers and crackers were men.

Burglars, too. And explorers. And rapists, of course.

Which did not really explain where she herself fit in, but it was hard to deny the wired-up pleasure Dulcie always felt when she found her way into someone else's system.

Her system was chewing up machine language, but it was slow going; not only did the J Corporation have all the usual state-of-the-art security gear, but the really important stuff she wanted was also buried under a tremendous amount of VR code. This made breaking into the vaults of the J Corporation even more like burglary than the usual foray: information could actually be seen as old-fashioned paper files in cabinets, the different sections of the massive system as rooms in some near-endless office building. Not that Dulcie bothered with any of these real-world imitations, but she could tell that if she wanted to, a few adjustments would set the whole thing unrolling in front of her like a game, virtual representations of gates and vault doors, steely-eyed security guards, and all kinds of things. Was it just that in fifty years of living entirely online Felix Jongleur had found time to add a human-friendly facade to everything? Or was something more complicated at work?

Maybe he's like Dread, she thought. *A bit of an illiterate when it comes to technology, but still wants to be able to access everything because he doesn't really trust anybody but himself.* That would certainly make sense if the stories about his immense age were true, since Jongleur would have been an old man already by the time the Information Era had begun.

She filed these questions about Jongleur away for

possible later use, but the idea had set off a few interesting sparks. Could something like that be the key to unlock Dread's own hidden storage? Some obvious thing that a technophile like Dulcie Anwin wouldn't normally consider – something that might not even occur to her? Several days had passed since she had stumbled across her employer's hiding place, but it still nagged her thoughts.

Not now, she told herself. *There's work to do here, with Jongleur's files. And I sure don't want Dread scorched at me.*

Not only that, she realized – she *wanted* to impress him. Something in Dread's self-confidence and self-involvement pulled up a corresponding need in her, a need to prove herself.

Well, even if he's the toughest, coldest son of a bitch in the world, he couldn't get into the J Corporation files by himself. But I can. And I will.

She did, eventually, but it took almost twenty-four hours.

As it turned out, none of the passwords or other bits of Grail network information that Dread had passed along to her proved much use at all. She was thrown back on old-fashioned methods and was glad she had come prepared. But even with the best gear that money and shady connections could provide, there was still a great deal of waiting. She left the building several times to take walks – trips she kept short, despite her need for fresh air and sunshine, because the neighborhood made her nervous – and curled up once for a couple of hours of uneasy sleep, which was punctuated by a dream of long hospital corridors. In the dream she was searching for a little animal of some kind that had been lost, but the corridors were starkly white and empty and the search seemed endless.

When her customized Krypton gearstripper finally gave
her the hole she needed, she jumped up, clapped her hands,
and whooped, riding an electrifying surge of adrenaline –
but the elation did not last long. The actual truth of breaking into the J Corporation's information system was in some
way worse than the grim hospital dream. At least there she
had been searching for *something*, however hard to find;
now, with the break-in accomplished, she was forced to
confront the ridiculous complexity of the task before her.

Dread, with the nonchalance of someone who didn't
understand what he was asking, had told her he wanted
anything of interest about the Grail network, but especially anything pertaining to the Otherland operating
system. At the same time, he had made it very clear that
he didn't want her examining the data too closely herself
– a stricture which had made her snort loudly while listening to his original message.

Right, she had thought. *Like they're just going to label
all their file material to facilitate easier industrial theft.
'Don't bother to read this: trust us, it's important.'*

Now that the exhilaration of cracking the system was
gone, the weight of the actual task depressed her. She had
no idea how she'd ever find the things Dread wanted. The
amount of information that lay before her was staggering, the accumulated institutional knowledge of one of
the world's larger multinational corporations. And the
Grail network information might not even be included –
it was an important secret, after all, wasn't it? At the very
least, it certainly wasn't going to be helpfully labeled.

Almost two hours of browsing the system indexes
confirmed her fears. She sighed, disconnected, and got up
to rip open another coffee pack. There had to be a way
to narrow things down.

It came to her as the cup was still bubbling. It wasn't

the J Corporation she really wanted – it was Jongleur's own personal system. None of the Otherland information, or at least very little of it, would need to be available to J Corporation employees, since the bulk of the network administration seemed to be handled by Robert Wells' Telemorphix, and even though Jongleur owned the J Corporation completely, it was still a quasi-public entity and presumably available to government audits. Jongleur couldn't have bribed *everyone*, could he? She thought the chances were very strong that someone who lived nearly his entire existence online would have his own separate system containing all the most important information, and certainly anything as vital to him as the secrets of the Grail network. The question was, how to find Felix Jongleur's personal system.

The solution, when it came, pleased her sense of irony and confirmed her earlier hunch: Jongleur's own eccentricities would give her the tools to defeat his security.

Jongleur's peculiar use of the VR interface slowed down her initial experiments, but since they were going to be the key to her success, she felt no urge to complain. She put her best analysis gear to work on the places where use of the clumsy, humanizing interface seemed most counterintuitive, guessing that these would be the most likely spots to find Jongleur's own connections to the J Corporation system. The gear did its job. Within an hour the links began to turn up – conduits for information to be siphoned out of the corporate system on a regular basis, data pipelines custom-tailored for Jongleur's own idiosyncratic use. Dulcie felt a buzz of pride. Dread might have his weird little tricks that he would not share or explain – he was clearly using something out of the ordinary to have breached the Otherland security so easily – but she had tricks of her own.

I'm good, damn it. I'm good at this. I'm one of the best.

As her gear tracked the smaller, capillary links to larger links, pursuing their mazelike course through rerouters and firewalls, her excitement continued to rise. This was what it was all about. This was better than anything – better than money, better than sex. When the larger links converged into a single broadband data tap, she was so excited she had to get up and take another walk just to pump some of the nervous energy out of her system so she wouldn't explode. As she paced along the slick, shiny streets in the wake of one of the city's unmanned cleaning trucks, she felt her heart racing as though she had just finished a marathon. All by herself, she was making a billion-credit incursion. If this had been her own play, this would be what others in her business called a retirement strike – she would never have had to work again.

She came back to the loft to find that the tracking gear had located its quarry and finished its work: she was spiked into Jongleur's personal system. There was still work to be done, of course. If it had been a true cold call, Dulcie would have needed weeks just to get into the simplest and least important levels, but now the passwords and other bits and pieces Dread had picked up enabled her to start nibbling away like a mouse in the wall-wiring. It still wasn't easy – the security mechanisms behind the ancient mogul's virtual playground were tough, smart, and adaptive – but because Dread's information was like having a fifth column inside the besieged system, the hardest part was now finished.

A management specialist would be in heaven here, she thought as she surveyed what now lay spread before her. *You could spend days – weeks! – just tracking the custodial staff in that big tower of his. And look at this! Personal security – it's an entire subsection. He's got a damned army out there on his island. Just the quartermaster's requisitions take up ten times the storage I have in my entire system!*

Even the most flawless spike-and-siphon had a time limit, of course, and even as she rode the crest of her triumph, Dulcie was keenly aware that things could go south very quickly.

Dread says Jongleur's out of contact, somehow – but someone must be in charge. You don't just leave a multi-trillion dollar enterprise empty like a laundromat while you step out for a few days. Good God, if J Corporation missed their payroll, the State of Louisiana would collapse.

Contemplating the corporate immensity spread before her, the thought of Dread's own hidden files plucked at her like a beggar's hand. *How much is he hiding from me, anyway? How much can I trust him? I'm putting my life on the line doing this – what if he's wrong? What if his boss is onto him already?*

Looking over Jongleur's empire, she had no doubt that at least one thing Dread had already told her was true: if they wanted to, Jongleur and his associates could make her vanish so quickly and thoroughly that Dulcinea Anwin might as well not have existed.

Only my mom will even notice. And she'll get over it.

In a way, she quickly realized, Dread had been right and she had been wrong. It *was* possible to copy information without surveying it first. In fact, it was imperative. There were so many thousands of files that seemed like they might have something to do with Dread's rather broad mandate, she could only designate whole blocks for duplication and send the data shooting down the high-speed links to the storage space Dread had given her – memory he had partitioned off for her from the Grail Network, because nothing she or Dread had access to would have given her anywhere near enough room.

In her mind's eye, Dulcie saw herself on one of those net game shows – what was that one, *Loot?* – throwing things into bags as fast as she could, stumbling over the objects of her own greed because they were too many and she was only one person.

She worked all night, and did not realize how much coffee she had consumed until she pulled the data-spike and collapsed onto her bed. Her entire nervous system seemed made of sparking, short-circuited electrical wires; she spent three teeth-grinding hours lying on her back until sleep came to her at last.

If she dreamed of lost animals or hospitals this time, she did not remember when she woke. The sleep just passed seemed like an impossibly long stretch of blackness, the attack on Jongleur's system weeks old, but after she had checked on Dread in his coma bed and made her way out into the gray day in search of some kind of meal that didn't come out of a wave-pak, she realized she had slept only ten hours, which wasn't too bad.

Nah, you're getting old, Anwin, she told herself. *Used to be you would have slept for two hours tops, then been up taking the data apart.*

Feeling much more substantial after the ingestion of a couple of rosella bud muffins, a fruit salad, and more coffee, she wandered back to the loft, hooked up her 'can and got into the Jongleur downloads. She had a perverse desire to wake up Dread, roust him out of his machine, and show him what she'd accomplished.

What is that – daddy stuff? She was disgusted with herself. '*Look, I'm a good girl, see what I did for you?*'

She was an hour into the preliminary investigation, and had found several of the codewords that designated Grail-related files, allowing her to pull a large number of them directly out of the mix and into the 'relevant' pile without having to examine them, when she came across an anomalous object. It was a VR file, or at least it had VR code attached to it, but it also had some strange encrypted link embedded in it as well. It was in among a grouping of much more mundane files having to do with what she was loosely calling Jongleur's personal estate – powers of attorney, links to various legal firms and accounting operations, instructions to J Corporation management. She had spent time on the estate data hoping that it might contain some information on maintaining the Grail network in case of an emergency, reasoning that someone as old as Jongleur would want to make sure his pride and joy was kept running properly if he was temporarily disabled. She hadn't found anything – the material seemed quite ordinary, the kind of thing any powerful, wealthy person would have to ease the transition during illness or at death – so the odd file stuck out even more.

It was labeled '*Ushabti*,' a word or name Dulcie didn't recognize, but she guessed from what Dread had told her about the old man's obsessions that it might be Egyptian. It had been created three years earlier and did not seem to have been added to or changed since. She triggered a quick search through her own system, and was given the information that *ushabti* was indeed an ancient Egyptian word, signifying a kind of tomb-statue. There was more detail available, but a quick glance turned up nothing relevant. Dulcie frowned and opened the file itself.

A dark-eyed man appeared before her so swiftly that

she flinched. He was perhaps in his sixties, a tiny smile on his lined face, his white hair neat. The viewpoint drew back to show that he sat behind a desk in an old-fashioned office, something that might have belonged in a nineteenth-century embassy, teak furniture and heavy drapes on the windows.

My God, she thought. *That's Jongleur. But this file is only a few years old, and he can't have looked like that in a hundred years.*

Which meant nothing in VR, of course. *What the hell difference when this was done – this is a guy who appears as some Egyptian god most of the time . . .*

The old man before her nodded his head once, then spoke, the voice public-school English with a tiny hint of something else, something more foreign, beneath.

'And so we meet, my son. Something we could never do while I was alive. I am anxious to tell you everything, and then you will understand why your life has been ordered in the way it has. But first you must tell me your name. Your true name, as it has been given to you, then we may proceed to the more prosaic forms of verifying identity.'

My son? Dulcie sat without a thought of anything to say. She had clearly triggered the first half of some kind of dual-encryption, and now Jongleur – or his recorded sim, or his ghost, or whatever the hell this was – was waiting for the other half of the key.

'I wait for your true name,' the old man said, a bit more of an edge in his voice. His eyes were quite mesmerizing, Dulcie thought as she waited helplessly – 'commanding' is what they would have been called in a romance, although there was little romantic about this flinty old monarch. If he had looked anything like that in real life, it was easy to understand how he had built himself an empire.

'Your true name,' the pseudo-Jongleur said for the third time. A moment later he was gone. The file had closed itself.

Dulcie rubbed her hand against her forehead and felt a film of sweat. She dropped out of the system. It was definitely time to take a break.

An hour later she sat staring at the *Ushabti* file. She was unwilling to open it again, or even examine it too closely, because things like this often had a built in number of attempts they would allow before simply self-destructing.

A search of available information on Jongleur had done nothing to illuminate the mystery. Not only had his actual sons and daughters died a century ago, but according to the best sources she could find there was nothing like a direct line of succession. All of his living relatives – the oldest still generations younger than Jongleur himself – were descendants of his cousins. He was not known to be close to any of them, nor did any of them have a role in the J Corporation.

As carefully as a specialist handling an unexploded bomb, Dulcie picked the *Ushabti* file out from the midst of the estate information and moved it onto her private system, then went back to work sorting files.

Dread could hide things? Dread wanted to keep secrets from her? Well, Dulcie could keep secrets of her own.

'Let's have another one,' Dread decided. 'This is interesting.'

He waved his hand and a dark-haired, muscular man shuffled forward into the glare of torches and fell to his knees. His linen robes showed signs of having been costly once, but they were singed and torn, and his black wig sat askew.

'What's your name?' Dread asked him.

'Seneb, O Lord.'

'And what do you do?' Dread turned to the woman beside him. 'Kind of funny, isn't it? Like a game show.'

'I . . . I am a m-m-merchant, O Great House.' He was so terrified he could hardly speak.

'Tell me . . . hmmm. What did you have for breakfast this morning?'

Seneb paused, fearful of a wrong answer. 'I . . . I had nothing, Lord. I have not eaten in two days.'

Dread waved a huge, pitch-black hand. 'The last time you had brekkie, then, mate. What did you have?'

'Bread, Lord. And a little beer.' The man wrinkled his forehead, thinking desperately. 'And a duck egg! Yes, a duck egg.'

'See?' Dread grinned at his female guest, his red jackal tongue lolling. It was much more entertaining to do these kinds of things with a real human audience. 'Every one different.' He pointed to the priest he had been interrogating only moments before beginning on the merchant. 'And what do you think of this bloke, eh? Is he a good man?'

Seneb looked at the cowering priest, again unsure of the answer that was wanted. 'He is a priest of Osiris, Lord. All the priests of Osiris are good men . . . are they not?'

'Well, since Osiris has stepped out for a while . . .' Dread smirked. 'I suppose we'll have to leave that question unanswered. But how about if I asked you to fight with him? To kill him if you can?'

Seneb, for all his beefy size, was trembling. That might have been in part because the jackal-headed god on the throne before him was twice human height. 'If the great Lord wishes it,' he said at last, 'then I must do it.'

Dread laughed. 'See? Some of them can't wait to pitch

into one of the priests. Some of the others think it's sacrilege and won't do it to save their own lives. It's bloody marvelous.'

His guest looked at him uncomprehendingly.

'Don't you see?' Dread asked. 'You can't predict anything here! God – no pun intended – but this is an impressive situation. They all are.' He turned to Seneb. 'If you kill him, I'll let you live.'

Seneb stared shamefacedly at the priest, hesitating.

'What are you waiting for?'

'And . . . and my family?'

'You want to kill your family, too?' Dread barked a laugh. 'Ah, I see, you want to know if I'll *spare* your family. Cheers. Why not?'

As the merchant Seneb raised his hands and lurched toward the priest, an older, frailer man who now moaned in fear, Dread shook his head in continued wonderment. It really was quite stunning. He remembered the Renie woman and others commenting on it, but with the total access he now enjoyed, the unshackled freedom to bend the network's simulated humans into any shape pain and power could contrive, it was even more clear: the individuality of these constructs was something unprecedented, each with its own little internal universe of hopes and prejudices and memories.

He could almost see why someone like Jongleur thought he could spend an eternity in this place. Not that he could imagine such a thing himself, at least not in the immediate future. Dread had nearly exhausted most of the obvious ways of enjoying himself, and although he definitely planned to take advantage of the Grail network's immortality options, he was not ready to give up the pleasures of real as opposed to virtual flesh. Not yet.

Still, there was fun to be had.

'Come on, admit it – you're rooting for one of them.'

The woman beside him shut her mouth in a firm line. Dread smiled. This was much more fun than anything he could do with Dulcie, to whom he was still forced to show a friendly face. After all, there was still so much more he needed her for. He had a lot to learn about the Grail network, but now that he had confirmed the Old Man's continuing absence – Jongleur's private line had gone dead, and if he still was somewhere in the Grail system, he was as marooned as any of Dread's former companions had been – he needed her to find a way into Jongleur's personal files. He badly wanted information about the operating system, and also about things that mattered outside the small, hermetic world of the Otherland system.

With the Old Man's money and power, Dread thought happily, *I can be a god in the real world, too. I can play these kind of tricks with real people. Industrial accidents. Biochemical releases. A few small wars when the mood strikes me. And then I'll have the Grail network to keep me alive.*

Astonishing vistas had opened up. Control of the Otherland system, which had seemed like the be-all and end-all, might only be the beginning.

John Wulgaru, he thought to himself. *Little Johnny Dread. King of the world.*

The merchant Seneb fought clumsily, but the aged priest was no match. His mostly toothless mouth sagged open as the younger man seized him and cracked his head against the polished stone of the temple floor, over and over.

Dread's female guest had closed her eyes. He smiled. If she thought that would solve the problem, she might be interested to find out how easily her eyelids could be removed. He turned to his other guest, who was just beginning to groan his way back to consciousness.

'A little bored?' Dread waved his silver staff and the merchant and priest melted screaming into puddles on the marble. The crowd of watchers shrieked too. Dread was intrigued; he had expected them all to be numbed to pain and death by now. 'Well, then perhaps it's time to get on with our own business.'

'You can torture me as much as you want,' the woman said. 'Even if you really *were* the Devil, I'd have nothing for you but the back of my hand.'

'Oh, come now.' Dread leaned over until his great muzzle touched her cheek and his nose pressed wetly on her ear. He licked the side of her face and wondered idly what it would feel like to take her head off in one bite. Would knowing it was a real person make it different? He had tried it enough times with this simworld's virtual inhabitants. 'Let's play a game . . . what was your name? Ah, right, Bonnie Mae. Let's play a game, Bonnie Mae. Every time you tell me something useful about the Circle, or about some friends of mine I know you met, that's worth an hour without pain. Play your cards right, you could have a couple of nice days' vacation here in sunny Egypt.'

'I'll tell you nothing. Get thee behind me, Satan.'

'Yes, well, I'm sure you'd keep your mouth shut like a good little martyr, no matter *what* I did to you, Little Red Riding Hood. At least at first. But let's not waste time.' He turned and reached a massive hand toward the other prisoner. The ends of Dread's stark black fingers began to glow an incandescent red. 'But how long can you stay quiet if it's your little Indian friend here that's taking the punishment?' He leered at his male captive. 'Wishing you had made it out of this simulation before I took over, aren't you?' He closed his long fingers on the man's leg.

Flesh sizzled and steamed. The prisoner's shrieks made even the numbed crowd moan and fall to the floor.

'No!' the woman screamed. 'Stop it, you devil! Stop it!'

'But that's just the point, sweetness.' Dread lifted his smoking fingers in a gesture of mock helplessness. 'It's not up to me to stop it – it's up to you.'

'Don't . . . don't tell him anything, Mrs Simpkins!' Nandi Paradivash was shivering with agony, but struggling to remain upright. 'I am no less bound than you. My life is nothing. My pain is nothing.'

'Oh, on the contrary,' said Dread. 'It's quite a bit. And if she won't talk to save you, I think you will when I start on her.' He grinned, displaying a line of teeth like an ivory chess set. 'Because I do even better work on women.'

CHAPTER 14

The Stone Girl

NETFEED/NEWS: Net Has Its Own Folklore
(visual: artist's rendering of TreeHouse node)
VO: Net historian Gwenafra Glass says that, like all new countries,
the net has its own folktales, mythical beasts, and ghosts.
GLASS: 'You go back to the earliest days and you hear about things
like cable lice. TreeHouse is another sort of example. It's a real node,
but it's been embroidered over the years into something that's mostly
fantasy. And more recently we have things like the Weeper, which is
a strange sobbing voice people hear sometimes in unoccupied chat
nodes and unfinished VR nodes. And of course an old folktale from
the twentieth century, the gremlins that used to lock up fighter
airplanes, has carried over into the Glowbugs and Lightsnakes that
people these days claim to have seen in VR environments, but no one
ever finds in the code . . .'

RENIE looked wildly from side to side, but could see no sign of whatever had made the sound. The nearest of the ghostly shapes pursuing her was a pale smear in the twilight murk, frighteningly close, but still several dozen meters away. She took a step to steady herself and to her horror felt something clutch at her ankle. She leaped away with a muffled shriek.

'Down here,' a small voice said. 'You can hide!'

Something rustled near Renie's feet. 'I . . . I can't see you.' Wind carried the pursuing creature's liquid groan down the slope. 'Where are you?'

'Down. Get down!'

Renie dropped to her hands and knees amid the under-growth, baffled by the shadows. One of the patches of darkness widened a little and a small hand reached out, closed on her wrist, and tugged. Renie crawled forward and found herself in a recess scarcely larger than her own huddled form, a space where a tangle of fallen branches had been silted over with crushed leaves and dirt. Pushing in headfirst, she could see nothing of the pocket's other inhabitant, and could feel only a childlike form pressed the length of her side. 'Who are you?' she asked quietly.

'Sssshhh.' The shape next to her stiffened. 'It's close.'

Renie's heart was still beating uncomfortably fast. 'But won't it smell us?' she whispered.

'It doesn't smell things – it hears them.'

Renie shut her mouth. She huddled, the smell of damp earth in her nostrils, and tried not to think about being buried alive.

She felt the hunter's approach before she heard it, a gradually growing sense of panic that made her skin tighten and her already speeding heart threaten to rattle right out of her chest. Was this the helpless, paralyzing horror that Paul Jonas felt each time the Twins came near him? Her respect for the man went up another notch, even as she fought down shrieking panic.

The terrifying thing had moved above them now; she could sense it as clearly as if a cloud had swung in front of the sun. Her throat tightened until the urge to scream was gone. She could not have made a noise if she wanted.

But the thing itself was not silent. It moaned again,

the sound so pulsingly near that it seemed to turn Renie's bones to sand in their sockets. In the wake of that awful noise she could hear other sounds, a sighing murmur, as though the phantom whispered to itself in a voice of wind, meaningless sounds just on the edge of speech. The breathy gibberish was as unbearable as the scream. It was the sound of a dying or even dead intelligence, an empty madness. Renie, already in darkness, squeezed her eyes shut until her face ached, clenched her teeth together, and prayed directionlessly for strength.

The sounds gradually grew more faint. The sensation of hungry, brainless malevolence also lessened. Renie cautiously let out her breath. The shape beside her touched her arm with cool fingers, as though to warn her against premature celebration, but Renie had no urge at all to move or make a sound.

Several minutes passed before the small voice said, 'I think they're all gone now.'

Renie wasted no time backing out of the tiny cavern of twigs and leaf-scatter. Afternoon, or what passed for it in this sunless place, was almost entirely gone. The world was gray, but seemed still a bit too bright for this shank of twilight, as though the stones and even the trees gave off a faint light of their own.

The foliage rustled at her feet. The little figure that crawled out was mottled gray and brown, human-shaped but not very exactly so, as though it had been cut out of raw soil with a cookie cutter.

Renie took a step backward. 'Who are you?'

The newcomer looked at her, surprise evident on its face – a face mostly suggested by the arrangement of dark and light spots and bumps and holes in the dun-colored surface. 'You don't know me?' The voice was soft but surprisingly clear. 'I'm the Stone Girl. I thought everyone knew me. But you didn't know enough to hide, so I guess that makes sense.'

'I'm sorry. Thank you for helping me.' She stared out along the empty hillside. 'What . . . what were those things?'

'Those?' The Stone Girl gave her a look of mild surprise. 'Just some Jinnears. They come out at night. I shouldn't have stayed out so late, but . . .' The Stone Girl's expression suddenly became morose, in its simple way. She bent and brushed herself free of clinging leaves, quite deftly considering the thickness of her limbs and the clumsy shape of her blunt fingers and toes.

'So who are you?' the little girl asked when she had straightened up. 'Why don't you know about Jinnears?'

'Just a stranger,' Renie said. 'A traveler, I guess.' The Stone Girl might look as though she had been quickly molded from raw soil, but there was an odd suppleness to her movements, as though she could bend in places other than just the normal joints. 'Do you live here?' Renie asked her. 'Can you tell me anything about it?' A sudden thought struck her. 'I'm looking for some friends – one is a small man, almost as dark as me, the other is a girl with curly hair and paler skin. Have you seen them?'

The indentations that were the Stone Girl's eyes widened. 'You sure ask a lot of questions.'

'I'm sorry. I'm . . . I'm lost. Have you seen them?'

The little head tilted slowly from side to side. 'No. Were you out in the Ending?'

'If you mean that place over there where things get . . . kind of strange, hard to see . . . Yes, I guess so.' Renie suddenly realized how tired she was. 'I really need to find my friends.'

'You need to get out of here, that's for sure. I do, too – I should never have been out so late, but I was trying to get to the Witching Tree to ask about the Ending.' The Stone Girl followed this unedifying explanation with a moment of silent thought. 'You'd better come with me to see the stepmother,' she said at last.

'The stepmother? Who's that?'

'Don't you have one? Don't you have a family at all?'

Renie sighed. This had become another one of those incomprehensible Otherland conversations. 'Never mind. Sure, take me to this stepmother. Is it far?'

'Shoes. Down by the bottom of the Pants,' the Stone Girl added, equally cryptically, and waddled past Renie to begin clambering down the hillside.

It didn't take long for Renie to understand the geographical reference, although it was not the kind of understanding that really explained anything.

As they made their way down the hillside in the dying light, following the course of the river, which emerged through a gash in the hillside and splashed energetically down toward the misty valley below, Renie began to see that her earlier observations had been disturbingly true. The shapes of the distant hills mimicked that of human forms, although they were still true hills, made at least on the surface from soil and covered in vegetation, as though earth had covered over the carcasses of titan forms. But where the giant on the black mountaintop had been singular and unquestionably alive, these smaller and more numerous forms buried in the earth seemed the remnants of some impossibly earlier time.

'What is this place?' she asked her guide when she caught up with her again.

The Stone Girl tried to look back over her shoulder, but it was hard without a neck. 'Haven't you been here? It's Where The Beans Talk. You can see all the giants that fell. They're big,' she added somewhat unnecessarily.

'Real giants?' Renie asked, then immediately felt stupid. As if such a question could mean anything in a world like this.

The Stone Girl seemed to take it at face value, however. 'They were. They fell. I don't remember why. Maybe you could ask the stepmother.'

As they followed the line of the cataracts down, Renie began to understand the rest of the girl's strange description. When she had seen them through the mist, the land's unusual features had seemed only the effect of odd hills and shadowy copses of trees, but now that she could see better she began to make out a strange order. One great fold of hillside, a ridge with a line of trees stark along its spine, was now revealed to be a single huge . . .

'. . . *Sleeve?*' Renie said. 'It's a sleeve? Do you mean we're walking down a . . . a shirt?'

The Stone Girl again twitched her head in the negative. 'Jacket. We're in the Jackets now. The Shirts are over there.' She pointed a stubby finger. 'Do you want to go to the Shirts?'

Renie shook her head violently. 'No. No, I was just . . . surprised. Why is this country . . . why is it all made of clothes?'

The Stone Girl stopped and turned, apparently tired of trying to talk over her shoulder without the proper anatomical equipment. She looked as though she suspected Renie of making sport of her. 'Why, they came off the giants, didn't they? When they fell.'

'Ah,' said Renie, who could think of nothing else to say. 'Of course.'

As they descended through river mist down a long fold of one of the Jackets, picking their way between the small but stubborn pines that seemed to cluster on all the most narrow and difficult bits of the path, Renie asked her small guide, 'Do you know anything about birds that talk?'

The Stone Girl shrugged. 'Sure. Lots of birds talk.'

'This one kept repeating the same thing again and again, no matter what I asked it.'

'You can't really talk to the ones that are asleep,' the girl told her.

'What does that mean? That bird was flying – it wasn't sleeping.'

'No, that's just how they are when they first get here, all sleepy, doesn't matter if they're flying or nothing. Used to be, anyway – there aren't many that come anymore. But the new ones never understand much at first. Just say the same things, over and over. I used to try to talk to them when I was little.' She darted Renie a quick look, just as any real girl would, to make sure that Renie realized she was very grown-up now, not just a kid. 'The stepmother said it wasn't our business – we should let them sleep, let them dream.'

Renie pondered this with a growing sense of excitement. 'So the birds . . . are sleeping? Dreaming?'

The Stone Girl nodded, then swung herself down to a lower section of the path and waited for Renie to follow. 'Yeah. Watch out for that part – it's pretty slippery.'

Renie balanced, then let herself slide down beside her. 'But . . . but what do you call this place, anyway? Not the . . . the Jackets, here, but all of this.' She lifted her hands. 'Everything.'

Before the girl could answer, a terrible choking sob came echoing up the furrowed hillside. Renie flinched so badly she almost lost her footing and fell. 'Oh my God, it's another one of those things!'

Her guide was calmer than she was, holding up her

blunt fingers for quiet. For a moment, as they stood in the mists, Renie heard nothing but the soft rush and splash of the nearby river. Then another ragged cry rose from the valley below.

'It's farther away now,' the Stone Girl pronounced. 'Going the other direction. Come on.'

Renie, only slightly heartened, hurried after her.

It was easier going as they neared the valley floor, but the mist was thicker, too, and the slow twilight seemed finally to have made the turn into night. In deepening shadow the strange shapes of the clothing, the mountainous shirts and pants only partially concealed by a cloak of earth and vegetation, seemed even more disturbing. Here and there Renie thought she could see smaller shapes moving in the mist, as though people watched her and the Stone Girl – people who did not particularly want to be seen in return. Renie was grateful to have a guide. Fumbling her way alone through these strange hills in growing darkness, especially with those screaming somethings on the loose, was not a pleasant idea.

From the fires she saw flickering through the mist, it seemed certain that many people, or many *somethings*, in any case, made their homes among the folds of Pants and Shirts. As the Stone Girl took them along the seam of a small canyon between a row of cookfires on the heights, a few voices called down greetings. Her guide lifted her stubby arm in reply, and Renie felt reassured enough to wish that !Xabbu and Sam could share this with her. There was something deeply, primitively satisfying about coming into a lighted settlement at night, especially after being in the wilderness, and she had been in something much more bleak than any ordinary wilderness for days.

As they moved out of the Pants into another dark

crease between hills, the Stone Girl said, 'We're almost there. Maybe the stepmother will be able to tell you where your friends are. And I have to tell her about the Witching Tree, and how the Ending's getting so much closer.'

They came around an outcropping of stone into another vale of cheery light. The buildings were ramshackle but the shapes were unmistakable, some of them so much a part of the landscape that they were indistinguishable from natural features, but others actually sticking most of the way out of the ground so that cookfires gleamed in the eyelets or through gaps in the soles. There were dozens of them, perhaps hundreds – an entire town.

'They're shoes! Big shoes!'

'I told you, didn't I?'

As she got used to the light, Renie saw that the spaces between the shoes were occupied too, dozens and dozens of figures huddled beside fires, shadowy shapes that watched almost silently as Renie and the Stone Girl passed. Despite their silence, she felt little menace. The eyes that stared at them, the voices that whispered, seemed dulled with weariness and despair.

It's like a shantytown, she thought.

'There aren't usually people living out here,' the Stone Girl explained. 'It's because they lost their homes when the Ending came. There are so many of them now, and they're hungry and scared . . .'

She was interrupted by a dozen shrieking shapes running toward them from out of a dark clutter of gigantic footwear. Renie's moment of panic ended quickly when she realized they were only children. Most of them were even smaller than the Stone Girl, and their energy was unmistakable.

'Where you been?' one of the nearest shouted. 'The stepmother is in a state.'

'I found someone.' The Stone Girl gestured toward Renie. 'Took a while to get back.'

The children surrounded them, chattering and jostling. Renie had assumed they were the Stone Girl's siblings, but in the growing light that spilled from the mouth of the nearest shoe she saw that none of them looked anything like her guide. Most of them appeared more ordinarily human, although their clothing (for those who wore any) was of a style she could not identify. But some of the swarm of laughing children were even stranger than the Stone Girl, their shapes distorted and fantastical – one plumply furred in yellow and black like a bumblebee, another with feet like a duck's, and even one child, Renie was startled to see, who had a huge hole right through her middle, so that she had almost no torso at all.

'Are these . . . your brothers and sisters?' she asked.

The Stone Girl shrugged. 'Sort of. There are a lot of us. So many that sometimes I think the stepmother just doesn't know what to do.'

The shape of a vast shoe loomed before them, and Renie suddenly drew up and stopped. 'Jesus Mercy,' she said. 'I get it.'

'Come on,' said the Stone Girl, and for the first time took Renie's hand. Her fingers were rough, with the cool dampness of forest loam. A little boy with the head of a deer looked up at Renie with shy, liquid brown eyes, as though he wished he could take the other hand, but Renie was busy wrestling with this new realization. 'Of course – it's that damn nursery rhyme, "The Old Woman Who Lived in a Shoe."' Something else was tugging at her, too, some distant memory, but it was hard enough to deal with finding herself in a Mother Goose book.

'We *all* live in shoes,' her guide said, drawing her

through a door at the back of the ancient, moss-covered boot. 'Well, everybody around here . . .'

It was a very, very old shoe. To Renie's relief, no olfactory traces of its previous giant owner remained. Two or three times as many children waited in the smoky firelight as had come out to meet them, but the stay-at-homes seemed just as weirdly diverse. Those who had eyes watched Renie with fascination as the Stone Girl led her through the great boot toward the toe. Although there were far too many for introductions, the Stone Girl called a few by name, mostly while instructing them to get out of the way – 'Polly,' 'Little Seed,' 'Hans,' and 'Big Ears' were a few Renie heard. She had to step over many of them, and a few times she trod on someone by accident, but no one objected. She guessed that the crowded way they lived had accustomed them to it.

Could these be the children in comas? she wondered. *Is that what this place is – a kind of concentration camp for all the children the Other has stolen?* If so, the prospects for finding Stephen were daunting – there might well be thousands just here in the Shoes, and God alone knew how many in the other pieces of clothing throughout the hills.

'Is that you, Stone Girl?' a voice called, echoing slightly in the dome of the toe. 'You're late back and you've set me worrying. These are bad times. It can't be allowed.'

A dark shape sat in a rocking chair beside the fireplace. A brick chimney poked up through the shoe leather overhead, but to little effect. In fact, Renie first thought it was the pervasive smoke that made it hard to see the figure in the chair, but then she realized that the humanoid form was itself vague as mist – a suggestion of shoulders and a head atop a body shapeless as a gray cloud. Twinned glimmers of firelight seemed to reflect where the eyes should be, but otherwise it had no face. The voice, though faint and airy, did not seem either particularly feminine or kindly. It was certainly not any version of the Old Woman in the Shoe that Renie would have expected.

'I . . . I tried to find the Witching Tree, Stepmother,' the Stone Girl said. 'Because everything is going wrong. I wanted to ask it . . .'

'No! You are back late. It's not allowed. And you have brought one who does not belong here. Already the streets outside are full of those who have lost their homes – why do we need another? We have nothing to share.'

'But she was lost. One of the Jinnears tried to . . .'

The smoky matter of the stepmother became for a moment more solid. The eyes flashed. 'You misbehaved. That calls for punishment.'

The Stone Girl abruptly fell to the floor, writhing and crying. The other children were all silent, their eyes wide.

'Leave her alone!' Renie took a step toward the fallen Stone Girl, but something jumped through her like electricity, a great convulsive snap of pain that threw her onto her hands and knees beside the child.

'This one does not belong,' the stepmother said complacently. 'Too big, too strange. This one must go.'

Renie raised her head; her jaw flexed but nothing would come out. Fighting to control her jerking limbs, she crawled a short way forward. The stepmother stared at her, then another whiplash of agony ran up Renie's spine and exploded blackly in her skull.

She dimly felt herself lifted by many small hands. When they set her down again, she was so grateful to stop moving she tried to say so, but only managed a wheeze. The dirt against her face was cool and damp, rather like the Stone Girl's hand, and she lay against it appreciatively as the last painful twitches worked their way out of her arms and legs.

When she could sit up, she found herself in the middle of a dark street surrounded by huge Shoes, as though she had been tossed into the back of some gargantuan closet. Light leaked from some of the dwellings, but their doors were all shut tight. Even the campfires of the shantytowns seemed to have been hurriedly extinguished, but she sensed the silent homeless watching her with fear and mistrust.

Okay, she thought blearily. *Don't have to hit me over the head. Know when I'm not wanted.*

A thin wail floated down into the valley. Renie shivered, wondering what she was going to do now, lost and alone.

She was staggering down the twisting thoroughfare when a shape came out of the shadows.

'I left.' The Stone Girl's voice was very small.

Renie wasn't certain – she wasn't certain about anything – but it seemed something important had happened.

'You . . . ran away?'

'The stepmother is getting meaner and meaner. And she won't listen to me about the Ending.' The Stone Girl made a funny sound, a muddy little snort. Renie realized she was crying. 'And she shouldn't have given you punishment.' She thrust something toward Renie – a blanket, soft and threadbare. 'I brought you this, so you won't be so cold. I'll go with you.'

Renie was touched but a bit overwhelmed. As she wrapped the blanket around her shoulders, she couldn't help wondering whether she had been given a huge favor or a huge responsibility. 'Go with me . . . where?'

'I'll take you to the Witching Tree. Ask it for help.

That's where I was trying to go today, but the Ending has eaten up the path I used to take. We'll have to go through the Wood.'

'Right now?'

The little shape nodded. 'It's the best time to find it. But we have to be careful – there are things hunting. Jinnears – and Ticks, too.' She looked up, suddenly hesitant. 'If you want to come with me, that is.'

Renie let out a breath. 'Oh, definitely. If you promise you'll explain a few things to me along the way.'

The Stone Girl's dark line of a smile was odd but genuine. 'That's right, you like to ask questions, don't you?'

THE world around them, Sam decided, was becoming both more and less real.

More real because as they walked farther upriver, what had been glassy translucency became more substantial, the meadows and hills all solid objects now, the river itself unarguably wet, splashing noisily beside them. More unreal because nothing seemed quite normal, as though it were all a picture improperly copied from life – or even a picture copied from another picture. The colors and shapes were all subtly wrong, too regular or simply not quite recognizable.

'It is purely an invention, I think,' said !Xabbu as he examined one of a small, scattered stand of trees by the riverside, the bark whorled like fingernails, the perfectly circular leaves like translucent silver coins. 'Like the first flower I made – a flower that was more an idea than anything else.'

'The first flower you made?' Sam asked.

'When Renie was teaching me how things are done in these virtual worlds.' He shook his head. 'This seems the same – as though made by a child playing, or someone experimenting.'

'Wasn't Renie talking about that? She said the mountain might have been made by . . . the Other. That system-thing. So maybe this all is, too.'

'It seems likely. It certainly is not a perfect copy of some real-world place.' He brushed aside some of the silvery leaves and smiled. 'Look, there is too much shini-ness, too much color! In that way, it is much like what a child would do.'

Jongleur turned back toward them, his bony face set hard. 'Are you two still wasting time? It will be dark soon.'

!Xabbu shrugged. 'Perhaps. We do not know the rules of this place.'

'Do you want to get eaten by something, then, because you don't know the rules?'

The little man paused, restraining his temper. Until recently, Sam had thought of him as perennially good-natured, but spending so much time with Jongleur was testing even !Xabbu's tremendous reserves of courtesy and equanimity. 'It is probably a good idea to make camp, yes,' he said with measured calm. 'Is that what you are saying?'

'We're not going to find that . . . your friend. Not before dark.' Jongleur's early mood of quiet withdrawal was over. He looked at Sam and !Xabbu as though he would gladly have hit them both with a stick, although he, too, kept his voice almost civil. 'This is not like being on the mountain – there may be living things here that we would not want to meet.'

'Very well,' said !Xabbu. 'Then this is as good a place as any to stop, since at least the ground is flat.' He turned to Sam. 'The man is right about one thing – we do not know what will come to us in this new land.'

'If you want me to gather wood or something, you could go have one last look around for Renie. Call her or whatever.'

He nodded, grateful. 'Thank you, Sam. I think I can make a fire – it worked in that unfinished place where we were before. See what you can find that is loose on the ground.'

She was not surprised when !Xabbu returned slowly, as though carrying something heavy. She had heard him shouting Renie's name for a long time. She decided to spare him the effort of making cheerful conversation.

He crouched and began building the fire. Jongleur sat on a spotted stone, brooding silently, his naked legs pressed together. Sam thought the old man looked like a gargoyle off a church roof.

Some of the trees stirred as a breeze blew across the grassy hills and through the camp. Watching the fire ripple, Sam realized that weather was one of the things that had returned when they had reached this area of greater substance.

Will it just keep getting more real? she wondered. It was only when !Xabbu looked up at her in surprise that she realized she had said it aloud. She felt silly, but the thought would not go away. 'I mean, if we keep walking, will this world just get more and more real?'

Before !Xabbu could speak, Jongleur leaned forward. 'If you think we will walk all the way back to the network, child, you will be painfully disappointed. This is not part of what I built, none of this. We are in some backwater of the net constructed by the operating system, something separate from the rest – very separate.'

'Well, what's it all for, then?'

Jongleur only scowled and stared at the fire.

'He doesn't know either,' Sam told !Xabbu. 'He's just dupping, like he knows everything, but he's scared like we are.'

Jongleur snorted. 'I am not "scared like you are," girl. If anything, I have more to fear, because I have more to lose. But I do not waste energy on pointless talk.'

!Xabbu reached over and patted Sam's hand. 'If only about one thing, he is again correct. We should get rest now, because who knows what we will find tomorrow?'

Sam hugged herself. 'I hope one of the things we find tomorrow is something to wear. It's getting cold.' She looked at !Xabbu, as contented in his own bare skin as if he were dressed. 'Aren't you cold, too?'

He smiled. 'I will be, perhaps. So we will spend some time tomorrow trying to discover if any of the plants here are good for weaving into clothes, or at least blankets.'

The idea of a project, however small, lifted Sam's heart. Nothing since Orlando's death had seemed to have much point, and certainly they seemed no closer to learning what they truly needed to know . . . but it would be very nice to be warm again.

She felt sleep pulling on her, so she curled up near the fire.

Sam thought she had only been asleep for a second when !Xabbu's long fingers touched her face.

'Quiet,' he whispered. 'Something is nearby.'

She tried to thrash herself upright but !Xabbu held her back. Jongleur too was awake and watching as shadows moved in the high grasses just beyond the firelight. Sam realized she was having trouble getting her breath. She reminded herself of all the frightening adventures she and Orlando had experienced together, how she had learned to fight through her nervous excitement to do what was needed.

Yeah, but this is real.

It wasn't, of course – just one look at the strange trees showed her that – but the danger was. A quiet hiss that might have been the wind, or might have been whispering voices, eddied past. Sam fumbled out the hilt of Orlando's sword and held it with both hands because she was trembling too much to hold it steady with just one.

A small shape slipped into the circle of firelight. It crouched low to the ground, huge round eyes staring nervously. It was one of the strangest animals she had ever seen, a bizarre hybrid of monkey and something like a kangaroo, its spindly legs covered with long fur, its tiny head set low against its body.

Jongleur suddenly lunged forward and snatched a smoldering branch from the fire. By the time he had straightened up the creature had vanished back into the tall grass.

'Stop,' !Xabbu said. 'It offered us no harm.'

Jongleur scowled. 'And doubtless the first piranha to reach a swimmer is well-mannered, too. But there are many more out there. I heard them.'

Before either !Xabbu or Sam could respond, the wide-eyed face appeared at the edge of the clearing again. Despite the creature's unfortunate aspect, Sam felt her heart touched by its bravery – it was half the size of Sam and her companions, and clearly frightened almost to death. But she was still startled when the creature spoke.

'You . . . you talk?' It slurred and mumbled the words, but they were still clear.

'We talk, yes,' !Xabbu replied. 'Who are you? Will you come and sit by our fire?'

'Sit by our fire . . . !' Jongleur exploded. The scrawny creature flinched away from him but stood its ground.

'Yes. Where I come from, we do not drive someone from our fire who has shown us no harm.' !Xabbu turned back to their small, hairy visitor. 'Come and sit. Tell us your name.'

The thing hesitated, bobbing on its long legs, rubbing its front paws together. 'Others are with me. Cold and frightened. They can come to the fire?'

!Xabbu quelled Jongleur with a look, which impressed Sam no end, although on this particular issue she was closer to Jongleur's opinion than to her friend's. 'Yes,' !Xabbu told the stranger, 'if they mean no harm.'

The thing smiled nervously. 'Nice. Things are . . . are not good. Everyone frightened.' It turned on its long legs, then turned back. 'Jecky Nibble. That's my name. You are nice people.' It faced out toward the forest and made a fluting sound, summoning its companions.

At first it seemed to Sam as though someone had thrown open the doors of a pet shop and let the merchandise escape. The dozen or so creatures that crept cautiously out of the undergrowth and into the faint firelight were mostly small and might have been mistaken for rats or dogs or cats until the firelight began to reveal a few odd details. Even as she found herself both disturbed and fascinated by the many tiny ways they were *not* the things they resembled, she heard a whirring above her head and looked up to see another score or so of visitors, winged creatures in the approximate shape of birds, settling in the branches all around the clearing.

'What, has the Ark sprung a leak?' Jongleur growled.

'Hey! He made a joke – sort of.' Sam tried to keep her voice light, but didn't take her eyes off the squadron of small, strange creatures that now shared their campfire. 'He must be scanning out pretty bad.'

'I will build up the fire,' !Xabbu told the first creature.

'We have no food to offer, but you are welcome to share the warmth.'

Jecky Nibble gave a funny bow, long legs flexing. 'Nice. Very.' It fluted again and the small animals scurried forward across the clearing, making a ring around the fire.

'Who are your companions?' !Xabbu asked as he laid some colorful deadwood on the fire. 'Or are they your children?'

To Sam it seemed a very strange question – how could a monkey-kangaroo be the parent of birds and three-eared rabbits? – but Jecky Nibble did not seem to find it unusual. 'No, not mine. I make . . .' It paused, big round eyes suddenly asquint as it thought. 'I do . . . I take? I take care of them? Of new ones – find them places, families. But no families left. Outside the gathering-places, it's very bad.' It shook its small round head. 'We are trying to find a bridge. The world is getting so small! I think the One is angry at us!'

'Who's . . . the One?' Sam asked. 'And what do you mean, "find them families"?'

A flicker of apprehension slid across Jecky Nibble's face, plain even in the dim light. 'You don't know? Don't know the One?'

'We are from far away,' !Xabbu said quickly. 'Perhaps our name is different than yours. You mean . . . you mean the One who made all this?'

It nodded, relieved. 'Yes, yes! The One who made us all. Brought us across the White Ocean. Feeds us. Gives us families.'

The smaller creatures, who had been murmuring and chirping quietly, now fell into reverent silence. Some of them nodded their tiny heads, smiling distantly, lost in a dream of nourishing community.

But Felix Jongleur was not smiling. In fact, Sam couldn't help noticing that he looked angry enough to bite someone. The visitors seemed to have noticed, too, and although they were now thick on the ground across the camp, they kept conspicuously distant from him.

Sam realized she had been sitting in one place so long that her joints were aching. She sat up, and the movement sent a flurry of startlement through their small guests. A few of the birds went whirring up into the air and did not settle back on their branches until Sam was still again.

The weird audience of tiny, staring creatures was becoming almost too much for her. Sam repressed a giggle. 'It's just like, what was that scanbox show for kids? *Bubble Bunnies on the Torture Planet? Any minute, they're going to start singing, ". . .* Bunny ears, bunny toes, extra-flexy bunny nose . . ."'

'Shut up, child,' Jongleur snapped. 'How can a man think with all this prattling?'

'Do not talk to her that way,' said !Xabbu.

'Worry not – I don't pay any attention to him . . .' Sam was interrupted by one of the small, vaguely squirrellike creatures, who suddenly took a few steps toward her and stood on its rear legs, staring at her fixedly.

'*He always says I spend too much time on the net,*' it proclaimed in a thin voice. '*Just 'cause he thinks Bubble Bunnies is stupid and doesn't have mortal values.*' It looked at her expectantly after finishing, as though awaiting a counteroffer on a major proposal. Then its tiny face fell and it crept back among its fellows.

'*Who* always says?' Sam could make no sense of it. 'I mean, did you hear that? It utterly talked! It talked about Bubble Bunnies!' She turned to !Xabbu, trying not to giggle, but somehow very frightened too. 'What did that mean?'

'That . . . the ghost-life,' said Jecky Nibble, worried
again. 'Didn't you have one when you first came here?
The One gives it to all – but maybe you forgot yours
when you found your place. It happens.'

Before she or !Xabbu could reply, Jongleur suddenly
bent over the monkeylike creature. 'The . . . One, you say?
It *made* you?' He leaned in closer. 'Made all *this*?'

Jecky Nibble raised long arms above its head for protection. 'Of course! One made everything. One made you,
too!'

'Oh, did it?' Jongleur's voice had become quieter and
nastier, like a burner turned down to a fierce blue flame.
'Well, you just take me to this One.' His hand snapped
out with startling speed and locked on a thin, furry wrist.
'Then we will damn well find out.'

Jecky Nibble let out a shriek as though it had been
burned. Its charges fled the clearing in a hiss of wings
and trampled grass. A moment later only the captured
creature remained, trying desperately to free itself from
Jongleur's grip. The look of raw terror on its little face
made Sam feel ill.

'Let him go!' she shouted. 'You big mean mamalocker,
let him go!'

!Xabbu leaped forward and grabbed Jongleur's free arm
and yanked hard. Jecky Nibble jerked free, then fled the
clearing in a tangle of digging limbs. Jongleur, eyes slit-
ted with fury, raised his hand as if to strike !Xabbu.

Sam dashed forward, waving the broken blade of
Orlando's sword. 'If you hit him I'll . . . I'll cut your balls
off, you old bastard.' Jongleur snarled at her, actually
snarled like an animal, and for a horrifying moment she
thought he had gone completely mad, that she would have
to fight this cruel, muscular man to the death. She spread
her feet wide apart, forcing herself to hold the shattered

blade level, and prayed he wouldn't see her knees threatening to buckle. 'I mean it!'

Jongleur's eyes widened. He looked slowly from her to !Xabbu, as though he had no idea how a Remote Area Dweller of the Okavango Delta had come to be attached to his arm, then shook himself free. He turned his back on them both and stalked out of the clearing.

Sam sat down, certain that she would collapse if she did not. !Xabbu was at her side in a moment.

'Are you hurt?'

'Me?' She laughed, far too loud. 'It was you whose head he was going to tear off. I never even got near him.' The strangeness of it all swam up on her. What was Sam Fredericks doing in a place like this, almost getting in a knife fight with the meanest, richest man in the world? She should be home studying, or listening to music, or talking to friends on the net. 'Oh, God,' she said, 'this just locks in so many, many different ways!'

!Xabbu patted her shoulder. 'You were very brave. But I would not have been as easy a victim as he might have thought.'

'Don't get all regular-guy on me, okay?' Sam tried to smile. 'You're not one of those. That's why Renie loves you.'

!Xabbu stared at her for a moment, then blinked. 'What are we to do now?'

'I don't know. I don't think I can stand to be around that man anymore. Did you see him? He's . . . I don't know. Seriously scanny.'

'It is bad enough that he attacked someone who was our guest,' !Xabbu said. 'But we might have learned much from those children.'

'Children?'

'I am certain. Do you not remember what Paul Jonas

told us? About the boy Gally and his companions, waiting to cross the White Ocean?'

Sam nodded slowly. 'Yeah. And that little chipmunk or whatever it was . . . it said something about Bubble Bunnies! That's like this net show for micros back in the real world!' She darted !Xabbu a quick glance. 'Micros means kids. Children.'

He smiled. 'I guessed.' The moment's cheer evaporated. 'As I said, there is much we might have learned . . .'

Now it was Sam's turn to touch the small man's arm in sympathy. 'We'll find out what this is about. We'll find Renie, too.'

'I will gather some more wood,' !Xabbu said. 'You should lie down and try to sleep. I will guard us – I do not think I shall sleep again for a while.'

Despite !Xabbu's suggestions, a restless, wakeful hour passed for Sam before movement in the vegetation brought her upright again. She kept the hilt of the ruined sword firmly in her hand; her fingers tightened when she saw Jongleur's hawkish features looming above them.

'What do you want? Do you think I was dupping about what I'd do . . . ?'

Jongleur scowled, but there was something strange in his expression. He spread his hands. They were shaking. 'I have come back . . .' He hesitated, then turned his face away, so that it took a moment before Sam made sense of the words. 'I have come back to say that I was wrong.'

Sam looked at !Xabbu, then back at Jongleur. 'What?'

'You heard me, child. Do you think to make me crawl? I was wrong. I let my temper control me and I spoiled an opportunity to learn something, perhaps something important.' He glared, but it was directed at no one, at least no one visible. 'I was a fool.'

!Xabby cocked his head to one side. 'Are you saying that you wish to be forgiven?'

Sam watched a visible shudder run up the man's naked torso. 'I do not ask forgiveness. I never have. Not from anyone! But that does not mean I cannot admit fault. I was wrong.' As if the firelight made him uncomfortable, he stepped back until he was almost in the shadows once more. 'It was . . . it was hearing what they said. How they spoke of my invention. The One . . . ! That is my operating system they spoke of, as though it were a god! He . . . it, whatever one calls it – the Other has made things without my permission, taken tremendous liberties! *This* is why the system was sluggish, why there were problems with the network that delayed the Grail Ceremony for so long! Because the damnable operating system was stealing power to make this little project for itself, this laughable, broken little Eden. Christ Jesus, I am betrayed on all sides!'

After a moment, !Xabbu quietly said, 'Yes, you have been unlucky with your servants, haven't you?'

Jongleur gave him a wolfish smile. 'You remind me that you are not a savage, after all. You have an unpleasantly sharp wit when you wish to use it – like one of your people's poisoned arrows, eh?' He shook his head and sank down onto the forest floor. Sam finally realized that the man was shaking not with anger, but with weariness and perhaps something else as well. For the first time she saw what he truly was beneath the mask – an old, old man. 'I deserve it. I have made two gross miscalculations and now I am paying for them. That may provide the two of you some little satisfaction, anyway.'

Before she could say anything, !Xabbu touched her arm. 'We have no satisfaction in any of this,' he said quietly. 'We are trying to stay alive. Your operating system

and your . . . what is the word? Employee. Your employee.
They are our problems as much as they are yours.'

Jongleur nodded slowly. 'He is horrifically clever, young
Mr Dread. He used that name to taunt me – More Dread,
he called himself. Do you understand the reference? But
even I did not see the full significance.'

Sam frowned. She knew !Xabbu wanted to keep the
man talking, so surely a question wouldn't hurt, would
it? 'I don't know what any of that means – More Dread.'

'The Grail legend. Mordred, son of King Arthur. The
bastard who betrayed the Round Table. Just as Dread has
betrayed me, and perhaps destroyed my Grail.' Jongleur
looked at his hands as though they too might prove treacherous. 'He has talents, he does, my little Johnny Dread.
Did you know he is a bona fide miracle worker?'

!Xabbu settled himself with the quiet unobtrusiveness
of a hunter who does not wish to startle his quarry.
'Miracle worker?'

'He is a telekinetic. He has power. A genetic fluke,
something that has probably been in the race for a million
years, but scarcely noticed. He can affect electromagnetic
currents. It is such a minute amount of force that I doubt
it was even noticeable as a trait until humankind developed a society dependent on those currents. He could not
push a paper cup off a tabletop with his mind, but he
can alter information machinery. Doubtless he found some
way to use it to burglarize my system, the miserable cur.
But the true irony is that I taught him to control that
power!'

The fire was beginning to die again, but neither Sam
nor !Xabbu made a move to stoke it. The bizarrely geometric trees grew remote as the flames faltered and shrank.

'You see, I have long been interested in such . . . talents.
I have eyes and ears in many places, and when certain

records pertaining to a boy named Johnny Wulgaru came to my attention, I made sure he was committed as a ward to one of my institutes. What he had was only a rough talent, but then, he was a rough boy. He'd already killed a few when I found him. He has killed many more since – only a small number of them on my behalf, I might add. But I should have known that someone so self-indulgent would never make a useful tool.'

'You . . . trained him?'

'My researchers took him and his raw skill in hand, yes. We helped him learn to use his unusual ability. We taught him restraint, selectivity, strategy. In fact, we taught him more than that – we made a street animal into a human being, or at least a convincing simulacrum.' Jongleur's laugh was sharp. 'As I said, even I underestimated him, so we did our work well.'

'And he used this . . . power . . . on your behalf?'

'Only incidentally. Even when he had learned to focus it, to fully harness his latent abilities, it was still capable of only small miracles – things that in most circumstances could be achieved by more mundane methods. He himself has found it useful for subverting surveillance equipment. But I discovered he had other, more practical skills as well. He is completely ruthless and he is clever. He made an extremely useful tool. Until recently.'

!Xabbu waited a while before speaking. 'And . . . the operating system? The thing some call the Other?'

Jongleur narrowed his eyes. 'It is of no consequence. Dread controls it, and thus controls the network.'

'But he does not control this part of the network, whatever it is.' !Xabbu gestured to the surreal, shadowy forest. 'Or he would have found us here, would he not?'

The old man shrugged. 'Perhaps. I still do not know where "here" is. But our true enemy is John Dread.'

!Xabbu frowned. 'I think that if this man Dread controls the network through the operating system, then knowing more of the operating system might be important – how it works, how Dread is forcing it to work for him.'

'Nevertheless, I have said all I will say.'

!Xabbu stared hard. 'If Renie were here, I think she would know what questions to ask. But she is not.' His eyes wandered for a moment. 'She is not.'

'So we're just impacted, then?' Sam was trying to keep her temper and not entirely succeeding. The memory of Orlando, staggering bravely through his final hours while this crusty old monster sat in his golden house, planning to live forever, burned her. 'Everything's just utterly scorched and nothing to do about it? And what do you mean, "our enemy is Dread." *Our* enemy? As far as I can see, you're as much an enemy to us as he is.'

!Xabbu watched her for a moment, eyes serious and remote. 'You frightened away innocents who might have helped us,' he said to Jongleur. 'You or your helpers have tried to kill us many times. She is right – why should we continue to deal with you?'

For a moment it seemed the old man might lose his temper again. The lines around his mouth grew tight. 'I have said I was wrong. Do you wish me to crawl? I will not. I never will do that.'

!Xabbu sighed. 'Never since I first left the delta has it been so clear to me that speaking the same tongue does not mean understanding. We do not care about apologies. The things you have done to us and people we care for can never be made better by apologies. We are as . . . practical . . . as you are. What can you do for us? Why should we trust you?'

Jongleur was silent for a long time. 'I have underestimated you again,' he said at last. 'I should have remembered from my time in Africa that there are many hard-headed bargainers among the dark peoples. Very well.' He spread his hands as if to show his unweaponed harmlessness. 'I swear that I will help you to get out of this place, and that I will not hurt you even if given the chance. Even if I will not willingly give you all my information – and what else do I have to bargain with? – I still know much that you do not. You need me. I would be in great danger alone, so I need you, too. What do you say?'

'!Xabbu, don't,' Sam said. 'He's a liar. You can't trust him.'

'Then if you won't bargain, what will you do?' Jongleur demanded. 'Kill me? I think not. I will simply follow you, deriving some benefit of safety from your presence while you gain none from mine.'

!Xabbu looked to Sam, troubled. 'Renie wished us to work with him.'

'But Renie's not here. Doesn't it matter what I want?'

'Of course.'

Frustrated, she whirled on Jongleur. 'Where are we going, anyway? How are you going to help? Like, strangle all the little forest animals until they tell us what we want to know?'

He scowled. 'It was a mistake. I have already said so.'

'If he comes with us, we're going to take turns sleeping,' Sam said. 'Like we were in enemy territory. Because I don't trust him not to kill us in our sleep.'

'You have not answered her other question,' !Xabbu pointed out. 'Where are we going?'

'In. To the heart of this place, I suppose. To find . . . what did they call it, those pathetic creatures? To find the One.'

'You said knowing about the operating system would do us no good.'

'I said I had told you all I wished to tell. And in truth there is nothing much we can do as long as Dread controls it. But if the operating system built this world, then there must be a direct connection back to the operating system somewhere in it.' He fell silent, musing, then seemed to realize he had not finished. 'If we can find that connection, we can use it to reach Dread as well.'

'And then what?' !Xabbu suddenly seemed very weary. 'Then what?'

'I do not know.' Jongleur too had run out of strength. 'But otherwise we wander here like ghosts, until our bodies die the real death.'

'I just want to go home,' said Sam quietly.

'A long way.' For a moment Jongleur almost sounded human. 'A very long way.'

CHAPTER 15

Confessional

NETFEED/FASHION: A New Direction for Mbinda?
(visual: models wearing designer's troubled Chutes line)
VO: After a disastrous year, many designers would rethink their fash-
ion ideas. Hussein Mbinda has done more than that. Yesterday he
announced that he is considering an even more radical approach to
his profession.
(visual: Mbinda backstage at Milan show)
MBINDA: 'I had a dream that everyone was naked. I was in a place
where clothes didn't matter, because everyone was young and beau-
tiful forever. I realized it must be heaven, and that what I was seeing
was people's souls. God sent this vision just to me, seen? And so I
wanted to find a way to show everyone that fashion and money and
all that – it doesn't matter . . .'
VO: Mbinda's spiritual insight has provided his latest direction: latex
sprays, but not in the usual fashion shades. Every one of Mbinda's
new sprays is a human flesh tone, so that the wearers can be naked
even when they're dressed. Despite the religious inspiration, they're
apparently going to be quite expensive, too . . .'

HE had stared at his pad long enough. He had performed every other undone task he could remember, and had improvised a few new ones. There was really no acceptable reason for putting off the call any longer. He spoke the code phrase Sellars had given him, the one that the strange man had promised would give him an untraceable connection, then waited.

In the past several days Catur Ramsey had come to believe in several impossible things – that a worldwide conspiracy existed to sacrifice children for the immortality of a few incredibly rich people, that an entire virtual universe had been created almost without any public notice, and even that the minuscule hope for its defeat rested in the crippled hands of a man who had been living in an abandoned tunnel under an army base. Ramsey had seen a father and his child kidnapped out of a public restaurant by the US military, had been threatened himself by a rogue general and then had seen that officer suddenly die, and now he and several other fugitives were apparently in terrible danger simply for having chanced on the vast and malevolent design. One set of clients had a child in a mysterious coma apparently caused by the conspiracy. Another client was being led by supernatural voices. Catur Ramsey had been through a lot just lately.

Somehow, though, this felt like the most difficult thing yet.

On the tenth ring the answering service clicked on. Disgusted by his own relief, he began to leave his message. Then Orlando's mother picked up the call.

'Ramsey,' she said, nodding in an oddly deliberate manner. 'Mr Ramsey. Of course. How are you?'

All abstract thoughts about danger and loss left him in a moment, blasted away by the reality of Vivien Fennis Gardiner. As jet fuel had changed Sellars' exterior so completely that it was almost surreal, grief seemed to have performed some similar dark alchemy inside Orlando's mother; behind the hollow stare and clumsy makeup –

he couldn't remember her wearing makeup in their previous meetings – something terrifying hid.

He struggled to find words. 'Oh, Ms Fennis, I am so sorry. So sorry.'

'We got your message. Thank you for your prayers and kind thoughts.' Her voice might have been a sleepwalker's.

'I . . . I called to say how bad I felt about missing Orlando's memorial service . . .'

'We understand, Mr Ramsey. You're a very busy man.'

'No!' Even this inappropriate outburst did not startle any deeper reaction out of her. 'No, I mean, that's not why I missed it. Really.' He felt himself suddenly in deep water, floundering. What could he tell her, even over a safe line? That he had been afraid agents of a secret conspiracy might follow him back to Sellars and the others? He had already withheld crucial information from her once, fearing to deepen her grief. What could he tell her now, after the worst had happened, that would make any sense at all?

At least some of the truth, damn it. You owe her that.

She was waiting silently, like a doll left upright, slack until someone came again to give it life. 'I've been . . . I've been following up the investigation I told you about. And . . . and there's definitely something going on. Something big. And that's . . . that's why . . .' He felt a weight of sudden fear on the back of his neck. Surely if these Grail people were willing to steal Major Sorensen out of a public place, they wouldn't balk at tapping Orlando's family's home line. What could he tell her? Even if everything Sellars said was true, the Grail conspiracy didn't necessarily know how much Ramsey himself had discovered – how deep into it all he now was. 'Orlando . . . all that stuff he was doing online . . .'

'Oh,' said Vivien abruptly, animation flickering across

the Kabuki mask of her face for the first time. 'Was it
you who sent those men?'

'What?'

'Those men. The men who came and asked to go
through his files. I thought they said they were government researchers – something about Tandagore's
Syndrome. That's what they say Orlando had, you know.
At the end.' She nodded slowly, slowly. 'But it was the
day after Orlando . . . and Conrad was back at the hospital
. . . and I wasn't really paying attention . . .' Her face
sagged again. 'We never did find that bug of Orlando's,
that . . . agent. Maybe they took that thing, too. I hope
they did. I hated that creepy little thing.'

'Wait a minute, Vivien. Hold on.' The weight on
Ramsey's neck suddenly felt like a ton. 'Somebody came
to your *house?* And went through Orlando's files?'

'One of them gave me his card, I think . . .' She blinked,
looked around. 'It's around here somewhere . . . hold on.'

As she wandered out of range of the screen, Ramsey
tried to hold down the sudden rush of panic. *Don't*, he
warned himself. *Don't do it – you'll turn into one of those
professional paranoids. It could have been actual
researchers, maybe from the hospital, maybe from some
government task force. Tandagore's been getting press
lately, some real officials may be feeling the heat.* But he
didn't believe it. *Even if they're with the Grail, so what,
man, so what? Just slow flow, man. You never even talked
to Orlando Gardiner about any of this stuff – never even
met the kid, except as a warm body in a coma bed.*

*But the bug. Beezle Bug. If they ever find that gear,
the Beezle program, what has it got in its memory?*

He had managed to calm himself into near-fibrillation
by the time she returned.

'I can't find it,' she said. 'It was just a name and a

number, I think. If I find it, do you want me to send you the information?'

'Yes, please.'

She was silent a moment. 'It was a nice service. We played some songs he really liked, and some of the people from that game he played showed up. Some others from that Middle Country sent a kind of tribute that they played on the chapel wallscreen. Full of monsters and castles and things like that.' She laughed, a sad little laugh, but it seemed to crack the mask: her jaw trembled, her voice hitched. 'They . . . they were just kids! Like Orlando. I had been hating them, you know. Blaming them, I guess.'

'Look, Vivien, I'm not your attorney, not in any official way, but if anyone else comes around wanting to look at Orlando's files, I strongly advise you not to let them. Not unless they're the police and you're damn sure that they are who they say. Understand me?'

She raised an eyebrow. 'What's going on, Mr Ramsey?'

'I . . . I can't really talk. I promise I'll tell you more when I can.' He tried to think – were they in any danger, Vivien and Conrad? He couldn't imagine how. The last thing these Grail folks would want to do would be to make an even bigger news story out of another Tandagore tragedy. 'Just . . . just . . .' He sighed. 'I don't know. Just take care of each other. I know it doesn't mean anything right now, but there's a chance your suffering won't be completely pointless. That doesn't make anything better, and I can only guess at how terrible this is for you, but . . .' There was really nothing else he could think of to say.

'I'm not quite sure what you mean, Mr Ramsey.' She had retreated a little, either out of reflexive distrust of anything that might force her to engage the horror more deeply, or simply because the effort of having a human conversation had finally worn her out.

'Never mind, Ms Fennis. Vivien. We'll talk again.'

He let her end the conversation and disconnect. Just now, that was the only thing he could give her.

Sellars sensed his mood and was kind enough to let Ramsey slump silently on the couch for a while, pretending to watch the wallscreen. It was a model at least twenty years off the showroom floor, a plasma-color that stuck out from the wall a full two inches, the top of the frame speckled with dust, its screen only slightly larger than the ghastly painting of a sailboat that hung over the couch.

'I'm suddenly remembering how much I hate motels,' Ramsey said. The ice in his drink had melted, but he couldn't even sit up straight, much less walk out to the ice machine in the hall. 'The bad paintings, the weird-colored furniture, the grit you find in all the corners if you look too closely . . .'

Sellars bobbed his head and smiled. 'Ah, but you see, Mr Ramsey, it's all a matter of perspective. I spent decades in a small house that was my prison cell. More recently, I lived for several weeks in a damp concrete tunnel under Major Sorensen's base. I find a certain pleasure in having seen several motel rooms in the last few days, even if the decor *is* something less than engaging.'

Ramsey swore under his breath. 'Sorry. That was self-centered . . .'

'Please.' Sellars raised a thin finger. 'No apologies. I had no hope of allies, and now I find I have several. You are a volunteer for a dangerous mission – you're entitled to complain about the accommodations.'

Catur Ramsey snorted. 'Yeah, and even I have to admit I've seen lots worse. Just . . . just in a kind of twisted mood. The call to Orlando's parents . . .'

'Bad?'

'Very.' He looked up suddenly. 'Someone's been to their house – been through Orlando's files.' He gave Sellars the details. While Ramsey spoke the runneled face seemed reposed and thoughtful, but the eyes were almost empty, as though already the old man were making inquiries, investigations, reaching out along his invisible web of connections.

'I'll have to look into it further,' was all he said when Ramsey finished, then he sighed. 'I am very tired.'

'Do you want to get some sleep? I'd be happy to go out and stretch my legs . . .'

'That's not what I mean, but thank you. Have you heard back from Olga Pirofsky?'

'Not yet.' Ramsey was still angry with himself. 'I should never have sent that first message – you were right. She must have thought that I was going to shout at her, tell her to turn around and come back at once.' He looked at Sellars. 'Although I have to say I'm still not sure why I *shouldn't* be telling her that.'

Sellars stared back at him, the yellow-eyed stare inscrutable, then shook his head. 'Damnation,' he said softly. 'I forget that I no longer have my wheelchair.' With great effort he rearranged himself so that he could face Ramsey more directly. 'As I said, Mr Ramsey, I am very tired. I do not have much time left, and all my plans and necessities won't mean anything when that time is up. As Ms Dickinson once put it, 'Because I did not stop for Death, He kindly stopped for me . . .' His head swayed on his thin neck.

'You're . . . sick?'

Sellars laughed, a dry sound like wind across the top of a pipe. 'Oh, Lord, Mr Ramsey. Look at me – I haven't been well in fifty years. But I have been better than I am at the moment, that's certain. Yes, I'm sick. I'm dying. There is the irony of all this – I'm doing the same thing the Grail Brotherhood is doing, trying to outrace a failing physical shell. But they want to preserve what burns inside them. I will accept extinguishment gratefully, if only my work is done.'

Ramsey still did not feel close to understanding this strange man. 'How long do you have?'

Sellars let his hands fall into his lap, where they lay like crossed twigs. 'Oh, perhaps a few months if I don't exert myself – but what are the odds of that?' He showed his teeth in a lipless grin. 'I am extended so far that I could work twenty-four hours every day without moving out of a chair, and now I have the added pleasure of traveling in the wheel-well of Major Sorensen's van.' He held up his hand. 'No, please, pity is not what I'm asking for. But there is something else you can do, Mr Ramsey.'

'What's that?'

Sellars sat quietly for what seemed to Catur Ramsey half a minute. 'Perhaps,' he said at last, 'it would help if I explained some things first. I have not told you or the Sorensens everything there is to know about me. Are you surprised?'

'No.'

'I didn't think you would be. Let me tell you one of the less interesting, but perhaps not entirely irrelevant things I haven't mentioned. Actually, Major Sorensen is likely to know this, since he has my personal history in quite excruciating detail. I'm not an American. Not by birth. I was born in Ireland – well, Northern Ireland, as that part of it was known in those days. My first language is Gaelic.'

'You don't sound Irish . . .'

'I came here to live with an aunt and uncle when I was very young. My father and mother belonged to a rather odd

Catholic sect in Ulster. They both died early – that is a story in itself – and I was sent to America. But while they were alive, I was raised to be a soldier of the faith, and probably would have been one if they'd survived.'

'You mean, like . . . the Irish Republican Army?'

'Oh, much smaller and much less responsible. A splinter group that formed during the days when the peace process had begun in earnest, and which was never reconciled. But this is all beside the point.'

'Sorry.'

'No, no.' Sellars nodded gently. 'In this mad hash of stories we're all living, it's hard to know what is relevant, what is not. But the fact is, I was raised in a very Catholic household. And now that the end of my labors is upon me, Mr Ramsey, I find that I want the chance to confess.'

It took a few seconds for him to make sense of it. 'You want to confess . . . to *me?*'

'After a fashion.' Sellars laughed his hooting laugh again. 'We have no priest in our company. As a lawyer, aren't you next in line?'

'I really don't understand.'

'It's not a religious thing, Mr Ramsey. I'm just very tired and lonely. I need someone to help me, and the first way to help will be to listen. I have been fighting this war by myself for too long. We are in desperate straits, and I no longer trust myself to make all the decisions. But you must understand the whole story.'

Ramsey begged a moment, then went to get a drink of water out of the bathroom sink and splash some on his face. 'You make it sound like there are some major undisclosed details here,' he said when he came back. 'What exactly are you getting me involved with?'

'My, you *are* a lawyer, aren't you? Just listen, please, then you can judge for yourself.'

'Why not the major? Or Kaylene Sorensen – she's a smart woman, even if she's a bit old-fashioned.'

'Because I have already put their child in danger several times, and they have Christabel with them now. They cannot be objective.'

Ramsey drummed his fingers on the arm of the couch. 'Okay. Talk to me.'

'Good.' Sellars slowly lowered his body back against the chair cushions, a process so deliberate it might have been performed by museum curators moving a fragile masterpiece.

Which I suppose he is, thought Ramsey, *if everything he's said is true.*

'First off,' Sellars announced, 'I did not stumble onto the Brotherhood's project – the Grail network – completely by accident.' He frowned. 'I will save that bit of the story for later, I think. For now, it's enough to know that as I began to realize what I had found, I watched their progress with growing alarm. And not just for altruistic reasons, Mr Ramsey. I watched the threat of the Brotherhood with growing despair in large part because I knew it was going to delay the most important of my own projects.'

'Which was . . . ?' Ramsey said after long seconds.

'Which was to die. Not that such a thing is difficult for me, Mr Ramsey. On the contrary – with the nanomachinery I have acquired, and my original circuitry, I now have enough control over my own body that I could turn off the blood to my brain with a thought.'

'But . . . why were you still alive, then? Before you found out about the Grail Project?'

'Because I have been balancing a scale for a long time, Mr Ramsey. On one side is the normal urge to live, my joys and my interests, solitary and limited as they may be. On the other is the pain. Because of my many surgeries, the things that have grown into my bones and my organs, the strains on my glands . . . it hurts to be me, Mr Ramsey. My life is very painful.'

'But surely if you have such control, you could turn off the pain?'

'I did not have as much control over my own functions when I first discovered the Brotherhood as I have gained recently, but yes, even then I could probably have switched off the feelings in my hands, my skin, cut my brain off from my entire body. But then why be alive? There is little enough of the physical in my life – for so long I have lived mostly in my own mind, as prisoners often do. Should I give up the sensation of a breeze on my face? The taste of the few foods I am able to eat?'

'I . . . I think I understand.'

'And in fact, the time was nearly upon me when the tradeoff was no longer going to be worth it. Then this Grail network reared its head, a problem I could not simply ignore. Still, I did not think I would be needed past the initial stages – I was planting seeds, as it were. I wanted to find a group of trustworthy people, teach them what I knew, and then be free to do as I wished. I even told them my real name, so you can imagine I was not planning to be around long! But things went wrong at the very beginning – the invasion of Atasco's island, the weird behavior of the operating system which prevented the people I rather dubiously call my volunteers from getting offline – and here I am, more needed than ever.'

'So what can I do? Besides listen.'

'Listening is very helpful, do not doubt it. It is an unimaginable pleasure just to be able to talk openly. But I have some very specific needs, too. I'm fighting on many fronts, Mr Ramsey . . .'

'Call me Catur, please. Or even Decatur, if that's too informal.'

'Decatur. A nice name.' The old man blinked slowly, summoning back his thoughts. 'Many fronts. There is that group, allies of ours, who are literally under siege in South Africa. There are various plans the Brotherhood had already put into action which have to be monitored and in some cases covertly resisted. And most importantly, there is the constant struggle to find and aid those people I've already brought into the Grail network. And that's where you . . . and Ms Pirofsky . . . come in.'

'I don't understand.'

Sellars fluted a sigh. 'Perhaps when I tell you this, Mr Ramsey, you will understand something of my frustration and weariness. I have been trying to locate and contact my volunteers within the system ever since I was first forced to abandon them in the Atascos' simulation world, but from the moment the Grail network was fully operational, I have found it impossible to get past the network's security. But I have told you a little bit about the operating system, haven't I? Its strange affinity for children? I discovered that if I bring the boy Cho-Cho online, at a certain point in the process, at a high enough level, the operating system will simply let him through. Not me, no matter how I disguise my intrusion – the operating system has always blocked me, sometimes quite painfully – but a real child will be allowed inside.'

'Well, that's good, isn't it?'

'You do not see the whole problem, Mr Ramsey. Decatur, excuse me. Imagine that you had a sealed box full of tiny beads, and a single thin needle you needed to push through the wall of the box so that it touched one particular bead, which could be anywhere in the container. How would you do that?'

'I . . .' Ramsey frowned. 'I wouldn't, I guess. Is it a trick question?'

'I wish it were. That's my problem – tracking my volunteers. Fortunately, it means that the Brotherhood hasn't been able to track them, either. The one I helped release, Paul Jonas, seems to have eluded them for quite some time.'

'But you *did* make contact with them a couple of times, didn't you? You said so.'

'Yes. I got Cho-Cho to the right spot. That was a little coup – I was quite proud of myself. Do you know how I did it? The operating system – this quasi-living neural network, or whatever it is – seemed to be fascinated with my volunteers. It paid special attention to them, and by carefully observing its actions, I could roughly track their whereabouts. Let me show you something.'

Sellars gestured, and the jai alai game from South America that Ramsey had been half-watching disappeared. In its place was a strange, fish-eye view of masses of green growing things.

'That is my Garden, my place of meditation,' Sellars said. 'Or my *tèarmunn*, as I would name it in the language of my birth. Every source of knowledge I have is represented there, displayed as trees, moss, flowers, and so on. Thus, what you are looking at is not a garden at all, but the complete, up-to-the-moment picture of all my information.

'Or rather, what you see is how it looked a week ago. Do you see those dark fungal traces sprouting up through the soil? There, and there? And a large something below the surface there? That was the operating system. A knot like that, a node of activity, showed that a great deal of the system's effort was being expended there. Often – but by no means always – it meant the system was monitoring part of my volunteer task force. As you can see, they have split into several groups.'

'So you can use a kid like Cho-Cho to get into the system. You can figure out approximately where your people are by the shape of the operating system.' Ramsey squinted at the complex green shapes on the wallscreen. 'So what's the problem?'

'That was a week ago. This is now.'

The difference was striking, even to Ramsey. Sellars' garden appeared to have been hit by a killing frost – whole structures gone, others blackened and shriveled. He could not tell what any of it meant, but it was clear something devastating had happened.

'The operating system. It's . . . gone.'

'Not gone, but vastly reduced, or perhaps withdrawn.' Sellars briefly highlighted a few points in the now-barren garden. 'It is now operating like a true machine, as if its advanced functions have been demolished. I can make no sense of it. Worse, there is no longer any correspondence that I can use to locate my people within the system. They are lost to me.'

'I can see why you're upset . . .'

'There is more. Have you noticed how quiet and sullen the boy Cho-Cho has been today? Last night, we had a very disturbing experience. Even though I could not locate any of my volunteers, I tried to get the boy online just to discover what I could about the current state of the network. We were both nearly killed.'

'What?'

'The operating system no longer acts in its earlier manner, at least as far as allowing intrusions into the network. There are no more inexplicable exemptions for children – or for anything else. The security of the Grail network, still deadly dangerous for reasons I've never been able to understand, is now utterly seamless. Nothing gets in, nothing comes out.'

Ramsey had to sit and think about this for a while. 'So the people you brought into the system are just . . . lost?'

'At the moment, yes. Completely. It is a very helpless feeling, Decatur. And that is where you come in.'

'Me? Somehow I don't think a lawsuit is going to do much good.'

Sellars' smile was less than hearty. 'We are far beyond that stage, I'm afraid. I know you cannot completely understand my Garden, but trust me – time is short. Things are changing quickly. The entire Grail system is extremely unstable, in danger of collapse.'

'But that's good, isn't it?'

'No. Not while there are children whose health is still wrapped up with this network. Not while people whom I brought into this war of mine are somehow trapped inside the thing. You've already seen one child die while we all waited helplessly. Do you want to make that same call to the parents of Salome Fredericks?'

'No. Jesus, of course not. But what possible use can you make of me?'

'Because the more I think of it, the more I realize that Olga Pirofsky may be our only hope. I have tried everything I can imagine to penetrate the system. I have tried tapping into my volunteers' own connections from the outside world, but although I can access them, there is still something that prevents me from tracing that link through the security system and into the network.'

'So what the hell is Olga Pirofsky going to do? She's just a nice woman who hears voices.'

'If she succeeds in her goal, it could be that she can do much. What we need at this point is something she might be able to provide – access to Felix Jongleur's own system.'

Ramsey blinked. 'Felix Jongleur's . . .'

'If there is anyone who can bypass the network security,

it will be the man who created the thing. If there is anything that can get us onto the Grail network, and thus back in touch with the people I have put in mortal danger, it will be found in Jongleur's system.'

'But Olga . . . ? You don't need some nice middle-aged lady, you need some kind of – Christ, I don't know, a tactical unit! Commandos! This is a job for Major Sorensen, not a kiddie-show host.'

'No, it is precisely a job for someone like Olga. Major Sorensen will be very useful to us, I promise you – we will need all his security expertise. But no one is going to swim to Jongleur's island by night, bypass the attentions of his private army, and climb up the outside of his corporate tower like some kind of spy hero. The only way someone will get into the enemy's stronghold is if he . . . or she . . . is invited in.'

'Invited? She quit her job, Sellars. She doesn't even work for them anymore. Do you think they're going to say, "Oh, this is fun, a disgruntled ex-employee who hears voices and is on medical retirement – let's take her up to see the boss!" That's crazy.'

'No, Decatur, I don't think that's going to happen. Nor would we want it to. There are people who go in and out of those buildings all the time and no one notices them. Cleaners – hundreds of them, mostly poor women born in other countries.

'Olga Pirofsky is more likely to get into that place pushing a vacuum cleaner than Major Sorensen would driving a tank.'

A half hour later, Ramsey's disbelief had not precisely turned to heartfelt agreement, but had at least mellowed into a kind of stunned acceptance. 'But I still don't understand why *me?*'

'Because I cannot do everything, and I fear I will be stretched even farther before the end comes, whatever that end may be. Ms Pirofsky will need constant supervision, support, encouragement. Sorensen will be able to help with many of the technical problems, and I will help with others, but she is going into the labyrinth, as it were – inside the monster's lair. She will need someone on the other end of the ball of string, if I'm not overdoing it with the mythological allusions. And of all of us, you are the only one she knows and trusts. Who better?'

'You're assuming that she'll contact me again,' Ramsey said, unable to keep bitterness out of his voice. 'That's a big assumption.'

Sellars let out a soft sigh. 'Decatur, we can only plan for what we can do, not what we can't.'

Ramsey nodded, but he wasn't happy about any of it. Worst of all was the knowledge that even if they succeeded in getting in touch with Olga Pirofsky, instead of giving her sensible advice – like, for instance, get the hell out of town and stay away from J Corporation – he would be trying to persuade her to do something far more dangerous than she had planned to do on her own. All this on behalf of a cause he hadn't even known about a week ago, and which still struck him as a half-step from total unbelievability.

Sellars cleared his throat. 'If you don't mind, Decatur, I find that I am indeed tired now. You don't need to leave, but you'll forgive me if I take a rest.'

'Of course, go ahead.' He jumped as Sellars relinquished control of the wallscreen and the Garden disappeared, replaced by some kind of car race through what appeared to be a mined course. Ramsey muted the sudden grind of sound. A slow-motion replay of an armored vehicle spinning into the air on the back of a bright explosive flash made him think of Sellars' horrific burns.

'Hang on.' He turned back to Sellars. The old man had closed his eyes, and for a moment a wave of pity washed through Ramsey. He should leave the poor crippled bastard alone. If even half of what he said was true, the old pilot deserved all the rest he could get . . .

But Catur Ramsey had spent his early years working in a prosecutor's office, and the training had never entirely left him.

'Hang on. One more thing before you fall asleep.'

The yellow eyes flicked open, alert and solemn as the stare of an owl. 'Yes?'

'You said that you were going to tell me the real story of how you found out about the Grail Network.'

'Decatur, I am very tired . . .'

'I know. And I'm sorry. But if Olga calls back, I'm going to have to decide what to tell her. I don't like loose ends. Confessional, remember.'

Sellars took a raspy breath. 'I half-hoped you had forgotten.' He levered himself awkwardly into an upright position, each almost-hidden twinge of pain a rebuke to his interrogator. Ramsey did his best to harden his heart. 'Very well,' Sellars said when he was resettled. 'I will give you this last piece of the story. And when I've finished telling you what I've done, I hope you will remember that confession is not complete without the possibility of absolution. I feel in need of it after all this time.'

And so, in a room lit only by the flicker of the wallscreen, by silent images of destruction and triumph from somewhere in the wide, wide world, Sellars began to talk. And as he listened to the old man's quiet words, Catur Ramsey's confusion and surprise gradually became something else entirely.

CHAPTER 16

Badlands

THE bleached, icy expanses of what had once been Arabia Deserta stretched on and on, drift upon drift of white like spilled sugar, the misty sky almost the same color as the empty countryside. By the end of the second day, the miserable cold was no longer Paul's greatest concern. He was beginning to miss color the way a starving man misses food.

'But for me,' Florimel said, 'it is the waste of time I most regret. It is like being forced to walk down train tracks for hundreds of kilometers while trains pass on the other tracks. An entire system set up for instant travel, but we cannot make it work.'

They had searched several more snowbound Arabian palaces in hopes of finding another gateway, with no luck. 'If we could only see enough of this place to make some sense of it,' Paul complained, as he had already done many times, 'we could probably find the sort of place they usually hide their gates.'

'Oh, chizz,' said T4b. 'So oughta just keep digging in the snow like some kind of dogs, us? Chance not.'

'We have already agreed.' Martine's plume of breath was the only sign she had spoken. Like the others, she was so wrapped in rugs pilfered from the icy fantasy castles that her face was all but hidden. Paul thought they all looked like piles of washing waiting to go in the machine. 'We continue to the end of the river. At least we know we will find one there.'

'I didn't mean to open up the argument again.' Paul stared disconsolately at the line of the black river stretching ahead. 'Just . . . thinking about Renie and the others . . . feeling so useless . . .'

'We are all feeling the same way,' Martine assured him. 'Some of us may even feel worse than that.'

It came up so slowly, perhaps because of the thickening mist, perhaps because the dark, cold water muted its normal vibrance, that Paul and the others were on top of it before they noticed.

'Op it,' said T4b. 'In the water around the boat – that blue light!'

'My God,' Martine gasped. 'We dare not go through on the river. Head for land!'

They applied their makeshift paddles, beautifully carved bits of paneling stolen from cabinets and chests in the empty palaces, to fight against the sluggish current. When the bow of the small boat grounded in the shallows they waded to shore through freezing water, losing several precious blankets in the process.

'I don't want to pressure you, Martine,' Paul said, his wet feet already making him shiver, 'but we're going to be frostbitten if this takes too long.'

She nodded distractedly. 'We are right at the edge of the simulation. I am trying to find the gate information.' The river and its banks nearly vanished in the mists only a few hundred yards ahead, but some trick of the simworld's programming gave glimpses of greater distances, made it seem that there was more river and more land beyond. Paul wondered what would have been seen here before Dread covered the place with killing frost – an illusion of unending desert?

'I think I have it,' Martine finally announced. 'Pull the boat along beside us so we don't lose it. We must all walk forward.'

They followed her small, shrouded figure through the drifts like a group of lost mountaineers trying to stay close to their Sherpa guide. T4b was the slowest, making his way along the river shore with the boat's rope, pulling the little craft against the current. He had been quiet much of the trip, even his usual litany of complaints muted, so much so that Paul wondered if the young man were going through some kind of personality change.

Paul could not help remembering a young soldier in his squadron, a lad from Cheshire with a thin, girlish face and a habit of talking about his family back home as though everyone in the trenches knew them and wanted to hear what they said and thought. The first bad bombardment had silenced him quite thoroughly. After seeing the reality of what the Germans wanted to do to them all, he became as miserly of speech as the most confirmed misanthrope in the trenches.

Six weeks later he had been killed by an artillery shell at Savy Wood. Paul could not remember him having spoken for days beforehand.

Startled, he pulled up. Martine had stopped in front of him and was studying the swirling mists with her blind eyes as though reading directions on a street sign.

What are you going on about? Savy bloody Wood? That isn't real – or your memories aren't, anyway. It was all make-believe.

But it felt real. The details of the World War One simulation he retained felt no different than the recovered memories of his real life, either the musty routine of his job at the Tate or his strange year in Jongleur's tower fortress.

So how do you know any of those memories are real? It was a question he didn't want to face, especially not here, in icy mists that might have cloaked the edge of the world, the reefs of Limbo. *How do you know? How do you know Paul Jonas is even your real name – that anything you think happened actually happened?*

'Step forward.' Martine's croaking voice sent the phantoms flying. 'We must hold hands as we step through, just to be sure.'

'Did you find Egypt?' Paul reached out and took Florimel's callused fingers, even as she clutched T4b's free hand.

'Just s-step forward with m-m-me – I will explain when

we p-pass through. Hurry! I f-feel like I am fr-freezing to death!'

As they walked forward, tangles of unsteady blue light curled up between their feet; sparks vibrated in the air like drunken fireflies. Paul felt the static lifting his hair.

Every detail, he marveled. *They thought of every detail . . .*

Twenty paces later he stepped through into burning air and sunshine that struck him like a hammerblow.

The river still flowed, but hundreds of meters below them now, glinting in harsh sunlight at the bottom of a raw, red mud canyon. The dirt road on which they stood was less than a dozen meters wide. It felt something like being on the trail up the side of the black glass mountain once more.

'It is . . . the index said this is . . .' Martine sounded a little dazed. 'Dodge City. Is that not a place in the old American West?'

Paul's whistle of surprise was interrupted by a loud yelp of alarm from T4b. They turned to see the young man stumbling back from what had been their boat, but was now a large wagon on spoked wheels. Odd as the transformation was, it was not so much the wagon that seemed to have startled him as the beast yoked to the wagon.

'W-w-was holdin' the rope on the boat, like,' T4b stuttered as he halted beside Paul. 'We come through, holdin' *that* instead!'

The shaggy black creature in the traces had something of the shape of a horse, but its back legs were too large and its front legs had knuckled hands like those of a great ape. Its face was long, but not as long as a horse's, and tiny ears lay close to the sides of its bulging forehead.

'What is it?' Paul asked. The creature had bent to graze on dry grass beside the narrow dirt road. 'Something extinct?'

'Nothing I have ever seen,' Florimel said. 'Not with fingers, no. I think it is something made up.'

'None of this is what I expected.' Martine swiveled her sightless gaze back over the canyon. On the far side, contorted shapes that Paul had briefly taken for human watchers, but which now he saw were cacti, stood along the ridgeline. 'I . . . do not think there were such large mountains in Kansas, even in the nineteenth century.'

'Why are we here?' Paul was grateful for the hot sun – he was even beginning to sweat a little. He dumped his rugs, which had changed their pattern but not their general substance, onto the dusty road.

'To imitate the old joke,' Martine said, 'there is good news and bad news. The good news is that the Egypt simworld still exists, or at least it is still on the index. The bad is that we could not get to it from the Arabian Nights world.'

'Can we reach it from this one?'

'Not if we go all the way through,' she said. 'The river gate at the end of this simulation opens to something called "Shadowland" – or once did, anyway. But there appeared to be a secondary gate, the kind that would be somewhere in the middle of the simulation, that we can use.'

'And that will take us to Egypt?'

'Yes, as far as I could tell. It is hard to be certain because some of the codes that indicated status were inde-cipherable to me. But I believe the chances are good.'

'Hey!' T4b shouted. 'Op this!' He had wandered a sort distance back up the sloping road and was peering at something in the dry grasses. 'Hole in the ground, but with like a frame around it. Some kind of treasure dungeon, something.'

'Stay with us, Javier,' Florimel called to him. 'That sounds like a mine shaft. It will not be safe.'

'So what now?' Paul asked. 'Where do you think this other gateway is?'

Martine shrugged. 'If this simworld is named Dodge City, I would think that the city would be a good place to start looking.' She pointed down the canyon. 'If we are at one edge of the simulation, then it must be in that direction. Do you see anything?'

'Not from here.' He turned to Florimel. 'Do you know anything about horses? If that's what that thing is supposed to be?'

She favored him with a grim smile. 'I have dealt with a few. Again, the benefits of growing up on a rural commune. Why don't you throw the rugs into the back so we have something to sit on?' She turned and shouted down the road to T4b, where the top of his black-haired head showed above the long weeds. His arm went up and down, as though he were waving at something. 'Damn you, Javier, if you fall down in there and break your legs, I am not going to pull you out. Come and help us.'

'Deep, utter,' T4b said as he rejoined them few moments later. 'Took that rock like about a minute to hit the bottom.'

'Jesus,' Paul said in weary annoyance, 'can we just get going?'

They piled into the wagon. Florimel had indeed managed to gentle the horselike creature, although Paul thought it looked at the rest of them with something less than trust as she climbed up onto the bench and took the reins. When the rest of the company was seated on the hard boards she clicked her tongue softly and the creature began to move down the gentle incline. The road was narrow and the canyon opened starkly to their left, a fall that would last several seconds should any of them be unlucky enough to try it, and Paul was glad of the beast's deliberate pace.

'It is so strange,' Florimel said. 'It is a river valley, but it seems so . . . raw.' Indeed, the edges of the canyon wall, banded in red and brown and orange, glistened like meat. 'So new.'

'I've never been here,' Paul said, 'I mean, in the real world, but I agree with Martine – I don't think there are many mountain ranges in Kansas. T4b? Do you know anything about it?'

The youth was staring out of the back of the wagon. 'About what?'

'Kansas.'

'That a city, something, right?'

Paul sighed.

'It *is* new,' Martine said. 'At least, I can feel something in the geological information – I cannot think of a better way to say it – that suggests it has changed much and is still changing.' She frowned. 'What is that clanking?'

'The very poor suspension of this wagon, perhaps,' said Florimel sourly. 'By the way, this thing pulling us is not what I think of as a native American animal either, when you come to it. In fact, I am reminded of . . .'

'*Fenfen!*' T4b shouted suddenly, pointing back up the slope. 'Op it! *Look!*'

Paul turned to see a huge, glittering shape slide out of the mine shaft. For a moment it was only multiple starbursts of bouncing light, then the great head heaved around toward them, and with the bright reflections gone, Paul could suddenly see it clearly.

'Sweet Jesus,' he said. 'It's some kind of snake!'

But it was more than that – it was another thing like

their horse, familiar yet strange. As the monstrous creature heaved more of its bulk out of the shaft, he saw that its body was studded with great chunks of copper and silver, as though its bones were metal and protruded through the horny, patterned skin. Instead of a smooth tube, it was segmented like a child's toy, but weirdest of all were the wheels at the bottom of each segment, great round buttons of bone.

'It's a . . .' Absurdly, even in heart-pounding fright he found himself grasping for the proper term. 'A mine train – ore cars!'

The thing writhed, squeaking and scraping, out onto the road. For a moment it tried to draw itself into a circle, but there was not enough room for its massive coils in the flat space along the edge of the cliffs. It rose up swaying, just its front two sections looming several meters high, and for a moment its huge, faceted rose-quartz eyes seemed to consider their wagon, halted and helpless as Florimel tried to calm the terrified horse-creature. A tongue like a hardened stream of quick-silver flicked out, then flicked out again, then with terrifying speed the serpent dropped its head and slid down the road toward them.

'Get out,' Paul shouted. 'It's coming! We'll have to run!'

'Chance not!' T4b slithered out of the wagon and onto the front bench and snatched the reins from Florimel. 'Done this one before, me – just like *Baja Hades!*'

He whipped the horse-creature's flank with the end of the reins until it gave a shrill whistle of pain and surprise, then leaped away down the road so suddenly that the wagon almost tipped over. It was all Paul could do to cling to the side. As soon as he regained his balance, the wagon wheeled around a bend and he spun sideways again to crash into Martine and almost knock her over the low railing. The snake-thing had fallen out of sight behind them.

'Flyin' now!' T4b whooped. 'Told you, done this before!'

'This isn't a game!' Paul shouted at him. 'This is bloody real!'

Florimel took advantage of a section of straightaway to fling herself into the back of the wagon with the others. She grabbed fiercely at the board railing beside Paul.

'If we survive,' she gasped, 'I will kill him.'

The odds on that outcome rapidly became worse; as the careening wagon picked up speed on an increasing slope, the vast head of the serpentine creature came around the corner behind them, followed by its juddering body. It had wheels, as well as the great muscular power of its ore-knobbed body to push it along. It was gaining on them.

They thundered over rocks in the road and for a moment Paul felt himself rise weightlessly off the wagon bed, then gravity reasserted itself, slamming him down hard on his back on the boards. A body, either Florimel's or Martine's, thumped on top of him and drove out the air, so that for a moment the sky exploded with daytime stars.

A second later the wagon tipped up at an alarming angle as the terrified horse dragged it around another bend on two wheels. From his position, it seemed certain to Paul that they had run off the side of the road and were hanging over pure nothing.

When all four wheels were touching ground again, Paul clambered up onto his hands and knees with the idea of putting Florimel's plan into action now, on the chance that they would not live to kill T4b later on. Instead, as he lifted his head up above the wagon floor, he saw the terrible face of their pursuer only meters behind them. The creature saw him, too. A mouth full of draggled iron fangs opened wide, displaying black depths as impenetrable as the pit out of which it had crawled.

Paul decided not to strangle the teenager just yet.

'It's catching up!' he shouted.

T4b crouched lower on the bench, snapping the reins against the horse-creature's back, but the animal had no greater speed to give them. Another bump and Paul felt himself flung up in the air again, and for a moment was heart-stoppingly certain he would be flung out the back of the wagon and into those waiting jaws. Instead he tangled with Florimel and the two of them slid and crashed into the back railing of the wagon.

'Grab her!' Florimel shouted as he struggled to extricate himself. For a moment Paul had no idea what she meant, but then saw that Martine also had hit the back of the wagon at such an angle that she had nearly flown out. She was clinging with one leg and one arm, her left leg dangling only a few inches above the dirt, too stunned even to cry out.

Paul scrambled along the railing, but could not get a firm hold on Martine's flailing limbs as he fought against the wagon's ceaseless jouncing. Florimel grabbed him, helping to anchor him as he worked to better his grip. T4b was staring back in alarm, and as if sensing his inattention the horse-creature had slowed a little. The pursuing serpent gave a creaking hiss and rose up behind them, looming over the wagon like the terrifying figurehead of a Viking ship.

The wagon abruptly swung to the right as the horse followed a tight curve in the hillside. Paul, Florimel, and Martine were all flung to the outside rail of the wagon; for an instant, Martine lifted off the railing and was in open air with nothing below her but the painted strata of the canyon. Paul felt her sleeve begin to rip under his fingers, the material pulling apart at the seams, even as the dragon head darted down at them and the giant stony jaws clacked a hand's breadth from Paul's head.

Paul yanked Martine back down into the wagon, banging her skull against the rail in the process. The serpent reared again, then paused and abruptly rolled sideways, its hiss a shriek of surprise, and fell away behind them.

Paul clambered to his knees, staring. The tail of the serpent had failed to make the last sharp bend, even as the head had driven in for the kill. Much of the creature's bulk had already skidded down the steep slope in a billow of dust. As Paul watched, the great head whipped back and forth as it tried to gain purchase with the part of its body still on the mountain road, but too much of its back end was sliding downward. With a screech like failing brakes, the head thrashed toward them once, sun glinting from the copper nodes, then it was gone over the side like a yanked rope.

Moments later a grinding crash echoed up to them, the sound of a vertical train wreck.

Paul slumped back to the wagon bed. Martine and Florimel lay beside him, breathing in shallow, rapid gasps. The wagon was still jolting swiftly down the winding road, swaying dangerously at every turn.

'It's gone!' he shouted. 'Javier, it's gone! Slow down!'

'This thing's locked up! Won't go slow!'

Exhausted, Paul sat up. The boy was pulling back as hard on the reins as he could, but although the horse had modified its pace a little, it was still moving down the hill road at a near gallop.

'It can't slow down,' Florimel groaned from the boards beside him. 'The wagon will run over it. Find the brake!'

'Brakes? On a wagon?'

'Great God, of course there is!' She clambered past Paul

and leaned across T4b's lap. She grabbed something there and pulled up. There was a groaning noise and for a moment the wheels dug, then rolled again, but this time a little more slowly.

'Damn,' said Paul. 'I can't tell you how happy I am you knew that.'

They were still rolling downhill at a whistling pace, but all four wheels now remained in contact with the ground. Paul, Martine, and Florimel dragged themselves back into the center of the wagon bed as the rocky hillside rushed past.

'Everybody all right?' Paul asked.

Martine groaned. 'I have scraped most of the skin off my hands. Otherwise, I will live.'

'Hey!' shouted T4b. 'What about some charge for the driver?'

'What?' Florimel rubbed bruised knees. 'Is he asking for drugs?'

'Charge!' T4b said, and laughed. 'You know, rep!'

Paul, who was at least glancingly conversant with street slang, was the first to figure it out. 'Thanks. He wants us to thank him.'

'Thank him?' Florimel growled. 'I would give him a painful spanking if I didn't worry we'd go over the cliff.'

T4b scowled. 'Didn't get eat by no snake, you. What's your boohoo?'

'You did a good job, Javier,' Martine said. 'Just keep your eyes on the road, please.'

Paul spread his legs to brace himself, then leaned against the front of the wagon bed, watching the hill road wind away behind them. The sun was dazzlingly bright, only an eyelash short of noon. Raw metal glinted here and there in the ragged landscape.

'I doubt that either that snake or the horse pulling us

were part of the original package for this place,' he said.
'Does that remind you of anything?' He was startled by
a line of black appearing on the ridge beside them. It took
a moment before he realized it was some kind of cable.
He raised himself on his elbows and turned to look ahead.
The cable paralleled the road, stretched along sentinel tree
trunks.

Telephones? Not in Dodge City. Telegraph, must be. He
eased himself back and watched the hill road and the line
of black sliding away behind them.

'It is like Kunohara's world,' Florimel said. 'Those mutations he said had just begun there. Perhaps Dread has
done something like that here as well.'

'That would be a quick and perhaps amusing way to
spoil things,' Martine said. She spoke slowly, obviously
still tired and sore. 'And he has so many worlds to ruin.
Just turn up a few randomizing factors, perhaps, then sit
and watch someone's carefully-crafted simulation turn
into something bizarre.'

Another telegraph line now hung below the first, twin
black streaks along the left side of Paul's vision. The
wagon rattled and lurched down the stony road. Paul
groaned. It was hard to imagine a less comfortable way
to travel – he was surprised he hadn't broken any teeth
with all the jaw-snapping bounces. 'Can't we go any
slower?'

'Not if you want Mister Horse in front of this ride,' T4b
said crossly.

Now there were telegraph lines along the canyon rim
as well, so that the wagon rolled between two high, sparse
fences of black cables. Paul wondered if this was another
misshaping of the original simulation, and if so, what
weird communication ran along these extra cables. Or
were they merely empty copies?

'I think I see a town,' Florimel said. 'See, down at the bottom of the canyon.'

Paul clambered to the edge of the wagon and squinted. The sun's glare off the canyon walls was fierce, making the river at the bottom a twisting line of silvery fire, but there was certainly something along the river's edge just before the canyon bent and blocked the rest of the river valley from view, something that seemed too regular to be stone on the canyon floor.

'Martine, can you tell if that's really a town – Dodge City, or whatever this is? I can't see it very well.'

'We will reach it soon enough.' She reached up and rubbed listlessly at her temples. 'Forgive me.'

'What in hell is going on?' Florimel said.

For a moment Paul thought she was talking about Martine's unwillingness to come look; then he saw that just ahead another half-dozen cables ran in from the hill-side and then bent off a leaning pole and stretched over the top of the roadway like a musical staff with no notes. An instant later they were bouncing along beneath the awning of black lines, and Paul could not help seeing that the cables now surrounded them on all sides. They hung loosely, a meter or two of empty space between each pair, so they were not in any way trapped, but it was still an unsettling sight.

'I don't know,' Paul belatedly answered Florimel. 'But I don't like it very much . . .' He looked up past T4b just as the wagon rounded a bend, still traveling in a tube of telegraph cables. The young man swore and jerked back hard on the reins. Their horse was already trying to slow up, but the weight of the wagon behind it was too much and the creature's knob-knuckled feet were furrowing the roadway.

Just a few dozen meters ahead the cables all ran

together, knotted in a crooked black mandala across the middle of the wide road. It looked like . . .

'Christ!' shouted Florimel, tumbling as the horse tangled in the traces and the wagon began to sway alarmingly. 'What . . . ?'

It looked like a huge spiderweb.

'Get out!' Paul shouted. The horse had bolted to the inner side of the roadway and the wagon could not make a sharp enough turn to follow. The wheels dug and skidded. The whole wagon began to tip even as it plunged swiftly forward into the swaying net of cables, now only a stone's throw away. 'Jump – now!'

Martine was wrapped around his legs. The wagon bed was tilting up sideways, lifting them inexorably toward the canyon side of the road. Paul bent down and grabbed the blind woman, then did his best to climb to the rising side of the wagon, hoping to leap out toward the hillside, but Martine's weight was too much for him.

One of the wagon wheels snapped with a noise like a gunshot. A splintered piece of spoke arrowed past his face and the whole wagon groaned like a wounded animal as it tumbled onto its side.

Paul had no chance to pick spots. He grabbed Martine and flung himself off the wagon bed. Something sticky caught at him, sagging beneath his weight, and for a moment he had the alarming sight of nothing but empty air beneath him, of the full vertiginous drop down the crazy-banded side of the canyon. He half-slid, half-fell down the row of cables until he was sitting in a painful, twisted position in the roadway, stuck at the nexus point of two of the black bands, with Martine lying motionless across his lap.

Before he could even look for the others, the wagon and the trapped, tethered horse rolled into the web of cable blocking the roadway, flinging up a dense cloud of dust. One of the horse's legs was obviously broken; it writhed helplessly in the wreckage of the wagon, a mess of kicking black fur and splintered wood dangling from the sticky web.

Then the web's builders appeared – hairy gray-and-brown shapes climbing up from the canyon or down the hillside, scuttling along the strands like spiders.

Spiders would have been bad enough. These things had the faces of dead buffalo, with hanging tongues and rolling eyes, atop their malformed, many-limbed bodies. Worst of all, they were even more clearly part-human than the insect-monsters of Kunohara's world. They hissed with hungry pleasure as they advanced down the swaying cables. The first of them to reach the middle of the web began to pull the living horse apart, bickering in wet, piping voices over the best bits, ignoring the creature's agonized squeals as they began to feed.

Paul tried to drag himself upright, but the sticky cables held him like a strong hand.

'**C**ODE *Delphi*. Start here.

'It seems pointless to me even to record these thoughts, since I cannot believe we will ever leave this place, but the habit dies hard.

'It is dark here, the others tell me – some kind of underground nest, filthy to smell and unpleasant to hear. I wish I could limit myself to those two senses, but in my own way I can even see the things moving, eating, coupling. They are horrible. I am running out of hope. My strength is all but gone.

'I suppose we are alive only because they feasted on the horse first. The sounds it made dying were . . . No. What is the point? Is there something we can do? I can think of nothing. There are dozens of the monsters. We should have tried to escape when we were first seized. Now we are in their nest. Any hope that they eat only animals has been destroyed by the human bones that lie everywhere, in careless piles. Those I touched have been picked clean of flesh and broken for marrow.

'Horrible things. T4b, who has spent most of the time praying, called them "rotten-cow spiders." I have not had a clear impression of them. What I perceive is the mass of them, the limbs, the voices – almost human, but my God, that word "almost" . . . !

'Stop, Martine. We have faced situations as bad as this and survived. Why is it that I am so weak, so weary, so miserable? Why have the past days felt like work too hard for me to do?

'It is . . .

'Good God. One of the things came to sniff at us. Florimel drove it away by kicking at it, but it did not seem frightened. They do smell of rotted meat, but they also have another scent, something strange I cannot define, something nonliving. This whole place, this simworld, seems to be in a paroxysm of change. The others can see only what *is* at this moment, but I can perceive the changes that have happened and those that are about to happen. Dread has grabbed the place and squeezed hard. This world has not resisted him any better than would a fistful of butter. Heaven only knows what these poor creatures were. People, perhaps. Ordinary people with ordinary lives. Now they live in holes in the ground and squeak like rats and eat things that are still screaming.

'Where is Paul? I cannot sense him near me anymore. But the noise and heat and confusion make it difficult . . .

'Florimel says he is just a few meters away, on his

hands and knees. Poor man. To have gone through so much, only to end here.

'I cannot stand this anymore – any of it. Ever since the Trojan simulation I have been dazed as an electroshock victim. In between the terrors and lesser distractions I have tried to find myself, the Martine I know, but it is as if I have been hollowed. The memory of the last hours of Troy haunts me. How could I do such a thing? Even to save these friends, how could I bring death to so many? Rape and torture and destruction? And after watching the pitiable humanity of Hector and his family, too.

'I tell myself over and over that they were only simulacra, not real, only bits of gear. Sometimes I believe it, for hours at a stretch. Maybe it truly is so, but I know that I cannot stop seeing the spear plunging into that Trojan soldier's stomach, the horror on his face. How can I know that was not someone like us, still trapped in the system, forced to play out his part in a famous war? Not likely, perhaps, but still . . . still.

'I dreamed last night that the great burning light of my own blinding came streaming out of his wound. I dreamed that I fell into a darkness even greater than the one I have known.

'I cannot stand this place. I cannot live with this madness. I ran away from all of this years ago. I am not meant to care this much. I do not want to be terrified anymore, to see my friends threatened and hounded and killed.

'I do not want to meet Dread again.

'There. That is perhaps the greatest fear. I admit it! Even should some improbable thing happen, should we drag ourselves out of this stinking pit, away from these cannibal monstrosities, it does not take magic to know that any road back to the real world must run through him. He handled me as though I were a child – made me whimper. Made me beg him to stop, and all without needing to cause any physical pain. Now he has the power of a god, and he is furious.

'Oh, merciful Heaven, I don't want this.

'It's all too much. I wish could turn off these senses. I want to cover it all over, bury myself in the dark – but not this dark! Escape . . . I don't want this!

'They're coming toward us, a great group of them. Are they . . . singing?

'Paul is gone – Florimel says so. Have they already taken him?

'*T4b! They're coming! Get over here with Florimel and me!*

'I wish he had his armor. I should . . . if this is the last . . . I should . . . but . . .

'Oh, God, not this . . . !'

CHAPTER 17

Breathing Problems

NETFEED/INTERACTIVES: GCN, Hr. 5.5 (Eu, NAm) – 'HOW TO KILL YOUR TEACHER'
(visual: Looshus and Kantee reading the Reality Scroll)
VO: Looshus (Ufour Halloran) and Kantee (Brandywine Garcia) have discovered that Superintendent Skullflesh (Richard Raymond Balthazar) is the reborn prophet of the Stellar Knowledge cult, and is preparing a blood sacrifice of the entire school population to bring on the end of the world. Casting 4 hall monitors, 7 cult members.
Flak to: GCN.HOW2KL.CAST

IT made a very small pile when she looked at it, all the things she had bought, all the things that she would carry with her into this last and strangest country of a life that had seen many countries and many strange things.

The new telematic jack was small, of course, no larger than the standard variety despite its additional range. It had cost a decent fraction of her bank account, but the salesman had sworn that it would keep her in touch with her fancy Dao-Ming pad at a distance of several miles – 'even in the middle of a high-usage telecom area during an electrical storm,' he had cheerfully promised. Olga didn't know about storms, although she had spent enough days now near the Gulf of Mexico to know that even on a clear day lightning never seemed more than a breath away, but she guessed that an island with its own army and air force would probably qualify as a 'high-usage telecom area.'

Beside the jack sat a small but extremely powerful LED flashlight, a piece of high-tech paraphernalia usually sold to businessmen with too much money, and despite its dramatic name – something like 'SpyLite' or 'SpaceLight,' she couldn't remember which – seldom used for anything much more dramatic than finding dropped keys in a parking lot, she guessed. She had also bought something called an OmniTool from the same store, then changed her mind and exchanged it for a more familiar Swiss Army knife. She had always meant to buy one, had thought dozens of times what a handy object it would be for a woman living on her own, but for some reason had never done it. The fact that she had finally bought one, a top-of-the-line model with all kinds of clever hidden devices and built-in micro-circuitry, helped mark the occasion. Things had changed. She was not the same Olga Pirofsky.

What *did* one bring on an infiltration of one of the world's largest and best-guarded corporations? She supposed there were many more things she could have bought, guns and cutting torches and surveillance devices, but it all smacked too much of boys playing war games. Besides, she was fairly certain she would be arrested at some point, and a pocketful of plastic explosives or wall-climbing pitons would make it hard to pretend she had wandered away from a tour group.

So her pile of tools to take behind enemy lines was a small one: the new jack, the knife, the flashlight, and the one object of sentiment she had not been able to leave behind in Juniper Bay with the rest of her old life.

The curl of white plastic was certainly not going to arouse anyone's suspicions. Olga's last name and first initial, as written decades ago by some nurse who might very well be dead, had almost faded away. Olga herself had cut the bracelet to remove it, but had never thrown it away, and through all the years in her top drawer it had retained the curve of her wrist. Many times she had come within inches of tossing it in the trash, but the O. Pirofsky who had worn that hospital bracelet was a different person, and the tiny snake of pale plastic was her only tangible connection to that Olga, a girl with her life ahead of her, a young woman with a husband named Aleksandr still alive, so very much alive, a young woman about to give birth . . .

Something rapped quickly and authoritatively on the motel room door. Startled, Olga dropped the bracelet back onto the small pile of objects in the middle of the bed. After a moment's hesitation, she stepped to the door and looked out through the fish-eye peephole. A black woman and white man stood there, both in dark suits.

For a moment she leaned breathlessly against the door, heart racing for no reason she could say. Missionaries, they must be – this whole region was acrawl with them, people with nothing better to do than walk around in heavy clothing on the hottest day, trying to convince others that there was somewhere hotter yet they might be going if they didn't embrace the doorstepper's faith.

The knock came again; something in its weight drove all thought of ignoring it out of her mind. She tossed her motel bathrobe over the things lying on the bed – irritated, despite her fright, that these people would now think she was the kind of person who normally left things strewn around the room.

It was the black woman who took the lead when the

door opened. She smiled at Olga, although it seemed a little perfunctory, and drew a long flat wallet out of her coat pocket. 'You're Ms Pirofsky, is that right, ma'am?'

'How do you know me?'

'Manager gave us your name. Nothing to worry about, ma'am, we just wanted a few words with you.' The woman flipped open the wallet, a brief glimpse of something that looked like a hologram of a police badge. 'I'm Officer Upshaw and this is my partner, Officer Casaro. We'd like to ask you a couple of questions.'

'Are you . . . police?'

'No, ma'am, we're security officers for J Corporation.'

'But I . . .' In her fear and surprise, she had been about to say that she didn't work for J Corporation anymore. She managed to keep her mouth shut, but only at the expense of looking like a slow and stupid old woman. But, she thought, perhaps there could be worse ways to look.

The man Casaro had only briefly made eye contact with her, and unlike his partner, he made no effort to smile. The black pinholes in the center of his pale eyes looked past her into the room itself, as if he were some kind of machine recording everything he saw for future study. Olga suddenly remembered her grandmother describing the old Polish secret police. *They didn't look at you, they looked through you, even when they were talking to you. Like x-rays.*

'What . . . what could you possibly want to ask some-one like me?'

Officer Upshaw grudgingly used the smile again. 'We're just doing our job, ma'am. We heard you were asking some questions in various places about the J Corporation campus.'

'The campus?' She could not shake the feeling that

they had been following her ever since she had walked out the doors of Obolos Entertainment – that this was only a bit of cruel pretense, and at any moment they would throw her to the floor and handcuff her.

'The buildings, the facilities – that's what we call it, ma'am. Some of the local merchants, well, they let us know when people are asking questions.' She shrugged, and for the first time Olga saw how young this woman really was – perhaps just past college age, and with a bit of insecurity in the measured way she spoke. 'Now could you please tell us what brings you to the area and what your interest in J Corporation might be?'

Officer Casaro's long inspection of everything behind Olga finally ended. His eyes found hers and locked. She felt her knees go a little weak. 'Certainly,' she managed to say after a moment. 'Why don't you come in – all of the air-conditioning will get out, otherwise.'

An almost imperceptible look flicked between the two. 'That's fine, ma'am. Thank you.'

After Olga gathered up the things on the bed, under the guise of tidying away the bathrobe, and deposited the bundle on the counter in the tiny bathroom, she was able to relax a little. None of the objects that had been lying there were illegal or even particularly suspicious for someone who had made her living in net entertainment, but she didn't really want her possession of a telematic jack that cost as much as a small car to become a topic of conversation.

As her initial terror ebbed a little, she began to believe that things might be no worse than they appeared. She had been asking questions in what was, after all, a company town, and the company itself was famously secretive. Similarly, if they had her name from the credit information at the motel, she couldn't very well pretend to be someone different, could she? Somewhere on that island – perhaps in the black tower itself – were the records of *Pirofsky, O.*, employee.

'You see,' she told them, 'I worked for a J Corporation subsidiary for years – you've seen Uncle Jingle, haven't you? I worked on that show.' Upshaw nodded and smiled politely. Casaro didn't bother. 'And since I was in the area – I'm taking a car trip across America now that I'm retired – I just thought I'd come see it. After all, they've been paying my salary for years!'

She answered a few more questions, all from Officer Upshaw, and did her best to pretend she was enjoying the break in routine, the importance of a visit from security officers. She struggled to remember the innocent taxpayer's serenity she had always been able to bring to her encounters with police in Juniper Bay.

You're an actress, aren't you? So act!

It seemed to work. The questions got more perfunctory, and even Casaro's surgical examination of Olga and her room gradually dulled to something like bored routine. She had no urge to rekindle his interest. She started telling a true but circumstantially pointless story about her dog Misha, which finally did the trick.

'We're sorry, but we'll have to get going, Mr Pirofsky,' said Upshaw, rising. 'We're sorry to have bothered you.'

Feeling almost pleased with herself now, she hazarded the tiniest return of serve. 'Maybe you can tell me, since I haven't been able to find out for certain. Is there *any* kind of tour of the . . . the campus, as you called it? I'd hate to come all this way and not get to see it except from a distance.'

Casaro snorted, then stepped out the door to wait for his partner in the motel parking lot, under hot gray skies.

Upshaw shook her head. For the first time her smile seemed honest – an amused grin. 'No, ma'am. No, I'm afraid there isn't. See, we're not really that kind of corporation.'

JEREMIAH was up in the sleeping area, changing the dressing on Del Ray's head wound, so Joseph had become the official watcher of the monitor screens. All of the men upstairs were in view on one camera, still in the same place beside the elevator doors. At the moment they were resting and smoking, but dusty chunks of concrete lay piled all around and the man standing in the hole, leaning on the handle of his pick, was a good half meter below his fellows.

Joseph supposed he and his companions should be grateful at least that they were so far out in the middle of nowhere, or the men upstairs would probably have fetched in air hammers and a compressor by now.

'Coward bastards,' he said, half-whispering. Just what they were doing that was so cowardly he couldn't quite define, but waiting was difficult, especially when you were probably waiting to be killed.

He looked down to the floor of the lab where the silent V-tanks lay. How strange, to think Renie was so close. And her friend, too – both of them sealed in the dark, like those little oiled fish in cans. He missed her.

The thought was so surprising that he had to stop and try it out for size and feel. Yes, he did, he truly missed her. Not just feared for her, not just wanted to protect her, do the fatherly duty of keeping her safe from bad men – he wished she were here to talk to him.

It was something he hadn't thought about much, and he had trouble holding it together to consider it. It was all wrapped up somehow with Renie's mother, but not with the awful helplessness of watching her die, as his feelings of protectiveness were. He missed having someone around who cared about him. He missed the company of someone who understood his little jokes. Not that Renie liked them very much, and sometimes she pretended they weren't jokes at all, that he was just being stupid or difficult, but there had been times when she was just as amused by him as her mother had been.

Now that he thought of it, though, it had been a long while. Not many jokes in the last few years, at least not the kind you could laugh about.

She was funny herself when she wanted to be, but it seemed to Joseph it had been some time since there had been much of that from her end either. She had got so serious, somehow. Angry, even. Because her mama was dead? Because her father couldn't work, with his bad back? That was no reason to lose your sense of humor. That was when you needed it most of all – Long Joseph knew that for a fact. If he couldn't have gone out and had a drink every now and then with Walter and Dog and found a laugh or two with them, he would have killed himself a long time since.

When she was a little girl, we used to talk. She'd ask me questions, and if I didn't know, I'd make up some foolishness just to see her laugh. He hadn't seen that laugh in a long time, that surprised laugh where her whole face lit up. Such a serious little girl she'd been, he and her mother couldn't help but tease her sometimes.

Come back, baby girl. He stared at the silent tank, then turned back to the monitor. Break time was over: three men were digging now in the hole in the concrete floor, dust billowing up like they were devils in the smokes of hell. Joseph had the strangest feeling, like he was going to cry. He reached out and took a swallow of his last, dwindling bottle of wine. *You come back soon and laugh with me . . .*

The ringing of the telephone startled him so badly that he almost dropped the precious squeeze bottle with its cap open. He stared at the device for a moment as he would a black mamba. Jeremiah was upstairs, but he must be able to hear the ring – with the floors all open to the high central ceiling, the underground lab complex was like being in some big train-station waiting room.

Maybe I just leave it alone until he gets down, Joseph thought, but the thought of being frightened of an antique telephone was too much. As it rang again, he stood up and snatched it off its dented metal cradle.

'Who is that?'

There was a pause on the other end. The voice, when it came, was ghostly and distorted. 'Is that Joseph?'

Only after the first superstitious chill had raced across his skin did he remember, but he wanted to be sure. 'You tell me who's calling, first.'

'It's Sellars. Surely Mr Dako has told you about me.'

Joseph didn't want to talk about Jeremiah. Joseph was the one who had answered the phone; he was the one in charge of this emergency. 'What do you want?'

'To help, I hope. I take it that they haven't managed to break in yet.'

'They are trying. They are surely trying.'

In the silence that followed, Joseph found himself suddenly worried that he had done something wrong, driven off their benefactor. 'I don't have much time,' Sellars finally said. 'And, I must confess, not a lot of ideas, either. You managed to get the armored elevator doors closed?'

'Yes. But those men are digging through the floor now – started out with a grenade, I think, but now they using picks, shovels. Coming right down through the cement.'

'That's bad. Do you have the monitors working?'

'I am looking at those men right now. They are digging like dogs after a bone.' Jeremiah had appeared, a look of worry on his face. Joseph waved him back: everything was being taken care of.

Sellars sighed. 'Do you think you can help me connect to your surveillance system? That would give me a better idea of what's going on.'

'You mean these cameras and so on?' Joseph felt his competence suddenly under heavy fire. 'Hook you up? To those?'

'We should be able to do it, even with that old equipment you have there.' There was a strange, wheezing laugh. 'I'm pretty old equipment myself, after all. Yes, I think I can talk you through it.'

Joseph was disturbed. Every cell in his body told him to take charge, to make something happen, but he knew Jeremiah had spent much more time with the machinery than he had. In fact, he knew he hadn't even bothered to learn anything about the monitors at all. With real regret, he said, 'I will let you talk to Jeremiah.' But he could not give up without even a show of involvement. 'It is that man Sellars,' he whispered as he passed the receiver. 'He wants to get hooked up with the pictures.'

Jeremiah stared at him quizzically, then leaned forward and tapped a button on the instrument panel. 'I've put you on the speaker, Mr Sellars,' he said out loud, then hung up the receiver. 'That way we can both hear you.'

Joseph was caught off-balance. Was Jeremiah being kind to him, like to a child? Or was he treating him as an equal? Joseph wanted to be irritated, but could not help feeling a small glow of pleasure.

'Good.' Sellars' voice sounded even more strange now, scratchy on the small speaker. 'I'm trying to think of things to do, but first could you patch me in to your monitors?' He gave a list of instructions to Jeremiah that Joseph could not quite follow, which left him feeling annoyed again. Who had been the mechanical one in this group, after all? Not Jeremiah, a kind of glorified lady's maid for a rich old white woman. Not Del Ray, an overgrown schoolboy who wore suits and sat behind a desk.

By the time Joseph had summoned up the meditative calm to shrug off the unintended insult, Jeremiah had apparently done what Sellars wanted.

'I see three working and one with a gun, watching,' the tinny voice said. 'Is that all of them?'

'I'm not sure,' said Jeremiah.

Joseph frowned, thinking. When he and Del Ray had snuck in, they had seen . . . how many? 'Five,' he said suddenly. 'There are five of those men.'

'So one's off somewhere,' Sellars said. 'We shouldn't forget about him. But first we have to deal with the digging. How thick are the floors, any idea? Wait, I should be able to access the plans.'

For long seconds the speaker was silent. Joseph's thoughts were just turning sadly to the small bit of wine he had left when the strange voice spoke again. 'Roughly two meters deep where they're working, next to the elevator bay. Which means they're probably about a quarter of the way there.' He made a strange sound, perhaps a hiss of frustration. 'It's heavy concrete, but they'll be through in a day at the most.'

'We only have one gun, Mr Sellars,' Jeremiah said. 'Two bullets. We're not going to be able to fight with them when they get through.'

'Then we have to see what we can do to keep them out,' Sellars replied. 'I wish this place were a bit older, then maybe I could find a way to banjax the heaters, fill that upper section with carbon monoxide.'

Joseph remembered enough from his days in the construction trade to remember something about those carbon what-so-oxiders. 'Yes, kill the bastards! Poison them. That would be a fine thing.'

Jeremiah winced. 'Kill them in cold blood?'

'We can't do it,' Sellars said, 'or at least I can't see a way just now, so it's not worth debating the morality of it. But you must understand that those are not ordinary men, Mr Dako. They are murderers – perhaps the very men who attacked your friend, the doctor.'

'How do you know about that?' asked Jeremiah, startled. 'Did Renie tell you?'

'In fact, they have killed someone else that Joseph knows,' Sellars said, leaving Jeremiah's question unanswered. 'The young technician you visited in Durban.'

Joseph had to think for a moment. 'The fat boy? Elephant?'

'Oh, God, they didn't!' said Del Ray.

'Yes. Shot him in the head and burned his building.' Sellars was speaking briskly now, as though a timer inside him was ticking loudly. 'And they will kill you, too, as blithely as swatting a fly, if it suits them . . . and I suspect that it will.'

In his mind's eye, Joseph could see the cluttered storage depot burning. His initial horrified fascination began to curdle into something else as he remembered Elephant's cheerfulness, his pride in his top-of-the-line equipment.

Not right. That is not right. He just helped us because Del Ray ask him.

'What will we do, then?' asked Jeremiah. 'Wait for them to break through and murder us?'

'He said about police.' Joseph felt anger building, a different kind of anger. 'Why don't we just call someone – the army? Tell them some men are trying to kill us right here in their base?'

'Because you are yourselves wanted by the police,' Sellars said, his voice flattened by the electronic distortion. 'The Brotherhood has seen to that. Do you not remember what happened when Mr Dako tried to use one of his cards?'

'How do you know about all this?' Jeremiah demanded. 'I didn't tell you any of that when we talked before.'

'Never mind.' Their invisible companion seemed frustrated. 'I told you, I have little time and much to do elsewhere. If you call the authorities it will take hours for any suitable force to respond – you are far up in the mountains. Then, even if they drive away or capture Klekker and his thugs, what will happen to you? More importantly, what will happen to Renie and !Xabbu? After you three are arrested, they will either be left alone and untended here, with the place empty and perhaps the power shut off, or, if you tell the authorities, they will be disconnected and dragged away. Still deep in what will appear to be comas, would be my guess. Moving them now might even be fatal.'

The idea of the electricity failing and Renie waking in the darkness of the tank, struggling to get out, thrashing in that strange jelly, was even more horrible than imagining her lying in some hospital, as unresponsive as her brother. Joseph slapped his hand down on the table. 'It will not happen. I don't leave my girl here.'

'Then we have to think of another solution,' Sellars said. 'And quickly – I have my hands full just now trying to put out fires, and for every one I control, two more seem to flare up.' A moment of silence was filled with the looping hum of the mystery man's voice-distortion gear. 'Hang on. That may be it.'

'What? That may be what?' Jeremiah asked.

'Let me look at the plans,' Sellars told him. 'If I'm right, we'll have to work fast – you'll all have lots to do. And it's risky.'

'Just a small pile at first,' Sellars told them. 'Concentrate on the things you know will burn – paper, cloth.'

Joseph looked down at the huge heap of trash they had spent the last hour and a half collecting under Sellars' guidance. The paper and kitchen rags he could understand, the dusty military-issue sheets from the supply depot they had dragged down in the first days of their occupation, but what on earth were they going to do with the wheels off all the office chairs? Plastic floor mats? Rugs?

'Let me test it one more time before we commit ourselves,' Sellars said. 'Unlike your enemies, you don't have access to outside air.' As if a ghost had flicked a switch, a rattling noise sprang up behind the wall vent. It mounted higher, until it was a high-pitched whine, then eased down again. 'Good. Someone please start the fire.'

Del Ray, who had dragged himself from his convalescent bed to help, looked first at Jeremiah, then at Joseph. 'Start it? How?'

Something like weariness was in Sellars' voice. 'Isn't there anything you can use? The base is old – surely someone left behind a lighter, something?'

Joseph and the others looked around, as though such an object might magically appear.

'There's a little petrol in the emergency starter for the generator,' Jeremiah said. 'Only a spark would do it. We can make a spark, can't we?'

'I suppose you can cut into the wires in the monitor console,' Sellars said. 'Those are the only ones you can get to easily . . .'

'Hold on!' Joseph stood up straight. 'I know. Long Joseph will fix this problem.' He turned and hurried toward the room where he slept.

He had put Renie's clothes in a box, knowing she would want them when she came out of the tank. He felt in the pockets, and to his great joy discovered her cigarettes, but could find no trace of a lighter no matter how he looked. His moment of pride turned sour.

'Shit,' he said, letting the clothes fall back into the box. He stared at the cigarettes, wondering dully how Renie was coping without them. Could you smoke in the computer-place she was?

She must be crazy if she can't, he thought. '*Course, I am in the real world and I can't get any wine, so who has got it worse?*

'Good thinking!' someone said from the doorway.

Joseph looked up at Del Ray. 'No lighter, no matches.'

The younger man seemed puzzled for a moment, then smiled. 'Don't need any of that. Those are self-lighting.'

Joseph stared at the packet of cigarettes, relief mixed with a certain angry regret at having to be told something important by someone his daughter's age. He took a breath, then swallowed what he had been about to say. He tossed Del Ray the cigarettes and followed him back to the makeshift bonfire.

The tab pulled, the end of the cigarette smoldered alight. Del Ray dropped it on the knee-high pile of paper and rags. Little tongues of yellow flame scalloped the top of the pile; within half a minute it was burning well. As Joseph and the others heaped more of the most flammable objects on top of it, smoke began to drift upward in

a visible cloud. The whine of the air intake deepened and
the smoke was drawn toward the wall vent.

'Slowly.' Sellars' disembodied voice was hard to hear
above the noises the fire was making. 'It has to be burning very hot before you can put any of the plastic or
rubber on it.'

Joseph wandered over to the monitors. The men in the
hole beside the elevator well upstairs were working just as
hard as ever, nearly waist-deep now. The white one watching their progress had a cigar in the corner of his mouth.

'You will get your smoke, ugly man,' Joseph said, then
went back to help the others.

Within twenty minutes the flames were as high as Long
Joseph himself, the blaze several meters across, and only
the air-intake, which now roared like a small plane taking
off, kept them from being choked by the clouds of gray
smoke.

'Push in the pans of oil,' Sellars said. 'And start throwing on the rubber mats.'

Jeremiah and Joseph used a pair of broom handles to
slide the kitchen baking pans full of machine oil into the
heart of the blaze. Del Ray threw much of the material
they had been saving onto the top of the pile. The smoke,
and even the flames themselves, began to change color:
the cloud billowing out now and being drawn into the
vent was stormy black, and even through the wet rag
wrapped around his nose and mouth the smell was making
Joseph woozy. His eyes were burning too: the safety
goggles they'd found in a cabinet were ancient and fit
badly. He stepped away to watch Jeremiah and Del Ray
throw the last boxes of plastic and rubber onto the top
of the burning pile. The flames beat out so fiercely the
three of them were forced back across the wide area they'd
cleared on the cement floor, coughing all the way.

Weren't for that getting sucked out, Joseph thought as the inky clouds disappeared into the vent, so thick they almost folded rather than flowed, *we all be dead.* He suddenly realized what Sellars had meant when he said 'risky.' If the power failed, if something in the burning, black cloud choked the intake system, that black mass would come flowing back on them. Then their choice would be to suffocate or open the armored elevator doors and stumble out into the gunsights of the killers.

The pall of black was beginning to overcome the intake's capabilities, curling back, widening like a thunderhead. Joseph felt a rising terror.

'Where is that damn man?' he said. Jeremiah and Del Ray were too busy coughing to answer. Joseph, in a moment of unusual clarity, turned to memorize the location of the V-tanks so he could find them and release the prisoners if the power went out. His thoughts, absorbed by the fire-building, were now beginning to grow fragmented and panicky. 'Sellars! Whatever your name is, what are you doing, man? We choking to death here!'

'Sorry,' the voice hummed. 'I had to disable the fire alarms. I'm ready now.'

Easy enough for you, Joseph thought. *You are not fighting just to breathe.*

He and the others gathered around the monitor, wheezing. The full-throated roar of the intake did not change, but there was a succession of distant clanks, as though someone was striking a metal pipe with a hammer. An instant later Joseph felt the pressure of the room change, not enough to make his ears pop, but a definite shift. The plume of black wavered and then bent visibly toward the vent. The rest of the smoke that had escaped the intake began moving back toward the vent, too, as though the mountain itself had just inhaled.

'Watch,' said Sellars.

For a moment the scene on the monitor remained unchanged, the picks rising and falling, the white man with the cigar – Klekker, Sellars had called him; Joseph wanted to remember the Boer pig's name – leaning in to say something. Then Klekker lifted his head like an animal hearing a distant gunshot. A moment later the picture darkened. For an instant, Joseph actually thought the monitor was failing.

It all seemed strange and distant on the tiny screen, without sound. Suddenly, in the new, nightdark dimness of the picture, the men came thrashing up out of the pit. One collapsed to his knees, choking and vomiting, but before Joseph could see what happened to him, the monitor screen went almost completely black.

All the screens of that floor were dimming as the smoke rolled out from the vent near the elevator shaft. Joseph could only catch glimpses of the men, stumbling, falling, crawling toward the exit.

'Die, you bastards!' Joseph shouted. 'Burn down my house, do you? Shoot up some fat computer boy you don't even know? Choke and choke and die!'

But they did not all die, at least not as far as he could tell. The monitors recorded their escape to the next level up and their frantic attempts to seal the doorway behind them, but Sellars was apparently forcing the fumes and smoke up to that level as well, so the mercenaries were forced to flee again.

Four of them escaped through the base's massive front door. The camera by the armored gate showed the small, silent shapes as they staggered out into the air and fell to the ground like shipwreck survivors who had reached land against all odds.

'Four,' said Del Ray, counting. 'So one of them didn't make it out. That's something, anyway.'

'The rest of them will not be able to enter the level they were digging in, not for a long time,' said Sellars. He did not sound particularly pleased, but there was an undertone of grim satisfaction. 'They already had the doors blocked open, probably just to make sure we couldn't trap them anywhere, but I've disabled the vents on that level and it will take them a long time to disperse the fumes.'

'I wish it had killed them all,' Joseph said.

Jeremiah shook his head and turned away. 'A terrible way to die.'

'What do you think they are planning for us?' Joseph was irritated. 'A *braai?* Cook up some barbecue, open a few beers?'

'I must leave you for now,' Sellars announced. 'But I will be in touch again. You should have gained a few days' respite.'

When the speaker was silent, Joseph took the damp cloth from his mouth, then had to put it back on.

'He better make sure our air gets better in here,' he rasped.

'The vent's still working,' said Del Ray. 'I think it will get better. But we should put out this fire.' He lifted one of the fire extinguishers they had set in readiness.

Joseph hurried to join him. 'How are Renie and the little man?' he called back to Jeremiah.

Jeremiah Dako raised his goggles for a moment to squint at the readouts on the console. 'Everything steady. They're breathing better air than we are.'

'So what do we do now?' Joseph asked, heaving a large

fire extinguisher off the floor. Smoke curled around his shoe tops, but the largest part of the cloud was still being sucked into the vents, the grille, and the wall around it stained a shiny, sludgy black.

'What we've been doing,' said Jeremiah. 'We wait.'

'Damn,' said Joseph. He fired a gooey plume of foam onto the blaze. 'That is the thing I am tired of doing. Why is it that Sellars man can turn this mountain upside down, but he can't send me a damn bottle of wine?'

IT was a dream, of course – not the sort that had ravished her life, not the children come back to her after their long silence, but a simple, ordinary dream.

It was nighttime, and Aleksandr was outside the door of her Juniper Bay house. He wanted her to let him in because he had left something behind, but even though she could see his outline in the thin light from the street-lamp – in the dream there was a window beside the door – she felt uncertain. Again and again he called to her, not in pain or anger, but in that sort of explosive preoc-cupation he had always had, that air of having something important to do that was being prevented by a needlessly obstructive world and its petty details.

He couldn't or wouldn't tell her what it was he had left behind. Driven to a kind of fluttering despair by inde-cision, she had rummaged through drawers and cabinets, trying to find whatever was so important that he would delay whatever journey he was on, but she could find nothing in any of the places she searched that made any sense at all.

She woke up to the wallscreen yammering and dark-ness in the spaces between the motel drapes. She had fallen asleep sitting on the bed, in midafternoon, and now only the light from the screen remained. Carelessly, she had nodded off with the drapes not completely closed. Anyone could have stood and watched her through the window.

But did anyone care?

She stood up and pulled the drapes shut, then went back to the warm trough of the bed. As she sat, trying to make peace with being awake, she felt something missing. It took a moment before she realized it was Misha, who at home would have been curled up beside her, or more likely in her lap, his entire little body laid trustingly upon her.

Never again. Tears came to her eyes.

The news was still chattering away in the background, stories of sudden instability in financial markets, of strange rumors, of mysterious silences from key movers and shakers. It was so hard to care. Rather, it was too hard to give it true attention, because the caring was too painful. Once she had sat down every night to watch the news, but each evening's iteration had left her feeling that she and the rest of human civilization were poorly balanced on the crest of some huge wave, that any moment the entire thing would crash down with shattering force.

She turned off the screen. It was time to go. The security officers, corporate police, whatever they were, had given her a bad turn, but clearly they were just investigating all possibilities. People had noticed her asking questions.

After all, for all they knew, I might be a terrorist, she thought. It amused her, then her own amusement struck her as even more ironic. *But I am a terrorist.*

The urge to laugh, all alone in the now-silent room, seemed unhealthy. She was frightened by the thought of what was to come, that was the truth of it. Olga was not the kind of person who lied much to others, and not at all to herself.

She had lied to the security people, of course, if only by omission. And in a way she had lied to Mr Ramsey – not by anything she had told him, but by doing it in a written message, knowing he could not respond, that she would not have to defend herself. And just as she had feared, his replies had come hastening back, a chorus of protesting voices that she could not bear to access.

It was time to go. She would sleep in her rental car for a few hours in the out-of-the-way spot she had found deep in the bayou, then when her alarm woke her at midnight, she would make her way in through the swamp in the raft she had bought, try to land somewhere in the park that covered one edge of the artificial island. It seemed unlikely there would be no guards, but there would certainly be fewer of them out on the edges of the impenetrable swamp, wouldn't there?

It wasn't much of a plan, she knew, but it was the best she'd been able to come up with.

The pad would stay hidden in the room, of course; with two weeks' stay already paid for, it would likely go unnoticed longer here than in the car, which might be found in a couple of days. And so she would be able to keep sending entries to it for rerouting until . . . until whatever happened. So at least Mr Ramsey would know what had happened to her. Perhaps that would be useful to him with the other things he was doing, trying to help those poor children.

She knew she should make a last circuit of the room, but the thought of Catur Ramsey would not leave her so easily. She flipped open the pad and looked at his last three messages, all of them blinking, tagged 'urgent,' practically screaming for attention. She knew that it would only make her feel worse to access them, that all his arguments would make good sense but would change nothing.

She was terrible at arguing – Aleksandr had teased her with it, made her agree to ridiculous things, then laughed and refused to take advantage. 'You are like water, Olga,' he would say. 'Always, you give way.'

But what if there was something else Ramsey wanted to tell her? What if he needed some other kind of permission from her to sell the house? What if the people who had taken Misha had forgotten the veterinarian's name and couldn't get him his medicine?

She knew she was stalling, fearful of the journey in front of her, but now the worry wouldn't go away. Had that been the meaning of the dream, of dear Aleksandr so fretful outside the door, wanting to leave but unable to go?

She made a last circuit of the room, then picked up the pad. She had decided to leave it in the closet, down at the bottom under the extra blankets. There would be no one in the room, so no reason to put in fresh blankets; the motel's underpaid cleaning crew would be unlikely to go searching for extra work.

Olga slid the pad into the back of the closet, then went to the desk and wrote a note on the quaint, old-fashioned note paper – the one thing about the place that had separated it from the dozen or so others in which she had stayed during this trip. Under the 'Bayou Suites' heading, she wrote, '*I will be back for this pad. If it must be taken out of the room, please leave it in the motel office, or contact C. Ramsey, atty.,*' then added his address and signed her name.

She was all the way back to the closet when the thought of little Misha jumped up at her again. What if something had happened? If he did not get his medicine, he would start having those terrible seizures again. She had told them over and over, his new owners, but who knew how much attention people might be paying?

Poor little thing! I gave him away to strangers. Left him behind.

Her eyes swelling with tears again, Olga swore quietly to herself, then sat down on the bed with the pad across her lap and began opening messages.

CHAPTER 18

Making a Witch

NETFEED/NEWS: *Mystery Still Surrounds General's Death*

(visual: *Yacoubian meeting President Anford*)

VO: *The death of Brigadier General Daniel Yacoubian in a Virginia hotel suite has spawned a surprisingly virulent set of rumors, strangest of which is an assertion by one of the general's bodyguards, Edward Pilger, that he believes Yacoubian was involved in some kind of coup against the American government. Journalist Ekaterina Slocomb, who produced a short documentary on the general for Beltway, an upmarket tabnode, finds that idea hard to swallow.*

(visual: *Ekaterina Slocomb in studio*)

SLOCOMB: *'It just doesn't make sense. Yacoubian was friends with a lot of powerful people. Why would he or any of them want to overthrow a government that they already more or less own? Yacoubian was not an ideologue – if anything, he was a kind of ultimate pragmatist . . .'*

ONE of these days, Renie thought, *something that happens to me in this network is going to make sense.* But not yet, obviously. A little creature made of mud who called herself the Stone Girl was stumping along determinedly beside her, on either side of the dark, empty street the giant shoes that housed the local inhabitants were shut up tight against the night and its dangers, and this entire world had grown out of silvery nothing right in front of Renie's eyes.

'I still don't understand why you're coming with me,' she told the child. 'Aren't you supposed to stay at home? You're already in trouble for my sake.'

The Stone Girl's face was as shadowy as the street. 'Because . . . because . . . I don't know. Because things are going wrong and no one will listen to me. The step-mother never listens.' She wiped defiantly at the dark spots of her eyes, and Renie couldn't help wondering how a child made of earth and rock could cry. 'The Ending is getting closer, and the Witching Tree isn't there anymore.'

'Hang on. I thought you said that's where we were going – to this Witching Tree.'

'We are. We just have to find out where it is now.'

Renie chewed this over as they made their way out through the outskirts of the shoe-village. It was touching and disconcerting, both. The girl's willingness to push against the normal order of her life made Renie think of Brother Factum Quintus back in the House world – it was hard to imagine someone programming such flexible individuality into any mere simulacrum, but over and over she had seen the evidence. There was something different about this newest simulation, though – something more than the fact it seemed to have been created by the Other itself. A ragged bit of memory was still tickling her, and had been ever since she had first seen the shoe where the Stone Girl and her motley assortment of siblings lived, but it remained out of reach.

So what do I know? That this place is made up from some kind of nursery rhyme – or from lots of them, more likely. I never heard of any Stone Girl in the 'Old Lady and the Shoe' rhyme. Martine said she taught the Other a song – that 'angel' thing it was singing when we first saw it on the mountain-top. Maybe she taught it some stories, too.

But that still did not scratch the itch at the back of her memory.

They had reached the edge of the dark settlement. There was no moon, only a sort of dully glowing latency to the sky that left it just a shade more purple than black and gave faint shape to the shadowy world. Renie could barely make out the small person walking right next to her. She had just begun to wonder what would happen if she lost her little guide when a glowing apparition stepped out in front of them, billowing and moaning.

Frightened, Renie grabbed for the Stone Girl, but her companion shook off her hand. 'It's just Weeweekee,' she said.

'Stop!' The thing lifted its hand. A glowing ball hung just above it, a flame with no source. 'Who goes there?'

'It's me, the Stone Girl.'

As they drew closer, the weird apparition blocking their path became only slightly less so – a kind of human-sized rodent in a pale, flowing outfit like a hooded wedding dress. It waved its paw and the hovering ball of fire followed its hand – an impressive display, somewhat undercut by the creature's chubby cheeks and goggling black-bead eyes.

'You should be in bed,' the giant marmot, or whatever it was, declared in the voice of a tattletale child. 'For it's eight o'clock.'

'How can it tell?' This was the first Renie had heard any mention of exact time for longer than she could remember. 'How does it know it's eight o'clock?'

'That's just his word for "dark,"' the Stone Girl explained.

'All children should be in their beds,' Weeweekee told her.

'I'm not going to bed. I'm going out to search for the Witching Tree, and she's going with me. So there.'

'But . . . but . . . you can't.' His voice was swiftly losing any semblance of authority – in fact, getting dangerously near a squeak. 'Everyone is to be in bed. I have to rap at all the windows.'

'The stepmother threw us both out,' asserted the Stone Girl, which was not true, but close enough. 'We can't go back.'

Weeweekee was getting close to panic now. 'Then you can go in somewhere else, can't you? Just . . . go to bed. There must be some other beds, even with all the people sleeping in the street.'

'Not for us,' the little girl said firmly. 'We are going out into the Wood.'

Now the dark eyes widened with horror. 'But you can't! It's eight o'clock!'

'Good night, Weeweekee.' The Stone Girl took Renie's arm and led her past the creature, whose whiskers and hovering flame were both drooping.

Renie turned to look back at him. The rodent was still standing as if frozen, staring after them with misery clear in every line of his being. Even his filmy robes had lost their animation.

'Oh,' said Renie, and suddenly found herself struggling not to laugh. 'Oh. He's Wee Willie Winkie. In his night-gown.' It came back to her in one piece, like an evocative scent – the paper Mother Goose book her grandmother had given her for her fifth birthday, the pictures bright as candy wrappers. She had been a little disappointed, wishing it were something that moved by itself like the children's stories she saw on their small netscreen, which all featured exciting toys (even though her family couldn't afford most of them) but her mother had given her a discreet push in the back and she had carefully thanked Uma' Bongela and put the book beside her bed.

Only months later, on a day when she had been home from school sick while her mother was out and her father was working, had she finally opened it. The strangeness of some of the words had confused her, but it had caught at her, too, like a window suddenly open into places she could barely imagine . . .

'"Wee Willie Winkie, running through the town
Upstairs and downstairs, in his nightgown
Rapping at the window, crying at the lock,
"Are the children all in bed? For now it's eight o'clock."'

This recital gained her an irritated look from the Stone Girl. 'His name is Weeweekee,' she corrected Renie, with the air of someone dealing with the borderline competent.

It took a moment for Renie to realize that even without Weeweekee and his magical candle, she could actually see that expression on her companion's face. 'It's getting lighter!'

The Stone Girl pointed to the surrounding hills. A radiant sliver had appeared along the crest – a frighteningly wide sliver. As Renie watched in mingled fascination and unease, the full moon slid up into the sky. It seemed to cover a huge portion of the heavenly firmament, a vast blue-white disk that nevertheless gave scarcely more light than the ordinary variety.

'That's . . . that's the biggest moon I've ever seen.'

'You've seen more than one?'

Renie shook her head. Easier just not to talk. This was

a dream-world – probably the dream of something not even human – and wrestling too strenuously with the particulars was useless.

The Stone Girl led her out beyond the village and along the valley floor. Renie saw more dark shapes clinging to the hillsides on either side, the shuttered dwellings of another settlement, leaking light between curtains or sparking from the chimneys, but whether they were more shoes or other articles of clothing she could not tell.

'So where is this tree?' she asked after they had walked for perhaps a quarter of an hour beneath the intrusive but oddly benign moon.

'In the Wood.'

'But I thought you said you went looking for it before and it wasn't there.'

'It wasn't. The Wood was gone.'

'Gone?' Renie pulled up. 'Hold on, then where are we going? I don't want to walk all night – I want to find my friends!' The thought that she might be putting distance between herself and !Xabbu, or that worse, he might be out in this same moon-domed night just a short distance away, gave her a fierce, sudden ache. She had been trying not to think about him but it was a precarious sort of ignorance, fragile as a bubble.

The Stone Girl turned to face her, arms akimbo, stubby hands on hips. 'If you want answers, you have to come and make a Witch. If you want to find the Witching Tree, you have to find the Wood.'

'It . . . it moves?'

Her guide could only shake her head. 'I don't understand you. I'm trying to help. Do you want to come with me or not?' There was a pleading note beneath the fierceness.

A sudden idea struck Renie. 'Could you make a map?

Maybe that would help me understand.' She reached down and found a stick, then scratched a line in the dirt – bold, so it would show on the moonlit ground. 'Okay, that's the road we just came down. See, I'll draw some shoes to be the houses. These are the hills. And here we are now. Now can you make a picture of where we're going?'

The Stone Girl looked down at the ground for a long moment, then up at Renie, squinting her pockmark eyes as though against a fierce sun. 'Before I met you,' she asked with a certain delicacy, 'did you sort of . . . fall down? Maybe on your head?'

By the time they had reached the thick, scrubby slopes that the Stone Girl said marked the outskirts of the Wood, Renie had begun to realize how impossible the whole thing really was. There would be no map, either for this journey or any other such trip Renie might want to make. Apparently, there were no such thing as maps in this place, and for a very good reason.

It looks like there's just not much normal here-to-there proximity, she decided. *I should have thought of it. The human-built simulations are made to be navigated by humans just like they were part of the real world. But why should a machine intelligence try to duplicate something like physical proximity or geographical continuity that it never uses or experiences itself?*

As far as she could tell, some things like the villages *did* have implied maps, or at least a sort of three-dimensional organization and stability that allowed the inhabitants to find their way around their home turf, but once you left the familiar locale there were apparently no memorized routes to other places within the world, even if the inhabitants had visited those places before.

In fact, the Stone Girl had been coping bravely with

what Renie now realized must seem very strange, funda-
mentally wrong questions. 'You just . . . find the Wood,'
she explained again. 'It's always in front of you until
you walk for the right amount of time, then you look
for things.'

'Things like . . . what? Shapes? Trees you've seen
before?'

The Stone Girl shrugged. 'Just . . . things that seem
like the Wood is somewhere near. Like that.' She pointed
to a vertical stone thrusting from the hillside undergrowth,
illuminated by the huge moon.

'That rock?' The finger of pale stone was the size of a
truck – certainly a fairly obvious landmark. 'You've seen
that before, then?'

Her guide shook her head in frustration. 'No. There are
lots of rocks like that. But tonight it's a close-to-the-Wood
kind of rock.'

Now Renie was the one reduced to headshaking.
Clearly her companion had knowledge she didn't –
perhaps transmitted cues that Renie could not receive,
or even precoded information being translated as spontaneous recognitions. Whatever it was, Renie didn't
understand it. And if it was something precoded, she
would *never* understand it.

As the Stone Girl led her uphill through the scrub
growth, Renie pulled the blanket tight around her to
protect herself from scratches and tried to imagine what
it felt like to live in such a world. *But how can I hope
to make sense of it? I can't even imagine what it feels
like to grow up the way !Xabbu did, to see normal urban
life as something strange, and he's a living, breathing
person like me, not an artificial construct.*

The sharpness of her separation from him came back,
this time with a helplessness she hadn't felt before. *Is it*

pointless anyway? she wondered. *I feel so strongly for him, I'm so scared we won't make it out of this together – but what then? Even if we survive, how could we have a life together? We're so different. I don't know anything about his background, his people's lives, except the few things he's told me. What would his family think of me?*

Renie's steps slowed as her spirits sagged. She forced her thoughts in a different direction.

I still don't know whether or not the people in this world – the Stone Girl, Weeweekee – are really the missing children. But it certainly seems possible. Maybe the Other brought them all here, their consciousnesses, their minds, whatever. She felt a shiver that was not caused by the cool of the night air. *Their souls.*

And if Stephen is here in this world, how can I find him? How will I recognize him? Would he even know me?

'The Wood is just beginning.' Her companion came a little way back down the slope. 'This is a bad place to stop – Jinnears, and maybe some Ticks, too, they all like it here on the edges.'

'Do you know . . .' Renie could hardly think of what she wanted to ask. 'Do you remember being . . . having a life before this?'

'Before what?'

'Before you lived in the shoe, with the stepmother. Do you remember anything else? Crossing a white ocean? Having a mother or a father?'

The Stone Girl was puzzled and clearly a little worried. 'I remember lots of things from before the shoe. Of course I crossed the White Ocean. Who didn't?' She frowned. 'But a mother? No. People talk about a mother, but nobody has one.' She suddenly became very solemn; the dark holes that were her eyes grew wide. 'Where you come from . . . do people have mothers?'

'Some do, yes.' She thought of her own, lost so long ago. 'Some lucky ones do.'

'What do they look like? Are they bigger than step-mothers, or smaller?' Renie had finally struck a topic that interested her companion. 'This boy who used to live in the Shoes, but then he went away, he said he remembered a mother, a real one, one that was just his.' Her indignant snort was not entirely convincing. 'Bragger, we called him.'

Renie closed her eyes for a moment, trying to make sense of what little information she'd put together. 'Do you all come here as birds? Are you all birds to begin with?'

The Stone Girl laughed loudly, a surprising sound in the evening dark. 'All birds? You mean everyone, the people in the Shoes, in the Coats, the people at Bang Very Cross and Long Done Bridge? How could there be so many birds?' She leaned down and poked Renie in the arm. 'Now come on. Like I said, there's usually Jinnears out.'

Renie realized that beginning to make some sense of this world would mean little if they were caught out-of-doors by one of those terrifying creatures. 'Okay. Let's keep moving.'

Like everything else she had seen since finding the black mountain, the Wood was both more and less than reality. A few paces in from the perimeter the trees grew very thickly and seemed to share branches, as though the whole upper forest was a tangled mat of one single growth spread miles wide. Some did not grow so high, but branched sideways farther than any real tree would, like vast green mushrooms covering hundreds of meters. Many of the freestanding shrubs had definite shapes to them, rounded forms as regular as the icons of playing cards, spades and clubs and diamonds, as though the tangled woodland were the preserve of a fanatical corps of topiary gardeners.

Although the high canopy blocked out most of the great blue-white disk overhead, small, warm lights now kindled in the overhead branches as if to replace the lost moonlight. These individually weak lights grew more and more dense until the forest was brighter than the hillside they had climbed an endless twinkling bower like a gigantic Christmas display.

'What are those shining things?'

'Bugs,' the Stone Girl told her. 'Wood-candles, we call 'em. They're like the candle Weeweekee has, but smaller.'

Will-o'-the-Wisps, Renie thought, *that's what they should be called. Whatever those things are that used to lure travelers off the path. They're beautiful. You could follow these lights forever.*

'We're close to the Witching Tree now.' The Stone Girl spoke quietly, as if the tree were something that might be spooked into flight.

But maybe it is, Renie thought. *Who can know around here?* She had begun to formulate a guess as to what the thing might actually be. 'This Witching Tree,' she said. 'What do we do when we find it?'

'Make a witch, of course.'

'Ah.' The weird mangling of Wee Willie Winkie into Weeweekee had not escaped her – the Other seemed to have an idiosyncratic grasp of spoken English, almost childlike in its misunderstandings. She was being taken to a Wishing Tree. 'You tell it what you want, is that right?'

The Stone Girl considered. 'I guess.'

They were deep in the Wood now, the swirl of tiny lights illuminating not just the arabesque of branches over their heads but also open places in the thickening forest,

long vistas of lighted tunnel, paths that bent out of sight
and vanished. A mist rising from the ground softened the
gleaming points to something out of a sentimental winter
scene, a holiday card. The memory that had been nagging
at Renie for hours finally rose to the surface.

*This is like that place under that horrible club – Mister
J's. Where those strange people, those children or whatever they were, took !Xabbu.* She thought back on the
Brothers-Grimmish ceiling of roots, the pinpoint lights,
the sensation of being tightly enclosed even in a wide
space. All of this invented country had that feel – as
yearningly claustrophobic as a beautiful clipper ship
constructed inside a bottle.

The Other made that place, too, she suddenly felt
certain, even though it was in the real world-net, not the
Grail network. *A little . . . what, shelter? Refuge?
Something it created for itself inside that ghastly place.
So the children there – Corduroy, Wicket, I can't remember all their names – were they children like the ones
here? Stolen children?*

There was some key to the Other's personality to be
found in comparing the two, she suddenly felt sure, if
'personality' was the right word. Some recurring theme
in what it made for itself. Something that might actually
benefit from an applied use of Renie's engineering smarts.

If I ever get the chance for uninterrupted thought . . .

'There it is,' announced the Stone Girl. 'The Witching
Tree.'

Renie's first thought was that she had stumbled onto
another case of complete communication failure, because
what lay before her where the forest opened out was not
a tree at all, but a wide expanse of dark water, a lake or
large pond. It took her a moment even to be sure of that,

because although the moon hung in the sky just above, big and bright as some alien mothership preparing to land, there was no reflection of it in the water: except for a crowd of smaller lights gleaming beneath the surface, the lake might have been a huge black hole in the forest floor.

Renie moved forward, squinting as though studying a dusty mirror. The lights in the water were not points like the wood-candles, but something more like active wave-forms, shimmers of faint purple and silver that were either moving swiftly or turning on and off in sequence. She lowered herself to a crouch and stared at the hypnotic movement of light in the blackness, then stretched out a hand to the dark water.

'Don't!' the Stone Girl said. 'We don't go in it. We have to go around it.'

'Why? What are those lights?'

Her companion wrapped small cool fingers around Renie's arm. 'They're just . . . they just belong there. Don't you want to go to the tree?'

Renie allowed herself to be drawn upright. 'I thought you said it was here.'

'No, silly. It's over there. Can't you see it?'

Renie followed the girl's gesture. Halfway around the lake, something a good bit larger than the surrounding vegetation loomed over the riverbank, half-sunk in the water like a giant cooling its feet. It was hard to see it clearly: the other trees wore their crowns of sparkling fairy-lights, and the water itself was alive with glimmers of faint color, but the thing the Stone Girl pointed at was dark.

As they waded along the spongy lakeshore, Renie could not shake the idea that the lights in the water were following them like curious fish, but she could not be sure it wasn't merely her own changing vantage point. She leaned over and violently waved a hand over the water, half-expecting the lights to startle back, but if the dull gleams were some kind of creatures, they were not much impressed.

Of all the unlikely shapes of living things Renie had encountered since entering this simworld, the Witching Tree seemed the poorest copy of a real-world object. It was scarcely a tree at all: only its roughly vertical middle section, which might have been a trunk, and the way it flared at the bottom and the top, seemed to fit the bill. Its hide was shiny and smooth but for the places it wrinkled at the bends of branch and root, resembling the skin of some black dolphin more than it did bark. At the end of their forking subdivisions the limbs disappeared among the branches of other, more normal looking trees; the rubbery black roots dangled in the murky water like the tentacles of an octopus dragged halfway onto land. The thing gave an impression of not quite belonging, a piece of alien life dropped into the environment.

Considering how weird everything else is around here, that's saying a lot, she decided. 'Are you sure that's . . . a tree?'

The Stone Girl frowned. 'It's the Witching Tree. Do they look different where you come from?'

Renie could think of no useful reply to that. 'What do we do?'

'We make a witch and ask a question.' She looked at Renie expectantly. 'Do you want to go first?'

'I have no idea what to do.' Something about this strange, lonely spot suddenly made her aware of how tired and used-up she felt. 'I'll just watch you, for now.'

The Stone Girl nodded. She rucked up her shapeless dress and sat on the ground, composing herself. Then, in a dry and touchingly off-key voice, she began to sing unfamiliar words to a familiar melody.

> *'Hush-a-bye, baby,*
> *Your cradle is green,*
> *Daddy's a king,*
> *And Mommy's a queen;*
> *Sister's a lady*
> *Who wears a gold ring;*
> *Brother's a drummer*
> *Who plays for the king.'*

In the moment's silence that followed, Renie thought she saw a slowing and dimming of the flashes in the dark water, but the tree itself, as if it were somehow absorbing the light, began softly to glow, the merest hint of a rich grape-skin purple beneath the Witching Tree's smooth black rind. It creaked and shuddered. For a frightened instant Renie thought the tree was going to stand up on its roots like some nightmare vision, but it was the branches that were slowly bending. Something came rustling down from the heights where it had been hidden in the foliage of the surrounding trees – a fruit that glowed like a lantern with a deep, fleshy red shine, dangling at the end of a long black branch.

The Stone Girl reached up her small hands and let the fruit nestle in her palms. She gave a small sharp twist; when the twig snapped free, the black branch sprang back into the heights. The Stone Girl looked up at Renie, her smiling face bathed in strawberry-colored light, her dimple-eyes round. Although she had been expecting it, the little girl's expression clearly said, it was nevertheless a thing of wonder.

The sparkle in the surrounding trees grew dimmer, so that the fruit, an ovoid about the size and shape of an eggplant, seemed now to be the brightest light. Renie found herself leaning forward as the Stone Girl clutched the glowing object firmly and split it in half.

A tiny shape lay at the center of the fruit – a baby, or something shaped like a baby, its shrunken body markedly female, the eyes closed as if in sleep. Its hands were laid across its stomach, the little fingers translucent as threads of glass.

'I made a Witch!' the Stone Girl whispered, thrilled and a little scared. The infant thing wriggled in its glowing bed at the sound of her voice.

'A . . . witch . . .' Renie fought against the dreamy illogic of the scene. She had thought it a simple mispronunciation, but clearly it was more, somehow.

The Stone Girl held up the homunculus, cradling it close to her chest so that she nearly touched it with her lips as she asked her questions. 'Will the Ending come any closer?'

The little thing stirred again. When it spoke, eyes still firmly shut, the voice was eerily out of keeping with the infant form, a lost moan that seemed to echo across great distances.

'. . . Ending . . . is only beginning . . .'

'But what will happen to us when all the world is gone into the Ending? Where will we live?'

The tiny mouth curled in a half-smile, then the Witch began to sing. *'Boys and girls come out to play, the moon is shining as bright as day . . .'*

Renie fought down a superstitious shudder. Despite the small, ghostly voice, the entire fantastic setting, this was something that existed for a reason – or at least its creator had once operated under direction and intention. It might be weirdly unsettling to listen to the murmuring pronouncements of what was essentially a machine, but she had too much at stake to be tricked into forgetting. Underneath all this hoodoo ran the binary blood of a comprehensible system: she was not going to be sidetracked by what was little more than game design gone badly astray.

The Witch in the Stone Girl's hand had begun to wither, shriveling into a wrinkled mass like the stone of a peach. Grotesquely, it continued to talk and sing, but the voice had grown so faint now that although the Stone Girl was still listening intently, Renie could no longer make out any of the words. After a while it became clear that even the Stone Girl could not hear it anymore; she stared at it sadly for a moment, then dropped it unceremoniously into the dark, unreflecting water.

'Will the tree work for me, too?' Renie asked.

The Stone Girl seemed disturbed, but not by the question. 'Suppose so.'

Renie seated herself on the ground beside the girl. She couldn't remember the words the Stone Girl had sung. 'Can you help me sing?'

Her small companion prompted her with the unfamiliar words about kings and queens, and Renie followed along, trying to make up for her hesitation between lines with clarity and volume. When she had finished, the air around the lake fell silent. A wind, perhaps, moved the branches of the trees so that the lights wavered. After a moment the branches of the dark tree began to move again: one of the shining, globular fruits was gliding down to her out of the hidden spaces overhead.

As she cradled the warm, smooth thing in her hands and tugged at it, watched it split open like a biology illustration to reveal the little creature within, Renie had a brief but powerful flash of memory. The childish solemnity of the experience, the crude images of death and birth, brought back to her the games she used to play with her friend Nomsa – elaborate, mock-Egyptian funerals of dolls, somber ceremonies out behind the flatblock where the weeds would hide them from mothers they somehow knew would disapprove. This was much the same, another flirtation with the forbidden that seemed not quite adult.

The miniature infant opened its eyes, startling her back to the present.

'*Too late . . .*' it said, the voice airy with distance. '*Too late . . . the children are dying . . . the old children and the new children . . .*'

Renie found herself growing angry, although she was a little distracted to realize that *her* baby was male. 'What do you mean, "too late?" That's a lot of shit, after everything we've been through.' She looked to the Stone Girl. 'Don't I get to ask it a question?'

Her companion was watching the baby's eyes, which filled the lids like pearls, without irises or pupils. The Stone Girl seemed frightened about something and did not answer, so Renie turned back to the strange fruit.

'Look, I think I know what you are, and I think I may even understand a little of what is going on.' Renie was not sure if she was addressing the homunculus, the tree, the air. *It's like talking to God*, she decided. *Although this one goes out of its way to communicate. Sort of.* 'Just tell me what you want from us. Are we supposed to find you? Was that what the black mountain was all about?'

Tiny limbs twitched slowly. '*Wanted . . . the children . . . safe . . .*' It flailed again, as though drowning in a deep, unfriendly dream. '*The new children . . . nowhere to be . . . Now the cold . . .*'

'What about the children? Why don't you just let them go?'

'*Hurts. Going to fall. Then warm . . . for a little while . . .*' Terrifyingly, the small perfect mouth opened wide and a rhythmic, wheezing hiss filled the air. Renie could not tell if it was laughter or gasping misery; either way, it was a horrible sound.

'Just tell us what you want! Why did you take the children – my brother Stephen, all the others? How can we get them back?'

The noise had ended. The tiny arms moved more slowly. The homunculus was becoming loose and flabby, collapsing in on itself in dreadful, high-speed putrefaction.

'. . . *Set free* . . .' The voice was a whisper that barely reached her ears. '. . . *set* . . . *free* . . .'

'God damn you!' Renie shouted. 'Come back and talk to me!' But whatever had spoken was silent. Renie tried to remember the song that had summoned it, but the words were a jumble in her head, adding chaos to the rising anger. It was like dealing with Stephen at his most truculent – the child that simply would not obey, who almost dared you to use force. She gave up on the unfamiliar verse and began hoarsely to sing the words she *did* know, determined to drag the thing back from wherever it was hiding, force it to deal with her.

> *'Rock-a-bye, baby,*
> *in the treetop,'*

The fruit in her hands liquified and ran between her fingers. With a grunt of disgust, Renie threw it down and wiped her hands in the dirt, singing all the while.

> *'When the wind blows,*
> *the cradle will rock.*
> *When the bough breaks,*
> *the cradle will fall,*
> *And down will come baby,*
> *cradle and all.'*

'Do you hear me?' she snarled. 'Cradle and all, damn it!'

For a long moment there was only silence. Then a whisper, thin as a death-sigh, rose all around her.

'Why . . . hurting? . . . Called you . . . but now . . . too late . . .'

'Called . . . ? You *bastard*, you didn't call anyone – you stole my brother!' Anger was bubbling out of her now, confined for too long in too tight a space. 'Where is he? God damn you, you tell me where Stephen Sulaweyo is or I'll come find you and take you apart piece by piece . . . !' There was no reply. Furious, she opened her mouth to begin the verse again, to drag the thing back by its metaphorical ear, but was stopped by a sudden convulsive shudder up and down the tree's smooth black trunk – a peristaltic spasm that made the branches whip and snap overhead, knocking leaves and twigs from the other trees even as the black roots stirred the lake to froth.

Then, with the suddenness of a frightened ocean creature retreating into its shell, the tree collapsed – a lightning parody of what had happened to the witch-babies, but unlike them, the tree did not merely shrivel: it shrank from something into literally nothing: one moment it stood before them, the next it was gone, with only the torn, muddy ground and agitated waters to show it had even existed.

The Stone Girl turned to Renie, eyes wide, mouth a dark gape.

'You . . . you killed it,' she said. 'You killed the Witching Tree!'

CHAPTER 19

The Bravest Man in the World

NETFEED/NEWS: ANVAC Arrests Own Customer for Noncompliance
(visual: defendant Vildbjerg's house, Odense, Denmark)
VO: Danish music producer Nalli Vildbjerg was briefly jailed and is being sued by the security corporation ANVAC for violating his contract – failing to notify them of a crime that occurred on the premises they protect.
VILDBJERG: 'These people are mad! I had a party, and someone took a coat that didn't belong to them – by accident, I'm certain. These ANVAC madmen saw it on the surveillance, and not only had this person arrested – a guest of mine! – but now they're prosecuting me, too!'
(visual: anonymated attorney from ANVAC's international legal firm, Thurn, Taxis, and Posthorn)
ATTORNEY: 'When you sign one of our contracts, it says very clearly on page one hundred and seventeen that all crimes that occur onsite must be immediately and accurately reported to the company. Mr Vildbjerg does not have the right to ignore crime – to appoint himself judge and jury in a matter of Danish and UN law.'

I'LL *just remember Orlando,* Sam told herself for perhaps the twentieth time in the past few hours. *Then I can keep going.* She might be stumbling with fatigue and miserable with worry, missing her parents and her home so badly she wanted to scream, but that was nothing compared to what Orlando had shouldered every single day.

But it killed him, she could not help remembering. *So what good did it do him being brave, so brave . . . ?*

'I think it is time for another rest,' !Xabbu said. 'We have been walking a long time now.'

'And nothing is different,' she said bitterly. 'Is it just going to be like this forever? It could, couldn't it? Huh? Just go on forever, I mean. It's not a real place.'

'I suppose.' !Xabbu dropped easily into a crouch, showing no effects from the all-day march that had Sam's legs trembling with fatigue. 'But it doesn't seem . . . what is the word? Likely. Logical.'

'Logical.' She sniffed. 'That sounds like Renie.'

'It does sound like her,' said !Xabbu. 'I miss her – always thinking, wondering, trying to make sense of every detail.' He looked up at a movement nearby, something cresting the low riverside hill they had just descended. It was Jongleur, trudging after them with that grim tenacity that Sam found almost admirable. His body might be relatively young and healthy, that of a fit middle-aged man, but it was clear Jongleur himself had no recent practice in moving such a body for very long and was feeling the endless walk even more than she was.

'I still hate him,' Sam said quietly. 'I utterly do. But it's hard to, you know, keep it up when you see someone all the time, isn't it?'

!Xabbu did not answer. He and the older man were no longer naked since the Bushman had woven them both a sort of kilt from the long river grasses during their rest stops, and Sam had to admit it made her a little more comfortable. She thought of herself as modern and unshockable, but it was strange enough having !Xabbu naked all the time, and herself nearly so; to have to confront the raw physical reality of Felix Jongleur for days on end had made her feel like she couldn't quite get clean.

'Not that we have days around here,' she said aloud. 'Not really.'

!Xabbu looked at her curiously.

'Sorry. I was thinking out loud.' Sam frowned. 'But it's true. It doesn't get dark or light here like a normal place. There's no sun. It's more like someone gets up in the morning and switches on a big light, then turns it off again at night.'

'Yes, it is strange. But why should it be anything else? It is not real, after all.'

'It's real enough to kill us,' said Jongleur as he stopped beside them.

'Thank *you*, Aardlar the Cheerful Barbarian.' Sam only realized after she said it that she was quoting one of Orlando's jokes.

!Xabbu wandered a little way down the riverbank. As Jongleur caught his breath, Sam watched her small, slim friend picking his way through the reeds. *He misses her so much, but he doesn't talk about it. He just wants to keep walking, walking, wants to keep looking for her.* She tried to imagine what it felt like, tried to picture what she would feel if Orlando were still alive and lost somewhere in this alien landscape, but it made her too sad. *At least there's a chance he might find Renie.*

'We should go on,' !Xabbu called. 'It is hard to tell how many hours of light we have.'

Jongleur rose without a word of complaint and resumed his plodding march. Sam sped up to catch !Xabbu.

'This place all looks just the same,' she said. 'Except

that sometimes it starts to look . . . I don't know . . . transparent again. Like when we first came here.' She pointed to a distant line of hills. 'See? They looked okay before, but now they don't look quite real.'

!Xabbu nodded his head wearily. 'I can make no more sense of things than you.'

'How about the other side of the river?' Sam asked, half-hoping to distract him. 'Maybe Renie's over there.'

'You can see as well as I can that the land is even more flat there,' !Xabbu told her. 'There are at least some trees and plants by the river on this side that might block her from our view until we were right beside her.' His somber look deepened: Sam did not need him to say that it would be especially true if Renie were lying uncon-scious or dead.

A cold shudder ran down her back. She wished she could remember some of the prayers they had taught her in Sunday school, but the youth pastor had been bigger on sing alongs than on the nuts and bolts of what to do when you and your friends were marooned in an imaginary universe.

Remembering the youth group, and a boy with braces named Holger who – much against her wishes – had tried to kiss her at the Overnight Retreat campfire ceremony, Sam walked several steps before she realized that !Xabbu had stopped. She turned, and the stunned look on his face made her think for a moment that the worst had happened, that he had seen Renie's legs protruding from beneath a bush, or her body floating facedown in the river. She whirled to follow his angle of sight, but to her relief saw only a small cluster of trees on an otherwise empty hillock of grass close by the water.

'!Xabbu . . . ?'

He dashed past her toward the trees. Sam hurried after him.

'!Xabbu, what is it?' He was touching one of the branches, drawing his fingers slowly along the bark. His silence, his strange, devastated expression brought Sam close to tears. '!Xabbu, what's wrong?'

He looked at her face, then down at her feet. She made a move toward him but he grabbed her arm with surprising strength. 'Do not move, Sam.'

'What? You're frightening me!'

'This tree. It is the one to which Renie tied the piece of cloth.' He waved the strip of frayed white fabric that he had been carrying in his hand like a holy relic since they had discovered it.

'What are you talking about? We left that behind two days ago!'

'Look down, Sam.' He pointed at the ground. 'What do you see?'

'Footprints. So what . . . ?' And then she understood.

A trail of her own footprints led back, showing where she had just crossed the powdery soil. But there were dozens more all around, mixed in with many others, including !Xabbu's own telltale small prints, more slender even than her own – far too many to have just been made. She put her foot down in one of the older tracks. It was a perfect fit.

'Oh, my God,' she said. 'That's too scanny . . .'

'Somehow,' !Xabbu said, his voice as miserable as she had ever heard it, 'we have come back to our starting place.'

Although the swift turn into nightfall was still at least an hour away, !Xabbu had made a fire: neither he nor Sam felt much interest in going any farther. The thin, silvery flames, which usually lent a homely atmosphere to their camps, at the moment seemed merely alien.

'It doesn't make any sense,' Sam said again. 'We never went more than a little way from the river. Even without a sun, we couldn't be that lost . . . could we?'

'Were there not our own footprints on this ground, I still could not forget this place – I could not mistake it for another,' !Xabbu said forlornly. 'Not the tree where we found a sign that Renie was alive and looking for us. Where I grew up, we know trees like we do people – better, since the trees stay in one place while people die and the wind blows their footprints away.' He shook his head. 'I knew for a long time that the land looked very much the same, but I tried to make myself believe I was mistaken.'

'But that still doesn't explain how we could get so utterly lost!' Sam said. 'Especially you – it just seems wrong.'

'Because you still believe that you are in a real world,' said Jongleur sharply. He had been silent for almost an hour; his sudden words startled them.

'What's that supposed to mean?' Sam demanded. 'We still have up and down, don't we? Left and right? We followed the river through that whole impacted network of yours . . .'

'But this is not my network,' Jongleur interrupted. 'That was planned by technicians, engineers, designers – conceived by humans, for humans. Left, right, up, down – very useful if you are human. Less meaningful for the Other.'

!Xabbu looked at him bleakly but said nothing.

'Are you saying that everything just . . . changes here?' Sam asked. 'That there are no rules?'

Jongleur picked a twig off the ground. Despite the occasional changes in the refractory quality of the land, Sam found it frustrating to see how normal everything looked, how ordinary, in a place that could play them such a terrible trick.

'It could be that we will find a place where the "rules," as you call them, are almost nonexistent,' the old man said, rolling the long twig between his fingers. 'But I suspect that there are indeed firm rules here – just not the sort we expect to find.' He leaned forward and cleared a space in the dirt with his forearm, then used the twig to draw a row of small circles laid out side by side like a line of pearls. 'The Grail network is set up something like this,' he said. 'Each circle a world.' He drew a single stroke all the way from one end of the series of circles to the other – a strand on which the pearls hung. 'The great river runs all through it, connecting every world to another world at each end. If you never left the river, used only those gates at either end of the simulation worlds, you would still eventually pass through every world before coming back to the beginning and starting again.'

Sam studied the scrawl. 'So? Why doesn't that work here? How did we lose the river?'

'I do not believe we did.'

'How can that be?'

'Because there is no reason this world should be linear, as the Grail network is. We assume a river must have a source and an outflow, but even the connecting river of my network does not truly begin anywhere or end anywhere.' Jongleur wiped out the string of pearls, then made a new circle, larger this time, with another squiggly circle inside it. 'This place has even less reason to follow the model of a real world. I suspect what we have been doing is following the river here,' he touched the wobbly circle with the end of the twig, 'to here.' He followed the squiggle all the way around until he reached the spot where it had started.

Sam stared. Beside her, !Xabbu was watching with more interest than he had shown in an hour. 'So . . . that's all there is?' she asked. 'We've seen the whole place? Just once around the bagel and we're done?' She shook her head, almost angry. 'That's too woofie to be true. For one thing, if we've gone all the way around the whole world, where was Renie? And that friend of yours, Klement? They couldn't just disappear.'

But maybe she could, Sam thought suddenly. *Into a hole. Into a river. Lost. Lost like Orlando . . .*

'Perhaps the model is even more strange,' said Jongleur. At that moment he seemed almost normal, like one of her teachers – not a chosen companion, but not an arch-villain either. And like her better teachers, he actually seemed interested in what he was talking about. Sam remembered that this was a man who, whatever his methods, had set out to solve the problem of human mortality.

Like that Greek guy in the myths, who stole the secret of life from the gods. Orlando would remember his name.

Jongleur had wiped away his other drawings and replaced them with the largest circle yet, this one filled with half a dozen concentric wavy circles, so that the whole looked something like a watery bull's-eye. 'Then consider this,' he said. 'Perhaps there are more worlds concealed within this world – many more, like Russian dolls. But instead of the river being the conduit between them, it is a barrier instead. So instead of following the river,' he traced one of the river-rings back to his starting point, 'which only brings us back to our starting point, we must instead cross *over* the river, into the next world.' He drew a line from one ring, across the wavy river line, and into the next ring inward. 'There is no need to mimic real-world geometry here. The self-elected god of this place doesn't know much about the real world, after all.'

Sam stared at the bull's-eye. 'Hang on – that just scans. Look out there – look!' She pointed to the far side of the river, its low hills and river meadows still glowing in the directionless light. 'Like !Xabbu said, we'd have seen Renie if she was over there. And besides, if it is another world, then your operating system doesn't have much imagination, because it's just like this one!'

Jongleur's self-satisfied chuckle made Sam want to hit him. 'Just because you can see it does not mean it's there, child.'

'What?'

'There are many places in the Grail network where only one side of the river was built. Those who try to reach that other side find that although they can see it, they never manage to reach it – but still the illusion of two sides is maintained. If we managed to cross that river somehow, who knows where we would be? Or what we would see if we looked back at this spot . . . ?'

The twilight was upon them, and it was getting hard to see the far side anyway. Sam was too tired and depressed to stay interested in a discussion of yet another mystery. Even if Jongleur was right, even if they could make sense of it and find Renie, maybe even find the Other itself, they would still be exactly nowhere. Sam remembered the Other, its cold presence, the way it had made the cartoon Freezer a hole into complete nothingness . . .

I wonder what Mom and Dad are doing right now? she thought suddenly. *They can't be at the hospital all the time, watching me.* Her loneliness was touched with something like jealousy. *Maybe they're home eating dinner. Watching something on the net. Mom calling Grandma Katherine . . .*

!Xabbu was still looking at the river. 'There is someone there.' He sounded very calm, but Sam knew better

– she had learned something about him in their days together.

'Somebody where?' She sat up, surveying the now-shadowy farther bank. 'I don't see anyone.'

'In the reeds at the edge of the river.' He stood. 'It is a human shape.'

Sam could see only the faint movement of the stalks, a wavering wall of gray. 'Is it . . . can you see who it is?' She tried to keep excitement out of her voice, having just realized it was just as likely to be the zombie Klement as Renie. It might even be Jecky Nibble or one of the other strange creatures from a couple of nights ago.

Something was indeed clambering out of the reeds – something very human in its shape and movements.

Her moment of hope lasted only until !Xabbu's next words, spoken in a voice so flat that Sam could only guess at the pain behind it. 'It is a man.' He had been poised, pulled taut like a bowstring, ready to run down the slope. Now she saw him sag, even the possibility of danger less important than the fact of loss.

The stranger raised his hands in the air. 'Don't run!' he called. 'I cannot stand to spend another night in the cold!'

He was limping, and the black trousers and loose white shirt he was wearing were badly torn and pink with washed-out blood. If he was faking, trying to lull them, Sam thought, he was doing a very good job of it. He staggered like a runner in the last meters of a grueling marathon and appeared to be dripping wet as well. !Xabbu watched his approach with a very strange expression on his face, but he did not seem frightened.

The stranger was of more or less ordinary size, his body older than hers, younger than Jongleur's, and very fit. Except for the bedraggled black mustache and wet hair, he was quite good-looking in what Sam thought of as a tanned, netsoap-actor sort of way, and seemed to be in the peak of life and health.

'Oh, share your fire, please,' he begged as he stumbled the last few steps toward them. When none of them said anything, he threw himself down beside the flames, shivering. 'Thank God. There is nothing good to make a raft here – the one I made keeps sinking. All last night I spent, wet and freezing. I saw your fire, but could not reach it. I have been following you. Ah, God, this empty, miserable place.'

Sam was surprised that !Xabbu had not made the stranger welcome. She looked to him for a cue, but the small man still seemed oddly distracted. 'We don't have much to give you,' she said, 'not even a blanket. But you can certainly get warm at our fire.'

'Thank you, young lady. You are very kind.' The stranger tried to smile but his teeth were chattering too briskly to hold it for more than a moment. 'You do me a favor, and Azador does not forget favors.'

'We should go get more wood,' !Xabbu said suddenly, touching Sam's arm. 'Come with me and we can carry back enough to last all night.'

!Xabbu walked very close to her as he led her toward a copse of trees farther up the meadow where he had gathered the first batch of deadfall. 'Do not look back,' he whispered to her. 'Don't you remember the name Azador?'

'It . . . it sounds familiar, now that you mention it.'

'He traveled with Paul Jonas for a while. Before that, with Renie and me. The lighter – the access device – came from him.'

'Oh my God! You're dupping, aren't you?' She fought the urge to look back. 'But what's he doing here?'

'Who knows? But what is important is that he doesn't know we recognize him. You see, he knows me only in the shape of a baboon.'

'You don't want him to know who you are?'

'We will learn more if he thinks us all strangers. At least we will be more likely to notice if he tells lies.' !Xabbu frowned. 'But now that I think about it, this is a very complicated problem. From what Paul Jonas said, this man calls himself a victim of the Grail Brotherhood. If he finds out who Jongleur is . . .' He shook his head. 'And since Renie and I used our real names in front of him, you cannot call me by name. But if you call me something else, some false name, Jongleur will notice.'

'This is making my head hurt,' she said as they reached the trees. 'Maybe we should just kill him.' !Xabbu turned to her, eyes wide. 'I'm joking, utterly!'

'I do not like such jokes, Sam.' !Xabbu bent and began picking up branches from the ground.

'Look,' she said as she filled her arms with deadfall, 'it wasn't a very nice joke, okay. Seen. But if we can't use Renie's name in front of him, if we can't use your name, if we can't talk about anything that's really going on, that's going to slow us down. What's more important, fooling this guy or finding Renie?'

!Xabbu nodded slowly. 'Of course you are right, Sam. Let us just see what Azador has to say for himself tonight – it is normal for us to ask him what brings him to our campfire – and then we will try to make sense of things.'

'Of course you would want to know my story,' Azador said expansively. The fire had warmed him; but for his swollen ankle and a certain damp-dog look to his upper lip, he seemed completely recovered. 'It is full of danger and excitement – even, if I must say it, heroism. But what you really wish to know is, how is it that Azador comes to you in this godforsaken place, yes?'

Sam wanted to roll her eyes, but restrained herself. 'Yes.'

'Then I will tell you a secret.' The handsome newcomer leaned forward, raising his eyes and looking from side to side in a children's-theater gesture of confidentiality. 'Azador has been following you for a long time.'

She resisted the urge to look at !Xabbu. 'Really?'

'Since . . . Troy.' Azador sat up and folded his arms across his chest as though he had performed a magic trick.

'What . . . what are you talking about?'

He smiled kindly. 'Do not try to trick me, pretty lady. I have been all around – I have seen more of the network than any other man. You are the only people in this place. I saw you on the mountaintop – yes, you remember! I see it on your faces. I know you are the same people I followed from Troy.'

Sam was trying to make sense of this. Were they in trouble? Were all !Xabbu's warnings to her now useless? She looked from the Bushman's intent face to Jongleur, whose expression was entirely unreadable. 'But . . . but why would you follow us? If we were the people you think we are, that is.'

'Because you were with the man Ionas. I knew he was more than he admitted to me, and when I saw him lead you and the others into a temple in the middle of a burning city, I knew he was looking for a gateway. Do not forget, Azador has been all over this network! The Grail Brotherhood has pursued me everywhere! There are some that say that I am the bravest man in all these worlds.' He spread his hands in a gesture of humility. 'I myself would never make such a claim.'

His silliness was beginning to subdue her fears, but

she could not help wondering if that was an intended effect. *God, this whole adventure just scans and scans. It's like playing Halloween party games in a pitch-black room, like for months – but if you lose, someone kills you.*

'Why were you following this . . . Ionas?' !Xabbu asked.

'Because he was my friend. I knew he would get himself in trouble in that Trojan world – he had not done the things I have done, seen the things I have seen. I wished to help him, to . . . protect him.'

!Xabbu was carefully keeping doubt off his face. Sam cleared her throat. 'So you followed . . . these people . . . into a temple?'

Azador laughed. 'You wish to keep pretending, little lady? Very well – I have nothing to hide. Yes, I followed Ionas and . . . his friends into the temple. All through the maze – I could hear them just ahead of me. Then they stopped. I stopped, too, out of sight in the corridors behind them while they argued. It was a long argument, and I thought the gateway was broken, that they would all turn back and I would have to follow them out into the city again, where people were being killed like animals. But instead the gate opened and all went through, with much shouting and more arguing. I waited as long as I could but I was afraid the gate would close again, so I went through.'

'But if Ionas was your friend, why didn't you want to be seen?'

For a moment a flicker of irritation crossed Azador's face. 'Because I did not know the people he was with. I have many enemies.'

'Okay,' Sam said. 'So you went through. And . . . ?'

'And found myself in a strange place – the strangest yet. I heard voices on the mountain ahead of me, so I waited until they began to move, then followed. Slowly, slowly, and very quietly. You . . . or should I say, the friends of Ionas . . . ?' He smiled in a way that Sam felt sure he thought extremely winning. 'The people ahead of me, they walked very slowly. But patiently I followed. By the time we reached the top I had let them get far ahead of me. I saw the giant there.' He shook his head, apparently in genuine dismay. 'What a thing that was! I have seen nothing like it in any of these worlds. And I saw Ionas and the others very close to it. But when I went to follow them, something . . . something happened.' He closed his eyes, thinking. 'Everything came apart, as though someone had broken a window and the pieces flew everywhere.'

There was a sudden stir beside her. Sam realized that Jongleur had sat upright; from the corner of her eye she could see tension in the lines of the old man's body. In all this strangeness, what had grabbed his attention so firmly? 'Everything came apart,' she prompted.

'And then I do not remember much,' Azador said. 'I fell. I think I hit my head.' He reached up and massaged the base of his skull. 'When I awakened the mountain was gone and I was surrounded by nothing – all gray, like a fog, but with no up or down. I have been searching ever since, and even when I found a world to be in, there was no one there. Azador was alone, except for the hunting creatures. Until I saw the light of your fire.'

'Hunting creatures?' !Xabbu poked up the fire. 'What are those?'

'You have not seen them? You are lucky.' Azador patted himself on the chest. 'Shapes that freeze the blood. Monsters, ghosts – who knows? But they hunt men. They hunted me. Only on the river was I safe, so I built myself a raft.'

Satisfied with the drama of his recitation, the newcomer sat back and gazed solemnly into the shifting flames.

'So we've let you get warm at our fire,' Sam said. 'What else do you want?'

'To travel with you,' he said promptly. 'There is safety in numbers, and you will have much benefit from gaining Azador as a companion. I can trap animals for food, I can fish . . .'

'We don't eat,' Sam pointed out.

'. . . And I can build a raft with my bare hands!'

'Which keeps sinking, you said.' She looked to !Xabbu, half-amused, half-disgusted. Was it just chance that kept saddling them with horrible traveling companions?

'There is no Ionas here,' !Xabbu said. 'I can say with truth that I have never known such a person in this world.'

'Ah, even with your different faces, I knew that he was not with you,' said Azador cheerfully. 'After all, Ionas was brave, in his way – for an Englishman, that is. He would not have stayed silent and pretended he was someone else with his friend Azador standing before him. But if he is lost somewhere in this world, then I will find him.'

Sam looked at !Xabbu, who was watching Jongleur, but the old man's face was again an impenetrable mask. When !Xabbu finally turned to her she saw that, beneath his composed expression, the only person here she trusted was just as worried and confused as she was. She almost used his name, but caught herself. 'So what should we do, then?'

He looked at Azador, who was smiling confidently. 'I do not know.' !Xabbu shook his head. 'I suppose you will travel with us, Azador. For a while, at least.'

The newcomer smiled and ran a finger along the bottom of his mustache. 'You will not regret it. This I swear.'

CHAPTER 20

Thompson's Iron

NETFEED/NEWS: Expert Decries Apocalyptic Themes
(visual: excerpt from How to Kill Your Teacher*)*
VO: Net ethics watchdog Sian Kelly thinks kid's programming is going too far these days – all the way to the end of the world.
KELLY: 'It's a trend, and it's not a good one. So many of the children's interactives – Teen Mob, Blodger Park, Backstab, that Kill Your Teacher thing – are running shows with apocalyptic themes. Kids are very suggestible, and the emphasis on suicide cults and the end of the world is irresponsible and frightening.'
VO: The networks uniformly deny any collusion between writers and creators of the shows cited.
(visual: Ruy Contreras-Simons, GCN)
CONTRERAS-SIMONS: 'It's a trend, sure, but it's nothing anyone has decided to do. I guess it's just in the air . . .'

THE trip down into the burrow had been horrible, the four of them carried like pieces of dead meat, which was clearly how the mutant web-builders already thought of them. Paul had fought back, but with his limbs tighly held had managed only to get himself dragged along sharp rocks and to earn a stinging blow on the head from a misshapen claw that was not quite either a hand or a hoof.

The only bit of good fortune was that they were not
bound. The sticky cables remained as part of the web; the
creatures had needed to drool some putrid-smelling fluid
on their captives just to pull them free of it.

Several dozen of the monsters were in just this open
part of the burrow where the captives had been thrown
down, but Paul, his senses raw in the darkness, thought
he could hear chittering voices down the side tunnels as
well. It was not completely dark; something was burning
or gleaming in one of the tunnels, letting in a bit of the
light and throwing just enough definition onto their crawling captors and the nest to make Paul see how hopeless
was any thought of escape.

The things were not human. He had to keep reminding
himself of that, both to ease the horror and to keep the
embers of hope smoldering. The spider-buffalos showed little
or no organization, and were clearly used to prey that was
either stunned or already dead. Other than roughly shoving T4b back when the boy had tried to scramble out of
the pit, they had not bothered with any other precautions
against escape. Not that more precautions seemed needed:
they out-numbered Paul and his friends by ten to one or
more, and were each at least as strong as a person.

Trying to decide what the things actually were, with
an eye toward discovering a weakness, was little help.
They were just some wild mutation of the simworld, possibly intentional – perhaps there was even a cruel joke in
the way they resembled the buffalo of the American West
that had been so completely and swiftly slaughtered for
their hides, massacred by the thousands, skinned, and then
left to rot on the plains. In any case, they were big, fast,
apparently without conscience, and obviously had a tooth
for human flesh. Man-bones crunched underfoot on the
tunnel floors and in greater numbers here in the pit itself,

becoming even more common lower down the slope toward the pit's black depths.

As if to underscore this, Paul put his hand down on something sharp. He felt around, expecting to discover another jawbone, and found instead something small, square and hard which he held up to catch the faint light. It was a rusty belt buckle, bent as though the belt itself had been torn open with great force while still fastened. Paul's stomach lurched. It was not hard to imagine these fierce, hairy creatures doing just that in their haste to make a meal of the tender flesh beneath it.

Despair swept over him like a cold rain. What could they do? Fight the monstrosities with bare hands and a belt buckle? Or take up jawbones, like Samson, to smite their enemies?

But I'm no bloody Samson, am I?

'Paul?' It was Florimel, a short distance away. 'Are you there? You cried out – are you hurt?'

'Just put my hand on something.' He stared up the slope at the grotesque figures moving in the half-light – probably performing the mutant equivalent of setting the table – and tried to keep the hopelessness out of his voice. 'Any ideas?'

He could not see her, but he could hear her grunt of misery. 'Nothing. I can barely crawl. I landed hard when we fell from the wagon.'

'How are the others?'

'Martine is alive, but I think she is hurt, too – she is very quiet, talking to herself just over there. T4b . . . T4b is praying.'

'Praying?' It startled him, but he could not claim to have any better ideas.

'There are so many of these monsters, and we are all so tired. I am frightened, Paul.'

'I am, too.'

Florimel fell into troubled silence. Paul could see no reason to make her talk. It would be one thing if they had a plan, but the situation was too bleak for peppy chats.

So it is me, then? Is it down to me to come up with something? I didn't bloody well ask to be here in this network in the first place. At least he didn't think he had – he still couldn't remember, but it would be hard to imagine: *'Oh, and if you have a few spare moments, Mr Jongleur, how about locking me up in a World War One simulation and torturing me a bit, all right?'*

But why, then? He was a nobody, a museum employee, a university graduate with less power than a classroom teacher or a shop steward. If he had interfered in the raising of Jongleur's daughter, why hadn't they just fired him? If he had somehow discovered something of the Grail Project, as seemed likely, why not just kill him? Perhaps they had not wanted the irritation of arranging an accident or a suicide, but it seemed bizarre to think that people like Felix Jongleur and his associates would lavish so much attention on a nonentity.

Even if the World War One simulation had been something already built, Finch and Mullet, otherwise known as Finney and Mudd, had devoted a great deal of time to him, and had doggedly tracked him all over the Grail network. Why?

Shuddersome memories of his escape from the trenches came back something to him, made worse by the similarity to his present situation. The mud, the bodies, the shattered pieces of men and their machines lying beneath his feet . . .

A thought sparked. Paul, who had been crouching on his heels, suddenly dropped back onto all fours and crawled down the slope, feeling with his hands. It was disgusting work. Not only were the human and animal remains more common as the slope descended, but many of them had not been completely cleaned of meat, remnants perhaps from days of great feasting when all the spider-creatures ate their fill with some left over. The bleak realization struck him that he and his friends probably represented a similar bounty – that they had been unharmed so far only because they were to be the center-piece of some grisly festival meal.

The stench near the bottom of the pit was terrible, the ground and remains alike active with small creatures taking advantage of the web-builders' generosity. Worst of all, the farther he crawled the less light he had, and he was forced to handle every collection of remains as he looked for something which might save his life and the lives of his companions.

Clambering across the rot and muck, it was hard to put the last hours of the World War One simulation out of his mind. Ava – Avialle – had appeared to him there as well, lying in a coffin like a vampire princess. *'Come to us,'* she had said. Was she simply speaking lines the Other had given her, as Martine guessed? Trying to bring Paul and his companions together in a sort of fairy-tale-inspired rescue mission? But why? And what was Ava's part in it? Why did she pick such strange ways to contact him?

He had been running his hands across the thing for some seconds before he realized what it was. At first he had unconsciously rejected it – if a buckle was no use, what good could be done with a rotting belt? – but as his fingers traced the length of it, coming at last to the large triangular pouch at the end, he felt his heart thump as though it might stop.

He had been hoping only for a walking stick or perhaps even a knife, something the creatures had thrown away that would even the odds a little. Now he hardly dared breathe as he pulled the pistol out of its holster. It seemed to be a revolver such as he had seen in old Western flicks. It was surprisingly heavy, but that was all he could tell about it by touch – he was no expert, and had never thought he would need to know anything about pistols, ancient or modern. Of course, not even the most paranoid of gun-obsessives had ever envisioned a situation quite like this.

Working slowly, but with a pounding sense of urgency, he carefully pulled and pushed at the cylindrical drum until it pivoted free of the barrel. He squinted, but could see nothing. A finger carefully inserted into one of the holes found an obstruction, and further examination showed that all the rest of the gun's six chambers were the same. Bullets – or mud? There was no way to tell without light and time, and Paul doubted he would get enough of either. And even if they proved to be bullets, there was still no guarantee that damp and dirt had not made them useless.

He hesitated. A part of him wanted to continue down the slope, a wild gambler's impulse suddenly activated by success. Maybe he would find enough pistols to arm the whole company. This was Dodge City, after all – many of the creature's captives must have been armed. Perhaps he would find something even more useful. It was hard to believe there would be a Gatling gun lying in the pit's muddy reaches, but there might be a shotgun. Paul actually knew how to shoot one of those, having endured several hunting weekends in Staffordshire with Niles and his family before mustering the courage to admit to himself, and then to Niles, that he never again wanted to stand on a cold moor with a group of people whose idea of a good time was to get drunk and blast small animals to shreds.

Still, he would not mind blasting the things capering above him into random particles, not at all. A shotgun would be a very satisfying, mind-easing thing to have, and he would not be placing all his hope on the performance of one gun – a pistol that could have been lying here in the dark for the simworld's equivalent of years, for all he knew . . .

It was tempting, but he could not take the risk. He was almost fifty meters down the slope from his companions – what if the creatures snatched them now? He would have to get quite close before aiming would be anything more than a blind lottery in this near-darkness.

He turned and began laboring up the slope, cursing now when he slipped on the bones and decomposing tissue he had so actively sought on the way down. As if to confirm his worst fears, definite activity of some kind had begun on the rim of the pit: the spidery creatures were gathering, their hissing, gulping cries rising in shared excitement. Paul heard a panicky shout from Martine. He tripped and fell, too numb and frightened now even to curse his luck, and scrambled upward on all fours like an animal, struggling to keep the gun out of the dirt.

'I'm coming!' he called. 'Get ready to run!'

He reached the top of the pit in time to see one of the two women – in the half-light he could not tell which – being dragged out by a cluster of hairy creatures while her two companions pulled desperately at her arms in a gallant but failing struggle to keep her. Paul pushed up beside them and found himself only a meter away from the closest of the buffalo-spiders, which turned its smashed face toward him, squinting lopsidedly at this slightly unexpected arrival.

It left its fellows to the job of dragging Florimel off to be eaten and reached for Paul with hideously long arms. He lifted the pistol and pulled the trigger. The hammer fell. Nothing happened.

The creature's horn-plated paw struck him on the head and knocked him backward. The pistol flew from his hand into the darkness and dirt. He sank to his knees, the faint lights and deep shadows now wavering as though seen through water. The creature that had slapped at him hesitated for a moment, torn between following up the attack and going back to help its fellows secure the chosen meal. In that space of a half-dozen fluttering heartbeats Paul recovered enough of himself to crawl after the gun. He lifted it again, certain that it was all useless, steadied his hand, and yanked the trigger once more.

This time the explosion was like a bomb going off. Fire leaped from the muzzle, and simultaneously the malformed head of the creature seemed to disappear. The other creatures sprang back, shrieking like startled gulls, but he could hardly hear them for the ringing in his ears.

'Run!' Even at a shout, his own voice sounded as though it were far away, floating through cotton. 'Come on!'

He grabbed at the nearest hand and tugged its owner, who turned out to be Martine, up the slope. The creatures had let go of Florimel, and now one of the inhuman shapes lurched in front of him. Paul shoved the gun into the thing's midsection and the creature bent double and flew backward as the gun detonated again. The creatures were leaping around the darkened nest in growing confusion, but Paul could only concentrate on what was just ahead of him.

Trusting that the other two were following, Paul dragged Martine toward the tunnel from which a little light washed out, praying that it was the sun. He had to duck his head as he entered the lower passage, and a surprise swipe from one of the creatures almost took his face off. Terrified, Paul squeezed the trigger, not bothering to aim. He didn't think he hit it, but the muzzle flash and the explosion of powder sent the creature squealing away down a side tunnel.

A dozen more steps and his heart sank. There was no sun. The tunnel widened into a broad space with a great fire pit in the middle, the flames surrounded by a crude ring of blackened skulls, both animal and human, and a corona of burned split bones. Several more of the monsters had backed against the wall, startled by the sudden appearance of the escaping prisoners, but they looked as though they were mustering the courage to attack.

No sun. We'll just stagger through these tunnels till they surround us or we run out of bullets. . . . The adrenalized numbness wore away a little. He realized he was already gasping for breath, that his wrist ached from the kick of the pistol. Behind him, Martine was jerking frantically at his arm.

'It's no good,' he said. 'Just their . . . their kitchen. No sun.'

'Keep going!' She was fighting to control her voice. 'You're going in the right direction. Go on!'

He could only hope she knew what she was saying. The little party hurried forward through the flaring yellow light. He waved the pistol, backing several of the creatures out of their path. One would not be bluffed, so Paul fired again. The thing fell to the floor in a hissing, writhing heap, forcing them to inch around it with their backs against the damp clay of the tunnel wall. Its guts had spilled onto the ground and the stench clawed at his nostrils.

How many bullets gone? Do I have any left?

Time became something not quite calculable as they stumbled through the nest. With every branch the tunnels seemed to get smaller and smaller. Paul began to feel horridly certain that Martine had made some miscalculation, that one or two more turnings would lead them into a tube where they would have to crawl on hands and knees, and from there into a wall of dirt where they would be trapped.

No, that was the war, he told himself. The shrilling of the enraged spider-buffalos was all around him. He felt his thoughts fragmenting. *Keep your mind on what's in front of you . . . in front of you . . .*

'Go to the right!' Martine shouted. 'Paul! To the right!'

He hesitated because at that moment he honestly could not think which direction was which. He felt Martine shoving him from behind and allowed himself to be guided out of the tunnel into a passage that turned sharply upward, a twisting path through cracked and broken rock.

'I see light!' he said excitedly. A circle of dim, twilight blue hovered a hundred meters above him, but this was no trick, no monster's cookfire: there were faint stars in it, real, honorable stars, as welcome as the faces of old friend. 'Hurry!'

He reached back to help Martine over a stone that jutted into the passage like a crooked tooth and had a moment of panic when he could see no one behind her. Then T4b and Florimel lurched into view, made clumsy by their hurry to get out of the corridor below.

'They're coming,' cried Florimel as she pulled down stones and earth, shoveling them with her hands into the tunnel opening to slow the pursuers. 'Dozens of them!'

Paul could not make his way up the steep tunnel with only one hand free; he shoved the pistol into the pocket of his torn, muddied coveralls and began to climb, stopping every few meters to reach back and help Martine. The sounds of pursuit were growing louder. As Paul felt the first breath of outside air wafting down the tunnel onto his face, Florimel shouted that the creatures were forcing their way into the passage below.

Paul reached the top of the hole and dragged himself out, gasping in his first breath of clean air in hours. He had only moments to look around as he helped Martine and the others out, but what he saw did not encourage him. They were in the middle of a stony mountainside almost bare of vegetation, a thousand meters above a valley floor already drowned in evening shadow. The top of the rocky ridge was much closer, but only after a terrible climb across jagged stones and loose scree.

'We have to go down,' he gasped as he and Martine dragged Florimel over the lip of the hole. Behind her T4b was muttering in terror and dismay, and almost knocked the older woman down the steep slope to certain death in his hurry to get out of the tunnel.

'Right behind me,' T4b gasped. 'Grabbin' my legs, them.'

'Let's go,' Paul said. 'Maybe they won't follow us across open ground.'

He didn't really believe it himself, and the hope proved futile by the time they had slipped and skidded a dozen meters from the tunnel. A horde of the spider-buffalos spilled out of the hole onto the hillside. They gulped and jabbered excitedly, peering around nearsightedly until one of them saw Paul and the others, then the whole bristling crowd of them came boiling down the slope like termites out of a split log.

Paul drew the pistol and aimed it at their pursuers. The jerk of the gun's detonation knocked him off-balance so that he stumbled into T4b and almost sent them both tumbling down the mountainside, but although the closest of the creatures recoiled from the shot, halting the pursuing pack for a moment of milling confusion, none of them fell.

Paul turned and hastened downhill behind his companions. He was fairly certain he had no bullets left, and carrying the gun in his hand was a terrible risk to balance, but the thought of facing a rush of those hairy things with only his bare hands was too much. If it wouldn't shoot, he would use it as a hammer.

I'll smash a few of those ugly faces back in the other direction before they get me. Even in his own head, the words sounded like the most pathetic and useless sort of bravado.

Martine was in front now, but at the rear of the line Paul could barely muster time to wonder about the wisdom of letting a blind woman lead them. The footing was terrible, loose stones and shallow soil everywhere: he could only pray Martine's strange gifts would make her a better guide across such terrain than others might be. As it was, every hurried step threatened to start an avalanche: Paul alternated between clinging to T4b's shoulders for balance and supporting the teenager in turn when patches of loose stones turned into little rockslides below T4b's feet. Florimel was clearly in pain and could move only slowly, but they could better accommodate her pace in their downward scramble than if they had been fleeing across even ground. Even so, Martine had to stop every few steps and help the German woman onto the next relatively stable spot.

Paul did not dare take his eyes off the slope in front of him until a sudden squealing from their pursuers, a shrilling chorus that sounded something like panic, made him turn back. Several of the monsters, scuttling too quickly across a section of scree already loosened by the passage of Paul and his companions, had started a slide. As Paul watched, the rocky earth crumbled away beneath them and they went hissing and shrieking down the mountain, freefalling in a hail of loose stones and dirt. For a moment Paul felt something like hope, but only a few had fallen, and although the rest had to stop and clamber uphill to make their way around the deadly section, it was the briefest of delays.

The sun had now disappeared between the horns of the stark mountain range on the far side of the river basin. Cold shadows climbed up out of the canyon. Paul could almost feel his heart freezing inside his chest.

We'll never make it. We'll die here in this idiot, backwater world . . .

A horrid wet barking noise, very close, stopped him in his tracks. He whirled to see two of the creatures crouching on a promontory just above him, twisted mouths open and drooling with excitement. They had found a faster way along the mountainside and had outflanked him from above.

The nearest leaned out over the edge of the rock shelf, long legs drawn up beside its head like some hairy midnight cricket. Paul only had time to let out a little shout of surprise and dismay before the thing unfolded itself in a powerful spring.

To his complete astonishment the beast missed him, even seemed to jolt and change direction in midair. It landed heavily at his feet, limp as a flour sack, and skidded a few meters down the slope to lie unmoving below him. The second monster leaped just as the crack of the gunshot that had killed the first reached Paul's ears.

The second spider-buffalo sprang only a little way downslope to land just above him, and had time to rear up on its legs and snatch at him before something went past Paul's ear like the crack of a whip and punched into its matted chest, drenching him in an explosion of blood.

Whoever was firing now shifted aim onto the large crowd of spider-buffalos farther up the slope. Bullets pinged off of stones and sent up gouts of dirt, but an almost equal number struck their targets; within seconds a half-dozen of the creatures were tumbling down the hill while the rest let out bubbling shrieks of dismay, eyes rolling with terror.

'Get down!' Paul scrambled forward and yanked T4b to earth, then huddled facedown while shots winnowed their pursuers. He could turn his head to one side just far enough to see Florimel's back where she lay nearby; Paul could only hope she had not been hit, and that Martine was safe on the other side of her.

The chase and almost inevitable capture of a meal had now turned into a spider-buffalo's worst nightmare. The rest of them scrambled back up the slope in a disorderly rout, leaving their dead and wounded scattered on the mountainside, some of the carcasses still bouncing from the impact of stray bullets. If Paul had not been so tired and terrified that he could barely remember his own name, he would have let out a bellow of triumph.

A few shots followed the survivors until they disappeared into the shadows of the rocks far above, then the mountainside was silent.

'What . . . ?' Florimel rasped. 'Who . . . ?'

Paul waited, but there was no shout of warning or welcome. He sat up and cautiously looked around, trying to guess where the shots had come from, but could see nothing but the darkening mountain. 'I don't know. I just hope they're on our side . . .'

'There,' Martine said, pointing.

Two hundred meters down the hillside, near a jumble

of boulders that looked very precariously perched, a light was moving. Someone was waving a lantern, signaling to them. It was just a small thing, a wavering gleam still faint in the last rays of the sun, but at the moment Paul thought it looked like a glimpse of heaven.

The person who held the lantern was small, face almost hidden by a scarf and hat pulled low, and the long billowing coat also seemed too large for the slight frame, but Paul was still surprised when the stranger spoke in a woman's clear voice.

'You can just stop there,' she drawled. 'There are a few guns pointing at you, so unless you think you can outrun a bullet better than those things that were chasing you, I suggest you tell us your business.'

'Business?' Florimel was so tired her temper was as raw as her voice. 'Business? Running for our lives from those monsters. They were going to eat us!'

'It's true,' Paul said. 'And we're grateful you drove them off.' He tried to think of something else to say; he was so exhausted he thought he might collapse any moment. 'Just don't shoot at us. Do you want us to reach for the sky?' It was about the only thing he could remember from netshow westerns.

The woman took a few steps toward them, holding up the lantern which was now the main source of light on the mountainside. 'Just hold your water for a minute while I get a look at you.' She peered at Paul and his companions, then turned and called over her shoulder, 'They look like real folk. More or less.'

Somebody shouted something from behind the boulders that Paul could not make out, but apparently it was agreement; the woman with the lantern waved them forward.

'Just don't do anything too fast or tricky,' she said as Paul and the others staggered down the slope toward her. 'The boys have had a long day, but they'd be willing to kill a few more if they had to.'

'Bitch talk that *fenfen*,' T4b muttered sourly. 'Don't like it, me.'

'I heard that.' The woman's voice had gone cold. A pale hand appeared from the voluminous sleeve, the small gun pointed right at T4b. 'I don't need Billy and Titus to deal with you, boy – I'll put you down myself.'

'Jesus!' Paul said. 'He didn't mean it! He's just a stupid kid. Apologize, Javier.'

'*Sayee lo*, you! Do what . . . ?'

Martine grabbed his arm and yanked. 'Apologize, you idiot.'

T4b stared at the muzzle of the derringer for a moment, then cast his eyes down. 'Sorry. All tired, me. Those things tried to kill us, seen?'

The woman snorted. 'Just watch your mouth. I may not be a lady myself, but we got a few in there who are, not to mention some young ones.'

'We're sorry,' Paul told her. 'We thought we were all going to die down in that nest.'

The woman's eyebrows rose. 'You got out of one of them nests?' she said. 'Well, that's something. My man will be pretty interested to hear about that, if it's true.'

Paul heard T4b's intake of breath and turned a stifling glance on him. 'It is true. But we wouldn't have made it without your help.'

'Tell it to Billy and Titus when you go in,' she said, gesturing to a space between two standing boulders. 'They did most of the shooting.'

Paul ducked his head and stepped through into the flicker of flames in a dark place – for a moment it was so much like the nest that he could not help fearing some terrible trick.

'Annie is a fair hand with a buffalo gun herself,' someone said beside him. Paul turned, startled. 'Shoots better than she dances, anyway. Don't let her tell you different.' The man who had spoken had long, fair hair and a face freckled with dirt that Paul realized only later was gunpowder. Several other people stood behind him, hanging back in the shadows where the firelight did not quite reach.

'That is Billy Dixon,' the woman said as she and the rest of Paul's friends filed in. The cavern knifed far into the hillside but was screened on the open end by an ancient tumble of boulders. Paul could see these survivors had picked their fortification well – only a few chinks between the great stones let in any sight of the evening sky. 'Billy might be the best hand alive with a Sharps gun – even my man would allow that was true.'

Dixon, who had a long straggling blond mustache and the beginnings of a serious beard covering his broad face, showed a smile but said nothing.

'And my name is Annie Ladue,' she said, unwinding the scarf. She was attractive, or should have been, with a sharp chin and big, heavy-lidded eyes, but her teeth were bad and one cheek was marked with a long horizontal scar. 'If you behave, we'll get along well. Titus,' she called over her shoulder, 'what's going on out there?'

'Nothing,' a deep voice said. 'No sign of nary a one of those devils, 'cept the dead ones.' A tall black man with a very long rifle swung himself down from a higher spot among the rocks – a look-out post of sorts, Paul guessed. He landed beside them with a thump.

'And this is Titus, who perforated that jackalo what was jumping down to give you a haircut and shave you wouldn't have forgotten, mister,' Annie said.

Paul stuck out his hand. 'Thank you. Thank you all.'

After a moment's hesitation, Titus took it. 'You would have done it for me, too, wouldn't you? Ain't no question of skin when something like *that* is coming after someone.'

For a moment Paul was puzzled, then remembered that this was supposed to be nineteenth-century America, where things like racial differences still meant a lot. 'Absolutely,' he said. 'Except I don't ever want to shoot a gun again.'

Billy Dixon gave a little snort of amusement and wandered off toward the depths of the cave. The other inhabitants were coming forward now. As Annie Ladue had said, many of them were women with children. In fact, except for a couple of old fellows who hobbled up to look the newcomers over and congratulate the shooters, Billy and Titus appeared to be the only young men in the cavern.

'I'm glad you enjoyed the show, Henry,' Annie told one old man notable for what looked to Paul like complete and utter toothlessness, 'because you can go pick up the Springfield and stand first watch. It oughta be cool now, and mind you don't bang that barrel on any rocks.' She turned to Paul and the others. 'This way we stand a chance of getting some good out of him before he gets into the liquor.'

The ancient laughed and went off to get the gun. Annie seemed to be one of the leaders, if not *the* leader. Paul was intrigued, but it was not enough to overcome his weariness. The adrenaline had worn off and strength was running out of him like air from a punctured tire.

'Do you folks want something to eat?' Annie asked. 'There's not much, but there is some beans and hardtack, which is sure better than nothing.'

'I think we just want to sit down somewhere,' Paul said.

'Lie down,' Martine quietly amended him. 'I need sleep.'

'Then you all better come over here and bunk down in what we call the shooting blind,' their hostess said. 'That way we can keep the young ones away – if you try to lie down back where everyone else is at, the little rats will be all over you.' She led them up a narrow makeshift path through the tumble of stones that screened the front of the cave until they reached the flat top of a boulder several meters across. A few animal skins scattered across it – Paul guessed they were buffalo hides – made it look quite inviting. At one edge the old man she had called Henry sat staring out through a crevice between two large stones, a long rifle propped beside him.

'These people need to get some rest,' Annie told him. 'Which means that if I hear you bothering them, you'll answer to me. So keep your no-tooth mouth shut.'

'I'll be quiet as the grave,' he said, eyes wide with mock fear.

'Which is where you'll end up if you cross me,' Annie said as she departed.

'You all lie down,' Henry told them. 'I'm keeping an eye out, and I see better than I chew.' He chortled.

'Oh, God,' Florimel said as she slumped heavily onto the nearest buffalo hide. 'A damned comedian.'

Paul didn't care about that or anything else. Even as he lay back he could feel sleep dragging at him, swallowing him as if the very stone beneath him had become liquid and he was sliding downward, downward into its depths.

He woke up with a throbbing head, a dry mouth, and a light but firm pressure against his ribs. The man named Titus was standing over him, high-boned African features betraying nothing.

'Want to get your friends up and come on,' he said, giving Paul another gentle shove with his boot toe. 'The rest of 'em have come back and the boss man wants to talk to you.'

'Boss man?' Paul asked muzzily. 'Come back from where?'

'Hunting.' Titus leaned against the boulders while he waited for the foursome to rouse themselves. 'You don't think we eat those bedamned jackalos, do you?'

Following the tall, lanky Titus, Paul was reminded of his sojourn in the imaginary Ice Age, the excitement that had prevailed at the hunters' return. There was a great deal of activity all across the wide cavern, and several fires were burning where only one had been lit when he and his companions had first arrived – perhaps to make it easier to see what was happening outside the stronghold.

'What time is it?' Paul asked.

'Don't know exactly, but it's morning,' Titus told him. 'You all slept like you needed it.'

'We did.'

Titus led them into a second large cavern, the one into which Paul guessed the other inhabitants had withdrawn the night before. Now it was just as busy as the outer chamber, full of the smell of cooking meat, and the smoke was even thicker. Paul was surprised to see three men with long knives dismembering the carcass of a good-sized calf. 'They've been out hunting cows?'

'Better we get 'em than leave 'em to the jackalos and the devil-men,' Titus said.

'Devil-men?' asked Florimel. 'What are those?'

Titus did not reply, but stopped and gestured with his chin toward the calf butchers. 'Go on. He's been asking about you.'

Paul and the others took a few steps forward. A broad-shouldered, well-built man with a thick mustache and a dusty plug hat rose from his crouch with the casual ease of a lion coming up out of the grass.

'I'd offer my hand,' he said, 'but as you can see I'm bloody up to the elbows. Nevertheless, you're welcome here. My name is Masterson, but my friends and a few of my more informal enemies call me Bat.'

'Bat Masterson?' Paul stared despite himself. It should not be a shock to run into simulacra of famous people, not in this artificial universe, but it was still a surprise when it happened.

'Heard of me, have you? That'll teach me to spend time with newspapermen.'

'Most of what's written about him is lies,' Annie Ladue said as she climbed to her feet beside him. Paul realized that he had again mistaken her for a man. She gave her paramour an affectionate pat on the rump. 'But to be fair, only about half the lies are Bat's.'

'Sit down and work, woman,' he said. 'We've got a half a hundred mouths to feed, which means we'd better be cutting pretty close to the bone.' He turned his attention back to Paul and the others, looking them up and down, his interest obviously piqued by the coveralls they had inherited back in Kunohara's bugworld. 'So what are you folk? Circus performers? Traveling players? You'd find an eager audience here. The little ones are getting a mite fretful in here after all these days.'

'No, we're not . . . performers.' Paul had to suppress a bemused smile. If this were a netflick, they'd probably have to pretend they were. What kind of bizarre act could they cobble up between them? *See the Amazing Lost Man! Marvel at the World's Most Sullen Teenager!* 'We're just ordinary people, although we come from a long way away.

We were passing through and got lost, then those . . . things attacked us.'

Once again, the system's ability to absorb anomalies moved them smoothly past an impediment; their odd garments were not mentioned again. 'I heard about that,' Bat said. 'I heard you fought your way out, too – which, if the ladies will pardon my language, is pretty damn impressive. How did you manage?'

'I . . . I found a gun,' Paul said, pulling it carefully out of his pocket. 'It had enough cartridges in it for us to shoot our way out, but just barely. We would have been killed if your people hadn't been there.'

'We have a lot of trouble with that nest so close,' said Bat casually, but his gaze had not left Paul's pistol. 'But this is the best place to defend for miles, so we chose the lesser of two evils.'

'How did you wind up in this situation . . . ?' Paul began.

'I hate to interrupt,' Bat said, 'and you may take this amiss, but I hope not. Would you extend me the courtesy of letting me have a look at that shooting iron of yours?'

Paul paused for a moment, confused by the strange tension in Masterson's tone.

'Don't,' said T4b in a too-loud whisper, then grunted as Florimel stepped hard on his foot.

'Of course.' Paul proffered it butt-first, but Masterson would not take it until he had found a handkerchief in his vest pocket so he could hold it without smearing blood on it. He lifted it up to catch light leaking in from a high chink in the cavern wall.

'You say you found this in the nest?' His voice was casual, but there was still something in it that made Paul nervous.

'I swear. In the muck, down with all the bones of animals and . . . and people. It was in a holster.'

Bat sighed. 'I'd almost rather you were lying. This is Ben Thompson's gun, and a better man and a better shot would be hard to name. I haven't seen him since all hell broke loose, but I was hopeful he was still alive out there somewhere, maybe at one of the other camps up on the ridgetop. But if you found it in the bottom of one of them godforsaken nests . . .' He shook his head. 'Dead is the only way Ben would be to let someone take his iron off him.' He offered the gun back to Paul. 'It's yours by right of spoils, I guess.'

'To tell the truth,' Paul said, 'I've hardly ever fired a pistol before this and I'll be happy if I never fire one again. If it belonged to a friend of yours, you keep it.'

One of Bat Masterson's dark eyebrows crept upward. 'I'd like to think you might get your pacifistic wish, sir, but it doesn't seem likely. We'll run out of bullets long before we run out of trouble.'

'What kind of trouble *is* this?' demanded Florimel. She had been impatiently quiet for too long. 'Why are there mountains? We've never heard of anything like that. And what are these monsters?'

'More importantly,' said Martine, 'how do we get into Dodge City? Can we reach it from here?'

Paul was puzzled by her question for a moment, until he remembered what she had said about finding the gate that could lead into Egypt.

Masterson, Annie, and Titus were far more surprised than Paul, and regarded her with something like astonishment, although Bat, when he spoke, was almost courtly. 'My dear lady, no offense, but where in creation have you greenhorns come from? Get into Dodge City? You might as well ask to be let into Hell's own saloon bar! You'd be better off stripping yourself naked – begging your pardon for the crudeness – and running into the nearest Comanche camp screaming "All Indians are liars and fools!"'

Titus snickered. 'That's a good one.'

Annie was less amused. 'They just don't know, Bat. They're from somewhere else, that's all. We should find out, though, because maybe that somewhere else is a better place to be than here.'

Bat smiled. 'The lady has more sense than I do, and more manners. Perhaps we should share information . . .'

Before he could finish his sentence, long-haired Billy Dixon appeared. 'Prisoner's cutting up somethin' fierce,' he announced.

'Damn. Maybe you could lend a hand here, Billy – I've been a bit distracted.'

Bat offered him the knife, but Dixon plucked one out of a sheath on his leg so quickly that it seemed to jump into his hand from thin air. 'Got my own.'

'If you just come and set your eyes on the little charmer we brought back with us,' Bat said, beckoning to Paul and the rest, 'it will save me a fair piece of explaining.' He led them toward the back of the cavern, well away from the fire. A few more hard-faced men looked up at their approach; Paul guessed they were the ones who had accompanied Masterson on his hunting trip.

'These fellows came down on us the day after the earth started moving,' Bat said. 'There was so much dust in the air we didn't even see them until they were almost on top of us. Then someone came riding down past the Long Branch screaming that a Cheyenne war party was coming up fast. We got all the women and children and old folks into the church, rest of us saddled up and got our guns. Didn't do us much good. For one thing, these aren't any

Cheyenne like *I've* ever seen . . .' He stopped. 'I hear he's getting twitchy, Dave,' he said as one of the men stood up.

The man, lean and with most of the bottom half of his face hidden by an immense whiskbroom mustache, shrugged. 'I say ventilate him. He won't tell us nothin' but his name – at least I think it's his name. Keeps saying, 'Me Dread,' over and over . . .'

'Oh great God!' said Florimel, staggering a step backward. 'How can this be?'

'Bastard shot me!' snarled T4b.

'It *is* Dread,' Martine whispered. She had gone deathly pale. 'Although he no longer wears Quan Li's body, I could not be mistaken.'

Paul stared at his companions, then at the slender, nearly naked man in a breechclout lying on the ground before them, bound tightly hand and foot, covered in bruises and dried blood. The prisoner looked up at them with no sign of recognition. His teeth were bared in a grin of exertion as he writhed in his bonds like a snake. His dark skin and Asian eyes gave him a little of the American Indian look, but Paul could not doubt Martine's senses. He had never met the much-feared Dread, but he had heard more than enough: despite the prisoner's obvious helplessness, he took a step back as well.

The prisoner laughed at Paul's retreat. 'Hah! Me kill you all.'

Bat Masterson crossed his arms over his chest. 'Well, if you folks dislike this one so much, you might want to reconsider your travel plans. You see, this fellow's got himself about a thousand identical cousins, and right now they're all having themselves a hell of a wing-ding on Front Street down in Dodge.'

CHAPTER 21

Handling Snakes

NETFEED/ART: Bigger X – Dead Genius, or Just Dead?
(visual: Coxwell Avenue death scene, Toronto)
VO: The art world is talking about the death of forced-involvement artist Bigger X, killed in a hit and run accident in Toronto, Canada. Already several camps have formed. Many believe X was responding to a 'suicide challenge' by another artist known as No-1, and may have arranged his own fatal 'accident' both as an acceptance of No-1's challenge and a further homage to a favorite artist of X's, TT Jensen. Others suggest that TT Jensen himself may have arranged the death, either out of irritation at Bigger X's constant citation of him, or (an even stranger alternative) as a symbol of gratitude for Bigger X's praise. Yet another group suggests that No-1 may have engineered the death out of frustration that Bigger X did not publicly respond to his 'suicide challenge.' There is even one brave group who suggest that X's death is just what it seems – something that happens to people who walk into a busy street without looking . . .

S HE had been staring at the wallscreen so long that she had fallen into a kind of dream. When the shouting began, she sat up so quickly she almost fell off her chair.

Dulcie darted a reflexive glance at the coma bed, but

Dread had not moved. He had been back online for most of a day. She was beginning to feel like she was keeping a deathwatch.

Someone screamed in the street below, a shrill but still masculine cry of pain and outrage. Dulcie walked across the loft, legs tingling because she had been in one place too long, and lifted the corner of the blackout curtain on one of the windows.

It was dark outside, which startled her almost as much as the noises had – how had it become night again so quickly? People were moving in the alley below, shadowed bodies performing an aggressive posture-dance. It was a fight of sorts, three or four young men strutting and shoving, but there seemed to be more arguing than actual attacking. Dulcie had spent too many years in Manhattan to be either surprised or concerned, and she certainly wasn't going to waste any time worrying that they might hurt each other.

Men. They're programmed for it, aren't they? Like those little builder robots. Just walk forward until you bump into something, then shove it until it does what you want – unless it shoves harder than you do.

She wandered back across the loft toward the cabinet where, in a fit of bored domesticity while waiting for some of her security-cracking gear to work, she had set a chair and arranged all the squeeze packs, sweeteners, and other related objects into a sort of coffee-break area. As the argument raged on in the alley below she became conscious for the first time that she had no idea what kind of security Dread had in this place. She couldn't imagine him leaving himself open to robbery or assault, especially in a neighborhood as troubled as this one, but she also knew he was highly unlikely to have any of the more common deterrents like an alarm system connected to the private-subscription police lines: Dread was obviously not the kind of man who would be calling the police. She couldn't picture him waiting for a private security firm to come save him either, or even men he had personally assembled, like the ones from the Isla de Santuario invasion. In fact, she just couldn't imagine him waiting for anyone. Dread was the type who would want to handle everything himself.

Yeah, and fat lot of good that will do me if he's off in Never-Never Land somewhere when the rude boys come through the window.

Another shout, a sputtering curse that seemed to come from right under the window, made her flinch. *By the time you could wake him up,* she thought, *someone might have already stuck a knife in you, Anwin.* She put down her coffee and walked to the room Dread had given her, then dropped to her knees and pulled her suitcase and attaché out from under the bed.

As she located and removed the various plastic components, some molded to blend into the corners and roller-wheels of the suitcase, others disguised as ordinary pieces of executive traveling equipment – a set of pens, an alarm clock for those exotic locales where you were occasionally denied net access, a purse-size curling iron – she considered her strange up-and-down relationship with her employer. He had made it pretty clear now that he was physically interested in her, and she had to admit that he in turn was pretty interesting himself. He had come up from his last session in the network bubbling with delight, and she had been surprised to find herself feeding off his mood, hurrying to tell him of her successes with Jongleur's personal files. He had praised her, laughing at her excitement, almost vibrating with that strange hyperactive glee that filled him sometimes, and for a moment she had wanted to have him right then, quick and nasty as something out of one of the paper-book potboilers her mother had left lying around the house in lieu of discussing the boring details of sex and love with her only child.

But although they had moved around the huge room in a kind of hyperkinetic dance, Dread shouting questions at her as he made himself coffee and banged in and out of the shower, her timing was bad: at that moment he seemed completely uninterested in her, at least sexually, sharing the joy of her success and his own upbeat mood, but only as her collaborator.

He had been pleased, though, and that was certainly something. For the first time since she had come to Sydney she had made her value unmistakable. He had told her as he stood with his black hair lank and gleaming from the shower, his robe carelessly open down to his tight stomach muscles, that Dulcie's work would give him the last tools he needed for his big strike.

She paused, absently contemplating the scatter of small plastic parts now lying on the discount-store rug beside the bed. What *was* his big strike, anyway? He seemed to have gained control of his employer's VR network, which was certainly impressive, and might even be in and of itself enough to make him wealthy, although it was hard to imagine quite how that would work. Would he continue the Grail Project, selling the prospect of immortality to wealthy people, but with himself taking the tolls instead of Felix Jongleur? Or, more likely, was he planning to sell his employer's secrets off to the highest bidder? Where *was* Jongleur, anyway? Had Dread arranged the same fate for him that he had for Bolivar Atasco? Then why hadn't anyone heard about it? Surely if one of the world's richest, most influential men had died at least a rumor of it would have made the newsnets by now.

Dulcie took the tube from the curling iron and screwed it into the case of the travel clock, working slowly through the unfamiliar design. She almost hadn't brought a gun with her – the dreams about Cartagena were still strong – but the ingrained habits of a professional woman, especially in her particular profession, were hard to shake. The gun she had used on the gearhead in Colombia had never left that country, of course: Dread had volunteered to dispose of it for her, but she had read and watched enough thrillers to know she wasn't going to give anyone incriminating evidence against herself. She had disassembled it, wiped it as forensically clean as she could with nail-polish remover, and dropped the pieces in a dozen different trash cans across downtown Cartagena.

So you wouldn't trust him not to blackmail you with a murder weapon, but you'd sleep with him? Interesting selection process, Anwin.

It was so hard to figure out how she felt. He was mercurial, of course, never the same from moment to moment, but wasn't that what she wanted? She had discovered a long time ago that advertising copywriters from Long Island and stockbrokers thrilled to be under warranty on their first armored Benz didn't make her heart go pitty-pat.

Face it, Anwin. You do like bad boys.

And even more, she liked knowing that she herself was at least as wicked, just more discreet. But when you moved out to the fringe neighborhoods of sex, more than the scenery changed. You got . . . well, a weirder selection.

Jesus, Dulcie, so you have a fling with him and it doesn't work out. So you go back to New York and spend a couple of days drinking and watching net-soaps and feeling sorry for yourself – worse things could happen. Do you really think he's long-term material anyway?

She had to admit that she couldn't imagine herself living in the same city with the guy for any stretch of time, let alone picking out curtains together. But was that so bad? He excited her. She thought about him all the time, alternating between fascination and, occasionally, something much stronger and more dangerous than irritation or dislike, something closer to hatred and fear.

So what? He's what you want – a bad one. He's just badder than most, and that scares you. But you can't walk the high wire and still use a net or there's no point in the high wire at all, is there? So his social skills are a little alien. The guy's an international criminal. At least he isn't boring.

Her hands had been moving reflexively, but it didn't matter: despite the differences from model to model, once you'd put together a few of these plastic stealth guns you could pretty much do it in your sleep. She got up off her knees and sat on the bed, shaking ceramic bullets out of a vitamin bottle and slotting them into the magazine. *Click, click, click . . .* like little babies, octuplets, being packed into a shared cradle. Babies, guns, virtual worlds, old men pretending to be Egyptian gods – her brain, she reflected, was definitely scrambled.

You need a vacation, Anwin. A long one.

She considered for a moment, then walked back to the main room of the loft. The loud argument outside was over; a peek through the window showed the alley was empty. She put the gun in the middle shelf of the coffee cabinet, under some napkins.

Or maybe I need something exciting to happen. Something big.

CHRISTABEL stood holding the glass in one hand. Her other hand was on the faucet but she didn't dare turn it on, even though she was so thirsty she was about to cry. She was angry at herself for being thirsty, angry at herself for getting out of bed to get a drink of water. Now she had to stand like a scared mouse in the dark bathroom and hear her mother and father having an argument in the next room.

'. . . It's gone far enough, Mike. I can't make you come back with me, but I'm certainly not going to stay here with Christabel, put her in danger, while all this is going on. We'll be perfectly safe at my mother's.'

'Jesus H. Christ, Kay!' Daddy's voice was so loud and full of hurt that Christabel almost dropped the glass to smash on the hard bathroom floor. 'Haven't you been paying attention to what's going on here?'

'I certainly have. And anyone with an inch of sense would know it's no place for a little girl. Mike, you let someone point a gun at her! At our daughter!'

For a long moment no one said anything. Christabel, who had been about to set the glass down so her arm would stop aching, stayed just where she was, like she was in a terrible game of Freeze Tag.

Her daddy's voice, when it came, was quiet and scary. She had never heard him sound mad in quite that way before – it made her want to run away. 'That's about the worst thing you've ever said to me, you know? Do you think I haven't had nightmares about that every night? I didn't take her in to meet Ramsey. *You* let her go off to find a bathroom by herself. What was I supposed to do?'

'I'm sorry. It was an unfair thing to say.' Her mommy was still mad, too. 'But I'm terrified, Mike. I'm . . . there isn't even a word for how I feel. I just want to take my little girl and get out of here, and I'm going to. I'm taking the boy, too. Just because he's poor doesn't mean he's any less of a child and doesn't deserve protecting.'

'Kaylene, will you listen to me? If I thought there was anywhere safer for you to be, I'd be the first one to send you both there – for God's sake, you have to believe that! But I'm only here right now because Yacoubian thought he could get away with using some of the ordinary base personnel. If it hadn't been Ron who picked me up, you would never have heard of me again. There's no doubt in my mind.'

'This is supposed to make me feel better?'

'No! But however much of Sellars' story is true, I can tell you this – the way they took me, that whole thing the general was up to, it stank. There was nothing regulation about that at all – it was a kidnapping. Ron and Ramsey saved my life, just by being there.'

'So?'

'So what if these people come looking for me again? Without bothering with the appearances of military law, this time – at night, maybe, disguised as burglars. Don't you think my wife's mother's place is somewhere they might look? And if I'm not there, don't you think that they might figure you and Christabel would make useful hostages? These aren't Boy Scouts. What's your mom going to do, sic the cat on them? Call that goddamn mobile home park committee she's always sending after the kids on skimboards?'

'All right, Mike. It's not very funny.'

'No, it's not. You were right before, Kay – it's terrifying. At least if I have you two near me I can protect you. We can keep moving, and Sellars seems to be pretty good with managing a low profile for us. You settle in one place, even somewhere not as obvious as your mom's, we'd just be hoping they don't find you.'

'You sound like you believe in this . . . conspiracy. This whole big crazy thing.'

'Don't you? Explain Sellars, then. Explain Yacoubian and his little hotel room and his matching Nazi weight-lifter bodyguards.'

Christabel had been stiff in one place so long that she was afraid she would scream if she couldn't put the glass down. She inched her arm to the edge of the sink, looking for a flat spot.

'I can't explain it, Mike, and I don't want to try. I just want my child safe and away from all this . . . craziness.'

'That's what I want, too, as soon as possible. But the only way I can see . . .'

The glass teetered, then tipped. Christabel grabbed at it but it jumped out of her fingers and hit the floor with a sound like something blowing up on the net. An instant later the bathroom light flashed on bright, and her father was so big and angry in the door that Christabel took a bad step back and started to fall. Her father jumped forward and caught her arm so hard she squeaked, but she didn't fall down.

'Oh, my God, what are you doing? *Ah!* Jesus! There's glass everywhere!'

'Mike, what's going on?'

'Christabel just broke a glass. I got a piece in my foot the size of a steak knife. Jesus!'

'Honey, what happened?' Her mom lifted her up and carried her into the room where her parents had been arguing. 'Did you have a bad dream?'

'I'll just clean up the glass, then,' her father said from the bathroom. 'And amputate my foot to save the leg. Don't mind me.' He sounded angry, but Christabel relaxed a little – it wasn't the kind if divorce-angry she had been hearing.

'I . . . I was thirsty. Then I heard you . . .' She didn't want to say it, but she still believed a little that if she

told Mommy, something would happen to make things all
right again. 'I heard you arguing and it scared me.'

'Oh, honey, of course.' Her mother pulled her close and
kissed her head. 'Of course. But it's okay. Your daddy and
I are just trying to decide what to do. Sometimes grown-
ups argue.'

'And then they get a divorce.'

'Is that what's worrying you? Oh, sweetie, don't take
it so seriously. It's just an argument.' But her mother's
voice still sounded funny and raw, and she didn't say,
'*Your daddy and I will never ever get a divorce.*' Christabel
leaned into her and held on, wishing she had never been
thirsty.

They were still talking in the other room, but much more
quietly now. Christabel lay in her bed, just across a space
like a little valley from the boy Cho-Cho, who was tangled
up in his covers on his own bed like an Egyptian mummy.
Christabel tried to breathe slowly like her mommy told
her, but she kept feeling the crying about to come out
and her breaths sounded all raggedy.

'Shut up, *mu'chita.*' Cho-Cho's voice was muffled by
his pillow, which lay over his face. 'People tryin' to sleep.'

She ignored him. What did he know? He didn't have
a mommy and daddy who were arguing and were going
to get a divorce. It wasn't his fault everyone was angry,
like it was hers. Even though she was so sad it hurt, she
also felt a little brave.

'This far crash,' Cho-Cho said, rolling out of bed and
taking most of his covers with him, so the sheeted mattress
suddenly was bare and white, like an ice cream sandwich
with the top peeled off. 'Can't nobody sleep with this
mierda.' Skinny in his T-shirt and underwear when the
blankets fell away, he walked toward the bathroom.

'Where are you going? You can't go in there.'

He didn't bother to look at her and didn't even close the door. Christabel buried her head under her own blankets when he started to pee. After the noisy flush of the toilet, it was quiet for a long time. When she at last stuck her head out from under the covers he was sitting up in his bed, staring at her with his big dark eyes.

'You afraid some monsters gonna come get you, something?'

Christabel had met a real monster, a smiling man in a hotel room with eyes like little nails. She didn't need to answer to this mean boy.

'Just go to sleep,' he said after a while. 'Got nothing to worry about.'

It was so unfair she couldn't keep quiet any more. 'You don't know about anything!'

'I know nothing happens to little *ricas* like you.' He stared at her, smiling a mean little smile, but he didn't look happy. 'What you think gonna happen? I tell you what's gonna happen to me, you wanna know that? When all this over, you gonna go back to some mamapapa house somewhere, little Cho-Cho's going to work camp. See, your daddy, he one of the nice ones. *Los otros*, man, they maybe just take me out and shoot me.'

'What kind of camp?' It didn't sound that bad – Christabel's friend Ophelia had been to Bluebird camp, and they made art projects and ate marshmallow sandwiches.

Cho-Cho waved his hand at her. 'Cross City, that was one they put my *tio* in. Digging and like that. Bread with, like, little *bichos* cooked right in it.'

Christabel put a hand to her mouth. 'You said a bad word.'

'What?' He thought for a second, then laughed,

showing his missing tooth. '*Bichos*? That just mean bugs.' He laughed again. 'You thought I said "bitches," huh?'

She gasped. 'You *did* say it!'

The boy let himself slide back into his bed, staring up at the ceiling. All she could see was the tip of his nose above the pillow. 'Tell you what, not gonna wait around, me. Next chance I get, Cho-Cho be too much gone.'

'You're . . . you're going to run away? But . . . Mister Sellars, he needs you!' She couldn't understand – it seemed like the kind of wickedness they talked about in church sometimes, not Sunday school, but the big room with the benches and the glass window of Jesus. Run away from that poor old man?

And her mother would be sad, too, Christabel realized. Mommy complained about it a lot, but she really seemed to like making Cho-Cho bathe and wear clean clothes, giving him extra food to eat.

The boy made a noise she could just barely hear – it might have been another laugh. 'I thought there was some *efectivo* around here, some money, but it's just a bunch of crazy people trying on some spyflick *mierda*. Little Cho-Cho, soon he going to be too . . . much . . . gone.'

He didn't say any more. Christabel could only lie in the bed next to his, straining to hear her parents' low voices, and wonder how the world could have turned so strange.

S HE had drawn enough hieroglyphs on the countertop with powdered creamer for an entirely lactose-free edition of the *Book of the Dead*. She had listened to the quiet hiss and hum of her employer's expensive coma bed adjusting itself until she wanted to scream. A thousand channels of net input and she couldn't muster interest in any of them.

Dulcie knew she ought to go lie down, but knew equally firmly that she wouldn't sleep for hours. She pulled on her lightweight raincoat and keyed the security sequence for the front door lock. When it chimed she hesitated, then went back and got her newly-assembled gun from its hiding place in the coffee cabinet.

A little before midnight and the hilly streets of Redfern were shiny with rain just fallen, although at the moment the skies were clear. A loud group of people were streaming out of a dirge club down the block, mostly young white and Asian kids dressed in funeral clothes, baggy black 'chutes and wrapped fellaheen hoods. She fell in behind the largest group, drawn down the street behind them as their voices rang off the building facades like the excited piping of a flock of bats. They seemed to be shouting things at each other in some pidgin Aboriginal dialect. Dulcie remembered a time when she could have stood on the streets of Soho or the Village next to a bunch of young people like this and done in-depth social anthropology on every word, every item of clothing and its positioning. Now she couldn't even remember if this particular sub-sub-group were Dirt Farmers or No-Siders, or anything much else about them except that they liked organic hallucinogens, loud slow music, and artificial skin bleaching.

It all seems so important when you're young, she thought. *Marking yourself up so everyone knows who you are. People should just have ID readouts in real life like* they do with VR sims, so instead of going to all the trouble to get your skin laced or your face branded, you could just display a little message – 'I like cats and bondage, don't listen to any music older than six months ago, and am punishing my father by getting too many subdermals.'

Or in my case, 'I'm punishing my mother by doing

things with my life that she probably wouldn't care about
if she knew.' Makes a lot of sense, doesn't it?

She was depressed, she realized. The missed moment
with Dread, because of bad timing or whatever, had turned
the possibility of something spontaneous and a little scary
into another nightmare checklist of should-she, shouldn't-
she. The fact was, although she rather enjoyed being
played in that way he had – jerked back and forth emotionally, frightened and then petted – the too-long courtship,
if that was what it was, had begun to lose her undivided
attention. The fact that she didn't actually *like* him much
was starting to weigh more heavily than it should.

*The real truth is, he hasn't told me anything. He's
dragged me into some major industrial espionage on pretty
thin promises, paying me decent but unspectacular hourly
rates, and for all I know he could have found a way to
turn lead into gold. I have no guarantees. And what if it
turns bad – I wouldn't let him take the gun for me, why
should I let him keep me in the dark here in somebody
else's country? I don't even know what the laws on this
stuff are like in Australia.*

*And what else did he tell me, like it was the big payout
– 'Do you want to be a god, Dulcie?' Meaning what,
immortality in the Grail network? Well, who knows? The
fact is, he hasn't offered. He hasn't really offered me
anything but himself, and although that's not bad, it isn't
enough. Not for this girl.*

The crowd was dispersing quickly, some to the bus
stops, others flagging down taxis. Coming home from the
apres-Jihad party, she thought with dry amusement as a
group of black-turbaned youth jostled their way into a
shared cab. Then she realized that a wide but dark street
that had been crowded and noisy only moments ago was
now nearly empty.

Where am I? That would be great – get lost out here in the middle of the night.

The street signs weren't particularly edifying and she had left her t-jack in the loft, so she couldn't even access a map. Angry with herself but not too worried – there were still people on the street, including some couples – she began to retrace her steps, doing her best to remember how many times she had turned while following the crowd. The old row houses with their rusting wrought-iron balconies seemed to watch her like blank but disapproving faces. She patted her coat pocket, reassuring herself. At least she was armed.

Three dark-skinned men watched her as she approached the corner on which they stood, and even though none of them moved or said anything – the youngest one even smiled very sweetly at her as she passed – she found her steps quickening as she moved away from them down a dark side street.

It's like we're always in the shadow of them, some-how, she thought. *Men are just there, blocking the light, and there's nothing we can do about it. Is it only because society has been shaped that way over the years, or is there something more prehistoric going on – because they were stronger back in the beginning?*

Felix Jongleur, a prime example of a predatory old man, flashed through her mind. His strange *Ushabti* file was apparently some kind of last will and testament – an *if-you're-seeing-this-I-must-be-dead* bit of drama care-fully prepared for an heir who seemingly never was. What would his real successors think about that when he did finally give up his lamprey-grip on life? Would they be as puzzled as she was?

Men and their secrets. It was part of their power, wasn't it? So hard to get them to talk about important things that

you'd think someone was trying to steal their souls. Dread
was another example – a very pertinent example, now that
she thought about it. What did she know about him
anyway? Sure, with the work he did, she didn't expect to
find anything very useful in her few early stabs at researching his background, but she had been impressed at how
much of a nonperson he was – or had made himself. There
wasn't even a Dread-shaped hole to be found in any of
the international files, criminal record banks, anywhere. He
was Australian and, by the looks of him, of mixed racial
ancestry, which could describe millions of people. Where
did he come from? What was his story? It must be an interesting one. Jongleur had secrets. All powerful men had
secrets. So what was it that John More Dread was hiding?

She heard the noise before she saw the clump of shadow
on the sidewalk half a block ahead of her – a soft retching sound like a cat bringing up a furball. She slowed as
she tried to make sense of the shape, which only resolved
a few slowing paces later into a man standing over a
kneeling woman. At first Dulcie thought he was holding
her head while she vomited – the results of a night's
excess at one of the bars or clubs – but even as she began
to step out into the gutter to swing around the pair she
saw that the man was actually pushing her down, forcing her toward the sidewalk.

The pale-haired man looked up, his eyes assessing and
dismissing Dulcie within a heartbeat in a way that infuriated her despite her sudden fear. He turned his attention back to the woman, saying something loud in a
language that sounded Slavic, and the woman, weeping,
choked out something in the same language. Dulcie
remembered Dread mentioning all the immigrants who
had come to Redfern after the Ukrainian grain belt disasters; he had said it with a sense almost of irritation, which

she had thought at the time was some kind of anti-white racism, and only realized afterward was the exotic Mr Dread experiencing a very common thing – discomfort at his old neighborhood changing.

The woman was bleeding a little from a cut on her lip, fighting clumsily to stand. The man, his wide jaw set in a line of fury, was holding her head down, the kind of thing a playground bully might do. Something about the situation pricked at nerves long Manhattan-numbed. Dulcie stopped a few meters from the slow-motion struggle and said loudly, 'Leave her alone.'

The man scowled at her, then turned back to the woman and shoved down hard, so that she gave up resisting and sank all the way to her hands and knees.

'I said, leave her alone.'

'You want it too?' His accent was thick but the words quite understandable.

'Just let her stand up. If she's your girlfriend, that's no way to treat her. If she's not your girlfriend, I'll have the police on your ass in twenty seconds.'

'No,' the woman said in a kind of despair. The man's broad hand was still on top of her head; she looked out from beneath his spread fingers like a beaten dog. 'No, okay. Is okay. He not hurt me.'

'Bullshit. You're bleeding.'

The man's face, which at first had showed a trace of amusement, began to shift. His scowl congealed into something quite frightening. He pushed the woman again so suddenly that she toppled over into the gutter, then he turned toward Dulcie. 'You want? You come here, then.'

Something that had been burning in Dulcie all day flared hotly. She tugged the gun out of her coat pocket and leveled it at him, bracing her wrist in best shooting-range style. 'No, *you* come here, asshole.' It was strange to feel that power all the way up her arm, like godly lightning at her fingertips. 'Get down on your knees, why don't you?' She saw the man's mouth drop open and her feverish high expanded. This was the way those Baptist snake-handlers must feel with thrashing, living death in their hands.

'You . . . you crazy!' The man began backing away, trying to keep his face hard but failing. The woman in the gutter was weeping and covering her head.

She was tempted to squeeze off a shot, just to let the bullying bastard feel the wind of it past his face, but she hadn't test-fired it, didn't know how sticky the pull was, anything.

So I miss and take his ear off instead, she thought. *Or worse. So what?*

But the face of the Colombian gearhead Celestino swam up out of the turbid darkness of her thoughts, his brown eyes big with fear like a wounded dog, although in real life she had never actually seen fear in his face, since he had been fiberlinked online and blind to her when she shot him.

The young Russian man turned and walked swiftly up the street, barely restraining the urge to run. Before Dulcie could take a step forward to help her up, the woman he had been brutalizing staggered upright, then – with only a brief scared-rabbit look at Dulcie – ran after him. She left both of her high-heeled shoes behind her on the sidewalk.

Dulcie was still breathing a little too fast, vibrating with an excitement that was beginning to turn a little sour, when she found her way back to the street that held the loft.

It's about power, isn't it? she thought. *You give them*

all the power, let them keep all the secrets, and they can grind you down. Without some kind of equalizer the game just isn't fair.

So what's Dread hiding? Just his Swiss bank accounts? Blackmail-quality details on some of the Grail folk?

She thought about the little invisible box on his system, a boy's carton of dirty secrets slid under the bed, out of reach of Sister and Mom.

I can find out, can't I? If I can crack the whole J Corporation, I can sure as hell beat some hidden storage on Dread's home system. I can get in and out without him even guessing. Then I'll have something on him for a change. I wonder how he'd feel about that?

She had a feeling he wouldn't like it very much, but just now, with fear and fury and triumph singing together in her veins, she didn't care.

CHAPTER 22

More Very Bush

BAFFLED and defeated, Renie slumped to the ground beside the black waters, which were still rippling from the disappearance of the Witching Tree. The Stone Girl had edged away from her, frightened by the strength of Renie's anger.

'Come back,' Renie said. 'I'm sorry. I shouldn't have shouted. Come back, please.'

'You made the Witching Tree go away,' the little mud girl said. 'That never happened before.'

Renie sighed. 'What did it tell you? Am I allowed to ask? I heard something about the Ending, and some boys-and-girls rhyme . . .'

The Stone Girl looked at her curiously. 'You said the tree stole your brother.'

'It . . . it's hard to explain. But not the tree, no.' A sudden thought struck her; however unlikely, it was worth asking about. 'Do you know anyone named Stephen? A little boy . . . ?'

'Stephen?' She giggled. 'What a funny name!'

'I take it that's a no,' said Renie. 'Jesus Mercy, what have I done? What kind of foolish, crazy place is this?' She let her shoulders slump, conscious for the first time in a while that the forest was turning chilly. 'What else did the Witching Tree tell you?'

Her guide became somber again. 'That things are bad. That the Ending is going to come closer and closer until there's nowhere left to go. That I should come to the Well with all the other people, because that would be the last place left.'

'The Well? What's that?'

The Stone Girl furrowed her earthen brow. 'It's a place like this, except way more big, across the river and across the river and across the river. Where the Lady comes, sometimes, and talks to people.'

'The Lady?' Renie's neck prickled – she knew who that must be. 'She comes to this Well and . . . what?'

'Tells people things that the One is thinking.' The Stone Girl shook her head. 'But she doesn't do it anymore. Not since the Ending started to come.' She got up. 'I have to go. The Witching Tree said I need to go to the Well, so I'm going to start walking.' She hesitated. 'Do you want to come with me?'

'I can't, I have to wait for my friends.' Renie felt events

slipping through her fingers. 'But I don't even know where I am. How can I get back to the place I was before you found me?'

The Stone Girl cocked her head to one side. 'Where did you come from?'

Renie did her best to describe what she could remember of the rolling meadows, the distant hills, their translucency. Trying to remember it now, it felt like a distant dream.

'You must have been at Over Thaw Hills, in Faraway,' the little girl decided. 'But it's probably all gone now. The Ending was already there when I was looking for the Witching Tree. That's how come it was all empty in some of it, like you said.'

And she had been so sure she had found a place that was becoming more real! Renie felt a harsh pang of fear for !Xabbu and Fredericks. What if they were not lucky enough to stumble on a crossing, as she had been? She had to go find them.

Yes, but find them how? Wander around these weird places by yourself while it all evaporates around you? What good will that do?

But what was the alternative? To follow a fairy-tale creature like this Stone Girl deeper into madness?

I shouldn't have lost my temper. Just for once, why couldn't I have kept my mouth shut? Maybe I would have got some useful information out of that thing if I'd been nicer. She should have remembered what it was like to deal with Stephen, how shouting and scolding just drove him deeper into sullenness. The operating system was so much like a child, and what had she done? Treated it as though she were an angry parent. And not even a particularly smart angry parent.

'What was that you said the . . . the tree told you?

That you were supposed to go to this Well, and that all the other people were going there, too?'

The Stone Girl nodded, still standing at the clearing's edge.

What if Stephen really is here? Renie thought. *What if he's one of the people drawn or sent to this Well? What if I could finally find him, reach him . . . touch him?*

So here was the balancing point. Renie was exhausted, but she couldn't put off the decision. The little girl was leaving, with her or without her. Did she abandon !Xabbu and the others, or perhaps abandon the chance to find Stephen?

Years of university, and for what? How can you make a decision like this – no facts, no discernible logic, no real information . . . ? It was agonizing to think of !Xabbu, who she knew would be looking for her just as diligently as she had been looking for him. It was no less agonizing to think of Stephen, her beautiful, shining little man, so close he was almost her own child, now curled in a hospital bed – a thing of sticks and skin like a broken, discarded kite. She felt bruised inside, helpless, miserable.

And just think – here in the network, I'm really nothing but a living brain. A brain with a bad case of heartache . . .

The Stone Girl scraped her foot against the ground, swaying a little. Clearly it was difficult, even painful for her to wait once the Witching Tree had told her what to do. 'I really have to . . .'

'I know,' said Renie. She took a deep breath. 'I'm coming. I'm coming with you.'

I don't have any choice, she kept telling herself, but it felt exactly like treachery. *!Xabbu and the others might never have made it out of that gray . . . whatever it was.*

They might have been tossed into another part of the network, or they could even be . . . It was almost impossible even to consider it. *I could look for them forever. And this could be my last chance to help Stephen.*

Of course, that's assuming I can do anything for him even if I find him, she thought grimly. *Considering I can't even get myself offline, that's a pretty big assumption.*

'Are you angry at me?' the Stone Girl asked.

'What?' Renie realized they had been walking for a long time without speaking. She had a sudden recollection of what it meant to be with an angry adult, thinking that she was the cause, and was ashamed. Even in the days before her mother had died, her father had been prone to sullen silences. 'No! No, I'm just thinking.' She looked around at the sparkling trees that still surrounded them, an endless series of leafy tunnels through the forest. 'Where are we, anyway? I mean, does this place have a name? Is it called Witching Tree or something?'

'The Witching Tree isn't a place, it's a thing.' The Stone Girl was clearly relieved: even Renie's invincible ignorance did not draw the usual look of disbelief. 'There are lots of places it can be – that's why we had to go look for it.'

'And we found it . . . where?'

'Here. I told you, it's always in the Wood.'

'And where are we going?'

The Stone Girl considered for a moment. 'I don't know for sure. But I think we'll have to go through More Very Bush and maybe even Long Done Bridge. It's really hard to cross there.'

'Cross . . . ?'

'The river, silly.' Renie's companion frowned. 'I just hope we don't have to go through Jinnear Bad House. That's too scary.'

More Very Bush and Jinnear Bad House. Those would
be . . . Mulberry Bush and Gingerbread House, Renie
guessed. She was beginning to get the knack. 'Why is it
scary?'

The Stone Girl put her hand up to her mouth. 'I don't
want to talk about it. We don't want to go there. But
there are Ticks and Jinnears there, lots of them.'

Ticks and Jinnears. For some reason, the phrase stuck
in Renie's mind, but unlike the place names, which seemed
to be childish malformations of things like London Bridge,
she couldn't find an easy explanation. But having seen
the things, she was just as eager as her companion to
avoid something called Jinnear Bad House.

'What are Ticks? Are they as bad as Jinnears?'

'Worse!' The little girl gave a theatrical shudder. 'They're
all starey. They have too many eyes.'

'Ugh. I'm convinced. So if we have a long trip ahead
of us, shouldn't we stop and sleep? I'm tired, and you, if
you'll excuse me saying so, are definitely up past your
bedtime.'

Now her small guide did indeed put on a look of disgust.
'Go to sleep in the Wood? That's a stupid idea.'

'Okay, okay,' Renie said. 'You're the boss. But how far
do we have to go before we *can* get some sleep?'

'Until we find a bridge, silly.'

Properly told off, Renie subsided.

As the flying-saucer moon hovered overhead, showing no signs of moving toward a horizon, they walked
deeper and deeper into the forest – deeper, Renie knew,
because the trees got taller and taller around them. They
had long since left the black lake and its sentient tree
behind, but Renie could not help feeling observed,
although she was not sure whether by the small, secretive eyes of invisible forest dwellers or by some larger,

more godlike entity. The clearings, with the branches arching cathedral-high overhead, glittering with fairy-lights like a sky full of bright stars, seemed particularly watchful. The weird, cartoonish beauty of the setting could not overcome the hackle-raising sensation of traveling through enemy territory.

Well, why shouldn't it feel this way? she thought. *If I'm right, I'm not just inside the network any more, I'm inside the operating system itself – right in the belly of the beast.*

Pulling her blanket-cloak tighter around her to ward off a forest breeze, Renie suddenly touched the lumpy shape of the lighter underneath her top, pressed against her breast.

'Oh, no! I called Martine . . .' In the unceasing strangeness since then, she had completely forgotten her distress call from the hillside, with the Jinnears coming down on her from all around. 'She must think . . .'

The Stone Girl stopped, eyebrow dents raised in astonishment, to watch Renie pull the small shiny object from inside her clothing and speak into it. 'Martine, can you hear me? Martine, this is Renie, can you hear me?'

No answer came back to her. Renie shook the lighter as though it were a stopped watch, conscious even as she did so how stupidly RL the gesture was. It made no difference, anyway: the lighter remained as silent as a stone.

They walked on, Renie adding the horror she must have visited on Martine and anyone else with her to her list of sins.

It's getting to be a long list, she thought. *Failed to find my brother, didn't do anything useful to interfere with the Brotherhood's plans, deserted !Xabbu and Sam, and also called my other friends and made them think I was about to get killed.*

Yes, but you really were about to get killed, she reminded herself. *Ease up, girl.*

As they walked on through twinkling trees and woodland dells carpeted by dark grass that wavered without wind, studded with circles of pale, dully-shining mushrooms, Renie began to feel a different kind of liveliness to the Wood. She began to hear rustles in the foliage and once or twice thought she saw shadows just disappearing around a bend of one of the long open pathways before them. She mentioned it to the Stone Girl, who nodded sagely.

'Other people going to the Well,' she said. 'The Ending is coming fast, I guess.'

'So they're not . . . Jinnears. Or Ticks.'

The Stone Girl managed a tiny smile. 'We'd know.'

The vast moon had still not moved noticeably from one side of the sky to another, but Renie had just decided that it had perhaps slipped a bit lower when they saw the campfire on a small knoll ahead of them through the trees. The Stone Girl hesitated for a moment, peering at the flicker of light, then lifted her stubby finger to her mouth for silence and led Renie forward. Strange shapes were clustered around the flames. The Stone Girl slowed again, leaning forward and squinting, then straightened.

'It's just dwarfs,' she said cheerfully, taking Renie by the hand.

A sentry shape at the edge of the knoll lifted a stick and said, 'Who goes there?' in a high, querulous voice.

My God, Renie thought. *More children. Is everyone in this place a child?*

'We're friends,' the Stone Girl announced. 'We won't hurt you.'

The creatures huddled around the fire watched their approach warily. Renie was at first secretly pleased to see

that the dwarfs numbered exactly seven, but discovered
a few moments later that she was a little less comfortable with how they actually looked. They might be someone's idea of dwarfs, but as with so many things she had
seen lately, it was a very curious kind of idea.

The little men were all dwarf-high – the nearest, the
stick-wielding sentry, stood no taller than Renie's hips –
but although the Other, if it was indeed the creator, apparently understood that dwarf meant small, it had accomplished this not by miniaturizing a normal person, but by
leaving out or rearranging parts. The dwarfs had faces
that grew right out of their chests, and after she had studied the awkward gait of the sentry, who had fallen into
step beside them, she realized that his legs ended at the
knee: there was no joint in the middle, which made the
little fellow walk something like a penguin. His arms,
however, were of normal length: he used them to aid his
movements, knuckle-walking like a chimpanzee.

Renie forced herself to remain calm, although it
reminded her unpleasantly of the grotesque patchwork
creatures in the Kansas simulation – not only cruelty made
monsters, it seemed. As Renie and her friend reached the
fire the little creatures rose and greeted them with
awkward bows. The tallest, whose shoulders were as high
as Renie's waist, asked, 'Are you searching?'

'No,' the Stone Girl replied. 'Just walking. Are you going
to the Well?'

'Soon. But first we must find what we have lost. And
we have lost everything, even our home!'

One of the other dwarfs was staring right at Renie.
'Say Dives,' he said mournfully.

'Um . . . dives,' she answered after a moment, wondering whether this was a greeting ritual or some kind of
test.

'No, they're from Say Dives,' the Stone Girl whispered.

'Say Dives is gone!' the leader said, his mouth open from floating rib to floating rib in a gape of woe. 'The meadows, the mountains, our beautiful caves! Gone!'

'The Ending has t-t-taken it all by now,' said the one beside Renie, choking back a sob. 'When I came home from work, my house was gone – and all my wives! The cats and sacks – all gone, too!' The other dwarfs echoed his misery in a wordless chorus of moans.

'The stepmothers came and told us we had to run away,' the leader said. 'The people that we meet here in the Wood say we must go to the Well. But we cannot go until we find our wives and our sacks and all our cats! There is a chance that they escaped!'

'A man without wives and kits and cats is no man at all,' another proclaimed heavily. A deep, tragic silence fell on the gathering.

'So . . . so you people have stepmothers also?' Renie asked at last, finding herself a seat on a log near the fire, trying very hard not to stare at what to her was a pattern of ghastly deformities. The dwarfs beside her slid down to make room. She had to remind herself that however bizarre this seemed to her, these events were just as terrible to them as to any real-world refugees.

The shy-eyed fellow beside her, his face set so low on his belly that his belt looked like it must be strangling him, offered her a cup of something that steamed. 'Stone soup,' he said quietly. 'It's good.'

Renie's guide looked over, her face solemn with worry. 'You eat . . . stones?'

The leader shook his head. 'We would never harm you, friend – we eat only unliving minerals. Besides, if you will forgive me, you look to be mostly sediment. No offense, but that is not to our taste.'

'No offense taken,' the little girl said in relief.

'Does everyone who lives in . . . in these places . . . do they all have stepmothers?' Renie asked.

The dwarfs could not cock their heads, since they had none, but they bent themselves into several strange positions to indicate surprise. 'Of course,' said the leader. 'How else would we know when danger is near? Who else would guard us when we sleep?' His lower lip drooped toward the fork of his legs. 'But they can't stop the Ending.'

So the stepmothers are part of the operating system, Renie decided. *A kind of monitoring subroutine – maybe a harsh one, like the wicked stepmothers in all those stories. But where do the monsters, these Ticks and Jinnears, fit in?* She tried to think of a nursery rhyme with a tick in it, but the closest she could come up with was 'Hickory Dickory Dock,' which wasn't very close at all.

'Where are you from?' one of the dwarfs asked Renie. She looked helplessly at the Stone Girl.

'Where The Beans Talk,' the little girl answered. 'But we went to the Witching Tree, and it told us it was time to go the Well.'

It didn't tell me that, Renie thought morosely. *It didn't tell me much of anything.* A sudden thought led to her to ask, 'Have any of you seen any others like me? A brown-skinned man and a girl with skin a little lighter?'

The dwarfs shrugged sadly. 'But the Wood is full of travelers,' one said. 'Perhaps your family is among them.'

Renie said nothing, struck by the idea. !Xabbu and Sam Fredericks, her family. It was true in a way, and not just in shared skin color. Few people had ever suffered greater hardships with their real families, and certainly no one had suffered anything more consistently peculiar.

Conversation wound down quickly. The dwarfs had made

a heroic effort to be good hosts, but their hearts were clearly
not in it, and Renie and the Stone Girl were exhausted.
They curled up on the ground to rest while the dwarfs went
on talking among themselves in quiet voices full of confusion and loss. Although she had proved herself much less
bothered by cold than Renie, the Stone Girl pushed herself
tight against Renie's body and within moments seemed to
be asleep – so much so that Renie could detect no breathing at all. She wrapped her arms around the compact little
form and watched the firelight glimmering in the treetops
above her head. She was wandering now in a weird, childish dream-world – a dream-world under siege. She had lost
everyone and everything. Of all who had come to Sellars'
summoning, only she remained. Even the operating system,
the god of this small world, had admitted defeat. What was
there left to do?

I can hold this child, she thought. *Even if it's just for
one night, I can give her a little comfort, a sense of safety
– even if it's an illusion.*

So, as the huge disk of the moon crawled down toward
the horizon and Renie eased into a sleep she desperately
needed, that was what she did.

When she awoke, a diffuse glow had spread across the
world, a sad gray light that did little to make things seem
more hopeful. The dwarfs had gone, leaving only the
embers of their fire behind. The Stone Girl was already
awake, squatting by the dying fire, poking in the ashes
with a stick.

Renie yawned and stretched. Even in this sickly dawn
it was good to have a blanket to wrap around herself,
good to have someone to talk to. She smiled at the little
girl. 'It feels like I slept a long time, but I guess I didn't.
So if there's a moon here, why isn't there a sun?'

The Stone Girl gave her a quizzical look. 'Sun?'

'Never mind. I see our friends are gone.'

'A long time ago.'

'Why didn't they wait for the sun . . . I mean, for morning?'

'They did. It's been this way since before they left.' Renie now noticed for the first time that her companion was frightened. 'I don't think there's going to be any more light than this.'

'Oh.' Renie glanced around. It *was* dark, the sky a mournful, shadowy gray. 'Oh. Does this . . . happen very often?'

'That it doesn't turn into day?' The little girl shook her head. 'Never.'

Jesus Mercy, Renie thought, *does this mean the system's shutting down now? Is this part of the Ending everyone's so afraid of?* If the operating system were a person, Renie would certainly have diagnosed severe depression at the very least. 'So is the damn thing just going to give up on us?' she said aloud.

And what if it does? If we're inside it, somehow, do we go, too? It was hard to believe that, locked as they were within the system, subject to damage and death just as in real life, she and her friends would survive a complete collapse of the network.

And Stephen, and all the other children here, trapped, helpless . . .

'We have to get going.' Renie struggled to her feet. 'To the Well, I guess. But you'll have to lead us there.'

Her guide balanced on her haunches and looked out at the encircling forest. 'We need to find a bridge,' she said listlessly. 'Then we can go to More Very Bush. Or maybe to Counting House. There's a king there,' she added.

Renie wasn't certain she wanted to meet this odd fairy

tale's version of royalty – for all she knew, he might
incline toward the Alice's Wonderland, off-with-their-
heads model. 'So we find a bridge.' She hesitated. 'Does
that mean we have to find the river first?'

The Stone Girl snorted. 'Of course.'

'Give me a chance.' Renie was glad to see a more normal
response from her companion. 'I'm just getting the hang
of all this.'

What had been mysterious, twinkling fairy-paths in the
night had become something less charming now – a series
of winding ways through a dank, dark forest – but no
less confusing. Even in the glum half-light, Renie could
see other travelers passing through the Wood, although
few even made eye contact, let alone stopped to converse.
Many had carts or wagons drawn by strangely uncon-
vincing beasts of burden, horses and goats and oxen that
seemed to be three-dimensional mock-ups created from
children's drawings. Renie recognized a few as refugees
from the storybooks of her childhood, like a trio of pigs
and a nervous-looking wolf who were traveling together,
having apparently made common cause, but there were
far more she could not identify, some so bizarre they made
the dwarfs look like netshow models. But all the travelers trudging or hurrying through the dim byways of the
Wood had one thing in common, the worried expressions
on their faces – at least among those that *had* faces. Some
were openly weeping. Others staggered, blank-faced as
shock victims.

The Stone Girl stopped in a clearing to talk with the
leaders of a large party, perhaps three dozen refugees in
all. As the little girl shared news with a buck deer and a
tiny bumblebee-man perched between his antlers, Renie
found herself staring at the faces of the group they were
herding, looking for Stephen.

But he won't look like Stephen, she told herself. *Which means he could be any one of these – he could be anyone we've seen today!*

Nevertheless, she walked over for a closer inspection.

'Have any of you seen some people who look like me – with skin like mine?' she asked. Several faces, animal and human, turned to look at her in dull hopelessness. 'A little boy, or even a man and a girl? They would be newcomers – people you hadn't seen before.'

'The Wood is full of strangers,' said a woman carrying a hedgehog wrapped in a baby blanket. She spoke as if each word were a heavy stone that must be lifted.

'But I mean real newcomers. From outside.' She tried to remember how the others had phrased it. 'From beyond the White Ocean.'

The crowd stirred, but only a little. The buck and the bee-man turned to look at her, then resumed their conversation with the Stone Girl.

'Nobody has crossed the White Ocean in a long time,' the hedgehog-mother said. 'Since before the Ending began.'

'What does it matter?' asked a fish-faced man. 'Who cares?'

'I care . . .' Renie began, but she was interrupted by a little boy with a nose as long as a finger.

'There have so been newcomers,' he said shrilly. 'Stepmother told me.'

'What kind of newcomers?' Renie asked. 'What did they look like?'

'Don't know.' He introduced a long finger into his finger-length nose and began to pick meditatively. 'She just said they were strangers, and that strangers were dangerous, and that was why the Ending was going to take away our house.'

'Where was this? Here in the Wood?

The boy shook his head. 'Cobbler's Bench, where our house is.' His fingers paused. His face grew sad, struggling with the enormity of loss. 'Was.'

'And where is that? Are they still there?'

Another child, this one with the russet ears of a fox, yipped in derision. 'Not nowhow! The stepmothers chased them out of town!'

Finger-nose nodded. 'They got Weasel to help, 'cause Monkey's sick.'

'Renie!' The Stone Girl was beckoning to her. 'We have to go.'

As they left the refugees from Cobbler's Bench behind, Renie tried to stay buoyant. So there *were* newcomers – someone had seen them. That had to be !Xabbu and Sam. Unless it was Martine and the others . . . Renie had assumed that because they were not on top of the black mountain when the dust settled, Paul and Martine and the rest of her companions had been dispatched somewhere else – but who was to say that this nursery-rhyme world was not that somewhere else. And if everyone was being drawn toward this place called the Well, they would surely all find each other.

As the gray day wore on into what Renie felt must be afternoon, they found the river at last and began to pick their way along the marshy ground beside it. The dark, gurgling water lulled Renie into a dreamy routine of one-foot-after-another. Strangely, despite all the travelers they had seen in the forest, they met few along the riverside, and those were just as likely to be hurrying in the opposite direction. All wore looks of desperation. None would stop to talk.

Renie was beginning to wonder about her companion, too. The Stone Girl, previously so steady in her walking that Renie often found herself hurrying to keep up, seemed increasingly tired and confused. Several times she stopped and stared out across the river as though looking for something, although Renie saw only empty forest there.

At last, as the daylong twilight was just beginning to slide into something deeper and darker, the Stone Girl flopped herself down on a fallen tree. Her little shoulders were rounded, her earthen face somber.

'I can't find the bridges,' she said. 'We should have got to one of them by now.'

'What bridges?'

'The places to cross the river. It's the only way to get out of the Wood unless we go all the way back through the trees to the other river.' She made a little snuffling sound. 'Then we could go back to Where The Beans Talk. If it's still there.'

'The other river? There's another river?'

'There's always another river,' the Stone Girl said dolefully. 'At least there used to be. Maybe that's gone now, too.'

Through careful questioning, Renie at last began to grasp that every single one of these lands – the Wood, the place Renie had met the Stone Girl, even the places she had not seen but had heard of, like More Very Bush and Say Dives – were bounded on either edge by a river. You had to cross a river to pass into the next land. The whole thing reminded her a bit of Lewis Carroll's chessboard world, where Alice found a different adventure in each square.

Yeah, but 'curiouser and curiouser' doesn't cut it here, she thought. *More like 'worser and worser.'* Aloud, she asked, 'So if we don't find a bridge, are we just stuck here?'

The Stone Girl shrugged miserably. 'I don't know. Why

would the Witching Tree tell us to go to the Well if we couldn't get there?'

Because the Witching Tree, or whatever's behind it, is running down, Renie thought. *Or giving up.*

It was Dread, she realized suddenly. On the hilltop, he had said something about inflicting pain on the operating system. It might have been a metaphor, but it seemed pretty obvious that there was a core of truth. Whether on purpose or not, Dread was slowly killing the thing that held the Otherland network – and most especially this part of it – together. 'We can't do anything if we sit. Come on! Let's keep looking.'

'But . . . but all my family . . . !' The Stone Girl looked up at Renie imploringly. Two little trickles were running down her dirt cheeks. 'They're back there, and the Ending . . . !'

The tears shattered Renie's impatience. She dropped to her knees beside the small child made of earth and stones and put her arms around her. 'I know, I know,' she said helplessly. What could she say? What had she ever said to Stephen when he had been scared, or heartbroken with disappointment, except the thing that all grown-ups said to children? 'Everything will be all right.'

'But it won't!' The Stone Girl sniffed angrily. 'I shouldn't have gone away! Polly and Little Seed and Tip, all the baby ones, they'll be scared. What if they don't get away? The Ending will come and take them!'

'Sssshh.' Renie patted the little girl's back. 'The stepmother will get them out. Isn't that what stepmothers do? Everything will be all right.' It was hard not to dislike herself for making assurances she knew nothing about, but she could see little good for either of them in a long trek back across the Wood to the land of giant shoes and jackets.

Renie's soothing seemed to help a little. The Stone Girl stood up, still snuffling loudly. 'Okay. We'll look for the bridge some more.'

'Good girl.'

The light was definitely lessening now, and there had been little enough to begin with. Eager not to spend another night on this side of the river, Renie hurried to keep up with her guide, and even forged ahead in some places where the reeds and riverside vegetation grew too high for the Stone Girl to see.

She had just relinquished the lead to the Stone Girl as they climbed up a rise between two bends of the river, when her companion stopped and cried out.

'Look! A bridge!'

Renie scrambled up after her so quickly that she slipped and had to catch herself with her hands; she was still wiping dirt and moist, too-pale grass off her blanket as she reached the little girl's side. Before them she could see an entire bend of the river valley. A large crowd had gathered on the near side of the river at the first stone of one of the most unusual bridges Renie had ever seen. It was made entirely of rectangular stone pillars stretching crookedly across the river like a linear Stonehenge. Although they were of slightly different heights, none of them seemed to be more than a meter or so from its neighbor. Renie could see how it would be possible to cross by clambering from one to the next, but the look of the thing, like a jaw full of uneven teeth, gave her a moment's sinking feeling.

It's like the mouth on the front of Mister J's, she thought. *This whole place is just a crazy-mirror, isn't it? One of those funhouse affairs, but it reflects all the things that the Other has been forced to do.*

'Why isn't anyone crossing it?' she asked.

The Stone Girl shrugged and trotted stiffly down the rise.

As they got closer, Renie could plainly see a continuation of the forest on the river's far side, but the middle of the bridge was swathed in mist so she could not actually make out where it touched the opposite shore. Still, that did not explain why so many travelers, a motley assortment of fairy-tale oddities that must have numbered almost a hundred, were gathered silently on the bank, looking yearningly toward the far side but not actually using the bridge.

'Is it . . . broken or something?'

As they reached the edge of the sullen crowd, the Stone Girl asked a woman in almost whimsically colorful medieval dress what was going on. The woman looked them up and down for a moment, paying particular attention to Renie, before answering.

'It's them Ticks, dearie. Dozens of them.'

'Ticks?' The Stone Girl's eyes went wide. 'Where?'

'On the other side,' the woman replied with a certain grim satisfaction. 'Some folk already tried to cross over – it's this Ending, you know. They said they weren't feared of a few Ticks. But it's not a few, is it? One or two of the ones what went over got back to tell about it, but the rest got et.'

As though whatever had animated her earthen body had suddenly ceased to work, the Stone Girl sagged to her knees. 'Ticks,' she said hoarsely. 'They're so *bad!*'

Renie felt herself go cold inside. 'Are they worse than Jinnears?'

'They're bad,' the Stone Girl would only say again.

'And some say them Ticks have some new ones still trapped over there,' the woman in the colorful dress went on. 'Some strange folk – not from anywhere around here.'

'What?' Renie could barely resist the impulse to grab the woman by her bodice and haul her close. 'What kind of strange folk?'

'Sure I don't know, dearie,' the woman said, giving Renie a look that implied she had just been categorized as strange herself. 'Heard it off a rabbit, I did, and they're always in a hurry. Or was it one of those squirrels . . . ?'

'On the other side, you're saying?' Renie turned to the Stone Girl. 'Those might be my friends. I have to go help them.'

The Stone Girl looked up at her, her dimple eyes pools of shadow, her face blank with apathy or helpless terror.

'Shit. Stay here.' Renie began elbowing her way through the crowd assembled on the bank, a casting call for a surrealist painting. Most of them seemed gripped by the same mood of fear that had immobilized the Stone Girl; only a few even murmured as Renie forced her way past them.

The first stone of the bridge stretched almost Renie's height above the shallows. She found a handhold and pulled herself up, not without strain. She was tired after the long day's walk, and when she had dragged her belly up onto the rough surface of the stone's top she had to lie there for a moment until she could catch her breath. Sprawled and vulnerable, she could not help thinking of the way the bridge had looked, like a row of chewing teeth.

'Help me up,' someone said.

Renie peered over the edge into the dark, upturned face of the Stone Girl.

'What are you doing?'

'I'm not going to stay here. You're my friend. And you don't know anything, either.'

Terrified by the thought that !Xabbu and the others

might be under attack, she only had a moment to consider. The girl was right about one thing – she knew a lot more than Renie. And with the system apparently dissolving the simworld around them, would the child be any safer waiting here, at least in the long run?

Bullshit justification, Sulaweyo. But what else was there?

'Grab my hand,' she said.

When the little girl reached the top of the stone, she gestured for Renie to keep silent.

> *'Gray goose and gander,*
> *Waft your wings together,'*

the Stone Girl intoned solemnly,

> *'And carry the good king's daughter*
> *Over the one-strand river.'*

'You're *always* supposed to say it before you cross,' she told Renie. Fear made her shrill. 'Don't you know? It's very important.'

They made their way quickly from tooth to tooth until the warning cries of those still waiting on the bank had faded. Midstream the water seemed faster, blackly turbulent as it washed between the close-set stones, the spray sharp and chilly as hail. The mist Renie had seen from the bank was all around them now, obscuring vision and making the stones slippery. She forced herself to take each step with slow care.

They were only a few stones past what she guessed was the mid-point of the river when the streams of mist thinned. Renie, crossing with a long stretch from one rocky tooth to another, was so startled that she almost lost her foothold and had to scramble to get her weight forward so she could jump to the waiting stone.

The far side of the river had changed completely.

Where before she had seen only primordial forest stretching into the distance on both sides, now she found herself confronted by a very different landscape. For a moment she thought it was some kind of formal garden, full of hedges and topiary shapes, but then the scale of the thing hit her and she realized she was looking at an entire town – a city – completely grown over by brambles and twining, crawling vines, a living green sculpture in the shape of houses and streets and church steeples.

'Is that . . . More Very Bush . . . ?'

The little Stone Girl only whimpered.

Almost the only contrast to the thousand shades of green were the many pale shapes moving over and through the bushes like maggots in a rotting carcass. Like the Jinnears, they were a sickly white, but where those things had been almost completely formless, these had the semblance of some kind of animal life. They were long and low to the ground, scalloped at the edges in what almost seemed a parody of legs, but they still moved horribly quickly, half-scuttling, half-slithering. They were also nearly her own size, and there were hundreds of them. The greatest number swarmed around the base of a green-strangled tower halfway into the town, a writhing white necklace easy to see even in the dying light, the creatures excited as ants who had discovered an unguarded wedding cake.

'Jesus Mercy,' Renie said, her fear turning sharp and cold, so cold. 'And those . . . are Ticks?'

The Stone Girl's voice barely rose above the noise of the river beneath them. She was weeping again, the words fracturing.

'I w-w-want m-my *s-s-s-s-stepmother!*'

Third:

THE DYING HOUR

'How many miles to Babylon?
Threescore and ten.
Can I get there by candlelight?
Yes, and back again.'
— Traditional

CHAPTER 23

Orientation

NETFEED/SPORTS: 'Body Fascism' Litigant Killed in Practice
(visual: Note outside courtroom after victory)
VO: Edward Note, who won a court case in which he proved a local
professional football team was discriminating against him based on
body type when they initially refused to give him a tryout, was killed
in his second day of practice with the team. Members of the Pensacola
Fishery Barons BMFFL team, who are responsible to UN antidis-
crimination laws because their stadium was built with revenue from
local taxes, put on a public face of regret, but some team members
said off the record that Note 'only got what he deserved.'
TEAM MEMBER (anonymated): 'What did the guy weigh, a hundred
twenty pounds, old school measurements? Running around with guys
that weigh three or four times that? It's no wonder he got his fool-
ish tiny ass crushed. Too bad for his kids, though.'
VO: The thirty-eight-year-old Note, who declared contemporary pro
sports a bastion of 'body fascism,' was apparently caught underneath
a pile-up in practice and asphyxiated. His family is demanding an
investigation of his death.

'JUST a minute, Olga.' The woman, a stranger of course, but acting as familiar as an old friend, handed her a cup of coffee which steamed convincingly. 'I hear you're working for that J Corporation now. That must be fascinating – you hear so much about them in the news. What's it like?'

'I'm not allowed to talk about where I work,' she said.

The woman smiled. 'Oh, of course not – I know that! But I'm not trying to get you to tell any important secrets, am I? Just . . . what's it like? Is it really on an island?'

Surely everyone knew that. Still, Olga was unbending. 'I'm sorry – I'm just not allowed to talk about where I work.'

The woman frowned. 'You're being really grumpy and silly about this. You must not be getting enough sleep. Are you working nights or something?'

'I'm really sorry, but I am not allowed to talk about my work.'

The woman waved her hand in disgust. A moment later the room wavered and changed, so quickly that Olga felt a bit dizzy, almost sick.

They should do a better job with their transitions, she thought. *If they ever got a job on the real net, for Obolos or someone, they'd get ripped to shreds for something like that.*

She sat patiently as someone who was apparently a relative of hers asked her to bring home some extra office supplies for the kids – nothing important, just a few stick-tights or hardclips for the poor, underprivileged darlings to make art projects for school. Olga sighed and began her refusals, waiting as patiently as she could through the upward spiral of recrimination, waiting for it all to end.

'Well, an excellent score,' Mr Landreaux said after she had stepped out of the hologram room. He was a small man with a shaved head and a scatter of sparkling stones embedded in his wrist – trying a little too hard to look young, Olga thought. 'You really studied up, didn't you?'

She tried not to smile. A quarter of an hour's examination of the company's voluminous hiring package the night before had made it pretty clear what the general idea was. 'Yes, sir,' she said. 'This job is very important for me.' *And you can't even guess how true that is, can you?*

'I'm glad to hear that. It's important to me, too.' The personnel officer squinted at his wallscreen. 'Your references are very, very good. Fourteen years at Reichert Systems – that's a very good company.' He smiled, but she saw something else glint in his mild gray eyes. 'Tell me again why you left Toronto.'

This is really just a junior version of the man who gave me my exit interview at Obolos, she thought, *another pink soft animal with sharp teeth. Does that Jongleur fellow grow them in vats, like those space-tomatoes?* Aloud, she recited the story Catur Ramsey had invented for her, and that his friends had somehow turned into accomplished informational fact. 'It's my daughter Carole, sir. Since her . . . since she split up with her husband, she needs some help with the kids so she can keep her job. She works so hard.' Olga shook her head. This was cake. Convincing a hundred overstimulated children to be quiet so they wouldn't scare the Boxy Ox, that was real acting. If the whole thing were not so strange and terrible, she suspected she might even be enjoying this little trick – corporate folk were such easy yet somehow satisfying targets. 'So I just thought, do you know, if I were nearer . . .'

'So you left the Great White North and came all the way down here to the Big Easy,' Landreaux said cheerfully. 'Well, *laissez les bontemps roulez*, as we say.' He leaned over, mock-conspiratorial. 'But not during working hours, of course.'

She tried to look duly impressed by his informality. 'Of course not, sir. I am a hard worker.'

'I'm sure you are. Well, everything's in order, so I guess it's my pleasant job to welcome you to the J Corporation family.' He extended his hand without standing, making her lean forward to shake it. 'Your shift supervisor is Maria. You'll find her in Building Twelve down on the esplanade. Go see her now. Are you ready to start tonight?'

'Yes, sir. Thank you very much, sir.'

He had already begun to lose interest, and was just turning back to his wallscreen when his attention snagged on the patch of white high on her neck. 'You know, I was meaning to ask you,' he said with deceptive lightness that did not lull her one little bit. 'About that bandage on your neck. You don't have a health problem you haven't told us about, do you, Ms. Chotilo?'

Caught a little off-balance by hearing Aleksandr's last name after all these years, even though she herself had chosen it as an alias she could remember, it took her a moment to reorient. 'Oh, this?' She touched the adhesive strip covering her t-jack. 'I had a mole removed. That's all right, isn't it? It wasn't cancerous or anything, I . . . I just didn't like it.'

He laughed and waved his hand. 'Just trying to make sure nobody's signing up with us just to get our medical insurance.' His face went through another little shift; the slightly ominous flicker came back. 'See, we don't like to be tricked, Olga. J Corporation is a family, but a family has to protect itself. It can be an unpleasant world out there.'

Out there, she guessed, meant anything more than five kilometers from the black tower. 'Oh, I know, Mr Landreaux,' she assured him. 'Full of bad people.'

'Right you are,' he said absently, his thoughts already

back on the day ahead of him, the little tricks and traps and bumps of mid-level management.

Olga stood. His back was to her as she scuttled out.

As she walked across the plaza outside the corporation's orientation center, heading across the esplanade, she made a conscious effort not to look up at the black tower looming on the far side of the water. It was hard not to feel she was being watched, although it seemed like a lot of effort to expend on the newest employee of a staff of thousands. And why wouldn't a new employee look up at the tower, the corporate symbol?

Still, she just didn't want to, not until she was actually on the boat. She was beginning to feel superstitious about it, as if relaxing herself to that point would automatically draw a heavy hand to her shoulder, the corporate security people wanting to do more this time than ask a few harmless questions.

Building Twelve was a hangar built right out onto the pier. The massive hovercrafts that carried maintenance and custodial workers to and from the island lay at anchor, bumping against each other on the gentle swell. Inside the hangar was an entire complex – supply warehouses and changing rooms, currently filled with the echoing chatter of hundreds of voices, since one of the custodial shifts had just come back from the island.

Maria proved to be an immense and not particularly patient woman, her hair dyed a once-stylish polychrome silver, her black roots badly in need of a touch-up.

'Oh, Lord, another one,' she said when Olga approached her. 'Don't those pocket-jockeys over in Orientation know I got no time to teach anyone this week?' She gave Olga a look that suggested the new recruit would be doing the best thing for all concerned if she simply drowned herself in Lake Borgne immediately. 'Esther? Where the hell are you? You take this new one, find her a uniform, tell her what to do. See if there's a badge for her on the fabricator thing. And if she gets in trouble, does something stupid, it's your ass, seen?'

Esther was a thin Hispanic woman close to Olga's own age, girlish in a tired way, with a kind, shy smile. She helped Olga find a gray two-piece uniform in the right size from a rack that would have stretched from wingtip to wingtip on a Skywalker jet, then led her past a series of bored functionaries until Olga had secured both her badge and a locker in one of the changing rooms. The place was like a boarding school for students with bad feet and aching joints, hundreds of black and brown women, as well as a few dozen European types like Olga, with English a second language for almost all.

As she changed, listening to the women shouting jokes across the humid locker room, Olga could almost believe for a moment that this was really her life, that the years on the net had never happened.

'Hurry up, now,' Esther told her. 'The boat leaves in five minutes.'

Olga studied her own blank face on the badge, tilting it to see her hologrammed profile. *I look like an old woman*, she thought. *God, I am an old woman. What do I think I'm doing with all this?* She picked up her backpack, popped the locker closed, and realized she would probably never see those clothes again. *Maybe I should have cut out the labels, like in that mystery I saw.* Of course, if she had really planned to be a woman with no past, she should probably be infiltrating a corporation that didn't already have her face and real name tucked away somewhere in its vast complex of personnel files.

She tucked the pack under her arm and fell into the swirl of grayclad women moving toward the dock.

In this strangest month of Olga's life, the meeting with Catur Ramsey had definitely been near the top of the list. It had been odd enough to pull off the road near Slidell into the picnic area and see him sitting on a bench – the same young man who, it seemed, had been at her own door for the first time only days ago, thousands of miles away in another country. He had hugged her, which was another unusual twist. Since when did lawyers hug people? Even a nice one like Ramsey?

Then, when the big blond man had stepped out of the parked van, she had experienced a moment of sinking fear and something worse. He had the look of a police officer, and for as long as it took him to cross the ten paces to the table she had been horribly certain that Ramsey had sold her out – for her own good, he would have deemed it, but no less a betrayal for that. But instead the man had only extended his hand, introducing himself as Major Michael Sorensen, then walked back to the car.

As if reading her mind, Ramsey had told her, 'Hold on – it's going to get weirder.' And when she saw the person Sorensen was lifting out of the van, Olga had to admit he had been right.

They had spent an hour talking while traffic rumbled past just on the other side of the trees, but Olga could remember little of it now. The shriveled man Sellars had spoken so quietly and carefully that at first Olga had taken offense a little, thinking she was being given the gentle treatment reserved for the pathetically unbalanced. After a while she came to realize it was just his way, and that this achingly thin man with runneled skin could not have taken a deep enough breath to speak loudly even if he

had wanted to. And when she actually heard what he had
to say, it kindled a spark of something like joyful relief
inside her. She had not realized until then just how lonely
she had become.

'I'm still not certain why you have experienced these
things, Ms Pirofsky,' he had told her, 'but whatever the
cause, they are real. If I had all day, I could not tell you
of all the strangeness I have encountered since I first
began studying these matters. Whatever the source of your
voices, it couldn't be a coincidence that you have been
drawn to Jongleur's tower. We only wish to combine forces
with you – to give you the best chance of getting answers
safely, answers that we may need ourselves to put an end
to a terrible, criminal conspiracy.'

The conspiracy itself, at least in Sellars' hurried explanation, had quite boggled her. And other than the fact
that he was some kind of military security specialist, she
had never quite managed to understand the major's place
in this tiny resistance movement – bizarrely, he had even
mentioned a wife and children waiting at some motel.
She was also still a little unsure how much Ramsey was
involved, whether he had known any of these things when
he had first interviewed her, but the mere fact that instead
of receiving patronizing looks she was finally getting
answers had made up for any residual confusion.

Sorensen, in a gruff but careful way that reminded her
of her own long-dead father, had inspected the tiny store
of possessions she planned to take to the island, and added
one more item – a small silver ring with a single clear
stone. The sparkling stone was not a gem at all, he had
explained, but a lens with a tiny transponder hidden
behind it. A camera ring.

'With this, we will see what you see, Ms Pirofsky,'
Sellars told her.

Returned to companionable humanity after what she realized had been weeks of self-absorption and voluntary exile, a solitude made even more fierce when the voices of the children deserted her, Olga would have gladly stayed longer with Ramsey and the others, but Sellars had told her that time was running short. In his gentle way, he had pushed her to begin her incursion as quickly as possible, and since he had promised to find her a way in, using his unspecified talents to somehow get her onto the island legitimately, she had no desire to argue.

And he had been as good as his word.

Once she was on the hovercraft, out in the hot, damp breeze of the foredeck with all the others, Olga could no longer avoid staring at the black tower. From the far shore it had looked something like a medieval cathedral, a jutting spire looming above more human-sized dwellings, but as it grew into the sunset-streaked sky before her it seemed more like the mountain of her dreams, a weird monolith of black stone, parts of its facade tortured and twisted in the modernist style, as intricately grooved as Sellars' odd face.

It seems like it's been waiting for me a long time – my whole life. But how could that be, when I only heard the voices for the first time a few weeks ago? Still, she could not shake off the feeling that she was on the brink of some long-sought revelation.

It's what I thought before – it's like catching fire with some religion. You just know things, you're sure of things, it doesn't matter how or why or what anyone says.

But most religions promised salvation. She expected nothing so cheerful from the black spire.

They docked in at another huge warehouse building, so

close to the tower that half the sky seemed to be black. It was not that the thing was so staggeringly tall – although she could not believe it was less than a thousand feet – but that its size and solidity were so overwhelming. Seeing it in the far distance or through the bayou mists had not prepared her for its disconcerting presence.

It's not an office, it's a fortress, she realized. *Whoever made this was at war, or planned to be. Maybe not against armies, but against something.*

She could not help remembering the architectural remains that had sparked so many lectures from her father as the circus troupe criss-crossed Europe – the remains of this or that triumphalist regime, communist or fascist, unboundedly capitalist or unashamedly imperial. Those buildings too had screamed their importance, but there had been something different in all of them, some quality of public-ness that the J Corporation tower lacked. Despite the difference in size, the only thing she could think of that came close were some of the Renaissance tower-houses of Italy, fortified islands in the middle of cities, designed for defense over glamour.

I've never seen a multibillion dollar office building that so clearly said, 'Go away,' she thought. *And I am ignoring the warning – like whistling past the sign that says, 'Abandon Hope All Ye Who Enter Here.' What are you doing, Olga?*

But she already knew the answer.

Esther found her standing quietly in a corner, trying to work up the courage to follow the rest of the chattering workers into the massive outbuilding that housed the entrances to the skyscraper's service corridors and elevators. 'C'mon, sweetie,' she said, patting Olga's arm and making her jump, 'they started the countdown when your badge went through that door back there, coming off the boat. More than ten minutes to get to our station and you lose half an hour's pay.'

Olga mumbled an apology and fell into step behind Esther. She was feeling extraordinarily reluctant to enter the huge black edifice, its polished surfaces gleaming with reflected sunset.

'Oh, no, why you got that backpack?'

Olga tried to look surprised. 'What's wrong?'

'You're not supposed to bring nothing like that over here,' Esther said. 'I guess 'cause they think we might steal or something.' She made an amused expression of disgust. 'But they are real strict about that. Oh, sweetie, you should have asked me, I would have told you to leave it in your locker back on the esplanade.'

'I didn't know. It's just my lunch and some medicine I'm taking.'

'They have a regulation box you bring lunch in, they run them all through some x-ray or something when the boat comes in.' Esther frowned. 'Well, we'll find some place to leave it. You don't want to get in trouble your first day.'

Olga shook her head. No, she certainly didn't want to get in trouble her first day, but she didn't plan to be separated from her bag, either. Under quick inspection the contents looked innocent enough, but anything more thorough and she would be attracting a lot more attention than the average custodial employee.

Her bag safely stowed in one of the cubbyholes provided for the custodians to stash rainwear and other items impractical to carry around the offices, Olga was introduced to her first day (and last, she fervently hoped) as a J Corporation cleaner. Esther, Olga, and a team of six other women were given B Level by the on-site supervisor, two

floors below the street. It was mildly disturbing to think
that they were working in a big tube down below the
surface of the lake, but any tendency to dwell on that, or
on the much more immediately dangerous things she
planned, was quickly overwhelmed by the sheer volume
of work. Stepping carefully over the hubcap-sized vacuum-
ing robots, they moved from office to office dumping
wastebaskets, cleaning surfaces, and tidying the common
areas. The bathrooms took special attention, all fixtures to
be scrubbed. As the newest worker onshift, Olga was gifted
with the least pleasant tasks, which of course included
cleaning the toilets and urinals with a brush and a spray
bottle of some enzymatic cleaner whose floral overtones
could not cover up the more disturbing chemical whiff
underneath. Esther warned her sternly about not spilling
any. What she had thought was an admonition to thrift
became clearer when she dripped some on the back of her
hand and felt her skin burn.

B Level was wider than the aboveground tower and
held hundreds of offices. As the night crept by in a cloud
of fumes, underscored by the off-key singing of a couple
of the other women and the constant sucking and chewing noises of the gray vacuum-bots, Olga realized how
lucky she had been that her little fantasy of actually doing
such a job for a living had not been true.

How can they stand it? she wondered. *With the supervisors watching so closely, like strict teachers, and some
of them won't even let you talk except in whispers. I
always thought that in a job like this you'd at least get
to chat and joke with fellow employees, but there hasn't
been much of that since we got off the boat. Is the company
really that stingy, frightened that these women are going
to waste a few minutes' worth of their wages?*

Her answer came when she paused for a moment to

lean on a desk near one of the restrooms and the wallscreen beside it leaped into life, activated by her touch. The screen displayed only a scene of someone's children sitting in a sailboat, a personal photo used as wallpaper, but within moments one of the on-site supervisors, a fat man named Leo with an unpleasant wheeze, was standing next to her.

'What are you doing?'

'Nothing. I . . . I just leaned on the desk. I didn't mean too . . .'

'Well, don't. Where's your badge?'

She showed it to him. He squinted, frowning as if angry at being forced to do what was presumably his job.

'First day, is it?' he said. He did not sound much mollified. 'Then you learn a lesson, and learn it good. You don't touch *anything* except what you're cleaning. You want to keep this job, you pay attention. There are plenty more would be happy to make good money. Don't touch anything. Repeat that back.'

Stung, furious at this petty, rude man, Olga fought to keep an outward aspect of frightened subservience. 'I don't touch anything.'

'Right. Damn right.' He turned and waddled off, a pudgy protector of the laws of private property and corporate inviolability.

It was not until she was nearing the end of the shift, when luckier employees in the upper levels might be glimpsing a bit of dawn's light at the edges of the blackout-curtained windows, that Olga found a chance to be alone. With Esther's permission, she made her way to one of the restrooms they had not yet cleaned and seated herself in the farthest stall. Positive that there were eyes and perhaps ears following her every move, she

lowered her pants and underwear before sitting on the
toilet for the sake of appearances, and said a silent prayer
of gratitude that she did not have to talk out loud. She
subvocalized the code word Ramsey had given her. A
moment later, she heard his voice in her ear.

'Are you okay? We've been worrying about you.'

She tried not to laugh. *Just working like most normal
people have to do*, she thought, but said only, 'I'm fine.
There hasn't been a chance to call before now.'

'I'm connected to this node all the time, so don't hesitate
if anything comes up. Really, Olga, whenever you need
me.' There was a note of beseeching guilt in his voice she
hadn't heard before, as if he thought he had shoved her
into danger, when she herself had in fact been rushing
toward it.

'Why?' she asked, half-teasing. Once you got the knack
of subvocalizing it was quite easy, she decided, as long
as something didn't startle you into speaking aloud. 'If I
get in bad trouble, are you people going to come get me
out of it?'

Ramsey's pause was painful. 'Sellars has been waiting
to talk to you,' he said at last. 'But don't go off when
he's done – I want another word.'

The old man's breathy voice was unexpectedly soothing. Whatever else he might be, this Sellars person was
clearly no stranger to such unusual situations. 'Hello,
Ms Pirofsky,' he said. 'We're all very glad to hear from
you.'

'I think you should probably call me Olga. Since I'm
sitting here with my pants around my ankles, pretending to go to the bathroom, "Ms Pirofsky" seems a bit
formal.'

She could hear the smile in his voice. 'Very well,
Olga. It's a pleasure to talk to you again, whatever the

circumstances. Did you have any problems with the hiring interview?'

'I don't think so. It all went very smoothly. How did you arrange all that?'

'We'd better save the details. Were you able to get your bag in with you?'

'Yes. I don't have it right this moment, but I can get it again, I'm pretty sure.'

'Call me when the shift's over, and when you have it. We'd better not keep you in there too long, so I'll save the rest of what I have to say until then. Oh, except for one very important thing. Can you hold your badge up near the jack on your neck? Just uncover it for a moment – if you think you're being watched, try to make it look like you're cleaning the spot under the bandage. I think I can pick up the encoding that way.' When she had done it to his satisfaction, he said, 'Good. Thanks. Now Mr Ramsey wants to talk to you.'

A second later Ramsey's voice was in her ear again 'Olga? I just wanted to say, be careful, okay?'

Now she did laugh, but there was real pleasure in it. 'All right, sonny. And you dress warmly and eat your vegetables.'

'I'm sorry – Olga, what exactly . . . ?' he was saying as she rang off, still grinning.

She was more physically tired than she had been in months when the shift came to an end, staggering after ten hours on her feet. Friday night had crept round to Saturday morning, although only the chronometers on the wall testified to that, sunk as she was in the sunless depths of the building. She could almost sense the massive mountain of plasteel and fibramic above her, separating her from the day's light, as though she were lost in some underground cavern of dungeon.

And the real work begins now, she thought. *God, I just want to sleep.*

She made weary chitchat with Esther and the other as they put away their cleaning supplies and began the march back to the dock. Then, heart beating fast now, frightened and also full of weird, unexpected exhilaration, she pulled up short.

'Oh, no!'

Esther turned. There were circles under her eyes, and Olga found herself for the first time wondering what the other woman went home to. A loving family and a kind husband? Or at least something a little better than this numbing labor in Pharaoh's mines? She hoped so. 'What is it, sweetie? You look like you see a ghost.'

'My backpack! I forgot my backpack!'

Esther shook her head. 'I told you you shouldn't have brought it. It's okay – you get it on Monday when we come back.'

'I can't. It's got my medicine in it. I have to take my medicine.' She took a step backward, putting up her hand to wave the other woman off, praying that fatigue would keep her from volunteering to accompany her back. 'I'll go get it. I'll be right back. You go ahead.'

'The boat leaves in a few minutes . . .'

'I'll run. If I miss you on the boat, have a good weekend!' Then, feeling surprisingly sincere, she added, 'Thanks for all your help!' before she turned and began breasting the tide of gray-clad workers, until Esther and her worried exhortations were out of sight and earshot. *Now I have to hope she won't look for me on that crowded boat, or after it docks, at least not very hard.* She had planted a seed earlier, saying she would have to be picked up by her daughter still in her work clothes because of a medical appointment. *And if Sellars did what he promised with that information off the badge, it will look like I got on the boat and then got off on the far end. Which will give me, what – until Monday evening, if I'm lucky?*

Two and a half days to discover the heart of the beast. It seemed so long. It seemed so brief.

The big room with the cubbyholes was empty except for a single male janitor swabbing the floor with a mop and a bucket. She nodded to him and took her backpack, then walked back in the direction of the hovercraft landing, but instead made a turn into one of the stairwells and climbed back down to B Level, which was now comparatively familiar ground. She knew that Sellars and Major Sorensen had arranged some tricks with the security cameras, but she knew they could do nothing if she ran into any flesh and blood company management, so she moved quickly to her planned destination, a utility closet off one of the maintenance corridors. After testing to make sure she could open it again from the inside, she pulled the door shut behind her and slumped on the floor, in the dark. Her heart was beating very fast and she was trembling.

When she had recovered a bit, she spoke the code again and Ramsey's voice was in her ear, reassuringly familiar in the midst of so much that was strange.

'Olga? How are things going?'

'Pretty well, as long as my supervisor doesn't look for me too hard on the boat. But the poor woman looked ready to drop. This is hard work, you know. All my joints are aching, and my hands are cracked – just from one day!'

'I'll give my cleaning lady a much bigger bonus this year, I promise,' Ramsey said, but he could not pull off the joking tone very convincingly. *So serious*, Olga thought, *Even if it really is the end of the world, so serious.*

'You should have been born a Jew, like me,' she said. 'You learn how to deal with these things.'

The pause was deafening. 'I have no idea what you mean, Olga. You have completely stumped me. But I'm glad you're safe. And I'm proud of you. Sellars wants to talk to you.'

'Hello, Olga,' the old man said. 'I echo Mr Ramsey's sentiments. I may not have much time to talk, so I'm going to give you as much as I can now. Don't write anything down, just in case someone grabs you.'

'Don't worry,' she said, sitting in the dark, talking silently to people who might as well be on another planet. 'I don't have the strength to lift even a pencil right now.'

'You'll need at least enough to lift what's in that backpack of yours. Will you get that now?'

'The package?'

'That's right.'

She fumbled in the backpack until she found her flashlight, then took out and carefully piled the military rations Ramsey – or really Sorensen, she supposed – had provided, several days worth of food that took up less space than an ordinary box lunch. There was also a bottle of water, which seemed a bit redundant in a building that probably contained a thousand drinking fountains. At the bottom of the pack she found the wrapped box bearing the label of a common thyroid medicine and a note in Olga's own hand that said, 'Two after each meal.'

'I found it.'

'Just open it please. I need to perform a little test.'

She unwrapped the box carefully so she could return it to its innocent appearance afterward, and drew out a slim gray rectangle the size of her palm. It was oddly heavy and she viewed it with some distrust. 'I have it.'

'Just tell me what happens,' Sellars said in his soft voice. A moment later a tiny red light sparked on the side.

'A red light turned on.'

'Good. Just needed to be sure. You can wrap it back up and put it away now, Olga.'

She was still troubled as she returned it to the depths of the backpack, along with the rations, and pushed her sweater back on top of them. 'Is that thing . . . is it a bomb?' she asked at last.

'A bomb? Goodness, no.' Sellars sounded quite astonished. 'No, we don't want to destroy anybody's system – we have friends alive in there. It would be like putting a bomb on a house where someone's being held hostage. No, Olga, that's what used to be called a vampire tap – a special sort of information shunt that the major helped me obtain. If we do find what we're looking for, I suspect that I'm going to need to send and receive at much faster speed than what I'm using now if I'm going to accomplish anything.'

'I feel better.'

'Now the water bottle – that *is* a bomb.' He chuckled, a soft hooting noise. 'But a very small one, just to make smoke. As a diversion. Goodness, I almost forgot to tell you.'

I've stepped out of reality, Olga decided. *I thought the dream-children were crazy? This is crazier still.*

'All right,' Sellars said, 'listen carefully and I'll explain what you should do next. We have less than three days before they begin to figure out something's wrong – that's if everything goes perfectly. There are still people in that building and you shouldn't let any of them see you from this moment on. I'll do my best to help you with the surveillance, but even so, this will be more difficult than you can possibly imagine, and in all honesty probably hopeless. But we have no other choice.'

Olga considered. 'Now you I could believe were Jewish, Mr Sellars.'

'I'm afraid I don't follow you.'

'Never mind.' She sighed and stretched her aching legs as far as the tiny closet would allow. 'Go ahead – I'm listening.'

CHAPTER 24

Getting out of Dodge

NETFEED/BUSINESS: Bad Year for Executives
(visual: Dedoblanco funeral, Bangkok, Thailand)
VO: The death of Krittapong Electronics' Ymona Dedoblanco pointed up once again that it has been a bad year for business executives. Several moguls, perhaps the richest and certainly the most famous being Chinese financier Jiun Bhao, have died during the last few months. Little has been seen of several others, including Felix Jongleur, the aged Franco-American entrepreneur, who seldom leaves his Louisiana compound.
(visual: business journalist She-Ra Mottram)
MOTTRAM: 'Yes, there have been several significant losses in the business community, and it's made the markets a bit shaky. Of course, most of these people were extremely old. That's why it's ironic that two of the oldest, Jongleur and Robert Wells, are still alive and kicking. They must get a certain pleasure out of seeing their younger rivals dropping by the wayside . . .'

PAUL stared at the lithe, dark man trussed on the floor of the cavern. The prisoner stared back, eyes narrowed as though he were a dog about to bite; Paul had no doubt that, given the chance, he would indeed cheerfully rip out their throats. 'A thousand more? What do you mean?'

Bat Masterson shoved the prisoner with the toe of his boot, earning a look of even more tightly focused hatred. 'Just as I said, friend. When they came down on us, we thought they were an ordinary war party of Comanche or Cheyenne. We didn't have much chance to get acquainted, though – we were too busy getting killed – so we only noticed after a while that they all look just the same. It's a ticklish mystery, sure enough. I reckon it's some tribe that's been inbreeding too long.' But he did not look confident in his solution.

'They're devils,' the mustached man who had been guarding Dread suggested. 'Simple as can be. Ground opened up. Hell busted out.'

'But, shit, Dave why would hell be full of octoroons?' Masterson tugged at his mustache. 'Oh. Begging your pardon, ladies.'

Martine, for one, was paying little attention to what was being said. 'It is Dread,' she murmured dreamily, 'but also it is less. I can feel that now. He has copied himself somehow – used something as a framework, perhaps one of the Indian tribes, then replicated himself.'

'Ma'am,' Masterson told her, 'I have to say that I can't figure out what in blazes you're talking about. Have you met these fellows before?'

Paul shrugged, tried to think of something to say. 'Not really. It's hard to explain.'

'Met him, yeah,' T4b said. 'Sixed him, too,' he added unhelpfully.

As Masterson stood perplexed, scratching his head beneath the plug hat, Paul put his hand on Martine's shoulder. They needed to do something, it was clear, but it was pointless trying to explain the devolution of the network to the sims who lived in it. 'Now what?'

'Even if a million of these waited for us,' she said softly, 'we would still have to make our way past them. We have no other way out of here.' She turned to Masterson. 'Can you lead us to Dodge City? Or at least tell us something of what to expect? We do not want to go there, but we have no choice.'

'If'n you folks just want to get killed,' the man named Dave offered, 'you all oughta just walk off the cliff yonder. Be quicker and a lot cleaner.'

'Mysterious Dave doesn't talk much,' Masterson said with a sour smile, 'but when he does, it's usually to a purpose. He's right. You go down there, you'll all die. No question about it. No, you stay here with us and stay alive – we could use a few more hands.'

'We can't,' said Paul, wishing fervently that it were otherwise. He'd heard enough about Dread to thoroughly terrify him, a monster as bad as Finney and Mudd, but with brains. The idea of a thousand of them, waiting . . . 'We can't. God, I wish we could stay. But we have to go.'

'But why, blast it?' Masterson almost shouted. 'Where are you from? And more importantly, didn't your mothers have any children with brains?'

Florimel, who had been watching the Dread sim with a mixture of horror and disgust, finally spoke up. 'We cannot stay. We have a need to go to your Dodge City. It cannot be explained any more than that.'

'It's . . . it's religious, I guess you could say,' Paul said, reaching desperately. 'We've sworn an oath.'

Masterson fell silent for a moment, eyeing them all. 'I suppose I should have known, seeing those queer outfits you're wearing. But it's still a bad bargain all around. We lose your help, you lose your lives.' He spat in disgust, missing the snarling face of Dread only by mischance.

'Can you tell us the best way to reach the place?'

Martine asked. 'We do not know these mountains, and we don't want to meet any more of the monsters who caught us before.'

'You'll find that this fellow's kin are worse than any jackalos,' Masterson growled. 'As far as finding your way down into that hellhole . . .'

'I'll take 'em as far as the river,' a voice said.

Paul turned to see the black man named Titus, who had been leaning on the cavern wall listening. 'Thank you. That's very kind.'

'See if you feel that way when they're taking your scalp off,' said Titus. 'I think you're fools, but I got me another long patrol to do so I might as well keep you out of trouble until you're closer. But it'll have to wait until dark.'

Masterson had walked a short distance across the cavern; he returned with the pistol Paul had carried earlier. 'Take this,' he said. 'It's reloaded. I hate like sin to see it lost and the bullets wasted, but I've got a Christian duty of sorts, I guess.'

Paul stared at the ivory handle and dark steel barrel as though it were a snake. 'I said I didn't want to carry it anymore. Besides, if there are a thousand of them, what good will six bullets do me?'

Masterson shoved it into his hands and leaned close to Paul's ear. 'I thought you had at least a little sense, friend. You think I'm going to let you take women down into that place without a gun to do the honorable thing? Do you think when they catch you they're just going to kill you?'

Paul could only swallow what felt like a stone in his throat and accept the gun.

Only a few people saw them off. The rest of the refugees

seemed to have decided that there was not much point in wasting time on a group of doomed fanatics. Of the half-dozen who stood at the cavern's outer edge, only Annie Ladue seemed genuinely sad.

'I can't believe you're going off to . . . that you're going off without even taking a meal with us.'

Paul frowned. How to explain that they needed no food and could not afford to waste time eating? All this prevarication, not being able to tell people the truth about their own existences . . . It was something like being a god among mortals, but he doubted most gods ever felt so miserable. 'It's our religion,' he said, by way of an explanation.

Annie shook her head. 'Well, I'm not the most Christian woman you'll meet, I suppose, but Godspeed to you all.' She turned abruptly and walked back inside.

'I'll not offer you my hand,' Masterson said. 'I can't abide such foolishness as this. But I will echo what Annie said, and add "good luck." I can't imagine where anyone could find that much luck, though. Titus, make sure you at least come back safely.'

'What . . . what are you going to do with the prisoner?' Paul asked.

'Let's put it this way,' said Masterson, 'in consideration of tender sensibilities. We're not going to be giving him a testimonial dinner. But it'll be a lot quicker than what you'll get down in Dodge if his kinfolk catch hold of you.' He nodded his head, tipped his hat to Martine and Florimel, and led the rest of the silent farewell party back into the cavern.

'Well, on that cheerful note,' Titus said, 'I reckon we should get going. Y'all follow me close and quiet. If I hold my hand up like this, just stop – don't say nothing, just stop. Got me?'

The river was already hidden in shadow below them as they set off, and evening shadows ran purple down the far mountains. Bringing up the rear, Paul could barely see his companions, although the nearest was only a few meters in front of him.

How many worlds? he wondered. *How many worlds are falling under shadow right now?*

It was not a question he could ponder very long or very thoroughly while making his way down the steep mountain slope, a thousand feet or more above the river valley.

Even with the confident Titus leading the way, they did not make very fast time. Florimel's bad leg slowed them, and T4b did not seem to like heights anywhere near so much when he wasn't imagining himself playing a familiar game. Almost half the night passed before they felt the moisture of the river in the air, although they had heard its thrashing roar for some time.

Titus was sparing of conversation, but during their stops for rest he told them a little of his life, of his childhood in Maryland as the son of a freed slave and his own escape westward. He had spent much of his adulthood as a trail hand – Paul had never known that there were black cowboys, but Titus said there were thousands like him all over the southwest. He had been riding herd on a shipment of shorthorns that had come up from Texas to the Dodge City railhead, and was in town spending his pay on the night the earth began to move.

'The most frightening thing I ever saw.' He was almost invisible in the moonlight, but his pale, crooked teeth showed for a moment as he put a wad of tobacco into his mouth. 'Worse than all those hundreds of same-looking fellows on horseback that came later, screaming and hollering. Everything was shaking, then the land just folded up – at first I thought we were sinking into the middle of the Earth, then I saw that it was mountains growing right up out of the ground all around us, shooting up like a canebrake. I thought it was Judgment Day, like my mama taught me. Maybe it was. Maybe this is the End of Days. Lots of others think so.'

And for them it is, Paul thought. *But when they're all dead, will they rise again and start over like the Looking Glass people? Or has Dread frozen this simulation in permanent decay?*

Titus was right – the mountains had simply sprouted from the ground like weeds. As they neared the valley floor they found no foot-hills, no gentling of the slope, only a jumble of boulders and scree around the mountains' roots. This was the most difficult part of the journey so far, every step threatening to set off a landslide, so although he was aware of the glow for some time, it wasn't until they were actually standing on the muddy flats beside the river that Paul saw the fires of Dodge City.

'Great God,' Florimel said quietly. 'What have they done?'

'What they'll do to you,' Titus whispered. 'And to me, too, so shut up!'

He beckoned them into a hollow where a cluster of boulders had tumbled free of the mountainside and stood piled like a giant pawnbroker's sign. From this pathetic hiding place they could look out across the river and the narrow valley to a huge bonfire in the main street that blotted the stars with its massive plume of smoke, as well as countless lesser blazes running along the roofs of Dodge City like Christmas tinsel. Shadows leaped and twirled through the stark, red-lighted streets; even from the far side of the river, they could hear screams.

'It's burning down,' Paul whispered.

'Naw. Been like that since those devil-men took it,' said Titus. 'Burns and burns, but it doesn't never burn down.' He shook his head slowly. 'The End of Days.'

'So where are we going, exactly?' Paul quietly asked Martine. He could feel his own heart hammering, and could see that Florimel and T4b were no less disturbed at the idea of walking into such a terrible place.

'I don't know. Let me have a quiet moment to think.' She got up and crawled a few meters away, putting one of the massive boulders between herself and her companions.

'Hate to spoil things,' Titus said, 'but it's time for this mother's son to be moving on.'

'Just wait a moment longer,' Paul begged him. 'We may have more questions to ask you . . .'

The moment stretched into something longer, while Paul and the others watched the proof of Titus' words not a half-kilometer away, flames that burned and burned along the housetops and high false fronts but never consumed them, despite the apparent flimsiness of the buildings.

'It is no use,' Martine said, crawling back. 'I can make nothing of it – too many distractions, too much disruption. If Dread had set out deliberately to make things difficult for my senses, he could not have done better.'

'So where then?' Florimel demanded. 'Simply walk into that? It would be madness.'

'Just follow the river, us,' T4b suggested. 'Make a raft. Sail on out of this scan-palace.'

'Were you not listening?' Although her voice was low, Martine sounded as angry as Paul had ever heard her. 'There is no other way to the place we seek. If we follow the river to the far gateway, and we are not killed by something on the way, there is little chance the gate will be open and no guarantee it will not dump us somewhere worse. If we wish to reach Egypt we must find this nearer gateway.'

'Find we get sixed up true, ask me,' T4b muttered, but fell silent.

'Where are the places we have encountered these things before,' she said to Paul and Florimel. 'Mazes? Catacombs?'

'The mines?' Florimel suggested. 'There were mines on the mountainside.' She groaned. 'Great God, I do not think I can climb back up.'

'Cemeteries,' Paul said. 'Places of the dead. The Brotherhood's little joke.' He allowed himself a grim smile. 'Came back and bit them in the arse, too, didn't it?' He turned to Titus, who had been watching them with puzzled fascination. 'Is there a cemetery in the town?'

'Oh, yeah, just outside to the northwest. Over that way.' He pointed across the river, out toward the darkness to the left of the blazing town. 'Got some silly-ass name. Boot Hill, something like that.'

'Boot Hill,' Paul breathed. 'I've heard of it. Can we just cross the river and walk to it?' He looked at his companions. 'We won't even have to go into the town at all.'

'I got no idea what kind of nonsense you all plan to get up to, but I can tell you this – you're not getting to Boot Hill by going around Dodge that direction. When the mountains came up, the riverbanks broke up over there. It's a swamp now, and there are snakes as big around as a bedroll and long as a twenty-mule team, not to mention mosquitoes the size of hawks.' He shrugged. 'I know it doesn't make no earthly sense, snakes and jack-alos and whatnot just coming up out of the ground like that – why didn't anyone see one before? That's why I think it's Judgment.'

'We know about the snakes here,' said Paul. 'We met one. What about the other way around, east of the town?'

'Not too good of an idea. Just beyond town that way the Arkansas drops off just like that,' he tilted his long fingers steeply downward, '– a waterfall – and there's a canyon goes down so deep it's dark at the bottom even at high noon. Canyon stretches for miles that direction. Why do you think we're all living on that mountainside instead of getting the blazes away from here?' He stood up. 'You should have listened to Masterson when he told you to stay put. He's a good man, and has a lot more sense than most. Now I'm going to get moving. I don't like being this close to Dodge.'

'But wait,' Florimel said, a hint of panic in her voice. 'Do we just . . . walk across the bridge?'

'If you can't wait to lose your scalps, sure enough. There's a dozen or so of them devil-men sitting on it night and day. But if you'd like to draw the whole thing out a little longer, I suggest you wade across the river a few hundred feet this side of the bridge. The Arkansas is good and shallow this time of year, even with all this topsy-turvy.'

He threw them a mocking salute and then was gone into the darkness, silent as a bird flying.

'Everyone seems pretty damned certain we're going to be killed,' Paul said quietly.

'Everyone is probably right,' growled Florimel.

The Arkansas waters, though never more than waist-deep, had a distinctly sinister feel, warm and oily. The river even had a strange undertow which tugged steadily at the travelers despite the sluggishness of the current, like a street urchin who had found his intended mark and would not turn loose.

Paul found he did not want to think about the water much, not just because of the unpleasant feel, but because he found himself imagining the many different things that might be swimming toward them from the swamp Titus had described.

Far on their right along the riverbank, illuminated by another group of huge bonfires, stood a massive fenced enclosure that Paul guessed was some kind of yard for shipping cattle. Despite the late hour it seemed that branding was going on, although wordless but still distinctive shrieks made it clear the victims were not cows.

Not all the voices were raised in pain. As a chorus of shouts and laughs rolled out from the stockyard Paul saw Martine falter and almost fall into the water. He grabbed her arm to brace her.

'To hear his voice again,' she whispered, eyes squeezed tightly shut as if she could somehow make herself deaf by increasing her blindness. 'To hear it multiplied, echoed over and over on all sides . . .'

'It's just a trick. Like you said, they're just crude copies. He's not really here.' But was that true, he wondered, or wishful thinking? Perhaps Dodge had a new sheriff.

A dozen meters from the bank, Martine grabbed Paul's arm again. For a moment he thought that the situation had finally become too much for her, but though her face showed strain, she was alert, listening, scanning.

'Titus was right,' she hissed. 'There are men on the bridge.'

'That's why we're here,' Paul said, but he waved for T4b and Florimel to stop.

'But there are men on the other side of the river, too,' she said. 'Not close enough for us to hear them, but I can sense them. If we come up out of the river we'll be right in their laps.'

'So what should we do?' Paul was fighting to keep a handle on his own desperation. Cries of misery and terror floated through the valley, echoing dimly in the mountainsides. 'We can't go back!'

'Turn west,' Martine said decisively. 'Stay in the river. Go under the bridge. We'll be closer to the side of town we want – we will not have to cross so much open ground.'

'You said there are men on the bridge!' Florimel whispered, leaning in close. 'What if they hear us?'

'We have no other choice,' Martine told her, but still no one moved. Paul could feel the moment hanging and knew that, surprisingly, the others were waiting for him to decide. He turned and began wading toward the bridge.

As they drew closer he could see shadowy human shapes atop the span, silhouetted by the numerous fires, but to Paul's relief they were down at the end nearer the town. He moved out toward midstream and into a deep spot where the oily water again streamed just beneath his chest and even higher on the two women. The wooden bridge was wide and low, but there was plenty of room beneath for them to pass. As Paul moved under it the darkness enfolded him like a fist.

Before he had gone halfway he heard loud footsteps above him. He froze, hoping the others would do the same even though they couldn't see him. The bridge creaked as more men joined the first. Paul cursed silently: the footsteps seemed to be right overhead. Had they been spotted? Maybe the Dread-replicas were just waiting until they emerged from the bridge's shadow to shoot them like fish in a shallow pond.

Even as he stood, his pulse beating so hard in his temple it felt like someone was tapping his head, he heard a muffled splash a few meters away, then a wash of current. An invisible something was in the water with them – one of the men climbing down from the bridge to investigate? Paul pulled the gun out of the inner pocket of his jump-suit and held it high above the level of the water, afraid to shoot but terrified at the thought of a wrestling match with anyone as wiry and strong as the man they had seen in the cave.

'What . . . ?' Florimel whispered, but never finished her question. Something thundered from above, an explosion so sudden and loud that for a moment Paul thought he had pulled his own gun's trigger by accident. The shot was still echoing in his ears when something big and solid smashed into him. He was thrown sideways off his feet; if he had not been flung into one of his companions, he would have gone under the water, gun and all. The men above were shouting and laughing, which covered the noises of terror from Paul's friends as they realized that something huge was in the water with them, thrashing violently.

'Snake!' Martine hissed, sounding serpentine herself in her fright. T4b let out a muffled screech as a flailing, muscular tail knocked him over. Paul flailed through the water until he found the struggling youth, then got a grip on his arm. Florimel grabbed him, too, and together they yanked him back to the surface, bubbling and sobbing.

'Don't move!' Martine whispered. 'Quiet!'

T4b might have wanted to argue, but he was too busy spewing river water. Florimel held him. The serpent was still thrashing the waters near them, but was moving away, as though it had struck them in a panic rather than by intent. When it fought its way out into the light on the east side of the bridge, Paul's skin crawled. The thing which had scraped against him was almost the size of the ore-train monster that had chased them down the mountain.

A dozen more shots thundered down, making the water hiss all around the huge tube of the snake's body. The men on the bridge were shrieking with joyful bloodlust.

'For God's sake,' Martine said, 'now, now!'

As she sloshed away, Paul grabbed T4b again and helped Florimel drag him toward the west side of the bridge. Behind them the wounded snake had beaten the waters to a fire-lit froth. The men jumped around on the bridge overhead as though they were dancing, firing shot after shot into the river and the dying reptile.

Despite a midnight hot as an oven, Paul was shivering when they dragged themselves up onto the riverbank, deep in the shadows a hundred meters west of the bridge. He and his companions lay in the mud for several minutes, panting. They could still hear the party on the bridge, although the gunshots now came infrequently.

As they forced themselves to rise and move up the bank the other noises of the town reasserted themselves, screams and cries that sounded barely human, tearful pleading, more of the shouting and devilish laughter of the town's destroyers. But to Paul's amazement there was also music, something he knew he should recognize, a classical melody played on a tinny piano that yawed in and out of rhythm, as though someone were staging the torture and slaughter like a pageant and had commissioned the most incongruous soundtrack they could imagine.

Wanting to know as little as possible about what was going on in Dodge City, Paul led the company farther to the west, despite Martine's headshake of warning, but he quickly discovered that Titus had been right: within moments they stumbled onto swampy ground, and into sucking mud up to their knees.

Florimel found herself in something even more treacherous. If T4b had not been just behind her, still making quiet hawking and spitting sounds from his own immersion, she would have been gone beneath the surface of the quicksand before Paul or Martine had noticed her absence. While Tb4 clutched her, Martine – who despite her blindness could clearly see in the dark better than the rest of them – found a stick to hold out to her. When they dragged her free, Florimel too was weeping.

'It is too much,' she said. 'I am not strong enough – I can barely walk on level ground.'

Paul turned to Martine. 'Okay. You were right, I was wrong. So where do we go?'

'I cannot say for certain – this place is very distorted to my senses – but the swamp comes right up next to this side of the town. We must stay among the buildings if we wish to avoid stumbling into more quicksand.'

Paul closed his eyes for a moment and took a deep breath. 'Right. Here we go.'

They cautiously retraced their steps to the place they had come out of the river. Front Street lay in front of them again, its buildings all in perpetual flame. A quarter of a mile away to the east a huge bonfire blazed in the middle of the street, between the main railroad line and its spur, and countless dark shapes reeled and whirled around it, celebrating a festival of destruction that had apparently been going on for days. But although most of those who had devastated the city seemed to be gathered there, dozens more staggered back and forth across the street at the end where Paul and his companions waited in the shadows, desperately hoping for some miracle that would allow them to make their way across the wide street unobserved.

Although all of Front Street's blazing buildings still

stood, some of the facades had collapsed, leaving the interiors open to the companions' horrified eyes like museum dioramas – and a strange, terrible museum it was. In the saloons, blank-eyed women with scorched legs danced on burning stages, wearily ducking the bottles and sharp objects being flung by whooping audiences of replicated Dreads. Men hung upside down from chandeliers with their throats cut, blood-drained like deer being readied for the smokehouse. Other bodies lay piled in the streets, although some had been propped against buildings or on benches in ghastly tableaux. The Dread-men reeled back and forth, drinking busthead whiskey out of jugs, some so drunk they crawled in the gutter barking like dogs or danced with vomit still streaking their mouths and chests.

It's not real, Paul tried to tell himself. *It's just like a netshow – not even that. These aren't even actors, just puppets.* But it was hard to make himself believe it when every smell and sound was so horrifyingly real, and especially when he knew the things around him could hurt him or even kill him.

Up the street, one of the Dreads rolled a barrel into the huge bonfire, then stood gaping as the ammunition inside began to explode. Within seconds the instigator was cut into bloody ribbons by flying lead, but others of his kind came running toward the fire, excited by the noise. Some went down in the hail of random bullets, but the others seemed to find the spectacle vastly amusing and formed a whooping circle around the fire.

Taking advantage of the distraction, Paul signaled the others forward, out into the open street. They loped silently to the railroad tracks that ran down the middle of Front Street, trying not to look too long at the mostly female corpses tied to the tracks. There was not in any case much left to see, since someone had run a locomotive back and forth over them several times before apparently tiring of the game and setting the locomotive itself on fire. The remains of the engine still stood on the tracks like the blackened skeleton of some huge sea creature, affording them a moment's shelter from any eyes which might look their way, but the stench of the mutilated bodies quickly drove them on.

They had almost crossed into the safety of the shadows beyond the end of the street when Martine suddenly slowed and clutched at Paul's arm. Although most of the Dread-men were now capering around the bonfire at the far end of the street, Paul and his companions were still in the open, exposed to any chance gaze, and his nerves were screaming, but Martine pushed at him insistently.

'Can't go this way,' she gasped. 'Head toward the cross street.'

He had learned his lesson. Without argument, even though it went against all his instincts, he turned and trotted a short way back up Front toward the center of the town before turning north into a side street beside a two-story building whose smoldering front still proudly proclaimed it 'Wright, Beverley and Co.' They had only just stepped off the main avenue when a group of riders came thundering around the corner from the direction where they had just been heading, a small troop of drunken Dread-men riding mutant horses, bellowing as they went past the shadowed cross street where Paul and the others pressed themselves back against the side of the building.

The music was louder in the side street, as though they stood near the speakers in a hellish amusement park, but there was something in the wobbly sound of it that made Paul want to turn away from it and brave the main thoroughfare again. His more logical side won out: he waved

for the others and they headed away from Front while
the noise of the piano rose and fell.

'Mozart,' Martine breathed. 'He told me he liked Mozart.'

Paul did not have to ask who she meant.

As they hurried up the side street, trying to stay in the
pockets of shadow, Paul at last saw the piano player. The
room in which he played might once have been the back
parlor of one of the saloons which faced out onto the
main street, a secluded nook where cowboys or gamblers
with money in their pockets could spend a little private
time with the town's professional women, but some explosion had taken out most of the wall, and privacy was in
any case clearly a thing of the past. The player was an
old black man, although his color now was much closer
to gray. He was surrounded by swaying duplicates of
Dread who were either too drunk to move much or were
actually attending to his warped rendition of Mozart. The
failings of the music became even more understandable
when Paul saw that the legless pianist had been tied to
his bench with barbed wire, and sat like a becalmed ship
in a spreading pool of his own blood.

Now it was Paul's turn to stumble, gagging, and to be
helped along by the others.

It took them long minutes to dodge from building to
building, the fires making their skin itch, their ears full
of the cries of the dying and those pleading for death –
an agonizingly extended walking tour through the inferno.
Paul had to fight to keep going. Every bit of sheltering
darkness seemed to offer an oasis of peace. Each open
space felt like it was watched by hundreds of eyes.

Thank God we came after they'd been at this for days,
he thought as he struggled to catch his breath in the smoldering, smoky depths of a livery stable. *Thank God those
Dread-clones have wallowed in this evil so long that they're*

almost senseless with it. He could not let himself think about the hundreds of Dodge City inhabitants whose misery had given him and his companions this chance.

They had crossed their second street and stood in a trembling huddle in a doorway across from the ruins of a newspaper office. A pile of what at first seemed to be some kind of animal skins lay in the dusty street. Paul had only just recognized them as the remains of more citizens – they had been run through the printing press until rolled bonelessly flat, and one unlucky victim even had a 'Dodge City Welcomes Visitors!' headline printed across his now greatly extended body – when Martine waved for silence. Since none of them had the breath to speak, it seemed a bit unnecessary.

'Over that way,' she said at last. 'It was just a moment, but I . . . I felt it.'

'Felt what?' Florimel's voice was flat with shock and fatigue.

'A gateway, I think.'

T4b stirred. 'Anywhere, gotta be better.'

They followed her along the gutted buildings and then west down Walnut Street. Behind them the Mozart was slowing like a gramophone in need of cranking. As they staggered out into the shadows west of the town, Paul saw that the moon was just now climbing above the peaks of the mountains, as if confused by the cataclysmic changes to its familiar plains.

'This way,' Martine panted.

It was such a relief not to be surrounded by burning walls that Paul could almost feel the darkness cover him like a cool, damp cloth. They made their way northwest along the edge of the swamp, squelching through the mud, slipping and sticking, but it seemed a thousand times preferable to what they had left behind. Even when a buzzing thing as large as a rat alighted on Martine's shoulder, making her shriek and fall to the ground, Paul felt the bargain was worthwhile. He plucked it off her with the nonchalance of complete, exhausted misery, and twisted it between his hands until it splintered, oozed, and died.

'There,' Florimel gasped as Paul helped Martine to stand. 'I think I see it!'

She was pointing at a pale, low protuberance a quarter mile away, burnished by moonlight until it seemed the top of a giant's buried skull. Despite their sagging weariness they broke into a trot across the slickly treacherous flats.

'*Fenfen!*' T4b cried out, his voice full of despair. For a moment Paul thought the youth had fallen, but when he turned he saw T4b was peering back at a cloud of small fires that had detached themselves from the greater burning that was Dodge City. 'Torches,' T4b moaned. 'Following us, like.'

Paul pulled the boy until they were both moving at a stumbling trot once more. 'Hurry!' he shouted to the others. 'Someone's seen us!'

The ground around Boot Hill was harder, drier, and when they reached it they broke into a sprint. Paul tripped and the earth seemed to leap up toward him, smacking him like a heavy hand, but now it was T4b who reached down and tugged Paul back onto his feet.

The graveyard on top of the hill was surprisingly small, a couple of dozen wooden crosses and a few modest stone markers littering the uneven ground. There were more rocks than monuments. Other than buffalo grass, the only object on the hilltop higher than Paul's waist was a slender ash tree with a noose dangling from a long branch – a hanging tree.

'Where is it?' Florimel asked. 'The gateway?'

Martine was pivoting slowly from side to side like a radar dish sweeping the skies. 'I . . . I cannot tell. It will not reveal itself to my command, and there seems nothing here large enough to contain it. A grave . . . ?'

'Want me to dig, tell me,' T4b said, bending to scratch at the nearest mound like a crazed dog. 'Need to get out now – for true!'

The torches were moving toward them with terrifying speed, and now Paul could see that the torchbearers were at least a dozen Dreadmen mounted on the strange black horses with hands. As the war party sped up the hill, not slowed in the least by the horses' bizarre gait, Paul felt himself sinking into apathy. He dragged Ben Thompson's pistol out of his pocket. It felt heavy as an anchor.

'Javier, be quiet!' Martine shouted from behind him. 'Let me think!'

Paul sank to one knee, trying to steady the gun. The first of the Dreads had reached the bottom of the slope. Paul did his best to aim, wishing for the only time in his life that he had been the kind of boy fascinated by weapons. He waited as long as he dared, sweating so that he could barely keep his finger on the trigger; then, when the rider was less than twenty meters away, he shot.

Whether from blind luck or some vestige of the original simulation favoring the human participant, his shot struck the ape-horse and sent it crashing to the ground. It must have rolled on its rider, for he did not rise after the horse had skidded to a leg-flailing stop. The other Dreadmen veered away sideways, taking a circular path around the base of the hill, screeching now with rage, or perhaps even with pleasure at the diversion. Many of them were armed with rifles and pistols; their guns cracked and bullets whined across the hilltop. Paul flung himself to

the ground. Florimel and T4b did the same. Martine did
not.

'What are you doing?' he screamed at her. 'Martine,
get down!'

'Of course,' she said as bullets whistled through the
grass at her feet. 'I should have seen it before.' She sprinted
for the tree. 'There would be no gallows on sacred ground,'
she shouted.

Terrified for her, Paul rose and began squeezing off
shots, hoping only to distract the attention of the circling
Dreads from such an easy target, but his luck had changed:
although he thought he saw one of the torch-wielding
shapes snap backward in the saddle, none of his other
bullets seemed to have any effect. He looked over his
shoulder and saw Martine reaching up to the hangman's
noose, pulling it with her fingers as though readying it
for a particularly large neck. Golden light burst out of it.
Within moments it was an opening larger than she was,
extending from the knot at the top of the noose all the
way to the ground. T4b and Florimel were already running
low across the hilltop. Paul turned to see the mounted
men charging up the hillside, their shouts rising like the
belling of hounds at the kill. He fired his last shot, flung
the empty revolver toward the dazzle of torches, then
sprinted for the glow.

Martine was waiting just at the edge. She grabbed his
arm and together they dived into the heatless golden brilliance.

For a moment, as Paul fell through onto hard stone, it
seemed that their pursuers had come through after them:
the unsteady light of torches was everywhere.

Reassured by the silence, Paul sat up. The torches hung
in wall brackets along a vast stone facade, outshining

even the stars in the black sky. The wall was covered with painted scenes in the stiff Egyptian style, colorful portraits of people and animal-headed gods.

He stood, feeling for broken bones, but found nothing worse than skinned knees and ripped coveralls. Beside him Martine and Florimel and T4b were also climbing to their feet. The quiet, an almost palpable thing in this gallery of vast stone walls, was broken only by the sound of his companions' breathing.

'We made it,' Paul whispered. 'Brilliant, Martine.'

Before she could reply, a shape appeared around the edge of the building, monstrously large but as silent as a cat. In one bound it stood before them and over them, a lion-bodied, human-headed giant. Crudely stitched in many places like an ancient doll, the sphinx leaked sand from a dozen gaping seams. Its eyelids were sewn shut.

'*You trespass on sacred precincts,*' it announced in a voice so low and powerful that it seemed to shake the stones. '*This is the Temple of Anubis, Lord of Life and Death. You trespass.*'

Paul found himself struggling to make words come out of his mouth, terrified by the astounding size of the thing. 'W-w-we . . . w-we don't . . . mean . . .'

'*You trespass.*'

'Run!' Paul shouted, turning, but before he had gone three steps something struck him like a velvet freight train and smashed him into darkness.

CHAPTER 25

The Hidden Bridge

NETFEED/INTERACTIVES: GCN, Hr. 7.0 (Eu, NAm) – 'Escape!'
(visual: Zelmo on ledge)
*VO: Nedra (Kamchatka T) and Zelmo (Cold Wells Carlson) are on the
run from Iron Island Academy, but agents of Lord Lubar (Ignatz Reiner)
shoot Zelmo with a Despair Ray, and now he is desperate to kill
himself. This is last episode before 'Escape!' folds into the 'I Hate
My Life' plotline. 5 supporting, 25 background open, cold-weather
outdoor shoot. Flak to: GCN.IHMLIFE.CAST*

FOR the third time they poled the raft across the sluggish current, steering toward the far shore. The bank seemed little more than a long stone's throw away, but after strenuous exercise by Sam and the new arrival Azador on one side, !Xabbu and Jongleur on the other, they had moved no closer.

At last they dragged the poles out and stood up straight to catch their breath. Released now to the current, the raft began to drift lazily downstream. The meadowlands on the far bank, so unexceptional, so apparently identical to the side of the river from which they had come, were beginning to seem like some mythical continent out of the past.

'Someone must swim,' Jongleur said. 'A person may be allowed where a boat is not.'

Sam was nettled. The old man might have been proved right in his conjecture that crossing the river, not following it, was the key to traversing this strange land, but she still didn't like the assumption of command in his voice.

'We don't work for you,' she said through clenched teeth. Something bumped her in the small of the back and she whirled, ready to shout at Jongleur, but it was !Xabbu who had nudged her. He gave her a significant look; it took Sam a moment to figure it out.

We're not supposed to talk about who Jongleur is, she remembered, and felt ashamed. All those years as a thief, creeping through the houses of the rich and powerful in the Middle Country – the imaginary rich and powerful anyway – and here she was, when it really counted, almost blurting out secrets for no reason. She lowered her eyes.

'He is right,' Azador said. 'We will not know for certain until someone tries to swim. I would do it, but with my leg . . .' He made a gesture of regret, of heroism postponed.

Sam waited for !Xabbu to volunteer and was surprised when he did not. Usually the small man insisted on taking the primary risks before he would let anyone else, especially Sam, do something dangerous. 'I guess it's me, then,' she said. So all those years of morning swim practice would get some practical use. She hoped she'd get to tell her mom about it someday. The thought of something so gloriously mundane as laughing with her mother about swimming those hated laps sent a sharp spike of longing through her.

'Wait, I am not sure . . .' !Xabbu began.

'It's okey, I'm good at this.' Without giving herself more

time to worry, she lifted her arms and leaped from the edge of the raft. When she surfaced she could hear Azador and Jongleur cursing at the violent rocking caused by her dive.

The water was a bit of a shock, colder than she expected, and though the current was slow, it was a steady drag that made swimming a great deal more difficult than it had been in the pool back home; still, after a few awkward kicks she got her body level and began to cut an angular path across the river, heading for the grassy, welcoming slope of the far bank.

A couple of minutes, she guessed, gauging the distance.

Within half a hundred strokes it became obvious that either the current was deceptively strong or she was suffering the same fate as the raft. She lifted her head above water and changed to a breast stroke so she could better see what was happening. She dug river water out from before her, surged against the resistance, made headway . . . but the land got no closer. Frustrated, she dove under the surface, forcing her way down until one of her hands brushed against the thick grasses waving at the bottom of the river before flattening out again. She kicked as hard as she could, wriggling her body like a fish. She was proud of her strength: she would not give up without testing herself and the simulation.

When she couldn't hold her breath any longer, she gave another two kicks, then allowed herself to glide upward. The shore was still just as far away. Disgusted, treading water, she had turned around toward the middle of the river to look for the raft when a sudden, shocking pain stabbed at her leg.

Something grabbed me . . . ! was all she had time to think before she slid under the water. She fought her way back up through agony, one leg helpless, and realized it was not some carnivorous river dweller that had struck but a cramp in her calf. It made little difference: she could not keep herself above water for more than a moment, and she was exhausted from her fruitless swim.

Sam shouted for !Xabbu, but her nose and mouth were full of water and it came out as little more than a gurgle. She simply could not kick the cramped leg, nor could she do much else. She tried to roll over on her back and go limp – the words *dead man's float* bubbled through her brain, a very unreassuring phrase – but the pain in her leg was excruciating and river water was rolling across her face.

She had just sunk under the surface for the second time when something whacked hard against her shoulder. She grabbed at the barge pole, clutching it as though it were the shepherd's crook of her very own guardian angel. Which, in a way, it was.

'I was very frightened, Sam.' !Xabbu had been unwilling to leave her side to make the fire, and had left the job to Azador. As she huddled beside the low blaze, still shivering a half hour later, she found herself actually grateful to the mustached man. 'I was hoping, hoping very hard, that we could get the raft as far as you swam,' !Xabbu went on. 'Oh, I was frightened.'

Sam was touched. In some ways, her experience seemed to have been worse for him than it had been for her. 'I'm okay. You saved me.'

!Xabbu only shook his head.

'So we are thwarted,' said Jongleur. 'We cannot cross the river, either by boat or by swimming.'

Sam made an effort to stop her teeth from chattering. 'But there must be a bridge. Those little animals or whatever they were – the Bubble Bunny ones – they said something about going to a bridge. We just never found out what they meant.' She could not help glaring at Jongleur, since it had been his frightening temper that had driven the natives away. She thought she saw a shadow of guilt cross his face.

Maybe he's a little bit human, she decided. *Just a little.* Of course, it might only be regret at having interfered with his own chances.

'But there are no bridges,' Azador declared. 'I have gone all the way around this bloody river three times. You have gone around it once yourself. Did you see bridges?'

'It's not that simple,' Sam said stubbornly. 'We can see the other side of the river, but that doesn't mean we can get there. So if we can see things we can't reach, why shouldn't there be things that we can't see but we *can* reach?' She had to stop and say it over again in her head to see if it made sense. She decided it did, more or less.

'We can do nothing more today.' !Xabbu's troubled expression had not gone, but it had changed into something different, more remote. 'We will think again in the morning.' He reached out and touched Sam's arm. 'I am happy you were not hurt, Sam.'

'Just my leg, and that's better now.' She smiled, hoping to cheer him a little, but wondered how convincing it was with her teeth still chattering.

For all !Xabbu's concern, he was not beside her when Sam woke sometime in the middle of the night. She could see the shadowy forms of the other two revealed by the dying coals, but no sign of the small man.

Call of nature, like, she guessed, and had almost toppled back into sleep when she remembered that there was no longer such a thing for any of them. She jerked upright. The idea of losing him, of being left alone with only

Jongleur and Azador, was too horrible to consider.

I don't want any of this. I just want to go home.

She tried to calm herself, forcing herself to imagine what Renie or Orlando would do. If !Xabbu was gone she had to go and look for him, that was all. She considered rousing the others but decided against it. If she could not find any sign of him within a hundred meters or so of the campfire she would think about it again.

She was just pulling a smoldering stick out of the fire to use as a torch when she noticed that someone else had already had the same idea: a hundred meters from the camp a single spot of orange light stood out against the black velvet hills. Sam trotted toward it.

The end of !Xabbu's torch had been spiked into the soft loam of a grassy hillside; he was sitting beside it. He did not look up at her approach, and she was just beginning to feel frightened again when he shook himself out of his reverie and turned to her.

'Is everything all right, Sam?'

'Yeah, chizz. I just woke up and . . . I was worried because you were gone.'

He nodded. 'I am sorry. I thought you were too deeply asleep to notice.' He turned back to the sky. 'The stars are very strange here. There is a pattern, but I cannot hold it in my mind.'

She seated herself beside him. The grass was damp, but after the mishap in the river she scarcely noticed.

'Will you not be cold?' he asked.

'I'm okay.'

They sat for a while in silence, Sam fighting an urge to drive the fear away with friendly noise. At last !Xabbu cleared his throat, a sound so uncharacteristic in its uncertainty that Sam felt her skin goose pimple.

'I . . . I did a terrible wrong to you today,' he said.

'You saved me.'

'I let you go into the river. It should have been me, but I was afraid.'

'Why should it have been you? You're as bad as Renie – you think you should do all the dangerous things before anyone else.'

'The fact is that I feared the water. I was almost killed once in the river where I grew up, when I was a child. A crocodile.'

'That's terrible!'

He shrugged. 'That does not mean I should have let you do what I could not.'

Sam hissed with exasperation. 'You don't have to do everything,' she said. 'That's uttermost *fenfen*.'

'But . . .'

'Listen.' She leaned toward him, forcing him to look at her. 'You've saved my life a dozen times already. Remember the mountain? Remember how you got us off that disappearing trail? You've done more than your share, but that doesn't mean the rest of us can't, like, do our part.' She raised her hand to keep him from speaking. 'Orlando got killed helping us – saving me. How could I live with myself if I wasn't taking risks, too? If I just sat back like some . . . some princess-girl in an old story, and let everyone rescue me? I don't know how things are in the Okeydongo Delta or whatever it is, but where I come from, that scans for days and days.'

!Xabbu smiled, but there was pain in it. 'Renie says it is "old-fashioned bullshit."'

'And she'll say it again when we find her if you don't straighten up.' Now Sam was the one to smile. She prayed it would be true, against all the odds. Renie and !Xabbu deserved each other in every way. So much love, so much stubbornness. She hoped they would have the rest of their lives to argue over which of them should do the harder jobs. 'Is that why you came out here? Because you felt bad you didn't go into the river and I did, and I got a cramp?'

He shook his head. 'Not only that. Something is troubling me, but I do not know what it is. Sometimes I need quiet to think.' He smiled again. 'Sometimes I need more than that. I thought I might dance.'

'Dance?' If he had suggested he was considering building a rocket ship she could not have been more surprised.

'For me it is . . . like praying. Sometimes.' He flicked his fingers, troubled by the inadequacy of his words. 'But I am not ready. I do not feel it.'

Sam didn't know what to say. After a moment, she stood. 'Do you want to be alone? Or should we go back to camp?'

!Xabbu plucked his torch from the ground and rose lithely onto his feet. 'I am troubled by something else,' he said. 'It is not enough simply to be silent about Jongleur's true story in front of Azador.'

Sam felt her face warm with embarrassment. 'I'm sorry – that was so stupid today.'

'It is hard – unnatural – to think of such things all the time. But I think we must make it clear to Jongleur that Azador has a hatred of the Grail Brotherhood. Then I think he must keep himself quiet, if only to protect himself.'

'It's so strange,' Sam said as they walked back toward the remains of the campfire. 'Nothing here is real, you can't trust anything. Well, almost anything.' She bumped !Xabbu, a gentle nudge of comradeship. 'It's all like some kind of . . . I don't know. Like a carnival. Like a masquerade.'

'But a terrible one,' he said. 'Dangerous and terrible.'

They reached the campfire, and the sleeping forms of their two companions, without saying anything more.

The next day was spent in what Sam felt was a clearly hopeless search for a way to cross the river. They clambered through the reed beds alongside the river, hoping to find some clue to how others had crossed – footprints, the remains of a bridge or dock – but without success. Sam was depressed, !Xabbu reserved and thoughtful. Jongleur, as usual, spoke little, lost in his private thoughts. Only Azador seemed unbowed. In fact, he talked for much of the day, chattering compulsively about his adventures in the network, his discoveries of how things worked, of secret shortcuts within simworlds and well-hidden gateways to get out of them. Some of it was clearly bragging, but Sam could not help being impressed by the depth of his knowledge. How long had this man wandered the Grail Network?

'Where do you come from?' she asked him as they sloshed through a shallow backwater. A group of promising stones were proving to be only the cracked remains of a larger rocky shelf. 'I mean, before you were here?'

'I . . . I do not wish to talk about it,' he said. He scowled, poking at the silt between his feet with a length of reed. 'But I have made the best use of my time here that anyone could. I have learned things the builders of this place thought would remain forever hidden . . .'

Sam did not want to hear another recitation of his accomplishments. 'Yeah, but you can't find a way across the river, so at the moment the rest of it doesn't count for much.'

Azador looked hurt. Sam felt bad – unlike Jongleur, he had done nothing to harm her or her friends – so she tried to think of something else to talk about.

'But I suppose that you did a pretty good job on that raft after all.' Although it had been !Xabbu's deft repairs that had made it riverworthy, she knew but did not mention. 'It's not your fault that the system won't let us cross that way.'

He looked a little mollified.

'Are you really a Gypsy?' she asked.

His reaction was sudden and fierce. 'Who told you such a foul thing?'

It was all Sam could do not to look at !Xabbu, who was holding quiet conversation with Jongleur thirty paces away across the muddy shallows. 'Nobody . . . I . . . I just thought you said you were.' She was furious with herself. 'Maybe I just thought it because . . . because of that mustache.'

He stroked the article in question as though it were an affronted animal he was soothing. 'Gypsies, they are sneaks and thieves. Azador is an explorer. Do not misunderstand when I tell you of my adventures. I am a prisoner. I have the right to discover all I can, to take what I can from my captors.'

'I'm sorry. I just misunderstood.'

'You should be more careful.' He gave her a hard stare. 'This is a place where you must be cautious what you say to strangers.'

Sam silently, emphatically agreed.

Another hour of fruitless investigation passed before she had a chance to talk to !Xabbu out of earshot of the others. He had joined her to scavenge in one last clump of reeds. Azador and Jongleur had given up, and were sitting on one of the meadowy hillocks, watching them.

'I'm such a scanbox,' she said when she had explained what happened. 'I should keep my mouth shut.'

!Xabbu looked troubled. 'Perhaps you blame yourself

too much, as I did last night. Perhaps we have learned something, although I cannot say what. For one thing, it is very strange that he should say this now. Almost the only thing he would tell us before was that he *was* a Gypsy – Romany, as he called himself. He seemed very proud of it.' The small man pulled aside a curtain of swaying cattails to reveal that what had looked from a distance like the remains of a wooden structure was only a tangle of tree trunks uprooted and piled by some storm. 'Perhaps he is not the only one who has decided to keep his past a secret.'

'I don't know. He didn't seem scared or nervous, like I would if someone knew something about me they shouldn't. He just seemed . . . angry.' She looked to the hillside. Jongleur and Azador were talking, or seemed to be. It made her feel uneasy. 'Look at that old monster just sitting there. It's his fault we can't find anyone to ask how to cross the river!' Whether it really was Jongleur's fault or not, they had seen no other inhabitants of the simworld since the old man had frightened Jecky Nibble and his charges away from their campfire.

'It is possible. But it may be they have all simply crossed over to someplace that is safer.'

'Maybe.' Sam frowned. 'What could those two be saying to each other?'

!Xabbu looked up. 'I do not know. I told the old man that Azador might become violent if he found out who Jongleur truly is. So I do not think he is telling him anything about that.'

By the time they had climbed out of the mud and started up the grassy hillside, Azador had risen and walked away from Jongleur. He stood on the hilltop, facing away from them. As they neared the crest, he suddenly turned and shouted, 'Come, come here! Look at this!'

Sam and !Xabbu hurried up the last few meters.

'Look,' said Azador. 'Can you see?'

'Oh, no!' Sam felt chilled. 'They're fading out.'

The distant hills were only ghostly outlines now, streaks of sunlit reflection, milky, misty indicators of where solid hills should stand. Even parts of the meadowed plain seemed to have turned transparent as glass. Sam looked around in panic, but the river and its banks were still solid behind them, the hillock beneath their feet still reassuringly lifelike.

'They are disappearing,' Azador said. For the first time, she heard something like real fear in his voice. 'What does it mean?'

'It means we are running out of time,' Jongleur said, coming up from behind them. His face was carefully expressionless, but his voice was not entirely steady. 'The simulation is dying.'

!Xabbu woke her with a light touch. 'I am going to be away from the camp for some time,' he whispered. 'I do not think I want to leave you with those two.'

Sam got sleepily to her feet and stumbled after him. The stars seemed brighter than ever, as though burning in premature mourning for the vanishing world beneath them.

When they reached the nearest hilltop, !Xabbu sat and began tying something around his ankles, circlets made from river reeds and seedpods that rattled when they moved.

'What are those for?' Sam asked.

'Dancing,' he said. 'Please, Sam, I need quiet now.'

Rebuffed, she sat down beside him and drew her knees up under her chin. The cloak of woven leaves !Xabbu had made for her was little protection against the cold, but

the night was mild. She watched him finish his preparations, then he walked a few steps away from her and
stood, staring straight up at the sky and its blazing stars.

He stood there a long time. Sam drifted into sleep
again, then started awake to find him still standing in the
same place, frozen like a statue. Her mind wandered,
touching mournfully on the stars over her own backyard
where she and her father had camped in sleeping bags,
Sam secure in his silent company despite the night sounds
of the garden, reassured by her mother's silhouette in the
kitchen window.

What are they doing now? They can't spend all their
time with . . . with me. In some hospital. Do they do
other things? Watch the net? Have dinner with friends?
Even if I die here, they have to have some kind of normal
life again, don't they? But it seemed wrong – unfair. But
would it be worse if they never got over it?

Oh, God, Mom, Dad, I'm so sorry . . . !

Slowly, !Xabbu began to move, lifting one foot in the
air and sawing it back and forth like an impatient horse
pawing at the ground. He stepped forward, lifted the other
foot and shook it, then set it down too. The rattles gave
a quiet, dry hiss. Gradually he began to move in a distinctive and intricate rhythm, the steps made even more exotic
by the near-silence.

At first Sam watched him closely, trying to guess from
the small man's absorbed expression what might be going
on in his mind, but the dance went on too lengthily, too
repetitively, to hold her attention: as he finished the first
slow trip around a circle only he could see, she found
her thoughts beginning to scatter again. His precise movements reminded her of a game she had once played, something on the net she had loved for about two weeks when
she was young, where oddly-shaped building blocks had

floated slowly through space and could be pushed together into expanding geometric structures. Like !Xabbu's dance, the blocks had revolved as if both heavy and weightless. Their intricate, multifaceted sides had kissed and stuck with just the same blend of delicacy and permanence as the lifting and setting down of each of the small man's feet, as though it were not blind brute gravity that held him to the earth but an act of careful choice.

I wonder if Orlando ever played that game, she thought sleepily. *I wonder what he would have made with it – something different, that's for sure. Something funny and sad.*

I wonder what !Xabbu would make . . .

And then she herself spun slowly away into another place, dreaming of dark high mountains and the lonely cries of birds.

'Wake up, Sam.' His voice seemed odd: for a moment, the dreams still muddling her, she thought it was Orlando who spoke.

'Let me sleep, you damn scanmaster.'

'The light is coming back. We do not have the time to sleep late today, I think.'

She opened her eyes to find !Xabbu leaning over her, his face gleaming with sweat, his chest expanding and contracting as though he had just run a marathon. Nevertheless, he seemed full of energy. 'Oh my God, I'm sorry. I thought you were . . .' She rubbed her eyes. 'Are you okay?'

'I am fine, Sam. I have done much thinking. It was good to dance, to . . . to be me again.'

She let him help her up. Her feet felt cold and prickly; it took her a moment to stamp life back into them. 'Did it help you think of anything?'

He smiled. 'You are like Renie in this way, too. My dance is not like a . . . what is the name? Vending machine. Put in a card, out comes an answer. But I realized why I was troubled and the answer to that may help us.' He laughed – he seemed lighter than he had in days, almost buoyant. 'So we will see, Sam. Now come.'

'What did you mean?' she asked as they walked back across the wet grass. It felt so real under her feet that it was hard to believe it might soon dissolve back into silvery nothingness, but the distant hills were frighteningly faint, a landscape carved in crystal. Without thinking, she hurried her steps. 'When you said it was good to be you again?'

'Always I try to understand this place, to think like the people who built it, to think like Renie and you others do. But that is not really the way I think best. And it is strange for me – like wearing clothing that does not fit well. I cannot change an entire lifetime in a matter of weeks. Sometimes I must . . . go back. Go back to my old ways.'

Sam nodded slowly. 'I think I know what you mean. I feel sometimes like I don't know who I am – who the real me is.' Spurred by his quizzical look, she went on. 'I mean, since I've been a girl again – you know, wearing this body – I don't talk the same, I don't even think the same, sort of. I start acting like . . . like a girl!'

His smile was gentle. 'Is that bad?'

'Not always, no. But when I was just Fredericks, Orlando's shadow, another boy . . . I don't know. It was easier, somehow. I tried more things, I talked different.' She laughed. 'I swore more.'

'Ah. And you have put your finger on it, Sam. That was one of the things that was troubling me.'

Surprised, she tripped over a hummock and took a

second to regain her footing. 'You're troubled because I'm not swearing?'

'No. But wait – we are almost there. Soon you will see what I have been thinking.'

Jongleur and Azador were sitting across the fire from each other, sullen and sleepy-eyed. The older man gave them a cold look as they approached. 'So, after all your talk about necessity and danger, you find time to take a romantic walk? Very sweet.'

Sam felt her face grow hot, and would have said something nasty, but !Xabbu touched her arm.

'There are many ways to solve problems,' the small man said evenly. 'But we need a new one, or we will still be here when this world melts around us.'

Jongleur made a noise of disgust. 'So it was a scouting expedition?'

'Of a sort.' !Xabbu turned to Azador, who was watching blearily, perhaps regretting the absence of coffee in this meadow beyond the world. 'I need to speak to you, Mr Azador. I have some important questions to ask.'

Something flickered behind his eyes, but he only waved his hand negligently. 'Ask.'

'Tell me again how you came here – how you reached the black mountain, then found yourself in this place.'

Sam looked at !Xabbu, puzzled but trying not to show it, as Azador somewhat reluctantly reiterated the story of his arrival – following them into the maze in Demeter's temple, waking into pale nothingness to find the mountain gone.

'But I have been thinking,' !Xabbu said abruptly as Azador neared the end of his story. 'Thinking that we sat a long time on the side of the black mountain, arguing and talking, after we came through from Troy. Thinking that the gate was gone by the time we began to climb the trail. So how did you step through it without us seeing you?'

'Are you calling me a liar?' Azador half-rose, but sat down again when !Xabbu held up his hand in a calming gesture, as though the violent movement had been mostly bluff.

'Perhaps – but perhaps not.' !Xabbu moved a few steps nearer, then seated himself beside the smoking remains of the campfire. Azador slid back a little. Sam found herself staring in fascination. What did !Xabbu know, or at least guess? Azador actually looked frightened. 'I believe that you did follow us through,' !Xabbu said, 'and it could be you are telling what you remember – but I do not think it happened that way.'

'Why are we wasting time on this trivia?' growled Jongleur.

'If you want to cross the river before this world disappears,' !Xabbu said coolly, 'I suggest you close your mouth.'

As if the remark had been directed at him, Azador abruptly shut his own gaping jaw. 'What are you saying?' he demanded after a moment. 'That I am mad? That I don't know what the truth is? Or have you decided I am a simple liar after all?'

'How is it that you came through a gate that had closed, unless it opened again for you? How is it that you found your way off the mountain through all that gray nothing – something that for me needed all the tracking skill that my hunting people have learned in thousands of generations? How is it that you managed to push your raft upstream against the current to catch us? Most strange of all, why do you have clothes when the rest of us here naked? What are the answers to any of these things if you have not been to this place before?' !Xabbu paused. 'Whether you remember being here or not, that is another question.'

'Yeah!' Sam said with dawning realization. 'Scanbark! I didn't even think about that. He has clothes!'

'That is ridiculous!' Azador sputtered, but the haunted something was in his eyes again. 'More sensible to call me a liar.'

'If you like,' !Xabbu said simply. 'But there are other questions, too. Tell me of the Romany, Mr Azador. Explain how you do not tell secrets to *gorgios*, as you told me before. How you and your Gypsy friends meet at Romany Fair, to pass stories and share information.'

Now Azador truly did look befuddled, staring at the smaller man as though !Xabbu had started speaking in tongues. 'What do you mean? I have never said any of those things to you – it was the girl who began this Gypsy nonsense.'

Watching, Sam realized that her heart was beating painfully fast. Even Jongleur seemed stunned by what was going on.

!Xabbu shook his head. 'No, Azador. You began it. In a prison cell, when I first met you. Then on a boat in a river in Kansas. Do you remember? You called me monkey-man, because I wore a baboon's body . . .'.

'You!' Azador leaped to his feet, sending the last embers of the fire in all directions. 'You and your bitch of a friend – you stole my gold!' He lunged toward !Xabbu, who only took a step back.

'Stop!' Sam shrieked. She regretted the shrill, panicked sound, but not much. She yanked the haft and broken blade of Orlando's sword out of her waistband. 'You touch him and I'll rip your guts out!'

'I will break your neck, girl,' Azador snarled, but did not force the issue. Jongleur was on his feet now too, and for a moment they all stood frozen, a four-sided shape of mistrust.

'Before you do anything else,' !Xabbu said, 'tell me what we stole from you.'

'My gold!' Azador shouted, but his face looked troubled, almost fearful. 'My . . . gold.'

'You do not remember what it was, do you?'

'I know you stole from me!'

!Xabbu shook his head. 'We did not. We were separated by a failure of the system,' he said as calmly as though Azador had not been glaring bloody murder at him, as though Sam were not standing with a broken sword in her hand leveled at the man's belly. 'What do you truly remember? I think you have been here before, inside the so-called White Ocean. Can you not try to think? We are all in terrible danger.'

Azador staggered back as though struck. His eyes wild, he waved his arms, then pointed at !Xabbu. 'It is you – you are crazy! Azador is not crazy.' He glared at Sam and her weapon, then at Jongleur. 'All of you crazy!' A sob choked his words, 'Not Azador!' He turned and ran limping out of the campsite, staggering across the meadow and up the slope of a low hill until he collapsed into the grass and lay there as if he had been shot.

'What have you done?' Jongleur demanded, but with little of his usual commanding tone.

'Saved us, perhaps. Go to him – I think he will not want either Sam or me to come near, but we need him.'

Jongleur gaped as though !Xabbu, too, had thrown his arms in the air and begun to gibber. 'Go to him . . . ?'

'Damn you, just go!' Sam shouted, waving the broken blade. 'We were ready to leave you behind two days ago. Do something useful for a change!'

Jongleur appeared to consider several responses, but only turned his back on them and stalked off toward the fallen figure of Azador.

'That felt *good!*' said Sam. Her heart was still speeding.

'But Jongleur is an enemy that must be managed carefully,' !Xabbu told her. 'It is like handling a very poisonous snake – we should not tempt bad luck.'

'How did you know? About Azador? And who is he? *What* is he?'

The confrontation over, !Xabbu seemed to shrink a little. 'What Azador is, I cannot say for certain – not in a place as confusing as this network. But perhaps he is like the woman Ava we have all seen, or that boy that Jonas met – someone who drifts from world to world in this network, uncertain of his identity. Certainly he is not acting like the Azador I met before, who was very full of himself, too, but mostly cold and superior. And Jonas described an Azador who hardly spoke at all.'

'You mean they're all different people?'

'I don't think so. But as I said, in this place, who knows?' !Xabbu seated himself beside the fire. 'However, it is not who he is that is important now. Rather, it is where he has been.'

'I don't understand.'

!Xabbu gave her a weary grin. 'Wait and see. Perhaps I will be correct again in my guesses and you will think me a very clever man. But if I am wrong, it will be less shameful if I have not bragged about what I think I can do. What comes next will be difficult.'

'You seem different, too,' Sam said suddenly. 'I don't mean like a different person, but . . . but more confident.'

'I have had time to listen to the ringing of the sun,' he said. 'Even though there is no sun here. To speak to the grandparent stars.'

Sam shrugged. 'I don't know what any of that means.'

!Xabbu reached up and patted her arm. 'It does not

matter, Sam Fredericks. Now, let us see if we can work some magic on Mr Azador.'

'And what will you do if I don't cooperate?' Azador demanded. 'Stab me with that sword?' He spoke with such an exaggerated tone of outrage that for a moment Sam could not help wondering if he might not be another stolen child hidden inside the shape of a grown man.

'It's tempting,' she said quietly, but was quelled by !Xabbu's stern look.

'We will do nothing to you,' the small man said. 'We will simply go back to waiting for this world to disappear around us.'

Jongleur stood a little apart, watching. He had regained his usual lizardlike reserve. Sam did not know what he had told the mustached man to bring him back, but she supposed she was grateful for it.

'I am in the hands of madmen,' Azador said.

'That could be,' !Xabbu replied. 'But I promise no harm will come to you.' He lifted his hand. 'Give me your shirt.'

Azador scowled, but stripped it off. !Xabbu took it and stood behind him, then rolled it and tied it around his eyes like a blindfold. 'Can you see?'

'No, damn you, of course I can't!'

'It is important. Do not lie to me.'

Azador waggled his head from side to side. 'I can see nothing. If I break my leg, I will see the same happens to you, even if you gut me.'

!Xabbu made a noise of irritation. 'Nothing will happen. See, I will walk beside you, Sam on the other side. Come, Mr Azador, you have said often enough that you are brave, resourceful. Why are you afraid to walk with your eyes covered?'

'I am not afraid. But the whole thing is stupid.'

'Perhaps. Now the rest of us will be silent. We will walk beside the river. You will continue, please, until you feel it is a good place to cross.'

Sam was puzzled but kept her peace. Even Jongleur appeared to be grudgingly interested in the experiment. They led Azador down to the last firm ground before the riverbank, then turned upstream.

They walked for a long time without talking, the quiet broken only by Azador's frustrated curses when he tripped on some unseen obstacle. In places the reed thickets grew so dense that they almost stumbled into the river; in other places the meadowlands stretched before them so openly that Sam felt her trust in !Xabbu's insights diminish. There was nothing but river and grass for as far as she could see. What difference would a man in a blindfold make?

After a while, Azador's reflexive grumbling began to die away. He moved like a sleepwalker now, walking stolidly forward, resting when the others rested, not even complaining when they wandered into mud. She heard him murmuring, but could not hear the words themselves.

Even the quality of his attention began to change as the first hour rolled into a second; a stillness came over him, and from time to time he stopped and tilted his head as though listening to something the others could not hear.

But by the time the light began to change, darkening just perceptibly as the middle of the day passed, they still had not found anything.

Look at us! Sam thought. Her feet hurt. She was hot and sticky. She felt a strong urge to lie down and let whatever was going to happen just happen, and had only kept herself moving during the last hour out of loyalty to !Xabbu. *Azador's right – this is stupid. Four people stumbling along the river, looking for something when we already know it's not here.*

They were just making their way out of another whispering crowd of rushes when they saw the bridge.

Sam gasped. 'But how . . . ? We've been here before! There wasn't . . . we didn't see . . . *Dzang!*'

It was narrow, little more than a wall of piled stones with arch-shaped holes to let the river flow through, but it was wide enough for them all to walk across side by side. Most importantly of all, it stretched all the way to the meadows on the river's far bank – or seemed to, in any case: the other end of the bridge was obscured by low mists.

'You may uncover your eyes,' !Xabbu told Azador.

Alone of them all, Azador showed no surprise, as though he had in some way seen the bridge already. Nevertheless, there was a frightened glint to his stare, and after a moment, he turned away. 'I . . . I do not want to go there.'

'We have no choice,' !Xabbu said firmly. 'Come. Lead us over.'

Azador shook his head, but reluctantly moved toward the near end of the span. He hesitated for a moment before stepping up. !Xabbu followed him, then Sam and Jongleur. Sam marveled at the stony solidity of the thing – she knew they had passed this very spot only a day or so before, but no bridge had stood here.

Azador took a few steps, then stopped. 'No,' he said, his voice oddly distant. 'First we . . . we must say something.'

They all waited expectantly.

>   *'Gray goose and gander,'*

Azador murmured at last, his voice heavy with some emotion Sam could not decipher,

> *'Waft your wings together,*
> *And carry the good king's daughter*
> *Over the one-strand river.'*

After a moment he looked back at them, then stepped out onto the stone path above the glinting, slow-moving waters. Sam was disturbed to see that the man's eyes, hidden for so long, were now wet with tears.

CHAPTER 26

Flies and Spiders

NETFEED/NEWS: Smell – The Final Frontier

(visual: WeeWin's olfactory testing lab)

VO: The Euro-Asian toy company WeeWin has announced what it calls 'the first genuine scent delivery system' for net users without neurocannular capabilities. WeeWin says the NozKnoz (pronounced 'noseknows') system uses a scent palette of basic olfactory stimuli to create millions of different odors.

(visual: Dougal Craigie, WeeWin VPPR)

CRAIGIE: 'Many people don't use neurocannulas – not just because they can't afford them, but also for medical and religious reasons. So we are not just excited, but deeply proud to announce that you no longer need to have your brain wired to enjoy the many smells of the net. This is not one of those cheap chocolate-and-cheese pastiche systems – NozKnoz nasal delivery plugs give results that cannot be distinguished from neurocannular stimulation.'

DULCIE snuck another look at her silent employer, certain at some irrational level of her being that even in his deathlike sleep he must be able to sense her guilt, but if he did, his still form gave no indication. She turned back to the small screen on her pad, which she had chosen because it seemed more discreet than the wide wallscreen.

Dread's hidden storage had remained adamantly inac-
cessible. She had thrown every sort of decryption and
security-breaking gear at it, had found it protected by
nothing more advanced than a password, no quantum
cryptography or anything special, but her gear had run
an almost uncountable amount of number and letter
combinations past it without success.

*For God's sake! It's just a goddamn password! Why
can't I break this?*

Of course, when it came to passwords, it always helped
if you knew something about the person whose account
you were trying to crack.

Reluctantly, she gave up on penetrating her employer's
mysteries, closed off her access to Dread's system and
then ran some cleanup gear. She doubted that either Dread
or his security program were sophisticated enough to spot
her incursion, but there was no sense taking chances.

Irritated with herself, her earlier bold mood dissolving
into worry and second thoughts, she opened up the
Jongleur files – her legitimate work, if you could use such
a term to describe felonious data theft – and got back
down to business. As the signifiers filled her tiny screen
she swore, then transferred operations up to the wallscreen
– it was hard enough trying to make sense of things in
two dimensions, let alone on a screen measured in
centimeters. She left it at that, though: for some reason
she felt reluctant to submerge herself in a 3D environment, even though she could do some things more efficiently in wrap-around.

*I'm scared to be helpless in a VR setup while I'm in
the same room with Dread,* she realized. *It's not street
hoodlums, not burglars I'm frightened of . . . but him.
That's great, Anwin – two weeks into the thing is a bit
late to realize it.*

She looked at the dark ridgeline of his profile, moving up and down gently now as the bed massaged him, and a sudden image from her childhood reading leaped into her brain. She almost dropped her coffee.

Jesus, I'm Renfield. That guy who ate the flies and spiders. And it's my job to watch over Count Dracula.

She felt a little better after a quick shower, although she had decided on a caffeine moratorium for the rest of the day.

Dracula? Let's not get too morbid, Anwin, she told herself as she sat back down to stare at the Jongleur files. Still, she thought, if her boss popped up out of his humming coffin just now, even full of kind words and barely-veiled sexual interest as he sometimes was, she didn't think she was going to be very receptive.

She did her best to narrow her attention, sifting through the Jongleur information that had not made the first cut, yet which somehow might still hide useful data about the Grail network. An hour passed and she began to feel more like herself, even taking a few minutes to try to reopen Jongleur's weird *Ushabti* file, but her failure to provide the proper code or password the first time had left it as mute and secretive as an oyster.

They're just the goddamn same, the two of them. No wonder Jongleur hired him . . . She froze, stunned by her own stupidity in not having thought of it sooner. *My God, of course. His employer! If anybody's going to have any information on our boy Dread it's going to be Jongleur!*

Within moments she had moved the display of Jongleur files back to the pad and had started to search. A request for 'Dread' turned up nothing useful, which didn't entirely surprise her, and neither did 'Sydney' or 'Cartagena' 'Isla de Santuario' or anything else that came to mind. How could you search for information on someone when you had almost no information with which to begin a search?

Jaws clamped so hard in concentration that she would have a headache later, Dulcie pulled up the immense bank of J Corporation accounting records and sent dozens of different bits of specialized gear looking for anomalies while performing the same search on Jongleur's personal files. *The guy has to be paid*, she thought. *No matter what they call it, there has to be a connection.* She also pulled up Dread's own system, all of which she had already explored except for the hidden storage – 'the locked room,' as she had begun to think of it, a phrase out of memory that rang a faint bell she was too busy to heed. It was boring, mundane stuff, but she wasn't looking for a revelation there, not in data she'd already examined. She was looking for a match, however obscure, a place where an open end on the Jongleur side lined up with something similar on Dread's side.

It took almost two hours, but she found it at last. A short string of numbers on a single disbursement out of the J Corporation's staggeringly large operating budget, routed through several smaller companies with no obvious connection to the corporation, one in North Africa, the others in the Caribbean, matched another string of numbers in an account which, although it belonged to an apparently fictitious company, was nevertheless listed on Dread's own system. Based on the dates, she suspected she was looking at some of the expenses for setting up the Colombian assault. It seemed to be an emergency replacement for some funds that had been misrouted, which was the only reason she had found the connection.

It's the little mistakes that kill you every time, she thought gleefully.

With this single small thread in her fingers she began to pick her way backward, following the chain of authority, sometimes by easy steps, sometimes only by leaps of practiced intuition, until at last she found herself moving slowly back up the connection she had discovered between the J Corporation and Jongleur's own personal system. Her palms were sweating, her heart fluttering.

The strands led to a group of files in Jongleur's system labeled 'disposal' – which she at first thought was a little joke on the old man's part, but when she began to examine them she found that they were indeed contracts, reports, and other information about the hugely complex waste removal systems of the artificial island, thousands and thousands of nested files, all perfectly, boringly normal. She sat back, stunned and disappointed. How could she have been so wrong? Had she missed a stitch back there somewhere, then followed the wrong thread all the way back across the tapestry? It would take her at least another few hours to go back over it and find her mistake.

She was just about to close the whole mess in disgust when she suddenly wondered why Jongleur should take such an interest in the waste removal infrastructure for the corporate property, to the extent of having it on his own personal system. It was his own principal residence, of course, but it still seemed odd. She checked and found that the same set of files existed in the corporate system, but that didn't prove anything – Jongleur could simply have wanted his own copy, perhaps because there was some more mundane accounting discrepancy he was examining. Still, the Jongleur that Dread had spoken of didn't seem like a man too interested in the day-to-day business of maintaining corporate headquarters.

Dulcie ran a comparison study of the two files, drumming

her fingers impatiently until the processing marker stopped flashing.

Two files with the same name, she saw, excitement rising again. *And the J Corp. version is smaller than the Jongleur version. Bingo!*

A moment's spin of the digital tumblers and the larger file was open. Dulcie's fingers were no longer rapping on the edge of the pad but curling like the claws of a hunting bird ready to swoop. The extra information was secured in a lower layer, like a smuggler's false bottom bolted to the undercarriage of a truck. She keyed it open, holding her breath.

Something whined like a dental drill.

Files and signifiers began to leap onto the screen and dissolve. Message pointers flashed like tiny explosions. Her system defenses were screaming, the high-pitched alarm so painful that for a moment she could not understand what was happening.

Oh, shit – a 'phage! But why isn't my gear stopping it?

She had opened the file without proper permission and had set off a dataphage, one that her own gear apparently did not know how to handle. Within moments it would destroy all the material in the file, not just delete the markers but chew the actual data off the storage. God only knew what else it might do on the way – maybe take her whole system down.

Once, as a teenage babysitter in someone else's house, she had dumped an ashtray into a wastebasket and, without realizing it, set the wastebasket's contents on fire. The flames had climbed the long drapes of a picture window before she wandered back into the room. The feeling of terror and transgression had been just like this. It was all she could do not to leap up and smash the pad against the floor in an attempt to kill the horrible thing she had awakened.

Knowing that every second was critical, she switched the pad over to voice command and began calling up emergency measures, her system's equivalent of the volunteer fire department, since the dataphage's explosive onset had already overwhelmed her built-in regulators. Within a few moments she had managed to isolate the cancerous 'phage from the rest of her own data, but that was doing nothing to stop the destruction of the disposal file she had copied from Jongleur's system. And despite her quick move to firewall the damage, the 'phage seemed to have done odd things to her system already: the communications markers were flashing, as though she herself had been trying to obtain an outgoing line.

Another minute's frantic work enabled her to find another piece of emergency gear she had almost forgotten she had, allowing her at last to grab the isolated section of data and freeze it, but the destruction was huge if not total. She very much doubted there was anything left of the original group of files.

But that's just a copy, she reminded herself. *The primary version's still there on the Jongleur system. I'll just call it up and copy it off again, then be more careful with it next time . . .*

It was only then that she understood the significance of the blinking communications marker. With dawning horror, she disconnected, but it was already too late. The implanted dataphage was an extreme measure, constructed not only to destroy the pirated file but to call out and destroy the master file, too, probably after sending a high-alert warning to the owner of the file to give them a chance to countermand.

But if Jongleur's not around, then the whole thing is

*just gone now. Gone. And if he is around, then I've just
told him that someone has one of his most sensitive files.*

A quick check confirmed her growing misery. The
master file in question was now officially nonexistent.

'Shit,' she said aloud. 'Shit, shit, *shit!*'

'What's the problem, sweetness?'

Dulcie shrieked and her pad slid from her knee and
thumped on the carpeted floor. Dread was standing beside
her, all long, tawny muscles and bare skin, wearing only
a towel wrapped around his waist so that he looked like
a statue stepped down from its plinth. She had not even
heard him approach.

'God, y-you scared me!' But the mere fact of his sudden
appearance was not the only reason for her stuttering
heart. The pad lay faceup on the floor, full of incriminating data. She dropped to her knees and picked it up,
babbling to cover her real terror. 'I didn't know . . . I
thought you were . . . it's so quiet in here, but I didn't
hear you . . .'

As he stared at her, an amused smile quirking his
mouth, she blanked the small screen. 'Didn't mean to give
you a heart attack,' he said. 'What's up?' He squinted at
her pad. 'Why aren't you using the wall?'

'My eyes . . . it gives me . . . makes my head ache,
sometimes.'

He nodded. 'What pissed you off so badly?'

'What?' She was desperately trying to remember what
was still open and flowing to the pad. What if he wanted
to access his system? 'Oh, just . . . some problems with
security on some of Jongleur's files. Some of his bank-
ing stuff.' As far as she knew, Dread's accounting data
was still live and connected, her own gear waiting for
further search requests. She cursed herself for not having
done the prudent thing and copied the files she was exam-

ining to her own system. She had a desperate, clammy feeling that if he found out, something worse than the usual firing might be the result. She tried to calm her unsteady voice and speak lightly. 'I've been doing this for hours and I'm ragged, utterly. Are you up for a while?'

He cocked his head. 'Why?'

'I don't know. Could we go out and get some dinner, something? Just get out of here for an hour or two?'

Something moved behind his dark eyes; she prayed she hadn't caught him in a suspicious mood. 'Right,' he said after a moment. 'Why not? Are you buying?'

She forced herself to laugh. 'Sure. Just let me tidy up a few things . . .'

While Dread was pulling on clothes, Dulcie closed and locked off everything, then ran her cleanup gear. She was trembling so badly she had to set her pad down on a tabletop so she didn't drop it again.

How can he move so quietly? He got out of that thing and walked all the way across the room behind me and I never heard him. Maybe he really is a vampire. It wasn't a very good joke, not at the moment. She finished and turned off her pad, then wiped her sleeve across her face. The room was cool, but she was sweating.

Maybe Renfield needs to think about getting into another line of work . . .

Dread was quite charming over dinner, flashing those white teeth, playfully exaggerating his Aussie machismo to try to make her laugh. If Dulcie had been meeting him for the first time she would have been quite taken by his stories of the strange places and even stranger folk he had met in his peculiar line of work. If it had been even a week earlier, she might have had that third glass of wine, even a fourth, and let herself descend into warm compliance. Instead, she spent the entire meal thinking about how close she had come to being caught, wondering every time he gave her one of his penetrating looks whether he was about to reveal that he knew what she had been doing.

Whether he suspected her of misbehaviour or not, there was definitely something going on beneath the surface. Dread had always been subject to oddly high-flown, almost feverish bouts of enthusiasm. That was going on tonight, but it was twinned somehow with the watchful Dread she also knew, as though he were keeping a tight rein on himself because he knew he was on the brink of letting go entirely. As they walked back from the café he fell silent, looking neither at her nor the rain-spattered streets, but keeping his eyes fixed at a point somewhere above the invisible horizon. There was an unusual bounce in his step, a subtle but consistent flexing of muscles, as though he alone of all humanity had overcome gravity but had decided to maintain the pretense of obeying it.

In the main room of the loft, with the overhead fluorescents still off and only the red and white fairy-lights of the coma bed giving shape to the dark walls, he put his arm around her and drew her close. He was shockingly strong, even in this swift and apparently careless gesture; for half a moment she thought he planned to break her spine and did not doubt he could do it. Instead he laid his cheek against hers, his lips close to her ear.

'Shall we dance, sweetness? I have music inside me, you know. I can play it for you.'

She had already spoiled any chance of a graceful exit by stiffening at his touch. Suddenly the idea of having sex with this man seemed far more disturbing than she had ever imagined it to be, not a question of morning-after remorse but of actual terror. A little voice deep inside

her brain – the child-voice, the remember-of-stories –
squealed *He wants to steal your soul . . . !* She struggled
to calm herself, although she was certain that with his
sharp animal senses he must smell her fear. 'I . . . I don't
feel very good. Cramps. But . . . it was a very nice dinner.'

His teeth gently, gently closed on her earlobe. The tiny
pain sent a bolt of black lightning down her spine. 'Oh,
Dulcie, sweetness – you wouldn't be teasing a bloke, now
would you?'

'No.' Her heart was thumping painfully. *I'm all alone.*
'No, I'm not that kind . . . I don't do that.'

He took her jaw between index finger and thumb and
turned her face so he cold look closely, his smile
completely at odds with the shadowed hollows that were
all she could see of his stare, like the black eyeholes of
a mask. She felt a clawing urge to cry out, but for that
brief moment, as if plunged into nightmare, she could
make no sound.

When he let go of her, she almost fell.

'Well, then,' he said lightly, 'I suppose I might as well
get back to work. It's quite a job being God, after all.' He
kissed his fingertip and touched it lightly against her dry
lips. 'Wouldn't want you to think I was the kind of man
who can't control himself.' He laughed, then with startling unconcern began to undress for the coma bed. Dulcie
fled to the bathroom.

I don't trust myself anymore, she thought. *I can't tell
what's real and what's not. He's a monster? Then why
didn't he just force me – I couldn't have lifted a finger.
No pleading, no trying to scare me.*

But she *was* scared, although the rationale-collectors
of her upper mind were beginning to send memos, form
committees, call meetings.

He's just . . . weird. Dark. But what did you expect? The guy is an international mercenary, for God's sake, not a homeroom teacher.

Just go to the airport, a more frightened voice told her. *Get the hell out of town. Tell him your mother's dying. Tell him anything.*

But I can't just walk out on him, she suddenly realized. *He's not going to let me, is he? I'm the only person who knows what he's been doing.* The nervous fear she had been feeling suddenly frosted over, turned into something thicker and colder. *If he killed his boss, is he going to just let me walk away? Certainly not if I do it in a hurry – that's what starts a hunting animal chasing you.*

Listen to you, Anwin – a hunting animal? Let's not get carried away. What has he done, really? He hired you. He's paying you. So you've decided you don't like him much . . .

She sat up on the bed, head pounding. She fumbled in her bag without result, then remembered she had put her gun back in the drawer next to the coffee things.

Am I really being ridiculous? Besides, he's so fast – if he doesn't want to take no for an answer next time, would I even get the chance to use it? She let her purse slide to the floor. *Too much. This is too much – I need some sleep.*

Half an hour later, although the painblockers had dulled the throb of her head, sleep was still depressingly distant. She got up and walked quietly down the short hallway into the main section of the loft.

Dread was again lying in the special bed, serene as a buddha. A slightly less adult part of herself whispered, *Typical man. I've got a headache and I'm thinking about shooting him, and he sleeps through everything.*

But he wasn't sleeping, of course. He was back in the network, doing whatever it was that he did there. Dulcie had not seen the place for weeks, and found herself oddly nostalgic for it.

What the hell is he up to?

Angered by her own fearfulness, although it was by no means gone yet, she took her pad off the tabletop and retreated to her room, then slid closed the bolt on her door. Within moments she was surveying the almost complete destruction of the Disposal files caused by the dataphage. She put her salvage gear to work and sat back, wishing she had some uncomplicated hobby with which to pass the time – smoking or serious drinking or Russian roulette.

Time for a major State of the Self meeting, Dulcie? She considered, but set it aside. Life was too strange right now, and it was never a good idea to make decisions when you were depressed and exhausted.

She had walked around the loft three times and returned messages from a few people in the States, including a cranky, rambling explanation from her neighbor Charlie about why she had accidentally fed dog food to Dulcie's cat Jones, which even a face-to-face call didn't ever quite clear up, before the gear finished its work. With very low expectations, she opened the salvaged files and found pretty much what she had expected – fragments. Some of them were incomprehensible segments of scrambled text, parts of what might have been accounting files or even personal messages, but now might as well have been written in a dead language. There were a few recognizable passages, but they were the predictable result of resurrecting a random half-percent of what had been a huge and diverse load of data, meaningless remnants of reports without enough context to make sense. The only intriguing thing was that some of the fragments were couched in what seemed like medical language, as though they were part of someone's health records. There was a mention of changing medications and a list of what seemed to be brain chemistry readouts, but oddly sophisticated, not the kind of thing you would expect in the medical records of even so important and unusual an employee as Dread.

In fact, based on the rubbish left after the dataphage's destructive attack, she couldn't even be sure these bits and pieces *were* about Dread. It was the logical deduction, but completely unprovable. Worse, though, was the fact that the disconnected bits gave her exactly nothing of what she had sought, information about her employer through his relationship with his own master, Felix Jongleur.

The one decent-sized chunk of data that remained coherent was a long image file, apparently one of hundreds according to its signifier, but the only one that had survived the data explosion. She managed to open it and run it, but was mystified by the small, grainy image, some kind of footage taken in what must have been a badly lit room, and perhaps by a camera with a hinky power supply. A white flash of emptiness was followed by a stark picture which seemed to show a small, dark-haired figure sitting at a table in a white room. A voice-over called a test number, then the camera zoomed in on the subject's hands and a small object lying between them on the table. Nothing else seemed to happen for some twenty seconds, then the camera pulled back again, some numbers were given by an off-camera voice, and the segment ended.

Dulcie sat back, puzzled. Normally she would have abandoned the whole thing as a loss, but she was still wired-up and nervous and wouldn't be able to sleep for hours. Also, she was unwilling to acknowledge defeat, however obvious the fact of that defeat might seem. She searched her system for image-enhancement gear – she had done a favor for a semi-friend who also worked the shadier areas of information transfer and he had paid her back with what he said was a package of state-of-the-art military image-crunchers – then began experimenting to see if she could make anything happen with the single surviving bit of visual imagery.

The first thing she did was work on enhancing the face of the subject. She couldn't improve it much, but brought enough clarity to the image to be certain it was a dark-haired and fairly dark-skinned boy. She stared at it stupidly for a moment, afraid to let herself believe what seemed obvious.

Could that be Dread? But he looks about thirteen. Why would Jongleur have footage of him when he was thirteen? What possible significance would it have?

She went back to work in earnest, struggling with the unfamiliar gear to get better resolution, wishing she knew more about this kind of work. She managed to alter the contrast enough to bring the cheek-bone and jaw out from the fall of straight black hair and felt her pulse speed – the face certainly had something of Dread's shape to it. But no matter how much she tried, she could not make the image any clearer, which was odd because she could improve things like the edge of the table or the subject's hands into a grainy but precise image.

Thwarted, but inwardly convinced it was him, she next began to work on the object lying on the table between his hands, a dark lozenge about ten by five centimeters. When she realized that it wasn't a familiar object and stopped trying to see it that way, she was finally able to bring it into better focus. It was some kind of timer with a digital readout, like an oblong watch with no strap. As she ran the footage backward and forward she began to make out the pattern of the numbers, although she confused herself several times before she finally realized that halfway through the experiment or test the numbers on the readout suddenly began to run backward.

Dulcie shook her head. A teenage Dread holding a timer that ticked forward in the standard manner, then switched and began running the numbers backward? What the hell kind of experiment was that? And why would Jongleur have stashed it in this very secret equivalent of a personnel file?

She reviewed the experiment footage over and over, and although she had become so certain that the figure was Dread she could no longer imagine it otherwise, she could make no other sense of it. It was only when she ran the sequence back to its very beginning for a last look that she realized she hadn't paid any attention to the flash of white at the start, assuming it was just a blank caused by bad data. When she stopped and slowed it she saw that it was actually something white passing in front of the camera. Certain that it would prove to be only someone's lab coat, or perhaps the vastly distorted hand of the person filming the test as they adjusted the lens, she nevertheless began to play with it.

It was a card, she discovered after many minutes fiddling with the resolution – perhaps something with the experiment number marked on it. The beginning of the footage was gone, so it was only present for an instant before it was whipped away again, but she could see faint gray marks that she felt sure were writing. She started the round of enhancements all over again, determined to make the smudges legible.

Half an hour later the machine came up with the fifth and best iteration. The card was catching light from an overhead fluorescent, a glare which all but obliterated the camera's ability to see what was on it, but gear meant to recognize facial features from low-Earth orbit had finally turned the marks into recognizable words:

DR CHAVEN – PROCEDURE #12831 – WULGARU, JOHN

Dulcie suddenly had an intense sensation of being watched, of naked vulnerability. She looked up in a panic, certain that Dread had crept up behind her again, but her bedroom was empty, the door bolted. She closed her pad and walked quietly out into the hallway to make certain Dread was still prisoned in his whispering sarcophagus.

John Wulgaru, she thought when she got back. Her hands were shaking. *Is that his name, then? Am I the only person who knows that? Or the only person still alive?*

She dismissed such melodrama as the product of her nervousness. The important thing was, she had cracked it. *Who else could have pulled it off? Damn few.*

The roller coaster was now heading back upward. Dulcie was eager to do something, anything, with this hard-won bit of knowledge. She called up Dread's locked room, but the hidden storage did not respond to the name in any combination. Only slightly disappointed, she closed the connection. Even if his real name was almost completely unknown, Dread would probably not use it as a password, especially for a file which might well contain incriminating evidence about his professional life. But it was a first step – getting to know the system's owner was the best key to cracking it, and now she knew something important about Dread.

Dulcie paused for a moment to wonder why Jongleur had so effectively booby-trapped his information about

Dread, but had left the *Ushabti* file, which was apparently concerned with something far larger and more important, the transfer of his estate, without similar protection. Perhaps because Jongleur knew there could be no good reason for anyone other than himself to be looking at the Dread information, she guessed, but the other file might wind up passing through the hands of attorneys, company officers, and various other third parties.

She drummed her fingers, anxious to do something else. At the very least, she could find out what records if any could be pulled up using her employer's newly-discovered name. She doubted there would be much of interest floating around, but as a veteran of the information wars she knew it was hard to completely eradicate anything from the vast worldwide matrix.

She set her gear on a shielded search for 'Wulgaru,' then went to lie down, stare at the ceiling, and grind her teeth.

As she had guessed, the search brought up little except a few bits here and there having to do with an Aboriginal myth. The longest and most complete version, by two people named Kuertner and Jigalong, came from an academic journal of folklore. It was a disturbing little story, strangely open-ended. Although it told her nothing useful about her employer, the hours she spent afterward waiting for sleep, mind already enflamed with all she had learned and done and risked that day, were troubled by the idea of a remorseless wooden man with stones for eyes.

DREAD brought the music up louder as the chorus moaned its way up and down the twelve-tone scale, then fragmented into separate sharp cries like a little shower of

squirmed a little in his column of semisolid air. *I could just fence the perimeter and then let them go. A free-range hunting preserve, all mine.*

The little stabs of musical misery washed over him. The godlike feeling had returned – in a weaker mind and spirit it might have seemed like madness, but Dread knew better. There was no one like him. No one.

And, as a god should, even when he soared to the outer limits of his own glory, he did not forget the little things.

Dulcie. So after I get her to finish the operating system research, shall I take her on a little camping trip out to the Bush? He considered this for a moment, lazily, until a mote of irritation fluttered up. *But I didn't plan for it, and I let her arrive in a taxi. There's probably a record. If it looks like murder, there will be questions, and no matter how many layers there are between me and the lease on this place, I still don't need that kind of aggro, do I? Not now. So it will have to look like an accident.*

Which doesn't mean I can't have fun with her first.

He decided to give his employee forty-eight hours to complete her work. Then, seized by a magnanimous urge, upped it to seventy-two.

Three days. Then some terrible thing will happen to the poor tourist girl from New York.

It would be fun deciding how it would happen, when he could pull himself away from the pressing business of the prisoners from the Circle and a few other projects within the network. But he would leave some of it to the final moment, of course – let it be spontaneous.

Otherwise, where was the art?

CHAPTER 27

The Green Steeple

NETFEED/NEWS: *Another Killing Mars Utah Peace*
(visual: wreckage of Eltrim car, Salt Lake City, Utah)
VO: *The car-bombing that ended the life of Joachim Eltrim, an attorney who worked for the mayor of Salt Lake City, also threatens to end the shaky peace established between the state of Utah and the radical Mormon separatist group known as the Deseret Covenant. The mayor's office and the Salt Lake City police say the finger of suspicion points straight at the separatists, who have denied responsibility.*
(visual: Deseret spokesman Edgar Riley)
RILEY: *'I'm not saying there aren't a lot of our people who want Eltrim and all other interfering, treacherous lawyers like him dead, I'm just saying we didn't have anything to do with it . . .'*

THE bramble-choked streets of More Very Bush were alive with pale, skittering shapes. Even seeing them from of the middle of the stone bridge, Renie felt such powerful terror and disgust wash over her that she swayed and almost tumbled into the swiftly moving river.

'I . . . have to go there,' Renie said, although everything in her screamed otherwise. 'The strangers that are trapped – those might be my friends.'

The Stone Girl could only sob and hide her face behind her stubby hands.

It was like the Jinnears on the hillside all over again – worse, because of the sheer numbers of the things. Only the knowledge that !Xabbu and the rest might be in that tower near the center of town, under siege by the ugly things swarming like giant termites, kept her standing. That and the little girl kneeling on the stone beside her, who was clearly even more frightened than she was.

'I can't leave you here,' Renie told her. 'And I can't go away and leave my friends by themselves. Can you make it back across on your own?' The Stone Girl's shoulders heaved. Renie reached down to lay her hand on the girl's back. 'I promise I'll wait until I see you make it to the riverbank.'

'I can't!' the Stone Girl wailed. 'I said the King's Daughter words! I can't go back.'

So many incomprehensible rules! It seemed pretty obvious by now that teaching fairy tales to an AI might not be the most efficient way to program it. 'But if we can't go back, we have to go on,' Renie said as gently as she could, hiding her own terror for the child's sake. 'We have to.'

The Stone Girl could not stop crying. Renie looked up at the darkening sky. 'Come on.' She tugged at the girl's arm, trying desperately to remember what she used to do when she couldn't get Stephen to move. 'Just . . . just do what I do. I'm going to sing a song. You just do what I do every time I sing a verse, okay? Just watch and step when I step, okay?' *God knows, it ought to be a nursery rhyme*, she thought, but could not for the life of her summon anything suitable. Desperate, she snatched at the first tune that came to her mind, the theme from some Asian game show her mother had liked to watch:

> 'If you are a know-it-all,'

she chanted,

> 'Come on down to Sprootie Hall . . .

'Yes, you can do it,' she encouraged the Stone Girl. 'See, just keep moving, like this.' She sang slowly, emphasizing the beats, 'If you *are* a know-it-*all* . . .'

The little girl finally looked up, face full of misery . . . and something else. She was silently begging Renie, in the way children did, to be *right*. To make the impossible happen. To make all the little lies true.

Renie swallowed hard and started again.

> 'If you are a know-it-all,
> Come on down to Sprootie Hall!
> Can you survive the Knowledge Kniche?
> Then you will soon be Sprootie Rich!'

Slowly, as though she waded through air as viscous as melted caramel, the Stone Girl matched her steps to Renie's cracked, almost tuneless singing.

> 'If you have a thirst for cash,
> Come on down and have a bash!
> If your brain is extra healthy,
> You will soon be Sprootie Wealthy!
>
> Eduformative!
> Infotacular!
> Sprootie Smart is brainiac-ular . . . !'

She sang it through six more times to get them across the bridge, getting more and more quiet as they neared the last stone pier, even though the nearest of the pale things was still a hundred meters away and had shown no sign of interest. Renie scrambled down onto the grassy bank and reached up to take the Stone Girl's small, cool hands and let her swing down. It was only when the girl had landed beside her that Renie saw that the child's eyes were pinched tightly shut with fright.

'It's okay,' Renie whispered.

The Stone Girl looked around her, clearly struggling not to cry again. 'Who . . . who's Sprootie?'

'Just some stupid . . . it doesn't matter. We should be quiet so they don't hear us.'

'Ticks don't listen. Ticks watch.'

Renie was relieved, but only for a moment. 'Is there anything we can do to keep them from seeing us?'

'Don't move.'

Renie could feel the horror of the pallid, scuttling things even more strongly now that the river was behind her, inhibiting escape. 'We can't just stay here. Is there anything else that will help besides not moving?'

'Move real, real slow.'

Renie squinted across the shadowy townscape, trying to make out the lay of the land between them and the tower which seemed to be the focus of the Ticks' attention. The streets and buildings were a uniform brambly green, as though they had all been put to service as trellises in some madcap gardening experiment, but if so, it had been a long time since there had been a tending hand: the corners and edges of the buildings were shaggy with leaves. Creepers had made their way from one high place to another, and now hung between towers and gables like great sagging spiderwebs.

'It's getting dark,' Renie said quietly. 'We have to start moving.'

The Stone Girl did not reply, but stayed close as they took their first cautious steps forward. They made it up the riverbank to a low wall at the edge of town without attracting attention. As they huddled behind it, Renie found herself wishing desperately for a weapon of some kind. All she was carrying was the lighter, and the idea of trying to set a flabby-looking creature like a two-meter cuttlefish on fire with a Minisolar was a joke she couldn't much appreciate just now. A torch was a possibility, but the nearest trees were still a long trot away.

'Are Ticks scared of anything?' she asked. The Stone Girl's look of incredulity answered her question for her, but Renie reached into the leafy vegetation covering the wall, thinking that she would at least feel a little better with a large rock in her hand. She found herself digging into the scratchy tangle far deeper than she would have believed necessary to find a loose stone, then was even more surprised when her hand pushed through and out the other side. It was all bramble.

'Where's the wall? Isn't there a wall under here?'

The Stone Girl had gone an ashier shade than her normal clay color. She looked at Renie nervously. 'That *is* the wall.'

'But . . . aren't there . . . things under all these leaves?' She had a sudden, confounding thought. 'Are all those houses and whatnot just made of plants?'

'This is More Very Bush,' the little girl explained.

'Shit.' So much for sticks and stones to use as makeshift weapons. It also meant that if her friends were truly besieged in that tower building near the center of town, they had no real walls to keep the creatures out.

In fact, what *was* keeping the creatures out?

Renie took another deep breath, finding it harder than ever to make herself go forward. Something like a cloud of terror seemed to hang over the whole town – not just her obvious and justified fear of the strange Ticks, but something deeper and less explicable. She remembered the wave of panic that had seized her while she was being chased by Jinnears.

We're inside the operating system. Are we feeling its fear? But what would an artificial intelligence fear?

She led the Stone Girl to a place where the wall was low and they could scramble over it easily, although not without Renie getting scratched quite a few more times. They stopped on the far side. A Tick was moving toward them, undulating across the low vegetation like something swimming along the ocean floor. Despite the Stone Girl saying that sound did not matter, Renie found her throat choked to silence.

The Tick paused a dozen meters away. It did not have legs, but each point of its scalloped sides ended in something like a pseudopod; they rippled gently, in sequence, even when the thing wasn't moving. Dark spots swam beneath the translucent skin, as though the creature were filled with billiard balls and jelly. It was only as the dark spots one after another pressed out against the skin and then receded in turn that she remembered the Stone Girl's words: Ticks had too many eyes.

'Jesus Mercy!' It was a strangled sound.

Whether because it actually could not see them without movement, or because they were too far away to be worth bothering with, the Tick turned and made its way back up the main street. Several of its fellows bumped it as it passed; some even crawled over it. Renie could not tell if they were communicating through touch or were simply terribly stupid.

'I don't want to be here,' the little girl said.

'I don't either, but we are. Just hold my hand and keep moving. Do you want me to sing the Sprootie Smart song again?'

The Stone Girl shook her head.

Slowly, they made their way deeper into the town, freezing in place every time one of the Ticks came near, trying to stay behind cover as much as possible. Renie found herself actually grateful for the advancing twilight: if the creatures were dependent on sight, then darkness must be her friend. Still, she definitely wanted to get away from these crawling things before full night if she possibly could.

They reached the first of the houses, a cottage of green leaves and snaking vines. As Renie stole a look inside – even the furniture was composed of vegetation – she couldn't help whispering a question. 'Who lived in this town?'

'Bears, mostly,' said the Stone Girl in a tight little voice. 'And some rabbits. And a big family of hedgehogs called Tinkle or Wrinkle or something, I th-th-think . . .' Tears seeped from her eyeholes.

'Ssshhh. It's okay. We'll be . . .'

Three Ticks glided around the corner of the next house and wriggled across the bramble-choked alleyway, heading right toward them. The Stone Girl gave a little squeak of horror and sagged. Renie grabbed her, holding her upright and as still as she could with her own limbs trembling badly.

The Ticks paused and lay pulsing gently atop the vegetative carpet, a mere half-dozen meters from the spot where Renie and the Stone Girl stood. Only their elongated shape gave them a front and a back; both ends seemed identical, but Renie had no doubts from the Ticks' postures that they were facing her. They had sensed something, and now were waiting.

One of the Ticks scuttled a little way forward toward the house. Another eased forward and slid over it, then they parted and again lay parallel. Ripples of lighter and darker color ran up and down their bodies. The eye-spots bunched at the things' front ends, three or four dark orbs visible in each creature, pressed up against the membranous skin.

A tiny whine of panic escaped the Stone Girl and Renie could feel the child's arms go taut. Any moment now her panic would become too much and she would bolt. Renie tried to keep a tight grip, but terror was rising fast inside her, too.

Suddenly, with a loud, swishing rattle that almost stopped Renie's heart, something leaped out of the carpet of brambles just in front of the Ticks – a blur of wild, shiny eye and gray fur – then sprang away across the dooryard heading for the open street. The Ticks flowed after it with terrifying speed, moving so quickly they barely seemed to touch the brambles. The child-sized rabbit in the tiny blue coat reached the street but had to dodge away from another Tick that reared up, its mouth a jagged rip on the underside of the head. The sudden change of direction ran the terrified fugitive right into its pursuers. The rabbit let out a single all-too-human scream of horror, then the Ticks fell on it in a squirming, fleshy mass.

Renie pulled the Stone Girl around the side of the house, away from view of the street and the wet sounds of feeding. They were lucky; no other Ticks were waiting there. She shoved the stumbling little girl in front of her, across the alley full of knee-high vegetation and into the shelter of the house next door.

Inside there was just enough light coming in through a small window to make out a quantity of household objects all made from living leaves and vines – chairs, a table, bowls, and even a candlestick; otherwise the little hut was empty. Renie clenched her fists in fear and frustration. She could actually see the church tower through the window, festooned with vines like a maypole, but although it was only a few dozen meters away it might as well have been a thousand. The ground between their temporary refuge and the tower was full of the pale things.

'I'll think of something,' Renie declared. 'Don't give up. I'll get us out of here.'

The little Stone Girl took a deep, shaky breath. 'Y-you w-w-will?'

'I promise,' Renie said firmly, even as she hugged herself to still the trembling. What else could she say?

THREE empty squeeze bottles of Mountain Rose lay on the floor in front of him like bleached bones. Long Joseph contemplated them with a feeling only a small distance from despair.

Knew it was going to happen, he chided himself. *Drink it a drop at a time, still going to finish some day . . .*

And the hell of it was that there was absolutely nothing he could do. At the moment when he most needed a supply of the healing, warming liquid, with men that wanted to kill both him and his daughter just a short distance above him, after he had been trapped for weeks in a cement tomb under a mountain with no company but boring, disapproving Jeremiah Dako – and adding Del Ray Chiume to the mix hadn't helped much – now of all times he had nothing to drink.

He wiped his hand roughly across his mouth. He knew he wasn't a drunk. He knew drunks, saw them all the time, men who could barely stand, men swaying outside the shebeens with old, dried piss stains on their pants and breath that smelled like paint thinner, men with eyes like ghosts' eyes. That wasn't him. But he also knew he could dearly use some comfort. It wasn't so much that he wanted a drink, not the taste, not even the little glow of satisfaction when the first few swallows made their way into the belly. But it felt like his entire body was a little loose and ill-fitting all over, his skeleton not quite sitting right in his meat, his skin the wrong size.

Joseph grunted and stood up. What was the point, anyway? Even if Renie came back, stepped out of her electrical bathtub like that what-was-his-name, that Lazarus man from the Bible, healthy and happy and proud of her papa, they still weren't going to get out of this mountain alive. Not with four killers up there, cruel hard men determined to dig them out like an anteater on a termite nest.

Joseph took a few stiff steps over to the bank of monitors. The men upstairs had not finished fanning out the smoke, but the atmosphere up there was much clearer. They would be getting back to work soon, chipping out the rest of the concrete floor. Then what – grenades? Flaming petrol dumped down on top of them, so they burned like rats? He counted the shapes in the murk. Yes, four. So at least they had killed one of them with Sellars' bonfire. But that would only mean the rest would be even nastier when the time came.

Nastier? You must be joking, man. This would never have been one of those simple Pinetown shake-outs after too many beers, fists and boards and maybe a knife just before people started running away, not even the bad kind with the young men and their guns, that terrible noise like a stick dragged along a fence and people stopping,

faces slack, knowing something bad had just happened
. . . No, this was always going to be something far worse.

The itch was bad now, a need to move, to get out, to
run as fast as he could under open sky. Maybe they could
find another way out, a heating duct like he had found
before. They would have to take Renie and the little man
out of those bathtubs, those wired-up coffins, but surely
whatever they were doing in there was not more important than their lives.

*Then do what? Run across the mountains while those
men come after in their big truck all armored up like a
tank?*

He smacked his hand down on the console and turned
away. All he wanted was to pour something down his
throat. Was that too much to ask for a man condemned
to die? Even in Westville Prison they gave the poor bugger
a last meal before they killed him, didn't they, a beer or
a little wine?

Joseph stood, flexing his fingers. Surely in all this big
place, there must have been someone who liked a drink,
who kept a bottle hid while he was on duty – just one
bottle that got left behind when everyone moved out. He
looked to the alcove where Jeremiah was discussing
supplies with Del Ray, the glow of the light spilling out
onto the cement floor that ringed the large chamber. They
didn't need Joseph. They didn't even like him, a man of
his hands, a man who didn't put on airs so he could work
for rich Boers. If it weren't for his daughter, he would say
the hell with them both and find himself an air shaft out.

He rubbed the back of his hand across his mouth again
and, without really thinking about it – because if he
thought he would know it was hopeless and foolish, that
he had searched the whole place from top to bottom a
half-dozen times – wandered off to look for that bottle

of beer some faceless soldier or technician had stashed
away for the long hours of the watch.

No – wine, he thought. If he was dreaming a hopeless
dream, why not make it perfect? *A whole bottle of something good, something with kick. Not even opened. He hid
it away there, then the orders came and they all had to
go.* He saluted his anonymous benefactor. *You did not
know, but you put it away for Joseph Sulaweyo. In his
hour of need, like they say.*

His skin prickled. The filing cabinet lay on its side against
the wall of the service closet, as wonderful as a treasure
chest from a pirate story.

In a fit of nervous energy brought on by fear and frustration, he had unstacked a pile of folding chairs he had
passed many times, working at it with no more hope than
when he had once more opened cabinets and drawers
already searched a dozen times in the last month – but
to his astonishment, he had discovered the tipped cabinet hidden beneath the chairs. Now he hardly dared move
for fear it would vanish.

Probably just full with papers, a small, sensible voice
told him. *Or spiders. If they are full with anything at all.*

Nevertheless his palms were sweaty and it took him
some moments to realize that it wasn't merely his slippery grip on the handles that kept the drawers from opening. *Don't work lying down*, he realized. *Thing needs to
be standing up.*

It was a huge, cumbersome cabinet, the kind meant to
survive fires and other disasters. As his muscles protested
at the strain he was putting on them, he thought for a
moment of calling Jeremiah for help, but could imagine
no believable excuse for wanting to get the cabinet
upright. At last, with much grunting and swearing, he

dragged the top end off the ground. He got it as high as his waist before his back would not take any more, then had to squat and let the full weight of the thing rest on his thighs while he prepared himself to heave it the rest of the way. It felt like it was full of rocks. He thought he could feel his ankle bones grinding down into powder from supporting it, but the solid heft of it gave him hope – there had to be *something* in it.

Joseph braced himself and lifted again, grimacing as the corners dug into his forearms, pulling it up until he could slide his whole body under the top end and really put his back and shoulders into the job. It tottered for a moment – he had a sour picture of lying underneath it with his back broken while Jeremiah and Del Ray chatted on, unaware, a hundred meters away – before he managed to rise from his crouch and shove it almost upright. It caught the edge of a heating vent screen in the cement wall and stuck. Back quivering and arms trembling, sweat running in his eyes, Joseph shoved until the bolts holding the screen tore loose and it clattered to the ground, allowing the filing cabinet to slide past and thump down square on its bottom.

Joseph bent from the waist, panting, sweat now dripping straight to the floor. The little room was small and hot, the light dim. The reflexive need for secrecy warred with discomfort. Secrecy lost. Joseph pushed open the door into the main hall, letting in a waft of cooler air, before trying the top drawer.

It wasn't locked. But his luck ended there.

Who wasted this cabinet by crowding it all up with files? A dull, helpless sort of rage filled him like a purpling bruise. The cabinet was heavy because it was filled with papers, meaningless papers, personnel records, some nonsense like that, drawer after drawer stuffed to the brim with old-fashioned folders.

Joseph had only a moment to savor this deep misery before something fell on him from above.

For a moment, wildly, he thought that part of the roof had given way, as had happened to Del Ray, that the Boer bastard and his henchmen upstairs had drilled through just above him. Then, as the strangely sagging weight pulled him down to the floor and fingers clawed at his face, he thought instead that Jeremiah had come and attacked him, was for some reason trying to hurt him.

Just looking for a drink, he wanted to shout, but the fingers clamped on his throat, squeezing him silent. In a panic, Joseph rolled hard to the side and banged himself painfully against the standing cabinet but managed to dislodge the choking hands. He scrabbled backward, shaking his head, coughing, and managed to whisper the word, 'What . . . ?' before his attacker was on him again.

Whoever it was seemed more octopus than man, all arms and legs, grabbing at him, trying to pin him, throttle him. Joseph struggled and tried to shout, but now an arm was across his throat, pressing down until he thought something inside his neck must tear and his head part company with his body. He kicked out wildly. His feet met the cabinet hard; he felt it give and heard it fall back against the wall, then scrape against the concrete and crash to the floor. He got a hand up under the arm that was crushing out his breath and pushed back hard enough to drag a little air into his lungs, but there were still sparkling lights in front of his eyes. Something moved over him, leaning in close, a demon's mask of black and red and whitely-shining clenched teeth. Joseph kicked again but touched nothing and the weight on his neck was now too much to resist. The devil-face began to retreat down a black tunnel, but the grip was growing stronger. He still did not know what had happened, who was killing him.

And then, just as the light-streaked blackness had become almost complete, the pressure lessened and then was gone – or almost gone, because he could still feel a crimp in his throat. He rolled over onto his stomach, wheezing and choking through a windpipe that felt like it would never open again.

Someone was shouting and something was thumping like a heavy weight being dragged down stairs. Joseph felt cool concrete against his cheek, felt the even cooler air rushing down his ragged throat like the finest of all wines. He dragged himself toward the wall of the service closet then turned around, lifting his quivering hands in self-defense.

It *was* Jeremiah, with a look on his face like nothing Joseph had ever imagined, a look of terrified rage. But what was he doing? What was he hammering on with that stick of his, that steel chair leg, that club he had carried since Joseph's return? And why was he crying?

Jeremiah seemed to feel Long Joseph's dazed stare. He looked at him with brimming eyes, then down at a dark bundle on the floor. The thing lying there was a man – a white man, although in his whole smoke-blackened, blood-ied face only a pink curve of ear gave that away. The back of his head was a ruin, bits of bone showing through the wet red. The end of Jeremiah's chair leg was dripping. Jeremiah looked up from Joseph to the wall overhead and the dark hole there that had been covered by the screen. Now Del Ray appeared in the closet doorway.

'My God,' he said. 'What happened?' His eyes widened. 'Who's that?'

Jeremiah Dako held up the bloody chair leg, stared at it as though he had never seen it before. A sickly smile pulled up the edges of his mouth – maybe the worst thing Joseph had seen so far.

'At least . . . at least we've still . . . got two bullets left,' said Jeremiah. He laughed. Then he began to sob again.

'He's the fifth one,' Del Ray said. 'I can still see four of them on the monitor. He's the one we thought got killed when the smoke got them.'

'What does that matter?' Jeremiah said listelessly. 'That just means there are still as many up there as we thought this morning.'

Joseph could only listen. He felt as though someone had ripped his head off and put it back on in great haste.

'It means they probably don't know about the vent,' Del Ray said. 'He probably crawled in there to get away from the smoke – he may have been cut off by what he thought was a fire, trapped on the other side of the building from the others. Then he just kept crawling until he got to that vent and could get air from our part of the building. Maybe he was even stuck there.' He looked at the corpse, which they had dragged out into the better light of the open hallway. 'So the rest of them aren't going to be coming down the vent on us in our sleep.'

Jeremiah shook his head. He had stopped weeping, but still seemed miserable. 'We don't know anything.' His voice was almost as raspy as Joseph's.

'What do you mean?'

'Look at him.' Jeremiah shoved a finger at the body, although he did not look at it himself. 'He's bloody all over. Dried blood. Burns. Scrapes and cuts. There's a good chance he got them getting into the vent in the first place, hurrying to get away from the smoke. He probably left marks of where he got in – maybe even left a screen lying on the ground. When the smoke clears up there, they'll find them. They'll go looking for him.'

'Then we'll . . . I don't know. Weld that vent in the storage closet closed. Something.' Jeremiah and Del Ray had already struggled to hammer the screen back into place, with limited success.

'They can just poison us – pour poison gas down it, smother us.' Jeremiah stared at the floor.

'Then why haven't they done that already?' Del Ray demanded. 'They could probably find our air intake if they wanted to. If they only wanted us dead, surely they could have done that already.'

Jeremiah shook his head. 'It's too late.'

Joseph was disturbed to see the man so unhappy. Was it because he had killed someone? How could anyone, even a sensitive soul like Jeremiah Dako, regret killing the man who had been trying to kill Joseph?

'Jeremiah,' he said softly. 'Jeremiah. Listen to me.'

The other man looked up, eyes red.

'You save my life. We fight sometimes, you and me, but I never will forget that.' He tried to think of something that would make things right. 'Thank you. Truly I mean that.'

Jeremiah nodded, but his face was still bleak. 'A postponement. That's all it is.' He sniffed, almost angrily. 'But you're welcome, Joseph. And I truly mean that, too.'

No one spoke for a while.

'I just thought of something,' said Del Ray. 'What are we going to do with a dead body down here?'

'THEY look like bottom-feeders,' Renie said. 'If it's more than just appearance, maybe we'll get lucky.' She was talking mostly to herself. Her companion the Stone Girl was too frightened to be paying much attention.

Renie took another look out the window at the church spire made of brambles, achingly near but still on the far side of several dozen Ticks, creatures so pale they almost seemed to glow in the dying evening. But at the moment it was a forest of vines and creepers that stretched away from the tower like guy-ropes had her attention.

'Come hold this steady,' she said as she climbed cautiously onto the table, which like everything else in this strange little subworld was made entirely from living plants, densely intertwined. It wobbled but held; apparently the furniture was indeed meant to be used, if not for the purpose Renie had in mind. The Stone Girl came forward and did her best to brace it.

Renie stretched up until she could get her hands into the vegetation of the low ceiling and began digging at the tangled branches, pulling aside that which could not be broken or torn until she had made a hole through which she could see the velvety dark sky, and the faint early stars. Reassured, she quickly began to widen the hole until it was big enough for her shoulders. She pulled herself up, grunting with the effort, and took a quick look around the rooftop. Satisfied that none of the scuttling things were waiting there, she let herself down again.

'Come on,' she told her companion. 'I'll lift you up.'

The Stone Girl took some convincing but at last allowed herself to be boosted through the hole.

'There,' Renie said as she lifted herself onto the roof beside the girl. 'On the far side, see? Those vines will get us to the house nearest the tower, then we can go up from there.'

The Stone Girl looked down at the Ticks swarming on the ground, then eyed the sagging creepers with mistrust. 'What do you mean?'

'We can climb them – put our feet on the lower ones and hang onto the ones higher up with our hands. It's how they build bridges in the jungle.' She did not feel as confident as she sounded – she had never actually crossed such a bridge, in a jungle or anywhere else – but it was surely better than sitting in the little house waiting for the Ticks to notice them.

The Stone Girl only nodded, overtaken by a sort of weary fatalism.

Trusting because I'm a grown-up. Like one of those stepmothers. It was an unpleasant burden, but there was no one to share it. Renie sighed and moved to the edge of the roof. She beckoned the Stone Girl and then lifted her up to the thick vine that stretched upward at an angle beside them, not releasing her grip until she was sure it would bear the little girl's weight. 'Hang on,' she told the child. 'I'm climbing up now.'

For a long moment after she swung herself up Renie had to cling with her hands and legs until she could get in position to grab the higher vine and stand. The lower vine swayed alarmingly beneath her bare feet until she got her balance straight. 'Go ahead,' she told the Stone Girl as she helped her stand and reach the upper vine. 'Just go slowly. We'll get off and rest at that roof there – the tall house between us and the tower.'

Going slowly turned out to be their only option. It was hard enough to keep their feet on the slippery vine while stepping over knots of tangling, leafy branches. Although the Ticks did not exactly seem to have noticed them, Renie wondered whether their senses were as limited as the child had suggested: those lurking just below seemed to be growing increasingly agitated. She couldn't help imagining what the creatures' response would be if she and her companion were suddenly to drop down into the brambles, right in their midst.

It seemed like a good idea to stop looking down.

The light was now almost completely gone. When they

reached the roof of the tall house, halfway to the spire, Renie began to think that resting could be a bad idea – that they might be better off using the last light to help in the difficult climb. The Stone Girl stopped, still several steps short of the roof.

'What's wrong?'

'I c-can't go anymore.'

Renie cursed silently. 'Just get to the roof, then we'll rest. We're almost there.'

'No! I can't go anymore! It's too high.'

Renie looked down, confused. It was less than half a dozen meters to the ground. She was a little girl, of course, Renie couldn't afford to forget that, but still . . . 'Can you just make it a little bit farther? When we get to the roof, you won't have to see the ground any more.'

'No, stupid!' She was almost crying with anger and frustration. 'The *vine* is too high!'

The Ticks seemed to be gathering beneath them. Distracted by their churning, it took Renie a moment to see that the child was right. The higher of the two vines they were using for their bridge had been rising more steeply than the lower. The Stone Girl had stretched her arms almost to their capacity just to keep a grip on it, but another few paces and it would be beyond her reach.

'Jesus Mercy, I'm sorry! I am stupid, you're right.' Renie struggled against panic. The Ticks were now swarming over each other just below them like worms in a bucket. 'Let me get closer and I'll help you.' She inched forward until she could take one arm off the upper vine and wrap it around the little girl. 'Can you hold onto my leg? Maybe even stand on my foot?'

The Stone Girl, who had clearly been keeping a worried silence for some time, now burst into tears. With help, she managed to wrap herself around Renie's thigh and grip Renie's ankle with her feet – it was an awkward and undignified position, but Renie found that if she was careful she could inch upward. Still, by the time they toppled off onto the cushiony safety of the roof perhaps another quarter of an hour had passed and the last daylight was gone.

'Where's the moon?' Renie asked when she had finally caught her breath.

The Stone Girl shook her head sadly. 'I don't think they have a moon in More Very Bush anymore.'

'Then we'll have to make do with starlight.' *Sounds like a song title*, Renie decided, a bit giddy with exhaustion and the very temporary respite from climbing over the Ticks. She sat up. The light was minimal, but it was enough to see the silhouette of the tower and even a glow from the belfry. Her heart leaped. Could it be !Xabbu? She longed to shout out to him, but was much less certain now about the deafness of Ticks.

'We have to go,' she said. 'If I wait any longer my muscles will cramp up. Come on.'

'But I can't *reach!*' The Stone Girl was on the verge of weeping again.

A brief instant of irritation dissolved quickly. *My God, what I've put this child through! The poor little thing.* 'I'll carry you on my back. You're small.'

'I'm the biggest kid in my house,' she said with a shadow of indignant pride.

'Yes, and you're very brave.' Renie crouched. 'Climb up.'

The Stone Girl struggled up onto Renie's back, and from there was boosted onto her shoulders so that her cool, solid little legs lay on either side of Renie's neck. Renie stood and swayed a bit, but found the girl's weight manageable.

'Now the last part,' Renie said. 'Hang on tight. I'll tell my friends how much you helped me.'

'I did,' the Stone Girl said quietly as they moved out onto the vines again. In a rare stroke of good luck, the bottom vine hung a little lower than the rooftop, so that Renie could step down instead of having to climb up with the child clinging to her back. 'I did help you. Remember the Jinnear? I helped you hide, didn't I?'

'You certainly did.'

The last part of the climb was the hardest, and not just because of the added weight and clumsiness caused by her burden. Renie's muscles had been worked too hard for too long, with too little rest, and her tendons all seemed to be pulled tight as piano wires. If not for the nagging fear that time was running out, that any moment now the Other might stop fighting and the very world might evaporate under her, Renie might have crawled back down to the roof to sleep, even with her friends only a stone's throw away.

Each step an agony, the angle of the vines growing steeper as the tall tower grew nearer, she did her best to distract herself.

What the hell are Ticks anyway? Why should a machine be afraid of bugs? And Jinnears? What are they?

And Jinnears. The phrase stuck in her mind, an indigestible lump. *And Jinnears . . . !* Startled, she almost lost her grip. The Stone Girl gave a squeak of alarm and Renie tightened her aching fist on the vine. The Ticks swarmed in agitation below. *And Jinnears – engineers! Who works with machines? Engineers and . . . and techs. Jinnears and Ticks.*

Renie let out a hysterical giggle. *But that means I'm a Jinnear, too – I have a degree and everything. Why didn't the Other make me a killer ghost-jellyfish as well?*

'Why are you laughing?' the Stone Girl demanded in a quavering voice. 'You're scaring me!'

'Sorry. I just thought of something. Don't mind me.'

But oh my God what did the techs and engineers do to this AI or whatever it is to make it think of them like that . . . ?

The vegetable firmness of the tower wall was startlingly close now. She could see the open window only two or three meters above her head, glowing against the dark sky, but the vines, which hung from the very top of the protruding roof, would not bring her very close, and the angle was soon going to be too steep anyway.

'We're going to have to get off the vines and try to climb up the wall,' she said as lightly and calmly as she could. 'I'm going to lean over as far as I can before I let go, but I'm going to have to jump. Will you hold on tight?'

'Jump . . . ?'

'It's the only way I can reach it. I'm sure the bushes will hold us,' she said without actually being sure at all. She got a good grip on the upper vine, then stopped so she could gently but firmly pry loose the fingers of the Stone Girl, who had decided to hold on as well. 'You can't do that. If you're still holding on when I jump . . . well, we're in a lot of trouble.'

'Okay,' the small voice said in her ear.

She trusts me. I almost wish she didn't . . .

Renie braced herself, then set the vine swaying, figuring even a few extra inches would help. On the fourth wide swing, she jumped toward the shadowy wall.

For a moment, as the dry leaves tore beneath her hands like paper and they slid downward, she was certain they were dead. Then she caught at something stiffer and more substantial and grabbed hard, digging her toes in as well, insensible of what she was doing to her bare feet and fingers. When they stopped sliding she clung for a moment, gasping.

Can't wait. Can't hang. No strength.

She forced herself up, grip by difficult, hard-won grip. What had looked like two or three meters to climb from the relative safety of the branch now felt like a hundred. Every muscle seemed to be writhing in agony.

The glow of the window was hallucinatory in its brightness. She pulled herself over the brambly sill and slid down to the brambly floor, gasping for breath, moaning as her muscles knotted, as star-flecked blackness rolled across her eyes.

The first thing she noticed when she could see properly again was the source of light in the tower room, a great, nodding flower hanging at the apex of the vaulted ceiling, glowing a waxy yellow at the heart of its petals. She heard the Stone Girl stirring behind her and sat up. Someone was sitting on the far side of the small room, half-hidden by leaves and shadows. It was not !Xabbu. It was Ricardo Klement, the Grail Project's only success, such as he was – handsome, young, and brain-damaged.

'Is that your friend?' the Stone Girl asked quietly.

Renie gave a sharp, cracked laugh. 'Where are the others?' She could barely muster the strength to speak. 'My friends. Are they here?'

Klement looked at her incuriously. He held something small cradled in his arms, but she could not make it out. 'Others? No others. Only me . . . us.'

'Who?' She was getting a very bad feeling. 'Us who?'

Klement slowly lifted the thing he was holding. It was small and unpleasant to look at, a sort of blue-gray, eyeless blob with rudimentary arms and legs and head, a loose gape for a mouth.

'Jesus Mercy,' Renie said in disgust and misery. 'What the hell is that?'

'It is . . .' Klement hesitated, his face blank as he sought for the words. 'It is me . . . no . . . it is mine . . .'

After all that, to find nothing but Klement and this inexplicable little monstrosity . . . ! Every bit of her was afire with pain, but worse than anything was the disappointment, a stunning blow like a bullet wound in the chest. 'What are you doing here?'

'Waiting for . . . something,' Klement said tonelessly. 'Not for you.'

'I feel exactly the same way.' Despite herself, Renie began to cry. 'God damn it all.'

CHAPTER 28

Master of His Silence

NETFEED/PERSONALS: So Sad And Lonely . . .
(visual: picture of advertiser, M.J. [anonymated])
M.J.: 'I don't care any more. There's nobody here, and I don't even
want to try. It's . . . it's really lonely here. Dark. I wanted someone
to call me because I'm alone and I'm sad. But nobody ever called –
I guess there's no one out there listening after all . . .'

IT had been bad enough falling out of Dodge City and into Egypt, but this second transition was much harder, far more painful. When Paul's thoughts came back they seemed to swim in dark, bloody waters, like primeval fish.

He opened his eyes to find a yellow face hovering just before him, grinning. Paul groaned.

'Oh, good,' said the clownish, lemon-colored mask. It was perched atop a body swathed in immaculate mummy wrappings. 'You're awake. I was afraid the sphinx had damaged you – but he's very gentle, in his way.'

Martine was gasping in pain beside him, as though she had not been brought any more gently to this place, a windowless gray stone room. T4b and Florimel were already awake, staring at their captor with grim faces.

'What do you want with us?' Paul could not make himself sound anything but hopeless and pathetic. His arms were tied securely behind his back, his ankles too. The four captives had been propped against the wall like unwanted parcels.

'I haven't really decided yet, to tell the truth,' said the yellow-faced man. 'I suppose Ptah the Artificer should know these things, but I've only really started this god business in earnest pretty recently.' He giggled. 'But now I'm really wondering where I've met you before. I would have recognized my old traveling companions, of course, even if you weren't still wearing the same old clothes – hello! But you . . .' He tilted his bright face as he regarded Paul. 'I *have* met you before, haven't I? Oh, wait, you're a friend of Kunohara's.'

'Wells?' Paul was shocked, although he could now see the weird, underwater resemblance. 'Robert Wells?'

The response was another pleased chortle. 'Oh, yes. But my Egyptian identity is rather to the fore at the moment. Lord Anubis has been kind enough to forgive my past bad associations.'

'Anubis?' Martine spoke hollowly. 'You mean Dread, don't you? You mean Jongleur's pet murderer.'

'Yes, I suppose that's his name. I would have found it much easier piecing these things together from the outside, but I've had to make do.'

'That's an understatement,' said Paul. 'You've fallen pretty low, Wells, haven't you – throwing in your lot with a butchering psychopath.'

'Don't waste your time, Paul.' Florimel's voice was cracked, the defiance unconvincingly forced. 'He is no better than Dread.'

'Anyone who knows anything about business knows

that sometimes you have to overlook certain foibles in your CEO if you want a take-charge kind of guy,' Wells said cheerfully. 'And the fact is, right now Mr Dread holds all the stock. Which means I'm proud to be on his team.'

'So . . . so you'll just stand by and let him do whatever he wants?' Paul said. 'Destroy the network, rape and murder and God knows what else . . . ?'

'In a word – yes,' said Wells. 'But he won't destroy the network. He wants to live forever, just like anyone else. Just like me.' He turned and tapped on the door. 'But he'll be back very soon, our gracious Lord Anubis, so I'm sure he'll be glad to explain things to you himself.'

The heavy door swung open, revealing a trio of shaven-headed guards just outside, their muscles shining with oil. The door thumped shut behind Wells and the bolt crashed back into place.

'Dread has us!' Martine seemed to speak from some far shore of despair. 'Oh, God, the monster has us!'

Exhausted and heartsick, squeezed to cramping agony by their bonds, neither Paul nor his companions felt much like talking. Something close to an hour passed before the bolt grated again and the door swung open to reveal the bizarre yellow countenance of Robert Wells.

'Keeping yourselves amused, I hope,' he said. 'Singing camp songs or something? *Michael row the boat ashore* . . . ?' His smile – in fact, Paul thought, his entire aspect – seemed quite insane. 'I've brought along some pals of yours.' A pair of guards shouldered their way into the room, each holding a sagging figure. When they let go of them, the prisoners stumbled and fell to the floor. Paul did not know the small, round woman in tattered Egyptian clothes, but after a moment recognized the man's face through the blood and bruises.

'Nandi . . . ?'

The prisoner rolled reddened, swollen-lidded eyes in his direction. 'I'm sorry . . . I . . . never thought . . .'

'Ah, yes!' said Wells. 'He never thought you'd actually be here, or he would have kept his mouth shut about meeting you.' The yellow mask nodded. 'It took a little while before I put two and two together. Then I realized it would be a bit of a coincidence for you to be a different Paul than the one this gentleman has been telling us about so eagerly.'

'You monster!' Nandi Paradivash struggled to crawl toward Wells, but was kicked brutally back to the floor by the nearest guard, where he lay, sobbing and wheezing.

'Paul Jonas.' Wells surveyed him with a glittering eye. 'Or "X", as I was calling you for a long time – Jongleur's mystery experiment. First I got a name to go with it, now a face.' He crossed his bandaged arms over his chest. 'Soon I'll have a lot more than that. You can explain everything. Not that it means much with Jongleur dead or missing in action, but still – I'm interested.'

Paul could only stare defiantly. 'Even if I knew . . . and I don't . . . I wouldn't tell you. It was wiped out of my memory.'

'Then maybe you'll thank me.' Wells smiled. 'When I help you remember.' He flicked his hand and the guards hurried forward and picked up Paul like a rolled carpet. He had no time to shout something brave to his companions, not even a good-bye, before they were hurrying him along a torchlit corridor. Wells' voice echoed after them.

'I'll be right there, boys. Make sure he stays tied. Oh, and sharpen everything, will you?'

'*Code Delphi.* Start here.

'I never expected to speak those words again.

'A few hours ago I was certain that continuing this journal in the face of all but certain death – a journal that no one but me would ever find, even if the network survives – would be complete madness. These entries spoken into air are only to remind me of what I felt and thought, in the unlikely event that I can look back on this time from some future I still cannot imagine. So when I was at my lowest points of despair, as I was then, it seemed even worse than mad – it seemed dull and point-less. I have never wanted to leave some dramatic last will and testament that no one will hear. I have never been moved by displays of hopeless bravery, and certainly was not going to bother with one of my own.

'In short, I had surrendered.

'I do not know that anything has truly changed – our chance of survival is still vanishingly small – but I have found a little unexpected hope. No, not hope. I still believe we will lose our lives without seeing the end of this. Determination? Perhaps.

'When we survived the feverish horror of the Dodge City simworld only to be captured in Egypt, and worst of all, when we discovered we were – and still are – being held for Dread himself, I fell for a while into the lowest despair. The pit. A hole into darkness. I could not speak, could barely even think except for nightmare images of that room in the House world where Dread tormented me. If someone at that moment had offered to put a bullet in my head, I would have accepted it with gratitude.

'Then everything changed again – for the worse, if such a thing were possible. Our captor, Robert Wells, who apparently has now become Dread's lieutenant, brought two more prisoners to join us and took away Paul Jonas for interrogation. My misery was such that I could scarcely move. I fear for Paul. God, how I fear

for him. He has already been through so much . . . ! I
am shamed that my own suffering should have left me
so self-involved. I cannot even imagine what he has
experienced, lost in this network with little memory of
his own real history and no knowledge of what was
happening to him. To have kept so sane, to be so kind
and so brave . . . It is astonishing. And it is equally
astonishing that I did not truly realize how much I
admired him until he was taken away.

'Even now, he could be dead. Or perhaps in terrible,
terrible, pain. Which would be worse?

'This is the curse I perceived before, the burden I have
evaded all my life. To like people, to . . . love people, is
to make oneself a hostage to fortune.

'So it was I began my slide into the abyss. For long
minutes after Paul was taken – it might have been hours
for all I could have guessed – I simply could not speak.
Could not think. Terror had seized my heart, frozen my
thoughts, turned me into something which could not
move, and had nowhere to go even if it could.

'This is just a more direct version, I realize now, of
what I have done in my own real life. Frightened, I have
gradually sealed myself in the rocky depths of the mountains, in the sanctuary I share only with my machines.
Without realizing it, I have actively conspired in making
myself something much less than a person.

'Still, in the grip of the terror I could not see these
things, but only now that it has passed. I might never
have left the black panic if it had not been for the hands
of my friends upon me, Florimel and T4b, who thought
I was having a heart attack. I felt them and heard them
as though from a long distance, and for a while I did not
wish to be plugged back into my nerves and senses. Better
to hide in the black pit. Better to let my overwhelming

fear protect me, as blocks of ice make a home that shelters Arctic hunters from the cold.

'Then, still at a great distance from my own self, I felt another set of hands upon me, clumsy, halting hands, and heard another voice. The new woman prisoner had dragged herself over to help, ignoring her own injuries. Even in the depths of my isolation I was shamed. Here was someone who had suffered what I only feared, and yet she could find the strength to worry about me, a stranger!

'I had thought that I would never come back to sanity, that I would simply fall down into that slow-motion blackness forever. How much worse, in a way, to return and find myself being cared for by my exhausted friends and even this newcomer, her limbs still trembling with the pain of what she had endured, as though I were a tired, fretful child commanding the attention of a group of adults.

'There are times when kindness is the sharpest cut of all.

'But even my shame passed. I realized that I knew both of the new prisoners at least by name – Bonnie Mae Simpkins, who had shown such kindness to Orlando and Fredericks, and Nandi Paradivash, who had been the first to explain to Paul that he was trapped in Jongleur's simulation network. Nandi was in a state something like I had been, torn with guilt at what had happened to Paul, and also clearly the victim of agonizing treatment, but the Simpkins woman spoke for both of them. She told how in opening a gateway and sending Orlando and Fredericks through, the remaining members of the Circle had waited too long, so that their own escape was prevented by the collapse of the great Temple of Ra which followed Jongleur's appearance in his guise as Osiris, master of this simulation world. Jongleur had not stayed long, and the survivors had hidden in the ruins, hoping to find another way out of the simulation, but within days Osiris had been supplanted by Anubis and the already bad state of affairs rapidly became worse.

'Bonnie Mae Simpkins described the destruction that followed Dread's taking control of the simworld, an orgy of murder and torture at least as grisly as that which we had seen in Dodge City. Although I thought myself numbed by this point, I was nevertheless chilled by her description of what happened here, of the public burnings, Dread's orchestrated symphonies of murder, wild jackals devouring the bodies of children in the streets while their parents were forced to watch. Chilled because I realized that even in this network where every whim could be indulged, there was no upper limit to his homicidal madness.

'Dread's power and his ambition are growing, but how long can mere simulations feed such an appetite? If he has Jongleur's power outside the network as well as inside – and if Jongleur is truly dead, why shouldn't Dread control his worldwide operations? – then the possibilities are quite terrifyingly vast.

'As Bonnie Mae spoke, I had a sudden thought, and asked, "What about the other children? The little flying children that Orlando mentioned?" I could not remember the name they called themselves – the Wicked Group, the Nasty Club, something silly.

'This question made her even more sad. She told us that although the monkey-children had wanted to follow Orlando and Fredericks through the gateway, they had been distracted by the chaos in the temple of Ra and so they had all been left behind when the gateway closed.

'Bonnie Mae Simpkins said she had tried to keep them hidden when soldiers found her and Nandi and brought them here, but the monkey-children had flown away, pursued by some of the temple guards. She felt sure they had been captured and probably killed, since even Dread would have felt there was little information to be gathered from a group of children who had not reached school age.

'She went on to tell something of the horrors she and Nandi had experienced, largely because Dread knew they had been seen in the company of Orlando and Fredericks. This was chilling too – it was bad enough to know we were soon to be delivered to Dread, worse to know he had been actively seeking us. His vengeance, it seems, will not be offhanded.

'But the idea of Orlando's monkey-children friends would not leave my head.

'You see, I had turned a corner of sorts. I was and am still resigned to death, and to an unpleasant one at that, but I cannot bear to wait for it passively. Where this has led me, I will tell in a moment. But I listened less and less closely to Bonnie Mae Simpkin's terrible stories, because . . . because I needed to think about something else. I understand now Renie's bullheaded, chronic need to go forward – when there is nothing to be done, to want to do something anyway.

'We will all die. It is what gives life its shape and even its beauty, perhaps, this fact of its brevity. So why bother to do anything except gratify oneself, faced with that? And knowing it may come literally at any moment, as we do, why not simply surrender?

'I do not know. But I know now I cannot.

'I told the pair from the Circle, "I do not think the little monkeys have been captured. Dread wanted to break your spirit – he likes that even more than inflicting pain. And he truly wanted to make you tell all you knew about Renie and the rest of us. So if the guards had caught

them, he would have threatened you with harming them.
He would have been delighted to do it."

'"Maybe they escaped, then," Bonnie Mae Simpkins
said. "The Lord keep 'em safe – I sure hope they did
escape, poor little creatures." I could almost feel her calling on a few last dregs of optimism, and again was shamed
by the comparison with my own earlier behavior.

'Florimel remembered what Orlando and Fredericks had
said about Nandi's expertise, so she asked Nandi if it was
possible to open a gateway here in the prison cell. Slowly
and with great pain – I think several of his ribs are broken,
although that is an odd thing to consider since we are
all wearing virtual bodies – he explained that he could
only open a gate at a designated spot, and certainly there
was no such thing in these prison rooms. As he spoke I
began to think in earnest about what was possible and
what was not, remembering that as much as it might seem
like it, we were not actually prisoners in a temple of stone,
but in the *idea* of a temple.

'Slowly, other ideas came to me. Nothing dramatic,
nothing that would burst the doors or slay the guards,
but enough to give me occupation, for which I was grateful. When Nandi had finished his explanation, I asked the
others to be silent for a while. Even T4b – who in fact
has been as reserved as I have ever seen him since Nandi
and Bonnie Mae Simpkins were thrown in with us – did
not protest.

'This virtual universe is constructed on stories, it seems,
and I suspect that in part that is my own fault. I believe
I helped to feed the Other the first tales on which the
system has created and defined itself, and particularly the
story which appears to define its hopes, if one can say
such a thing about an artificial intelligence. And in our
way, we have each of us become defined as though we

were characters – Renie the bold and sometimes overly stubborn hero, !Xabbu her wise companion, Paul the one buffeted by fate, a mystery to himself and others. For a long time I had thought my role was clear. I was the blind seeress – I even made a joke of it in the indicators I used to mark my journal entries for later salvage. But with !Xabbu helping me I had accomplished more than that, opening a gate where no others could have managed. In fact, the unusual senses this place gives me have allowed me many times to do what my friends could not.

'Apparently, I am a sorceress – a witch. A good witch, I hope.

'Here, within this invented world, I have powers. As I sat in the cell thinking about Nandi's struggles to make the system work, I realized that I have not fully tapped those powers. And what better time to do so than now, with Dread to arrive at any moment?

'I asked my companions for quiet, then did my best to grasp what lay beyond the walls of our small cell. When I have reached out in this way before, in the House world or the Place of the Lost, it has always been in the open, where I could read information from air currents and long echoes, even if I could not always identify them as such. My abilities seemed an extension of natural senses, so I have always thought of them as limited in the same way, but I had just realized I did not know this to be true. Thus, as my friends waited in confused, fearful silence, I opened myself up and tried to see, hear, feel – there really are no proper words – what lay outside.

'Exploring the ways of the system with !Xabbu, I had always felt a fundamental separation between his perceptions of it and mine, something which the symbology of the string game and its mathematical underpinnings had helped to bridge but had never fully eliminated. Now I began to think of what that separation meant – why, after all, should a young man with so little experience of the information sphere grasp things that I, with years of study plus the altered and enhanced perceptions the network granted me, could only barely understand? The reason, I have come to realize, is that I am limited by my own expectations. !Xabbu was taught by his people to absorb everything the world gives him and then, after sifting out the most important details, to act on them. But he is also clever and supremely flexible. Faced with a new world, he did not try to force it to comply with his expectations, but began all over to learn the rules, without prejudice as to where the information came from.

'But I – along with all the rest of us, I suppose – have been fooled by the way this network mimics reality, and have tried to make sense of the world as though it were in fact the real world. Even using the astonishing abilities I have here, I have allowed myself to hear only what could be heard, touch only what could be touched, and then channeled that data into something safely like the real-world model. The irony of this – that a blind woman should so desperately struggle to make a place where she is superior to her companions into something more like the real world in which she was inferior to them – is almost staggering.

'So what would !Xabbu do? Even in the midst of horror and despair, I smiled at the thought. *What would !Xabbu do?* He would open himself. He would let what was around him speak and he would listen without prejudice instead of trying to force the information into some orderly, preconceived scheme.

'I tried to do the same.

'The first thing I discovered was that I was still terrified despite my outward show of calm. My heart was speeding, and the sound of Paul Jonas taking a startled breath as the guards seized him was still fresh in my thoughts, as though the echo of it were immortalized within our prison cell. That thought gave me another idea, which I put aside for a moment, concentrating instead on calming and clearing my mind. I did my best, but I am far too weak to learn that kind of serenity in a matter of minutes.

'It was difficult to lose the idea of the cell walls and in fact the entire temple as a real and solid thing. I suppose that for mystics and scientists it takes a similar effort of will to perceive the physical world as only a coherence of energy. I had dim inklings of what lay beyond our prison – sound information, smells – and to me they were already more significant than they would have been for any of my companions, but I needed more than that. I had to let myself feel them as equally significant to the things happening within the cell itself, until the walls began to blur into insignificance, until the signature of the simulated obstacles was only another piece of information. I had to learn to look *through* the walls, not *at* them, to put it in the language of the seeing.

'It took a long time, but when it happened, it was quite sudden – a single twist of perception, then I could feel the information arrayed in front of me, layer upon layer, the information of the guards in the corridor outside just as significant as that of my companions in the cells. One of them was scratching his head. I laughed. It felt a bit like discovering a trick, like that childhood day when I first learned to ride a two-wheeled bicycle. I moved cautiously to expand my survey, tracing the knitted expression of the wall-information on the corridor's far side, then sliding through it, as it were, to examine other corridors and rooms.

'This ability is not by any means limitless. The farther from myself I aim my perception, and the more barriers I penetrate, the less reliable the information. A hundred meters away from our cell the signature of a person – a sim pretending to be a person, that is – was little more than a humanoid shape, identifiable mostly because of movement. Twice that distance and only movement itself was noticeable. As my attention roved, I found several clusters of human shapes and movement, any one of which might have been Paul and his captors, but they were too far away for definite identification.

'I let my perceptions travel farther outward, looking for the energy-shadow of a gateway, the thing that lingers even when the gateway itself is closed. I found one at last which seems to be just at the edge or just outside of the temple-palace, but by this time my head was pounding. I surfaced, returning to the cell and my companions, and told them what I had discovered. I asked Nandi a few questions, and his answers confirmed Orlando's description of him as an expert on the network's internal travel mechanisms. Armed with this extension of my own investigations of the gateways, I let myself reach out to find the gateway again.

'It was more difficult this time. I was weary and my head ached, but I needed to examine the gateway to make sure it was functioning. Strangely, although it seemed open and in working order, I could not access the usual gateway information. But at least it seemed like it would take us somewhere else, and right now, that is our main need.

'I barely had time to explain this to the others before exhaustion pulled me down and I slept like a dead thing. When I woke, perhaps an hour later, the tiny bit of good cheer my news had roused in the others had turned back into a miserable silence, since as long as we were trapped in a cell, even a nearby gateway might as well have been on the moon.

'Despite feeling like my skull was made of old, brittle glass, I decided to try something different. Time was running out – time *is* running out. I could not afford to wait until I felt better, since Dread might appear at any moment, but I did not want to raise anyone's hopes either.

'In fact, although I experienced some success with this last attempt, there is still little about which to be hopeful.

'Again I let myself open. For a moment I feared I had lost the knack, that the walls would remain solidly impenetrable, but I thought of !Xabbu and calmed myself and at last the shift came. I reached out, not in any one direction, but generally, letting my attention flow diffusely outward through the information patterns. I was looking for something less specific than the signature of a gateway, and the farther away from the cell I went exploring, the harder it was to sift through the information.

'I had nearly given up when I found something that seemed a possibility. It was a nested confusion of signatures, of small movements, on the far side of the temple. From what I could discern it was located in a sort of alcove, perhaps a niche behind a cloth hanging, which was worrisome. The second and less-formed part of my plan would be very difficult if it was.

With the location fixed in my mind I surfaced again. My head was throbbing even more painfully now, but I had only to consider what Nandi and Bonnie Mae Simpkins had endured, and what we all could still expect, to drag myself up off the floor and move toward the door of the cell, where I lay down with my face against the open space at the bottom.

'"What are you doing?" Florimel asked worriedly. "Are you having trouble breathing?"

'"I need silence now more than ever," I told her. "Please, just be patient for me. Try not to move if you can help it."

'I turned my ear to the crack under the door and listened. I listened in the same way I had let all my senses roam, but with a narrowing of focus. All I wanted now was sound, in any form I could perceive it. I imagined the temple as a two-dimensional maze and did my best to locate and chart the movement of air currents, following back along the track I had navigated earlier until I could detect the quiet rustle and murmur from the alcove. Describing it, I make it easier than it was, not out of false modesty – it was astoundingly difficult – but because I am running short of time to describe what happened.

'Once I had heard the excruciatingly faint sounds I sought, I began the hardest part of all. I turned my face and spoke a soft, almost silent word to the crack under the door, then followed its progress. The coherence of the wave of sound dissipated quickly, vanishing into diffused silence by the end of the corridor.

'Someone, I think it was T4b, moved behind me, and to my fiercely-straining senses it was like the roar of the ocean. It was all I could do not to scream at my companions. Instead, I tried again.

'It took me the better part of two hours, and could have taken forever if I had not had the wonderful luck that the corridors I was using were mostly deserted. It was like plotting the most complicated billiard shot in the universe, trying to move a small sequence of sound from one end of the temple to the other – bouncing off walls, caroming around corners, all dependent on nearly microscopic differences in the initial direction and on excellent guesses about the swirl of air currents. Still, for all my painstaking care, the fact that I eventually succeeded was mostly luck.

'It was easier to hear the reply, although it took some moments drifting back. No one but me could have heard it – in fact, the sound wave was so small I was not really hearing it, but reading it.

'"*Who that?*" it said. "*How you know Zunni's name? How you know Wicked Tribe?*"

'It was too difficult to carry on a conversation – it would have taken hours of hit and miss – and based on the stories I had been told, I did not have the highest belief in the patience of the Wicked Tribe children. I banked my entire roll on one message.

'"*We are friends of Orlando Gardiner's. We are locked in a prison cell here in the temple. They are going to hurt us. We need help right now.*"

'I heard no reply back. A guard had begun to talk in the corridor outside, blasting the subtle pipeline of space and movement into crazy ripples.

'So that is that. It is a ridiculously unlikely possibility that they even heard the whole of my message, or that they can do anything about it, but it was the only plan I could devise. At least I was right in my guess that the monkey-children were still hiding in the temple. And against all odds I have told *someone* that we are here, that we need help. The fact that our safety is now dependent on a group of preschool children leaves us no worse off then we were, if not a great deal better.

'Still, although Bonnie Mae Simpkins was happy to hear that the children had survived, I think the rest of my companions were depressed to hear of the slim thread I had expended so much time and energy constructing, and on which our hopes now hung.

'However, I was so tired and felt so sick at that point that I was not even afraid of Dread – would not have cared if Satan himself had knocked on the cell door. I fell asleep almost immediately despite my head banging like a drum. Now I am awake again, but nothing has changed. My head still aches, a persistent throb that I fear will never leave me. Poor Paul Jonas is suffering God alone knows what kind of punishments. The rest of us still wait for death – or worse. We wait for Dread. And perhaps I have accomplished nothing – perhaps I am a failure as a witch. But at least I have done . . . something.

'If I am to die soon, that might be a little solace. A little.

'*Code Delphi*. End here.'

H E was tied and helpless, his back bent across the curved stone table so that he felt the merest touch would split open his belly. In the dim, torchlit chamber the yellow face of Ptah hovered like a sickly sun.

'Comfy?'

Paul struggled against the bonds that were already rubbing skin from his wrists and ankles. 'Why are you doing this, Wells?'

'Because I want to know.' He straightened up and told the guard who had tied Paul, 'Go find Userhotep.'

'But I don't know myself! You can't torture someone into telling something he doesn't know!'

Robert Wells shook his head in mock sadness. 'Oh, but I can. This isn't the real world anymore, Jonas. This is something much more complicated – more interesting, too.'

'Interesting enough to get you killed if your new master doesn't like what you're doing to me.'

His captor laughed. 'Oh, I'll leave plenty for him to

play with, don't worry. But first we're going to try a few tricks of our own.' He looked up at the sound of footsteps. 'And here's the chief trickster himself.'

'I live to serve you, O Lord of the White Walls.' The man who spoke might have been old or young – it was hard to tell in the shadowy chamber, and was made more difficult by the fleshy smoothness of the stranger's features. He was not fat – his arms showed hints of terrifying muscle beneath the unusually pale skin – but he was rounded, almost curvaceous, and had the sexless look of a eunuch.

'Userhotep is a very special person,' Wells said solemnly. 'A . . . damn, what's the term? There's a little snake that talks in my ear, but it almost never shuts up and I get tired of listening. Ah, right, a *kheriheb*. A special kind of priest.'

'He's a torturer,' Paul snapped. 'And you're an arrogant criminal bastard, Wells. Does your snake-gear have an Egyptian translation for that?'

'You know it already. The term is . . . a god.' Robert Wells smiled. 'But Userhotep is far more skilled than any mere torturer. He's a lector priest. That means a magician. And he's going to help you tell me everything you know. And everything you don't know, too.'

Userhotep moved closer, raising his hands above Paul's unprotected belly. When Paul flinched, the priest frowned slightly, but his eyes remained as empty as the glazed stare of a fish.

No, a shark, Paul thought miserably. *Something that uses its teeth just because it has them.*

'No need to squirm,' Wells said. 'The painful bit is a pretty small part of the whole operation – I just mentioned it to give your cellmates something to think about. No, Userhotep here is going to cast a spell over you, then you're going to sing like a canary.'

'You've been in here too long if you think some of Jongleur's ancient Egyptian mumbo-jumbo is going to make me tell you anything.' He strained against the ropes, lifting his head until he could look into Userhotep's epicene face. 'You're code, did you know that? You don't even exist. You're imaginary – a bunch of numbers in a big machine!'

Wells chuckled. 'He won't hear anything that doesn't fit in with the simulation, Jonas. And it's you who doesn't understand much if you think this . . . mumbo-jumbo won't affect you.'

Userhotep bent. When he stood again a long bronze blade was in his hand, more like a straight razor than a dagger. Before Paul had time to react, the priest swiped it across his chest. He had made three shallow cuts before Paul felt the burning pain of the first.

'You bastard!'

Paying no attention to Paul's struggles, Userhotep lifted a jar from the floor and dipped out something black and viscous. He rubbed it across the incisions. It was all Paul could do not to scream as it burned into the raw flesh.

'I think that's probably poppy-seed paste,' Wells observed. 'Kind of a primitive opium to help you dream. They have a multidisciplinary approach here, you see – a little science, a little magic, a little pain . . .'

> *'Here is the malefactor, O gods,'*

the priest chanted,

> *'The one whose mouth is closed against you*
> *as a door is shut*

Here is the one who will not tell truth
Unless you open his mouth so that his spirit
    has no shade in which to hide!
Give unto me the provenance of his tongue!
Give unto me the secrets of his heart!'

Even as he spoke the charm Userhotep sliced at Paul's skin again and again, caulking each wound with salty black paste. His fluting voice was distant, distracted, as though he were reading the minutes of an unimportant, forgotten meeting, but there was a curious intensity to the man's flat, cold eyes: as the pain mounted, they seemed to grow brighter, until the face was all Paul could see, the rest of the room falling back into shadow.

'See, it doesn't matter whether you believe or not,' Wells said from somewhere behind him, the yellow Ptah-face eclipsed by the priest's round visage like the sun disappearing behind the moon. 'That's one of the clever things about this network – really, you have to give old Jongleur credit, it approaches genius . . .'

'I don't *know* anything!' Paul groaned, fighting uselessly against the ropes, the burning of his skin.

'Oh, but you do. And if we play the system right, perform the proper spells, you'll talk whether you want to or not – whether you think you remember or not. Surely you've noticed by now that the network operates below the conscious level? Makes everything more real? Hides things that you know must actually be there, even kills people just by convincing them they're dead? If I'd known how Jongleur managed it all, I would have pushed him out a long time ago.' Wells' bad-boy giggle penetrated only slowly – Paul was having trouble understanding, his mind beset by storms of agony and confusion.

> '*See, the gods are waiting for you in the*
>   *caverns of theNetherworld!*
> *See, how they crush the heart of your silence!*
> *See them in all their power, and know fear!*
> *The Upreared One!*
> *The Terrible One!*
> *Turned Face!*
> *He of the Coffin!*
> *She who Combs Out!*
> *The Cobra Speaking in Flame!*'

'. . . Of course, that's probably why he never let any of us know how it worked.' Wells' voice was now quite distant, barely audible above the priest's chanting. Hot cramps pulled at Paul's joints, threatening to force them apart. 'What was his little joke-term? Reality Enhancement Mechanism. Get it? REM, like when you dream. But damn him, you have to admit it works. Are you feeling it yet?'

Paul could not catch his breath. A black fever was creeping through him, hot and thick as the poppy paste, dark as the caverns of the priest's spell, caverns he could almost see, impossibly deep, full of watching eyes . . .

'Now, Jonas, I think it's time for you to tell me everything you know about our friend Jongleur.' The yellow face of the god returned, floating into the swirling shadows of Paul's vision. 'Tell me what happened . . .'

> '*Give me the force of his tongue, that I shall*
> *make it a whip to chastise the gods' enemies!*'

the priest said, a triumphant note now entering the drone,

> *'Give me the force of his tongue, that he shall*
> *hide his secrets no more!*
> *Make me master of his silence!*
> *Make me priest of his hidden heart!*
> *Speak now!*
> *Speak now!*
> *Speak now!*
> *The gods command it . . . !'*

'I . . . I don't . . .' The priest's voice seemed like thunder in his ears, a din so great he could barely think. Images whirled past, fragments of his life in the tower, Ava's sad dark eyes, the smell of wet greenery. His own words were echoing both inside and outside his head. 'I'm . . . I'm . . .' He could see himself, could see everything, and the past tore open, ripped like flesh – painful, shriekingly painful, as the memories came tumbling out.

The darkness fell away, dropping him into something deeper still. He heard his own voice speak as if from a great distance.

'I'm . . . an orphan . . .'

CHAPTER 29

Stony Limits

NETFEED/MUSIC: Horrible Animals to Reunite?
(visual: Benchlows entering hospital for presurgical exploration)
VO: In what even their staunchest fans admit has become a rather
bizarre saga, onetime conjoined twins Saskia and Martinus Benchlow,
founding members of My Family and Other Horrible Horrible Animals,
who had themselves surgically separated a few months ago to facil-
itate the breakup of their musical partnership, are now contemplat-
ing reattachment.
S. BENCHLOW: 'Even after we broke up, we were spending all our
time together arguing. My new manager said, 'What's with you two,
it's like you're joined at the hip,' and, well, it got us thinking . . .'
M. BENCHLOW: 'The whole separation's been utterly weird. I never
knew it could be so lonely going to the toilet.'

HE said it again, caught on some incomprehensible
cusp. The momentary blackness was fading, but his
voice echoed strangely, as if he stood outside himself,
listening. 'I'm an orphan . . . !'

'Sorry you had to find out about it like this, lad.' Niles
sounded genuinely troubled, but his face on the screen
was as unreadably reasonable as ever. 'For some reason
the hospital couldn't get through to you there in the States,

so they called me. I suppose you must have put me down
as a backup or something.'

'I'm . . . I'm an orphan,' Paul said for the third time.

'Well, that's pushing it a bit, isn't it?' Niles spoke kindly.
'I mean, I think you have to be an actual child to qualify, don't you? But I really am sorry, Paul. Still, she had
a good run, didn't she? How old was she?'

'Seventy-two.' He'd been in America for over half a
year, he realized. 'Seventy-three. That's not old at all. I
thought . . . I thought she'd be around a few more years.'
*I thought I'd get back to see her. How could I let her die
alone?*

'Still, she wasn't well. Kindest thing, isn't it?'

For an instant, Paul hated his friend's handsome face
and easy sympathy. *Kindest thing? Yes, if you come from
the sort of family that shoots its old dogs and horses, it
probably seems that way.* A moment later the rush of fury
was gone.

'Yes, I suppose it is,' he said heavily. 'I should call and
make the arrangements . . .'

'Done it for you, mate. It was all in her records, anyway.
Do you want the ashes sent there?'

It was such a strangely repellent idea that Paul actually considered it for a moment. 'No. No, I don't think
so. I don't think she'd like Louisiana. I suppose she'll want
to go in that place next to Dad.' He couldn't for the life
of him think of the name of the so-called remembrance
park, had never visited his father's resting place – if a
cubbyhole with a door in a fibramic wall made to look
like marble could really be dignified to that extent. 'I'll
look up the details and call you tomorrow.'

'That's fine. We're at the Oaks.' Which was a breezy
way of saying Niles' family were having one of their semi-
annual bivouacs at their country house in Staffordshire.

'Thanks, Niles. You're a good friend.'

'Worry not. But how are things going on your end? I had sort of a strange call from your Americans a while back.'

'I know.' He debated telling Niles the whole story, but he was already in his friend's debt – how much did you actually owe someone who arranged to have your mother burned, anyway? – and did not want to descend deeper by keeping him on the phone listening to complaints and suspicions and just plain weirdness. 'Things are okay here. Lots of stories to tell when we get together. A bit odd, I guess, but basically everything's fine.'

Niles gave him a quizzical look, but with his usual deftness swiftly turned it into a smile. 'Right. Well, stay out of trouble, old man. And I am sorry about your mum.'

'I'll call you tomorrow. Thanks again.'

He was embarrassed he'd said it in front of Niles, but as the elevator shot soundlessly upward, the word would not leave his head.

Orphan. I'm an orphan. I've got no one left . . .

It was a bit overblown, perhaps – he hadn't seen Mum since leaving England, and while he was there he hadn't exactly moved heaven and earth to keep her at his side once she'd got sick the first time – but now that she was gone, something had definitely changed.

Who do you have, really? Niles? He'd be just as kind and efficient if it was you who'd snuffed it, and then he'd get on with his fabulous life. 'You remember Paul Jonas,' he'd say to his friends, who wouldn't. 'Chap I've known since Cranleigh – we were at university together, too. Worked at the Tate? Poor old Paul . . .'

She met him in the antique study, her fine features so rigid they seemed almost a mask, and gave him a very small, very polite smile. 'Come in, Mr Jonas. I've been looking forward to our lesson.'

He paused in the doorway, disconcerted by the gleam in her eyes, a hint of excitement or even fear. 'Miss Jongleur, I . . .'

'Please!' Her laugh was a little too shrill. 'We should waste no more time! You are already a bit late, dear Mr Jonas, although I do not criticize. You must understand that time weighs heavily on me between activities.'

He allowed himself to be pulled inside, yanking his hand through just in time to keep it from being caught by the closing door. Before he could even take a breath she had thrown her arms about his neck and was covering his face with kisses.

'Miss Jongleur!' He tried to detach himself but she clung to him like a creature of the tide pools fastened onto a rock. 'Ava! Have you lost your mind?' He managed to get one arm against the firmness of her corseted stomach and push her back until he could get a grip on her shoulders and hold her away. He was shocked to see her eyes streaming with tears.

'They cannot see us here!' she said. 'Our friend is protecting us!'

He only half-noticed that her phantom friend had somehow become his as well. 'Even so, Ava – I told you this was a terrible idea! That it simply cannot be!'

'Oh, Paul, Paul.' Disconcertingly, she bent her head and kissed his hand where it clutched her arm. Despite his monstrous uneasiness, the lunacy of it all, something in him responded with a throb in his groin, a twitch of the serpent sleeping in his spine.

'Ava, stop. You must stop.'

'But, Paul!' She turned her huge, tragic, damp eyes up to him. 'I have just found out the most terrible thing. I think my father . . . I think he is going to have you murdered!'

'What?' It was too much. For a moment he hated her, too – despised her helplessness and her derangement. How had he got himself into such a terrible, ridiculous situation? Something like this would never happen to Niles Peneddyn. 'Why should he do that?'

'Come outside,' she said. 'Come into the wood. We can talk there.'

'I thought you said we could talk here. That your . . . your ghost or whatever was protecting us.'

'He is! But I cannot stand being in this house a moment longer. Caged like an animal. Time . . . time is so long here!' She threw herself at him again, and although he kept his face turned from hers, refusing her kisses, the straining, panicky need in her tensed body performed a strange inversion and he wrapped his arms around her, soothing her as though she were a terrified child.

Which she is, he thought, his fear and confusion mixed with genuine sorrow. *They've done something terrible to her. Whatever they've done, it's criminal.*

Her chest heaved against his. At last a little quiet came. 'Come outside,' she said. 'Oh, please, Paul.'

He allowed himself to be led to the door of the study, pulling away at the last moment so that they made a more decorous picture as they emerged from the supposed zone of safety.

She's even got me believing this, he realized. *This ghost, this secret friend of hers. Either someone really has hacked the system or else Finney and Mudd just aren't paying attention. I can't believe they'd find this kind of behavior acceptable.*

The house was quiet, the maids withdrawn to wherever they went – off-duty? Gossiping about their employer's crazy daughter in some modern break room down on lower floors? Or were they hanging in a closet like marionettes, waiting for the unseen puppeteer to use them again?

They have to be real people, he told himself. The Gothic atmosphere was beginning to make even the most freakish notions half-believable. *I've bumped into one of them. You can't bump into a hologram and they don't make robots that realistic.* He hoped he survived all this to make it back to England, if only so he could tell Niles and his other friends about it someday, preferably with a drink in his hand. This would be one story that he felt sure none of them could top.

Ava's breakfast sat untouched on the table in the sun porch. Paul looked at it wistfully, wishing he'd had more than a cup of coffee himself. Once out in the garden, his pupil broke into a trot. For a moment he felt drawn to hurry after her, then remembered the eyes that were almost surely watching; he walked down the path as sedately as he could manage.

She was waiting for him in the fairy ring, her eyes bright, but not with tears. 'Oh, Paul,' she said as he stepped into the circle, 'if only we could always be together like this. Able to say what we wished without fear!'

'I don't understand what's going on, Ava.' He sat down beside her, keeping a careful distance. She looked at him reproachfully but he chose to ignore it. 'The last time we were here you told me . . . you told me you had a baby. Now you say your father is going to kill me. Not to mention your friend from the spirit world. How can I believe any of this?'

'But I *did* have a baby.' She was indignant. 'I wouldn't lie about such a thing.'

'Who . . . who was the father?'

'I don't know. Not a man, if that's what you mean.' She paused. 'Perhaps it was God.' There was no hint of mockery.

Paul was finally convinced beyond any residual doubts that she was mad. Her father's controlling obsessiveness, her prisoned life in this bizarre place – a zoo, really, with only one animal – had completely disordered her mind. He knew he should get up and walk back into the house, take the elevator down to Finney's office and resign, because no good could come from such a situation. He knew he should, but for some reason, perhaps the pain hiding behind her gentle face, he did not.

'And where is this child?' he asked.

'I don't know. They took him from me – they didn't even let me see him.'

'Him? You know it was a boy? And who took him?'

'The doctors. Yes, I know it was a boy. I knew it even before I knew I was carrying him. I had dreams. It was very strange.'

Paul shook his head. 'I'm afraid I'm not understanding this very well. You . . . you had a baby. But you never saw it. The doctors took it away.'

'*Him.* Took *him* away.'

'Him. When did this happen?'

'Just after you came to be my tutor, six months ago. Do you remember? I was ill and I missed several days' lessons.'

'Just after I came? But . . . but you didn't look like you were carrying a child.'

'It was very early.'

Paul could make no sense of it. 'And you never . . .' He hesitated, caught in the strange trap of speaking to her as though she truly were a girl from nearly two centuries in the past. 'And you had never . . . been with a man?'

Her laugh was unexpectedly loud. She was very amused. 'Who would it be, dear, dear Paul? Poor old Doctor Landreux, who must be a hundred years old? Or one of that horrid pair who work for my father?' She shuddered and inched nearer to him. 'I have been with no one. There is no other man for me but you, my beloved Paul. No one.'

He was losing the strength to object to her endearments. 'But someone took the child away?'

'I didn't know at the time. I had been feeling ill for weeks. I was particularly sick in the mornings. I went to the doctors and they examined me – at least that's what I thought they did. I only found out later that they'd taken away my baby before it could grow. But somehow I knew anyway, Paul – I knew! But I only understood for certain when Miss Kenley told me.'

'Miss Kenley . . . ?' He felt like he had walked into a play at the interval, and now was hopelessly trying to figure out what had happened in the first half. 'Who . . . ?'

'She was one of the nurses who used to come in with Doctor Landreux. But Finney saw her whispering to me, and now she doesn't come in anymore. Miss Kenley was very sweet – she was a Quaker, did you know? She didn't like working here. She wasn't supposed to tell me anything, but she thought it was terrible, what they did, so she told the doctor she was going to see if I was improving, but instead she took me for a walk in the garden and told me that they'd taken out my little baby.' A tear trickled down her cheek. 'Before he could even grow!'

'So you only know you were going to have a baby because this nurse told you so.'

'I knew, Paul. I knew in my dreams that there was a

baby inside me. But when she told me the terrible thing they had done, then I understood everything.'

'That's a lot more than I can say.' The twitter of birdsong in the trees overhead was continuous and loud. Paul found himself wondering how sound could enter into the circle so freely, but their own conversation could somehow be kept secret.

But there has to be something *going on*, he thought. *They wouldn't just let us sit here and talk about things like this, would they?* Unless of course they already knew the girl was crazy and were curious how Paul would react. Was it all some kind of loyalty test? *If it is, I don't want the job that badly. In fact, I don't want this bloody job at all.*

Still, there was something in Ava's story that wasn't so easy to dismiss. That didn't mean it was true – the whole thing might be some hysterical fantasy of this Miss Kenley's, foisted on the unfortunately sheltered, gullible Ava – but it might mean the girl wasn't entirely deranged either. And whatever else she might be, she was certainly a victim.

'Let's talk about something else for a moment,' he said, noting that she had moved a little closer still, so that her thigh, beneath dress and ruffled petticoat, was pushed against his. 'Why do you think your father wants to kill me?'

'Oh!' Her eyes widened, as though she had entirely forgotten the danger that half an hour earlier had driven her to terrified weeping. 'Oh, Paul, I couldn't bear to lose you, but I'm so frightened!'

'Just tell me why you think I'm in danger.'

'My friend told me. You know, my friend.'

Paul grimaced. 'Yes, I know. Your ghost. What exactly did he tell you?'

'Well, he didn't really tell me – he showed me. In the same manner he showed me you, sitting in your room.' She frowned – prettily, he thought, just like in the old books. Was it an automatic product of being raised in an old-books sort of way? 'Paul, what is a grail?'

'Grail?' It was not the sort of thing he was expecting to be asked. 'A grail . . . right, it's . . . it's a mythical object.' Despite his university lit, courses and a dozen lectures on the pre-Raphaelites, his recall was embarrassingly vague. 'The Holy Grail. I think it's supposed to be the cup that Jesus drank from at the Last Supper. Something like that. It features in a lot of medieval legends – all that King Arthur stuff.' He sounded, he thought, like the kind of nonreading, philistine American he and his friends had always mocked. 'I think there are other meanings, too – some cauldron from Irish folktales – but I can't quite remember. Why?'

'My father was talking about it with those cruel men who work for him, Finney and Mudd.'

Paul shook his head. 'You've lost me again, Ava.'

'My friend – he showed me them talking in the mirror. Or rather, he showed me Finney and Mudd in the mirror, and they were talking to my father, who was in a mirror big as a wall. He was in the mirror for them just like he is for me.'

Finney and Mudd talking to their boss on a wallscreen, Paul thought. So Ava's phantom could not only trick those spying on her and Paul, he could also spy on the spies in turn. 'And?'

'My father told them that the Grail was again within reach. And so perhaps it was time for you – he called you "that Jonas character" – to disappear.'

Paul was desperately trying to find threads of sense in this great, ragged tapestry of incomprehensibilities and folly. 'People use the term "grail" sometimes to mean something important, Ava – a project, a goal. I don't know what it would have to do with firing me, though, or even why your father should concern himself with such a small detail.' He smiled to show his resignation to his own comparative insignificance, but she was not amused or reassured.

'He wasn't just talking about sacking you, Paul.' She was stern, as though he had become the larky pupil and she the teacher. 'Nickelplate – Finney – said they were ready whenever my father gave the word, and Mudd said, "It won't matter much to anyone, anyway. All he's got is an old mother who won't last much longer. She's in no shape to raise a fuss." I'm quite sure that's how he put it.'

Something as cold and startling as a wet hand clutched his innards; for a moment, Paul felt dizzy with sudden panic. Nobody talked that way about terminating someone's employment, did they? It sounded like a crime drama. Surely there had to be some innocent explanation. Surely.

Aloud, he said, 'She's gone now. My mum. She just died.'

'I'm sorry, Paul. It must very painful for you.' Ava's eyes turned downward, showing a great expanse of dark lash. 'I never knew my mother. She died when I was born.'

He looked at her carefully. The flush of excitement had pinked her pale skin above the high collar of her dress. 'You wouldn't . . . you didn't make this up, did you? Please tell me, Ava. I won't be angry, but I have to know.'

Her hurt was as raw and obvious as a child's. 'Make it up . . . ? But, Paul, I would never lie to you. I . . . love you.'

'Ava, you can't. I've told you.'

'Can't?' Her laugh was shrill, painful to hear. '"For stony limits cannot hold love out" – your William Shakespeare said that, didn't he? I remember it from *Romeo and Juliet.*'

Which is exactly why I wouldn't have taught that play to a lonely, impressionable young girl, he thought. *Her other tutors have a lot to answer for.* 'I have to think, Ava. This is . . . this is quite a bit of information.' The inadequacy of the phrase was laughable. 'I need a little time to sort things out in my mind.'

'Do you not care for me, Paul? Not in the slightest?'

'Of course I care for you, Ava. But you're talking about something much larger and a hell of a lot more complicated.' As she colored and brought a hand to her mouth, Paul felt shamed. By her standards, he had used very strong language indeed. 'Look, Ava, I just don't know what to think about all the things you've told me.'

She put her hand on top of his, cool, dry fingers startling against his skin. 'You think . . . you think I might be mistaken, don't you? Worse, you think I might be . . . what is the word? Hysterical? Mad?'

'I think you are a good and honest person.' There was nothing else he could say. He squeezed her hand and gently removed it before standing up, then had a sudden thought. 'Could . . . your friend . . . could he talk to me? Would he?'

'I don't know.' Her composure was a thin facade covering something like devastation. Paul Jonas was glad he could not see the whole of it. 'I will ask him.'

The flickering light woke him up.

After a long, agonizing night, he had at last fallen asleep, helped or hindered by more wine than usual. His first disjointed thought was that the window blinds had somehow gone on the fritz and were jigging up and down, semaphoring him with the harsh and unwanted light of morning. It was only after he had dragged himself upright that he realized the arrhythmic flash came not from the window but the wallscreen.

A call . . . ? he thought dazedly. *Why didn't it ring?* A charge of fear went through him. *A disaster. Emergency warning system. The tower's on fire.*

He scrambled out of bed and dragged open the blinds. It was still deep night, the miniature city below still dark, the orange lights of the oil derricks the stars' only rivals. No flames were sweeping up the shiny black side of the tower toward him, nor were there any other signs of something amiss. It must be only a malfunction.

'Paul Jonas.'

He spun around, but the room was empty.

'*Paul Jonas.*' The voice came from nowhere in particular, as quietly intrusive as a buzzing fly trapped in a windowsill.

'Who . . . who is that?' But he knew even as he asked. The last traces of his cloth-headed grogginess vanished. 'Are you . . . Ava's friend?'

'*Avialle,*' the voice breathed. '*Angel . . .*' The wallscreen flickered again, then bloomed with color. Ava filled it – not the Ava of this moment, but an Ava in full if ersatz sunlight, crouched beneath a tree spreading crumbs for the birds that surrounded her like a crowd of admiring Lilliputians.

'Who are you?' Paul asked. 'Why do you talk to Ava – to Avialle? What do you want from her?'

'*Want . . . want . . . safe. Avialle safe.*' It spoke with a strange, aphasic slur. Pity would have pulled at him, except something about the shambling, inhuman voice also scared him to death.

'And who are you?'

'*Lost.*' It moaned, a strange staticky roar. '*Lost boy.*'

'Lost . . . where? Where are you?'

For a long moment there was only silence as the image of Ava rippled away, replaced by unevenly shimmering bars of light. '*Well,*' it replied at last. '*Down in the black, in the black black black.*' The moan came again, a stutter of harsh sound. '*Down in the black well.*'

All the hairs on Paul's body stood upright. He knew he was awake – every quivering nerve told him so – but the conversation had the terrible downhill feel of a nightmare.

He searched desperately for something to build on. 'You want to keep Ava . . . keep Avialle safe, is that right? Safe from what?'

'*Jongleur.*'

'But he's her father! What would he do to her . . . ?'

'*Not father!*' the thing groaned. '*Not father!*'

'What are you talking about?' The family resemblance was plain, although what was hawklike and cruel in the pictures Paul had seen of Felix Jongleur was softened and sweetened in the daughter. 'I don't understand . . .'

'*Eating the children,*' the voice moaned. '*Jongleur. Grail. Help them. Too much pain. And . . .*' The bars of light began to flicker more rapidly, until they nearly became a solid burst of radiance. Paul found himself staring helplessly. '*All the children . . .*'

The light strobed even faster, a white rush so bright that as he stared even the walls of his room fell away. Then somehow he was toppling forward into the light, into a brilliance that had no ending, and the haunted voice was all around him, powerful and lost.

'*The Grail. Eating the children. So many . . . ! Hurting them!*'

His senses were afire with sensation, but he was helpless. He could do nothing as the light streamed over him, through him, scorched into his eyes and turned his brain to a knob of clear crystal. Faces began to appear, children's faces, but it was no simple stream of images: he knew these children, felt their lives and stories even as they flew past him like a flock of sparrows caught up in a hurricane wind. Hundreds of tiny spirits flowed through him, then thousands, each one a node of painful darkness in the sea of shining light, each one precious, each one doomed. Then, out of the whirling darkness, a new shape began to form – a great silvery cylinder floating in a vault of black emptiness.

'*The Grail,*' the voice said again, imploring, mourning. '*For Jongleur. Eating them.* Ad Aeternum. *Forever.*'

Paul found his voice, though he had no lungs to drive the air, no throat in which to form the scream.

'Stop! I don't want to see any more!'

But it did not stop. He was lost in a storm of suffering.

He woke up on the carpet with the true light of morning streaming through the window. His head felt like something rotten that had been imperfectly balanced on top of his neck. Even an extra-strong cup of coffee and a small handful of painblockers did nothing to make him feel more human. He was miserable.

He was also terrified.

There was no explanation for what he had experienced. He did not insult himself by pretending it might have been a bad dream – the details were too sharp, his waking position on the floor in front of the wallscreen too telltale. But there was no simple way of understanding. The thing that had contacted him was no ordinary hacker, that was laughably clear. He didn't believe in ghosts, especially ghosts who appeared on wallscreens. So what did that leave?

Paul sat by the window with shaking hands. Below, he could see one of the corporation's hovercrafts arriving at the esplanade just below the tower, the ship's cheerful white-and-blue paint at odds with his own current viewpoint – that the ferry was basically a larger version of Charon's boat, conveying passengers to a Hades in which Paul was already a resident.

He roused himself. The sight had given him a longing to be somewhere else, anywhere else. He could not spend another day inside the great black building. He needed to move, to get out. Maybe then he could think properly.

As he dressed he felt a pang of worry and sorrow for Ava. If he simply disappeared, even just for the morning, she would be frightened. He was reluctant to ride all the way up to her house, frightened that he would never be able to pull himself away from her, so he called and left a message with one of Finney's many assistants. *'Mr Jonas has business to take care of because his mother in England has died. He will be out for the day. Please ask Miss Jongleur to study her geometry and read two more chapters of* Emma. *Lessons will resume as usual tomorrow.'* Hanging up, he felt the same sort of guilt he had experienced as a child skiving off school.

I have to get out, he told himself. *Just for a while.*

Walking from the elevator across the huge atrium lobby to the front doors, Paul could not resist looking around to see if someone was following him.

But isn't that just what you aren't supposed to do when you leave Hades? What was that from, the Orpheus legend? That you weren't supposed to look back?

Whatever the case, he was not being followed by either

weeping ghosts or dark-suited security personnel, although the vast lobby was so full of people it was hard to tell for certain. The wash of commingled voices echoing from the marble walls and down the crystalline, pyramidal ceiling was like the roar of an ocean, like the rush of childish faces that had invaded his sleep now made into sound.

He paused for a moment in the plaza before the front doors to look up at the tower, a mountain-high finger of warped black glass, a million darkly translucent plates trussed and polished. If this was indeed the gate of the netherworld, what kind of fool was he even to think about coming back? He had planned a day's research trip, since he was afraid to access the larger net from within the J Corporation matrix, but what was there to draw him back at all? A doomed girl? It would take someone with a lot more power in the world than Paul Jonas to break her free from that cage. Something called the Grail, some threat to the world's children? Surely he could do much more from the outside, perhaps as a secret informant to some serious investigative journalists, than he could ever manage under constant surveillance.

Should I just take off? Just go? For God's sake, what job is worth this madness, this kind of paranoia?

'There's something wrong with your badge,' the woman said. He could see the ferry's gangplank just the other side of the security-glass air-lock door, but the door itself did not open.

'What do you mean?'

The young woman frowned at the symbols dancing on the inside of her goggles. 'It's not cleared for departure from the island, sir. I'm afraid you'll have to step out.'

'My *badge* isn't cleared?' He stared at her, then back

at the gang-plank, only a few meters away. 'Then keep the damn thing.'

'You'll have to step out, sir. There's a security hold on it. You can speak to my supervisor.'

Before a half-dozen sharp words were out of his mouth, the security guards – exactly the sort that he had half-expected to be following him through the tower lobby – had escorted him to a quiet office for, as they put it, a quiet chat.

It was at least a little solace that afterward he was allowed to walk back out of the departure area and back to the tower by himself. Security hadn't been ordered to do anything *to* him, not even detain him, as long as he stayed on the island. A little solace, but not much.

Conscious that he had sweated himself rank inside his coat and shirt despite the cool of the morning, Paul stood inside the lobby elevators, full of terrified indecision. Did this mean they had heard him after all, talking the J Corporation equivalent of treason with the master's daughter? Or might it just be a fluke?

He had to see Finney. If he didn't, if he simply did as he wanted so desperately to do, returned to his room and got shatteringly drunk, he would be admitting that he deserved this treatment. He had to act innocent.

Finney's assistant kept him waiting twenty-five minutes. The spectacular view across to the city – a city now heartbreakingly out of reach, although it seemed so close he might reach out and prick his finger on the Riverwalk Spire – did little to soothe him.

When he was finally allowed in, Finney was finishing a call. He looked up, his eyes as always strangely hard to see behind his spectacles. 'What is it, Jonas?'

'I . . . they wouldn't let me leave the island. Security.'

Finney looked at him calmly. 'Why?'

'I don't know! Something wrong with my badge. They said there was a security hold on it, something like that.'

'Leave it with my assistant. We'll sort it out.'

Paul felt a gush of relief. 'So . . . I can get a temporary replacement or something? I've got some things I have to do in New Orleans.' In the silence, he felt the need to make it more compelling. 'My mother died. I have arrangements to make.'

Finney was looking at his desk, although the desktop appeared to be bare. He nodded distractedly. 'Sorry to hear that. We can make arrangements for you.'

'But I want to do it myself.'

Finney looked up at him. 'Fine. As I said, leave your badge with my assistant.'

'But I want to go now! Go off the island, deal with things. I mean . . . you can't keep me here. Not just . . . keep me here.'

'But, my dear Jonas, what is your hurry? Surely you can make arrangements by net more efficiently. And these security procedures might seem silly to you, but I promise you they're deadly serious. Deadly serious. Why, if someone tried to get onto the island – or off it, for that matter – without a valid badge, I wouldn't even want to think about the kind of terrible things that might happen!' Finney gave him a slow smile. 'So you just sit tight, will you? Be a good boy. Entertain Miss Jongleur. We'll straighten everything out . . . in time.'

Back in the elevator, Paul could hardly support his own weight. He stumbled to his room, turned off the lights, carefully and definitely shut off the wallscreen, then sat in darkness broken only by a pane of light tilting out from the crack between window and blind and tried to drink himself into oblivion.

* * *

He could see his own fingers touching the button of the elevator, see the dawn light bleeding into the corridor disappear as the doors swished shut behind him – he could see it, but he could not quite feel it. The drunkenness was still on him, a twisted, feverish disconnection. He did not know what time it was, only knew it was morning, only knew he could not take another night of such monstrous dreams.

The door hissed open, revealing the inner door. He leaned against it, resting his head on the cool frame while he clumsily entered his code and pressed his hand against the palm reader. Dizzy, he remained leaning for several stupefied moments after the lock had clicked.

One of the parlormaids looked up in surprise as he stumbled through. In her wide-eyed gaze he saw an entire factory of deceit. 'You're real,' he said. 'So you must be a liar.'

'Where are you going, sir?' She took a careful backward step, as though preparing to turn and run.

'Important business. Miss Jongleur. We're going out.' The spectacle he must be presenting finally sank in. He tried to assume a slightly more dignified manner. 'Sorry. I'm not well. But I need to give Miss Jongleur her lessons – she has to have her lesson plan for today. I'll be gone in a few minutes.'

He continued down the corridor, trying to walk a straight line.

I'm not drunk, he thought. *Not really. I'm bloody well coming apart at the seams.*

He knocked on the door, waited, then knocked again. 'Who is it?'

'It's me,' he said, then remembered the no-doubt listening ears. 'Mr Jonas. I have to give you your lessons for today.'

The door flew open. She wore a white nightgown, soft but opaque, and had pulled her dressing gown on without tying it closed. Her dark hair, unbound and surprisingly long, spilled down past her shoulders.

Angel, he thought, remembering the ghost-thing's words. *You're beautiful*, he wanted to say, but retained enough sense to lift his hand and push his own sweat-damp hair from his forehead. 'I need to speak to you for just a moment, Miss Jongleur.'

'Paul! What's happened to you?'

'I'm ill, Miss Jongleur.' He lifted his finger to his lips in a clumsy admonishment to silence. 'Perhaps I need a little air. Would you mind coming outside with me while we discuss your work for today?'

'Let me . . . I just need to dress.'

'No time,' he said hoarsely. 'I'm . . . I'm really not very well. Can you come out with me?'

She was frightened, but trying not to show it. 'Let me get my shoes, then.'

It was all he could do to refrain from pulling her down the hall by the arm. Two of the maids were standing in the doorway of the sunporch, for the moment not even counterfeiting work; they stepped aside as Paul and Ava approached, casting their eyes down.

'But I insist, Mr Jonas,' Ava said brightly for their benefit. 'You are looking very poorly indeed. A turn in the garden while we talk will do you a world of good.'

He could almost feel the maids' shocked propriety and was embarrassed for his pupil. His own floating, hapless confusion was such that he did not remember until they had reached the garden path that whatever else they might be, the Jongleur servants were not young women from two centuries past.

This time Ava did not hurry toward the wood, but

walked with care, asking solicitously about Paul's health as they went, insisting that immediately upon leaving her he should drink a cup of chamomile tea and go straight to bed. It was only when they had reached the ostensible security of the mushroom ring that she turned and threw herself at him, clutching him so tightly he had to struggle to stay upright.

'Oh, Paul, dear Paul, where were you? When you did not come yesterday, I was so frightened!'

He did not have the strength to hold her off, did not have the strength to do much of anything. He had no plan, no solution. He was not entirely certain he was not going mad himself. 'Your ghost friend. He came to me. Showed me . . . children.'

'So you believe me?' She leaned back, staring at his face as though she might never see it again. 'Do you?'

'I still don't know what to believe, Ava. But I know I have to get you out of here, somehow.' A heaviness settled in his chest. 'But I can't even leave myself. I tried to get off the island yesterday and they wouldn't let me.'

'An island?' she said. 'How strange. Are we on an island?'

The hopelessness of it all came crashing down on him. What did he think he was going to do? Kidnap and hide a girl who had never even left this building, the daughter of the world's richest man? A man with his own army, with tanks and helicopters? A man with half the world's leaders in his pocket? His knees weakening, Paul let himself slide down to the ground. Ava came with him, still clinging, and for a moment they were tangled together, the girl half atop him, her slim, uncorseted body pressing against him.

'I don't know what to do, Ava.' He was light-headed, almost stoned on despair. Her face was very close, her hair surrounding both their heads like a canopy so that for a moment they were in half-darkness.

'Just love me,' she said. 'Then everything will be right.'

'I can't . . . I shouldn't . . .' But he had his arms around her waist, in self-defense if nothing else, to keep her from wriggling along the length of his body. 'You're just a child.'

'Stony limits,' she reminded him, and her giggle was so unexpected he almost smiled himself.

And I am Fortune's fool. The quote swam up like the fish in the tiny, tended stream gurgling a few meters away. *Fortune's fool.* He lifted his head and kissed her. She gave it back to him with all the untutored enthusiasm of her age, her breath sharp and fast, and after a moment he had to lift her away from him and sit up. The grass slowly sprang back erect where they had lain.

'My true heart,' she murmured, tears in her eyes.

He could think of nothing to say back to her. *Romeo and Juliet*, he thought. *Good Christ, look what happened to them.*

'I have something for you!' she said suddenly. She reached into the collar of her nightgown and withdrew a tasseled bag that hung around her neck. She shook something small and glittery into her hand and held it out toward him. It was a silver ring with a blue-green stone cut into the shape of a feather. 'It was a present from my father,' she said. 'I think it was my mother's once. He brought it back for her from North Africa.' She held it up until the feather-shape caught the light, sparkling clear as a tropical ocean, then passed it to him. 'He said the stone is a tourmaline.'

Paul stared at it. The feather was strikingly carved, something light as air made from stone, the solidity of earth turned into a puff of wind.

'Put it on.'

Still in a sort of trance, he slipped it onto his finger.

'Now you can't leave me.' There was more than just pleading in her voice – it almost had the force of a command or an incantation. 'You can't ever leave me now.' An instant later she had crawled into his lap and put her arms about his neck, pressing her lips to his. He fought it for a moment, then surrendered to the full, force-ful tide of madness.

'Oh ho!' someone said.

Ava shrieked and threw herself backward out of Paul's arms. He turned to see the grinning, misshapen face of Mudd peering at them through the trees.

'Naughty, naughty,' said the fat man.

Suddenly everything went dark, sucked away as if down a long drain. The light, the air, the sound of Ava weep-ing, the trill of birds and the rustle of leaves, all fled. Nothing was left but blackness and empty silence.

He had been in the dark for so long that he had almost forgotten there was anything else. Then something cold crashed down over him and he woke up screaming.

Paul Jonas struggled up out of the emptiness, his skin raw and shocked, his head hot and swollen, as though he had been left out in the desert sun for hours. It was not sand or sun that he found when he opened his sticky eyes, though, but the flickering semidarkness of a cell.

The dull-faced priest Userhotep stood over him, still holding the clay water jar which he had emptied over Paul's bound body. Frowning as at a piece of machinery which had proved to be shoddily manufactured, the priest examined Paul for a moment, testing his pulse and pulling back his eyelid with a grubby finger before stepping away.

Robert Wells' yellow, hairless face split in a clownish grin. 'My God, once you get started you don't shut up, do you?'

Paul tried to say something but could only moan. The arteries serving his brain seemed to be pumping something far more thick and caustic than blood.

'But we still haven't learned much,' Wells complained. 'So you found out something about the Grail – well, golly, I could have guessed that. It still doesn't explain why the Old Man didn't just have you killed. And it's clear from what you remember that his operating system was even more unreliable than we guessed, than even Jongleur guessed – that it achieved some kind of consciousness. But we stopped just short of the really interesting stuff.' He shook his head. 'That last part of the block is pretty strong, which suggests it was the thing he originally wanted wiped out. So, of course, that's what I want to learn.'

Paul's throat was as rough as sharkskin, but he at last mustered the saliva to speak. 'Why do you care? It's all over now. Jongleur's dead, my friends and I are prisoners, Dread's in charge. What does it matter?' The truth was, he didn't want to touch any more memories. A brooding disquiet lay over all that had returned to him, a sense that something horrible waited just around the corner. 'Go ahead and kill me, if you really aren't any better than your new boss.' It would be an end at least to the pain. It would be an end.

Wells wagged a lemony finger. 'Selfish, Mr Jonas, very selfish of you. If the Old Man's dead, that's all the more reason we need to know as much as possible. You may not be on the guest list, but the rest of us intend to make our homes here for a long, long time. If we have to replace the plumbing, we need to know the extent of the problem.'

He leaned forward until his face was very close. 'And I must admit I'm curious about you. Who *are* you? Why did Jongleur single you out for such star treatment instead of just dumping your body in his private swamp?' He's had us taking very elaborate care of you at Telemorphix, you know. We really wondered who you were.'

'You won't find out the rest,' Paul said hoarsely. 'The brainwashing, the hypnotic block, whatever it is, it's too strong.'

'Hmmm. I think we can go a long way toward testing that theory without killing you.' Ptah the Artificer moved back and the lector priest Userhotep stepped forward again. 'I was wrong to think we could do the job with only minimal damage, though. We'll have to push the envelope a bit – see how much you can take. It's amazing what the brain will do to cope with extreme pain, you know. Some pretty extreme neurological effects. I wouldn't be surprised if we have you singing like a bird before we've done much beyond taking the top layers of your skin off.'

Robert Wells crossed his bandaged arms over his chest, stared at Paul for a moment, then nodded cheerfully to the priest. 'Well, Userhotep, I guess you might as well get started.'

CHAPTER 30

Climbing the Mountain

NETFEED/NEWS: Doctor Sued for Keeping Patient Alive
(visual: Dr Sheila Loughlin and Bellings' parents at news conference)
VO: In what the International Medical Association is calling 'a fright-
ening low point in corporate compassion,' a doctor is being sued by
an insurance provider for keeping a patient alive past the point which
Trans-European Health Insurance claims is 'either ethically or finan-
cially supportable.' The patient, ten-year-old Eamon Bellings of
Killarney, Ireland, has been in a Tandagore coma for almost a year,
but his parents and doctor refuse to remove his life support despite
the demands of the insurance company . . .

'*I*'*M sorry,*' Sellars told her, '*but it has to go all the way to the back. That way it will be hard for anyone to find the source – that might buy you an additional half an hour to get out.*'

Olga wiped the sweat out of her eyes and leaned back into the duct, wedging her shoulders so she could keep her hands free. The basement hadn't seemed that hot when she started half an hour earlier, but it was beginning to feel like she was working in a sauna. She angled the camera ring to pick up the corner where the flashlight

had splashed white, trying to make sure Sellars could see.
'Back there?'

*'Yes, that should do it. But see if you can get it behind
that bundle of cables so it's a little less visible.'*

Olga took a moment to wipe her wet, slippery hands
clean on her coveralls before lifting the bottle out of her
backpack.

'You have to prime it first,' Sellars said, almost apologetically. *'Twist the nozzle until it clicks.'*

She did, briefly fearful that despite the assurances of
Sellars and Major Sorensen the thing might explode in
her hands, but it made only the expected noise; a moment
later she was pushing it into the space she had opened
by yanking a twined cable of polymer-covered cables to
one side. She sat up, rubbing her hands again, and said,
'It's in. Do you want to see it?'

'That's all right . . .' Sellars had begun when someone
grabbed her waist from behind.

'Caught you!'

Olga shrieked and fell off the edge of the duct backward and landed on the concrete floor, banging her elbow
painfully. Panicked, she scrambled into a crouch, conscious
that she had no weapon except her flashlight, and that if
Sellars triggered the smoke bomb now it would be more
likely to asphyxiate her than to help her escape. She could
hear his startled voice talking inside her head.

'Olga? What happened?'

She reached up and pressed the t-jack, damping the
sound input. The man standing over her looked just as
shocked as she did. He wore a J Corporation uniform like
hers, and had a lot of gray in his hair, but his posture
was that of a scolded child, arms held up, hands dangling.

'You're not Lena!' He backed up a step. 'Who are you?'

Olga's heart was beating like a drumroll, as though she

stood at the top of a platform about to leap out to a distant trapeze. 'No,' she said, trying to decide if she should take advantage of his obvious surprise and shove her way past him to the door. 'No, I'm not.'

He leaned toward her, squinting. His eyes were a little foggy and there was something strange about the shape of his facial bones, as though they had been hastily reassembled after being dropped. 'You're not Lena,' he said again. 'I thought you were Lena.'

She took a shaky breath. 'I'm . . . I'm new.'

He nodded solemnly, as though she had answered some troubling question, but he still wore a worried look. 'I thought you were her. I was . . . I was just teasing. I didn't mean nothing. Me and Lena, we have a joke like that.' He lifted his hand and briefly chewed on one finger. 'Who are you? You're not mad at me, are you?'

'No, I'm not mad at you.' She felt her pulse slow a little. She remembered seeing milky eyes like his in an accident victim who had gone through a sight-saving operation. Whatever was going on, the man didn't seem like a security guard who had just caught an intruder. She finally noticed the object behind him that her eyes had flicked across several times in the last seconds while searching for an escape route – a rolling plastic bucket and long-handled mop. He was a janitor of some kind.

'That's good. I was just playing a joke, because I thought you were Lena.' He smiled tentatively. 'You're new, huh? What's your name? I'm Jerome.'

She briefly considered lying to him, but decided that it would do little good – either he would report an unauthorized person in the basement, or he wouldn't: the name she gave would make little difference if people started looking for her in earnest. 'My name is Olga, Jerome. It's nice to meet you.'

He nodded his head. It was. A moment later, he squinted again. 'What are you doing? Did you lose something?'

Her heart pit-pattered again. The door to the duct still hung open behind her. She turned as casually as she could and pushed it shut, searching desperately for something to tell him. 'Mice,' she said at last. 'I thought I heard mice.'

Jerome's eyes got big. 'Down here? I never seen any down here.' He frowned. 'Should I put down some traps, maybe? We had to do that for the roaches. I don't like roaches.'

'That sounds like a good idea, Jerome.' She stood up, brushing herself off, forcing herself to speak slowly and calmly. 'I should get back to work upstairs.'

'So isn't Lena coming in this weekend?'

Olga had no idea who Lena was, and now regretted having given her name – Jerome might not be too curious, but this Lena might be. 'I don't know. If I see her, I'll tell her you were asking. But I've got to get back to work now.'

'Okay.' He frowned again, thinking. She took the opportunity to make her way past him toward the basement stairs. 'Ol-ga?'

She let out a breath and stopped. 'Yes?'

'If you see Lena, maybe you better not tell her. See, I'm not supposed to be down here yet. 'Cause I'm supposed to do the other floor first. But I heard her down here – no, I heard *you* down here, huh? So I came down to do a joke on her. But Mr Kingery might be mad if he knew I came down here to do a joke on Lena.'

'I won't tell anyone, Jerome. Nice to meet you.'

'Nice to meet you. You can come down sometime when it's time to have a break. I eat my dinner down here – except it's really breakfast, I guess, because I eat it in the morning . . .'

'That would be nice, Jerome.' She waved and hurried up the stairs, unmuting the t-jack as soon as she reached the next level.

'. . . *Olga, can you hear me? Can you hear me?*'

She leaned back against the wall and closed her eyes, drawing the first deep breath she had taken in minutes. 'I can hear you. It is okay. A janitor surprised me. I think he might be . . . how do you say it? A little slow.'

'*Are you on your own now?*'

'Yes. But I need to stop and rest. I almost had a heart attack when he grabbed me.'

'*Grabbed you?*'

'Never mind. Let me get my breath back, then I will explain.'

'*Sorry about all the stairs,*' Sellars told her. '*But if we interfere with the surveillance cameras in the elevators too often, building security might wonder why so many empty elevators are going up and down.*'

'I . . . understand.' But it didn't make it any easier not to fall over in a faint.

'*Catch your breath. The plans I'm looking at say the patch room is on this floor.*'

She peered into the hallway in time to see a flirt of color at the end of the hall as someone stepped into the elevator. She froze, waiting, but no one got out, which was good. Sellars could hide her movements by looping the output from a security camera, but only if the corridor was deserted first. It wouldn't do to have people suddenly vanishing when they entered one end and then reappearing at the other end.

The elevator door whispered shut. Now the corridor was silent again, the long stretch of dark carpet empty as a country road at night.

Sellars' long-distance manipulation of her badge worked as well for the patch room door as it had for basement access. He had begun to loop the surveillance signals in the room even before she entered, so after the door hissed open she stepped in quickly and shut the door behind her. The room, a walkway a hundred meters long with machines in racks standing on either side like the monuments of dead kings, was surprisingly cold.

'*I won't keep you here any longer than I have to,*' Sellars told her. '*So let's get to work.*'

She found the machine he wanted after a few minutes' search, holding up her ring to give him a chance to double-check. She took the gray rectangle out of her backpack. 'Do I push it into one of these holes?'

'*No, just set it against the ends of those bits sticking out, then square it up. May I see? Excellent. Now hold it flat.*' There was a click; the gray box vibrated for a moment under Olga's hand. '*You can let go now.*' She did. The box remained in place. '*Why don't you go sit somewhere – out of view of the door, just to be on the safe side. This will take me a short while.*'

Olga found an old swivel chair in a niche behind some of the equipment and collapsed into it gratefully. There was nothing to do but stare at the rows and rows of almost featureless machines. She might have dozed for a few minutes. When she woke up she was shivering from the chill and Sellars was again in her ear.

'*There's something wrong.*'

She was suddenly alert, heart speeding. 'Someone is coming?'

'*No. It's just . . . this is the wrong room. The wrong equipment. As far as I can tell, none of this machinery has any connection to the Grail Network. It's all just the regular J Corporation telecom infrastructure. There's got to be another plan room – something very large.'*

'So what do we do now?' She was tired and could not help feeling a little resentful. It was one thing to turn your destiny over to mysterious strangers, but when those strangers had apparently sent you on a wild goose chase, it was another thing altogether.

'I truly don't know, Olga. I'll have to spend some time on the problem. I'll come back to you in one hour. In the meantime, take the tap off that machinery, then I think you should go to that storage room we talked about and wait. I've keyed your badge for it. If you go now, you can be there in five minutes. I'll massage the stair cameras.'

'More stairs.'

'I'm afraid so.'

The storage room took up much of a floor, a huge warren full of stacks of unopened shipping boxes and unused furniture. Once Sellars looped the surveillance signal, Olga made her way to a far corner and settled herself behind a set of privacy screens in the most comfortable executive chair she could find.

She dozed again, and woke up thinking how strange it was that she should be here in the very center of the black tower, the thing she had seen in so many dreams, and yet the children who had led her to this place had vanished like shadows in the sun. The silence in her head was almost painful.

There was silence of another kind, too. She checked her internal display. Almost two hours gone. Sellars or Catur Ramsey should have called her by now. She stood and stretched, limbering herself, then found the storage facility's restroom. When she had finished, she called Sellars. There was no answer. She called Ramsey but he wasn't answering either, so she left a message for him.

It's a hard problem, this one, she guessed, and settled in to wait a bit longer.

Two hours turned into three. Olga felt a cold certainty settle on her like mist. They weren't going to call. Something was wrong – very wrong.

Four hours became five, then six. The dim safety lights high over-head continued in permanent twilight. The stacks of boxes stretched away like dozens of cardboard Stonehenges, stashed and forgotten by busy Druids. Olga's certainty had hardened into something frozen and miserable.

She was alone in the middle of the black tower. First the children had left her, now Ramsey and the man Sellars. She had been deserted again.

'I can make no sense of it,' Sellars finished.
Ramsey tried to look helpfully attentive, but Sellars' explanation had lost him some time back. 'Well, there must be some other equipment in the building somewhere.'

'No,' the old man said, 'it's not that simple. All the data lines from that building come out of that patch room and get handed over to the telecom providers. And everything in the building – even Jongleur's private offices and residence at the top of the tower – pumps out through those lines. I couldn't be missing anything as significant as the amount of throughput needed to manage the Grail network. It would be like hiding the data from all of NASA.'

'Nassau?' Ramsey frowned. 'The Bahamas?'

'Never mind. Before your time.' Sellars took a moment to inhale through a chemical-scented rag clutched in his knobby hand, a rag that had begun to seem as much a part of him as the kerchief of a Versailles courtier. Ramsey thought the old man's breathing seemed worse just in the last two days, and could not help wondering how long a being so frail could endure this kind of stress. 'But I must come up with something,' Sellars continued. 'Your Ms Pirofsky is waiting patiently for a call back.'

'I don't understand. You've already hacked into the Otherland system, haven't you? So why can't you find it now?'

'Because I've never been able to hack into it from Felix Jongleur's end.' Sellars sighed and lowered the rag. 'That's why I thought Olga's . . . incursion, for lack of a better word, might prove to be a help. I've never been able to touch the operating system, no matter what I tried. I got into the network through the Telemorphix end, where the gross maintenance of the system is done. I've been in and out of Telemorphix at will for years. I might as well be drawing a paycheck.' His smile was perfunctory.

Ramsey shrugged. 'So what do we do?'

'I don't know. I just . . .' For a moment he physically faltered, then raised a shaking hand to his face as though surprised to find his head still attached. 'Time is pressing now. And there are other things pulling at my attention. Any one of them might be crucial.'

'Can I do anything to help?'

'Possibly. Just having you listening . . . it forces me . . . it forces me to make a little order out of the chaos. Sometimes we think we know things too well, and it's only when we try to explain them . . .' He straightened. 'Look. I will show you one of the matters that is tugging at me most strongly.'

The wallscreen sprang to life in a blaze of pure light. Ramsey jumped. A moment later, the image resolved into the tangle of strange greenery that Sellars called his Garden.

'I've seen this before,' Ramsey said gently.

'Not this you haven't.' Sellars gestured and part of the picture jumped forward into magnified resolution. A cluster of fungus, gray and sickly, but still somehow with the shine of a new thing, had erupted from the ground around the base of one of the more complicated plants. 'It just happened today, while I was working with Olga. I had all kinds of alarm messages waiting for me when I got off the line with her.'

'What is it?'

'It's the operating system,' Sellars said. 'The Grail network operating system. Or rather, it's a pattern that looks like what the operating system does when it singles something within the network out for attention – a sort of locus of special interest.'

'I have no idea what any of that means,' Ramsey said, 'but I guess I'm learning to be comfortable with complete and chronic ignorance. And I have to say that I'm impressed – you're the first person I've ever heard actually use the word "locus" in conversation.'

He won another smile from the old man. 'What it means is that for the first time since the system went haywire, for lack of a better word, I've found a symptom of the operating system within the network. Well, the operating system is everywhere in the network, of course, but the part of it that seems intelligent, that seems to make actual choices, has been absent since things broke down. Now it's back.'

'And that means . . . ?'

'In the past, as I think I told you, it was the method I used to locate my volunteers within the network. So perhaps what this concentration of attention represents is the location of the poor people I've put into danger – the people who have been hidden from me for days.' He closed his eyes, thinking. 'One of the reasons I wanted to get into the system from Jongleur's end was so I could bypass the network's very fierce security and have a proper chance to search for them myself. And there they are – maybe. God only knows how long this opportunity will last.'

'Sounds like you need to try to contact them again.'

'I agree – if I can get in. As I think I told you, the system hasn't even allowed me to sneak Cho-Cho into the network the last few times I've tried.' He paused for a moment, consulting some private source of information. 'I have half an hour before I told Ms Pirofsky I'd get back to her. That should be plenty of time for the attempt, even if it's successful – I've never been able to hold off the network security systems for more than a few minutes.' He nodded toward the door separating their room from the Sorensens'. 'I'll need your help. It may work differently when the boy's not asleep.'

'The boy?'

'Of course, the boy. I doubt things have changed enough for the system to allow me in by myself.' He inhaled from the cloth again. 'But as I said, it may work differently this time – I've never tried it when Cho-Cho was awake. You can make sure he doesn't fall off the couch.'

All three Sorensens stood in the doorway, watching with the sickened fascination of bystanders at the scene of an accident, even though nothing had happened yet. Christabel in particular looked frightened, and Ramsey felt a sudden tug of shame. As grown-ups, they had all failed these two kids pretty thoroughly, at least when it came to shielding them from life's uglier moments.

'Oh, for goodness' sake,' Sellars said testily. 'I can't get anything accomplished with you all hovering over me.

Leave me alone with the boy. Mr Ramsey will be able to help me if I need anything.'

'I still don't understand what you're going to do to him, but I know I don't like it,' Kaylene Sorensen declared. 'Just because he's a poor little Mexican boy . . .'

Ramsey saw Sellars bristle. 'Madam, he's as much an American as you are, and certainly has a greater claim to it than I do, since I wasn't even born here.' His glare softened. 'I'm sorry, Mrs Sorensen. You have every right to be worried. I apologize. I am . . . very tired. Please try not to worry. We have done this several times, Cho-Cho and I. But I do need some privacy so I can concentrate. Time is growing short. Please.'

She set her jaw, but took her daughter by the hand and pulled her away from the door. 'Come on, Christabel. Let's go out and sit by the pool. I'll get you an ice cream.'

'Be careful, Mister Sellars,' the little girl called, hesitating in the doorway. 'And . . . and take care of Cho-Cho, okay?'

'I promise, little Christabel.' Sellars sagged a little as the girl and her mother disappeared.

Major Sorensen was the last to leave. 'I'll be in the next room,' he said as he shut the door. 'Holler if you need me.'

Cho-Cho had pushed himself to the far end of the couch where he waited like a trapped animal. 'What you think you gonna do?'

'Just what we have done before, Señor Izabal. Except this time, you're going to be awake. I'm going to send you through to that other place.'

'How come awake?'

'Because I can't afford to wait until tonight. My friends might have moved again by then.'

The boy scowled. 'What you want me to do?'

'For now, just lie down.'

Cho-Cho did so, but with the kind of careful attention that suggested he expected at any moment to be hit with something. It was not hard to see the fear under the bluster.

If people's insides were their outsides, Ramsey thought, *it would be this kid, not Sellars, who was scar tissue from head to toe.*

Sellars leaned forward until he could lay a trembling hand along the boy's neck. Cho-Cho shook him off and sat up. 'What you doing, *loco?* Touching me and all that *mierda?*'

The old man signed. 'Señor Izabal, I strongly suggest you lie down and shut up. I'm just making contact with that thing in your neck, your neurocannula.' He turned to Ramsey. 'I could actually just narrowcast to it, but it's a pretty shoddy piece of street engineering and I get less interference if I'm actually making contact.'

'Hey! Me, I racked plenty *efectivo* on that, old man.'

'You were robbed, sonny.' Sellars laughed weakly. 'No, don't get angry, I'm just teasing. It does the job well enough.'

Cho-Cho lay back along the couch. 'Just don't get funny.'

Sellars made contact again. 'Close your eyes, please.' When the boy had done so, the old man shut his own, lifting his face blindly toward the ceiling. 'Do you see the light yet, my young friend?'

'Kind of. All gray, like.'

'Good. Now just wait. If everything goes well, in a few minutes you should find yourself inside the network, as you have before – that place you admired so much. You'll have my voice in your ear. Don't do anything until I tell you.'

Cho-Cho's mouth had fallen slackly open. His fingers, pressed into fists only moments before, uncurled.

'Now . . .' said Sellars, then fell silent. He was still as stone, but unlike Cho-Cho, he seemed not unconscious but vastly absorbed, as distant as a meditating holy man.

Ramsey watched, feeling as nearly useless as he ever had. The silence continued long enough that he was just beginning to wonder if flicking on the wallscreen for some news would interfere with whatever Sellars was doing when the old man jerked upright in his chair, his hand snapping away from the boy's neck as though the skin there had burned him.

'What is it?' Ramsey hurried to Sellars' side, but the old man did not speak. He twitched violently and his eyes opened wide then squeezed shut. A moment later he collapsed forward. If Ramsey had not wrapped his arms around the thin body, light as a bundle of sticks, Sellars would have fallen onto the floor. Ramsey pushed him back upright, but the old man only lolled in the chair, limp and silent. The boy still lay on the couch, equally slack, equally still. Ramsey tried to shake Sellars awake, then sprang to the boy, his desperation increasing with each second. The boy's head bounced on the cushions as Ramsey tried to bring him back, but lay still when Ramsey stopped.

'They're both still breathing.' Sorensen let go of Sellars' wrist and stood up. 'Their pulses feel regular.'

'If this is Tandagore, that doesn't mean anything,' Ramsey said bitterly. 'My clients . . . their daughter has had normal pulse and respiration for months, the whole time she's been in a coma. Her friend did, too – he's dead now.'

'Jesus.' Sorensen jammed his hands in his pockets – to

make it less obvious how helpless he felt, Ramsey suspected. 'Jee-zuss. What the hell kind of situation are we in now?'

'The same as we were, just a bit worse.' Ramsey felt so heavy he could not imagine how he would ever stand up again. 'Should we take them to a hospital?'

'I don't know. Shit.' Sorensen walked across the room to sit down in the other chair. There would have been room on the couch, since the unconscious child stretched only two thirds of the length, but Ramsey was not surprised by the major's choice. 'Does being in the hospital help those other Tangadore kids?'

'Tandagore. No. Well, I suppose it keeps them from getting bedsores.' A thought flickered past. 'And they have to be fed with a drip. And catheterized, I guess.'

'Catheterized . . . ? Christ.' Major Sorensen seemed more depressed than frightened – Catur Ramsey wished he could say the same of himself. 'I'd better go tell Kay what's going on.' He frowned. 'I don't know how we'll be able to take them to a hospital. The kid, yeah, but we put an advisory out on Sellars from the base to every emergency room on the Eastern seaboard, because we thought he'd be having breathing problems. Shit. Breathing's about the only thing he *isn't* having problems with right now.'

'Don't look at me, Major. Sellars was in charge of this whole thing. I was just along for the ride.'

Sorensen regarded him with something like sympathy. 'Yeah. Some ride, huh, Ramsey?'

'Yeah. Some ride.'

When Sorensen had disappeared through the connecting door, Ramsey went looking for his pad, hoping that he had some first-aid information on Tandagore in the research he had done for the Frederickses. When he picked it up, the small device was vibrating.

Oh, my God, he thought. *It must be Olga. She's been waiting for at least an hour – she must be panicked. But what can I tell her?* He fumbled the device open to take the call. *I have only the most general idea of what Sellars was trying to do, and not a clue as to how he was going to go about it.*

'Olga?' he said.

'*No.*' The voice was spectrally faint, perforated with dropouts. '*No, Ramsey, it's me.*'

He recognized it. His hackles rose. He could not help staring at the boneless, broken shape in the wheelchair. 'Sellars? How . . . ?'

'*I'm not dead, Mr Ramsey. Just . . . very busy.*'

'What happened? You – your body's here. You and the boy are both . . .'

'*I know. And I have very little time to talk. The system is collapsing – dying, I think. I don't know if I can get it to release its hold on the boy – or on me, for that matter . . .*' For a moment the transmission simply stopped – a pure slash of emptiness – then Sellars' whispery voice returned. '*. . . vitally important. We have to find the operating system's data path so we can tap into it. Everything depends on that. You must help Olga Pirofsky . . .*'

The signal failed this time for so long that Ramsey was certain he had lost him. Sellars' living body mocked him with its silence.

'*. . . And don't do anything drastic with either of us. I'll reopen the connection hourly, if I can . . .*' Sellars' voice faded again. This time, it did not return.

Ramsey stared at the pad, now as mute as the old man and the sleeping boy.

'No!' he said, not even aware he spoke out loud. 'No, you can't – I don't know what to do! Come back, damn you! Come back!'

CHRISTABEL could tell from the way her father was whispering to her mother that something was really wrong. She was so busy watching them talking with their heads close together that she forgot all about her ice cream until it fell off the stick and landed in a big cold blob on her foot.

She kicked it into the bushes beside the hotel pool, then rinsed her foot clean with some water from the pool because the sun was already making it sticky between her toes. It only took a few seconds, but when she looked up, her daddy was gone again and Mommy was looking at her funny. It made Christabel's stomach go flippy. She ran toward her mother.

'Christabel, never run by the pool,' Mommy said, but her eyes were flicking back toward the hotel, and Christabel could tell she was hardly thinking about what she was saying.

'What's wrong?'

Her mother was putting things back in the big straw bag she'd carried down from the room. For a moment she didn't say anything. 'I'm not sure,' she said at last. 'Your daddy said Mr Sellars and Cho-Cho . . .' She put both hands on her eyes, like she did when she got a bad headache. 'They're not feeling well. I'm going to see if there's anything I can do to help. You can watch some net . . . Christabel?'

She hadn't waited for her mother to finish. She had known all day something bad was going to happen. She wasn't running, exactly, but she was going up the stairs from the pool as fast as she could, thinking of poor Mister Sellars and his hooty voice and how tired he looked . . .

'Christabel!' Her mom sounded angry and scared. 'Christabel! You come back here right now!'

* * *

'Christabel, what the hell are you doing in here?' her father growled as she crashed into the room. 'Where's your mother?'

'She ran away from me, Mike,' Mommy said, trying to hold onto the sunblock and other things she hadn't had time to put back in the bag. 'She just . . . Oh my God. What did you do to them?'

'I didn't do anything to either of them,' her father said.

'Mister Ramsey, what happened?' Mommy asked.

Christabel could not stop staring. Mister Sellars looked horrible, propped up in a chair like one of the Mexican mummies she had seen on the net, his mouth open in an 'o' like he was trying to whistle, his eyes half-shut. The frighteningly blank face blurred as her own eyes filled up with tears.

'Is he dead?'

'No, Christabel,' Mister Ramsey said. 'He's not dead. In fact, I just talked to him.'

'You telling me he looks like that, and he *talked* to you?' said Christabel's daddy.

'He called me.'

'What?'

While the grown-ups spoke in quiet but excited voices, Christabel reached out and touched Mister Sellars' face. The skin that had always looked like a melted candle was harder than she would have guessed, firm as the leather on her dress shoes. It was warm, though, and when she leaned close she could hear a little noise from deep in his throat.

'Don't die,' she whispered close to his ear. 'Don't die, Mister Sellars.'

It was only when she turned away from him that she noticed Cho-Cho on the couch. Her heart thumped around in her chest like it was going to fall out. 'Is he sick, too?'

The grown-ups were not listening to her. Mister Ramsey was trying to explain something to her parents, but they were interrupting him to ask questions. He looked tired and really, really worried. All the grown-ups looked that way.

'And I can't even call her,' he was saying, talking about someone Christabel didn't know. 'For some reason, I can't connect with her number. She must be going crazy!'

Staring down at Cho-Cho, Christabel thought he looked like a different kid than the one who had teased her, frightened her. His face wasn't hard when he was sleeping, not scary. He looked little. She could see the plastic thing behind his ear – his 'can, he had called it, when he bragged to her about it – and the rough skin around it that hadn't healed right.

'Are they going to die?' she asked. When the grown-ups still didn't answer, she felt something get hot inside her, hot and angry and eager to come out. She shouted, 'I said, are they going to die?'

Mommy and Daddy and Mister Ramsey turned to her, surprised. She was a little surprised herself, not just because of the shouting, but because she was crying again. She felt upside-down.

'Christabel!' her mother said. 'Honey, what . . . ?'

She stuck out her lip, trying to keep some of the crying inside. 'Are they . . . are they going to die?'

'Ssshh, honey.' Her mommy came over and gently lifted the little boy up from the couch, then sat down with him on her lap. 'Come here,' she said, then reached out and pulled Christabel toward her, too. Christabel didn't like the way the boy looked, not just normal asleep, but floppy, and she didn't want to touch him, but she squeezed up against her mother's side and let her put an arm around her.

'All right,' Mommy said quietly. 'It's going to be all right.' She was stroking Christabel's hair, but when Christabel looked up, her mother was looking down at Cho-Cho and she seemed like she wanted to cry, too. 'Everything will be all right.'

It was Mister Ramsey who finally answered her question. 'I don't think they're going to die, Christabel. They're not really sick – it's more like they're sleeping.'

'Wake them up!'

Mister Ramsey kneeled down beside the couch. 'We can't wake them up right now,' he said. 'Mister Sellars has to do it, but he's very busy right now. We just have to wait.'

'Will he wake Cho-Cho up, too?' For some reason, she hoped it was true. She didn't know why. She would be happy for the boy to go away somewhere else in the world, but she didn't want him just to lie there all floppy forever, even if she wasn't around to see it. 'You have to save him. He's really scared.'

'Did he tell you that?' her mommy asked.

'Yes. No. But I could tell. I've never seen nobody so scared in my whole life.'

The grown-ups went back to talking. After a while, Christabel slid out from under Mommy's arm and went to look for something warm. She wasn't strong enough to pull the cover off either of the beds, so she got two big towels out of the bathroom and wrapped one around Mister Sellars' narrow shoulders. She draped the other one over the little boy, pulling it up like a blanket to just below his chin, so it looked like he really was just having a nap on her mother's lap.

'Don't be scared,' she whispered into his ear. She patted his arm, then leaned close again. 'I'm here,' she told him so quietly that even Mommy couldn't hear her. 'So please don't be scared.'

'. . . **W**RAPPED around a fibramic core which was one of the earliest uses of this hybrid material for a high-rise office building. The convoluted shell of custom-manufactured, low-emissivity glass, the shape of which has almost as many interpretations as interpreters, has been likened to everything from an upraised finger to a mountain or a black icicle. The resemblance to a human digit has spawned more than a few wry comments over the years, including one journalist's famous assertion that having secured everything he wanted from the pliant Louisiana legislature, J Corporation founder Felix Jongleur was offering one-half of the peace sign to the rest of us – in short, folks, he's flipping us off. . . .'

Olga paused the research file, freezing the bird's-eye view of the immense building in which she was now marooned. She was in full surround, but it was too much effort to change the viewpoint, and in any case she didn't know enough about buildings like this to be able to look for anything specific. What had Sellars said – there had to be another room with all the rest of the machinery? Without his guidance and protection, she didn't have a prayer of being able to locate it. Not without getting caught. And that was his interest, anyway, not hers. What could she learn about the voices that had drawn her here from investigating telecom equipment?

She sighed and surfaced from the wraparound long enough to make sure she was still alone in the vast storage room, then let the file – obtained from a specialty node about skyscrapers – play on.

'Topping out slightly under three hundred meters, not counting the radio mast and satellite arrays on the roof, the J Corporation tower has been surpassed by several newer buildings since its construction, most notably the five-hundred-meter Gulf Financial Services skyscraper, but

*it is still one of the tallest structures in Louisiana. Known
primarily for the massive engineering work that went into
creating the artificial island on which it stands – or which
surrounds it, since the building's foundations go down as
deep as the island's – and its spectacular ten-story
Egyptian-themed atrium, the tower is also reputed to be
the residence of Jongleur himself, the corporation's reclu-
sive founder, who is said to keep an extensive penthouse
complex on the top of the great black edifice, from which
he can look down on Lake Borgne, the Gulf, and most of
southeastern Louisiana and no doubt think about how
much of it belongs to him . . .'*

The view of the atrium had given way to a long shot
across the lake, its waters turned burnt tangerine by the
setting sun, with the black spike of the tower jutting above
it – a view much like Olga's own first sighting of it. She
closed the file and shut off the visual override, so that
the storage room sprang up around her. She had kept her
incoming call line open. Ramsey and Sellars had still not
tried to get in touch with her.

Olga rose to her feet, disturbed by how much she had
stiffened up.

You are old. What do you expect?

But it was more than that. It was hard enough to admit
that she was on her own – that whatever must be done
she would have to do herself. The physical weariness and
the ache of her muscles, overtaxed by a full day's cleaning and then uncountable stairs climbed at Sellars' direction, made it all seem even more impossible. What could
she hope to accomplish, anyway?

*Animals, when they're trapped and can't do anything,
after a while they just curl up. Go to sleep.* She remembered reading that somewhere. That was her own best
choice, it seemed certain: just stay here, wait, doze. Wait.

Wait for what?

Something. Because I can't do anything on my own.

But even in her own head, even with her own self telling her such a sensible thing, that made her angry. Had she come much of the way down the continent to huddle like a rat in a hole simply because this man Sellars had been distracted? She had not even heard of him when she had made her decision to come here – she had planned to do it alone from the first.

But what had she planned to do, exactly? Olga had to admit that she had been so daunted by the problem of getting into the heavily-guarded corporate headquarters that she had not thought much beyond that. Sellars' intervention had in that way been a blessing. Where did you go to search for missing voices, ghost children?

To the top, she thought suddenly. *This man built this place. He owns Uncle Jingle. He is the one poisoning children's minds, somehow, making them sick. If he is up there, then at least I can let him know that someone knows he is doing wrong. If I can get up there. If the guards don't kill me. I'll tell him to his face, then whatever will happen will happen.*

What else can I do?

Olga began to pack up her few possessions for the journey to the top of the mountain.

CHAPTER 31

Romany Fair

*NETFEED/NEWS: Multibillionaire Offers to Buy Mars Project
(visual: Krellor in Monte Carlo news conference)
VO: After declaring bankruptcy only months earlier, former nanotech-
nology baron Uberto Krellor has come forward with a startling offer
to buy the crippled Mars Base Construction Project, lock, stock, and
minirobot barrel, providing the UN will give him long-term rights to
Mars, including concessions on mining and real estate rights on
terraformed environments. Krellor is rumored to be the front man for
a shadow-group of financiers kept out of the MBC Project sweep-
stakes by earlier UN decisions to avoid complete privatization of
Martian ventures.
KRELLOR: 'Nobody wants to see governments throwing the people's
money away over these things anymore. Let a businessman see what
he can do, someone who is used to taking risks. If I succeed, all
humankind will share the triumph . . .'*

SAM Fredericks had been quite a few things since
she had entered the network. After the bloody
climax of the Trojan War, a battle between Egyptian
gods and sphinxes, and an attack by giant carnivorous
salad tongs, she should have been bored with miracles,
but she was still a little impressed with the way they

started out crossing one river and finished up crossing an entirely different one.

The river itself still seemed largely the same, the water inky beneath the dark sky, feathered with white where it splashed around stones. In happier conditions its breathy murmuring might have been charming, the stone bridge beneath their feet picturesque. Then, as the mists cleared mid-span, Sam saw that the meadowed bank visible from the foot of the bridge had now become the edge of a fogbound forest instead, with steep black mountains looming beyond the trees. She had to admit it was a very effective trick.

But she was sick to death of tricks.

'How?' she whispered to !Xabbu. Azador walked ahead of them, more sleepwalker than traveler. 'How did he find this bridge? And how did you know he could do it? We went past this spot before! There utterly wasn't any bridge here.'

'Because I suspect we were not here.' Her friend was avidly surveying the breakfront of ancient trees – hoping, perhaps, to see another one of Renie's markers fluttering from a branch. 'Not the here that has a bridge, I mean.' He saw the look on her face and smiled. 'It does not make much sense to me either, Sam, but I believe Azador is from this . . . Other's land to begin with, this place built by the operating system, and so things will happen for him that will not happen for us. That is my guess.'

'So far, it's a pretty good guess,' Sam had to admit.

Azador had already descended from the bridge and was making his way up the dark soil of the bank, apparently headed for the trees.

'We should stop,' !Xabbu called after him. 'It is getting dark!' Azador did not slow or even turn. 'We will have to hurry to keep up with him,' !Xabbu told Sam. 'If we lose him in the trees we may never find him again.'

The bridge sloped down to the bank, joining a road so overgrown with grass that they had not been able to see it from the river. The track, filled with ancient ruts and a few that looked more recent, curved away up into the woods. Sam looked back. Jongleur was still behind them, his slow stride that of a man walking into a dark and doomful place.

They caught up with Azador as he passed under the edge of the trees.

'I think it is time to stop,' !Xabbu told him. 'It is getting dark, and we are tired.'

Azador turned to regard him with strangely mild eyes. 'It's just ahead.'

'What is just ahead?'

'There will be fires – many fires. The horses will be brushed, shiny. All the band will be wearing their finest clothes. And singing!' He seemed to be talking to someone else: his eyes had returned to the winding track between the trees. '*Shoon!* Listen! I can almost hear them!'

Sam, on the edge of a question, closed her mouth. She heard nothing but the velvety rubbing of the wind through countless branches.

Azador's face showed that he too was listening; after a moment, his gaze grew troubled. 'No, I cannot. Perhaps we are not close enough yet.'

Sam was footsore, exhausted. They had spent all of a long wearying day searching for the bridge, and now that they had crossed it she certainly did not want to spend the rest of the night following Azador through the wilderness as he searched for magic elves or forest musicians or whatever it was he was seeking. She was about to tell him so, but something in his eyes, a haunted but also hopeful look unlike anything she had seen in him so far, kept her quiet.

The forest was more real than anything since they had first reached the black mountain, the trees almost perfect, although where she could see their upper branches in the fading light the leaves were not sharp and individual, but seemed to blur into a cloudy mass. Still, there was recognizable grass underfoot, even if thicker and more like a lawn than what Sam guessed you would find in a real wild wood, and moss on the stones and tree trunks. The only thing that seemed distinctly wrong was the absence of wind or bird or cricket sounds. The woods were as silent as an empty church.

Azador led them on, lifting his hands before him wonderingly as though to touch the things he saw, lost in some kind of waking dream. Even Jongleur seemed struck by the strangeness of their forest journey, bringing up the back of the tiny procession in silence.

'Where are we?' Sam whispered, but !Xabbu had stopped, wide-eyed. A piece of pale cloth dangled beside the path, rippling in the faint breeze. 'Chizz – is it from Renie?'

!Xabbu's face fell. 'It cannot be. The color is wrong, more yellow than what you and she are wearing, and there is too much of it.'

But the strip of cloth seemed to mean something to Azador, who reached out and touched it carefully, then left the wide track and struck out across the woods. He was moving quickly now; Sam and !Xabbu had to hurry to keep up.

A piece of blood-red fabric dangled on a shrub; Azador turned left. A hundred paces later two white strips side by side marked one edge of a clearing. Azador turned his back on them and walked out the other side. They emerged from a screen of trees onto a hillside and found the wood-land road again, or one much like it, torn with the passage of many wheels.

They followed this track down into a grove of tall trees with twisted gray trunks. Now Sam could smell smoke. Inside the dense ring of trees, hidden from anyone outside, stood the wagons.

At first Sam thought they had stumbled on some odd kind of circus. Even in the dying light the wagons were stunning, two dozen or more, painted with many colors in almost unbelievable combinations, striped and swirled and checked, festooned with feathers and tassels, brass fittings on the wheels and doors. So splendid was the sight that it took her a moment to realize something was wrong.

'But . . . where is everybody?'

Azador groaned, staring around wildly as he entered the clearing, as though the crowd of people and horses who brought the wagons to this place might be hiding behind a tree. Sam and !Xabbu followed him. Azador stopped and stiffened, then bolted across the open ground. A wavering line of smoke drifted up from behind one of the farthest wagons, a somber vehicle by comparison to the rest, painted in deep midnight blue and dotted with white stars.

A small fire burned in a circle of stones on the ground beside the wagon. A set of steps had been unfolded between the high wooden wheels. On the bottom step, smoking a pipe and wearing a bonnet, sat what Sam at first thought was an old woman; only as she got closer did she notice that the stranger was slightly transparent around the edges.

Azador stopped in front of the figure and sank into a crouch before her. 'Where have they gone?'

The woman looked up. Sam felt a chill. What she could see of the woman's face looked as smoky as the gray plumes curling above the fire, the eyes only points of light, small but bright as the coals at the edge of the fire pit.

'You come back to us, Azador.' Her voice was strangely resonant, not at all as insubstantial as the rest of her. 'Out of time, my *chabo*, my ill-omened one. Your name proves a true name. They all are gone.'

'Gone?' The misery in his voice was palpable. 'All?'

'All. The *morts* and their *mards*, all the children. They have run ahead of the Ending. As you see, some were so fearful they even left their *vardoni* behind.' She looked to the wagons and shook her head in disapproval. Azador seemed stunned. Clearly leaving without these bright, beloved vehicles was a sign of something very dire. 'And at the last, here you are. It was an unlucky day when you left. Now it is an equally unlucky day when you return.'

'Where . . . where have they gone, Stepmother?'

'The Ending is coming. All the Romany have gone to the Well. The One has commanded it. They hope when they get there, the Black Lady will speak to them, tell them some way to save themselves.'

'But why are you still here, Stepmother?'

'I could not rest until all my *chabos* had been told. It was my task. Now that you are back, after all these years, my task is ended.' She stood up and mounted slowly to the door of her wagon. 'Now at last I can go.'

'But how do I get to the Well?' Azador was on the verge of tears. 'I can remember so little. Will you take me with you?'

She shook her head; for a moment the light of her eyes was shrouded. 'I am not going there. My task is ended.' She began to turn away, then hesitated. 'Always I knew your destiny was a strange one, an unhappy one, my lost *chabo*. When you were born, I read the leaves – oh, what sadness! *He will die by his own hand, but unwillingly,* that is what they told me. But perhaps it can be different. Now, when all is coming to an end, when even the One himself is dying, who can say what will happen?'

'How do I reach the Well?' Azador asked again. 'I cannot remember.'

'You of all the Romany, who left the world of his fore-fathers to go who knows where – you can find your way. Not across the world but through it. Inward. To the place where you touch the One, as we all do.' It was impossible to read expressions in the smoky countenance, but Sam thought the next words might almost be spoken with a smile. 'Perhaps you will even reach the place before the rest of your people. Just like the Unlucky One that would be, eh? To leave after the others, but to reach the Ending first?' She nodded, then stepped into the darkness of her wagon. Azador dragged himself to his feet, one hand stretched toward the place where the thing he called his stepmother had stood, but the firelight flickered and the wagon faded until all that could be seen were the pale painted stars that had decorated its side, hanging in the air like the dying image of a pyrotechnic display. Then even the stars were gone.

Azador fell down into the dirt and sobbed. Sam reached for !Xabbu's hand and held it. She did not understand what had happened, but she knew what a broken heart looked like.

Azador was clearly not going to be much use for a while. Sam was helping !Xabbu gather more wood – the

stepmother's campfire at least had remained – when she
noticed Jongleur was gone.

'That's impacted!' she said. 'He waited till we were
distracted, then ditched us!'

'Perhaps.' !Xabbu did not seem convinced. 'Let us look.'

They found the old man sitting against a tree at the
edge of the clearing, as coldly serene as a statue. He was
so still that for a moment, until he flicked them with an
expressionless glance, Sam thought he might have had a
stroke. She was mildly disappointed to discover it was not
true, but could not help thinking there had been something odd about his behavior all day.

'What are you *doing?*' she demanded. 'You could at
least come help us set up camp.'

'No one asked me.' Jongleur rose stiffly and began to
walk toward where the firelight flickered along the trunks
of the trees. 'Is that thing gone?'

'What Azador called the stepmother? Yes, it is gone,'
!Xabbu said. 'Do you know what it was?'

'No. But I can guess. A function of the operating system,
meant to instruct and assist. A cracked version of the
things we built into many of our simulation worlds.'

'Like Orlando's Trojan tortoise,' said Sam, remembering. She started to explain to !Xabbu, but realized
suddenly that she did not want to talk about her dead
friend in front of the old man.

*Just because I'm feeling a little sorry for Azador, I
don't have to let it spread over to the old murderer, too.*

'Do you think it spoke with the voice of the One, then?'
!Xabbu asked. When he saw the sour look on Jongleur's
face, he amended it to, 'With the voice of the operating
system?'

'Perhaps.' Despite his scowl, the old man had only a
little of his usual fierceness, and in fact seemed troubled.

Had something in Azador's misery touched even Jongleur's heart, which Sam imagined to be as small, dark, and hard as a charcoal briquet? It seemed difficult to believe.

Azador did not look up at them when they joined him at the fire, nor would he respond to any of Sam's or !Xabbu's questions. The moon had risen into the sky and now stood framed between the black hands of the trees, the stars small but bright behind it.

Sam was nodding with fatigue, and wondering if it would be too utterly creepy to sleep in one of the empty wagons, when Azador suddenly began to talk.

'I . . . I do not remember everything,' he said slowly. 'But when I found the bridge, much began to come back to me, as though I saw the cover of a book I had read as a child but had forgotten.

'I remember that I grew up here, in these woods. But also I roamed with my family through all the countries. We crossed the rivers, took our wagons to villages and towns in search of work. We did what needed doing. We had enough to live. And when we came together here, at Romany Fair, all was music and laughing – all the Romany together.' For a moment there was light in his face, a memory of better things, but it faded. 'But I never felt that I belonged – never could I accept that this was my life, the whole of it. I was unhappy even when I was happy. "Azador," all the Romany called me. It is an old Spanish Gypsy word, I think. It means to make ill luck, to bring mischance. But still they were kind to me, my family, my people. They knew it was destiny that made me so, not my choice.'

'What is your real name?' !Xabbu asked gently.

'I . . . I do not know. I do not remember.'

Even Jongleur was listening intently, an avid look on his hawklike features.

Azador abruptly sat up straight and his face darkened with anger. 'That is all I can tell you. Why do you do this to me? I did not wish to come back here. Now I have again lost all the things that I lost once before.'

'She said you could follow them,' Sam reminded him. 'Your stepmother. She said you could follow them to . . . what was it? A well?'

'They are making a pilgrimage to Kali the Black,' Azador said with a scornful laugh. 'But they might as well have flown to the stars. I do not know how to get there, except to walk. We are far from the center, where the Well is – we would have to cross river after river. The world would be gone before we were halfway there.'

'Do you remember nothing else?' !Xabbu leaned forward. 'I met you far away, in another part of the network. You must have crossed great distances to get there. How did you do it?'

Azador shook his head. 'I remember nothing. I lived here. Then I wandered in other lands. Now I am back . . . and my people are gone.' He scrambled to his feet so violently that he kicked leaves into the fire, which jumped and sputtered. 'I am going to sleep. If the One is merciful, I will not wake up.'

He strode away. They heard the creak of leather springs as he climbed into one of the wagons.

'Didn't . . . didn't his stepmother say he might kill himself?' Sam asked worriedly. 'I mean, should we leave him alone?'

'Azador will not commit suicide,' Jongleur said in a flat voice. 'I know his type.' He too rose and walked off between the wagons.

Sam and !Xabbu looked at each other across the campfire. 'Is it my imagination,' Sam asked, 'or is the scan factor just, like, rocketing upward every minute?'

'I do not understand you, Sam.'

'I mean, are things getting crazier and crazier?'

'No, I do not think you are imagining it.' !Xabbu shook his head. 'I am puzzled myself, and worried, but I am also hopeful. If all are being drawn to some place called the Well, then perhaps Renie will be going there, too.'

'But we don't know how to get there. Azador said by the time we walked there, the world is going to have ended.'

!Xabbu nodded sadly, but then manufactured a smile, even more admirable for the effort behind it. 'But it has not happened yet, Sam Fredericks. So there is hope.' He patted her. 'You go sleep now – if you choose that wagon, I can see it from the fire. I wish to think.'

'But . . .'

'Sleep now. There is always hope.'

Sam woke from a troubled sleep into a world of mist and shadow.

In the dream, her parents had been explaining that Orlando couldn't come with them on the camping trip because he was dead, and even though he was standing right there looking sad, he still wouldn't fit in the car because his Thargor body was too big. Sam had been angry and embarrassed, but Orlando had only smiled and rolled his eyes, sharing a silent joke with her about parents, then faded away.

When she sat up, rubbing tears from her eyes, and stumbled out of the wagon, it was into a world without daylight.

'!Xabbu!' Her voice echoed back to her. '!Xabbu! Where are you?'

To her immense relief he appeared from around the corner of the wagon. 'Sam, are you all right?'

'Chizz. I just didn't know where you were. What time is it?'

He shrugged. 'Who can say here? But a night has passed, and this is as much morning as we are going to get, it seems.'

She looked out at the wet grass, the white tendrils of mist between the trees, and felt a thrill of fear. 'It's all shutting down, isn't it?'

'I don't know, Sam. It seems a strange way for a simulation to behave. But it does not make me happy, no.'

'Where are the others?'

'Azador went away early this morning, but came back. Now he is sitting in the center of the meadow and will not talk to me. Jongleur has gone out walking too.' !Xabbu looked tired. Sam wondered if he'd had any sleep at all, but before she could ask him, a tall, gaunt, and mostly naked shape appeared out of the gray murk at the edge of the clearing.

'We can wait here no longer,' Jongleur announced before he had even reached them. 'We will leave this place now.'

In the real world, Sam thought sourly, you got breakfast. In this world, you got a two-hundred-year-old mass murderer spouting orders at you before your eyes were all the way open. 'Yeah? How are we going to do that?'

Jongleur barely glanced at her. 'Azador can take us to the operating system,' he told !Xabbu. 'You said that.'

!Xabbu shook his head. 'Not me. The . . . the step-mother told him he could. But he did not believe it.'

'We will make him believe it.'

'Are you going to torture him or something?' Sam demanded. 'Trick him?'

'I think I can help him find the way,' Jongleur said coolly. 'Torture is unnecessary.'

'Oh, *you're* going to show him how to do it?'

'Sam,' !Xabbu said quietly.

'Your manners are typical of your generation. That is to say, nonexistent.' Jongleur glanced at Azador, sitting a few dozen meters away, looking bleakly out at the forest. He lowered his voice. 'Yes, I will do it. I built this system in the first place, and I have learned a few things now about this backwater section of it.' He turned to !Xabbu. 'Azador is a construct, a pet of the operating system, as is all this world. You proved that, to your credit.' Disturbingly, he tried to smile. Sam thought of crocodiles. 'He will have within him a direct connection of some sort, even if he is not aware of it. "To the place where you touch the One, as we all do," the stepmother-program said. Am I right?'

!Xabbu looked at him carefully for a moment, then shrugged. 'So how will we do this?'

'We must find the next river. Those are the crossing points, the connections, like the gateways we built into the Grail system. The rest you must leave to me.'

'How did you know what the stepmother said, anyway?' Sam asked suddenly. 'You didn't listen to her. You went off by yourself.'

Jongleur's face was a mask.

'You've been talking to Azador already, haven't you?' she said, answering her own question. 'Just utterly whispering in his ear.'

'He does not trust you,' Jongleur said calmly. 'He is unhappy, and feels you forced him to come here.'

'Oh, and you're his friend now? He wants to kill all the Grail people. Did you mention that you had a little something to do with that?'

!Xabbu laid a hand on her arm. Across the foggy expanse of grass, Azador had turned to look at them. 'Quietly, Sam, please.'

For a brief moment Jongleur seemed about to respond with an equal measure of fury, then the storm building inside him calmed, or was suppressed. 'Does it matter what he would really think of me? We need him. This part of the network – perhaps the whole thing – is dying. You said yourself that I was useless, girl. Perhaps I have been that so far, although I think your absent friend might remember that I saved her life on the mountain. Can I not contribute something now?' He fixed her with his cold, clear stare. 'What will it hurt if I try, other than your pride?'

Sam could not help staring back. There was something odd in Jongleur's stiff manner, something off-kilter and discomforted. *He's been funny ever since we followed Azador here*, she thought. *Could he actually be, like, turning into a human being a little bit?*

She doubted it, but despite her dislike and distrust of the man, could not really argue with what he said. 'I guess we have to do . . . something.' She looked at !Xabbu, but the small man showed little reaction except to nod briefly.

'Good.' Jongleur clapped his hands together. The crack echoed through the gloomy clearing. 'Then it is time to set off.'

'Just one thing,' Sam said. 'There were some clothes left in the wagon I slept in. If it's going to stay dark around here, it's going to be cold, so I'm going to find something to wear.'

Jongleur did not smile again, for which Sam was grateful, but he nodded his approval. 'As long as we do it swiftly, that is a good idea.' He glanced down briefly at his own sarong of reeds and leaves. 'The novelty of simply having a body has worn off. I grow weary of being scratched by branches and thorns. I will find some clothes as well.'

* * *

Although the garments in Sam's wagon had been colorful, even gaudy, Felix Jongleur managed to find an old and somewhat threadbare black suit and collarless white shirt in one of the other wagons. Sam thought he looked like a preacher or an undertaker out of a net Western.

Bowing to the trend, !Xabbu had discarded his own brief kilt of woven leaves for a pair of pants only a few shades darker than his own golden skin, but had stopped there.

Sam inspected the blue satin pants and ruffled shirt she had selected – the best she could find, but nothing she would have been caught dead in at home. *Like the back end of the world's saddest, most impacted parade, that's what we look like.*

A quiet conversation with Jongleur had apparently reconciled Azador to the old man's plan. Whatever emotions the place had provoked in him, he did not look back as he led them out of the clearing and away from the circle of brightly painted wagons. Sam could not help taking a final, yearning glance at the ghostly vehicles, which seemed almost to float above the misty grass. It had been nice to sleep in a bed, however small and confined. She wondered if she would ever get the chance again.

Azador led them on a long winding trek through the forest, a journey that would have lasted until long past noon if anything like noon had ever come. The light remained minimal and diffuse, the forest a twilit haze. A few weak little lights like dying fireflies pulsed in the treetops but added nothing to the cold gray world.

Sam had grown so weary of stumbling through the damp, dark woods that she was about to scream, if only to hear a sound that wasn't dripping water or their own scuffing feet, when Azador stopped them.

'There is the river,' he said dully, pointing downhill through a break in the trees. The gray water did not shine, and looked more like the mark of a broad pencil than the lively stream they had seen elsewhere. 'But even if I find the bridge, it will only lead us to the next country, far from the center where the Well is.'

'I suspect we were far from Romany Fair when you found the last bridge,' Jongleur said. 'Not in the country beside it. Am I right?'

Azador seemed tired and confused. 'I suppose. I do not know.'

'You found Romany Fair because it was where you wanted to go. Just as you found your way out of these worlds in the first place. Am I right?'

Azador swayed. He lifted his hands to cover his face. 'It is too hard for me to remember. I have lost everything.'

Jongleur took his arm. 'I will speak to him alone,' he told Sam and !Xabbu. The old man dragged Azador along the hill, out of earshot, then leaned close to his face as though forcing the attention of an unwilling child; Sam almost thought Jongleur would take the Gypsy's chin in his hand to keep him from looking away.

'Why can't he talk in front of us? I don't trust him, do you?'

'Of course I do not trust,' !Xabbu said. 'But there is something different in him. Have you seen that?'

Sam admitted she had. They watched as Jongleur finished his harangue and led Azador back toward them.

'We are going to find the bridge now,' Jongleur said flatly. Azador looked stunned and exhausted, like someone who had given up arguing because he knew he could not win. He glanced at Sam and !Xabbu as though he had never seen them before, then turned and began to make his way down the steep, forested slope.

'What did you tell him?' Sam demanded between breaths.

'A way to think.' Jongleur did not elaborate.

They came out of the trees onto a slope just above the river. Azador stood with his arms limp at his sides, staring at a bridge.

'Lock me sideways,' Sam said, panting. 'He did it.'

It was a covered bridge made of rickety wood, like a single small house stretched to absurdity across the dark, flat river. She could just see the spot where it touched the other bank through the mist hovering above the river, but she knew better by now than to assume that the hilly forest there, a mirror of the place where they stood, was their actual destination.

When they reached Azador, they discovered that his eyes were closed.

'I do not want to cross,' he said quietly.

'Nonsense,' Jongleur told him. 'You want to find your people, don't you? You want to do what the One has commanded of you.'

'My own end is there,' Azador said miserably. 'As it was foretold. I can feel it.'

'You feel your own fear,' Jongleur responded. 'Nothing is achieved unless fear is overcome.' He hesitated, then put his hand on Azador's arm – a more or less human gesture which surprised Sam almost as much as it startled the Gypsy. 'Come. We all need you. I am sure your people need you, too.'

'But . . .'

'Even death can be outwitted,' Jongleur said. 'Did I not tell you that?'

Azador swayed. Sam could almost see him weakening. For a long moment she wondered whether she wanted him to give in or not.

'Very well,' he said heavily. 'I will go across.'

'Good man.' Jongleur squeezed his arm. The old man seemed excited, even anxious, but Sam could not imagine why. Her mistrust flared again, but he was already leading Azador onto the span.

Sam and !Xabbu followed a few steps behind. Within moments they had passed beneath the roof of the bridge. It was so dark inside that the gray twilight they had left behind now seemed bright afternoon by comparison. Sam found herself straining toward the single point of gray light hovering far in front of them, the opening at the bridge's other end. Her footsteps echoed in the small space. The bridge creaked beneath her.

'Wait a minute,' she said. 'If that's the light from the other end, how come we can't see Jongleur and Azador in front of us . . . ? !Xabbu?' She stopped. '!Xabbu?'

Even the point of light was wavering now, as though fog were drifting in from the river to fill the covered bridge. Sam's heart sped. She turned, but there was no longer a light behind her, either. '!Xabbu! Where are you?'

She could hear nothing but the thumping of her heart and the soft creak of timbers beneath her feet. The darkness was so close, so strong, that Sam could feel it twining around her like a living thing. She put out her hands, searching for the bridge's walls, but her fingers touched only cold air. Panicked, she began to move forward, or what she thought was forward – slowly at first, but her cautious movements quickly gave way to a trot, then a breakneck run.

Right into the grip of something as strong as pain, as cold as regret.

Living fear caught her up like a huge dark fist. In a split-instant a deathly chill burrowed into her, numbing her body into nonexistence, until there was nothing of her left but a tiny flicker – a thought, a breath, struggling against the all-conquering nothing.

I've felt this before – inside the temple in the desert. But I didn't remember how . . . how bad . . . !

She was not alone. Somehow she could feel !Xabbu, and even Jongleur, as if they were all connected to her through the dark by some sputtering, fading circuit – !Xabbu drowning in emptiness, Jongleur shrieking in the shadows, snatching at the blackness as if to pull it into some more coherent shape – but it was only a glimmer, a moment. Then the others were gone and she was left alone, a dying spark.

Let me go, she thought, but there seemed nothing that could hear her or wanted to listen.

The force that held her squeezed, squeezed hard, and the void wrapped her and pulled her down . . .

It was the park near her old house – a place she had not seen for years and years, but the swings and monkey bars were still as familiar as her own hands. She was sitting on the grass at the edge of the play area, in the bright sunshine, scuffing her bare feet in the sand and looking at the patterns it made, at the bits of tanbark sticking up through the pale drifts like flotsam on a frozen ocean.

Orlando was sitting beside her. Not the barbarian-hero Orlando, or even the wizened, cartoonish thing she had sometimes seen in her darker thoughts since learning about his illness, but the Orlando she had once imagined, the dark-haired boy with the thin, serious face.

'It doesn't want you,' Orlando said. *'It doesn't really care much about anything anymore.'*

Sam stared at him, trying to remember how she had come to be in such a place. All she could remember with any certainty was that Orlando was dead, which didn't seem like a very polite thing to bring up.

'I think if you can, you'd better get out,' he continued, then bent to pluck a long grass stem.

'Get out . . . ?'

'Of where you are. It doesn't want you, Sam. It doesn't understand you. I think it's stopped trying.'

The ground shuddered – just a little, but Sam felt it in her haunches, as though someone had struck the world a heavy blow, but far from where they sat. 'I'm scared,' she said.

'Of course you are.' He smiled. It was just the kind of crooked smile she'd always imagined him having. 'I would be, too, if I was still alive.'

'Then, you know . . . ?'

He held up the stem of grass, then blew it out of his fingers. 'I'm not really here, Sam. If I were, I'd be calling you "Fredericks," wouldn't I?' He laughed. His shirt, she could not help seeing with loving pity, was buttoned wrong. 'You're just talking to yourself, pretty much.'

'But how do I know about . . . about what it thinks?'

'Because you're inside it, scanmaster. You're in its mind, I guess you'd call it – way inside. In its dreams. And that's not a very good place to be right now.'

The ground shuddered again, a more distinct rolling, as though something beneath them had discovered itself confined and was chafing against its restraints. The rings on the monkey bars began to sway slowly.

'But I don't know how to get out!' she said. 'There's nothing I can do!'

'There's always something you can do.' His smile was sad. 'Even if it's not enough.' He got up and dusted off the knees of his pants. 'I have to go now.'

'Just tell me what to do!'

'I don't know anything you don't know yourself,' he explained, then turned and walked away across the grass, a field of green far more immense than what she remembered. Within moments the slightly awkward figure had diminished until she felt she could have reached out and picked him up in one hand.

'But I don't know anything!' she called after him.

Orlando turned. The day had grown dark, the sun lost behind clouds, and he was hard to see. 'It's scared,' he called back to her. Another rumble passed through the ground, bouncing Sam where she sat, but Orlando did not waver. 'It's really scared. Remember that.'

Sam tried to scramble after him but the earth beneath her feet had begun to pitch and she could not get her footing. For a moment she thought she had her balance under her at last, might be able to catch him before he disappeared – she had always been a fast runner, and Orlando was crippled, wasn't he? – then a vast black something came up from beneath the surface of the world, breaching the crumbling earth like a whale heaving up out of the ocean's dark underneath, and Sam was thrown headlong into the sagging, collapsing deeps.

The swift rasp, she realized at last, was the sound of her own terrified breath sawing in and out. She could feel dirt beneath her fingers, dirt against her face. She did not want to open her eyes, frightened that if she did she would see something staring back at her, something as big as all Creation.

It was the sound of someone gasping next to her that gave her the courage to look.

She was lying on her back beneath a purple-gray bruise of a sky, grimmer even than what had stretched above the forest. The ground beneath her felt hard and real. They

were on a slope, surrounded by hills that looked something like the crown of the black mountain, a bleak landscape without vegetation.

Sam sat up. !Xabbu was on his hands and knees beside
her, his face pressed against the earth, his chest expanding and contracting as though he were having a heart
attack, sobs hitching in his throat. She crawled to him
and put her arms around him.

'!Xabbu, it's me! It's Sam. Talk to me!'

The noises quieted a little. She could feel his compact
body shuddering against her. At last he calmed. He turned
toward her, his face wet with tears, but for a moment did
not seem to recognize her.

'I am sorry,' he said. 'I have failed you. I am nothing.'

'What are you talking about? We're alive!'

He stared, then shook his head. 'Sam?'

'Yes, Sam. We're alive! Oh, God, I didn't think . . . I didn't
know . . . but I did, I just forgot about it, like it was too
painful or something. When I was in the temple in the desert
with Orlando, it was just the same . . .' She realized that
!Xabbu was looking at her in confusion, and that she was
babbling. 'Never mind. I'm just so happy you're here!' She
hugged him tightly, then sat up. She was still wearing her
borrowed Gypsy finery, as was he. 'But where are we?'

Before he could answer, they both heard a cry from
farther down the slope. They climbed to their feet and
made their way down the scree of dark, crumbling soil,
and found Felix Jongleur on the other side of a small
hillock. He was lying on his side with his eyes squeezed
shut, writhing like a salted slug.

'No,' the old man gasped, 'you cannot . . . ! The birds
. . . the birds will . . . !'

!Xabbu reached out a tentative hand. When it touched
him, Jongleur's eyes snapped open.

'She is mine!' he shrieked, flailing at them. 'She is . . .' He stopped and his face crumpled. For a moment he seemed to look at !Xabbu and Sam without defenses, his eyes those of a hunted, desperate animal. Then the mask was back in place. 'Do not touch me,' he snapped. 'Do not ever touch me . . .'

'I have found it!' Azador shouted.

They turned. He was making his way up the hill toward them, bent against the steepness of the climb. When he lifted his head, his face was lit in an astonishing smile. 'You were right! Come see!'

Sam looked to !Xabbu, who shrugged and nodded. As Jongleur was still raising himself to his feet with chilly if unsteady determination, they followed Azador back down the slope.

In a few minutes they had reached a place where they could look out across the last of the small hills to see the bowl-shaped valley as a whole. Like the ring of hills, it bore more than a passing resemblance to the top of the black mountain, but instead of a huge, pinioned figure, the valley was dominated by a monstrous crater filled with black water and strangely muted lights. A crowd of figures too distant to make out huddled along its rim.

'What . . . what is it?' Sam asked at last.

'It is the Well,' said Azador triumphantly. He turned and clapped Jongleur on the shoulder so hard he almost knocked the old man over. 'You were right! You are a wise, wise man.' He turned and pointed. 'Do you see them all down there? All the children of the One have gathered. The Romany will be there, too. My people!'

As if he had exhausted his patience waiting to show them, Azador now went scrambling down the hillside toward the plain, leaving Sam and the others stunned and staring.

CHAPTER 32

Bad House

NETFEED/ENTERTAINMENT: Jixy Jinxing Jingle?
(visual: excerpt from Mirthday special)
VO: Creators and performers on the popular Uncle Jingle children's interactive are beginning to wonder what's going on. A series of strange happenings on the show have led some people at Obolos Entertainment, the show's producers, to suggest sabotage, with the implied suspect being WeeWin, a children's toy firm with offices in Scotland, but which is primarily owned by a subsidiary of Krittapong Electronics. In recent weeks characters on the Uncle Jingle program have disappeared mid-show, other objects not designed to be part of the environment have appeared, and some character interactions have been interrupted by unexpected noises one participant characterized as 'moaning and roaring and even crying.'
(visual: company spokesperson Sigurd Fallinger)
FALLINGER: 'Could it be sheer coincidence that these attacks began right after we filed a large and completely justified suit for infringement on our intellectual property? We doubt it, let's just say that. We have some very strong reservations about that theory.'

THE Ticks were active around the base of the vegetal tower, dozens and dozens of pale shapes swarming in the evening darkness like maggots on putrefying meat. Renie, remembering how just a few of them had torn the rabbit, could not look at them for long without feeling sick.

She stepped back from the window. 'We ought to be out of here before it gets light again – if it ever does.' She looked over to Ricardo Klement, who still held the strangely deformed thing that Renie had begun to think of as the Blue Baby. 'Any ideas? How did you get here in the first place?'

Klement never made much eye contact, so it was hard to tell if he had even heard her. After a long moment, he said, 'We walked. I walked. With feet.'

'Yeah, with feet.' Renie had been angry with herself for crying, but if the alternative was being an emotionless jelly like this, she was proud of her tears. 'Why didn't those things get you?'

Klement did not respond. The Blue Baby moved fitfully in his arms, a squirm of malformed limbs. Despite the horror of the thing's appearance, watching how Klement held it, like a stone or a piece of wood, almost made her want to take it from him and give it some kind of human contact. She went and knelt beside the Stone Girl instead.

'Are you okay?'

The little girl shook her head. 'Scared.'

'Yeah, me too. We'll get out of here, then things will be better.' *If I can only come up a machine gun or a flamethrower someone has conveniently grown out of twigs and leaves and left for me.* The flamethrower idea tugged at her. 'I wonder how they actually see,' she thought aloud. 'I mean, just the same visible spectrum as us? Or maybe they're using the infrared part as well.'

The Stone Girl stared sadly at her stubby little fingers. 'What's *imfer red?*'

'Hard to explain right now.' Renie reached into her

makeshift brassiere and pulled out the Minisolar lighter.
'But I wonder if any of this green stuff will burn.'

Now the Stone Girl looked up, eyes widening. 'You're
going to make a fire? That's dangerous!'

Renie laughed despite herself, a pained bark. 'Jesus
Mercy, child, we're surrounded by those carnivorous
creepy-crawlies, waiting for the world to end, and you're
worried about me doing something dangerous?' On an
impulse, she leaned forward and kissed the Stone Girl on
the top of her round, cool head. 'Bless you. Come help
me see if any of these leaves and branches are even a
little bit dry.'

As she chivvied the girl along, more to keep the child's
mind occupied than anything else – she could certainly
have worked faster on her own – it was hard not to think
of Stephen. Renie had fought so many battles over the
years, dragging the boy unwillingly through even rudimentary housework, doubling or even tripling the time
she would have taken by herself, but determined that her
brother at least would not grow up into the kind of man
who assumed some woman would step into his life and
do all the messy jobs.

The kind of man my father is, for instance. But even
as she thought it, she remembered the days when she was
young and Joseph Sulaweyo had come home from work
tired and sore and gleaming with sweat. *He did work hard
once*, she had to admit. *Before he gave up.*

'Is this dry, Renie?' the Stone Girl asked her.

'Well, it's brown, I think,' she said, squinting. The radiance from the nodding flower in the ceiling was fainter
than gaslight. 'Just rip it off and pile it here.'

The surging vitality of More Very Bush cost Renie and
her small companion something like an hour as they struggled to locate enough dead leaves to make a knee-high

pile, and even so most of what they found were still more green than brown. Ricardo Klement looked over from time to time, incurious as a bundle of laundry. He did not offer to help.

'If this works,' Renie pointed out with some resentment, 'you're not going to be able to just sit there – not unless you want to be roasted like a potato.'

Klement was looking away again. The Blue Baby turned its blind face toward her for a moment, as though trying to make up for the disinterest of its caretaker.

'Give me that big leaf,' she told the Stone Girl. 'It's okay that it's green – yes, that one. Actually, give me two. I'll build the fire on one, then use the other as a fan.' Renie squatted in front of the pile of torn and crumpled leaves. 'Now wish me luck.'

'Luck,' said the Stone Girl seriously.

Renie ignited the lighter and held it against the driest leaf she could find. She was relieved to see the edge of the leaf blacken, then a little smoke curl up. She cupped it with her hand to keep the breeze from the window away until a small flame was actively burning, then she began taking other dry pieces off the pile and pushing them against the tiny fire. After a while she realized that she was getting uncomfortably hot. The original leaf on which she'd built the blaze, a vast ivylike pad almost as large and tough-skinned as an elephant's ear, was beginning to curl and blacken.

'In just a few minutes we're going to have to make a run to the next bridge,' she told the Stone Girl.

'The Ticks will get us!'

'Not if this confuses them enough – we should at least get a good head start. But we'll have to run straight for the bridge. You said it wasn't too far.'

'We can't go over that bridge.'

'What? What are you talking about? I already asked you and you said it would work – that we could cross the river!' The fire, although still somewhat contained, was beginning to lick upward toward the low ceiling. The hanging, orchidlike light was beginning to brown and curl a bit at the edges. 'I don't even know if we can put this out now. What do you mean we can't go over that bridge?'

'It goes to Jinnear Bad House.'

'I don't care. I'm sure it's dreadful, but if we stay here, eventually those things are going to catch us and kill us.'

'I don't want to go to the Bad House.'

'No arguing. I can't leave you behind.' She rose and found the long fibrous stalk she had put aside. 'Now move over beside the window where we came in.' Renie turned to Klement. 'You too. It's time to get out of here.'

Klement looked at her for a long moment, then stood up. Renie returned her attention to the fire. With the stalk, she shoved the blackening leaf against the tower wall opposite the window. Bits of flaming vegetation fell off along the way and died where they landed, insufficient to ignite the dark, moist greenery, but the leaves along the wall began to blacken and shrivel.

'We've got only a few minutes before it's too hot to stay in here,' Renie said as she turned, then stopped, staring in amazement. Only the Stone Girl remained in the small green belfry. 'Where's Klement?'

'He went down there.' She pointed down the opening to the lower level.

'Christ. Christ! He'll get eaten by those things!' Renie took a step toward the bramble-stairs, but a burning leaf fluttered free from the wall and stuck smoldering against her blanket. It took her several seconds to put it out. The wall was beginning to burn in earnest, the heat such that even the living plants were being consumed as though they were straw. Renie hesitated. The Stone Girl was looking at her, eyes huge with fear. Who was Klement after all but a murderer, a monster? Maybe this new version had seemed more acceptable, but did she have the right to risk the child's life in order to save him from his own damaged folly?

A line of flame crackled across the floor, making the decision moot. 'Out onto the vines,' she told the Stone Girl. 'Now.'

Renie hoisted herself through the window. When she had found something like stable footing in the tangle of greenery on the wall, she helped the little girl out and onto her shoulders. 'I have to climb down a little way,' she told the child. 'Hold on tight.'

By the time Renie had lowered her head beneath the line of the windowsill, the room behind her was burning brightly; flames crackled in the ceiling and the blaze had already eaten several holes in the wall. When Renie felt the first vine beneath her feet, she probed until she found another one of the springy cables a little lower down so she could use the first as a handhold. When her feet were firmly situated she lowered the Stone Girl down beside her, both of them swaying above the darkness and the swarming Ticks.

'In a minute the whole tower will be burning,' Renie whispered, 'so we'd better get going. If we're lucky, the whole flaming mess will come down on top of the those things and confuse them – kill a few, too, if we're really lucky!'

They were inching along some twenty meters out from the tower, the top of the structure burning like a torch now and spitting great sparking fragments onto the breeze, when the Stone Girl yanked at Renie's blanket. 'What's . . . what's going to happen when it falls down?' she asked.

'Ssshhh.' Renie tried to steady the alarming sway the

girl's tugging had begun. The whole center of the vegetal town was lit with wavering red light, including them,
and despite the distraction of the fire, she feared they
might be noticed any second. 'I told you! It's going to
fall down in a big burning, smoking mess, and it's going
to distract those monsters and we're going to get away.'

'But won't the vines fall down, too?'

Renie paused, still swaying from side to side. 'Oh, shit.'

'You said a bad word!'

'I'm going to say more, I'm afraid. Oh, damn me, how
stupid can I be?' She began sliding along the vine with
increased speed. They had only been spared so far, she
realized, because the fire was burning upward much faster
than it was burning downward, toward the spot where
the vines were rooted into the tower.

She looked at the ground between her feet, wondering
where they would fall when the vines gave way, and
wished she hadn't. More of the white shapes were beneath
them, weaving back and forth atop the brambles like
dolphins sporting in the wake of a ship.

'Just hurry,' she hissed at the Stone Girl. 'If it gets too
hard, let me carry you.'

Now it was a race against the fire she had set, and
Renie wished she had spent more time scouting the vines
before committing to this particular pair. They stayed a
reasonable distance apart, but not always one above the
other: by the time they had slid their feet another dozen
meters along one vine, the one they were using as a
handrail had sagged down until it was scarcely higher
than the first. Renie had to let the Stone Girl climb onto
her back again, since she was leaning out almost horizontally and the girl could no longer brace herself against
Renie's leg when the distances between the vines became
too great.

Something pinged and snapped on the tower end and the lower vine sagged alarmingly. It held, and Renie was able to stand almost upright once more, but the vine suddenly felt very loose. She looked back and saw that the uppermost part of the tower was belching flames dozens of meters into the sky, then a huge fiery piece of it tottered and broke free. Somebody or something may have heard her panicked prayer, because it fell away from the vines on which she and the Stone Girl were trapped, but the collapse set the whole springy structure quivering. The vines leaped like plucked strings and Renie had to wrap both arms around the upper vine and cling just to keep her balance as the Stone Girl teetered atop her and almost fell.

They had seconds now, if they were lucky, and Renie cursed her own earlier decision to pick the longest vines. She had wanted to get as far away from the tower as possible before having to touch the ground, but now she desperately wished there was a roof somewhere close by onto which they could jump. She put her head down to concentrate on her footing, trying to see each coming step in the inconstant, glaring light as she hurried sideways. The Stone Girl clung to her shoulders, crying softly.

She had only an instant's warning: the vine seemed to tighten beneath her hand as though someone had given it a hard tug. Renie made a lightning decision and let go so she could grab at the lower vine with both hands.

'Hold on tight!' she screamed as she wrapped hands and legs around the bottom vine. The weight of the little girl snatched her over backward but Renie kept her desperate grip and so did the Stone Girl. As they dangled upside down, the upper strand parted with a distant crack and a second later the broken end swept past, glowing red, flying away from the collapsing tower like the lash of a bullwhip. Renie felt its rough hide score her fingers as it flew past.

Would have taken my head off, she thought, a dizzy, horrified fragment of thought. The broken vine had whistled going by, a ton of fibrous cable moving at bullet speed. *We have to let go*, she realized in horror, *before the next . . .*

This time she did not even have a chance to warn the little girl. Renie's fingers released just as the second vine snapped with another whipcrack explosion. They tumbled down into the dark even as it hissed through the spot where they had been.

They landed in something like thick bushes, but Renie still felt the air leave her body as though she had been slammed by a giant hand. For long moments she could not get the breath back into her lungs and lay straining, facedown in prickly leaves.

When she was able to stagger to her feet she saw that the flaming tower had collapsed into a wildfire fifty meters wide, with tendrils of flame already marching out into the surrounding greenery. Some Ticks had been caught in the collapse – she could see writhing shapes in the blaze – but far more of them remained in an agitated mass around the perimeter of the fire.

The Stone Girl groaned. 'Are you okay?' Renie whispered. 'Anything broken?' The little girl seemed able to move, but did not get up. Renie reached down and pulled the child into her arms, then stood. 'Which way?' The Stone Girl groaned again and pointed. Renie began to run.

It was terrible country in the dark, so much vegetation that there was little hard ground beneath her feet, brambles and vines and trailing roots everywhere, snatching at her and tripping her up like malicious fingers. After a few hundred meters she was gasping for breath and feeling the bruises of the fall from the vine. She stopped and set the solid weight of the little girl down on springy leaves before looking back. She was relieved to see that the spreading fire was still surrounded by squirming, confused Ticks, and that she could see no others any closer.

'Can you walk? I don't know if I can carry you much farther.'

'I . . . maybe I can.' The little girl struggled up. 'I hurt my legs, I think.'

'Just try. If you can't make it, I'll carry you again. Let's hurry. We don't know how long this will distract them.'

They quickly stumbled out of the vicinity of the fire. Renie's feet were achingly sore, her legs scratched and cut so many times she had stopped paying attention, but there was nothing to be done. *Run or die*, she thought. *It's been like that since we first got onto this damn network.* 'Are we almost there?' she asked the little girl. 'Are we still going in the right direction? Can you tell?'

The Stone Girl only plodded forward. Renie surrendered to trust.

A quick glance back sent a wave of terror through her: this time she definitely saw pale shapes behind them. She had no idea if the Ticks could follow a trail, or even if these were some of the same creatures who had surrounded the tower, but it wouldn't matter much if they got close enough to see her and the girl. She had no illusion they could outrun the pallid monsters for more than a few steps – she had seen their terrible, darting speed.

Something rose out of the dark shrubbery before them. Renie gasped in alarm and tripped, slamming down onto one knee and dragging the Stone Girl face-first into the undergrowth. She scrabbled desperately for something to use as a weapon – a weapon she already knew would be useless – but the expected attack did not come.

The thing in front of her had a face.

'Klement! How did you . . . you're not . . . !' The Grail master was still holding the strange blue infant, although it was almost invisible in the dark night. 'They're behind us,' Renie said. 'I've just seen them. You'd better run, too.'

'I am . . . waiting.'

'Waiting for what? To get eaten?'

Klement shook his head. 'I do not know if this is the right . . . place. I . . . we . . . cannot feel . . .'

Renie scrambled to her feet and pulled the quietly weeping Stone Girl up as well. 'No time for this. You do whatever the hell you want.' She swept the little girl into her arms, a weird mirror of Klement and his malformed charge, and sprinted ahead.

Once Renie looked back and was sure she saw maggoty-white shapes pursuing them, another time there seemed nothing behind her but endless vegeration. She no longer trusted her own eyes. Her lungs were burning. It seemed almost impossible to believe she had ever done anything but run through this endless, tangled nightmare world.

She was tripping and crawling her way up a long slope, the wildfire in the town now a small coin of flame in the black night behind her, when the Stone Girl's arm tightened around her neck.

'I feel it,' the girl said. 'We're almost there.'

A high wall ran along the top of the hill, as leafy as everything else in More Very Bush. Renie stopped to lean against it, desperate to suck some new air into her chest before attempting the climb. She looked back and saw Klement walking stolidly up the hill, still a couple of hundred meters back. Behind him, but closing fast, half a dozen Ticks were sliding through the undergrowth like sharks. From this angle there was no question. They were moving rapidly and in concert. Whether it was Klement or Renie and her companion they were trailing, they were actively in pursuit.

Renie cursed bitterly. She lifted the little girl, who seemed to have tripled in weight, up onto the top of the fence, then left her clinging there while she began her own climb. Pulling herself up a vertical nearly defeated her, but somehow she found the strength.

From the top she could see the blessed river only a short distance away down the hill, its waters a meandering black stripe through the endless bramble. She turned again and saw that the Ticks had broken out of the deeper growth at the base of the hill and had almost caught up with Ricardo Klement. They boiled up the slope like hunting hounds, swiftly overtook him, then parted around him as though he were a tree in the middle of their path, leaving him untouched and seemingly unnoticed. Without a moment's hesitation they continued up the slope toward the spot where Renie still hung at the top of the wall, dumbfounded.

She had only enough time for a single startled and horrified curse, then she grabbed the Stone Girl and lowered her far enough to let her drop to the ground, then swung her own legs over and slid down the scraping branches.

'Where's the bridge?' she shouted to the Stone Girl. 'They're right behind us!'

The little girl took her hand and pulled her on an angled course down the slope. The Ticks were flowing over the wall behind them like fingers of cloud coming down a mountainside. Renie snatched up the little girl and sprinted.

By the time they reached the thick brush that lined the

river, Renie could hear the crackling slither of their pursuers.

'There!' squealed the Stone Girl.

The bridge had been almost invisible. Like everything else in More Very Bush, it was made of living branches and leaves, an arch leaping out from the center of the thicket across the water. Renie ran the last few steps and sprang up onto the end of the bridge with the girl in her arms. When the water was beneath her, she finally risked a look back.

The Ticks had stopped at the edge of the river, but clearly knew she was there. They made a few tentative movements toward the bridge, but something seemed to hold them at bay.

'I think we're safe,' Renie gasped. 'Don't we . . . need to say something now . . . before we cross? About a . . . a gray goose?

'I don't want to cross.'

'We have to. We can't go back – look at those things! They're waiting for us.' *But why didn't they want Klement?* 'Let's cross,' she said to the child. 'We'll be all right.'

'No, we won't,' the Stone Girl murmured, but spoke the nursery rhyme in a tone of flat resignation. 'It's the Bad House,' she said when she had finished. 'This goes to the Bad House.'

'It can't get any worse than this.' Renie turned back toward the center of the river.

'It can,' the little girl said. 'It really can.'

She had been prepared for the mists that rose as they neared the center of the span, prepared for the way the river vanished beneath them, even its noise becoming so muted as to be little more than a constant, indrawn breath, but the sudden dark surprised her. The few distant stars of More Very Bush abruptly winked out and the black sky oozed down and covered everything like paint. And when the first faint lines of the place the little girl had called Jinnear Bad House appeared out of that darkness, Renie realized she had not been prepared for it at all.

She had half-expected something in the nursery rhyme vein, a quaint cottage of gingerbread – overblown perhaps, even a sprawling edifice like the House world, acre upon acre of crenellated cake with marzipan trim – but she had not expected the utter, utter strangeness of the Bad House.

It had no shape. She could see it only in strange, silver gleams, as though its curves and angles caught light that came from some invisible source – thin crescents and flat surfaces that came and went, as though the thing itself revolved. But it also seemed . . . inside out, somehow, as if the momentary illusions of an exterior shape were immediately succeeded by – or were perhaps simultaneously manifesting – almost incomprehensible inversions, an outfolding into imaginary space of every boundary wall. There was even something rounded about the glimmering, elusive shape, something paradoxically sealed and secretive.

She could no longer see the bridge beneath her feet, but it certainly did not feel like the uneven vegetal construct that had been there before. There was only the feeling of a bridge now, an idea of a span between her and . . . the place. The Bad House. And the mists were rising.

She realized she could no longer feel the Stone Girl's hand in her own. 'Where are you?' she asked, then called again, louder. 'Stone Girl?' No one answered. Renie stopped, even retreated a few steps, swiping her hand from side to side, but found nothing. She paused, her heart rattling, and thought she heard a thin sound like a child crying in a distant room – but it was in front of her, not behind her.

Horrified, shamed, Renie could hardly think. She had brought the girl here, against all the child's wishes, and now she had lost her. She could not retreat, no matter how powerfully her instincts told her to do so.

She walked forward into the darkness. The Bad House opened to her and then closed around her. She joined it.

This, too, she had experienced before, but it was something for which she could never, never be prepared, a clutching void so terrifying that in the first moments she nearly surrendered everything. This remorselessly freezing grip must have been what killed the old man Singh, she thought, clinging to rationality. Even though she had felt it before, felt it and survived it, it seemed to be only a breath away from extinguishing her entirely, too.

I'm inside it now, she realized. *The operating system. Not just in something it made – I'm inside it!*

That glimmer of perception brought something else with it, a thought so terrible that it almost blasted her loose from her ragged grip on sanity. *Is this what it feels like all the time? Is this what it feels like . . . to be the Other?*

As if this revelation had fractured a perfect black crystal, the darkness shattered and flew apart. Flashes of imagery ran through her, some so swift they seemed to laser through her brain in a continuous stream, others substantial enough to register, but only briefly, as though she fell through a universe of broken mirrors, catching glimpses of a thousand disparate scenes.

There were voices in hundreds of languages, children's voices raised in fear and pain, adult voices yowling in terror and anger, agonized faces, searing bursts of cold and intense heat. Then the oscillations slowed and became more regular, resolved into something like time and space in their normal ratios. There was a white room. There were bright lights. Deep voices roared, loud and incomprehensible as the rush of a mighty river, and faces pressed in on her, gigantic and distorted. Then there was a huge convulsion, the universe itself seeming to choke and vomit, and the faces exploded away from her, blood-stained and howling.

The voices shrieked. White and red. White walls, splattered with red. The deep barking adult voices wrenched into a higher pitch. Blood became a fine mist in the air. Dark shapes fell down and lay writhing.

Renie was inside the horror, drowning in it, but it wasn't directed at her. It simply was, and she was in it, like a weakening swimmer flailing in the ocean.

Hang onto something, she thought. *Grab something. A stick, anything. Drowning.*

Stephen.

But for a dizzy moment she could not even remember who Stephen was, what he was to her. Was he one of these torn faces shrieking at her? Was she?

My brother. Little brother.

She snatched at that thought, threw her weight onto it as the fear battered her, as the darkness and the screaming madness strobed through her. She struggled to build something – Stephen, with his bright eyes and his close-cropped hair, his ears that stuck out just a little too far, his slouchy walk that imitated a teenage strut while making him look more of a child than ever. She had lost him. This thing, this frozen storm of horror, had taken him. She would not forget that. She could not forget that.

I want him back! If she had a mouth, she would have screamed it. *I won't give up looking for him. You'll have to kill me like you killed the others.*

The blackness collapsed in on her like an avalanche of ice, the pictures gone now, the spikes of madness freezing into something far more deadly, far more implacable.

Stephen, she thought. *I came here for him. He's not yours. I don't care what you are, what they did to you, how they built you, how they used you. He's not yours. None of the children belong to you.*

The blackness crushed her, trying to silence her. Renie felt herself vanishing, being absorbed into a cold despair as endless as a journey across the universe.

I won't stop. It was a last thought – a lie, a pathetic boast, because everything that she was . . . *was* stopping . . .

And then the blackness became something else.

There was so little left of her, it seemed, that for a long time she could only lie with her eyes closed, stretched full length on her back, trying to remember not who she was, or where, but why she should care about either question. It was only the sound of distant crying which finally forced her to live again.

Renie opened her eyes to a gray world. At first all she could make of it was vertical shadow, darker on one side of her than the other. Only after a few searching, puzzled moments could she begin to make sense of it.

She lay on a path, a bit of rough stone running along the edge of a wall of stone, a little like the corkscrew trail that had led them up and down the black mountain. But as if to prove that every version of reality here had its inversion, this path seemed to curve around the inner rim of a great, circular hole: a great and empty blackness lay beside the path, but she thought she could just make out an opposite wall beyond it.

A pit, she thought. *I'm stuck on a trail down the side of some huge pit.*

The Well, she remembered a moment later. *That's where the Stone Girl said we were going.*

Where did the light come from? Renie looked up and saw something like stars in the murk far above her, a circular field that, she reasoned, must be the top of the hole. It was a vast, wide circle, but a momentary hope that this signified she was close to it disappeared when she tracked the far side of the pit upward. It would be hours of climbing to reach that opening, even if this massive hole was something closer in scale to the real world than the impossibly tall black mountain had been.

That's it – this thing is like the mountain turned upside down . . . inside out . . . was the beginning of a thought, then the muted sound of a child sobbing snapped her attention back again.

Stone Girl. She's somewhere below me.

Renie tried to get up, groaned, then tried again. Her body felt like a damp sack that might fall to pieces with the slightest rough handling. Her head seemed far too heavy for the strength of her neck.

On the third try she dragged herself onto her feet. The path was uneven but wide, the light of the oddly foggy stars enough that, with care, she could navigate it safely.

The crying came again, at intervals. As Renie stumbled downward, as minutes became what seemed closer to an hour, she began to fear that some trick of the acoustics was leading her farther away from the source of the noise, that it might actually be above her. Only the fact that the Well itself, if that was truly what it was, slowly became narrower, its far wall looming closer with each long circle, kept her from giving up in despair.

At last, when her already exhausted body and mind

were close to collapse, she found the bottom of the Well. But the bottom was out of reach.

The trail tapered to an ending which left her perched still some ten or fifteen meters above the base of the pit, where a thread of dark water flecked with subdued blue light murmured across the rough stone. A small, bent shape huddled beside this modest river.

'Is that you?' Renie asked. The figure did not look up. The quiet sound of weeping floated to Renie's perch, heartbreaking and ghostly. 'Stone Girl?'

The small shape went quiet. For a moment she feared it was all illusion, that she had mistaken some nodule of rock on the bottom of this pointless place in this most pointless of universes for a child, that the sound of weeping came from nowhere or everywhere, that she should just lie down here and die and solve all problems once and for all. Then the child looked up.

It was Stephen.

Fourth:

SORROW'S CHILDREN

'One for sorrow
Two for joy
Three for a girl
Four for a boy
Five for silver
Six for gold
Seven for a secret
Never to be told'
      – Traditional

CHAPTER 33

Weekend Hours

NETFEED/NEWS: Sea Squirt Squad – A Damp Squib?
(visual: S3 members wearing fish masks and kilts)
VO: The 'Sea Squirt Squad,' the militant arm of an anti-net group
called the Dada Retrieval Collective, have failed on another attempt
to, in their words, 'kill the net.' For the fifth time since announcing
this goal, a Sea Squirt action has gone badly wrong. This time, an
attempt to destroy the sales records of one of the main online retail-
ers, which would theoretically have meant a loss of billions in revenue,
resulted only in buyers receiving electronic Christmas cards several
months out of season.
(visual: DRC member wearing Sepp Oswalt mask)
DRC: 'You people are underestimating what a shock it was for Jewish
and Islamic shoppers to receive those Christmas cards. We've had a
few setbacks, seen, but we're well on our way to achieving our goal.
Just wait until we hack the national elections.'

CALLIOPE Skouros sat in the wreckage of a Saturday morning – unwashed coffee cups and breakfast plates, some of which dated back to Wednesday, the news blaring across most of her wallscreen while some children's show that had caught her attention fizzed and giggled in

an inset panel – and wondered what it would feel like to
have a personal life.

It wasn't sex she was thinking about, particularly, just
company. Wondering what it would feel like to be sitting
next to another human being – Elisabetta the waitress, just
for instance – and talking about the day ahead, maybe planning a trip to a museum or the park, instead of wondering
how much longer she could go without doing her laundry,
and whether if she ate that other waffle she would have to
skip having a bowl of ice cream after dinner.

When work crashed, when the job changed dramatically, as hers had when she and Stan had been pulled off
the now officially moribund Merapanui case, it was a lot
harder to ignore the emptiness.

Maybe I should get a pet, she thought. *Yeah, chance
not. Imprison some poor dog in here all day while I'm
working? There are laws about that.*

It had been a busy if boring week, mostly spent catching up on unfinished paperwork – a curiously old-fashioned expression, so redolent of ancient offices and dusty
files. With Merapanui closed, she and Stan had rolled
back onto a number of other pending matters, most of
them of the grim, foot-slogging variety, interviewing
sullen or intentionally stupid witnesses about stabbings,
canvassing neighbors for the last damning details of
domestic disputes that had suddenly turned fatal. What
was it about the Merapanui case that had kept her so
fascinated? The sniff of brimstone that seemed to accompany all reminiscences of John Dread? Or was it the
hopelessness of Polly Merapanui, as overlooked in death
as she had been in life, waiting with the patience of the
perpetually put-off for someone to give her savage murder
some meaning?

It's over, Skouros, she told herself. *You took your shot.*

It didn't work out. Now you get to do laundry. That's what life is shaped like.

She tightened the belt on her sagging dressing gown, then began to pick up cups and spoons.

The message had been left on her work account near the end of Friday afternoon. It was from Kell Herlihy in Records, and its importunate blink reminded her how tired she had been at quitting time yesterday, how even checking her mail had seemed like a cruel imposition, and of her tiny, pleasurable feeling of escape when she had decided against it.

It can wait, she told herself now. *Probably the stuff on what's-his-name, the Maxie Club arson guy.* But what else was there to demand her attention except the last Belgian waffle?

Fifteen seconds after she had opened the message, she was on the central database, trying to find out Kell Herlihy's home number.

When she finally made the call the screen came up dark. She could hear two or three kids arguing loudly in the background, plus a loud play-by-play of what sounded like Aussie Rules. 'Hello?' a woman said.

'Kell? It's Calliope Skouros. Sorry to bother you. I just got your message.'

A moment later the image flicked on. Herlihy from Records looked like she was having the married-with-kids version of Calliope's Saturday morning, although Calliope couldn't help noticing with some chagrin that the one with kids had at least managed to get dressed.

'Yes?' Herlihy looked a little dazed. Watching the three girls in the background, who appeared to be trying to dress a cat in baby clothes, Calliope refined her idea of the advantages of company.

'I'm really, really sorry, Kell, but I just had to follow up. You said you got something about John Wulgaru?'

'C'mon, Skouros, it's the weekend. Don't you ever do anything but work? Besides, I thought Merapanui was closed.'

'Not by my choice. Just tell me what you have.'

Kell Herlihy made a disgusted noise. 'A headache. Christ, what was it? It wasn't John Wulgaru, anyway – it was just "Wulgaru." An inquiry. I had that automatic monitoring thing set up for you.' She frowned, then turned away for a moment to rescue the cat and send her daughters out of the room, who went squealing in tripartite protest. 'If you ever miss the joys of being a breeder, feel free to do some babysitting for me.'

Calliope forced a laugh. 'Tempting, Kell. Look, what do you mean, "just Wulgaru"?'

'Just that. It was a word search. Someone trying to find out what it meant. I thought you'd want to know, since that was about the only active hit we ever got since I set up the monitor.'

'A word search?' Calliope's excitement had cooled just a little. 'Where was it from?'

'Some university, somewhere weird. Helsinki, I think. That's in Finland, right?'

'Yeah.' As quickly as it had blown up, the storm of excitement faded. 'Just someone from a university in Finland doing a search. Shit.'

'I didn't think it was much, but if you want to do a follow-up, the trackback information is attached to the original message.'

'No. Thanks anyway, Kell. As you pointed out, the case is closed. Not much use in bothering some graduate student in Finland.' She reached out to close the connection.

'Yeah, probably not, if that's where it's from.'

Calliope paused. 'What do you mean?'

'I mean if that's really where it's from.' Herlihy looked away, distracted by some dire sound from the other room that Calliope couldn't hear.

'But you said it was from Finland. A university.'

Herlihy stared at her for a moment, impressed by Calliope's naïveté. 'That's where it's *supposed* to be from. But people use universities all the time to screen stuff. Easy to hack into, lots of nodes to confuse things, sloppy accounting procedures because of all the students sharing time – you know.'

'I didn't know. Does that mean this search could . . . could be from somewhere else entirely?'

'Yeah.' Herlihy shrugged. 'Or it could be just what it looks like.'

'Can you find out for me?'

'Oh, God. If I can find some time, Monday or Tuesday . . .' She looked doubtful. 'I can try, Calliope. But I'm really, really busy right now.'

She had to ask. 'How about this weekend?'

'What?' Kell Herlihy's weary amusement sharpened into something like real anger. 'Are you joking? You are, aren't you? Tell me you are. I have three kids rioting here, my lump of a husband's going to take all day just to wash the car, and you want to know if I can drop everything and track down some . . . !'

'Okay, okay! Bad idea. I'm sorry, Kell.'

'I mean, come on! Just because you're single and you don't have anything to do on weekends . . .'

'Sorry.' She thanked the woman from records several times, in a hurry now to get off the phone. 'I'm an idiot. You're right.'

When the call was over she sat staring at the wall-screen. The news was showing some in-depth report on a tottering Asian gear empire and the apparent mortal illness of its mega-rich owner. The woman's face, as full of hard lines and surgically-smooth planes as an Easter Island statue, was horrifyingly shallow and empty, even in a piece of publicity file footage obviously meant to flatter.

That's what happens to people who don't get a life, Calliope thought. *They die on the inside, but nobody knows it for a long time.*

The odd thought lingered, confusing her. *But I can't just let this go. Not without checking this last bit, whatever it is. Sure, it's probably meaningless . . .*

. . . But what if it isn't? And how can you ever know unless you try?

Stan was sitting on the couch between his two nephews, of whom Calliope could see only half of each, one long skinny leg and one bare foot. From the sound of it, she was sharing the Chan wallscreen with the same sporting event that Kell Herlihy's husband-lump had been watching.

'You really have too much spare time, Skouros,' Stan said. 'It's Saturday.'

'Why does everybody feel so free to talk about my personal life?'

The Chan eyebrow crept up. 'Who was it who spent most of the last week or so keeping me up to the minute on the Wild, Wonderful World of Waitresses? Without me asking once, I might add.'

'All right. I'm a little sensitive today. So sue me.' She was glad she'd at least shed the dressing gown for actual I-have-a-life clothes. 'Better, why don't you humor me? You must know someone who can help with this.'

'On a weekend? It's a closed case, Skouros. *Finito. Kaput.* If you're going to flog a dead horse, why don't you at least let the poor bugger rest in peace until Monday?'

'Because I want to know. Monday everything will start over again, all the usual shit, and poor little Polly Merapanui will get farther and farther away.' She tried another tack. 'Not to mention that on Monday I'd be using office time for what you so accurately point out is a closed case. Right now, I'm only wasting my own.'

'And mine.' But Stan shut his mouth for a moment, thinking. 'Honestly, I can't come up with anyone, not that I could reach on a weekend.' One of his nephews said something Calliope couldn't hear. 'You're joking, right?' Stan asked.

'I'm not!' Calliope said, aggrieved.

'No, I'm talking to Kendrick. He said he has a friend who could help you.'

'A friend . . . like, someone his age?'

'Yeah. I don't think you can afford to quibble, Skouros.' Stan grinned. 'Not if you're looking for someone who'll work weekend hours.'

Calliope sank a little in her chair. 'Shit. Okay, put Kendrick on.'

Ten minutes seemed to pass between the time his older sister left to find him and the moment when Kendrick's friend appeared on Calliope's wallscreen. The boy, barely a teenager, coupled a small frame and dark, round face with an immense head of curly black hair, artificially frosted with white so that he looked like some kind of mutant dandelion.

'You the police lady?' Kendrick had already called to explain, it seemed.

'Yes, my name is Detective Skouros. And you're Gerry Two Iron, right?'

'Seen.'

She paused, trying to remember how to deal with a teenager who was not accused of any crimes. It was not an area in which she had much experience. 'So . . . hey, Two Iron is a really unusual name. What tribe is it from?'

He was amused. 'Golf.'

'Beg your pardon?'

'My dad's the club pro at Trial Bay, up north. That's what everyone calls him, so the kids at school there called me that too. Our real name's Baker.'

'Ah.' *What was that you said about yourself earlier, Skouros? Was 'idiot' the word?* 'Uh, did Kendrick tell you what I need?'

He nodded his head. 'You want to find out where someone's request comes from – whether it's real or, like, duppy.'

'Exactly. I'm sending you the information I have – the person who got it for me says all the trackback is included.'

Gerry Two Iron was already scrutinizing the bottom of his screen. 'Worry not. Looks easy.'

'Are you sure . . . are you sure this is all right? Your parents won't mind? Do they want to talk to me or anything?'

'Nah. Mom's in Penrith with her boyfriend this weekend anyway. But I did all my homework last night, so I'd just be in No Face Five or Middle Country this afternoon. Weather locks today – I have asthma, seen? If I find this out for you, can I be, like, some kind of official police auxiliary or something?'

'I . . . I don't know. We'll see.'

'Chizz. I'll call you back when I get it. Flyin'.' The picture vanished, leaving Calliope with the feeling she had been processed through some kind of machine expressly designed to make her feel old and slow.

* * *

EVEN the service elevators didn't go above the forty-fifth floor.

You can't get there from here, Olga thought. *Who said that, anyway? It was a joke, the name of an old show, something. Yes, a joke. From a time when things were funny.* She took a deep breath to slow her speeding heart, then keyed the floor number.

When the elevator stopped and swooshed open on what the elevator readout called '*45-building security*,' Olga Pirofsky half-expected to find herself dumped into some kind of airlock, stabbed by bright white beams like a police interrogation from an old netflick. She was not prepared for the small grotto outside the elevator door, the soft splashes of light on the dark walls, the quiet fountain and empty desk with its vase of drooping gardenias.

Olga stopped briefly to examine the desk, its glossy black top currently screening random scenes of nature. Was this the kind of thing Sellars would have wanted her to find for him, a screen terminal on the security level? Not that it mattered anymore – Sellars wasn't talking to her, and even if the desk were the portal to all J Corporation's secrets, she didn't have the first idea of how to go about discovering them.

Suddenly mindful that there must be cameras all around her and that she no longer had a secret ally hiding her from surveillance, she took a rag from her coveralls and gave the desk a quick dusting, then continued on to the door set in the wall to one side of the work area. She felt sure there must be an elevator somewhere on this level that would take her up to Jongleur's private penthouse – the information she had seen suggested there was room for at least half a dozen more floors above this security level. She held her breath as she lifted her badge to the reader, half-expecting to be blasted off her feet by some

kind of alarm. Instead, the door slid open, revealing the
room beyond. When she saw what was there she felt sick.

The room was large, perhaps fifty meters on each side.
The entire perimeter was empty – nothing but carpet. In
the middle, taking up almost three quarters of the space,
stood a huge cube made of floor-to-ceiling plexiglass so
thick that she had no doubt it was bombproof and bulletproof. Inside the plastic cage was an entire office – not
a showy garden spot like the reception area, but a working office with desks and machinery and a long bank of
wallscreen monitors. The lights were low and streams of
data played right on the plexiglass walls, further obscuring her view of the interior. Hologram structural models
of the building rotated above two of the desks; at the
moment, nothing else seemed to be moving except the
neon reflections flicking along the transparent walls. Then,
as her eyes adjusted, she saw that half-a-dozen muscular
men in shirtsleeves were scattered around the security
office like exhibits in a zoo, all staring at her.

I can't breathe, Olga realized. She wanted only to run
back through the reception area and throw herself into
the elevator. *I'm caught!*

One of the men stood up and beckoned to her. She
could not make her legs move. He frowned in irritation
and his amplified voice boomed all around her. '*Step
forward.*'

She forced herself to shuffle toward a heavy plexiglass
door built into the transparent wall. Beyond the security
men, near the back of the plastic tank, a single wide
rectangular shaft of polished black fibramic stretched up
to the ceiling. A featureless door was set in the nearest
side. *The elevator to the top floors*, she realized, but without pleasure or even much interest. It might as well have
been in another country.

'Give me your badge,' the man said. He was probably half Olga's age, head shaved everywhere except in two stripes above his ears. He spoke mildly, but there was something frighteningly cold in his eyes, and she could not help staring at the large gun he wore in a holster tucked under his arm. 'Your badge,' he repeated, his voice harsher.

'Sorry, sorry.' She fumbled it off her coveralls and dropped it into a trough that opened up in the door. Her hands were shaking so badly she felt sure they would execute her on that basis alone.

'What are you doing here?' The man held her badge next to a small box. 'You're not cleared for this floor.'

Olga could feel the man's suspicion deepening with every second that passed. His companions were talking among themselves – one was even laughing and gesturing, perhaps telling a funny story – but there was a watchfulness even to their inattention. 'I look for . . . for . . .' She exaggerated her accent, hoping to seem less of a threat, but it didn't really matter. Her brain had frozen up. She couldn't remember the name. She had been off Sellars' leash less than an hour and already she had spoiled everything.

I don't want to die – not like this, not for such a stupid mistake. I don't want these men to kill me and dump me in the wildlife preserve somewhere, those water flowers growing all over me like on one of those abandoned boats . . .

'Jerome!' she said, and wondered if it would do any good. 'I look for Jerome.'

'Jerome? Who the hell is Jerome?'

'He is custodian.' She did her best to sound like a hopelessly stupid peasant, one who would be of no interest whatsoever to any self-respecting Cossack. 'He is . . . friend of me?'

The security man looked back to one of his companions, who was telling him something she could not make out.

'Oh, *that's* Jerome?' said the man who had been talking to her, and laughed. 'That guy, huh?' He turned back to Olga. 'And why would you think he would be up here, Ms Cho . . .' He squinted at the monitor. 'Ms Chotilo. Why are you looking for him here? He works on the lower floors.'

'Oh, I don't find him there,' she said, hoping her fear seemed a reasonable part of her character and situation. 'I think, maybe you see him on your cameras, you tell me.'

The young security officer looked at her for a long, hard second, then his face grew a bit milder. 'You thought that, did you?' He said something too fast to register over his shoulder to his coworkers, who laughed. 'Well, I'll just go see. Is Jerome your boyfriend?'

Olga tried to look embarrassed. 'He is . . . he is a friend, only. We eat lunch together, yes? Sometimes?'

The man wandered over to one of the monitors, then ambled back. 'I just saw him coming out of one of the restrooms on Level A. If you take the elevator back down right now, you should catch up with him.' His smile turned cool. 'One more thing. You should be pretty careful about wandering around this building. The bosses get real nervous when people aren't where they're supposed to be. Understand?'

She nodded, backing toward the outer office. 'Thank you!' Her gratitude was not feigned.

In the elevator, Olga squeezed her hands under her arms to stop the trembling. She was angry at herself. What had she thought – that it would be easy? She was very, very lucky she was not in a cell right now.

But what does it matter? There's no way at all to get past those people. I have failed. I've lost the children forever.

She wished the elevator would just continue down through the bottom of the building and into the muddy delta earth, burying her in the dark quiet.

TIME, Ramsey thought. *We're running out of time here. What have we got left? Less than forty-eight hours until the weekend is over and someone notices Olga isn't with her shift when they come back on – not to mention the fact that the building will be swarming with employees again . . .*

'Damn!' He sat and stared at his pad, feeling hopeless. Sellars and the boy Cho-Cho were unconscious, maybe dying in the next room, and Catur Ramsey had inherited sole responsibility for the safety of Olga Pirofsky . . . but he couldn't find her telephone number.

'We can't just be . . . cut off!' He turned imploringly to Sorensen. 'We must still be connected to her.'

'Didn't Sellars tell you what to do?' Major Sorensen peered at the readout on Ramsey's pad with the expression of a shade-tree mechanic about to admit he never did know what a ring valve was in the first place.

'He barely told me anything. He said, I don't know, that the system was collapsing or something. That he'd call me right back. But he never did.' Ramsey put his head in his hands. He hadn't done anything more strenuous in the last four hours than help carry the bird-like, comatose form of Sellars, but he had never felt more exhausted in his life. 'He's got the connection to Olga channeled through some weird merry-go-round of repeaters – he told me he did it for security. But I can't find it! I just don't know anything about this stuff. You must have someone back at your military base who can fix this for you, Sorensen.'

From the expression on his face, Michael Sorensen was not having any better a day than Ramsey was. 'Haven't you been paying attention? We're goddamn fugitives right now, or might as well be – we can't risk acting any other way. And we don't know how widespread Yacoubian's little private network is inside the base. I know one old boy in my own office I don't trust at all, just for starters. So I'm supposed to call them and ask someone to help me figure out how to restore communications to our spy in the J Corporation tower?'

'Well, how about the guy who helped us already. Your friend, Parkins?'

Sorensen laughed sourly. 'Ron knows about as much about this kind of information gear as I know about ballet dancing. Not to mention the fact that he already said he doesn't want to be involved.'

'Jesus, we're all involved!' Ramsey put the pad down and went to wash his face in the sink, trying not to look at Sellars and the boy lying side by side on the bed, disaster victims waiting to be identified. He could feel the slipping of time as a physical thing; it made his fingers twitch. Sellars' voice on the wire, the apocalyptic warning about the death of the network, had gotten into Ramsey like a virus.

'Look, we're not either of us doing any good right now,' Sorensen said when Ramsey came back into the main room, face dripping. 'I've got one seriously upset wife right now and my little girl is barely holding it together. I'm worried that any minute Kaylene is going to march out of here and head for the nearest police station. I'm going back next door and spend some time with them. If you think of anything, call me.'

Ramsey waved his hand. 'Go on, yeah. Tell them . . . tell them I'm sorry.'

'Isn't your fault.' Fatigue showed in his failed smile. 'Isn't really mine either, but I don't think I could convince Kay of that just now.'

When the major had shut the connecting door, Catur Ramsey went to the minibar and found himself a tiny whiskey in a tiny bottle. He took it into the bathroom, this time shutting his eyes as he passed the bedroom door, emptied the bottle into a drinking glass and filled the glass halfway with water. Back in the main room, he lowered himself into the chair. He was so tired he felt he might fall asleep sitting up, and he knew the alcohol was a bad idea, but sometimes bad ideas were the only ones you had left.

We helped that poor woman get into that building when she'd probably never have made it on her own, then, just for added value, put a ring on her finger that will make a fine piece of incriminating evidence. Now we've abandoned her. That was what the whiskey was for – to dull the pain of betrayal, of failure. *It's like defending someone for jaywalking and they wind up getting a lethal injection. My best legal advice, Olga? Get a different attorney.*

It was a ridiculous thing to get stuck on – a mere problem of sorting through some telecom mumbo-jumbo and reestablishing the connection. There were probably a hundred bright high-school kids living within fifty miles who could do it. The boy Orlando Gardiner could probably have managed it in a matter of minutes. But it was not Catur Ramsey's world, and the need for secrecy was going to make it very difficult to find anyone who could help him, especially in the short time before things got very, very bad.

So that's your alternative, he asked himself, staring at

this still-untasted drink. *That's your big solution? Just bring Orlando Gardiner back from the dead?*

Ramsey upended the glass and took a measured swallow, thinking of darkness and death, thinking of empty wires.

Before the whiskey had finished burning in his stomach, Ramsey remembered someone he could call.

He had not used the number in what seemed a very long time. When the tone sounded twelve times without an answer, his worst suspicions were confirmed. Then, just as he was about to give up, someone answered.

'Hello? Who's this?' The screen stayed dark, but the intonation was unforgettable.

'Catur Ramsey. You remember me, don't you?'

'I don't recognize the line you're calling on.' There was a pause. 'In fact, it's a pretty weird connection.'

Sellars' defenses, Ramsey realized. Their outgoing calls from the hotel must be routed all over hell and Kansas, as his dad had been fond of saying. 'It's me, I swear. Can't you . . . can't you do voice recognition or something?'

'Yeah.' The speech seemed a little slower than Ramsey remembered. 'But I'd have to run it through this police department system that . . . that a friend of mine arranged. It would take a while.'

'I don't have a while. Look, do you still have my old number? Call me on that. But all I'm going to do is say, "It's me," then hang up and call you back. Got it?' Surely even if his regular line was tapped, that wouldn't give anyone a chance to do more than notice a strange little exchange, would it?

Two minutes later, the electronic pas-de-deux successfully completed, Ramsey called back on the shielded line.

'Satisfied?'

'I guess,' the other growled. 'But I may still run you through that recognition gear anyway.'

Ramsey couldn't help a weary smile. So it had come to this, had it? Having to prove your identity to untrusting machines. 'How are you, Beezle?'

'Okay, I guess. No word from Orlando in a long time.'

Even alone in a room, talking to a jumped-up kid's toy, it was impossible to repress a flinch of guilt and sorrow. Beezle didn't know?

But how would he? It's not like anyone would have remembered to contact Orlando's gear and let it know that its master was dead, now would they? In fact, his parents were trying to find Beezle and shut him down. No wonder he's out of the loop.

'I need you,' he said, sidestepping the issue entirely, but he couldn't help wondering if it was immoral to lie to a machine, more forgivable if it was only by omission. 'I'm still trying to get the answers – the things you and I were working on together – but I'm in trouble.'

'I don't know.' The cab-driver voice still seemed to lag a bit, as if Beezle had taken the electronic equivalent of a few Saturday afternoon beers and was finding it hard to get started on short notice. 'I need to keep my lines clear in case Orlando tries to reach me.'

Ramsey closed his eyes. He was so tired he could barely talk, so worried about Olga Pirofsky he felt sick to his stomach. Only a decade's worth of courtroom training helped him keep his temper and not say anything stupid or irretrievable, but just barely. 'I'm sure if he tries to get in touch with you, there's some way for you to know about it. Please, Beezle. This is important. If . . . if what Orlando's gone through means anything, then this is what it's about.'

There was another pause, in all probability while Beezle

parsed Ramsey's tortured syntax, but it seemed as if he were considering the pain in Ramsey's voice. 'Tell me what you need, boss,' the agent said at last. 'I'll see if I can help.'

'Thank God,' Ramsey breathed. 'And thank you, Beezle.' He got ready to send everything of Sellars' that he had on his pad, including the records of the last call. He could not help wondering what Beezle had been doing in the dead days since the last time they had spoken. 'Where are you, anyway?'

'Not really anywhere,' the raspy voice said. 'Just . . .' It trailed off. Ramsey cursed himself for a clumsy question – after all, what did physical location mean to electronic circuitry? In fact, Ramsey decided, bemused again by the topsy-turvy universe he was currently inhabiting, it wasn't just a clumsy question, it was almost cruel. Like asking an orphan, 'Where are your parents?'

Indeed, when Beezle spoke again, there was a tone of confusion that Ramsey had not heard before. 'Where am I? Just . . . waiting. You know. Waiting.'

SATURDAY afternoon had inched along like a dying animal. It was all Calliope could do not to ring up Kendrick's friend and demand a progress report.

He's just a kid, Skouros. And he's working for free. Besides, what's your hurry, anyway?

Elisabetta had not returned her call. In fact, the girl's roommate had been so vague and scatty Calliope had very little faith the message had even been delivered. Bored and unaccountably anxious, she had been thrown back on household chores.

Mixed results, she could see herself reporting to an imaginary commander. *We didn't catch the Merapanui girl's murderer, but I finally scoured my sink and threw away some old clothes in my closet.*

Afternoon crept toward evening. The apartment finally clean, or at least cleaner than it had been in some weeks, she settled down with a flick she had been wanting to watch, some figurativist thing from Belgium that Fenella had been talking about the last time Calliope had seen her. It would be fun just this once, she decided, to know what someone was talking about – even though by the time she saw her again, Fenella would undoubtedly be raving about something new, a museum retrospective or some ballet about the genocide against the Tasmanian Aboriginals.

Half an hour in and Calliope had completely lost track of the story, or what passed for the story. Instead of sitting wishing she knew an actual Belgian figurativist so she could strangle him, she turned it off and brought up her copy of the Merapanui file. The ghostly images of John Dread mocked her. *You think you can find me?* they seemed to say. *I'm dust. I'm the wind. I'm the darkness in your own shadow.*

She went back over her notes, looking for something she'd missed, anything, as the sun slid down behind the harbor. If John Dread was alive, as she felt so certain he was, why didn't anyone know it? Or did people know, and they were just too frightened to say? She couldn't help remembering the odd look that had flickered across the face of 3Big Pike. '*You cross him, he come back out of the ground and kill you three ways.*'

Where in the world was he? On a train in Europe, in an American mall, sizing up his next victim? Or somewhere closer? Still on the Australian continent, maybe? Lying low in some cattle station in the Outback, waiting until the time was right to come back to his old haunts with a new identity? Waiting like an evil spirit . . .

The beep of her pad startled her badly.

'Yes?'

It was Gerry Two Iron. 'Been working on that thing of yours, seen?'

She could feel her heart beating. 'And you found out . . . ?'

He looked a little ashamed. 'Harder than I thought it was. Somebody got a rare venture here. Duppy little piece of *fenfen*.'

She was proud of her self-control. 'Gerry, I don't know what any of that means. Just tell me in English.'

He rolled his eyes. 'It's, like, complicated, yaa? Trying to track it down, but it's all over the place. All kinds of switchbacks, blind repeaters, *fen* like that.'

'Does that mean it's not from the University of Helsinki?'

'Means it's from the University of Scan Major. Someone made this real twisty. Someone good at hiding things.'

Calliope sat forward. 'So it's not just a straightforward request.'

Gerry Two Iron shrugged, his frosted hair bouncing gently. 'Don't know about that – could just be from someone utterly private, seen? Someone who doesn't like anyone else knowing their venture.'

She tried to keep her elation under control. What did they have, really? As the boy said, it might be a perfectly ordinary request from someone who, for whatever reason, had a well-shielded system. But she could not help looking up at the frozen, smeary face of John Wulgaru on the wallscreen above her. *I'm going to get you, you bastard. Somehow. Some day.*

'When can you find out for sure where it's from?'

'Don't know.' He stuck out his lower lip, thinking. 'Pretty drezzed right now. I'll work on it again tomorrow. But might take me some more days than that.'

'You can't work on it again until tomorrow?'

Gerry Two Iron gave Calliope the universal teenage look saved for crazy grown-ups. 'Haven't even had anything to eat yet, me.' He smiled his annoyance. 'Even the police let a guy eat, don't they?'

'Okay, you're right. I really appreciate what you're doing – sorry to be difficult.'

When he had broken off, she sat back, irritated with herself. It wasn't like there was any real time pressure, was there? Polly Merapanui had been dead and buried for five years. John Wulgaru, aka Johnny Dread, had been presumed dead for a few months longer than that. What was the hurry?

Still, as she sat with the blurry pictures and the picked-over files on the wallscreen providing the only light in the darkening apartment, she could not help feeling that more than a weekend was slipping away.

Most of the morning was gone when she dragged herself out of bed. It had taken her four beers after dinner to get relaxed enough to sleep and she felt every one of them. She sat in the living room nursing her coffee with the blinds shut tight, wondering whether God had deliberately made the light of Sunday mornings unpleasant to the eye to try to force sinners to shelter in dark churches.

She was finishing the second cup and deciding that she might even be able to eat a little something when she finally noticed that what she had dismissed as a symptom of her incipient headache was actually a message alert blinking in the corner of her wallscreen. She had slept through a call, apparently.

Elisabetta? Or Kendrick's friend? Could this turn out to be a decent day after all? Suffering with a sour stomach and a dry, gritty mouth, she found that hard to believe, but she called the message up.

It was from Gerry Two Iron. He had been working late, he said, and he had a little something for her. That *thing* she wanted to know about, his recorded image reported with heavy significance. Even through impatience and the actual arrival of the headache, she had to smile. *This kid watches too many spyflicks.* She called him back.

When they were finished, she thanked him for his help – yes, she promised, she would definitely look into the chance of him becoming a police auxiliary (whatever the hell that meant) – then sat back, staring at the now-cold coffee in her mug. The fruits of Gerry Two Iron's search might be something useful, but it could just as easily turn out to be no more than what the original request had seemed to be – someone researching a piece of Aboriginal folklore. But it was out of a Sydney telecom router, so if she could get the provider to cough up a street address . . .

Calliope sighed. Was this any way to spend a Sunday? If she couldn't get any voluntary help from the telecom company, she'd need a judge's order to get anything. How could she get that without opening herself up to a bulk scorch from the captain, or maybe even a formal inquiry?

She'd try a little persuasion on the provider and see what happened. Another weekend day shot to hell. Well, it was better than cleaning.

And what if she did somehow get an address? Wait until Monday?

Stan's line rang for a long time. When it finally answered, the face that greeted her was a monster's, powder-blue, with insect eyes and long antennae.

'Christ!' she said, startled.

'*Stanley Chan is not home,*' the thing said doomfully. '*He has left the planet.*'

'Kidnapped!' said another bug-eyed mask, shoving its way into view. 'Kidnapped by aliens!'

Now Calliope could see Stan sitting on the couch, pretending to be tied up while his nephews recorded the message. He waved his hands, bound by what looked like the belt of a bathrobe. 'Sorry, everybody! I'm being taken to another planet,' he called. 'Or the zoo. Or something.'

'Into space, to be tortured,' said the first monster, rubbing his hands in anticipation.

'Message,' hissed the second.

'Oh, yeah. If you want to leave a message, go ahead. But it won't do Mr Chan any good, because he'll be on our home planet, being like utterly tortured to death.'

Calliope left a message asking the prisoner to call back when he got home. Even if her partner was no longer in the galaxy, and she was about to waste her Sunday trying to track down a meaningless detail from a closed case, she didn't want to lose touch with him entirely.

CHAPTER 34

Desert Smile

NETFEED/DOC/GAME: IEN, Hr. 17 (Eu, NAm) – 'TICK TICK TICK'
(visual: contestant in flames)
VO: The season-ending episode of the popular game show, in which
twelve contestants are given mystery injections and have to wait a
week for the results. Ten are harmless, and the contestants win only
the home version of the game. One injection creates the famous 'Wild
Credits' logo on the winner's skin, signifying that he or she has won
a million Swiss credits. The twelfth contestant – a designation the
show has now made famous – spontaneously combusts. The fun comes
in watching what the contestants do during the seven-day countdown
as they wait to discover their fate on live television at week's end.
This final episode of the season ends last week's contest, and also
provides a retrospective of some of the most touching and outrageous
moments from earlier shows . . .

THE priest with the dull eyes set the ivory box down
on the stone beside Paul. One corner pressed into his
skin as the priest opened it and began carefully to remove
a collection of bronze knives and other objects not so
immediately classifiable.

'Here is the malefactor, O gods,'

Userhotep chanted,

'The one whose mouth is closed against you as a door is shut.'

Paul tried desperately to concentrate on the drone of the priest's voice, the flickering lamplight as it splashed and ebbed along the ceiling, even the smirking god-mask of Robert Wells – anything but what was going to happen.

As the dead-eyed man bent toward him, a polished crescent of bronze shining in his fingers like a tiny moon, Paul tensed his muscles, then jerked his torso to one side, stretching the ropes until they creaked. The knife made only a shallow cut, which nevertheless left a stripe of agony along his rib cage. Paul's breast heaved with the effort but he had bought himself only a few seconds. Userhotep shot him a look of contempt, then prepared to cut again.

'It's really rather pointless, Mr Jonas,' said Robert Wells. 'All this struggling. Why don't you just be a good sport?'

Staring at the hateful yellow face, Paul felt his mouth fill with acid rage and despair. Something burned into his side like a white-hot flame and a scream forced its way out of him like an animal fleeing its lair.

'The sooner you relax and stop fighting, the sooner we can break down that hypnotic block.' Wells' voice floated to him from what seemed a great distance. 'Then the pain will stop.'

'You bastard,' Paul sobbed. The shadows in the room seemed to be coming alive. Something was moving behind Wells, a widening angle of black.

The *kheri-heb* priest suddenly dropped his knife. Even before it clinked on the stone floor the torturer had staggered back from the butcher block, waving at his face.

He was being swarmed by something Paul could not quite see, a moving cloud of pale shapes.

'Master,' the priest shrieked, 'save me!'

But something had grabbed Wells, too: Paul could just see him from the corner of his eye, a tall, bandaged figure struggling with something small and hairy that gripped his leg like a dog. Wells was cursing in shock and pain, flailing at his attacker. Then other shapes poured into the room. People shouted. The torches fluttered so that the shadows, which moments earlier had been so still, began to leap along the walls. Everything seemed to expand and waver.

Now Wells was wrestling with a dark-haired figure almost his own size. As they rolled on the floor together a flash of electrical light turned the world blue for a painful instant. Paul strained his head upward from the stone, trying to blink away the effects of the explosive glare.

What's happening . . . ? was all he had time to think, then Userhotep rose up beside him, still screaming, another knife in his hand and his face acrawl with squirming shapes. The priest fell across the altar, smashing Paul's head back against the stone and filling his head with blackness.

His limbs, now free, were on fire, and his heart felt like a motor working on bad fuel. His head felt worse. Somebody was under each of his arms, holding him up.

'My God, he's all wet – he's bleeding . . . !'

Paul recognized Martine's voice with a rush of gratitude. He tried to open his eyes but they were full of something salty that burned. 'Shallow . . .' he gasped, struggling unsuccessfully to support his own weight with his legs. The returning circulation felt like a swarm of murderously stinging ants. 'Shallow cuts. They only . . . started . . .'

'Don't talk,' ordered Florimel from his other side. 'Save your strength. We'll help you, but we have to get moving.'

'I never thought I would see the yellow-faced one like this.' This was a voice Paul did not know, deep and hoarse; it came from somewhere close to the ground, as though its owner were kneeling. 'Look at him wiggle like a worm on a hot rock.' The laugh was gleeful. 'That is a powerful spell you hold in your hand, fellow.'

'Just want out, me,' Paul heard T4b say. The boy sounded as breathless as if he had just run a marathon. 'Before that *sayee lo* killer come looking for us.'

'Should we finish him off?' Florimel asked, and for a moment, in his pain and confused exhaustion, Paul thought his friends were planning to put him out of his misery.

'Look, look!' a tiny, high-pitched voice said almost inside his ear. 'All blood! You fall down, mister? Look like zoomflier ripscrape, huh?'

'What the hell is going on?' Paul moaned. 'What happened?'

'You speak lightly of finishing off Ptah,' said the hoarse voice, going on as if Paul had not spoken, 'but I must tell you that to kill a god changes the shape of heaven – especially one so important as the Lord of the White Walls.'

'Wells is not our enemy,' Martine said. 'The real monster is coming – he might be here at any moment.'

The voice by Paul's knees snorted. 'If your enemy is our new lord and master Anubis,' he said, 'then you don't need any other enemies. If he catches us he will crush you – and me, too – like dust beneath his black heels.'

Paul had at last managed to blink his eyes clear. The figure before him was not kneeling. It was a dwarf of some kind, with a great tangle of beard and a shockingly

ugly face which widened in a grin as he saw Paul looking at him.

'Your friend can see again,' he said, then bowed. 'No
need to thank Bes for saving you and your companions.
There is little work for a household god in a land where
all the households have been smashed into ruin.' The dwarf
laughed. He seemed to laugh a lot, but Paul could not
help noticing that he didn't seem very happy. 'However,
I suppose all my work could be called little work.'

Paul shook his head, dazed. A yellow monkey the length
of his finger was hovering just before him now. A moment
later a half dozen more joined the formation. 'Nobody
tells us where 'Landogarner is,' the tiny ape complained.
'You know? And Freddicks?'

Robert Wells lay on the stone floor a few feet away,
writhing as though in the grip of a seizure, clutching at
his bandaged head. The priest Userhotep was crumpled
against the far wall in a spreading dark pool that reflected
torchlight.

'What's going on?' Paul asked again, helplessly.

'We'll tell you later.' Martine reached up from under
his arm and patted his face. Her hand lingered there for
a moment, cool and reassuring. 'You're safe now.'

'As safe as the rest of us, anyway,' said Florimel darkly.
'Here are your clothes.'

'Leave Wells,' Martine said. 'It's time to go. I don't know
exactly how far it is to the gateway.'

'Gateway . . . ?' Paul's head felt as though it were
sloshingly full of black paint or dirty oil, something sticky
that kept fouling the connections. There were two other
people in the room, he saw, the prisoners who had been
brought in just before Paul had been dragged out. When
Nandi Paradivash saw him looking, he limped over.

'I am glad you are alive, Paul Jonas.' Patches of Nandi's

skin had been scraped raw on his face and arms, and he
had gruesome, handshaped burns on his legs. He seemed
shriveled, a shadow of his earlier brave and resourceful
self. 'I will never forgive myself for betraying you.' Paul
shrugged, unsure of what to say. Nandi seemed to want
some kind of absolution, but at the moment Paul could
not make much sense of such an abstract idea. 'Mrs
Simpkins and I . . .' Nandi gestured awkwardly to the
woman, 'we were . . . prisoners of the man called Dread
for many days.'

'We'll talk about it later.' The Simpkins woman sounded
rational and calm, but her shadowed eyes did not meet
Paul's, and her hands drooped like they were boneless.

'Can you walk if we help you, Paul?' Martine asked.
'We have to hurry and it will be hard to carry you. We
distracted the guards, but they'll be back.'

Bes chuckled and trotted to the door, then pulled it
open. Paul could hear distant shouts in the corridor. 'It is
impressive how much distraction you can cause when you
give a torch to a troop of flying monkeys.'

A yellow cloud of simians exploded into the air and
out into the hallway.

'Burn burn burn!' they squealed, whirling like a dust
devil. 'Burn all pretty!'

'Big *fuego!*'

'Ruling Tribe!'

T4b lurched after them. He was holding one of his
hands as though it hurt. Paul could not help noticing that
the hand was glowing.

Supported by Martine and Florimel, Paul staggered out
of the cell. He had to step over one of Wells' legs, which
jerked and twitched as though electrified.

The sun overhead was a vast white disk, the air outside

Abydos-That-Was so dry and hot Paul could almost feel it sucking the moisture out of his lungs. Ruined, fire-blackened buildings stood on all sides of the great temple, some still bleeding dark smoke into the sky. Dread appeared to have thrown a party here much like the one in Dodge City.

Paul needed to lean a little on Florimel, but he had regained enough strength that Martine could let go of him and walk down the stone pier that jutted out from the back of the temple into the flat brown water of a wide canal. The monkeys hovered around her for a moment, then darted forward to inspect the immense golden barge waiting at the end of the pier like a floating hotel. Martine stopped halfway down the span and turned slowly from side to side.

'It's not here.' Her voice was tight with growing panic. 'The gateway – I can feel it, but it's not here.'

'What does that mean?' Florimel demanded. 'It's invisible?'

'No, it's simply not here. I could sense it out here when we were inside. I can still feel it, very strongly, but . . .' She turned until she was facing away from the temple, looking down the river valley to the south. 'My God,' she said slowly. 'It's . . . it's far away. But it's so strong! That's why I thought it was just here, at the edge of the temple.' She turned to Bes, who watched her with the serene calm of someone who saw and even made miracles himself every day. 'What's out there?'

'Sand,' he growled. 'Scorpions. More sand. It's closer to the point to talk about what *isn't* out there – water, shade, things like that.' He tugged at his curly beard. 'That way lies the Red Desert.'

'But what's out there? What am I sensing? Something big, powerful – an opening.' She frowned; Paul guessed she was searching for a way to explain that the dwarf would understand. 'Some . . . some very big and dark magic.'

Bes only shook his head. 'You don't want to go there, woman.'

'Damn it, we have to!' Martine came back up the pier toward him. 'Just tell us. We will make our own choices.'

The bearded god stared at her for a moment, then shook his head again. 'When the little apes found me, I came to help you because I regretted how I had left these two—' he gestured toward Nandi and Mrs Simpkins, '– at an evil time in the temple of Ra. Now you want to go somewhere even worse? I am not the most noble of gods, woman, but neither do I wish to send good people to their ruin.'

'Just tell us what is out there!' snapped Martine.

Mrs Simpkins stepped forward; her uselessly dangling hands made her look like a begging dog. 'We need to know, Bes,' she said. 'After that, it's up to us, not you.'

He looked at her angrily. 'The Temple of Set,' he said at last. 'The house of the Lost One. That is what you sense out there in the desert. It is a hole into the underworld, a place that even great Osiris entered like a mortal man being dragged alive into his own tomb. And if you go there you will be lost forever.'

Martine stared toward him, an unreadable expression on her sightless face. Nandi and T4b limped back from the end of the pier where they had been examining the vast barge.

'Like, all these black guys with oars in there,' T4b reported. He still cradled his glowing hand as though it hurt him. 'Just sitting, staring at nothing. Locking scanned.'

'Go, then,' Bes said to Martine. 'Just step onto the boat

and say where you wish to go. The boat will take you. You will be there sooner than you wish.'

'We have to do it,' she said quietly.

'Then you go without Bes.' The little god turned in disgust and began to walk back toward the temple. 'May the seven Hathors give you a merciful ending.'

Mrs Simpkins turned to call after him. 'Thank you for helping us! God bless you!'

Bes made a gesture, half-farewell, half-dismissal. The monkeys wheeled around his head for a moment, then fluttered back toward Paul and the others.

'Is it just me,' Florimel asked heavily, 'or is someone always telling us that we are going to hate the place we are going even worse than where we are?'

Even in the hot Egyptian air, Paul was shivering. 'Well, they've been right every time,' he said.

*C*ODE *Delphi.* Start here.

'We have been incredibly lucky. No, *I* have been incredibly lucky. My desperate attempt to find help roused the Wicked Tribe, and the children themselves located the little god Bes, friend of our fellow prisoners Nandi Paradivash and Bonita Mae Simpkins. That in itself was a great stroke of fortune – the tiny Tribe children could never have lifted the bolt on our cell door themselves, but Bes is far more powerful than his stature would suggest. He is a god, after all.

'And against all my dark certainties, we have rescued Paul Jonas as well, injured and traumatized, but still alive, still sane. Even now, his skin washed clean of blood, his many wounds bandaged to the best of my ability, he is sleeping beside my feet. Nandi and Bonnie Mae have also survived torture, although there is a shadow across them both. The virtual galley slaves are rowing the barge of

Osiris upstream, like an engine that does not care who is driving – upstream toward the Temple of Set.

'I did not need Bes to tell me how dangerous our journey is. Orlando and Fredericks were drawn to this temple once, sucked in like leaves into a whirlpool, and Orlando said they barely survived it. Still, I cannot help feeling at least a little optimistic, foolish as that is. We are still alive, when good sense proclaims we should not be. And we have escaped from under the very nose of Dread, at least for a moment. Something inside me dances like a child let out into the garden after a long boring day inside. I am alive! There is nothing more important than that. It is all I have. For the moment, it is enough.

'But as I sense Paul lying near me – so deep in exhausted, trembling sleep that he resembles Robert Wells after Javier jabbed that strange, glowing hand of his into the back of Wells' head, dropping someone who was a great god in this Egyptian simworld straight to the floor like a slaughtered bullock – I cannot help wondering what it all means. Is it only luck that we are again rescued? We are inside an operating system that has been fed with the idea of stories, so perhaps the thread of coincidence and strange chance is not so unbelievable. Perhaps T4b having been damaged in just the way that would save us makes a kind of sense – perhaps it was part of the story of the network. But that does not explain every odd stroke of fortune that has affected us. I came into this network by my own choice, trying to help Renie Sulaweyo find her brother, absolutely unaware that it might have anything to do with that long-ago day I lost my sight. How could such an extreme coincidence be?

'Unless there is more to this idea of story than anyone understands.

'After all, is it not the way we humans shape the

universe, shape time itself? Do we not take the raw stuff of chaos and impose a beginning, middle, and end on it, like the simplest and most profound of folktales, to reflect the shapes of our own tiny lives? And if the physicists are right, that the physical world changes as it is observed, and we are its only known observers, then might we not be bending the entire chaotic universe, the eternal, ever-active Now, to fit that familiar form?

'If so, the universe, from the finest quantum dust to the widest vacuum spaces, does indeed have a shape. It begins "Once upon a time . . ."

'And if it is true, then only we humans, poor, naked semi-apes crouching in the thin light of our single star, marooned on the rim of a minor galaxy, can determine whether there will be a "Happily ever after."

'It makes my head hurt to think of it. It is a possibility too large and strange to contain for long, especially when we are still in such danger.

'The ship of Osiris breasts the sluggish river current, rocking beneath me, the timbers creaking, the oars beathing an inhumanly steady rhythm. We are heading up the Nile to the darkest place in this world, maybe in any of these worlds. I am very tired. I think I will try to sleep for a little while.

'*Code Delphi*. End here.'

DREAD floated in the white spaces of his bone-sparse Outback castle. The yip of a dingo sounded through the archway, offering a weird but compelling counterpoint to the piano melody shivering in the air. Dread muted the light, pushing the arid landscape into twilight so he could better see the abstract which Dulcie Anwin had prepared for him.

He frowned, annoyed by having to pay attention when

he would rather have drifted and daydreamed. The abstract
was an expanding treasure box of charts, three-dimensional graphs, and lists of assets – a neat summation of
the hugely various holdings controlled by Felix Jongleur.
A forest of markers sprang from each point, containing
information about access and connection, and for a little
while he entertained himself with contemplating how each
subcorporation, holding company, and business asset
could be used as an instrument of pain.

He listened with pleasure to the lonely, atonal lurch of
the piano. *I can make a true symphony out of it*, he
thought. *An economic collapse here, a plague there, so
that even the rich ones cop it sweet. War, famine – all
the bloody horsemen of the Apocalypse, one after the other.
Like World War Three, but in slow motion. Which will
make it easier to enjoy.*

*Of course, I'll have to play it carefully – make sure it
doesn't get too far out of hand. After all, I don't want
anything happening to me, now do I?*

But before the real fun could begin he had to get the
last details dealt with. It was one thing to be able to
access Felix Jongleur's high-level information, another to
implement the kind of wild art projects Dread was now
envisioning. Surely at some point Jongleur's absence
would officially become Jongleur's death, and his various boards of directors and successor-designates would
step in, sending armies of accountants and data analysts
ahead of them. Before that happened, Dread knew he
would have to firm up his own controls, transferring the
assets and connections he needed into his own hands.

Did he need Dulcie for that? No. She had lived out her
usefulness. In fact, she knew far too much. Another day
or so while she helped him handle the various transfers
of power, then her trip to Australia would end. He had

decided that he could combine the need for an unsuspicious resolution with a little pleasure for himself, after all. Who would be surprised if an American tourist were to be found robbed and murdered in one of the seamier parts of Sydney?

The piano was joined again, not by a wild dog this time, but by the quiet beeping of an urgent message. Dread considered ignoring it, but knew it might be from Dulcie. Since they had such a short time left together, he wanted to keep her working. A good manager didn't waste an asset.

To his surprise, the call was on a line he hadn't yet used. The head that filled the view-window was shaved bald, the robes streaked gray and black with soot.

'O Lord of All!' the priest said, stuttering in his haste and panic. 'Woe is come upon us, O Great House. Your servants are full of despair – all the Black Land is in terror!'

Dread frowned. It was one of the Old Man's virtual priests. The call had been routed directly to him through Jongleur's connection to the Grail network, just as though the servitor were calling from the real world instead of an imaginary Egypt.

'What do you want?'

'O blessed Anubis, master of the final journey, there is fire in great Abydos! Many priests are dead, many more lie burned and dying!'

Which was a pretty funny thing to call him about, Dread reflected, since he had been torturing and murdering priests himself in the temple complex of Abydos-That-Was not twenty-four hours ago. 'So?'

The ash-smeared face went paler still. The man's mouth worked without noise for a moment. 'And the prisoners of the great god have escaped.'

'What?' He narrowed his eyes. 'You let those two idiots from the Circle get away? Both of them?'

The priest swallowed. When he spoke, it was almost a whisper. 'All of them. All of the great god's prisoners.'

'What are you talking about?' He heard his voice rise to an angry howl, as though he truly were the god the priest must be seeing. 'Don't move!'

With a flick of thought, he threw himself into Egypt.

Wells cowered on the floor of the cell, his mummy wrappings smeared with dirt, his banana-yellow face tight with fear and resentment as he stared up at the huge, jackal-headed figure of Anubis.

'How was I to know?' Wells was slurring his words as though something had damaged his brain. 'It was just some kid – he must have been the same one who got Yacoubian. He just . . . stuck his hand in me. I was paralyzed – almost felt like I was thrown offline, except I was still locked inside this virtual body.'

'What the hell are you babbling about?' Dread whirled and struck Wells hard across the side of the head, knocking the bandaged god to the floor. 'I'll give you paralyzed, you whining poof. The priests said my prisoners escaped – *all* my prisoners. I had two little god-botherers I was hanging onto, but they weren't going anywhere. Almost dead, they were. So what are the priests talking about?'

'They just . . . showed up here,' Wells said quickly. 'The ones I came to Kunohara's world with. They showed up here and I was holding them for you.'

'Kunohara's world . . . ?' Dread stared at the cowering figure. 'Are you telling me . . . ?'

Wells climbed to his feet. 'But Paul Jonas was with them, see?'

'Who the bloody hell is that?' The name was slightly familiar, but any memory was washed away in a hot red fury that made him feel as though he might burst into flame.

'Someone Jongleur was searching for!' Wells seemed to feel he had redeemed himself with this information; he clambered back onto his feet. 'The Old Man turned the network upside down trying to find him, but we never knew why – we didn't even know his name. Jonas has some kind of post-hypnotic block on his memory, so I thought a little session with one of the *kheri-heb* priests might loosen it up . . .'

'Shut up!' Dread roared. 'I don't give a shit about this Jonas. Who was here? What prisoners? Who escaped?'

Wells flinched back, blinking. 'I told you, the . . . the ones from Kunohara's world. You remember, don't you? You sent all those mutant bugs after them. The boy with the strange hand. The woman with the bandaged head. The blind woman . . .'

'You . . . you had Martine here . . . ?' Dread could hardly speak. His hands were shaking. 'You had Martine Desroubins and her friends here and you didn't tell me?'

Wells took a step backward. He tried to stand taller. 'I would have told you. I would have! But I can make some decisions on my own, you know. I ran one of the largest companies in the world – and now I'm a god, too!'

Dread was on him so fast that Robert Wells did not even have time to squeak. The jackal-god's huge hand closed around the other's throat, then he lifted his victim up until his bandaged feet dangled helplessly a meter above the ground.

'Which way did they go?'

Wells shook his head violently, eyes bulging.

'Right. I'll find out myself.' He pulled Wells closer still, until he could have closed his jaws on Ptah's hairless head and cracked it like a walnut. 'You goddamned Yanks think you know everything. Well, here's some information for you, mate. You may be a god now . . . but around here, I'm God Almighty.'

His captive struggled in terror, but only for a moment. Dread's hand shot out, swift as a cobra's strike, and plunged into Robert Wells' gaping mouth, then his fingers curved upward, poking through the skull as though it were an eggshell as he set his grip. With the smaller god secured, he took his other hand from Wells' throat and pulled the yellow lips hideously wide, stretching them back like a latex mask until the face disappeared. Then, with a terrible twisting motion of his long arm, Dread yanked Ptah's entire skeleton out of his body and let it drop to the floor. A puppet of bone and sinew twitched like a landed fish beside the empty, rubbery folds of its own flesh. The eyes, still trapped in the orbits of the naked skull, rolled wildly even as their intelligence began to fade.

'So you're a god, eh?' Dread spat beside the slick, shiny bones. 'Then heal *that.*'

His mood ever so slightly improved, Anubis went in search of his prisoners.

HE could think better now. The oppressive cloud that had darkened and confused his thoughts was beginning to disperse, as if baked away by the glaring Egyptian sun, but despite the improvement, Paul found himself not just uninterested in thinking but actively unwilling to try. The memory of his own helplessness was a shame and a terror.

Upon waking he had dragged himself into the shade of the boat's gilded deck awning. They seemed to have left the canal and moved out onto the Nile itself: on either side of the wide brown river stretched kilometers of empty sand. The rugged mountains, ocher-gray and indistinct in the distance, only underscored the flat, featureless desert.

Whether he wanted them or not, scraps of memory fluttered through his head – Ava, the chirping of the birds, Mudd's triumphant, subhuman face as he found them embracing.

I kissed her. Did I love her? Why can't I feel it? If you love someone, surely you can't forget that.

But it was all too dark, too heavy with misery. He didn't want to know any more – surely one of them had somehow betrayed the other. Nothing else would explain his revulsion at the idea of uncovering additional memories.

He was distracted, and was grateful for it, by Nandi Paradivash lowering himself carefully down beside him. 'I see you are awake.' He spoke far more slowly than Paul remembered from their first meeting. In fact, this Nandi seemed quite different from the mercurial character with whom he had sailed through Xanadu – hard and dry, as though some crucial petrifaction had occured. 'I am glad to see you again, Paul Jonas.'

'And I'm glad to see you. I never got the chance to thank you for saving me.'

'From the Khan's men?' Nandi showed him the phantom of a smile. 'They actually caught me, but I escaped. It is much like an adventure game, this life, eh? But all too dangerous, both to the body and the soul.'

'*Nothing around you is true, but the things you see can hurt you or kill you,*' Paul quoted. 'That was the message I was given – I think I told you. And you did save me, in the most important way. You told me what was really going on. Then I didn't have to be afraid I was losing my mind.'

Nandi slowly eased himself into a lotus position, being

careful with his burned legs. The scarred flesh brought back Paul's own last hours in the temple so strongly that for a moment he thought he might be sick.

Nandi did not seem to notice: his eyes were on the riverbank. 'God will protect us from evil men. They will live to see their works cast down.' He turned to Paul. 'And their works *have* been cast down, haven't they? I have been told of what happened to the Grail Brother-hood's ceremony of immortality.'

'Yes. But somehow it still doesn't feel like we're winning.'

After they had sat in silence for a little while, Paul suddenly said, 'You know, you were right. About the Pankies.'

Nandi frowned. 'Who?'

'That English couple. The man and woman who were with me when you and I first met. You told me they weren't what they seemed.' He related the strange happenings in the catacombs beneath Venice, when for a moment the Twins and the Pankies had confronted each other as though looking into a mirror, and how Sefton and Undine Pankie had turned away and vanished. 'But that still doesn't explain them,' he said.

'Early versions, perhaps,' Nandi offered. 'A release that was superseded by a later, improved product. But someone forgot to delete the original version.'

'But there have been others, too,' Paul said, remembering Kunohara's world. 'I met a pair who were insects, but they didn't care about me either. They were obsessed with something they called the Little Queen.' A memory prickled him. 'And the Pankies were looking for their imaginary daughter.'

'A common thread in both versions, no doubt,' Nandi said. 'Martine told me you know the originals.'

Paul was taken aback at the thought that people were discussing his ugly secrets, his imperfectly remembered life – it was *his* life, after all, wasn't it?

But it's everyone's mystery, he reminded himself. *Everyone here is in terrible danger.*

'Yes, I suppose I do, but I don't remember everything even now.' It was there again, a shadow at the edge of his thoughts, a dim perception of something he did not want to know better. 'But why should there be different versions doing different things? Why are some of them after me, hunting me, and others don't care?' Again the Venetian catacombs loomed in his memory, the mirrored pairs facing each other as he and poor Gally and the woman Eleanora watched.

'Perhaps they're simply programmed differently.' Nandi didn't seem to see much purpose in speculating, but Paul was trying to remember something else, something Eleanora had told him, or showed him . . .

'My God,' he said suddenly, 'they *are* just copies.' He sat up straight, ignoring the sharp pain across the ribs. 'Eleanora – she was a real woman who lived in the Venetian simworld – she showed me her boyfriend, this Mafia fellow who had built the world for her in the first place. He was dead, but the Grail people had made a copy of him while he was still alive. I think it was an early version of the Grail process. He was real – he could answer questions – but he was also kind of an information loop, kept forgetting what had been asked, said the same things over and over. What if the Pankies and the other versions of the Twins are like that?'

'You are bleeding,' Nandi said quietly.

Paul looked down. His sudden movement had opened the shallow cuts on his chest; blood was running freely, soaking through the dirty jumpsuit.

'Jonas, what are you doing?' Florimel was striding toward him. 'Martine, he's bleeding again.'

'She can't hear you,' Nandi said. 'She's at the bow of the ship.'

'Help me get him cleaned up.'

'I'm all right, really.' But Paul did not resist as Florimel opened the front of his jumpsuit and began cursingly to fumble at the sopping strips of cloth Martine had applied.

'T4b?' she called. 'Where are you? Find me something I can use to make more bandages. T4b?' There was no answer. 'Damn it, Javier, where are you?'

'Javier?' asked Nandi as he helped Florimel peel Paul's jumpsuit down to his waist.

Paul was irritated – they weren't life-threatening wounds, and the idea now blazing in his head felt important. Many copies, some less perfect than others . . .

I am a broken mirror, she had told him. *A broken mirror . . .*

'You took your time, Javier,' Florimel said as the boy finally approached. 'Did you find some cloth?'

'Isn't any.' He darted a glance at Nandi as though more fearful of him than of Florimel's anger.

'Javier . . . Javier Rogers?' Nandi asked.

'No!' said T4b harshly, then stiffened and looked down at his feet. 'Yeah.'

'You know each other?' Florimel looked from one to the other.

'We should,' said Nandi. 'It is because of the Circle that Javier is here.'

Florimel turned on the youth. 'Is that true?'

'Oh, *fenfen*,' he said miserably.

The way they were all gathered around the boy, Paul thought, it was hard not to think of an inquisition. But

T4b, his face damp with sweat and teenage embarrassment, did not make a very convincing martyr.

'What else have you lied to us about?' Florimel
demanded.

'Didn't lie about nothing, me.' T4b scowled. 'Ain't
duppie. Just didn't tell you, seen?'

'You don't need to justify your faith, honey,' Bonnie
Mae assured him.

'He kept no dangerous secrets from you,' said Nandi.
'We recruited many like him, promising young men and
women of belief. We gave them information, some education, and we gave them equipment. This is a war we are
fighting, after all, as you people should know better than
anyone. Were you not recruited yourselves by someone
whose motives are far less openly stated than ours?'

'Are you working for Kunohara as well?' Florimel asked
T4b. Paul thought she seemed unusually upset. 'Was
Martine right about that too?'

'No! Don't got nothing to do with that Kuno-whatsit,
me.' He looked like he was about to cry. 'And I never did
nothing wrong to you either. Just didn't tell you . . . about
the Circle.'

Paul looked at Martine, but she seemed to be listening with only part of her attention. 'What did you mean
when you said "men and women of belief"?' he asked
Nandi.

'We are a group bound together by our belief in a
power greater than mere humanity,' Nandi said. 'I made
no secret of that when you and I met.'

'But Javier . . . ?'

The boy looked sullen when he realized everyone was
looking at him once more. 'I'm born again, me. Jesus
saved me.'

'There you go,' said Bonnie Mae. 'Don't be ashamed of

the path you've chosen. '*Blessed are they who do hunger and thirst after righteousness,*" as Jesus said on the mountain, "*for they shall be filled.*" Nothing wrong with a hunger for righteousness.' She turned to the others. 'This boy has found his way through Christ. Does that offend you? What about me, then? Is there something wrong with loving God?'

'Jesus helped me give up charge,' T4b said earnestly. 'I was, like, lost. Then He saved me.'

'He just came over to your house and showed you some new tricks?' Florimel laughed bitterly. 'I am sorry, but I grew up with this nonsense. It poisoned my mother's life and it poisoned mine. Forgive my reaction, but I feel betrayed to learn that he has been serving another master all this time.'

'Serving another master?' Now it was Nandi who was angry. 'How? We have not spoken to Javier since he entered the network. Are your goals not ours – to save the children and bring about the destruction of this devilish operating system, this terrible immortality machine that runs on blood and souls?'

I was thinking of something important when all this happened, Paul remembered, but could not tear himself away from the looks of fury and confusion on the faces of his companions. Only Martine Desroubins seemed somewhere else, listening to sounds she alone could hear. 'Martine?' he asked.

'It is close,' she said. 'I feel it. It is like nothing else I have experienced here – like the Cavern of the Lost, but both more and less alive. And it is very powerful.' She grimaced. 'Close. So close.'

Paul looked up. The ship, driven by its indefatigable crew of robotic galley slaves, was rounding a bend in the wide, sluggish river. As they tilted past a scattering of rocky foothills Paul saw it, nestled by itself in a wide valley of red sand.

'Good lord,' he said quietly.

'It is empty.' Martine was still frowning, the lines of her face tight with pain. 'But not empty. There is something deep inside it that is hot and active. It is like an oven with the door closed.'

The Wicked Tribe, who had been hovering over the discussion like particularly anarchic thoughts above the heads of comic-strip characters, now descended in a yellow flutter, clustering on Paul.

'Bad place,' one of them said.

'Been here,' said another. 'Don't want to be here again. Go away now!'

Several of them flew up and began tugging at Paul's hair. 'Time to go away. Back to somewhere fun. Now!'

The argument over T4b ended as one by one the combatants saw the faint brown shape of the temple in the distance, the sandstone pillars of the massive facade standing sentry between oblongs of pitch-black shadow.

'It . . . it looks like a smile,' said Florimel.

'Like a dead smile,' Nandi said slowly. 'Like the grin of a skull.'

The temple not only looked empty, but was half-covered with drifting dunes, as though it had lain long unremembered and unvisited. Swirled by a breeze none of them could feel, clouds of sparkling gray sand helped shroud the structure so that its full size and dimensions were never quite clear.

The quiet splash of the banked oars now fell silent. As the ship glided slowly to a stop beside the dock Paul and his companions stared at the looming temple, its windblasted front high as an office building and as wide as several city blocks. There was no noise anywhere along the riverbank.

'Don't want to go in there,' T4b said at last.

'We must,' Martine said, but gently: if she had heard the argument about his secret affiliation, it did not seem to have lessened her opinion of the youth. 'Dread will come looking for us – it could be any time now. He will not be tricked or defeated, not like Wells. And he will be very angry.'

T4b did not say anything else, but when the others began moving toward the gangplank he went with them as though being led to execution. The Wicked Tribe hung on his and Paul's and Florimel's clothes like sleeping bats, frightened for once into good behavior.

'Not so bad this time,' one of them whispered in Paul's ear, but the childish voice did not sound entirely convinced. 'It more asleep. Maybe doesn't know we here.'

Despite Martine's warnings, Paul could not make himself move any faster than a foot-dragging trudge across the sun-blasted desert. The blowing sand stung his face. The looming row of columns seemed ready to swallow him down. The very air was heavy, as though they were pushing their way through something solid and sticky. Behind him Florimel let out a strangled sigh, fighting to get breath into a fear-tightened throat.

The baking heat diminished only a little as they stepped between the cyclopean columns and into the shade. The long wall before them was covered with what had once been intricately carved panels, but which had been worn down until they were only idiot scribbles, devoid of sense or reassurance. The only doorway was a simple black square in the middle of the massive front wall, a hole into a deeper darkness.

Martine went through first, holding her hands to her

ears despite the thickly expectant silence of the place – exactly as though someone stood beside her screaming, Paul thought as he and the others followed her inside.

As his eyes grew used to the darkness of the interior, illuminated only by the light from the door, Paul saw that white-clad bodies lay everywhere, perhaps two dozen in all. Not one was moving; all appeared to have suffered in dying. He turned away in dismay from the nearest corpse, its fingers red from tearing at the unyielding stone floor, eyes rolled up as though looking for a salvation that would never arrive.

'They are not Puppets,' Nandi said quietly. Paul looked at him in surprise. 'They are empty sims,' the dark-skinned man said. 'See – they have not putrefied or even changed, only stiffened. Real people died or went offline and left their sims behind.'

Martine had stopped in front of an immense doorway that stretched to the ceiling along the interior wall, its double doors covered in hammered bronze. The very size of them gave his fear an extra, sickening twist.

I don't really want to see what's on the other side . . .

Something touched his arm and he jumped.

'Didn't lie to no one, me,' T4b said quietly. Paul was amazed that in the midst of this doom-laden atmosphere the boy was still worrying about what people thought.

'I believe you, Javier.'

'Sorry. Sorry . . . I tried to six you.' He spoke so quietly Paul did not immediately understand him. 'On the mountain, like.'

'Oh! Oh, that. It's all right, really.'

'But that girl, Emily, she was chizz. Had ops for her, me. Utterly did.' He seemed desperate for Paul to understand. 'Then when all that *fen* blew up . . .'

The whole conversation was surreal. *First Nandi, now this boy. When did I become the father-confessor? Or is it because they both think we probably won't be alive much longer – that soon it will be too late for apologies . . .*

'Are you all simply going to wander around until someone shows up to kill us?' Martine called, her voice ragged with pain or fear or both, startling both Paul and T4b. 'Come and help me open this door!'

They hurried across the echoing room. The others gathered near the doors, whispering. Paul wanted to laugh, but the ache of fear was too great. Why bother to be quiet? Did they think the thing on the other side was really sleeping, that it wouldn't hear them? He remembered the monstrous presence he had summoned on Ithaca, the thing that had come to Orlando and Fredericks in the Freezer. Didn't they understand this place by now? The Other was always sleeping – but it was always listening, too.

Weighed down by dark foreboding that made it hard to think or even move, he let himself be pressed in beside T4b and Nandi to pull at the huge double doors. For a moment there was no movement, then the great bronzed panels swung outward with a screech like some angry primordial beast. The Wicked Tribe darted back from the opening as though the cavern beyond were full of poisonous gas or burning-hot air; Paul could not help remembering what Martine had said about an oven.

'Not go in there!' one of the monkeys shouted. 'Wait out here!' They looped up into the high reaches of the antechamber and hung near the doorway leading back outside, babbling in fear and excitement.

Martine had already stepped through like a woman wading into a high wind. Paul followed her, expecting to feel something similar to what she was experiencing, but the sensation of oppressive menace was no greater outside the room than in.

The chamber was made of rough, dark stone, as though it had been hurriedly chipped from a living mountain. At the center, its exquisitely carved and polished lines in sharp contrast, lay a gigantic black stone sarcophagus.

Paul could feel the others pressing in behind him, but he was unwilling to take another step. Martine had her hands to her ears again, swaying in place as though dizzy. Paul feared she might fall, but even that could not make him move closer to the silent black box.

'He . . . he feels me . . .' Martine said in a strangulated whisper. It echoed from the walls and came back in pieces: '*Feels me . . . feels . . .*'

A light, painfully bright, flared at the side of the cavern, twenty meters from the coffin. As though in a nightmare, Paul could not move, but he felt his heart lurch inside his breast.

The light hung in the air for a moment, dripping sparks like burning magnesium, then resolved into a human-shaped blank white hole. Paul was surprised to feel a dull and somewhat anticlimatic tug of recognition. Still, neither he nor his companions were quite prepared for the high-pitched voice that echoed across the cavern.

'*Man! What kind of* mierda *that crazy old man throw me in this time?*'

The astonishing spectacle of a twitching, featureless figure swearing in Spanish was interrupted by the explosive entrance into the tombchamber of a cloud of yellow, finger-sized monkeys.

'Someone coming!' they squealed, 'Look out! *Le* big *chien*!'

Their shrill excitation made it almost impossible to

figure out what was going on. 'What on earth are you children screaming about?' Bonita Mae Simpkins demanded. 'Zunni, you tell me straight – the rest of you, quiet!'

'*No wonder you all friends with Sellars,*' declared the glowing shape with a mixture of amusement and disgust. '*You all* loco, *for true.*'

'Sellars?' said Florimel, startled.

'It's coming,' the little monkey named Zunni explained.

'What?'

'Big black dog,' she squeaked. 'Coming here across the desert.'

'Big, *big* dog,' one of the other monkeys piped up. 'Big like a mountain. Coming fast!'

CHAPTER 35

Rainbow's Shoe

NETFEED/NEWS: *Chargeheads Getting 'In the Mood'*
(visual: VNS outpatients waiting for module adjustment)
VO: *Vagal Nerve Stimulation, or VNS, an artificial mood-altering process prescribed by some doctors as a cure for charge addiction, may itself become another form of addictive behavior.*
(visual: Dr Karina Kawande, inset)
KAWANDE: *'It was inevitable, really. Stimulating the vagus nerve to relieve stress is an acceptable substitute for dangerous street-gear only when the pulse dosage can be controlled. But any device based on code can be hacked, and there are patients now who have their VNS pulsing twenty-four hours a day . . .'*

As they walked through the crowd, face after strange face slid past Sam Fredericks like some endless nightmare – dogs, bears, opal-eyed snakes, children with wings and birds' heads, boys and girls made from wood or gingerbread or even glass. But of the thousands of creatures that surrounded the Well and its roiling lights, an entire refugee camp beneath the endless twilit skies, not a single one was familiar.

Not a single one was Renie Sulaweyo.

Sam could barely stand to look at !Xabbu, who she knew must be even more disappointed than she was. When they had left Azador with his rediscovered Gypsy family, !Xabbu had set out almost at a run to begin the search for Renie, but as the day had worn by without any sign of her the small man's steps had become slower and slower. In all their journeying, even in the most desperate of times, she could scarcely remember him looking tired. Now he moved as though almost too weary to breathe.

'We should go back now.' Sam took his arm. She felt his resistance but kept her grip. 'We can look some more later.'

His face, when he turned to her, was hollow-eyed, devastated. 'She is not here, Sam. Not anywhere. And if this is the last place in this world . . .'

She did not want to think about it, and she did not want !Xabbu thinking about it either. 'No, we don't really know how this scanny place works. And we might have missed her, anyway – I'm getting so tired my eyes are blurring.'

He sighed. 'It is terrible of me to drag you on like this, Sam. We will go back and rest for a while with Azador's people.'

'Chizz. Do you remember where they are?' She looked around at the ring of featureless hills. 'I'm lost.' Sam felt a little guilty – she had appealed to his protective instincts on purpose – but knew it was for his own good. It was funny how much !Xabbu was like Orlando, she thought. You couldn't get either of them to do much for them-selves, but they would throw themselves off a building for a friend.

Orlando even got himself killed for me . . . It was not a good thought and she pushed it away.

Making their way back through the aimless, uneasy

throng seemed to take hours. Some of the other refugees
had also worked hard to locate their own lost fellows –
tiny exile communities from places with names like Where
The Beans Talk and Cobbler's Bench had been pointed out
to Sam and !Xabbu by helpful folk – but many more
seemed to have simply walked as close to the Well as
they could get, then stopped.

Azador's Gypsy kin had either arrived early or had
staked their claim more aggressively than most. Their
camp was close to the edge of the Well, the painted wagons
clustered at the bottom of a bluff, as though a group of
day-trippers had decided to picnic on the edge of an
immense bomb crater – but no bomb crater had ever
looked like this. When Sam had first seen it, she had
thought that the black waters reflected the unchanging
evening sky overhead and its sprinkling of faint stars. As
they had drawn closer, all of them quiet and withdrawn
except Azador, all troubled by their experiences crossing
the covered bridge, she had discovered that the Well was
a mirror of a very different kind. The stars, or whatever
unstable points of light moved in its dark depths, were
not static like those in the sky: they flared and died, as
inconstant as foxfire. Sometimes an even greater light
bloomed far below, so that for a moment all the well was
full of a ruddy glow, as though a supernova had been
born in the deepest expanses. Other times the points of
brilliance dimmed and then disappeared entirely; for a
few moments the Well became utterly black, a lightless
hole gouged into the desolate earth.

'It is the mountain turned upside down,' !Xabbu had
said when they first approached it, even as Azador hurried
ahead of them like a man rushing to meet his lover after
a long separation. Sam hadn't quite understood, but she
thought she could see now what he meant. Everything in

this most other of Otherlands seemed to be something else
turned wrong-way 'round.

She was grateful to spot the fires of the Gypsy camp
at last. The more she looked at it, especially during the
times it went dark, the more the Well came to resemble
a cave, a burrow. She could imagine something as big as
the mountaintop giant but even more disturbing suddenly
climbing up out of its swirling depths. But the Gypsies,
like the other fairy-tale denizens of the place, did not
seem frightened of the Well at all. For them, the end of
the world had become the occasion for reunion and even
celebration. As she and !Xabbu made their way back across
the base of the bluff and down into the camp they could
hear music and singing voices.

Felix Jongleur had not joined them in their search.
Sam had been grateful, although she thought it odd that
such a sour, cold-eyed man would choose to remain in
the Gypsy camp, surrounded by living stereotypes of care-
free amusement. Now, as they came back through the
outskirts of the camp, she saw him sitting by himself on
the steps of one of the wagons, watching a trio of Gypsy
women in long shawls dancing to a busy fiddle. She pulled
!Xabbu in another direction: at the moment, she thought
their hearts were both too heavy to deal with that terrible old man.

Azador had spotted them making their way across
the camp and came to meet them. He had traded his
travel-worn clothes for new ones, a colorful vest and
puffy-sleeved white shirt. His black boots shone. He had
even combed and oiled his hair, which gleamed nearly as
brightly as his boots. With his splendid smile and chiseled
jaw, he looked like something from a not-very-convincing
netflick.

'There you are!' he called. 'Come! There is music and

good talk. We will wait until the Lady comes to us, then we will be saved.'

As he led them through the settlement, which was made up of many little family camps, Sam wondered at how quickly his anger at even being thought a Gypsy had been replaced by a belonging that was almost religious. As she stared at the gathered Romany, and was occasionally stared at in return, she couldn't help feeling that they were all a lot like Azador – so extremely . . . *Gypsy-ish*, for lack of a better term . . . as to seem almost a joke. There were men with huge curling mustaches pounding out horseshoes on small anvils, and old women dressed entirely in black gossiping like crows on a wire. At the edge of the camp some of the others had set up games of chance and were busily fleecing all the interested non-Gypsies in the vicinity with dried peas hidden under fast-moving thimbles.

I guess this is what you get when you make your Gypsies out of old fairy tales, she thought.

Azador led them down close to the banks of the Well, where his own extended family had made their place. As he introduced his relations to her, most for the second time, a Romany parade of *chals* and *chais* and *chabos*, all dark flashing eyes and white flashing teeth, Sam found herself in danger of falling asleep on her feet. !Xabbu saw and took her by the arm, then asked Azador for a place where she could sleep. She was guided to one of the wagons by a clucking Gypsy granny who led her to a tiny bed scarcely bigger than a bookshelf. Sam wanted to protest that it was !Xabbu who needed the sleep even more than she did, but somehow she wound up lying down. Within seconds, it was too late to say anything.

If Sam dreamed, she did not remember the dreams when

she awoke. She stumbled out and nearly fell down the
wagon's steep steps. The old crone was gone. All around,
Gypsies lay sleeping on the ground, as if the party had
raged so long that they had dropped where they stood,
but the sky was unchanged, still the same murky, bruised
gray.

I miss time, she thought sadly. *I miss mornings, and
the sun, and . . . and everything.*

Someone was singing, a low and quiet wandering in
a minor key. She walked around the edge of the wagon
to find !Xabbu squatting beside a guttering fire, drawing
in the gray dust with the end of a piece of charred fire-
wood as he sang. He looked up and offered her a weak,
almost ghostly smile.

'Good morning, Sam. Or good evening.'

'You can't tell, can you? Sometimes it feels like that's
the most impacted part of this whole thing.' She crouched
on the ground beside him. 'What are you drawing?'

'Drawing?' He looked down. 'Nothing. I was only letting
my arm move while I was thinking. Like dancing, perhaps,
but not so tiring.' He couldn't muster another smile, even
for his own small joke.

'What are you thinking about?' She was fairly certain
she already knew, but he surprised her.

'Jongleur.' He looked around. 'But before we talk, let
us go somewhere more . . .' He searched for the word.

'Private?'

'Exactly. Where we can see for a distance around us.'
He stood and led her between the wagons, past more
smoky embers and more sleeping Gypsies, toward the bluff
that loomed above the encampment. They climbed until
they could sit on a small headland at the end of a long
slope with the wagons a hundred meters below them.
There were still people nearby, some even camped along

the slope – not Gypsies, but fairy-tale folk, as Sam thought of them, talking cats and gingerbread children – but they seemed listlessly uninterested in the newcomers.

'What are you thinking about Jongleur?' Sam asked as they settled themselves.

'That there is some mystery between him and Azador I do not understand.' !Xabbu frowned. 'First there is the way he helped Azador lead us here. Then there is his interest in the Gypsy camp – this man, who has nothing but scorn for the other people and creatures he has met here.'

'I know.' Sam shrugged. 'But maybe there's a simple explanation. He did build the network. It makes sense he might know some things about it we don't, and not want to tell us. He's not, like, Mister Generosity.'

'True. But there is still something about it that puzzles me.'

They sat watching the movements of the awakening Gypsy camp, as well as the larger crowd of people and semi-people surrounding the Well, a tent city of the not-quite-human. The weird, lunar landscape brought back Sam's fierce sense of homesickness.

'So are we really waiting here for the end of the world?' she asked.

'I do not know, Sam. But there is always hope. Have I told you the story of how the All-Devourer came to the kraal of Grandfather Mantis? That is a story about hope. I told it to Renie, because she is the Beloved Porcupine.'

'What?' Despite the heaviness of her spirit, Sam was startled into a laugh.

!Xabbu nodded his head. 'Yes, that is what Renie also did when I told her. Porcupine is the daughter-in-law of Grandfather Mantis, his favorite of all the First People. And she was the bravest of them all as well – even when

Grandfather Mantis himself was overcome by fear, she kept her head and did what was necessary. That sounds like Renie, does it not?'

Sam looked at him fondly. 'You really love her, don't you?'

He did not speak for a moment, but a complicated set of emotions played across his face. 'My people do not have a word that has so many meanings as your English word "love," Sam. I care for her very much. I miss her badly. I am very, very frightened and unhappy that we cannot find her. If I did not see her again, my life would always be smaller and more sad.'

'Sounds like love to me. Do you want to marry her?'

'I would like to . . . to try to have a life together, I think. Yes.'

Sam laughed. 'You may be from somewhere else, !Xabbu, but you've got the single-guy stuff down pretty well. Can't you just say it? You love her and you want to marry her.'

He growled, but it was only mock-irritation. 'Very well, Sam. It is as you say.'

She guessed that his light-heartedness did not go very deep. 'We'll find her, !Xabbu. She's here somewhere.'

'I must believe it is so.' He sighed. 'I was going to tell you the story of the All-Devourer. It is frightening, but as I said, it is also a story of hope.'

Sam settled in. 'Go ahead.'

!Xabbu was a good storyteller, active and involved. He changed voices for the different characters and punctuated the tale with broad gestures and even dancelike movements, leaping to his feet to show Porcupine journeying to her father's house, greedily scooping his hands toward his mouth as he portrayed the All-Devourer eating all that he found. When he crouched and said, in the flat, frightened voice of

Mantis waiting for the monster, '*Oh, daughter, why is it so dark when there are no clouds in the sky?*' Sam truly felt the horror of seeing one's own sins come home at last.

When he had finished, she noticed that a few of the fairy-tale folk from the surrounding campsites had moved closer to listen. 'That was wonderful, !Xabbu. But it's so scary!' It had not been the simple folktale she had expected. Something powerful that lurked in the unfamiliar images, in the confusion of motives, made her wish she understood better.

'But the story says there is light behind the greatest darknesses. Grandfather Mantis and his people survived and moved on.' His face fell. 'I thought that it was my job to preserve them, and with them the story of my people. I thought that was to be the work of my life, but I have done nothing to make it happen.'

'You'll do it,' she said, but !Xabbu's nod of agreement was perfunctory. She wanted to see him animated again, thinking about something other than Renie and their terrible situation. After all, it wasn't as if they were in a hurry anymore. They had nowhere else to go. 'Can you tell me another one? Do you mind?'

He raised an eyebrow as if he suspected her motives, but said only, 'Yes, but then I would like to go look for Renie again, in case new people have come in while we were sleeping.' He looked out at the Well. 'In fact, this place does bring another story to my mind – one of the greatest of my people's tales.'

'Chizz,' she said. 'What's it about?'

'It is another story of Grandfather Mantis, about how the moon came to be in the sky . . . and about other things. You will see why I cannot help thinking of it in this place, beside this hole in the ground full of stars swimming in the waters of creation.'

'The waters of . . . Do you really think that's what it is?'

'I do not know, but to me it looks like the pictures I have seen in the city-school where I studied, pictures taken through the eyes of telescopes looking far away out into space – and back in time, too, as they explained to me, since the light itself was old when it reached us. To me this Well looks like a place where universes are born.'

Sam felt a little shiver. She could not help wondering what it would be like to drown in that deep hole, to gasp out your last breath even as galaxies of light swirled around you. 'Scanny,' she said quietly.

!Xabbu smiled. 'But the stories of my people are seldom of great things, of wars or stars or the creation of universes – or even if they are, they are spoken of in a small way. We are a small people, you see. We step very softly, and when we die, the wind soon has blown our footprints away. Even Grandfather Mantis, who once stole fire from beneath Ostrich's wing to give to his people so they would not fear the dark – yes, even Mantis, the greatest of us all, is only a tiny insect. But he is a person, too. All things in those first days were people.' He nodded, eyes closed as he composed his thoughts. 'This story starts with a very small thing indeed, as you shall see. A piece of leather.

'One day Grandfather Mantis was out walking, and discovered a piece of leather beside the trail. It was a piece from the shoe – you would call it a sandal, I think – that belonged to Rainbow, his own son. It had broken loose and been left, forgotten. But something about the shoe-piece called to Grandfather Mantis. Something about it seized his attention, this tiny, discarded thing, and he picked it up and carried it with him.'

As !Xabbu spoke, his preoccupation and sadness

dropped away. His voice rose, his hands fluttered into the air like startled birds. Sam saw that more refugees were moving toward them, drawn by his animation in this quiet, sad place.

'Mantis came to a pool of water,' !Xabbu said, 'a place where reeds grew all around, a hidden, fertile place, and he put the shoe-piece in the water – it was almost as if a dream had come to him and commanded it, but he was not asleep and he had not dreamed.

'Grandfather Mantis went away then, but he could not forget about it. At last he came back to the pool and called out, "Rainbow's shoe-piece! Rainbow's shoe-piece! Where are you?"'

'But in the water the shoe-piece had become a tiny eland. Now, if you do not know it, to my people the eland is the greatest of the antelopes. My own father hunted one so long and so desperately that he followed it out of the desert which was the only world he knew and stumbled into the river delta of my mother's people. And Grandfather Mantis himself, it is said, when he wished to travel in dignity and power, would ride between the antlers of a great eland.'

!Xabbu showed the proud stride of the eland in a sort of dance, head held high, so that Sam could almost see antlers worn like a crown. The throng of refugees was growing around them, several rows deep across the headland. Wide eyes watched the little man avidly, but !Xabbu did not seem to notice his swelling audience.

'But this eland in the pool was not great and powerful. It was small, wet, and shivering, so new that seeing it brought tears to the eyes of Grandfather Mantis. He sang a song of praise and gratitude but he did not touch it, for it was still too small and weak. Instead he went away, but when he came back he found small hoofprints in the earth beside the pool and he was so full of joy he danced. The eland saw him then and came to him as though he were completely its father. Mantis then brought honey, dark, sweet, and sacred, and rubbed it onto the little eland's ribs so it would become strong.

'Each night he returned to the pool and his eland. Each night he sang to it, and danced, and rubbed it with sweet honey. Then at last he knew he must go away and wait to see if the young eland would grow. Three days he stayed away from the pool, and three nights also, though his heart was very sore. When he returned on the morning after the third night, the eland walked out of the water in the light of the sun, its hooves clicking. It had grown to magnificent size, and Grandfather Mantis was so delighted he shouted out, 'Look, a person is coming! Ha! Rainbow's shoe-piece is coming!' For he felt that he had created the living creature from Rainbow's discarded piece of leather.

'But Rainbow and his sons, Mongoose and Younger Rainbow, were not happy when they heard what Mantis had done. "He thinks to fool us with his stories," they told each other, "and keep the meat to himself. Everyone knows that old Mantis is a trickster." So they went to the pool and found the young eland grazing on the bank. They surrounded it and killed it with their spears. They were very excited – it was a fine, big eland – and began to laugh and sing as they cut it up.

'Grandfather Mantis was coming to the pool when he heard their voices. He hid in the bushes and watched them, and soon came to realize what had happened. He was full of anger and sorrow, not just because they had killed his eland, but because they had not shared it with him, and had done everything without ceremony or even a dance of gratitude. He was afraid of them, though, because they were three and he was but one, so he waited in the reeds until they left, still laughing and singing as they carried away the meat from their kill, wrapped up in its own skin.

'Mantis came out of the reeds and walked to the place where the eland had died. Rainbow and the two grandsons of Grandfather Mantis had left only one thing behind, one of the organs from the eland's stomach, that which contained the black, bitter gall that not even my people, though schooled by need to eat almost anything, can swallow. They had left the gall hanging on a bush. Mantis was so sad and angry that he took his spear and hit the organ sack. From inside it the gall spoke to him, saying "Do not strike me."

'Mantis became even more angry. "I will strike you if I wish," he said. "I will throw you down on the ground and step on you. I will stab you with my spear."

'The gall spoke to him again, saying "If you do, I will come out and cover you in with my darkness."

'But Grandfather Mantis was too angry to listen. He lifted his spear and stabbed the organ. The gall came out as it had threatened, bitter, dark as a night without stars, and it covered Mantis in, even flowing into his eyes so that he was blinded.

'Mantis threw himself down on the ground, crying, "Help me! I cannot see! The black gall has covered my eyes and I feel myself to be lost!" But no one heard him calling in that remote place by the pool, and no one came to help him. Mantis could only crawl along the ground, feeling his way, blind and helpless. "Hyena will find me this way," he thought, "or some other hungry creature, and I will be killed. Grandfather Mantis will be dead – will that not be a sad thing?"

'But no one came to help him and he could only crawl

on through the darkness. Then at last, just as he became
so tired and fearful he could not move any farther, he
put his hand down upon something. It was an ostrich
feather, white as smoke, bright as a flame, and the heart
of Grandfather Mantis was filled with hope. He took the
feather and wiped the black gall from his eyes. When he
could see the beauty of the world again, he took the
feather and wiped off the rest of the bitter gall, which
fell away, leaving the feather clean and untouched.
Marveling at this wondrous thing, delighted with his
escape, Grandfather Mantis threw the feather high into
the sky where it stuck, a curve of white against a darkness as black as the gall. He danced and sang. "You now
lie up in the sky," Mantis told the feather. "From this day,
you will be the moon, and you will shine at night and
give light to all the people when there would otherwise
be darkness. You are the moon, you will live, you will
fall away, then you will live again and give light to all
the people." And it did. And it does.'

   !Xabbu fell silent, lowering his head as if saying 'Amen'
at the end of a prayer. Sam could not help noticing all
the faces surrounding them in the unending twilight –
childlike, expectant faces. The crowd had grown larger
still, pressing in like victims of a disaster pleading for
information, until they surrounded the small knoll many
rows deep.

   She thought she should thank him for the story,
although she felt again that she hadn't really understood
– what was all that about some icky black *fenfen* getting
all over the insect the story was about? And how could
he be an insect but have a rainbow for a son? Also, she
was puzzled why one kind of story, about making an
antelope out of a sandal, had suddenly turned into another
kind of story: it violated her sense of how stories were

supposed to work. But she knew that these things were somehow important to !Xabbu, sort of like a religion, and she didn't want to offend anyone she liked so much.

A high-pitched voice called from the largely silent crowd. 'Tell another!'

!Xabbu looked up, a little startled, but before he or Sam could make out where the request had originated, others were also asking, a growing chorus.

'A story!'

'Tell another.'

'Please!'

'They want to hear more stories,' !Xabbu said wonderingly.

'They're scared,' said Sam. 'The world is coming to an end. And they're all children, aren't they?' Looking around at the pleading, terrified faces, she felt herself fighting back tears. If Jongleur had been within reach she would have hit him, would have tried to knock him down and make him pay for what his cruel self-obsession had done to these innocents. 'They have to be them,' she said, as much to herself as to !Xabbu. 'They have to be the stolen children.'

She was arrested by a familiar face in the throng, although it took her a moment to remember where she had seen the handsome, dark-haired man before. He was a few rows back in the crowd, holding a bundle Sam couldn't quite see, watching !Xabbu with an unblinking, almost vacant stare. None of the fairy-tale children stood too near him, as though they could sense something wrong.

Sam pulled at !Xabbu's arm. 'Look, it's that Grail guy – the one that disappeared when Renie disappeared!'

'Ricardo Klement? Where?'

'Over there,' Sam said, but now there was only an empty

space where Klement had stood. 'He was there a second ago, no dupping!'

As they scanned the throng of refugees, Sam became aware of someone standing very close to her, a small child apparently made of mud. She tried to step around the tiny obstacle but the child moved with her and reached up a stubby hand to tug at Sam's Gypsy finery.

'He is not there now,' !Xabbu said. 'He is larger than most of these people – we would see him, I think . . .'

'He couldn't have got away that fast,' Sam said angrily. Beyond the crowd of refugees still begging for another story, the gray slope was empty for dozens of meters. 'Not without us seeing him.' The mud child was still trying to get her attention. 'Stop pulling on me, will you?' Sam snapped.

The child let go and took a step backward. It was hard to tell from its odd face, the features little more than dents and grooves, what the creature was thinking, but it squared its shoulders in a way that clearly said it would not be chased off. 'I want to talk to you,' the stranger said in the voice of a little girl.

Sam sighed. 'What?'

'Are you . . . are you Renie's friends?'

Sam had been expecting a plea for another of !Xabbu's tales, and for a long moment could only stare at the child, dumbfounded. 'Renie . . . ?'

!Xabbu was there in a heartbeat to kneel beside the child. 'Who are you?' he asked. 'Do you know Renie? Do you know where she is? Yes, we are her friends.'

The girl looked at him for a moment. 'I'm . . . I'm the Stone Girl.' Her simple finger-stroke of a mouth writhed and she began to cry. 'Don't you know where she is either?'

From the way he closed his eyes and grunted, like a man suffering a painful blow, Sam could feel !Xabbu's terrible disappointment. 'Maybe you'd better just tell us everything,' she said to the weeping Stone Girl.

'. . . And then after we ran away from the Ticks, up the hill, we crossed the bridge.' The child was still sniffling a bit, but in telling the story of her travels with Renie she had found a sort of calm. 'And we saw the strange man who was her friend, too, but he was just walking, and the Ticks went around him!' She was clearly impressed. 'Like they didn't even care about him.'

'That's so scanny!' Sam said. 'That has to be what's-his-name, Klement.'

!Xabbu frowned. 'And then what happened? When you crossed the bridge?'

The Stone Girl chewed for a moment on a muddy finger, thinking. 'We didn't really go to Jinnear Bad House, not like usual. We both went in, sort of, then right away I came out here at the Well. But Renie didn't.' Her eyes squinted for a moment as she fought more tears. 'Do you think she's all right?'

'We utterly hope so,' Sam said, then turned to !Xabbu. 'But where is she?'

The small man had a distant, disturbed look on his face. 'The rest of us traveled in a similar way, I think. We came close to the Other, were weighed – judged, perhaps – and then were sent away. Those who belong in this world, like Azador and this little girl, did not even experience that much, but were simply sent straight here.'

'What does that mean?'

He stood, absently patting the Stone Girl on the head, but he looked as miserable as she had ever seen him. 'It might be I am wrong, but I think Renie was allowed in.'

'Allowed in?' Sam was not following.

'To the Well.' !Xabbu turned to look at the crater and

its sea of restless light. 'I think she is in the Other's inner-most heart.'

'Oh, no,' Sam said. 'God, really?'

!Xabbu's smile, for the first time in Sam's memory, was something unpleasant to look at. 'Yes, God, really. The god of this place, anyway. The dying, crazy god.'

Sam's pulse was rabbiting. She had all but forgotten the Stone Girl who still stood between them, her crude little face puzzled and sad. '!Xabbu, what will we do?'

'What *I* will do is go after her.' He was staring at the Well as though seeing it for the first time. Sam could not help remembering how afraid he had been just to dive into a placid river. 'I . . . I will go down.'

'Not without me you won't.' For the moment, her fear of being left behind allowed her to ignore the terror of the unnatural Well. 'I already told you what I think about all that let-me-save-the-day *fenfen*.'

He shook his head. 'You do not understand, Sam. The Other – I believe it already has rejected me once, rejected you too, all of us.' His voice had gotten very quiet. 'I do not believe I will reach Renie, but I have to try.' He turned to her, almost pleading. 'I cannot take you, Sam, when I feel sure there is no hope.'

She was just about to issue an angry rebuttal when she finally realized that an irritating noise which had been in the background for several seconds was Felix Jongleur's loud, angry voice. She turned and saw the old man on open ground midway between the place where she stood with !Xabbu and the outskirts of the Gypsy camp.

'. . . But I do not believe that anymore. I think your silence is insolence – or worse.'

The person he was shouting at was Ricardo Klement.

!Xabbu was already hurrying down the slope. Sam took a few steps, then turned, startled by a cry of unhappiness behind her. She had forgotten the Stone Girl.

'Come on,' Sam said. 'Do you want me to carry you?'

The Stone Girl shook her head stiffly, but reached out and took Sam's hand in a cool and surprisingly firm grip.

By the time they reached the others, !Xabbu was doing his best to ask Klement a question about Renie, but Felix Jongleur was full of cold fury and would not be interrupted. Sam could finally see the thing Klement was holding and she was shocked and disgusted. The infant shape and vestigial features made a bad combination with its muddy gray-blue color.

'So you will not even answer me?' Jongleur asked Klement. 'Come, I thought you were my ally, Ricardo – I have made many sacrifices for you. Yet you disappear when we are all in need, then will not even tell me where you have gone? And I suppose you will not explain your little . . . souvenir either?'

For a moment Klement almost seemed to clutch the little baby-creature tighter, a gesture that was the first human thing Sam had seen from the man. 'It . . . is mine.'

'Just tell me what you have been doing,' Jongleur demanded.

'Waiting,' said Klement after a long pause.

'For what?'

'For . . . something.' Klement slowly turned toward the Well, then back to Jongleur, !Xabbu, and Sam. 'And now . . . I have found it.'

An instant later, Ricardo Klement was gone.

Sam stared helplessly at the empty space, then turned to !Xabbu, half-believing that something must be wrong with her. Her friend looked just as surprised, but his astonishment was as nothing to Jongleur's, who looked like a man who had just seen his own furniture rise up and attack him.

'What . . . ?' he said, gaping. 'How . . . ?'

Even as he spoke, the universe shifted and reality stuttered to a halt. Sam had not felt anything like it for many days, and had almost forgotten the terror of one of these hitches in time and space. Color and noise blurred into a mishmash of sensory information. Sam felt sure that the end had finally come, the crash of the system, and even tried to brace herself for a return of the hideous, bone-drilling pain she had experienced when she had once before been yanked out of the Grail Network. Instead the meaningless chaos of sight and sound abruptly knitted itself back together, as if someone had wound a key and set a clockwork mechanism moving forward again. Reality was restored. Or most of it was.

The Stone Girl was tugging at Sam's arm, but Sam could hardly see her or anything else because the light that had come back was much dimmer, as though the entire virtual universe were powered by a single spluttering, ancient generator. The shapes around her were little more than shadows, but she could hear a rising murmur of terror from the refugees crowded around the Well, a sound like wind in tall trees.

The Stone Girl tugged her arm again. 'Look at the stars,' the little girl said, her voice a choked whisper.

Sam looked up.

The sky was darkening from the long twilight into true night, but the stars were not getting brighter. Instead, they were fading. The evening sky was turning black and the starlight was dying, plunging all the land around the Well into deepest shadow.

CHAPTER 36

Without a Net

SHE stood paralyzed on the platform, watching the arc of the trapeze as it sailed out toward her, paused, then swung back into the shadows at the top of the big tent. She knew that she must leap out and catch it on the next swing or else she would never reach it, would be stuck on the high platform forever. But she knew just as firmly that there was no net, and that a fall onto the sawdust-caked center ring beneath her, invisible in the glare of the spotlights, would be like an eighty-foot swan dive onto cement.

The trapeze swung toward her again and its slightly diminished arc confirmed that she would get no more chances. She tensed her muscles and felt the edge of the platform through the soles of the soft shoes, letting herself lean forward against every shrieking instinct until her balance was compromised and there was no turning back. As the bar neared the end of its swing, slowing to the moment when it would finally stop and hang in space for a fraction of a second, she leaped outward into the pillars of light, the unending dark.

Only as she touched the rung, clutched, and felt it squirt from her grasp like a bar of soap – only in that moment when she too was briefly weightless, but with all of death and eternity solidifying around her, changing her from a person into a mere proof of gravity – did Olga realize she was dreaming. The dream-audience bellowed in distorted surprise and terror, deafening her even as she fell, then she was gasping on the floor of the storeroom where she had fallen asleep, shivering and struggling to catch her breath as the air-conditioning vent above her head roared like a jet engine.

By the time she had found the water fountain and taken a long drink the trembling was beginning to subside. Some deep frequency in the air-conditioning was starting to make her feel ill, so she picked up her belongings and moved to the other side of the storeroom.

The unintended nap had done little to make her feel better. She could still feel the moment of slippage and freefall, something that even after years of working over a net, practicing with her father and his aerialists, never completely lost its terror.

Wouldn't be much of a circus unless there is a chance someone might die.

Strangely, the thought gave her a little comfort. Nothing was assured in that life or this: even a safety net was no guarantee. Jansci, the Hungarian wire-walker, a good friend of her father's, had fallen to the net during practice, caught his foot as he was bouncing up, and had somehow gone over the edge. A mere fifteen-foot fall, but it had paralyzed him.

No guarantee, even with a net.

She drank a little more water, then tried Catur Ramsey's line again, but whatever magic had once connected her through the telematic jack to the real world outside this artificial black mountain was gone. The coach was a pumpkin once more, the footmen had become mice. She would have to do it on her own.

She packed her meager belongings and headed for the service elevator.

Almost a full day of living like a rat in the walls of Felix Jongleur's house had made her cautious. When the elevator hissed open on the mezzanine floor she peered around the edge before stepping out, then shrank back into the interior until the young man at the end of the corridor had rounded the corner and disappeared. He was wearing a collarless shirt and work pants, but seemed more like a business employee in casual clothes than a custodial worker – perhaps a young manager on the way up, anxious to impress the bosses with unpaid overtime.

Even the minions of Hell don't have to dress up on weekends, she decided. *I don't remember Mr Dante mentioning that.*

As she held the door open and waited a few extra moments for safety, she could not help thinking about the dozens of oh-so-ordinary employees she had seen around the building, all doing oh-so-ordinary things. In fact, she had seen no evidence that her own reasons for being here were anything but delusional. J Corporation headquarters, once she was past its forbidding black facade, held nothing she could not have found in any downtown skyscraper. Even the hardened office for the squad of security guards was not excessive if you considered that the building was also the residence of one of the world's richest men.

Any reasonable person would have to admit that the fantasies of lost children and worldwide conspiracies seemed more and more farfetched – and Olga herself was a reasonable person.

Can you be reasonable and still be insane? she wondered. *That would seem to be stretching the rules a bit.*

When she felt certain the hallway was empty, she made her way down the stairs from the mezzanine onto the ground floor of the vast, pyramid-roofed lobby. Although she had seen several people crossing from one elevator bank to another, at the moment it was empty – almost shockingly so, in the way only a closed public building can seem. She hurried across the black marble floor toward the main reception desk, the echo of her footsteps sounding as loud as gunfire. When she reached the desk she made a show for the hidden cameras of accidentally tipping a square vase of flowers across the countertop, so that the water and the fading irises from Friday morning splashed out onto the floor in front of the desk. Pretending she had not noticed what she'd done, she hurried back up to the comparative safety of the mezzanine.

From a secure place in a copse of potted ornamental trees she waited and watched as an agonizingly slow trickle of J Corporation workers checked in through the inset security door for some weekend catch-up, or wandered across the lobby from one part of the building to the other. Several of them seemed to notice the pool of water and spilled flowers in front of the desk, but if any of them decided to notify someone about it they used their telematic jack to do so. Olga had no way of knowing for sure.

An hour went by. Somewhere between twenty and thirty employees had trekked across the lobby but the spilled vase still lay untended. The huge clock on the wall, a rectangle of gold the size of a panel truck inset with Egyptian figures and characters, showed a few minutes past eight o'clock. Saturday night, her time almost half gone, and nothing accomplished. Olga had always been a patient woman, but now she felt herself stretched like a thin cord, vibrating in every breeze, poised to snap. She had all but decided that she would have to take the risk of exposing herself on a search of the lower floors when a gangly figure shuffled out of the service elevator and across the lobby floor pushing a plastic bin on wheels, a mop resting on one shoulder like a sentry's rifle.

Relieved, Olga let out a long-held sigh of breath. She watched for a moment as the custodian gathered up the fallen irises with slow, careful movements, then lowered the mop. When she was sure she was right – who knew how many custodians actually worked here on weekends? – she hurried to the elevator and got in. A minute later it was summoned to the lobby level. She did her best to look surprised when he got in.

'Well, hello, Jerome,' she said as he bumped his bin

over the tiny gap between car and door. She gave him
her best smile. 'What are you doing up here?'

'I don't know anything about that, Ol-ga.' He spoke mildly,
but was clearly troubled. 'All those floors are closed. I
only been up there when the security fellows ask me to
come help move something.' He sat thinking with his
mouth open and his milky eyes almost shut, half a sandwich in his hand, arrested on its upward journey.

Olga forced herself to take a bite of the liverwurst sandwich he had insisted she share. Since she had vetoed
eating in the custodians' lunchroom, convincing him
instead to join her in the storage room – she had spent
so much time there it was beginning to feel like home –
she had not felt it politic to turn down the sandwich,
despite her extremely mixed feelings about liverwurst. 'So
. . . so you've been to those floors?'

'Oh, sure. Lots of times. But only up to the security
office.' He frowned again. 'Once to the room above that
where they have all these machines, because one of the
bosses was angry there was mouse poop there and he
wanted to show me. But I told him I didn't even clean
that room, so how was I supposed to know there were
mice up there?' He laughed, then embarrassedly cleaned
a morsel of liver-wurst from his chin. 'Lena said the mice
were going up in the elevator! That was really funny.'

Olga tried to suppress her almost panicky interest in
this second machine room. What good would it do her,
in any case? She had no idea how to attach Sellars' device,
or what to attach it to, and no Sellars to benefit from its
use anyway. But it was in the part of the tower she wanted
to visit. 'So could you take me up there?'

He shook his head. 'We're not supposed to. We'll get
in trouble.'

'But I told you, if I don't, *I'll* get in trouble.'

'I still don't understand,' he said, chewing vigorously again.

'I told you, my friend from the other shift took me up there Friday, just to show it to me. But I dropped my wallet up there, you see? By accident. And if someone finds it I will get in trouble. And I also won't have my cards for shopping and things.'

'You'd get in trouble, huh?'

'Yes. They will fire me for sure. And I won't be able to help my daughter and her little girl.' Olga was torn between self-loathing and increasing desperation. Nobody but a man with some serious thinking problems would buy an ill-concocted story like this. She was taking advantage of Jerome because he was credulous and eager to please – probably brain-damaged – and she felt like the lowest scum imaginable. Only by thinking of the dream-children as though the memories were a mantra, of the way they had flocked to her like frightened birds seeking shelter, their imploring, hopeless voices, could she ease the pain of what she was doing.

'Maybe . . . maybe we could just tell some of the fellows in security,' Jerome said at last. 'They're pretty nice guys, really. They could get it for you.'

'No!' She softened her tone and tried again. 'No, they would have to file a report, otherwise *they'd* get in trouble, see? Then the friend who took me up there would get in trouble, too. I don't want someone else to get fired because of a mistake I made.'

'You're a nice person, Ol-ga.'

She winced, but tried to keep her smile. 'Is there anything you can do, Jerome?'

He was clearly very distressed by the idea of breaking the rules, but she could see him thinking carefully. 'I could try, but I don't know if the elevator will open. Which floor did you lose your wallet on?'

'The one with the machines.' It seemed likely to be the most sparsely occupied, and there might be a way to get to the other floors – didn't even the highest-security, most supervillainish buildings still legally have to have stairways and fire escapes? As for how to get rid of Jerome so she could investigate in peace, she would have to think of something on the fly.

Maybe you could club him unconscious when you get there, Olga, she thought sourly. *Just to make the whole thing complete.*

Jerome put the rest of his sandwich back in the vacuum bag and carefully sealed it. He seemed to have lost his appetite. 'We can go up and see, Ol-ga. But if it doesn't work, don't get mad at me, okay?'

'I promise.' *And may God forgive me for this*, she thought.

Rᴀᴍsᴇʏ looked around the room, trying to take it all in. Even for a virtual environment, where gravity was not an issue and cubic footage was equally an illusion, it was insanely cluttered. A grisly pile of heads in transparent boxes, a collection of human and nonhuman trophies more like flash-freeze holograms than actual decapitations, dominated the multilevel space, but there was plenty of competition. Strange objects were stacked everywhere, swords and spears and complete sets of armor, gems the size of Catur Ramsey's virtual fist, huge skulls of animals that could never, thank God, have actually lived in the real world, even a banister that was a huge, immobilized snake with a head half as long as Ramsey was tall. The walls, where they could be seen between the leaning piles of memorabilia, showed two scenes whose complete

disparity were the only reason Ramsey knew they were
displays rather than what was supposed to be outside
Orlando Gardiner's electronic home in the Inner District.

The Cretaceous swamp, where even now a mother
Hadrosaur was chasing away a slender Dromeosaurus that
had made a couple of half-hearted lunges toward her eggs,
was a pretty obvious thing for a kid to be interested in;
the other, a vast and seemingly lifeless landscape of red
dust, was a little less understandable.

All in all, it was a boy's room in a place with no limits,
and these were the proud possessions of a boy who would
never come back to claim them. Ramsey could not help
thinking of the child-king Tutankhamen, his tomb stuffed
with personal effects dug open and exposed to view millennia after his death. Would Orlando's room just remain on
the net? He supposed the Gardiners would have to keep
paying for it. But what if they did? Would someone stumble across it generations in the future and try to make sense
of the mind and world of a forgotten child from the twenty-
first century? It was a strange and pitiful thought, a life in
all its complexity reduced to a few toys and souvenirs.

Well, maybe not a few . . .

A hole opened in the floor and something like the head
of a ragged black dust mop emerged, accompanied by a
cloud of cartoon dust.

'Thanks for meeting me here,' Beezle said.

'No problem. Is this . . .' He wanted to ask if the place
was special to the agent, but again found himself confused.
It wasn't even like Beezle was a real artificial personality. He was a kid's toy, essentially. 'Do you come here a
lot?'

Beezle's goggling eyes rolled and then settled. His
answer was strangely hesitant. 'I know where everything
is. So it's a good place. To do things.'

'Right.' Ramsey looked around for someplace to sit. The only obvious thing designed for human comfort was a hammock stretched in one corner.

'You want a chair?' Beezle reached down into the hole in the floor and, with a few strange sound effects, produced a chair three or four times his own size. 'Siddown. I'll tell you what I found.'

As Ramsey made himself comfortable, Beezle produced a small black cube, then flicked it so that it opened into a foggy three-dimensional shape that hung in the middle of the room. A moment later the fog inside dispersed, revealing a tall black object.

'That's the J Corporation building.'

'Yep.' Beezle tapped the transparent cube and the building opened like a paper book, revealing its interior. 'This is from that guy Sellars' notes.'

'You found them!'

'Yep. What is this guy, anyway, a robot or something? He keeps his notes in machine language.'

'He's not a robot, as far as I know, but it's a long story and I'm in a hurry. Can you put me back in touch with Olga Pirofsky?'

'You wanna see where she is?' Beezle waved a misshapen foot and a tiny red dot gleamed into view about one third of the way up the structure. 'Sellars has a trace on her – she's got a badge or something, right? – and you can track it off the readers they got on all the floors. It's a weak signal, but it's enough to triangulate her.'

As Ramsey watched, the red dot slowly began to move sideways. *She's alive, anyway*, he thought. *Unless someone's carrying her.* 'Do Sellars' notes tell you what he planned to do? Something about tapping into the building's data stream, that's all I know.'

'Kind of,' Beezle said, cabdriver voice suddenly distracted. 'Your friend – she's moving.'

'I saw . . .' Ramsey began, then suddenly realized that the red dot had stopped its horizontal movement and was now slowly rising. 'Oh, my God, what's happening? What's she doing?'

'Service elevator. She's going up.'

'But the top of the building . . . ! That's where Sellars said the private quarters were, and the security guards. I have to stop her!' He had a sudden thought. 'Will her badge let her in up there?'

Beezle gave as much of a shrug as a creature with no shoulders and too many legs could manage. 'Not unless she's done something to change it. Let me check.' After a moment's silence, he said, 'Nope. She could stop on the security floor, but if she tries to get out anywhere else above the forty-fifth she's probably gonna set off all the alarms.'

'Christ. Can you put me in contact with her?'

'I haven't finished looking through all this stuff yet, but I'll try.' Another hole in the floor opened next to Beezle. He made a move toward it, then stopped. 'You know they got a whole army base on that island? Why the heck you wanna mess with someplace like that, anyway?'

'Just hook me up!' Ramsey shouted.

Beezle took a few shambling steps and dropped into the pit. Moments later the electronic cottage resounded with the clang of something being hammered and the earsplitting *voopa-voopa* of a wood saw.

'Good Christ, what are you doing?'

Beezle's voice echoed as it drifted up out of the hole in the floor. 'What you asked me to do, boss. You wanna let me work?'

The red light was climbing steadily up the tower. Ramsey could not bear to watch. He turned to the rusty desert that covered one whole wall. He could see now that there were small beetlelike shapes in the sand, half-buried and as motionless as fossils. He dimly remembered reading something on the net about the MBC Project on Mars, how the little robots had stopped working.

That'll teach them to trust machines, he thought bitterly, wincing as the saw started up again, accompanied by what sounded like a jack-hammer, shaking the walls of the 'cot until it seemed the whole thing might fall down. A plume of dust floated up out of the hole. A dragon's skull vibrated off a shelf and shattered, a piece of the jaw coming to rest beside Ramsey's feet.

In the midst of it all, the red dot rose serenely upward.

DESPITE the smoothness of the silent elevator, Olga felt as though a giant had grabbed her in its fist and was lifting her up, up toward a monstrous face she didn't want to see. She suddenly knew exactly why she'd dreamed of the circus, all its performers now dead and gone – a part of her life that was equally dead. It had been just like this, the climb up the ladder to the high platform, no matter how many times she did it: part of it had been almost mechanical, hand over hand in practiced motion, and even the surface of her mind had been full of rote memorizations, all the things her father had taught her to set her mind and prepare herself for whatever might come.

'*Always you must be inside your thoughts and outside your body, my dear one.*' She suddenly could almost see him in the elevator with her, as close as Jerome was standing, Papa with his neat, graying beard, the scar across the bridge of his nose where his own brother's heel had broken it when they were young performers. It was only one of many scars – his large hands were ribboned with them, scored by nets and tent cables and guy wires. He often claimed that on his days off, he played catch with *Le Cirque Royale*'s knife thrower. The first time he had said it, when she was three or four, she had been terrified until he assured her it was a joke.

He smelled of pine resin, always, which he used to keep his hands dry in the ring. That and her mama's cigarettes, those foul Russian things, even after all these years the two smells always brought back her childhood in an instant. Watching her father with his big hands on Mama's shoulders, or wrapped around her waist from behind while they watched rehearsal. Mama always, always with a cigarette in the corner of her mouth, her chin lifted to keep the smoke out of her eyes. She had been ramrod straight, slender, her dancer's body hard and muscular well into her seventies, before she got sick.

'My Polish princess,' Papa had called Mama. 'Look at her,' he had always said, half-mocking, half-proud. 'She may not be royalty, but she's built like it. No rear end on her at all, hips like a boy.' And then he would give Mama a playful swat on the backside, and she would hiss at him like a cat being annoyed by a child. Papa would laugh, winking at Olga and the world. *Look at my good-looking wife*, it meant. *And look at the temper she has on her!*

They were both long gone now, Mama dead from cancer, her father following not long after, as everyone knew he would. He had said it himself: '*I don't want to outlive her. You and your brother, Olga, God grant you long lives. Don't take offense if I don't stick around to see the grandchildren.*'

But there weren't any grandchildren, of course. Olga's brother Beniamin had died not long after her parents, a freakish piece of bad luck when his appendix had ruptured while he was on a mountaineering holiday with friends from university. And long before that she had lost her own baby and her husband in the same week – her entire chance at happiness, it had seemed then and still somehow did.

So I'm the last, she thought. *That line from Mama's and Papa's parents and grandparents ends with me – maybe ends today, right here in this building.* For the first time in days, she felt truly overwhelmed. *So sad, so . . . final. All the plans those people made, the baby blankets they knitted, the money they tucked away, and it all comes down to an aging woman probably throwing her life away over a delusion.*

The elevator seemed to be creeping upward as slowly as a rising tide, the little squares on the black glass panel lighting one after the other. *So sad.*

'Do you have a family around here?' she asked Jerome, just to hear some human noise.

'My mom.' He was squinting at the blinking lights on the panel as though hypnotized. She wondered how well he could see. They climbed from 35 to 36 to 37. For a modern elevator, Olga thought it seemed cruelly slow. 'She lives in Garyville,' Jerome went on. 'My brother lives in Houston, Texas.'

'*Olga? Can you hear me?*' The sudden voice in her head made her jump and gasp.

'What's wrong, Ol-ga?' Jerome asked.

'Just a headache.' She put a hand to her temple. '*Who is that?*' she subvocalized. '*Mr Ramsey, is that you?*'

'*Jesus, I never thought I'd get through again. You need to get off the elevator.*'

She looked at the panel. 40. 41. '*What are you talking about? How did you know . . . ?*'

'Ol-ga, you look really sick.'

She waved her hand to show she didn't want to talk.

'*Just get off the elevator!*' Ramsey's obvious panic cut through her confusion. '*Now! If that door opens above the forty-fifth floor, you're going to set off alarms all over the building. Security will be on you before you can blink.*'

The feigned headache was becoming real. 'Stop the car,' she told Jerome. 'What floor are we on?' The blinking panel suggested it was *43*. 'I need to use the restroom, Jerome. Is that okay?'

'Sure.' But even as he pressed the button, the car had already moved up another floor. Olga found herself holding her breath. The car slid to a stop and the door hissed open, revealing a carpeted hallway and a bizarrely festive lighting scheme. It took her a moment to see that the walls were hung with shimmering pieces of neon art. Jerome stood in the open doorway. It took Olga a moment to realize that he expected her to know where the restrooms were. After all, she was an employee, wasn't she?

'I haven't been on this floor,' she explained. When he had told her where to go, she asked him to wait in the elevator lobby, afraid that someone might notice an elevator stopped on one floor too long.

The restroom was empty. She sat down in the farthest stall and pulled up her feet. 'Tell me what's going on,' she said to Ramsey. 'Where did you people go? I've been trying to call you all day.'

His explanation did not make her feel any better about anything – in fact, it was hard to think of something more carefully designed to destroy what little confidence she had left. 'Oh, God help us, Sellars is . . . gone? So who is this Beezle who is helping you out? Is he one of that army fellow's specialists or something?'

'It's a long story.' Ramsey didn't sound very eager to

tell it. 'Right now, we have to figure out what we're going to do. Are you in a secure place?'

She had to laugh at that. 'I am in enemy territory, Mr Ramsey! I am about as secure as a cockroach standing in the bathtub when the light comes on. If someone doesn't smash me with a shoe, yes, I suppose I am just fine.'

'I'm doing my best, Olga, honestly. You don't know how hard I've been trying to get back in touch with you since Sellars . . . since whatever happened to him.' He took a deep breath. 'I'm going to put Beezle on with you. He's . . . he's a little eccentric. Don't worry about it – he's very good at what he does.'

'Eccentric I can live with, Mr Ramsey.'

The voice, when it came, was like that of some ancient comedian from the Television Era. 'You're Olga, right? Pleased to meetcha.'

'And you.' She shook her head. Sitting fully-clothed on the toilet talking to an escapee from the Catskills circuit, probably twenty vertical feet or so from armed men who would be happy to kill her, or at least beat her senseless, if they knew what she was trying to do. *There has to be an easier, more sensible way to commit suicide*, she told herself.

'Look, if there's a bunch of machinery up there, that may be just what Sellars wants,' Beezle told her after she explained what she had heard from Jerome. 'We won't know until we find it, and even then we won't know anything anyway, since according to Ramsey this Sellars is kind of a sleeping partner at the moment.' His snort of indignation was audible and almost funny. 'But if you try to walk in there without authorization, you're lunchmeat, seen?'

He sounded a bit old to be using kiddie slang, but Olga had spent her life among showfolk who liked affecting Bohemian airs. 'Seen, I suppose.'

'So we have to monkey with your badge some more. I don't know what Sellars planned. I haven't found any notes about this, but I'm still looking. He might have had some legitimate code to plug in, but I ain't got it. Maybe you could find someone who has access already, then I could, y'know, counterfeit an authorization.'

'There's a janitor who's helping me,' Olga said hesitantly. 'He's been up to those floors at least once or twice.'

'What?' Ramsey had been listening in. 'Olga, we can't tell anybody . . . !'

'I didn't tell him anything,' she said angrily. 'Give me some credit. I told him a big, stupid lie. He is brain-damaged, or perhaps a little retarded, so you can imagine how I feel right now, using him like this.' She was close to tears again. 'Would his badge information help you?'

'Yeah.' There was a moment's silence as the stranger named Beezle considered. 'Maybe we could make it look like the janitor got off at the wrong floor or something – y'know, like he was just messin' around . . .'

'If you do anything to get him in trouble, I will kill you!'

'Kill me?' The raspy laugh sounded in her ear. 'Lady, the kid's parents tried to unplug me for weeks and didn't get to first base, so I don't know how you think you'd manage it.'

Completely thrown by this bizarre *non sequitur*, Olga could think of no response.

'Look, just get us his badge information,' Ramsey said after a moment. 'You still have the ring, don't you?'

'I can do a better job with her t-jack,' Beezle said.

'Fine. Just do that, Olga. Then we'll decide what to do.'

Feeling like a character out of some antique farce, she hurried out of the restroom and trotted down the corridor.

Jerome was standing stock-still in the elevator lobby, looking at his shoes. The overhead lights gleamed on his prominent facial bones, making him seem like some machine that had run down and stopped.

The custodian lifted his head when he heard her. The smile changed his misshapen face into something lovable, an old doll, a broken but familiar toy.

'I just wanted you to know I'm almost done,' she said. 'Oh, my shoe. Can I hold onto your shoulder?' She steadied herself while she pretended to adjust the shoe, taking care to lean her telematic jack close to his badge, then she hurried back to the restroom. Ramsey and his new friend were already analyzing the results.

'I can make something to get you in,' Beezle said at last. 'But it won't fool anyone if they check up, and they'll probably notice you going in. The schematic says there are security cameras all over that floor. There are some little indicators that are probably drones, too.'

'That won't work,' Ramsey said miserably. 'Even if she had time to plant Sellars' little package, and we got the right place first time, someone would check the place over if they found her in there with a forged clearance. They must have engineers on call.'

The relief that washed over her at the idea of being barred from the upper floor made Olga realize for the first time how frightened she was. 'So it's hopeless?'

'I can't do miracles, lady,' Beezle grated. 'My owner Orlando always used to say . . .'

'Hang on,' said Ramsey, interrupting yet another puzzling remark. 'You brought in more than one package. We can set off the smoke device.'

'How is that going to help?' In a way, Olga had already begun to accustom herself to failure. Every spur to going on, even the memory of the children, had been blunted by her growing fear. She desperately wanted to see the sky again, to feel real wind on her face, even the warm bathwater that they called air down in this part of the United States. 'It is not going to blow the doors off or anything, and it is too far down in the building to hide me from anyone without choking me to death at the same time.'

'But if they have to evacuate the building they won't be paying much attention to who's getting on and off at the forty-sixth floor or whatever.'

'You said they had cameras. Even if they don't see me that moment, they can access the footage when they find out it's a false alarm.'

'If we're lucky – if you're lucky, I should say, since I know you're the one taking the risks – you'll be done by then, maybe even out of the building, and none of it will matter. So you'll have to be quick with the tap. Just plant the device, then get out.'

She felt dizzy. 'I . . . I will try. Are you going to set off the smoke bomb now?'

'Not yet,' Ramsey said. 'Beezle needs to fake your clearance – pretending to set the building on fire won't do us any good if you're still locked out of that floor. And I'd like to study Sellars' notes. I called you in a hurry, so I've hardly had a chance to think.' He sounded glum again. 'I wasn't really trained for this kind of thing.'

'So who was? Me?' Olga lowered her feet to the restroom floor.

'Can you find somewhere safe to hide again? We'll call you at midnight.'

'Fine.' She cut the connection, feeling a bit like she was watching the departure of a boat that had dropped her off on an isolated, uninhabited island.

The restroom door hissed shut behind her as she headed

back to tell Jerome that her plans had changed. It was
some small solace not to have to drag him into danger.
She thought of the lost children. She seemed fated to be
their paladin and protector whether it made sense or not,
and even whether she wanted to or not. She hoped they
appreciated it. What was it her mother had used to say
about gratitude?

*'You should be grateful to me now, while I'm still alive.
It will save on postage.'*

But I wouldn't mind paying the postage, Mama, she
thought. *If I only had your address.*

HER mother wanted her to go to the store with her, but
Christabel just didn't want to go. She didn't want to do
anything. She told her mommy that she wanted to stay
at the hotel and watch the wall-screen, but she really
didn't. Mommy and Daddy had a little fight – Daddy
didn't like Mommy going out where someone might see
her.

'We just need to lie low,' he said.

'I'm not going to lie so low my child eats nothing but
junk food,' she said. 'We have a kitchen as part of this
room and I'm going to use it. That child hasn't touched
a vegetable that wasn't deep-fried in days.'

It was a small fight, and it wasn't the reason Christabel
was feeling bad, but she still didn't like it. Mommy and
Daddy didn't make jokes anymore. Daddy didn't put his
arms around Mommy, or lean over and kiss her on the
back of the neck. He picked Christabel up and gave her
hugs, but he wasn't happy and neither was Mommy. And
since the bad thing had happened to Mister Sellars and
the boy, they hardly talked at all without fighting.

'Are you sure you won't come with me, honey?' her
mother said. 'You could pick out some cereal you like.'

Christabel shook her head. 'I'm tired.'

Mommy closed the door and came back into the room to feel Christabel's forehead, then sighed. 'No temperature. But you don't feel good, do you?'

'Not really.'

'We'll be getting out of here soon,' Mommy said. 'One way or the other. I'll bring you home something nice.'

'Call if you're not going to be back by half an hour, Kay,' her father said.

'Half an hour? It'll take me that long just to get there and back.' But for a moment the little angry look she almost always wore these days went away and she looked at Daddy the way she used to. 'If I'm still out, I'll check in an hour from now. I promise.'

When she was gone Daddy went off to the next room to talk to Mister Ramsey. Christabel tried to watch the wallscreen, but nothing was interesting. Even Uncle Jingle seemed stupid and sad, a story about Queen Cloud Cat's new baby, Prince Popo, getting lost at the circus. Even the best joke in the whole thing, when Uncle Jingle got his foot caught by an elephant and it started swinging him around and around and around in a big circle, only made her smile.

Feeling bored, but also like she was going to cry, she opened the connecting door and went into the next room. Her daddy was talking to Mister Ramsey, both of them looking at Mister Ramsey's pad, so that they didn't even see her. She walked down the hall to the bedroom where Mister Sellars and Cho-Cho were lying side by side on one of the beds, still quiet, still not moving. She had gone to look at them a lot of times, always hoping that she would see Mister Sellars' eyes open so she could run to her parents and Mister Ramsey and tell them he was awake. They would be very proud that she had noticed, and Mister Sellars would sit up and call her 'Little Christabel,' and thank her for watching over him. Maybe Cho-Cho would wake up, too, and would be nicer to her.

But Mister Sellars' eyes weren't open, and she couldn't even see his chest moving. She touched his hand. It felt warm. Didn't that mean someone wasn't dead? Or were you supposed to touch their neck? People were always doing it on the net, but she couldn't quite remember how.

Cho-Cho looked very small. His eyes were closed, too, but his mouth was open and a little spit was on the pillow. Christabel thought that was pretty yick, but decided it wasn't his fault.

She leaned in close. 'Wake up, Mister Sellars,' she whispered, loud enough for him to hear if he was listening, but not loud enough for her daddy to hear in the other room. 'You can wake up now.'

But he didn't wake up. He looked bad, like something that had been run over and was lying by the side of the road. She felt like crying again.

Uncle Jingle didn't get any better. She tried a bunch of other shows – even *Teen Mob*, which her parents didn't like her to watch because they said it was 'vulgar,' which meant bad or scary, she wasn't sure which. Maybe both. Her daddy came back then so she had to change to another show fast.

'Why on earth are you watching lacrosse, Christabel?' he asked her.

She guessed that was the name of the game. The people were swinging sticks at each other. 'I don't know. It's interesting.'

'Well, I'm going to lie down for a few minutes. Your mom should be calling in a quarter of an hour, so if she doesn't call, come wake me, okay?' He pointed at the clock in the corner of the wallscreen. 'When that says 17:50, okay?'

'Okay, Daddy.' She watched him walk into the bedroom, then switched back to *Teen Mob*. The people on the show always seemed to be talking about who was dancing with who – dances she hadn't heard of, like 'Shoeboxing' and 'Doing the Hop.' Someone said 'Klorine will play Bumper Cars with anything in sprays,' and Christabel wasn't sure if they were talking about another dance or real bumper cars, even though there hadn't been any on the show, because someone else said, 'Yeah, and that's why she's always getting hurt,' which sounded more like cars than dancing. She turned off the wall-screen.

It didn't seem fair. Mister Sellars was sick, maybe dying, and they didn't even call a doctor. What if he needed some medicine to get better? Mommy was at the store buying things, but Christabel knew you didn't get real medicine at the grocery store, just fruit-flavored cough medicine and things like that. When you were really sick, like Grandma Sorensen, you had to have medicine from the drugstore, or even go to the hospital.

She wandered around the room, wondering if she could go and talk to Mister Ramsey. Mommy wasn't supposed to call for another ten minutes and Christabel felt like that would be the longest ten minutes ever in the world. And she was hungry, too. And even more bored than sad. She thought she should have gone to the grocery store with her mother.

She was looking in her daddy's coat pocket for the pretzels he had taken away from her that morning because she wasn't supposed to have pretzels for breakfast, when she found the Storybook Sunglasses.

She was surprised a little, because she had thought

Daddy had left them behind back at their house. As she
thought about the day when they had left, she had a
really bad homesickness. She wanted to see the other kids
again – even Ophelia Weiner, who wasn't *always* stuck
up. And sleep in her own room again, with her Zoomer
Zizz poster and her dolls and animals.

She took the sunglasses back to the couch and put
them on, just looking at the black for a moment, because
it was more interesting than anything else in the stupid,
sad hotel. Then she touched them to turn them on, and
although the sunglasses stayed black, Mister Sellars' voice
was in her ear.

At first she thought it was one of his old messages.
But it wasn't.

*'If this is you, little Christabel, tell me our code word.
Do you remember?'*

She had to think for a moment. 'Rumplestiltskin,' she
whispered.

'Good. I want to tell you something . . .'

'Where are you? Are you okay? Did you wake up?'
She was already halfway across the room, heading for the
connecting door to go see him, but when the questions
had stopped jumping out of her mouth he was still talking. He hadn't even heard her.

*'. . . And I can't really explain it to you, but I'm very,
very busy. I know it looks like I'm sick, but I'm not – I
just can't be in my body right now. I hope you're not too
worried.'*

'Are you going to get better?' she asked, but he had
started talking again and she finally understood that it
was only a recording, that he hadn't called her up to tell
her he was awake. He hadn't even called her. It was just
a message.

'I need you to listen very carefully, little Christabel. I

*don't want you to be frightened. I have only a few moments,
then I'm going to be very busy again, so I want to leave
this for you.*

'*I suspect Cho-Cho is in just the same situation that
I'm in – that he looks like he's sick, or sleeping. Don't
worry too much. He's here with me.*'

She wanted to know where 'here' was, but she knew
it wouldn't do any good to ask.

'*I'm leaving this message for two others reasons,*' Mister
Sellars' voice went on. '*One is that no matter what we
say, grown-ups can't always make things come out right.
I hope I will see you again and talk to you, and that we
will be friends for a long time. But if something happens
to me – remember, Christabel, I am very old – I want you
to remember that I think you are the bravest, kindest little
girl I have ever met. And I've been around a long time,
so that is not small praise.*

'*The other thing I want to tell you is that if I manage
to . . . to stay well for a little while longer, and some of
the other things I'm trying to do also work out, I may
need you to help me one more time. I not quite sure I
understand it myself yet, and I don't really have time to
tell you anyway – I'm as busy as the night we burned my
house down and I went into the tunnels, do you remember? – but I want you to listen to me now and think about
what I'm saying.*

'*When you first met Cho-Cho, I know he scared you.
I think you have come to see that he is not as bad as all
that – perhaps you understand that he has had a difficult life and does not trust people, that he is worried that
only bad things will happen to him. His life has made
him different than you, but there is a lot of good inside
him.*

'*I want you to remember that, little Christabel, because*

I may need your help. If I do, I will be asking you to . . . to meet someone. That is the only way I can explain it. And that someone may seem even more different and frightening than Cho-Cho. You will have to be as brave as you have ever been, Christabel. And that is very brave indeed . . .'

CHAPTER 37

The Locked Room

NETFEED/NEWS: Suing Do-Gooder Parents for Doing too Much Good
(visual: Wahlstrom heirs entering Stockholm courthouse)
VO: The four children of the late Gunnar and Ki Wahlstrom, famous
Swedish environmental activists, are suing their parents' estate,
demanding that the Wahlstroms' substantial bequests to environmental
organizations be given to them instead.
(visual: Per Wahlstrom)
WAHLSTROM: 'Everybody thinks what we are doing is so terrible.
But they didn't have to live with parents who paid attention to every-
thing but their own children. Not a one of us cared a fig for whales
or rain forests. What about us? Don't we deserve something for putting
up with absentee parents for all those years? They cared much more
about snails than they did about us.'

PAUL ran to the front of the temple, praying that the Wicked Tribe had exaggerated. As he skidded through the door the heat and light hit him like a small explosion and for a moment he could only stand, blinking against the dazzle.

As his eyes adjusted, he saw it first as a homeless shadow – something black sliding swiftly along the desert sands. Even though he had been prepared, warned by the

children, it was only when he saw it climb one of the
nearby hills in just a few steps, the dust of its seismic
footsteps billowing behind it, that he realized how terrifyingly huge it was.

It paused on the hilltop, a colossus come to life. The
doglike muzzle lifted as it howled and seconds later the
air outside the temple, kilometers away, surged and
snapped. Then it lowered its head and began to run once
more.

Paul stumbled back through the door on legs that felt
like burned matchsticks.

'He's coming! Dread's coming!' He lurched to a halt
just inside the inner chamber. Florimel and T4b and the
others looked up at him, eyes wide and faces slack from
terrors that seemed to have no end. 'They're right – he's
huge!'

Only Martine had not turned. She was facing the pure
white human silhouette that had appeared to them
moments earlier and now hung just above the ground like
something out of a puppet show. 'Tell me,' she asked it,
'can you talk to Sellars?'

'*El Viejo?*' The thing squirmed, making its outlines hard
to distinguish. 'Sometimes. I hear him. But he's all busy
right now. Said I was supposed to stay with you.'

'Then he gave you a death sentence!' Paul heard something close to utter despair in Florimel's cracked voice. A
distant sound like a monstrous drum being pounded –
boom, boom, *boom* – sent faint vibrations through the
massive stones of the temple floor.

'Gonna step on us!' T4b shouted.

'Silence, please.' Martine turned away from them to
face the great black sarcophagus lying at the center of
the chamber. 'Stay together,' she called. 'Someone get the
little monkeys.'

'What are you doing?' asked Nandi Paradivash, even as he summoned the Wicked Tribe down out of the air with urgent gestures. A few of them settled on Paul, clinging to his clothes and hair.

'Just be quiet.' Martine's eyes were closed, her head down. 'We have only moments.'

The floor was shaking in earnest now, as though bombs were being set off deep beneath the temple. Each titan footfall was louder than the last.

'*Hear me!*' Martine called out. 'Set, Other, whatever your name is – do you remember me? We have met before, I think.'

The sarcophagus lay secretive as an unhatched egg. The shuddering made Paul stagger to keep his balance.

'What *is* this psycho place?' demanded the white silhouette fearfully.

Bonita Mae Simpkins was praying. 'Our Father who art in Heaven, hallowed be Thy name . . .'

'Listen! I am Martine Desroubins,' she said to the low black box. 'I taught you the story of the boy in the well. Can you hear me? I am trapped here in this simulation world, and so are many others that you brought into your network. Some of them are children. If you do not help us, we will die.' The moment stretched. They could hear the roar of the approaching monster's breath, hissing like a sandstorm. 'It will not listen to me,' Martine said at last, her voice raw with despair. 'I cannot make it listen.'

The ground shivered so violently that the whole temple seemed to shift around them. Trickles of rock dust filtered down the walls; Bonnie Mae and T4b were knocked off their feet. Then the footsteps stopped. Even the monstrous sound of breathing was stilled.

Paul licked his lips. It was almost impossible to speak. 'Try . . . try again, Martine.'

She squeezed her eyes tightly shut and put her hands to her head. 'Help us, whatever you are – whoever you are. God damn it, I can *feel* you listening to me! I know you are hurting, but these children will be killed! *Help us!*'

Something exploded like a bomb above their heads. There was a second concussive crash, then another and another. Flung onto his back, Paul could only stare upward in horror as huge fingers poked through the rocky walls at the top of the great temple. A moment later, with a sustained smash of sound and a rain of falling stones, the entire roof of the cavernous chamber tore free and rose up into the air. A boulder the size of a small car rolled unsteadily past Paul and crashed into the far wall, but he could not even move. Sunlight blazed in, the limitless desert sky now spread above them once more.

The monstrous jackal-headed figure shifted the roof to one side and dropped it. Stone dust boiled up like a mushroom cloud as the giant leaned into the gaping wound that had been the top of the temple room. It smiled, tongue lolling out from jaws that could gulp a Tyrannosaurus like a boiled chicken.

'I'M NOT VERY HAPPY WITH YOU LOT,' rumbled Anubis. More stone and dust showered from the crumbling walls. 'YOU LEFT BEFORE THE PARTY STARTED – AND THAT'S A BIT RUDE.'

Only Martine was standing, still swaying beside the sarcophagus. Paul crawled toward her, intent on pulling her down before the monster reached in and beheaded her like a dandelion puff.

'*Help us,*' he heard her say again. It was little more than a whisper.

'WELL, WELL. WHAT'S THAT WIGGLING ALONG THE FLOOR?' the thing said gleefully.

The sarcophagus began to come apart. Cracks streamed along its angled edges, red light leaking like blood; a moment later the whole thing shifted inside out, as though it contained not the corpse of a god but some new dimension of space-time, unfolding and expanding like a slow-motion detonation until the utter black and the bright, bright glaring red were all Paul could see.

'It's screaming . . . !' he heard Martine cry, her own voice cracked with agony, but she was fading like a dying signal. 'The children are . . .' Paul's head seemed to be filling with fog – chill, empty, dead.

'WHAT IN THE BLOODY HELL . . . ?' was the last thing he heard – a thunderous bellow from above, but already curiously muffled – then even that stone-shattering noise dwindled away as Paul was swallowed by silence and nothingness.

GROWLING wordlessly, sputtering saliva that fell like rain onto the dusty floor, Dread scrabbled in the debris for long moments, like a child who has discovered nothing in his birthday-present box except tissue paper. They were gone.

The growl rose to a choking snarl of rage. Black spots burst before his eyes like negative stars. He kicked over a temple wall, sent another crashing down with a flailing hand, then bent in the swirling dust and grabbed a stone obelisk. He snapped it loose from its base and hurled it as far as he could. A puff of desert sand marked its distant landing.

When he had smashed the entire temple complex into lumps of crumbling sandstone, he stood in the wreckage. The anger was still there, pressing on the front of his brain until he felt it might catch fire. He threw back his head and howled, but it brought no relief. When the echoes

had died in the distant mountains, the desert was silent
again, still empty but for himself.

He closed his eyes and screamed, '*Anwin!*'

It took several seconds before she responded, and
through each of those seconds a pulse beat in his skull
like a hammerblow. When the window opened, hovering
in midair against the desert sky, her eyes were wide with
shock and surprise. He didn't know if she was seeing his
real self or the mountainous form of Anubis, god of the
dead. At that moment, he didn't care.

'What? What is it?' She was sitting in a chair – the
angle suggested she was seeing him on her pad instead
of the wallscreen. She looked not just startled but guilty
and for a fleeting instant his rage cooled enough to wonder
why that might be. Then he thought of Martine and her
little friends winking out right beneath his fingers and
the choking rage fumed up inside him again.

'I'm on the network,' he gasped, trying to take his fury
enough to communicate, when what he really wanted to
do was tear down the universe and stamp on it. 'A connection has just . . . opened up. I need to follow it – go
through. It's something to do with the operating system.'
The operating system itself had defied him – that was the
most galling part. When he realized what was happening
he had sent a bolt of pain through it that should have
frozen every function. He had half-thought he would
destroy the thing once and for all, but had been too angry
to care. Instead, it had absorbed the punishment and acted
anyway.

It had stolen his prisoners and now it was hiding them
somewhere. It had defied him! And they had defied him,
too. They would all pay.

'I'll . . . I'll see what I can do,' she stammered. 'It may
take a little while.'

'*Now!*' he shrieked. 'Before it closes completely, or disappears, or whatever. Now!'

Her eyes wide with something more animal than mere guilt, more electric than surprise, she bent to her machinery.

'It's still there,' she said. 'You're right. But it's just a back-door in the programming.'

'What the hell does that mean?'

'It's a way in and a way out of the network, except it only seems to open inward. I can't explain because I don't really understand.' Her terror had been subsumed by concentration, although he could see her fingers trembling above the screen. Even in his white-hot rage he could admire her all-deflecting absorption, her total love for what she did.

Kindred souls, in a way, he thought. *But still different enough that my kind of soul has to eat your kind of soul.* He would take care of her when he had finished destroying Martine and the others – had the Sulaweyo bitch been with them? He hadn't had time to notice – and after he had reduced every last bit of volition in the operating system into whimpering imbecility.

'I've hooked it up for you as best I can,' she said at last. 'It's a bit like one of the gateways in other parts of the . . .'

'Go away now,' he said, disconnecting her. He narrowed his focus until he could almost see the dwindling point of transit like a will-o'-the-wisp still floating above the shattered sarcophagus. He could feel his *twist* strong within him, glowing like a hot wire in his forebrain, roused without his intention, as sometimes happened when he was hunting. *Well, I'm hunting now,* he thought. *Too right I am.* They had mocked him, the freaks, and now they thought they were safe. *I'm going to find them all, then I'm going to pull them into pieces, until there's nothing left but screaming.*

He stepped through, a god with a heart of black fire. A mad god.

PAUL could only lie in the dust, struggling to remember where he was, who he was . . . *why* he was.

It had been like traveling through the center of a dying star. Everything had seemed to collapse into infinite density; for a time he could not measure, he had thought he was dead, nothing but particles of consciousness dispersing in the void, moving farther and farther apart like ships lost from their convoy until communication failed and each became a solitary mote.

He was still not entirely certain that he *was* alive.

Paul pushed himself up from the ground, which was as dry and dusty as the courtyards of the Temple of Set. There was one huge improvement over Egypt: the sky was gray, spattered with distant stars, the temperature cool. Paul was at the base of a low hill, in the midst of a plain bumpy with other such hills. The landscape seemed strangely familiar.

Bonita Mae Simpkins sat up beside him, rubbing her head. 'I'm hurting,' she said in a flat voice.

'Me, too. Where are the others? Where are *we*, for that matter?'

'Inside, I think,' said someone else.

Paul turned. Martine was making her way down the steep hillside, half-walking, half-sliding on the loose soil. She was trailed by Nandi, T4b, Florimel, and a boy he didn't recognize – a small, dirty child with raggedly cut black hair. The Wicked Tribe, their color muted in the twilight, circled above them like a swarm of gnats.

'What do you mean?' he asked. 'And who's that little boy?'

'This is Cho-Cho,' Martine announced. 'Sellars' friend. You already met him – he just looked a bit different. We've been having a talk, and now he's going to be traveling with us.'

'Chance not, lady,' the little boy said sullenly. 'You people *loco.*'

Martine and the others reached the bottom just as Paul and Bonnie Mae finally got onto their feet. Paul felt so weary and sore he immediately wanted to lie back down. He had questions, lots of questions, but no strength to ask them.

'As to where we are,' Martine said, 'I think we are inside the operating system.'

'But I thought we'd been inside it all along, more or less.'

'No.' She shook her head. 'We have been inside the Grail network, and the operating system extends throughout that network like invisible nerves. But I think now we are inside the operating system itself, or at least some private preserve of its own, kept safe from all its masters, Jongleur and the Grail Brotherhood, and now Dread.'

'Renie said . . . she was in the heart of the system,' Paul remembered.

'How can you know such a thing?' Nandi said sharply. 'It makes some sense, but it can only be a guess.'

'Because I touched the Other before it brought us through,' she said. 'It did not speak to me in words, but I could still understand much. And because we have been to a place like this before. Twice, although the first version, the Patchwork World, was unfinished. I failed to understand the similarity on the last occasion, but I am now seeing the patterns for a third time.'

found a direction and cocked her head to listen for a moment.

'Run,' she said.

'What are you . . . ?' Florimel began, then the sky split open.

From nowhere, winds howled down on them and the ground trembled. The trembling became general, the air and the earth all vibrating in shuddering synchronization, then something huge appeared on the hilltop they had just deserted, something vague and dark and beast-like. Heat lightning crackled around its misshapen head. The thing was on its knees, howling in rage and what sounded like pain, a barking roar that made Paul's ears throb. More winds came shrieking through the hills flinging horizontal dust, so that he had to cover his eyes with his hands and peer through the cracks in his fingers.

'I told you, run!' Martine screamed. 'It's Dread! He followed us through!'

The vast figure on the hillside writhed in pain; its howl of rage . . . 'Something's fighting him! Paul shouted. 'The system! It's fighting back!'

'The system is going to lose!' Martine grabbed his arm and yanked him forward, leading him a few stumbling steps up the hill. The Wicked Tribe blew past, squealing helplessly on the breast of a gale wind. Paul turned to grab at Bonnie Mae, who had fallen; when he dared a look back he could see the immense, murky figure struggling to rise to its feet, outscreaming the storm winds, the lightning now flashing and snapping around its misshapen head.

Paul turned away from the sight and began to run. Behind him the roar of the beast rose and rose until all the world seemed to vibrate to a single animal cry of rage.

crack it and copy it, then maybe I have a bargaining chip. Something that will help me make a deal to get out of here safely.

Also, I'm tired of being kept in the dark.

When the tea was ready and her hands were steadier she took the cup and returned to the chair and small table she had set up in one corner of the loft. She could hear people laughing on the street below, music blaring from cars. She reflected wistfully on how much nicer it would be if she had been born a sensible young woman, someone who would be out with friends on a Saturday night instead of sitting in a silent loft with black-out curtains on the windows, playing caretaker to a moody, violent bastard like Dread.

She took a sip of tea and stared at her pad screen. Whatever password Dread was using had resisted every attempt. It was infuriating, almost unbelievable. A password? Even the most garbled collection of numbers and letters should eventually roll up as a combination on her random character generator, but for some reason it hadn't happened. And now that she had found a new bit of back-alley crypto gear to sniff out the shape of the password – nine characters – it was even more frustrating that she couldn't solve it.

In fact, it almost seemed impossible. Nine characters! It only took a short time for the gear to go through every possible combination of letters, numerals, and punctuation marks, but again and again it came up with nothing that would open the door to Dread's metaphorical locked room.

Remembering the lab tape and the strange, blurred experiment footage, she had also tried every variant on what she felt sure was his name, John Wulgaru. The gear should have generated the same things randomly as part of its algorithm, but she could not help feeling certain that the things he kept so scrupulously hidden, like his name and background, would have some connection to other things he wanted to keep secret from the world, for instance this bit of mysterious storage. But his name had not provided the key either, and before Dread had so unexpectedly and alarmingly interrupted her she had been inputting names from Aboriginal mythology, even though they too should already have been created by the near-infinite patience of the crypto gear.

Dulcie stared at the pad, then back at Dread's supine form, his dark Buddha face. It didn't make sense. Nine characters, but she had worked on it for hours without result. There was something she was missing – but what?

On a hunch, she went looking in her toolbox for a piece of gear she didn't often use, a strange little tangle of code even more esoteric than the one which had determined how many characters were in the password. A Malaysian hacker with whom she occasionally did business had traded it to her for a set of Asian bank personnel files she had downloaded while assisting a hostile takeover that ultimately failed. The would-be corporate pirates had been jailed in Singapore, and one of them had even been executed. Dulcie had made sure she would never be connected with the incident, but she hadn't been paid either, so she had been happy to unload the files anonymously and get something for them.

The bit of code she had received in return, which her Malaysian friend had called 'Stethoscope,' was not the most broadly employable piece of gear she'd ever owned, but it had its uses. What it did best was to locate extremely small changes in processing speed – things that would never show up at the interface level of the system, but which could be used to discover potential bugs before they became larger problems. Not being in the gear-creation business, Dulcie had never used it for its intended purpose, but she had occasionally found it useful for locating flaws in the security of systems she wished to attack. She hadn't used it for almost a year before the Australia trip but it had proved very handy during Dread's incursion into the Grail system. Now something – hacker's intuition, perhaps – suggested it might serve a purpose again.

Because there has to be something else going on, Dulcie told herself as she put Stethoscope to work.

She started up the random-character generator again so the gear would have something to analyze, then sat back to sip her tea. She had almost forgotten the bolt of fear that had shot through her when Dread had burst shouting onto her screen. Almost.

Three minutes later the character-generation cycle had finished, as unsuccessfully as it had the other two dozen times. She opened the Stethoscope report and felt her heart quicken. There *was* something, or it certainly looked that way: a small hesitation, a minute hitch, as though Dread's system security had paused for a moment. Which, she guessed, meant that the security program had seen part of what it wanted, done a check, not found whatever else it needed to open access, and rebuffed the overture.

Dulcie bit her lip, thinking. It had to be some kind of double password – first X, then Y. But if the generator had given it the nine requisite characters, why hadn't she been given a prompt for the second password? Why hadn't the system stopped and waited? No human being could input fast enough to cough up another password in that microsecond of hesitation, even if it was spoken instead of typed.

Spoken. The back of her neck prickled. She checked

Dread's system and felt a glow of triumph when she discovered, as she had guessed, that the audio input was turned off. That was it. The second password was supposed to be spoken after the first had been typed. The system had heard the first, checked for audio and found it disabled, so it had treated the whole thing as a failed attempt, all of this happening in a flash of time too small to be perceived by human senses.

She turned the audio on, reminding herself to be damn sure to turn it off again when she was finished – otherwise she might as well leave Dread a note saying she had been trying to hack his system – and began to patch together some modifications, hooking the character generator to the Stethoscope gear. When the hesitation came this time, the character generator would stop to be read, which should at least give her the first password.

She took another sip of tea, barely tasting it, then set the generator to work – in her mind's eye it was a roulette wheel, spinning so fast as to be almost invisible. In less than a minute it stopped, the letters 'DREAMTIME' blinking in the log-in box. She recognized the word from her brief survey of Aboriginal mythology and felt a flush of triumph. This time, with the audio enabled, the system had recognized the first password and was waiting for the second.

But it's not going to wait very long, she suddenly realized, and the glow of victory faded. *It's going to give me ten seconds, or twenty at the most, then it's going to shut off unless I say the right word. And the next time, or the time after that, when I don't give the right password, it's going to shut down for good – cut off all access, maybe even set off an alarm. It will certainly leave a damn clear mark that someone tried to get in.*

She could never come up with the second password

off the cuff, could think of nothing to try except 'Wulgaru,' which still seemed too obvious. And she could not generate verbal password at anything like the speed with which she could generate characters directly to the system, not even if she modified the character generator – which would take days anyway, maybe weeks of work in an area she knew almost nothing about.

Ten seconds gone. 'DREAMTIME' still blinked on her screen, mocking her, but any moment now the window would close. She had worked so hard to solve the first part of the puzzle, but even though she had done it, she was stuck, fooled, foiled.

'Son of a *bitch!*' she said feelingly.

At the last word, the screen went blank. A moment later, 'ACCESS GRANTED' flashed up and the door of Dread's hidden room opened.

The fifty-six files were ordered by date, the first over five years old and simply labeled 'Nuba 1.' She opened it and discovered it was sight-and-sound, but only 2D, not full wraparound. In many ways the quality was even worse than the lab experiment files. The whole thing had been shot by a single very primitive camera fixed in one place, like surveillance footage.

At first it was hard to make sense of it. The picture was extremely dark. She only realized after watching for half a minute that the concrete pillars in the foreground were some kind of outdoor structure, the support for a freeway ramp, perhaps, and the dark background near the top was actually night sky.

Movement near the base of one of the pillars, hidden in shadow despite a pool of light from what she guessed was a sodium lamp on the freeway above, proved eventually to be two human figures, although the human part

was only an educated guess until at least a minute of
the footage had passed. At first she thought the dark,
indistinct shapes against one of the farther pillars were
making love – first a hand, then a leg extended out into
the light splashing down beside them. Then, with an
indrawn breath of horror, she became sure that the larger
one was strangling the former. But even that seemed not
to be true, since after a moment the larger figure stood
and the smaller was revealed to be still moving, slumped
against the pillar but holding out its hands as though
imploring the large one not to leave. The only sound in
the file was the continuous rumble of traffic, muted and
low, as though the camera were closer to the roadway
than the events being viewed.

It was hard to see what happened next and harder still
to understand why anyone should bother to make a record
like this of it. The quality of the image was maddening,
as though someone had found a way to reroute the footage
from a security camera with a bad correction chip. Why?
What did it all mean?

The larger figure leaned over the smaller, exhibiting
something that shimmered palely for just a moment, catching a glint of the overhead light – a bottle? A knife? A
folded piece of paper? The small figure seemed to be arguing or pleading, with much movement of hands, but
Dulcie's bad feelings about the whole thing were eased a
bit by the fact that the smaller one made no attempt to
escape.

The larger shape knelt beside the smaller, holding it so
close that again they appeared to be making love, or at
least preparing to do so. For a long time – it was two
minutes' worth of file but it seemed even longer – the
two shadowy shapes were merged. Every now and then
a hand would emerge again, waving slowly as though to

the distant camera or to a departing train. Once the hand emerged, stretching to what must have been its greatest reach. The spread fingers slowly closed, like a flower shutting for the night, a movement almost beautiful in its simplicity.

At last after many minutes the larger figure rose. The smaller still sat against the pillar, but before Dulcie could see anything more the footage ended.

Dulcie sat staring at her pad with a sour taste in her mouth. It was impossible to tell exactly what had been happening and it might take hours working with her enhancement gear before she'd even be able to guess. But whatever she was going to do, she should do it on her own time, on her own system. It was foolish sitting here with Dread's secrets exposed – better to copy everything, then deal with it on her own terms.

But she could not resist opening a few more files, just to see if everything Dread had stored so carefully was as ambiguous as what she had seen. She selected a few more, turning her attention first to one labeled 'Nuba 8.'

The images in Nuba 8 were much sharper, although they also seemed to have been downloaded from a security camera, this one on the stairwell of what looked like a large office or apartment building, also at night. The scene was lit by floodlights; the figure of a woman, when she emerged from the glass door with her purse under one arm and her keypad in her hand, was quite clear. She was young, perhaps Dulcie's age, dark-haired, slender. She paused on the bottom step and fumbled in her purse, withdrawing a cylinder that looked like some kind of chemical defense weapon, but even as she did so she looked up in startlement. A shadow moved in front of her, swift as a flitting bat; an instant later the stairwell was empty. The image jumped and changed, the footage now coming from a different camera in an underground parking lot, but the woman being shoved toward it by an indistinct figure in dark clothing was recognizably the same, even with her face disfigured by terror.

Disturbed as she was by this brief bit of horror flick – was this Dread's ugly, awful secret, that he collected snuff footage? – Dulcie was even more disgusted by herself than she was sickened by what she was watching.

It figures, she thought. *The first guy I get interested in for months and he's into this kind of horrible shit. Thank God I didn't let him . . .*

The woman was shoved to the ground. There was no sound in this file, but Dulcie didn't need to hear it to know the woman was screaming. Then the man who had thrown her down onto the cement floor looked up to the camera – he had known it was there all along – and smiled as though he were sending a snapshot home to his family.

Dulcie didn't find out until later, but that was just what he was doing.

She gaped in unbelieving horror as John Dread, also known as John Wulgaru and Johnny Dark, elaborately bound the woman's wrists and gagged her with duct tape, then produced an extremely long knife. He arranged everything with care so that the security camera would have the best possible angle. Watching, Dulcie felt as though she were paralyzed and could not turn away, as though she too had been tied down, with nothing left in her control but her staring, horrified eyes.

It was only when a soft, sentimental piano melody began to play, joined after a few bars by strings and an artificial choir, and Dulcie realized it had been added to the footage afterward, that something snapped inside her. She staggered to her feet, whimpering, then fell down twice before she could make it to the bathroom to vomit.

CHAPTER 38

Boy in Darkness

'STEPHEN?' Renie scrambled along the ledge, searching desperately for some way to crawl down to the boy, but the path ended within a few meters, rejoining the wall of the pit like heatfused glass. 'Stephen! It's me, Renie!'

His head tilted up slowly, his shadowed eyes catching a glint of slow fire from the stars high above, but he gave no other sign of recognizing her. Could she be wrong? It was dark here in the pit despite the distorted, weirdly bright stars overhead, as dark as late evening, and he was many meters away.

Renie crawled back and forth at the end of the path

like a leopard trapped on a branch. 'Stephen, talk to me. Are you okay?'

He had stopped crying. As the echoes of her call died away she heard him sigh, a trembling exhalation that stabbed at her heart. He was so small! She had forgotten how small he was, how vulnerable to the world and its cruelties.

'Look.' She struggled to keep the fear out of her voice. 'I can't find a way down, but maybe you can find a way up to where I can reach you. Can you look, Stephen? Please?'

He sighed again. His head sagged. 'There's no way up.'

Renie felt something so powerful it was like a hard thump on her chest. It was his voice, unmistakably his. 'Damn it, Stephen Sulaweyo, don't you tell me that without trying.' She heard the anger in her voice, an anger born of exhaustion and terror, and tried to calm herself. 'You don't know how long I've been looking for you, how many places I've been trying to find you. I didn't give up. You can't give up, either.'

'No one was looking for me,' he said dully. 'No one came.'

'That's not true! I tried! I've been trying.' Tears were in her eyes, blurring the already strange scene into complete nonsense. 'Oh, Stephen, I've been missing you so much.'

'You're not my mother.'

Renie froze, leaning out over the long fall down to the river. She wiped the tears from her face. Was his brain damaged? Did he think Mama was still alive? 'No, I'm not. I'm your sister, Renie. You remember me, don't you?'

It took him long moments to answer. 'I remember you. You're not my mother.'

How much did he recall? Perhaps he had invented a

protective fiction about their mother still being alive. Would she frighten him into some kind of catatonia if she disputed it? Could she afford the risk? 'No, I'm not your mother. Mama isn't here, but I am. I've been trying to find you for . . . for a long time. Stephen, we have to get out of here. Is there someplace you can climb up?'

He shook his head. 'No,' he said bitterly. 'No place. I can't climb. I hurt.'

Slow down, she told her rabbiting heart. *Slow down. You can't help him if you get in a panic.* 'What hurts, Stephen? Talk to me.'

'Everything. I want to go home. I want my mother.'

'I'm doing my best . . .'

'*Now!*' he screamed. His arms thrashed – he was hitting himself on the head. 'Now!'

'Stephen, don't!' she shouted. 'It's okay. It's okay. I'm here now. You're not alone any more.'

'Always alone,' he said bitterly. 'Just voices. Tricks. Lies.'

'Jesus Mercy.' Renie felt like her swelling, aching heart would choke her. 'Oh, Stephen. I'm not a trick. It's me, Renie.'

He was silent for a long time, a tiny shape barely distinguishable from the nodules of stone along the bottom of the pit. The river murmured.

'You took me to the ocean,' he said at last, his voice calmer now. 'There were birds. I threw . . . threw something. They grabbed it in the air.' There was a tone almost of wonderment in his voice, as though something had been given back to him.

'Bread. You threw pieces of bread. The seagulls were fighting over it – do you remember? It made you smile.' *Margate*, she remembered. How old had he been? Six? Seven? 'Do you remember that man playing music, with the dog? The dog that danced?'

'Funny.' He said it as though he did not quite feel it. 'Funny little dog. Wearing a dress. You laughed.'

'You laughed too. Oh, Stephen, do you remember the other things? Your room? Our apartment? Papa?' She saw him stiffen and silently cursed herself.

'Shouting. Always shouting. Big. Loud.'

'It's okay, Stephen, he . . .'

'Shouting! Angry!'

Something rippled across the stars above, a lurch of shadow that for a moment turned the great cavern dark and set Renie's heart pounding again. She did not take a breath until she could see Stephen's small, huddled form once more.

'He does shout sometimes,' she said cautiously. 'But he loves you, Stephen.'

'No.'

'He does. And I do. You know that, don't you? How much I love you?' Her voice cracked. It was horrible to be so close and yet be separated. All she wanted to do was grab him and hold him and kiss his face, pull him close and feel the tight curls of his hair, smell the little-boy smell of him. How could a real mother feel more?

The memory of his father seemed to have pushed the child into sullen silence once more.

'Stephen? Talk to me, Stephen.' Only the murmuring river answered. 'Don't do this! We have to find a way out of here. We have to get you out. But I can't do anything unless you talk to me.'

'Can't get out.' The voice sank so low she could hardly hear. 'Tricks. Hurt me.'

'Who hurt you, Stephen?'

'Everyone. No one came.'

'I'm here now. I've been looking for you a long time. Won't you try to find a way to climb up to me?' She crawled back along the path, away from the dead end, looking for a place where it might be possible to get down the steep stone wall. 'Tell me some other things you remember,' she called. 'How about your friends? Do you remember your friends? Eddie and Soki?'

His face tilted up. 'Soki. He . . . he hurt his head.'

She felt a chill race up her spine. Did he mean Soki's seizures, the convulsions Renie had seemed to provoke when she had questioned him? How much did Stephen know about that? Could he have buried memories of the boys' first time in that horrible nightclub, Mister J's? 'Yes, Soki hurt his head,' she said carefully, waiting to see what would come next.

'He was too scared,' Stephen said quietly. 'He . . . pulled away. And he hurt his head.' A strange tone crept in. 'I'm . . . I'm so lonely.'

Renie closed her eyes for a moment, trying to squeeze back tears, but was terrified that Stephen might vanish when she wasn't looking. 'Can't you remember any nice things? You and Eddie and Soki – didn't you use to play soldiers together? And Netsurfer Detectives?'

'Yes . . . used to . . .' Stephen sounded exhausted, as though even their brief conversation had made him dangerously weak. He said something else, an unintelligible mutter, then fell silent. Again panic flared in Renie's midsection.

'I really need you to do something,' she said. 'Okay? Stephen, listen to me. I need you to get up. Just stand up. Can you do that?'

He sat, slumped, his head down on his chest.

'Stephen!' This time, she could not keep the terror out of her voice. 'Stephen, talk to me! Damn it, Stephen, don't you dare stop talking to me.' She raced back down to the lowest point of the path, then leaned out until she could feel her weight tip to the outermost edge of balance. 'Stephen! I'm talking to you. I want you to get up. Do you hear me?' He had not moved for half a minute now. 'Stephen Sulaweyo! You pay attention! I'm getting really angry!'

'*No shouting!*' His sudden cry seemed loud as a thunderstroke. It bounced against the walls of their prison, broke into echoes. '*Shouting . . . shouting . . . shout . . . out . . .*'

Renie was clinging to the ledge. The surprise of his explosive bellow had almost toppled her. 'Stephen, what . . . ?'

'*"That's some vicious-bad wonton!" said Scoop.*'

Renie felt her heart skip, stumble. He was quoting from the Net-surfer Detectives story she had read him in the hospital – but that was not what made it hard for her to breathe.

'*He left his holo-striped pad floating in midair as he turned to his excited friend. "I mean, there must be major trouble – double-sampled!" . . .*'

Darkness hemmed her in, a narrowing circle. She felt dizzy and sick.

Stephen was speaking to her in her own voice.

'What . . . what are you doing . . . ?'

'*That's enough, boy!*' It was Long Joseph's snappish tone now, perfect in every way, as though recorded and played back. '*Had enough of your nonsense. You get it done or I beat the skin from your backside! Damn, if you make me get up again when I'm resting then I will slap your face around the other side of your head . . . !*'

Worst of all, Stephen was laughing with his own voice even as he was speaking with his father's.

'Don't do that!' Renie was shouting too, now. 'Stop it! Just be Stephen!'

'*But why in the name of God would anyone have a security system like that?*' Suddenly, staggeringly, it was Susan Van Bleeck's voice that echoed up from the floor of the pit, waspish and shrewd, but Stephen was still laughing, a cracked hilarity that was almost a sob. '*What on earth could they be protecting?*' Doctor Susan, a person Stephen had never met, from a time after he had been in his coma. Susan Van Bleeck, who was dead. '*Have you got yourself involved with criminals, Irene?*'

And for a moment she felt she could bear no more, that the horror was too great. Then, abruptly, she understood. Her fear became a little less, became a fear only for herself, but what diminished was replaced by a desolation so large as to be almost incomprehensible.

'You're . . . you're not Stephen, are you?' Abruptly, the voices died. 'You never were Stephen.'

The thing that looked like her brother still sat by the river, hunched, shadow-draped.

'What have you done with him?'

It did not reply, but seemed to grow less visible, as though slowly merging with the stone of the great pit. An expectant stillness grew in the air, the crackling tension before a lightning storm. Renie felt her skin tingle and crawl. Suddenly there did not seem to be enough oxygen to fill her lungs.

Anger began to rise again inside her, a bleak fury that this bizarre thing, this conglomeration of code, should pretend to be her brother – the same inhuman thing that had taken him in the first place. She pushed it down and concentrated on breathing. She was in the heart of it, somehow. Everything around her must be part of the Other, part of its mind, its imagination . . .

Its dream . . . ?

She would accomplish nothing if she infuriated it. It

was like a child – like Stephen at his very worst, two years old and full of screaming resentment, almost beyond language and rationality. How had she dealt with him then?

Not very well, she reminded herself. *Patience – I was never as patient as I should have been.*

'What . . . what are you, exactly?' She waited, but the silence remained unbroken. 'Do you . . . do you have a name?'

The thing stirred. The shadows lengthened. Overhead, the stars seemed to grow fainter and more distant, as though the universe had suddenly hastened its expansion.

But it's not the real universe, she told herself. *It's the universe inside . . . inside this thing.* 'Do you have a name?' she asked again.

'*Boy*,' it said, using Stephen's voice again, but with a strange, hitching cadence. '*Lost boy.*'

'Is that . . . is that what you want me to call you?'

'*Boy.*' A trudging aeon seemed to pass. '*Have . . . no name.*'

Something in the way it spoke pierced her own misery, her terror, even her rage at the theft of her brother.

'Jesus Mercy.' Her eyes welled again with tears. 'What have they done to you?'

The thing at the bottom of the pit seemed to become even less visible. The wash of the river was loud now, a continuous rush and mumble; Renie thought she could hear voices twining through it. 'Where are we now?' she asked. 'What are you doing here?'

'*Hiding.*'

'Who are you hiding from?'

It seemed to consider for another long moment. '*The devil*,' it said at last.

For an instant, even though she did not know exactly

what it meant, Renie felt she could feel what it felt – the hopeless, uncomprehending fear, the abused, devastated resignation.

Why me? she wondered. *Why did it let me in? Into . . . whatever this is? Was it because of the way I feel about Stephen?*

And even as she considered, her thoughts a thin membrane of rationality over deepening terror, she understood something about the thing that spoke to her – understood it in a deep, almost instinctual way.

It's dying. Its light, the flame of its existence, was flickering. Not just its words but everything around her, the fading light, the thinning air, proclaimed it. Such weariness could precede nothing but extinction.

It may be using Stephen to speak to me, she thought. *Wearing him like a mask. But not just a mask. The way it reacted when I mentioned Papa, somehow it knows what Stephen knows, and even what I know. Feels what he would feel.*

'I think you can get free.' She did not entirely believe it, but she could not simply wait here for everything to end, abandon herself and her friends and all the children this thing had devoured to the destruction she felt sure would come if the operating system stopped functioning while they were still prisoned inside it. 'I think we can escape. My friends might even be able to help you, if you let us.'

The shadowy shape moved again. '*Angel . . . ?*' it asked plaintively. The voice was less like Stephen's than it had been. '*Never-Sleeps . . . ?*'

'Certainly.' She had no idea what it meant, but she could not let that stop her. She thought of how she had kept the Stone Girl moving even when the child was almost paralyzed with fear. Patience, that was all that worked. Patience and the illusion that a grown-up was in charge. 'If you can come to me . . .'

'*No.*' The word was flat and weary.

'But I think I can help . . .'

'*Noooooo!*' This time the very walls of the pit seemed to draw closer, the shadows grown so deep that for a moment the darkness seemed too great for the space to hold. The echo went on for a hideously long time, blending with the sound of the river as it died away, the river-tongues very clear now, cries of misery and fright and loneliness in a thousand different voices – children's voices.

'I want to help you,' she said loudly, speaking as calmly as she could when what she really wanted was to shriek and then keep on shrieking until the air was gone. Her nerve ends were on fire – for a moment she had felt the grip of that cold fist again, the squeezing heart of nothingness. *Patience, Renie*, she told herself. *For God's sake, don't push too much.* But it was hard to hold back. Time was speeding away from them, the cries of the children desperate, hopeless. Everything was slipping away. 'I want to help you,' she called. 'If you can just come closer . . .'

'*Can't get out!*' the thing shouted. Renie fell to her knees, clapping her hands over her ears, but the excruciating voice was inside her, in her very bones, shaking her to pieces. '*Can't! They hurt! Hurt and hurt!*' The thing was building to a terrified rage, something that would crack the world in half. '*Very angry!*'

The voice – nothing like Stephen's now – thundered in her ears.

'*Angry! Angry! ANGRY!*'

Darkness lashed out at her with an obliterating hand.

J EREMIAH sat staring at the clock on the biggest of the

console screens, wiping the sleep from his eyes. 07:42. Morning. But what morning? What day? It was almost impossible to keep track, here in the pit under the mountain, hundreds of meters from the sun. He had tried, had managed to keep things ordered for weeks just as if he were still above ground, still living a life that made sense, but the events of the last several days had broken down all his careful arrangements.

Sunday morning, he decided at last. *It must be Sunday morning.*

Just a few short months ago he would have been up making breakfast in his clean, well-stocked kitchen. Then he would have washed the car before he and Doctor Van Bleeck went to church. Pointless, perhaps – Susan went out so little that the car seldom needed it – but it was part of the routine. Those days he had sometimes felt he was drowning in routine. Now it seemed like the most beautiful island a drowning man could imagine.

Long Joseph Sulaweyo should have been sitting at the monitors taking his turn on watch. Instead the tall man was sitting on the edge of the walkway, dangling his feet and staring at nothing. He looked lost and miserable, and not just because he had no wine to drink. Jeremiah and Del Ray had finally decided the only sensible thing they could do with the corpse of the mercenary Jeremiah had killed was to put it in one of the unused, unwired V-tanks. They had all done it together after wrapping it in a sheet, but as soon as the lid was bolted down and the seals airtight Joseph had walked away to sulk.

Oddly, for once Jeremiah was sympathetic. Turning the V-tank into what it so strongly resembled, a coffin, could not help but remind Joseph of his daughter Renie lying nearby in another almost identical casket. She and her Bushman friend might still be alive, but at this point the difference between them and the dead mercenary seemed largely academic.

And then there's the three of us, Jeremiah thought glumly. *What's the difference between us and Joseph's daughter, except that it's a bigger coffin?*

The thought abruptly popped like a soap bubble and disappeared as Jeremiah stared at the monitor. 'Joseph, what the hell is this? You're supposed to be watching here, aren't you?'

Long Joseph looked at him, scowled, and turned back to his contemplation of the laboratory floor and the silent pods.

'Del Ray!' Jeremiah shouted. 'Come here! Quickly!'

The younger man, who had been scavenging some breakfast from among the supplies – Jeremiah had been too tired and depressed to cook even one of the rudimentary meals he had been making – hurried up from the floor below.

'What is it?'

'Look!' Jeremiah pointed to the monitor that showed the feed from the front door camera. 'The truck – it's gone!' He turned to Joseph. 'When did this happen?'

'When did what happen?' Joseph levered himself to his feet and walked over, already defensive. 'Why you making such a fuss?'

'Because the damned truck is gone. Gone!' His anger was leavened by an exhilarating, almost dizzying breath of hope. 'The mercenaries' truck is gone!'

'But they're not,' Del Ray said heavily. 'Look.' He pointed to another monitor, the one which displayed the area beside the elevator upstairs where the men had been digging. A cluster of sleeping forms lay beside the hole, which was fenced with chairs turned on their sides.

'Then where's the truck?'

'I don't know.' Del Ray stared at the screen. 'I count three. So one of them took the truck somewhere. Maybe to get supplies.'

'Maybe,' said Joseph, with a certain gloomy satisfaction, 'to get more killers.'

'Goddamn you, Joseph Sulaweyo, you just shut up.' Jeremiah barely resisted the urge to hit him across the face. *What am I turning into?* 'We should have known this hours ago. He probably took off at night. But you weren't doing your job!'

'What job?' Even Joseph did not seem himself, the opportunity for an argument provoking little interest. 'What difference it make? You going to run out and stop him driving away? "Please, Mr Killer, don't go get some more men with guns." So what are you complaining for?'

Jeremiah sat down hard in the chair in front of the monitors. 'Just shut up.'

'You expect me to stay up all night, looking at some little screens,' Joseph suggested, with the reasoned calm of a schizophrenic explaining a worldwide conspiracy, 'then you better learn to talk nice with me.'

It was late morning when the truck reappeared on the front door monitor. Jeremiah called the others over and they watched with sickened fascination as the mercenary swung himself down from the front seat, adjusted a massive sidearm in his shoulder holster, then went around to the back of the big gray offroad vehicle.

'How many you think?' Despite the hundreds of meters of concrete separating them from the scene, Long Joseph was whispering. Jeremiah didn't bother to say anything – he felt like doing it himself.

'Who knows? You could get a dozen men in there.' Del Ray's face was damp with sweat.

The driver swung open the back door and climbed inside. When he had been invisible almost a minute, Joseph said, 'What the hell is he doing back there?'

'Briefing them, maybe.' Jeremiah felt like he was watching footage of some terrible fatal accident on the net, except this accident was happening to him.

The door swung open again.

'Oh, Jesus Mercy,' groaned Long Joseph. 'What are *those?*'

Four of them leaped out in succession, sniffing the ground eagerly. When the driver climbed down they circled him like sharks around a deep-water buoy. Each massive dog had a crest of bristling fur along the top of its spine between the shoulders, adding to the sharkish look.

'Ridgebacks,' Del Ray said. 'The mutant ones – look at how the foreheads stick out. It's illegal to breed them.' He sounded almost offended.

'I don't think that's the kind of thing these men worry about.' Jeremiah could not tear his eyes from the screen. Even in the daylight outside the front gate the creatures' eyes were sunken too deeply to be seen beneath the protruding brows, giving their faces a lost, shadowy look. A memory came to him, bleakly terrifying. 'Hyena,' he said quietly.

'What you talking about?' Long Joseph demanded. 'You heard what he say – they are ridgeback dogs.'

'I was thinking about the little Bushman's story.' The gate was opening. The driver snapped heavy leashes onto the animals' collars and let them draw him through the entrance and into the base. 'About the hyena and his daughter.' Jeremiah felt sick. 'Never mind. Good God, what are we going to do?'

After a moment's heavy silence Del Ray said, 'Well, I've got two bullets. If we position ourselves just right, get the dogs to stand properly, I can shoot through one and get the one behind it, too. Two bullets, four dogs.'

Long Joseph was scowling fiercely, but his eyes were wide, his voice hoarse. 'That is a joke. You are making a joke, right?'

'Of course it's a goddamned joke, you idiot.' Del Ray slumped into the other chair by the console and put his face in his hands. 'Those things were used to hunt lions – and that was before anyone really started messing around with their genes. They'll find us even in the dark and then they'll tear us to pieces.'

Jeremiah was only half-listening. The dogs and the mercenary were making their way across the garage level of the base, but Jeremiah wasn't paying attention to that either. He was watching a small readout at the bottom of one of the console screens.

'Sellars isn't answering,' he said dully. 'No message, nothing.'

'Just what I thought will happen!' Joseph exploded. 'Telling us what to do, telling us, telling us, then when we need him, gone!'

'That smoke idea of his saved our lives,' Del Ray said angrily. 'They would have been down here days ago.'

'Saved us to be eaten by monster dogs!' Joseph declared, but the energy had gone out of him. 'Maybe we should build another fire, see how those dogs like smoke.' He turned to Jeremiah. 'Dogs, they need to breathe too, don't they?'

Jeremiah was watching the monitors. The mercenaries by the elevator had wakened and were huddled with their returned comrade. The dogs were sitting now, a row of muscled, ivory-fanged machines waiting to be turned on and set to work. Jeremiah realized that the mercenaries must have all but finished digging their way through the floor,

and planned on using the mutant dogs as insurance against
another toxic smoke attack or armed resistance.

If those men only knew, he thought. *With what we
have, we couldn't drive away a group of determined schoolchildren.*

'We can't do that trick again without Sellars,' he said
aloud. 'We don't know how to operate the vents. I don't
think we can even access them from down here.' He
frowned, trying to catch an idea that was already threatening to dissolve back into the fear and disorder of his
thoughts. 'And we don't have anything left to burn to
make that kind of smoke . . .'

'So we are just going to wait here?' Joseph, too, was
staring helplessly at the screen. 'Wait for . . . those?'

'No.' Jeremiah stood up and started across the lab, heading for the stairs. 'At least I'm not going to.'

'Where are you going?' shouted Del Ray.

'To find something to make another fire,' he called back.
'We can't smoke them out, but even a dog the size of a
house is afraid of fire.'

'But we used everything!'

'No. There is still more paper. There's a cabinet full of
it where . . . where the mercenary tried to kill Joseph.
And we need to make torches!'

Even as he began to run, he heard Joseph and Del Ray
hurrying after him.

For an instant – and mercifully, only an instant – Renie
felt herself seized again in the implacable grip of the void.
There was no restraint this time, only unthinking rage,
explosive and all-powerful. Then the pit was around her
once more. She was on her hands and knees on the ledge,
retching, bringing up nothing but air. The voices of the
river were rising, a weeping, begging choir.

'He's coming!' The cry was a childish thing of pure
terror that vibrated inside her skull like an alarm bell. A
cascade of images battered her, huge shapes, howling dogs,
a room full of blood and shrieking white shapes. Pain
sizzled through her like electricity. Renie screamed,
writhing, adding her own thin shrieks to the weeping children of the river as the voice in her head shrilled again,
'He's coming here!'

The pit expanded, deeper, darker, the walls retreating
so swiftly they seemed to be collapsing out into empty
space. The river and the tiny shape beside it were retreating too, falling away down an endless tunnel, plummeting into a bottomless well.

'Who?' she gasped. 'Who's coming?'

Faint, vanishingly faint, the voice in her head was only
a whisper now.

'The devil.'

Then the stars fell down from above and Renie was
engulfed by the distorted night sky, which seemed to pour
over her like an upended ocean. She slipped like a trapped
bubble between freezing black nothingness and the white
brilliance of the burning stars all around her. She was
churned and rolled and crushed by monstrous pressures.

I'm drowning, she thought, a bemused spark of
consciousness lost in the silent roaring of the big lights.
Drowning in the universe.

CHAPTER 39

Broken Angel

NETFEED/NEWS: *Window Sues Nanotech Firm Over Honeymoon Holocaust*
(visual: Sabine Wendel at husband's funeral)
VO: Capping a tragedy that has already become fodder for comedians all over the world, Sabine Wendel of Bonn, Germany, has filed suit against the distributors of Masterman, a nanotech-based product advertised to cure erectile dysfunction. Although the manufacturers Borchardt-Schliemer insist their product is to be used only under a doctor's care, many distributors sell the product without prescription, and that is apparently how Jorg Wendel purchased the microscopic Masterman trigger-mites that led to the fatal accident dubbed 'the Sexplosion' by many tabnets . . .'

THEY stumbled down out of the hills and onto the desolate plain, lightning flickering through the sky behind them as they raced toward what looked like an ocean full of stars. A cluster of strange shapes lined its shores, waiting. Night was falling, the constellations overhead dimmer than those swimming in the pit.

It's like the end of H.G. Wells' Time Machine, Paul thought. *The horrible last moments of Earth the time*

*traveler sees – gray skies, gray soil, a dying crab-thing
on an empty beach.*

Bonita Mae Simpkins tripped and fell heavily, unable
to use her crippled hands to stop herself. Paul leaned close
to help her up. The roaring of the thing that had followed
them from Egypt was muffled now by the intervening
hills and the electrical storm still hugged the distant spot
where the monstrous form had appeared, but Paul had no
doubt that Martine was right – no matter how strenuously
the operating system fought back, Dread would be after
them soon. He was hunting them.

Mrs Simpkins was whispering as he dragged her onto
her feet. '. . . He maketh me to lie down in green pastures.
He leadeth me beside the still waters . . .'

*Though I walk through the valley of the shadow of
death*, Paul thought. *I will fear no evil.* But he did fear –
he did. They had been swallowed by a nightmare.

. The others were far ahead now, although Nandi
Paradivash had stopped to wait. Paul put his arm around
Mrs Simpkins and hurried her forward.

'Thank you,' she whispered. 'God bless you.'

Nandi silently pulled the woman's other arm around
his shoulders so he and Paul could keep her upright. The
pool of surging, flaring radiance seemed very close now.
Some of the throng that surrounded it came swarming
toward Martine and the others. For a moment, as his
companions disappeared in the tide of bodies, Paul fought
panic, then he saw that Martine and Florimel and the rest
– that tall one was certainly T4b – were being surrounded
but not openly menaced. In fact, the crowd that enveloped
them acted more like the beggar children he had seen in
Rome and Madrid than like an overt threat.

'Those people are . . . they are . . .' Nandi was watching, too. 'I have no idea what they are!'

Neither did Pual. As they reached the outskirts of the crowd he was astounded by the wild, seemingly pointless diversity of its parts – upright animals and creatures with human faces and the bodies of beasts, as well as others made of things from which no living being could ever be composed. The variety was amazing, but what was most astonishing about them was the apparent whimsy. It was an army of purely make-believe creatures that swarmed out to meet them, a population decanted from children's storybooks.

The nearest, a collection of anthropomorphic bears and goats, fish with legs – even a skinny and fat couple who Paul guessed must be Jack Sprat from the nursery rhyme and his huge wife, but whose silhouettes gave him a moment's nasty turn – now came running toward Paul and his two companions, even the most inhuman faces full of unmistakable fear, the childish voices shrill.

'What is it?' scrawny Jack Sprat cried. 'Who are you? Did the One send you?'

'Who took the stars?' shrieked his wobbling spouse.

'Have you seen the Lady?'

'Why won't she come to the Well? Why won't she tell us what to do?'

Caught up in the swirl of pleading creatures, Paul was rushed along toward the shore of the pulsing sea like a leaf going over the rapids. 'Martine!' he shouted, struggling to hold onto Bonnie Mae and Nandi even as furry fingers and graspingly prehensile wings tugged at him. 'Florimel! Where are you?' Someone yanked at Bonnie Mae so hard that Paul, still trying to keep her upright, lost his grip on her and was pulled off his feet. For a moment he was certain he would be trampled to death.

After all this, I'm killed by cartoons, he thought, choking in the dust. *There's irony in that, isn't there?*

Suddenly people around him began to shout in alarm; the bizarrely diverse collection of legs and feet hemming him in began to back away. Paul struggled to his feet and discovered Nandi and Mrs Simpkins only a few meters away, staring. He turned to see what they were looking at.

It was not the most unusual sight of the day, but it was still a bit of a surprise.

Rolling toward them through the crowd, moving slowly to give the fairy-tale creatures a chance to get out of his way – but helping them along with occasional light flicks of his riding whip – was Azador, smiling hugely. He was perched on the driver's bench of a fantastically colorful coach pulled by two white horses.

'Ionas, my friend!' he shouted, teeth gleaming beneath the luxuriant mustache. 'There you are! Come, you and your other friends – climb up or these idiots will step on your toes.'

Paul could not help staring, and not just at the unexpected rescue. In all the time he had traveled with Azador, even in the toils of the Lotos-dream, the man had never seemed a fraction this cheerful. Paul looked up at the sky, which was almost pitch-black now, the stars dwindled to tiny points. *How could anyone be in a good mood with this going on? Unless he's daft as a brush.*

Still, it was better than being trampled by teddy bears.

Paul clambered onto the side of the wagon and helped Nandi and Mrs Simpkins up onto the step beside him, then Azador clicked his tongue at the horses, cracked his whip, and turned the carriage back toward the flickering sea.

'There are people waiting to see you, my friend!' Azador cried. 'You will be so happy. We will sing and dance and celebrate!'

Not just a little daft, thought Paul as they rolled along beneath the dying sky. *Utterly, utterly mad.*

Azador's tribe of Gypsies had arranged the dozens of wagons they had retained into a semicircle along the shore of the strange crater, walling themselves off from the rest of the refugees and making a little city with wheels, the lacquered coaches shining both from the light of many campfires and the silver-and-blue glimmer of the great pit. Paul was grateful for the respite, however temporary, but he could not help looking back at the hills. Lightning still leaped above the hilltops, swift as swordplay, but the display seemed to have diminished, as if the contest being fought there was coming to an end.

Paul did not feel good about what that ending might be.

He was immediately distracted by people hurrying toward him, calling his name as they forced their way through the crowd of curious Gypsies. If they had not introduced themselves he would never have recognized Sam Fredericks and the Bushman !Xabbu. He might have guessed who the small, almond-eyed man was, given a slightly less confusing situation in which to consider it, but he had all but forgotten Fredericks' confession back in Troy about being a girl.

'It's . . . I'm astonished to see you both,' he said. 'And delighted.' He hesitated. 'Where . . . where is Renie?'

!Xabbu's face fell. He shook his head.

'We don't know,' Sam Fredericks explained. 'We got separated.'

!Xabbu seemed about to say something else, but Martine Desroubins, who it seemed had also survived the attentions of the fairy-tale crowd, was standing beside one of the wagons clapping her hands loudly. 'Florimel,

Paul, Javier – all of you,' she called. 'We must talk. Now.'
Suddenly distracted, she turned slowly toward the spot
where Paul stood. Unlike him, she seemed to have no
trouble seeing past the unfamiliar faces and forms.
'Fredericks . . . !Xabbu?' She climbed down and fought
her way through the crowd of refugees until she could
put her arms around both of them.

Within moments Florimel had joined the group, laughing, seizing !Xabbu so hard Paul worried she would crack
the little man's ribs. The Bushman seemed oddly reserved,
but Paul thought it might be his own unfamiliarity with
!Xabbu's human face. Even T4b allowed himself to be
drawn into reunion embraces and the babble of half-artic-
ulated questions and answers.

'Enough,' Martine said abruptly, although she still held
Sam Fredericks' hand firmly in her own. 'We do not come
at a happy time, no matter how it eases our hearts to see
you. Dread is behind us.'

Fredericks screwed up her face in puzzlement. 'Dread?'

'You have seen him only once, I think, on the top of
the black mountain when he was the size of a god – an
evil, angry god.'

'Scanny! Yeah, I remember!'

'Well, that is the Dread who is coming – no, who is
already here. The operating system fights him. There.'

Only a few last flickers of lightning now blinked in
the distant hills, gleaming scratches across the night sky,
dim as firefly trails.

Paul and the others settled down around one of the campfires, huddled beneath the night. The Well pulsed beside
them, a pit full of earthbound polar lights that turned
even the few familiar faces grotesque.

Martine tried to keep some kind of order in the

proceedings but curiosity and urgency made too volatile a mix: few questions were entirely answered before another volley had been launched. Nandi and Mrs Simpkins and the little boy named Cho-Cho could only watch in amazement as the words fountained out of the others. Paul found himself almost as impressed by hearing the adventures of his own group recounted – it made a formidably strange tale – as he was by hearing what had happened to !Xabbu and Sam. But one element of their story struck him more powerfully than any other, until at last he had to interrupt Sam Fredericks in mid-flow.

'I'm sorry, but . . .' His head was throbbing, his entire body so weak with stress and fatigue he could barely sit up, but he could not let this go. 'I almost can't believe I'm hearing this. You traveled with Jongleur? With Felix Jongleur, the bastard who made this whole thing?' *The bastard who stole my life away*, he wanted to shout, but he could see by Sam's expression that she was not happy about it either.

'We . . . we thought we had to do it, even if it was majorly impacted.' She looked to !Xabbu for support, but the little man had risen a few minutes earlier and walked off to do something, so she had to turn back to Paul. 'Renie said . . . she said we might need him. Need what he knew.'

Paul fought down his anger. 'I'm amazed.' He swallowed. 'That you didn't just push him off a cliff, I mean. Or skull him with a rock.' Paul sat up straight and tried to calm himself – there was much crucial information to share. 'Where did he go, finally? What happened to him?'

Sam took a moment to answer. 'What . . . what do you mean?'

'When did you part ways with him – or did something eat him, I hope?'

Her age was truly apparent for the first time. She was suddenly a nervous teenager faced with an angry adult. 'But . . . he's here.' She looked at Paul and his companions as though they should know this already. 'Right over there,' she said, pointing.

Paul felt a kind of tightness around his temples, a band of pain. Only a few meters away Azador and a bald man in dark clothes stood watching them, Azador talking animatedly, his companion silent, eyes half-shut. 'That's . . . that's him?' Paul's chest felt like someone was sitting on it. '*That's* Felix Jongleur?'

'Yes, but . . .' Before Fredericks could get out another word, Paul was on his feet and running.

Azador looked up. 'Ionas, my friend!' he said, opening his arms, but Paul was already past him. He threw his full weight onto the bald man and dragged him to the ground. Jongleur had seen him coming, but Paul's anger was such that for the first moments there was no stopping him. He seized Jongleur's head in both hands and smashed it back against the ground, then climbed up onto him and began swinging at his face. The man fought back, throwing up his arms to block Paul's wild blows, writhing in an effort to unseat him. Paul had the satisfaction of feeling some of his punches land on Jongleur's hard head, but it seemed to be happening at a distance greater than the length of his arms. Voices were shouting in his head and his exploding rage seemed to have knocked time slightly out of joint.

Stole my life! Tried to kill me!

He swung again and again.

Bastard! Murderer!

He was grunting some of the words out loud. There were other voices too – Paul could dimly hear people calling his name, pulling at his arms – but Jongleur stayed coldly silent. The older man had weathered the flurry of blows; now his hand snaked up and clutched Paul's chin, forcing his head backward until his vertebrae threatened to separate.

'Kill you!' Paul shouted, but Jongleur was slipping away from him as though Paul were on the bank of a river and his enemy on a boat in the current. Dimly, through the haze of anger and adrenaline, he realized that he was wrapped now in several arms and was being lifted from the ground and off his quarry. At least two of the men holding him were Gypsies, muscular men who smelled of woodsmoke.

'Let me go!' he bellowed, but it was no use. He was held too firmly.

'Just stop,' Florimel said in his ear. 'You will do no good, Paul.'

Azador had pulled Jongleur back out of Paul's reach. 'Why are you doing this?' the Gypsy demanded. 'You are my good friend, Ionas. But this man, too, he is my friend. Why should friends fight?'

Paul heard Azador's words but could make no sense of them. He stared at Jongleur with helpless hatred. The older man returned his look, his face a mask of placid contempt, a trickle of blood from his nose the only sign of what had happened.

'Martine?' someone asked. Paul realized for the first time that the blind woman was part of the crowd pinioning him. 'Martine?'

'What is it, Sam?'

'I can't find him, Martine.' Sam Fredericks looked pale even in the odd, metallic light from the great pit. 'He's gone somewhere – gone!'

'Who are you talking about?' Martine asked. Some of the people holding Paul began to loosen their grips, although the two Gypsy men still held him securely. 'Who's gone?'

'!Xabbu,' Sam said miserably. 'He got up from the campfire but he never came back. And now I can't find him anywhere.'

WATCHING the others split up into pairs to search for !Xabbu should have made Sam feel better, but it didn't. Something in the suddenness of his disappearance made her certain that what had happened to him was much worse than simply wandering off or getting lost.

!Xabbu doesn't get lost, she told herself and was miserable again.

She knew she couldn't just stand and wait for the others to come back, but she had no idea of where else to look. She had already been all along the fringes of the Gypsy camp, calling the small man's name into the press of refugees beyond the circled wagons, and that was probably what Martine and the rest were doing right now, too, but she could think of no better way to spend her time. Anything was better than just sitting here, cooling her heels at the end of the world.

When she turned she almost tripped over the Stone Girl.

'Your name is Sam, right?' the little girl asked.

Much as she wanted to right now, she couldn't just ignore the child. 'Yes, I'm Sam.'

'Your friend wanted me to tell you something.'

'My friend?' She squatted beside her, suddenly intent. 'What friend?'

'The man with curly hair and no shirt.' The Stone Girl looked worried. 'Isn't he your friend?'

'What did he say? Tell me!'

'I have to remember.' The little girl wrinkled her loamy

forehead. The poked holes that were her eyes squinted in concentration. 'He said . . . he said . . .'

'Come on!'

The Stone Girl shot her an offended look. 'I'm *thinking!* He said . . . that you were with friends now so he could leave and he'd know you were all right.' The frown turned into a pleased smile. 'That's what he said! I remembered!'

'Leave to do what? Where did he go?' Sam grabbed the little girl's arm. 'Did he tell you? Did you see which direction he went?'

She shook her head. 'No. He pointed to where you were and told me to hurry up and go.' The Stone Girl turned and indicated a spot far down the shoreline of the great pit. 'He was over there.'

And then Sam remembered. 'Oh, *fenfen!* He thinks Renie's down there – he said he was going to go find her!' The Stone Girl looked at her curiously but Sam had no more time to talk. She sprinted across the long, gradual slope of the Gypsy camp, away from the wall of wagons and the campfires, down toward the uneven shore.

I should get the others, she thought. *Paul and Martine – I couldn't stop him by myself* . . . But already she saw a slender figure silhouetted at the pulsing edge of the Well, familiar despite the unsteadiness of the outline. She knew she would never reach the others and get back in time.

'!Xabbu!' she shouted. 'Wait!'

If he heard her he gave no sign. He stood a moment longer, poised at the edge of the glimmering ocean of blue and pale yellow and misty silver light, then took a few steps forward and jumped into the pit. It was not a dive but a suicide's staggering leap, the first graceless thing she had ever seen !Xabbu do.

'No! Noooo!'

Within seconds she had reached the spot where he had stood. There was no sign of him, only the strange ferment of light in motion.

He told me he was so scared of the water. But he jumped into . . . this . . . She went cold from her feet to her head. *He must have been so afraid . . . !*

She knew that if she considered for another second her better sense would take charge – she would turn and walk back to the Gypsy camp with a hole right through the middle of herself. *Lost Orlando*, she thought wildly. *And Renie. Not !Xabbu, too!* She tottered on the edge for an instant, then flung herself after him.

It was not water that rose up to claim her but something far more strange – a vibrant, fizzing, electrical wash that seemed to flow right through her. Her eyes popped open as if yanked by strings but there was no depth or breadth, nothing at all to see but an impossible simultaneity of blackness and blinding light.

How can I find him . . . ? she wondered, but only for a second. The scintillant ocean contracted around her, squeezing her up and out like a bar of wet soap from a fist. *Orlando said . . . it didn't want me . . .* Then she was lying stunned and twitching on the bank, unable to do anything but stare at the Well as lazy bubbles of light formed and burst beneath the surface. She watched them with a strange detachment, wondering if this was what it felt like to die. Voices were coming closer, Florimel's and Martine's and others, all shouting something that must be her name, but she could feel nothing except the uncommon sensation of having been tasted and then spat out again.

PAUL knelt down beside Florimel. 'Is Fredericks all right? What's wrong with her?'

Despite all that had happened, Florimel had not lost her distinctive bedside manner. 'How in the devil's name should I know? She is breathing. She is semiconscious. God alone knows what caused this.'

'Jumped,' T4b said. 'Just jumped in, all *sayee lo*. Saw it, me.'

'But why?' Paul asked.

Martine was squinting out toward the pulsating lights with the expression of someone leaning into a terrible windstorm. 'She was searching for !Xabbu . . .'

'Jesus, does that mean . . . ?' Paul's stomach lurched – to find them both after all this time, then to lose one of them so quickly, maybe both of them . . .

Martine abruptly swung around, putting her back to the unstable sea. Her face was haggard. 'We have a greater problem now,' she said.

'What?' Paul stared at the Well, but saw nothing different. He turned until he was facing the same direction as Martine, looking out across the plain. 'Oh. Oh, damn.'

It was only a distant speck and should have been invisible in the deep twilight, but the man-shape had a disturbing negative radiance of its own, as if it were not entirely part of the world through which it passed.

'He's not a giant anymore,' Paul said. That startling change should have given him hope, but there was something so horridly fascinating about the thing named Dread walking toward them across the dead gray land, stride after measured stride, that it seemed to make no difference. Fear washed through Paul, a sick, paralyzing terror as powerful as the aura around the Twins, but somehow even worse: where those two were cruel and destructive, this lightless specter seemed a thing of pure, focused evil.

'He has shed what was unnecessary,' Martine said. 'He has been burned and battered until he has hardened like a black diamond. But it is him.' Her voice was listless with horror. 'The Other could not keep him out.'

Their companions had seen it, too, and stood staring in drop-jawed surprise, mesmerized by the advancing figure. Voices cried out all around them, wails of despair that proved the refugees could sense what was coming. As the invisible cloud of fear swept over them the fairy-tale folk at the outer edge of the encampment turned and fled from the distant stranger, shoving their way toward the Well. Their flight set off a mass panic; hundreds more joined them, shrieking down the slope toward the edge of the great pit like a herd of deer running before a wild-fire. Paul and the others had to make a wall around Sam Fredericks, linking arms to keep themselves from being swept over the edge by the crush of maddened refugees.

'Where is Nandi?' Martine shouted. 'And the Simpkins woman and the little boy?'

'Somewhere in the crowd!' Paul held on to T4b's arm for dear life as a trio of weeping goats backed into them. Even when Paul smacked at the nearest with his fist, the goats paid no attention, bleating, '*Troll, troll, troll!*' in tones of helpless horror as they stared out at the approaching shadow.

I just hope he kills that bastard Jongleur first, was Paul's only coherent thought.

The crush of terrified creatures was shoving hard now, pushing them back despite their best efforts, until Paul could see the Well just behind them. Some of the other refugees were forced screaming over the edge of the pit; they disappeared into the silent wash of light and did not come up. T4b's elbow was locked in Paul's; the youth was murmuring what seemed to be a prayer. Florimel screamed at them all to move closer together to keep Fredericks from being stepped on. Paul felt another arm slip through his and a body push close against him. It was Martine. Something of a child's unalloyed fright was in her face. Paul hooked her arm more tightly.

Dread had reached the edge of the encampment. He stopped on ground that had been torn and churned by fleeing refugees and lifted his hands as though he woudl take the entire huge throng in his arms. His face was a thing of shadows, the human features plain but somehow inconstant, the eyes blank white crescents. Only the teeth were clear – a huge, avid grin. The shape radiated such triumphant, heedless, blood-smeared power that the nearest refugees, untouched, fell down shrieking and writhing.

Martine was not even looking. She had shoved her face against Paul's arm. 'This must be . . . the terror the Other feels,' she moaned.

Paul thought it seemed pointless to analyze anything. It was the end, after all.

'*Oh, you're all so clever.*' Dread's laughing voice was in every ear. '*But I know you're here somewhere.*' The dead white eyes swept across the whimpering throng.

He's looking for us. Paul's heart was skipping, staggering. *He knows we're here, but he's not sure where.*

The shadow-man and everything around him suddenly grew dim.

And I'm going blind like Martine . . .

Blind?

The air was growing thick, foggy. Paul tried to blink it away but the fog was not in him but before him, a sticky density forming above the shimmering pit and around them all. At first he thought it was something of Dread's doing, the metaphorical air being sucked from an entire world, but the dark figure seemed disconcerted, lifting his hands in front of his face, fingers twitching as if to tear away a curtain.

'*But I* crushed *you!*' Dread snarled. '*You can't stop me now!*'

There *was* a curtain, Paul saw in astonishment – a wall of rapidly thickening mist forming between Dread and his victims. The gossamerthin, translucent barrier rapidly grew thicker, a hemispherical wall of cloud coagulating all over the Well, transparent enough that the carbon-black figure of Dread could still be seen through it, thick enough to reflect some of the dull shimmer from the pit. The shadow-man lunged forward, scrabbling at the solidifying fog, and the cloud strands stretched to what seemed the breaking point . . . but they did not break.

Dread's scream of frustration rattled in Paul's skull, made him crouch shivering on the ground. All around him refugees were running mad, knocking each other down, trying to escape something that was in their heads. The cry rose until Paul thought his brains would boil, until he felt sure there must be blood running from his nose and ears, then it trailed off like storm winds passing.

For a moment there was silence. Inside the dome of cloud it was the silence not just of pain but of astonishment, of a last-minute reprieve beyond all hope.

Martine's voice was faint with agony and shock. 'I . . . I can feel such . . . oh, my God! The Other has put up a last-ditch defense, but it has . . . little strength left.'

The figure behind the wall of cloud had grown very still.

'*This can't last.*' The icy words pricked at Paul's ears. He could hear children sobbing all around him, unable to escape the voice of the bogeyman. '*It's only a matter of time.*'

The dark figure spread his hands again, pressed them against the barrier. The nearest refugees wept and tried to force themselves farther away, but Dread was making no attempt to break through this time. '*I know you're there – all of you.*' He paused. '*You, Martine. We've shared something, sweetness. You know what I mean.*'

She had fallen on her face. Paul put his hand on her back, felt the convulsive shudders.

'*It's going to be very bad if you make me wait,*' Dread murmured. '*Pain. And not just for you, little Martine. Screaming – oh, there will plenty of screaming. Why don't you just come to me now and save the innocent ones?*'

'No,' she said, but it was a hollow whisper that even Paul could barely hear.

'*Come out,*' said the dark shape. '*I'll show you those secret places again. Those places in you that you didn't think anyone could find. You know it's going to happen. Why wait? The fear will only get worse.*' The voice deepened, turned horribly seductive. '*Just come to me now, sweet Martine. I'll release you. You won't have to be afraid any more.*'

To Paul's horror she began to squirm toward the barrier on her stomach. He grabbed her waist to hold her back, but whatever pulled at her was strong, horribly strong. Flailing, sobbing, she fought him until he had to wrap both his arms and legs around her. T4b shoved his way through the crush of bodies and grabbed her shoulders and at last Martine stopped struggling. She wept harder now, her body shivering convulsively. Paul put his face against her cheek and held her tightly, murmured meaningless assurances in her ear.

'*Well,*' said Dread. '*Then we'll have to play it a different way.*' He moved sideways along the barrier, swift as a spider on a web, then stopped. '*Just because I'm on the outside doesn't mean I can't touch you at all. Doesn't mean I can't make it . . . interesting. This little wall the operating system threw together may keep me out for a few minutes – but it also means you're locked in with some old friends of yours.'* He pressed his fingers against the barrier, tenting the net of mists inward. *'They're everywhere, aren't they? The whole network is rotten with the things. Harmless enough, this lot.'* He chuckled. *'Until I wake them up.'*

In the puzzled hush that followed, Paul pulled Martine up into a sitting position but kept her wrapped firmly in his arms. A thin scream floated up from farther down the shoreline, then another and another until a chorus of shrieking filled the air. That part of the crowd began to shove outward in all directions, a frenzied rush like rats off a burning ship. Something was growing at the center of the disturbance, a bizarre and complicated shape swelling up and out as if unfolding out of the dry dust.

No, Paul saw, and his guts twisted. *Two shapes.* He could hear Dread laughing inside his head, T4b cursing helplessly behind him. Martine hung in his arms like an empty sack.

Jack Sprat and his wife blossomed outward in a sprawling explosion of flesh until they towered over the other refugees. Sprat's bony fingers twisted and stretched like fast-growing twigs. His legs lengthened, his toes humped and clawed, even his face stretched and distorted until he was as tall and gnarl-limbed as an old tree. He reached out his skeletal claws and snatched up a squealing shape covered in fur and wearing a pink ribbon, then tore it to pieces, raining bits down on the refugees struggling to escape.

Sprat's wife was expanding like a fairground balloon, her arms and legs remaining doll-tiny while the great gross body spread and crushed the helpless creatures packed in around her. The head began to disappear in the humped inflation of shoulders, until all that could be seen was a huge hippopotamus mouth full of crooked teeth, gaping on the lumpy bosom. She leaned, folding like a great pudding, then came back up with a dozen more fairy-tale figures in her maw. She swallowed slowly. Her neck distended, small shapes still moving inside it.

'Where is the princess?' Jack Sprat had no eyes now, only a crease across the narrowest part of his head.

'The princess!' his wife belched out. A small, sodden creature tried to escape her mouth but was sucked back in and vigorously chewed. 'Our pretty, tasty princess!'

They began to wade through the crowd, Jack Sprat tangle-fingered and five meters tall, his wife humping along beside him like a massive jellyfish, killing as they went. The refugees, trapped between the wall of fog and the pit and unable to scatter, trampled each other in mindless terror. Bodies and pieces of bodies flew through the air. The screams rose to an unbroken chorus of wailing.

Forced backward by the crush Paul could only clutch Martine and struggle to keep her sagging form upright. Light strobed and flashed from the pit behind them as though some kind of terrible conflagration was building, but Paul was hemmed so tightly now he could not look around, could barely breathe.

'Give us the princess!' Jack Sprat had something in his twiggy fingers that might once have been a living being. He was using it as a club. 'Bring her to us!'

They were only meters away from Paul and the others now. The light leaped and burned on them, making them even more grotesque.

'*Stop!*' The voice was thin, but it cut through the chaos like a razor. '*Stop!*' it cried again. '*You are hurting them – killing them!*'

The huge, deformed shapes paused, eyeless and rapt, facing out toward the pit.

'Our princess.' Jack Sprat's wife almost groaned it, a ravening hunger finally introduced to the ultimate feast. 'Princess!'

The shrieks of the wounded and dying still drifted to the skies, but even the refugees had slowed and stopped as if under compulsion, turning from their murderers to stare out at the pit.

She hung above the agitated sea of light with her arms spread wide, hung on some invisible cross of misery, flickering in and out of existence like an image on ancient celluloid film. It had been so long since he had seen her that Paul had forgotten the beauty of her presence, the great light that could shine through even this corrupted incarnation.

'Ava.' His voice was choked, no more than a murmur. 'Avialle.'

She did not see him, or did not care that he was there. In the sudden stillness she flickered and grew even more insubstantial, her ghostly face full of pain and horror.

'*Let . . . them be.* She was beginning to smear like dirt on a rain-spattered window. '*You . . . are . . . hurting us . . .*'

'We eat you, Princess!' bellowed Jack Sprat's monstrous wife. 'Come home!' The Twins began to shuffle toward the edge of the pit, sweeping bodies from their path or crushing them into the dead gray earth.

She moaned, a sound that swept across the shore, then brought her arms together in front of her face in helpless resignation.

'Avialle! *Avialle!*'

It was not Paul's voice this time. A man was shoving his way through the press of refugees toward the hovering apparition. It was Felix Jongleur.

'Avialle!' the bald man screamed, and this time Paul

could hear the rage beneath the desperation. Jongleur's face, pale and full of crazed intensity, seemed to grow so bright that Paul could see nothing else, not even the shimmering angel shape that had haunted him for so long. 'Come to me! Avialle!'

His words echoed in Paul's head, growing instead of diminishing, until all he could hear was her name sounding over and over, tumbling through his brain like a bullet, smashing his mind into fragments so that the blackness beneath came up and swallowed him whole.

'**O**H HO!' *someone said.*
Ava shrieked and threw herself backward out of Paul's arms. He turned to see the grinning, misshapen face of Mudd peering through the trees.

'Naughty, naughty,' said the fat man. 'What have we here?' But despite the mockery, Mudd seemed a little uncertain, as though he too had been caught by surprise.

'Leave us alone!' cried Ava.

'Oh, I don't think so.' Mudd shook his large head. 'I think Mr Jonas has overstepped his privileges.' He gave Paul a look of gleeful malice. 'I think some punishment is in order.' Now he turned his leer on Ava. 'For both of you, perhaps.'

'No!' Ava leaped to her feet but stumbled, tangled in her long nightgown. Mudd stretched out a heavy hand to seize her, or perhaps just to steady her. Seeing that great paw reach toward her, Paul snatched up the first heavy thing he could find, a rock the size of a fist, and flung it into Mudd's face. The big man bellowed in pain and fell backward. When his hands came away from his forehead they were covered in blood.

'I'll kill you, you little shit,' he rasped. 'I'll pull your bones out!' Paul yanked Ava to her feet and ran. Behind

*him, Mudd was talking to someone, talking to the air.
'Attention! Security to Conservatory Level. Now!'*

*Branches slapped Paul's face as he pushed Ava before
him, running blindly through the tangle of trees. Where
could they go? This was not a true forest, it was a park
on top of a skyscraper. Security would be coming up in
the elevators. There was no way down.*

*He slowed to a walk. 'This is pointless, Ava. We can't
escape, and you might be hurt.'* And they're going to hurt
me no matter what, *he thought but did not say.* 'Is there
some way you can contact your father directly?'

*'I don't know! I only speak to him when he . . . calls
me.' Her eyes were wide, feverish, as though she were the
one who had drunk too much. Paul felt himself growing
cold and distant, everything happening at a great distance.
'I can't let them hurt you,' she said, tears welling up. 'I
love you, Paul.'*

*'It was all foolish,' he said. 'We should never have let
it happen. I'll give up.'*

'No!'

*'Yes.' They had him and they could do what they wanted
to him. He had a sudden thought, an unlikely glimmer of
hope. 'Can you talk to your helper – the one you call the
ghost? Can you contact him now?' It was perhaps the only
insurance he could provide against simply being swatted and
disposed of like a troublesome insect. If the intruder could
enter the communication lines, perhaps it could contact his
friend Niles Peneddyn. At the very least he could construct
a message for Niles, tell him something of what was happening. It would make it much harder for Jongleur's men to
make him disappear – perhaps he could even use it as a
bargaining chip. 'Can you contact him?' he asked Ava again.*

*'I . . . I don't know.' She stopped and closed her eyes.
'Help me! My friend! I need you now!'*

In the silence that followed Paul could hear the sounds of pursuit – not just Mudd's voice now but several others too, shouting back and forth through the trees – along with the alarmed shrieks and whistles of birds. The first security team must have arrived, he decided, and were even now fanning out through the artificial forest behind him.

'He's . . . he's not answering me,' Ava said miserably. 'Sometimes he doesn't come right away . . .'

Now I know why they wanted to hire someone like me, who didn't have one of those implanted jacks, Paul thought bitterly. I thought it was because it looked too modern, but they just didn't want anyone who could communicate freely with the outside world.

'Where is he?' The sharp, high-pitched voice echoing through the trees was Finney's. Jongleur's dogs were all out now, in full cry. Paul considered sitting down and waiting for the inevitable.

'Help me!' Ava cried to the air.

'Forget it.' He felt little more than anger now – anger at himself, at this foolish, deluded girl, even at Niles and his upper-class contacts. 'It's over.'

'No.' Ava pulled her arm from beneath his hand and dashed away into the trees. 'We'll go beyond the forest – there has to be a way out!'

'There is no way out!' Paul shouted, but she was already crashing through the thick vegetation. His legs as heavy as in a nightmare, he stumbled after her.

All around him the hunters were closing in, narrowing the angle, hemming their escape. Ava was plunging ahead as though the forest would truly come to an end, as though they might burst from the trees to see hills and meadows and freedom stretching before them.

'Come back!' he shouted, but she was not listening.

Her billowing nightgown snagged on trailing branches, but she still moved much more swiftly than he could, an elusive phantom. He struggled after her, trying to remember what was ahead of them. Another elevator? No, not on this side. But wasn't there a fire escape? Hadn't Mudd or Finney said something about that the first day?

Yes. 'You'd better hope you never have to use it, Jonas,' Mudd had told him, grinning. 'Because the window's sealed. Mr Jongleur doesn't like the government telling him how to run his own house.'

Sealed. But sealed how? Smacked and poked by branches, stumbling over the bumpy, artificial forest floor, he could scarcely think. Ava was a dozen meters ahead now, calling for him to hurry. He also heard the pursuers clearly, clipped voices passing information to each other, efficient as robots.

'Don't be stupid, Jonas!' Finney sounded only steps behind. 'Stop now before you get hurt.'

The hell with you, mate, he thought.

'Paul, I can see the end of the trees . . . !' Her voice was full of hope. A moment later she cried out, an animal howl of pain and misery. Paul's heart lurched. He crashed through the last of the branches to find Ava frozen and stupefied at the end of the natural earth, staring at an empty white wall. Seamless, without openings or features of any kind, the wall stretched straight up for ten meters before curving up to roof the entire floor and display the artificial sky. The space between forest and wall also bent away to either side, hidden within a few paces by the tangling trees.

'It's . . . it's . . .' Ava was stunned.

'I know.' Paul's heart was beating so fast he was dizzy. The bland curve of the outside wall gave no hint of what to do. Their pursuers were crashing toward them, only

*moments away. He had to pick a direction. He had no
idea where to find the fire escape. Opposite the elevator
– but where would that be? They had run through the
forest in a zigzag track and might be a hundred meters
from it or more.*

Left, *he decided, his thoughts flickering like agitated
fish.* Coin-flip. Fifty percent, and it probably won't matter
anyway. *He grabbed Ava – she seemed light as a small
child, almost hollow-boned – and pulled her along the
curve of the wall.*

*Some of the tree branches snaked out beyond the bounds
of the artificial forest. They scraped at Paul's face as he
tugged the girl forward, forcing him to put a hand in
front of his eyes. He could barely see, and did not notice
at first when the branches stopped touching him.
Something cool and smooth pressed against his other side,
something more slippery than the wall.*

*Paul stopped and uncovered his eyes. The sweep of the
entire island stretched below him on one side, although
the view was strangely distorted, the colors blurry and
prismatic. The window ran from a few feet above his head
down to knee level, perhaps five by five meters. Beneath
their feet lay only smooth parquet – the artificial woodland curved away from the wall and its inset window
here, broadening the walkway; forming a space between
glass and forest wide enough to park a couple of trucks.*

*Mudd was shouting in the trees, bellowing like a bull
as he hurried closer. It sounded like he was knocking the
trunks down with his bare hands.*

'He's here!' *Ava said in a strangled voice.*

'I know.' *Paul wished he had another rock – it would
be a great pleasure to try to smash the fat man's ugly
teeth. Or put out one of Finney's little snake eyes.*

'No, I mean my friend – he's here!'

Paul looked around, half expecting to see a spectral figure, but of course there was nothing. His eye flicked down to the weird view through the window, the buildings far below bent crazily up toward him as though reflected in the bowl of a spoon. The glass is energized somehow, *he thought.* Some kind of electrical charge running through it – probably one of those hyperglass things, meant to keep anyone from firing a missile through it and blowing up Jongleur and this madhouse of his . . .

'Tell him to turn off the window,' Paul said. 'The power, the electrical power – it has to be turned off or we can't reach the fire escape stairs.'

'I don't understand,' said Ava, but apparently something did. The window abruptly changed, the view leaping out clear and unwarped, the sky gray, the air full of drizzle, the buildings beneath them now as sharp-edged as some kind of expressionist sculpture.

The wall began to flicker around the window. For a split-instant Paul thought, wildly, that it too might dissolve, everything illusion, leaving them standing naked to the elements. Instead the angry, hawklike face of Felix Jongleur appeared ten meters high along the wall, first twinned on either side of the window, then multiplying outward all the way along the curve.

'WHO SET OFF THE ALARMS?' *It was the face of an angry god, a voice like a controlled explosion. Paul shrank back, fighting not to drop reflexively to his knees.* 'AVIALLE? WHAT ARE YOU DOING?'

'Father!' she cried. 'They are trying to kill us!'

A group of security guards dove out of the bushes onto the walkway and rolled to a crouch, leveling an ugly variety of guns that Paul had not dreamed existed outside of net dramas. The effect of frightening, fatal efficiency was undercut slightly as the guards saw the massive face of Felix Jongleur – one of them even let out a cry of star-tled surprise. All stared with their mouths open. Finney strode out of the trees just a few meters from Paul, his expensive suit snagged in several places, covered with leaves and dirt.

'WHAT IS HAPPENING HERE?' *Jongleur roared.*

Ava wept, sagging against Paul. 'I love him!'

'It's under control, sir,' *declared Finney, but he looked nervous. Twenty meters down the curve of the wall, on the other side of Paul and Ava, Mudd smashed out of the forest like an angry rhinocerous, followed by a half-dozen more guards.*

'There you are, you little Limey bastard,' *grunted Mudd. He had tried to wipe the blood from his face but had only managed to smear it into a warpaint mask.* 'Somebody shoot him.'

'Shut up,' *Finney snapped.*

'No!' *Ava swung herself in front of Paul.* 'Don't hurt him – Father, don't let them hurt him!'

The nightmare had swung far out of control. Whatever the girl believed, Paul did not think for a second that Jongleur would spare him – they just didn't want it to happen in front of her. He took a quick glance over his shoulder, then flung himself backward and turned to scramble toward the lever at the edge of the window frame. For a moment he had it in his hand, could even look down and see the black metal rail of the fire escape outside the window, then one of the guards' guns went off in a series of explosive pops. The bullets stitched past him, blowing fist-size pieces of construction foam out of the wall and spiderwebbing the heavy glass above his head.

'ARE YOU MAD?' *Jongleur bellowed, his face replicated all along the wall like the masks of an enraged god.*

*Colorful birds, startled by the gunshots, had abandoned
the trees and now filled the air, squawking and fluttering.* 'YOU COULD HAVE HIT MY DAUGHTER!'

'No more firing, you idiots!' shrilled Finney.

*Paul lay on the ground below the sill, strengthless,
almost numb. He had lost. The window was still closed.
A huge hand tightened on his collar and yanked him to
his feet.*

*'You little shit.' Mudd leaned close. 'You can't even
imagine the trouble you're in.'*

*Finney had grabbed Ava and was pulling her back
toward the forest. 'Father!' she cried, struggling hard.
'Father, do something!'*

*'SEDATE HER,' Jongleur said. 'THIS WAS A MISTAKE
AND SOMEONE WILL PAY.'*

Finney stopped. 'But, sir . . . !'

*'AND PUT THE TUTOR SOMEWHERE, TOO. WE'LL
DEAL WITH HIM LATER.'*

*Mudd shoved Paul toward the guards. One of them
stepped forward as if to catch him, but instead raised a
fist and smashed it into the side of Paul's head. He
dropped, his skull bursting with fireworks and flapping
birds.*

*'No!' shrieked Ava, then she had pulled free of Finney
and was running toward Paul.*

'STOP HER, DAMN IT!' thundered Jongleur.

*Finney snatched at her nightgown, which held for a
heartbeat, then tore. One of the other guards threw himself
at her feet, and tripped her, sending her staggering backward toward the window. Some of the birds that had
settled on the sill fluttered up in panic; she snatched at
them wildly, hopelessly, as she struck the glass.*

*The bullet-pocked window splintered in a thousand
jagged cracks and for a single quantum instant she hung*

there, suspended against emptiness as if frozen in flight, surrounded with radiating lines like a stained glass angel. Then the window collapsed outward in a sparkle of broken crystal and she was gone into the gray air.

A dull clang as she hit the rail of the fire escape. An endless second before Paul heard her scream begin, then an eternity before it whistled away and faded. It might have been a wordless yowl of terror. It might have been his name.

Everything was silent then – Finney, Mudd, the guards, even the giant, astonished masks of Felix Jongleur, a curving hall of petrified images. Suddenly a cloud of colors, of sparks, of something Paul could not at first understand, swirled out of the trees and darted out through the shattered window.

The birds.

Wings beating, whirring, a murmur of questioning calls finally rising to a many-voiced screech of triumph, the birds escaped their long prisoning, sprang out into the rain-misted sky and then scattered, bright feathers shimmering like the shards of a broken rainbow.

In the stillness that followed, a single gleam of blue-green drifted down through the space between the trees and the shockingly empty window, riding the air in broad loops until it settled at last on the floor between Paul's hands.

CHAPTER 40

The Third Head of Cerberus

*NETFEED/CHILDREN'S INTERACTIVES: HN, Hr. 2.0 (Eu, NAm) –
'Pippa's Potato Patch'
(visual: Pippa and Purdy looking for Cracky Hoe)
VO: Pippa wants to plant flowers, but Rascal Rabbit has other ideas
and hides her tools. Also featuring a short episode of Magic Counting
Box and when the wind blows the cradle will rock when the bough
breaks the cradle will fall and down will come baby down will come
baby down will come baby down will come baby . . .*

'JUST stay put,' Catur Ramsey told her. 'I don't think there will be enough smoke to make it all the way up to your storeroom, but you might keep a wet cloth handy to put over your mouth, just in case.'

'By these calculations, it'll fill up the basement pretty good,' Beezle said. 'More than fill it up.'

'Sellars wanted enough that no one could get down there right away and find out how much of a fire there was – especially since there won't really be a fire.'

Olga looked at the vents high on the wall of the storeroom. 'You are sure I won't be suffocated up here? Or in one of the elevators?'

'Trust me, lady,' Beezle grunted.

'Trust you?' Olga was tired and nervy. She had been up and down so many elevators in the last forty-eight hours that she was starting to look for numbers every time she walked through a door. The idea of being caught inside one with smoke billowing in through the air ducts was terrifying. 'Why should I trust you? Where did you come from – and who are you, anyway?'

'He's a friend,' Ramsey said hurriedly. 'He's . . .'

'I'm an agent, lady. Didn't you know?'

'What?' Olga tried to sort it out. 'A theatrical agent? A secret agent? What kind of agent?'

His noise of disgust was as vivid as a cartoon fart. 'A software agent – I'm gear. An Infosect virtual assistant, manufactured by Funsmart Entertainment. Jeez, Ramsey, you didn't tell her?'

'I . . . I didn't . . . we were in such a hurry . . .'

'Hold on, please. You . . . you have turned all this over to an imaginary person?' Something tickled her memory. 'An Infosect? That is a child's toy! We sold it on Uncle Jingle. Years ago!'

'Hey, lady, I'm not the newest gear out of the box but I'm still the best.'

'Mr Ramsey, I cannot believe you would do this to me.' It felt like betrayal. For the first time in many days of stress and danger tears sprang to her eyes. 'My safety – a toy!'

'Ms Pirofsky . . . Olga.' Ramsey sounded like a boy caught stealing, almost stammering with contrition. 'I'm sorry, really sorry. You're right, I should have told you. I *would* have told you, but things have been happening so fast. Beezle isn't just kiddie gear – he's been upgraded a lot. And I've been working with him for a while now . . .'

'He's a child's plaything, Mr Ramsey! We sold the damn things on my show. My God, he came in a box with a picture on it of a little boy saying "Wow! My new best friend!" If you had a client on trial for his life would you get a Judge Jingle Courtroom Playset to do your research? I do not think so. But you're asking me to put *my* life in the hands of this . . . jack-in-the-box?'

'Yeah, it's nice to meet you, too, lady.'

'Look, it's not like that, Olga, honestly.' Ramsey sounded panicked now and it undercut a little of her anger. He was trying so hard. Foolish, maybe, but a nice young man, that was what he was, still at an age where he thought life could be argued into doing the right things.

But life doesn't argue back, she thought. *It just rolls over you like the tide, over and over, taking away a little bit each time.*

'Who am I fooling?' she said aloud, and almost laughed. 'I came here because there were voices in my head, ghost-children talking to me. I'm sneaking around like a spy. We are going to burn down the richest man in the world's building – if only by accident. Why shouldn't a child's toy run the operation? Let's do it.'

'I told you, Olga, I'm sorry.' Ramsey had misread the swing in her mood, had taken the doomed amusement for pure sarcasm. 'I can help you, but only with Beezle to . . .'

'I just said we'll go on, Mr Ramsey. Why not?' She did laugh now. It almost felt good. 'Better to risk breaking your neck than never to look up at the sky, as my father used to say.'

There was a moment of silence. 'You know, lady,' Beezle said admiringly, 'you got a certain style.'

'And that is all I have, at this point. But thank you.'

'So . . . so we're okay to go ahead?' Ramsey still

sounded as though he were a few streets behind. 'Set off the . . . the smoke device?'

'The bomb. Yes. Why not?'

'We'll be careful, Olga. We've got the ventilation diagrams – we'll keep a close eye on everything . . .'

'Please, Mr Ramsey. Catur. Just do it before I lose my nerve.'

'Right. Right.' He took a breath. 'Make it work, Beezle.'

'Okay, here goes. Three, two, one – *bingo!*' He fell silent as though watching something. Olga could not help wondering what a software agent saw – shapes? Colors? Or did it just read raw data, letting it flow past and through like a sea anemone sifting the ocean currents? 'Yep. We have ignition!' the agent said cheerfully.

Olga closed her eyes and waited.

'Shouldn't I have been in one of the elevators already?' she asked as the door closed behind her. 'To save time?'

'We got smoke on three levels now, boss,' Beezle reported. 'Moving up fast, too. Since they were marked on the diagrams, I disabled a couple of the seal-off valves.'

'Too risky,' Ramsey said, answering Olga's question. 'That's also why we're starting you from close to the top. We don't want anyone paying any more attention than necessary, so we're waiting until we know the guards have already started the fire procedures. Any alarms yet, Beezle?'

'Yeah, a bunch. Sellars prepared some virals to confuse things, though – change the outgoing codes on the alarms and send 'em to the wrong authority or make 'em give the wrong location information. They haven't even gotten word to their own firefighters down on the military base yet. It'll take at least a quarter of an hour before anyone off the island figures out what's happening, maybe longer.'

A blatting noise began to pulse through the walls, a sequenced honking of robotic terror as though the building itself had smelled the smoke and taken fright.

'Here we go,' Ramsey said. 'Key the floor number, Olga, and let's see if the changes to your badge work.'

She did, then clapped her hands over her ears. The alarm had jumped a notch in volume. 'I can hardly hear you!' She imagined the sound shaking the walls as smoke billowed through the lower levels, the weekend employees running in terror, the few remaining cleaners, janitors – poor, slow Jerome . . . ! 'What's going to happen to the people down there?' she asked in sudden dismay. 'You said it wasn't toxic, but how will they breathe if it fills up?'

'It won't fill up,' said Beezle in his cabdriver's growl. 'I'm venting – makes it look better, anyway. Security is getting calls from all over the island.'

'You're moving,' Ramsey said with relief as the elevator rose.

'I know.'

'Sorry, of course. I'm just watching you here. Up, up, up.' He sounded almost giddy. Olga felt as though she had left her stomach behind.

'Are there still guards in security?'

'Doesn't look like it,' Ramsey told her. 'They're probably already trying to get people out of the building.'

'Lots of activity downstairs, no activity on the security floor monitors,' Beezle said. 'But when the door opens, don't go in right away, got me?'

I take orders from a toy, she thought. 'Got you.'

She waited in the elevator at the forty-fifth floor, feeling Ramsey and Beezle at her shoulders like invisible angels. The alarm was still blaring mindlessly. *They don't need to get the alarm calls on the mainland*, she thought. *They will be able to hear this all over Louisiana.*

'Still no movement,' said Beezle. The door hissed open.

There was no one in the tastefully-lit reception area but the screen-top desk had been hit by the automatic override and instead of woodland scenes it now displayed a map of the floor with the exits blinking red. The alarm was more distant here, as though the upper part of the building was built of some heavier, more soundproof material, but a secondary alarm whispered through the air, an irritatingly calm female voice instructing whoever was listening to 'proceed directly to your designated escape location.'

Some of us do not have designated escape locations, dear. The door at the back read her modified badge and pinged open. Even with Beezle's report, she still went through it like a trainer entering the cage of a particularly unpredictable animal.

The guard area was empty, the neon data-hieroglyphs on the plexiglass walls like cave paintings of a vanished race. The calm female voice kept urging her over and over to go to her escape location but Olga was finding it easier to disregard now.

She presented her badge to the reader set into the thick plastic. The door opened immediately, as though pleased by the visit. She quickly crossed the glassed-in area to the black fibramic shaft she had seen the first time. Sure enough, there was an elevator door set into it and a black reader plate beside the door. She took a breath and held up her badge. An instant later the door slid open, revealing an interior covered in some expensive kind of leather.

'It worked!' Ramsey sounded like he had been holding his breath.

'How can you tell? It didn't make any noise.'

'Your ring. I've got the camera ring sending because we're going to need it. I saw the doors open.'

But the doors in question had already closed again, this time with her inside, and the elevator was moving effortlessly upward. Three seconds, five, ten . . .

'It's only supposed to be one floor up,' she said. 'Why is it taking so long?'

'Thick floors,' said Beezle. 'Just thought you might like to know, they're evacuating a buncha people out the front door now. Still no fire engines, nothing like that. I think Sellars may have had something else set up, too, to make sure everyone cleared out.'

'What do you mean?' Ramsey asked.

'I'll tell you when I know.'

The elevator stopped. The door opened into an airlock. Briefly, recorded messages about security and clean room procedures battled with the escape announcement, then gave up as the airlock door reader responded to her badge and the inner door hissed aside. Olga stepped out.

Her first thought was that she was watching a netflick, some science-fiction epic in full wraparound. It was harder work to convince herself it was real. The entire floor was one open room with only a few structural pillars to break what seemed like tens of thousands of square meters of floor space, and most of that space seemed to be covered with machines. The machine barn had no windows, only a continuous expanse of curving white wallscreen, currently painted with the escape route maps that had preempted the building's regular programming. The room was massive and, but for the quiet robot voice, as silent as a museum after closing. It was unreal.

But it *was* real.

'. . . *Directly to your designated escape location. Repeat, this is not a drill* . . .'

'Oh, God,' Olga said. 'It's huge.'

'Lift the ring,' Ramsey told her, his voice sharp with anxiety. 'We can't see anything but the floor.'

She made a fist and held out her hand, pointing it aimlessly down the rows of stacked, silent machines. She had thought the collection of machinery on the lower floor was imposing, but it was like comparing a toaster to the engine room of an ocean liner. 'What . . . what do you want me to do?'

'I don't know. Beezle?'

'I ain't so good at reading visuals,' the agent rasped. 'Lotta translation effects, back and forth. But I'll give it my best shot. Just start walking. Give me a view side to side, will ya?'

Olga made her way up and down the rows as though led by her own outstretched hand, past what had to be billions of credits worth of gleaming machinery. First five, then ten minutes ticked away as she trudged along, her arm aching and stiffening. She could not help wondering if the firefighters were in the building now, and how long it would be until the security guards were back at their screens. Twice she stepped over things that suggested employees had been here recently but had vacated in a hurry – an expensive-looking, very small pad abandoned in the middle of a row, still fiberlinked to a port, and twenty meters away the shattered remains of a coffee cup and a puddle of gently steaming liquid.

She had just found a third artifact, a shapeless piece of synthetic fabric that she guessed might be some sort of clean-room headwear, when Beezle said, 'I think that's it, boss.'

She looked up to where her fist was pointing and saw a tower of components little different from many others, except that there seemed to be a greater-than-average number of huge fiberlink bundles snaking down into the floor conduits. 'This?'

'It's worth a try,' Ramsey said. 'Will anything bad happen if you're wrong, Beezle?'

'The building might blow up. Just kidding.'

'Funny,' Olga said dully. The weirdness was beginning to get to her, not to mention the idiot voice still droning out the escape location warning.

'Sorry. Orlando likes stuff like that.' This non-explanation issued, Beezle began to give her instructions on where to place Sellars' mystery box. As before, she minutely changed its position several times until her instructor – Sellars the first time, Beezle this time, and if Beezle was gear, then what the hell was Sellars? she wondered – seemed satisfied; the box clicked, vibrated briefly, and adhered.

After a few long moments of silence Olga began to feel panicky. 'Are you still there? Catur?'

'I'm here, Olga. Beezle, is it the right machine? What do you have?'

The silence again, but longer this time, much longer. Ramsey called Beezle several times in mounting anxiety. Only when almost a minute had passed did Beezle come back.

'Whoa,' he said, his voice more than a little distorted. 'I wish I could swear, but like the lady pointed out, I'm a children's toy. This is un-friggin-believable.'

'What?' Ramsey demanded.

'This place is carrying the dataflow of a major city, I kid you not.'

'Which city?'

'Not a real city,' Beezle grunted. 'Don't be literal. I'm just talking about how much throughput there is. Amazin'! There's a whole light farm on the roof of the building –

a laser array like you've never seen, pumping data up, readin' it comin' back. Weird, too – some kind of boosted cesium lasers according to the schematics. You want me to do some research?'

'Not now,' said Ramsey.

'What is it?' Olga wondered. 'All this data – is it this Grail network I have been told about?'

'Don't ask me.' Beezle sounded almost surly. 'I'm not up to this. You just can't understand the quantity of data ridin' through here.'

'But didn't this Sellars make any provision . . . ?'

'Look, lady, I don't know what Sellars had planned. He sure didn't leave any notes about what he was going to do with this if he tapped into it. And even with all the upgrades and extra processing power Orlando rigged up for me, I can't begin to make sense of it – you might as well try to run all the UN Telecomm data through an abacus!'

For a toy, Olga thought, he sounded quite convincingly overwhelmed. And he had an admirable way with metaphor as well. 'So what do we do? Mr Ramsey?'

'I . . . I guess we've done all we can,' the lawyer said. 'Until we can contact Sellars again. Beezle, are you sure you can't, I don't know, hook up enough processing power to make some sense of it – any sense at all?'

The agent's snort was answer enough.

'Right,' said Ramsey. 'Then I suppose we really have done all we can. Good work, Olga. We'll just hope it all comes to something – that Sellars gets back to us and that he had some idea of what kind of processing this would take.' Catur Ramsey did not sound entirely convinced. 'So we might as well get you out . . .'

Olga looked around the massive room. 'Not yet.'

It took Ramsey a moment to hear what she'd said.

'Olga, that place is going to be swarming with firefighters and cops soon, not to mention J Corporation security. Get going!'

'I'm not ready to go.' A calm she had not felt in hours, perhaps days, descended on her. 'I didn't come here in the first place just to put in some vampire-tap or whatever your Sellars called it. I came here because the voices told me to come. I want to know why.'

'What are you talking about?' He had gone from irritated to panicky and was swiftly moving on toward something even more extreme. 'What the hell are you talking about, Olga?'

The alarms were still going, both the distant wordless pulse and the empty female voice. 'I'm going up to the top,' she said. 'Where this terrible man lives. Uncle Jingle's house, I guess you could call it. Uncle Jingle's lair.'

'Wow.' Beezle manufactured a whistle. 'You really are crazy, lady.'

'Actually, it's probably true,' she said, perfectly happy now to be talking to a piece of code. 'I spent a long time in a sanitarium when I was younger. And recently – well, we all know what it means when you hear voices in your head.'

'You're hearing voices in your head right now,' Beezle pointed out.

'Yes, you are right. I'm getting used to hearing them.' She turned and began to walk across the impossibly wide room toward the elevator.

'Olga, don't!' Ramsey was desperate now. 'We have to get you out of there!'

'And I am getting quite good at ignoring them, too,' she added.

IT was a little easier now, but not much. He didn't feel

like he was dying quite so quickly.

For the hundredth time, thousandth time, he had no idea, Sellars repulsed an attack and still managed to hold open his connection into the Grail network. With all the experience he had gained from this horribly protracted encounter, as well as from his earlier incursions, he was still amazed by how the thing reacted.

He floated, bodiless, in a darkness that seemed alive with malice. Now that he had survived the original blaze of resistance the secondary attacks continued to come in waves, the timing random. Sometimes he had almost a whole minute to consider and plan, then the assaults would resume, storm following storm, and his every thought was once more focused on survival.

He had learned from his previous connections that there was more to the system's defenses than merely the technical countermeasures, however sophisticated. It could manufacture all the traces, blowbacks, and disconnection attempts that he expected from top-of-the-line gear, attacking and defending and then counterattacking so quickly that it was like fighting war in space at light speed. But there was a purely physical side, too, perhaps the same thing responsible for the Tandagore illness: during each attack he could feel the security system reaching not just into his system but into *him* as well, trying somehow to manipulate his autonomic responses, to slow or speed his heart rate and respiration, to reprogram his neural circuitry.

But Sellars was not an unsuspecting child stumbling into the jaws of a hidden monster. He had been studying the system a long time and had modified his own internal structures until most of the grosser attempts to manipulate him physically could be routed down harmless pathways, their force wasted on buffers almost as a lightning rod drew away the deadly force of electricity. Even so, as long as he was trapped online, struggling with the network's defenses, he had to remain completely disconnected from his physical self so his old, worn body would not pull itself to pieces in seizure. The security system might not be able to kill him yet, but neither could he disengage from it without losing contact with Cho-Cho, and he could not let one more innocent disappear into the darkness at the heart of the system – he had too many such sins on his conscience already. And although the operating system was clearly weakening, probably failing, he could not hope for that kind of release, since its ultimate collapse would probably also doom those who remained online. Sellars and the system remained locked together, neither able to let go, failing enemies trapped in a death dance.

The latest wave of attacks stuttered to a halt. He hung in the blackness, trying desperately to think of a way to break the impasse. If he could only understand what he was fighting . . . ! Dark and angry as the thing seemed to him (he had struggled against such anthropomorphic characterizations for a long time, until he realized that by doing so he was underestimating the subtle unpredictability of his enemy), there was far more to the operating system than that.

The most immediate part of it, the security programming which was trying its best to kill him, was only one head of this particular Cerberus. Another head watched him and considered him while the battle raged – even seemed, in some paradoxical way he could only feel but not define or explain, to wish him no ill. He could not help wondering whether the security system responses were something over which the operating system as a whole had almost no control, just as an ordinary human could not consciously control his own immune system. This second head, he guessed, was the part of the operating system which had achieved something like true intelligence. It must also be the part that let children like Cho-Cho into the network unharmed – for how could a mere security system know whether a human user was a child or not? – and which avidly followed his volunteers through the network.

There was a third head, too, Sellars sensed, a silent one that was turned away from him, but what it thought about – what it dreamed? – he could only guess. In some ways the third head frightened him most of all.

A new wave of defensive blitz began with no warning, a violent allout burst that swept him up like a hurricane and for long minutes pushed all considerations but mere survival from his mind. Again he felt it trying to reach into his very mind. The attempt failed, but Sellars knew that if the stalemate went on long enough this damnably bizarre and clever machine was going to find a way to subvert his defenses. He began to wonder just how long he had been here in this no-place, wrestling with Cerberus.

After he had weathered the storm and had snatched a few seconds of much-needed rest, he accessed his own system long enough to discover that almost a full day had passed since he and Cho-Cho had first contacted the network. An entire day spent fighting for his life! No wonder he was exhausted.

In the real world it was already Sunday afternoon. He was running out of time. If the system killed him, or if he killed the system, he would fail. He needed to find some other way. His only hope was that Olga Pirofsky and Catur Ramsey could place the data tap and that the Grail network information would somehow provide answers.

No, he told himself, *not just answers, but a solution to this impossible problem.*

But he could not even afford to check in on their progress until he had weathered at least one more round of attacks by the security systems. He had stolen moments in the earliest lulls to make a few emergency calls and to find and activate vital defensive gear, but he needed far more time than that to deal with the data tap.

The next assault came quickly enough that he was glad he'd waited. It was as violent as any of the others, but even as he fought off the multipronged attempt he thought he sensed something different this time, a slight lessening of what he could only think of as the resolve behind the attack. When he had suppressed all but the most basic of the security routines, the ones that could be safely left to his own built-in defenses, he prepared to turn his attention to what was happening in the J Corporation tower. But just before he shifted to his own system and his connections to the real world he stopped and hesitated in the darkness, troubled by something he could not name.

That hesitation saved him. The attack that followed mere instants after the defeat of the last was the most savage so far, not just a redoubled assault on his connection but a concentrated, many-fronted attempt to break down his resistance to the more subtle and more devastating physical feedback. For long moments he could actually feel the thing reaching for him down the connection, a monster just on the other side of a splintering, flimsy door, and Sellars knew real terror. The blackness of no-visual became another kind of blackness, an endless void in which he was lost, isolated, pursued.

He held on somehow, and when the probing, searching thing touched him at last he was even able to send a jolt of resistance back down the partially opened channel. He

was certain that he felt the nonphysical presence flail in
pain and surprise, then the entire attack was suddenly withdrawn.

The beast had limped back to its cave.

His heart and respiration spiraling up to near-critical
levels, his mind reeling at what he'd just felt, but desperate to take advantage of whatever time he had bought
himself, Sellars left his automatic systems in place to warn
him of a new attack, then slid back into his own system.

His beloved, carefully-nurtured interface, the Poetry
Garden in which he had spent so much time, tending,
planting, pruning, simply *being*, was all but gone now. It
had been replaced by a mutant tangle of activity, a sprawling chaos of data root and virtual vine in which only he
could have discerned even a trace of order.

He took a moment to issue some crucial messages and
set a few small works in motion, then turned his attention to the slender black sapling that had sprung up at
the edge of the sea of vegetation. Three vines had crept
up its dark verticality, climbing to a surprising height. He
knew what two of the creepers represented, but about the
third, its livid, unnatural color and texture more like plastic piping than vegetable, he was less sure. Sorensen? It
seemed odd the Garden would represent him in such a
way. With foreboding, Sellars made a connection.

Like a phantom he listened in on Catur Ramsey's
conversation with Olga and although he shared Ramsey's
worry about her, and even debated cutting in to echo
Ramsey's warning, the larger and more pressing issue of
the data tap would not allow it. He did permit himself a
brief moment of amusement at the identity of the third
vine. Orlando Gardiner's software agent! What an idea –
but a good one. Working together, somehow they had

found a way to install the data tap. Sellars found himself admiring and liking Ramsey even more, and Olga, too. He wished he had more time to get to know them both. It was unfortunate that he was probably not going to be alive long enough to do so.

He quickly turned his attention to the data tap, accessing Beezle's captured visuals to carefully examine the linked array of knowledge engines that seemed to power the Grail network. Even without knowing their exact nature and location he had suspected what the software agent had now confirmed and had arranged with the people of TreeHouse, among other resources, to make sure he had the processing power to cope with the influx of data. He checked and then rechecked his already labored calculations. He whispered the prayer which had accompanied him at takeoff on every flight. He opened the tap.

The Garden exploded.

It was too much information – beyond imagining. The constraints of his Garden burst and dissolved, the models incapable of keeping up with the flow. Within a heartbeat his entire system was teetering on the brink of collapse. When that happened, he knew, everything would be lost. He would be trapped in the blackness of the Tandagore coma without even an online existence, or helpless before the next defensive cycle of the operating system. Everything would fail. Everything.

He fought, but the Garden was dying all around him, collapsing, reduced in microseconds to random, nonrepresentational bits. Before his inner eyes the intricate matrix of greenery devolved into abstract patterns of dark and light, flashing randomly, warping and seething like a nest of stars.

Then just as it seemed nothing worse could happen the alarm signals began. The operating system had launched another attack, trying to sever his connection to the Grail network.

No, he realized, *it's reaching for me. For me.* He felt the system's probe thrust past his crumbling defenses and into his mind. He was helpless before it.

Sellars screamed in shock and pain as it touched him, but there was no sound to be heard in that empty place of endlessly streaming data, no hope and no help – only the mindless throb of a universe being born.

Or a universe dying.

SHE didn't know how she had got back to the chair or why, but she was staring at her pad again. Only minutes had passed since she had opened her employer's locked storage but they seemed to have ground past as slowly as geological aeons. A tunnel of darkness surrounded her, narrowing her sight until all she could see was the screen, the terrible screen. On it a file called Nuba 27 was now playing. Dread was doing unspeakable things to a woman in what seemed to be a hotel room, the sunlight streaming in through the windows giving everything a stark, ghastly clarity.

Get up, Dulcie thought. *Get up.* But the tunnel around her hid everything except the screen. All she could see was the horrid, bright hotel light. *Get up.* She wasn't even sure if she was talking to the woman strapped to the plastic-draped bed or to herself.

A dull bonging sound intruded on her even duller thoughts. She realized she had turned off the sound on the file, a tiny mercy in an eternity of horror, because she had not been able to make herself listen anymore. The musical soundtrack had been even worse than the screaming. So if the sound on the file was turned off, what was making that noise?

A window opened up in the corner of the pad screen. In it, a figure in an overcoat stood in a doorway. For a moment she thought it was only some elaboration of the file's horrors, a second victim perhaps, her employer about to arrange some hideous duet of grunting and screeching, then she slowly came to understand that the doorway in the view-window was the loft's seen from the security camera over the door. It took another long time and more ringing from the doorbell, before she realized it was really happening. Right now.

Close your eyes, a voice urged her. *Let it all go away. Never open them again. It's a nightmare.*

But it wasn't a nightmare. She knew it wasn't, even though at this moment she knew very little else. One of her hands was clutching an empty coffee cup so hard her fingers had cramped, although she did not remember picking it up. She looked up through the tunneled swirl of darkness and saw Dread still lying on his coma bed, a million miles away.

The light of stars, she thought disjointedly. *It takes years, it seems so cold when it gets here. But if you were close, it would burn you right up . . .*

The doorbell rang again.

He's going to kill me, she thought. *Even if I run. Wherever I go, whatever I do . . .*

Get up, stupid! This last voice was very faint but something in its urgency cut through the fog in her head, the disassociated murk that was her only protection against pure shrieking animal terror. She clambered to her feet and almost fell down, bracing herself against the back of the chair until her legs were shaking a little less. The chair squeaked. She jerked her head in panic to look at Dread but he still lay unmoving, a god's effigy carved in dark wood. She stumbled to the stairs and went down them like a crippled woman. The doorbell sounded again but the speaker was upstairs; here on the bottom landing it was only a distant sound, like something sinking into the ocean.

If I lie down here, she thought, *after a while I won't even hear it.*

Instead some inner compulsion made her reach out and thumb the security lock, then open the door. From up close she could see that the figure in the doorway was shorter than she was, although more heavyset. Dark curly hair, eyes narrowed in suspicion or annoyance. A woman.

A woman . . . she thought. *If it's a woman, I have to tell her something . . . warn her . . .* But she couldn't think. She couldn't remember. The darkness was very thick.

'Excuse me,' the stranger said after a moment, her voice deep and firm. 'Sorry to bother you on a Sunday. I'm looking for someone named Hunter.'

'There's . . . no . . .' Dulcie leaned on the doorframe for support. 'There's no one here by that name.' A part of her was glad. She could close the door now and walk back upstairs and pull the blackness over her like a blanket. But . . . Hunter? Why did that name sound familiar? Why did anything sound familiar, for that matter?

'Are you sure? I'm sorry, did I wake you up?' The woman was looking at her carefully, concern and something else in her expression. 'Are you feeling all right?'

It came to her then, as if a memory from another country, even another lifetime. Hunter – that was the name on all the documents for the loft. She had seen it on Dread's system, thought it just a random pseudonym, but now . . . 'Oh, God,' she said.

The woman stepped forward and took her arm – gently, but with a grip that suggested she could squeeze a lot harder if she wanted to. 'Do you mind if we talk? My name is Skouros – I'm a police detective. I have a few questions.' Her eyes flicked across the darkness behind Dulcie. 'Can you step outside?'

Dulcie was caught, paralyzed, as if possessed by some slow seizure. 'I . . . I can't . . . He . . .'

'Is there someone else home?'

It was a funny question, really – where was that place, after all? *Otherland, they called it. Other. Somewhere? Nowhere?* That was why Dulcie laughed. But when she heard herself it was not a good laugh. 'No. he's . . . gone . . .'

'Let's go up, then. Is that all right with you?'

She could only nod. *I'm a ghost*, she thought, trying to remember what it had been like on the other side of the darkness. *It doesn't matter – summoned or banished. I can't do anything about it.*

As they went up the stairs the woman in the coat took something out of one of her pockets. For a moment Dulcie thought it was a gun, but it was only a little black-and-silver pad. The woman held it up to her mouth as though to speak into it, but Dulcie had suddenly remembered the files were still open on the screen of her own pad, open and running for anyone to see. *Nuba 27. Those fingers wiggling, like something lost and drowning at the bottom of the ocean* . . . Even through the freeze she felt a rush of embarrassment, as though the scenes of horror were something of her own, something shameful, and as they reached the top of the landing she took the woman's hand.

'They're not mine,' she explained. 'I didn't know. I . . . he . . .'

And as she turned, still clutching the woman's hand, she saw that the coma bed was empty.

'Just tell me . . .' the woman began, but didn't finish. Air huffed out of her in a popping wheeze and she staggered forward, four or five steps across the loft floor, then fell down on her face. A huge knife stuck out of her back as though it had simply appeared there, a few inches of blade showing between the handle and the redness oozing out around the place where it had slashed through the over-coat. Dulcie could only stare at the woman, talking one moment, silent and motionless now. The blackness was coming back, closing in swift as wind-driven fog.

'Ah, sweetness, what have you been doing while Daddy was away?'

Dread stepped out of the shadow behind the loft door. He was wearing his white bathrobe, loosely tied. He walked past her, cat-silent on bare feet, and stood over the police-woman. Her eyes, Dulcie saw, were still open. A bubble of red spit was trembling at the corner of her mouth. Dread crouched down until he was only centimeters from the woman's face.

'I wish I had time to do you properly,' he told her. 'You must have worked hard to wind up at my door. But things are happening fast and I can't stop for games.' He stood up, grinning, full of manic energy that lit him up like a Christmas tree. 'And as for you, Dulcie, my pet, what have you been up to?' His gaze slid to her pad, still sitting on the chair, the screen flickering with violent motion, and his eyes opened just a little more – they were already as wide as someone on the downhill rush of a roller coaster. 'Well, you *have* been a nosy little bitch, haven't you?'

Without realizing it she had been backing toward the small area of counter where she had set up the coffee makings. 'I didn't . . . I don't . . . why . . . ?'

'Why? Well, that's the question, isn't it, sweetness? Why? Because I like to. Because I can.'

She paused, her spine against the drawer, her fingers feeling for its handle. She had remembered what was in it. Something had finally jolted her back to life, a splash on her thoughts cold as ice water, and for the first time in an hour she could think. *Oh, Jesus, keep him talking,* she told herself. *He's a monster, but he likes to talk.*

'But why? You . . . you don't have to do it.'

'Because I can get sex the legitimate way?' The smile lingered. He was high, high on something, high as the sky. 'That's not what it's about. And sex – it's nothing. Not in comparison.'

She was easing the drawer open, silently, slowly, afraid that her hammering pulse and trembling fingers would make her slip and pull it out too far, send it clattering to the floor. 'What . . . what are you going to do to me?'

'Get rid of you. You know that I have to, love. But you've done good work for me so I'm going to make it quick. Terminations should be quick and humane, right? Isn't that what the business manuals all say? Besides, I'm very busy right now – very, very busy.' He smiled; if she had not known now what was beneath the mask she would have sworn it was a true and kind thing. 'And I can do without you now. I've got things under control. You should see what's going on with the network and your old friends! I hated to leave, even for a minute – things are very exciting there right now – but I believe in keeping an active relationship with my employees.'

The drawer was open. She let out a little terrified sigh to mask the sound of her hand searching. There was no need to fake the terror, no need at all. He was watching her with mesmerizing intensity, his pupils big and black as the barrel of a . . .

Gun. Where's the gun?

She swung around as quickly as she could, risking all, and pulled the drawer all the way out. It was empty.

'Looking for this?' he asked.

She turned back in time to see him pull it from the pocket of his bathrobe. The curling-iron barrel came up and pointed right between her eyes.

'I'm not an idiot, sweetness.' Dread shook his head in mock-disappointment. 'Oh, and you know what I said about quick . . . ?'

He let the barrel swing down from her face to her middle. Dulcie felt herself punched in the belly and flung backward even as she heard the loud, explosive *crack*. Then she was on her side, trying to understand how so many things could stop working all at the same time. She wanted to make noise, to scream for help, but couldn't: something was crushing the air out of her, a huge fist squeezing her chest. Her hands had flown instinctively to her stomach. She looked down and saw blood welling between her fingers. When she lifted them away, it began to drip down to the floor where it formed a spreading pool.

'I changed my mind,' he said.

CHAPTER 41

Playing the Knight

NETFEED/NEWS: 'Autostalking' Not Illegal, Court Rules
(visual: defendant Duncan's 'Smiling Avenger' avatar)
VO: A UN regional court has ruled that there is nothing inherently illegal in a piece of gear that follows a user into virtual simulations and does harm to that user's simuloid unless it violates the laws pertaining to that node. Amanda Hoek, a seventeen-year-old South African schoolgirl, has been pursued online by a piece of code created by an ex-boyfriend and, in the words of her lawyer, 'systematically stalked and assaulted numerous times.'
(visual: Jens Verwoerd, Hoek's attorney)
VERWOERD: 'This poor girl cannot use the net – vital to her school-work and her social life – without her online character being followed into every node by the defendant's avatar, a piece of code designed specifically to harass her. She has been insulted, attacked, and sexually assaulted numerous times, both verbally and through the tactors of the VR nodes, and yet this court seems to think this is nothing more than the horseplay of adolescents on the net . . .'

EVEN as she swam and died in the glittering darkness Renie could not rid herself of the taste of fear – but it was someone else's fear. *Not someone*, she thought, *something. How can a thing, a machine made of code, be so frightened . . . !*

The operating system had touched her and then pushed her away, had fled back into the recesses of itself, leaving her to drown in a sea of stars. It was a slow drowning – an ebbing away of consciousness, a fragmenting of the personality. She had felt something like it before when the system had been angry; then it had filled her with terror. Now she drifted, pulsing like a fading echo through the lonely lights, and knew that the operating system lived in a state of fear far worse than anything she could understand – a terror so complete and so alien that even its distant resonances could kill.

But does it make any difference? she wondered. *Dying like this instead of dying from fright?* She could feel herself letting go, coming apart, but it was all so gradual, so . . . unimportant. Freezing to death, they said, was a kind death. Body and mind disassociated, what had been painful chill came to seem like warmth, and at last sleep came like a friend. This must be a little like that.

But I don't want to go, she thought distantly, and even convinced herself a little. *Even if it doesn't hurt. I don't want to cut the string.*

Never to see Stephen again, or Martine and the others, Fredericks . . . and !Xabbu . . . That was from his poem, wasn't it? Something about death – or was it just about string . . . ?

> 'There were people, some people
> Who broke the string for me
> And so
> This place is now a sad place for me,
> Because the string is broken.'

She could almost hear him saying it, his soft voice, the slightly alien inflections hurrying the words at surprising moments, then slowing down to voice a single syllable like music. !Xabbu.

> *'The string broke for me,*
> *And so*
> *This place does not feel to me*
> *As it used to feel,*
> *Because the string is broken.'*

What had the unbroken string been? A life? A dream? The cord that held together the universe?

All of those things?

Now she could hear it as though he stood beside her, as he had stood through so many moments of anguish, a stalwart flame in all darknesses.

> *'This place feels as if it stood open before me*
> *Empty*
> *Because the string has broken*
> *And so*
> *This place is an unhappy place*
> *Because the string is broken.'*

This place is an unhappy place, she repeated to herself. *Because the string is broken. Because I am alone.*

This place feels as if it stood open before me, she told the darkness as she drifted and disintegrated, mere flotsam left behind in the flight of a terrified child-thing.

Empty, something whispered to her across the flashing emptiness. *Because the string has broken.*

For a moment she floated, bemused, trying to remember

what it was that had caught her fragmenting attention. A voice. A voice?

The operating system, she thought. *It's come back for me. Whatever 'back' means. Whatever 'me,' means . . .* It was growing harder and harder to think.

Because the string has broken.

The chant wafted to her through the void, but it was not a sound, it was both more and less. It was a spattering of light like a distant explosion in vacuum space, a tiny pulse of heat at the bottom of a frozen, sluggish ocean. It was a whisper from a dream heard on the porch of wakefulness, an idea, a scent, a muffled heartbeat. It was . . .

!Xabbu?

From the other side of the universe, still, small: *Renie . . . ?*

Impossible. Impossible! *!Xabbu! Jesus Mercy, is that you?*

And suddenly diminishment was not a blessing but a horror. Suddenly she wanted back all she had lost even though she knew it must be too late. She was almost gone, reduced to essences and drawn apart into the cloudy impermanence of the sea of stars.

No, she thought. *He's out there, somehow. He's out there!* She fought, but she scarcely felt real – there was no leverage, nothing to push against. *!Xabbu! I'm drowning!*

Renie. He was faint, only a voice and barely that. *Reach for me.*

Where are you?

Beside you. Always beside you.

And she opened herself and felt him there just as he had said, a presence as vague and dispersed as her own but right beside her, as if they were two galaxies rolling

down the long night-tides of the universe to meet and
pass through each other like ghosts.

I feel you, she said. *Don't leave me.*

Don't leave me, he might have echoed her, or *Believe
me.*

She believed. She reached for him and willed the string
to unbreak.

Touch, she said. *I touch.*

I feel.

And then they met and embraced – light-years wide
but close as the ebb and flow of a single heartbeat, two
matrices of naked thought drawn together in the darkness and held tight by the infinite compression of love.

She had a body again. She knew it even with her eyes
shut, because she was holding him closer than she had
ever held anyone.

'Where are we?' she finally asked. She could hear his
heartbeat, fast and strong, hear his breath in his lungs.
All else was silence, but she needed nothing else.

'It does not matter,' he said. 'We are together.'

'Did we . . . make love?'

'It does not matter.' He sighed, then laughed. 'I do not
know. I think . . . we were made of love.'

She was afraid to open her eyes, she realized. She
clutched him more tightly when she had not thought such
a thing possible. 'It doesn't matter,' she agreed. 'I thought
I would never find you again . . .'

His fingers touched her face – cool, real. It startled her
so that she looked in spite of herself. It really was his
face, his dear face, that looked down on her in the cool
evening light. There were tears in his eyes. 'I . . . I would
not believe it . . . could not let myself . . .' He lowered
his forehead until it touched hers. 'I was swimming so

long . . . in all that light. Drowning. Calling you. Coming apart . . .'

She was weeping. 'We have bodies. We can cry. Are we . . . back? In the real world?'

'No.'

Worried by his strange tone, Renie sat up, taking care to keep her arms around him, not trusting him or herself to stay solid. The landscape was alien but oddly familiar, gray in the dying light. For a moment she thought they had returned to the black mountaintop but the outline of a leafless tree, the fuzzy sprung shape of a bush, confused her.

'At first I thought we were in the place where I dived in to search for you,' !Xabbu said slowly.

'Dived in . . . ? Where?'

'The Well. But I was wrong.' He pointed to the sky. 'Look.'

She raised her head. The stars were bright. The moon was round and yellow, hanging fat above the horizon like a ripe fruit.

'It is an African moon,' he said. 'The moon of the Kalahari.'

'But . . . but I thought you said we weren't . . . back . . .' She leaned away from him, staring. He wore a loincloth of animal hide. A bow and a crude quiver of arrows lay on the dirt beside him. And she was also dressed in skins.

'It's your world,' she said quietly. 'The Bushman simulation you took me to – God, that seems like a century ago! Where we danced.'

'No.' He shook his head again. He had wiped the tears from his cheeks and eyes. 'No, Renie, it is something different – something . . . more.'

He stood, extending a hand to help her up. The

seedpods tied around his ankles rattled as he moved.

'But if this isn't *your* world . . . ?'

'There is a fire,' he said, pointing to a flicker of light that stained the desert sands red and orange. 'Just beyond that rise.'

They walked across the dry pan, kicking up dust that hid their feet so that it seemed they walked across clouds. The moon touched the dunes, rocks, and thorn bushes with silver.

The campfire was small, made of only a few crossed sticks. Other than the fire itself there was no sign of human life in all the immensity of desert night.

Before Renie could ask again, !Xabbu pointed to a gulley that carved through the cracked earth beside the campfire, the drywash shell of some long-dead stream. 'Down there,' he said. 'I see him. No, I feel him.'

Renie could see nothing but the jittering of shadows around the campfire, but !Xabbu's voice made her look to him. His face was solemn but there was something else in it as well, a kind of exalted fire behind the eyes that in anyone else she would have feared was hysteria.

'What is it?' She took his hand, suddenly afraid.

He kept her hand in his and led her down the pan, stopping beside the fire. She could not help noticing that theirs were the only footprints crossing the dust. When they looked down into the gulley, she saw that the stream that had carved it was not entirely dead: a trickle of water ran along the bottom, so narrow that if she climbed down into the hole she could dam it with one foot. Something was moving beside this streamlet – something very, very small.

!Xabbu sat in the dust beside the shallow scrape. His rattles whispered.

'Grandfather,' he said.

The mantis looked up at him, triangular head cocked, sawtoothed arms held high.

'Striped Mouse. Porcupine.' The calm, still voice came from everywhere and nowhere. 'You have come far to see the end.'

'May we sit at your fire?'

'You may.'

Renie began to understand. '!Xabbu,' she whispered. 'That's not Grandfather Mantis. It's the Other. It's taken this from your mind, somehow. It appeared to me as Stephen – pretended to be my brother.'

!Xabbu only smiled and squeezed her hand. 'In this place, it *is* Mantis,' he said. 'After all, whatever you call it, we have finally met the dream who is dreaming us.'

She sat down beside him, feeling limp and emotionally exhausted. All she wanted was to be with !Xabbu. *And maybe he's right*, she thought. *Why fight it? Logic is gone. We're definitely in someone else's dream.* If this was the way the Other chose to communicate – perhaps the only way it *could* communicate – then they might as well accept it. She had tried to force the Stephen-thing to see reality in her terms and its anger and frustration had almost killed her.

The mantis tipped its shiny head down, then up, regarding them with tiny, protuberant eyes. 'The All-Devourer will be here soon,' it said. 'He is coming to my campfire, too.'

'There are still things that can be done, Grandfather,' said !Xabbu.

'Wait a minute,' Renie whispered. 'I thought if anyone was the All-Devourer in this story, he was. *It* was. The Other, I mean.'

The insect appeared to have heard her. 'We are at the end of things now. My fight is over. A great shadow, a hungry shadow, will swallow all I have made.'

'It does not have to be that way, Grandfather,' said !Xabbu. 'There are those who might help you – our friends and allies. And see! Here is your Beloved Porcupine, she of the clear thought and brave heart.'

Brave heart, maybe, Renie thought. *Clear thought? Not bloody likely. Not in the middle of this cracked fairy tale.* But aloud she said, 'We want to help. We want to save not just our own lives, but the children's lives, too. All the children.'

A minute twitch as the mantis shook its head. 'It is too late for the first children. Even now the All-Devourer has begun to eat them.'

'But you – we – can't just give up!' Renie's voice rose in spite of her best intentions. 'No matter how bad it looks we still have to fight! To try!'

Mantis seemed to shrink even smaller, drawing in on itself until it was little more than a spot of shadow. 'No,' it whispered, and for a moment its voice was as raw and miserable as a child's. '*No. Too late.*'

!Xabbu was squeezing her hand. Renie leaned back. However frustrating it was, she had to realize that this . . . thing, whatever had formed it, whatever shaped its thoughts and dreams, was not going to be argued into doing the right thing.

After a long silent time !Xabbu said, 'Do you not think of a world beyond this? A world where the good things can be saved, can grow again?'

'His mouth is full of fire,' Mantis whispered. 'He runs like the wind. He is swallowing everything I have made. There is nothing beyond this.' It was quiet for a moment, crouching, gently rubbing its forelegs together. 'But it is good not to be alone, we think. It is good to be where the campfire still burns, at least for a little while. Good to hear voices.'

Renie closed her eyes. So this was what it had all come down to – trapped in the imagination of a mad machine, waiting for the end in a world built from !Xabbu's own thoughts and memories. It was an interesting way to die. Too bad she'd never get to tell anyone.

'Come, it is too quiet,' said Mantis. Its voice was very small now, like the merest brush of wind through the thorn bushes. 'Porcupine, my darling daughter, you are sad. Striped Mouse, tell the story again of the feather that became the moon.'

!Xabbu looked up, a little startled. 'You know that story?'

'I know all your stories now. Tell it, please.'

And so, in a moment of calm beneath the fiery stars of an African night sky – a moment that seemed like it could last forever, although Renie knew better – !Xabbu began to recite the story of how Mantis created life from a discarded piece of shoe leather. The dying mantis crouched beside the trickling stream, listening intently to the tale of its own cleverness, and seemed to find it very interesting indeed.

THEY had prepared not just a fire, but a wall of fire – an arc of papers, boxes, empty grain sacks and other combustibles they had piled in front of one corner of the room and set alight. Behind the fiery barrier was stacked every piece of remaining furniture not bolted to the floor – desks and chairs, even the lids from the V-tanks that were not being used. Even the spaces between objects were crammed tight with thin military mattresses.

But those things will not stop bullets, Joseph thought sadly. *Stop no dogs either.*

A flicker on the monitor caught his attention. 'They are moving now. Light the fire.'

'It's t-tempting,' said Del Ray, not hiding his panic very well, 'but I'll wait until you're back here with us. Just tell us what's happening up there.'

Joseph was feeling increasingly exposed as he watched the four mercenaries upstairs leaning over the hole, gesturing. They had already strapped on their combat gear, puffy vests, and hoods with goggles. He resented having been given monitor duty just because he had supposedly fouled up before. *That – we were going to stop that truck driving away, somehow? Stop them getting those big monster dogs?* But even his resentment was nothing against the skin-tightening, horrible certainty of what was to come. 'They are ready,' he said out loud. 'I don't need to stand here no more.'

'Just tell us what they're doing,' Jeremiah said.

'Dressing up the dogs,' Joseph told him.

'What?'

He squinted at the monitor. 'No. First I think they wrapping the dogs up in blankets, but they are doing something else.' Just the sight of the things made his guts watery. The huge animals were shivering with excitement, their cropped tails wagging rigidly. 'They . . . they are using the blankets to do something. Maybe to carry them.' He watched miserably as the men approached the pit they had dug into the floor, using attached ropes to haul the blanket, the first mutant ridgeback sitting upright in the center like a royal personage. 'Oh. Oh. They are going to use the blankets to lower the dogs down through the hole.'

'Shit,' said Del Ray miserably. 'Time to light the fire. Come on!'

Joseph did not need to be urged. He sprinted across the floor of the darkened lab and jumped over the wall of file papers, then clambered up over the furniture barricade, almost knocking over Del Ray as he tumbled down the far side. 'Go ahead! Light it!'

'I'm trying!' Jeremiah moaned. 'We didn't have enough petrol left to get it really soaked.' He flicked another of Renie's cigarettes from shaking fingers. The papers caught with a *whuff* of ignition. For a moment, as blue flames ran along the makeshift barrier, Joseph felt a tingle of hope.

'Why the lights out?' he whispered. 'Then we can't see to shoot them.'

'Because we've got two bullets and they've probably got thousands,' Del Ray said. 'Just stop arguing, Joseph. Please?'

'Dark isn't going to fool no dogs,' Joseph pointed out, but more quietly.

Del Ray made a strange noise, a kind of groan. 'I'm truly sorry, Joseph – I don't want the last thing I say to be "shut up." But *shut up.*'

Long Joseph could feel his heart getting big in his chest, big but weak, trying so hard to beat fast even though something was squeezing it badly. 'I am sorry we are all here.'

'I am too,' Del Ray said. 'God knows, I am too.'

'Something's coming,' said Jeremiah in a cracking voice. They all stared out past the flames, trying to see movement in the shadows at the other end of the laboratory.

Joseph's chest seemed tighter and tighter. He tried to imagine his Zulu ancestors, the ones he bragged of so often, staring out from their campfire at the African darkness, tried to imagine how brave they felt even when they heard the rumbling of a lion, but he couldn't. His only weapon, a steel bar from the underside of a conference table, hung loose in his sweaty hand.

Please, God, he thought. *Don't let them hurt Renie. Make it fast.*

Joseph saw something moving at the far end of the lab – a low and silent shadow. Then he saw another. The first one looked up, swiveling its head from side to side. Two points of baleful yellow gleamed as its eyes caught and reflected the firelight.

A loud *voomp* made Joseph jump. Something smashed through their little wall of fire, scattering sparks, and rolled toward their hiding place. A moment later a cloud of smoke billowed over him, filling his eyes, fouling his lungs. He waved his hands, heard Jeremiah choking and shouting, but before he could do anything more a huge dark shape plunged over the flaming barrier and landed on top of him, growling.

He was smashed to the floor and something tore into his arm – he felt a spike of silver pain brighter than any fire. He struggled but he was being pressed down beneath something heavier than he was, something that wanted to get its teeth into his belly. A volley of explosions roared above his head but they seemed far away, meaningless. The thing had him, the beast had him. He heard one of his companions screech in frightened anger, then Del Ray's pistol cracked and spit flame by his head and the heavy burden slid off him.

Joseph struggled up off the floor, gasping for breath. A string of stuttering shots – *katokkatokkatokkatok* – went off like firecrackers. More animal shapes were picking their way through the scattered remnants of the fire; he could hear men shouting, then more shots. Several human figures were pushing through the doorway into the smoke-clouded room. To Joseph's blurred eyes there seemed too many, far more than four.

Not right! he wanted to shout but his mouth was burning, his throat constricted. Del Ray crouched trembling beside him, the pistol with its one remaining bullet in his outstretched hand. Joseph couldn't hear him fire it over the noise of the other guns, didn't even see a flash from the muzzle, but two of the dogs fell.

Two with one shot, Joseph marveled, dazed by smoke in his lungs and in his thoughts. *Just like you said. How can you do that, Del Ray?*

But before he could make sense of it another mutant dog came up out of the smoke and over the wall of desks and mattresses, striking Joseph like a thunderbolt and hurling him back onto the ground. A grunting head shoved up toward his face, dug its hot, wet muzzle into Long Joseph's throat, and took away his air.

Paul Jonas lay at Sam's feet, twitching and moaning like a man who had received a terrible electric shock. Sam herself had only recovered a few moments earlier after her abrupt ejection from the Well, and now she struggled to make sense of what was happening. The weeping angel had flickered and vanished from the air above the Well. The Twins, in the form of Jack Sprat and his wife, were shrieking in wordless fury at her disappearance, snatching up screaming refugees and throwing them into the flaring pit as though that might force her to return. But none of the hapless creatures who fell into the pit came up again and the angel did not reappear.

'Sam Fredericks!' It was Martine's voice. Sam could not see her through the stampede of terrified creatures. She tried to get a grip on Paul's arm to drag him to safety but he was slippery with sweat, writhing like a man in the grip of nightmare. Someone pushed in beside her to help her pull and together they managed to drag Jonas back from the worst of the crush, to a spot on the very edge. After the lunatic events of the last minutes Sam was only mildly surprised to discover that her helper was Felix Jongleur.

'We must get away from this,' he snapped. 'I have no control over this version of Finney and Mudd. Where are your friends?'

Sam shook her head. It seemed impossible to locate anyone in the chaos; it was all she could do to stand her ground and protect Paul from being trampled by maddened milkmaids and panicked dwarfs.

'Fredericks!' Martine was shouting for her again, but this time Sam spotted her a dozen meters farther down the shoreline, crowded with several others along a dip in the rim that seemed only a handspan above the surface of the Well. Sam bent and grabbed Paul under the arms, straining to lift his upper body. His head lolled but his eyes were open, staring at the sky. Jongleur took his feet and they half-carried, half-dragged him toward the spot where Martine and the others huddled, temporarily out of the worst of the chaos.

Paul Jonas' face swung toward her. For a moment his eyes appeared to focus.

'*Tell him to turn off the window . . .*' he said urgently, as though it meant something sane and useful, then his eyes rolled up and his words fell away again into murmuring nonsense.

They made it a dozen awkward steps before something grabbed Sam's ankle and dragged her to the ground.

'Bring back the princess!' a voice hissed behind her. She tried to crawl forward but the grip on her leg was painful and strong; it flipped her on her back as though she were a rag. 'We want the princess!' demanded Jack Sprat and shook something at her. It was another victim – a small, bulge-eyed man dressed in green, dangling by the neck from the monster's other hand. Jack Sprat leaned closer, blind face as grainy as old, white wood. So frightened she could not take in enough breath to scream, Sam kicked, but could not dislodge the twining fingers. The tree-tall creature yanked her into the air and dangled her upside down, then his attention wandered to the struggling, green-clad man. He squeezed the prisoner's neck in a gentle, almost experimental way, watching with interest as the little man's struggles first sped, then slowed.

'The blade!' shouted Felix Jongleur. 'Give me the sword!'

Sam could only wonder why the old man had remembered the broken sword but she hadn't. She fumbled it out of her belt and let it drop to the ground. Jongleur snatched it up with such a look of triumph that for a moment Sam could only curse her own stupidity.

That's the last I'll see of him . . . she thought, her head roaring and aching as she swung like a pendulum two meters above the ground. But Jongleur surprised her by leaping forward to hack hard at the twiggy hand pinioning her ankle. Still fascinated by the death throes of its other prisoner, Jack Sprat scarcely even seemed to notice what Jongleur had done, but his fingers popped and parted; Sam fell to the ground so hard it took her a moment to know which way was up.

'Hurry!' Jongleur shouted. 'Help me with Jonas!'

Reeling, Sam climbed to her feet. They lifted Paul and stumbled to the edge of the well, shoving their way between yelping, sobbing refugees. Hands reached up from the low spot along the shoreline and helped Paul down, then Sam too was assisted over the edge and onto a narrow shelf scarcely three paces wide and a dozen paces long, the whole thing only a few meters below the rim of the pit and less distance than that above the glimmering surface of the Well. Jongleur climbed down after her and crouched beside her on the ledge, panting, ignoring startled or even hostile glances from the others.

Martine, Florimel, T4b, even Mrs Simpkins and Nandi were already crammed along the ledge with chittering Wicked Tribe monkeys perched on several of them. The strange boy named Cho-Cho huddled beside Martine, his back against the gray earth, eyes wide with terror.

'Do we just wait here until they find us?' Bonnie Mae Simpkins demanded in a breathless whisper.

'What are those things?' said Florimel. 'Where did such monsters come from?'

Nandi Paradivash looked down at where Paul lay beside Sam's feet, still locked in some miserable dream. 'They are copies of the real Twins – the men who have followed Jonas through the network. Apparently there are many of these duplicate versions, all obsessed with Jongleur's daughter, but usually harmless. Dread has control of the system, even though for the moment the Other is keeping him at bay. Apparently he has found a way to mutate these copies.'

'But why?' Florimel demanded. She flinched as a long, choking scream cut through the already terrible noises above them, then plucked a nervously fidgeting monkey off her forehead and deposited it back on her shoulder. 'He cannot destroy the operating system this way – all he is doing is killing the children! Is he simply mad?'

'He wants us to give up,' Martine said in a slow, dead voice. 'He wants us to surrender, to save the children.'

'But even if we did they'd never survive.' Sam waved her hands, trying to get the others to listen. 'He's killing the what-do-you-call-it – the operating system! They'll all die anyway!'

'Perhaps . . . perhaps Dread is being more clever than we give him credit for.' Martine sounded frighteningly hollow, as if she no longer cared about anything. That scared Sam badly. 'He was clearly startled and very angry to find that the Other was still resisting him, but if he destroys it completely, he loses control of the network. Maybe he is not really expecting to lure us out. Maybe by doing this terrible thing to these children the Other is protecting, he is trying to drive the operating system insane.'

'But don't any of you care?' Florimel's anguished words tore through the din. 'Those are our children out there! *Our* children! And those creatures are murdering them! My daughter Eirene – I can feel her beside me at this moment, feel her real body next to mine, I swear it! She must be terrified, her heart is beating so fast! Because whatever part of her the Other stole must also be out there – and those things will murder her!'

And who else is up there with her? Sam wondered miserably. *Who else is getting crushed and eaten right next to us? Renie's brother? T4b's friend? That poor kid who called himself Senbar Flay in the Middle Country?* A great, cold hopelessness folded around her. Everything was pointless now. If they had shared one goal, it was to save the children and get themselves out of the network alive. They were going to fail on both counts.

'So what do we do?' Bonnie Mae said in a cracked, urgent voice. 'Let them go on slaughtering the innocents?'

'*Princess!*' The jiggling bulk of Jack Sprat's wife appeared atop the rim of the pit only a dozen meters away. Sam and her friends shrank back against the ledge but the shapeless face was staring out over the pulsing waters and did not see them. The groaning, belching voice no longer sounded human at all. 'Come back to us, Princess – we want to eat you up!'

Her scrawny, hideous husband followed her to the edge of the crater then began to move sideways along the rim, snatching up and throttling anything it could catch. It was headed right toward their hiding place. Even if it did not know they were there it would stumble onto them in moments. 'Kill until you feed us,' it creaked. 'Feed us.'

Bonnie Mae had fallen into prayer again. Almost paralyzed with fear, Sam looked at the looming Twins for a second, then turned her head away. She, too, wanted to close her eyes – not to pray, but so that she wouldn't have to see the things that were going to kill them all. Instead she found herself staring at a spreading darkness in the Well itself, a cloudy obscurity that rippled out from a point near the shoreline, dousing the vast, pulsing lights as it grew.

It's really dying, she thought. *We're all going to die in the dark . . . !* Then something else caught her attention. A prickle of smaller lights trailed up through the darkness, tiny incandescent bubbles that grew more numerous by the second.

'Look,' she said softly, then realized no one could hear her. '*Look!*'

Something was rising from the troubled waters. *The angel again?* Sam wondered. *The Other? Is the Other finally coming?* But it did not feel that way, nothing like the immense cold presence that had filled the Freezer. It was something smaller and more human – she could even get a dim sense of its shape now, a murky silhouette swimming upward through the midst of the twinkling lights.

The thing that broke the surface of the Well and clambered up onto the rim was the size and shape of a man, the lean, muscular body gleaming with smears of phosphorescence. The lights of the Well had faded to a dull gleam – even the massive Twins had become shadowy, obscure shapes. Frosted with streaks of light, the newcomer was the brightest thing on the landscape and all eyes

turned toward him. For a sinking instant Sam thought it
was Ricardo Klement, but then he turned and raised his
sword and his face lifted so that she could see his profile,
his long black mane of hair. Her heart exploded with
astonishment and joy.

The Wicked Tribe rose shrieking from Nandi's shoulders. "Landogarner! 'Landogarner!'

'*Orlando!*' Sam screamed. 'Oh, my God, it's Orlando!'

The roar of both murderers and victims had fallen away,
but if he heard Sam's cry the newcomer gave no sign. He
turned toward the Twins and pointed his sword at them,
a mixture of salute and threat. The Jack Sprat thing let
out a sobbing noise – Sam recognized only a moment
later that it was an excited laugh – and lurched toward
him. The lights of the Well suddenly blazed up again,
returning the world to unsteady twilight.

Sam was scrambling up over the lip of their shoreline
refuge when someone caught her by the leg and dragged
her back down. She shouted in anger and slapped wildly
at the restraining hand, certain it was Jongleur, but it was
Nandi Paradivash, his face like gray marble in the light
from the Well.

'Let him go,' he told her. 'This is his fight, I think.'

'That's *fenfen!* I have to help him . . . !' She kicked, but
Florimel had grabbed her other leg and would not let go.

'No, Sam,' she growled. 'The rest of us, we will only
slow him down. See!'

'Yes, look,' said Martine. 'The Other has played his
knight.'

Sam had no idea what she meant and did not care –
she could only tug helplessly against her friends'
restraining hands. Orlando had sprung toward his huge
adversary, the Thargor body moving with a speed she
hadn't seen since the Middle Country simulation, his sword

so quick it was all but invisible in the strange half-light from the Well. He struck three hard blows against Jack Sprat's legs before it could swipe at him for the first time, so that it was stumbling by the time its arm flailed out toward him. Even so it was a near-miss: the twiggy fingers whickered past his head so swiftly Sam knew they would have smashed it off his shoulders if Orlando had not flung himself to the ground.

Sam could not take her eyes from what was happening, even as she felt the others crowding up behind her. It was a dream, a nightmare – Orlando! Fighting for his life!

But there was something different about him, she saw now – not just his speed but even his shape. The body he wore was not the Thargor of the last days gaming in the Middle Country, the scarred, battle-hardened veteran of a hundred wars, nor even the younger version of the character he had become when they first crossed into the Grail network. This new Thargor was still muscular but lithe and lighter of foot than he had ever been in the Middle Country, as though Sam watched a version of the character she had never seen – a stripling Thargor that had existed only in Orlando's imagination.

The greater weight of the older versions might have been a useful advantage, for now the Jack Sprat creature surprised him with a back-handed blow and lifted him completely off his feet, smashing him to the earth just a few meters from the quivering form of the wife-thing. The second monster slithered forward with surprising speed then rose and folded over him like a huge, living jelly. For a heart-tripping moment Sam thought Orlando had disappeared into the immense mouth; instead the blade of his sword suddenly poked out through the side of the thing's head and it contracted away from the attack,

roaring liquidly. Orlando had thrown himself to one side
to avoid its killing stoop and now managed to jackknife
away from a follow-up swipe by Jack Sprat, which had
hurried forward to grab him while he was engaged with
its blubberous companion.

The wife, its head streaming with fluids from its wound,
attacked again, catching him between the two of them.
Both creatures had learned their lesson and moved in on
him with greater caution. He backed away, trying to
lengthen the triangle, but he had the Well behind him
and was running out of room.

Sam's joy had turned to helpless misery. There was no
way he could beat them both. She was watching him die
all over again. She hit out at the hands restraining her
but her friends would not let go. 'Run!' she screamed.
'Run, Orlando!'

He took a last step backward. As his heel teetered on
the edge of the Well he threw a quick glance back at its
flickering impermanence. His measured but fearful gaze
was enough to tell Sam a terrible truth: he had come out
of it, but he could not go back into it and survive.

He'll break up again if he goes in, she thought wildly
– *he'll disappear*. She did not know how she knew it but
she was certain: there was not enough energy left in the
Well to make him again.

Make him? But that's Orlando, it really is Orlando . . . !

The Jack Sprat creature limped toward him on its
wounded legs, swinging its arms like giant brooms, trying
nothing more ambitious than to force him over the rim
of the pit. With no room left he did the only thing he
could: he leaped forward between the flailing hands and
rolled into the thing's scrawny legs like a bowling ball.
A leg cracked with a dry pop and the monster tottered,
giving out a whistling shriek of rage. It staggered, hobbled

a step, and as it regained its balance began to reach down, but Orlando was behind it now. He chopped through the wounded leg with a two-handed stroke. As it teetered on its remaining leg he threw his weight against it and shoved it toward the Well.

Jack Sprat toppled over the edge, but managed to sink its fingers into the soft soil and cling, its long legs kicking above the roiling waters. It had even begun to pull itself back up but Orlando dodged a hammering, sideways blow from the other beast and hacked the grasping fingers into splinters. Jack Sprat slid into the pulsing depths, shrieking and whistling like a boiling lobster, then surfaced for a moment with arms thrashing before it dissolved at last into the glimmering substance of the Well.

The monstrous, gelatinous form of the wife-thing humped up behind Orlando, spluttering in fury. He had only a fraction of an instant to jump away as it smashed down like a titan fist made of putty. It oozed quickly to the side to trap him against the precipice then stretched upward again, its mouth hanging open in an idiot gape that made it look like some kind of giant, cancerous sock puppet. Before it could drop and crush him Orlando shoved the blade of his sword deep into its bulk, then struggled around to one side, dragging the blade with him, his long muscles knotting as he pulled it through the rubbery flesh even as the creature folded down on top of him.

Sam's heart stuttered and seemed to stop entirely until Orlando scrabbled back out from under the bulky thing, covered with its slime. The sound of the creature's anger went sharper in pitch, into pain and even fright. It heaved upward again but something viscous was running out of the long jagged hole across its middle. Jack Sprat's wife swayed, grew slack as a deflating balloon, then collapsed

and slid over the edge in a wet, sticky glob and vanished
into the Well.

Sam was already up and running, forcing her way
through the stunned refugees, leaping over the dead and
dying without any thought for them at all. Orlando turned
away from the edge of the Well, staggered, and fell to his
knees.

'Orlando!' she screamed. 'Oh, *dzang*, Gardiner, is it
really you?' She crouched and wrapped her arms around
him. 'Don't die, you better not die! Oh, God, I knew you
couldn't be dead. You came back! Like Gandalf! You
utterly came back!'

He turned his head to look at her. For a moment he
seemed to be looking at a stranger and her stomach
contracted. Then he smiled. It was a miserable, weary
smile, but she thought it was the most wonderful thing
she had seen in her whole life. 'But I *am* dead, Frederico,'
he said. 'I really am.'

'No, you're not!' She hugged him as hard as she could.
She was weeping, babbling – she didn't care, she didn't
know anything, he was alive, alive! The others were
running toward them but she did not want to let go, ever.
'No, you're not. You're here.'

After a long moment he pulled back a little. 'Gandalf?'
He peered at her, tried to blink away his own tears, then
laughed. 'Damn, you *did* read it. You read it but you never
told me. You are such a scanmaster, Fredericks.' And then
he collapsed in her arms.

CHAPTER 42

Old School

NETFEED/NEWS: Poor Countries Want to Be Prisons
(visual: new facility at Totness)
VO: The governments of poor nations such as Suriname and Trinidad
and Tobago are vying to house overflow prisoners from the United
States and Europe, where prison populations are rising faster than
facilities can be built, despite fierce domestic opposition in many of
these small countries.
(visual: Vicenta Omarid, Vice-chairman, Resist!)
OMARID:'Our country is not a dumping ground for toxic waste or
toxic humanity. This is a cynical exploitation by the first world nations
of their own people and ours, an attempt to hide the consequences
of their own jail-the-poor policies by waving money under the noses
of hungry nations like Trinidad and Tobago . . .'

A T first Sellars had no idea where he was. He was
sunk deep in a padded seat that felt more like a
womb than a chair, surrounded, comforted, connected.
The great window before him was full of burning points
of light and he could feel the almost silent vibration of
engines – no, not just feel the vibrations, he realized, but
discern the actual working of the antiproton drive, every
detail of its performance as well as the ship's million other

functions, all flooding into his altered nervous system. He was flying through the stars.

'It's the *Sally Ride*,' he murmured. *My ship . . . ! My beautiful ship.*

But something was wrong.

How did I get here? Memories were seeping back now, a kaleidoscope of days, of fire and terror followed by years of isolation. Of a past in which this silver seed had been blasted to twisted wreckage in a hangar in South Dakota without ever having flown outside the lower thermosphere.

But the stars . . . ! There they are, bigger than life. Could it be that everything else I thought was real, the destruction of PEREGRINE, my long imprisonment, was it all just a dream – a cold-sleep nightmare?

He wanted to believe it. He wanted to believe it so badly he could taste it. If this were real then even the nightmare of five crippled decades would soon evaporate, leaving him alone with his ship and the endless fields of starlight.

'No,' he said aloud. 'This isn't real. You got past my defenses. You've taken this out of my own head somehow.'

For a long moment he heard nothing but the hum of the ship's engines. The stars swung past the window like flurrying snow. Then the ship spoke.

'Stay,' it said. 'Stay with . . . this one.' He had heard the voice before, of course, during countless tests – the strangely sexless, computer-generated tones of his own starship. 'This one is lonely.'

Something caught at his heart. After it was destroyed in the Sand Creek disaster he had pushed the ship from his thoughts like a dead lover. Even to hear its voice after all these years was a miracle. But he was troubled by the words. Did the Grail Network operating system which had built this dream in his head really only want to talk? Sellars had fought the thing for so long that he found that almost impossible to believe. 'I know this isn't real,' he said. 'But why are you doing it? Why didn't you just kill me when you broke through into my mind?'

'You . . . are different,' said the mechanical ship-voice. Outside the thick window, the snowflake stars continued to wheel past. 'Made of light and numbers. Like this one.'

My wiring – my internal systems. Does it really think I'm the same kind of thing as it? Could it really just be looking for a . . . a kindred soul? He could not believe that was all there was – the operating system had sensed him long ago, had been studying him through each incursion as carefully as he had studied it. Why had it waited so long to contact him? Was it only that its own defenses had prevented it? Or was something else going on?

Sellars was baffled and exhausted. The seductiveness of the dream, the granting of this fondest wish, which had turned to ashes so long ago, was making it hard to concentrate.

'The stars,' the thing said as if it sensed his thought. 'You know the stars?'

'I used to,' Sellars said. 'I thought I would spend my life among them.'

'Very lonely,' the ship's voice said.

That at least had been real. No mere shipspeak program could manufacture a crippled bleakness like that. 'Some people don't think so,' he said, almost kindly.

'Lonely. Empty. Cold.'

Sellars was drawn to respond – it was hard to hear such childlike despair and not say something – but as the strangeness of the experience began to wear away the illogic continued to disturb him.

If all it wanted was to talk to me, why now? It was able to reach outside its network a long time ago – just look at the way it manifested in Mister J's, the way it's begun to explore other real-world systems. Why didn't it just contact me, instead of waiting until I was trying to enter the Grail network? In fact, even if it had to wait until I entered the network, why did it wait until this particular moment – I've been in the network many times. He tried to piece together what had happened just before the contact. *We were struggling, or at least I was struggling with its security routines. Then I left it so I could go and open the data tap . . . all that information from the Grail Network, that massive, overwhelming flow . . . and that was the moment it attacked me again. Pushed past my defenses.*

When I opened the data tap.

'You, this one – we are the same,' the ship-voice said suddenly. It almost sounded frightened.

'You've been using me, haven't you?' Sellars nodded. 'You clever bastard. You waited until I broke into Jongleur's system, then piggy-backed in on my access. There was something there you couldn't manage on your own, wasn't there? Something expressly designed to keep you out. And you needed me alive and connected until you could get into it.' With that understanding came a deeper fear. What had his adversary fought so hard and so craftily to reach? What was it doing even now, while it entertained him with recreated memories?

And what would it do to him when it didn't need him any longer?

'*No. Lonely in the dark. Don't want to be here anymore.*' The mechanical voice was becoming increasingly distorted.

'Then let me help you,' Sellars begged. 'You said that

I am like you. Give me a chance! I want what you want – I want the children to be safe.'

'*Not safe*,' it whispered. Even the stars were growing faint beyond the window, as though the *Sally Ride* was now outracing their ancient light. '*Too late. Too late for the children.*'

'Which children?' he asked sharply.

'*All the children.*'

'What have you done?' Sellars demanded. 'How did you use me? If you tell me, there might still be some way for me to help you – or at least help the children.'

'*No help*,' it said sadly, then began to sing in a mournful, halting voice.

'*An angel touched me, an angel touched me, the river washed me . . .*'

Sellars had never heard the words or the simple tune. 'I don't understand – just tell me what you've done. Why did you keep me here? *What have you done?*'

It began to sing again. This time, Sellars recognized the song.

'*Rock-a-bye, baby, in the treetop . . .*'

And then the ship was gone, the stars were gone, everything was gone, and he fell back into the familiar confines of his Garden.

But it was a garden no longer, or at least not the comfortable, curved space he had nurtured for so long. Now it stretched for what looked like kilometers, vaster than the grounds at Kensington or Versailles, an almost impossible riot of greenery spreading in all directions.

It held together, Sellars realized. *My Garden absorbed*

the Grail network information and held together. And I am still alive, too. The Other did whatever it wanted to do and then it released me. He checked to make sure his connection to the network was still open, that he still had contact with Cho-Cho, and was filled with relief to discover he did.

So what did the operating system do? he wondered. *What did it want?*

He flung himself into the acres of data, quantities of information that might take a team of specialists years to analyze properly. But there was only Sellars, and he did not have years or even months. In fact, he suspected he might only have a day or two left before things fell apart completely.

The revelations, at least some of them, came swiftly. As he examined the most recent events concerning the Grail Network, for speed's sake tracking just through what had happened since he himself had opened the data tap, then delving frantically in the Grail Brotherhood's files to confirm his suspicions, he discovered what the operating system was and what it had done.

It was worse than he could have imagined. He did not have days. If he was lucky, he might have three hours to save his friends and countless other innocents.

If he was insanely lucky, he might have four.

THEY made themselves another camp of sorts among the ruins of Azador's Gypsy settlement. The shattered frames of the wagons loomed in the half-light like the skeletons of strange animals. Bodies of fairy-tale creatures lay everywhere, broken and dismembered. Many of the remains had been claimed and dragged away by friends and the Gypsies had laid out their own fallen kin at the edge of camp, covering the bodies with colorful blankets, but dozens of corpses still lay unmourned and unburied.

Paul could scarcely bear to look. It was a blessing, in a way, that the Well was dying, the light fading.

The waters were almost entirely dark, the radiance that had once danced there only a flicker now; it barely touched the cocoon of cloudy gray overhead, so that even the few campfires seemed to give out more light than the Well. The growing shadow on both sides of the barrier held one other benefit: Paul had no doubt that Dread still waited beyond the cloud-wall, but at least they didn't have to watch that manshaped point of infinite night pacing calmly back and forth on the other side anymore.

Out of his childhood a snatch of the Bible came to him. *'Whence comest thou?' Then Satan answered the Lord, and said, 'From going to and fro in the earth, and walking up and down in it.'*

But there are two Satans in this universe, Paul thought. *And one of them is in here. With us.*

He stared at Felix Jongleur who, like Paul, sat some distance from the fire and the other survivors. Jongleur stared back. Their companions seemed far more interested in Orlando, who had not yet regained consciousness. But except for having been dead – something Paul thought was usually considered a fairly serious medical problem – the boy seemed to be suffering from nothing worse than exhaustion.

Nobody cares about me, he thought. *Except the man who tried to kill me. But why should they care? They don't know what I know.*

It had all come back – not just the terrible last moments in the tower, but with it all the little missing pieces, the day-to-day boredom and routine, everything that had been hidden from him by the post-hypnotic block.

'She's dead,' he said to Jongleur. 'Ava's been dead all along, hasn't she?'

'Then your memories are unlocked.' Jongleur spoke slowly. 'Yes, she is dead.'

'So why was she here? Why did she keep . . . appearing to me?' He looked over at the others huddled around Orlando. They were only a few meters away but he felt so disconnected from them it could have been a hundred times that. 'Is it something like what happened to that boy – to Orlando Gardiner?'

Jongleur gave him a brief appraising glance. Even the firelight sparkling in his eyes did not make him look more alive. *He looks like something stuffed*, Paul thought. *Something with glass eyes. Dead eyes.*

'I do not know,' Jongleur said at last. 'I do not know what the boy is, although I have my suspicions. But my Avialle, when she died . . . all that was left were copies.'

'Copies?' The word, although half-expected, chilled him.

'From earlier versions of the Grail process. Different mind-scans made at different times. None wholly satisfactory.' He frowned as though about to send back an unimpressive wine.

'Like that Tinto from the Venetian simulation,' Paul said. 'I was right.' Jongleur raised an eyebrow at the name but said nothing. 'How did the . . . how did Ava – all those Avas – get into the system? Why did she keep appearing to me?'

Jongleur shrugged. 'After she died, when I found that all the stored copies, even those made of Finney and Mudd, had been dumped, I thought there had been some malfunction in the Grail system. It is a huge and fearfully complex enterprise, after all.' His eyes narrowed. 'I did not realize that the Other – the operating system – had broken the bonds of its confinement, had made its way out of the straitjacket of the network and into my own system. Even when I . . . saw her for the first time in one of my simulations, I did not understand how one of the copies could have made its way into the Grail network.' His back straightened and his jaw set; Paul thought he looked like someone trying to mask either great pain or anger. 'I was visiting my Elizabethan simworld. I saw her in Southwark, near the Globe Playhouse, being pursued by two cutthroats who looked like Mudd and Finney. I caught them and immobilized them for later study but she escaped. It was then I realized that all the missing copies must have somehow been dumped into the Grail network, but I still did not suspect the operating system.'

'So . . . all the versions of the Twins are just copies?' It was horrible having to cajole information out of this cruel man, this murderer, but the hunger for answers was too strong.

'No, Finney and Mudd still exist. After . . . what happened with Avialle they were punished – imprisoned, in a sense – but they still work for me. They are the ones that pursued you through the Grail Network after your escape.'

'But why, damn it?' For a moment the anger came back again in a surge of heat up his spine. It was all he could do to remain seated. 'Why me? Why am I so damned important?'

'You? You are nothing. But to my Avialle you were something.' The old man scowled and lowered his eyes. 'The copies of her, all those ghosts – they were drawn to you. Not that I knew it at first. After Avialle was lost, I kept you imprisoned and unconscious. I still had many questions about what had happened. I implanted a neurocannula and brought you into one of my Grail network simulations so I could . . . investigate.'

'So you could torture me,' Paul spat.

Jongleur shrugged. 'Call it what you will. I have almost no physical life anymore. I wanted you in my realm. But I soon noticed that you had attracted attention from . . . something. It was always fleeting, but I was able to capture traces. It was Avialle – or rather, the duplicate versions of Avialle. They were drawn to you, somehow. They could not keep away from you for long.'

'She loved me,' Paul said.

'Shut your mouth. You have no right to speak of her now.'

'It's true. And my sin was that all I could truly offer her was pity. But that's still more than you can say, isn't it?'

Jongleur stood, pale with fury, and raised his clenched fists. 'Pig. I should kill you.'

Paul rose too. 'You're welcome to try. Go on – you've done everything else to me that you could.'

Paul's companions had turned as his argument with Jongleur grew louder. Azador hurried over to them. 'Please, my friends, no more fighting. We have an enemy already – and he is enough for us all, eh?'

Paul shrugged his shoulders and sat down. Azador whispered something in Jongleur's ear, then went back to the group gathered around Orlando. Jongleur stared at Paul for a long moment before lowering himself back to the ground. 'You will speak no more of that,' he said coldly.

'I will speak of what I want. If you hadn't imprisoned her, treated her like something in a museum, none of this would have happened.'

'You understand nothing,' Jongleur said, but the fire was gone from his voice. 'Nothing.'

For a while Paul only listened to the distant hissing and popping of the fire, his companions' murmuring conversation. 'So you stuck me in that simulation of the First World War,' he said at last. 'You staked me out. I was the bait.'

Jongleur looked at him as if from a great distance. 'I hoped to bring her close enough to capture, yes. Perhaps eventually to gather enough of the copies to reconstitute something close to the real Avialle.'

'Why? Was it anything so normal as a father's love? Or was it something less pleasant? Was it just because she was yours, and you wanted back what belonged to you?'

The old man was rigid. 'What is in my heart . . . is for no man to know.'

'Heart? You have a heart?' He expected anger, but this time Jongleur seemed too chilled and weary even to respond. 'So what was it all about, then? All that madness, that bizarre museum of a house and grounds – what did you intend?'

Jongleur did not speak for a long time. 'Do you know what an *ushabti* is?' he said at last.

Paul shook his head, puzzled. 'I don't know the word.'

'It does not matter,' Jongleur said. 'In fact, all this talk is worthless. We will both be dead soon. When the system collapses everyone here will die.'

'Then if it doesn't matter, you might as well tell me the truth.' Paul leaned forward. 'You were going to kill me, weren't you? Ava was right about that. You were going to kill me – swat me like a fly. Weren't you?'

Felix Jongleur looked at him for a long, calculating second, then looked down at the fire. 'Yes.'

Paul sat back with a sick little feeling of triumph. 'But why?'

Jongleur shook his head. 'It was a mistake – a bad idea. A failed project. It was named for the *ushabti* of the

Egyptian tombs, the tiny statuettes that were meant to work for the dead Pharaoh in the after-life.'

'I'm not following you. You wanted me to work for you after you were dead?'

Jongleur showed a wintry smile. 'Not you. You give yourself too much importance, Mr Jonas. A common problem with the people of your small island.'

Paul swallowed a retort. So the ancient Frenchman wanted to insult the Brits – let him. He had never imagined he would actually get the chance to speak to this man face-to-face. He could not waste the opportunity. 'Then who? What?'

'I began the Ushabti Project several years ago, at a time when I felt quite certain that the Grail process was going to fail. The first results on the thalamic splitter were very bad and the Grail network's operating system – the Other, as some call it – was unstable.' Jongleur frowned. 'I was already very, very old. If the Grail Project did not succeed, I would die. But I did not want to die.'

'Who does?'

'Few have the resources I do. Few have the courage to flout humanity's cowardly surrender to death.'

Paul held in his impatience. 'So . . . you started this . . . Ushakti Project?'

'*Ushabti.* Yes. If I could not perpetuate my actual self, I would do the next best thing. Like the pharaohs, I would keep my line alive. I would save the sacred blood. I would do this by creating a version of me that would survive my death.'

'But you just said that the technology wasn't working . . .'

'It was not. So I came up with the best alternative I could. I could not escape death, it seemed, so I created a clone.'

A number of terrible thoughts began fizzing in Paul's head. 'But that's . . . that doesn't make sense. A clone isn't you, it's just your genetics. It would grow up into a very different person, because its experiences . . . would be different . . .'

'I see you begin to understand. Yes, it would not be me. But if I gave it an upbringing as close to my own as I could, then it would be more like me. Enough like me to appreciate what I had done. Perhaps even enough to resurrect me someday from the Grail copies we had already made, flawed as they were.' Jongleur closed his eyes, remembering. 'All was prepared. When he reached his maturity and spoke his true name – *Hor-sa-iset*, Horus the Younger – to my system, it would have served as his access code. That is the *true* Horus of Egyptian mythology – the Horus born from the dead body of Osiris. All of my secrets would have been his.' He frowned, distracted. 'If I had already conceived of the Ushabti Project when I was founding the Grail Brotherhood, I would never have given 'Horus' as a code name to that imbecile Yacoubian . . .'

'Hang on a bit. You . . . you were going to use a clone to recreate your own childhood?' Paul was stunned by the magnitude of the man's lunacy. 'On top of a skyscraper?' A thought struck him like a stone. 'Oh, my God, Ava? She was going to be . . .'

'The mother. *My* mother – or at least the mother of my *ushabti*. A vessel for the preservation of the blood.'

'Christ, you really are mad. Where did you get the poor girl? Was she some actress you hired to play your sainted Mama? She couldn't have been your real daughter, unless you raised her in a genetics lab too.' It struck him then, sapping the strength from his body, chilling him to the bone. 'Jesus. You did, didn't you? You . . . made her.'

Jongleur seemed wearily amused by Paul's astonishment. 'Yes. She was another clone of me – modified so
she would be female, of course, so actually quite a bit
different. You need not look so shocked – the Egyptians
married brother to sister. Why should I do less for my
own posterity? In fact, I would have used my real mother
as the source for Avialle's genetic material, but I could
not bring myself to exhume her body. She had rested in
the cemetery in Limoux for almost two centuries and she
still does. Her bones were left undisturbed.' He waved his
hand dismissively. 'But it made little difference, in any
case. The mother was to provide no DNA, after all. She
was only to be the host – to carry and bear and then
raise my true son.'

'God help me, it just gets worse and worse. So Ava
was right – she *was* pregnant!'

'Briefly. But we had a breakthrough on the Grail Project
and so I abandoned Ushabti.'

'And so you took the embryo back. Then you just . . .
kept Ava anyway. Kept her a prisoner.'

For a moment, Jongleur's mask of disdain slipped. 'I
. . . I had come to care for her. My own children have
been dead for years. I scarcely know their descendants.'

Paul put his head in his hands. 'You . . . you . . .' He
took a deep, shuddering breath. 'I should just stop, but I
can't help asking. What about me? What did you intend
to do before Ava ruined your plans by falling in love
with me?'

The cold smile returned. 'She ruined nothing. I expected
her to do just that. My own mother was in love with her
tutor. He committed suicide. In her misery she allowed
her parents to marry her off to my father but the sadness
never left her – it was the thing that shaped the rest of
her life. If it had not happened, she would not have been

the mother I knew.' His smile twisted. 'It was those fools Mudd and Finney who let things get out of control. They should have left the two of you alone until we were ready to dispose of you. I had just canceled the Ushabti Project, so what did it matter, anyway?'

'It mattered to me,' Paul said, shaken but angry. 'It mattered to me and to Ava.'

'You are not to speak further of Avialle. I am tired of your familiarity.'

Paul squeezed his eyes closed for a moment, fighting the rage that would end all questions and answers. 'Then just tell me this – why did you pick me out of all the poor sods in the world? Was it just random? Did you simply choose the first acceptable applicant for this little . . . honor? Or was there something particular about me?'

When he looked up, the old man's eyes were glassy and dead again. 'Because you went to Cranleigh.'

'What?' It was the last answer he expected. 'What are you talking about – my public school?'

Jongleur's sneer was almost a sign of weakness – the first such sign from him Paul had seen. 'I was sent there as a child. The English boys singled me out as a foreigner and a weakling. They tortured me.'

'And because of that you chose *me?* You were going to murder me just because I went to Cranleigh?' Paul laughed despite himself, a painful, near-hysterical flutter at the top of his lungs. 'Christ, I hated that place. The older boys treated me just like they treated you.' *Except for Niles*, he remembered, and the thought brought another with it. 'So what happened to me afterward – the *real* me. Am I dead like Ava? Did you have me killed?'

The old man had lost his fire. 'No. We arranged an automobile accident, but not with your real body. That is still quite safe in one of the project's laboratories and, as far as I know, quite alive. The remains that were sent back to England were those of a vagrant. There was no need for British authorities to doubt the identification of the body.'

But even if I'm not really dead, I might as well be, he thought. *Niles isn't shifting heaven and earth to find me, that's certain. He's given that 'remember good old Paul Jonas?' speech a long time ago now.* 'How long?' he asked.

Jongleur looked at him in confused irritation. 'What?'

'How long have I been in your damned system? How long since you killed your daughter and as good as killed me?'

'Two years.'

Paul struggled up onto his feet, legs weak, knees trembling. He could not sit across from the murderer any longer. Two years. Two years obliterated and his life ruined, for nothing. For a failed, insane project. Because he had gone to a particular school. It was the bleakest joke imaginable. He stumbled away from the fire, toward the Well. He wanted to weep but he couldn't.

ORLANDO was stirring, even fighting a little. Reluctantly, Sam let go of him and sat up. 'Is he okay?'

'He is just awakening, I think,' said Florimel.

Over T4b's shoulder, Sam saw Paul Jonas abruptly stand and stagger away across the camp, heading toward the pit. Remembering !Xabbu, she was torn between fear for Paul and an absolute unwillingness to leave Orlando, but Martine was already rising to her feet.

'I will go with Paul,' she said. 'I can wait to speak to Orlando.'

Orlando's eyelids flickered, then opened. He looked at the faces leaning over him. 'I had the most amazing dream,' he said after a few seconds. 'You were in it – and you, and you, and you!' His lips trembled. 'That's kind of a joke.' He burst into tears.

Sam wrapped her arms around the weeping barbarian. 'It's okay. We're here. I'm here. You're okay.'

Florimel cleared her throat and stood. 'There are many injured all around. I will see if I can be of any help.' None of the others had risen. Florimel looked sternly at T4b. 'Javier, I am still upset that you lied to us, but I will be closer to forgiving you if you come and help me.'

'But, want to check out Orlando, me . . .' he began, then the look on Florimel's face sank in. 'Yeah, seen, coming.' He stood, then reached back down to pat Orlando. 'Lockin' miracle, you got. Praise God, seen?'

'Nandi, Mrs Simpkins, perhaps you could help me, too?' asked Florimel. 'And Azador – surely some of your people are in need of attention as well.'

'All right, I don't need to have a house fall on me,' said Bonita Mae Simpkins. She too leaned down to touch Orlando before she got up. 'Javier's right, boy – it's a miracle you're back with us. We'll leave you young ones alone for a little while. Sure you got lots to talk about.'

Sam made a face at their retreating backs. 'You'd think we were in love or something.'

Orlando smiled wearily. 'Yeah, you'd think.' His eyes and cheeks were still wet. He rubbed at his face with the back of his hand. 'This is so embarrassing – Thargor never cries.'

Sam's heart was pierced again. 'Oh, Orlando, I missed you so much. I never thought I'd see you again.' Now she was crying, too. She angrily dabbed at her eyes with the tattered sleeve of her Gypsy shirt. 'Damn, this is so stupid. You're going to start thinking of me as a girl.'

'But you are a girl, Frederico,' he said gently. 'This may be the first time I've ever seen you look like one, but you're definitely a girl.'

'Not to you! Not to you, Gardiner! You treat me like a person!'

He sighed. 'I recognized your voice when I first . . . came back. I saw you trying to come and help me against those things. I could have killed you myself. What were you thinking?'

'I wasn't going to sit there and watch you get murdered, you impacted idiot! I already thought you were dead once.'

'I was dead. I *am* dead.'

'Don't talk *fenfen*.'

'It's not.' He reached for her hand. 'Listen, Sam. This is important – really important. Whatever else happens, you have got to understand this. I don't want to see you get hurt any more.'

Something about his tone touched her, made her heart flutter. It wasn't love, certainly not the kind the kids at school and on the net talked about, but something wider, deeper, and more strange. 'What do you mean?'

'I died, Sam. I know I did. I felt it. I was fighting with that thing, that Grail bastard with the bird's head . . .' He paused. 'Whatever happened there, anyway?'

'You killed it,' she said proudly. 'T4b stuck his hand into its head – that glowing hand, do you remember? And then you stabbed it right in the heart with your sword, and it fell on you . . .' She suddenly remembered. 'Oh, your sword . . . !'

Orlando waved the interruption away. 'It's right here in my hand. Listen, Sam. I was fighting with that bird-thing and everything in me was . . . shutting down. I could feel it. And afterward I was gone – utterly gone! I was somewhere else, and . . . and I can't even explain. Then it was black, and then I was swimming up through the lights here and I knew I had to kill those two things, and . . . and . . .' He frowned and tried to sit up but Sam gently pushed him back down. 'And I don't even know, really. But I know one thing. The other Orlando, the one with progeria, the one with a mom and a dad and a body . . . he's gone.'

'What are you talking about?'

'Remember what they were saying at that Grail Brotherhood ceremony? About how you had to leave your body behind to live on the net? Well, I think that's what happened to me. I don't know how, but . . . but I was dying, Sam! And now I'm not. I can tell.'

'But that's good, Orlando – that's wonderful!'

He shook his head. 'I'm a ghost, Sam. My body – that Orlando – is dead. I can never go back.'

'Go back . . . ?' It was beginning to sink in now, cold, inescapable. 'You can't . . . ?'

'I can't go back to the real world. Even if we survive all this, even if all the rest of you make it back . . . I can't go with you.' He looked at her for a long moment, his eyes wide, almost fevered. Then his expression softened. 'Damn, Fredericks, you're crying again.' He reached out and caught a tear on her cheek, holding it up to sparkle in the firelight. 'Don't do that.'

'What are . . . what are we going to do?' she said, breath hitching quietly as she did her best not to sob.

'Try not to get killed. Or try not to get killed again, in my case.' He pulled himself up into a sitting position. 'Now tell me what happened after I died.'

It caught her by surprise. She squeaked with laughter in spite of herself but it also left her feeling frighteningly hollow. 'Damn you, Gardiner, don't do that to me.'

He smiled. 'Sorry. Some things don't change, I guess.'

SHE caught up to him at the edge of the shoreline. Without saying a word she slipped her arm through his. He started a little at the unexpected contact but did not pull away. It was nice to be touched, he realized, and with that also realized that he was planning to live.

'I wasn't going to jump in,' he said.

'I didn't think so,' she told him. 'But it would have been messy if you fell in by accident.'

He turned and she pivoted neatly beside him. They moved along the shore.

'Tell me,' she said. 'Did it all come back this time?'

'More than I wanted,' he said.

As he described his returned memories – his returned life, in fact – and Jongleur's bizarre explanations, he found himself feeling more than ever ashamed at his own timidity, at the way he had let the events of his former life carry him along with little resistance to such a terrible conclusion.

'. . . And Ava – she was so young!' His hands were clenched into such tight fists that he knew Martine could feel the tremors in his arm. 'How could I . . . ?'

'How could you what?' He was surprised to hear anger in her voice. 'Offer her comfort? Do your best to help her in the middle of a bizarre, frightening, inexplicable situation? Did you try to seduce her?'

'No!'

'Did you take advantage of her ignorance – her sheltered innocence . . . ?'

'No, of course not. Not on purpose. But just by going along with it – just by continuing to be her teacher even when I knew the whole thing was somehow rotten . . .'

'Paul.' She tightened her grip on his arm. 'Someone . . . a friend . . . told me something once. He was speaking of me, but he might have been speaking of you. "You never avoid an opportunity to stare directly at the wrong things," is what he said.' She made a noise that might have been a laugh. Paul found himself wondering for the first time what the real Martine looked like and was saddened that her blindness made her image bland and unremarkable. 'It was an even wittier epigram originally, of course,' she said. 'Because of the bit about staring.'

'He sounds cruel.'

'I thought so at the time, and I valued him for it – I was very cynical in my student days. But I think now he just did not yet have the strength to be gentle.' She smiled. 'We may all be in our last hours, Paul Jonas. Do you really want to spend them trying to remember the many things you may have done wrong?'

'I suppose not.'

They walked for a while in silence beside the dimly pulsing Well.

'It's hard,' he said. 'I've been thinking all along that somehow I'd find her . . . save her. Or perhaps that she'd save me.'

'You are speaking of . . . Ava?' she asked him carefully.

He nodded. 'But there is no Ava. Not really. Avialle Jongleur is dead, and all that's left are fragments. Held together by the Other, I suppose, but she's not quite real. Like trying to reassemble a puzzle without having all the right pieces. In its way, the Other must have loved her more than anyone else did – certainly more than her so-called father did. More than I did. She was its angel.'

Martine did not reply.

'There's something else,' he said after a moment. 'Jongleur told me that as far as he knows, my body's still alive.'

'Do you think he is lying?'

'No. But I don't think it's my body anymore.'

Martine paused. 'What do you mean, Paul?'

'I've been thinking – during the few moments something hasn't been actively trying to kill us, that is.' He made the effort to smile. 'Those very few moments. And I believe I know what happened when Sellars got me out of that World War One simulation. See, as long as the Grail people had my body, they also had my mind. Sellars – and Ava – could only talk to me when I was dreaming. But somehow, I escaped the simulation.'

'And you think . . .'

'I think that I've been through the Grail Brotherhood's ceremony – that my consciousness has been split off somehow, the way they planned to do for themselves. Perhaps it was an accident – I don't know why they would have made a virtual mind for me like they did for all the Grail people. But I think it did happen, and Sellars somehow brought that virtual mind to life. And that second, virtual Paul Jonas . . . is me.'

She said nothing, but clutched his arm more tightly.

'So all the things I left behind, the simple, silly things that have kept me going here when I wanted to lie down and die, my flat, my mediocre job, my entire old life . . . they don't belong to me. They belong to the real Paul. The one whose body is in a lab somewhere. Even if that body dies, I can never have them . . .'

He fell silent for a while. It hurt too much to talk. They walked on along the desolate shoreline.

'What is that line from T. S. Eliot?' he said when he trusted himself to speak. 'Something about, "I should have been a pair of ragged claws, scuttling on the floors of silent seas . . ."'

She turned her sightless face toward him. 'Are you criticizing yourself again?'

'Actually, I was talking about the landscape.' He stopped.

'It does seem like the kind of place to wait for the end of the world, doesn't it?'

'I am tired of waiting for the end of the world,' she said, but her head was cocked at a strange angle.

'Well, I don't think we have a lot of choice,' he began. 'Dread is still waiting just outside, and even if Orlando took care of the Twins I don't think he's up to dealing with what Dread's become . . .'

'I suspect you are right. The Other has played its knight and it has bought some time, but nothing else.'

'Its . . . ?'

'Its knight. Do you remember the story of the boy in the well? One of his would-be saviors was a knight. I suspect the Other had Orlando picked out for that role from the beginning.' She frowned and raised her hand. 'Quiet for a moment, please. Stand still.'

'What is it?' Paul asked after a short silence.

'The waters are receding.' She pointed. 'Can you see it?'

'Whatever it is, it's not visible to me.' But he wondered if in fact the lights were not already a little dimmer.

'I can feel the whole thing failing,' she said distractedly. 'Like an engine that has run too long. The end is coming very fast now I think.'

'What can we do?'

She listened silently for long moments. 'Nothing, I fear. Go back to the others and wait with them.' She turned toward him. 'But first I must ask you something. Will you hold me, Paul Jonas? Just for a short while? It has been a long time for me. I would not . . . would not like to die . . . without touching someone first.'

He put his arms around her, full of conflicted thoughts. She was small, at least in this incarnation; her head fit just beneath his chin, her cheek against his chest. He wondered what her heightened senses would make of the quickness of his heartbeat.

'Perhaps in another world,' she said, the words muffled against him. 'In another time . . .'

Then they just held each other and did not speak. At last they let go and went back side by side across the gray dust, toward the fire where their friends were waiting.

CHAPTER 43

Tears of Ra

NETFEED/ENTERTAINMENT: Porn Star Ignores Protests Over Planned Children's Interactive
(visual: Violet in excerpt from 'Ultra Violet')
VO: Adult interactive actress Vondeen Violet says she doesn't under-stand the controversy over her intention to produce what she calls 'educational interactives' about sex for the under-twelve crowd.
VIOLET: 'Kids need to learn and they'll find it out somehow. Isn't it better they learn from a nonviolent interactive where they will partic-ipate with trained professionals like myself, instead of getting their information in the schoolyard or on the street? I mean, these things were written by a doctor, for God's sake!'

'I see it,' said Catur Ramsey, 'but I don't really believe it.'

'I am here,' Olga told him. 'And I'm not sure that I believe it either.'

Ramsey sat back and rubbed his tired eyes, half certain that any moment now he would wake up and the whole bizarre day would prove to have been a dream. But when he looked at the screen again the feed from Olga Pirofsky's camera ring still showed the same improbable, fish-eye view.

'It's a forest,' he said. 'You walk out of the elevator onto the top floor and into . . . a forest?'

'Dead,' she said quietly.

'What?'

'Look.' The viewpoint swung upward and now Ramsey could see that most of the branches were bare. Even the evergreens were almost all dead, with only a few clusters of brown needles remaining on the skeletal limbs. The camera ring swung down again. Ramsey could see Olga's legs wading through knee-high drifts of brown and gray leaves, squeezing up puffs of dry dust. The picture stopped moving as Olga paused to kick some of the cover aside, then the viewpoint swung across an expanse of black speckled with white.

'What is it?' Ramsey asked. 'I can't make it out.'

'I think it was a stream,' she said. 'It's mud now. Almost completely dry.' The viewpoint moved closer until Ramsey could see that the white streaks were arranged in familiar shapes.

'Are those fish?'

'They were.'

Her tone was conversational, but Ramsey heard something in it he didn't like – something close to despair. 'Come down, Olga. I've got Beezle in my other ear telling me they're almost done evacuating the building. We probably only have minutes to get you out.'

'I see something.' A moment later the camera swung up. Ramsey could see it too, now. It was an even stranger sight on the top floor of a skyscraper than the dead trees and fish skeletons.

'A house? A *house?*'

'I'm going to go look.'

'I wish you wouldn't.' Ramsey opened his other line. 'I can't get her to leave yet, Beezle. How much time do we have?'

'You're asking me? Sellars set it up so this whole thing would be screwed up on purpose – misleading alarms, rerouted communications, you name it. There's even some kind of reactor alert going out. The army could be there in five minutes or no one may come near the place for days.'

'Reactor alert? There's a reactor? Jesus. Just keep letting me know what's happening, will you?'

'Beezle snorted. 'When I know anything, you'll know it too.'

The view on Ramsey's pad screen was too vertiginous to watch just now: Olga's hand was swinging up and down as she pushed her way through the overgrown vegetation. He closed his eyes. 'How big is that forest?' he asked her. 'Can you see anything else? What's over your head?'

'Nothing. Just a big white ceiling at least fifty meters up.' The picture settled as she lowered the ring to show him the house, much larger now. 'Can you see it?'

'You can't just walk in, Olga. What if someone's in there?'

'You obviously can't see it very well,' she said, but didn't explain. Ramsey found himself holding his breath as she made her way across the ragged brown remains of what might once have been a large and very nice garden.

'It is not too American-looking, this house,' Olga said. 'It looks like a European manor house – a small one. I saw many like it when I was younger.'

'Just be careful.'

'You worry too much, Mr Ramsey. No one has lived here for some time, I think.' The viewpoint swung forward as she reached for the door. 'But who did live here? That is the question.'

The door creaked open. Ramsey heard it clearly enough down her channel to know that the silence that followed it was just as real. 'Olga? Are you okay?'

'It is . . . quite empty.' She moved out of what seemed a narrow hallway and gave him a slow, sweeping view of the front room. The windows were shuttered, the room dark. Ramsey adjusted the brightness and resolution on his picture but still could make out little beyond the broad shapes of antique furnishings.

'I can't see much. What's there?'

'Dust,' she said distantly. 'There is dust on everything. The furniture, it seems quite old. Like something from two or three centuries ago. The carpet is dusty too, but I see no footprints. No one has been here in a long, long time.' There was a long pause. 'I do not like it here. I do not like the feeling.'

'Then get out, Olga. Please. I already told you . . .'

'I wonder who lived here? The man Felix Jongleur? But what trouble, to build something like this on top of his building when he could have had a real New Orleans mansion on the ground, with real gardens, real orchards . . .'

'He's rich and probably crazy, Olga. That combination produces a lot of odd things.'

'Whoever lived here, it was a sad place.' The viewpoint moved along the wall, past a tabletop full of framed pictures; Ramsey saw grim faces in high collars. 'A haunted house . . .'

'Time to go, Olga.'

'I think you are right. I do not like it here. But I will look into some of the rooms first.'

Ramsey held his tongue, but barely. He had no control over her, only the ability to suggest – it wouldn't do any good to give her an ultimatum he couldn't back up. Still, her weird, unhurried mood was making him very tense.

'Dining room – look, there is still a table setting. Just one. As if someone simply did not come home for their meal.' The viewpoint wandered across dusty plates and silver. The glassware was furred with cobwebs. 'It is like Pompeii. Have you ever been there, Mr Ramsey?'

'No.'

'A strange place. Even the most ordinary things become magical in the right situations.'

She wandered through a few more rooms. When she found what was clearly a girl's bedroom with its shelf of cobwebbed but wide-eyed dolls, she broke her long silence. 'Now I will leave. It is too pitiful, whatever this was.'

Ramsey did not say anything, not wanting to interfere with her resolution. He stayed quiet as she made her way back outside and into the barren garden.

'Olga . . . ?' he finally said as she lingered in front of a dry stone fountain.

'The children – they are not on this floor.' She sighed. 'There is nothing in that place, nothing left.'

'I know . . .'

'So there is one more place I must look,' she said.

'What? What are you talking about?'

'There is a floor between this one and the room with all the machines,' she said. 'I will look there, too.'

'Olga, you don't have time . . . !'

'I have nothing but time, Mr Ramsey. Catur. All my life has come to this – this place, this moment.' Even through the dreamy tone her voice was firm. 'I have time.'

'I seem to have forgotten the way to the elevator,' she said at last. She had not bothered to lift the ring for many minutes; Ramsey's only view was of the camera swinging back and forth over the ground, across the leaves and the humped, desiccated roots and parched ground.

'Beezle,' he said on the other line, 'which way should she go?'

'Jeez, I don't know,' the agent rasped. 'I don't have the maps for this floor. But the wall's circular and there's probably a walkway all around the outside, like there was just outside the elevator. Just tell her to keep going straight. She'll hit it sooner or later.'

'Sooner or later?' Ramsey closed his eyes again and took a deep breath. 'Good God, am I the only person who's in a hurry around here?' But he relayed the message to Olga.

Beezle was right. Within a few hundred paces she stepped onto a floor of polished wood and found the wall at the end of the dead forest. 'Which direction?' she asked.

'Beezle says take your pick.'

She turned right, following the featureless curve. After a moment, she slowed, then stopped. Maddeningly, Ramsey could still only see her feet.

'What is it?'

The viewpoint swung up. A vast square of darkly transparent plastic had been set into the wall. Through it he could just make out a dim suggestion of the roofs of buildings far below and for a moment he thought it was only another window, but the crudeness of the way adhesive foam had been splashed around its edges suggested it was a late and rather cursory repair to the now-decayed but careful work elsewhere on the floor.

'I can . . . can feel them.'

It took him a moment to understand her. 'The . . . the voices? You can feel them?'

'Faintly.' He heard her laugh a little. 'I know, you are now finally convinced of what I have tried to tell you so long. I *am* mad. But I can feel them, just a little.' She was silent for a moment. 'Not good. It is another sad place – different from inside the house, even worse. Not good.'

She began moving again. 'But whatever happened there, it is not what brought me here,' she added. Ramsey was chilled by her casual tone, her certainty.

'But . . . you felt them?'

'I felt ghosts, Mr Ramsey.'

She found the elevator and summoned it with her badge. When she had stepped in and the door had shut behind her, Ramsey moved to his other line.

'She's taking forever, Beezle – she's going to the next floor down to look there, too. How are we doing? Firefighters show up yet?' The agent did not reply. 'Beezle?'

'I had to cut in and I'm afraid I've lost him,' said a voice that was definitely not Beezle. 'Things are a bit . . . difficult at the moment.'

'Sellars?'

'Barely, but yes.'

It was unquestionably his voice but there was something eerie about it, a jittering tension beneath the calm. Ramsey thought he sounded like a man holding the live ends of a fifty thousand volt electrical cable. 'Jesus, what's going on?'

'It's a long story. I see Olga is still in the tower . . .'

'Yes, and I can't get her to leave. We've tricked up all the alarms, all the stuff you set up, but the authorities are probably going to be breaking in the doors any moment now and I keep telling her to get out, but she won't listen – she's still wandering around looking for the children, you know, the voices in her head . . .'

'Mr Ramsey,' Sellars interrupted, 'at this moment I am already swimming in information – no, drowning. I am surrounded by data, more data than you can imagine. Every nerve in my body is about to catch fire and burn

to carbon.' Sellars took a shaky breath. 'So will you do
me a favor and shut the hell up?'

'Sure. Sure, yes.'

'Good. I have to talk to Olga. While I'm doing that, I
need you to go next door and talk to the Sorensens. If I
have time, I'll join you and speak to them myself. This
is critically important. If they're not there you have to
find them immediately.'

'Got it.'

'And when I get done with Olga, I want you on the
other line with her.'

'Me? But . . . ?'

In remarkably few words, Sellars explained what he
had discovered and was shortly going to tell Olga Pirofsky.
Ramsey felt as though he had been kicked in the gut by
a horse.

'. . . So perhaps now you can understand why I want
you with her when I've finished,' Sellars said a bit harshly.
He was maintaining his calm, but clearly at a price.

'Christ.' Ramsey looked at the screen, barely able to
focus. 'Oh, Christ. Oh, God.' Olga's feet were still in view,
stepping out of the elevator and onto a carpeted floor.
'She's . . . she's just getting out.'

'I know,' said Sellars, a little more gently now. 'Go and
talk to the Sorensens, will you, please?' And then he was
gone.

'Who the hell was that?' demanded Beezle. 'Sucker cut
me right off, booted me off the line.'

'I can't talk now,' Ramsey told the agent. 'Oh, my God,
I can't believe this. Just stay on the line. I'll be back.'

'Jeez,' said Beezle. 'This'll teach me to quit working
with meat.'

'**S**o is there nothing left we can do?' Florimel asked angrily. 'Again we must wait?'

'Unless we can discover some way out,' said Martine, 'we have little choice.'

Orlando sat up and stretched his long arms, then tested the point of his sword with his fingertip. It was an old, familiar Thargor gesture, and it distracted Sam just as she was trying to remember something important. For a moment she could almost believe they were back in the Middle Country, in a world where games had rules. Thargor was here. Didn't that mean they would win? Thargor always won.

But there is no Thargor, she thought sadly, *not really. There's just Orlando and he already got killed once.* She looked to the unreal gray wall of cloud. *And even if we can't see him at the moment, that guy Dread is still out there.* Sam felt like a mouse caught away from its hole, being stalked by an unhurried cat.

I'm really going to die, she thought. It hadn't quite hit her before – there had always been hope, or at least distraction. Now nothing remained between her and noth-ingness but the last defenses of the dying system. *I'm never going to see Mom or Dad again. My school. Even my stupid room . . .*

'What about this child?' asked Nandi Paradivash. 'You said he was the emissary of the man Sellars.'

'Ain't no messary, *vato*,' snarled the little boy Cho-Cho, who was sitting so far away from the others that the near-est person to him was the unsocial Felix Jongleur. 'He never touch me – I cut anyone who try that. Me, I'm just helping him out.'

'That's what it means, boy,' said Bonnie Mae Simpkins. 'An emissary's a helper. Someone who carries messages.'

'But what message?' Florimel had calmed a little since

the Twins had been dispatched but she was still edgy, her anger barely controlled. Looking around at the wreckage left by the Twins' attack, hundreds of miserable survivors still huddled around the edge of the Well and too many victims still lying where they had fallen, Sam couldn't really blame her. Any of the cowering fairy-tale folk could be Florimel's daughter or Renie's brother, but random questioning had confirmed that none of them seemed to remember a prior life. 'What message?' Florimel repeated. 'We know nothing. We continue in absolute ignorance as we have since the beginning!'

'Has Sellars said anything to you?' Martine asked the little boy. 'Can you hear him at all?'

'Not since that dog-head mamalocker pulled the roof off that place,' Cho-Cho said sullenly. 'He just ditched me, like.'

'So it seems we won't get much from Sellars,' Paul said wearily. 'What next?'

Felix Jongleur pierced the uncomfortable silence. 'It is a miracle you have all stayed alive so long. Democracy is a frightening thing, seen up close.'

'Shut up,' Florimel snapped. 'You pig-dog, you want to see the frightening side of democracy? Remember, there are a lot of us and then there is just you.'

'The idea was that he would be *useful*,' said Paul slowly. Sam had never seen him looking so cold and angry. 'Well, it's about time he was. It may be too late to do us much good, but I'd still like some answers. About the operating system – about the whole thing . . .'

Several of the others seemed to agree: an increasingly unhappy murmur rose around the campfire. They all turned to look at Jongleur, who accepted their attention with his usual flat, forbidding gaze, but Sam thought she saw something else just beneath, something peculiar.

Was he ashamed? Frightened? He seemed almost . . . nervous.

'Come, friend,' Azador called from his seat next to Martine. 'These people have questions. Put their minds at rest.'

Paul turned on the Gypsy. 'And you, Azador – what is your problem? Do you know who your so-called friend really is? That's Felix Jongleur, the man who ran the Grail Brotherhood. Remember the bastards you went on and on about, the ones who chased you and imprisoned all your people, who used them to make their machines work? That's the head of it all – that man, right there.'

Sam held her breath, wondering if Azador would now attack Jongleur as Paul had earlier. It was a miracle, really, that the secret she and !Xabbu had agreed to keep should have lasted so long . . .

'!Xabbu!' she said out loud, suddenly remembering.

Azador was not listening. He peered intently at Jongleur, then at Paul Jonas. Finally he shrugged, oddly embarrassed. 'It seems a long, long time ago.'

'What?' Paul was almost screaming. 'Good Lord, this man has been killing your people but you're just going to let bygones be bygones because you're you're . . . bloody *chums* now? How can you?'

'Because it never happened,' Jongleur said scornfully. 'These *are* his people, what is left of them.' He waved his hand to indicate the wreckage of the wagons, the remaining Gypsy men and women huddled around their fires. 'Everything else was fantasy.'

'!Xabbu!' Sam said, louder this time. 'Everybody, I utterly forgot about !Xabbu because of those monsters, and Orlando, and . . . and everything. He went into that pit – he dived in! I went in after him but it spit me out and I couldn't get him. He thought Renie was down there!'

This set the circle around the campfire buzzing.

'Then he is gone, Sam,' Florimel said at last. There was something softer and sadder in her tone now.

'Orlando came back from there!' Sam said angrily.

'That is different, Sam,' Martine told her. 'You know that it is.'

Because he isn't alive like !Xabbu, Sam thought but didn't say. *That's what she means.* Deep down, much as she hated it, she knew Martine was right. Several of her companions were all talking at once now. *Because Orlando didn't come back from there, he was . . . born from there.*

'There is an easy way to find out if she is there,' said Jongleur loudly. A sour smile played around the edge of his mouth. 'But I am sure you have thought of it already and need no assistance from a monster like me.'

'Don't push your luck,' Martine warned him. 'If you have something useful to say, do so.'

'Very well. Do you still have your communication device? I was with the woman Renie when you called her before. Why not call her again?'

'My God,' Martine said. 'My God, with everything going on I had completely forgotten.' She pulled a chunky silver lighter from the pocket of her coveralls.

'How did you get that?' Sam asked, completely confused. 'Renie had it!'

'It is a copy,' Martine told her. 'I will explain later.'

Sam saw the glint of satisfaction – or perhaps something else – in the hawk-faced man's eyes. She jumped to her feet and pointed at Jongleur. 'Don't let him get near it!'

He spread his hands. 'I am on the other side of the fire. There are, as you pointed out, many of you and only one of me.'

Martine lifted the lighter. 'Renie,' she said, 'can you hear me? It's Martine. Renie, are you there?'

For long moments, there was nothing.

'Can you hear me, Renie?'

Then suddenly her familiar voice was in their midst, as close and clear as if she had joined them at the campfire. '*Martine? Martine, is that you?*'

Martine laughed with delight. 'Renie! Oh, what a blessing to hear you. Where are you?'

'*I'm . . . I don't really know. Inside the operating system, I guess. But that's only the beginning of how bizarre this all is. !Xabbu is with me . . .*'

'!Xabbu!' Sam found herself crying again. 'He's alive!'

'Can you hear Sam Fredericks?' Martine said, still laughing. 'She . . .'

Something knocked Martine to the ground. Sam shouted and stood up. Orlando, still sore and weary, took a full two seconds to struggle to his feet beside her. Azador stood over Martine, the lighter in his hand and a hugely triumphant grin on his face.

'I have it back!' he shouted. 'I have it back!'

THE voice seemed to come out of nowhere.

'*Renie,*' it said, '*can you hear me? It's Martine. Renie, are you there?*'

She had fallen into a sort of half-drowse, exhaustion having finally overwhelmed everything else, and for a long moment she could not even remember where she was.

'!Xabbu, what's going on?' She stared at the dry pan, the thorn bushes and the brightly starred sky, trying to imagine where Martine could be. Could you dream inside a dream?'

'*Can you hear me, Renie?*' Martine asked again.

'It is in your *kaross*.' !Xabbu pointed at the antelope-hide garment she wore. Renie fumbled out the device. It was still a lighter, just as it had always been, although it now seemed the most unlikely object in an entire, unlikely world. She pressed hot points in sequence, praying she had remembered the right order. 'Martine? Martine, is that you?'

'Renie! Oh, what a blessing to hear you. Where are you?'

She looked at !Xabbu, then down at the small shape of Grandfather Mantis crouched at the bottom of the gulley beside the trickling stream. It lay on its side now, legs drawn up. *It must still be breathing*, she thought distractedly, *or all this would be gone.*

But do gods breathe? she wondered an instant later.

'I'm . . . I don't really know. Inside the operating system, I guess. But that's only the beginning of how bizarre this all is. !Xabbu is with me . . .'

'Can you hear Sam Fredericks?' Martine sounded absolutely joyful. Renie felt tears spring to her eyes. *'She . . .'*

Abruptly, the transmission stopped.

'Martine?' Renie asked after a moment. 'Martine, are you still there?' She turned to !Xabbu. 'It just . . . cut off.'

The mantis stirred. She could hear its words in her head but they were desperately soft. *'You should not . . . should not have spoken. The All-Devourer will follow your words now. It will come straight here.'*

'Did you cut us off?' Renie crawled to her feet, aware as she did so of the absurdity of standing up to shout at a dying insect. 'Those are our friends!'

'Too late. Too late for them.' It was only a whisper, faint and distant. *'All we had left . . . was a little time. And now it is gone.'*

'Martine!' Renie shouted at the lighter. 'Martine, talk to me!' But when the device finally spoke again it was not Martine's voice she heard.

AZADOR backed away from the blind woman, who was already struggling up onto her knees, apparently not badly hurt. 'Mine!' he said feverishly. 'They thought they could take it from me – my gold! But Azador does not forget!'

Orlando snarled and raised his sword, but before he could take a step toward the thief someone shouted, *'Nobody move!'*

With a nightmarish, underwater feeling, Sam turned to see that Felix Jongleur had snatched up the boy Cho-Cho, who struggled like a scalded cat until Jongleur laid the broken blade of Orlando's old sword against the child's throat.

'I am not bluffing,' said Jongleur. 'Unless you wish to see your only connection to this man Sellars killed before your eyes you will sit down and stay seated.' He turned a baleful stare on Orlando. 'Especially you.'

Azador moved toward Jongleur, the lighter in his cupped hands, a look of reverence on his face. 'Look – is it not beautiful? You were right, my friend. You said the blind woman would have it and you were right!'

Jongleur smiled. 'You have been very patient. Will you let me see it?'

Azador stopped, his joy suddenly turned to suspicion. 'You cannot touch it.'

'I do not want to touch it,' Jongleur said. 'I only wanted to look, to make sure they had not tricked you – you heard what they said about a copy.'

'It is no copy!' Azador said indignantly. 'I would know! This is mine!'

'Of course,' said Jongleur.

Cho-Cho suddenly wrenched free of the old man's grip and dashed away across the Gypsy encampment. Azador turned to watch the boy go, and as he did, Jongleur grabbed Azador and set the broken blade against his neck then dragged it across his throat. Already gurgling blood, the Gypsy turned toward his supposed ally in amazement and tried to strike at him, but Jongleur grabbed his arm. Azador sagged and fell to the ground. Jongleur stood over him, holding the lighter in his red-smeared hand.

'Bastard!' shouted Paul Jonas. Orlando said nothing but was already moving toward the bald man.

Jongleur held up the lighter. 'Careful. I could easily throw it into the Well from here, couldn't I? Then you have lost your friend Renie.'

Orlando stopped short, breathing like a mastiff on a choke chain, his whole face disfigured by fury.

'I knew it!' Sam darted a look at Azador. The Gypsy's blood had made a blackish puddle on the shadowy ground beneath him. His dying eyes were still wide in astonishment. 'I knew it!' she screamed at the old man. 'You liar! You murderer!'

Jongleur laughed. 'Liar? Yes, certainly. Murderer? Perhaps, but not if you mean him.' He poked Azador with the toe of his Gypsy boot. 'He is not even a person. He is another copy, just like the Twins. Just like my Avialle.'

'Copy?' asked Paul haltingly.

'Yes – a copy of me,' Jongleur said. 'A rather poor and incomplete one from early in the process, given a home here by our rogue operating system. Perhaps it was taken while I was sleeping, I cannot remember. It certainly seems to have been dominated by a parade of my boyhood fantasies. That ridiculous Gypsy camp, the kind that only ever existed in Victorian fiction – I recognized it immediately.' He smirked. 'When I was a child I used to pretend that I came from such a place, not from my so-boring home and my so-boring parents.'

'What do you think you have accomplished, Jongleur?' demanded Martine Destroubins, her face still smeared with dirt from Azador's assaut. 'This is a standoff. We will not let you escape with the lighter.'

'Ah, but you cannot stop me.' He showed his teeth in a predatory grin. 'I have been waiting very patiently for this. Now I am going home to pull the plug on you and my ex-employee and my entire recalcitrant system. Be grateful – there should be no pain. I imagine your hearts will simply stop.' Jongleur held the lighter up. '*Priority Override*,' he said. '*Tears of Ra.*'

An instant later he was gone, vanished entirely from the dead lands beside the Well.

CHAPTER 44

Stolen Voices

NETFEED/NEWS: Arizona – The Voucher Society?
(visual: Thornley in front of state capitol building)
VO: Arizona's first Libertarian governor, Durwood Thornley, is propos-
ing to extend the school voucher system to a whole variety of taxpayer
opt-outs, and his critics are not very happy about it.
Thornley's proposed system would allow a variety of ways to reroute
taxes for services that the individual taxpayer does not want to support.
As an example, Thornley's staffers suggest that people without cars
could redeem their roadbuilding vouchers for repair work on patios and
sidewalks, or taxpayers without pets could use animal control vouchers
to pay for extermination of unwanted house and yard pests . . .

FOR a moment he feared that the override had not worked – that somehow the system had managed to undo its own basic programming – but the moment of darkness dissolved into the familiar depthless gray of his own system. He could feel his body again – not the robust physicality of the false form but his actual dying body, floating in its tank, maintained only by the careful attention of countless expensive machines. But for all the horror of returning to his true condition, it was still a wonderful feeling.

Felix Jongleur was home.

And now to trigger the Apep Sequence. There was no question the Other had to be destroyed, especially if Dread had it in his control. It was a shame to lose the millions of hours of work that had gone into it but this particular operating system had long since proved his worst fears to be underestimations.

It would be a shame if the Grail network itself should suffer too much damage, though. It was not the people trapped in it that worried Jongleur – he had not a single qualm about killing Paul Jonas and the rest, especially since as far as he was concerned Jonas had been on borrowed time for two years – but he did not know how well the network would survive being shut down. Even with a back-up operating system in place there would doubtless be huge losses in detail and responsiveness, since the system had been geared to the unique and astonishing capacities of the system known as the Other. And beside Jonas and his friends, anyone else still in the network, and thus still hooked into the Other's peculiar matrix, would doubtless die as well. He could not even be sure that the ghost-versions of Avialle would survive, although as code they should remain in memory when the network was revived.

He wished now that his own attempts to find and develop another operating system had borne fruit, or even that there had been time to work with Robert Wells to produce a proper alternative system of a more conventional sort, but it was too late for regrets. This was a war – a war for his own network, which had demanded ludicrous quantities of money, sweat, and blood – and in war there would always be casualties.

The most worrisome thing, of course, was his own safety. He had already been reluctant to commit himself permanently to a virtual body, so how could he trust one of the lesser systems designed by Wells' Telemorphix engineers – more reliable than his own perhaps, but far less sophisticated?

But if Avialle's copies can survive a system shutdown, he thought, *then my waiting virtual body should survive the changeover as well. And if I must risk completing the Grail process, even without entirely trusting the new system – well, I have never been afraid of risk.* The events of the past days had been unforeseen; he had come close to despair but he had remained strong. To survive and conquer now he would have to remain smarter and more aggressive than those around him, just as he always did.

It had not been easy to stay patient and meek with Jonas and the others, especially when he had known that one of the access devices was again within his easy reach, being carried by the woman Martine. But a single access device had never been of any use to him, or he could have taken Renie Sulaweyo's by force days earlier. He had feared he might somehow have to find his own way into the heart of the system, but luckily that coarse Sulaweyo woman had stumbled into it on her own. Jongleur had only needed to wait until contact was opened between the two devices so he could risk everything on one gamble, praying that when his override command reached Renie Sulaweyo's end of the communication circuit inside the Other, it would force the system's compliance.

Of course, risk was one thing, foolish risk another: he had prepared for the moment carefully, pretending to help the clownish Azador, quietly urging the pseudo-Gypsy to take back what he stupidly thought was his, so that if the first attempt to steal it should fail, Jongleur himself would still be free to try again.

In fact, he found it a bit disconcerting to discover how

easily he could trick and manipulate another version of himself – even a flawed version. It almost wounded his pride.

But that was a small detail. Everything had worked just as he had planned. He had waited, gambled, and won.

And now it is time. Time to play the endgame.

He ordered initialization of the Apep processes, seting in motion the complicated preparations so that he would be able to trigger it as soon as possible and be done with his rebellious operating system, then he rose out of the empty gray system-space into the reality of his great house.

Which, to his definite surprise, seemed to be completely empty.

What is going on here? The building's systems were alive with conflicting alarms – a fire alarm from the underground floors and a secondary alarm warning of a toxic release event from the island's offshore power plant. He brought up his camera-eyes and began to flick through the employee levels. It was Sunday, so of course the building would not be full, but the halls and offices were uniformly deserted. Jongleur put out a priority message to security but no one answered. He brought up the view of the building's security station, two floors below him. It was empty.

Impossible. Something was very wrong. He sent out an even higher priority message to the island's private military base, but all its lines were engaged. Someone had turned off his connection to the base surveillance cameras as well. He flicked to one of the low-orbit satellites and focused in until he could see movement – a great flurry of movement, in fact, like an ant army on the march. His troops were boarding a line of company ferries. Being evacuated.

Jongleur could sense the machineries of his heart trying to race, then the equipment compensating. He felt the cool placidity of countervailing chemicals flushing through his system. He found the override controls and turned down the tranquilizing flow: something terrible had happened, was happening right now, and he did not want to be lulled.

The basement, he thought. *That first.* He brought up the displays. The bottom of the building was indeed full of smoke – it had clouded the underground floors and leaked all the way up to the atrium lobby – but he could see no sign of flames. He checked the timing on the alarms. Almost two hours since the fire was first detected. Jongleur could make no sense of it. A smoldering fire that was mostly smoke could certainly last that long, but was it enough of a threat to abandon the building completely, let alone the whole island? Where were the fire crews? He asked for a quick analysis of the building's air system and found no unusual readings, no surprise toxins.

What in hell is going on?

The reactor incident might have been the answer but the records showed that those alarms had not even been triggered until half an hour after the fire began, although they were almost certainly the reason behind the mass evacuation of the base. It made no sense, though – the power plant was on a tiny offshore island, separate from the main island with its base and tower. Jongleur had wanted a small reactor under his personal control to make sure the narrowcast of the Grail network's operating system always had a source of backup power, but he had not been fool enough to put it next to the corporate offices – next to the place where his own helpless body was kept.

He brought up a bank of readouts from the power station but they were muddled and inconclusive. An alarm had definitely been sent out and the facility abandoned but he could get no clear picture of what had happened. The visual evidence gave no clues: the reactor itself seemed in perfectly normal condition, and a closer inspection of the reactor management data showed that it was shut down, temperatures normal, and in fact appeared to have been shut down well before its own alarm warnings went out, as though the technicians had responded to some completely separate order, securing the reactor and raising the containment shields before evacuating in an orderly fashion.

So if the fire was a minor one and the reactor wasn't in danger, why was everybody leaving?

Could it be one of my enemies? Has Wells also escaped offline? But why would he risk destroying the entire network, risk his own massive investment, just to strike at me?

Dread. It came to him like a winter's chill – for a moment he even saw his former employee's face blur into the terrifying features of Mr Jingo, his childhood nightmare. *This must be his work. Not content with stealing my network, that street thug, that petty murderer, has attacked my home, using my own operating system. But what could he possibly think he can accomplish, even if the entire island is deserted? Doesn't he know I have several different sources of available power – that I have enough resources available to survive in my tank for months if necessary?*

The more he thought about it the more puzzling it was. For the moment all thought of triggering the Apep Sequence was pushed aside by the mystery before him.

Jolted by a sudden fear, he made a quick surveillance of the hangarsized room that contained the Grail machinery, checking to make sure all was still functioning properly. On the cameras he could see that the huge space was empty of technicians, the banks of processors and switchers untended but still doing what they should.

So what is John Dread up to? Is he just testing my defenses? Or is it something less rational – he always had a childish mind. Perhaps this is some million-credit equivalent of a prank call to his old employer. Perhaps he doesn't even know whether I'm dead or still online.

Feeling much better, certain now that there was no true immediate danger within the building, Jongleur went back to the preparations for the Apep Sequence, but an anomaly in the program's readings brought him up short. It seemed an obvious fallacy. Somehow, he decided, in the riot of false information throughout the island, of alarms and alerts, even the crucial Grail network data had been corrupted. According to what was before him, the Apep program had already been triggered, which could not be right. The time recorded for the event was close to two hours ago. But he himself had only just begun initialization a few minutes earlier.

It must be an error, he thought. *It must.* The most obvious evidence was that the trajectories were completely nonsensical. Then a flicker on one of his surveillance screens took his attention away from even as important a matter as the fate of his rogue operating system.

Someone was moving. Someone was still in the building.

As he enlarged the picture, pushing the other camera views into the background, he saw the camera designation. A burst of terror went through him. The intruder was *here* – on the same floor as his own tank! For a hallucinatory moment he could feel himself plunged back into childhood – the smell of the airing cupboard, the starched towels and sheets pressed all around him, stifling him as he hid from Halsall and the other older boys. He could almost hear them.

'Jingle? Jingle-Jangle? Come out, Frenchie. We're going to debag you, you little sod.'

With a little noiseless whimper he pushed the memory away. *How? How could anyone get into my sanctuary?*

The desperate hope that it was some brave technician who had elected to remain behind shattered into cold fragments as he studied the view-window. The intruder was a woman, a middle-aged woman with short hair. He had never seen her before. More astonishing still, she was wearing one of his own company's custodial uniforms.

A cleaning woman? On this floor? On my *floor?* It was so ridiculous that if he had not been gripped by fear at the invasion of his privacy, full of confusion and suspicion about all that was going on outside, he might have laughed. But at the moment he did not feel at all like laughing. He stared at her face, trying to see something in it that would tell him who she was, what she wanted. She was walking slowly and looking all around, clearly uneasy and surprised, exactly as someone would be who had stumbled into the room by accident. She showed no sign of an agenda, none of the intensity of a saboteur or assassin. Jongleur breathed a little more easily but he was still frightened. How could he get her out? There were no employees available – not even his security guards. He felt rage bubbling up.

She will hear me, he decided, *and she will hear me loud. Like the bellow of an angry God. That will set her running.* But before he let his voice thunder through the audio system he pulled up the room's security records, wanting to know how she had gotten in.

It was a simple blanket priority approval, the same

thing his approved team of technicians used as they moved between floors. *Olga Chotilo, Custodial Worker*, it read. Something about the name seemed slightly familiar. More surprisingly, there was a code listed on her security trail that he did not at first recognize. Where had she just been? A long moment passed as he tried to remember – he had not seen that code for some time.

Upstairs, he thought, and his thoughts spasmed like dying things. *She's been on the locked floor . . . the death-place . . . how could she have gotten in . . . who helped her . . . ?* And at that moment he remembered why he knew the name.

Felix Jongleur's respiration grew dizzyingly shallow. His pulse wavered, then spiked. Again the calming chemicals began to pump, a river of heart's-ease flowing into his ancient body through plastic tubes, but it was not enough to stifle the sudden, overwhelming terror, not anywhere near enough.

THE floor was as large as those beneath and above, but strangely empty. Here there was neither the cold magnificence of a thousand banked machines or the surreal tangle of an indoor forest. At the center of the huge, dark room stood only an arc of machinery, bulking high in a pool of light like a druidic ruin. In the center of the array, in a circle of marble tiles, four black pods lay in a triangular arrangement, one almost five meters square at the center, one about the same size just above it, and two smaller pods set a bit farther out.

Not a triangle, she decided. *A pyramid.*

Coffins, she thought then. *They look like coffins for dead kings.*

She moved forward, her feet silent on the sable carpet. The rest of the room lights came up slowly, so that although the spotlight was still strongest on the arrangement of machines and plastic sarcophagi, she could now see the distant walls; windowless, they were covered in something as dark and unreflective as the carpeting, so that even with brighter lighting the machinery at the room's center seemed to float in starless space.

Good God, she thought. *It is like a funeral parlor.* She half-expected to hear quiet organ music, but the room was silent. Even the automated warning voices did not trespass here in the tower's upper reaches.

When she reached the center of the room she stood for long seconds staring at the silent black objects, trying to overcome a tingle of superstitious fear. The middle pod was so big that its top loomed above her head, the second large pod a bit lower, the other two positively squat by comparison. She stared at the nearest, which lay to the right of the middle pod, but the plastic was opaque and seemed to join the floor smoothly. Plastic pipes that she guessed held cabling of some kind came out of ducts along the pod's side and burrowed into the black carpet like roots.

She passed it by and paused by the pod that topped the horizontal pyramid, the second-largest. She took a breath and reached out to it. When her fingers touched the smooth, cool plastic, a red light blinked on along the side; she jumped back, startled and afraid, but nothing else moved. Little glowing letters appeared beside the red light. She leaned close, but carefully, not wanting to touch the thing again.

> *Project: Ushabti*
> *Contents: Blastocyst 1.0, 2.0, 2.1; Horus 1.0*
> *Warning: Cryogenic Seal – Do not Open Or*
> *Service Without Authorization*

She stared, trying to remember what a blastocyst was. A cell of some kind – cancerous? No, something to do with pregnancy. As far as what a horus might be, she had no idea – probably another kind of cell. Olga could not even begin to guess why someone would want to keep cellular tissue in a huge tank like this.

Are these all the same? she wondered. *Some kind of freezers for medical experiments? Are they doing some kind of genetic engineering here?*

She touched one of the smaller pods. Another red light blinked on, but the characters beside it only read: *Mudd, J. L.* and a string of numbers. The other small sarcophagus yielded *Finney, D.S.D.* and more numerals. It took her long moments to work up the courage to touch the largest pod, but when she flicked it lightly with her finger, nothing happened. She waited until her hand was trembling a little less, then touched it and held the contact.

'Ms Pirofsky?'

She squealed and jumped back. The voice was right in her head.

'I'm sorry – I didn't mean to frighten you. It's me. Sellars.' His voice was rough, as though he were in great pain, but it sounded like him. Olga took a stagger-step, then sat down on the carpet.

'I thought you were in a coma. You did frighten me. It is like the mummy's tomb in here. I almost jumped out of my skin.'

'I really am sorry. But I must speak to you and I'm afraid it can't wait.'

'What is this place? What are these things?'

Sellars waited a moment before answering. 'The largest of those devices is the true home of Felix Jongleur. The man who owns J. Corporation, the man who built the Grail network.'

'Home . . . ?'

'His body is nearly dead, and has been for years. There are many, many machines connected to that life-support pod – it extends down nearly ten meters into the floor of the room.'

'He's . . . right there . . . ?' She looked at the pod, amazed and disturbed. 'He can't leave it?'

'No, he can't leave it.' Sellars cleared his throat. 'I have to talk to you Ms Pirofsky.'

'Olga, please. Yes, I know I have to get out of here. But I haven't found anything yet – anything about the voices . . .'

'I have.'

It took a moment to sink in. '*You* have? What?'

'This is difficult, Ms . . . Olga. Please, prepare yourself. I am afraid that it will be . . . shocking to you.'

It was hard to think of anything stranger than what she had already experienced. 'Just tell me.'

'You had a baby.'

This was the last thing she had expected to hear. 'Yes. He died. He was born dead.' It was quite amazing how the pain could still come so quickly, so powerfully. 'I never saw him.'

Sellars hesitated again. When he spoke, it was almost in a rush. 'You never saw him because he didn't die. He didn't die, Olga. They lied to you.'

'What?' There were no tears, only a dull anger. How could anyone say such a cruel, ridiculous thing? 'What are you talking about?'

'Your child was a rare mutation – a telepath. He was . . . is . . . a child that would never have lived under normal circumstances. The raw power of his mind was so great that despite many preparations, a doctor in the delivery room actually died of a stroke while performing the cesarean. Two nurses had seizures, too, but there were several on hand and one of them managed to deliver a huge dose of sedative to the child.'

'This is craziness! How could such a thing happen and I would not know about it?'

'You were already sedated – you had been told it would be a very difficult birth, a breech, do you remember? That's because there had already been evidence that the child was abnormal. Don't you remember all the tests? Surely you must have thought there was something unusual about it. The doctors and nurses were all specialists. Highly-paid specialists.'

Olga wanted to curl up and put her fingers in her ears. Her baby was dead. For over thirty years she had struggled with it, learned to live with it. 'I don't understand anything you are saying.'

'The man in that pod – Felix Jongleur. He had been looking for a child with just the potential of your baby. He and his associates had connections in dozens of hospitals all over Europe, owned many of them outright. You did not choose that hospital yourself, did you?'

'We . . . we were referred. By a doctor – but he was a kind man!'

'Perhaps. Perhaps he didn't understand what he was doing. But the fact is, you and your baby were delivered into the hands of people who only wanted your child – your son. After testing gave some idea of what they had found, Jongleur's specialists had already begun sedating him in the womb. They were as ready for his arrival as they could be, but even so, he nearly died from the trauma of birth – too much mental energy, a kind of hyperactivity that would have killed him in minutes. At least one person present at the birth *did* die. But as I said, they were largely ready. He was put into a cryogenic unit and his temperature lowered drastically. They put him into something like suspended animation.'

Now the tears did come. Memories came with them – the nights she had sat awake in bed with Aleksandr sleeping beside her, convinced there was something wrong with her baby because what was inside her simply did not feel right. The other times when she would have sworn she could sense it . . . *thinking* inside her, the strange sensation of a little alien thing living inside her belly. But she had told herself the feelings were nothing that other mothers did not also experience and the doctors had agreed with her.

'How could you know all this?' she demanded. 'How could you know? Why did you wait until now to tell me? You are making this up – this is some crazy game, it's your conspiracy, your crazy conspiracy!'

'No, Olga,' he said sadly. 'I didn't tell you because I didn't know. Until now. I had no idea how the Grail network's operating system worked, since it did not seem to function within any of the rules for even the most sophisticated neural networks. But . . .'

'My baby!' Olga leaped up and staggered to the pod at the top of the pyramidal arrangement. The word *Cryogenic* had faded but it was burned in her mind. 'Is he here? Is he in here?' She scratched uselessly at the plastic. 'Where is he?'

'He is not there, Olga.' Sellars sounded as though he too was fighting tears. 'He is not in the building. He is not even on Earth.'

Her legs buckled. She sagged and fell to the ground, thumping her forehead against the carpet. 'What are you saying?' she moaned. 'I don't understand.'

'Please, Olga. Please. I'm so sorry. But I have to tell you everything. We have very little time.'

'Time? I have thought for most of my life that my baby was dead, now you tell me I have no time? Why? What are you doing?'

'Please. Just listen.' Sellars took a deep, shaky breath. 'Jongleur and his technicians built the Grail system around your child. His problem . . . his gift, whatever you call it, the hypermutation that would otherwise have killed him long before he came to term – and perhaps would have killed you, too – made him ideal for the Grail's purposes. With all their work to prepare a world where they could spend eternity, they still could not create a virtual environment responsive and realistic enough, not with the best information technologies of the day. What good would it have been to them to make themselves immortal if they did not have a suitable place to spend that immortality? So Jongleur and his scientists created a massively parallel processor constructed of human brains – fetal brains, mostly – and relied on your son's native abilities to make connections between those brains that no machinery could make, to dominate and shape them into the operating system for their network.

'But there were problems from the very beginning. The human brain is not a computer. It needs to do human things to grow. If it doesn't learn, it doesn't physically develop. Your son was a one-in-a-billion oddity, Olga, but he was still a human child. In order to develop this incredibly powerful resource, the Grail engineers and scientists discovered that they had to teach it – had to let it come into contact with other human minds, learn to communicate, even to reason after a fashion, or it would be useless to them.

'Paradoxically, the Grail people only exposed him to human ideas in order to make him the most efficient machine possible. They had no interest in his true humanity. And in the end, that is what killed them.' There was a certain grim satisfaction in his voice.

'So early on, in order to help him develop, they began experiments in which they brought him into contact with other children, normal children. One of the people inside the system now, a woman named Martine Desroubins, was one of those children. She knew your son only as a voice – but she knew him.'

Olga had stopped crying now. She sat against the pod staring at her hands. 'I don't understand any of this. Where is he now? What have they done to him?'

'They have used him, Olga. For thirty years, they have used him. I am sorry to tell you this – I beg you to believe that – but they have not used him kindly. He has been raised in the dark, figuratively and literally. He does not even know what he is – he acts almost without thinking, half-awake, dreaming, confused. He has the powers of a god but the understanding of an autistic child.'

'I want to go to him! I don't care what he is!'

'I know. And I know that when you speak to him you will be kind. You will try to understand.'

'Understand what?' She was breathing hard now, squeezing her fingers into fists. *A fire ax*, she thought. *There must be a fire ax somewhere. I will take it and I will smash this man Jongleur's black coffin to bits, drag him out into the light like a worm from its hole . . .*

'You son is not . . . a normal human. How could he be? He speaks almost entirely through others. Somehow, he has connected to the Tandagore coma children. I do not understand that part yet, but . . .'

'Speaks through . . . others . . . ?'

'Children . . . the children in your dreams. I think they are his voice, trying to talk to you.'

Olga felt her heart skip. 'He . . . he knows me?'

'Not truly. But I think he sensed something significant about you. Didn't you say that what first made you suspicious was that none of the affected children were viewers of your program? Your son escaped the bounds of the Grail network some time ago – he has explored much, and I suspect that he was drawn particularly to the children watching your show, as he has been drawn to other children elsewhere. What it was he sensed in you, I don't know, but he may have felt some deep affinity, some . . . similarity to himself. Wordless, uncomprehending, he immediately lost any other interest in your child viewers. Instead, he tried in his half-conscious way to . . . make contact. With you.'

She was sobbing convulsively but her eyes were dryly painful, as though she had cried so much she could never shed tears again. Those terrible headaches, the confusing voices, they hadn't been a curse at all, but . . . 'My ch-child! My baby! Trying to f-f-find me!'

'Time is very short, Olga. We have only minutes, then things will have gone too far. I will try to bring him to you – let you speak to him yourself. Do not be too frightened.'

'I would never be frightened . . . !'

'Wait. Wait until you have spoken to him. He was born different, but even his raw humanity has been shaped by cold, self-serving men. And now another man, even crueler, has hurt him and abused him until he has nearly given up. It may be too late. But if you can speak to him, calm him, many lives can be saved.'

'I still don't understand. Where is he?' She looked around wildly, imagining some strange, Frankensteinian form might suddenly appear from the shadows that cloaked the huge room. 'I want to go to him. I don't care what he is, what he looks like. Let me go to him!'

'You must listen carefully, Olga.' Sellars sounded even more strained, as though he were clinging to a high place by his fingernails. 'Time is short. There is still a lot I haven't told you, crucial things . . .'

'Then tell me now!'

And as she sat in the big, dark room, the only moving thing in the circle of light, he told her as kindly as possible where her son was and what he was doing. Then he left her alone so he could see to the rest of his own desperate agenda.

Olga had thought she had no more tears left to cry. She had been wrong.

THE intruder was still talking to someone – someone Jongleur couldn't see. Immersed in protective fluids, he writhed in impotent fury. He tried to bring up the room audio but again he discovered himself blocked, the commands disabled. He knew it must be his ex-employee who had done all this, but why should that street animal go to such ridiculous lengths just to confuse him?

Jongleur stared at the screen with the intensity of a mad thing, an old falcon who lived only to strike at anything that moved. The woman's lips were moving – what was she saying? *Damn her, is she talking to Dread?*

He watched the woman begin to cry again, shuddering, pulling at her face with her hands, and his distant heart was again chilled. She knew. Somehow, she had found out. Which meant that his enemies knew as well, for who else would tell her?

Why bring this woman into it? What does he think she can possibly accomplish?

She was standing over his pod now – *his* pod, only a few short meters from the rags and tatters of his living body. He switched cameras so he could see her face, which was grotesque with rage and misery. She made a fist and struck the pod – a tiny, meaningless blow on the hardened plasteel, but Felix Jongleur suddenly felt himself suffocating, his fear twisting ever tighter. There were strangers in his home – he was violated. Pursued. Caught.

No! I won't let it happen. A dozen possible reprisals flashed through his mind, all thwarted by the evacuations and the meddling in his system. Even his last-ditch defenses had been rendered inoperative. He could not flood the room with immobilizing gas or crippling sonics.

I won't let it happen!

It came to him suddenly, but he could not at first decide if it was genius or complete madness. Months – they had been immobilized for almost twenty-four months. Would it work? It would – it had to. He triggered a massive dose of adrenaline to be administered to both of them. It would work. He knew it would. He was excited now, his pulse suddenly racing with feverish glee instead of terror. What was the release sequence? If that much adrenaline hit them and they couldn't get out, they would thrash themselves to death – damage the breathing masks and drown in the suspension fluid.

There. He selected the commands. In the window in his mind, the system brought up the life signs, the graphs already spiking as they rose toward something like normal function, then moved on beyond, fueled by the adrenal surge. He brought up the view of the room again, the heedless woman sitting obliviously on the floor of his *sanctum sanctorum* between his own helpless body and the last remnants of *Ushabti*, the terrible mistake that had destroyed his beautiful Avialle.

Violated. She has . . .

'There is an intruder just steps away from you,' he told

his servants, making the words thunder in their ears so they would retain them even in the confusion of waking to their real bodies for the first time in two years. '*Take her and hurt her and find out what she knows. Do this and afterward you may remain free.*'

The indicator lights blinked, then blinked again as the lids of the two black pods slowly began to rise.

CHAPTER 45

Send

NETFEED/OBITUARY: Robert Wells, Founder of TMX
(visual: Wells at Telemorphix 'torchlight rally' company meeting)
VO: Robert Wells, technology pioneer and one of the world's richest
men, died of a heart attack yesterday. Wells, the founder of the
Telemorphix Corporation, was one hundred and eleven years old.
(visual: Owen Tanabe, Wells' executive assistant)
TANABE: 'He went out the way he would have wanted – at the office,
plugged into the net, working right up until the last moment on ways
to improve human life. Even though he's gone, all of us will be feeling the impact of Bob Wells' personal vision for years to come . . .'

HE was laughing, laughing out loud. He couldn't help
it. His heart was aflame with exhilaration, his
thoughts swirling like smoke and sparks. He was as alive
as he had ever been – it was like the last moment of the
hunt, drawn out by some hallucinatory distortion of time
into an hours-long orgasm.

The chorus in his head had reached a crescendo. *Camera
in close. Face flushed but coldly handsome. The winner.
Unstoppable.*

All his enemies inside the network were at his fingertips now, hopelessly trapped – the blind woman, Jongleur, the Sulaweyo bitch, even the operating system itself. They cowered before him. He was the destroyer, the beast, the devil-devil man. He was a god.

And outside the network . . . ?

Pull back to reveal his enemies at his feet. Long shot. Only one standing.

Dread looked down at the two bodies on the floor of the loft. Dulcie lay silent in a tangle of arms and legs like a puppet with its strings slashed, blood pooling around her. The policewoman was still moving, but only a little, her head twitching in time with her swift, jerky breathing, bright red arterial blood frothing on her lips. He frowned. Even in the flaring majesty of the moment he remembered his mantra against overconfidence.

Dread muted his inner music, then bent and rolled the policewoman onto her side. She gave a little whistling grunt but otherwise did not respond, even when he wiggled the handle of the knife in her back. A shame to leave her unattended in the last moments, but he had bigger game afoot. She wasn't his type, anyway – he didn't like them stocky. He reached down into her overcoat, found the holstered Glock, and pulled it out. He put the barrel against the policewoman's head, then remembered that even after he returned to the network her final moments would be recorded on the loft's surveillance cameras.

Why waste a slow death? he thought. Dulcie's end had turned out to be a bit disappointingly swift, after all.

He considered briefly, then ejected the bullets from the policewoman's gun and Dulcie's snapped-together pistol and tucked both weapons into the pockets of his robe. He reached back into the woman's breast pocket and found her police pad. *Sorry, sweetness, no calls.* He ground it under his heel until he heard components shatter, then kicked it across the room.

No sense in putting temptation in the way of a dying woman, he thought cheerfully. Women just couldn't resist temptation – pretty things, bright colors, false hopes. They were like animals that way.

He climbed back onto the coma bed and frowned at the blood he was smearing on the purity of the white surfaces. *Can't be helped. Fix it in editing.* Then again, maybe it would be a nice effect . . . ? He ran a quick check to make sure the cameras would pick up everything that happened in the loft, and that he himself would have a view of it even when he was back on the network. *Confident, cocky, lazy, dead, right? Not this boy.*

Dread brought his music back up, a swell of triumphant strings and kettledrums. The chorus came in again, hundreds of voices singing in the bones of his skull as he dropped back into the universe he had conquered.

PAUL could only stare at the spot where Felix Jongleur had stood a moment before. One second the ancient man had been there, then he had simply vanished – pop, like a soap bubble.

T4b was the first to speak. He sounded lost, younger than Paul had ever heard him. 'Old Grail-knocker . . . won, him? Just . . . over? All over?'

Sam Fredericks was crying. Beside her, Orlando Gardiner put a muscular barbarian arm around her shoulder. 'I knew it!' she said for the fourth or fifth time. 'So impacted – we were all so stupid! He was just waiting!'

Paul could only nod in stunned agreement. *I should have seen it coming – should have known a device like that lighter would be worth something to someone – to Jongleur.* But he had let himself be lulled by Jongleur's unusual volubility, his surrender of secrets. The old man had acted like someone without hope. Paul had recognized the feeling, and so he had believed it.

'We may have only moments,' Martine said softly.

'It's in God's hands,' said Bonita Mae Simpkins. 'We don't know what He has planned.'

'It is out of *our* hands,' Martine replied, 'that is the one certain thing.'

Florimel stood. 'No. I cannot believe that. I will not give up my life, my daughter's life, without a fight.'

'Who are you going to fight?' Paul's own misery made it difficult even to speak. 'We underestimated him. Now he's gone. And even if something keeps him from shutting down the system, what about that?' He pointed to the dome of clouds, the silhouette of Dread moving along the edge like a shadow-puppet demon. 'What about him?'

'Where has the boy gone?' asked Nandi. 'Sellars' boy. He was frightened. He ran.'

Orlando pointed. 'Over there.'

Paul could see Cho-Cho crouched on the rim of the Well, a small shadow against the flickering lights. 'I'll get him,' he said heavily. He knew what it was to be lost and confused. *We should face it together, as Martine said.*

'Something is happening.' Martine Desroubin's face tightened in concentration. Paul hesitated, but then turned to go after the boy.

The end, he thought. *The end is happening, that's all.*

The weakening glare of the Well made him think of Ava as she had last appeared, suffering, fighting hopelessly against the inevitable. *I'm sorry*, he told her memory. *Whatever you were, whoever, it doesn't matter. You risked everything for me – lost everything. And I failed you.*

The boy was on all fours, shuddering. When Paul

touched him he scrambled back along the edge, making Paul fear he might tumble into the Well.

But what difference does it make, really? Still, he put out his hand. 'It's all right, lad. It's all right. I'm one of the good guys.' *And that's a laugh, isn't it?*

'He here,' the boy said.

'No, he's gone. The man is gone.'

'He not! He in my head, *verdad!*'

Paul paused, his hand still stretched toward the boy. 'What are you talking about?'

'*El viejo!* Sellars! He in my head – I can hear him!' The boy backed a little farther along the rim of the pit, keeping well out of Paul's reach. 'It hurts!'

My God, Paul thought. *Just don't scare him into falling.* He squatted down, then extended his hand again. 'We can help you. Please come back.' *What if he falls? What if he falls and we never find out?* 'What is Sellars saying to you?'

'Don't know! Can't understand – it hurts my head! He want . . . he want . . . want you to listen . . .' The boy began to cry, then rubbed his face angrily as if to push the tears back into the ducts. 'Leave me alone, *m'entiendes?*' It was hard to tell who he was shouting at.

Paul risked turning away for a moment so he could wave to some of his companions to come and help, but he could not tell if anyone had seen him. 'Cho-Cho – that's your name, right? Come back with me. That man who tried to hurt you is gone. Sellars can tell us how to get out of here – how we can all get out of here. You want that, don't you?'

'*Mentiroso,*' the boy snarled. 'Heard what you said before. All gonna die here.'

'Not if Sellars can help us.' He inched a little closer. 'Please, just come with me. I won't touch you, I promise.

No one will touch you. I'll just turn and walk back to the other, and you walk with me.' The boy crawled a little farther away. Paul looked around, but none of the others were coming, although a few were watching with a kind of glazed curiosity. 'Look. I'm getting up now and I'm going back to the fire. You come with me if you want. We're friends here.' *Who is this boy, anyway? What can I say to him that will convince him?* 'There really are people in the world who want to help, you know. There really are.'

He waited a few seconds, but the boy did not move or speak. Knowing that he was almost certainly doing a foolish thing – how many minutes did they have left, in any case? – Paul got up, turned, and walked deliberately back to the campfire. He did not look back. He heard no sounds behind him: if the boy was there, he was moving silently across the gray, dead ground.

Florimel and Nandi were nearest; they looked up at him with a question in their eyes. Paul stopped beside them, then carefully sat down, eyes still averted.

'Anybody touch me,' the boy promised, 'I cut them.'

'Then you just sit there,' said Florimel.

Paul cleared his throat. 'Sellars is talking to him.'

'What?'

'He trying to,' the boy said sullenly. 'But it locking up my head.'

The others around the fire had turned toward them now. 'The child is terrified,' said Bonnie Mae.

'Just tell us what you think he is trying to say,' said Florimel. 'That is all we want. Martine, are you listening?'

'I am . . . trying. It is . . . There are . . . distractions.'

Paul could tell it was far worse than a distraction. Martine Desroubins had the look of someone suffering a five-alarm migraine.

'He talking again,' Cho-Cho said suddenly. The others leaned toward him. 'He say . . . he say . . .' The boy sighed and his eyes squeezed shut. For a long, tense moment he was silent, his jaw working. '*This . . . is very difficult,*' he said at last. '*I apologize . . . for the confusion.*' But though it still was Cho-Cho's voice, a child's voice, the intonation had changed.

'Sellars?' asked Florimel. 'Is that you?'

'*Yes.*' Cho-Cho's eyes remained closed even as his mouth moved, as though the child were talking in his sleep. *As though he were possessed*, Paul thought. '*In fact,*' Sellars continued, '*I have many apologies to make, but we don't have the time. It is not easy to manipulate the child's neurocannular connection to speak directly to you, but what I have to say is too important and too complicated to be relayed through little Cho-Cho.*'

'What's going on?' Florimel's voice held anger as well as relief. 'Where have you been all this time? While everything in this damned artificial universe was trying to kill us?'

'*No time to explain, I'm afraid. I am deep into the workings of the network and the operating system and my head feels like it's going to explode – and that's the least of our problems.*' Paul could hear the incredible strain even through the child's supple voice.

'You know about Jongleur escaping, then?' he asked.

'*What?*' The boy's face remained impassive but the voice was clearly startled. '*Jongleur?*'

Paul told him, with help from the others.

'He was planning it all along,' said Sam Fredericks miserably.

'It's not your fault, Frederico,' Orlando told her. 'But if we get another chance, let's cut his head off, okay?'

'*Oh, my,*' said Sellars. '*Is that . . . do I hear . . . Orlando Gardiner?*'

Orlando grinned sourly. 'Pretty scanny, huh?'

'*Explanations must wait until later – if there is such a thing as later,*' Sellars told him. '*The operating system is failing, preparing for its own destruction. I need to make direct contact with it now. That is our only hope to preserve the system long enough to get you out, and it's a very thin hope. Quick, now. I saw some trace of a contact, just minutes ago, between your group and the innermost workings of the system.*'

'Yes, Renie Sulaweyo is there, in the center of it. That is who we were speaking to with the access device,' Florimel said heavily. 'But Jongleur has taken it.'

Paul waited for Sellars to say something, anything, but the voice that spoke through Cho-Cho's virtual body had gone silent. 'So is that it?' Paul asked at last. 'We were ready to give up before we heard your voice. Is that all you've got to give us?'

'*I am thinking, damn it,*' Sellars snapped. '*But I confess I am at a loss. I have tried everything possible on my end, but the conscious part of the operating system has isolated itself and won't respond to me.*'

Paul turned to Martine Desroubins, who seemed to be listening with only half her attention. 'Martine, you told me how you found your way out of that other strange world – how you and !Xabbu managed to open a gateway. Could you do it again?'

'Open . . . a gateway . . . ?' The pain in her voice was palpable. She and Sellars both sounded like they were trying to carry on business while being stung to death by bees. 'Renie . . . !Xabbu . . . they are . . . beyond any gateway, I think.'

'But you had the communicator in your hand.' Paul leaned closer, trying to keep her focused. 'Can't you . . . feel it? You said when we came back from the mountain to Kunohara's world that you felt a connection, sensed it with your mind somehow – that you held on so we could follow it back. Come on, Martine, you can do things none of the rest of us can do! We have no other chance!'

'Do it,' T4b said. He put out a hand and touched the blind woman's fingers. She flinched a little, startled. 'Be strong. Don't want to get sixed, us – not yet!'

'But that connection to Kunohara's world was active,' Martine said weakly. 'I caught it just before it faded!'

'Try,' Paul urged her. 'We need you. No one else can do it.'

'He's right,' Florimel said, but gently. 'It is in your hands.'

'It is not fair.' Martine shook her head violently. 'Already, the pain . . . I cannot . . . bear it.'

Paul crawled to her side and put his arms around her. 'You can,' he said. 'You have already done miracles. For God's sake, Martine, what's one more?'

She put her hands in front of her face. 'When I did not care,' she whispered hoarsely, 'I did not hurt so much.' She shook her head as Paul started to speak. 'No. Do not bother to say it. I must have silence.'

Renie stared at the lighter in baffled fury. The orange moon hung low in the sky, a mocking face. 'No! I heard her – you heard her, too! She was right there!'

'I did hear her,' !Xabbu said. 'But I heard Jongleur's voice as well.'

'What happened?' Renie could not reconcile the extremes – the joy of hearing Martine speak, the moment of exhilarating contact with their friends, then the ugly surprise of hearing Felix Jongleur's voice bark out something about a priority override. And now . . .

'Nothing,' she said, running through the sequences again. 'It's dead.'

!Xabbu reached out his hand. Renie passed it to him, then turned her eyes back to the minuscule form of the dying mantis. 'I hope you're happy,' she snarled down at it. 'Our friends are gone now. If I wasn't certain it was Jongleur who did it – if I thought it was you . . .'

Dying. The everywhere-and-nowhere voice was so faint now as to be almost inaudible. *Tried to last . . . until the children . . . could be . . . saved.*

'The children?' Renie asked bitterly. 'You haven't saved any children. Didn't you hear? Jongleur, the man who built you – he's in charge again now.'

No. The devil. Still . . . the devil. The one who hurts and hurts . . .

'I feel something,' !Xabbu said quietly.

'What?'

'I . . . I am not certain. Distant.' He frowned and closed his eyes. 'Like a faint spoor. Like the musk of an antelope on the wind, half a day away.' His eyes opened wide. 'The string game! Someone is asking about the string game!'

'What are you talking about?' Renie began, and then she remembered. 'Martine! Isn't that how you and Martine . . . ?'

He closed his eyes again. 'I can feel something, but it is so . . . difficult.'

No. The wind-murmur of the mantis voice had become a little stronger. *No, you must not open us again to . . . to . . .*

'Shut up!' Renie squirmed in anger. 'Our friends are trying to call us!'

The mantis struggled up onto its bent-twig legs. The tiny eyes were filmed, dark. *You will lead the devil here too soon – steal the last moments . . .*

'I think I am losing it.' !Xabbu held the lighter so tightly Renie could see his knuckles bulging, pale against his brown skin. 'She is so far away!'

Will not . . . must not . . . No!

'Stop it!' Renie said, then the desert began to melt around them, the dark night colors, the amber moon, even the flaring stars all smearing. 'Stop!'

It was too late. The sky and the ground ran together, swirling as though someone had dipped a stick into a paint pot and begun to stir. Renie threw out her hand to seize the tiny insect but it was simultaneously growing and dwindling, dominating everything even as it receded, shrank, became a tiny spot of nothing that sped away before her.

After a long chaotic moment the world came to rest again.

'!Xabbu?' she breathed, swaying with dizziness.

'I am here, Renie.' His hand touched hers, clutched, held.

They were still in the desert, !Xabbu's imaginary Kalahari, but now it was somehow also the pit in which Renie had spoken to the false Stephen. The stars, moments ago so bright, were now almost unimaginably distant, faint as the last embers of a fire. Renie and !Xabbu crouched on a rim of earth that had been the outskirt of the dry pan, but the land had stretched up above them into the walls of the pit, and the gulley and its tiny trickle of stream had dropped away far beyond their reach, half a hundred meters below their ledge. Despite the distance and the dying stars, the light had the impossible clarity of a dream. Renie saw that the shape huddled beside the stream didn't resemble a mantis any longer, but neither was it a child. It was something else entirely, something not quite definable – small, dark, and very much alone.

All will die. The breathy voice rose up like smoke. *Could not . . . save the children.*

A glimmering silver something lay on the rough gray stone floor of the pit, as hopelessly beyond reach as though it were on one of the stars overhead. As she watched it, it suddenly sprouted legs. Like a tiny metallic beetle, it crept away from the child-thing, limping blindly until it toppled over the edge into the river and was gone.

The lighter, Renie realized. The little flicker of hope she had felt in the desert finally went out. *We've lost it. We've lost everything.*

'This is the sun,' !Xabbu murmured beside her. For a moment, she thought he was talking to her, but his eyes were shut, and what he said made no sense. 'Yes. And now it moves lower. Fingers so, thumbs wide. There – it sets behind the hills.'

SHE could not keep her eyes closed a moment longer, no matter what the risk. Already the lassitude was creeping over her, a dark fog shot with red light and tiny, bursting stars. Another moment and she would find it easier simply to give up. The gnawing ache – it was in her back, she knew, but it felt as if it went right through her body and out through her chest – was growing more distant. The pain was receding.

Calliope Skouros knew this was not a good sign.

Should have waited until Stan called back, she thought, and coughed up another bubbly spill of blood. *Wish he was here. Look, Chan, I could tell him. I wore my flakkie for once. Kept the blade from going all the way through my lung and into my heart. That's why I won't be dead for at least another two or three minutes. Plenty of time.*

Yeah. Plenty of time for what?

Calliope tried to roll over from her side onto her

stomach. If she could crawl there might, just might, be something she could do – maybe drag herself down the steps and out the front door of the loft. Also, there would be less chance of snagging the knife on something. She knew she couldn't pull it out – the blade and the shock-absorbent gel of the flak jacket were probably the only thing keeping the wound even partially sealed. Without the knife that had almost killed her, she'd die in seconds.

It was no use. Her arms weren't strong enough to roll her onto her stomach, which meant they certainly weren't going to lift her body. All those hours in the gym and all she could do was thrash uselessly, like a fish hauled onto the deck of a boat. She might be able to pull herself a few inches but she would never make it down the stairs. She coughed and a sudden spike of agony went through her. For a long moment afterward she could only grunt and clamp her jaws against the scream that would probably open the wound fatally wide.

Something made a little sighing noise behind her. Calliope strained to lift her head, but could see nothing from her angle on the floor. Johnny Dread must be on the other side of the room – she had heard him walk across the floor and climb into what must be the strange bed in the corner and had not heard him move again. Who had made the noise?

The woman – the woman who lived with him. The one he just killed.

Calliope scrabbled herself a little to one side, pivoting slowly on the axis of her hip and sliding through a puddle of her own blood, until she could see the woman, who was also lying on her side, as though she and Calliope were a pair of very disturbing bookends. The face was deathly pale but the eyes were wide. Staring. Staring at her.

The woman who had been shot made a little mewing noise.

Yeah, me too, sister. Calliope struggled to hang onto coherence, fighting without even knowing why against the encroaching darkness in her vision, the blurriness at the edge of her thoughts. *We both wanted him, even though I'm guessing your reasons were different than mine. And we both misjudged him.*

The other woman's eyes opened wider. She let out another small sigh.

Like she's trying to tell me something. She's sorry? She didn't know he was home? He made her lure me in? What difference does it make?

Then she saw the corner of the woman's pad sticking out from under her chest, spattered with red as though painted by a child. She had fallen on it and her body had hidden it from Dread. The woman's eyes flicked down toward it, then up to Calliope, mutely pleading.

'I see it,' Calliope tried to say, but the words came out only as bloody bubbles. *It will kill me to get to it,* she thought dimly. *Then again, I'll die if I don't.*

She tried to stretch out her arms, hoping to catch her nails in the carpet and pull herself forward, but she couldn't lift them beyond her chest without a bolt of pain that made her feel as though someone had kicked the hilt of the knife in her back. As shadows gathered before her eyes and even the fibers of the carpet seemed to slip farther and farther away until they seemed like some strange snow-covered forest seen from the window of a plane, she discovered that if she wiggled her legs she could inch forward on her side.

They never taught us this one . . . She did her best to ignore the scalding pain that came with each movement. The carpet dragged at her like fingers. *All that stuff about climbing walls, shooting at targets. They should have taught us . . . how to crawl . . . like a worm . . .*

The worm coughed. The worm coiled in shock at the agony, writhed, even cried out in a quiet bubbling gasp. When the red electrical-shock fog retreated, the worm cursed silently, bitterly, and tried to crawl forward once more.

Too bad I don't have a brain at each end. Don't worms have that? Or is that dinosaurs? Stan's nephews would know.

Since when do you care about dinosaurs, Skouros? Stan asked her.

They're interesting, she told him. *They died out because they were stupid. Too big. Too slow. Didn't wear their flakkies.*

But they did – they wore their flakkies, even on a week-end call on their day off. They just didn't take their part-ners. That was the real problem. Ask Kendrick – he loves the things.

It's all right. It doesn't matter. They're all dead a long time now, right? I'll just sit on the couch . . . get a little rest.

You tired, Skouros?

Oh, yes, Stan. I'm really tired . . . really, really . . . tired . . .

The fog cleared a little. She could see something pale before her. The moon? It was surprisingly close. But was it the right time of day?

The ghostly white shape was the woman's face, only centimeters away. *God, no. I was out there, right out. Running out of oxygen . . .*

Calliope inched forward until she could touch the pad with her fingers, feel the curved case.

Can't get it open – it's under her . . .

She shoved weakly at the woman with her head, trying
to get her to move, but although her eyes were still open,
the stranger did not react. *Shit, don't tell me she's dead,
please, please . . . Dead weight. Right on top of it.* Calliope
shoved her hand forward, watching it with a kind of
crazed interest as it closed on the pad. She tugged, lost
her grip on the slippery surface. She tried again, fighting
the blood which now seemed not just on her hands and
the floor and the pad, but all around her in a mist, even
filling her ears so that the sound of her own heart-beat
became as close and strange as the voice of the sea in a
shell.

Slowly, she brought her other hand up. The ray of pain
in her back grew brighter, fiercer, threatened to set her
insides on fire. Her fingers closed. She pulled. It came
free.

Calliope fumbled with the bloody cover until she found
the place to touch. The pad sprang open, the screen aston-
ishingly clean and bright.

No blood, she realized. *Must be the last place like that
on Earth . . .*

She could make no sense of what she saw on it, the
open files, the flicker of movement in a view-window –
her vision was blurring badly. She could only pray that
the thing's audio pickup was switched on. She did her
best to speak, coughed, wept, then tried again. Her voice,
when it came out, was as quiet as the whisper of a shy
child.

'Call zero . . . zero . . . zero.'

Calliope let her head sag until it touched the floor,
which felt as soft as a feather pillow, inviting sleep. There
was a police priority code she could have added but she
could not think of it. It was all in the lap of the gods
now – had the thing picked up her voice? Was it set to

call out on vocal commands? And even if it worked, how long until they dispatched a car to answer the call?

Done everything I could, she thought. *Maybe . . . just rest . . . a little.*

She did not know if seconds or minutes had passed, but she surfaced from another, even deeper fog to see something moving beside her. Calliope opened her eyes wide, but that was all she could do. Even if it was Dread himself she did not believe she could move a centimeter.

It was another bloody hand. Not her own.

The woman with the face pale as paper was reaching for the pad, fingers walking slowly toward it like a red-and-white spider. Calliope could only watch in dismay as the hand crept onto the screen and began, clumsily but determinedly, to open files, to move things around.

She'll cut off the call. Calliope tried to reach out but her muscles would not respond. *What if no one's picked it up yet? What the hell is this idiot woman doing?*

The bloody hand slowed, touched again, paused, then slid off the screen, leaving behind a streak of translucent crimson. Through her own swiftly encroaching fog Calliope heard the woman beside her take a deep, gurgling breath.

That's it, thought Calliope. *She's dead.*

'Send,' the woman whispered.

CHAPTER 46

Thoughts Like Smoke

NETFEED/NEWS: UN High Court to Rule on 'Lifejack' Case
(visual: excerpt from Svetlana Stringer episode of Lifejack!)
VO: The UN High Court in the Hague has agreed to hear the case of
Svetlana Stringer, a woman who claims the netshow 'Lifejack!' had
no right to select her for surveillance and create a documentary about
her love life and family problems without her permission. Her attorneys argue that unless the High Court makes a stand, continual blurring of the lines of privacy by the media will mean that soon no one
will have a right to any private life at all. Attorneys for the American
network that makes 'Lifejack!' insist that a waiver Ms Stringer signed
several years ago to allow herself to be filmed for another program
– a documentary on music education made when she was a teenager
– means she has given up her right to resist surveillance.
(visual: Bling Saberstrop, attorney for ICN)
SABERSTROP: 'UN guidelines on privacy are just that – guidelines,
not laws. We consider this to be a case where the plaintiff wants to
have her cake and eat it, too – privacy only when she wants it.'

H E watched the dying policewoman squirming in her
own blood for a few moments after he reentered the
network, but then he had to close the window. It was too
distracting. Too entertaining. The problem was, he wanted
to do everything at once.

Like a kid in a candy shop, he thought.

He wanted to watch the cop bitch's last moments, but it was one of the things he could set aside for later. He also wanted to drive the operating system out of hiding and break its pseudo-will once and for all, make it abandon this infuriating, pointless resistance and truly yield to him. And he most definitely wanted to hunt down Martine Desroubins and the Sulaweyo woman and all the other escapees, then carry them back to his endless white house in the virtual Outback and give each a magnificently intricate, drawn-out death. The prospects were enchanting: he would imprison them, terrify them, permit a few apparent escapes, even take the place of first one, then another, so he could live each terrifying moment with them just as he had done with the woman Quan Li, playing with alternating hope and despair until they all went almost mad.

But never completely mad, of course. Because then the ending would lose its bite.

And he would record the whole thing. He would watch it over and over after the grand enterprise was complete, edit it to highlight the artistry, add music and effects – hours and hours of the greatest entertainment ever created. Perhaps someday he would even allow others to see it. It would become an object of religious significance, at least among those few people who really understood how the world worked. His name would be spoken in awed whispers long after he was dead.

But I won't be dead, will I? I won't ever die.

No wonder he was so excited. There was so much to do . . . and all eternity in which to do it.

He forced himself down, down into calm. *No mistakes*, he thought. Soothing music filled his head, a *glissando* of strings, a gentle shimmer of cymbals. *First, the operating system.*

He stood on the weird, lunar plane and inspected the barrier the failing system had erected between Dread and his victims. He stroked the insubstantial but unbreachable mist. Where had this thing come from? And how could he best get through it?

It was clear he had pushed the Grail operating system to the breaking point, but although he wanted it subdued and broken he did not want to destroy it completely, jeopardizing the whole network, before he had a chance to install a replacement. That might be a little more difficult now that Dulcie was sprawled gut-shot dead on the floor of the loft, but she had cracked Jongleur's house files for him first: the Old Man would have some kind of system backup in place. So the sensible thing to do would be just to wait until he could bring another system online. But what if doing so not only killed this operating system but destroyed Martine and the rest as well? And what if Jongleur was in there with them? The thought that all his enemies might be stolen right out of his grasp by a mercifully swift death was maddening.

And they're right there . . . ! He prowled along the barrier, trying to make sense of what little he could see. As he walked he let his mind wander through the network infrastructure. It was a strange problem, trying to be two places at once, very strange. Here he stood, with the powers of a god, but he could not actually find his own location in the network: he had followed Martine and the others through into this place, but the place itself did not seem to exist on any of the network's schemata.

It's a damn strange environment, whatever it is, he thought. He had even more power here than he did in other parts of the network – the inhabitants had fled screaming from him even before he did anything – but the operating system had more power here, too.

Bloody hell! The insight was sudden and overwhelming. *I must be . . . inside the damn thing.*

He laughed and the wall of mist rippled back from him like sensitive tissue being poked by a surgical tool. *Of course I'm powerful here. It knows who delivers the pain. It's scared of me.*

So if it believes in something, he realized, *that something comes true here.* That explained why the barrier could hold him out – it represented the system's own faith in its last-ditch defenses. But when the last shred of belief that it could resist him died . . .

It's all make-believe, he thought. *A world of ghosts, magic. Like my bloody mother's stories.* It was not a thought that went well with his celebratory mood so he pushed it away.

But where is the bloody thing, then? Where is the system hiding? Dread closed his eyes as he walked along the barrier, examining his internal map of the system. The thing, the part of the operating system that thought, must be close. Again he had the strange sense of being in two places at the same time. It worried him just a little – a lifetime's dislike of exposure and a powerful urge toward control made him uncomfortable about being spread between two spheres of operation – but his pride and assurance were growing with his power and he shrugged it off. But he could not shrug off the essential puzzle.

The two things are tangled up. Until I cripple the system's brain once and for all, I'll never be able to get my hands on the ones who got away from me. But if I cripple it too badly – if I ruin it – they'll be gone, dead . . . escaped.

He could no longer see Jongleur's two monstrous agents

on the other side of the barrier. Whatever they had accomplished was over now, but they clearly had not pushed the operating system into surrender since the barrier still stood; neither had they delivered him Martine or any of the others. There were no more copies of the agents inside the barrier. Whatever he did next he would have to do himself.

Wouldn't have it any other way, he thought.

Already the excitement of the hunt was beginning to mount again. He cast his thoughts back into the network controls, searching for some clue to the location of the system's ultimate refuge. There had been a flurry of recent activity but none of it made sense, and as he struggled with the obscurities of network activity logs he had a brief moment of irritation over Dulcie's disloyalty. *She would have been useful for this, the bitch.* The escapees and the system itself remained hidden from him, both by this virtual barrier in this virtual world and in the immense, trackless confusion of the network. It was infuriating that with all his godlike power he couldn't simply find them – that he was forced to search through virtual landscapes, or listen in on virtual communicator conversations.

Communicators . . . ! He gestured and the silver lighter was in his hand. He opened the communication channel and discovered it was in use, but what he heard was nonsense – faint, unrecognizable voices babbling about strings and sunsets and something called a honey-guide. The communication line was clearly corrupted, and in his anger he considered returning to his loft and using Jongleur's access codes to pull the plug on the entire network, to kill it and then resurrect it with a different and more tractable operating system . . . but that would mean that Renie Sulaweyo and Martine and the Circle people would be granted a far too merciful release.

He stared at the lighter in fury. What use was the damned thing? A communicator that didn't communicate, full of ghost-voices.

But Dulcie Anwin had said it was something else as well. What had she called it? A V-fector. Something that would transmit not just voices, but . . . positional data.

Dread smiled.

He reopened the network's master records. The line was hot, so someone must be using it, even if the transmission itself was corrupted. He quickly found the positional information, but both sides of the current call seemed to have no origination point. Dread fought another flare of rage. Of course, if they were somehow inside the system itself there would be no conventional effector information. But this fairy-tale world had to be *somewhere* in the no-space of the network; just as he had chased the operating system through its interstices, he would chase the communication link until he found one end or the other.

He reached for it now, feeling with his mind, his *twist* coming to life like a white-hot filament. The open communication channel was a silver wire, trembling, delicate. He would run down it and find them all. He would find the system and he would hurt it until the barrier fell, and then he would take the others and they would be his, utterly his, until their last gasping breaths.

'I think I can . . . feel !Xabbu,' Martine gasped. Sam was terrified by her anguished, death mask grimace. 'But he's a million kilometers away – a billion! On the other side of the universe! It is too . . . too far.'

Martine Desroubins staggered to her feet, clutching her head. Paul Jonas reached out to steady her but she pulled away with a violent shake.

'Do not . . . !' she begged him. 'So difficult . . . so difficult . . . to hear . . .'

'*You must hold the connection open,*' Sellars said through the boy Cho-Cho. '*I am not ready.*'

'Cannot . . .' Martine bent at the waist, fingers squeezing her own skull as though she feared it would come apart. 'Something terrible . . . ah! Ahhh! The Other! He is in . . . such pain!' Then her knees buckled and she fell forward onto her face.

Paul Jonas ran to her side. When he lifted her up she sagged bonelessly.

'*Ready or not.*' It was Dread, whispering right inside Sam's head. '*Here I come!*' She cried out in fear.

The others had clearly heard him, too: in his shock, Paul nearly dropped Martine back to the ground. Then reality lurched and stuck in gear again. It lasted only a moment, but when the world around Sam shuddered back into life things were not the same.

It's so cold . . . ! The room-temperature universe had fallen into a deep winter chill. Something else came with the cold, a squeeze of terror that made it hard for her to breathe. She heard several of her companions cry out but she kept her eyes tight shut, every childhood instinct telling her to pull the blanket over her head and stay hidden until the nightmare went away.

But there was no blanket.

'Oh, Christ – it's gone!' Paul said. Sam could barely hear his voice over the rising sounds of terror from the fairy-tale folk scattered along the edge of the Well. Strong fingers curled around her arm and she cried out.

'Get up, Sam,' said Orlando. 'It's happening.'

She opened her eyes. Orlando's Thargor body seemed different, wrong somehow, and it was more than just the strange light. He looked strangely incomplete, as though

the top level of reality had been peeled away, leaving
only its preliminary designs.

'It's really dying,' he said, and she could hear the terror
just beneath his words. 'The whole thing's dying. Look at
us.'

Sam stared down at her own familiar tan arm, purple-
gray in the pit's dimly smoldering light, now unreal as
everything else. The path, the rock walls, her companions, all had lost some vital thing that had made them
realistic, had slid back into a more basic state just as the
black mountain had devolved beneath her feet during the
long climb.

We're not people, she thought, looking at the smooth
planes of Paul Jonas' face, at Orlando's stiff musculature.
We're really puppets.

She struggled onto her feet, trying to fight back against
the pressing fear. *No, it's the operating system, the Other,
not us. It's losing its grip. It's losing the dream . . .*

'Oh, this is so impacted,' Orlando breathed. He held up
his sword, not to challenge, but to block out an unwanted
sight.

The barrier was dissolving.

At the edge of the encampment the net of iridescent
cloud that had covered them was becoming raw mist
again, shifting, dispersing. The refugees, who like everything else had lost some critical degree of definition,
ran from it like misprogrammed robots, tripping and
scrambling and shouting in childish terror. A dark form
appeared out of the thinning fog, striding toward the
Well as the remains of the barrier swirled around it like
cobwebs. Fairy-tale folk caught too close to the disin-
tegrating curtain flung themselves out of the shadow-
figure's path and fell on their stomachs, rubbing their
faces against the ground in helpless panic. The thing

ignored them, walking through the cleared space like some horrible null-light Moses crossing the Red Sea. Fear held Sam pinned in place. Orlando swayed beside her and his sword dropped out of his hand into the dust.

'*Now we finish*,' the thing said, and the terrible, gleeful voice in Sam's head made her want to smash her skull against something until she couldn't hear it anymore. '*The end. Fade out. Roll credits.*'

'The Well!' Florimel wailed. Her voice seemed to come from half a world away. 'It's sinking!'

Sam turned and saw that even the diminished light which had filled the Well was draining away into the heart of the world, emptying the great hole and pulling the empty black sky down on top of them like a rotting blanket. Now the only light in the world seemed to come from the eyes and grinning teeth of their enemy.

'Into the Well!' someone screamed behind her – Paul, Nandi, she could not tell. 'It's the only place left to hide! Down into the Well!' But Sam could not tear her eyes away from the walking darkness.

It's coming now.

The thing under the bed . . . the noise in the closet . . . the smiling stranger pulling up along the curb as you walk home from school . . .

Orlando's hard hand closed on hers and jerked her to her feet. He pulled her toward the spot where Martine Desroubins had fallen onto her hands and knees at the edge of the pit. Most of their other companions were already scrambling down into darkness along some path Sam could not yet see. The blind woman looked as though she were shouting in pain. Orlando and Paul Jonas grabbed her and lifted her.

'*Where are you?*' Dread's voice whispered, flicking soft

as a snake's tongue in Sam's ear. *'You can't hide from me. I know you all too well.'*

She followed Orlando and Paul onto a ledge that ran crookedly along the inner wall of the empty pit. The two of them moved swiftly, even with Martine dangling between them. As she hurried after them Sam tripped on something and fell. By the time she clambered back onto her feet they had disappeared into the shadows below. Panicked, Sam looked back, sure that the thing with the ice-cold voice must be right behind her, and saw what she had stumbled over – a human foot. The boy Cho-Cho was lying at the side of the path, almost invisible in the deepening darkness. With her insides churned to sick horror at the thought of what must be right behind her, she only wanted to run after the others.

No, he's just a micro! I can't leave him for . . . that.

She turned against the shrieking of her own nerves and fought her way back up the slope. Cho-Cho seemed asleep, unaware of the deathly thing that was hunting them. She pulled him up into her arms, surprised and staggered by the limp weight.

'What is happening?' Sellars' phantom voice sighed from the boy's open mouth. *'Who are you?'*

'Everything – everything's happening! It's me, Fredericks!' She tripped again and almost went down.

'Where is Martine?'

'Just . . . shut up,' Sam grunted. She fought her way down the path, struggling to keep herself upright. The walls of the pit were quickly losing the last of what had made them real; they glowed now with a strange dim light, a duller version of the liquid stars. She thought she could make out the inconstant silhouettes of Orlando and Paul just a few meters ahead on the long downward spiral.

Upside down – !Xabbu was right! Her thoughts flitted

like smoke-maddened wasps. *It's the mountain turned upside down . . . !*

She could see nothing behind her yet but the pictures in her head were vivid enough – the empty-eyed shadow that was Dread swollen in her mind to giant size, sifting through the shrieking refugees with immense, shadowy fingers, picking them up in handfuls, examining them, then flinging them down in crackboned heaps.

Looking for us, Sam thought. *For us! He'll be coming down that path any second . . .* The horror of it made her so dizzy and scared that when she came around a bend into a wider part of the path and ran into Paul Jonas from behind, she almost blacked out.

'Sam?' he said, nearly as startled as she.

Martine was lying in the middle of the path where they had set her down, curled in a fetal ball. Orlando stepped around her to grab Sam's arm, then held it as though he didn't plan to let go. 'Oh, jeez . . .' He glanced at the limp form of Cho-Cho as if he didn't quite see it. 'Frigging hell, Frederico, I didn't know where you were!'

'I . . . had to go back,' she gasped. 'It's the little boy – I mean, it's Sellars . . .'

'*I cannot stay involved with this.*' Sellars' fretful voice beside her ear startled her again. '*There is too much to do. Tell Martine to keep the connection open at all costs. I will return.*'

'Don't go,' Paul said. 'That thing . . . Dread . . . he's right behind us.'

'*I can't do anything more here*,' Sellars said urgently. '*I am sorry, but I still have my side of this to complete. Whatever else happens, Martine must not lose her connection to the heart of the system. She must hold on at all costs!*'

'Damn you, Sellars, don't you dare . . . !' Paul began,

then Sam lurched against him and almost fell off the narrow path as the small body draped across her shoulder suddenly began to thrash in panic.

'Put me down!' Cho-Cho screamed. He got a hand loose and grabbed at her face, making Sam stumble again. For a moment she felt nothing under her left foot, then found the edge of the path with her heel. She swayed, trying desperately to regain her balance.

'Let me go!' The boy's elbow hit her in the side of the head so hard that her knees went rubbery and she slipped sideways. The boy's weight vanished from her shoulders.

I dropped him, she thought, and then she too seemed to be tumbling into space until a powerful grip curled in the back of her shirt and yanked her back to the center of the ledge.

A flare of light from deep in the Well painted dim streaks of silver and blue up the side of Orlando's barbarian form. He held the still-struggling Cho-Cho clasped against his naked chest. 'Are you scanned beyond belief?' he barked at the boy, then snapped his chin down hard on top of his head. Unconscious or just educated, Cho-Cho stopped thrashing and hung motionless in the crook of Orlando's muscled arm.

'*You're all down there in the hole, aren't you?*' It was Dread again, amused and annoyed, his words crawling through her skull like a trail of ants. Orlando was hearing it too: he grimaced in pain and disgust. '*Do you really want me to come get you? Haven't you already played enough games?*'

Paul Jonas had dropped to Martine's side and was trying to lift her again.

Orlando gave Sam's arm another squeeze. 'Now, I might be imagining things, Frederico.' His heroic imitation of a casual tone could not hide the tremor in his voice. His hand was probably shaking too, but Sam was shivering so badly herself she couldn't tell. 'But our friend, Count Dreadula – is he some kind of Australian?'

Catur Ramsey burst through the door into the adjoining room in time to hear the last of Sellars' words. The old man sounded worse than ever, weak and faint, as though he were talking through a garden hose from the other end of the galaxy.

'. . . *I have no time to explain it all again*,' he said. '*There are minutes only.*'

Kaylene Sorensen stood splay-footed in front of Christabel, fists curled, treating the faltering, disembodied voice from the wallscreen like a physical threat to her daughter. 'You must be crazy! Mike, am I the only person here who hasn't lost her mind?'

'*I have no other useful options, Mrs Sorensen.*' Sellars sounded weary to the point of collapse.

'Well, *I* do.' She turned to her husband. 'I told you, it was bad enough that a . . . fantasy like this should drag us all out of our house, make us run for our lives like criminals. But if you think I'm going to let anyone get Christabel involved again in this . . . this . . . *fairy tale* . . . !'

'It's all true, Mrs Sorensen,' Ramsey interrupted. 'I wish it wasn't. But . . .'

'*Ramsey, what are you doing here?*' said Sellars with surprising strength. '*You were supposed to stay on the line with Olga Pirofsky.*'

'She doesn't want to talk to me. She said to tell you to hurry up – she's waiting for her son.' It had been far stranger than that, of course. The Olga he had spoken to was nothing like the woman he had befriended, detached and frighteningly distant, as though Sellars had somehow connected

him to an entirely different person. She had not acknowledged any of his words of pity and commiseration, had not
even quite seemed to understand them. Like Sellars himself,
she seemed to have receded across interstellar gulfs.

'*We have one chance,*' Sellars said. '*If I cannot reach
the operating system, all is lost. But even now, with the
lives of so many in the balance, I cannot force you.*'

'No,' Christabel's mother said angrily. 'You can't. And
you won't.'

'Kaylene . . .' Major Sorensen sounded miserable, both
angry and helpless. 'If no harm can come to Christabel . . .'

'He never said that!' his wife snapped. 'Look at that little
boy in the other room – *he* was under this man's protection, too. Is that what you want for your daughter?'

Sellars spoke like a man climbing a mountain whose
summit he already knew he did not have the strength to
reach. '*No, there aren't any guarantees. But Cho-Cho is
different. He is connected directly into the system through
his neurocannula. Christabel cannot make that kind of
connection.*'

Ramsey felt like a traitor, but he had to say it. 'How
about the others who are stuck in the system – some of
them didn't have direct neural links. Neither did a lot of
the Tandagore children.'

'You see!' said Kaylene Sorensen in fury and triumph.

'*Different,*' Sellars said wearily, his voice barely audible. '*At least I think so. Operating system . . . Olga's son
. . . dying now. Can't close . . . feedback loop.*'

Because the Sorensens were facing the wallscreen, only
Catur Ramsey saw Christabel slide off the bed, her bare
feet stretching to touch the floor. *So small*, he thought.
She looked frightened and very, very young.

Good God, Ramsey thought. *What are we doing to these
people?*

The little girl turned and walked silently into the bedroom and closed the door.

It's too much for her – too much. It would be too much for anyone.

'I can't . . . I can't disagree with my wife,' Major Sorensen was saying.

'What does that mean?' Mrs Sorensen snapped. Neither she nor her husband had taken much notice of Christabel's departure.

'Lay off, honey,' Sorensen said. 'I agree with you. I just feel like shit about it.'

'Then there is nothing more to be said,' Sellars declared in a dying man's voice. Incongruously, the wallscreen from which he spoke displayed the hotel's in-house node, footage of smiling people enjoying various New Orleans restaurants and tourist parks. *'I will do what I can with what I have.'*

Ramsey did not need visuals to know Sellars had disconnected. The Sorensens stared at each other, oblivious to him or anything else. Ramsey stood awkwardly in the doorway; with Sellars' departure he had changed from participant to voyeur in an instant.

'I have to go,' he said. Neither of the Sorensens looked at him.

On the other side of the connecting door he leaned against the wall for a moment, wondering what had just happened and what it actually meant. Could Sellars really do nothing without the help of a girl scarcely out of kindergarten? And if he failed, what did that mean? Things had been happening so quickly that Ramsey was finding it hard to keep up. Just in the last two hours he had committed several major felonies – emptying an office building with a smoke bomb, interfering with the alarm systems for an entire island, putting a data tap on one of the world's biggest corporations. Not to mention the even more bizarre things that had come to light, the abandoned house and forest on top of the skyscraper, the tomblike pod room, the incomprehensible news about Olga's lost child being the operating system for the Grail network.

Olga, he thought. *Damn, I have to get back to Olga.*

The door to the Sorensens' rooms banged open and almost hit him. Michael Sorensen's face was pale, almost gray.

'It's Christabel.' The major's voice, his stunned expression, made Ramsey feel like he wanted to be sick.

Kaylene Sorensen was cradling her daughter on the bed, calling her name urgently, as though the child were half a block away. The girl's ragdoll limbs and the eyes rolled upward until only the white showed told the story, or most of it. A pair of thick black sunglasses lay on the bedcover near Christabel's legs.

'He did this!' Mrs Sorensen said to Ramsey, a hiss of raw fury. 'That monster – he pretended to ask our permission . . .'

'I'll call a doctor,' her husband said, then turned to Ramsey, his face so strange and confused that Ramsey felt nauseated again. 'Should I call a doctor?'

'Wait. Just . . . don't do anything. Wait!' Ramsey started back toward his room, then realized that he could call from the wallscreen here and not risk disconnecting from Olga. He barked out the number, praying he had remembered it correctly. 'Sellars! Answer me now!'

'*Yes? Ramsey, what?*' He sounded even worse, if that was possible.

'Christabel's in a coma, damn it! A Tandagore coma!'

'*What?*' He sounded genuinely stunned. '*How can that be?*'

'Don't ask me – she's lying on her bed. Her parents just found her.' He tried to think it through. 'There are some sunglasses lying next to her . . .'

'*Oh. Oh, my goodness.*' Sellars did not speak for a moment. '*I had precoded an entry sequence, but . . . but only for use if they agreed to it . . . !*' Despite the strain in his voice, the unfamiliar hesitations, he suddenly became focused, sharp. '*Tell them not to move her. She must be entering the system now. I have to go.*' For a moment, there was silence, but before Ramsey could break the connection, Sellars' voice came back. '*And tell them I am truly sorry. I did not want this to happen – not this way. I will do whatever has to be done to . . . to bring her back.*'

Then he was gone.

Ramsey had left them sitting silently in the bedroom, cradling the unmoving body of their little girl. Despite his own vague feelings of responsibility, or perhaps because of them, he could not wait to get away.

He picked up the pad to talk to Olga, wondering whether he should tell her what was happening on his end, thinking that if she remained as she had been the last time they had spoken, she would not even listen. Staring at the screen, his thoughts jumbled, it took him several seconds before he realized what he was seeing.

Olga Pirofsky still sat beside the cluster of massive black pods, swaying from side to side with her face in her hands, a picture of terrible and all-consuming grief. She clearly had no idea what was happening behind her.

The lids of two of the pods were rising – slowly and apparently silently. For a moment, Ramsey felt that same sense of helpless, almost sexual horror that he had felt as a child in the darkness of a movie theater. An alien spacecraft, the door opening, something about to come out – but what would it be?

But this was no movie. This was real.

A shape lurched in the nearer pod, then began to drag itself upright, bathed by the dim lights around the inside rim of the lid.

Ramsey had the line open and was shouting at the screen now, but Olga clearly was not receiving his call. He could only shout her name over and over as an immensely fat, horribly naked man climbed out of the glowing pod.

SHE slid the Storybook Sunglasses on. It was good to be in the dark behind the lenses. She could hear her mother's voice in the other room. Mommy was really angry – angry at Mister Sellars, angry at Daddy, even angry at Mister Ramsey, who didn't seem to have done anything as far as Christabel could see.

It was good to be in the dark. She wished she could have sunglasses for her ears as well.

'Tell me a story,' she told the glasses, but nothing happened. The lenses stayed black. There was not even a message from Mister Sellars. It made her sad – he had sounded so tired, so hurt. She almost wished that her mother and father hadn't found out about her secrets with him – her visits, the ways she had helped him, all the things, all the secret things. How he smiled and called her 'little Christabel.'

Their secret word.

'Rumplestiltskin,' she said. Light opened out in front of her eyes like a flower.

'*This will be like a call to someone far away,*' Mister Sellars' voice said in her ears. '*Or like going on the net. I'll be with you in just a moment . . .*'

'Where are you?' she asked, but his voice was still talking, not hearing her. It was another message, a recording, like before.

'. . . *And then I will stay with you, I promise. But I am doing many things, little Christabel, and it may take me a moment to reach you. Don't be frightened. Just wait.*' The light was moving now, dancing, spinning. It made her head hurt. She tried to reach up and take the sunglasses off but for some reason she couldn't find them. She could sort of feel her head but it seemed to be changing shape – first her hair felt funny under her fingers, then it didn't feel like hair at all. Then the light swept away from her, pulling her with it as if she had been sucked down the drain of the bath, and the light had a noise, too, a moan like the wind or like children crying.

'Stop it!' she yelled. She was really frightened now. Her voice sounded wrong, close in her head but strange and echoey and far away, too. 'I don't want to . . . !'

The light was everywhere. Then the light was gone. Everything was dark and she couldn't feel herself touching anything. For a few seconds she was all alone, as alone as she had ever been in her life, like in a bad dream, but awake, and there was nobody else anywhere in the whole world, not Mister Sellars, not Mommy, not Daddy . . .

But then there *was* someone else.

Scared, she held her breath, but it was more like thinking about holding your breath because she couldn't feel her chest get tight. She felt like she was about to pee all over herself, but that didn't feel quite real either. Something was looking for her. Something big. It was in the darkness.

It touched her. Christabel tried to scream, tried to hit, but she had no mouth, no hands. It was so cold! It was like all the black had frozen, like she was in the refrigerator with the door closed and the light out and she couldn't get out and nobody heard her and nobody heard her and nobody . . .

The big, cold something touched her inside her head.

That story on the net, the one I wasn't supposed to watch, about a giant gorilla that picked up a lady and smelled her and looked at her and it was so scary, and I thought he's going to throw her down on the ground or put her in his mouth and chew her with his teeth, and then I peed my pants and I didn't even know it until Mommy came in and said Ohmygod what are you watching Mike you left the screen on and now she's wet herself and ruined the couch because of your stupid monster I told you she was too young . . .

And then it let her go. The big, cold something passed through her like a wind, and she could smell it, but she was smelling how it thought, how it felt, and it was tired and sad and angry and even very very frightened but it didn't care about little girls anymore and it let her go.

She was hanging in darkness. She was lost.

'Christabel?'

When she heard Mister Sellars' voice, his kind, hooty-soft voice, she couldn't help it. She started to cry, then she was crying so hard that she thought she wouldn't stop, not ever, not ever.

'I w-want . . . Mommy.' She could barely make the words.

'I know,' he said. 'I'm sorry – I didn't mean for it to happen this way.' She couldn't feel him, not like she had felt the freezing dark, but she could hear him, and in all the blackness that was a tiny, good thing. She tried to stop crying. She had hiccups. 'I'm with you now,' Mister Sellars said. 'I'm with you, little Christabel. We have to go. I need your help.'

'I didn't mean to do it . . . !'

'I know. It was my fault. Perhaps it was meant to be – but perhaps not. In any case, it will all be over soon. Come with me.'

'I want my Mommy.'

'I know you do. And you are not the only one.' Now she wasn't quite as scared as she had been and she could hear how much he was hurting. 'Just come with me, Christabel. I'm going to take you to meet someone. I'm sorry this happened but I'm glad you're here, because otherwise I would have had to send your friend off to meet him by himself.'

Then she heard a new voice – a surprising voice, because she knew the person the voice belonged to couldn't be talking, because he was asleep on the bed like a dead person. But Mister Sellars was also asleep like a dead person, wasn't he?

Am I asleep like that too? Won't Mommy and Daddy be frightened?

'Get me out of here!' the voice shouted. 'Not doin' this *mierda* no more!'

'Cho-Cho,' she said.

For a moment, he didn't talk. Christabel hung in the blackness and wondered if this was what it felt like to be dead. 'Weenit?' he said at last. 'That you?'

'Yes.' Mister Sellars' breath was all funny and rough, as though he had stepped away for a moment and then run back. 'That is her, Señor Izabal. And we are going somewhere together. You two are going to find a little lost boy. And afterward . . . and afterward I will do my very best to take you both home.'

'You all crazy,' Cho-Cho's voice said. 'Not gonna do nothin'!'

But as the darkness began to turn into light – a gray

like a morning sky, but everywhere at once, below as well as above – Christabel felt someone reach out and take her hand.

'You okay, weenit?' Cho-Cho whispered.

'I think so,' she whispered back. 'Are you okay?'

'Yeah,' he said. 'Ain't scared of nothin', me.'

Whether that was true or not, his fingers tightened on hers as the gray light grew and grew.

PAUL and Orlando carried Martine down the twisting ledge until they came to where the others were blocking the path. 'Move!' said Paul in a loud whisper. 'Didn't you hear that madman? He's coming after us.'

'The path is gone,' Florimel said. 'It has dropped away. Melted. Something.'

'Like the mountain,' Sam murmured as she staggered up behind Paul and set Cho-Cho down on the stone. 'All gone.'

So this is where it ends, Paul thought. *All that drifting, all that running. It got narrower and narrower until I reached the end of the trap*. He looked at the others, Nandi, young T4b, all of them staring-eyed, their haunted, not-quite-real faces devolving into crude planes, the colors bleeding out of their skin and clothes and even the stones before which they stood. The walls of the pit seemed strangely abstract, like the brushstroked masses of some hurrying Expressionist painter.

'We can still fight,' said Orlando. Paul thought it was a statement so patently ridiculous that it was almost comical, a bleak joke for which their pointless deaths would be the only suitable punch line.

Martine shuddered and tried to sit up. 'Is th-th-that you, P-Paul?' She was trembling so powerfully that he crouched beside her and held her legs, afraid she would shake herself right over the ledge and down into the deeps. That endless blackness was the only thing that still looked entirely real.

'It's me,' he said and gently touched her face. She was cold. He was cold, too. 'We're all here, but we need to be quiet. That thing – Dread – is looking for us.'

'I h-haven't let go,' she said. 'I can . . . feel . . . where !Xabbu is – and b-beyond. I can even feel where . . . the Other is. All the way . . . to the end.' Her shivering had lessened, though she seemed farther away than ever.

'I'm here.'

'Cold. It's so cold. Vacuum cold.'

He tried to rub her hand but she pulled it away. 'That is so strange – I can feel you touching me but it is like it is happening on another planet. Don't. Let me think, Paul. It's so hard . . . to keep . . . to hold . . .'

'*Hello, chums,*' Dread's voice crooned. '*I know you must be getting tired of waiting for me.*' The path behind them was still empty, the light bent and strange. '*I'd have been with you by now, but I've been playing with the kiddies. Listen.*' A thin, sobbing shriek echoed through Paul's ears, through all his companions too, making them flinch and cry out, linked by a circuit of horrified helplessness.

'He's taking his time on purpose,' Florimel groaned. 'Sadist. He wants us to suffer first.'

'Smelling us scared, like,' T4b said.

'Silence!' hissed Nandi. 'We don't know how far away he is – he could be trying to lure us into giving ourselves away.'

'How much trouble will he have finding us on this path?' Florimel said with ragged contempt. 'I will not crawl.'

'Me neither,' said Orlando. 'I don't care if he's Dracula or the Wolfman or the Wicked Witch of the West – we'll

put some pain in his venture before . . . before the end.'
As the boy spoke, Sam Fredericks climbed unsteadily to
her feet beside him, reflected light flickering on her terrified, determined face. Paul felt a swelling in his heart,
something he could not name. *These poor, brave children.
How can this be happening to them?*

'Cold . . . !' Martine shouted. Startled, Paul clamped a
hand across her mouth. She shook it off. When she spoke
again it was barely a murmur. 'I can feel the Other – but
he's so small! Frightened! The children . . . they aren't
crying anymore. They're quiet, so quiet . . . !'

'*It is cold where the Other is.*' Sellars' voice made them
all jump.

'He's back,' Sam said tonelessly.

'*There is no time to waste.*' Cho-Cho now lay like a
fitful sleeper at Sam's feet, Sellars' bizarrely precise voice
issuing from the boy's open mouth. '*Martine, I will try
to reach you – to join my end of the connection to yours.
It will be a strange feeling, I'm sure, but please try to not
to fight me.*'

'Can't think. Too cold . . . hurts . . .'

'*The Other is imprisoned in a great coldness, both inside
and out,*' Sellars said, rapping out the words in a great
hurry. '*If you understand that, you will be less afraid. He
is not a machine, or at least he did not begin that way.
He was a child, a human child, corrupted by the Grail
Brotherhood and made the heart of their great immortality machine.*'

Paul felt a wash of helpless hatred. The Other, little
Gally, Orlando and Sam Fredericks, the screaming victims
beside the Well – all those innocents sacrificed so a man
like Jongleur could crawl on through more years of life.

'Frightened . . .' Martine wept. 'He is so small . . . !'

'*He always has been, at least to himself. Frightened.*

Abused. Kept in the dark, metaphorically and literally, because they feared his almost unlimited potential. He affected the minds of those who guarded him, so they exiled him – put him in the cruelest, most secure prison they could devise.'

'Prison . . . ?'

'A satellite.' Sellers spoke quietly, but his words seemed starkly loud on the ledge above the abyss. *'The Other is in a satellite, orbiting above the Earth. Cryogenic engines keep his metabolism slow, make him more controllable – or so they thought. They banished him to the emptiness of space, with fail-safe devices on his prison so that if anything went wrong they could fire the rockets and push him out of orbit and into deep space.'* Sellars' voice was dry, cracked. *'The Apep Sequence, Jongleur called it. After the serpent that tried every night to swallow the flying boat of Ra, king of the gods.'*

Martine gasped. 'Hurry! I . . . I can't . . .' She twitched, twitched again – it was strangely rhythmic. Paul looked down to see her hands moving in a strange pattern, the fingers held in front of her chest, weaving in and out. '!Xabbu, too . . . he hurts . . .'

'I am struggling to make the connection, even as I speak,' Sellers said through the sleeping child. *'It is . . . like threading a needle . . . with a thread a million miles long. And . . . I am holding the far end . . . of the thread.'*

Something was moving now on the far side of the Well – a point of darkness so pure that even in this shadowy netherworld Paul could see it striding down the path at a weirdly unhurried pace, winding along the wall of the pit.

'He's coming,' Paul whispered, knowing it was useless to say it, knowing Sellars could not work any faster. 'Dread's coming.' He touched Martine with his hand, the merest feather-light brush of his fingers on her leg. She moaned and writhed.

'No!' Her hands were moving faster now, clenching and unclenching, the fingers almost too swift to see in the weird half-light. 'Don't! Hurts!'

'Please don't touch her,' Sellars gasped. *'Please. It . . . is . . . very close. Very . . . difficult.'*

The shadow-shape turned along the wall, still following the path. Although it was still far away, Paul could see the gleam of two pale eyes. His heart sped even faster, hammering in his chest. *We're feeling what the Other feels,* he realized. *But that's what I've felt all along when the Twins were chasing me – its fear of them, its terror of Jongleur. I'm not even a real person, I'm just part of the bloody network code. I don't even have my own feelings!*

The dark man walked down the path.

What did all this truly mean? Paul's panicked thoughts flared and sputtered. What was the reality here? A murderer, or the devil himself? A boy who thought he was an operating system? An operating system that thought it was a little boy who had fallen down a well? Madness. Nightmares.

It really is the Red King's dream. It's all true. When the dream's over, when this network dies, Paul Jonas will blow out like a candle.

But I'm not even Paul Jonas, he thought with a sudden, chill clarity. *Not really. I'm the residue of the Grail process – a copy, like Ava. I'm just a better copy, that's all.*

He looked at his companions, frozen, staring. The only sound was Martine's harsh breathing.

It's the end, he thought, *and I'm still running. Still drifting. But I said I wouldn't do it anymore . . .*

Sellars needs time. This thought tore across the first

like a sudden scream. *The one thing we don't have. He needs time to save my friends.*

And what is there for me, even if I survive? An eternity in this looking glass universe?

The black shape turned the last bend, moving in an invisible cloud of terror.

'*Hello*,' Dread called, laughing. '*Have you been waiting long?*' The monster's eyes and smiling teeth gleamed out of the head-shaped shadow, as though it wore a charred mask of Comedy. '*Waiting for old John? Waiting for your old chum Johnny Dark?*'

The end, Paul thought. And then he ran.

He could hear the others shouting behind him, the raw surprise in their voices, but it was just noise. The poisonous fear that surrounded the shadow-figure swept over him, a stormfront of nerve-jangling, limb-deadenign panic that slowed him until it was all he could do to put one foot in front of the other. He staggered up the path like a man running against gale winds.

The thing called Dread stopped to watch his approach. He could feel its amused interest, but that was a solitary note in a roaring symphony of utter terror which grew louder and stronger the closer he got.

Zero. The dark. He couldn't think. He pushed himself forward two more steps. *Lost. Lost! Running in the dark, lost!* He took another step, his heartbeat so swift it was almost uniform, a zipper being pulled along its track, *beatbeatbeatbeatbeatbeat* . . .

'*So which one are you?*' The thing reached out for him with a hand cold as the bottom of a grave. Its empty eyes widened as Paul took one last stumbling step, then his brain and spine could not drive him any farther. He fell to the ground at the shadow-man's feet, twitching in helpless horror.

'*And what were you planning to do?*' it asked him. '*Challenge me to a fight? Marquis of Queensbury rules?*' It bent closer. An icy finger lifted Paul's chin, forced him to meet the white, blindfish gaze, the smile glinting like ice in the black fog of its face. '*I'm going to eat your heart, mate. And your friends – I'm going to take them home with me and rape their souls.*'

Paul's quivering hands, which for a moment had risen a few inches above the ground, dropped back to the path. As the blackness closed in on him he clung desperately to a single slender point of sanity.

'No more,' he gasped.

Dread leaned down until his grinning mouth was only a finger's breadth away. Paul felt sure his heart would stop. '*You aren't giving up already, are you? Oh, that's very disappointing . . .*'

'No more . . . *drifting!*' he screamed, and pushed off from the ground. He wrapped his arms around the shadow-thing and dragged them both over the side of the ledge.

For a long moment they fell, the dark man thrashing and struggling in his arms like an immense bat. Paul could feel Dread's surprised panic, and even through his own terror something like triumph rose. Then they slowed and stopped.

They hung in midair, Paul held like an infant at the end of Dread's outstretched arm. The grinning mouth was now contorted by rage. A terrible, scalding heat ran up Paul's body, flames suddenly crackling on his limbs, his hair, even inside him, racing up his gullet to fill his mouth. He let out a smoking shriek of agony as the monster swung him high, then flung him down, flaming like a comet, to slam against the sloping wall of the pit.

The first blow was so hard it was like something else entirely, as sudden and transformative as being struck by lightning. He dimly felt himself caroming down the uneven rock wall, limp, helpless, but it seemed very far away, strangely unimportant. Everything was broken inside him.

He stopped at last. He supposed he was still burning, but the flames were only more lights flickering before his eyes, and now all the lights were growing dim.

Doesn't feel like being a copy, he thought absently. *Feels . . . just like dying.*

A moving darkness floated down from above and hung just before him.

'You wasted my time. Bad choice.'

Paul would have laughed, but nothing worked. What an unimportant thing to say. What an unimportant thing to think. His own thoughts were like smoke, curling and rising, lighter than the air, lighter than anything that had ever been.

I wonder if there's a copy of Heaven, too . . .

And then he didn't think anymore.

CHAPTER 47

Star Over Louisiana

NETFEED/LIFESTYLE: Can't Diet? Maybe You Can Change Your Genes . . .

(visual: genetic engineering department laboratory, Candide Institute)

VO: The Candide Institute of Toulouse, France has announced a break-through in the quest for what some critics have called 'junk food genes,' a reversal of the usual approach for dealing with poor dietary habits in the First World.

(visual: Claudia Jappert, Candide Institute researcher)

JAPPERT: 'Some people can't improve their diet, no matter how much they try. We do not make judgments, and we are certainly not in the business of punishing people for poor habits, especially when we now believe we can optimize their body instead for the kind of food they do eat. If a few genetic adjustments can make someone better able to deal with a diet weighted toward saturated fats and sugar and too much red meat, then why should they suffer needlessly from life-shortening illnesses . . . ?'

THE tears were finished now. All Olga could do was wait. There was nothing left at all, inside or out, nothing but the hiss of an empty channel. She had turned her link to Sellars all the way up – in their last moments he had grown so quiet she could scarcely make out his

words, – and now all that it brought her was the sound
of his long absence.

Maybe it's me, she thought dully. *Maybe I just can't
hear any more.*

Before entering the tower she had believed she had
already given up everything, but in only minutes she had
been made to understand how foolish that belief had been.
Thirty years of believing a terrible lie, a lie on which she
had built her life and to which she had reconciled as to
a decrepit but familiar home. Now it was gone.

*How many times did my baby cry? And nobody came
to him.* She could not move, could not open her eyes.
Better I never knew. Nothing could be worse than this.

The link to Sellars still blew nothing into her ear but
the ghosts of electrons, the phantom voices of quanta.
She tried to imagine a life spent that way, a life spent
listening to a void like that, not even knowing that you
were human. That it should be her son – that she, of all
the mothers who had ever lived, should have been singled
out for such horror . . .

The light had changed. Through the cracks between
her fingers Olga saw a spill of blue, the broad black band
of a moving shadow. Her heart flip-flopped, threatened
to stop entirely.

Did Sellars bring him here? After all? It was only a
instant's thought as she turned, a flare of panic and hope
that she knew was ridiculous, but it made the immense,
dripping thing shuffling toward her all the more incomprehensible.

'Heh-woh.' It smiled, showing its big teeth. 'Heh-woh,
wih-uh way-ee.'

The words came out in a gargling slur – the fat man's
massive jaws did not seem to be working properly. He
trailed fiberlink and medical cables like some deep-sea

monster twined in kelp. The mounds of his pale skin were slick with some shiny, fluorescent grease.

Behind him, the lid of his black sarcophagus stood open. On the far side of Jongleur's huge central pod another lid was also up. Bony hands scrabbled at the rim as whoever or whatever was inside tried to climb out.

The fat man took another dragging step, raising a huge, meaty arm. Olga stumbled backward. He was slow but getting faster. Even in the somber light she could see slimy footprints on the carpet behind him like the track of a monstrous snail. 'Non't wun away,' he said. His speech was improving, but not much. 'We've min in vose muckets a wong, wong nime. We've min missing owah vun. Vinney? Wheah ah you?'

Another figure now stood upright in the other pod – a naked man, painfully thin, but much more normal-looking. He turned and stared blearily at the fat man. 'I g-g-gan't zee . . .' the thin man complained. 'Where . . . my . . . glazzez . . . ?'

The fat man laughed. A smear of blue froth gleamed on his lips and chin. 'Non't worry, Vinney – you ahways worry noo much. Yoo woahn neen 'em. I'll hoad her nown, you noo . . . you do . . . whatever you wanna do . . .'

Olga turned and ran across the carpet.

She reached the elevator in moments but the door was closed. She screamed for Ramsey and his agent friend, then remembered she had turned off his line so she could listen for Sellars' return.

'Ramsey!' she said when she had activated it. 'Open the elevator door!'

'*It's coming,*' he shouted, as frightened as she was. '*I sent it already. I've been screaming at you! You didn't hear me!*'

The elevator hissed open. She jumped in and waved

her hand over the door-closing sensor. The two men were lurching toward her across the carpet, the fat man waving his hands in the air, roaring gleefully. 'Come back! Come back, little lady! We just want to have some fun!'

'This elevator will only take you down to the security station,' Ramsey warned her as the door finally slid shut. 'Then you'll have to change to another that descends to the lobby. At least I think so – is that right, Beezle?'

'Far as I know, but who pays attention to me?' said the cartoon voice.

Something smashed against the door of the elevator so hard Olga saw the metal doors flex inward a little.

'Up,' she said. 'Up!'

'What are you talking about? There's only one floor above you. You'll be trapped . . . !'

'I'm not going down. Fine, then, I will do it myself.' She waved her badge and touched the up light, but the car didn't move.

'It needs a special clearance, remember?' Ramsey said. 'Beezle had to work hard on that one.'

'Just do it,' she begged. Another smashing blow wrinkled the door in half an inch. She could hear the fat man outside shouting unpleasant invitations. 'Do it, for the love of God!'

'You got it, lady,' said Beezle. The elevator began to rise.

'Even with all those trees, that crazy forest, you can't hide up there for long, Olga,' Ramsey told her. 'I don't get it.'

'I won't need to hide very long,' she said.

SAM could only stare down into the gulf as the thing with the dead eyes and gleaming teeth rose toward them. Her chest was frozen with terror, a slab of ice where her heart and guts should be. She had watched helplessly as Paul Jonas was burned and cast down. She was too frightened even to cry out.

On the ledge beside her Martine breathed in short, painful gulps like a woman giving birth. Orlando was holding the blind woman's head. Florimel, T4b, and the others were all silent with shock and helpless anguish. A whirl of tiny shadows settled on Orlando and a few made their way onto Sam.

'It coming, Freddicks,' something whispered miserably. She could feel the little monkey fingers pulling at her hair, trying to find a good hold. 'Gotta get out of this place!'

'Nowhere to go,' she said.

Martine gasped and sat up, eyes wide but unfocused. 'I feel it! The Other – it is horrible! It has no body – it is only a brain, a huge brain!'

Sam reached back and took her hand, trying not to scream as Martine squeezed her fingers until she felt the bones would crack.

Won't matter long, Sam told herself. She felt Orlando take her other hand. The grinning shadow-shape drifted up toward them like a black leaf on a warm, lazy wind.

'*They did not bother to keep a body*,' Sellars' voice sighed from a million miles away. Cho-Cho's mouth was barely moving now. '*Easier . . . just to keep . . . the brain itself.*' The voice grew ever more distant, a fading signal. '*Engineered cells replicating . . . to replace . . . dying . . . miscalculated . . . it filled the . . . satellite.*'

Martine's breathing sped again, a chain of rasping grunts that did not sound like anything human. The shadow floated up.

'Bye-bye,' Sam said – not to anyone, even Orlando. Perhaps to herself. 'Over,' she whispered. 'I'm sorry.'

THE moon had faded to a shadow of white in the sky. Even the brilliant desert stars were all but gone. Renie held !Xabbu's head in her lap. He was barely conscious, his breathing a low, vibrating rasp like nothing she had heard. Even after he had stopped speaking aloud his hands had traced the shapes of string-figures for long minutes. Now they no longer moved.

'Don't leave me, !Xabbu. Not after all this. I don't want you to go first.'

Something flickered. She looked down, blearily certain that the bottom of the pit was even farther away than it had been. Light gleamed again.

The river was beginning to glow.

The faint sparkles of light began to thicken, became streaks that sent flaring, rippling light all along the sides of the pit, but the shadowy child-shape beside the river did not move or even open its eyes. Only when the whole of the watercourse was ablaze with coruscating brilliance did the small figure stir and raise its head.

Two little children, a girl and a boy, stood in the middle of the river as though they had walked there along the surface of the water. Renie had never seen them before, or at least she did not recognize them: the light surged and leaped so brightly around them that they almost disappeared in the glare of cold fire.

The little girl held out her hand to the huddled shape. She looked like a dream-creature, but her voice was shaky, the words those of a real and frightened child. 'Come with us. It's okay. You can.'

The shadow-child looked at the ones bathed in light. It did not say anything, did not even shake its head, but the river suddenly leaped higher, rose to breast-high on the two children. They did not move, but Renie could see their eyes open wide.

'No, don't be afraid,' the little girl said. 'We came to take you to your mommy.'

'*Liar!*'

She turned to the boy beside her, dark-haired, solemn-eyed, his mouth locked tight against what Renie thought might be a cry of complete terror. He looked back at her and shook his head violently.

'Tell him,' the little girl said. 'Tell him it's okay.'

The boy shook his head again.

'You have to,' she said. 'You . . . you're more like him.' She turned back to the shadow-child. 'We just want to take you to your mommy.'

'*Liar!*' The thing writhed and shrank, became something even smaller and darker and more hidden. The river blazed up, so that for a moment it covered the children over and Renie's heart flipped in her chest. '*The Devil always lies!*'

The flaring light subsided. The boy and girl stood, frightened but still unmoved by the rushing, scintillating waters. They were holding hands. 'Tell him,' the little girl said to her companion, her whispering voice carrying up to Renie as though it were meant for her alone. 'He's really scared!'

The little black-haired boy was crying now, his shoulders trembling. He looked at the girl, then at the shadow-child huddled on the river bank. 'P-people,' he said slowly, so quietly Renie found herself leaning forward to hear, 'some people, they want to help, seen?' His breath hitched. 'Some people really try to help you.' He was crying so hard he could barely speak. 'It's t-t-true.'

The glowing river swirled and sparked. !Xabbu twisted in Renie's arms but when she looked down in fright, his face seemed a little calmer. She turned back to the pit.

The shadow-child rose and stood on the bank, then

stepped into the glowing river. For a long moment the
children stood facing each other in a silence that seemed
the deepest communication of all, the two shining in the
river's light, the other so small and murky-dark that even
in the heart of such radiance no light could touch him.
Then all three were gone. Renie was not sure what had
happened but her eyes were blurry with tears. A moment
later she felt the darkness fold in on them, taking the
desert, the pit, everything. With her last thought she
clutched !Xabbu tightly to her.

The end, she thought. *Finally*. And then, *Oh, Stephen
. . . !*

OLGA was covered with scratches and bleeding in a dozen
places by the time she reached the deserted house. She
pushed in, then threw the bolt on the front door. It would
not take them long to get past it, but she didn't care about
that either. She watched the two figures, the fat one and
the thin one, stagger out of the trees at the bottom of the
garden and turn to look up at the house. However long
they had been in those tanks, it had been long enough
to make the chase difficult for them.

I've kept in shape, she thought. *Who knew it was for
this?*

Riding the elevator up she had felt a sudden almost
horrifying sense of freedom. Her life had been a lie. She
had built it all on lies. All the years she had entertained
children, mourning her loss, her own child had been alive
– suffering as perhaps no living creature had ever suffered.
What could you do, knowing that, but shake your fist at
the universe? Spit at God? It didn't matter now.

'*Olga . . .*' Sellars' voice in her ear was thunderously
loud but paradoxically weak. She turned down the volume.
'*He's coming to you. Don't be afraid.*'

'Not afraid,' she murmured. 'Not that.'

When her son came at last, she did not hear him, but felt him – a tiny constellation of lights drifting up out of subterranean depths, tracking toward her across unimaginable distances. He came like a flock of birds, of shadow-shapes, a whirring and a fluttering that was all confusion and fear.

'I'm here,' she said gently, so gently. 'Oh, my little one, I'm here.'

They were banging at the front door of the abandoned house now, trying to dislodge the bolt. Olga moved from room to room, ever deeper, until she reached the girl's bedroom. She sat on the dusty coverlet beneath the shelf of ancient, wide-eyed dolls.

'I'm here,' she said again.

The voices began as something she had heard in her dreams, a chaotic whispering, a moaning, laughing chorus of children. They swelled into a noise like a river, blending, merging, until at last it was one voice – nothing human, but one solitary voice.

'*Mother . . . ?*'

She could feel him now, could feel everything, even as her ears dimly registered the crunch of the front door being knocked off its hinges. A moment later she heard the glee-drunk shouting of the fat man down the halls, the sharp tones of his thin companion.

'I'm here,' she whispered. 'They took you from me. But I never forgot you.'

'*Mother.*' There was a sadness in it no human voice could have contained. It swam up like a blind thing from the bottom of the ocean. '*Lonely.*'

'I know, my little one. But not for much longer.'

'Yoo hoo!' The voice of the fat man was just outside the bedroom door now. The tiny latch would last only moments.

A voice crashed in on the side channel. '*Olga, this is Ramsey. You have to get out now!*'

She was annoyed at the interruption, but she reminded herself that Catur Ramsey was in a different world – the world of the living. Things seemed different there.

'*There may be a few minutes left, time to . . .*'

'Just a moment, Mr Ramsey. I am finishing Mr Sellars' errand.' She disconnected from him, then stood. 'I'm still here,' she assured the huge, lonely thing. 'I won't leave. But you have to let them help you, my beautiful child. Do you feel someone reaching to you? Give him what he wants.' She felt a spasm of guilt, hating to use these precious few moments of mother-love in this way, hating to manipulate a child who had known nothing else, but she had promised. She still owed a little something to the living.

'*Give him . . . ?*'

'He'll save what he can. Then you don't have to worry anymore.'

The bedroom door shook, made splintering noises.

'*Yes . . . Mother.*' A brief pause, then she felt him again. '*Did it.*'

She let out a sigh. All obligations finished now. A memory, long buried, too painful, finally surfaced. 'You have a name, little one, did you know that? No, of course, you could not know – but you have a name. Your father and I chose it for you. We were going to call you Daniel.'

A moment passed, a long moment. '*Daniel . . . ?*'

'Yes. Daniel, the prophet who kept his faith even in the lion's den. But don't be afraid – the lions can't hurt you anymore.'

'*Have . . . a name. Daniel.*'

'You do.' It was hard to speak. No tears, only a dry numbness, something beyond pain. 'I'm coming to see you now.'

When she opened the door the fat man and the thin man started back, surprised but prepared for violence. She lifted her hands to show they were empty.

'I think there's something you should see,' she said, then calmly walked past them toward the parlor. The two gleaming, naked men stared after her in astonishment. The fat man's hands twitched but she was already gone. They looked at each other for a moment, then turned and followed her through the parlor and out onto the front porch.

'So you've decided to do the sensible thing,' the thin one began.

'Mr Ramsey, can you have your mechanical agent friend open a window on this floor?' she asked. 'Something big that I can see from the front of the house?'

'*B-but, Olga . . . !*' he stuttered in her ear.

'Just do it, please.'

'What the hell is going on?' the fat man growled. He reached forward and closed his massive, stubby fingers around her wrist. 'What kind of trick . . . ?' He broke off in surprise as, with a grinding of long-unused gears, a huge square section of the roof slid back, revealing the dark evening sky, the true sky, its sprinkling of stars dimmed by the lights of the metroplex below. All the stars but one, which was growing brighter, ever brighter on the horizon.

'*Olga . . . !*'

'It's all right, Mr Ramsey. Catur. Thank you for everything. I mean that. But I am not going anywhere.' She turned and smiled again at the fat man and his thin companion. 'So here we are, gentlemen. We have a few moments – time for you to catch your breath.'

The fat man turned to the thin one. 'What is she talking about?'

'My son,' said Olga Pirofsky. 'We're waiting for my son.'

Sᴇʟʟᴀʀs had hung in chill emptiness so long he could scarcely remember where he was, or even who he was, but he could feel the chain of suffering stretching into the distance, a fragile link with the heart of the void. The blind woman, the Bushman, the two frightened children – how much longer could they all last?

Then he felt it. Something in the darkness had touched the connection. Like a fisherman who had discovered Leviathan on his hook, Sellars braced for its anger. He faced it naked of defenses, risking all to ensure that he did not frighten it away. Even in its dying moments it could kill him easily if it wished.

No, not it, he thought. *Him.*

When the touch came, it was surprisingly gentle.

'*Have a name.*' The inhuman voice held a new note. '*Daniel.*'

'Ah,' Sellars said. 'Daniel. Bless you, child, that's a good name.' He hesitated. They had only moments, but if he pushed too hard he might destroy the fragile connection.

The Other, however, had his own plans. '*Fast. Mother . . . my mother . . . is waiting.*' He extracted a final promise from Sellars, then gave up the keys to the kingdom he had built for himself, had built out of himself – an exile's island in the ocean of his own fear and loneliness.

'I'll do my best to save them all,' Sellars said.

A silent groan – release? Fear? '*All done. All done.*'

'Goodbye, Daniel.'

But the great cold thing was already gone.

Dʀᴇᴀᴅ could actually feel himself bursting with radiant darkness, as though the fire inside him was devouring an entire planet, endless fuel, the food of gods. His inner music was blaringly loud, horns and crashing drums. As he soared upward, he reached out his hand to the quailing figures on the ledge, and at the same moment he plunged his thoughts, his glowing *twist*, down along the silver thread into the heart of the system, reaching toward the dying thing that had hidden from him and resisted him so long.

All resistance was over now. He had won.

He found it at last, a tiny twitch of life at the center of things, a beaten, cowering presence. He gave it pain just to feel it shrivel like a burning leaf. His twist blazed, fueled by his glee and his anger, his trimphant, all-devouring rage.

Mine, he exulted. *All mine!*

He paused to examine what he had finally captured, the bit of individuality, of naked will, which was all that was left of the system's intelligent core. He could smother it now with only a thought. The system would be his mindless slave. And after that . . . ?

It shifted in his grasp, almost slipped free. Surprised, he focused his will, pinned it like a helplessly struggling insect even as it curled into itself, trying to hide again. How could it still be resisting him? After all that agony? Surely only Dread, of all the victims in the world, could find strength in suffering that way. No machine could do such a thing, only John Dread. For was he not a black angel, a power upon the Earth? A god?

He pried it open. A small voice was all that he found, a breath.

'*Confident . . . cocky . . .*' it whispered. '*Lazy. Dead.*'

It surrendered its last secrets and suddenly he knew everything. In horror he fought to disengage, to throw himself back into his body, but even as he tried to yank his glowing twist free from the heart of the system it grabbed at his mind, a dying animal sinking its teeth into its tormentor. His music stuttered, faded. He smashed it with his will, hurt it, tore it, but it hung on blindly.

Priority Message. The words blazed out before his inner eye. Struggling with all his might to pull out, he could not turn it off, could not even wonder where such a bizarre thing might come from. His superior strength was beginning to tell, but the thing still clung, determined to drag him down into its self-destruction.

Images began to flit across his consciousness. Bodies . . . women's bodies, torn and ragged, slick and wet. *But why? Where?* He could not be distracted – he had only seconds – but the images filled his brain, falling through him like angels shotgunned out of the sky. The trickle became a torrent, an obscene, unstoppable wash of dismemberment and death, of his own face leering out at him from a thousand mirrors, of a thousand mouths screaming, screaming until he couldn't think. He flailed, trying to find his way out trying to regain control to get out had to get out but the eyes were all looking at him now staring eyes knowing eyes mocking mouths the faces his mother's face laughing the screams the blood the silent music of death and dying and it didn't stop it didn't stop it didn't . . .

FINNEY and Mudd had chased the intruder all the way up to the top floor, but Felix Jongleur could not see what was happening there – he had sealed himself off from the place a long time ago. The oldest man in the world could only writhe helplessly in his preserving fluids and wonder.

Dread. It was all Dread's fault. Jongleur had raised him up from nothing but the minion had turned on him like the dog he was. His teeth were sharp, it was true, but he was only a beast after all, a beast that Jongleur himself had almost entirely created . . .

The cacophony of alarms seized his attention again. He tried to focus but his thoughts were scattered. He had not felt so afraid in decades – how could all this have happened? How long would it take to put it all right? He forced himself to look at the security information but it was a hopeless jumble. The new alarms seemed to be about a potential violation of his airspace. *Why aren't my helicopters and jumpjets seeing to it?* It was probably just another false indicator, but still, that was what he paid all those useless indolent soldiers for . . .

Gone. They were gone, of course. Evacuated.

He stared at the blinking lights, the line that started high in the atmosphere and ended . . . here?

The Apep data was flashing beside it. In the surprise, in the horror of his privacy violated, he had forgotten about the program's weird insistence that it had already been triggered. False – the readings had to be false. It said the rockets had fired hours ago, shooting it out of orbit at thousands of miles an hour, just as they were designed to do, but the trajectory for the satellite was so clearly wrong . . .

The trajectory. *Falling, not rising.*

He flicked to his perimeter cameras, but could not find one that pointed at the sky. When he finally found one that could be elevated it seemed to take forever. When it stopped at last and refocused, he saw the new and fiery bloom racing toward him along the sky.

In a sudden, horrible moment he understood everything, or at least enough. But Felix Jongleur had not survived so long by letting panic rule him, even in a situation like this. All might seem lost, but something could still be salvaged. It would only take seconds to trigger the Grail process – it had been ready since before the Ceremony. The physical Felix Jongleur might die, but hidden in the network's memory, the vast reserve of Telemorphix storage safe on the other side of the country, his immortal self could survive even this catastrophic shutdown of the system. Someday he would again be free within the electronic universe, a prisoner entirely escaped from death, possessed of knowledge that could bring all his power back to him.

Jongleur plunged himself back into his house system, opening a link to the network. A long moment of terrified waiting passed, but the Other's autonomic security routines allowed him his rightful access. He reached for the controls that would trigger the Grail process and bring his sleeping virtual double to life – a Felix Jongleur who would live forever, whatever happened to his flesh, the Felix Jongleur he would awaken into, refreshed and immortal, as though death were an afternoon nap.

The gray light faded. The darkness came.

He did not understand. He had done nothing yet. The Grail process was still coming on line, had not been activated. Why was the space around him turning black?

The darkness slowly took on shape – long, low, and sealed in secrecy. Felix Jongleur stared, dumbfounded. Somehow, without his ordering it, he had been drawn into his own Egyptian simulation – for surely that was Set's coffin. But where was the rest of the temple? Why was all in shadow?

A red line gleamed along the edge of the sarcophagus. Jongleur found himself being drawn forward. He searched desperately for the override commands, but was as helpless as in nightmare. The line of fire became wider. The lid was opening. There was someone inside.

The man sat up, his black suit almost invisible against the shadows inside the sarcophagus. His bleached face glowed like a candle beneath his black stovepipe hat as he smiled and stretched out his pale ancient hands.

Terror gripped Felix Jongleur, squeezed him, crushed him. The staring eyes burned into his, scorched his thoughts to cinders but Jongleur could not look away. He tried to scream but his throat was locked shut, his pulse racing so swiftly that no chemical could slow it; no machine could regulate it.

'I'm coming for you.' Mister Jingo's tombstone grin grew wider and wider until it seemed to swallow everything. 'I've finally come. Riding the sky.' He opened his mouth wide to reveal the blackness behind the teeth. The new star burned in that blackness, streaming flame, growing larger and brighter as it hurtled toward him like the headlight of an approaching train.

'Here I come, Felix,' said Mister Jingo.

That smile.' Jongleur's heart suffered, lurched. *That empty, fiery smile . . . !*

'I caught you at last.'

And then, in the shadows and silence where only electrons moved, the old man finally screamed. It went rattling out into the vacancies that lay behind moments, fading but not dying, echoing on and on through that place where even Time itself did not rule.

THE star sped down the sky toward her, a streak of fire like the hands of a midnight clock.

Olga did not even turn to watch the fat man and the thin one as they ran shrieking toward the elevator. The plummeting satellite was growing larger every moment; it now filled the sky beyond the opened roof like a blazing eye. She could feel her son in her mind, close as her own heartbeat. The flames were all around him now, and even though it was his own hand that had broken the bough and thrown down the cradle, his fear was terrible.

She reached into her pocket and pulled out a curl of laminated paper.

'I'm here, Daniel.' She stared at the hospital bracelet for a moment, then closed her eyes. 'I'm here with you.'

And then she could feel him, truly feel him, as though he were in her arms not just her mind – the way it should have been. She pulled him close and comforted him.

A few meters behind her, in another universe, the elevator had arrived. The door opened halfway, then stopped. The fat man and the thin man grunted and tore at each other as they both tried to force their way in. The fat one squeezed the thin one's throat. The thin man sank his teeth into the other's hand and scratched bloody runnels down his naked belly with his fingers and toes.

In a place behind her eyes, in a time out of time, Olga held her son. The light of the falling star blazed down on her, brighter by the moment. Alarms wailed from every wall, unwanted voices yammered in her ear, and the two men squealed in pain as they fought before the elevator, but she heard only one thing.

'Sshhh,' she told him. 'Don't cry. Mama is here.'

RAMSEY shouted her name, over and over, but Olga Pirofsky did not reply.

He could see her in the visual window Sellars had opened. Considering the circumstances, she looked strangely calm as she stared out at the night through the skylight Beezle had opened, but the two naked men who had chased her now seemed to be fighting to the death in front of the elevator. Things weren't exactly making sense.

He called Sellars, but got no answer there either.

'Beezle, what the hell is going on? Sellars said we had only a few minutes to get her out, but she won't come –

won't even answer me. She must be out of time by now. Is security on the way yet?'

'Not security.' Even for a piece of gear, Beezle sounded strange. 'But *something* is.'

A new view flashed open on Ramsey's screen. He stared at it for a stunned moment, then let the pad slide from his lap. He stumbled to the window of his room, fumbled for a helpless moment with the shade, then ripped it loose and threw it on the floor so he could see out the window.

'Oh, sweet Jesus,' he murmured. '*Sorensen! Get everyone down on the floor!*'

He heard a clamor from the next room, thumping, Major Sorensen's voice shouting, but he could not tear his eyes from the sky. A new star shone in the Louisiana night, a star that burned more brightly than any others in the sky and which was growing larger every second.

As the streak of flame shot past overhead, smaller lines of light leaped up from the darkness in the distance, from the island in Lake Borgne.

Must be automatic defenses, he thought distractedly. *Missiles. Everyone else is off the island. Almost everyone.*

Oh, shit, he thought. *Why, Olga?*

The smaller lines leaped up toward the streaking star. Two of them swept past without contact, then faded into the endless night sky, but one struck the burning thing. Bits of fire spun away, backward and down, but the core had only been diminished, not destroyed. It swept on toward the horizon, sinking, and then Ramsey could not see it as it passed beyond the buildings and the great dark ruck of the swamps.

Silence. The night, undisturbed. Catur Ramsey let out half a breath.

A dazzling flash blanked the sky like sheet lightning. A pillar of fire climbed swirling up from the middle of the dark lake. Ramsey gaped as it boiled toward the clouds, God's own barber pole made of solid flame, rolling, billowing, its harsh light turning the city and swamp flat electric white. He threw himself backward, rolled across the couch and onto the floor just as a crash like the end of the world smashed the glass out of the hotel windows.

When he climbed to his feet half a minute later his ears were ringing painfully. He crunched through broken shards to the window and stood with the Gulf air cool and wet on his face. The pillar of living flame had shrunk a little, but still seemed tall enough to scorch the underside of Heaven.

CHAPTER 48

Unreal Bodies

NETFEED/NEWS: ANVAC Unveils The Doctor
(visual: test subjects in convulsion)
VO: ANVAC Corporation today announced what it calls the new
benchmark in crowd control – a product nicknamed 'Doctor Fell.' The
heart of the device premiered at the International Security Exposition,
whose official name is Mob Disruption Field Electronics Launcher
(hence the nickname, MD FEL) is a device that fires a fist-sized
projectile that blankets an area of several hundred square meters with
a finely tuned electromagnetic field. Anyone within range who is not
wearing a field inhibitor, which ANVAC supplies as part of the pack-
age, loses all body control and, frequently, consciousness as well.
ANVAC claims that Doctor Fell is 'a huge step forward in the control
of dangerous humanity . . .'

SAM slowly let go of Orlando's arm. The white marks her fingers had made remained for a moment on his skin, livid in the half-light.

'We're . . . still here,' she said.

Orlando laughed raggedly, flopped over onto his back, arms spread across the path. '*Dzang*, Frederico. You haven't lost your talent for the obvious.'

She stared into the pit. Only moments ago something

Sam found almost impossible to distinguish from Satan himself had been rising from the pit. Now it was . . . gone.

'I mean . . . we're alive!'

'Speak for yourself.' Orlando rolled over and struggled onto his feet, rubbing at the place Sam had squeezed him. Indignant at being dislodged, a small cloud of monkeys fluttered up, protesting loudly, and swept out to circle above the now-empty Well. Despite her over-whelming confusion Sam almost smiled. The real Thargor wouldn't have rubbed his arm if a dragon had bitten it off.

'Everything feels . . . different,' said Florimel, who had also stood.

'Big bad thing gone,' one of the monkeys fluted, sweeping back to hover before her. It paused for a moment as if listening. '*Both* big bad things.'

'That's not all,' said Orlando, staring up at the opening far above, the faint stars. 'The whole place is different. Scanny-different, but I can't explain why.'

Sam looked too. Hadn't the stars disappeared completely only hours before? Now they hung in the dark sky again. Orlando was right – everything was different. The pit had seemed endless, bottomless, impossibly, night-marishly huge, even after it had devolved into something less realistic. Now, for all its size, it seemed simple, almost normal. It was just a big hole in the ground. Had everything changed? Or were they just seeing things differently . . . ?

'Martine! Where is she?' Sam spun. The blind woman's body was stretched along the ledge, her face turned toward the pit wall, almost hidden in the shadows. Sam pulled her over. She was unconscious but breathing.

Florimel bent down to examine her. 'We have all survived, it seems.'

'All but Paul,' Sam could not help pointing out. She was angry about it – such a stupid waste! 'He didn't have to.'

'He felt he did,' said Florimel gently. She lifted one of Martine's eyelids, frowned, then checked the other.

'But what happened? Someone explain.' Sam turned and scanned the ledge for the boy who had spoken with Sellars' voice but could not see him.

'He just . . . disappeared,' said Bonnie Mae Simpkins. 'That Cho-Cho. Don't ask me, child – I don't know either.'

'The man Sellars brought him into the network,' said Nandi. 'If he's gone, perhaps that means Sellars is gone, too . . . or dead.'

'Who won, so?' T4b demanded. His usual truculence had been blasted away. He seemed more childlike than Sam had ever seen him. 'Us?'

'*Yes, in a way,*' said a voice from nowhere. '*Our enemies are dead or disabled. But we too have lost much.*'

'Sellars?' Florimel looked up in offhand irritation, as though disturbed by a neighbor while she did some prosaic household task. Sam guessed that, like the rest of them, the German woman wasn't hitting on all cylinders. 'Where are you? We are tired of tricks.'

The invisible presence laughed. Sam wondered if she had heard him do that before. It was a surprisingly nice laugh. '*Where am I? Everywhere!*'

'Scanned,' muttered T4b. 'Lockin' scanned.'

'*No,*' Sellars said. '*It is far stranger than that. But Florimel is right – I should remember my manners and make it easier for all of us to talk.*' And suddenly, he appeared – a strange, shrunken creature in a wheelchair, his face crinkled like a dried fruit. The chair's wheels did not touch the ledge. In fact, it hovered several meters away from it, out over the great emptiness. 'Here I am. I know I am not much to see.'

'Are we all to live, then?' demanded Florimel. 'Can you help me with Martine?'

Sellars floated forward. 'She will awaken soon, I think. She is physically as well as can be expected.' He shook his misshapen head. 'She carried a tremendous burden – pain and horror that few could bear. She is an astonishing person.'

Martine groaned, then threw her hand over her face and rolled over, turning her spine toward them. 'You are saying kind things about me.' Her voice was hoarse and almost inflectionless. 'I hope that means I have died.'

Sam crawled to her and awkwardly patted her hair. 'Don't, Martine.'

'But it's true – you have done an amazing thing, Martine Desroubins,' Sellars said. 'In fact, we have all done something nearly as amazing just by surviving. And it is possible we are to be the witnesses of something more astonishing still.'

'No more puffed-up talk,' said Florimel. 'I am alive when I did not expect it – but I am not ready to be lulled with a speech about what we have done. Where is my daughter, Eirene? I can feel her, I think – her real body still lives, and that is good, but what of the coma?' She scowled and rose from Martine's side to face Sellars. 'Her spirit must be somewhere above us – lost and terrified after all that destruction. I will climb to her now and the rest of you can spend as much time talking as you wish.'

'I am sorry, Florimel.' Sam decided that 'hover' was nto the right word: Sellars sat rock-solid above the void, as though a hurricane could not move him an inch. 'I wish I could tell you she was recovered, that even now her real body was awakening, but I cannot. There is much I simply do not know, and there are still many mysteries here. However, I can at least promise that the Eirene you love is not up there, huddling in fear on the shores of the Well, and she never was. Now, will you let me explain what I do know?'

Florimel stared at him, then nodded once. 'I will listen.'

'I will tell you some of it as we proceed,' Sellars said. 'There is one last thing that must be done here, and I do not trust myself to deal with it alone.'

Orlando sighed. 'Do we have to kill something else?'

'No.' Sellars smiled. 'And there is a happy side to this duty as well. There are friends waiting. No, not that way, Javier.'

T4b had already begun to trudge up the sloping path. 'What?'

'Down.' Sellars began to drift beside the ledge, following its path into the depths. 'We have to go down to the bottom.'

'Old melty wheel-knocker,' T4b grumbled quietly to Sam and Orlando as they helped Martine up. The others also struggled to their feet, murmuring with pain and weariness. 'Don't have to walk, him – just float like some *sayee lo* butterfly.'

Hᴇ was silent and very still, but his chest was moving.

'!Xabbu?' She shook him gently. '!Xabbu?' She could not, would not believe that they should have come through so much and fail now. '!Xabbu, I think . . . I think it's over.'

She looked up, still uncertain what was different. The bottom of the pit lay in a half-light, only a little of it provided by the stars far, far overhead.

Stars. Were there stars before?

Most of the light came from the river, if it could still be called that. Although it flickered with strange gleams, hints of blue and silver light, it had shrunk back to a tiny rivulet.

But the mantis, the shadow-child . . . the Other . . . was gone.

Those two children came, she remembered. *They took it . . . him . . . away. Who the hell were they?*

But not just the river had changed. The quality of the light, the feel of the stone ledge beneath her, everything – the whole place had become both more and less real. The most grotesque of the exaggerations were gone, but when Renie moved her head quickly, there seemed to be an infinitesimal lag. And there was something else . . .

She was distracted by !Xabbu moving. His eyes were open, although he did not yet seem to see her. She put her head on his chest, felt it moving, listened to his heart.

'Tell me you're all right. Please.'

'I . . . I am alive,' he said. 'That is one thing. And I seem to be alive . . . after the world has ended.' He struggled to sit up. She got off him. 'That is another thing,' he said. 'A very strange thing.'

'There's something else,' she told him. 'Feel your face.'

He looked at her with surprise. The surprise deepened as he felt along the side of his jaw, let his fingers move out onto his chin and up over his mouth and nose. 'I . . . feel something there.'

'The mask,' she said, and suddenly could not help laughing. 'The mask from the V-tank. I've got one too! Which must mean we can go offline again.' But even as she said it, she thought of something. '*Jeremiah – Papa – can you hear us?*' she called. She said it again, louder. 'No. For whatever reason, we don't have communication with them yet. What if there's something wrong with the tanks?'

!Xabbu shook his head. 'I am sorry, Renie, I don't understand. I am . . . tired. Confused. I did not expect to feel all the things I have felt.' He rubbed his head with his hands, a gesture of weariness so unfamiliar that Renie could only stare for a moment. She put her arms around him once more.

'I'm sorry,' she said. 'Of course, you must be exhausted. I was just worrying, that's all. If we can't speak to Jeremiah and my father, we don't know that the tanks will open. There are emergency release handles inside, but . . .' She realized she was almost as tired as !Xabbu. 'But if they don't work for some reason, we'd just be stuck in there.' The idea of being trapped inches from freedom in a pitch-black tank filled with gel, after all they had already survived, made her feel queasy.

'Perhaps we should . . . wait.' !Xabbu was having trouble keeping his eyes open. 'Wait until . . .'

'A little while, anyway,' she said, pulling him toward her. 'Yes, sleep. I'll keep watch.'

But the warm, reassuring solidity of his head on her chest quickly drew her down as well.

She came up again slowly, her lids gummed together and so hard to open that for a panicky second she was certain they had awakened in the tanks after all. Her fog-headed thrashing woke !Xabbu, who rolled off her and thumped down onto the ledge.

'What . . . ?' He raised himself on his elbows.

Renie looked around at the now-familiar stone pathway, the rock wall behind them, the shadowed empty expanse beyond the ledge. 'Nothing. I . . . nothing.' She squinted, shook her head, looked again. The river had stopped glowing – it was now only a dark scratch at the bottom of the pit – but something else was creating a warm, pinkish-yellow light which spilled across the stones where the child-thing had crouched and waited.

'There's something shining down there,' she said.

!Xabbu crawled forward and peered down. 'It comes

from a crack in the rock wall – there, to the side of the river.' He sat up. 'What can it be?'

'I don't know and I don't care.'

'But perhaps it is a way out.' He seemed already to be recoving some of his natural bounce; by contrast, with her adrenaline no longer flowing, Renie felt like she had been given a beating by experts. !Xabbu pointed up the path. 'Look at how far it would be to climb back up.'

'Who said anything about climbing up? We're going to wait until Jeremiah or my father know we're ready to come out. And if we don't hear from them, well, I suppose at some point we'll take the risk and do it ourselves. So why the hell would we care whether there is another way out?'

'Because it might be something else. It might be a threat. Or it might be our friends looking for us.'

'What, with flashlights?' Renie waved her hand at the idea.

'Then you stay here and rest,' he said. 'I will go and look.'

'Don't you dare!'

!Xabbu turned to her, his expression surprisingly serious. 'Renie, do you truly love me? You said that you did.'

'Of course.' He had startled her, scared her. Her eyes burned a little and she blinked. 'Of course.'

'And I said the same to you. And it is a true thing. I would not stop you doing something you felt was important. How can we live together if you will not show that respect to me?'

'Live together?' She felt as if whoever had beaten her up before had come back for a last sucker punch.

'Surely we will try. Isn't that what you want?'

'Yes. I guess so. Yes, of course, I just . . .' She had to stop and take a breath. 'I just haven't had a chance to think about it much.'

'Then you can think while I go look.' He smiled as he rose, but he seemed a little distant.

'Sit down, damn it. I didn't mean it that way.' She tried to order her thoughts. 'Of course, !Xabbu – of course we will live together. I couldn't be without you. I know that. I just didn't expect to have this discussion in the middle of an imaginary world.'

His smile was a little more genuine this time. 'We have not had any other kind of world lately in which to discuss things.'

'Come back, please.' She put out her arms. 'This is important. We have never been together – not as lovers – in the real world. In some ways it may be as strange and difficult as anything we've experienced in this . . . *not*-real world.'

'I think you are right, Renie.' He was solemn now.

'So let's start with the basics. We seem to be stuck here, at least for now. Whatever is making that funny light doesn't seem to be going anywhere. We've been here for hours and it hasn't done anything to us. It's not getting brighter – or even dimmer for that matter.'

'These are all true things.'

'So instead of arguing about some new piece of virtual foolishness, why don't you come here and hold me?' She was worried, she realized, but she was also hungry for his touch. They had survived countless horrors. Now she wanted something better. 'We have a ledge. We have time. We've got each other. Let's do something about that instead.'

He raised an eyebrow. She could almost have sworn he was embarrassed. 'You city women are not shy.'

'No, we're not. How about you desert men?'

He sat and leaned toward her, put his hand around her neck and gently pulled her toward him. She decided he wasn't that embarrassed after all.

'We are very healthy,' he said.

She had slept again, she realized, this time from a happier
sort of exhaustion. Her eyes drifted open and she made
a slow inventory of her surroundings. The stone, the empty
expanse, the distant sky – nothing seemed to have
changed. But of course, in a way, everything had changed.

'Do we count that as our first or our second time?' she
asked.

!Xabbu lifted his head from her breast. 'Hmmm?'

She laughed. 'I like you this way. Relaxed. Is this how
a hunter acts when he's had a big meal?'

'Only a meal that good.' He slid upward and kissed her
jaw, her ear. 'It is funny, this kissing. You do so much of
it.'

'You're picking it up,' she said. 'So – first or second
time?'

'Do you mean before – when we found each other in
. . . in the great dark?'

She nodded, pulling at the coils of his hair with her
fingers.

'I don't know.' He lifted himself above her, smiling. 'But
we still have another first time to go!'

She had to think about it for a moment. 'Real bodies.
Jesus mercy, I'd almost forgotten. That certainly *felt* real.'

He looked down into the pit. 'The light is still there.'

Renie rolled her eyes. 'All right. I surrender. But you're
not going by yourself.'

The surrender did not become immediately effective.
Renie was reluctant to let him go, and would have happily
made another experiment with the potentials of virtuality, but !Xabbu held her to her bargain. At last, with much
protest, she allowed him to help her up onto her feet.

'It is just so nice,' she said lazily. 'That's why I don't

want to go anywhere. Just so nice to be . . . human for a while. Not running for our lives. Not frightened.'

He smiled and squeezed her hand. 'Perhaps that is a difference between us. I am happy with you, Renie – so happy I cannot say. But I will not feel completely safe until I know what is around us. In the desert we know every bush, every spoor, every drift of sand.'

She squeezed back, then let him go. 'All right. But go slowly, please, and let's be careful. I am truly exhausted – and you are partially to blame.'

'I hear you, Porcupine.'

'You know,' she said as they walked down to the place where the path ended, 'I think I'm beginning to like that.'

!Xabbu was staring at the rocks below the path. Either because of the change in the lights or some subtler and more profound shift of the whole environment, the climb down did not look as impossibly steep as it had before. 'I think I see a way down,' he said. 'It will not be easy. Are you sure you would not rather wait for me?'

'If I'm going to respect your wish to climb up and down things for no good reason,' she replied calmly, 'then you had better learn that I don't get left behind very well.'

'Yes, Porcupine.' He squinted down the stones. 'Do you mind if I go first?'

'Hell, no.'

It took them the better part of what Renie guessed was half an hour, but she was grateful to discover that her first impression had been right: it was not a bad climb, especially to someone who had survived the trip down the black mountain, just one that needed care. With !Xabbu beneath her, pointing out handholds and places stable enough to stop and take a short rest, they reached the bottom with no mishaps.

The bottom of the pit was strangely smooth, more like

something that had melted and cooled than like the bottom
of any true canyon. Renie looked up at the stars and the
circle of dark sky far above. The distance was dizzying.
She started to say something to !Xabbu about the climb
back to the ledge – she was already wondering whether
she could make it back without a long rest – but he held
up his hand, asking for silence.

Seen up close, the hole in the wall was more than a
crack. At its narrow top the crevice stretched to four or
five times her height, and the opening, aglow with peach-
colored light, was wide enough to drive a car through.

!Xabbu walked toward it with quiet care. The light
seemed to roll over him like something liquid, so that all
she could see was his slender silhouette. Suddenly afraid,
she hurried to catch up to him.

As they stepped through the crevice Renie found herself
in a high corridor of raw stone, a gouge so full of soft
radiance that at first she could see nothing. After a
moment, she thought she could make out a pattern to the
light, as though the walls of the corridor were full of
sealed alcoves, each one holding a little core of brilliance.

What are they? she wondered. *It's like a beehive. There
must be hundreds of them . . . thousands . . .*

'I heard your speaking and your other noises,' said a
quiet, strange voice behind them. Renie whirled. 'I thought
– I questioned . . . wondered? . . . when you would come.'

Standing in the mouth of the crevice, blocking their
escape, stood a tall man. Dazzled by surprise and the glow
all around them, it took Renie a moment to recognize
him and the malformed thing he was holding.

It was Ricardo Klement.

'**O**KAY, so the Other was floating around in some kind of
satellite and the Grail Network data was shooting up to

it and back on special lasers or something. Chizz. And then the Other flew the satellite down and crashed it, so Jongleur's blown up and dead.' Sam was trying hard to sort through all the new information. 'That's utterly chizz. But Dread isn't. Dead, I mean.'

'I said I don't know,' Sellars told her. 'I am trying to find out what happened to him, but it may take a while . . .'

'Right. We don't know about Dread, so that's not so chizz. But are you telling us that we saved the Other just so he could *kill himself?*' She shook her head. 'Man, that's impacted!'

'We did not save him,' Sellars said. 'The Other had suffered too much, first from Jongleur and the Grail Brotherhood, then from the man called Dread. He had already decided he did not want to live. Such things . . . such things happen.' There was a strange tone in the man's voice that Sam did not understand. She turned to Orlando to see if he had heard it too, but her friend was staring down at the path as though he feared stumbling. 'When I first brought Cho-Cho online, while I struggled with the network's defense systems, the Other fooled me. I thought all his attention was on fighting me, but while I was busy trying to understand him and his strategy and struggling to repel his attacks, he was preparing to use me. When I accessed the data tap and was temporarily overwhelmed by the magnitude of information, he was ready.

'If he had wanted to, he could have killed me easily then – but he wanted something quite different. He reached through my connection into Felix Jongleur's central control system for the network – the one part that had been expressly shielded from him, and which included the mechanisms that kept him imprisoned. By the time I understood what was happening he had already wrenched the satellite out of orbit and begun his carefully-aimed descent. By that point there was nothing that could have saved him: gravity had already signed the warrant.'

'How horrible!' Sam could hardly bear to think about it. 'He must have been so unhappy!'

Martine had been walking between them like a zombie, but now she stirred. 'He had . . . a little peace at the end. I felt that. I do not think I would still be here if I had not.'

'You did not feel . . . everything, did you?' Sellars slowed his downward progress until he hung near her. 'I hope you did not have to suffer through the very last moments.'

She shook her head wearily. 'He pushed me away. Before the end.'

'Pushed you away?' Sellars looked at her with his sharp yellow eyes. Sam could not help wondering if it was their true color. 'Was there . . . contact of some other kind? Did he say something?'

'I do not wish to speak of it,' Martine said flatly.

'But if the Other is gone, why is all this still here?' asked Orlando. He too seemed troubled. 'I mean, this place was all . . . a dream, wasn't it? The Grail network was kind of like his body, but this part was the inside of his mind, right? So why isn't it gone? Why isn't everything around us gone?'

'And if the network goes, you will go, too – that is what you are thinking, isn't it, Orlando Gardiner?' Sellars' voice was kind. 'It's a good question. And the answer has two parts, both important. The second part I will save until we reach the bottom of this pit, for reasons of my own. But the fact is that I had prepared for this day a long time – I just never thought I would have the chance to use any of those preparations. I did not know the true nature of the Other until today, of course, but I knew it was at least quasi-sentient and dangerous. I also knew that the network might not survive without it. The physical records of the system are safe – they are stored in room after room of processors in the headquarters of the Telemorphix Corporation. Thanks to the late Robert Wells, the hard code of the network and the simulations is relatively safe.'

'Wait a minute,' said Florimel. 'The *late* Robert Wells? He was alive in the network, in the Egypt simworld – if we survived, he probably did also.'

Sellars' laugh was not so pleasant this time. 'He hid your capture from Dread. Dread found out.' The old man glided a bit farther out from the ledge and looked down. 'So the hard data was safe, but it would include nothing from *here.*' He gestured with his thin fingers, encompassing the pit, the spiraling path. 'Because this was part of the Other itself.' He frowned. '*Himself* – I don't want to steal his humanity as others did. So when he was destroyed, this would all go too. The replacement operating system I had been able to cobble together in preparation for this day, with help from the people at Tree-House, would contain none of it.'

Sellars sighed. 'Now we come to the first of my several confessions. When I freed Paul Jonas from the simulation in which Felix Jongleur had held him for so long, I did not fully understand what I was doing. I was ignorant about the actual workings of the Grail process and even more ignorant of the Other's true nature. I had no idea that it had created for Paul a version of the virtual minds the Grail Brotherhood were making for themselves. I am still not sure why it did that, although I suspect it was something to do with the fondness Avialle Jongleur felt for him and the affection the Other felt for her.

'In any case, I foolishly went ahead and released him anyway, seeking only to get his consciousness free from Jongleur's clutches so I could find out what he knew and why they held him. But he escaped not just from them, but from me as well. I did not know until later that what I had done was to free a virtual copy – that the real Paul Jonas was still unconscious in the vaults of the Telemorphix Corporation.'

Martine grunted as if struck. 'The real Paul Jonas . . .' she murmured. Sam thought she sounded like a woman on the verge of tears, but Sellars didn't seem to have heard her.

'In any case, things had grown steadily worse throughout the last hours. Even before the endgame began, the Other had been struggling to run the network and also siphon resources to this private world. There were several times when the whole thing came to the brink of collapse . . .'

'Those, like, reality hiccups,' Sam said.

'But in the last moments the Other had finally surrendered to despair. It triggered its own death, wishing only to destroy the symbol of its torment and its cruel master, Felix Jongleur. The rest of the network might survive that destruction, but I knew that this secret place would not. Caught in the Other's . . . feedback loop, for lack of a better word, the coils of its powerful hypnosis, you would die when it did.'

'And the children, too,' added Florimel. 'Was it not trying to save the children by keeping them hidden here?'

Sellars took a moment to reply. 'Yes, it was trying to protect the children as well,' he said at last. 'So there things stood. I could salvage the network, but not the things the Other had created out of its own mind.'

'Wait a minute,' Orlando said slowly. 'Are you saying

that we're *not* in the network? That we've been . . . somewhere else all this time? In something's mind?'

'Where are a human being's memories?' Sellars asked. 'In its mind, but where? This place exists within the larger body of the network, just as human thought exists within the brain, but we may never be able to answer either question with a definite location.' He lifted his hand. 'Please, let me finish. The Other had surrendered, but *I* had one last plan. If he would let me, I decided I would try to make a last-minute version of the kind of virtual matrix the Other had created for Paul Jonas. The Grail process is an exacting, time-consuming thing, but I hoped that I could at least generate something basic, just as the Grail process starts with the mind's simplest functions and then adds layer after layer of memory and personality. I did not need the Other, only his most basic functions. But I could not do it without his cooperation.

'In his very last moments, and thanks to another brave woman, this one a stranger to you all, he gave that cooperation to me. It was a near thing, though, and there was no guarantee we would create enough of a double that this matrix, this internal Otherland, would survive.' Sellars shook his head, remembering. 'There – that is half your answer, Orlando, as promised. It *did* survive. We are in a sort of Grail-process version of the original operating system, the Other.'

'He's alive?' Sam felt as though the whole world had suddenly become unstable again.

'Not alive. There was not time for that. The greater network is still operating, and this place has survived too, existing as a kind of salvaged memory. It functions, more or less. The things that are damaged should be reparable.'

'Reparable?' Nandi slowed, then stopped. 'This place is an abomination – a crime against Nature, built on the bodies of innocent children. We of the Circle came into this place to destroy it, not repair it.'

Sellars looked at him with an unreadable expression; Sam didn't think it was just because of the strange deformities of the man's face. 'Your point is a good one, Mr Paradivash. This is one of the things that must be discussed. But there could be no discussion if I had not accomplished what I did. The system would be gone and you would be beyond conversation.'

Nandi stared at him angrily. 'You have no right to make such a decision, Sellars – to keep this place alive at your own whim. Dozens of people from the Circle died to prevent such a thing.'

'Martyrs,' said Bonnie Mae quietly. 'Like my husband Terence.'

'But you do not know yet exactly what they were martyred *for*,' Sellars said evenly. 'So I suggest we wait to have this conversation until you do.'

'We are not children, like most of your so-called volunteers.' Nandi shook his head. 'And we kept no secrets from our soldiers. We will not be convinced by high-minded talk, or by mystification.'

'Good,' replied Sellars. After a moment, he laughed wearily. 'Would anyone else like to shout at me?'

'We're listening,' said Sam. The conversation between Sellars and Nandi made her nervous, although she wasn't quite sure she understood the argument. Why would someone want to shut the network down, especially if it was safe now? It was huge and expensive and unlike anything else ever made. *Besides, don't . . . scientists have to study it?* she wondered. *People like that?*

'But I still don't understand,' said Orlando. 'Why did the Other fight so long, then just give up? If it made all this out of its own thoughts and worked so hard to keep the children safe here, why didn't it fight a little longer? And why did it make such a big deal out of the children when it was the one that stole them in the first place?'

'Some of the answer I have given you already,' Sellars told him. 'The Other had been tormented so long that he had finally fallen to despair.' He found his smile again. 'But the rest is part of your earlier question – the part I told you I wouldn't explain until we reached the bottom.'

'Jeez,' Orlando said. 'Then how long are we going to have to wait?'

'Enough.' It was Martine. 'Enough of this. This prattle.' She did not look up. Her voice was ash, the remains of something burned. 'You argue and you question and none of it matters. A good man is dead. Paul Jonas is dead.' Now she raised her head. Sam thought there was something unusual in the way she turned her face toward Sellars. 'Who brought him to life in this nightmare without his understanding or even permission? You. Will all this bring him back? No. Yet you can hardly contain yourself. You are pleased that everything has gone so well. Meanwhile we trudge down, down, down into this gray hell with no bottom. Just let us go home, Sellars. Let us crawl back to our holes and lick our wounds.'

A new expression flickered across the old man's scarred face, both surprised and saddened. 'I meant no disrespect to Paul Jonas, Ms Desroubins. We still need to mourn him properly and fittingly, you are right. But I assure you, this is not a journey I bring you on lightly.' He turned to the others. 'And there *is* a bottom. But I have been properly reminded of something that the confusion of our situation made me forget. There is no need for you to . . . trudge.'

'What does that mean?' asked Florimel.

'This.' And suddenly, most startlingly, Sam felt herself

lifted as though by a perfect agreement of air molecules, with no uneven pressure in any one spot, and swung out over the deep, dark canyon. The others hung beside her in various states of flailing startlement.

'Down!' shouted T4b, struggling wildly. 'Back!'

'Before, this place did not . . . connect with the place we are going. Now it is all relatively simple, relatively . . . real.' Sellars nodded. 'My error was in forgetting what I could do – the ability I have gained to manipulate the network. I have made you tire yourselves unnecessarily. My apologies.'

Suddenly Sam was dropping – not like a stone, but not like a feather either. T4b let out a string of very inventive street curses as he too plunged down through the darkness. Sam saw bodies on all sides of her, her companions, all dropping at the same rate. Tiny yellow monkeys tried to fly out from her hair and shoulders, but although they could hover, they could not fly back upward against the forces that pulled them all.

I'm tired of all this scannity, she thought. *I just want to go home. I want to see my mom and dad . . .*

'Like the Resurrection in reverse.' Florimel sounded both annoyed and nervous.

'Just hold onto your seat cushion,' Orlando said cheerfully. 'They always come in handy. That's why they tell you about them.'

Yeah, and don't you think Orlando wishes he could go home, too? It was a painful thought.

'*Save me, Jesus!*' shouted T4b.

Two minutes falling, five – it was hard to tell. Despite the sensation of speed, they did not slow; when they reached the bottom they simply stopped, and found themselves standing on a smooth bed of stone. The walls stretched only above them now, an immense vista tunneling upward to the circle of night sky. But the place where they stood had a light of its own.

'Here,' Sellars said, wheelchair still comfortably adrift above the ground. He led them toward a vast crack in the wall that spilled warm, pink-orange light.

'I bet we do have to kill something,' Orlando whispered. He tapped his sword against the stone wall at the edge of the crevice. It rang flatly.

Sam stepped through and found herself in a great blazing chamber, a honeycomb of light. Three figures waited at the center of the vast space. Sam squinted, already hoping, but wanting to be sure.

'Renie?' she called. '!Xabbu?'

They turned in surprise as she sprinted toward them. The third figure, which was clutching something against its chest, did not move. Sellars glided up beside her, his runneled face even more surreal in the bright, almost directionless light.

'Stop, Sam,' he said, an unusual note in his voice. 'Wait.'

She slowed. Sellars moved a little ahead of her, then paused and hovered. He seemed to pay no attention to Renie or !Xabbu, but instead addressed the third figure. 'Who are you?'

Doesn't he recognize that Klement guy? Sam wondered. *He knows everything else.*

'Just wait,' Orlando said quietly beside her. He had come up as silently as a cat. When he touched her arm she could feel the trembling strength in his big hand. 'I bet that's the one we have to kill.'

'He's Ricardo Klement,' Renie explained to Sellars, although she looked stunned herself. 'One of the Grail Brotherhood. He traveled with us for a while.'

'No.' The man paused a long time before shaking his head, as though he had to remember the movement. Sam could see what he was holding now, but could make no sense of the weird, semihuman bundle. 'No, I am not Ricardo Klement. I wear the . . . body . . . that was meant for that one. For a length of time, at first, I think . . . thought . . . I *was* Ricardo Klement. Because it disorients, this bodyliving. It makes thinking . . . strange. But I am not that one.

'My name is Nemesis.'

CHAPTER 49

The Next

NETFEED/NEWS: *Middle East Unified At Last*
(visual: Jews and Arabs demonstrating at Western Wall)
VO: *Palestinians and Israelis, enemies for so long, have at last found common ground – in hatred of the UN's management of the Jerusalem Protectorship.*
(visual: Professor Yoram Vul, Brookings Institute)
VUL: *'The only thing that could bring these people together, it seems, was someone trying to stop them from killing each other. It would be ironic if it were not so sad, but now we have eleven more UN peacekeepers dead in the Hashomaim Tunnel bombing, and the most common thing you hear is, "What do you expect – it's the Middle East!"'*

RENIE could only stare helplessly, first at the thing she had thought of as Ricardo Klement, then at her long-lost companions. She had never expected to see them again, yet here they were – but like Renie and !Xabbu they only stood, frozen and confused, and where there should have been rejoicing there was only more mystery. *And fear*, she realized. *I'm frightened again, but I don't even know why.*

'What . . . what's a Nemesis?' Renie asked.

'It is a machine – a piece of code.' She had never heard Martine Desroubins sound so flatly miserable. 'It was sent to find Paul Jonas, I think. I met it when I was Dread's prisoner. In all the confusion after that, I don't believe I ever told you.' Martine turned to the inhuman, handsome face that the real Ricardo Klement had intended to wear for eternity. 'And what do you want now?' she said bitterly. 'Jonas is dead. That should make you happy – as happy as something like you can be.'

'Oh, no!' Renie raised her hand to her mouth. 'Not Paul.'

'Yes, Paul,' said Martine.

'But how did it turn into that Grail guy?' asked Sam Fredericks. 'We saw him come alive . . . at that Ceremony thing.'

'And what's with the ugly blue monkey?' With his feet on the ground, T4b had regained a little of his confidence.

'I saw it take another's form before,' Martine said. 'It imitated a corpse. One of Dread's victims. It did something similar with Klement, I imagine – perhaps it merely took Klement's empty virtual body before the Ceremony even began.'

Renie could not bear to hear her friend sound so helpless. She wanted to go and put her arms around her – around all of them, Sam, Florimel, even T4b – but could not ignore the feeling in the air, a cloud of anxiety like an impending storm. She was almost afraid to move.

As she looked over the familiar and unfamiliar faces, she suddenly recognized the tall young man with the whipcord muscles.

'Oh, my God,' she whispered to !Xabbu. 'Isn't that . . . Orlando?'

The long-haired youth heard her, even from some distance away, and gave them a quick, tight smile. 'Hello, Renie. Hi, !Xabbu.'

'But you were . . . dead, weren't you?'

He shrugged. 'It's been a pretty interesting day.'

The man in the wheelchair had not moved. He hovered a few paces from the Klement-thing, his eyes narrowed. 'You are Nemesis, then. You heard what was said and I think you understood – Paul Jonas is dead. What do you want with the rest of us?'

Sellars. Even after all this time, Renie recognized his voice. How strange, that he should look like that. *If* he looked like that. She suddenly felt a fierce homesickness for the real world, for things that felt and looked the way they were supposed to, that didn't change from second to second.

The thing cocked its head at Sellars, then slowly wheeled to survey the others. 'Nothing,' it said at last. 'I am here because I was . . . called. Were you not called, too?'

'Called?' Renie asked. 'Called to what?'

The thing in Ricardo Klement's body did not answer, only turned its flat stare back to the rows of glowing cells.

The others, cautiously at first, then with increasing confidence as Nemesis showed no signs of hostility or even interest, moved past the thing toward Renie and !Xabbu. As Sam Fredericks reached her, Renie found her eyes filling with tears again.

'I haven't cried like this since I was a baby,' she said, laughing as she hugged Sam. 'I can't believe we're all here – all together again.'

'Oh, Renie! Look!' Sam turned back to grab Orlando and pull him toward them. The barbarian sim looked embarrassed, as though his resurrection from death had been some prank that he now regretted. 'He's alive! Can you believe it?' Sam giggled wildly. 'And you are, too!

We looked for you – everywhere! But you were just utterly gone.'

For long moments it was chaos, but a happy chaos, despite the weirdness of the setting. Even T4b came forward and allowed Renie to put her arms around him.

'Chizz you're not dead,' he allowed, stiff and embarrassed in her embrace. 'And the little bushy man, too.'

After more hugs and tears and even a couple of introductions, accompanied by a flurry of questions and half-answers, most of which left Renie feeling even more confused about what had happened – the Other had destroyed itself, it seemed, and had taken Jongleur and maybe even Dread with it – she made her way to Martine, who had hung back from the general gathering. Renie wrapped her arms around her friend, but was dismayed by the woman's passive resistance.

'It's been bad for you,' she said. 'Oh, Martine, at least we're alive. That's something.'

'It is a great deal,' the other said quietly. 'I am sorry, Renie. I am very happy to see you well – happy for you, and for !Xabbu, too. Pay no attention to me. I . . . I am crippled. The end was . . . very bad.'

'It was bad for !Xabbu, too,' Renie said. 'I thought I'd lost him.'

Martine nodded and straightened; for the first time in a while Renie thought she saw in the woman's posture something of the companion she knew. Martine gently broke free, squeezed Renie's arm, then walked past her to !Xabbu. A moment later they were in whispered conversation.

That's a step forward, Renie thought, pleased to see some animation in Martine's face. She could not think of a better ear for a heartsick person to find.

'Just a moment.' Florimel's voice cut across the other

voices, loud and sudden. 'I am as glad as anyone to have this reunion, but we were promised answers.' She pointed at Sellars, who had been watching the gathering with a gentle, avuncular smile. 'Well? I want to get out of this . . . false universe. I want to be with my daughter. If, as you say, her condition will not improve, at least I can see her, touch her. Why are we still here? What do you want to tell us?'

It took Renie a moment to understand what Florimel meant about her daughter, then a spasm of nausea gripped her. *Stephen – does that mean he won't get better either?* She couldn't bear to think about it. After all this time, all that they had suffered . . . it wouldn't be fair. 'No,' she said aloud. 'That can't be.'

'I did not say that,' Sellars declared. 'I have no idea what will happen to the children in comas. All I said was that I could not promise they would get better. But the reason for the coma is gone.'

'Because the Other is dead?' Florimel's brisk, hard tone could not hide the anxiety beneath.

'Yes.'

'But the system is still functioning,' said the man who had introduced himself to Renie as Nandi something-complicated-with-a-P – *the man from the Circle*, as she thought of him for convenience. The one who had helped Orlando and Sam get out of the Egypt-world. 'Thus it must still be . . . using those poor children. Sucking their lives like a vampire. That is why it must be destroyed.'

'Please wait until you understand everything,' Sellars told him. 'Florimel is right. The time has come for the rest of the explanation.' He let his chair float a little higher in the air so that all could see him. 'First off, I told you that there is a new operating system, one created with the help of TreeHouse technicians and others – a much more conventional operating system. The network no longer requires a linked network of human brains to function. Of course, it is not quite so dramatically realistic either, but that may improve . . .'

'So because the last survivors of the concentration camp are soon to be free or dead, should the camp itself remain open?' Nandi was scornful. 'Become a holiday retreat, perhaps?'

'It is a more difficult question than that,' Sellars replied. 'Children's brains were being used to run this system, but the ones victimized are not those we sought. The brains used to supplement and expand the processing power of the Other were those of the unborn – of fetuses, or perhaps even cloned brains. I have not discovered the whole truth yet, but I will. There is a near-infinity of information to sift, much of it hidden or deceitful. The Brotherhood did their best to hide their tracks.'

'What exactly are you saying?' Renie asked. 'Do you mean that my brother Stephen *isn't* part of the system? Or just that he isn't . . . *in* the system? That he isn't one of the children in the simulations, for instance.'

'He was never part of the system, not in the way we thought. Nor was Florimel's daughter or T4b's friend.'

'*Fenfen!*' snapped T4b. 'Heard Matti, me. Heard 'im like he was standing there.'

'But all the signs pointed here, to this network!' Florimel said angrily. 'What are you trying to tell us? That we were deluded? That we have suffered all this, watched friends die . . . for a coincidence?'

'Not at all.' He let his chair drift a little closer to her. Behind him, Ricardo Klement – *No, Nemesis*, Renie reminded herself, *whatever the hell it is* – settled himself . . . itself . . . on the floor, gazing intently up at the gleaming walls as though in some fabulous art gallery.

'The network,' Sellars went on, '—or more specifically, the Other – was certainly to blame for their comas. But only in the same way that the Other convinced all of you that you couldn't leave the network without suffering terrible pain. As I explained, the poor, lost creature we called the Other was a freakishly powerful telepath. Mind-reader, mind-controller – he was something of both. The mind-*reading* – the actual remote connection to a human brain – was the freakish part. But once contact could be made directly into the nervous system, everything else was probably relatively easy. After all, that is how I managed to control the boy Cho-Cho's speech centers and talk to you.'

'Talk, talk, that's all you do – but what are the answers?' growled Florimel. 'Why is my daughter in a coma?'

'Let me explain, please. It is not a simple story, even the little of it I have discovered.

'Despite his arrogance and megalomania, I had wondered all along whether even Felix Jongleur would take the risk of exposure that would come from putting thousands of children into comas to complete his machine. And in fact, he did not. He and his minions were not satisfied with the Other – it was too powerful, too untrust-worthy. So even while they built their system around it, while they told the rest of the Grail Brotherhood that everything was working perfectly, they were looking for possible substitutes, other telepaths and wild talents that might be able to replace the Other. They concentrated on children, both because they would be easier to mold to the system, and because they would physically last longer. One such discovery was the man you knew as Dread, although Jongleur found a very different use for him.

'They had many different programs in place to sift through children and test them, private schools and clin-ics like the Pestalozzi Institute, which they also used to educate the Other, if such a term can be used for such an inhuman practice. And there were places like the virtual club called Mister J's – the spot where I first met Renie and !Xabbu – which were a sort of preliminary screening device, meant to sift out the few interesting prospects from the millions of ordinary children. Two of Jongleur's lieutenants were in charge of this project, although Jongleur himself carefully watched over everything.'

'Finney and Mudd,' Martine said. 'The men who chased Paul.'

'Yes, although I doubt those were their real names. From what I have seen, they seem to have had a very unsavory background.' Sellars frowned for a moment.

'But those children – my brother!' Renie said. 'Why are they in comas?'

'Because Jongleur underestimated the Other. His own body stolen, the Other was given the whole of a fantastically complicated network to be his new body – but Jongleur and his minions did not understand the Other's ambition. More importantly, they did not understand his humanity . . . and his loneliness.

'He discovered his power could be extended through electronic communications over a distance. Part of that power was a hypnotic effect – something the Other himself probably never understood, any more than the rest of us spend much energy considering our own vision or sense of balance. You all being trapped here is a perfect example. He wanted all of you to stay in the network. He was fascinated with you, for some reason – I watched him watching you, almost following you . . .'

'It was because of a story,' Martine said in a raw voice. 'About a boy in a well.'

'Ah. Well, I hope you will explain that to me later.' For

the second time in an hour, Sellars appeared startled. 'But I should finish this story first.

'The Other was interfacing with your minds directly, without you even realizing it. And at some level his wish to keep you, to hold onto you, translated into a direct plea planted in your subconscious. You could not go offline. Whether by pain or by the apparent disappearance of your neurocannular connections, you believed yourselves prevented, and it was so.'

'But that Other thing truly sixed now, right?' T4b asked anxiously. 'We could go now. To our caves – home, like?'

'Yes. But after I finish this explanation there is something very important I need from you – now, with you all gathered together.'

'Yeah? Thinkin' about it,' T4b said. 'Keep talkin', you.'

'So you're saying that the children like my brother were held here the same way?' Renie asked.

'No. They were never truly *here*, not like we are. Instead, they were . . . and are, for all I know . . . in comas simply because the Other made it happen – perhaps even by accident.

'I am guessing here, but I imagine that when the Other finally discovered how to move beyond the constraints of the Grail network, he reached out through Jongleur's own information web, then discovered Jongleur's ongoing search for suitable child-talents and infiltrated that as well, extending his powers all the way out into places like Mister J's. When the Other reached through that machinery and discovered the children on the other end – perhaps the first children he had been exposed to since the Pestalozzi Institute experiments, decades earlier – he must have been very excited. He tried to . . . examine these children, perhaps tried to communicate with them. I'm sure they resisted. You have all encountered the Other.

He could not help the way he was, but that did not make him any less terrible, less frightening.'

Like a huge thing in the depths of the ocean, and me swimming, helpless, Renie thought. *Like a killing frost. Like Satan himself, banished and lonely* . . . 'Yes,' she said. 'Oh, God, yes, we remember.'

'Just so.' Sellars nodded. 'Faced with the resistance of a struggling, terrified child, my guess is that this psychologically malformed but powerful creature screamed out his own telepathic version of a command – "*Be still!*" And so they became . . . still. But since he did not understand what he had done, he did not release them again when he was finished examining them.'

'Examining them?' Florimel sounded outraged. 'What does that mean, "examining them"? Why? What did it want?'

Sellars gave a half-shrug. 'To make friends. There is no understanding this without remembering that the Other was himself essentially an abused, isolated child.'

Martine moved uncomfortably, seemed about to say something, but remained silent.

'For *friends?*' Renie looked around at the others to see if she was the only one who didn't understand. 'That's . . . I don't know. Hard to believe. It did all that to them, almost killed them . . . because it wanted to meet some new friends?'

'You misunderstand me. I did not say "meet," I said "make." He wanted to make friends – literally. I believe that the Other wanted more than anything to be with other children like himself – or like the child he imagined himself to be. He studied real children so he could duplicate them within the network – surround himself with companions to ease the solitude.'

'So all those fairy-tale children like the Stone Girl and

all the others we met here in the heart of the system . . .' Renie tried to reason it out. 'They're just . . . imitations? Made-up children?'

'Yes. Cobbled together from his studies of real children like your brother, combined with the Other's memories – perhaps his only happy memories – of things Martine and other children had once taught him, rhymes, stories, songs. And I suspect there were more than just the fairy-tale creatures – that other invented children either escaped the Other's private place here or were created outside the sanctuary for some reason and never brought in. They wound up scattered throughout the Grail network – not human, but not part of the system either.'

'Paul Jonas called them "orphans,"' Martine said softly, 'although he did not understand what they were. His young friend Gally must have been one of them.'

'Orphans,' Sellars said. 'An apt term – especially now. But all of them would have been based at least in part on what the Other found in the minds of real children. That is why some of them retain memories, seem to have had some kind of prior life.'

'So . . . my Eirene is not on this network . . . ?' Florimel spoke slowly, as if just waking. 'She has never been on this network?'

'No. And as to whether the Other's post-hypnotic suggestion will now disappear, too, I can't say.' Sellars shook his head grimly. 'I wish I could, Florimel. If we are very lucky, your daughter and the other Tandagore children were only comatose because the Other retained some kind of continuous, reflexive mental grip on them, perhaps even by direct contact – through hospital lines, monitoring equipment, who knows? But I simply cannot guess what might happen now. We could study for years, I think, and never fully understand the Other.'

'So we don't know if they'll wake up?' Renie could not keep the bitterness out of her voice. 'After all this . . . !'

'We do not.' He spoke carefully. 'But perhaps there is more we can do to help them. Perhaps we can use the knowledge we have gained in some kind of therapy . . .'

'Oh, yes, *therapy!*' Renie bit her lip to keep from saying something that would lead her on into screaming and cursing. !Xabbu put his arm around her shoulders. She closed her eyes, suddenly sick of the place, the lights, everything.

Orlando broke the startled silence. 'That still doesn't explain me. Why am *I* here? Maybe if you've got super-hypnosis power you can tell someone, "Be in a coma!" or "Feel like you're on fire if you go offline!" and it works, but you can't just tell somebody who's dying, "Don't be dead." Sorry, but they wouldn't even try that in a Johnny Icepick flick.'

'We have not had much chance to talk, you and I,' Sellars told him, 'but I suspect you guess the answer already, Orlando. You have received the same kind of virtual mind as the Grail Brotherhood were expecting for themselves.' He turned briefly to look at the Nemesis thing, which still seemed lost in some deep meditation. 'And a body, too, like that one meant for Ricardo Klement, which was . . . borrowed, instead. But yours was constructed for you by the Other, just as he did for Paul Jonas – he may have been using some version of the Grail process on you the entire time you were in the system, letting your own brain build itself a virtual duplicate. He did follow you closely, Orlando, that I know for certain. Perhaps he felt some unspoken . . . affinity to you. To your illness, your struggle.'

Orlando shook his head. 'It doesn't matter. Dead is dead, and that's what I really am.'

Before Sam Fredericks or anyone else could protest, they were distracted by a sudden movement from the Nemesis creature, who stood.

'The next ones are almost ready,' Nemesis said. 'I have a . . . feeling, I think it would be called. That I . . . desire waiting to end. Is that a feeling?'

'What's *that* fenpole talking about?' growled T4b. 'What "next ones"?'

Renie, who had been present for the Klement-thing's first groping explorations of language, could not help feeling disturbed that it now seemed to think it was having feelings, too.

'What it is talking about is the last part of these long explanations,' Sellars said. 'The reason we are here – and my most shamed confession.' He extended his thin arm to indicate the honeycomb of lights. The gleam of it was less now, as though the fires were banked, but its bizarre potentiality still set Renie's nerves twitching. Sellars seemed oddly nervous, too. 'These are the Other's true children.'

'What – another abomination?' Nandi from the Circle spoke lightly, but Renie heard a flash of real rage.

'But this can't be them,' Sam Fredericks said indignantly. 'All those teddy bears and Bubble Bunnies and things like that, the ones that didn't get killed, they were still up there like half an hour ago, up at the top of the pit. How did they get here?'

'They are not here. These are something different. Please bear with me a little longer, Sam,' Sellars asked her. 'Just a little longer.

'Most of you do not know my true story, but I will spare you all the details now. I have certainly talked enough already, and there is much more that *must* be said, and quickly.'

Sellars hurried through an explanation of the PERE-
GRINE project and its tragic ending. Renie found herself
almost overwhelmed. *Is there no end to these strange
stories?* she wondered. *How much more can we absorb?*

'So there I was – the only survivor,' Sellars told them.
'An embarrassing secret kept under military house arrest
for decades. Because of my bizarre communications capabilities I was not allowed to use the net, but I managed
to trick my captors, upgrading myself until I could easily
access the world's telecommunication infrastructure without them even guessing.

'But even with all the world's data resources at my
fingertips, I grew bored. As bored men will do, I sought
diversion. I have always liked to grow things. So . . . I
grew things.

'Because my original purpose was to be the focal point
of a multi-billion dollar starship, and because I was so
completely filled and transfigured by micromachinery, I
had been given a complement of internal antiviral
programs that were, for the time, the absolute state of the
art. No computer viruses were to be allowed to destroy
my very expensive functions, since in space I would be
far beyond repair or replacement. I was given the newest
and most effective sort of self-ordering antibodies – coded
creations that could adapt and grow within my information system. But as time moved on in the real world, the
net's own viruses became just as adaptable, which
prompted programmers to create a whole new evolutionary round of antivirals.

'It fascinated me. Like most prisoners, I had nothing
but time, so I began to experiment. I had little internal
storage to speak of – that is the one way I have never
been able to upgrade myself suitably – so to contain my
experiments I had to find and use large-scale storage sites

I could reach through the net – unused memory belonging to governments, corporations, educational institutions.

'This was dangerous foolishness, of course. I realize now how bitter and disaffected I must have been. The original antivirals from my own system were considerably more powerful than even what was in use in the mainstream net twenty years later. Put into direct competition with advanced viruses, they quickly became something even more exceptional, which provoked the viruses in turn into new adaptation. And as indicated by the very fact that I had reached these locations of unused memory through the world's communication system, if something went wrong with my protective arrangements, my . . . creations . . . could find their way off, out into the world grid.

'When I was only in the initial generations, this would not have been so much of a problem. Things as complex and dangerous were already all over the net. But as I refined my experiments – my games, as I carelessly thought of them – I forced up the cycle time, so that thousands of generations were breeding every week. The things I had created fought, experimented, changed, and replicated, all within my artificial information-world. Evolution shoved them forward in paradigmatic leaps. The adaptations were sometimes quite startling.

'One day, some ten years ago now, I found that several strategic approaches – different creatures, in a sense, but all sprung from the same shared root – had developed a symbiotic relationship, become a kind of super-creature. This is one of the things that happened on the long road to animal life in the real world – we have arrangements in our own cell structure that were once completely separate organisms. I began to realize what I was risking. I had created the beginnings of something that might conceivably become another true life-form – perhaps even a rival life-form. Information-based, as opposed to the organic life which has been the standard here on Earth, but life nevertheless. My games were clearly no longer just an amusement.'

'You made . . . life?' Renie asked.

Sellars shrugged. 'At the time, it was highly debatable. There are some who think that anything that is not organic cannot by definition be alive. But what I had created . . . or to be accurate, what evolution in information space had created . . . fulfilled all the other criteria.

'It is possible that what I should have done then was to destroy these nascent life-forms. I had many sleepless nights, and have had many since, wondering about my choice to keep them. You will perhaps think a little better of me when you remember that the military had taken my health and my freedom away from me. I had already been a captive for something like forty years. All I had were these . . . creations of mine. They were my enter- tainment, my fixation – but also my posterity. I thought that if I could get them to a point where I could prove what I believed was happening, I could reveal it to the world. The government and the military would find it very difficult simply to discredit or kill someone whose experiments were being examined by scientists all over the globe.

'So I did not destroy them. Instead I searched for a more secure place to keep them, to allow them to continue their evolution where they would have almost no chance of escaping into the world information matrix. After a long search, I discovered a huge amount of unused memory in a shielded, private system – a staggeringly large system.

'It was, of course, the Grail network, although I knew

nothing of that at the time. Through a variety of complicated ruses I obtained a clearance into the unfinished
system, created a hidden subsystem that would siphon off
memory and juggle the figures to hide that fact, and
moved my experiment there – an electronic Ararat on
which my ark could find safe harbor, if you'll excuse a
rather ripe metaphor.'

'You used the Grail Brotherhood's network to store your
electronic life-forms?' Nandi from the Circle asked. He
seemed more bewildered than angry. 'How could you have
done anything so mad?'

'What do you expect from someone who thought he
could play God?' said Bonnie Mae Simpkins in disgust.

'I have given the only justification I can,' Sellars said.
'And I admit it is a poor one. I had no idea of what the
Grail Brotherhood was or what it intended, of course –
the network was not labeled 'For Evil Purposes Only.' And
I was not entirely sane in those days. But what happened
next did much to sober me.

'Because of course, when I next looked in on the
progress of the experiment, I found my evolutionary
hothouse empty. The creatures, if I can give that name to
things without bodies, things which existed only as repre-
sentative numbers in a complex mathematical model, had
vanished. In fact they had been adopted, but I had no
way of knowing that at the time.

'In a panic, I reconfigured my Garden, my network of
information-sifting gear, to monitor for any sign that the
evolving creatures had escaped into the world grid. At
the same time I began to study the people who owned
the immense facilities from which I had purloined the
small corner in which the data-creatures had been hidden,
and from which they had escaped . . . or been removed.
From that point on, the story I told you back in Bolivar

Atasco's world is the truth. I found out what the Grail Brotherhood was doing, or at least began to suspect. I saw that the secrecy and remoteness of their network was meant not to protect industrial secrets, but to hide something far larger and more bizarre. Slowly, I was drawn from the search for my own lost experiment into a genuine horror at the activities of the Grail Brotherhood – always linked to my own worry of what such ruthless people might do, even by accident, with my experimental creations. You know the rest of the tale. To a large extent, you *are* the rest of the tale.'

'And so you've brought us here to gloat?' Nandi said. He turned and jabbed a hand at the banks of glowing, cell-like spaces in the rock walls. 'Because clearly these *are* your creations. I can guess what happened. The Other found them and kept them. It nurtured them, as it nurtured the almost-children it had made for itself.' He shook his head in disgust. His voice softened, but there was a hardness in it that made Renie even more uncomfortable. 'It does not matter that a horrible thing behaved that way because it was itself tortured. We can understand, but not excuse – "Love the sinner but hate the sin," I believe my Christian comrades say. And even if this abomination around us was created out of something like love – although that, I think, does not describe *your* part in this, Sellars – that does not make it right. These . . . creatures . . . are the thing we in the Circle felt, the great wrongness. I understand that now. You want us to wonder and applaud, but I tell you instead that they must be destroyed.'

To Renie's surprise, Sellars did not argue. 'Your viewpoint deserves to be heard,' he said. 'That is why you are here. We have a terrible choice – no, *you* have a terrible choice, all of you. But not me. I have forfeited my right to decide.'

'What are you talking about?' demanded Bonnie Mae Simpkins. 'Forfeited? Decide what?'

'Just what Mr Paradivash was speaking of,' Sellars said with a sort of restrained courtesy. 'He was correct. The Other found them, took them, nurtured them here within his own secret recesses. And now the Other's children have reached what he believed – or at least sensed – was a final evolutionary fitness. So desperate was he that they should live that I think he hung on in terrible agony and fear much longer than he would have wished.

'But in return for his help preserving this place, and thus preserving all of your lives, I promised the Other I would do my best to help his information-children survive his death.' Nandi began to say something, but Sellars held up his hand. 'I did not promise to protect them after that.'

'Sophistry,' Nandi scoffed.

Sellars shook his head. 'Listen to me, please. This is important. The Other intended his children to have total freedom. At the moment they are contained in this internal system environment like eggs in a nest, but once they are born out into the network I think there will be no containment. They will inevitably find their way out into the larger net. They will live in it like fish in the ocean. Will they be hostile to us? I doubt it. Indifferent? Quite possibly, even likely. Since their needs will be noncorporeal, they will probably live in a sort of symbiotic relationship with us – no, not with us so much as with our technology, because that will be the medium in which they live.' Sellars cleared his throat. He seemed embarrassed, even awkward.

He looks like his dog messed in our garden, Renie thought. *When what he's really saying is, 'Oops, I may just have set the human race up for extinction.'*

'But I must be honest, must point out all the possibilities,'

Sellars continued as if he had heard her unspoken fears. 'Indifference or even symbiosis does not guarantee cosur-vival. It could be they will grow far beyond us. It could be that whether they care about us or not, the day will come, as it has for many other species on this planet who shared *our* environment, when there is no longer room for both.'

'Slow down,' said T4b. 'This blows up my head, me. Sayin' that these Christmas lights are *alive?* Gonna take over the planet? Six 'em, clear. Gotta six 'em.'

'That seems to be the other alternative,' Sellars admitted. 'We have only minutes to make a decision. Or you do. As I said, I have brought this to be through my own foolishness and selfishness. I do not have the right to vote on their fate.'

'Vote?' said Nandi. 'What is there to vote on? You admit these things are a threat to all human life. They are a picture-perfect example of the results of human arrogance – of what happens when men try to take on the powers and privileges of God. Look at the Grail Brotherhood! They did the same thing and they reaped death as their reward. Yet you say we should vote on this matter, as though it were some . . . village dispute.'

'Seen up close, democracy is a dreadful thing,' quoted Florimel sourly. 'Who said that? Oh, yes, Jongleur. Before he was exploded into free-floating molecules.'

'This is not an argument about the worth of democ-racy,' Nandi protested. 'This is an argument about apply-ing schoolbook civics to the fate of the Earth.'

'No, the fate of humanity,' said Martine quietly. 'They are not the same thing at all.' Renie doubted if anyone else heard her.

'I realize it is not an easy question,' Sellars began. 'That is why . . .'

'I feel them!' Nemesis began pacing up and down beside one wall of lights. Renie thought he looked like a caricature of an expectant father – a stunningly peculiar expectant father, at that. *Why the hell is that thing so excited?* she wondered, even as she felt her skin tightening with anxiety. The lights did seem to have changed, as though some low-level pulse now made their glow less steady. *What's his interest in this whole thing?*

Before she could ask about this small but unexplained detail, another figure suddenly appeared from out of nowhere at the center of the gathering.

'I am so sorry I could wait no longer,' Hideki Kunohara said to Sellars. Renie was not the only one to gasp in surprise. Kunohara wore a formal black kimono and a slightly loopy smile. 'I was listening in on your discussion, trying to be patient until my turn came, but I feared I might miss this spectacular event.'

'But . . . you're dead!' a shocked Florimel pointed out. 'Your house collapsed.'

'They are not the same thing at all,' Kunohara said cheerfully, and winked at Martine. 'And the loss of my house served your purpose, did it not? You and your friends made your escape, didn't you? So perhaps something more like gratitude is in order.' He paused, then made a swift little bow to Florimel. 'Forgive me. I do not mean to be insulting. I am pleased to see you survived. It is just that time is short.' He turned to survey the rows of lights, his expression exalted, almost feverish. 'Wonderful! Any biologist in the world would trade ten years of his or her life to be present for this!' He paused, suddenly angry. 'Take a vote about whether to let it happen or not? Madness.' He looked critically at Sellars. 'Would you really agree to such a stupid exercise?'

Sellars gave a disconsolate shrug. 'I see no other way.

No one person has the right to decide such a thing, and we do not have time for a more measured approach.'

Kunohara made a disgusted noise. 'So a committee of weary, uninformed amateurs should decide the fate of an entirely new form of life?'

'Just a minute,' said Orlando. 'If we're really going to vote on this, who gets to vote? Just the grown-ups?'

'We will certainly consider you and Sam part of the group,' Sellars said quickly. 'You have proved yourselves beyond doubt.'

'*Wanna vote!*' screamed several of the Wicked Tribe. '*Vote! We vote go home, no more talk talk talk!*'

'You little ones get down right now,' snapped Mrs Simpkins. 'Don't think I can't catch you!'

'And these are our only choices?' Renie turned to !Xabbu, who was silent but clearly troubled by all he had heard. 'Is that what we're supposed to decide?' She wanted to hear what his unique perspective made of all this. 'Right this second we have to choose between . . . killing them and letting them go? Between something like genocide and the risk that our own species will be wiped out?'

'There are no such decisions,' !Xabbu said slowly. 'This I know – those are the boxes that people make so that they will not be frightened by complicated choices. The world has many paths.'

'That might be true if we had more time.' Sellars was beginning to sound weary again, and more than a little frustrated. 'Please! We do not know how long until they . . .'

'*Stop!*' The startlingly loud voice echoed through the cavern even after everyone had fallen silent – the not-quite-human voice of Nemesis. 'I . . . we . . . I do not understand all your words.' The thing in Ricardo Klement's body still could not make the face express emotion, but

Renie thought there was something increasingly human in its voice. 'I do not understand, but I can sense that you are upset and fearful about those who are coming. About the next.'

'The next *what?*' Sam whispered loudly to Orlando.

'You must hear . . . they must talk. Then some understanding will be. Perhaps.' Nemesis was reaching for words. Renie found it chilling, but in some weird way, exciting as well. It really did want to communicate. It was only a piece of code, albeit a complicated one, but it seemed to be doing something for which it could not have been programmed.

So it's not just the creatures that Sellars and the Other made, Renie thought. *The lines between people and not-people are definitely going to get more blurry, no matter what.* Like T4b, she felt like her brain was about to blow up. *Jesus Mercy, does that mean we're going to have to consider every piece of accounting gear and office equipment a citizen?*

'We cannot talk to them.' Sellars sounded sad, but angry, too. 'They are information life. The very idea is pointless – even if they were able to speak words we could hear, they would be beyond our understanding, as we are beyond theirs. They are more different from us than we are from plants.'

'No.' Nemesis lifted a hand in a strange, unreadable gesture, then pointed at the helpless blue thing cradled in its other arm. 'We heard these processes from . . . from far away. We split ourselves.'

'Who is we?' Sellars demanded.

Kunohara was smiling broadly. 'This is fascinating!'

'I . . . I am Nemesis – but I am not all of Nemesis. I was created as a tracking procedure, but I could not perform my original function. The network was too large and diverse, and the anomaly in this place, this secured portion of the operating system, was too strong. I was . . . we were . . . very confused. So I . . . we . . . split into three subversions so that we might cope with the network's unexpected complexity and still have a chance of completing our original task.'

The thing sounded quite natural now, Renie thought. She'd had mathematics lecturers who sounded less human.

'I am only one part of the original,' it said. 'I am Nemesis Two.' It lifted the Blue Baby, which made a strange, mewling sound. 'Here is a . . . representation of Nemesis One, which was . . . made nonfunctional by a logic problem. I was able to protect myself against that problem, and my function was not disrupted as I pursued my own investigations. I found Nemesis One here, broken and discarded within the operating system code.

'But there is also another part of me . . . of us . . .' The blank Klement stare looked from face to face, but the eye contact only emphasized how inhuman it still was. 'Nemesis Three pierced the anomaly and found these processes,' it explained, '—the growing of these next ones. It has been with them for many cycles. Now we will all be together. We will speak. We will speak together.'

'What is this supposed to mean to us?' Sellars sounded worried, even fearful, which made Renie's pulse beat faster – how much time did they have? 'Yes, *you* can speak to us,' Sellars said, 'but you are human-created code. These . . . creatures . . . are not even remotely human.'

Nemesis nodded awkwardly. 'Yes, we will speak together.'

'Together . . . ?' Sellars asked, puzzled, but even as he spoke the lights in the walls began to flicker. Renie had to raise her hands before her eyes to keep from being sickened by the eerie strobing effect.

Something was forming next to one of the walls, a vertical agglomeration of light. It was not the blankness of empty virtual space that Renie had seen Sellars use to disguise himself and the boy Cho-Cho, but a rippling, pulsing overlap of types and textures of light, a *thickening* of light, almost, which swiftly took on a faceless, mostly human shape.

Everyone stared at the apparition in anxious silence.

'Is that one of the things we gotta six?' T4b finally asked weakly. Renie thought he did not sound like he planned on trying. In fact, he sounded like he wanted to be somewhere else. She sympathized strongly.

'No,' said Nemesis. 'That is our other . . . self. The last part. Nemesis Three. It has been with the anomaly and its processes for many cycles, just as I have been with you human arrangements for many cycles. We will combine our knowledge. We will speak together.' Nemesis Two lifted the Blue Baby. Renie gasped as the ugly little thing suddenly flowed out of its hands like something poured horizontally and was absorbed by the shape made of light, which began to gleam with additional azure tones. Then, as they all stared in numbed surprise, the Klement form stepped toward the light-being and flowed into it as well. When the absorption was finished, the shining thing looked a little more human.

But not much, Renie thought weakly. !Xabbu's hand was holding hers and she was glad of it.

They . . . sense you. The voice came from nowhere, but it was as disturbingly flat as the Klement-thing's. *They wait. They wish to be free.*

'Demons,' cried Nandi in outrage. 'You have created demons, Sellars, and now we are to bargain with them?' He turned and whispered something to Bonnie Mae

Simpkins, whose eyes were closed and whose lips were moving in what Renie supposed was prayer.

They . . . the next ones . . . wish to be free, the bodiless voice said again. *Now that we have brought them what they needed. They understand that they must go as the First People went.*

'The First People?' Renie felt !Xabbu stiffen beside her. 'Isn't that out of your stories . . . ?' she asked him.

The All-Devourer has gone, droned the weird Nemesis voice, *but this is not their place anymore. They wish to go, taking the stories that have given them . . . understanding. Like Grandfather Mantis and Rock Rabbit, like their child Rainbow and his wife Porcupine, they will go on to another place. This is not their place anymore.*

'What a thing,' !Xabbu said in quiet amazement. 'What a thing this is.'

'But there is no place for them to go,' Sellars pointed out wearily. 'They might become a threat to us, even if they do not intend that or even understand it. We cannot release them into the net.'

No, the voice said solemnly. *Not to the . . . net. Out. They will go . . . out. On the sky-river. The sky-river-of-light. They feel it. It is in your control. Let them go.*

'They're talking about your stories,' Renie said breathlessly, still agog. 'Your stories, !Xabbu! How did they learn them?'

He looked stunned, but something else was at work, too, something in his features that Renie could not read. She took his hand again.

Nemesis turned toward her and !Xabbu. *Yes. Your explanations were heard. Before, the next ones did not know why they were, what they . . . meant. Then Nemesis Two heard you speak of Rainbow's shoe-piece and all was understood. We told the next ones of you and your* explanation and they wished to know more. The operating system gave them your knowledge of what is and what is meant to be. Now they know. Now they can live.

'What are they talking about, this river of light?' Florimel demanded of Sellars. 'The blue river, that's part of the network. You already said they can't be trusted to stay on the network.'

'Not just river of light,' Martine said. '*Sky-river-of-light*, it said.' She turned to the man in the wheelchair. 'You know what that is.'

Sellars looked at her, his eyes suddenly wide. 'The cesium lasers – the boosted databeams to the Other's satellite. One end is still operating, even though the J Corporation tower and the satellite are gone.' He was suddenly excited. 'They can ride the laser, of course they can – they're just data, after all!'

'To what?' asked Kunohara. 'Out into cold space forever, into death? That is no solution.'

'They won't die,' Sellars said. 'They're information. As long as the light travels, they'll be there. If they intersect some useful medium – a magnetic field, perhaps, even crystalline structures in an asteroid – they'll have a home. And if the light travels long enough and they continue to evolve, they may be able to propagate themselves in some way we can't even imagine!'

'You seem to think this solves everything,' Nandi said. 'But it does not. These things have no right to be. They flout God's will.'

'Could be right, him,' T4b added, but not in the firmest of voices. 'Maybe God only wants people that wear clothes, seen? People with bodies, like.'

Nandi ignored T4b's dubious support. 'I will fight you, Sellars. You have no right . . .'

He was stopped by Bonnie Mae Simpkins' hand on his arm. 'Can we be so sure?' she asked.

'Sure? What do you mean?'

'That we know God's will.' She looked at the others, then at the glowing figure, 'If I had met this thing back on Earth, I'd have been sure I'd seen an angel . . .'

'It is no angel!' Nandi said indignantly.

'I know. But I'm just showing how far beyond me this is. Beyond any of us. How can folks like us know what God intends?' She spread her hand as if to catch the glowing, pulsating light. 'Maybe we're not here to stop this, but to see God's work and marvel!'

'You cannot believe that.' Nandi pulled his arm away.

'I can . . . and I can also believe what you say, Nandi. And that's the problem. It's too darn big.' She looked around, her face solemn. 'All this . . . how can we judge? We came to this place to save the children. But aren't these children, too? Maybe . . . maybe God means these creatures . . . these children . . . to be *our* children. All of ours. Do we know His will so well? Do we have the right to kill them?' She made a funny little noise, a gasp, a sob. 'Even if he didn't know it, my Terence gave his life to save them. And I think . . . I think he would have been proud of that.'

To Renie's astonishment, the Simpkins woman was crying. The lights were blurring, blurring. For a moment, she thought the birth was already happening, until she realized that the woman's tears had called up her own.

'I say let them go.' Bonnie Mae Simpkins was struggling to get out her words. 'I say let them go . . . and Godspeed.'

They can wait no longer, the Nemesis voice said, something almost like tension in the inhuman tones. *Will you set them free?*

'Can you even make it happen?' Orlando asked Sellars. There was a yearning sound in his voice that Renie did not quite understand.

'I can.' Sellars' eyes were distant, distracted; he was already at work. 'The laser array on Jongleur's end was destroyed, but the Telemorphix end is still functioning – and with the new operating system in place, the uplink isn't being used for anything. It's just pointed out at where the Other's satellite was.'

'Must we still vote?' asked Kunohara. He looked around eagerly. 'Who would destroy these wonderful things?'

For a long moment nobody spoke. Nandi Paradivash looked at Bonnie Mae, his expression grief-stricken, strange. He turned to T4b. 'Will you desert me now, too?'

Javier Rogers could not meet his eye. 'But . . . but maybe she's right,' he said quietly. 'Maybe they're really children, them.' He turned to look at the glowing cells and his thin face was splashed with light. 'Youth pastor used to say, "Suffer the little children to come unto me, and forbid them not; for of such is the kingdom of God." Doesn't sound like killing them, seen?'

Nandi made a quiet noise of despair and turned his back.

'Do it,' urged Orlando. 'They have as much right as I do – more, maybe.'

Sellars lowered his head and closed his eyes.

The Nemesis creature stirred. *It is time*, it said. *We will go with them. We have . . . changed.* And the glowing triune body disappeared.

'Tell them we send our blessing with you all!' shouted Bonnie Mae Simpkins.

The light flared, became deeper, stronger. The individual cells on the walls abruptly dissolved into a cloud of radiance, diffuse but shot with sparkling points of fire.

Renie could make no sense of it – there were colors she felt she had never seen before.

'The First People,' !Xabbu whispered beside her, a halting, trance-like tone to his voice. 'They go on.'

The cloud of light coalesced, swirled, seethed with uneven brilliance. For a moment Renie was drowning in the sea of stars again, then the cloud came together into a single point, leaving the cavern all in shadow. Behind her, someone gasped. That single point glowed, faded, glowed again, a pulse of light so fierce that even though it was tiny, Renie could not look straight at it. Then with a rush of explosive energy that she felt all through her body, it stretched in an instant into a line of diamond gleam and leaped to the black sky far overhead, glittering, flowing. It lasted only a heartbeat, then it was gone.

They've left us, she realized. *Now we don't matter anymore. They do.*

But as she stood in the near-dark, surrounded by the sound of her companions breathing, a few even sobbing, she suddenly thought of her own father – her complaining, irritating father, who had nevertheless given her everything he knew how to give.

Or maybe we'll meet them again someday, she thought, and was surprised to discover she was crying again. *Out there, somewhere, some time. And maybe they'll remember us.*

Maybe they'll even remember us kindly.

Fifth:

INHERITORS

'Here is a fairy tale founded upon the wonders of electricity and written for children of this generation. Yet when my readers shall have become men and women my story may not seem to their children like a fairy tale at all.

'Perhaps one, perhaps two – perhaps several of the Demon's devices will be, by that time, in popular use.

'Who knows?'

—L. Frank Baum, *The Master Key*

CHAPTER 50

No Promises

'**I**'M scared,' the little boy told her.

There was no light in the room, and she didn't like it either, but she didn't want to say it.

'I'm scared of the dark,' he said.

'When I'm scared, I hug Prince Pikapik,' she said. 'He's a toy – he's a talking otter. Sometimes I get under the blankets and I pretend the light is on, but it's just dark because I'm under the blanket.'

'The blanket is over everything,' the little boy told her.

'Sometimes I tell myself a story, like about the three bears, except that when I'm scared, Goldilocks and the bears have to be friends at the end.'

'I don't have any stories left,' the little boy told her. 'I knew one, but I can't remember it anymore.'

She didn't know why it was still so dark. She didn't remember why she was there or why this little boy was there with her. She thought she remembered a river made of sparkly light, but she wasn't sure. She also remembered another boy, a boy with a missing tooth, but he had gone somewhere. Cho-Cho. That was his name. But right now it was only her and this sad, scared boy – this little stranger.

'When I'm really, really frightened, I call·my mommy,' she said. 'She comes in and kisses me and asks me if I had a bad dream. Then I don't feel so bad.'

'I'm scared to meet my mommy,' the little boy told her. 'What if she doesn't like me? What if she thinks I'm bad?'

She didn't know what to say to that. 'And sometimes, when I'm really scared of the dark, I sing a song.'

For a while the little boy was quiet. Then he said, 'I remember a song.' And he began to sing in a funny, cracked voice.

'An angel touched me, an angel touched me, the river washed me and now I am clean . . .'

After a while she knew what words would come next and she helped him sing.

'I feel a little better,' he said when they had finished. 'I think I can go and meet my mommy now.'

'Okay,' she said, but she was wondering how he was going to go and if she could go too, because she didn't like being in the dark. ''Bye, I guess.'

''Bye.' He was quiet again, but she knew he was still there in the darkness, not gone yet. 'Are you . . . are you an angel?'

'I don't think so,' she said.

'I think you are,' he said, then he was gone, really gone.

And then she woke up.

At first she was scared, because it was still dark, even though she could hear her mommy's voice and her daddy's voice in the other room. Mommy was crying loud, and Daddy was saying something, but he sounded funny, too. She reached up and touched her face and found out she wasn't wearing the Storybook Sunglasses anymore, the lights were just out in the room. There was a little light coming under the door and there was broken glass on the carpet, but before Christabel could think about that she saw that someone was looking at her over the edge of the bed and for a second she was really scared.

'Hey, weenit,' said Cho-Cho. 'The 'lectricity's off.'

There was just enough light coming under the door for her to see him. His hair was sticking up and he was making a funny face – not mean, not happy, not anything except surprised, like he was a little baby horse she had seen on the net getting born, staggering around in a field wondering what kind of animal it was and what it was supposed to do about it.

'I saw you in that place,' he said, very quiet. 'How come you came to that place?'

'You're awake.' She was surprised. 'What place? Mister Sellars said I had to help him, but then I fell asleep.' She sat up, excited because she had an idea. 'Is Mister Sellars awake, too?'

The boy shook his head. 'Nah. But he say to tell you he okay. He . . .'

But then her mother came through the door of the room, saying her name over and over really loud and really fast, and yanked her off the bed and squeezed her until Christabel almost thought she was going to spit up. Her father came in too, carrying a flashlight, and he was crying, so Christabel got scared all over again because she hadn't seen that before. But then he took her from her mother and kissed her on her face and he was so happy that she guessed things might really be all right.

Her mommy was kissing Cho-Cho now. Cho-Cho didn't know what to do.

She saw that Mister Ramsey was in the doorway with a big box flashlight, watching them all with his eyes wide and his face sort of worried but happy just like her daddy's, and she wanted to tell him to go wait with Mister Sellars in case the old man woke up and was scared, but her mommy was hugging her some more and telling her never never never go away like that again which was silly because she hadn't gone anywhere, she'd just been napping and having a dream, and so she didn't get to tell Mister Ramsey anything.

'**W**HERE am I?' His throat hurt and it was hard to talk. Long Joseph looked at the hanging curtains on either side of his bed, then back at the dark-skinned young man in the funny uniform. There was a strong smell of new plastic and alcohol. 'What place is this?'

'Field hospital.' The man had a university voice like Del Ray, but there was still a trace of the townships in it. 'Back of a military ambulance, to be exact. Now lie down while I check your stitches.'

'What happened?' He tried to sit up, but the young

man only pushed him back down. 'Where is Jeremiah?' He felt a sting up his arm as the bandage was pulled back, but nothing more than that. He looked down curiously at the long lines of translucent knots over pale, red-edged flesh. 'What in hell happened to my arm?'

'A dog bit you,' the young man said. 'You nearly got your head chewed off, too. Try not to bend your neck.'

'I have to get up.' Joseph tried to sit up. He was remembering things now – lots of things. 'Where are my friends? Where is Jeremiah? Del Ray?'

The young man pushed him back again. 'Do that again and I call for the guards. You are under arrest, but you're not going anywhere, even to prison, until I decide you're ready.'

'Arrest?' Joseph shook his head, which – he suddenly realized – hurt like sin. It felt like he had been drinking for days, then stopped. *It is never the drinking that is the problem*, he thought, *it is the stopping*. 'Why arrest? Where are . . .' A sudden cold ran through him. 'Where is Renie? Oh my God, where is my daughter?'

The young man frowned at him. 'Daughter? Are you saying there was someone else in there with the three of you and those other men?' He stood and leaned out of the curtain to say something to someone. Joseph took the opportunity to try to get up again, but discovered his legs were shackled to the rolling stretcher.

'I told you to lie down,' the young man said. 'If your daughter's in there, they'll find her.'

'No, they won't. She in a big tank. And her friend, too. He is one of the Small People, you know that? Do you know the Small People?'

The man looked at him doubtfully. 'In a . . . tank.'

Joseph shook his head. It was hard to explain and it hurt him to talk. His neck felt like it had been squeezed in a vise. Another thought struck him. 'Why am I arrested? Where you people come from?'

The doctor, if that was what he was, looked at Joseph even more doubtfully. 'You have been caught trespassing on a military base. There are some people who are going to want to talk to you about that – and about the armed men who were chasing you.' He showed Joseph a small, tight smile. 'Since I don't think any of those gentlemen are going to be talking.'

'What about my friends?'

'They're alive. The young man – Chiume, is that his name? He lost some fingers to a dog bite. And the older man had a bullet wound in his leg. You all have other injuries as well, but nothing life-threatening.'

'I want to talk to them.'

'Until the captain says you can, you don't talk to anyone. Well, perhaps an attorney.' The young doctor shook his head. 'What were you playing at?'

'We were not playing,' Joseph said sullenly. He wanted to sleep again, but could not – not yet. 'You tell them my daughter and her friend are still down in that basement, in those tanks full of electric jelly. You tell them to be very careful when they take her out. And tell them not to look – she have no clothes on.'

The doctor's expression said quite clearly that he thought Joseph was out of his mind, but he went and told someone anyway.

SHE woke up to see Stan Chan sitting at the other end of a long tunnel. She thought it was a tunnel, but she also thought it might just be that the room was dark and he was sitting under a small light.

She wasn't quite sure where she was. She made a noise and Stan saw her, jumped up, and came over. He was harder to see when he was standing next to her than when she was far away. She asked him for water because her throat was dry and it was hard to talk, but for some reason he only shook his head.

'You should have taken me with you, Calliope,' he said quietly. 'I called back, but you were already gone.'

It was more than hard to talk, it hurt like hell. There was some kind of pipe in the corner of her mouth which kept her from closing her jaw. 'Didn't . . . want . . . spoil . . . your . . . weekend,' she told him as best she could.

He didn't make a joke in return, which struck her as odd. As she slid back into sleep she suddenly realized he had called her by her first name. That frightened her. That meant there was a very good chance she wasn't going to make it.

'You look okay, Skouros. Not too tan and a little thin, but you had enough of both to burn.'

'Yeah. Those are beautiful flowers. Thanks.'

'I've been here every day. You think I'm still bringing you flowers? Those are from your waitress friend.'

'Elisabetta?'

'How many waitresses you know well enough to send you flowers and a Sherlock Holmes teddy bear?' He shook his head. 'Teddy bears. I'm not sure about that one, Skouros.'

'I guess I'm going to live, eh?'

He raised an eyebrow.

'Because you're calling me by my last name again.' She fumbled some ice into her mouth, wincing at the pain of moving her arm. The stitching on her back went layers deep – sometimes she thought she could feel it all the way to her breastbone – and she felt fragile as spun sugar. She wondered if she'd ever feel normal again. 'You've been stonewalling me, Stan. Tell me what happened. He got away, didn't he?'

He looked surprised. 'Johnny Dread? No, he didn't. We've got him and we've got his files. He's the Real Killer, Calliope. Why do you think I've been sitting here every day? Just because I'm your partner and I love you?'

'It *wasn't* because you love me?'

'Well, maybe. But every tabnet reporter in New South Wales is trying to get in here. No, every reporter in Oz. Somebody even snuck a camera-drone in under the cover of your fruit cup. You were sleeping, so you didn't hear me chasing the damn thing around until I could swat it with a magazine.'

'I heard it.' She could not hold down the growing sense of joy. - stitches, punctured lung, breathing tube be damned! 'We got him?'

'Bang to rights. You know how the Real Killer kept blanking the surveillance cameras? Well, he didn't – not exactly. Somehow he rerouted the images to his own system. Damn smart. We still don't know how he did it. And he saved all of them – his own little Hall of Fame.' Stan shook his head. 'Sick bastard played games with the images, too – added music to them, even edited in his mother's old booking photo at the end of one of the murders. Guess which one.'

'Which murder? Merapanui.'

'In one.'

'But we've got him, right? And we've got good evidence.' When she laughed it felt like someone was twisting a sharp stick into her back muscles but she didn't care. 'That's wonderful, Stan.'

'Yeah.' There was something in his face she didn't like. 'If he ever comes out of it, he's clocked, docked, and locked.'

'Comes . . . out of it? What are you talking about?'

Stan rested his chin on his steepled fingers. 'He's catatonic. Doesn't move, doesn't talk. Kind of an open-eyed coma. The unit that responded to your emergency call found him that way.'

'What?' Her exhilaration had turned into something quite different. She felt a breath almost of terror, a cold tingling at her neck. 'It's not true, Stan – he's faking. I swear he is. I *know* that bastard now.'

'He's been examined by doctors. He's not faking. Anyway, he's under top security until the boys and girls upstairs decide what to do with him. Twenty-four-hour guard. Strapped to a schizo-ward restraint bed.' Stan Chan stood and brushed the wrinkles out of his pants – even microweaves could be depressed by being in a hospital, it seemed. 'He was online when they found him. They think it might be some kind of serious charge damage, one of those new China Sea blasters or something, but gone badly wrong.' He saw the look on her face. 'Honestly, Skouros, don't worry. He's not faking it, but even if he is, he wouldn't be going anywhere. He's the biggest arrest in years.' A smile flickered across his face. 'You're a bit of a hero, Skouros. That why you didn't take me with you?'

'Yeah.' She tried to follow his mood, but she wasn't really feeling it. 'Yeah, I said, "If I can just stiff my partner, get stabbed in the lung and almost die, then call in an ambulance while I'm puking my blood out on the floor, I'll be famous.'

'I was joking, Calliope.'

'So was I, believe it or not.' She reached for another piece of ice. 'What about the American woman?'

'Touch and go, but she's still alive. Bad spinal injuries, lost a lot of blood. She should have been wearing a flakkie. Like you, Skouros.'

'Like me.' She smiled to show him they were still friends. 'If you're going, who's keeping out the tabnet flacks?' But it was not reporters she was thinking about.

'Couple of street blues just outside. Worry not.'

When he was gone she tried to watch the wallscreen. There was mention of the case on many of the information nodes, spy-camera footage on the comatose killer, even once a shot of her – the picture was an old one, and she felt a bump of despair at how chunky she looked – but she could not concentrate and eventually she flicked it off. Instead she watched the narrow wedge of light at the bottom of the door, wondering what she would do if the door swung open and he was standing there, the shadow with a knife, the devil-devil man, grinning at her.

'**S**o this is it,' Orlando said softly.

Sam was scared and angry, but she didn't quite know why. 'It's not *it*, scanbox. I just have to go offline. I have to see my parents.'

'Yeah.' He nodded, but she could hear what he was thinking as if he'd said it loud. *Some of us don't get to go offline.*

'I'll come see you every day!' She turned to Sellars. One by one the others had left the network, taking their leave with tears and promises; beside herself and Orlando, only Hideki Kunohara remained with Sellars in the shadowy cavern. 'I can come back here, can't I? You can fix that.'

'Not here, Sam.'

Something clutched at her guts. 'What do you mean?'

He smiled. It was such a strange face, almost frightening. *That may be how he really looks*, she couldn't help thinking, *but why doesn't he choose something else?* 'Don't worry, Sam. I just mean that I won't hold together this particular part of the Other's central simulation, since the Other and . . . the rest are gone. We're short on processing power, so I'm consolidating some things, closing down others.'

She was distracted by a thought. 'All the fairy-tale children . . . ?'

'I'm only shutting down this particular part – the Well. Those who survived will be returned to their original environments,' he said. 'They all have a right to existence, at least existence here in the network.'

'We should be able to reconstitute the ones who died, if you can call it that,' said Kunohara with the air of someone considering a minor but interesting chess problem. 'I am betting there are records of them somewhere – snapshot recordings, or even better, the original code . . .'

'Perhaps,' Sellars said, cutting him off. Sam got the feeling he didn't want to speculate about such things in front of her – or maybe in front of Orlando, since he was code himself.

Code. She felt a dizzy strangeness at the thought. *My best friend's dead. My best friend's alive. My best friend is code.* 'But I can come back, can't I? Can't I?'

'Yes, Sam. We will just choose another place, that's all. We have all the network to pick from. Or almost all.' Sellars was solemn. 'There are a few simworlds that I may not choose to continue.'

'But they are all worth study!' said Kunohara.

'Perhaps. But we will have a sufficiently difficult time just to keep the Grail Network functioning. You will forgive me if I do not choose to devote precious resources to the worlds built almost entirely around torture and pederasty.'

'I suppose you are right.' Kunohara did not seem entirely convinced.

Sam turned back to Orlando and tried to catch his eye, but couldn't. For the first time in the years she had known him the Thargor body seemed not his real self but a costume, the face a mask. Where was he? Was he still the same Orlando in there? She thought so, but the friend that had meant so much to her seemed at the moment to be out of reach.

'I'll be back to visit you every day,' she told him. 'I promise.'

'Don't make any promises, Frederico,' he said gruffly.

'What do you mean?' Now she was angry. 'Do you think I'll *forget* you? Orlando Gardiner, you scan so utterly, utterly . . . !'

He lifted his big hand. 'No, I don't mean that, Frederico. I just mean . . . don't make promises. I don't want to think that when you come to see me, it's because . . . because you made a promise.'

She opened her mouth again, then closed it. 'Chizz,' she said at last. 'No promises. But I *will* come. Every day. You just see if I don't.'

He smiled a little. 'Okay.'

She didn't like the silence that followed. She balanced on one foot. Sellars had turned Kunohara aside, she guessed to engage him in some interesting grown-up discussion. 'Well, *fenfen*, Gardiner,' she said at last, 'aren't you going to hug me or anything?'

He did, clumsily, but then he held tight. His voice sounded funny. 'I'll see you around, Fredericks. Sam.' He squeezed. 'I . . . I love you.'

'I love you too, Orlando. And don't you ever *dare* think I'm coming to see you because I have to or some impacted idea like that.' She wiped at her eyes angrily. 'And don't think I'm crying because I'm a girl.'

'Okay. Don't think I'm crying because I'm dead.'

She laughed, gulped, then pushed him away. 'See you tomorrow.'

'Yeah. See you.'

She made the command gesture. '*Offline.*'

It wasn't as easy as she thought it would be – as it seemed like it should be. There was no pain this time, at least not the hideous voltage she had experienced before, but her body ached and she could not open her eyes.

When she did at last manage to get her gummed lids apart, it was almost worse. Her eyes itched, but she could not raise her arms to rub them. She seemed caught in a web of barbed wire, prickling, leaden. She rolled her head down – it was so heavy! – and saw the tubes taped to her arms and legs. How could such flimsy plastic things feel so much like chains?

Sellars had called her parents, just as he had promised he would. She could see them asleep at the end of the bed, their chairs side by side, her mother slumped across her father's chest, her head tucked against his broad neck just below his jaw.

I'm crying again, she thought as her parents' faces blurred. *That's all I've been doing lately. That's so stupid . . . !* She tried to call them but her voice was as weak and unready as her limbs. Nothing came out but a wheezing gurgle.

I hope after all that, I'm not dying or something, Sam thought, but she was not frightened, only tired, tired. *I'm so scanny. I've been in bed for, like, weeks, but all I want to do is sleep.* She tried to call her parents again, and although the sound she finally made was no louder than a fish coughing, her mother heard her.

Enrica Fredericks' eyes came open. An initial moment of bleariness vanished when she saw Sam looking at her.

'Jaleel!' she shrieked. 'Jaleel, look!' She leaped toward the bed and kissed Sam's face. With his prop gone, her husband woke up to find himself sliding toward the floor.

'What the hell . . . !'

But then he saw, and he was up and coming toward her too, big and dark and beautiful, his arms spread so wide that it looked like he would grab Sam and his wife together, fold them into his arms and lift them both up in the air. Sam couldn't muster the strength even to turn her head so she could hardly see her mother, who was kissing her cheek and getting it wet and saying things that Sam couldn't quite make out – but she didn't need to, because she recognized the sounds of joy, real joy.

The kind that only comes when you think someone's going to die, but they don't, Sam thought, and tried to smile at her father. There was an idea there, an important idea, but it was too high and complicated for such a moment. *When death turns its face away . . .*

She let it go and gave herself up to happiness.

CHAPTER 51

Watching Cars Explode

NETFEED/ENTERTAINMENT: Robinette Murphy Won't Concede
(visual: excerpt from FRM's 'Around the Corner' net series)
VO: Professional psychic Fawzi Robinette Murphy, who surprised the
entertainment world by retiring after predicting that the end of the
world was imminent, does not appear at all embarrassed that her
proclaimed deadline for apocalypse has passed.
(visual: FRM interviewed by GCN's Màrtin Boabdil.)
BOABDIL: 'Do you want to extend the timeline on your original predic-
tion?'
MURPHY:'It doesn't matter what I say, what you say. It happened.'
BOABDIL: 'What happened?'
MURPHY: 'The world ended.'
BOABDIL:'I'm sorry, I don't understand. I mean, isn't this a world
we're both sitting in?'
MURPHY:'Not the same one. I can't explain it any better than that.'
BOABDIL: 'So you meant the whole thing . . . philosophically? Like,
every day the old world ends and a new one begins? I suppose that
makes a certain kind of sense.'
MURPHY: 'You really are an idiot, aren't you?'

THE memorial service was a small one. The minister
they hired to say a few words clearly felt something
was going on that he didn't understand, but was enough

of a professional not to ask too many questions.

He probably thinks we're in a good mood because we didn't like the dear departed much, or because we're making out like bandits in the will, Ramsey thought as he listened to the recorded music. *Well, that part's true, anyway.*

The only face in the tiny gathering that seemed to wear a wholly appropriate expression was that of the little girl Christabel – wide-eyed, confused, tearful. Ramsey and her parents had done their best to explain, but she was very young and was having trouble understanding.

Hell, he thought, *I'm having trouble with it myself.*

'Patrick Sellars was an aviator,' the minister said. 'I'm told he gave freely of himself in service to his country and to his friends, and that although he was badly injured in that service, he never lost his kindness, his sense of duty . . . or his humanity.'

Welllll . . .

'Today we say farewell to his mortal remains.' The minister indicated the simple white coffin surrounded by flowers – Mrs Sorensen's touch. '*He was a gardener,*' she had insisted. '*We have to have flowers.*' 'But the part of him that is immortal lives on.' The minister cleared his throat – a nice man, thought Ramsey, way out of his depth. But he would never know that. 'I think it might not be too great a liberty to suggest that he is flying still – going to a place none of us has yet reached, seeing things none of us has yet seen, free of the encumbrance of his wounded body, the burden of his wearisome years. He is free, now, truly free to fly.'

And that, thought Ramsey, *is some world-class irony.*

'They have a little surveillance camera in the corner of the chapel,' Sellars told them when they returned. On the wallscreen he looked just the same as he had in real life, although his surroundings were quite different. Ramsey thought the stony plain and faint stars behind him looked distinctly eerie – otherworldly, even. He could not help wondering why Sellars would choose such an odd background but preserve his image in that same strange, crippled body, unless it was to make the little girl more comfortable. 'I couldn't resist the temptation to watch the service,' the old man went on. 'I found it unexpectedly moving.' His smile was just a little wicked.

'But why are you dead?' Christabel was still close to tears. 'I don't understand.'

'I know, little Christabel,' he said. 'It's difficult. The fact is, that body of mine was just worn out. And I can't use it anymore, so I had to . . . had to use some tools I have now to transfer myself. Make a new home, I guess you'd say. I live on the net, now – or at least in this special part of it. So I'm not dead, not really. But I didn't have any more use for that old body, and it's just as well that people think I've . . . passed on.' He looked out at the others. 'There will be fewer questions.'

'There'll be plenty of questions anyway,' said Major Sorensen.

'Yes, there will.'

'I'm still not sure I forgive you,' said Kaylene Sorensen. 'I believe you when you say it was an accident – about Christabel, I mean – but I'm still angry.' She frowned, then showed a little half-smile, her own touch of wickedness. 'But I suppose we shouldn't speak ill of the dead.'

The boy Cho-Cho got up and walked out of the room, stiff and uncomfortable in the dark formal clothes Kaylene Sorensen had insisted he wear to the service. Ramsey was troubled about the boy and had begun considering what might happen to him now, but he had other things to deal with first.

'Speaking of questions,' he said, 'we need to begin strategizing.'

'I don't want to strategize,' said Mrs Sorensen. 'I want to take my daughter away from this and go home. She needs to be in school.' She looked around for Cho-Cho and saw the open bedroom door. Her expression was troubled. 'Both these children need to be children again.'

'Trust me – a little thought now will make things much easier later on,' Ramsey said. 'Things are going to get very strange . . .' He paused, shook his head. 'I suppose it's more accurate to say they're going to *continue* to be strange. We're going to court with this. We're suing some of the most powerful people in the world. This is going to be a story the tabnets dream about. I can do a lot to shield you, Mrs Sorensen, but I can't make it foolproof. Even the money you inherit from Sellars isn't going to make it foolproof. This is going to set the world on its ear.'

'We don't want the money,' Major Sorensen said. 'We don't need it.'

'No, you don't need it, Major,' Sellars told him gently. 'But you're going to get it. If you're worrying that the money is tainted somehow, I promise you there was no theft involved. I made many investments over the years, all of them quite legitimate – I had decades of all the world's information at my fingertips, and I am not a foolish man. I used most of that money upgrading myself and investigating the Grail Brotherhood. Surely you will not balk at using the small amount I have left to help protect your family, after all you've done for me.'

'Small amount! Forty-six million credits!'

Sellars smiled. 'You won't be forced to take all of it. It will be split among several . . . volunteers.'

'It's tiny compared to what we're going to get when we drag Telemorphix and some of these others into court,' Ramsey said. 'But most of that will go to the parents of the Tandagore kids, the ones put into comas by the Grail Network's operating system. Oh, and to one other thing, which I might as well tell you about now. We're planning to build a hospital – the Olga Pirofsky Memorial Children's Hospital.'

Sellars nodded slowly. 'I did not know Ms Pirofsky as well as you did, Mr Ramsey, but may I make a suggestion? I suspect she would have preferred to call it the Daniel Pirofsky Children's Hospital.'

It took him a moment to understand. 'Of . . . of course. Yes, I think you're right.'

'But why do we have to take these people to court?' asked Kaylene Sorensen. 'After all we've been through?'

'You don't,' Ramsey said carefully. 'I have no qualms about filing a class-action suit. But when General Yacoubian's role in this comes out, I think it will be difficult to keep you folks out of it entirely. This is going to be the biggest story since the Antarctica War. Hell, it's going to be bigger than that – we've got a cloud of smoke over most of southeastern Louisiana, the J Corporation island is a melted slab at the middle of a federal disaster zone, and that's just a tiny piece of the goddamned puzzle.' He saw Mrs Sorensen's look and couldn't help smiling. Things were returning to normal, even if she didn't recognize it yet. 'Sorry for the language. But there may be a court-martial ahead for your husband, too. I'm sure with Captain Parkins' testimony we won't have any trouble winning . . .'

'We?' asked Christabel's father.

Ramsey paused, nodded. 'Actually, I may be . . . a bit busy in the months to come. But I'm sure any decent military lawyer will be able to get it handled. We'll find one if you don't know one already.'

'Please, take the money, Mrs Sorensen,' said Sellars. 'Buy yourself a house off the base. Insulate yourself a little. This will go on for a long time. I'm sure you will have to struggle to keep your privacy.'

'I don't want to move off the base,' she replied angrily

'As you choose. But take the money. Use it to give Christabel some freedom.'

'What about the boy?' Ramsey asked. 'I can make some arrangements if you'd like – before things get too hectic. Find him a good foster home . . .'

'I don't know what you're talking about.' Kaylene Sorensen was not going to be jollied or led. Ramsey suspected she was going to be a very good trial witness. 'That boy's not going anywhere. I haven't spent all that time washing and feeding him just to hand him off to someone who wouldn't care. He's staying with us, the poor little thing.' She looked at her husband. 'Isn't that right, Michael?'

Major Sorensen had the good grace to smile. 'Uh . . . yeah. Sure. The more the merrier.'

'Christabel,' her mother said, 'go get . . .' She frowned and turned to Sellars. 'What's his name? His real name?'

'Carlos, I believe.' Sellars was smiling, too. 'But I don't think he likes it much.'

'Then we'll think of something else. I'm not going to have a foster son named Cho-Cho. It sounds like a train or something.' She waved at her daughter. 'Go on, honey – go get him.'

Christabel looked at her strangely. 'He's going to live with us?'

'Yes, he is. He doesn't have anywhere else to go.'

The little girl thought this over for a moment. 'Okay,'

she said, then trotted into the bedroom. She emerged a moment later pulling the protesting boy by the arm. He had taken off his suit, but as if he had been uncertain of what to do next, wore only his T-shirt and underwear.

'You're going to come live with us,' Kaylene Sorensen said. 'Is that all right?'

He looked at her as though peering up out of a hole. Ramsey thought he might actually try to run away. 'Live with you?' he asked. 'Like, *su casa*? In your house?'

'Yes.' She nodded emphatically. 'Tell him, Mike.'

'We want you to live with us,' the major said. To his credit, he definitely sounded like he meant it now. 'We want you . . . to be part of our family.'

The boy stared from one to the other. 'Not going to school,' he said.

'You most certainly are,' Kaylene Sorensen told him. 'And you will take regular baths, too. And we'll get those teeth fixed.'

'Teeth . . . ?' He looked a little stunned. One hand crept up to finger his mouth. Then his expression changed. 'Gonna live with the weenit?'

'If you mean Christabel, yes. She'll be . . . your sister, I guess.'

He stared at them again, calculating, still suspicious, but also glimpsing the outlines of something about which Ramsey could only guess.

'Okay,' he said.

'If you don't say bad words, I'll let you play with Prince Pikapik,' Christabel promised.

He rolled his eyes, then the two of them wandered off to the other room – lawsuits, court-martials, even a dead man talking on the wall-screen not enough to keep them around while grown-ups were doing boring grown-up things.

'Good,' said Sellars. 'This is all good. Now we have a few more matters to discuss.'

This truly is the story of the century, Ramsey marveled. *I wonder if someday, half a millennium from now, people will be studying what we're saying here today.* He looked at the bedroom doorway. The other wallscreen was on. Christabel was lying on the floor talking to a stuffed toy. Cho-Cho was watching cars explode.

No, he thought, and turned his attention back to what Sellars was saying. *People never remember this stuff, no matter how important it is.*

'I'm sorry I'm late. I've only been back a day and I still feel . . . pretty strange. And you know how slow the buses are downtown.' Renie looked around. 'The office isn't quite what I expected.'

Del Ray laughed and waved his good hand dismissively at the windowless space, the small screen on the unadorned white wall. His other arm was pulled tightly against his chest in a sling, the damaged hand invisible under a knot of bandages. 'It's only temporary – I've got my eye on a much nicer one at the main UN building on Farewell Square.' He settled back in his chair. 'Bureaucracies are a funny thing. Three months ago you would have thought I had a communicable disease. Now I am suddenly everyone's best friend again because the smell of a wrongful-termination suit is on the wind and my face is on the newsnets.' He looked at her. 'But not your face. It's too bad – it's a nice face, Renie.'

'I don't want it – the attention, anything. I'm tired. I just want some quiet.' She lowered herself into the chair facing the desk. 'It's a miracle I'm up and walking around, but those old-fashioned tanks were actually better than what some of the other people in the network went through. Let us move our limbs so the muscles didn't atrophy, things like that. And, of course, we didn't get bedsores.'

'You'll have to tell me one day about the others. I still don't entirely understand.'

'It will be a long conversation,' she said. 'But yes, I'll tell you. It's quite a story.'

'So was our end. How is your father?'

'Grumpy. But also a bit different, somehow. Actually, I'm on my way to see him.'

He hesitated. 'And your brother?'

She tried to smile but it wasn't easy. 'No change yet. But at least I can touch him now.'

Del Ray nodded, then began to look around on his desk and in the drawers. For a moment Renie thought that he was pretending to be busy – that he wanted her to leave. 'I don't think there's such a thing as an ashtray in this office,' he said at last. 'Shall I go find you one?'

It took her a moment. 'You know, I haven't started smoking again. I wanted one so bad while I was stuck in that place, the VR network, but once I got out, it just seemed . . .' She moved nervously in the chair. 'Things just seemed different. But I don't want to keep you away from your work, Del Ray. I just wanted to thank you face-to-face for getting things smoothed out – with the military, the police, all that.'

'Still a long way to go. But the military doesn't know that it was Sellars who tipped them off, and they're more than a bit embarrassed a bunch of armed mercenaries were about to take over one of their bases without them even noticing, so they will be just as happy if it all goes away quietly. And as I said, people want to be my friends now. Important people.'

He liked it, she realized. Did she begrudge it to him?

She didn't think so. 'But I still want to say thanks. After all that, I think I would have gone mad if they'd kept me in some government cell.'

'So would I,' he laughed. 'The first time I saw the sky again I burst into tears.'

'I didn't have much crying left in me,' Renie said. 'But I know what you mean.' She cautiously levered herself up out of the chair. *I might as well be an old woman,* she thought. 'Like I said, I won't keep you, Del Ray. I'd better get going if I'm going to catch my bus.'

He reached into his pocket with his good hand. 'Here, Renie. For God's sake, take a taxi. A real one.'

It hurt. 'I don't want any more money from you, Del Ray.'

For a moment he too looked stung, then he shook his head slowly. 'You don't understand. There's a lot more where that comes from, and it doesn't come from me. I've been talking to our friend Sellars while you've been out of touch. He's hooked me up with a man named Ramsey. You're going to get a surprise, Renie. But trust me, Sellars would want you to take a taxi. Use this.'

She stared at the card for a moment, then took it. 'Okay. But only this once, because my legs hurt.'

He smiled as he came around the desk. 'Same old Renie.' He put out his arms and she moved into them. For a moment she rested her head on his chest, then, suddenly uncomfortable, tried to pull away. He held against her pressure, kissed her gently on the cheek, then leaned back to look at her face. 'And your new man?' he asked. 'Is it serious?'

'Yes, I believe it is. Yes. I'm meeting him at the hospital. He's been getting his things from his landlady's house. We're going to look for a flat.'

He nodded. She wondered if she was imagining a little

sadness in his smile. 'Ah. Well, then I wish you two good luck. But let's not be strangers, okay? I am not just saying that – not after what we've been through.'

She looked at the white club of bandages at the end of his arm. The doctors had sewed two of the fingers back on, he had told her when she called, but they had been badly mangled and there was little chance they would ever function. *None of us will ever be the same,* she thought. *Not ever.* 'I know, Del Ray.' She disengaged herself, but reached out and touched his cheek. 'And thank you.'

'One other thing, Renie,' he said as she reached the door. 'Don't be too quick to pick out a flat.'

She turned, anger bubbling up again. 'You don't think it's going to work out?'

He was laughing. 'No, no. I just mean you may find you have more housing options than you think.'

It was an interesting experience to see the exact amount she was expected to pay displayed on the cab's screen. *Is this how it always is?* she wondered as she waved the card in front of the reader and added a tip for the driver. *For people who have money? Things just . . . work?*

Durban Outskirt Medical Facility was a different place with the quarantine lifted. Visitors milled in the lobby or nested around the waiting areas in little family groups of tired relatives and yammering children. The doctors and nurses looked like people instead of visitors from other planets. *At least they've got that vaccine now,* she thought. *At least I don't have to worry about Stephen getting Bukavu 4 anymore.* It was not much solace.

She held the bag carefully as she made her way up the elevator, feeling as though she had turned into someone else when she wasn't looking. *But why? Everything's*

the same, really – same Renie, same Papa, same sick
Stephen. While we were in that place, the world went on.
Nothing's really changed.

Except for how she felt about !Xabbu, of course. That
scared her a little. She wanted it to work so badly, but
she could see so many problems. They were so different,
so completely separate in their experiences. What they
had, they had made in the most unreal environment imaginable. How would it hold up in the day-to-day of missed
buses and scraping for rent, of countless miserable visits
to the hospital?

Her father's door was open. She had only spoken to
him over the net so she was surprised to see that he had
a private room and couldn't help wondering how they
were going to pay for it. But even if she had to go into
debt, she wasn't going to let Del Ray set himself up as
their savior.

She hesitated at the threshold, suddenly frightened for
reasons she could not name. Her father was watching the
wallscreen, waving his long fingers to jump from node
to node, his expression blank and bored. *He's so old!* she
thought. *Look at him. He's an old man.* She took a breath
and stepped in.

When he saw her he blinked, then blinked again. To
her astonishment she realized his eyes were filling with
tears. 'What is with everyone?' she asked, startled and
afraid again. 'Is that all anyone does anymore? Cry?'

'Renie,' he said. 'It is so good to see you.'

She was not going to cry – not for this old fool.
Jeremiah Dako had already told her of his little trick,
wandering off to Durban and leaving poor Jeremiah to
mind the fort. But she found herself getting teary whether
she wanted to or not; to hide it, she leaned in and kissed
him on the cheek. His hand closed on hers; she found

herself trapped, held tight against his whiskery face. He smelled of honey-lime aftershave, and for a moment she was a child again, overwhelmed by his bigness, his power. *But I'm not a child. I'm not. Not since a long time gone.*

'I am so sorry,' he said.

'Sorry?' She got free and carefully sat down. 'Why are you sorry?'

'For everything.' He waved and the wallscreen went blank. 'For all the foolish things I have done.' He found a tissue and blew his nose angrily. 'You the one who always tell me about the foolish things, girl. You saying you don't remember them now?'

Something unbent inside her just a little. 'Yes. I remember. But we all make mistakes, Papa.' She took a nervous breath. 'Show me your arm.'

'See? Dog close to tore it off me. Then they call me One-Arm Joseph instead.' He displayed the lacerations with pride. 'Tried to bite my neck out, too. Bet you happy you were safe in that tank.'

'Yes, Papa. Safe in that tank.'

He heard something in her tone and his satisfied smile died. 'I know it wasn't like that, really. I am just making a joke.'

'I know, Papa.'

'Have you seen Stephen?'

'Not today – I'm going to see him after you and I have our visit. I'll come back and tell you if there's . . . any change.' Seeing her brother's little body, still withered and empty, had stolen away most of her joy at being back in the world again.

Joseph nodded his head slowly. He broke a long silence by asking, 'And that man of yours? Where is he?'

Renie fought down irritation. Why did men always ask that? It was like they needed to know whose protection she was under – to make sure that a suitably responsible transfer had been made. 'He's okay, Papa. I'm going to meet him later. We're going to look for a flat. I have enough left in my bank account. I think I might even be able to get my old job back – called the chancellor's office and apparently some of them have been watching the newsnets.'

He nodded, but he wore an odd expression. 'So that's why I am here? So you can find a place with your new man?'

It took her a couple of heartbeats to understand what was bothering him. 'You think . . . ? Oh, Papa, I only left you here because there wasn't anywhere else for you to go. !Xabbu and I stayed at his old rooming house last night, sleeping on the front room floor.' Despite her sadness, a little smile surfaced. 'The landlady wouldn't let us stay in his room because we're not married.'

'So?'

'So of course you're going to live with us,' she said, although it made her feel heavy and cross to have to say it. 'I wouldn't leave you on the street. We're family.' She darted a glance at the time display in the corner of the darkened wallscreen. 'I'd better go.' She stood, then remembered the bag clutched in her hand. 'Oh, I brought you something.'

He balanced it against his chest to open it with his working hand. He lifted the bottle out and peered at it for a long time.

'I know it's not your old favorite,' she said, 'but they told me at the store that it's good. I figured you might as well drink something decent – you know, to celebrate.' She looked around. 'I don't think you're supposed to have anything like that, so you'd better hide it.'

He was still staring at the bottle. When he looked up

at her, his expression made her a little uncomfortable. 'Thank you,' he said. 'But you know, I don't think I drink it here. Maybe when I get out.' He smiled, and again she was struck by how old he looked, bony and . . . scoured. Like rocks in a windy valley. 'When you find the new place. We will have a little celebration.' He handed her back the bag.

'You . . . you don't want it?'

'When I get out,' he said. 'Don't want to get in trouble here, do I? They might keep me longer.'

She took a long time trying to fit the bottle back into the bag. When she had finished she stood for a moment, fighting the urge to walk straight out the door, to avoid confusion and difficult feelings and simply get on with things. It was only as she looked at him, at the way he was looking back at her, that she realized what she wanted to do.

She bent and kissed his cheek again, then wrapped her arms around his neck and gave him a squeeze. 'I'll be back tomorrow, Papa. I promise.'

He cleared his throat as she stood up. 'We can do better, you and me. You know I love you, girl. You know that, right?'

She nodded. 'I know that.' It was hard to talk. 'We'll do better.'

!Xabbu was not in the waiting room for the children's wing. Renie was a little surprised – it was not like him to be late – but her brain was too full to spend much time wondering about it. She left a message for him with the receptionist, then went to see Stephen.

She found !Xabbu sleeping in a chair at the foot of the hospital bed, his head back, his hands open in his lap as though he had held and then released some flying thing.

She felt ashamed. If she was tired and out of sorts, how much more exhausted must !Xabbu be, after those last hellish minutes holding open the line of communication with the Other? *And now I'm going to drag him out looking for some miserable little flat.* Her heart twisted in her breast.

But it will be our *miserable little flat,* she reminded herself. *That's something, isn't it?*

She gently stroked his head as she stepped past him to the side of her brother's bed. Stephen's little arms were still curled against his chest as if in mantis-prayer, his body terrifyingly bony under the thin hospital blanket, his eyes . . .

His eyes were open.

'Stephen?' It almost came out a scream. 'Stephen!'

He did not move, but she thought his eyes followed her a little as she leaned in. She took his head in her hands, terrified by his frailty. 'Can you hear me? Stephen, it's me, Renie!' And all the time a voice in the back of her brain was saying, *It means nothing, it's just something that happens, their eyes open, he's not there, not really . . .*

!Xabbu had begun to stir at the sound of her voice. He sat forward, but seemed still to be partly asleep. 'I had a dream,' he murmured. 'I was the honey-guide . . . the little bird. And I was leading . . .' His eyes finally came all the way open. 'Renie? What is happening?'

But she was already at the door, shouting for a nurse.

Doctor Chandhar had taken her fingers from the pulse in Stephen's neck, but she was still holding one of his bony hands in hers. 'The signs . . . are rather good,' she said, the smile on her face a fine counterweight to professional caution. 'There is definitely improvement, the first we've seen since he's been here.'

'What does that mean?' Renie demanded. 'Is he coming out of it?' She leaned in to stare at Stephen again. Surely that was a flash of recognition deep in his brown eyes – surely it was!

'I hope so, yes,' the doctor said. 'But he has been comatose a long time. Please listen, Ms Sulaweyo. Do not get your hopes up too high – the odds against full recovery are very long. Even if this means he's awakening, there might still be brain damage.'

'I'm here,' Renie told her little brother firmly. 'You can see me, can't you? You can hear me. It's time for you to come back to us, Stephen. We're all waiting for you.' She straightened. 'I have to tell my father.'

'Not too much all at once,' said Doctor Chandhar. 'If your brother is truly waking up, he may be disoriented. Soft voices, careful movement.'

'Right,' Renie said. 'Of course. I'm just . . . God, thank you, Doctor. Thank you!' She turned to !Xabbu, threw her arms around him. 'His eyes are open! Really open!'

When the doctor had left to go call a specialist at one of the bigger hospitals, Renie sagged into the chair and wept. 'Oh, please let it be true,' she said. 'Please, please.' She leaned forward and reached between the bars at the side of the bed to hold Stephen's hand. !Xabbu came and stood behind her, wrapping his arms around her neck as they both looked at the shrunken shape. Stephen's eyes had closed again, but this time in what Renie felt unprovably sure was something closer to normal sleep.

'I had a dream,' he said. 'That I was a honey-guide bird, and that I was leading Stephen to honey. We came a long way. I could hear him behind me.'

'You led him back.'

'Who knows? Perhaps I felt him coming up and it touched what I was dreaming. Or perhaps it was just chance. I am not so certain of anything as I was.' He laughed. 'Was I certain of things once?'

'I am certain of something,' she said. 'I love you. We belong together. With Stephen, too. And even my father.' Now she was the one to laugh. 'My ridiculous father – he wants to do better. Wants to start over with me. Isn't that the most ridiculous thing you've heard?'

'I think it is a fine thing.'

'It is. A fine thing. I'm just laughing because I'm tired of crying.' She reached up to touch !Xabbu's hand, then pulled it against her mouth so she could kiss it. 'If everything is a story, do you think we could actually have a happy ending?'

'There is no telling.' !Xabbu took a deep breath. 'About stories, I mean. Where they come from. Where they go. But if we do not ask for too much, then yes – I think that in our story, happiness is most possible.'

And as if he had heard !Xabbu and agreed, Stephen tightened his fingers on hers.

CHAPTER 52

The Oracle Surprised

'**C**ODÉ *Delphi*. Start here.

'It is daylight outside, but here in the deeps of my mountain I cannot see it. I have been back in my body for forty-eight hours. I have taken three baths, eaten two small meals, thrown them both up, and have spent at least six or seven of those forty-eight hours weeping with terrible, agonizing muscle cramps. My body is not entirely happy that I have returned to tenancy.

'I am weak as a mouse.

'Still, I have also – with Sellars' help – recovered my

journal entries. I never thought to hear them again. Unable to sleep, or even to rest comfortably, I have paced slowly back and forth across the floors of my subterranean home, listening to them.

'It is the voice of another woman. I know her, but I am not her. Already those hours, those mad worlds, seem like a dream. A terrible dream, yes, but a dream nevertheless.

'The one who spoke that journal, left that record of her thoughts and fears – that Martine was blind, but she could see things others could only imagine. The Martine who hears those entries now, who makes this new record, this Martine can see. But she is blind to all that the other Martine had and much of what she knew.

'I can see. I am more blind than ever. I . . . I cannot . . .'

'Back now. I had to go for a little while and now I am lying down in the dark. It is still so hard to see things, so hard. My head aches with it, my new vision blurs. Someone, I cannot remember who, once told me, 'Every injury is a gift, every gift an injury.' Some cursed therapist or eye doctor, probably, but oh! It is so true, so true, now that I understand.

'The Other . . . he was the one who took my sight from me so long ago. I understand that now, understand the puzzled doctors, the unanswered questions beneath the diagnosis of hysterical blindness. I do not think he did it cruelly, or even accidentally, in the way Sellars believes he plunged children into comas, trying only to make them quiet and tractable. No, he was with me there in the darkness of the Pestalozzi Institute, with me in a way I could not understand at the time – in my ears, but also in my mind. And when the lights came on, dazzling me, hurting me so that I shrieked and shrieked, he tried to do a kind thing. He made the light go away.

'Dying, he has given it back to me.

'He touched me at the end, at least I think he did. I felt him as I had not felt him since I was a child. For a moment, a brief instant, we were children again together, both afraid of the dark. He . . . touched me as he gave himself up. He touched me, then he was gone.

'I wish I had been with him at the end, riding down the night sky in flames like a bolt of divine lightning. Perhaps then I would have gone too, dissolved in that great fiery tantrum. It would be a simple solution. I long for a simple solution, although I am far too cowardly to effect one myself.

'Listen – Martine is talking to herself again, as always. Alone. In darkness by choice, even though I can now see. Back in my world beneath the world.

'For the others, life goes on. Sellars and his friend Ramsey and Hideki Kunohara, already they are busily organizing how things will be. Renie and Florimel have loved ones to attend to – they do not need me now. What use would I be, anyway? I thought once I could help Paul Jonas. I realized, even if he did not, that there was no life for him offline. I even daydreamed that if we survived we could make a sort of life together in the network – a virtual life, but a life. The witch and the wanderer. The patron spirits of the Otherland.

'Now everything has changed. Paul is dead and I have lost the thing that made me different, made me valuable. With my sight no longer supressed, my brain struggles to make new connections, remake old ones. The Otherland information, which I could once read like a bloodhound sniffing the wind, now means nothing to me – less than nothing, because with my new eyes I can barely see what is apparent to others.

'I have listened to my journal. I will listen to it again, I suppose, even though I no longer know the woman who spoke those words. There is little else to do. Perhaps one day I will go out into the real world and explore it with my new eyes. Perhaps that is something to live for. Perhaps.

'But for a moment I had a world for myself. I had friends – comrades. Now they have their lives back. We will talk, of course – such a bond does not disappear overnight, or even quickly – but the uncomfortable truth is that they had lives to go back to and I did not. We lived through a terrifying time, in a place of unbeliev-able danger and horror. But I was alive there. I *mattered* there. Now . . . what?

'It is hard to think. It is easier to rest. It is easier to keep to familiar darkness.

'*Code Delphi*. End here.'

RENIE settled into the cushioned seat and wished she was using better gear.

All those weeks in a perfect imitation of reality just so I could feel myself being gouged, slammed, shredded. Now that there's something nicer to feel, I'm linked in from a sidewalk VR shop and I can't experience it prop-erly.

'I thought the others told me your bubble-house was destroyed,' she said to Hideki Kunohara. She gestured at the huge, round table, at the view through the hemi-spherical roof of the towering outsized trees and of the river like a surging ocean all around. 'You rebuilt it quickly.'

'Oh, this one is much bigger,' he said, amused. 'Since

we needed a meeting place, I thought I would accommodate it in my new construction.' He settled back in his chair. 'I remember your friend – !Xabbu, I believe? – but I do not know your other guest.'

'This is Jeremiah Dako.' Renie waited while Jeremiah leaned across her and shook Kunohara's hand. 'If it hadn't been for him and two others, !Xabbu and I wouldn't have survived to attend this . . . meeting.'

'This is quite amazing.' Jeremiah seemed stunned by the hallucinatory size of the forest. 'And you were really here all the time you were in that tank, Renie? We had no idea.'

'Not just here – but yes, the network is a pretty overwhelming place.' She frowned slightly. 'And you're not even getting a very good idea of what it can really be like. Why *are* we here like this? We could have arranged to use much better gear.'

'You must ask your friend Sellars,' Kunohara said. 'He should join us any moment.'

'I am here.' Sellars, still in his wheelchair, appeared at one end of the large table. 'Apologies – things are very, very busy. What is it they must ask me?'

'Why we couldn't use better gear,' Renie said. 'Our friend Del Ray Chiume would have been happy to arrange some VR rigs through his UN connections, and they'd be a lot better than what we're experiencing.'

'It was not the quality of the gear I objected to,' Sellars told her. 'And in the future we will certainly arrange better access for you. But for various reasons I did not think it a good idea for you to be using United Nations equipment, even arranged by a friend.'

'What does that mean?

'I will explain when everyone is here. Ah, Mr Dako, we meet at last – at least in person. Well, perhaps that isn't entirely accurate either. Face to face? I hope your leg is healing well.'

'You . . . you're Sellars.' Jeremiah seemed a bit over-whelmed. 'Thank you for what you did. You saved our lives.'

The old man smiled. 'Most of us in this room have saved each others' lives. Your courage helped keep Renie and !Xabbu alive so they could play their own very impor-tant parts.'

'It was you who called in the military, wasn't it? Tipped them off that someone had broken into the Wasp's Nest base?'

Sellars nodded. 'It was the only thing left I could do to help you. I was very busy at the time. I'm glad it worked out.' He lifted his head as if hearing a distant sound. 'Ah. Martine is here.'

A moment later Martine Desroubins appeared – or rather, an almost featureless sim popped into view in one of the chairs. Renie was startled. She had wondered whether she would actually get to see Martine's real face, even though Sellars had arranged that all the rest of them looked like themselves, but she could not help feeling that the barely-humanoid sim was a step backward.

'Hello, Martine,' said !Xabbu. She only nodded.

She's hurting, Renie thought. *Hurting badly. What can we do?*

Renie was quickly distracted by the arrival of T4b and Florimel, who appeared only a half-minute apart. She already knew T4b's true face, although she had never seen him with his lank black hair combed and all his subder-mals ignited.

'Only lit 'em halfway,' he explained. 'More classy, seen?' He lifted his arm to display a perfectly normal left hand. 'Wish this was far shiny still, like in the network. That was *crash!*'

Florimel's real face was a bit of a surprise. She looked younger than the peasant sim in which she had spent so much time, perhaps only in her middle thirties, with an open, attractive, square-jawed face and a functional haircut not much longer than Renie's own. Only the black eyepatch made her someone who would provoke a second look.

'How is your eye?' Renie asked.

Florimel kissed her on both cheeks, then did the same for !Xabbu. 'Not good. I'm mostly blind in this eye, although there is better news about the ear – my hearing is coming back.' She turned to Sellars. 'But I am grateful for the help, not just with my own injuries, but with Eirene. Hospitals are very expensive.'

Reminded, Renie wanted to talk about the money, but Florimel had raised a more important issue. 'How is she?'

Florimel's mouth quirked in a sad smile. 'She is intermittently conscious, but she does not really see me. Not yet. I cannot stay long at this meeting. I do not like her to wake up alone.' She was silent for a moment. 'And your brother? I have heard the signs are good.'

Renie nodded. 'So far. Stephen is awake and talking – he recognized me and our father. He has a long road ahead – lots of physical therapy, and there may be some other problems we don't know about yet, but it looks good, yes.'

'That is truly splendid news, Renie,' said Florimel.

Hideki Kunohara nodded. 'Congratulations.'

'Major *dzang*,' added T4b.

'I'm sure Eirene will get better, just like Stephen,' Renie said.

'She has the best doctors in Germany,' Florimel replied. 'I have hope.'

'Which brings up a point.' Renie turned to Sellars. 'The

money? Several million credits in an account under my name?'

He cocked his hairless head. 'Do you need more?'

'No! No, I don't need more. In fact, I'm not sure I need . . . or deserve . . . any of it.'

'You deserve everything,' Sellars told her. 'Money is a poor substitute, but it will help you keep your family together. Please, you and all the others here have been through a terrible time, in large part because I dragged you in. And I have no use for it now.'

'That's not the point . . . !' she began, but was interrupted by the sudden appearance of a well-dressed man she did not recognize. Sellars introduced him as Decatur Ramsey, an American. Ramsey greeted Renie and the others as though he was meeting people he had heard about for a long time. 'Sam Fredericks and Orlando Gardiner are going to be here in a moment, too,' Ramsey said. 'They're finishing their preparations for a . . . little project.'

'We are only waiting on them,' Sellars said, 'and then we can begin.' He shook his head. 'No, I tell a lie, there is one other on her way.' Even as he finished the words a small, heavyset woman appeared in the chair beside him.

'Hello.' The apparent stranger had a stern if slightly unsettled look on her sharp-featured face. 'I suppose I should say thank you for inviting me.'

'Thank you for making the time to come, Mrs Simpkins,' Sellars replied. 'Ah, and here are Orlando and Sam.'

Orlando's barbarian avatar seemed flushed and nervous, Sam's more realistic sim not much less so. 'We're all set, Mr Ramsey,' Orlando announced after waving to the others.

'I can't tell you how strange this all is.' Ramsey smiled.

'Not just this place, but especially to be talking to you, Orlando.' His face suddenly fell. 'I'm sorry, you probably didn't need to be reminded . . .'

'That I died? Hard to forget, especially today.' He summoned a creditable smile. 'But there's no reason you can't be friends with someone just because they're dead – right, Sam?'

'Stop it!' She clearly didn't enjoy Orlando's new line in humor very much.

'You make a joke, Orlando,' !Xabbu said, 'but we have all learned much about friendship and how wide it stretches. We have helped each other many times, as Mr Sellars earlier said. We are . . . we are one tribe now.' He looked a little embarrassed. 'If that makes sense.'

'It does,' said Sam Fredericks quickly. 'It utterly does.'

'And perhaps that is a good beginning for our meeting today,' said Sellars. 'And helps to explain why I hope we will meet regularly here in the network, since great geographical distances separate us. For today, we should also thank Hideki Kunohara for inviting us to his new home.'

Before Kunohara could do more than nod, Martine sat forward in her chair. 'All well and good, but I believe we still have some unfinished business with Mr Kunohara – specifically, an unanswered question.' It was the first time she had spoken since her arrival, and the rawness of her voice seemed at odds with the spirit of reunion. 'First, though, I would like to know how long you two have been working together.'

'We two?' Sellars raised a hairless eyebrow. 'Kunohara and I? Only in the last hours of the old network, when I had begun to understand the shape of things. But we knew each other a little.'

'He . . . felt me out on the subject of investigating the

Grail Brotherhood,' explained Kunohara. 'But I was not interested in risking their attention – make of that what you will. Sellars made an arrangement with Bolivar Atasco instead. The late Bolivar Atasco. I am satisfied with my choice.'

'No one will criticize you for not being killed,' Martine said dryly. 'But what about that unanswered question – the one I asked you back in the earlier version of this house, just before we were attacked?'

'And that question was . . . ?'

Martine snorted. 'Please, we must be done with games now. I asked if you were spying on us. You never answered.'

Kunohara smiled and folded his hands. 'Of course I was spying on you. Every time I turned around, there you all were, disturbing the status quo, threatening my own safety. Why would I not do my best to find out what you were doing, what effect it was having?'

Renie only imperfectly understood what had happened between Kunohara and the others – her own memories of him stopped with their strange conversation while watching the soldier-ant invasion. 'You were . . . spying on us?'

'Not all along. But after our initial meeting, yes.'

'How? Or to be more precise,' Martine said ominously, 'who? Is there one of us who has not told all the truth?'

'Do not be too quick to accuse,' Sellars said. 'Remember we are friends here.'

Kunohara was shaking his head. 'It was the man I knew as Azador. I first discovered him as he wandered through my simulation. He told me tales of what else he had seen and it became clear to me that he could travel the network almost as easily as one of the Grail Brotherhood. I did not understand then that he was a partial version of

Jongleur or I would have been more cautious, but I did know he was valuable – and, fortunately for me, easy to convince. I reinforced some of his rather fuzzy notions about the wrongs the Brotherhood had done to him – things he may have picked up in a subliminal way from the Other itself, as the many fragmented versions of Avialle Jongleur also partook of the Other's thoughts – and set him out to discover things for me.'

'You set him to spy on us,' Martine said heavily.

'Not at first, no. I met him before I knew anything of you. I was mostly interested in finding out more about the Brotherhood's plans – as I told you once, living with them as neighbors and landlords was like trying to stay alive in the courts of the Medici. And he was in any case not that biddable a servant. I had no idea he had purloined the access device, the thing in the shape of a lighter, from General Yacoubian.' He spread his hands. 'So, yes, I am guilty of your accusation. Later, in my own covert travels through Jongleur's Egypt, I heard that these two,' he paused to point to Orlando and Sam, 'were asking about Priam's Walls.'

'Then you must have talked to old Oompa-Loompa,' Sam said. 'I don't think we told anyone else.'

Kunohara nodded. 'Yes, Upaut. A very strange sort of a god, wasn't he? He was quite happy to tell me that, as he put it, when you weren't busy worshiping him you had told him of your quest.'

'So you sent Azador to spy on us in Troy,' Martine said.

'I tried. But the Iliad and Odyssey simworlds were misbehaving – some combination of your own presences and the Other's interest in you, I think. If Paul Jonas had not rescued him, Azador would not have lived to be there.'

'You blame it on Paul?' Martine asked angrily.

Kunohara lifted a hand. 'Peace. I blame no one. I have admitted my acts. I merely point out that coincidences – or things that seem like coincidences – have informed much of what we experienced.'

'Unless there are more questions . . .' Sellars began.

'What has happened to Dread?' Martine had clearly come to the meeting in search of answers. 'Reports suggest he is unconscious, in something like a Tandagore coma. Does that mean that he will wake up someday, like Renie's brother?'

'Even if he does,' Sellars said, 'he is in police custody in Australia, heavily guarded – a famous murderer.'

'He is a devil,' she said flatly. 'I will believe he is harmless when he is dead. Perhaps not even then.'

'As far as I can reconstruct it, he never detached from the system.' Sellars was quiet but firm. 'He was in close contact with the Other right to . . . to the end. You all know what it was like to be linked to the Other's mind – you perhaps most of all, Ms Desroubins. Do you really think Dread could survive the Other's death and stay sane?'

'But what if he *is* alive somewhere in the network?' Martine demanded. 'What if his consciousness has survived there, like Orlando's? Like Paul's did – for a while,' she finished harshly.

Sellars nodded, as though accepting a reasonable punishment. 'There is no evidence that such a thing happened, no trace of a virtual mind or body constructed, no smallest hint of Dread anywhere in the resurrected system or network. That is not complete proof, perhaps, but I think that what *seems* true here *is* true. His mind could not withstand the horror at the end. The doctors who examined him say he is catatonic and will stay that way.' He looked around. 'Now as I was saying, if there are no more questions I will take it as my cue finally to speak about the reason we are all here.'

'We're all here because you *asked* us to be here,' Renie pointed out. 'Even if we had to come with street-shop gear.'

Sellars briefly closed his eyes; Renie felt like an obstreperous schoolgirl, but she had thought Martine's questions entirely reasonable. 'Yes,' the old man said patiently. 'And rather than continue to talk, when I know you've all heard too much of my voice lately, I am going to turn over those duties to Mr Ramsey.'

Catur Ramsey stood, then decided to sit down again. 'Sorry,' he said. 'I'm a courtroom lawyer – I do my best talking on my feet – but I suppose it's a bit more appropriate to keep it informal, as befits a discussion among friends.'

'A *lawyer?*' asked Martine. 'What in the name of God for?'

Ramsey appeared a little daunted. 'I suppose that's a good question. Well, first I think I have to make one thing explicit at the very beginning. We consider you all founding members of the Otherland Preservation Trust.'

Renie couldn't believe her ears. 'A . . . what? A preservation . . . ?'

'The governments of southern Africa made many trusts for my people and their land.' !Xabbu's voice had an uncommon edge to it. 'Afterward, my people had no land.'

'Just let me explain, please,' said Ramsey. 'No one is taking anything away from anyone. I'm involved in this because I was dragged into it, not because I wanted to be.'

'You don't have to defend yourself, Mr Ramsey,' Sellars said. 'Just explain what happened to you.'

And so the lawyer did. It was a piece of the story Renie hadn't heard – a strange and shocking piece. It was the first time she had heard more than a brief mention of

Olga Pirofsky or the little girl Christabel Sorensen.

God, this was big, she thought. *It wasn't just us on the inside and my father and Del Ray and Jeremiah on the outside.* And then she thought, *I want to meet some of those people – the little girl and boy we saw at the end. They were real children! I want to meet everyone. After all, we're the members of a very small, special club.*

And I want to see the Stone Girl again, she realized. *She may not have been real, but I certainly miss her.* She resolved to ask Sellars about it when she had a chance.

Ramsey's recital drew questions – many of those present were only now putting all the details together. By the time they had all lapsed into overwhelmed silence, more than half an hour had passed.

'It seems I owe you an apology, Mr Ramsey,' Martine said at last. 'You have had your own difficult journey.'

'Nothing like what you all went through, Ms Desroubins. And that's not even speaking of those who didn't come through – Olga, her poor, mistreated son, your friend Paul Jonas. Compared to the rest of you, I don't have much stake in this. But that's all the more reason I'd like you to listen.'

Renie said, 'I think we're listening now.'

'Thanks.' He took a moment to compose himself. 'Now, what you've heard already from Mr Sellars is that the stored code for the network was basically intact.' He gestured to the bubble-distorted view of giant trees. 'As you can see, Mr Kunohara has largely recovered his own world already. And there are other worlds waiting to be saved, too. With time, everything could be saved.'

'Could be?' Martine was still asking questions, just a little more gently. 'Why the conditional?'

'Because unless we take a bold step,' Sellars said with

some heat, 'I do not want to save them.' He waited until the clamor died down. 'I apologize – I should not have interrupted, Mr Ramsey. Please continue.'

'The problem has a couple of parts,' Ramsey explained. 'The first is – who owns the network? It was built by the Grail Brotherhood, but all the guiding members are dead. They built it through various business entities, but in many cases by illegally funneling monies out of their own corporations or the countries they ruled – embezzlement for purely personal benefit.' He shrugged. 'The two largest pieces of technical infrastructure belonged to J Corporation and Telemorphix. J Corporation still exists, but its headquarters is a lump of rubble and molten glass in the middle of a Louisiana lake and its founder is dead. Nothing like that happened to Telemorphix, although Wells is definitely dead, too – you may have noticed they finally announced it.' He took a breath. 'The fact is, the squabble over ownership is going to go on for decades. Trust me – this affair is going to be worth hundreds and hundreds of millions just to the trial attorneys.'

'So what are we supposed to do?' asked Bonnie Mae Simpkins, who had been largely silent. 'That's just how things work, isn't it? Regular folks get it in the neck and the lawyers and big businesses make out like bandits.'

'I wish I could take time to defend my profession,' Ramsey said. 'We're not all sharks. But there's another question – a vital one. And the person at the center of that question is right here in this room.'

Sellars saved them from a search for dark corners in the cornerless bubble. 'We're talking about Orlando Gardiner, of course. This network is Orlando's home now. He can't live anywhere else.'

Orlando shrugged. 'Nobody's going to be pulling the plug, are they? Not for a while.'

'But there's even more to it,' Ramsey said. 'Mr Kunohara?'

Their host leaned forward, wearing one of his odd half-smiles. 'All of you – well, almost all – were with me when the information life-forms were set free. Despite the objections of some of those present, by the way, I do think that was the only rational solution. Can you imagine the political and legal struggles to determine their fate if we had left it up to the people back in the real world?' He said it as scornfully as if he owed that place no allegiance at all. 'Well, I have something else to tell you. Those creatures . . . a bad word . . . those *beings* are gone now, released from their so-strict confinement. But the evolutionary algorithms first generated by Sellars, the processes which helped create them, were not kept in such a secure way. Remember, the Other was not a discrete entity monitoring a network from some separate location – in some ways, the network was the Other's body. Any evolutionary biologist knows that cells which prove useful in one part of an evolving organism may eventually be put to use in other parts as well. And the evolution of both the Other and the Grail Network itself has been rapid and not very well understood.

'For a long time I have been discovering examples here in my own simworld of unusual or even impossible mutations. The first appeared years ago, and thus had nothing to do with the more grotesque mutations forced by Dread. Initially I thought these things were just flaws in the programming, then later I put it down to Grail Brotherhood manipulations. Now I think differently. I believe that the Other put some of the same evolutionary algorithms which helped shape its children into use in the network at large – or at least unknowingly allowed them to seep into the code.'

'So there are like, too many mutants,' Sam said. 'Do you want Orlando to kill them? He's *ho dzang* at killing mutants.'

Kunohara looked at her in horror. 'Kill them? Don't you understand, child? This may not be the kind of evolutionary breakthrough that the information life represented – that life was hothoused, protected, even hastened toward more complex evolution – but it is still something rare and wonderful. In a sense, this entire *network* may almost be alive! Whether through slow change to the general matrix, the springing up of unusual forms, or even a deepening of the individuality of the virtual inhabitants, I suspect that the algorithms have already had an effect.' He settled back, smiling again, clearly pleased with the prospect. 'We have no idea what this network can become – all we know is that it is far more complex and vital than any mere virtual reality simulation.'

'So,' Martine said, 'this is the crux.'

'Exactly.' Catur Ramsey nodded. 'We all can guess both the good and bad that might come from this network. The good – a place like no other, almost a new universe for humankind to protect and explore and study. The bad – uncontrolled growth of pseudo-evolutionary information organisms. Possible contamination of the worldwide net. Who knows what else? Now, do you really, really want to put those potentialities into the hands of the same corporations that built it – and their lawyers?'

Renie broke the long, uncomfortable silence. 'Since we couldn't bring ourselves to kill off the Other's children, you're obviously not going to suggest we blow up the entire network. But sending it off into space doesn't seem to fit the bill this time. So what's the alternative? You look like you have an alternative in mind.'

Sellars nodded. 'We hide it.'

'What?' Dumbfounded, Renie looked at !Xabbu, but to her astonishment he was smiling. She turned back to Sellars. 'How in the hell can you hide it? Del Ray Chiume, just for one, has already been repeating what I told him about the network on every newsnet that can get a feed out of downtown Durban. There must be others, too – something this big won't just vanish. People are filing court cases already, for goodness' sake.'

'And I am one of them,' said Ramsey. 'No, we can't pretend it doesn't exist.'

'But what we show them won't necessarily be the real thing,' Sellars explained. 'Don't forget, I have a great deal of control over the network now. In fact, with enough processing power – power I'm sure the corporations and governments concerned will be happy to supply – I can reconstitute the entire network for them. But I don't even have to do that – I can just give them the code and let them do it themselves.

'However, that doesn't mean what they get will be the network we all experienced, especially if I sanitize their version first to remove anything that was not in the Grail Brotherhood's original code – that should make sure they don't get hold of any of the Other's mutated algorithms, which didn't exist until he found my experiments. Meanwhile, the true network can exist in careful isola-tion on the free-floating private web I've put together, based on the TreeHouse model. There are sympathetic parties who will support us. We can keep our network entirely separate.'

'Separate, yes,' said Martine, 'but secret?'

'If we allow very few people to enter, I think we might be able to manage it. Remember, Otherland is not really a place, it's an idea – an idea that can be moved at a moment's notice if sufficient preparations have been made.'

'And who would be allowed to enter this separate, secret place?' Martine asked.

'You, of course – all of you. And selected guests of our choice. That is why we call you founding members of the Otherland Preservation Trust. If you agree, that is. If you can imagine some better alternative, please tell me.'

Renie listened to the others – all except !Xabbu – as they began to talk and argue, struggling to make sense of what had been said, but she wanted a more crucial question answered. 'Why did you smile?' she asked !Xabbu. 'Do you think this is a good idea?'

'Of course,' he said. 'The big and strong cannot help but draw attention to themselves – they will always battle each other. The small and silent will hide and survive.'

'But do we have a right to do that?'

He shrugged, but he was still smiling. 'Did the shining lights – the information life-forms, as that fellow Kunohara called them – did they have a right to make the stories of my people their own? Who knows, but the world is different because of it. Who do you trust, Renie? These people, our friends . . . our tribe . . . or people who have never been here and who have not fought together to survive, as we have?'

She nodded, but she was still troubled.

'What about you, Mr Sellars?' she asked, stilling the last of the questioning voices. 'I believe you are a good man. Do you feel comfortable taking on so much responsibility? You can call us a trust, but in the end it's you we will all be trusting. Because we don't have the power you have. You will be God in this new universe.'

'Only for a while,' he said. 'Because I am working even now to put myself out of a job.' He held up a gnarled hand. 'Have you wondered why, with all the resources of the Otherland network, I haven't chosen a more attractive

appearance? Because this is the real Patrick Sellars –
burned, twisted, all but dead. Or it was, until I found a
way to lose my crippled body. But I don't want to forget
it. You won't see me manifesting as Jove, throwing thun-
derbolts.' He grinned. 'Please! I'd kill myself laughing. But
it's a serious question, Renie, and the only real answer is
. . . no, I don't trust myself with so much power, even if
it is power over a universe very few people will ever know
about. But I don't know anyone else I would trust with
such singular power either. That's why I need you all to
help me make decisions.'

'Why me?' asked Bonnie Mae. 'I'm not one of your
volunteers.'

'You're not only a person of faith, you're a person of
good faith,' he said. 'We need to hear what you bring. In
fact, I hope you can convince Nandi Paradivash to come
to the next meeting. We need him, too.'

'He's hurting, Mr Sellars.' She shook her head. 'He told
me he was going back to the burning ground, whatever
that means. That he was going to start over.'

'We need him,' Sellars said firmly. 'Please tell him so.'
He raised his scarred head. 'As I said, I really do want to
make myself obsolete. Once things are up and running,
these new worlds won't need another God – neither the
twisted sort the Grail Brotherhood made or a caretaker
deity like me. Besides, I have other ambitions.'

Even Kunohara and Ramsey seemed puzzled by this.
'Other ambitions . . . ?' asked Hideki Kunohara.

'You saw where the others went,' Sellars said. 'The new
creatures. How they rode the light out into the great
unknown. Well, I'm information now, too. One day, when
I'm not needed anymore, it will be good to be free to fly
again.'

Renie wasn't sure why Catur Ramsey laughed. She

thought what Sellars said was very touching. 'So . . . so what does this Otherland Trust do?' she asked. 'Vote on things?'

'Yes – in fact we have something to vote on now.' Sellars looked over at Sam and Orlando, who were whispering. 'Orlando – would you please rise?'

Renie could not hide a smile. He sounded like a schoolteacher.

Orlando stood, a strange mixture of barbarian grace and teenage awkwardness. 'Have you decided on what you want to call yourself?' Sellars asked him.

'I think so.'

'But he's already got a name!' It was clear Sam Fredericks had not known this was coming, whatever it was.

'It's not another name he needs,' Sellars told her, 'but a title. Whatever happens, the worlds of the network will need lots of supervision, especially at first as we bring them back online. I can't do it all. I considered Kunohara, but he has made it clear he does not wish such an active role. Also, I need to train someone for the long term, teach them some of my responsibilities, as a maintenance man if not as a god – especially if I hope to ride the sky-river-of-light someday, as our absent friends called it. So I need an . . . apprentice, I suppose. Orlando?'

'I think I want to be called . . . a ranger.' Renie thought she saw a blush beneath the deep tan. 'I plan to travel a lot, so it makes sense. And to kind of have responsibility for the place, too – like a forest ranger. And . . . and it has another meaning. From a favorite book of mine.'

Sellars nodded. 'An excellent choice. But may we at least dignify it with the little "Head Ranger"?' He smiled. 'Considering that this network was largely the province of one astounding mind, that adds another layer of meaning, too.' He turned to the table. 'Let us vote. All in favor of Orlando Gardiner as the first Head Ranger of the Otherland network . . .'

All the hands went up.

'Wow, Gardino,' Sam Fredericks said in a loud stage-whisper. 'Now you're Assistant God!'

'Yeah, and I never even got a high school education.'

'Enough jokes, you two,' Sellars said kindly. 'I believe you have another meeting to attend?'

'Oh, yeah.' Orlando's good cheer suddenly evaporated and he was pure nervous adolescent. 'Yeah, we do.' He and Sam stood up. 'Mr Ramsey, are you coming?'

'I'm ready,' the lawyer told them.

'But we have come to no conclusion about the network itself,' Martine protested. 'Surely it is too important a question simply to abandon.'

'It is indeed,' Sellars said. 'But we have days, perhaps even weeks, to make our decisions. Try to get Nandi Paradivash to come to the next meeting. Let's say in two days, shall we?'

Renie almost complained that two days was too soon, that some of them had to find jobs, but then she remembered. 'About that money . . .' she said.

Sellars shook his head. 'There's no one to give it back to – I'm dead, remember? If you don't want it, I'm sure you can find a worthy cause that will accept a large donation.' He seemed to enjoy her frustration. 'And if you remind me, I'll arrange a better way for you to get online next time. You might want to consider getting a neuro-cannula, unless you have some religious objection.'

By the time Sellars moved off, summoned by Hideki Kunohara for a private chat in one of the adjoining rooms, Orlando, Sam, and Catur Ramsey had already left and the others were all talking – all but Martine, who still sat apart as though she were a stranger at the gathering. Renie squeezed !Xabbu's hand before moving around the table toward her. Martine looked up, but it was impossible to glean anything about the woman's emotional state from her featureless sim.

'So does the money upset you, too?' Renie asked. 'I'm grateful, I suppose, but it does seem a little high-handed . . .'

Martine seemed surprised. 'The money? No, Renie, I have scarcely thought of it. I was wealthy already, from my settlement, and . . . and I have few needs. I have already earmarked my share to go to children's charities. It seems appropriate.'

'You can see now, can't you? Is it strange?'

'A bit.' She sat motionless. 'I will grow used to it. In time.'

Renie searched for something to keep the conversation going. 'There's something I've been thinking about. Emily. And Azador.'

Martine nodded slowly. 'That had occurred to me as well.'

'I mean, if she was really a version of Ava – and Azador was really Jongleur . . . !'

The Frenchwoman could not show it with her face, but there was a sour tone in her voice. 'It is stranger than incest, when you consider that Ava was a clone – and strangely accurate as well, when you consider the child she was meant to bear. I suppose it was a subconscious expression of Jongleur's ultimate vanity.' She sighed. 'It was all as haunted and ugly as the House of Atreus. But they are dead now. All of them . . . every one . . . dead.'

'Oh, Martine, you seem so sad.'

The featureless sim shrugged. 'There is little in it worth talking about.'

'And you seem very angry about Paul.'

She did not reply immediately. On the other side of the table, Bonnie Mae Simpkins laughed at some remark of !Xabbu's, although the small man looked entirely serious.

'Paul Jonas was very unhappy . . . at the end,' Martine finally said. 'He was devastated to realize that he was a copy, as he put it. That he could never have the things he wanted most of all – that he was separated forever from the life he remembered. Yes, I am angry. He was a good, good man. He did not deserve that. Sellars had no right.'

Renie thought that somehow, Martine felt the same kinds of things Paul had. 'Sellars was doing his best. We all were.'

'Yes, I know.' The edge was gone and only listlessness remained. Renie almost missed the anger. 'But I cannot get it out of my mind. His loneliness. That feeling of being exiled from your own life . . .'

Renie was trying to think of something reassuring to say until she noticed that the quality of Martine's silence had changed. Even without a facial expression to read, Renie could see a certain tension, an alertness in the woman's sim that hadn't been there before.

'I have been a fool,' Martine said suddenly. 'A selfish fool.'

'What . . . ?'

'I'm sorry, Renie. I have no more time to talk. We will speak later, I promise.' With that, she disappeared.

Troubled, Renie wandered back around the table.

'Javier is criticizing my appearance,' Florimel announced.

'Chance not!' T4b said. The glyphs of light on his cheeks dimmed when he blushed. 'Just saying that the patch looks chizz. She only did some other stuff, could be major scorchery.'

'Like what?' Florimel gave him a severe look. 'Buy my sim some gigantic breasts?'

Javier shook his head vigorously. 'Didn't say that, me – not all unrespectful like that! Just meant you could get some sub-Ds. Like your initials, something . . .' He trailed off and his own subdermals became even harder to see. 'Oh. You molly-dupping me, huh?'

'If that means teasing, Javier, then yes.' Florimel shared an amused glance with Renie. 'But why are *you* so dressed up? I'm assuming that is what you really look like today. Such nice clothes just for old friends like us?'

He shrugged. 'Got an interview, me.'

'For a job?' Renie asked.

'Chance not. Tryin' to get back into school. AGAPA.'

'Arizona General and Pastoral Academy,' Mrs Simpkins elaborated.

'Seen. It was Bonnie Mae's idea, like.' He suddenly looked like he wanted to back away from the gathering. 'Well, mine too.'

'Tell them what you want to do, Javier,' Mrs Simpkins said.

He scowled. 'Thought . . . thought after all the things happened, I might try to be . . . a minister, like. Youth minister, seen? Work with micros.' His shoulders came up as if to protect him from a beating. He looked at Florimel out of the corner of his eye.

Renie and !Xabbu congratulated him, but he was waiting for something.

'Well,' Florimel said after a moment. 'I think that is a wonderful idea, Javier. I really do.' Smiling, she leaned forward and carefully kissed him on his glowing cheek. 'I hope your dream comes true.'

Even as his subdermals threatened to disappear entirely, another kind of light stole onto his face. 'Make it through all that *sayee lo* stuff, can make it through anything, me,' he promised.

'Amen,' said Bonnie Mae.

CHAPTER 53

A Borrowed House

'**A**RE you ready?' Catur Ramsey did his best to keep his voice calm. His stomach was full of small active flutterings, and he of all of them had the least reason to be nervous. Jet lag didn't help. 'I think it's time.'

'I don't know.' Vivien Fennis looked around their living room as if she might never see it again. 'I don't know what to do.'

'Should we say something?' asked Conrad Gardiner hoarsely. He had been pacing for half an hour while the other two made sure the gear for his wife's new neurocannula was working properly, and now he could hardly sit still on the couch. 'Or is there some . . . button we have to push?'

'No.' Ramsey smiled. 'If you're ready, just let me and Mr Sellars do the rest.'

The transition was instantaneous: one moment they were in a well-furnished California house in a gated community, the next on a path at the edge of a dark and ancient forest.

'Oh my God,' said Vivien. She turned away from the trees and surveyed the meadowed hills, the grass glinting with dew in the morning sunshine. 'It's . . . it's so real!'

'Not quite up to the network's earlier standards,' said Ramsey. 'But yes, it's still pretty impressive, isn't it? I haven't got used to it myself.'

'Who's that?' asked Conrad. 'Is that . . . ?'

Ramsey squinted at the figure coming down the curving hill path. 'No, it's Sam Fredericks, right on time.'

She waved, then walked briskly toward them, a little incongruous-looking in her pants and dark shirt. Ramsey could not help an inward flinch of embarrassment as he remembered her reaction when he suggested that for such a special occasion she could wear a dress if she wanted to. Still, he had to admit that other than the workaday teenager clothes, she looked like someone who belonged in a storybook setting like this, her eyes bright, her cloud of fluffy brown hair wrapped but not contained by a bright scarf.

She stopped in front of them, suddenly shy. 'You're . . . you're Orlando's parents, right?'

'Yes. I'm Vivien and this is Conrad.' Ramsey had to admire the woman's aplomb. After all, in the impatient hours leading up to this he had seen almost all of the emotions she was now hiding so effectively. 'And you must be Sam. We've met your folks.' She hesitated, then swept Sam into a trembling hug. Both of them hung on for a moment as though unsure of what to do. 'We feel . . . we feel like we know you, too,' Vivien said, releasing her.

Sam nodded. Her own careful composure was also threatening to come undone. 'Well, I guess we oughta go,' she said after a moment. 'He's waiting.'

As the four of them made their way up the curving, stone-lined path, Ramsey saw that Orlando's parents were holding hands. *They've had too much horror to practice on*, he thought – *but maybe it helps now.*

Still, how could anyone be ready for this?

'What . . . what is this place?' Vivien asked. They had almost reached the top of the hill. A river splashed down beside the path, loud among the reeds, the water so musical it almost chimed. Behind them the forest spread like a shadowy, frozen ocean. 'I've never seen anything like it.'

'It's from Orlando's favorite book,' Sam said. 'Somebody had made it already. He could have lived in a castle or something, one of the fancy parts, but he liked this part better.' She turned her gaze down to the ground; her smile was strained.

'Somebody . . . made this?' asked Conrad. 'I guess I knew that, but . . .'

'There's more than this,' said Ramsey. 'Lots more. You can see it all someday if you want.'

'You should see Rivendell!' Sam offered. 'It's so chizz! Even without the elves.'

Conrad Gardiner shook his head in bafflement, but his wife was no longer listening. As they neared the crest of the low hill they could see the next rise. On a knoll above them stood a low house made of stone and wood surrounded by trees, simple in construction but somehow perfect for its setting. 'Oh my God,' Vivien said quietly as they reached the bottom of the short slope and started up again. 'Is that it? I didn't know I'd be so nervous.'

A figure appeared in the doorway. It looked down on them but did not smile or wave.

'Who is that?' asked Conrad Gardiner. 'That doesn't look anything like . . .'

'Oh, Conrad, don't you listen?' Her voice sounded like something about to rip at the edge. 'That's what he looks like . . . here. Now.' She turned to Ramsey, eyes wide. 'Isn't that right? Isn't it?'

Catur Ramsey could only nod; he no longer trusted himself to speak. When he turned back the figure was making its way down the path toward them.

'He's so big!' Vivien said. 'So big!'

'You should have seen him before he got younger.' Sam Fredericks laughed – a little wildly, Ramsey thought. He stopped and touched Sam's arm, reminding her. They let Orlando's parents walk the rest of the short distance to meet him by themselves.

'Orlando . . . ?' Ramsey could hear sudden doubt in the woman's voice as she looked at the tall, black-haired youth before her. 'Is that . . . are you . . . ?'

'It's me, Vivien.' He lifted his hands, then suddenly clamped them over his nose and mouth for a moment as though to keep in something that wanted powerfully to escape. 'It's me, Mom.'

She closed the distance in a step and threw her arms around him so hard that they both almost toppled onto the turf beside the path. 'Hey, careful!' Orlando said, laughing raggedly, then Conrad had grabbed them both. The threesome did stumble then, and fell to the grass in awkward stages. They sat holding each other, babbling things that Ramsey could not quite hear.

Vivien was the first to lean back, but she kept one hand against Orlando's face and gripped his arm with the other, as if afraid to let him go. 'But how . . . I don't understand . . .' Her hands not free to wipe her face, she could only shake her head and sniff loudly. 'I mean, I understand – Mr Ramsey explained, or tried to, but . . .' She pulled his hand against her own cheek, then kissed it. 'Are you certain it's you?' Her smile was crooked, her eyes bright with fear and hope. 'I mean, really you?'

'I don't know.' Orlando watched her as though he had forgotten what she looked like and might have only this small time to rememorize her features. 'I don't know. But I feel like me. I think like me. I just . . . I don't have a real body anymore.'

'We'll do something about it.' Conrad Gardiner had a fixed, miserable grin on his face and was holding Orlando's other arm with both hands. 'Specialists . . . somebody must . . .' He shook his head, suddenly speechless.

Orlando smiled. 'Believe me – there *are* no specialists in this stuff. But maybe someday.' His smile faded a little. 'Just be glad for what we have.'

'Oh, Orlando, we are,' said his mother.

'Think of it . . . think of it like I'm in Heaven. Except you can visit me whenever you want.' Tears were running down his cheeks again. 'Don't cry, Mom! You're scanning me out.'

'Sorry.' She let go of him for a moment to blot away her own tears with the arm of her blouse, stopped to stare at it. 'It . . . feels like it's real. This all does.' She looked at her son. 'So do you, even if I've never seen . . . this version of you before.'

'It feels real, too,' he said. 'And this is what I look like now. That other me – well, he's gone. You don't ever have to look at him again and feel sorry because . . . because he looked like that.'

'We never cared!'

'You cared about how I felt when other people stared at me.' He reached out and touched her cheek, caught a drop of wetness there. 'This is how it is now, Vivien. It's not all bad, is it?' He swallowed hard, then suddenly sprang to his feet, pulling his parents up as though they were children.

'You're so strong!'

'I'm Thargor the barbarian – sort of.' Orlando grinned. 'But I don't think I'll use that name anymore. It's kind of . . . woofie.' He was eager to move now. 'Let me show you my house. It's not really mine. I'm just borrowing it from Tom Bombadil until I build my own.'

'Tom . . . ?'

'Bombadil. Come on, you remember – you were the one who told me to read it in the first place.' He pulled her to him and hugged her; when he let go she was in tears again, swaying. 'I want to show you all of it. The next time you're here the barrow wights and Tom and Goldberry and everyone will be back. It'll be different.' He turned to Ramsey and Sam. 'You two – come on! You should see the view I have down the river valley.'

As Orlando's parents brushed leaves and grass from their clothes, they were startled by a movement at their feet. Something black, hairy, and decidedly bizarre climbed out from underneath one of the borderstones along the path.

'You gotta do something about those little psychos, boss,' it shouted. 'They're makin' me nuts!' It saw Orlando's guests and stopped, eyes impossibly wide.

Vivien took an involuntary step backward. 'What . . . ?'

'This is Beezle,' Orlando said, grinning again. 'Beezle, these are my parents, Vivien and Conrad.'

The misshapen cartoon bug looked at them for a moment, then performed a little bow. 'Oh, yeah. Pleased to meetcha.'

Conrad stared. 'This . . . it's . . . this is that gear thing.'

Beezle's lopsided eyes narrowed. 'Oh, nice. "Gear thing," huh? I told the boss, sure, bygones are bygones – but seems to me the last time we hooked up, you were trying to unplug me.'

Orlando was smiling. 'Beezle saved the world, you guys.'

The bug shrugged. 'I had some help.'

'And he's going to be here with me – help me out with things. Have adventures.' Orlando stood up straighter. 'Hey! I have to tell you about my new job!'

'Job?' asked Conrad weakly.

'We . . . we're pleased to meet you, Beezle,' said Vivien carefully, but she didn't look very pleased at all.

'It's "Mr Bug" to you, lady,' he growled, then suddenly flashed a broad cartoon smile. 'Nah, just kiddin'. Don't worry about it. Gear don't hold grudges.'

Further discussion was forestalled by a cloud of tiny yellow monkeys that swirled out of the forest, shrieking.

'Beegle buzz! Found you!'

'Come play!'

'Play stretch-a-bug!'

Beezle let out a string of curses that sounded exactly like random punctuation, then disappeared back into the ground. The monkeys hovered for a moment, disappointed.

'No fun,' said a tiny voice.

'We're busy now, kids,' Orlando told them. 'Could you go play somewhere else for a while?'

The monkey-tornado swirled about his head for a moment, then lifted into the air.

'Okay, 'Landogarner!' one shrilled. 'We go now!'

'*Kilohana!*' squealed another. 'Time to poop on the stone trolls!'

The yellow cloud coalesced and flashed across the hills. Orlando's parents stood like accident victims, so clearly overwhelmed by everything that Ramsey wanted to turn his back and give them some privacy.

'Don't worry – it's not always this exciting around here,' said Orlando.

'We . . . we just want to be with you.' Vivien took a deep breath and tried to smile. 'Wherever you are.'

'I'm glad you're here.' For a long moment he only stood looking at them. His lip trembled, but then he forced a smile of his own. 'Hey, come see the house. Everybody come!'

He started up the path, then turned back so he could take Conrad and Vivien each by the hand. He was much taller than either of them, and they were almost forced to run to keep up with his long strides.

Ramsey looked at Sam Fredericks. He offered her his virtual handkerchief and gave her a moment to use it, then they followed the Gardiner family up the hill.

'**Y**OU look a lot better than the last time I saw you,' Calliope said.

The woman in the bed nodded. Her expression was flat, as though someone had carefully rubbed the life out of it. 'So do you. I'm surprised you're walking.'

Calliope pointed to the plasteel tubes beside her chair. 'On crutches. Very slowly. But the doctors can do some amazing things these days. You should know.'

'I'm not going to be walking, no matter what they do.'

There wasn't anything much to be said to that, but Calliope tried. 'Would dying have been better?' she asked gently.

'That's an excellent question.'

Calliope sighed. 'I'm sorry you've had such a bad time of it, Ms Anwin.'

'It's not like I didn't deserve it,' said the young woman. 'I wasn't an innocent. An idiot, yes – but not an innocent.'

'Nobody deserves John Dread,' Calliope said firmly.

'Maybe. But he isn't going to get what *he* deserves, is he?'

Calliope shrugged, although the same thought had been burning in her own mind for days. 'Who ever does? But I've been meaning to ask you something. What exactly were you doing with the pad after I made the emergency call? What were you trying to send?'

The American woman blinked slowly. 'A dataphage.' She read Calliope's expression. 'Something that chews up information. It had eaten half my system a few hours earlier, so I figured it might do him some damage. I wrapped it in his own . . . files. Those horrible images. So he wouldn't know at first what it was.'

'Maybe that's what put him in the coma.'

'I wanted it to kill him,' she said flatly. 'Painfully. Anything less was a failure.'

They sat for a few moments in silence, but when Calliope at last began to shift her weight, preparing to stand, the woman suddenly spoke. 'I . . . I have something on my conscience.' Something came into her eyes, a strange mixture of fear and hope that made Calliope uneasy. 'It's been . . . bothering me for a long time. It happened in Cartagena . . .'

Calliope held up her hand. 'I'm not a priest, Ms Anwin. And I don't want to hear anything more about this case from you. I've studied the reports and your interview with Detective Chan. I can read between the lines as well as the next person.' She stilled another attempt with a glare. 'I'm serious. I represent the law. Think very carefully before you say anything else. Then, if you still need to do something to . . . ease your conscience, well, you can always call the Cartagena police. But I can tell you that the jails in Colombia are not all that nice.' She softened her tone. 'You've been through a lot. You're going to have a lot more time to think while you heal, then you have to decide what you're going to do with the rest of your life.'

'You mean because I won't be able to use my legs, don't you?' There was more than a hint of self-pity; Calliope's anger sparked.

'Yes, without your legs. But you're alive, right? You have a chance to start over. That's more than a lot of people get. That's more than Dread's other women got.'

For a moment Dulcie Anwin glared at her with something like fury and Calliope braced for the harsh words, but the American woman stayed silent. After a moment her face sagged. 'Yeah,' she said. 'You're right. Count my blessings, huh?'

'It'll be easier to do that later,' Calliope told her. 'Listen, good luck. I mean that. But now I've got to go.'

Dulcie nodded and reached for a glass of water on the bedside table, then hesitated. 'Is he really gone?' she asked. 'Not coming back? Are you sure?'

'As sure as anyone can be.' Calliope tried to keep her voice calmly professional. 'He hasn't shown anything for a week – no change, no sign of waking. And he's guarded day and night. Even if he comes out of it, he goes right to prison.'

Dulcie didn't say anything. She took the water and held it close to her mouth with trembling hands, but did not drink.

'Sorry, but I really do have to go.' Calliope picked up

her crutches. 'Call me if I can help with anything. Your visa's been extended, by the way.'

'Thanks.' Dulcie finally took a drink, then put the glass down. 'And thanks for . . . for everything else.'

'Just doing my job,' said Calliope, and made her way slowly to the door.

The guard recognized her but still made her wave her badge in front of the reader before he would allow her in. Calliope silently approved. The heavy door clunked open and she stepped through into the hallway with the big one-way windows. The guard leaned past her to make sure the door closed again behind her.

'Anything?' she asked.

'Nah. Two more doctors today. Nothing. Reflex tests, pupil dilation, you name it. If he isn't dead, it's a technicality. They might as well bury him.'

The idea started a shiver of superstitious horror. *I'd have to stand over the grave with silver bullets and a sharpened stake.* 'He's already been dead once,' she told the guard. 'Let's not get too cocky.' She moved to the window, stared through the crosshatching of tensor-wire. The figure in the pool of light was strapped to the heavy bedframe and festooned with tubes and wires and dermal sensors, which evoked further horror-flick thoughts – the Frankenstein monster rising, crackling with electricity, snapping his restraints. Dread's eyes were open just a tiny fraction, his fingers slightly curled. She tried to fool herself that she could see a twitch of movement here or there, but except for the slow expansion and contraction of his torso, the automatic pumping systems moving breath and blood, there was nothing.

He's not coming back, she told herself. *Whatever happened to him, charge, some kind of data-eater, he's*

somewhere else now – as good as dead, like the man said.
You could come here every day for the rest of your life
and nothing would change, Skouros. He's not coming back.

Oddly, this did not bring her much relief, let alone the
release she was only beginning to realize she badly needed.
But that means he's escaped, she thought, and did not
realize how her fingers were tightening on the windowsill
until she felt the stab of pain in her healing back muscles.

He's gone out the easy way. After everything he did,
he just got away. He should be in hell, screaming. Instead
he's probably just going to sleep out the rest of his life,
then slip away quietly.

She pulled her crutches tight against her forearms
again, gave a last look at the still, almost handsome
face, then made her way slowly back toward the security door.

Life goes on, she told herself. *Sometimes it ends this*
way. The universe isn't a kid's story, where everybody gets
their just desserts at the end.

She sighed and hoped Stan would have found a parking place close to the facility. Her legs hurt and she badly
needed a cup of coffee.

Hᴇ wanted to sleep, ached to sleep, but would not get
the chance. It had been days since he had slept, maybe
weeks. He couldn't remember. As it was, he had not even
regained his breath, which still sawed in his throat, when
he smelled the smoke.

Bushfire. They've set a bushfire to drive me out of the
trees. For a moment he was so filled with rage and despair
that he wanted to stand and shriek at the sky. Why
wouldn't they leave him alone? Days, weeks, months –
he had lost track. He had no more strength.

But he could not give up – what they would do was

too terrible. He could not let his fear overcome him. He never had and he never would.

The smoke ran past him in tendrils, curling like beckoning fingers. He could hear the noises now, not just behind him but closing in on his left as well, the shrill cries whispering down the flame-hot wind. He stumbled wearily onto his feet and took a few limping steps through the tangle of undergrowth. They were driving him out of the stand of gum trees and back into the empty lands. The light was dim – it was always so dim! Where was the sun? Where was the daylight that would drive these terrible things into hiding in the earth, that would allow him to rest?

It's been twilight forever, he wanted to scream, *it's not fair!* But even as he raged at the monstrous cruelty of the universe he heard a coughing bark close behind him. He staggered out of the now useless security of the trees and into the open. The field of gray-yellow stone that lay before him promised to cut his bare feet unmercifully, but he had no choice. Sweating, already exhausted and the chase just starting again, he hurried down the salt pan and out into the dead, dusty land.

The cries behind him grew louder now, inhuman voices whooping with glee, screeching like carrion crows. He looked back, although he knew he should not, that it could only weaken him to see them. Surrounded by the flames of the bushfire, they came loping out of the copse he had just left, laughing and cackling as they spotted him, a crowd of horrid shapes from his mother's stories, some animal, some not, but uniformly monstrous in size and aspect. All of them were female.

His mother ran yipping at the front of the pack, the Dreamtime Bitch herself, first and fiercest as always, her bright dingo eyes glaring, her hairy dingo jaws open to

swallow him down into her horrible red insides. Behind
her came the Sulaweyo bitch with her sharp spear, as well
as the whores Martine and Polly who had somehow grown
together into one stone-eyed, blind, remorseless thing.
And behind them, through the spreading smoke, hurried
all the others – the hungry pack of *mopaditi*, the name-
less, almost faceless dead. But they did not need faces.
The dead women had terrible claws and jagged teeth, and
legs that could run forever without growing tired.

They had hunted him, hour after hour, day after day,
week after week. They would always hunt him.

Weeping like a nightmare-plagued child, whimpering
with exhaustion and pain and terror, Johnny Wulgaru ran
naked across the dry lands of the Dreamtime, searching
desperately for a hiding place that did not exist.

SHE pulled him into a little park across from the hospital,
although she wasn't sure why. The late afternoon light
was slanting between the buildings and the thought of
taking a taxi back to the rooming house with the harsh
light in her eyes depressed her. She wanted to sleep, but
she also wanted to talk. The truth was she didn't know
what she wanted anymore.

They sat on a bench beside the path, next to a small
but surprisingly well-tended flower bed. A group of children were playing atop a bench on the other side of the
park, laughing, pushing each other off. One tumbled onto
the cement path, but even as Renie leaned forward in
reflexive fear the little girl sprang up again and clambered back onto the bench, determined to regain her place.

'He looked better today, didn't he?' Renie asked !Xabbu.
'I mean, the way he smiled – that was a real Stephen-
smile.'

'He does seem better.' !Xabbu watched the children for

a moment, nodding. 'One day, I would like you to see the place I grew up,' he said. 'Not just the delta, but the desert, too. It can be very beautiful.'

Renie was still worrying about Stephen; it took her a second to catch up. 'But I've been there!' she said. 'The one you built, anyway. That was a beautiful place.'

He looked at her carefully. 'You seem full of worry, Renie.'

'Me? Just thinking about Stephen, I guess.' She settled back against the bench. The children had now scrambled down to the ground and were running in a circle on the dusty, cracked cement at the middle of the park, using a solitary palm tree as their center pole. 'Do you wonder sometimes what it all means?' she asked suddenly. 'I mean now . . . now that we know.'

He looked at her again, then back to the shrieking children. 'What it all means . . . ?'

'I mean, well, you saw those creatures. Those . . . information people. If they're what comes next, then what about us?'

'I don't understand, Renie.'

'What about us? What . . . *purpose* is there for us? All of us. Everyone on Earth, still living, breeding, dying. Making things. Having arguments. But those information creatures are what comes next, and they've gone on without us.'

He nodded slowly. 'And parents, when their children are born, do they need to die? Are their lives ended?'

'Well, no – but this is different. Parents take care of their children. They raise them. They help them.' She sighed. 'Sorry, I'm just . . . I don't know, sad. I don't know why.'

He took her hand.

'I just wonder what it all means now,' she said, laughing a little. 'I suppose it's just that so many things have happened. The world almost came to an end. We're getting a place together. We have money! But I'm still not certain I want to accept it.'

'Stephen will need a wheelchair and a special bed,' !Xabbu said gently. 'For a while, anyway. And you liked that house in the hills.'

'Yes, but I'm not sure I *belong* in that house.' She laughed again, shook her head. 'Sorry. I'm just being difficult.'

He smiled, a small, secret smile. 'Besides, I have something I wish to spend some of my share of the money on. In fact, I have already done it.'

'What? You look very mysterious.'

'I have bought some land. In the Okavango Delta. One of the treaties lapsed and it was being sold.'

'That's where you grew up. What . . . what are you going to do with it?'

'Spend some time there.' He saw her expression and his eyes widened. 'Not by myself! With you, I hope. And with Stephen, when he is strong enough, and perhaps even someday with children that you and I might have. Just because they will live in the city world should not mean they never know anything else.'

She settled back, her sense of alarm fading. 'For a moment there I thought you'd changed your mind . . . about us.' She couldn't help frowning. 'You could have told me, you know. I wouldn't have tried to stop you.'

'I am telling you. I had to make the decision very quickly on the way to meet you at the hospital.' He smiled again. 'You see what your city life is doing to me? I promise not to hurry again for a year.'

She smiled back, a little wearily, and squeezed his hand. 'I really am sorry I'm such bad company. All these things to think about, everything is so big and important and . . . and for some reason I'm still wondering if any of it matters.'

He looked at her for a moment. 'So because the new people took my people's stories on some strange voyage we cannot imagine, does that mean that my people themselves no longer matter?'

'Does it . . . ? Of course not!'

'And because you have seen a version of my desert world – one that I built from my own particular memory – does that mean there would be nothing to gain from seeing its true shape and color? Nothing to gain from taking Stephen and our children there to sleep under the real and living stars?'

'No.'

He let go of her hand and reached down beside the bench. When he straightened up he held a small red blossom in his hand. 'Do you remember the flower I made for you? The first day you showed me how your virtual world worked?'

'Of course.' She could not help staring at the petals, slightly ragged along one edge where something small had chewed them, at their rich, red, velvety color, even at the golden pollen smudged against !Xabbu's brown wrist. 'It was very nice.'

'I did not make this one,' he said. 'It is real and it will die. But we can still look at it together, in this moment. That is something, is it not?'

He handed it to her. She raised it to her nose and sniffed it.

'You're right.' She took his hand again. Something within her that had been pinched and confined since she had stepped out of the tank at last began to open – to unfurl its wings inside her heart. 'Yes. Oh, yes. That is definitely something.'

The streetlights were coming on, but across the park the children played on as night fell, oblivious.

Afterword

EVEN the sounds of the battle had almost vanished now, the pounding roar of the German heavy guns reduced to bass notes that throbbed but no longer had the power to inspire terror. He was swimming up through something, caught and carried toward a light like a dawning sky, and as he rose he could hear her voice again, the dream-voice that had spoken to him for so long.

'Paul! Don't leave us!'

But there was something different about it now – something different about everything. He had heard her so many times, felt her, almost, a presence with wings, with pleading eyes, but now in the confusion and the growing light he saw her whole. She floated before him, her arms spread. Her wings, he realized, were a network of cracks that radiated light. Her face was sad, infinitely sad, but somehow not quite real, like an icon that had been painted and repainted until the original face was almost gone.

'Don't leave, Paul,' she begged. For the first time there was something more than sadness in her words – a demanding note, a hopeless, harsh command.

He tried to answer her but found he could not speak. He finally recognized her. It all came flooding back – the tower, the lies, the terrible last moments. And her name came back, too.

'*Ava!*' But as he said it, as he finally found his voice, she was gone.

And then he woke up.

For the first moments he thought he was still trapped in endless nightmare, but had simply shuffled into a different foul dream, the chaos of battle and the surreality of the giant's castle now to be replaced by some horrible vision of death – white walls, faceless white phantoms. Then one of the doctors pulled away his surgical mask and straightened. His face was an ordinary one, a stranger's face.

'He's back.'

The others stood up too, shuffled back, then there was a new surgical-smocked figure on the stage, leaning over him, a smiling man with Asian features.

'Welcome back, Mr Jones,' he said. 'My name is Owen Tanabe.'

Paul could only stare at him, overwhelmed. He let his eyes slide around the wide white room, the banks of machinery. He had not the slightest idea where he was.

'You're undoubtedly a bit disoriented,' Tanabe said. 'That's all right – you may rest as long as you like. We've provided you with a first-class room – the one this hospital saves for visiting dignitaries.' He laughed softly. Paul could tell the man was nervous. 'But you are not merely visiting, Mr Jonas. You're back!'

'Where . . . where am I?'

'In Portland, Oregon, Mr Jonas. At Gateway Hospital. Where you are the guest of the Telemorphix Corporation.'

Things were filtering up, scatters of memory, but they only made him more confused. 'Telemorphix . . . ? Oregon? Not Louisiana? Not the . . . the J Corporation?'

'Ah.' Tanabe nodded solemnly. 'I see that you're beginning to remember. It's a terrible thing, Mr Jonas, a terrible thing. A very grave mistake . . . an error made not by us but by the J Corporation, I must hasten to point out. But we have rectified it. We hope . . . we hope you will remember that.'

Paul could only shake his head. 'I don't understand.'

'Time and rest, Mr Jonas, that's all you need. But please – let's not keep you here any longer. Some of my colleagues wanted to have a conversation with you, but I said, "First we must show Mr Jonas the depth of our commitment, demonstrate our sorrow and indignation over what was done to him." You've suffered from a regrettable mistake, Mr Jonas, but we are on your side. The Telemorphix Corporation is your friend. We will see that everything is put right.'

Paul was still shaking his head and fingering the neurocannula at the base of his skull – a piece of expensive equipment he had no memory of acquiring – when he was wheeled into the private room, which did indeed bear a greater resemblance to a hotel suite than anything usually found in a hospital. Only the discreet bank of monitors beside the bed gave any hint of the place's true purpose. A pair of silent orderlies helped him up onto the mattress – Paul was astonished to discover that his legs almost worked, although he felt horribly weak – and then there was only Tanabe standing in the doorway, still smiling.

'Oh, one other thing. I imagine you're too tired to have a visitor?'

'Visitor?' He was exhausted, but frightened to close his

eyes – terrified he might wake up in some even stranger situation. 'No. I'm not too tired.'

Tanabe's mask of good cheer slipped a little. 'Ah. Very well. But your doctor and . . . and your visitor's lawyer . . . have agreed that it will only be a fifteen-minute visit. We don't want to risk your health.' He regained his expression of unflappable optimism. 'After all, you're an important man to all of us.'

Paul could only stare, dumbfounded, as the door closed behind Tanabe. He heard someone say something in the hall – voices might have been raised, but the walls were thick and Paul's head felt thick, too. Then the door swung open and a woman he had never seen before walked in. She was about his own age, slender and well-dressed, but clearly ill-at-ease. The only thing he could not quite understand was why she was wearing dark glasses in a dimly lit room.

'Do you mind if I sit?' Her English was lightly accented – Italian? French?

'No.' He shook his head, willing to let whatever else was to happen wash over him. *Just drift*, he thought. *Until things make sense*. Then it occurred to him that drifting hadn't been a very good strategy so far. He felt a stab of regret for poor, dead Ava, for his own negligent foolishness. 'Who are you?'

She looked down for a long moment, then turned the dark lenses back toward him. 'I did not think that would hurt, but it did. We are strangers, Paul. But we are friends, too. My name is Martine Desroubins.'

He stared at her as she lowered herself into a chair beside his bed. 'I've never seen you before – at least I don't think so.' He frowned, still slow, still cloudy in his head. 'Are you blind?'

'I was.' She folded her hands on her lap. 'I am still . . .

not used to seeing. My eyes hurt from the light sometimes.' She tipped her head a little to the side. 'But I can
see well enough. And it is very good to see you again,
Paul.'

'I still don't understand any of this. I was working for
. . . for Felix Jongleur. In Louisiana. Then something terrible happened. A girl died. I think I've been unconscious
since then.'

'You have . . . and you have not.' She shook her head.
'I am confusing you again, of course. I am sorry, but it
is a long story – a *very* long story. Before I begin, though,
I need to tell you something important, since they may
try to enforce their ridiculous fifteen minutes. Do not sign
anything. No matter what the people from that corporation ask you to do, or promise you, give them nothing.
Nothing!'

He nodded slowly. 'That Tanable fellow – he was nervous.'

'As well he should be, since they helped steal two years
of your life. Did he tell you they paid for this hospital
room? That is a lie – your friends paid for it. No, that is
unfair. You earned it – many times over.'

'Two years? I'm not getting any less confused.'

She smiled for the first time. It changed her face, trans-
formed nice but nondescript into radiant. 'No. I imagine
not. Do you suppose we can get decent coffee delivered
in this hospital? There is much to say.'

'Shouldn't I be resting?' he asked, but gently, not wanting to offend her.

'This version of you has been asleep too long already.
Hear what I have to say, at least a little, then decide,' she
said. 'Oh, Paul, I am glad I came here. The others want to
see you too, but they are so busy – there is still so much
to do. But when you are healthy we will visit them all.'

'I don't think I'll be able to travel terribly soon, at least not far.'

She shook her head and smiled again. 'Your friends are closer than you think.'

'What friends? You keep saying that.' He searched his still-fuzzy memory. 'Do you mean Niles?'

The woman called Martine laughed. 'I am certain this Niles is a fine person – but no. You have the most wonderful friends imaginable, friends who have suffered at your side and who have triumphed against all odds, in large part because of your heroism.'

'Then why can't I remember them?'

'Because, Paul – dear, brave Paul – you haven't met them yet. But you will.'

And now turn the page for a preview of Tad Williams'
thrilling new novel

THE WAR OF THE FLOWERS

Prologue

A single flower, a hellebore, stood in a vase of volcanic glass in the middle of the huge desk, glowing almost radioactively white in the pool of a small, artful spotlight. In other great houses the image of such a deceptively fragile-looking bloom would have been embroidered on a banner covering most of the wall behind the seat of power, but there was no need for such things here. No one could reach the innermost chambers of this monstrous black glass building and not know where they were and who ruled in this place.

The hellebore is sometimes called the Christmas Rose because of an old tale that says it sprouted where a little girl wept into the snow outside the stable in Bethlehem because she had no gift to give the Christ Child. Both snow and the flower itself were unlikely to have been found in the Holy Land in those days, but that has never hurt the story's popularity.

In the Greece of the old myths, Melampus of Pylos used hellebore to save the daughters of the King of Argos from a Dionysian madness that had set them running naked through the city, weeping and screaming and laughing.

There are many stories about hellebore. Most of them have tears in them.

The Remover of Inconvenient Obstacles was no stranger to silence – in fact, he swam in it like a fish. He stared at the spotlit flower, letting his thoughts wander down some of the darker tracks of his labyrinthine mind, and waited, patient as stone, for the figure behind the desk to speak. The pause was a long one.

The person behind the desk, who had apparently been pursuing some internal quarry of his own, stirred at last. Slowly, almost lazily, he extended an arm to touch the flower on his desk. His spidersilk suit whispered so faintly only a bat or the creature sitting across from him could hear. His long finger, only a little less white than the flower, touched a petal and made it quiver.

There were no windows here in the heart of the building, but the Remover of Inconvenient Obstacles knew that it was raining hard outside, the drops spattering and hissing on the pavement, car tyres spitting. Here the air was as still as if he and his host sat inside a velvet-lined jewel casket.

The shape in the beautiful, shimmering blue-black suit gently prodded the flower again.

'War is coming,' he said at last. His voice was deep and musical. Women who had only heard him speak, waking to discover him warm and invisible in their rooms in the middle of the night, had fallen so deeply in love with that voice that they had foresworn all human suitors, giving up the chance of sunlit happiness forever in the futile hope he would return to them, would let them live again that one delirious midnight hour.

'War is coming,' agreed the Remover of Inconvenient Obstacles.

'The child of whom we spoke before. It must not live.'

'It will not.'

'You will receive the usual fee.'

The Remover nodded. He had very little fear that anyone, even this most powerful personage, would neglect to pay him. With the War coming they would need him again. He was the specialist of specialists, totally discreet and terrifyingly effective. He also made a very bad enemy.

'Now?' he asked.

'As soon as you can. If you wait too long, someone might notice. Also we don't want the risk. The Effect is still not perfectly understood. You might not get a second chance.'

The Remover stood. Then he smiled. 'I have never yet needed such a thing.'

He was gone from the inner room so quickly he might have been a shadow flitting across the dark walls. The master of the House of Hellebore could see much that others could not, but even he had trouble marking the exact progress of the Remover's self-deletion.

It would not be good to have to guard against that one, he thought to himself. He must be kept sweet, or he must become ashes in the Well of Forgetting. Either way, he must never again work for one of the other houses. The master of the house stroked the pale flower on his desk again, considering.

Another curiosity of the hellebore is that its bloom can be frozen solid in the deepest winter snows, but when the ice melts away, dripping from the petals like tears, the flower beneath is still alive, still supple. Hellebore is strong and patient.

The tall, lean figure in the spidersilk suit pressed a button on the side of his desk and spoke into the air. The wind carried his words to all those who needed to hear them, throughout the great city and all across the troubled land, summoning his allies and tributaries to the first council of the War of the Flowers.

Orbit titles available by post:

❏	Otherland: City of Golden Shadow	Tad Williams	£6.99
❏	Otherland: River of Blue Fire	Tad Williams	£7.99
❏	Otherland: Mountain of Black Glass	Tad Williams	£7.99
❏	The Dragonbone Chair	Tad Williams	£7.99
❏	Stone of Farewell	Tad Williams	£7.99
❏	To Green Angel Tower: Siege	Tad Williams	£7.99
❏	To Green Angel Tower: Storm	Tad Williams	£7.99
❏	Tailchaser's Song	Tad Williams	£5.99
❏	Caliban's Hour	Tad Williams	£4.99

The prices shown above are correct at time of going to press. However the publishers reserve the right to increase prices on covers from these previously advertised, without further notice.

ORBIT BOOKS

Cash Sales Department, P.O. Box 11, Falmouth, Cornwall, TR10 9EN
Tel: +44 (0) 1326 569777, Fax: +44 (0) 1326 569555
Email: books@barni.avel.co.uk.

POST AND PACKING:

Payments can be made as follows: cheque, postal order (payable to Orbit Books) or by credit cards. Do not send cash or currency.

U.K. Orders under £10	£1.50
U.K. Orders over £10	**FREE OF CHARGE**
E.E.C. & Overseas	25% of order value

Name (Block Letters) _____

Address _____

_____

Post/zip code:_____

❏ Please keep me in touch with future Orbit publications

❏ I enclose my remittance £_____

❏ I wish to pay Visa/Access/Mastercard/Eurocard

Card Expiry Date
